COLONEL JACK;

OR, THE

LIFE OF A HIGHWAYMAN.

A HISTORICAL ROMANCE

OF THE TIME OF

GEORGE THE SECOND.

LONDON:

H. LEA, WARWICK LANE, PATERNOSTER ROW.

COLONEL JACK;
OR, THE
LIFE OF A HIGHWAYMAN.

CHAPTER I.

THE ROAD—STOPPING THE OXFORD COACH —DESPERATE ENCOUNTER.

IT is night! a few fleecy clouds are chasing their way across the heavens, occasionally obscuring the silver moon in their transient passage. A sharp, frosty, November air braces the limbs of the traveller, and induces him to locomotion. The same opaque, old-fashioned oil lamps, cast a dim light along Piccadilly, and that human tide which ebbed and flowed through this main artery of London are materially decreased in their numbers, for the hour is late, and the new police, those watchful guardians, were, at the time we write, unknown to the metropolis. Among the few equestrians, a handsome, well-appointed, gentleman might be observed mounted on a horse of perfect symmetry. He wore a blue

No. 1.

coat with the deep turned up cuffs of the period, and had on his head what appeared to be a long flowing wig, so much then in vogue, and, however, was not actually the case, for his long locks were his own natural hair—his features where cast in what would be termed an aristocratic mould, and indeed his whole appearance would have led a casual observer to conclude that he was a gentleman of considerable note, although upon a second glance there was the air of the *roué* stamped upon his features, and that almost undefinable expression about them that would lead to the supposition that he was a man of strong passions, and had possibly led a life of dissipation. He was accompanied, or rather followed, by a dog of a mongrel breed, more like a bull terrier than any other species. Gently walking his horse along the road he gazed leisurely at the passers by in apparently an abstracted mood. After traversing Piccadilly he arrived at that spot where Apsley House now stands, and crossing over the bridge from which Knightsbridge takes its name, he paused not until he had arrived at the door of a low old-fashioned inn, with seats in front, known as the " Old Cromwell " posting house ; here he halted, and dismounted, flung the reins of his horse into the hand of an obsequious groom or ostler, to whom he seemed to be well known; for, by a gesture, which was immediately understood by that worthy, he seemed to indicate that his visit would be of a short duration, upon which the ostler wetted some hay and gave it to the animal he held without further enquiry. Hastily entering the old-fashioned parlour, he flung a hasty glance around until his eye lighted upon a figure smoking a pipe in the chimney corner, at the sight of whom he uttered a satisfactory "Humph!" and, taking a chair, seated himself by his side, and called for a can of hot-spiced ale.

"It's all right, I suppose?" he said, addressing himself to his companion.

"Yes, master," was the reply, in a mysterious whisper; "Hackett and t'other chaps are at the appointed place."

"Good! where did you leave them ?"

"At the 'Badgers.'"

"Oh! they've not passed yet, I suppose?"

"No, gone another road."

"That's as well."

"Yes ; so Hackett thought."

"Good night, my friend," said the other, carelessly, as he rose from his seat and abruptly left the apartment; upon emerging from which he was met by a plethoric obese individual, who was the landlord of the house. He came out of his bar-parlour rubbing his hands, and asked if there was anything he could do for his honour. The landlady also presented herself in front of the bar, with one of her most bewitching smiles; taking a parting drain with the two, the traveller wished them a cordial good night, and hastily mounted his steed, when, dropping a crown into the hand of the ostler, he trotted off at a good pace. The clatter of his horse's hoofs were heard sharp and clear upon the crisp earth. He no longer wore the negligent air when we first made his acquaintance in Piccadilly, but appeared now to be a man intent upon some pressing business, while his horse seemed prescient of his master's intent; for he pricked up his ears and was impatient to get over the ground. Kensington was soon passed through, and then Hammersmith. After which there was a dull, gloomy piece of road without a vestige of light; and as the moon had now become obscured it was enshrouded in a pitch-like darkness. Our traveller slightly slackened the pace of his steed, when, as he gently trotted along, he thought he heard the sound of horses' hoofs behind him; he held his rein with a still firmer hand and listened attentively. He was soon overtaken by a stout, farmer-looking personage on horseback, who, as he came up, wished him good night; the salutation was returned, and the two rode side by side for some minutes, when the new comer said to his companion as the moon's light now more distinctly revealed the form of the other.

"Your servant, sir! with your permission we'll travel together as far as we can for safety; there are some ugly customers about these parts sometimes."

"As you please, my friend ; any company is better than none to a solitary traveller," was the reply.

And after this, the two went on together chatting familiarly. The farmer, for so he turned out to be, being the most loquacious. The state of the crops, the markets, politics, all formed themes for conversation; besides which, he descanted upon the exploits of several highwaymen, at which his companion smiled. Arriving at a narrow bridle-road which led to the farmer's house, the two parted, and our first traveller hastened on the high-road at an increased speed, followed by his faithful dog, who ever and anon, cast furtive and enquiring glances up towards his master. Nothing occurred to break the monotony of the journey, save an occasional passenger, until the horseman arrived within a short distance of Hounslow Heath. Lying some little distance out of the road, were some ruined barns and granaries. As he neared there, he halted and took a careful survey, after which he produced a small whistle from his coat pocket, and blew it sharply. An answer was immediately returned, and two or three figures emerged from the barn; they were masked, and armed with pistols thrust into the belts which encircled their waists.

"Is that you, Hackett?" said the traveller in an under tone.

"All right, colonel," was the reply; for the individual whom we have followed, was no other than Colonel Jack himself. He hastened at once to join his companions, and like them, proceeded to conceal his features with a mask. The whole party then ensconced themselves in the interior of the barn.

"By the Lord, but it's cold work this waiting about," said Hackett. "I have got them to knock up a bit of a fire; for this nipping air is apt to take the pluck out of a man when not in action," and he warmed himself by the flames of several sticks of wood which had been ignited.

"Have you been here long?" asked the colonel.

"More than an hour," answered Hackett, as he drained a glass of brandy, and handed another to his companions, "and we shall have to wait another half hour at least for this lumbering old drag. Curse me, if I like this waiting about. How's ———— All well at home, colonel?"

A nod in the affirmative was the reply to this latter question.

"What's to be our game, colonel?" said another of the party who rejoiced in the name of Crawley, "when we hear her coming?"

He said *her*, but he meant a coach, it was a peculiar characteristic of this individual, to use the feminine gender, in speaking of inanimate objects.

"What's to be our game when we hear her coming?" he again asked of his superior.

"Why, out and on to business, of course," was the reply; you and Galdie can stand behind the hedges on each side, letting this rope lay across the road, watch your time carefully, and, as it passes, you can lift up the rope and manage to throw the leaders; now, do you understand? The rest you leave to me."

"All right," colonel, "I'm fly."

Colonel Jack paced up and down the barn in moody silence, a prey to his own dark thoughts; when in these humours his companions seldom ventured to address him. He was abstracted for some minutes, when he turned sharply round, and addressing himself to Hackett, he said,

"Are the barkers all primed?"

"All's ready for instant duty," was the answer.

"Well, success my friends!" said the colonel, "success to bold hearts and steady nerves," and he drained off a bumper.

The toast was drunk by all present. It is a trying time to most men, however bold they may be, when they have to wait for any expected event, their nerves are strained to the utmost degree of tension, and used as the occupants of the barn had been to scenes of danger, the period they passed while waiting for the Oxford coach was a painful one.

Two of them were outside attentively on the watch, and in a short time they thought they detected the sound of an approaching vehicle; laying their heads close to the ground they listened for some minutes, and the rarefied air brought to their ears the sound of horses' feet and revolving wheels.

"Hist! she's a comin', Colonel" said Crawley, in a hoarse whisper, while at the same time he motioned to his superior by an expressive piece of pantomime; Colonel Jack, Hackett and two others, whose names were Knapp and Warrington now mounted their horses, and stood concealed behind a clump of trees which were contiguous to the spot; Crawley and Galdie lay crouched down behind the hedge on either side of the road, holding in their hands the rope, and the whole party waited with eager anxiety the appearance of the Oxford stage, which they knew was nearly due according to its usual time; Slott (Colonel Jack's dog) pricked up his ears, and looked knowingly at his master,

As yet the Oxford stage was not in sight, but it was toiling up a hill some half-mile distant from where the expectant party of free-booters watched; the offside leader was slightly lame having cast a shoe, and his smoking sides and snorting nostrils gave indications that he was what is termed distressed. The coach was heavily laden with luggage and passengers, it was named the "Comet" from its meteoric and rapid course, for it actually did the journey from London to Oxford in something less than seven hours, which was a great thing in those days, and was looked upon positively as a wonder; as yet the giant steam and all its various appliances was unknown to the world, and the fair land of England was guiltless of those iron girdles which now encompass her prosperous isle. The coach carried two lights in front, although they were hardly needed, for by this time the scudding clouds in the sky had entirely dispersed, and the moon's light shewed mead, hedge-row, and road as clear and distinct as in broad day; descending a gentle declivity the coach halted for a moment, and became for the first time visible to the party who were so anxiously waiting its appearance.

"There she is, colonel," said Crawley, who could scarcely conceal his delight.

"Hush! silence!" said the colonel. "What are they staying for?"

"Stopping to unskid, I think," said Warrington.

The latter surmise was correct, for again the sound of wheels were heard, and the coachman was driving merrily along unconscious of those who lay in ambush. The first indications he received was the rearing and stumbling of the leaders. The rope had been drawn taut by Crawley and his companion, and raised about two feet from the ground. It was a wonder it did not throw the two fore horses, as it was they kicked and plunged furiously. The coachman, who was an experienced whip, had the greatest difficulty in managing his team. The guard dropped down to see what was the matter, but before he got to the horses' heads, the dog, Slott, sprang furiously upon the near side leader and seizing him by the throat brought him to the ground. In another instant, Colonel Jack and his companions surrounded the coach with their loaded pistols, and demanded a passive obedience to their demands. Colonel Jack and Hackett went to the windows of the coach and presented their pistols to the occupants, while Knapp, Warrington, and his companions made a foray upon the outside passengers.

"Resistance would be worse than useless, gentlemen," said Knapp, in his usual firm business-like tone. "We will trouble you, sir, if you please." This was addressed to the passenger nearest to him, who was a man in a military cloak with a thick heavy moustache.

"Resistance be d——d," was the reply given by this individual, "Take that, you scoundrel! do you think a captain in his Majesty's service is going to be bullied by a cut-throat bragadocia like you? Take that!" and with these words he discharged his pistol full in the face of Knapp, who, however, bore it unflinchingly—people can do so when they know the charge has been drawn. Wild with rage at observing the harmless effect of his fire, the officer, for such he was, flung his discharged pistol full in the face of the highwayman, who reeled from the force of the blow, and whose face became immediately covered with blood; other pistols were now discharged. The guard let fly his blunderbuss, several piercing shrieks were heard from the interior of the coach. Appeals for mercy in a female voice, cries of rage, and a confused babel of sounds were heard.

The officer who had resisted Knapp, jumped from his seat, and called upon his companion to follow him; the two drew their swords, and prepared for a stout resistance.

"That's right! that's right! gentlemen," said a man's voice from the interior of the coach; "capture the scoundrels. I am one of his Majesty's justices of the peace, and am bound to vindicate the majesty of the law;" and with these words he drew himself in the interior of the carriage, being under the impression, perhaps, that a representative of the law was too precious an object to be exposed to danger.

"Have at them!" said the officer in the military cloak; and he rushed upon Colonel Jack with his drawn sword.

"Move one step and you are a dead man, our pistols never miss!" said the colonel, as he pointed his weapon full at the chest of his assailant, and there was that in his eye which spoke of his determination; but the officer was a brave man, had looked a yawning cannon in the mouth, and he rushed on towards the colonel.

"A curse upon your obstinacy!" exclaimed the latter; "but you force me to it;" and with these words he aimed at the sword arm of his antagonist, whose limb dropped uselessly by his side, while his sword fell from his grasp.

By this time several other passengers had dismounted from the coach, and a terrible melée ensued. The officer's companion, seeing his friend so severely wounded, instantly rushed upon the colonel, and by main force dragged him from his horse. He fell with a heavy weight to the ground, but instantly rose to his feet and grappled with his opponent. A desperate struggle ensued. The colonel had received a severe contusion on his knee from the fall, and was, therefore, had at a disadvantage. His antagonist threw him, and pinned him to the earth; but he struggled desperately to release himself, while, at the same time, he shouted out to Hackett.

"Fire, Ned!" he called out; "d—n it, Ned, why don't you fire?"

But, in the struggle with the two combatants, it was difficult to aim with anything like certainty, and Ned Hackett was afraid of hitting his friend; besides which he was engaged with some of the other passengers and guard, who had set upon him.

"Yield!" shouted out the officer, who was engaged with our hero; "yield, and trust to our clemency, ere it be too late!" said the officer, as he fixed an iron grip upon the highwayman's throat.

"Never! I yield to no man while I have life," was the reply.

The naked sword of the officer was presented to the throat of the colonel, who in vain endeavoured to release himself. And in another minute, the probability is, that his career would have come to a close, had he not with difficulty managed to call out,

"Slott!" The faithful hound bounded to the spot, and in an instant fixed his fangs in the up-raised arm of the officer, who roared with rage and pain, and endeavoured to beat off his canine assailant, who however held on with the tenacity of a bull-dog.

"The dog! curse the hound," exclaimed the officer, writhing with pain. "Help! help!"

"Oh, mercy, gentlemen," exclaimed an elderly female; "oh, mercy! there'll be bloodshed, I'm sure there will. Take all we have—but mercy. Oh! oh! oh!" and she relapsed into a series of sobs.

By this time, the colonel managed to gain his legs, and throwing himself upon his adversary, succeeded in pinioning him.

"Mullins!" he shouted out. "A rope! quick man! Do you hear? A rope! some of you——"

"You'll have a rope, some of these days," exclaimed the representative of the law, from the interior of the coach. "You'll have a rope, you scoundrel, as sure as you'r born."

"Here she is," said Crawley, as he came to the side of his superior.

"Slip it round his arms, then; look sharp, man!" said the colonel; and in a few seconds the officer's arms were firmly fastened to his side.

The colonel took his opponent's sword, and commenced an onslaught upon those engaged with his companions; when after a sharp struggle, and several severe wounds, the highwaymen succeeded in obtaining the mastery.

"My friends," exclaimed a quaker, whose head now was presented to the window. "My friends, thee be'st violating both the laws of God and man. Pass on thy way in peace, I pray thee——"

"Shell out first, old broad brim," exclaimed Hackett, who now went again to the window of the coach.

"Come, shell out! All fighting and no swag, ain't the thing at all, you know, to agree with the constitution."

The quaker shook his head ominously, and said in a solemn voice, "Friend, thee be'st going the wrong road."

"Oh, that's a matter of opinion, you see," answered Hackett. "We think we've come the right road, if it's only to meet with such lovely company."

"Leave them alone," exclaimed a voice belonging to the magistracy of the law. "Good words are thrown away upon such scoundrels."

"Ah, ah! my worthy friend and well-wisher. Is it your dulcet voice I hear?" exclaimed Hackett, as he made a mock reverential bow to the party in question.

"Now, gentlemen," exclaimed the colonel, as he trotted up, and presented his re-loaded pistol to the occupants of the interior of the coach.

"Now, gentlemen and ladies," he continued, as he gracefully raised his hat to the only female occupant. "You have given us a great deal of trouble, and time presses. Come, your money, without further bloodshed."

The quaker handed him a well-filled leather purse with a sigh.

"You may as well give me your watch," said the colonel, as he observed some heavy seals depending from his waist. This was handed without a word.

"Ah! A man of business, I perceive. Thank you, sir! And you?" This was addressed to the magistrate.

"This is wrong," exclaimed that worthy. "Very wrong; you'll suffer for this some of these days. Repent ere it is too late."

"The rhino first, and repentance afterwards," was the reply. "Come, look sharp, man!"

More valuables were thrust into the hand of the colonel.

"And now, madam, I must trouble you," said our hero, addressing himself to what appeared to be a young, and pretty female, although her features were hardly distinguishable through the heavy veil she wore. She made no reply, but gave her purse and jewels. And the colonel gently squeezed her hand as he received them.

It would appear that the inside passengers had not been nearly so valorous as the outside occupants of the coach, for the colonel observed another male passenger beside the young lady, who had escaped his notice upon the first occasion of his appearing at the coach window. He appeared to be a gentleman rather advanced in years, and to the demand made upon him, he like the rest, gave the contents of his pockets. Our hero was about to turn his horse's head and leave, when his eye was attracted by something shining in the corner near to where the last-named gentleman sat. Upon a second glance, it presented the appearance of an ordinary cash box, such as is usual in the present day, only somewhat larger in its dimensions. Turning back to the window, the colonel said to the elderly gentlemen—

"Pardon me, sir, but I think I must trouble you for that box by your side."

A visible paleness came over the features of the party addressed, and as he nervously clutched at the box in question, he said in broken accents—

"Oh! no—no—no, I pray you. It is of no value to anyone but myself—not the slightest. I swear to you that it contains only papers which do not interest anyone but my own family or myself."

"I am always sorry to be importunate, but I am afraid I must insist upon having it in my possession," said our hero gently, but in a firm tone.

"No, no! I cannot—will not part with it."

"Nonsense," said Hackett. "Hand it over at once," for by this time, he and his companions concluded naturally enough, that it contained valuables to a large amount.

"I swear to you that it is of no value."

"Open it then and show us its contents," said the colonel.

"Alas, I have not the key with me."

"Oh, indeed!" exclaimed both the highwaymen; and Hackett turning the rays of his dark lantern on the object in question, opened the door of the coach, and snatched it from the grasp of its possessor. The lady uttered a scream, and the gentleman leaped from the coach, and was earnest in his appeals for its restoration. Then the lady spoke in imploring accents.

Her voice was low and sweet, in its tones, and fell upon the ear of Colonel Jack, as something which reminded him of past events. He turned pale, and uttererd a half suppressed exclamation which came involuntarily from him; and a visible tremour now for the first time shook his iron frame.

"Great heaven! can it be possible!" he exclaimed to himself, in an under tone, and for a few moments he seemed lost. Hackett was leaving with the prize-box, when the lady addressed our hero now more passionately.

"Dear, kind gentlemen," she said; "you cannot, will not be so cruel as to rob us of that which is to us of inestimable value, but to you none. You are evidently more gentle in your nature than these your lawless companions. Have pity on a poor female! Have pity, sir, for mercy's sake!"

"Lady," answered the colonel, "it pains me much to refuse so fair and graceful a pleader as yourself, but my duty to my comrades necessitates me to be firm. I really have not the power to grant your request."

"Oh, yes, you have; I'm sure you have! take anything, do what you will, but pray return this box to its rightful owner; I'm sure you will; nay, do not turn away; there is yet some touch of human sympathy in your breast—I'm sure there is."

"I hope so," answered our hero, as he turned away his head, for he was moved now by some indescribable feeling more than was his usual wont.

"We will send you a handsome reward —a princely reward—if you leave us the box, Let us know where we can send; I promise you that in two days you shall have a large sum of money forwarded; only I pray you to grant this request now. It contains family papers which are to us of the most vital importance.

The colonel hesitated, when the voice of Hackett was heard calling him to be off.

"Nay, do not go," continued his fair suppliant; "do not leave, I entreat, without granting this one boon, and heaven will reward you for the good act—heaven will reward you."

The colonel was touched; there was an eloquence in the silver tones of the speaker which he found it difficult to resist.

"I promise you," he said, somewhat suddenly. "that this same box shall be restored to you provided you will let me know your address, or where I may send it. If it contains as you say only family papers they can be of no service to me or my comrades; when we are once assured of this fact they shall be returned on the honour of a gentleman."

"A gentleman!" exclaimed the justice derisively.

"Yes, sir," was the curt answer.

"Oh! that I might trust you, sir," exclamied the lady.

The highwayman bent down and whispered something in her ear. She uttered one piercing scream and fainted.

A shrill whistle was now heard, and Colonel Jack, clapping spurs to his horses' sides, trotted off in the direction from whence the sound had proceeded. While all this had been taking place the other members of the gang had rifled the other passengers and had proceeded to a place which had been originally appointed for their meeting.

"Confound it, colonel," said Warrington, "what could induce you to extend your parley with that damsel? there's three of our chaps wounded, and, by my soul, I hear the sound of coming horsemen."

"The devil!" exclaimed the colonel, "Yes, I hear them plain enough."

"What's to be done?" said Hackett

"Take a circuitous route to London as fast as we can."

"And the wounded? Galdic and Knapp are severely scratched."

"We must make for old Blogg's, and drop them there."

"Good! then let's be off at once."

CHAPTER II.

THE FOX HUNTING PARTY—THE FLIGHT— THE CHASE

THE highwaymen were right in their surmise respecting the sound of horsemen, the party who were destined to arrive at the scene of action, were a roystering lot of fox hunting gents, who had been out with the hounds in the early part of the day, and had dined at Sir Harcourt Fullerton's, who was a famous sporting baronet, and whose fame for good runs and princely feeds, was known and appreciated for miles around ; there had been a grand gathering of two sections of these gentry, one of which was known as the buffs, and the other section as the flat hats ; in the company was the coroner and under sheriff of the county ; they had all been keeping it up late, and partaking pretty freely of the baronet's choice wines, and were consequently in exuberant spirits, and our highwaymen were made acquainted with the presence of the new comers by a loud view halloa. The colonel thought it advisable to direct his party to halt, as the noise of their horses' feet would necessarily declare to the new comers the road they were taking ; in the clear air and in the stillness of the night, every sound could be heard with the utmost distinctness.

"Yoicks ! Tally ho !" sung out several of the fox hunting party, " Yoicks ! Tally ho !" was succeeded by a crashing of branches, and the sound of more than one horse's feet after a heavy leap, for they found it quite impossible to trot along the road without taking a gate or hedge or two. Crash went the underwood, "hurrah !" shouted the riders in perfect ecstacy.

"Halloa, what's been the row here I wonder !" exclaimed the foremost of the party ; "why here's the Oxford coach—a break down, I suppose."

A dozen questions were asked at once by the different riders, and an explanation took place as to the state of affairs.

"Highwaymen ! robbery, and murder ! perhaps," said the sheriff in unfeigned horror, "the scoundrels, how long since ?" The old lady on the top of the coach said they were only just gone.

"Which way ? shall we follow them my lads ?" said another.

"Aye, sure, let's make a night of it ; by the Lord, but that would be glorious."

"Ah, gentlemen, if you could overtake them and secure my box from their hands, it would indeed be an inestimable favour," said the old gentleman who was the owner,

of the article in question. A general explanation took place as to the position of affairs, and the probable road they had taken, and they all expressed their determination of " hunting the game down," as they termed it. The officer who had been bound by Crawley insisted upon accompanying them, but there was no horse for him to ride, without one of the party chose to lend him one ; eventually a gentleman, who happened to be near his own home, proffered his steed to the officer, which was immediately accepted with many thanks.

" Which road have they taken, think you ?" asked the sheriff. The guard pointed to where he had last seen them, but while they were discussing this point, one of the party observed the colonel and his companions creeping cautiously along, under cover of a hedge-row, some few fields off. He pointed out their figures to his companions, who observed through the interstices of the foliage the figures of horsemen, gently walking their steeds, so as to make as little noise as possible.

" Bravo !" shouted several, "we shall unearth them yet." And taking what firearms could be found handy, the fox-hunters dashed off in full pursuit, loading their pieces as they went along.

The colonel was soon made acquainted with the fact of the pursuit, and presuming that his position had been discovered, he set spurs to his horse, and bid his companions to push on their utmost speed. He knew the ground pretty well, but not nearly so perfectly as did his pursuers. He had taken a turning which led to a cross road, and intended to reach London by Bagshot Heath.

"Curse it," said Warrington, "we shall be overmatched. They are fox hunters, and know every road of the country ; shall we turn and face them ?"

"Not yet, at all events," said the colonel; "by the noise they are making there must be a goodish lot of them."

Gallop, gallop ! on, on ! both parties went at their fullest speed. They were not as yet within sight of each other.

"Can't we double them in some way or other ?" asked Hackett.

"We'll try," said the colonel, " but in any case when we come to the three roads at the end of this lane, we had better divide ourselves, and go in three separate parties."

"Unless you mean to turn and face them," said Knapp.

"I'm afraid there are too many, and we have already three wounded ;" whilst he said this, they came to a part of the lane which, as it turned sharply round at an angle, ascended into a small acclivity.

Upon turning this point of the road our hero for the first time caught sight of his pursuers. There appeared to be some dozen of them, including a straggler or two, whose horse-flesh had refused to keep pace with their wishes.

"By the Lord! but there's too many to be pleasant," said Hackett, as he observed the party, who, on catching sight of the highwayman, set up a shout which was echoed for miles around.

"Hurrah! we shall be on them presently," screamed out several voices. "Hurrah! this is glorious sport. Flap hats for ever—Hurrah!" And away dashed their steeds at increased speed. The highwaymen urged their horses on to the utmost. Hackett, Warrington, and the colonel were splendidly mounted, indeed of such superior stuff were their horses made, that they did not doubt being able to distance any pursuer, but the others were not quite so well up to the mark, consequently, when they arrived at the end of the lane, which was the place were three cross-roads diverged off, the colonel directed his company to divide themselves.

"Now," he observed, "if you take the left-hand road, and you this other, Hackett, Warrington and myself will wait the appearance of our friends, thus you will find time to get greatly in advance on each of your respective courses, when leave the rest to me—the devil take the hindmost, as the saying is." They did as he desired, and gently trotted forward. Quietly waiting the appearance of the fox-hunting party Colonel Jack proceeded to light his pipe, down which he puffed a thick cloud of smoke. In a short time the pursuers appeared with loud demonstrations of joy.

"Ah! ah! my friends; it's as I wished, said our hero; follow in welcome; you'll have your work to do, I promise you." And as the party of horsemen appeared in sight, elated with the prospect of a speedy capture, Colonel Jack gave the word of command, and himself and companions set off at headlong speed.

"Now for it," he exclaimed; "they are following us that is evident, and the weaker portions of our gang are safe."

It was, as he said, the fox-hunting party had not given a thought beyond capturing those in sight, and one and all followed the colonel and his two companions. Mile after mile was passed, but the highwaymen as yet had distanced their pursuers, several of whom had become worn out with the chase and had fallen into the rear. No matter, there were plenty to follow. The sheriff and coroner still formed part of the company, and urged on their companions to fresh exertion, and they became still more elated as they found they were gaining upon their enemies. The colonel saw this, and an expression of deep anxiety was observable upon his features.

"By my faith, but they must be well mounted, though," he exclaimed.

"There's no mistake about that," said Hackett.

"We shall be at the turnpike presently," answered the colonel, "and then we shall perhaps be able to square matters."

His companions laughed at the idea. When they arrived at the pike the gate was immediately opened at our hero's bidding, and a couple of guineas were placed in the man's open hand.

Keep those chaps as long as you can," said the colonel. "Do you understand, Bryent?"

"All right, master," was the reply; and away dashed the horsemen as the gate closed after them with a heavy swing. It had scarcely recoiled back upon its hinges when the fox-hunting party appeared.

"Holloa!" exclaimed several. "Open the gate. Do you hear, you old fool?"

"Clear it!" shouted out another.

"Easier said than done, I'm thinking," exclaimed a third.

The old turnpike keeper detained the party as long as possible, who were impatient at the delay.

"Some scoundrels! some highwaymen! have passed through this gate but just now" said the sheriff.

"Law! you don't say so," said the pike man, opening his eyes in well-feigned astonishment. "Highwaymen! Dear me! Who would have thought it? I wish I had known they had been such."

"And what good would that have been, pray?" asked the coroner.

"I wouldn't have let them through, sir," said the man, assuming a look of injured innocence.

"Get out! Which way did they go?"

"Oh! they took to the road, sir, as is their wont, I suppose. Highwaymen! dear me! highwaymen!" he continued to repeat as he went into his wooden habitation. This little divertisement was of essential service to Colonel Jack A minute or two was of consequence when so closely run, and he trusted by distancing his pursuers to thereby induce them to give up the chase; and the probability is, he would have succeeded had not the sheriff and coroner been amongst them, for, to say the truth, although our fox-hunting friends had started in such good spirits, and had hoped to effect an immediate capture, now that seemed to be as far distant as ever, and the efforts of the wine began to wear off, they were not quite

so enchanted with their task, still they held gallantly on their way, and the officer who formed one of their company, urged them on to renewed action. After a few more miles had been passed, Colonel Jack and his companions reached Bagshot Heath.

"Heaven be praised! that we are here at any rate," said the colonel, "but they've held on bravely, though."

"In truth they have," said Hackett, "more than I should have given them credit for. I wonder if old Dabbs is open."

"I fear not, and if he is it would be hardly safe to seek shelter there," answered the colonel.

"They are evidently bent upon following us to the world's end, if needs be."

"Yes, those who are left of the party are stickers at their work, but they havn't put salt on our tails yet," said the colonel. "Let me see, I think we will try my old friend the mayor; yes, that will be one dodge, under the protecting wing of that great legal functionary, it is just probable that we may give our friends here the double."

He turned his horse's head, and went down a broad open turning, followed by his two companions. At the distance of a few hundred yards down this turning, was situated a large old-fashioned mansion, or gentleman's seat as it is called, but whence the name of seat we could never divine; a lofty avenue of chesnuts sheltered the broad carriage drive which led to the habitation; a pair of massive gates of wrought iron, surmounted by an heraldic device, were at the commencement of the carriage

No. 2.

drive; on the right side of the mansion there was a circular road-way, which led to the stables of the establishment, they were at some little distance from the house itself.

Bow reverentially, my son, for this palatial dwelling was the habitation, or country seat, of no less a person than Ephraim Gubbins, Esq., lord mayor of London; here it was, that occasionally that great civic functionary would unbend, in those hours when the state did not require his services. Here it was that those flashes of wit, pungent satire, and forensic wisdom fell from the lips of his lordship, in his more social moods; it was not often he came down here, it is true, for his mind was occupied between his magisterial duties, and the price of hides and tallow, for by the two latter articles it was, that he had realized a large fortune, indeed a princely fortune; he would have told you, that it was by his own indefatigable industry, and how, when an errand boy he had to sweep out the shop; how, even then he saved half-pence, and bought and sold with other boys; how, after then he put a little of his savings in the candle-making business; he might have run the duty, in fact did, but he forgets to mention this. Well then, the man in whose firm he had been a sleeping partner, became a bankrupt; as the business was carried on in his name, Gubbins slips quietly out of the affair, and had not the honor of appearing before the Mr. Commissioner Holroyd, of that period. Ah, no, he has made himself quite safe, long before affairs had come to their present crisis; clever man, Gubbins, but their are hundreds such, my friend, in the city of London now, as then, thousands such. It's a curious history, that of trade; I am afraid dodgery, quackery, and chicanery forms three of its most important elements; yes, I'm afraid so, not that it is possible that any of these three qualities ever entered the compositions of Gubbins, it's perfectly preposterous to suppose such a thing; it was, as he used to say, by industry, integrity, punctuality on—ly, that he rose to his present position. Be that as it may, we shall presently see, that his rural mansion was of infinite service to our hero, who by the way, we do not put upon the highest pinnacle of moral rectitude. Like lord mayor Gubbins, Colonel Jack turned down the circuitous entrance, which led to the stabling, and quietly taking a key from his pocket, opened the door of the latter, and led his and his friends' horses in, and then closed the door, and locked it on the inside; having done this, he indulged in a sly laugh, as he observed his companions' astonishment.

"Well!" exclaimed Hackett, "Lord bless your check; why, this place belongs to the lord mayor."

"Of course, my friend, there is no place so safe as that which is protected by the law."

"Why, how did you manage to obtain an entrance here, and if we should be discovered, what then?"

"Listen!" said the colonel, "I have stalled my horses here more than once before. Old Fleetwood, who does all his lordship's jobbing carpentering, did the door and wood-work of these stables, he's a relative of—that is—no, not a relative of mine, but I know him, so I managed to obtain a key to this door without his knowledge."

"Well, but the groom?" enquired Warrington.

"Oh! matters can be squared with him on a pinch; besides, I know his lordship is engaged in London, and does not happen to be down here just now; of course, if he were, (and he said this with marked emphasis,) if he were, why, he would be too happy to provide us beds for the night."

"Yes, in the cage," answered Hackett, with a grin.

While this conversation was taking place, Colonel Jack had proceeded with the greatest *sang froid*, to tie up each of the horses in separate stalls, and given them a feed of corn, taking care at the same time of that portion of the booty which they carried in leather bags; it was in one of these bags, that the dog Slott had been ensconced; he had trotted behind his master until fairly worn out, when he was taken up by the colonel. When the horses of the three highwaymen were stalled, they heard the sound of voices, which came from the pursuers.

"I tell you it was just here I missed sight of them; I'll swear it," said some one in shrill tones.

"No banting" said another, "they have gone down the lane."

"I tell you I saw them turn in here," obstinately persisted the first speaker; "it was here they disappeared, and no where else."

"But this is some gentleman's mansion," said another of the party.

"Yes, evidently so, they cannot have gone here. Where does this road lead to?"

"To the other main road which leads to London."

"Then it is that which they have made for."

"How can you be so obstinate, Boodle," exclaimed the first speaker pettishly; "did we not hear the sudden cessation of the horses' feet; you've not been on the road all these years to be deceived upon that point."

"Clearly not," said the military gentleman who had accompanied them. "It is quite certain, that either here, or somewhere about this spot they came to a halt, and in my opinion they are lying concealed in close proximity to where we are now standing; I vote we undertake a thorough search, for that they halted here, or somewhere near, I am quite certain."

"I do not believe there can be any doubt upon that point," said the sheriff.

"Of course not," said the first speaker, nobody but such an obstinate buffer as Boodle, would ever contradict such a proposition.

"Well, I vote we search at once in the grounds of this house. Who does it belong to I wonder?"

The heavy lumbering sound, as of an approaching vehicle was now heard, and the tinkling of the bells, at once made the listeners acquainted with the fact, that it was in all probability a waggon; in a few more minutes the hooded head, broad wheels, and heavy footed horses were discernible, as also the horn lanthorn which swung in front of the vehicle.

"Come," said the sheriff, "this fellow will be able to put the matter at rest; he will be able to tell us if any horsemen have passed down the road, for in all probability he has entered it himself from the commencement."

"Hillo, my friend," called out the sheriff. "A word with you."

The waggoner was walking by the side of his team, whip in hand, but he did not seem to take any notice of the sheriff's salutation; he either could not, or would not hear it, although it was loud enough to have awakened one of the seven sleepers; but I believe it is proverbial, that the waggoner and watchman of the olden time considered it a matter of duty, to either be, or appear deaf.

"Seen any horsemen pass down the road my man?" said the military gentleman, as he trotted up to the waggoner; the man opened his mouth and stared at the questioner. That's another theory I have; I believe the waggoner of old used literally to walk sleeping, it may be an erroneus impression, but it will suggest itself to the imagination notwithstanding.

"Has any gentleman on horseback passed you on the road?" again asked his questioner.

"E'es, since I first started, a goodish many.'

"Oh, indeed; when?"

"Weel, let un see; why yesterday there moight 'a been"—

"Yesterday!" exclaimed the other in a rage at the man's manner, "I don't mean yesterday, of course."

"Oh, oh! may happen ye mean the day afore then," said the other, looking as if really a light had broken in upon him.

"Zounds! man, no! I mean within this last half hour, or so."

"What down along the road, aye."

"Yes."

"No'a I arn't a seen noa un; what be they like?"

"Why, highwaymen to be sure," exclaimed the coroner.

"Oh! ye doan't mean that; highwaymen! the Lord preserve us."

"Highwaymen!" exclaimed a shrill voice in the interior of the waggon; "Pringle, wake up, here's highwaymen," but the person addressed did not seem disposed to either move, or awake from the deep sleep in which he had evidently fallen, he only answered with a grunt, and then relapsed into his original state of somnulency.

"We have nothing, I assure you," said the female voice, peering out from the canvass awning which enclosed the waggon; "we are all wretchedly poor, I assure you," she continued, fully believing that the vehicle had been stopped by robbers of some sort; when upon observing our military friend, she gave a slight scream, and drawed her head in again.

"Quite safe, madam," said the individual, "you need not be under the least apprehension, I assure you."

By this time, two persons habited as countrymen, with that ungainly slouching walk, which is peculiar to the inhabitants of the rural districts, now made their appearance, coming along the road, they stared at the waggoner and the party of horsemen, in stupid surprise.

"Seen any horsemen pass, as you came along?" said the sheriff, with magisterial authority.

"Aye, sure, I should just think we have Baukins, eh?"

"E'es," was the answer, and the party addressed, grinned, as the saying is, all round his face.

"What description of men?" was the next question.

"Ah, they had nation good cattle that they were mounted on, and seemed to be masked."

"Masked! the devil! It is them, sure enough," exclaimed the military gentleman; "sure enough, which way were they going? where did you see them? eh?

"They were travelling round the road, which goe by farmer Ilford's five-acre field."

" Where is that, my friend ?"

" Oh, it lays at the back of the house, only you must go round to get at it."

" They've forced a passage through here, some how or other," said the sheriff. Whose mansion is this, my friend ?"

" The lord mayor's—Squire Gubbins."

" Is it possible ?" said the sheriff, as he bowed reverentially to the building.

" Well, let us waste no more time, but be after them ; I'll never give up the chase while my horse has a leg to stand on," exclaimed the military gentleman.

" Never ! come on my friends !"

" Perhaps you and your companion wouldn't mind showing us where you saw these horsemen," asked the sheriff of the two countrymen.'"

" Aye, surely," was the reply, " that un doe wi pleasure."

Away trudged the countrymen towards the rear of Squire Gubbin's house, while the waggon lazily proceeded on its journey, which the Lord willing, and weather permitting, it might reach London in a couple more days ; such my friend was the rate of progression of our forefathers ; happy son of mine to live in so fast an age as this, be thankful that you were not born when steam, gas,. and crinoline were unknown ; in those good old days, when gentlemen in big wigs, stiff buckram coats, knee breeches, with buckles and ruffles, were conveyed about by two stalwart fellows in a sedan chair ; when ladies wore hoops, beauty spots on either cheek, and indulged in the use of large fans ; when those watchful guardians of the night the "old Charlie's" were our only protectors.

The two countrymen accompanied their sporting companions, and pointed out the exact road taken by the highwaymen, when, after receiving a reward for the information, the party of horsemen galloped off at their utmost speed. As soon as they had got out of ear-shot the supposed countrymen burst out in a loud and uproarious fit of laughter.

" Well done, Warrington—admirably performed ; you'll be a great actor in time," exclaimed Colonel Jack, for the two countrymen were no other than our hero and his comrade, who had thus put their pursuers on the wrong scent. In the stable of the Mayor's house they had heard the discussion and altercation with the waggoner. The colonel soon made up his mind as to his course of action. The key of which he had become possessed opened another door belonging to the stable which led to the gardens in the rear of the house. To run across these vault, over the oak fence was the work of but a few moments to the colonel and his companion. Beyond this

was the heath, and here were encamped a tribe of gipsies, who were on excellent terms with the colonel ; betaking themselves to the tents of these pedatory class a sufficient disguise was furnished to the highwaymen for them to complete a perfect metamorphis in their appearance. The colonel and Warrington, the former of whom had tied up his long locks, and donned a flaxen wig ; they run round to the road through which the waggon had passed, and then walked leisurely along as though they had been chance wayfarers. It has been seen already how admirably their ruse had succeeded. After the departure of their sporting pursuers, the colonel betook himself again to the stable, saddled his horses, and trotted off to the heath, where he rejoined Hackett.

" It has answered admirably," he observed to the latter.

" So I imagined when I saw our legal and red-coated friends trot off so gaily," was the answer, accompanied by a burst of hearty laughter ; " what is our next proceeding ?"

" I think," answered the colonel, " that you had better at once proceed to town with the swag ; whilst myself and Warrington will do ourselves the pleasure of waiting to see if our friends return, for I must confess I should like to quietly observe their chagrin."

Then the matter was arranged, and Hackett went off to London in a handcanter. The colonel and Warrington partook of the fare provided for them by the gipsies, which they washed down with a cheering potation or two, and quietly waited the result. For a short time they had the satisfaction of observing from the interior of the gipsies' tent the party of horsemen return after a fruitless search for the fugitives. The colonel and Warrington indulged in an immoderate fit of laughter at the chap-fallen visage of their pursuers. They had now arrived at that period known as the small hours of the morning, so after the departure of the sheriff, coroner, and their sporting companions, the colonel and Warrington stretched themselves upon some rude couches which their friends provided for their accommodation, and slept the sleep of the weary.

CHAPTER II.

THE FASHIONABLE PHYSICIAN—THE NIGHT ATTACK—A DEED OF MYSTERY.

IN the aristocratic locality of Brook-street, Grosvenor-square, dwelt, at the time we write one Doctor Loftus Carruthers, famous for the extent of his practice, his aristocratic patients and his skill in pharmacy, surgery, and midwifery. Week in week out, ran the eminent Doctor Carruther's carriage rattling along the west-end of London, where notabilities most do congregate. The doctor himself was an easy going, sleek, elderly gentleman, whose whole time was devoted to curing or alleviating the ailments of suffering humanity.

He was a very prosperous gentleman, doing an extensive and profitable practice, and enjoyed a fame which was perhaps one of the highest in the profession. But a wearisome hard life is that of a medical man, however high his position, for him there is no repose, no cessation from the endless whirl of visits. On the night on which we are about to make his acquaintance the doctor had to attend a consultation upon a difficult and intrinsic case, an elderly gentleman residing in what was then the little village of Kilburn, had been a subject to attacks of the malady for many years of his life. In the last one of which a variety of other symptoms presented themselves, which were of such a conflicting character that his life was despared of. At the suggestion of a friend he determined upon calling upon two physicians to meet the country apothecary who had been attending him. One of these was the celebrated Doctor Loftus Carruthers— poor patient, if his constitution would hold out against three sons of Esculapius he must have been a most wonderful man indeed. Behold then Doctor Carruther's carriage journey down the Edgeware-road and proceed to a locality that to him appeared almost out of the world, for the doctor's practice was chiefly confined to the west-end of London, and he seldom ventured so far a field, save in especial cases as in the present instance. Nothing but a large retaining fee would have prevailed upon him to undertake the unpleasant task, for unpleasant it was to him, as he had a great repugnance to go out of his own particular circle. Wrapt in his own meditations the doctor rolled along in his carriage towards Kilburn, arrived there the consultation lasted some time, for the patient was rather irascable, and would insist upon detailing all his symptoms himself, after his medical attendant had already gone over the ground. The learned triumvirate shook their heads, looked wise, but were quite at a loss to comprehend the nature of the malady, although, of course, they took excellent care not to say so. The consultation over, the learned Doctor Carruthers esconsed himself in his carriage, and became deeply absorbed in a book of

science. The interior of his carriage was furnished with a light to enable him to peruse such works as he usually carried with him for the purpose of consultation, for in the days of which we write, the profession had not attained that degree of perfection which it has done by the aid of a few brilliant luminaries at the present period. The doctor's vehicle had arrived near to an old fashioned road side public house in Edgeware-road, near to where old Paddington Church now stands. It was then a deserted locality scarcely inhabited, save an occasional house here and there badly lighted or rather not lighted at all, and but few wayfarers on the road. The docter was aroused from his studies somewhat suddenly by the stoppage of his carriage. Outside all was darkness, for the night was getting late and no moon was visible in the heavens. The first intimation the doctor received, as to how affairs stood after the halting of the carriage, was the sight of a figure on horseback masked, who presented a pistol at his head, while in a deep toned masculine voice said in a determined tone.

"Doctor Loftus Carruthers, attempt to raise the slightest alarm, and you are a dead man."

He recoiled at the sight of the shining barrel which was made painfully distinct by the light in his carriage.

"What would you?" said the docter. Take what I have in welcome and let me pass on."

The figure by a gesture of his hand indicated that he did not desire his worldly wealth.

The doctor looked astonished and stared enquiringly at the mysterious stranger— who said, in answer to his looks of surprise,

"We do not want your gold, Doctor Carruthers. We want your skill and services; and these we must have."

"Nolens volens."

"Tell me how I can be useful?" answered the man of medicine.

"By passive obedience."

Mr. Carruthers bowed his head and said, "I suppose I am in your hands, gentlemen;" for by this time, he observed another figure similarly mounted, habited and masked.

The man who had spoken to him, now gave orders for the carriage to be driven down a bye-lane, which was immediately done, for the coachman had been already overpowered and pinioned, while one of those who had stopped the carriage, mounted the box and took charge of the reins. The vehicle halted some three or four hundred yards down the lane in question, which was situated where Church-street Paddington now stands. When the carriage again stopped, the first speaker again addressed its owner thus—

"Doctor Carruthers, you must consent to submit to such terms as I dictate."

The party addressed, bowed an affirmative.

"Your attendance is required in a case where secrecy, despatch, and skill are needed. You must consent to be driven by my companion to an appointed place blindfolded."

"Gracious heavens! What for? Would you murder me?"

"Certainly not, if you do my behest; but if you refuse, we certainly shall. Now, do you understand?"

Mr. Carruthers turned pale with fright. "Blindfolded!" he exclaimed.

"Yes. Upon no other terms can you be of service for what is required."

"Well, and what is expected of me?"

"That you will learn all in good time. But I pledge my word as a gentleman, and a man of honour, that no harm is intended you. That we shall convey you to a place where your services are required, as I before said, blindfolded. Having performed your mission, I promise, that we will convey you uninjured to your residence in Brook-street, Grosvenor-square. More than this, you shall be handsomely paid for your time."

"But, gentlemen—really——"

"No faltering, or else——" and the pistol was again presented at the head of the doctor.

"Oh! no—no; pray don't," he exclaimed, in fear and trepidation. "I will submit to your wishes—believe me I will without a murmur. What will they think of my absence at home," he continued, as the thought crossed his mind of the anxiety of his wife at his prolonged absence.

"That has already been provided for," answered the man, whose bearing was that of a superior person to a robber or highwayman. "We have already apprised your lady, Mrs. Carruthers, that you are detained by a dangerous case at some short distance from town, and consequently she will not be surprised at your absence. "Come, sir, we will proceed to business, if you please." And so without further parley, the speaker and his companions proceeded to blindfold the trembling doctor; which being accomplished, one of the man's comrades placed himself on the opposite seat to the medical man, and kept guard over his actions, while the two horsemen rode beside the windows of the carriage.

While all this was taking place, the doctor's coachman, who was an old man that he had had in his service for more than a quarter of a century, was taken from the box, and carried off under the escort of two of the attacking party towards the doctor's own residence. When after conveying the old coachman for a mile or two on the road, they unloosed him, and bid him make what haste he could home; and at the same time, charged him to keep a still tongue respecting the whole transaction, or it would be worse for him: but more particularly, not to mention the circumstance to either his mistress or any of the household.

After the departure, the doctor was driven along the Edgeware road, when arrived at its termination, his conductors took that road by the side of the park, which leads to where Bayswater now stands; all this however, at the time these circumstances took place, was waste ground and fields. Rumble, rumble went the carriage, and to its unfortunate owner's imagination, it appeared to have already gone miles and miles, when in point of fact, it had as yet only reached Kensington gravel pits. But few words were spoken, and these were only in whispers, and the doctor could not possibly divine the road he was being driven, he however, made up his mind to passively submit to the wishes of those who had made him their prisoner; in all his professional experience, he had never met with so terrible a drama, in which he now found himself a prominent, although certainly most unwilling actor.

Past Kensington gravel pits, along that dreary road which runs to shepherd's bush, dreary enough now, but doubly wretched at this period; along this gloomy road did the carriage of the west end phisician take its way. To its owner the time appeared an age, for he was in a state of miserable suspense, as to what would be the result of the night's proceeding, and his own ultimate fate; dark suspicions crossed his mind, but he knew himself to be utterly helpless, and entirely at the mercy of his gloomy and taciturn conductors; the slightest movement of his hand, towards the bandage which blindfolded him, called forth an exclamation of discontent, from him who sat opposite to him in the carriage, and the doctor crossed his arms in passive obedience.

This night's proceedings served him to talk about for the remainder of his life; they were sufficiently mysterious in themselves, but to him awful, but the darkest night has a dawn—the longest day has an end, and the occupant of the carriage found some relief, from the fact of the vehicle coming to a halt, be it for good or for ill, he supposed he should soon know his fate.

When his conductors came to a full stop in their course, the man who had been spokesman from the first, directed him to alight, politely informing him, that he need be under no apprehension of coming harm, for that he would soon now know, for what purpose he had been conveyed hither.

The person who had been his companion in the carriage now took his hand and guided him out of the vehicle, when, upon alighting upon the ground, he found himself taken by each arm and guided by two persons as conductors. He heard the sound of a deep-toned bell, which he supposed belonged to some mansion into which he was about to be conducted; and he heard, at the same time, the distant barking of some large dog, which, from its note, suggested to his mind that the animal was in all probability of the mastiff breed. Such thoughts will run in the head at times without our being able to account for the same. He then heard the unbarring of some ponderous bolts or locks, upon which his progression was hastened forward by his two conductors; he then found himself, as he supposed to be, on a gravel walk, and heard the tramp of the horsemen who had accompanied him following immediately behind; he also heard the sound of voices in a subdued tone, which he supposed to be addressed to some domestics of the establishment, for he heard their replies given in strange voices to the questions. Arriving at the end of this walk he ascended a short flight of, what he supposed to be, stone steps; after which he traversed, what he imagined to be, the hall of the mansion—then down some half-dozen more steps, which were wood this time—then through some apartment—then along some winding passage, when another and longer flight of steps had to be ascended; having accomplished this another passage was passed through, then more steps, when he imagined himself to enter an apartment, for his guides directed him to halt, and gently released their hold, when the same voice which had previously spoken addressed him thus:—

"Doctor Carruthers, perhaps the most painful part of this night's proceedings, as far as you are concerned, is past. I now require one other favour of you—"

"What may that be, sir?" asked the doctor.

"It is necessary to fulfil properly the duty which has been assigned to me for you to take an oath, and that, too, a solemn one—that you will not divulge to any living soul the purpose for which you have been brought here."

"I do not know it myself yet," he answered.

"No; but you will; and it is, therefore, for that reason that I require you to bind yourself to a solemn oath."

"I certainly object to bind myself to what I am at present in utter ignorance of. Really I think it is too much to ask of anyone. If your purposes are honourable, why this secrecy?"

"That is our business. Only you must bind yourself by the required abjuration."

The doctor hesitated. He then felt the cold muzzle of a pistol presented to his temple, as the holder thereof called out in an angry voice—"Swear! Unless you hold your life so cheaper, that——"

"Oh, dear, yes; I'll swear," answered the man of science. "Tell me what you wish me to say, and I will at once obey you."

"We require you to swear by your hope of peace hereafter, never to divulge whatever may take place here, or the purpose for which you have been brought hither."

"I will swear of course," answered the doctor, hesitatingly; "but I make an entry of all my transactions in a day, and——"

"Well, you can put in attended Foots for a sore throat; that would be a plaster to your conscience. No one need know who Foots is—a very respectable man no doubt."

Several of the man's companions laughed at the latter observation. When the doctor said—

"Oh! then there is a patient in the question?"

"Certainly, else why should we have brought you here?"

The doctor took the required oath. Upon which, he was conducted by his guides for several yards further, then he ascended a few more steps, descended again two or three more, and after then, he felt beneath his tread something soft as though he were walking over a thick carpet, which was in reality the case. He then came to a halt, and the bandage which had so successfully blindfolded him, was taken from off his eyes. It is hardly possible to describe the relief he felt, when this act was accomplished; but still at the same time, he felt the sudden rays of the light dazzling to his vision. He stared round in some surprise. He found himself in an elegantly furnished apartment, the deeply twined windows with their diamoned panes of glass of many hues, gave to the place a monastic appearance. The walls were hung with costly tapestry, and all the appointments gave evidence of material wealth. At the farther end of the room, which was of very large dimensions, the doctor observed a bed, the hangings of which were lace over blue satin. Situated as he was, where he at present stood, he could not see the occupant thereof, but he was made acquainted with the fact of there being some one there by the groans and moans he heard as of a female in pain. As he took a second glance, as his eyes become more accustomed to the light, he observed an elderly female moving about near to the bed-side of the patient. As the doctor's eye met hers, she came forward and dropped a low curtsey.

"This is the gentleman who will attend upon your mistress," said the man who had brought the doctor to the home in question; "you will remember, Bridget, to obey all the instructions you have received, and, above all, not to——"

He did not finish his sentence, but nodded significantly to the old nurse, for such in reality she was. She seemed to understand his meaning, for respectfully addressing the doctor she said in a mild voice—

"Will it please you, kind gentleman, to see my poor mistress, for she is at present in great suffering?" and with these words she led the way to the bed-side of the patient.

Mr. Carruthers started in astonishment as he observed a slender female stretched upon a costly bed, but his surprise was increased when he observed that she was masked, so that her features were not recognizable, except a small delicately-formed chin, a pair of ruby lips disclosing a set of pearly teeth of dazzling whiteness. Mr. Carruthers observed her eyes look through the holes in the mask, and stare upon him with an enquiring expression; she was evidently in great pain, as he judged from her moans and uneasy movements, but wherefore was the mask worn upon her features. Altogether events so thickened in their mystery that our learned son of Esculapius was well nigh distracted with the startling incidents. The nurse, Bridget, informed the doctor of her mistress's state, and he, with his accustomed skill, proceeded to meet the exigencies of the case. Whilst performing his professional duties he was left in the apartment with no other occupants but the patient herself and Dame Bridget. Doctor Carruthers thought it would be imprudent to ask any more questions of the nurse than those which were absolutely necessary. In a short time, after much suffering, the lady gave birth to a fine boy. A child brought into the world under such extraordinary circumstances struck the doctor as something ominous; he felt that he was being made the instrument of some species of deception or chicanery, the nature of which it was impossible for his imagination to conceive, or his mind suggest some double dealing, he

did not for a moment doubt was being practised; his own professional experience as well as that of his brethren, did not furnish a parallel for such a case.

"It will be necessary for you to see my mistress again, I suppose?" said Dame Bridget to the doctor.

The latter hesitated, looked at the patient, and, motioning her to hold out her arm, he felt her pulse. He watched the beatings of life's current, while his eye glanced towards the form and face of the patient. Something attracted his notice; with an involuntary exclamation he said, in a half-suppressed tone, but still loud enough to be heard all over the apartment, while his cheek blanched, and a tremour shook his frame,

"Gracious heavens—the lady!——" he paused just in time, perhaps, for his hair lifted itself up in perfect horror, and his blood seemed curdled as he beheld the figure of a tall man emerge from a deep recess which he had not before observed; so sudden, mysterious, and noiseless was the appearance of this figure, that to the doctor's bewildered imagination he appeared to have sprung from the air. He, too, was masked; he said in a solemn repulsive voice,

"Doctor Loftus Carruthers!"

The party addressed stared in mute surprise, and indeed, so great was his astonishment, that his faculties seemed to be for the time suspended, and the power of volition denied him; he was, however, recalled to a sense of his own position by the new comer, motioning him with his hand to come forward, the doctor obeyed the summons, when the other pointed to a dark passage, which was only lighted by the moon's rays, through a stained glass oriel window. The mysterious visitor had in his manner, something which was in itself so imperious and commanding, that the doctor found himself following him in mute silence, without precisely knowing why or wherefore; at the end of the passage, there was a carved massive oak door, the masked individual opened this, and pointing in gloomy silence for the other to enter first, upon which he closed it with a loud slam, and the doctor found himself alone with his mysterious visitant, in an apartment which appeared something like the library of the establishment; his companion motioned him to a seat at the end of the room, where a bright cheerful fire was burning; the furniture in the room was what might have been termed massive, old-fashioned, gloomy and grand; however, the doctor took one of the ponderous high-backed chairs, and seated himself thereon, in obedience to the other's offer; his companion

seated himself immediately opposite him, and leaning his chin upon one hand, while his elbow rested upon the library table, he said, staring at the doctor with a pair of hawk-like eyes, which peered through his mask, simply these words—

"Lady,———who?"

"Sir," stammered forth the doctor, who withered beneath the basalisk gaze of his tormentor.

No. 3.

"Lady—who?" again said the other, without moving a muscle of his face or body.

"I beg your pardon, but I thought—that is I supposed the patient resembled—that is, it was in all probability only a supposition—resembled some one I attended years ago."

"Indeed, sir, your faculties of perception are something marvellous, but that is not lady anything, that you have been attending, but simply a poor peasant girl, whom I have befriended, and consequently I wish to conceal her shame from the eyes of a too curious world; hence this mystery, and your attendance."

"Oh, said the accoucher, I understand clearly;" he did nothing of the sort, but he thought it best to keep quiet upon the subject.

"How does your patient?" asked the other.

"I think she bids fair to go on rightly enough," was the response.

"There will be no need of further attendance, I suppose."

"Umph, I am hardly prepared to say at present."

"Do you know where you are?"

"No, sir."

"Have not the slightest idea?"

"Not the faintest notion."

"And that lady."

"Who?"

"Ah! I mean—the lady—who—doctor —eh?"

The other winced under the searching gaze of the man in the mask, but made no reply.

"Doctor Carruthers I know you, as is sufficiently evident, and I am not a man to be trifled with; that lady whom you have but just left, is, you think, of gentle blood— eh?"

"I do not know — I thought" — he stammered and hesitated, for he observed the kindling force in the other's eye as this subject was broached--"I thought she resembled an old patient of mine; but of course I am mistaken. I see so many in the course of my career, that I must be pardoned if sometimes I trace an imaginary likeness, which after all is likely to be erroneous, as in this instance it seems."

"S' death man! likeness? indeed you have not seen her features. Have you— eh?"

"Ah! no—no—no—indeed I have not."

"Swear it!" said the other sententiously, as he laid down a pistol upon the library table with a heavy sound. "Swear it, sir."

"I do most solemnly——"

"What was the name of this patient of yours?"

"What?"

"The one you imagined this lady resembled."

"Lady Reichbeck."

This questioner started to his feet and seemed moved in no ordinary degree. He paced the apartment with hasty strides, then paused and looked again mysteriously at the doctor.

"Reichbeck; I have heard of such a name. Yes, of course, from the Rudhall family. Well, sir," he said, as he came to a full stop before the doctor, and endeavoured to look him through as the common saying is.

"What!"

"Ah! what? You are mistaken that is all. If you blab or tell any absurd story about this night's proceedings; nay, more, if you ever mention the fact casually to any of your extensive circle of acquaintance, I swear by the Lord above, that you will be found a lifeless corpse either in your own house or carriage before three days are past over your head. I swear it." And here he uttered an oath which we do not think it worth while committing to paper, suffice is it that it was terrible in its earnestness; and the doctor was doubly appalled at his situation, and the unpleasant circumstances in which he found himself so unpleasantly mixed up.

"Do you understand me, Doctor Loftus Carruthers? I have agents in all parts. It is impossible for you to escape me if I am once betrayed—a terrible revenge will follow, as surely as you are here present."

The doctor looked at the speaker with an expression of fear upon his good-natured features. There was that in the man's manner which left no doubt about the certainty of his carrying his threats into execution.

"For the future I am mute upon this subject, and all the incidents of this night. They are, to say the truth, anything but agreeable ones to reflect upon, and I should, therefore, wish to bury them in oblivion. You have no right to fear respecting me; I have no wish to pry into your secrets, all I desire is safe escort home as speedily as possible."

"Good!" answered the other; "spoken like a discreet man. What am I indebted to you, Doctor Carruthers?"

"Nothing; I have not come here upon my own free will and shall not make any charge for my attendance. I assure you I I shall be sufficiently thankful to be permitted to again reach my own domicile in safety."

A silver bell was touched by he whom the doctor supposed to be the master of the establishment, and a servant in livery appeared. Wine and refreshments were ordered, and shortly placed upon the table, which were offered to the doctor, who declined to partake of anything.

A dark shade of suspicion crossed the features of the master of the house as his guest declined. He poured himself out a glass of wine, pledged his companion, and drank off the contents.

"You need be under no apprehensions," he said, coldly; "of drinking with me, we are not poisoners here."

The doctor drew back a pace or two, and looked at the speaker, and then said somewhat more assured,

"Such a thought, sir, did not cross my mind. You do me an unjustice, believe me; to prove which I shall have the pleasure of drinking your very good health," saying which he drank up a glass of the liquor. The stranger bowed courteously.

"If I thought, Doctor Carruthers, that you intended to play me false, I, to deal frankly with you, would not allow you to leave this house alive."

There was something so cool in the manner in which these words were uttered that the unfortunate doctor found all his worst fears again aroused. It was with considerable difficulty that he was enabled to put anything like a bold face upon the matter.

"I do pray you, sir, to believe in my sincerity. I have been brought hither for a certain purpose, that being accomplished, I neither seek to enquire, or care to know further about the matter——"

"Enough, so be it then; your resolution is a wise one."

The speaker stamped his feet upon the oak flooring of the room, the sound of which reverberated in the vaulted apartment; and in a few seconds the masked figures who had accompanied him on his journey appeared. The owner of the mansion pointed to the wine, and they all partook of the proffered refreshment in silence.

A conversation then took place in a whisper at the farther end of the room, out of the doctor's hearing. After which, the two men who had been his guides, proceeded to again blindfold him, and shortly afterwards, he was borne under their guidance out of the room. As he emerged from the door, the voice of the owner of the mansion was heard calling to him—

"Remember your oath, Mr. Carruthers."

"I shall not forget, sir; you may depend upon my discretion," was the reply.

"Good night, sir."

"Good night," was the doctor's ready rejoinder, too glad to be quit of his gloomy and mysterious employer.

His guides seemed to be conducting him a different way to the one which they had previously taken, for to judge by his previous sensations, the road did not, to his imagination, present the same features. He, however, was made aware of his safe egress from the house by the fresh night air blowing upon his feverish and throbbing temples. He again heard the deep bark of the mastiff, or such as he supposed to be one; and he heard also the stamping of the horses' feet outside the gateway of the mansion. With what joy did he find himself again an occupant of his own carriage —or what he supposed to be such, for after all it was only a conjecture. He, however, was fully aware that another occupant was in the carriage besides himself, in all probability, the same one who had accompanied him on his journey, for he seemed to be as cautious as ever, and the doctor was not disposed to break the silence, for he became lost in the contemplation of the whole mysterious circumstances of the extraordinary transaction in which he had played so conspicuous a part. The carriage rolled on at a rapid pace, and the passage back did not seem nearly so tedious as it did upon his first being taken to the unknown locality. When it had arrived at the top of Piccadilly there was a halt. The door of the vehicle was opened; a head was thrust in, and some orders were given to the man inside, who was the doctor's companion. In another minute Mr. Carruthers found himself released from the bandage which had so effectually blindfolded him, and he was enabled to observe that he was not very far from his own residence, felicitating himself upon the circumstance he turned towards the individual who had opened the door, and who seemed from his manner to be in command of the equipage.

"We shall leave you now, Doctor Carruthers," observed the man, "and I am desired by my principal to thank you for your services, and, at the same time, to give you the enclosed;" presenting, as he spoke, a small paper package, which the doctor took in silence. "You will be driven by one of my companions safe home to your residence, and I caution you not to endeavour to detain him, or make any unnecessary inquiries, or it will be worse for you. Good night;" and, with these words, he slammed the door, and the vehicle drove off at a rapid pace.

As it proceeded, the doctor's curiosity prompted him to open the paper which the man had placed in his hands. He found it to contain a fifty-pound note, which he immediately transferred to his pocket-book. Shortly afterwards he had the gratification of seeing his carriage stop at his own door. A loud knock and a violent ring at the night bell was given, and, when the man-servant came out with extended eyes to let his master in, no one besides the doctor was seen on or near the carriage in question.

Doctor Carruthers was true to his word, or rather the oath, which he had taken.

He maintained an impenetrable silence as to all the events of the night, although the whole circumstances preyed upon his mind, and continually harassed him whenever, in those periods of which were but few and far between, he reflected upon the mysterious events. There was one circumstance which troubled him considerably—that was the discovery, or supposed clue to the identity, of the lady whom he had attended. The reader will remember his involuntary exclamation when by the bedside of the patient. This was occasioned by his observing the mark on the thick part of her arm—it was the cicutrix of a wound which had been by all probability healed for some years. Nevertheless its position and form was remarkable, and the doctor remembered to have operated many years previously upon a lady of title for cancer in the arm, and from the position and form of the cicutrix he did not doubt but that the masked lady in question was the same individual. Hence his involuntary exclamation; and hence, also, the sudden and mysterious appearance of the masked figure from a recess in the apartment. All these circumstances troubled the doctor the more he reflected upon them; but in the continual whirl of his professional practice, and the gradual progression of time the circumstances lost a good deal of their intensity, and were only recurred to occasionally, as some trifling event like a faint glimmer would light up a recollection of the past.

It will be necessary now to return to the mansion where the strange scene already described was enacted.

In the village of Acton, lying a few hundred yards out of the main road, there stood an old, substantial, brick building, or custellated mansion. Its grounds, park, and meadow-land were altogether on an extensive scale. It was the country seat, or rather one of the country seats of Sir Richard Fleetwood, Bart. Here it was, then, that the scene we have described was enacted; and, for the better understanding and elucidation thereof, we must hasten to another chapter.

CHAPTER III.

SCENE IN THE LIBRARY—SIR RICHARD FLEETWOOD AND HIS LAWYER, THEIR DIABOLICAL PLOT — INTERVIEW WITH COLONEL JACK.

AFTER the departure of Doctor Carruthers from the mansion, Sir Richard Fleetwood, its owner, who was now unmasked, paced the apartment which was known as the library, with uneasy strides. He was apparently lost in deep meditation, as with folded arms and knitted brows, his looks were bent on the oak floor, which was, however, in the centre, covered with a thick matting. Having continued in his reflective mood for some time he made a sudden pause, after which he walked to the library table and touched a silver bell. In a few seconds a domestic appeared, when his master said, with some suddenness—

"Tell Mr. Sharpthorne I desire his presence;" the man disappeared, and in a few minutes a little old man, dressed in a suit of rusty black, made his appearance. He bowed obsequiously as he rubbed the palms of his hands together, and a hideous grin showed itself on his wrinkled parchment features.

"So far all progresses well, Sir Richard Fleetwood," said the lawyer, for such in reality was Mr. Sharpthorne.

"I suppose so," was the reply of his employer.

"A child has seen the light?" asked the other, as a still more sardonic grin distorted his fox-like visage.

"Yes, sit down." The lawyer obeyed in silence, looking up at his employer to see what next was to follow, with that peculiar stealthy glance which was habitual to him. Sir Richard did not, however, seem communicative, and was, for a minute or two, apparently unconscious of the presence of the attorney.

"Are—our—are our friends gone?" asked the latter, in a sort of supercilious whisper.

"No! They are down stairs having refreshment."

"Ah! ah! I see," exclaimed the man of parchments, in a still small voice. "How is Lady Fleetwood?" he enquired again, after another pause.

"Well, I believe quite well; that is, as well as can be expected under the circumstances."

"And the child?"

"Seems a fine healthy one, so Bridget says."

"Umph!"

"Well—what?" said the baronet, as he turned sharply round upon the speaker, and looked him in the face.

"Oh! nothing, Sir Richard, nothing. Only it must be cared for, that's all," answered the lawyer, in accents half husky and half oleagenous.

"Unquestionably; and that as soon as possible, I suppose."

"Ye—es. It's likely to live, I suppose?"

"S'death! man. How do I know? I suppose so."

"Ah! you suppose so. I see."

"It's a matter of doubt, of course, when life is so young in the frame; but the child appears healthy. That is all we can tell at present."

"What are the next proceedings, Sir Richard?" asked his companion, as he continued to rub and squeeze his hands as though he were kneeding therefrom some choice rare idea. "Must be put out to nurse, I suppose, eh?"

Mr. Sharpthorne quickly wetted his forefinger with his tongue, with which he moistened a spot of dirt or grease upon the cuff of his coat; and then with his nail began to remove the same in a quiet reflective manner, while he seemed as though he were ruminating to himself.

"Yes—put out to nurse under the name of—let me see, suppose we say, Girdley. Yes, that would do I dare say, or any other equally euphoneous. It might be in infancy children are soon carried off. It might die you know; and have a grand funeral from —ah, let me see—here, for instance."

"What do you mean?" asked Sir Richard, with some warmth. "It might die! of course it might; so may you or I. What of that?"

"Why, then——" he paused, and looked up at the baronet through his spectacles from under his thick grey eyebrows, and said, in continuation —"And then you know there would be no further trouble in the matter."

It was not exactly the words he had uttered, although they were suggestive and significant enough in themselves under the circumstances of the case, but it was the manner of the man which struck the baronet, that he started back a pace or two, and looked with a severe expression of countenance upon the speaker for some seconds.

"There would be no further trouble to us. No, perhaps, not. What then."

"Oh, nothing, Sir Richard," answered the other, as he placed his hands between his two knees, and began to chafe them still more vigorously. "Nothing, only certainly there would be a complete end of the matter then."

The baronet looked at the speaker as a hightened colour suffused his features, and a curl of scorn was observable on his lip.

"An end of the matter I should suppose so, Mr. Sharpthorne." Most assuredly. What then, sir?"

The lawyer nodded, and went through some pantomime evolution with his hands and arms, nay, with his whole body. The baronet turned pale now as he observed the others movements.

"If you mean, Mr. Sharpthorne——" —he paused, as though unwilling to proceed further, and then continued, more firmly—"If you mean, sir, to suggest the destruction of my brother's child——"

Oh, no, no—no! my dear Sir Richard. Pray do not suppose me capable of such a suggestiou," exclaimed the other, as he saw a gathering storm on the features of his employer.

"You had some such thought, sir, I do verily believe," answered Sir Richard, still in angry accents.

"I should be sorry if my meaning were misinterpreted," answered the attorney, mildly, now looking at the buttons of his long plush waistcoat, and brushing therefrom some stray dust. "Very sorry with so excellent a gentleman and client as yourself. I was merely making a chance remark, and must ask pardon if my words were deemed offensive. All has been I think managed with caution and complete decision. Bridget, we know, can be relied on. The doctor does not, I suppose, know either the place or the name or position of the parties for whom he has attended: and our friends below?"

"Do not know for what purpose he was required," answered the baronet."

"All is then as we could desire. Lady Fleetwood will not object to part with the child, I suppose?"

"She must!" was the curt answer.

"Ah! true she must; that is certain. Well, then you have nought to fear. Of course, it will be well taken care of, and in the due course of time, be placed in a good position. What more can be required? Nothing!" and again the man of parchments began to kneed his hands.

"Mr. Sharpthorne," said Sir Richard Fleetwood, solemnly, and with an air of considerable dignity, "it is at your suggestion this course has been adopted; not a pleasant one or a particularly honorable one perhaps; but——"

"But the only alternative left under the circumstances,—I believe the only one," chimed in the party addressed, as he gazed like a lynx at his questioner.

"Possibly so, at any rate it is now adopted, and our future proceedings must be in consonance to the course of action we have chosen out for ourselves."

"It is certainly too late now to retract."

"Lady Fleetwood," said the baronet, "is fully persuaded that the marriage of my late brother with herself was a mock ceremony; but at any rate she possesses no proof of such a marriage having taken place; consequently she thinks the child is illegitimate. Let her remain in happy ignorance of the same to the end of the chapter."

"Amen!" said the lawyer, assuming a solemnity upon the occasion. "But there are proofs, nevertheless, you know—but they will never reach her, and even if they did, the proof of this child's birth can never now be established, that is, assuming that she wished to put forward a claim, which under the circumstances is not at all probable, for poor dear lady she seems of a gentle compliant nature." He uttered this last sentence with a degree of mock pathos which would have told well at one of our metropolitan theatres. "Consequently you will find I think, Sir Richard, that the course I have advised has been a wise one, however repugnant it may have at first appeared to yourself."

The baronet bowed his acquiescence, and the speaker continued, as he placed the ends of his fingers together while demonstrating the position.

"Your brother, Sir Reginald Fleetwood, has left behind him papers proving the legality of his marriage, and also other documents connected with Reichbeck property and estates. This I have good reason to know, but where those papers are now I am at present unable to say; but they must and shall be found. I have, as you are already informed, set two knowing hands, Grime and Flimby, at work to ferret them out. If it is possible to light upon them they are the men who will do so. Once in possession of those we may defy everything."

"Yes," answered Sir Richard Fleetwood, in evident impatience, "but without them——"

"Well," answered the lawyer, who let fall his words like drops of cold water, "even without them the identity of the heir can never be established seeing that there will be no proofs of its birth, no proof of its identity. Another name is assumed, and as years advance, which they soon do, Sir Richard—which they soon do." Here he shook his head prophetically. "The difficulties will amount then to an impossibility, if they are not already so. Sir Reginald was cut off suddenly; if not in the flower of his youth, in the full flush of his manhood. I say he was cut off so suddenly, and under the circumstances attending upon this run away marriage, there is little left behind as evidence. He was a different man to you, Sir Richard," said Mr. Sharpthorne, contemplating the party he was addressing in a meditative manner, as the baronet turned away from his gaze.

"Yes," continued the lawyer, "he was a very different man—ingenuous, trusting, headstrong, perhaps, and with but little notion of the business affairs of the world. He was hurried on by his feelings and passions, believing all that men said as truth: his was what I call a trustful nature; but when men have seen as much as I have they will be mistrustful of even their own especial friends or relatives."

Sir Richard turned at these observations.

"Lady Fleetwood," continued the same cold and business like tone he had assumed throughout, "will not object to the course, I suppose?"

"Oh! no, I should say not."

"Ah! that is well; she, too, is trusting."

"She is gentle," answered the other, "and as you have pointed out to her the wisdom of the course she is adopting, why I do not imagine she will depart from it now, however great a pang it may cause her."

"Yes, she has confidence in me, poor dear lady," answered Mr. Sharpthorne with an hypocritical sigh, "great confidence, poor soul," and he looked up to the ceiling as though he expected some cherub to appear and approve of his proceedings and sentiments.

"I will see the colonel," observed Sir Richard Fleetwood to his companion. "It will be as well, perhaps, that I should bring him in here, as a word or two from you may serve to——"

"Precisely," answered the other. "Let me see him by all means; I should wish to do so."

The baronet then left the library to seek out our hero, who was in a room on the basement of the house with his companions, partaking of Sir Richard's good cheer.

"So, ah! Sir Richard Fleetwood," soliloquised Mr. Sharpthorne, "you want those papers, do you; so do I; when they are once obtained they can be sold to the highest bidder. I wonder whether that scoundrelly valet really did part with them as he says. The fellow is such an inherent scoundrel, and so incorrigible a liar that it is impossible to put any trust in a word he says; Grimes and Flimby have augres at work— I've promised them a handsome reward, and sooner or later I shall have them in my hands, and then——. Ah! we shall see after that. We shall see. When once in my possession they are mine till I see justice done. Justice! what am I saying?— bah! always that word when we have our own interests to serve. Justice, forsooth, and to whom I wonder? Let me see Lady Reichbeck's property and estates ought by right to go into that lady's own family; but they never will. Ah, ah, no never! Then there is this child; in common justice he ought to have the baronetcy if he lives, but he never will. While the plot thickens—becomes more and more entangled—some day or other I shall have to unravel it—very likely."

"Mr. Sharpthorne, allow me to introduce you to Colonel Jack," while at the same time the baronet ushered in the last mentioned personage. The lawyer rose from his seat, adjusted his spectacles, and gazed curiously at the highwayman. They were quite a contrast, the two, the lawyer and the lawless. The former with his slender form, shrunken limbs, and shrivelled features, and the latter of whom was the very personification of manly daring. His fine proportions were set off in the gentlemanly habiliments of the period. His long flowing hair fell in natural curls on his shoulders, and his countenance was open and frank in its expression, although perhaps there was something of the roué in its character. Colonel Jack, as he entered with the baronet, was accompanied by his inseparable companion, his dog Slott. This canine quadruped almost deserves a chapter to himself. He was an animal who appeared to think he was playing an important part in the world. So he was in the select circle in which he moved. There was a haughty independent bearing about him which seemed to say that he was not to be trifled with. It was not, nor never had been his custom to play with other dogs in a loose desultory manner; he appeared to think that he had a mission. He was right; and a very important one it was to his master. As he entered the baronet's library he was a study. He held up his head as he stretched out his fore legs, which were bowed, and came from a chest of wide and ample dimensions, and pricked up his ears as though he were master of the place, and was desirous by a rapid survey to make himself acquainted with the occupants of the apartment. I am sure if he could have spoken, his words would have been short and sententious—there would be nothing superfluous about his observations. He was a grave animal, and seemed very chary of making new acquaintances. He seldom indulged in great demonstrations of joy, even towards his master, whose very look, however, he seemed to comprehend and appreciate. Amongst his own kind—that is his fellow dogs—he might have been considered a misanthrope, or rather a cynic—a veritable canine Diogenes. If annoyed by them beyond endurance, he would let them know by one sharp, angry growl, that they had gone to the length of their tether; and as he was an animal who certainly did not stand upon trifles, and had such a mouth of such terrible dimensions, furnished with a

set of teeth which could find their way through a bullock's tanned hide, those animals who fell in his way were cautious in their dealings with him, although no doubt treated him either as a bully or a churl. Perhaps the only being he was patient with beyond his master, were children; these he would allow to tease him with impunity, seldom or ever evincing impatience with those who might chance to test his forbearance.

I am convinced he knew well his master's occupation, and gloried in it; and am equally confirmed that should the colonel have the misfortune some day or other to be placed in the dock of the Old Bailey, to take his trial for stopping the Balleraggon stage, or Lord Loftanrour's carriage, an injustice would be done him if he was not placed beside him for the same purpose. In his attacks he never gave notice by a bark. Oh, no! he was too business-like a quadruped for that; but when he did bite, it was what our transatlantic brethren would term a *screecher*.

When his eyes lighted upon the lawyer he cocked up his nose and assumed a most contemptuous expression of countenance. Lawyer persons, and all gentlemen of that description, he held in sovereign contempt, and he showed by the expression of his countenance, for he certainly had an expression which to say the truth was anything but amiable or becoming to its character. As to his eyes they were always red and bloodshot; and as to his nose, it was short and snuffy. His tail, too, was short, and stuck out defiantly. In fact, all his characteristics were suggestive of defiance. His coat consisted of a dirty white, the hems of which run in all sorts of ways, for he certainly did not take much pains with it, being a brute who did not think it worth while to sacrifice to the graces. He was a character! the colonel's dog; and I am convinced dogs have characters, and very wicked ones too. The lawyer did not seem prepossessed in his favour, for he eyed him with no very pleasant glances: he hated dogs of every description, and the present one in particular. Nevertheless he bowed several times towards Colonel Jack, as though he were desirous of propitiating men.

"This is the gentleman," observed Sir Richard, addressing himself to Sharpthorne, "to whom I am beholden for the appearance of Doctor Carruthers here this night. It was through his boldness and skilful management that we have been enabled to avail ourselves of the Doctor's invaluable services. —*nolens volens*."

"Sir Richard has cause to thank you, sir," answered Sharpthorne, in his most oily accents. "You see in consequence of a quarrel of no ordinary nature Doctor Carruthers had determined upon never visiting the family again. It was a foolish and unjust resolve perhaps, but so it was."

"So Sir Richard informed me," answered Colonel Jack, "my principle is that when a man will not give what is desired of him, my usual practice is to make him."

"Ah! ah! ah!" laughed the attorney in well-feigned mirth; "an excellent practice—too excellent! Ah! ah! Well, in this instance, it has been most especially advantageous, for the lady who is now so dangerously ill, had made up her mind that had Doctor Carruthers failed to have seen her or given his advice, she of a surety would die. It may be fancy. I don't say it is or not, nor do I altogether say it is, for with a nervous patient the slightest thing will produce a mischievous effect, and we have all our prejudices, you know; and really under the circumstances of the case, I thought it advisable for Sir Richard Fleetwood to adopt the course he has; and in my opinion a very justifiable one it is—for where life is at stake—and particularly the life of a beloved relative, it is pardonable to swallow a few scruples. I do not use the word scruples in a mechanical sense—in a moral one—rather. Eh! eh!" and the lawyer laughed, as though he had actually tumbled over a piece of wit. "Not that I am, as a general principle, justifying brute force to attain our ends," he put in as a demurrer to the proposition he had just propounded."

"Sir Richard Fleetwood has needed my services for a certain purpose, which I hope has been effected to his satisfaction," answered Colonel Jack, who, with all the lawyers sophistry, plainly saw that he was endeavouring to throw a blind over the transaction. "If, continued the highwayman, I have performed my mission satisfactorily, that is all that is needed, and I neither desire or care to know the object of the doctor's visit."

"No, no, certainly not!" answered Sharpthorne, who, man of the world as he was, plainly saw that the other was not to be blinded by his specious tale so readily as he had imagined.

"I suppose," he continued, addressing himself to the colonel, "that the night's proceeding is in full confidence between ourselves—I mean that there will be no blabbers."

"Oh dear, no. Both myself and my companions have always discretion enough to keep things dark. We have too much practice at that sort of game to *blow* the *gaff*. First because we are of a retiring disposition, and have no desire to occupy a prominent position," answered the colonel with a smile.

"Ah! ah! I suppose not!" laughed the lawyer.

A large roll of notes were now counted out on the library table by Sir Richard Fleetwood, which the colonel examined carefully, and then transferred to his breast pocket; and making a graceful bow to the lawyer, Colonel Jack left the apartment, accompanied by Sir Richard Fleetwood, who courteously saw him and his companions mount their horses, and in a few minutes their hoofs were heard clattering along the hard Acton Road towards London. Sir Richard watched them till they were lost to sight, and then returned again to his library—still in a ruminating mood.

"A bold man!" said Sharpthorne, as the baronet entered, "but doomed some day or other to a hempen noose, I suppose. Such men are useful though, at times. Where did you meet with him, Sir Richard?"

"I did him a good service many years ago," was the answer, "before he was what he is now, and the fellow has not forgotten it. He possesses gratitude, and has his feelings, despite the lawless life he is at present leading."

"Ah, I suppose so," answered his companion, as he still continued to clean the cuff of his coat with his nail. "So have we all, even to the most debased: there's some touch of human nature left in the most hardened. Have known him a long time then?"

"Well, yes. On and off."

Ah! Sharpthorne was curious to ascertain the particulars; but, well accustomed as he was to endeavour to interpret and read the thoughts of men by their countenances, he saw very plainly that this was a subject upon which the baronet was in no humour to be communicative, and, although his curiosity had become aroused, he abstained from pressing his companion further upon the subject.

The incident detailed of Doctor Carruther's visit is not a fable or fiction. Such an one did actually occur in the neighbourhood of London many years ago. A doctor's carriage was stopped, its owner taken therefrom, and forced to attend upon a sick or dying person. The perpetrators of this outrage, were, however, brought to justice, and received a heavy sentence.

———

CHAPTER IV.

THE SCENE IN THE TEMPLE—THE LAWYER'S
OFFICE—THE FERRETS AT WORK.

It was in one of the gloomiest courts of the Temple that the firm of Sharpthorne and Bags—attorneys at law—held their court, when engaged on business matters. Most of us know the appearance which the Temple now assumes; but it was far different in the days when Messrs. Sharpthorne resided there. Quiet it is now, certainly—painfully quiet in some parts, like most inns of courts, but it is positively uproarious compared to what it was in the days of yore. In the least sunny part of this inn, where the crops and grass began to vegetate, and gave indications of

damp, where the iron rails were partially corroded with rust, and the wood-work of the stairs were worm-eaten and creaked beneath the tread of the visitor; there it was that the chamber of Messrs. Sharpthorne and Bags were situated. We have most of us had occasion to visit the abode of those learned in the law. We have most of us, I dare say, in common, felt that depression of the spirits and sinking of the heart when we have placed our foot upon the first step which led to a lawyer's office, knowing well that our visit, be it of short or long duration, would be sure to find its way in the bill of costs, which, as time advances, generally assumes a form of gigantic proportions.

A "cute," hard-dealing man was the senior partner of the firm in question. In

No. 4.

truth, a man would have to get up early indeed in a morning who would get the blind side of Mr. Sharpthorne. Mr. Bags, the junior partner, was many years younger than the principal; he had been originally common law clerk in the establishment, when, from his business-like habits and indefatigable perseverance, Mr. Sharpthorne deemed it advisable to take him in as a partner in his prosperous establishment. He did all the in-door toiling and drudgery work, whilst his senior's whole time was employed in seeing clients and holding audiences in the innermost penetralia of his establishment. In this juncture Mr. Sharpthorne was seated in a reflective mood, as he turned over several papers and carefully received their contents; he had left the mansion of Sir Richard Fleetwood on the night previous; presently his ruminations were brought to a close by a clerk putting his head in at the door, and saying, in an under voice—

"Mr. Grime and Flimby, sir."

"Oh, ah! show them in," answered the lawyer quickly.

"Yes, Sir."

In a few seconds the two individuals found themselves in the presence of Sharpthorne, who eyed them attentively. They slid into the place so quietly, making so little fuss or noise in their movements, that to a stranger they would have suggested the thought that their feet were muffled or padded. The lawyer motioned them to a seat which they did not seem anxious to accept, it being one of the characteristics of these men to prefer standing during their interviews.

"Well!" said Mr. Sharpthorne, looking in the countenance of each, but more particularly in that of Grime, who generally acted as spokesman for himself and his companion, for he generally had one, as these worthies generally hunted in couples.

"Well," said Grime, as he carefully brushed round the hair or nap of his hat with the cuff of his coat, "we're on the scent, guv'nor."

"Indeed! that's a fine fellow," answered the attorney, well pleased.

"Yes, but not as yet hunted down the game, you see."

"'Cause why, it ain't to be got at jest yet."

"Ah! how's that?"

"Why we had it almost within our grasp, when we have lost sight of it, and are for the present at fault."

"Explain yourself," answered the attorney.

The man squared his elbows, and prepared himself for a burst of eloquence.

"Well," began Mr. Grime, "it appears

to me from what this Styant says that the late Sir Reginald Fleetwood was more careful in this business than you imagined. He left the proofs of his marriage, the papers connected with the Reichbeck affair, and other documents in a strong iron fire-proof box which, when on the continent, he never lost sight of or parted with."

"Yes, yes, so we have had every reason to believe," answered the lawyer respectfully, "we know that—or at all events we assume it. Where are they now? that is the question."

The man shook his head—both continued:

"I and my pal saw Styant, and did as you requested, offered him a handsome reward, in fact a very large reward, if he would place them in my hands, for you must know we were of opinion—" and here Mr. Grime gave a knowing jerk of his head, as though he were trying how dislocation would agree with him—"we were of opinion that Mr. Styant was gammoning, and that he had them in his possession after all."

"Well, did you ascertain this for certain?"

"We did," said Mr. Grime with a flourish of his dexter hand."

"And has not got them I suppose."

"No, no," that's fortune."

"Umph."

But he has given us the history of the whole affair. It appears that after Sir Reginald's death that this Styant had the management of the deceased baronet's affairs, his lady being, as you might say, almost a child, leastways, in the affairs of the world. Her ladyship came over to England leaving Styant to follow and bring the luggage, and whatever personal property the baronet possessed abroad. He started for England, and amongst other things this said iron box was to be brought over under his charge."

"Well,—yes," said Mr. Sharpthorne, fidgetting on his chair."

"It appears that on his passage a violent storm came on, the vessel was in danger of being wrecked, and eventually she did strike upon some rock; but by the timely assistance of life-boats from the shore, her passengers, or at all events most of them, were saved."

"Well, and the vessel?"

"Broke to pieces and went down, and everything was lost then, and those papers lay at the bottom of the sea."

"They did do so," answered the man with another dislocating jerk, and bending his forefinger in the shape of a reaping hook. "They did, but they have been recovered."

"Ah! by whom? and how?"

"Styant was unwilling to say: he seemed inclined to be dark upon this subject, for he is a shickery sort of a card at best. However, we managed to work the oracle so as to press the affair out of him."

"Good!" said the lawyer: "very good my friend. Go on."

"It appears," continued the astute Mr. Grime, "that Styant was not aware, or at any rate, said he was not aware what the box contained, neither do I think he did. But they were supposed to be papers of some consequence to the family. However, he gave a history of the miraculous escape as he called it, and the foundering of the vessel, and her ladyship took but little pains about them, and——"

"Well," said the lawyer, impatiently.

"It appeared after this," said Mr. Grime, still holding up his reaping hook finger, "that some members of Lady Reichbeck's family paid a large sum of money for a vessel to go out, and a diver to go to the bottom of the sea and endeavour to recover the missing property, but more particulary the box in question."

"Did they succeed in their endeavours?"

"It appears they did, the box and its contents were safely brought to shore and came in possession of an elderly gentleman whose name I have not been able to ascertain, but he was a relative of the late Lady Reichbeck."

"Confound it. Then we are done after all," said Mr. Sharpthorne, and his exclamation was this time perfectly genuine.

Again the reaping hook finger was brought to bear upon the attorny, as its owner shook his head and gave another still more desperate jerk.

"We ain't queered yet, guv'nor." answered Mr. Grime, as he grinned and glanced at his companion, Flimby.

"Not quite," answered that individual.

"Everybody seems to have wanted that box," continued Mr. Grime. "It appears that the gentlemen who had succeeded in obtaining possession of it, after it had been fished up from the depths of the sea, was doomed to lose it again. He was travelling inside the Oxford coach, accompanied by a young female, when the coach was stopped by highwaymen, and the box amongst other things was handed over to the robbers."

"Then it is lost to us as much as ever?" exclaimed the lawyer.

"Not altogether," answered Grime, "my mate here," nodding towards Flimby, "thinks he will be able to get scent of where it is at present."

"How?"

"Ah, that's his business," answered Mr. Grime; "every man to his own calling, you know."

"Well, I have no wish to ask more than you feel justified in making known," said the lawyer; "all I am anxious to learn is what probability there is of your ultimately obtaining possession of these papers."

"I can't promise," answered Grime; "but we are at work, and sha'n't leave a stone unturned to accomplish our object;" and with this assurance he rose from his seat and prepared to take his departure.

"I shall leave the affair entirely to you, then," said Mr. Sharpthorne, as he shook the hands of his two emissaries. Mr. Grime bowed, and said as he departed—

"The moment we have anything fresh to communicate—I mean if anything turns up—you may rely upon seeing either one or both of us."

"Thanks! thanks my friend," and the two worthies were bowed out by Mr. Sharpthorne with great politeness.

It will be necessary for the better understanding of the events which have taken place, to give a brief recital of the more immediate antecedents of the Fleetwood family: Mr. Reginald Fleetwood, the elder brother of the present baronet, had been a free-hearted man, taking but little heed of business matters; and he had, to use a common saying, "been picked up" on more than one occasion. Being a man of impulsive nature, he was therefore a more ready prey to clever persons. He led for some years what is called a gay life, until one day he chose to fall madly in love. The object of his attachment was a mere girl, many years his junior. She was a distant relative of Lady Reichbeck's, and had been adopted and brought up by that lady. Sir Reginald met her in society, wooed and won her, which, under all the circumstances, was perhaps the most imprudent thing he could do, for the Reichbeck and Fleetwood families were, and had been for years past, the most bitter enemies. When Lady Reichbeck learnt the fact of Sir Reginald's attentions to her adopted daughter, her rage knew no bounds, and she positively forbid her to ever think any more of her lover, which, as the young girl was of a complacent nature, she promised to endeavour to fulfil. Eventually, however, Sir Reginald, whose impetuous nature was always prompting him to bold steps, determined, as there was no other course, to make a run-away match of it. He succeeded in inducing the simple-minded girl to consent to the course he proposed, and precipitately carried her off to the continent, where they were married. There were supposed to be some informalities in the marriage by some parties, whether the supposition was a right one or not it might have been hard to determine. At any rate the bride herself was afterwards fully persuaded that the ceremony was a mock, or, rather, not a legal one. Some few months after Sir Reginald's wedding the baronet's career came to a sudden close. Riding out one day his horse ran away, fell over some rocks, throwing off its rider, and dislocating the neck of the unfortunate Sir Reginald Fleetwood. His wife, who was distracted at her sudden bereavement, came to England. Thus it was that Sir Richard Fleetwood, who had succeeded at his brother's death to the title, commenced putting in practice his schemes respecting the future management of his brother's wife. He almost by force compelled her to come under the charge of an old domestic of the family, the nurse Bridget. Mr. Sharpthorne had been the legal adviser of the late Sir Reginald. This worthy limb of the law had the full confidence of the dowager Lady Fleetwood, and when it became known that her ladyship would in the due course of time, give birth to a posthumous child of the late Sir Reginald, he laid down the course of action for the present baronet to adopt, who, in conjunction with Mr. Sharpthorne, succeeded in persuading his brother's widow to consent to a clandestine accouchment, telling her that the child would in any case be illegitimate, and that it would be better for all parties that the affair should be kept a secret. Poor Lady Fleetwood had at first great repugnance to this course of action, but she was of such an easy disposition, and possessed of such little strength of character, that eventually, by threats and entreaties, the two worthies, Sir Richard and Sharpthorne, succeeded in obtaining her consent to their proposition. The reader has already seen how they carried out their project by the aid of Colonel Jack and Dr. Carruthers. No wonder the latter should have uttered the exclamation he did at the sight of the cicatrix on the arm of his patient. He had attended her when a girl, under the charge of Lady Reichbeck, and performed the operation himself, and therefore felt convinced, or at any rate nearly so, that the lady was no other than the adopted daughter of the late Lady Reichbeck.

CHAPTER V.

THE PARTY AT OXFORD — THE LOVERS — COLONEL JACK IN DISGRACE — THE FRAIL FAIR ONE.

WE have already seen in our first chapter how Colonel Jack and his companions suc-

ceeded in stopping the Oxford coach, and eventually made good their retreat from their obstinate pursurers. It will be now necessary for us to journey to the classic town of Oxford itself. In this city nearly opposite to where the martyrs' memorial now stands, resided an English gentleman of considerable property, moving in the highest society. He was proud withal, as many of our English gentlemen frequently were, and are still for the matter of that, and was known by the inhabitants of the town as Squire Langford. He possessed wealth and position, it is true, but he had a still richer treasure—namely, one lovely daughter, Honora Langford by name, who of course, as is usual in such cases, was beloved by all who knew her. There were many suitors for her hand—sighing swains who passed sleepless nights and agonizing days when she frowned upon them. Many were the harmonious verses that were composed by the young collegians in her praise—verses breathing poetic love, and descriptive of her varied charms—suitors came and sued, and sighed, and sighed, and sued again; but still Honora had not as yet positively declared who was the favoured man. There were one or two of whom her father approved, and whose addresses he wished her to encourge, but these did not seem to altogether meet with her approval.

There are lights in Mr. Langford's house, blazing in all the windows, at the time when we are just about to introduce ourselves in the interior thereof, for its worthy owner has numerous guests partaking of his hospitality. Honora Langford is seated at the harp, as her fingers stray carelessly over the strings, while she chats to the knot of swains who are continually hovering about her. Nearest to her, leaning with one arm upon the back of her chair, may be seen the figure of a young man, who seems to have found it utterly impossible to leave her side. If a casual observer were to hazard a guest upon the matter, it is more than probable that he would surmise that this was the favourite suitor, for although but little passes between the two in the shape of conversation, there is that indefinable expression and manner which seldom fails to show some latent lurking fondness towards each other. The individual who is so continually by her side, and pays her those delicate and graceful attentions which most women know how to appreciate, is a student at Christ Church College, Oxford,—Henry Osborne by name. He was what is termed at the college, " on the foundation"—that is, he received his education gratuitously, and if studious would be enabled to take degrees the same as the more wealthy competitors, for academic honours; for Henry Osborne was unquestionably poor, although universally respected and esteemed for his unobtrusive manners, and the integrity of his character.

"Will Mith Langford oblige us with a thong?" drawled out a young exquisite, by name Farnaby, as he lounged rather than walked towards Honora. "My friend Osborne, I fear, has been engrossing her whole attention."

A heightened colour was observable upon the features of the latter, as this observation fell from the lips of Faraday. "Pardon me," said Osborne, "I should be sorry to engage the whole attention of Miss Langford, where there are so many others who would fain bask in her sunny smiles."

"You are flattering, Mr. Osborne," observed the lady.

"Ah, it's his usual way," drawled out the exquisite. "I wish I had the eloquence of my friend Osborne. I am quite sure I shall never succeed with the ladies without. By the way, Miss Langford, have you ever heard about the box you had stolen from you?"

"No, never!" answered Miss Langford. "Strange to say the highwayman who promised so faithfully to return it has never communicated with my father, although a large reward was offered, and—and he promised so faithfully. A paleness came over her features as she referred to the subject, which, from some cause or other, appeared to be a painful one.

"Never put trust in men's promises," said a sonorous voice. The speaker was a tall, dark, handsome man, with a profusion of long flowing hair, which fell in natural curls upon her broad and ample shoulders.

"Ah! Mr. Halford," exclaimed Honora, as she offered her hand, which the other shook warmly, "I was not aware that you were here, still less that you were party to our conversation."

"I have but just come," answered the gentleman who had been addressed as Mr. Halford. "Harry, my boy, how are you?" he continued, as he turned towards Osborne; and a warm greeting took place between the two, for they were perhaps the oldest and best of friends of the whole party.

"Never put your trust in men's promises," repeated Halford, as he turned again towards Honora.

"I should have thought where their interest was concerned you had a right to do so," said Osborne.

"Or where there was any spark of honour left in their composition," answered Honora somewhat bitterly, "and I will never believe that even the most hardened are destitute of some latent sparks, which by nurture can be kindled into a flame."

"Bwavely spoken," exclaimed Farnaby, "Miss Langford would be a match for our senior wrangler."

The eye of Halford glanced towards the last speaker, as he now for the first time became aware of his presence; his look had in it something of contempt.

"Your observations do credit both to your head and heart Miss Langford," answered Halford, "I entirely coincide with the sentiments you have but just now uttered; and depend upon it some day or other you will find this highwaymen has some sparks of goodness left in his composition, depend upon it my words will come true."

The lady started as he was speaking, something seemed to strike her, some tones or accents for which she was at a loss to account. She looked at Halford with enquiring eyes, and said after a pause.

"Then why caution me not to put my trust in man's promises?"

"As a general principle only," answered the other, "in two cases out of three the chance is that you would be doomed to disappointment, and, therefore, it were best at all times to be cautious."

The lady bowed, and then said, "You talk like a worldly man."

"Say rather like one who has seen something of the world," was his answer.

"As you please—its a distinction without a difference, to my thinking."

"There is a vast difference nevertheless," answered Halford, whose haughty bearing, and scornful curl of the lip, together with that serious impressive manner which he at times knew so well how to assume, had put an end to the light badinage which had been going on previous to his entrance. Mr. Langford, himself, who was a quiet elderly gentleman, now made his appearance amongst the assembly, and greeted merely those who were new comers to his salons, amongst whom was Mr. Halford. There was a constraint in the host's bearing towards Osborne, whom, as a suitor to his daughter, he viewed with no very favourable eyes. Soon after this the conversation was at an end, from the fact of many of the guests standing up for a dance. Amongst the assembly there was a showily dressed voluptuous looking woman—a Mrs. Swansdown by name — she had on Halford's first entrance, to use a common phrase, made eyes at him, which he was not long in returning. When it became a question of partners for the dance Halford begged of his host an introduction to the lady, which was readily acceded to by Mr. Langford. The gentleman came out with his best bow, and the lady curtseyed as is usual in such cases. "Might he have the honour of becoming her partner for the next quadrille ?"

A slight simper—and "With pleasure" was the answer.

The dancing commenced, and Halford found that the varied charms he clasped in the mazy dance were by no means of a contemptible or insignificant character. The lady looked languishing and lovely. The round and supple arms, bare shoulders, which were, as well as her neck, of dazzling whiteness, and the partially revealed beauties of her bust, were fascinating to the eyes of her partner, who did not fail in the next waltz to squeeze her voluptuous form towards his own in a close embrace. Matters went on thus during the greater part of the evening—Halford danced with but few other partners. He was obliged, to save appearances, to now and then take another lady, but Mrs. Swansdown was the chief attraction to him. As the evening advanced, and the heat of the rooms had become oppressive, Halford escorted his charmer to a balcony or terrace which lay at the rear of Mr. Langford's home. This contained several evergreens intermixed with some exotics, and thither did several stray couples wander as they became fatigued and exhausted with the heated atmosphere of the ball room.

One of these was our amorous pair, namely Langford and Mrs. Swansdown.

"My dear lady," said Halford, as he squeezed her hand, "with your sweet presence, this place is indeed rendered an Elysium."

"Ah! Mr. Halford," exclaimed the lady, endeavering to put on an injured look, "what flatterers you men are."

"He must be utterly dead to a sense of female beauty, who could pass by unnoticed such fascinating charms as Mrs. Swansdown possesses," said Halford, as he fastened on her one of those looks, half of admiration and half of desire, which women are seldom at a loss to interpret

A blush spread itself over the features of Mrs. Swansdown, as her eye met that of her companion, which made her look still more lovely in the eyes of her admirer. And as he saw the crimson current tinge the face and neck of the lady, he became still more amorous in his glances. For say what you will, a natural blush upon the features of girl or woman, possesses an indescribable charm to most of us.

"My most charming Mrs. Swansdown," continued Halford, as he led his companion to a remote part of the terrace, immediately behind a gigantic yucca, "you see before you a captive to love. May I hope?"

"What!" enquired the lady suddenly.

"You are, I presume, your own mistress ?"

"Nay," she answered; "I own a liege lord."

"Whew!" exclaimed Halford with surprise, who thought he had to do with a widow.

"You have then——"

"Yes, a husband," was the reply, as the speaker turned her head away. There was a pause, when the gentleman said deprecatingly.

"And can he leave so lovely a wife for a single evening. It's monstrous."

"All men do not view a woman with the same eyes, perhaps as yourself," she answered.

"They must be utterly devoid of feeling, of sense, of sentiment."

"Hush! don't speak so loud, sir. Mr. Halford, they'll hear you."

"Ah, true, I forgot. I am incautious, Mrs. Swansdown. I love you," continued Halford, as he went down on one knee, and clasped her person passionately towards him. You will say it may appear strange that at this, our first meeting, that I should be so completely enraptured by your presence, that the very atmosphere I breathe seems intoxicating to my senses."

"Ah! Mr. Halford, don't—pray don't— you hurt me," exclaimed his charmer, struggling to release herself from his too fond embrace.

He rose from his kneeling position, and covered her face and neck with warm and passionate kisses. Half resistant and half willing, she endeavoured to release herself from his ardent grasp, but in vain!

He drew her towards him, and again and again, embraced her cheeks, her lips, neck, and hair with a savage fervour. It would be difficult to determine how far matters would have gone, had they not have been suddenly brought to a close by Halford observing through the leaves of the yucca, which had provided so excellent a screen for his operations, Miss Langford and Osborne walking arm-in-arm towards the spot occupied by himself and his fair enamorato. With the ready tack of a man well versed in intrigue, Halford conducted his lady round the balcony or terrace, and sauntered leisurely as though they were but admiring the collection of plants, and indulging in a cool and refreshing stroll."

"We shall be the scandal of the whole house," said the lady reproachfully, as she glanced at her companion.

"Pshaw!" he exclaimed. "And wherefore? No one has shamed us, and if they had, is it a sin to embrace one of the fairest and loveliest of Eve's daughters.

No, Mrs. Swansdown, I should only be the enemy of those who saw, even assuming there were any such."

Assuming as indifferent an air as possible, the pair returned to the ball-room, where they were shortly joined by Osborne and Miss Langford. And in the due course of time, the guests took their departure, some singly, and others by twos and threes at a time. Halford was about the first to leave, upon the plea of an early engagement on the following day, which necessitated his return home at a reasonable hour. He had been a frequent guest at Mr. Langford's, and was supposed by him to be a gentleman living on his own means, and he had also been an intimate friend of Osborne's, for the greater part of the latter's life; they having known each other from boyhood, and they had formed a strong and lasting attachment for each other.

Mrs. Swansdown's liege lord resided a mile or so on the London side of Oxford at a little village called Headington. That lady had been escorted to the party by her cousin, a young man of the spooney class.

As her husband was a quiet old card, many years her senior, and little given to that species of pleasure so frequently indulged in by his better half, his lady was forced to enlist anyone she could obtain as her conductor to the numerous entertainments she was in the habit of visiting. She had her own, or rather her husband's vehicle to convey her home to Headington. And it was something like an hour past midnight, while her husband was quietly drinking at home, that the chariot which contained his lady and her cousin left the hospitable mansion of Mr. Langford. Slowly it crept along through High-street, Oxford. After which, it took that dark road which led direct to Headington Hill. It had just got about a quarter of a mile, or rather more on the road in question, when its progress was brought to a sudden halt. The horse stumbled over some large stones and fell, while the hind wheel of the vehicle came off, and the carriage broke down, jolting its occupants severely. In vain the coachman endeavoured to raise his horse, he dismounted from his seat, and proceeded as well as the darkness would permit to see what was the matter. There were several heaps of large stones lying along the road, which were certainly not there when he had conveyed his mistress from Headington in the earlier portion of the day. How the wheel had come off, he was at a loss to conjecture; but his attention was now taken up by his horse who began to kick and plunge, as though he was bent upon breaking the whole affair to pieces. By this time, the lovely Mrs. Swansdown had sufficiently recovered from the first shock, to indulge in a series of screams—the usual resort of a woman in distress. As to her cousin, he seemed speechless with fright, and sat pale as a parsnip, shivering and shaking in every limb.

"Dear me, Hodges, what is the matter?" asked the lady, as her pretty features were thrust out from the window of the chariot.

"A break down, marm, and no mistake," answered her coachman, "and how its to be put straight is more than I can tell."

By this time another carriage was heard coming along the road; as soon as it arrived at, or rather near, the scene of the catastrophe, it halted and its owner alighted and offered whatever assistance he could afford under the circumstances. Upon learning how matters stood, he at once offered to take Mrs. Swansdown home while her cousin and the coachman could see what could be done to bring the carriage home. Mrs. Swansdown observed upon the first glance that the new comer in her carraige was no other than Mr. Halford himself. She gladly embraced the offer he had made, and he handed her into his carriage, which immediately drove off at a rapid pace. It would have been as nearly as she could calculate about a mile and a half from the place of the accident to her husband's residence; and she was much surprised, therefore, when she had gone as she imagined considerably more than double that distance to find no symptoms of a halt—and yet the carriage was going at a rapid pace.

"When shall we arrive at our destination?" asked Mrs. Swansdown of her companion, "Dear me, how late we shall be."

"If it were all night it would be too short a time for me while I have such a lovely and fascinating companion," answered Halford, as he tenderly embraced her who was by his side. They were alone now and in the dark, with no listeners or curious eyes to give enquiring glances at their proceedings; and so if the lady found the journey long, her companion did all he could to cheer her. With all this, however, she began again to fidget and ask which way they were going, when upon endeavouring to catch a glimpse of the road they were taking she was appalled at observing that they were taking their way through the High Street again.

"Mr. Halford!" Sir—what's the meaning of this? Mercy on me—we are coming away from my husband's home—I shall be ruined—pray turn back."

"Dearest Mrs. Swansdown," said her companion gently, and in his most winning accent, "you must pardon a devoted and ardent admirer—I love you!—no eastern worshipper of the sun bows down to his divinity with greater reverence than I do to you, who are to me my life, my sun, my light, my existence; nay, turn not from me, do not grudge me this hour or two's gentle converse—for oh, Mrs Swansdown, how devotedly I love you." Again he covered her face and neck with passionate kisses. "This is wrong, it is cruel," exclaimed the lady, who although she did not actually repulse his embrace, nevertheless made a show of doing so. "Let me at once return home, sir," she continued, now more firmly, as the thought of flying hours rushed through her mind.

"My fair name will be gone for ever—you surely cannot be a gentleman, or you could never have had recourse to such unfair means as these. I must and will go home at once! I insist upon it, or I will raise an alarm."

"Pray do not talk thus; do not endeavour to bring me into disgrace, for oh, Mrs. Swansdown, consider, fairest of womankind, that it has been your beauty which has driven me well nigh distracted. Is it sinful to be a humble worshipper at the shrine of woman's surpassing loveliness? Is it a crime? You cannot deem it such. Listen! Until I saw you I scoffed at the mad-brained youths who sighed away their existence over some fair enchantress. I had never then had stirred within me that mighty and master passion which men call love. For your sake I would dare anything, give my very existence provided some time were left me to bask in your smiles. Ah, Mrs. Swansdown, forgive a too-devoted and ardent admirer of you!" He hurried on with a torrent of eloquence, until they had passed again through the High Street. Having passed through which, some pangs of conscience or remorse seemed to sieze hold of Mrs. Swansdown, for she exclaimed in more passionate tones than she had previously assumed, that unless she was driven home she would scream out for assistance. It had been the object of her companion to convey her to a road-side home in the neighbourhood where he was well known, but, finding she resisted so pertinaciously, he was compelled to make a compromise of the matter, and therefore gave orders for the driver to take the coach back to Headington. When this was done, the frail Mrs. Swansdown became more pacified, and returned the embraces of her betrayer. What excuse to make at home for the time consumed, she was at a loss to suggest. However, her companion proposed as an excuse, his man mistaking the road, and such was the course she ultimately made up her mind to

pursue. Her conductor left her at her own door, and told the conchman and her cousin, who had arrived home some time previously, that his man had mistaken the road, and had driven miles out of the way. And as soon as the lady was safely deposited in her own home, and her lover's vehicle was fairly out of ear-shot, its occupant indulged in a violent fit of laughter at the success so far of his ruse; for the breakdown of Mrs. Swansdown's carriage had been all a planned thing with himself and his companions; and the so-called Mr. Halford, was no other than our hero, Colonel Jack. Halford was, by the way, his real name, that is, the one he was known by in the respectable portion of society before he had assumed his present calling.

CHAPTER VI.

THE LOVERS—THE DECLARATION.

LIKE many other men, our hero Colonel Jack had two sides to his character. Under his real name of Frank Halford he moved in respectable society, and attached to himself a numerous circle of friends and acquaintances. Perhaps one of the most endearing and sincere among the former class was his old companion and schoolfellow, Harry Osborne, who was, however, some ten years his junior. Osborne had not the slightest suspicion or knowledge that the companion of his boyhood was the celebrated Colonel Jack, who had, in the days of which we write, won for himself a world-wide reputation. Being, in fact, one of the most celebrated highwaymen of his day. Halford possessed a sincere respect and esteem for his quondam companion Osborne, and had too great an opinion of his integrity to ever seek to dispel the illusion by declaring his own mode of existence. A diligent, studious, painstaking pupil Osborne had been during the period he was at school, so much so that in his progress he distanced all his companions.

Colonel Jack, or rather Frank Halford as he was then called, was altogether of a different type. From his earliest youth he had been of an impetuous nature. For his sphere of character he required action—clever he certainly was, but he wanted steady application; and altogether his course might be termed erratic and lawless enough now. Colonel Jack remained in Oxford, or rather in and about the neighbourhood, for some days after this leisure with Mrs. Swansdown, and he had the gratification of listening to the recital of the exploits of

himself and his companions in the circle in which he moved as Mr. Halford.

While our hero was plying about the country on various expeditions, the ardour of Harry Osborne's passion was hourly consuming. This was a virtuous love, deep seated, and springing from the well-springs of the heart. He had viewed Miss Langford with eyes of admiration for some three or four years past, but had considered her too far above him in worldly position for him to ever hope she would look so low for a husband. He who had youth, beauty, talents, and no inconsiderable amount of worldly wealth, that charming amalgam which gilds over so nicely the matrimonial pill. By degrees, as he met Miss Langford about at evening parties—for in a provincial town like Oxford, one meets the same round

of faces—by degrees he managed, by delicate and respectful attentions towards her, to engage some share of her notice, and gradually as they became more and more familiar with one another, and used to each others' ways, he thought he observed, or at any rate flattered himself that he perceived, that she viewed him with certainly not unfavourable eyes. Oh, that moment! who shall describe it, when the belief first dawns upon us that the object of our adoration is awakening to a tender emotion towards us? Then comes the doubts, the hopes and fears, the sleepless nights; then comes those long draughts of sweets and bitters, mingled together. All this Harry Osborne had already gone through, as most of us have, my friend, at one time or another of our lives. Harry, although he had been persevering in his respectful attentions, and studiously polite towards Miss Langford, he had not as yet entered the charmed ring of love's circle; he was not either a declared lover or an accepted suitor of Miss Langford's. An event occurred, however, which hastened on this catastrophe, if it could be so termed. Most persons know that at Oxford the Thames, or rather the Isis, is a pure and glassy stream, the water being as clear as crystal; unlike our own metropolitan river, so redolent of filth of every description. Pleasure parties and aquatic excursions were then, and, indeed, are still of frequent occurrence amongst the inhabitants of the town. On one of these occasions, a party was formed to take a trip up the river in what is called a house-boat. Mr. Langford and daughter, with several friends, and some of the young collegians—amongst whom was Harry Osborne—proceeded down the stream in the house-boat, carrying provisions and a plentiful supply of refreshments on board. Having journeyed down the river for some miles a few of the party expressed a wish to land on one of the banks; and, as the house-boat drew too much water for them to effect their object, those who desired to reach the shore put off in a small four-oared cutter. In stepping into this the foot of Miss Langford slipped, and she was precipitated into the water amidst the screams of those on board the house-boat. Her form was carried away rapidly by the strong tide which was running at the time, and, before the spectators had recovered from their first panic, Harry Osborne had divested himself of his coat and waistcoat, and, leaping in, was seen to strike out vigorously towards the still floating figure of Honora. He succeeded in reaching her in time, and, by skilful management—for he was a strong and expert swimmer—he had the satisfaction of bearing her in his arms safe to the shore. A shout of joy and thankfulness rose from those on board the house-boat, and all were profuse in their expressions of gratitude for his gallantry. Honora said but little, but her looks were more expressive than words.

On the following day Harry called to inquire how the lady was, and her father again expressed his gratitude towards her preserver. This little incident drew the lovers closer together, and a few days after the occurrence the two were taking a stroll in Christ Church meadow. The day was unusually fine, and birds were carolling from every bough. A shade of nervousness was visible upon the features of Osborne, and his companion was not a whit the less triste in the expression of her countenance.

They had been talking upon indifferent subjects, certainly nothing to evoke sorrow or a dejected mein, but there was that in their hearts which as yet had not found utterance. Presently the gentleman led his companion to a rustic seat placed round the trunk of a gigantic chestnut. There was a pause after they had seated themselves—an awkward one to both. Osborne seemed a thought paler than was usual with him, and there was an uneasy bearing about him which is scarcely definable by any written description. However, after several efforts, he managed at last to find his tongue. It is hardly fair, but we will listen to what he has to say.

"Miss Langford," he began, in an undertone, "it is not that you possess beauty only, or that you have talents, amiability of disposition, and all those many graces which adorn and elevate the female character. It is not all these, but your gentle spirit and goodness of heart which have taught me to admire, respect, and—love you!"

"Mr. Osborne!" she exclaimed in some trepidation.

"Yes Honora, if I may dare call you by so familiar an appellation. I feel awake within me that mighty and mysterious spirit which men call love. I feel that yearning to be all in all to her from whose smiles I draw my very existence. You will think my words presumptive—think perhaps that I am forgetting our relative positions when I am addressing you thus: but alas, is human love the growth of human will? Is it a fault of mine to be sensible of your many graces and sweetness of disposition?

The lady blushed as he proceeded thus, but made no other answer, but a slight tremor shook her frame.

"In my lonely college life—for lonely enough it is, seeing that my so called companions have no sympathy with the poor student. In my lonely life, therefore, the only hours of comfort—of happiness unalloyed, and perfect happiness which I have had—have been those which have been past by your side, or in your presence. It is your sweet ministry which has shed a light upon my path. Listen! Miss Langford, I shall perhaps be deemed egotistical if I expatiate upon my own troubles and vexations. Let it suffice, therefore for me, to declare that they have been of a nature, which had it not been for the knowledge that I was near you, I should have left this town long ago. But enough of this: I have said as sincerely, truly, and honourably as ever man said to woman, that I love you. Ah, Miss Langford, have pity on me—have mercy for one whose very life and existence rests upon your word or dictum."

He was on his knees by this time, and took her hand in his own, and looked up beseechingly in her face. She, however, made no reply, although she gently returned the pressure of his hand. This gave him hope. He again appealed to her in more passionate accents.

"Nay," he continued, "you are too good—too kind—too noble in disposition to say aught that might wound the feelings of even an enemy, and I am sure I am at least considered as a friend. I know you have other and more wealthy suitors, and it may appear selfish on my part to wish to engross your affections. If you have set your choice upon any one of such, say so, I can bear it. It is my duty to do so: for oh, Honora! I love you so; that even your lightest word would be to me an imperative command——"

He broke down here, and covered his face with his hands. He certainly was dreadfully serious poor man. So, I suppose most of us are under similar circumstances.

"If it is my love you want," said Honora Langford, "you have had it long ago."

He rose to his feet, and embraced her tenderly. Her words had been but few, and yet were so expressive, that he was delerious with joy.

He hurried on with a torrent of expressions which would be perhaps found tedious to record in this chapter; for love making, delightful as it is to the parties concerned, does not possess the same attractive features to a third party.

"Although we now sufficiently understand our mutual feelings towards each other, Henry, my heart misgives me, when I reflect upon my father; my duty to him as his only daughter demands some counsel taken of his wishes in this matter. And there I fear we shall find an obstacle."

"Say, not so," answered Osborne. "I will myself state the whole case to his better judgment. He surely would never oppose your wishes, upon a subject which so deeply concerns your happiness."

"Happiness is, as we view the matter. I am afraid he will object."

"Ah! he wishes you to marry some one of his own choosing?"

"No doubt that would be his desire."

"And would you consent?"

"No. I will never give my hand to anyone without he takes with it my heart. It is the worst of all deceptions to do so: a cruel mockery which seldem goes unpunished. My belief is, that a woman loves but once, thwart her in her first choice, and there is nothing then but bitter dregs for her to swallow for the remainder of her life. We are not creatures of reason, Henry, so much as you men. We act more from instinct of an innate sensibility. And are therefore, incapable of coldly reasoning away our fancies. Consult my father, dearest, and hear what he has to say: but be patient with him, for he has, I fear, built up schemes and theories which he will not be pleased perhaps to find fall to the ground."

It would be kind to say, how long the lovers sat exchanging mutual vows, and future schemes of happiness, but the chilly night air told them that their converse must for that evening come to an end, and Osborne was compelled to take a relenting leave of his enchantress, after he had seen her to the gate of her father's mansion. A day or two elapsed, before he could muster up courage to seek an interview with Mr. Langford, which was a task he had a great dread of. However, he was compelled to screw his courage up, and he hastened to pay him a formal visit. His name being announced, he was ushered into the old gentleman's library, and was politely handed to a seat,

"Mr. Osborne does me the honour to come and have a chat with such an old proser as myself," said Mr. Langford with something of a sneer lurking about his tone and utterance.

"Ahem! yes!" stammered his visitor, "it is not exactly, Mr. Langford, it is a matter of business—no—that is, I mean—a matter which deeply concerns my interest, happiness and future welfare, which has prompted me to wait upon you."

"Ah! indeed!—your own welfare—you know, Mr. Osborne, that you are a young man for whom I entertain a great esteem, and if I can be instrumental in forwarding your interests in any way, of course, why of course, I need hardly say you may command me. Tell me what it is now," said Mr. Langford, as he crossed his knees and settled himself in his easy chair.

"I have come—that is—I dare say sir you will think me very presumptuous—but the fact is, that—that—I love your daughter."

"Oh, is that all," was the cool rejoinder, as the speaker indulged in a quiet laugh, "really my friend I do not see how that can possibly forward you in the world; it will only distract your mind from your studies, unhinge you from following your usual avocations; sir I have always found in my experience that a lover was always a most useless member of society, being in fact just fit for nothing."

This was to Osborne a most unpleasant way of receiving his announcement, which he had not made without an inward struggle.

"All that may be true enough, Mr. Langford, but it is past my controul. I love your daughter with as sincere an attachment as it possible I believe for man to entertain for a woman."

"Ah, so we all think—did so myself—found out my mistake, though, afterwards—but go on, I beg your pardon for interrupting you."

"I hope you will do me sufficient justice to believe me incapable of heartlessly winning the affections of your daughter for the purpose of any worldly gain that might accrue therefrom."

"Pshaw man ! who has accused you of winning her affections," exclaimed his listener with considerable impatience; "but you must pardon me again, go on I pray."

"I wish," continued Osborne, "that the case was reversed. I wish that I were a rich man, and Miss Osborne the daughter of a less prosperous gentleman than yourself."

"Thank you, sir, for the suggestion."

"Well I don't mean exactly that, perhaps, but I wish I had a sufficient amount of wealth to entitle me to become a suitor for her hand."

"Ah! that's better—spoken like a sensible man; I wish you had, and then, perhaps, we might consider this matter seriously; but as you have not, and as she is in no want of admirers, why, you see Mr. Osborne, I think you had better think no more of the matter, for it will only occasion you a vast amount of useless trouble and annoyance."

"That is all past now," answered Henry; "it is impossible for me to ever think of any one else but Miss Honora."

"Ah, you have gone off your head as clean as that, eh! Have you consulted my daughter herself in this matter?" asked Mr. Langford quietly as he looked hard at his visitor."

"Yes, sir, and she has given her consent conditionally, of course, that it meets with your approval."

"Oh!" exclaimed Mr. Langford, now somewhat more seriously, "Oh, you have declared your passion to Honora, and she consents conditionally—of course—ah !"— There was a long pause after this, and Osborne sat watching the features of his companion, endeavouring to see some gleam of hope in their expression; but their expression could not be easily interpreted; presently Mr. Langford said quietly—

"I now fully understand, then, the purport of this visit : it is to obtain my consent to your visits here as an accepted lover of my daughter."

"Yes, sir, precisely."

"Well, now, Mr. Osborne ; you must, upon reflection, see the impossibility of my consenting to such a course. Personally, I can have no possible objection to you, but you must know, that your own position—I mean in a worldly sense—does not warrant you to aspire to become a candidate for my daughter's hand."

"I acknowledge that."

"Very well. Then, as an honourable man, you ought not to press the matter; indeed, you ought, in my opinion, never to have broached it either to her or me."

"I can hardly see that."

"But I do. We all take our own view upon this question. I say you ought never to have broached it. You know, and have known for some time past, that she has, or is likely to have at any rate, several eligible offers, and you had no right, therefore, as my guest, to endeavour to estrange the affections of my daughter. If your own position had warranted you in doing so, why of course you might have taken your chance with other competitors, but as it is, you have not to my thinking pursued a right and proper path."

"I am sorry to hear you say that, sir ; I hope I am incapable of doing a mean or dishonourable action; still more so towards Miss Langford or yourself."

"Well—well. There, I do not want to hurt your feelings," said Mr. Langford, more kindly. "Let us understand each other, and talk this matter over like two sensible men. You must understand, Mr. Osborne," continued Mr. Langford, now more confidentially, "that it is essential that my daughter should make a good match. I do not wish to enter into the particulars of my affairs, but the fact is, that I am not by any means the wealthy man people suppose me. Quite the contrary. There is a considerable amount of property gone from our family owing to the disastrous circumstance of which we were but alluding to the other evening—I mean the loss of that box which contained papers, deeds, and will of the late Lady Reichbeck, by which we should have inherited a considerable amount of property, all of which, are now in all probability, lost to us for ever. And what renders the matter more annoying, I had spent a considerable amount of money in obtaining these documents. Consequently, I am, for my position in society, decidedly a very poor man. And what is still worse, a great portion of my present income goes away to other members of the family at my death. I don't wish to mention all these circumstances to anyone, they are spoken to you in confidence ; and I am thus explicit, that you may at once see the impossibility of the tenour of the position you would endeavour to assume with regard to my daughter."

"I am much pained to hear this account of your affairs, more for yourself than any other cause. May I hope, sir, that, if in the course of a few years, I earn for myself a better position, may I hope then to obtain your consent?"

"Young man," answered Mr. Langford, "sands are running. A few years, indeed. My daughter, although young at present, cannot wait for you 'till her bloom of youth is faded. Besides which, who likes to have a girl or woman who is supposed to have had a prior attachment—a sort of second-hand love? No, that would never do. We soon get old, Osborne. You'll find that out if you live long enough."

"Well, sir, I will not press this subject upon you. Consider it over, and perhaps you may take a different view of the question—upon a little reflection. I love your daughter sincerely, and my life would be devoted to her."

"Ah—ah! that's the way we all begin," said Mr. Langford, smiling. "The old story. We most of us begin much the same, and believe in what we say, but time—time! Ah! Good night. Good night!" And he bowed his visitor out with great obsequiousness.

Poor Osborne, he was terribly chapfallen at the result of his interview with his charmer's father. He did not doubt for one moment but that the old gentleman had been speaking the truth when discoursing upon his own affairs. And so indeed he had. Osborne saw that there really was an almost insurmountable obstacle to his union with Honora. He returned to the college, and shut himself up in his rooms, consuming his grief alone and in silence. He gave orders to his servant to admit no visitors, as he was at his studies. Poor fellow, study was out of the question. While reflecting upon those events which had so recently transpired, he heard a loud altercation in the passage, and the well-known voice of Halford, in angry conversation with the college scout. He instantly flung open the door of his apartment, and called out for his friend to enter.

"Why, Harry, my boy," exclaimed Halford, "I knew you would never box yourself up from me. I have had the hardest job in the world to persuade this chap that you would see me whatever might be the case."

"Come in—come in, my boy," exclaimed Osborne. "My doors are never barred against you, that I need hardly say."

Osborne closed the outer door, when his old schoolfellow had entered, and seated himself in a chair by the side of the fireplace.

"We don't so often meet, I am sure," said Osborne, "and I take it kindly, that you have popped in just now; for to say the truth, I am rather hippish."

"Ah! what's up."

"Oh; a good many things," was the reply.

"Not a woman in the case, eh?" said Halford.

"Yes," said his companion, sighing.

"Oh, dear! Anything wrong, Henry?"

"Most confoundedly so."

"What she refused you—has she?"

"No, not so bad as that; but her father has."

"Oh, is that all," answered the other contemptuously.

"All! My dear fellow, it's everything.

"Well, come tell us all about it. But first of all, what have you got to drink, for these stories make a man feverish and thirsty."

Glasses and liquors were placed on the table.

"Now then, Harry," said Halford, after he had drained off a bumper, "proceed with your tale of woe, for such, damme, it must be from your countenance."

Henry Osborne, detailed to his friend all those circumstances which have been described in this chapter. Halford listened to his tale with interest—he saw how deeply moved his companion was during the recital of all the incidents."

"Umph!" exclaimed Halford. "I suppose Langford is not rich. Of that there can be no doubt."

"In that case," said Osborne, "it is hoping against hope, to ever dream that I shall obtain his consent to wed his daughter. And to tell you the truth, Frank, my life will be for ever embittered; for oh! I do love that girl, and I sit thinking here in these solitary chambers, of my unhappy fate. Why was I ever thrown in the way of one so far removed from my own sphere?"

"It is generally the fate of man—either that thing or something worse," answered Halford.

"Ah, yes; you can make light of these matters, I know. Frank, I wish I were a man of your mould."

"Pshaw! don't wish any such thing," answered the other pettishly; "you are much better as you are."

"It may be so; but you have mixed so much more with the world; have such a happy knack of throwing off anything of this sort, with——"

"Philosophy! eh?" said his companions, laughing.

" With that easy way, Frank, which was always peculiar to yourself."

" Well, now, I tell you what you shall do," said our hero with a manner which he was wont to assume when he had made up his mind positively upon any subject.

" What?" was the eager inquiry of the distracted lover.

" Don't break your heart!"

" Well, is that all?"

" No; something else remains behind—listen. The story old Langford has told you I have no doubt is a true one; now, mind what I am going to say. You shall have this girl after all."

" My dear, dear Frank!" exclaimed his companion, passionately, as he grasped both his hands in ecstasy.

" Don't be in too great a hurry—I think I may, perhaps, be of service in this matter."

" Then I am sure you will."

" Unquestionably. If these papers, or box containing them, could be obtained and restored to Mr. Langford, I think you might stand a good chance of obtaining his consent."

" Very likely; but how are they to be got at?"

" Well, that we must see about. I think, from a legal person in London, that I myself may obtain a clue as to their whereabouts; should I succeed in doing so, and once obtain possession of the same, why I can, you know, give them to you; and then——"

" Well, what?"

" Why, you can, if you like, make your own bargain for their restoration. No daughter no papers—do you see?"

" Oh, that would never do; I would never consent to barter for Miss Langford."

" Well, that's the business view of the question; but I know lovers ignore business or common sense either."

" Don't be too hard upon me, Frank."

" Now, you must mind and keep a still tongue upon this subject; I am off to London to-morrow, and if I learn anything of advantage to you, which I doubt not, I will drop you a line; and we can advise as to your future conduct, only keep dark at present! Do you understand?"

" I leave it entirely to you. Oh, how much I am beholden to you, Frank; you were always ready with your superior tact in getting me out of any scrape or difficulty."

" Nonsense man, there's nothing done at present, so you have nothing to thank me for; keep your spirits up—don't break your heart for the finest woman in the world—they are not worth it—and when you have lived as long as I have you will come to the same conclusion. There, no thanks—good bye, I shan't see you any more before I go, but you may rely upon my not forgetting. Adieu," and the two friends parted.

The clattering of Colonel Jack's horses' hoofs might soon afterwards have been heard as he rattled over Magdalen bridge, and, after a smart gallop of some dozen miles or so, he was joined by Hackett, Knapp, and Warrington; and this choice trio were on " business thoughts intent." They were about to work their way up to London, and took the Henley road, meeting with what they termed several good " hawls" before they reached the metropolis. As it is not our purpose to follow them this night on their professional duties, we will proceed to another chapter.

CHAPTER VII.

SCENE AT THE " COW AND CAULIFLOWER" —" THE BRISTOL BADGER "—" THE BOOZING KEN."

IT will be remembered, that mention was made in our opening chapter of the " Badgers." When Colonel Jack called in at the " Old Cromwell" Posting House, at Knightsbridge. he was informed by the individual in the parlour, that his companions had been last seen at the " Badgers." In fact, it was from that respectable establishment, that the whole of them had started. The house so called by its more familiar frequenters, was a large, low old-fashioned public house, or " boozing ken," situated in the classic locality of Rochester-row, Westminster. The sign of the famous hostelry, was the " Cow and Cauliflower." In front of the house, there swung a huge sign, upon which there was a dun cow rudely painted, with a large cauliflower in her mouth. What was the origin of so ridiculous a sign, it would be difficult to determine. Some said it originated in an old legend, and others, that the original owner of the property was a farmer and cowkeeper. Be this as it may, it is a matter of duty and pleasure for us to pay the house a visit, and introduce ourselves to the landlord, who was rather an important person in his way. He had been—let me see—what? I should be almost insane to say what he had not been. Bill Dyson, or as he was more familiarly termed, the " Bristol Badger," was the landlord of the " Cow and Cauliflower," and in his day, he was a remarkable character. He had originally worked in an iron smelting factory at Bristol, which was his native place. Here he became distinguished for wrestling and his pugilistic encounters, and in fact, owing to many gentlemen backing him, he became for a long time, a professed pugilist, until he encountered a man by the name of "Bandy-legged Ben," which cut short his career for a time. His opponent practised some new style of fighting, in which he meant, as he termed it, to draw out the "Badger," who, however, knew too much, and fought a cautious game. The fight was protracted beyond all reasonable limits, for both were good men, and fought with considerable caution; "Bandy-legged Ben," who was a lighter and younger man than his opponent, thought to wear him out as the saying is. He worried and tormented the "Badger" to such an extent, that at last he got savage, and went into his opponent in good earnest. Some terrible knocks were exchanged on both sides, and the two combatants closed. Poor "Bandy-legged Ben" was seen to rise in the air, as though he had been tossed by a bull. The "Badger" had thrown him fairly over his shoulders, and he fell to the earth speechless and motionless.

The fight was over, for the man remained senseless, and was conveyed from the spot to the nearest surgeons. He lay in a state of syncope for fifteen hours, and then expired.

A warrant was issued for the apprehension of the "Badger," but that worthy thought it best to "step it," as the common saying has it. He took his passage in one of the vessels trading with Hamburgh, and escaped thence to the continent. Here he got a precarious existence by buying and selling, and attending fairs, and hawking goods in the meanwhile. After this, he did a little in the smuggling line, in conjunction with some Frenchmen, for by this time, he had learnt to "patter a little of their lingo," as he termed it — contraband goods, some of not a very respectable nature, conveyed to the shores of England by the instrumentality of the "Badger," and he found this, he used after to say to his customers, a profitable game. In it he made a good deal of money, but unfortunately for himself and his companions, he was caught one fine day, and sentenced to three years imprisonment in the Tuleet. He served nearly half his time, when he managed some how or other to escape—no one ever seemed to know how this was managed—but escape he certainly did, and started after this, as a hawker of Bibles and Testaments; but his taste for contraband goods remained still strong upon him; and with his Bibles, he took round what he called smuggled brandy, which, however, was a misnomer, the spirits he hawked being in

fact, nothing else but the produce of several private stills which were kept by some of his choice companions.

The "Badger" did not find this so profitable a speculation as he desired; he ran great risks, and worked hard, and did not, as he considered, reap a sufficient harvest for his labours. So to use his own phraseology, he "cut that game," and took a place in Bucklersbury, and started as auctioneer. He was not particular what he bought or what he sold, so long as he could reap a profit. Bankrupt stock, goods come by "on the cross," damaged goods, made up goods, anything and everything—it was all the same to the "Badger," and here he made a vast deal of money, for he had a large connection with what he called "the suppliers." There, however, he was doomed to come to disgrace, for unfortunately, some goods he sold, were traced as stolen property from a Scottish house, and the Lord Mayor was unreasonable enough to request him to account for his possession of them. He informed his lordship, that he had bought them in the course of business of a gentleman of the Hebrew persuasion, of the name of Nathan. His lordship did not deem his explanation perfectly satisfactory, and consequently, the "Badger" was compelled to receive board and lodging at the expense of his Majesty for six calender months.

At the expiration of that period the "Badger" embarked in a new line of business. He had always had a taste for "the fancy," as it was termed, and as cock fighting was then much in vogue he took to training these description of birds, and bet largely upon the same. This he found sufficiently profitable, besides which it was in accordance with his own peculiar taste. He, at the same time, rented an archery-ground at Raverlust; "anything to turn an honest penny," as he used to observe. It would be an endless task to follow him through all his various adventures or callings. These were, however of a sufficiently mixed character to content any enterprising man. We will take him up were we now find him, namely—as the landlord of the "Cow and Cauliflower."

Here we find him in first-class circumstances. Not over particular in his associations, for, to say the truth, his house was the resort of a mixed assembly of vice in various forms; but, with all this, the "Badger" had the reputation of being what is generally understood to be one of the right sort; and, to do him justice, he was kind to those who were "out of luck;" he gave a helping hand to many when completely "down upon their luck." At the time we are about to make his acquaintance he was oracular in his large parlour, which was filled, as it usually was, with an heterogeneous mass of visitants. At the end of the room is a gigantic fire-place, with boiler and oven, all attached thereto. Here it was that the cooking operations for his customers was performed. Gentlemen who brought their own viands could have them boiled or fried gratuitously. The "Badger" is at the fire-place, while Peg, his handy maid, is superintending the cooking department under his own humble directions, for the "Badger" was a rare one to see to things himself. Observe him! he is no beauty to look at, certainly. His nose appears to have been broken at one time or another, and one of his eyes is a little askew. There is also on his dexter a huge and ugly scar. A short cropped head, a wide mouth, dilated nostrils, a bull-neck, and a pair of shoulders of gigantic proportions complete the appearance of the man, which, take it altogether, is such as to make you rather cautious of picking a quarrel with him. He had on a velveteen shooting jacket and a white apron. The company which may be seen round the room, disposed in various groups, would have been a study for Hogarth. Rogues of every degree were in the habit of visiting the establishment. A general burr may be heard proceeding from the various guests, who mostly converse in whispers, or else in very low tones. There is, however, a general hush in the whole assembly, as two figures enter the establishment several members of the company exchange significant looks, and some depart immediately upon urgent business. Many of those who remain do not appear to be so much at their ease as they were some half hour before.

The two new comers are Messrs. Grime and Flimby. They steal into the room like cats, as is their usual practice, and assume a soft, bland manner as they sidle up to the farther end of the room, near to where the "Badger" stood. The latter gentleman looked at them inquiringly, as a shade of displeasure passed over his swarthy features.

"Morning, gentlemen," said the "Badger," sulkily, as they approached near to where he stood.

"Morning—anything I can do for you?"

"I thank you—no" said Mr. Grime, "no, believe not, eh?" this was addressed to Flimby, who shook his head.

"On business?" said the "Badger."

"Well, not exactly," answered Grime; "only waiting for a party, that's all."

"Oh!"

"Expect him here presently."

"Nobody wanted?," was the short inquiry of the "Badger."

"Oh, dear no, not at all! Oh, dear no!" quickly answered Grime.

"What's your game, then?" flourishing the toasting fork he had in his hand, with which he had been turning some chops on the fire.

"Got a reward to offer for some lost property."

"Oh, I see. Come out handsome?"

"I believe you; a good round sum."

Down went the "Badger's" toasting fork, and, leaving directions for Peg to see to the cooking, he motioned the two comers to follow him, which they immediately did. The three proceeded to the landlord's back parlour. Upon which the "Badger," placing his hands in the pockets of his shooting jacket, while he turned a piece of a splint in his mouth, as he stared hard at the two who had followed him.

"Come, what's your game?" said the "Badger."

"We want to recover some missing property, that's all," answered Mr. Grime.

"How was it lost?"

"Prigged," was the expressive answer.

"Oh, want to trace 'em. What was it? a mix up affair?"

"No, a chance robbery," answered Grime, who did not at all relish these straight forward questions. As for the "Badger," he generally managed to make matters as smooth as he could for both parties—but he set his face against handing any of his customers over to the mercy of the law—which, by the way, was carried out in rather a singular manner in the days of which we write.

"You see, Mr. Dyson," said Mr. Grime, in his most winning tones, "this is a matter which is left entirely to myself and my friend Flimby. Do not imagine any harm is intended. We have a party, (he now came out with his reaping hook fore-finger, as he was about to become demonstrative) whom we think may put us on the right scent. As to tracing the robbers or anything of that sort, why, that you know, is out of the question."

"Very well," said Mr. Dyson. "You know your own business, gentlemen. I have no right to enquire what it is, perhaps—only you see I can sometimes square matters when nobody else can. I knows a goodish lot, one sort and another."

"Oh! certainly—most unquestionably," said Mr. Grimes. "Much oblige to you for your consideration—I'm sure—much obliged."

"Quite welcome—take a glass of wine

or brandy, gentlemen. Come, what's it to be?" said their host.

"Thank you, you're very kind. What say you to a toothful of brandy, Flimby?"

"Wery good."

The "Badger" turned his back to a three-cornered cupboard to reach therefrom a bottle of choice Cognac, when Mr. Grime made a significant motion to his companion, who in reply thereto, frowned and shook his head. His meaning was immediately understood by his brother fox.

Glasses were filled and emptied — the liquor was declared to be of the right sort, and no mistake, as indeed it was. When the "Badger" said—

"Think it over, gentlemen. It's very likely I may be able to do this job cheaper

No. 6.

than you can yourselves. Just think it over, and let me hear."

"I thank you. "We will," said Grime. "We'll just see this party, and can afterwards consult our principal upon the matter. I am much obliged, Mr. Dyson for the offer, very much obliged," and the two foxes then betook themselves to the parlour again.

"Dash it all," said the "Badger," "I wish I knew their game."

Grime and Flimby quietly seated themselves again in the parlour of the "Cow and Cauliflower." Several furtive glances were again cast at them upon their entrance, for they were pretty well known to the majority of those present.

Near to the fire-place, a man was on his legs, pipe in hand, whilst he was indulging in what for him, must have been an oratorical flourish. He gave a significant look at Grime and Flimby as they neared the spot where he stood, and then proceeded with his discourse, which their entrance had for the moment interrupted.

"I say, no, Jim," continued the man. "I don't envy the Marquis of Badstock, or the Duke of Rockingham all their wealth. What comfort have they known compared to us? They do not know what it is to have a pair of boots with never a bit of a sole what let in the water at every step you took. They never knew the value of a new pair. When you went into all the puddles to just to defy 'em like. Nor the luxury of a meal after eight-and-forty hours fasting, when you just could walk into a tidy allowance and no mistake. That's what I call real enjoyment. Happiness, indeed! Go without your grog for a while, and then see how you enjoy it when you do chance to lay hold of any. It ain't them as have plenty of everything, as are the happiest. It's the variety and chances of life which makes it charming. Your nobs are not half so happy as us. They haven't the same freedom or independence."

And at these words, he gave a graceful flourish with the pipe he held in his hand, to impress the force of the sentiments he had been propounding upon the understandings of his hearers. To say the truth, the speaker would not impress the beholder with a perfect picture of happiness. He was dressed in miserable rags. His boots were what might be termed of the ventilatory description. And a grimy face and unshorn beard completed his appearance, which was certainly in direct opposition to that of an aristocratic personage.

"Ah, that's all very well," said another of the company, who was smoking his pipe at one of the tables near to where the last speaker stood. "But I mean to say, as how I should like to have an independence —leastways, I should like to try it for a time, if it only were for a change."

"You'd soon be sick of it now," answered the first speaker, contemptuously. "Very soon. Don't you think so, sir?"

This latter observation, was addressed to Mr. Grime.

"Can't say," said that individual; "but I think with your friend here, that I for one should like to try it."

A murmur of applause proceeded from several of the occupants of the room at the latter observation, from which it was evident that the theory propounded by the man with the pipe, was not a popular one.

The conversation was cut short by the entrance of an individual who came direct to where Grime and Flimby were seated, and without a word took his place beside them.

He was evidently the party whom they had been waiting for. The three conversed in whispers, and in a few more minutes, they rose to take their departure. They had scarcely gone out, when the oratorical individual followed them.

"Well," said Grime, when they had got some fifty or sixty yards from the "Cow and Cauliflower." "What's your news?"

"The colonel's stuck to it," was the brief reply.

"Ah! I thought so. Have you got scent as to where it is at present?"

"Yes."

"Umph! you have. So far so good. Where is it?"

"At a lawyer's, named Baintree."

"In London."

"It was in Bedford-row, but Loftby has found out through the clerk, that it's at the old gentleman's private house at Dulwich. He took it home to examine the papers at his leisure."

"Who is this Loftby?"

"Oh! he's a genteelish sort of a youth we employ upon the quiet. He looks so blessed innocent, that you'd suppose he was the son of some parson. But he's a knowing card, I can tell you."

"Then how do you propose getting it?" asked Grime.

"Ah!" exclaimed the man; "There's no other way, but——"

"Well; go on. We don't care how it's managed; there's the five hundred pounds the moment it is placed in our possession. We don't care how it is obtained."

"Oh, don't we though! Well, then," and here he sunk his voice to a whisper; "it must be a pull up job."

"Oh, a burglary."

"Xactly."

By this time the man who had stood by the fire-place overtook the three who were conversing together, and spoke to Grime and Flimby, by whom he was well known.

"One of us," said the party who had been conversing with the two officers, "is in this affair."

"Oh, indeed."

"You see," continued the man, "I ain't altogether up to this affair myself. It's the 'Nobbler' as is a going to do this ere job. If a crib is to be 'cracked' it's the "Nobbler' as will do it to rights, so I thought you'd jest like to see him, to come to an understanding."

"Very good," answered the two ferrets; and with this the man led them down one of the most ruinous streets in Westminster, where the houses, which were chiefly of wood, were nodding to one another. In one of the most ruinous of these did Grime and Flimby, with their two companions, enter. The passage was pitch dark, but the man who had conducted them thither blew a peculiar whistle with his lips, which appeared to be readily understood, for a door was opened at the farther end, and the figure of a man emerged therefrom; he was a broad-shouldered, square-built, ill-conditioned individual enough; and there was a savage ferocity and determination about his countenance which made it anything but agreeable to look upon. This person was no other than the "Nobbler," one of the most celebrated "cracksmen" of his day.

"The gentleman of whom I was a speaking to you about," said the man to the "Nobbler," by way of explanation to his looks of inquiry."

"Oh," answered the individual addressed; "walk in, gentlemen." They did as he desired, and found themselves in a dingy apartment, lighted by a solitary candle, which was placed on a small oaken table. Several housebreakers' implements lay about the room, such as "jemmys," skeleton keys, a dark lanthern, &c., &c.

"You want the chest in the possession of Mr. Baintree?" said the "Nobbler," looking at his visitors under a pair of bushy eyebrows.

"Y-es; there are five hundred pounds offered as a reward for it, which are yours, the moment it is obtained."

"Umph! and worth it," answered the "Nobbler."

"Well, it's a good round sum, I should suppose it's enough," said Grime; "but we sha'n't stand about giving a trifle more, you know."

The "Nobbler" nodded significantly.

"It must be a put up affair, and will want a deal of planing; however it must be done."

"And if you think the sum hardly sufficient I dare say our principal won't mind springing a little," said Mr. Grime."

"Oh, as to that we can see about extras afterwards," answered the other. It won't be enough, only I shall be able to do a little on my own hook, I dare say."

After some further conversation the parties seemed fully to understand one another, and Messrs. Grime and Flimby left, fully satisfied with the result of their interview.

CHAPTER VIII.

THE BURGLARY—DESPERATE RESISTANCE— THE SANGUINARY STRUGGLE.

WHEN Colonel Jack arrived with his companions at the "Badger's," after stopping the Oxford coach, which was recorded in our opening chapter, he and his companions retired to a private room, which Mr. Dyson kept for their especial use—and here it was that the plunder was divided. It then became a question about the box, and it did not take our highwaymen long to break it open. Hackett and Warrington uttered exclamations of disgust when they found it contained nothing else but musty old parchments, as they termed them; so Colonel Jack, who was mindful of the promise he had given to the young lady in the coach, took it under his own especial care. When more at leisure he hastily scanned the nature of its contents. There was a will of the late Lady Reichbeck, proofs of the marriage of the late Sir Reginald Fleetwood, and numerous other papers, the precise nature of which he was at a loss to determine. He, however, had seen enough to be made aware that there were many conflicting interests hanging upon the documents now in his possession; and he hesitated, therefore, in returning them to their supposed owners so soon as he had originally determined.

Mr. Baintree was a respectable solicitor. with whom he had been long acquainted. To him the colonel was known only under his right name of Frank Halford. Colonel Jack lost no time, therefore, to consult him upon the nature of the documents, and get that gentleman, to translate their contents to him; for law papers to the uninitiated require translating as much as Greek or Arabic MS.; more especially at the time of which we are writing, for verbose as the language of the law is even now, it is as nothing compared to what it was some centuries ago. Mr. Baintree, as the "Nobbler's" pall had truly observed, had conveyed to his private residence at Dulwich the papers our hero had entrusted to his charge. He had done this to be able to examine them more at his leisure, for Mr. Baintree had "declined into the vale of years," and did not visit his chambers quite so often as was his wont. His son attending to the more active duties in town.

The reader has already seen how many persons there are who take so deep an interest in the contents of the box, which so singularly should have come into the possession of our hero. Sir Richard Fleetwood wanted it, if it were for no other purpose than destroying the proofs of his brother's marriage. The astute Mr. Sharpthorne had an eye to its possession to obtain the highest terms he could for it, no matter from whom; hence it was that the services of that daring pair of foxes, the Messrs. Grime and Flimby, were called into requisition. A traitor is generally to be found in everybody's camp is an old saying, and it proved so in the present instance. One of the colonel's odd men, as he might be termed, was sent as proof against Mr. Grime's gold. He informed that worthy the whereabouts of the desired chest. Then it was that the youth Loftby was employed to call at the lawyer's office, and, by several indirect questions, artfully designed, he was enabled to ascertain that it was safely deposited at Dulwich. This ascertained, the services of the "Nobbler" were brought into requisition, and that gentleman being a first-rate master of his craft, set to work in his usual business-like way—for the "Nobbler" was not a man to do his work bunglingly. His plans were laid with great care before any great "crack" job came off. Having ascertained the locality and residence where the desired prize was concealed, the next steps were to become acquainted with the interior of the house, and, if possible, where Mr. Baintree placed this description of valuables.

The "Nobbler" sent efficient emissaries down for his purpose. A smart young fellow—of course, an arrant rascal, or else he would not belong to the "Nobbler"—was instructed to make love to one of Mr. Baintree's servants. This was soon accomplished, for the fellow took lodgings at the nearest public-house, and, when the girl came for beer or anything else for the household, he endeavoured to pick an acquaintance with her, and eventually was declared to be "her young man;" then it was that he obtained an entry into the house, and, of course, all the information required for the "Nobbler's" purpose.

All his plans being matured, our celebrated cracksman, went himself down to take another survey of the premises, with a view to making his final arrangements. Facing the lawn of Mr. Braintree's house, was what they called the drawing-room, which nevertheless was on the basement with a verandah in front, with French windows opening on the lawn. This was the room "the cracksman" chose to make his entrance. He had obtained from his emissary an exact description of the shutters and fastenings; in fact he was furnished with a rough sketch of the same.

As this room abutted out from the house itself, and was joined by two other parlours before the passage was reached, it was sufficiently far removed from the sleeping apartments for the "Nobbler" to work his housebreaking instruments with safety, without fear of waking the inmates. The shutters were fastened with bolts, the exact position of which had already been ascertained. These bolts were held by screws. The skilful cracksman had an instrument made which was capable of turning the screws from the outside, that is he proposed to bore with a centre-bit until he reached the end of the screw, and then insert his instrument and turn them one by one until the bolt was fairly released.

Darkness enveloped the house and grounds of Mr. Baintree. Darkness also enshrouded the Dulwich, which, in these days was almost guiltless of lamps—unless those miserable old fashioned oil lamps could be called luminaries. These were placed here and there at about the distance of a quarter of a mile apart, and even then every second one was out, in all probability having succumbed to a passing breeze. It was a fitting night for deeds of darkness, and well adapted for the "Nobbler's" work. The household of Mr. Baintree have long since yielded to the drowsy god, and there is no watcher there for the coming outrage, save Mr. Baintree's faithful dog, who will, however, by the time the burglars arrive, be no longer numbered with the things of this earth, for already has he partaken of poisoned food, which one of the burglars gang had caused to be placed in his way for the purpose of destroying him. It is past midnight by nearly an hour; one of the distant watchmen is comfortably snoozing in his wooden habitation, and, with the exception, perhaps, of a market cart or two, neither passenger or vehicle is to be seen or heard on the Dulwich road. Hark! there is a cart coming now—yes, rumble go the wheels—it is from London apparently—it contains the "Nobbler" and five of his choice companions, with the implements of their vocation. It stops at a small cottage down a lane not far distant from Mr. Baintree's house; here the horse is stabled and the party of housebreakers alight from the vehicle, and, armed with the necessary implements, they proceed with stealthy steps towards the "crib" they intend to crack. They soon reach the garden rails of Mr. Baintree's house, and to vault over these is the work of only a few seconds, then they creep through the shrubbery, and arrive at the lawn, which faces the dining room—this is at the rear of the house. The "Nobbler" proceeds to business. Had the inmates of the house been awake or near enough, four long scratches might have been heard, and then a sudden jingle as a plate of glass was removed; then came a grinding sound, low, and continuous. Something is moving close to the fastening of the bar which goes across the shutters —ah! it falls—it is a screw. The same process is gone through with another, and so on till the bolt, into which the pin is inserted, is about to fall, the iron bar would then go with it and make a great noise in so doing, but the skilful cracksman has provided against this. He thrusts a thin shining blade through one of the chinks in the shutter, upon which, as the sixth screw falls, the bar, deprived of its support, sinks, but is received on the blade and allowed to sink slowly down, the shutters part and the fingers of a hand appear at the edge of the nearest—the shutters are thrust apart, and, with a cat step the burglar enters the room, followed by his companions. Cautiously shading the dark lanthern he held in his hand, the "Nobbler" took a hasty but careful survey of the apartment. All was as still as death, they then took their way into the room adjoining, beyond which was another. Having passed through these they found themselves in the passage; here they paused. The man who had been doing the amatory to the servant, and whose name was Dabbs, now led the way. He was well acquainted with the house. Two bedrooms had to be passed through—with inmates in each—before the room could be reached which contained the coveted treasure. The first one was the servants, which led to an empty room, beyond which was the bed-room of young Mr. Baintree. It was necessary to pass through this to reach the room beyond, in which the elder Mr. Baintree kept the majority of his papers, title deeds, &c., &c.

When the party of burglars entered the servant's room they beheld her fast asleep; and the man who carried the only dark lanthern with which they had provided themselves carefully concealed it beneath his coat. He had not proceeded many steps before his foot struck against something, when he stumbled and fell to the floor, putting out his lanthern with the fall, and upsetting some small piece of furniture, which in the stillness of the night made a loud clatter.

A muttered curse issued from the lips of the robber, and the girl awoke, and uttered a loud scream; and when she observed the figures of several men in her bed-room, she huddled on what clothing she had on, and would have made her escape through the open door, had not one of the burglars, foreseeing her intention, sprang forward and firmly grasped her by the arm. She was about to send forth another scream, when the man who detained her stopped her utterance by placing his hand over her mouth.

"Curse you," he said, "if you utter one word I'll scatter your brains."

He presented at her head the muzzle of a large pistol, from which she recoiled back in horror. In another moment one of the other burglars tied a handkerchief round the mouth of the girl, and bid his companion who had hold of her keep her quiet.

While this scene had been taking place, it will be necessary to take a glance at young Mr. Baintree. That gentleman, upon the burglars' first entrance into the girl's apartment, had been sound asleep, but the noise occasioned by the man's fall, added to which was the girl's scream, together with the smothered voices of the men, these various noises awoke him. He slipped on his trowsers and listened attentively at his bed-room door. In spite of all their caution he could detect the sound of shuffling feet and hoarse whispers. Mr. Baintree then felt fully persuaded that there were robbers in the house.

To spring out upon them without a weapon would be worse than madness, as there was evidently several of them. Although the night had been dark when the housebreakers originally started upon their expedition, there was sufficient light admitted into the sleeping apartment of Mr. Baintree to admit of his seeing pretty plainly about his room. In vain his eyes wandered about in search of some weapon of defence. The only thing he could find for his purpose was a small species of carving knife, which luckily for him, by the merest chance, had been left in his apartment, for he said afterwards that he was totally unable to account for its presence. He instantly armed himself with this. To comprehend the position of the respective parties, the attacking and repelling, it will be necessary to explain the nature of the stage on which the present tragedy was performed—for it was a tragedy, as will be seen hereafter. Upon entering Mr. Baintree's room there was opposite to the door a large wainscoated recess, which in all old fashioned houses were very common. It was through this recess that it was necessary to pass before the room could be reached which contained the required treasure; there it was that Mr. Baintree took up his station, determined, if needs must be, to sell his life as dearly as possible. Armed with his knife he awaited patiently the issue. He was not long kept in suspense. He observed the "Nobbler" enter first; he could in the dark recess where he had taken up his position observe with tolerable accuracy the actions of his opponents. They looked round the apartment and observed that the bed was unoccupied, although it had evidently been laid upon. The "Nobbler" uttered an exclamation of surprise and discontent as he made this discovery, and looked about the apartment for its occupant, but in vain. In the recess where Mr. Baintree stood concealed it was impossible to discern anything, it being enshrouded in complete darkness; he could see his opponents, but they were unable to observe him. There was but one entrance in this recess, and that was through a small door, which would only admit one person to enter at a time.

"Now Dabbs," said the "Nobbler," "What's to be our game now? You know the way; on with me at once!"

"Yonder's the door," answered Dabbs, as he pointed to the partition.

"That!—why it appears a sort of closet or store room. Sure you are right—eh?"

"Yes; quite sure. When inside there you will find another door, which leads to"—he nodded significantly.

"Lead the way, then; look sharp, men!" said the Nobbler.

Dabbs was the first man to enter. He had scarcely put his foot inside when he found himself in the grasp of a powerful man, who struck him with the knife, which entered his chest.

"D——n!" he exclaimed; "I am a murdered man!" and he fell to the floor bathed in his blood.

The burglars recoiled back in horror at the evident fate of their companion. It was impossible for them to tell with certainty how many persons were concealed in the recess; however, another of the party ventured in. He was received upon his entrance with a blow from the knife—this time not a fatal one, as he raised his arm and secured the blade on the thick part thereof. A deep flesh wound was the consequence, and the men groaned in agony. He then grappled with his assailant, and struck at him in the dark at random. Again and again the knife found a passage in his body, and after repeated wounds he fell from exhaustion and loss of blood. The burglars now hesitated; two of their companions had fallen by the same mysterious agency. The "Nobbler," to use his own phraseology, found himself *queered*.

"Fire in!" he exclaimed, "and be d——d to them. Fire; give them an ounce of lead!"

He snatched a blunderbuss from one of his companions and pointed the muzzle of it to the open doorway.

Baintree saw the end of it plain enough and calculated the chances; these were in favour of escaping from its contents; should these spread much, the probability was that he would receive a portion of the contents; however, being a man of inflexible resolution and iron nerve, he made up his mind to avert the result. Placing his back against the wall, to get as far removed as possible, he scarcely breathed lest by doing so he might give any indication as to his whereabouts. The panel was found—the shot was scattered in various directions, but Baintree found himself unhurt. After this, a death-like stillness prevailed; no sigh, or groan, or falling body gave indication to the burglars that the contents of their guns had found a home in human flesh. After this two other pistols were discharged with a like effect.

In the stillness of the night and enshrouded in darkness the operations of their concealed foe had in it, to the minds of the burglars, something awful. In a few minutes, however, another of the party ventured in the fatal recess. A desperate stab was made at him, which struck his shoulder, and the weapon striking against the scapula, or shoulder bone, it gleamed downwards, opening the flesh in its passage, causing a long wound, but not one which disabled the burglar from further action. He closed with his antagonist, and, by a desperate effort, endeavoured to throw him, in which, however, he was unsuccessful. Two more wounds were given by his determined opponent, and he was compelled to succumb, and fell senseless beside his companions in crime.

By this time the burglars found themselves shorn of half their numbers; six in all had entered Mr. Baintree's sleeping apartments while one was engaged in keeping the servants in check, consequently, out of their party there were but the "Nobbler" and two of his companions. The former made up his mind to have a rush for it—and they all then entered, one after the other in quick succession. The first man received a desperate wound—the second, which was the "Nobbler" himself, grappled with his unseen adversary. A most fearful struggle now ensued, the "Nobbler," with his prodigious strength, lifted his adversary fairly off his legs, and endeavoured to dash out his brains against the partition—but Mr. Baintree held firmly on to the throat of the housebreaker, and made repeated and desperate plunges with his weapon, and was surprised to find that it took no effect. He became aware that the point of the knife had become bent from coming in contact with the ribs or chests of his assailants.

During a slight pause in the struggle, he

contrived to straighten it by stamping upon its end with his foot. Having partially accomplished this, he dealt the "Nobbler" a terrible blow, which laid open his cheek, and finished by inflicting a severe wound in his left shoulder.

"Hell's curses," roared the ruffian, as by a vigorous effort he threw his companion from him with terrible force.

The boards had become by this time so slippery with gore, that it was with some difficulty that the combatants had been able to keep their feet.

Mr. Baintree, when thrown by the "Nobbler" with such force, slipped along the floor, and fell against the partition, striking his head so severely, that he, what with his exertions and the blow, was rendered for some time senseless. The "Nobbler" did not wait after he had fairly shook off his determined antagonist. He rushed immediately into the room where he had been told the chest lay concealed, and he was followed by his only remaining companion.

Immediately upon their entrance into this apartment, they found means to fasten up the door with screwes they carried in their pocket. The "Nobbler" and his companion then proceeded to break open desks, drawers, cupboards, safes; in fact, everything which they thought contained valuables, and discovered amongst other things the desired box. Securing this, and hastily ransacking the apartment, the housebreakers now bethought themselves of how they were to make their escape. To return through the recess was not to be thought of. The "Nobbler" opened the window of the room, and saw that by laying hold of the vine and trellis work, there would be but little difficulty in reaching the ground in safety. The "Nobbler's" descent was, however, painful, owing to the severe wound he had received in his conflict with Mr. Baintree, which he had hastily bound up as well as the circumstances would admit. He had, however, lost a considerable quantity of blood.

The two housebreakers, when they had reached the lawn (which fronted the house) in safety, blew a whistle, to let their companions know that they were about to depart. Not that they imagined any of those in the recess would be even able to answer any summons again in this world. But the man who it will be remembered was left in charge of the servant girl, had not been in the desperate affray already described. He, however, did not appear to the summons of his companion in crime.

It will be necessay now to return to Mr. Baintree. When he had been thrown so violently by the housebreaker, he lay for some minutes senseless—partly from sheer exhaustion, and partly from the blow. When, however, he did recover, he tried the door which the "Nobbler" had so effectually screwed up. This he found impossible to open. He then made for the other part of the premises, upon which he caught sight of one of the burglars presenting a pistol at the head of the unfortunate servant girl; who, the moment she caught sight of her young master, clasped the wrist of her tormenter, and made a desperate struggle to release herself from his grasp.

The pistol went off in the conflict, happily without any mischievous effect. The ruffian drew a clasp knife, which he placed between his teeth, while with his hands he endeavoured to pinion the girl preparatory to giving her a final blow. Muffled as her mouth was, she uttered a half-stifled scream. Mr. Baintree rushed forward to her assistance, and struck at the man with his avenging knife.

"Hell's curses," exclaimed the burglar, as the blade of the knife entered his upraised arm. He turned like a tiger upon his foe; his wound was only a surface one after all, and he flung himself like an infuriated animal upon his antagonist. Weak as he was, Mr. Baintree found himself no match for the burglar, who held him firmly in his grasp, while with his upraised knife he was about to implant a fatal wound upon the young lawyer. In another minute his career would in all probability have come to a termination had it not have been for the heroism of the servant girl, who seeing the imminent danger of her master, with an energy which the softer sex are sometimes able to call forth upon great emergencies, rushed upon the assailant, and with the butt-end of the pistol, which had fallen on the floor, and struck him a terrific blow on the temple. He reeled beneath its effects and was nearly stunned. Mr. Baintree wrested the knife from his grasp, and opening the window shouted loudly for assistance.

The groom and gardener slept in two rooms over the stable. Hearing their master's voice they were awakened from their slumbers, and lost no time in making for the interior of the house. In crossing the lawn they came in contact with the "Nobbler" and his companion, at whom they discharged their two pistols, wounding the former in the leg and the latter in the shoulder. However, the two housebreakers managed to get clear off the premises, followed by the groom and gardener, who gave chase to them for some distance, but under the cover of the darkness of the night they were enabled to conceal themselves from their pursuers, and the two men thought it best to repair to the assistance of their master, and succeeded in making the other burglar a prisoner.

By the following morning the whole neighbourhood was in the greatest state of alarm when the incidents of the previous night became known. All those who were in the recess were found to be dead. It is true that one of them survived for three or four hours, but he never recovered his consciousness. An inquest was held on the bodies of the deceased men, and a verdict returned of justifiable homicide.

The "Nobbler" and his companion when they had escaped from the two men, made the best of their way to the cottage where they had put up their horse and cart and started upon what might be termed to them an unfortunate expedition. Here they remained concealed during the night, and in the morning endeavoured to drive with their "swag" to town, which was an important thing to have risked under all the circumstances; for by this time the events of the previous night was in everybody,s mouth; and the "Nobbler" and his companion had not got very far upon their road when the former observed, at some distance, one of the district constabulary coming along on horseback. He much feared that his person was known to this officer. What was he to do? It would look suspicious to turn back, and there was no immediate turning out of the road they were taking. The "Nobbler" thought, under these circumstances, that it would be advisable to drop himself from the cart and let his companion drive on. This expedient he adopted, and watched the result from behind a thick clump of foliage. He saw his companion halt and the parish constable enter into conversation with him. While this was taking place, another constable made his appearance, and the contents of the cart being examined, the two took the housebreaker and his vehicle into custody. The burglar was too much crippled with his wound to give a thought of offering any resistance against two well-armed men, and with a bitter oath the "Nobbler" beheld his companion, with all the booty, marched off to the district gaol.

It was with great care and difficulty that he was himself eventually able to make his escape to London and reach the "Cow and Cauliflower," whither he had made an appointment with that sapient pair the Messrs. Grime and Flimby.

The two prisoners were conveyed to London in the prison van, and had the honour of appearing for examination before no less a person than Lord Mayor Gubbins, and were by that great dispenser of justice fully committed to take their trial for burglary with violence, and attempted murder.

A day or two after the prisoners had been taken to Newgate, there to await their trial at the ensuing sessions, the astute Mr. Sharpthorne made his appearance at Guildhall, and begged a private interview with Ephraim Gubbins, Esq. He was admitted into the apartment where that great legal functionary was wont to see a favored few upon private business. Sharpthorne had been intimately acquainted with the great Gubbins before he had attained his present giddy height in the social scale, and consequently found no difficulty in gaining his lordship's "ear"—to use a common phrase. The chief magistrate actually extended his hand to the little lawyer, as he entered the hallowed precincts of his private audience chamber.

"A terrible affair—shocking affair I may say," said Mr. Sharpthorne, knocking his hands. "I mean the late burglary at Dulwich. In the dead of the night, the sanctity and peace of the private home of one of the most worthy members of the profession I have the honour of belonging to, has been most ruthlessly violated."

"Yes," said Gubbins, oratorically, "but the law is all powerful, and happily does not allow such miscreants to escape unpunished."

"It is lucky we have such able administrators of the law, who are enabled to mete out justice with such an even hand," said Mr. Sharpthorne, bowing towards the Lord Mayor with profound respect. When it was needed, he could for the *nonce* assume a flattering and obsequious manner, and could act the bully as well when it answered his purpose. The Lord Mayor twirled the heavy chain which hung round his chest and looked potentially wise.

Mr. Sharpthorne eyed him with an admiring gaze, and then said very quaintly——

"The property!"

"Oh, that which has been taken from the house of Mr. Baintree, do you mean?"

"Yes; precisely."

"It is in our possession."

"And will be, I suppose?"

"Yes; till after the trial."

"Part of it is stolen property."

"It's all so, I should suppose, seeing that it was taken from the burglars."

"No; I don't mean that. Of course we knew it was taken from Mr. Baintree's house, but part of it was previously purloined. I allude to the iron box, containing family papers of same importance. This belonged to a client of mine, of which he was robbed by a highwayman."

"Indeed! that is singular. How came it then in the possession of Mr. Baintree?"

"That, perhaps, is hard to say; but my present object in seeing your lordship is to inquire if this can be given up to its rightful owner, Sir Richard Fleetwood."

"Oh, it belongs to Sir Richard Fleetwood, does it?" said the Lord Mayor. He had a great respect for a baronet or titled person. The lawyer nodded assent.

"From whom it was stolen," he said in continuation.

"Well," said the Lord Mayor, "Sir Richard will have the satisfaction of recovering back his property after the trial."

"Yes; no doubt, but you see," said the lawyer, mysteriously, "there are several contingencies hanging upon these papers. It is necessary that they should be kept as secret as possible. There are proofs of a marriage of Sir Richard's brother, a will,

No. 7.

and a variety of documents which it is necessary for the more perfect ends of justice to be met, that they should lie in obscurity. Then again, I, as Sir Richard's legal adviser, require the documents in my possession at once."

"I do not see that I should be justified in giving up those papers before the trial, although, of course, I should be too glad to do anything to oblige either yourself or Sir Richard Fleetwood."

"Umph! Not justified. Ah, perhaps not; but you perhaps might lend them for a while, merely for legal purposes. *Sub rosa.* Eh?"

The Lord Mayor hesitated, and then desired his visitor to wait a few minutes, while he consulted the city clerk. After which, he returned and informed Mr.

Sharpthorne, that he could not consistently with his duty part with any of the property which had come into his hands.

The little lawyer was chagrined at this refusal, as he was particularly desirous of making himself fully acquainted with the documents, without consulting Sir Richard in the matter, who was quite in ignorance of his attorney's proceedings.

"Umph!" exclaimed the lawyer, as he cut his finger nails. "That is awkward, I particularly wanted this property, my lord; or at any rate, the loan of it for a day or two. But if it is against your rules, why of course I must bow to you decision. You could not, I suppose, let me see them in your presence? Say for half an hour or so."

"Well, as a matter of personal friendship," answered the mayor, pompously; "that might possibly be arranged. I tell you what can be done, Mr. Sharpthorne. We have known each other a few years, you know——"

"We have, my lord—we have indeed. Ah, ah! I should think so; and every year has added to the respect I have towards your lordship."

"I am much flattered, I am sure. Now as a matter of personal friendship between ourselves, I will let you consult these documents at my private residence. I shall be leaving here when the court closes, and shall drive down to Bagshot to-morrow. If you like to pay me a visit there then, and be my guest for the night—for it will be too far for you to return home in the evening—you can then have a glace at what you please amongst these documents, for I will take them in my own carriage for the purpose, and bring them back with me upon my return to my official duties. There can be no harm done by that proceeding, and nobody will be any the wiser."

"I am much bounden to your lordship for your lordship's consideration and kindness evinced on this occasion, as in many others," said Mr. Sharpthorne, in a burst of overwhelming gratitude. "I will do myself the pleasure of waiting upon your lordship at Bagshot to-morrow. Let me not intrude upon your valuable time any longer," and shaking the Lord Mayor by the hand warmly, the lawyer took his departure.

CHAPTER IX.

AT THE "COW AND CAULIFLOWER."

In a dingy private room of the "Cow and Cauliflower," sat the "Nobbler" after his return to town. His features had never at any time been prepossessing, but now they appeared perfectly demonical—rage, hate, and desperation were observable upon his ill-favoured visage. He bent his head down upon his hands, and bit his nails as he ruminated upon his disastrous expedition. He was the very picture or personification of every evil passion. It would have been rather a dangerous thing for a stranger to come across him in his present mood. His liquor remained untouched—he was too absorbed in his own immediate trouble to care much for his creature comforts.

Presently the "Badger" entered the room, and being of a philosophical temperament he generally sympathised with those customers who had the honour of sharing his confidence. The "Badger" had a straw in his mouth, which he twisted about as he reflected upon mundane affairs.

"You've been queered Jem, this time, and no mistake," said the "Badger," looking through the dingy window of the apartment at a fives court which lay at the back of the premises.

"Ugh! Queered! Should think I had, and no mistake. Queered! Come to a regular smash!—done up!—two palls in quod, and the remainder sent headlong to the devil, and all the swag gone."

"And palls likely to be scragged."

"Ugh! likely! Certain you mean."

"Will, they split?"

"How the devil do I know! 'Spose not—may though.

"You'll hook to somewhere till all this is over, I suppose. Eh?"

"'Shall keep as dark as I can of course."

"Well we are safe here we know. Here's the trap," said the "Badger" as he pointed to a trap-door in the floor, which, however, would never be observed by a stranger, as it was in a dark corner of the room, which was covered with an old stained piece of matting nearly the colour of the boards.

"Down here leads to the cellar, Jem," continued the "Badger." "After going through one or two cellars, you come to that subterranean passage, or what was originally a sewer that, as I told you before, leads to the vaults or arches by the side of the Thames. When you are once underneath here I'll forgive them if they find you or anyone else."

"Thanks, Bill. All right," answered the "Nobbler" a little mollified.

"Not that there's any probability of any on 'em coming here; but I don't admit strangers into my private rooms."

"No," answered the housebreaker, "but

they do come sometimes notwithstanding."

"They does," answered the "Badger." "They does so certainly, Jem, but not without my being able to give a bit of a notice to my more peculiar friends, and then they know what to do."

"All right," answered the "Nobbler." "Have those pair of beauties shown head yet?" This was in allusion to Messrs. Grime and Flimby.

"No," was the answer.

"No, don't intend and be d—d to them. They know the game is up, and have namassed."

"Small blame to them for that," answered the landlord.

"Ah, that's as thinking goes. I wish I had never seen their ugly mugs. Should'nt if it had not been for that gipsy chap, who's as big a humbug as the rest." The "Nobbler" was in a mood to carp and find fault with all the world.

"Well, Jem, it ain't of no manner of use showing the down-hearted over what can't be helped. You acted for the best as you thought; we've all our misfortunes and trials in every line. Cheer up man and take a sup of that, it's some of the right sort," and he pointed to the untasted liquor which stood before his customer.

The "Nobbler" uttered a grunt, and drained off the contents of the tankard savagely.

"Well, now I'll leave you, Jem, 'cause o' business. You aint a going yet."

"Should think not," was the prompt reply.

"Well, then, I'll just lock you in, for safety's sake."

The man nodded his assent to the course, and the landlord of the "Cow and Cauliflower" retired from his moody companion. Betaking himself to his own private bar-parlour, he found it occupied by Colonel Jack, Hackett, and Warrington, who were seated on the table thereof, while they beat their boots with the riding whips they held in their hands.

"Servant, gentlemen," said the "Badger," as he caught sight of the new comers. "Hope as how things are all going smooth and square with you. Got one cove here down upon his luck, and no mistake."

"What's been his game?" asked Hackett.

"Cracking a crib."

"Oh! Got the ferrets after him?"

"Xpects to have."

Hackett looked at the colonel significantly, but made no reply. Some further conversation ensued; after which the three highwaymen retired to a room they generally went to when visiting the establishment.

In the course of an hour a mean-looking little man made his appearance at the bar, and inquired for Colonel Jack. He was immediately shown up into the room where he and his companions were seated. The colonel rose and left the room with his visitor. When in the pasage he said quickly—

"Any information?"

"Ye-es, m-aster;" the man had an evident impediment in his speech, which was habitual with him. "Yes-es; th-ee lawyer goes to the mayor's home to-m-morrow."

"Well, what of that?"

"The mayor takes the—ch!—chest down with him in his own carriage."

"When?"

"To-night. He said to Mr. Sharpthorne as how it was to be to-morrow, but I found out at the stables that the coachman has orders to drive his lordship down to-night."

"At what time do you suppose?"

"Can't tell xactly, but should say he would start at about six."

"Very good. You've done well—there, take this with many thanks," said the colonel, as he handed the man several pieces of money, which he quickly deposited in his pocket.

"Have anything?" said the colonel.

"No, thank you, master."

"Yes, take something. Call for what you like at the bar, and say it's for me. Do you hear?"

The man nodded assent, and departed. The colonel returned to his companions.

"Well," said Hackett, as he entered the apartment.

"Is it business or no business to-night?"

"Business," answered the colonel.

"When?"

"The sooner the better. Our worthy friend and well-wisher starts with my property. Ah! ah! at about six o'clock this evening."

"The devil!"

"No not him; the Lord Mayor."

"Ah, I see! It's a distinction without a difference. Ah! ah!"

"Precisely; but with your consent we will be off and away as soon as possible. No matter how long we have to wait, we can do business on the road and take our time."

In a short time their horses were saddled, and the colonel, Hackett, and Warrington, left the streets of London far behind them, as they galloped along the road leading to Bagshot, and, after some "hauls" from a stray passenger or so, they reached the mayor's house, but as yet had not been able to catch a sight of his carriage coming along the road.

"Are you sure you are right in your information?" asked Warrington of the colonel.

"Quite sure; that chap you saw come in at the "Badger's" is a sort of understrapper at Guildhall. He serves summonses and warrants, and is a general odd man under the clerks. He knows most what's going on, and keeps his mouth shut until he is well paid for opening it."

"He's a 'cute sort."

"Yes! Although he looks spoony enough, I generally find him right in his information, and should we be disappointed to-night depend upon it his lordship has, for some reason or another, altered his mind. Great men are fitful."

"They are so;" and little ones, too, sometimes."

"But it's no use our loitering about here," said the colonel, as he ran his eye along the distant road in his endeavour to catch a sight of any coming vehicle. "Let us trot gently back towards London;" and with this the three took their way along the road; two, three, four, eight miles had been past, and still no signs of his lordship's carriage. The three highwaymen halted under the shadow of some trees; and, taking their pipes and tobacco pouches, commenced smoking with the greatest *nonchalance*, and quietly awaited the appearance of the party for whom they were on the watch.

After some considerable time had past, Colonel Jack had the pleasure of observing the carriage of the Lord Mayor making its way along the road at a good round pace.

"Here it comes!" he exclaimed to his companions. "We have, after all, not waited for nothing; I thought my information could be relied on. Here it comes, and no mistake; keep quiet till it nears us!"

The three highwaymen were upon the alert with pistols, ready primed and at half-cock. As the carriage came up, Hackett and Warrington sprang to the horses' heads and stopped the vehicle. In vain did the coachman endeavour to lash his horses on. Warrington rode up to the side of the box upon which he was seated, and presented his pistol at him, demanding at the same time his instant obedience to his commands on pain of immediate death. The old coachman recoiled at the appearance of the barrel of the weapon and let go his reins, in mute obedience to the man's desire. By this time the colonel had ridden up to the carriage window, which he opened, and demanded all the valuables possessed

by the occupant. A shrill scream was the only answer he received. This emanated from the Lady Mayoress, who was with her husband in the interior of the vehicle. There were two stalwart footmen behind, but all they did was to gaze in speechless horror upon the highwaymens' proceedings.

"Scoundrels! villains!" exclaimed the Mayor. "I shall have the pleasure of paying you out for this some day or other; you'll find the law too powerful for you—a terrible day is in store for you. Do you know, sir, that you have the audacity to stop the chief magistrate of London?"

This was addressed to the colonel, whose masked visage peered in at the window.

"Can't help it, my lord," said the colonel. "Every man to his business."

"Business, you rascal! Do you call highway robbery a business?"

"As much as you do swindling," was the reply.

"You highway thief!" exclaimed the Mayor, "you'll swing for this as sure as you are a living man."

"Very possible; but that's not to the purpose. Come, out with your cash! I am in no mood to hear sermons. Come, your money at once! or—I'll show you as little mercy as you show the unfortunate wretches who are brought before you. Your money at once! I'm rather in a hurry, my lord!"

"Oh, good Mr. Highwaymen!" exclaimed the Mayoress. "Pray have mercy on us; take what we have in welcome!" and here she thrust in the hands of the colonel her watch, chain, purse, brooch, and rings.

"Take all, although"—and here she hesitated.

"What, madam?"

"Although that ring was the gift of a dear friend, and consequently highly prized."

"Then I beg your acceptance of the same," said the colonel, as he took off his hat and returned it to its owner.

"Thanks—many thanks; I'm sure you are very good. After all, really, quite a gentleman, I declare," she continued, addressing herself to her husband.

The Lord Mayor directed upon her a withering and magisterial glance, such as he was wont to direct towards some juvenile culprit who had the misfortune to appear before him. His glance, however, failed to strike with awe his better half, who appeared perfectly impervious to it.

"Now, then," said the colonel, "Quick! I will trouble your lordship for a few small articles by way of a keepsake, which, of course, I shall duly treasure up in recollection of the honour of the present interview."

This was said in a mocking tone. With many muttered anathemas, the chief magistrate of London handed over his property to Colonel Jack, who, after he had taken possession of the same, still remained at the window of the carriage. The Lord Mayor stared with some surprise at his pertinacity.

"I am afraid there is something else I shall require," said our hero, quietly. His lordship looked aghast at the latter observation.

"What more do you require? You have all we are possessed of," said the mayor.

"Not quite," was the cool reply. "There is another article—a small iron chest or box."

"Zounds, man!" exclaimed the Mayor, "Would you rob the law of its rights. I cannot nor will not defraud innocent persons of their property, and shall require to hand over the same. Besides which it can be of no service to you, as it only contains legal deeds—only legal deeds, which are valueless—though the only deed you will ever require will be your own death warrant, and that you'll have sure enough some of these days."

"Possibly so," answered the colonel. "Nevertheless, you see I require this box; and more, I must and will have it. Now do you understand? It happens to be my property, having been stolen from me."

"Stolen, indeed! And where did you get it from?"

"By the exercise of my profession," answered the highwayman with a sneer.

"You may take all I have, indeed! Indeed, I have given you already what I possess. But that which is entrusted to me in my judicial capacity, I persist in refusing to the last," said Mr. Gubbins, firmly.

"Then we must have it by force," answered the colonel, "by fair means or foul. "What! oh, oh! Hackett!"

In a moment, his companion was by his side in answer to his comrade's summons.

"Mercy! gentlemen, mercy!" screamed out the Lady Mayoress. "Let me entreat of you to show mercy."

"We wish not to offer any violence—always regret being compelled to do so, but in this instance, do not intend to be thwarted." The colonel opened the door of the carriage, and pistol in hand, forced an entrance. The mayor grappled with him, but Colonel Jack pinioned him firmly against the back of the carriage. His lady uttered several piercing screams, which called forth an oath from Hackett, who also entered, and sought for the desired property. The Lady Mayoress, who wished for peace at any price, directed his attention to where it lay concealed under the seat. Hackett lost no time in securing it, and left the interior of the carriage, whilst the mayor, breathless, and almost half strangled, endeavoured to call upon his footmen to come to the rescue.

Those valiant worthies did manage to descend from the rear of the carriage, and seized hold of the colonel, as he alighted. Who with one blow from his fist, sent one of them sprawling full-length upon the earth. The other man let go of our hero, and began shouting lustily for assistance.

"Hold your row," said Warrington, as he dealt the man a tremendous blow with his heavy riding whip; upon which, he ran off at a good round pace, and continued to call for assistance.

Slott, who had hitherto contented herself with watching the proceedings of her master, and wait to see if her services would be required, now seemed to have lost that admirable patience which usually characterised her. She sprang towards the fugitive flunkey, and seized him by one of the calves of his legs. The man yelled with pain, and his delicate white stocking became stained with a copious flow of blood from the wound inflicted by the dog's teeth.

"Hold your cursed row, you fool," said Hackett, "or I'll blow your brains out. That is, if you have any."

Slott shook the man violently, and he fell to the earth groaning and rubbing his wounded leg, while he kicked and rolled over in agony. The colonel's dog then left him to his fate, and trotted after his master, who by this time had got some little distance from the scene.

The colonel and his companion took a bye road to town, and galloped on at full speed. They had done enough for that night, and did not consider it worth while risking the chance of a capture by being detained on the road in the exercise of their vocation. Once more the colonel found himself in possession of the box, which had awakened the interest of so many individuals who have at present been introduced. How its contents bear upon the various characters, it is for us hereafter to see.

CHAPTER X.

THE LOVERS PARTING — THE JOURNEY TO LONDON — SIR RICHARD FLEETWOOD IN LOVE.

AH! unhappy is the wretch who ships his hopes upon a woman's smile. At the mercy of the wind and waves, his frail shallop is tempest tost, and threatened to founder at every passing wave. He finds his happiness anchored in quicksands. So thought Henry Osborne. Not that he had any reason to complain of Honora, who, to say the truth, appeared, and indeed, was true and constant towards him; but she was about to leave him. Her father had determined upon a residence in the metropolis, and for a time at all events, he had determined to leave the classic ground of Oxford.

When Miss Langford made her lover acquainted with this fact, he saw in it the possibility of an estrangement between himself and Honora. In the giddy vortex of London fashionable society, the pale Oxford student might be forgotten. He did not dare to hint such a supposition to his enslaver, but in the lonely hours spent in his own rooms at Christ Church College, such thoughts as these obtruded themselves upon his notice, which he in vain endeavoured to dispel. Ah! unhappy he, who waits upon a woman's smile!

Osborne was of a sensitive nature, and knew that he had made a great demand upon Honora, in which he called sacrificing herself for his sake; and he foresaw the possibility of suitors making their appearance. And then when he was absent, and her father's persuasion, what might be the consequence. However, with mutual vows of constancy, the lovers parted. Mr. Langford and his fair daughter fixed their abode in Harley-street, Cavendish-square. Some months had passed since the removal of Mr. Langford to the metropolis. Months of anxiety and heartbreakings to Henry Osborne. And during this period, by one of those singular coincidences which will occur to many of us, Sir Richard Fleetwood met Mr. Langford and his daughter in society, and became a frequent guest at their house. He knew well how to play the part of a finished gentleman, and paid all those delicate and flattering attentions to Honora which would hardly fail to be acceptable.

Time went on, and, impossible as it may seem, Sir Richard Fleetwood—the callous, and cold hearted—the unprincipled, and grasping—the rake, the debauchee—the man of iron will and strong resolve, actually fell in love! Yes, and with Honora Langford; and his passion had something of a high tone about it, it was neither gross or sensuous in its character; it, perhaps, was the only bright spot in his character. Many years older than Honora, his love had in it something of that deep and lasting character which men of more mature years feel, for the first time perhaps, for a young

beautiful, and virtuous woman. His attentions became gradually more marked. Honora did not fail to observe this, and she trembled when she reflected upon what was, in all probability, coming. At first she had not for a moment looked upon him as a probable suitor for her hand, having only received those attentions which, he had, in the first instance, offered as a gallant gentleman would do generally to the softer sex; but now, as they had gradually become more pointed, and as her father saw with joy the turn affairs were likely to take, poor Honora was in as much, if not more, trepidation than Frank Osborne. More days and weeks pass, and still Sir Richard is a more constant attendant at the house of Mr. Langford. We will take a glance at them ourselves.

Honora is seated in the first floor with an embroidery frame before her, over which she is bending, while she plys her needle upon some piece of work, which, in fact, is intended as a present to her own Harry Osborne.

Sir Richard is in the apartment alone with her—Mr. Langford being out. A deeper shade of thought is upon the features of the baronet; thoughtful as they were at most times but now, more especially so. He has a book in his hand which he has been reading occasionally aloud to Miss Langford. Placing his arm round the back of the chair he leans over her and asks about her work, which, as a matter of course, he does not fail to admire. His voice is mellow and soft; when he chooses to tune it so, it can be harsh enough in his strong passion.

"Miss Langford," he said, and Honora started as he spoke these two words, she had a presentiment of what was to follow; it was not that there was anything so remarkable in his pronouncing her name, but the tone and manner was solemn, and so entirely different to that which he was wont to assume in the ordinary course of conversation. He gazed at her with some surprise as she started, and a flush came over her beautiful features. Perhaps he himself was quite unaware of the difference in his own intonation.

"Miss Langford," he repeated again with some slight hesitation, for although he had been used to make love, as it is termed, to many sorts of women, he found himself slightly at fault in declaring this, his only pure passion, perhaps.

"I should suppose that you have been at no loss to divine the cause of my visits here. You can readily guess, I dare say, the magnet which has attracted me."

She bent more over her embroidery

frame, and ingenuous as her nature was, it would not admit of her even prevaricating, and she said gently, almost in a whisper—

"I might have my own thoughts or ideas upon the subject.

"I should have supposed so," he answered in the same deep quiet tone in which he had commenced,

"I should have supposed so," he reiterated; and then seemingly at a loss to know how to proceed, he paced the apartment once or twice, and then halted near to where she was seated.

"I am not about to tell you that you are the only woman in the world that I have admired, or that I have paid attention to. It would be an insult to your better sense to suppose that I have lived so long in the world without seeing some grace and beauty in the other sex. I am many years older than yourself, but still in the prime of life, so let that pass." He paused here, and seemed to have lost himself, so to speak. He, however, approached nearer towards her, and again placed his arm and hand on the back of the chair upon which she was seated, and said in a still lower tone of voice—

"What I would wish to express to you, my dear young lady, is this, that you have awakened within me feelings and springs of affection I have never known before. In your presence I have found myself chastened. Your gentle sweet loving nature has so won upon me, so wound its fibres round my heart"—— He paused here, and then said suddenly, and with increased energy—

"Oh, Miss Langford! I am almost afraid to tell you how deeply, passionately, and devotedly I love you."

He was on his knees now at her feet, and looking up beseechingly in her face. A death-like paleness came over the features of Honora, and she trembled at the precipice on which she found herself.

"Sir Richard!" she exclaimed, as with difficulty she restrained her tears. "I pray you rise. Do not kneel to a poor mortal like yourself; keep it for Him who knows and sees all hearts."

"Oh, Miss Langford! let me pay my adoration to one I worship as a divinity, for it is in your sweet society alone that I have had awakened within me the best and purest thoughts I have ever known. I cannot but choose to adore one who has taught me to love."

"Taught to love, Sir Richard! How so?" she said in some surprise.

"By being the most enchanting of her sex, Miss Langford, is nothing to say—that I who have seen so many, have mixed so much in Continental and English society,

that I, who have wandered from flower to flower, never as yet found your equal, and as Heaven is my judge"—he rose up at these words—"and as Heaven is my judge I have never known what love is till I have known you."

"Oh, Sir Richard!" exclaimed the unfortunate Honora, as her lips actually trembled, as the exclamation escaped them. He misinterpreted the meaning of her observation, and continued now more passionately.

"No never. I feel stirred within this breast that subtle essence, that mysterious agent, that indescribable and magic influence which men and women call love, Nay more, the hours passed out of your presence are miserable ones, and in it I have supreme bliss."

"I am sure I ought to feel myself flattered," stammered forth Honora, who hardly knew what reply to make to all these fine speeches.

"Miss Langford," continued Sir Richard now in a more subdued, quiet, and serious tone, "to say that I love you is perhaps only to to tell you what amongst the multiplicity of the admirers which you must of necessity have had you have already had said to you on more than one occasion. But to say to you as I do most sincerely, and with truth, that in all my acquaintance with the best and most accomplished women of my day, I have never seen one at all comparable to yourself."

"Sir Richard!" she exclaimed reprovingly.

"No never!" he said more firmly. "Never knew one upon whom my heart was set till I knew you."

She sighed as he uttered these last words.

"You may sigh, Miss Langford, but alas, until I know your verdict it is for me to sigh and groan, to pass hours and days of torture and agony, for"—and here he approached close to her again—"it may appear to you, a young, fresh, and blooming girl, I say it may appear strange to hear from the lips of a man who has attained a ripe and lusty manhood, that he cannot live without you, and that the remainder of his life would be one long draught of bitterness and despair if he thought he was obnoxious to yourself or might not have a chance of ingratiating himself in your good graces. It seems strange to you that I should say this."

"I certainly did not guess or ever dream that"—

"That, what, Miss Langford?" he inquired eagerly.

"That the attentions you have offered me were tending towards a declaration."

"You must surely have been blind then."

"Lately, it is true, I did imagine so," said Honora.

"Ah! so I should have thought."

There was a long pause after this. Honora trembled from very excitement. The pale Oxford student rose before her imagination, and looked on her reproachfully. She knew not what to say, hardly daring to have the courage to give Sir Richard a direct refusal. She knew him to be a man of strong and violent passions, and in fact, with all his gentleness of manner towards her, she had an undefined fear or sort of dread of him. She could not find it in her heart to make an immediate reply. He contemplated her for some time as her little trembling hands endeavoured to ply the embroidery needle.

"You have heard my confession," he said, sorrowfully. "It is no fable or fiction—neither is my love a brief transitory flame, which might exhaust itself by its own intensity. In my case, it is destined to last a lifetime, be it for good or for ill. It is too late to retract now, or endeavour to call back the past. Young woman, around this heart," he continued, as he placed his hand upon his heart, "you have wound a series of meshes, deep rooted and immovable—they can never be displaced. In the long category of human ills—there is perhaps none so poignant, so intense, so diastrous as an unrequited love. Think of that young lady, and answer this appeal, for oh! I do love you," he continued, now more passionately, as he clasped his hands and looked up to heaven. "I do love you, how much it were impossible for mortal man to tell."

There was a deep earnestness in his tone which carried conviction of the truth of his words. Honora was pained more and more, as the depth of his attachment became so self-evident.

"I do not dream or guess that I had inspired you with so—with—so strong a feeling," said Honora, hesitating, and stammering over her words in evident trepidation.

He took a chair, placed it beside her, and sat down; then taking hold of one of her hands, which she found it impossible to resist, for there was a firmness of decision and command about Sir Richard, which overawed the young girl for the time.

"Now, hear me, Miss Langford," he began, argumentatively. "You know I am no boy who imagines himself in love with every pretty and fascinating woman with whom he meets. And you know also, at least, I suppose you will do me the justice to believe, that I am not simulating in the declaration I have been making. Now hear me, for I would give up house, home, wealth, title, all I am possessed of in the world. This is no fancy—no idle dream—it's sober, solemn truth. A truth, my dear young lady, I have found it difficult to believe myself, but truth nevertheless. I have examined my own heart, communed with myself at all hours, asked myself those questions which men ask themselves when they find they are under the potent sway of an unseen and mysterious power. The thraldom in which I find myself held, has in my imagination, something marvellous in it. I am under that unseen power for the first time."

"For the first time, Sir Richard?" murmured forth Honora, as she turned away her face, which was suffused with blushes.

"Yes; for the first time in my life. It is true," he said in continuation, in the same quiet, argumentative tone he had assumed. "It is true that I have seen many of your sex which may have in some measure excited my admiration but not love! Oh, no; not such an enduring and deep-seated passion which fate has reserved for you to evoke. Gentle, pure-minded, guileless—of a soft, sweet, and fascinating disposition, how was it possible for me to be insensible to all these various amiable qualities which I find centered in yourself.

"Oh, Sir Richard!" exclaimed Honora, as she burst into tears, for she was quite overwhelmed by his pleadings, and found herself at a loss to compete with him.

"In tears," he said quietly; "is it possible that by some unguarded expression I may have touched this too soft and sensitive heart. Say dearest Horona, if I may dare so call you; say, have I wounded or hurt your feelings by some chance observation; —say dearest. He bent over and gently kissed her forehead. She retreated from him as he did this, and hid her face in her hands.

Sir Richard Fleetwood was at a loss to interpret the precise meaning of her actions, but a shadow seemed to cross his imagination, and an expression of doubt passed over his features.

"Does the declaration of my strong attachment evoke sorrow, Miss Langford; am I to understand that I am repulsive to you?"

"Oh, no, I do not say that," answered Honora; "but I should have thought——"

"What?"

"That you had some other lady who, perhaps, was more worthy of your love."

"Say not so. It is impossible. Tell me—why this hesitation—this sudden expression

of grief. Have you any prior attachment?"

She was silent, and he, too, as he remained contemplating her with many mixed feelings, which he found unable to disentangle.

"You do not answer me, Miss Langford. Am I to interpret your silence to consent to my proposition. Come, now, let there be no disguise between us. Have I a rival?" He said this so sharply that she became again alarmed. She, however, recovered a little of her usual composure, and said in her own gentle manner—

"I beg of you, Sir Richard, not to urge this matter further! I esteem and respect you, nay more, for your many excellent qualities I admire you, but as to promising my love——" she paused here,

No. 8.

and then said—"a woman loves but once."

He reeled back a pace or two at the latter observation a dark shade past over his features, and all those smothered, violent passions, which had hitherto been hid, seemed to be at once made manifest. He did not speak for some minutes, but chafed and fumed as he paced the apartment now with hurried steps.

"A woman loves but once," he ejaculated, apparently to himself. "No! that may be, and no doubt is, true enough. Never but once! What of that? my fondest hope has been that I might have been the first to awaken this passion in your breast, but now, I see my folly, my mistake. Ah! Miss Langford, do not in mercy tell me that your heart is already engaged—do not, in mercy. Great Heaven! have I been wasting the whole of my thought upon an unsubtantial dream? Have I set my life, my whole hopes of happiness, upon that which never can be mine. Listen to me, you may have had a lover, some youthful swaine, who has fawned or feined a flame, but never—oh! never, could you have had a man who offers a love like mine—never!" he continued, more passionately. "Miss Langford, reflect! examine your own heart, I proffer you a love, deep, passionate, endearing—one that will last for a life-time. Do not doom me to despair. Do not doom me to torture and anguish for perhaps many painful years. I love you! oh! how fondly, is more than I can tell. Have mercy on me, miserable sinner that I am—Have pity on me—say something that is kind—only one word—for oh! I am driven to destruction already." He knelt at her feet and passionately pleaded his cause—so much so that she felt herself too weak to stem the torrent of his eloquence. Honora, nerving herself as best she could, said slowly—

"Tell me, Sir Richard, if you had known a woman to whom you had plighted your truth, could you appeal thus to another?"

"Mercy on me, no! I should be the veryest wretch to do so—but I never have known one such—never! as Heaven is my judge."

"I do not say you have, I would not do you the injustice to suppose such a thing but I——"

"You what?"

"I have known one to whom I have plighted my troth."

"Oh, mercy, mercy! is this so?" he exclaimed, in accents of such terrible anguish that she actually pitied him.

He paused for some time and paced the apartment with hurried steps, whilst the expression of his countenance was indicative of utter despair and anguish.

"Miss Langford," he said presently, "you cannot, you surely will not doom me to that unattainable amount of human misery, which surrounds and enshrouds the path of him who has nursed a hopeless passion. Consider what nights of untold agony await the wretch who eats the bitter fruits of ruined hopes. Unsay the words you have but now spoken, for oh! they sound like a funeral knell to all my happiness. Say, my dearest young lady, it is not so, let me hope that time may teach you to alter your resolve, and oh, let me hope that in time also, you may learn to love me." He paused here and gently knelt at her feet. Honora was pained to see the evident earnestness and depth of his passion.

"Say," he continued, "am I then objectionable to you?"

"No, Sir Richard," she gently replied, "I do not and can not say that, far from it, I am, and ought to be, flattered at your evident preference of me, and, had we met earlier, or were I disengaged, I should have been able, perhaps, to have returned you a different answer to that, which, in honour, I am compelled to assume now."

"Are you so engaged that it does not admit of some reconsideration?" asked her lover.

She gently shook her head in reply to this interrogatory.

He rose up and covered his face with his hands, and was again silent for some time.

"If these walls could speak, they would say, indeed here is a most unhappy man," he suddenly exclaimed, "oh! so unhappy that life is stript of all its charms, and existence a misery—of what avail is it to him the sun—the air—the beauty of the external world, if the sun that lights up his main life is enshrouded in darkness, and for him shines no more?"

"It is sad, Sir Richard," said Honora, "very sad to nurse a hopeless passion."

"Hopeless!" exclaimed the baronet, in a paroxysm of passion, "hopeless! Have mercy Heaven!" and he rushed from her apartment apparently under the influence of a sudden frenzy. So rapid, and unexpected had been his movements, that Honora had no time to endeavour to restrain him, even if she had had the presence of mind to have made the attempt. She heard the street door close suddenly, and became aware that Sir Richard had left the house. A sort of tremor seized the frame of the delicate girl, her susceptible nature was touched at the evidences of Sir Richard's passion. He had left in so distracted a state that uneasy fears and doubts came across her mind and she half regretted her own candour in answering his fervent appeal. So gentle and kind was the disposition of the sweet Honora Langford that the thought of having been the innocent cause of pain to a human creature, was, in itself, agony to her.

As to Sir Richard himself, he rushed home and shut himself up in his own apartment, refusing to see any one, the canker worm was at his heart, and rage, disappointment, and wounded pride, all tended to lash him into fury.

Shut yourself up Sir Richard Fleetwood! bolt door and bar window, for you have to wrestle with yourself, and quaff a long and bitter draught alone and in silence.

It is, and has been, the fate of man for centuries past to learn that human affections and sympathy are not always to be called forth at his bidding, and that woman's love is not a thing to be commanded, and often flies from us when most sought after. Shut yourself up Sir Richard, callous, stern willed, and imperious man, as you have been throughout your life, accustomed to command and receive implicit obedience, you are overmatched now and are mortally wounded by a weak and gentle girl, the shaft has found a home in, perhaps, the only vulnerable part of your hard and callous organization; better men than you, have succumbed to the magic of woman's spell, other enchantresses besides sweet Honora, have played their part, other men besides you have sighed to feed upon the honey dew of woman's lip, and yearned to have a heart which lived, beat, and throbbed for them alone.

Flinging himself into his library chair, Sir Richard rested his elbow upon the library table and buried his face in his hands. His temples were hot and feverish. The life current coursed rapidly through his frame, and his strong and muscular form trembled with excitement. To be foiled thus! To be baffled by some love-sick, empty-pated puppy! for such, he doubted not, was his rival. He, the hearty Sir Richard! who was wont to win the smiles of so many fair ones. He, whose strong will bore with it as rushing torrents all obstacles and impediments. He, to have the best and purest passion he had ever known flung back into his teeth, the thought was madness! but he would find out this much—yes! as he reflected upon them he rose up from his chair and paced the apartment. Yes, he would find him out and then take summary vengeance. There was some comfort, too, when he reflected upon this. It suited his disposition to arouse himself to action, and, when once this thought had entered his mind he cogitated with himself as to how it would be possible to find out the name, station, and residence of his rival. She had come from Oxford, in all probability it was there that she had formed the attachment. Yes, he felt assured of this the more he reflected upon it. He then considered and reconsidered the matter over as to who amongst his acquaintance it would be best to seek for the desired information. Then the thought occurred to him of seeing Mr. Langford himself, and declaring his attachment towards his daughter, and enlisting his authority on his behalf, for he did not for one moment doubt but what Honora's father would entertain the suit; in fact, he had enough evidence given of that during the progress of his preliminary attentions; but the baronet found his nerves too much unstrung to wait upon Mr. Langford, and, therefore, deferred his visit till he was a little more calmed down.

CHAPTER X.

JONATHAN WILD—THE SCENE IN NEWGATE.

THAT ancient magistrate erudite scholar and great legal authority, Ephraim Gubbins, Esq., Lord Mayor of London, felt himself dishonoured, his moral person treated with disrespect, the law outraged, the whole substrata of society undermined. It seemed incredible to him that any one should have had the audacity to arrest the progress of the chief magistrate of London. A more disastrous circumstance it was hardly possible to conceive, as it was, of course, entirely extra-judicial, his lordship having in his possession the property which Colonel Jack had so dexterously purloined. Lord Mayor Gubbins was a sadder and wiser man as he rose the following morn. A matrimonial dispute took place between himself and the self-willed Mr. G——, who insisted upon the highwayman being a very gentlemanly, well-conducted sort of personage. This exasperated Gubbins, who commenced heaping a torrent of abuse upon the head of our hero, whom he hoped some day or other to have the pleasure of seeing him hung at Tyburn. In no very pleasant mood he left his home for Guildhall, he detailed to his chief clerk the particulars of the previous night's proceedings. Dismay and horror sat upon the countenance of that individual as he heard the account which fell from the lips of his unjust master.

"Would it not be possible to trace the perpetrators of the outrage?" suggested the chief clerk.

His lordship was afraid not, but there would be no harm in trying.

At the time of which we write the great man, in all cases of this sort, was no other than the celebrated Jonathan Wild.

After the business of the court was over that worthy had an interview with the Lord Mayor.

He informed his lordship that he was on the track of the man who had been the chief in the burglary at Mr. Baintree's; but as to the highwayman he was at present at fault, but he promised to ferret out all the information it was possible under

LIFE OF A HIGHWAYMAN.

the circumstances; and, with this assurance, the renowned thieftaker took his departure to follow up all the necessary inquiries. He bent his steps towards old Newgate, in the woman's ward of which prison there was a female awaiting her trial, from whom he supposed some information could be extracted respecting the whereabouts of the "Nobbler."

The great city bell had just struck ten, as the turnkey of Newgate, whose turn it was to take charge of the outer gate, with two of his coadjutors and a friend, sat down to play a game of cribbage in the ante-room. A two gallon can of beer stood like a tall giant beside a half-pint pewter pot at one corner of the table.

"The beer is in, and all is right for the night," said the turnkey. "All is locked up, and the clock has struck ten. No more commitments to night, so if we have no country lags, we shall have a snug game. Governor out, too, so we shall not have him again."

The several wards were indeed locked up, and all except the female prisoners' ward were shrouded in darkness; but many tales of daring and suffering were being related to beguile the slow foot of time, as he paces with heavy foot-steps the interior of a prison.

In the female wards, as we have said, there seen only a faint glimmering light. Both the upper and lower compartments of this portion of the building, were so much thronged, that as the inmates laid themselves on the floor to rest, the feet of some were near to, and opposite to the door which led to the ward.

The prisoners as was their wont, had assorted themselves into portions of similar ages and congenial minds, the young whispering to their companions, episodes of their first love for Bill or Jack, and their subsequent adventures with Harry or Joe. Those more advanced in life, were openly relating aloud, tales and anecdotes of London scenes on the *pave*, even numerating the number of liberals they had met with in their time, also how many swindlers and bilks they had suffered by in their career. The more reckless and wholly abandoned of the lowest class, were vieing with each other, which should most outrage decency, or use the coarsest language. All were talking, excepting about seven or eight servant girls, who had been committed for petty thefts while in service, these being comparatively novices in crime, laid on their mats, marvelling at the extent to which moral depredation was carried. Such was the state of the prison, as Jonathan Wild was about to pay it a visit.

"I shall peg you four," said the turnkey.

"You're taken fourteen, when you are only ten, and cannot show four."

"I'll bet a crown of that," rejoined the other, "and write about it to the 'Public Ledger.'"

"Done! Done!" simultaneously exclaimed the disputants, as at the same moment a knocking was heard at the outer gate.

"Who have we here at this time, I wonder? Hope there ain't a ward to open at this hour," growled the turnkey, as he rose and enquired who was there.

"Open the gate, I want to see a prisoner in the females' ward," said a man's voice.

"You are too late. It is past the hours," said the turnkey, not at first recognizing the speaker's voice to be that of Jonathan Wild.

"Then I'll see the governor," said the thief-taker.

"Oh! begs pardon, it's Mr. Wild," said the man, as he immediately flung open the gate, when he became aware who it was addressing him.

Mr. Wild entered, and received courteous salutations from the turnkey's companions.

"What's her name?" asked the turnkey of the new comer.

"That I can't tell you, but she's a young woman, and has only been received here some half hour since," was the reply.

"Ah!" exclaimed the turnkeys, simultaneously.

"Ah! the last new comer, a young woman in black, of genteel appearance."

"That's her; but 'll just step in and see the governor first," said Mr. Wild, "and then go round the women's ward with you," and with these words he took his way into the governor's house. It appeared that the prisoner had only been received in the prison some half hour previously. Bradshaw, the turnkey, had been disturbed at his game then, as at the appearance of Jonathan Wild, and he harshly thrust the female prisoner in as he unlocked the ward door, and left her to seek a place of rest unassisted with any forms of introduction by calling to the ward's woman.

"There," said he, "you will find plenty of company, and he gave her a thrust to remove her from the door. While Jonathan Wild was closeted with the governor, the turnkeys proceeded with their game.

"I say, Bradshaw," said one of his companions as he again took up his cards, "she was a likely looking sort, that last new comer. She aint a fancy wench of old Jonathan's, is she?"

"Never yer mind about fancy ladies, but attend to your game. See, we wants twenty holes, and it's their deal, so if it's a fine morning, cut along. I'll take two half bulls to one we wins it."

"But Bradshaw," continued the man, "if I had been on duty I should have put that girl up in the infirmary ward; there's a ruffish lot in now, and after that mill to-day, Moll Smash was brought down to the bottom. I hope you ain't put her in there?"

"Hold your cheek," replied Bradshaw, angrily. "You'll make me loose the game. Only eight, partner, eh? Well, take them, carefully, because I'm out to a hole. Now tip up, gentlemen, and mind you are in for all the half-and-half."

"Holla, there, in the woman's lower ward. What game are you at? Now stow it I say. Bradshaw, Bradshaw! do you hear that shindy?" called out one of the watchmen on the top of the prison.

Bradshaw pocketed his money, snatched up his keys, and repaired to the yard into which the barred apertures of the ward looked.

"I say galls," he called out, "what's this all about? Some of yer will knab it. What, must we get the darbies down for women? Come, stow it, stow it."

Admonitions and remonstrance from without were, however, all lost and drowned from the noise within the ward. To any unaccustomed to similar scenes of riot, the violence of the screaming was such as to carry terror in their sounds, and it seemed as if the women intended to have a gala night of confusion, spreading alarm even around the vicinity of their locality; volley after volley of screams assailed the ear, while the contention and confusion among the female prisoners below appeared to be at its acmé. The upper ward, however, soon caught the panic, and presented a scene of increased alarm. The prisoners there, unacquainted with the cause of the screams from below, rushed simultaneously to the door and windows, calling out fire! fire! fire! and in their precipitancy and fright trampled on and seriously injured each other. Thus scream after scream followed as fire to the flash, and one ward sympathetically or spasmodically responded to the other.

It subsequently appeared that when the unhappy girl, whose name was Lucy, was thrust into the ward, she, for a moment, found support against the door, and, in this situation, dressed as she was in black was only just discerned by some young girls lying immediately opposite the door.

"What is that black figure?" said one to a companion. "A nun," was the reply. "No its the devil," said another, and at the same instant, the unfortunate Lucy, overcome by the effluvia of the crowded apartment, fell prostrate across the girls as heavily and lifeless as one actually deprived of existence. The screams of fright that this incident elicited acted on the whole party like an electric shock. The black inanimate figure was pushed from one to the other amidst the cries of "the devil," "the devil."

During the uproar which ensued, some more thoughtful than the great body of the prisoners, brought the candle from the other end of the ward, and seeing a delicate creature of their own sex likely to be trampled to death, made an effort to drag her from the scene of action. This attempt ultimately divided the ward into two parties till all became involved in the contest, some exclaiming——

"Whose afraid of the devil? send him down here."

Others said, "What do you mean by a nun? ain't we all nuns? why else be ve locked up here within stone walls?"

"I say, Bet," called out a muscular copper-coloured countenanced female from the upper end of the ward, "devil or nun mind they pays footing, and grab the veil as security."

"Footing, footing!" cried out several voices, at the same time rushing forward to secure the veil; while another party, which stood over Lucy, prepared to resist the aggression and a general melée was the result, during which, the only candle they had, was frequently extinguished, the belligerents pausing with the hair of their opponents head in their hands, each maintaining their position till the light again heralded them on to a renewal of the contest. All the time the turnkeys were standing in the yard hesitating as to the policy or propriety of opening the door of the ward. At length, Bradshaw, waiting his opportunity, made a faint of entrance by inserting the key in the lock, when the cry of, "the keepers are coming in," instantly changed the melée into a regular blockade. Moll Smash seized the poker; making her way over the fallen, reached the door of the ward where, in a voice resembling a cracked bugle, she exerted herself to effect a suspension of hostilities among her fellow prisoners.

"Cheese your milling," she screamed out, "come here and defend yourselves like women, the rascals don't enter here."

Bradshaw essayed another faint by rattling the wards of the lock and calling, "We must come in, then, I see you won't be quiet without interference."

"Oh, oh! that's you Mr. Screwsman Bradshaw is it?" exclaimed Moll. "Now lets you and I understand one another, you ain't a going to ill use these innocent girls, there's a poker to crack your empty scull. It may be very well out there, but we women ain't a going to let such blackguards as you Newgate birds have it all your own way I can tell ye, t'other side of the door is your place and there you may bounce it, but, you hang dog, it's no go here. You dare to put your ugly mug in here, you villain, I'll crack your scull with this ere poker as easy as I would one of Billy Walkers heavy crabs."

"Go it, Moll, give it him, take him by the leg and drag him in, we'll sarve him out. He dare to come in here, and we all naked. Only let him try it on, a vagabond," called out several voices rallying round their leader.

"I say Moll," replied the keeper, from the passage coaxingly. "Come no hard words, you know in all your trouble I have been a friend, and why should you and I quarrel now? I only want's the young woman in black."

"The young woman in black is it Mr. Bradshaw? then send the undertaker for her corpse in the morning, you've been at some foul work to night, Muster Bradshaw," continued Moll, winking to those around her, "a delicate morsel to come into the hands of your kidney, and so you thought after you had murdered her you would poke her corpse in here slyly and lay it on us innocent creatures, did you. God forgive us all, these screwsmen are worse than the prisoners."

One of the girls now stepped up to Moll, and whispered that the young woman was not dead. There, indeed, laid Lucy, looking more like death in reality, than in counterfeit."

"Dead," exclaimed Moll, that resounded back from the staircase, "Don't all the galls know that the villain throwed her in here a corpse. We'll all swear to it," continued Moll, turning round to her backers.

"We'll all swear that she was pushed in here a corpse," exclaimed some forty voices.

"Nonsense, women," exclaimed Bradshaw, in evident trepidation. "Nonsense! the girl is all right I dare say."

"Who blowed the candle out?" enquired Moll. "Light it directly, or by the holy powers I'll smash the heads of some of ye. There, stick it up against the wall over the corpse," she continued, as it was brought to her."

The turnkey made a third faint to open the door.

"Oh, you desperate dog, you want to come in, do you, and take advantage of poor girls. Stand up behind here, all of you. We are ready for him. Bet Glib and Sall Stunt close up there, and you, Long Jane, throw a rug over the corpse, it's shocking to look on. As it is there, let It lie, for the sheriff. All dead bodies in Newgate belong to the sheriff."

Lucy had now become an object of interest to all in the ward, as indeed, it is probable she would have been from the first, had she been properly introduced. Moll, however, owed the turnkeys a grudge, and therefore would not let the opportunity slip of aluring their fears and bringing them into disgrace. She had previously been many times in Newgate, and was now there under sentence of transportation for passing bad money.

The parley between Moll and the keeper, Bradshaw, was broken up by the arrival of the governor and Jonathan Wild, the latter of whom was observed looking into the ward through the bars of the window. At the sight of the thieftaker's face, another general scream proceeded from the inmates of the female ward, causing a response from the ward above. Moll now shifted her position, ordering the forms to be brought up, one of which she mounted, so as to command the opening of the yard.

"So, ho! It's you, is it, Mr. Grabbing Wild," said Moll, as she placed her arms akimbo, and stared impudently at the thieftaker. "You ugly mugged wretch. It was you as lagged Joe and the Darkun. The devil will get his own when he lays hold on you, and no mistake, and the sooner the better, say I. Let me catch sight of your ugly peepers a looking in here again, that's all." And herewith, she assumed a threatening attitude, defient and valarous.

"Dress yourselves, women and girls," said the governor. "The men must come in and take the woman in black."

"This is very improper, and very immodest," said a female prisoner, "to bring a parcel of fellows round galls at this time of night. You can't deny that, can you? And, as to the corpse in black, it can't make much difference whether it is taken out now or in the morning. It's decently covered over for the sheriff to see it just as that villain Bradshaw throwed it in on the poor girls, frightening them out of their senses. Some of them too may die before the morning through his villainy."

"Then you are sure," said the governor, mildly, "that the female in question is dead?"

"Dead!" exclaimed Moll. "Think I've lived all these years, and don't know a deadun from a liveun."

Turning round and winking at her forces in the rear, who could not resist a laugh at her manner of treating the affair. These movements did not escape the searching eye of Jonathan Wild.

"I see how it is," exclaimed that individual. "A footing is a custom here. See, this is for something to drink," and he held up a sovereign, that the coin might be seen. "Lead the women to the further end of the yard, while we take out the female in black, and it's yours. All shall be done modestly with due consideration to your feelings. There, take it," he continued, "I'll trust to your honour," throwing the coin in at the window, which Moll adroitly caught in her hand, and then set up a loud shout of exultation.

"Hoorah," she exclaimed, "old grabby Wild has *blued* a shiner, and has thrown in a canary bird. Hoorah! galls, fall back, and let one of the guv'nor's men in; but there's one thing we bargains for, that fellow Bradshaw sha'n't enter here."

"Don't be afraid of that, Moll," said the governor, "for his conduct I have given orders that he shall be suspended."

"Hurrah," cried Moll, "A'fore you opens the door let us have one loud hurrah for that Bradshaw to be scragged. There's news for you—hip, hip, hip, hurrah!"

"I said suspended," continued the governor, smiling.

"What's that but scragging?" answered Moll.

It cannot be said that peace was that night restored in either of the women's wards; there were too many discoloured faces to be looked to, and too many hand's-full of hair to discuss, and moreover the monotony of a prison life cannot afford to suddenly pass over any cause of excitement. Moll, however, now as much excited herself for the restoration of order as she had before done for even exulting in her triumphs of having obtained a sovereign from that rascal Wild, and causing the suspension of the turnkey Bradshaw.

The unhappy girl Lucy, bruised and insensible was conveyed up to the third or infirmary ward then in charge of an aged female offender whose infirmities unfitted her for any other species of employment than that of attending upon the sick. This woman, together with three convalescent girls received the unhappy cause of the confusion; beneath she was laid on a mattress, and a messenger dispatched for the surgeon to attend her, and in the interim the woman was supplied with restoratives for her patient, but changing her opinion as to their efficacy, she appropriated them to her own use.

"Here's better luck and plenty of it," said she to the three girls as she drained off the glass. Now depend on it seduction is at the bottom of the affair. Oh them men! It puts me in mind of other days, deary me, galls, if you knew how I've been deceived. Oh! it would make your heart bleed. You must know that I was brought up for a lady, but I was too good for one—too good natured for your fine, inoffensive, cold-hearted lady. Bless me, galls, the fellows used to come round me like flies round a honey pot. No stalling 'em off no how. Well, well, everyone has their day, and the poor thing's, pointing to Lucy, is likely to be a short one, I suppose.

While Lucy was under the tender care of the old woman, Jonathan Wild had followed the governor into his own house.

"Confound the women," said the governor, "there's no end to the trouble and bother they occasion. You will not be able to get much from the girl to-night, that's quite certain."

"S'pose not," said Wild; "but I'll wait till the doctor comes, at any rate, and see which way the feline quadruped is likely to mizzle."

"What is it you want of this woman?" asked the governor. "She's committed upon a charge of forgery."

"So I heard," answered Jonathan Wild. "Well, you see this is how the case stands. This ere girl's been connected with a flash cove, whose done a good deal on the cross in various ways. Indeed, the fact is, he was manager of a large mercantile house at one time, but he's been playing a queerish game for some three or four years past—passing forged cheques, obtaining goods upon false orders, purporting to come from respectable people. Lord bless you, there's no end to the dodges he's been up to, and, although he has had two or three narrow escapes, he, for the present, has managed to evade the law."

"What has he to do with this girl, then; or, rather, she to do with him?"

"She's his mistress, I suppose. At any rate she has passed some forged notes and cheques upon Crash, Bunglam and Co. She seems an innocent sort of a person enough, and so I'm giv'n to understand she really is, but this chap has tutored her in crime."

"You want to worm out from her something about the fellow, then?" said the governor.

"No, that would be useless. I'm thinking unto him she's as true as steel. No, my dodge is this—her chap is connected with the chief housebreaker, who escaped out of that burglary at Dulwich. I don't want to ask her directly about him, but by promising her to intercede in her behalf, it is just possible that I may learn where to pitch upon the "Nobbler," as we call him."

By this time the surgeon came, upon which he immediately went up into the infirmary ward and returning therefrom after an inspection of Lucy, he pronounced her state to be such that she could not possibly be seen by Jonathan Wild—for that night at any rate—and so the renowned thief-taker was compelled to take his departure and await the result. On the following day he again visited the prison, and was permitted to have an interview with the unfortunate girl Lucy, from whom he contrived to worm out what were to him very important facts, but as to criminating her paramour that she studiously avoided doing, and notwithstanding all Wild's finesse evinced in his artfully devised questions, she proved in this instance more than a match for him, and maintained an imputurbable silence.

CHAPTER XI.

AWKWARD POSITION OF THE " NOBBLER "—
JONATHAN WILD ON THE TRACK — DES-
PERATE STRUGGLE.

THEY were dark days which the "Nobbler" spent during that intergerment of time which elapsed while his palls awaited their trial at Newgate. Every day brought some fresh alarm, and the "Nobbler" felt himself like some wild beast who lay in ambush, concealed from view whole days, and hunters were on his track in some lonely prairie. Bill Dyson advised him to leave London altogether, and seek refuge in some remote part of England, but the housebreaker was obstinate. His old haunts had too many attractions for him, and he was loth to leave for any strange locality. It has been often said, that the best place for concealment is in London, and without doubt, to a considerable extent this is true, for in the metropolis a stranger is not so much observed as in the rural districts or small provincial towns, where everybody wants to know the business of a new comer.

It will be necessary now to take a glance again at that respectable hostelry, the "Cow and Cauliflower." In the bar-parlour of which, sat the "Nobbler" and the landlord.

"You'd better hook it, Jem," said Mr. Dyson. "Take my advice, and cut altogether, or they are sure to ferret you out, old boy. Disguise yourself as a countryman, and go to field labour."

"Ah, gammon and all," said the housebreaker. "I should like to catch myself at that dodge. I ain't fit for it. It's too slow work for one of my kidney."

" Better than being lagged or scragged," was the answer.

"S'pose it is; but it don't suit me, and I'd rather run my risk here in London."

"You run very great risks, mind you. How do you know that one of your palls hasn't already blowed the gaff?"

"Ah, it's like enough, and if they have, it can't be helped," observed the "Nobbler," despondingly, for he was sore oppressed in his mind, and felt himself driven like a rat to its hole. He was reflective—abstracted—and sententious in his observations. He had numerous haunts it's true, but could not feel assured that any of them were safe from the mermidons of the law, and he was fully aware that the burglary at Mr. Baintree's, was of that description which attracted a more than wonted public attention. In fact, it was one of the most remarkable affairs that had happened for many years. The "Nobbler" felt all this, and became painfully impressed with the fact that every effort would be made to effect his capture.

While he was ruminating upon all these disastrous incidents, Mr. Dyson sauntered to the window out of the dingy panes of which he contemplated the horse trough and hay rick in front of his premises, while doing this he gave a low exclamation of surprise—

"What's the row?" asked the house-breaker, whose eyes and ears were on the strain and indeed were continually so.

"A stranger," said Mr. Dyson, also in a suppressed tone.

"After no good, I dare say," said the "Nobbler," "what's he like? Coming this way."

"Are sure enough, that he is. You'd better hook it, Jem, to the vaults below; but stay, I'll see if the coast is clear."

He had scarcely uttered the last observation, when he became aware that there was the shadow of one or two men to be seen in his passage, this shadow was caused from the light in the public parlour and he could pretty well judge from its situation, that the individuals, whoever they were, must be standing in front of the door which led into the public room. It would be, therefore, supposing those in the passage to be enemies, for the housebreakers to make good his retreat to the back room, from which, as the reader has been already informed, there was a secret way into vaults beneath. The Badger's mind was troubled, assuming that the new comers were enemies, there was no mode of escape open to the housebreaker.

"I tell you what you must do, Jem," said

Mr. Dyson. "You must manage to creep in here till I see how matters is."

And with this, he opened a three cornered cupboard, in which were hung towels and cloths of various descriptions used in his establishment. The place was so small that it was with difficulty that the housebreaker could contrive to pack his muscular, broad-set frame in the place at all, and when the door was about to be closed, the idea of suffocation immediately occurred to his imagination.

"It won't be for many seconds, Jem," said the Badger. "All right, keep quiet, and I will soon let you know how matters lay,"

And Mr Dyson cautiously strolled into the passage to reconnoitre, and very soon saw the state of the case, for an universal panic seemed to have seized his parlour customers;

this was caused by the appearance of no less a person than Jonathan Wild, at the glance of whose eye the occupants of the parlour of the Cow and Cauliflower found themselves as much under the fascinating gaze of the rattle-snake.

Jonathan Wild himself was in the parlour while two of his men kept guard in the passage, two more outside, in front of the house, and immediately facing the bar parlour window. It was one of those who had just attracted the Badger's notice, and given the alarm, so, even with all his cunning, Jonathan Wild showed his cards, as the saying is.

Had he at once gone into the house, and walked boldly up to the bar, he must have seen the Nobbler conversing with the landlord, but he was over cunning, and played generally a cautious, and, when needed, a desperate game. Mr. Dyson, the landlord of the Cow and Cauliflower, strolled into his parlour, and observed the august Jonathan Wild peering round the room with an inquiring glance. Several of the occupants quailed before his gaze.

He, however, seemed satisfied with his observations of those present, for he turned round upon his heel and, for the first time, noticed the Badger.

"Umph!' said Jonathan Wild. "It appears the bird has hopped on to another twig."

"Somebody's wanted, I suppose," asked the Badger.

"Your'e right, mate," answered the thieftaker, as he followed the landlord into the passage, "very much wanted? We'll go over the house, if you please."

"Oh, certainly, gentlemen—certainly," said the Badger. "You can go into all the public rooms at once, the racket-court and skittle-ground included."

"Yes, Mr. Dyson, and private rooms as well," said the thieftaker, significantly.

"Oh, as you please; you have a search warrant then, I suppose. I hope you don't imagine that I harbour people who are wanted."

The thieftaker smiled, and followed the Badger over the house, while he left his men below to keep guard at all the ports.

There was no help for it. Badger found it absolutely necessary to accompany Wild over the premises, and consequently could not have an opportunity of communicating with the unfortunate housebreaker, whom he left stifled up in the small cupboard beside the fireplace in his own little bar-parlour.

Every nook and cranny of the establishment was searched, and, of course, no Nobbler was there."

"I hope you are now satisfied, Mr. Wild? Always ready to aid you, I'm sure."

"Ah!" said the thieftaker, "I should be much more satisfied, my friend, if I had found my man, seeing as how I know he was in this house a few minutes ago.''

"Indeed!" exclaimed the Badger; "sorry he ain't here now."

Jonathan Wild eyed the speaker with one of those half suspicious and half inquiring looks which were peculiar to that well known character.

"Dare say you are," he said. "You can't play a double game, Mr. Dyson. Of course not,"

"If I can't, I knows some one as can—do you see."

"Ah, perhaps. Well, Mr. Dyson, you have not lent him one of your empty vats to creep into, I suppose?"

The Badger felt uncomfortable. He saw from the manner of Jonathan Wild, that he suspected the unfortunate Nobbler was concealed in the house.

As they came down stairs in front of the bar, the thieftaker deliberately walked round on the other side of the bar, and from thence into the little parlour.

"A word with you, Mr. Dyson," said Jonathan Wild, as he entered the bar parlour, followed by the Badger. "We must unearth this fox somehow or other, Mr. Dyson," said the thieftaker, as he seated himself in a chair.

"Now you've your duty to perform to your particular customers. Of course, that's all plain enough; but still, Mr. Dyson, this man is wanted, and must be had. Now do you understand," he continued, as he adjusted a large patch which covered his dexter eye.

"In course, I understand," said the Badger, as he twisted the straw in his mouth, and looked anything but comfortable at the turn affairs were taking. He, however, tried to put as good a face upon the matter as possible, and repeated again—"In course, I understand, Mr. Wild. Every man to his business, and if I could aid you in any way, you can command me."

He said this falteringly, in spite of his usual self-command.

"Well, then," said Jonathan Wild, suddenly, "what s gone of this chap?"

"I don't know who you mean, or who it is you are looking after," said Mr. Dyson.

"Oh, don't you though. Well, then, it's the Nobbler, as is wanted."

"Oh, indeed!'

"Yes, 'tis," said the other, significantly, and nodding at the party whom he was addressing. "And now where is he?"

"Really, Mr. Wild, I cannot say," exclaimed the Badger. "I do not take any account of my customers arter they leave here."

"No, not after they leave here—but when they haven't left, Mr. Dyson—how then?"

"But he has. I should think you have sufficiently satisfied yourself upon that point."

"No we arn't," was the short and meaning reply.

"Well, I don't know what more I can do, then," said the Badger, who was in a state of feverish surprise, as he reflected upon the terrible position of the housebreaker, who was in the cupboard, immediately at the back of Jonathan Wild's chair. He feared the unfortunate man would undergo all the horrors of suffocation, and Wild's quick eye detected in the expression of Mr. Dyson's countenance, a troubled look, which at once declared that there was something lurking behind which had been at present concealed from observation."

"I don't know what more I can do for you," Mr. Wild."

"Unearth him," said Wild.

"But I can't, when I don't know where he is."

"Oh, can't you," said the other with a sort of Ethiopian whistle. Ethiopians, by the way, had not been imported in this country at this time, but it gives us of the present period, a tolerable good notion of the nature of Mr. Wild's manifestations of doubt.

While this part of the conversation was taking place, the Badger was horrified at beholding the door of the cupboard immediately at the back of Jonathan Wild, slightly open, and part of the features of the miserable Nobbler, were visible through the aperture. The fact was, that the wretched housebreaker, found himself nearly suffocated. Jonathan Wild caught the Badger's eyes directed to something immediately behind, and he turned his chair sharply round, glanced suddenly at the cupboard. By the time he had done this, the housebreaker had withdrawn into his hiding place and closed the door, but Jonathan Wild's suspicions were aroused upon the instant—he flung the chair on one side, and exclaimed in a loud voice—

"Rats hides in holes, sometimes, Mr. Dyson," and on the instant, he flung the door of the cupboard wide open, and disclosed the form of the Nobbler.

The housebreaker had endured an agony of suspense in his small prison house, and now saw the game was a desperate one.

With a yell, more like the howl of a wild beast than anything human, the Nobbler rushed upon the thieftaker, and dealt him so terrific a blow with his fist between the eyes, that Jonathan Wild was laid on the instant prostrate on the floor. He rose up, however, and caught his assailant by the tail of his coat. Another and another blow was dealt by the Nobbler in quick succession, returned by Jonathan Wild.

In a paroxysm of rage and despair the housebreaker succeeded in disengaging himself from the firm clutch of Jonathan Wild, and rushed out into the passage. Wild shouted out to his companions, and as they caught sight of the flying man, they immediately sprang upon him to effect a capture. Then came a struggle of a desperate and fearful description. Winding his fingers around the throat of his first assailant, he bent his form back till his body seemed to be threatened with dislocation.

The contortions of the struggling combatants were fearful to behold. The Nobbler was seeking in the breast pocket of his coat for a clasp knife. It was some time before he could succeed in obtaining it, owing to being so engaged with his adversary. He

however did manage, after repeated and desperate efforts, to release it. Taking it with one hand, as with the the other he held his adversary with a firm grasp, he placed the blade between his teeth, by which means he managed to open the weapon.

By this time the other officer, seeing the intentions of the housebreaker, sprang upon him, and caught him by the collar of his coat from behind.

A still more desperate struggle now ensued, and the Nobbler made several stabs with his weapon at his second assailant, and two flesh wounds were the consequence. The Nobbler then, with almost superhuman force, lifted up his first antagonist by one of his legs, and canting him over, actually flung him into the public room through the open door.

He fell bruised and bleeding over one of the tables, and by this time the passage was chocked up by the occupants of the parlour, who now became anxious for the Nobbler to get clear off.

"Two upon one isn't fair play, master," said a burly occupant of the public room, as he went to the rescue of the housebreaker.

"More it ain't," shouted out several voices, who now the ice was broken, were anxious to join the fray against the representators of the law.

"What's all this about, eh?" exclaimed another, as he rushed about, and created still greater confusion.

"Can't you let the man alone?"

"Do your duty!" said Jonathan Wild, as he made his way in the passage, which he found choked up with persons. "We must clear the place," and he proceeded to collar hold of one or two nearest to him, and thrust them forcibly on one side. "Don't lose sight or hold of your Loxton," he called out to his men—but as to getting near the combatants Wild found was now an impossibility.

"Mr. Dyson, clear the passage," said one of Wild's men.

Jonathan Wild, who was very much vexed before, was now doubly irritated at the turn affairs were taking.

The landlord made a show of clearing the premises—he made desperate efforts to effect the most unruly of its occupants, but he suffered himself to be thrown nevertheless, and screamed out to Wild for assistance, who in his turn, shouted to the men outside the Cow and Cauliflower.

These gentlemen endeavoured to effect an entrance, which they found next door to an impossibility, for no sooner were their intentions manifested when an heterogenous mass of persons rushed out towards the doorway, and, by the very weight of the moving body, the officers were forced out again and cut off from approaching to the assistance of their companions.

Those who had been pushed out of the house by the occupants of the passage, were now engaged with the officers outside, and a capture and two or three rescues were the consequence. All this time, in the midst of the crowd, the Nobbler was fighting his way with his antagonist, panting and snorting like some savage animal, which to say the truth, he certainly was—indeed nothing else. So great had the confusion and uproar now become, that it was impossible to distinguish what were combatants and what spectators. Jonathan Wild threw himself in the midst of the persons in the passage, and made another desperate effort to reach the centre of the affray, and catch hold once more of the belligerent Nobbler, who to do him justice, was fighting tooth and nail to make his escape. Wild was hustling about from one to the other, and although he struck out on all side, and inflicted severe punishment upon those near him. He was not, however, able to fight his way through the crowd, although he struck out right and left with his staff, and in a short time, might in all probability have effected his object, but before this took place, there was a new turn in affairs.

The Nobbler had been struggling desperately in the midst of the crowd against two of Jonathan Wild's officers. Prodigious as was the strength of the housebreaker, he found it difficult to throw his assailants completely off. They would cling to him in spite of all his struggles and efforts, however, chance at length turned up in his favour. One of his enemies was tripped up from behind by the crowd, and the other, he struck down by repeated blows from his fist. Once clear, he was jostled in the midst of those in the passage. The people parted like two waves of the ocean, and free egress was allowed to the Nobbler, who rushed out of the Cow and Cauliflower at headlong speed.

The officers outside sprang forward immediately upon their observing him emerge from the doorway of the public house. The first man that reached him received a stunning blow from the housebreaker's fist, which laid him prostrate; he, however, picked himself up, and joined his companions in giving chase to the fugitive.

Loud shouts of stop thief resounded from all quarters. The housebreaker took his course along the middle of the roadway, for there were but few vehicles to intercept his passage.

Jonathan Wild had by this time managed to get clear of the crowd, and emerging from the house, he joined in the chase.

"Twenty guineas to the man who captures him—twenty guineas!" shouted out Jonathan Wild, in a stentorian voice, and staff in hand.

The Nobbler was a considerable distance ahead of his pursuers, but several passengers joined in the chase.

"Twenty guineas to the first man who collars him," the thieftaker continued to shout out to those ahead.

Excited to exertion by the prospect of this reward, one of those ahead pushed forward. The Nobbler heard them like a pack of wolves at his tail, and it was surprising how a man of his heavy build could have continued to keep up at the pace he had hitherto done, but now he heard the clatter of the feet of the man who seemed bent upon earning the twenty guineas; he found it but added wings to his own speed, and he strained every nerve to distance his pursuer, who was both a younger and lighter man, and, in spite of all the Nobbler's efforts, he found his pursuer was gaining on him.

Loud shouts from Jonathan Wild and his companions reached the ears of the housebreaker, and added to the confusion.

The man who headed those behind the unfortunate Nobbler now redoubled his speed, and there seemed a certainty that he would succeed in overtaking the hunted man.

There was but a few yards between them, and the housebreaker was well nigh exhausted—nothing but the exigency of the case would have enabled him to have held on so long.

Seeing the impossibility of his holding out much longer, the Nobbler had recourse to a feint.

As his pursuers rushed on at full speed the housebreaker stopped suddenly, and stooped down low—the man who had made certain of a capture could not stop himself in his career, and as the housebreaker let his body down lower than the other's knees, his determined pursuer fell over the body of the housebreaker, and was sent sprawling on the hard flag stones in Tothill Street, Westminster.

So serious had been his fall, that he was bruised and half stunned therefrom.

In an instant the Nobbler darted down a small court, which led out of Tothill Street, and entered a marine store shop, kept by a Jew, with whom he had occasionally transactions in the way of business.

Rushing into the shop, he made known his position to the owner of the shop, and sought concealment in the rear of the premises.

Taking his way through these, he became lost in a labyrinth of wretched, squalid habitations.

In a few minutes Jonathan Wild and his men were, like a pack of hounds, on the scent, and filled the marine store shop—the proprietor of which they collared and threatened with summary punishment.

He declared his innocence of the transaction, and obstinately declared that he knew nothing of the Nobbler.

Every room in the house was rapidly examined—as also the court and adjacent houses—but, with all their search, no Nobbler was discovered.

He had fairly given them the double—and Jonathan Wild was breathless, and well nigh frantic with rage, but he was compelled to give up the chase as hopeless.

Jonathan Wild reluctantly enough left the locality and proceeded back to the Cow and Cauliflower, there to vent his spleen upon everybody, and, more especially Mr. William Dyson.

"Look here, you double dealing rascal," said Wild to the Badger upon his return; "I'll not only have your license stopped, but give you a turn in the pillory besides, for encouraging and concealing one of the biggest rascals in all London."

"It's very hard, Mr. Wild, to be knocked about in one's own house," answered the Badger.

"It is, indeed," said Wild in a mocking tone.

"And be abused in the bargain," continued Dyson.

"Very hard," said Wild, in the same mocking strain.

"Besides, it ain't no fault of mine if you didn't catch the man."

"No fault?—Who concealed him in that cupboard?"

"Not me," answered the Badger, whose face, by the way, was covered with adhesive plaster.

"Oh—not you—who then, if I may be so bold as to ask?"

"I am sure I don't know—not me I'll swear!"

"Psha,—you'd swear to anything, and say anything but your prayers."

"I declare most positively that I know as little about his being in the cupboard as yourself—he must have crept in there while we were up stairs—that's how he worked it, depend on it."

"You'll have to answer for this, Mr. Dyson—you'll have to answer for it, but of that hereafter," said Mr. Wild, in a decided tone.

"I hope as how you ain't agoin' to be hard upon a poor chap, who endeavours to get an honest living. I always have done the thing what's square, as you know afore now," said the Badger.

The Badger produced some of his best brandy, and then placed it before the thieftaker.

"Now, look here, you Jesuitical rascal," said Wild, "had it not been for you we should have had that chap to a certainty—but your cursed intriguing has completely baffled us."

"I'm sure I tried my hardest, and got terribly knocked about, as you see," he said, pointing to his face which was covered with contusions, and which he had, to do him justice, made the most of.

"Well, the only reparation you can make is to put us on the scent when this fellow makes his appearance again here—that is if he ever does—which, to my thinking, is not at all likely."

"That you may rely on," answered the Badger, "I pledge my right down honest word to it."

"You do?"

"I do."

"Very well. When he comes here send round to Boscow—he lives only a few streets off."

"I will, Mr. Wild."

"Do you understand me?—I'll leave you his address."

"It shall be done, Mr. Wild," answered the Badger.

"Enough!—that's an understanding;—mind I'll make it worth your while," said Jonathan.

The Badger made a deprecating gesture, to intimate that his actions were not to be influenced by filthy lucre.

After a few minutes more conversation, Jonathan Wild took his departure, battered, bruised, and chapfallen, not without, however, taking three of the most riotous occupants of the passage prisoners.

We must now follow the footsteps of the Nobbler.

After his escape through the marine store shop, he crept into one of the houses in the rear of the premises.

It was a notorious thieves' house, and there were so many places of concealment, that it was next door to hopeless to ever expect to find him,

Indeed, he lay concealed in an aperture, made on purpose, beneath the dustbin—the secret hiding-place of many, who, like him, were keeping safely out of the reach of the officers of the law.

Here he escaped detection—and when a sufficient time had elapsed for the owner of the house to feel satisfied that the coast was clear of the thieftaker and his myrmidons, and that all had departed, notice was given to Nobbler.

The unlucky housebreaker did not feel at all certain that Wild and his companions would not return, so he shifted his quarters to another thieves' house some few streets off.

In this second house he lay concealed till night—under the cover of whose dark mantle he took his way to his own home, fearing every step he heard might be that of the parties who were in search of him.

The Badger's position was, indeed, not an enviable one.

His house was situated in the then lawless locality of Whitefriars.

In a dingy, gloomy apartment, in one of the most ancient houses in Whitefriars, sat the Nobbler. His appearance was the personification of woe and despair. Repulsive as his features were at all times, they were doubly so now.

The ugly scar which he had received in his conflict with Mr. Baintree, was visible on his face; and besides this he was covered with contusions both on body and face in his struggle with Jonathan Wild's officers.

A solitary candle cast its feeble rays around the apartment—whose darkness it, however, sought in vain to dispel.

Near to the Nobbler sat an old woman, who had evidently once possessed no inconsiderable amount of beauty, but her features were worn and thin, and lines of care were visible upon her pallid cheeks.

From the expression of her face, a superficial observer would have divined that she had been possessed of many womanly attributes as well as female beauty.

Alas, poor thing—her connection with the housebreaker had sadly altered her character, although it had not entirely shut out that light which even the most abandoned have at times still burning, with a pure fire, within them.

She cast several furtive glances towards the face of him, who years ago, in the first blush of youth, she had learnt to love as dearly and devotedly as woman only can.

A dear penalty she had paid for the same as she afterwards found to her cost.

"Be thankful you are safe thus far, Jem," said the woman soothingly.

"Thankful—for what?" he asked, while at the same time he kept his eyes fixed upon the floor.

"Things might have been worse," she replied.

He made no reply but sat gloomy and glumpy as before.

"Things might have been worse—and the affair will blow over after the trial, and be no more thought of," said the woman, with a sad smile.

"Stop your magging," he answered, savagely, "I don't want to be preached to by a woman. What do you know about the matter? Mind your own business, will you."

She was immediately silent, and cast a frightened look towards the housebreaker, and then proceeded with some work she was about

There was a long silence after this, the burglar not deigning to vouchsafe another observation.

"Odd rot him!" exclaimed the housebreaker, after a pause of some minutes' duration. "I wish I had him here alone, the warmint; I'd bet a crown he wouldn't trouble either me or my palls again, the white livered hound!"

This was said in allusion to Jonathan Wild.

"He'll get his deserts himself some day, Jem, depend on it," said the woman, mildly, who, in her own inverted code of morals, deemed the thief taken much the most culpable of the two.

Such is the false notion with which so many view those who happen to be in antagonism to themselves.

The figure of a gaunt man now entered the apartment on tiptoe. His costume was quaint and curious, and made up of odds and ends, not even one garment fitted its owner.

The coat was ridiculously short, and his waistcoat as absurdly long; and his long legs, which were much attenuated, gave you an idea of a daddy long legs—these said legs were encased in close-fitting smalls, ending in worsted stockings, and shoes with buckles, then unusually worn.

If one were to hazard a guess, we should be disposed to form the opinion that the lanky individual had bought his garments at the marine store shop, through which the Nobbler had escaped, and moreover, that he had not been particularly happy in the selection of his habiliments.

The man came into the room so noiselessly that his presence would hardly have been observed, had not the Nobbler's quick ears been continually on the strain to catch the least sound.

He turned towards the new comer, and uttered a satisfactory exclamation.

"Well, Long Sam, what news?" said the housebreaker.

"The hawks are in the air," said that individual, in a hissing whisper. "Mizzle's the word!"

"The devil! What do you mean?" said the housebreaker.

"The downy one's on your lay," replied the other.

"How do you know?" asked the housebreaker

"Charley Springer heard 'em a talking about it."

"Curse them!—a long and a bitter curse cling to them and their's," said the Nobbler, as he rose and threw his seat, in a paroxysm of rage, from him.

"Hush! Don't make such a clatter," said Long Sam, "or it—"

He had no time to finish his sentence for he was interrupted by a loud and piercing scream from the woman, whose alarm was occasioned by the appearance of the head of a man peering through the window of the apartment.

In another moment the window was thrown quickly open, and the man endeavoured to force an entrance.

The Nobbler waited not for him to effect his object, but he instantly levelled a pistol and fired.

The man dropped on the outside, with a deep groan.

This had scarcely taken place, when the door of the house was split in two with a tomahawk, and in a few more seconds Jonathan Wild himself rushed hastily into the room.

"Hell and devil!" exclaimed the Nobbler. "Your life's blood!"

And he sprang upon Jonathan Wild with the howl of a wild beast, his knife twice found a home in the body of the thieftaker, after which he flung him with terrible force to the earth.

By this time a number of constables entered, and were about to rush forward and capture the Nobbler, who stood like a tiger at bay, eyeing them with savage and ferocious looks.

Long Sam had by this time seized hold of a long spear or halbert, such as was used by the beefeaters at that period. He made a desperate charge at the new comers with this weapon, from whose point they recoiled back in some confusion.

Some two or three entered the room sideways, when Long Tom again charged them at the doorway.

"Hook it—hook it, master!" shouted out Sam.

Under cover of Sam's weapon the Nobbler rushed into the passage, and like a panther tore up the old, crazy staircase, followed by several of the constables, some of whom, however, Sam managed to trip up in their passage, and these falling over their companions caused some confusion, and enabled the Nobbler to reach the top of the house in safety.

A few agonising seconds of breathing time are allowed to the Nobbler, which to him are invaluable. Above the landing is the trap-door which leads to the loft.

The burglar flew into the adjoining apartments to possess himself of some piece of furniture by which he might reach the trap-door, but none was there.

He heard the shuffling footsteps of his pursuers, and, with a violent effort, he sprang, or rather leapt to the loft.

He gave his hands a terrible blow against the door, but he heeded it not; escape was uppermost in his mind, and he succeeded in clasping the side of the trap-door—drawing himself up by a vigorous effort, he managed to get one knee on the side, and with his head he pushed back the trap, which, for him, was luckily unbolted.

In another moment he found himself safe in the loft.

His pursuers came up on the landing like a pack of bloodhounds. The Nobbler observed them, and hurled in their midst a large billet of wood, which he found in the loft.

It struck two of them with terrible force, and called forth oaths and curses of pain and rage.

The Nobbler then shut down the trap with a loud slam.

Jonathan Wild's men procured a short ladder, and in a little time they found themselves in the loft.

By this time the burglar had opened the other trap which led to the roof, and commenced climbing cautiously over the slanting tiles.

It was a high-pitched roof, and it required the utmost caution in taking a passage over it. The house itself was very high, and a panoramic view of the ancient city of London lay disclosed to view, if the housebreaker had had either time or inclination to survey it."

"There he goes," said one of the officers, "He can't escape us after all; follow, lads—follow!"

True enough, there indeed was the object of their search, climbing like a cat over the tiles.

The officers, bent as they were upon effecting a capture, found themselves in no very pleasant position, when they began to crawl upon their hands and knees along the tiles. It was a giddy height, and the holding was so insecure, that a sense of dizziness came over one or two of the officers.

They began to think that they had not acted wisely in thus venturing their lives in this dangerous undertaking.

Still they kept on in their determined search.

By this time the Nobbler had gained the roof of the adjoining house, which was similar to his own, or, if possible, worse to pass over.

Having arrived at the summit or apex of this, he dislodged one of the round tiles and threw it among his pursuers. It struck one who started with fright, and it was a mercy he did not loose his balance. The tile then run down the roof with a sharp grating noise and then descended into the street, and was shivered into a hundred pieces.

The officers shuddered as they heard it fall on the pavement, and trembled with fright.

There is always something very jarring to the senses to hear a falling body hurled from some high eminence upon which we find ourselves placed. So thought the officers; but they persevered in the chase.

One of them then drew a pistol, and presenting it to the housebreaker, demanded his passive surrender. The only answer to this was a derisive laugh, and the housebreaker laid himself down upon the roof of the house so as not to present too good a mark to the officer.

A flash—a sharp report—which sounded doubly loud to the surrounding neighbourhood, and the housebreaker found himself as yet unhurt."

"Yield, man!" again shouted out the officer.

The Nobbler did not condescend to reply, but crawled now more cautiously towards a neighbouring stack of chimneys, having reached which, he found himself under cover from the enemies fire.

He now searched in all his pockets for something which seemed to be of vital importance, for cold drops of perspiration stood upon his forehead as he thrust his hand hastily from one pocket to the other. At length a satisfactory expression passes over his features—he has found what he was so anxiously in search of. This proved to be a coil of rope, having obtained which, he proceeded to make a slip knot, while he passed the other end of the rope round the stack of chimneys, and made it thoroughly secure.

"Heavens, he contemplates a descent!" exclaimed the foremost officer.

"He is going to let himself down into the street, as I'm a living man. On to him—he's behind the chimneys—I can see his hands—there!"

"I see them," said another, "fire, and disable him."

Another report of a pistol followed these words, but the Nobbler had heard them, and very prudently withdrew his hands behind the chimneys.

It is very probable that we should have done the same thing under similar circumstances.

The officers saw the inutility of their last proceeding.

"Great heaven, he will escape after all," exclaimed one of the company. "Follow on and secure him before he has time to lower himself into the street by the means of the rope."

The foremost man, urged on by a strong desire to have the honor of first laying hold of so celebrated and determined a ruffian, now made a rapid passage towards the stack of chimneys occupied by the sanguinary Nobbler, who, from behind his breastwork, took a survey of his actions.

Deliberately watching his proceedings, the housebreaker became aware that it would be impossible for him to trust himself to his rope with an enemy so close at hand, for before he could possibly reach the ground, the officer would have gained the chimney, and could cut the rope, and the burglar would have a fall of a hundred feet or more, which would crush him into a shapeless mass.

He calculated all these chances, and made up his mind immediately what course to pursue.

He quietly waited till the ill-fated officer came within close range, and then carefully sighted his piece, and covered the approaching man.

For a few moments an almost death-like silence prevailed amongst them, disturbed only by the stealthy, cautious foot steps of the officer who was foremost in approaching the stack of chimneys to capture the Nobbler.

Now a third sharp report was heard—this time with horrible results.

The unfortunate man who was pursuing the burglar, received a death wound from the latter's piece.

The unfortunate man gave one piercing shriek—flung his arms in the air—fell backwards—slid along the slanting roof—and fell with a deadening and sickening sound into the street below.

His brother officers were pale with fright as they observed the fate of their unfortunate companion—a fate so horrible, that in their present precarious position, it had in it something too dreadful to think of.

They could not repress a shudder as they glanced towards that part of the roof over which the unhappy man had fallen but a few moments previous.

They paused panic struck, and were so appalled at the awful fate of their companion, that they could not find it in their hearts to proceed immediately.

The Nobbler took advantage of their hesitation, upon which, indeed, he had calculated, and swinging himself down by the rope, proceeded to make good his perilous descent.

The rope swayed to and fro with his weight, and his hands were jagged against the rough brick work during his passage; but it was a question of life and death, and what will not a desperate man undertake when driven to the last extremity?

By this time the whole of the surrounding neighbourhood had become thoroughly aroused, and a motley crowd of anxious and

inquiring faces were in the street, gathered round the house, and as this locality was chiefly occupied, or, indeed, wholly inhabited by the most lawless class, they sympathised with the Nobbler, and cheered him during his descent. Most of them were at no loss to divine the state of the case.

He slowly began to descend from the giddy height.

When he had reached about half way down from the top of the house, the officers began to recover from the surprise and panic in which they had been thrown by the sudden and terrible fate of their companion. Two of them reached the stack of chimneys, when one, more precipitate than the other, was about to cut the rope, but he was hastily stopped in his proceeding by his fellow officer, who immediately commenced descend-

No. 10.

ing by the rope, and called upon his companion to follow.

"We shall have the scoundrel yet," exclaimed the officer ; " follow, Bill, and avenge poor Martin's death."

The Nobbler had by this time reached the ground in safety, and would in all probability have made good his retreat ; but two of Jonathan Wild's men were outside the premises keeping watch, and those on the top of the house called to them to effect a capture of the burglar, who immediately upon his alighting on the ground, found himself set upon by both the men.

Wild, infuriated, and driven to desperation, the Nobbler maintained an obstinate and determined struggle with his two fresh assailants, in which no doubt, however, he would have been ultimately overpowered, had not the lawless multitude rendered him some assistance.

It would have been hard to tell what would have been the result of the conflict, for the men were determined, and although severely handled by the crowd, they fought bravely, and stuck to their man with bull-dog tenacity.

By this time the two officers had succeeded in descending from the top of the house, and rushed forward to the assistance of their brethren. One, however, was tripped up by one of the crowd, and fell on the pavement with terrible force, cutting his temple and severely wounding himself thereby. The Nobbler was in the hands of one of the officers, who clung to him with the utmost determination. He struggled to release himself, and the contortions of the two combatants was something dreadful to behold. The burglar fought for life and liberty. If taken, certain death he knew awaited him, and consequently he fought with desperation. In vain he endeavoured to remove the hand of the officer, which maintained still a firm grasp of his throat. In vain he struck at him right and left with his clenched fists, until the man's face presented to the beholders one mass of contusions. Seeing the other officers coming on to the rescue of their companion, the burglar foresaw the probability of being overpowered, and with one desperate effort at escape, he bit the hand which was at his throat so severely, that the man roared with pain and agony, and almost swooned from the effects of the bite, he found his hand was cramped and powerless, and it fell by his side bleeding profusely. The Nobbler, with herculean strength, flung him off, and rushed down Whitefriars Street at headlong speed.

"See, he's off! follow my men, follow!" exclaimed the chief officer, and the three rushed on in hot pursuit of the burglar. Two pistol shots were discharged after him without any other effect than knocking off the hat of an old gentleman who happened to be turning the corner of the next street at the time. Poor man, he believed himself to be mortally wounded, and his senses were completely scattered, as he found himself in the midst of a scene which baffles description.

Away rushed the Nobbler, and after him the officers, followed by a vast number of the crowd, who were anxious to witness the termination of the exciting affair.

As the burglar hurried along, his pursuers called out to the passengers to stop him. One or two of these did make a snatch at him to endeavour to arrest his progress, but there was a ferocity upon his wild and distorted features which made them cautious of hazarding a close contest. Nevertheless, the offi-

cers were gaining upon him, and it is probable that they might have overtaken him if the run had been a longer one; but it was destined to come to a termination. The burglar made for the banks of the Thames. Arrived there, he rushed madly into the river. Anywhere to escape.

It is an old saying, that he who is born to be hung can never be drowned. It appeared so in this instance, for the men who were in pursuit, upon seeing him rush into the water, exclaimed simultaneously—

"Merciful heavens, he is going to drown himself rather than be taken alive."

The burglar had now become submerged in the water nearly up to his chest. He had walked, or rather, run in, and in a few more seconds his pursuers observed him strike out and swim for his life.

"He must perish," exclaimed one of the officers. "Encumbered as he is with his clothes, and well nigh exhausted, it will be impossible for him to keep afloat long. Never mind, we will after him at all events."

And with that they rushed towards the banks of the river, and proceeded to unloose a small boat. In this they put off in pursuit of the escaped prisoner.

"We must have him now, at any rate," observed one of the occupants in the boat. "The fellow must have nine lives if he manages to escape this journey."

"Most probably he seeks death rather than be taken and tied up at Tyburn. Small blame to him for that, I'm thinking. Ah, see, there he is!"

It was true enough; the Nobbler was in the centre of the river swimming with the tide, although his strokes seemed feeble and faint. He was evidently making for a coal barge which was drifting down the river.

Jonathan Wild's men pulled lustily at their oars to endeavour to overtake him. He was, however, many hundred yards ahead of them, and before they could reach the object of their pursuit, the Nobbler had hailed the man in charge of the barge, and the officers observed him assist the burglar from the water, and lift him into the barge in safety.

"Pull away, lads, and we shall have him yet," exclaimed the steersman of the boat.

The men laid too with their oars in a masterly manner, and very soon shot ahead and came up with the coal barge which contained the burglar, whom, however, they had not as yet got safe into custody.

Shooting the head of their boat alongside of the collier, they would have effected a landing on the vessel, but the burglar's eyes were intently watching their proceedings, and he stood with the large bow oar of the collier in both hands waiting the attack. No sooner did their boat near the collier, than he poised the large oar in both his hands and striking the officers' boat violently with the end of it, he endeavoured by one terrible lunge to upset their craft. He nearly succeeded in this object, for the off side of the boat dipped in the water, and would have capsized, had not its occupants shifted their positions, and by the weight of their bodies on the other side, succeeded in righting their small craft. As it was, they found themselves some distance in the rear of the vessel by the force of the blow, and their boat three parts full of water.

"Curse the fellow," exclaimed the steersman; "it's only by a miracle we have ourselves escaped a watery grave. Egad, but that was a well directed blow. But we'll on to him again, and manage better the next journey."

"We must bale out the water first, or the chances are that we shall find ourselves 'nowhere,' to use a sporting phrase."

They now proceeded to bale out the water as they best could by means of their hats, leaving the boat to drift gently down with the tide as they did so.

It proved a longer job than they had at first anticipated, and their position was anything but a pleasant one.

While so engaged, the report of a pistol was heard, a flash gleamed on the surface of the water, and a shot struck the head of the boat, from which it glanced off and struck one of their oars and broke it short off.

"D—n the fellow, he means to show fight to the last," exclaimed one of the occupants of the boat. "Here is for a return of casualties," said the man, as he was about to prime his pistol, when to his great mortification he found both powder and weapon had become saturated with the water, and it was consequently for the present useless. His companions' weapons were in a similar condition.

"The brute has managed to keep his own powder dry, somehow or other," said one of the men, sulkily.

They shortly after this had the satisfaction of getting their boat tolerably free from water, and again pulled after the collier with lusty strokes. As they neared the collier they observed the indomitable Nobbler awaiting their coming, with his terrific weapon poised above his head, at the stern of the vessel.

The officer in command of the wherry called out to the man in charge of the collier to give up the burglar to the officers of justice. The man did not condescend to make any reply to this request, but either did not or would not hear them.

"Ay," shouted the officer, in a still louder tone; "do you hear, you sir? You are protecting and abetting a murderer."

"You be d—d," said the man, in a Cornish dialect. "Arter I've saved the life o' a poor

crow, I ain't a goin' to gi' 'em upe to ony o' your kidney."

"You blackguard, you shall suffer for this, as sure as my name's Ruddick," exclaimed the officer, with indignation. "Pull away, men," he continued, "and we'll take them both yet."

The stalwart form of the Nobbler, as his large proportions loomed ominously at the stern of the vessel, did not look very encouraging to the attacking party, who were certainly had at an advantage, as they were without the use of their fire-arms. Nevertheless Ruddick determined to make another attempt, and as his boat neared the collier, the Cornish man, who was in charge, called out and said—

"You'd bette'n nought coome arter him, or you may happe'n to find yoursel' capsized as sure as fate—"

"Never mind what the fellow says," answered Ruddick. "We know our duty; and if such a scoundrel as that is allowed to escape, it's a disgrace to the force, that's all I have to say. On, men, on to him, and make a safe job of it this time."

But it did not appear quite so easy to those who were pulling at the oars. It was quite certain that the Nobbler, with one stroke of his gigantic weapon would be well able to scatter the crew of the boat before they could effect a landing, and it seemed almost a foolhardy thing to even attempt it. Nevertheless the officers were determined men, and were moreover irritated at seeing their companion meet with so dreadful a death from the roof of the house.

"You'd better be off about your business," said a female voice, addressing herself to those in pursuit; "you'd better be off about your business, and let poor unfortunate folks alone, what's got into trouble, and ought to be protected, poor souls. Me nor my husband ain't a-goin' to give up the poor soul, I can tell you; and all the good you'll get will be a ducking and a cracked crown. Now be off, or it will be the worse for you."

As the boat approached the lighter, the woman who had addressed the officers threw some missile at the crew, at which they only laughed.

Their countenances, however, assumed a more serious expression as they observed the burglar grasp the oar with his left hand, while with his right he cocked and presented a pistol at the approaching party. Affairs assumed a serious character, and the attacking party now hesitated in their onward movement.

The countenance of the burglar was determined, desperate, and ferocious. There could be no doubt but that he was likely to take his stand in his present position to the last, and would never be taken alive, however the contest might terminate. This fact was fully impressed upon the minds of the attacking party, and it made them hesitate in their course of action.

"Yield," shouted out Ruddick, as he observed his men hesitate.

A shot from the pistol of the burglar was the only answer to this demand. It struck one of the men on the shoulder, and knocked him over, wounding him severely, although, as it afterwards turned out, not mortally. Ruddick now thought it a good opportunity to push forward towards the collier before there was time for his enemy to reload. He urged on the men at the oars, and they pulled towards the vessel with promptitude and decision.

They had now come within reach of the long oar wielded by the burglar. He swung it round with a force which seemed a marvel of strength, and the end of it came dashing in the very midst of the boat's crew. Two of them were knocked almost senseless by the force of the well-directed blow, and the boat spun round and was nearly capsized therefrom. Three of the oars were unshipped and drifted away with the tide, and the crew were in the utmost state of confusion. To mend matters, Ruddick observed the Nobbler quietly reloading his pistol, and under these circumstances he backed water to get the boat out of pistol range. Besides the two men who had been nearly stunned, a third had received a severe wound in the right arm which incapacitated him from active duty.

Ruddick inwardly cursed the unfortunate turn affairs had taken. To follow now would be an act of madness. But as he was upon doing his duty, and effecting a capture by any possible means, it would have been worse than useless to follow in the present crippled state of his men, more especially as there did not seem the the most remote probability of his ever attaining his object : besides which, it almost amounted to an impossibility, for he had but one pair of oars left. He therefore immediately attended to his wounded comrades, and pulled as well as he could back to shore, and gave up the chase as hopeless.

CHAPTER XII.

HONORA LANGFORD AND HER LOVERS.—HENRY OSBORNE ARRIVES AT THE METROPOLIS—HIS INTERVIEW WITH MR. LANGFORD.

HONORA LANGFORD, the gentle, trusting, Honora—with all her guileless innocence, unsophisticated manners and demeanour—would need a chapter to define her character, and expatiate upon her many and varied graces. Poor, simple-hearted girl, her mind was sorely troubled since the declaration of Sir Richard Fleetwood. He had not called or taken any notice of her since their last interview, in which he had so passionately declared his love. She did not for one moment doubt the genuineness of that declaration. There generally is a truthfulness in the outpourings of the human heart which can hardly fail to carry conviction with it to those who listen to its natural promptings. And Sir Richard, although stained in his character by many dark qualities, was nevertheless truthful in his declaration to Honora. There is a halo surrounding a young, lovely, and virtuous girl, which chastens and purifies the most hardened when they come into her presence. The worldly man and debauchee often finds himself at fault, and stands abashed as dishonourable thoughts arise.

Not that any such had been called forth in Sir Richard, for, to do him justice, and he cannot afford to be defrauded of the few good qualities he might be possessed of—to do him justice, his attachment to Honora had been honourable and pure from the first. Had it been otherwise, he would not, in all probability, have suffered so much as he had done.

Honora had fully expected to receive some communication from her father, being under the impression that Sir Richard would, in all probability, lay the state of the case before him, and endeavour to induce him to use his parental authority in persuading his daughter to listen to his suit.

But Mr. Langford did not mention the subject. It is true, he appeared reserved and grave, the cause of which Honora could not determine.

Under the circumstances she thought it better to mention to her father the fact of Sir Richard Fleetwood's declaration, and having come to the conclusion that this was the best course, she proceeded to consult a young lady by the name of Staunton, who was staying with her, and had, indeed, been one of her choicest companions.

Edith Staunton was generally consulted upon all Honora's private affairs, and might be said to be her confident. She had already been made acquainted with the particulars of Honora's last interview with Sir Richard, and evidently from her manner, although she said but little, viewed his suit with rather favourable eyes.

"Edith, dear," said Miss Langford, "I'm thinking that my father will consider it rather sly of me if I do not let him know about Sir Richard Fleetwood. What say you ?"

"He must know of it sooner or later, dearest, if he does not already, and I am sure the information had better come from yourself, for you may be sure Sir Richard will broach the subject to him."

"So I have thought ; but, do you know, I think he will be sure to view the suit of Sir Richard with favourable eyes, and I almost dread naming it to him."

"It would be a good match," said Miss Staunton ; "and I am sure, for my part, I think Sir Richard in every way a gentleman."

Honora darted upon her friend a troubled look, which was not lost upon the latter.

"There now," she said, in continuation. "don't let me hurt your feelings, dearest Honora, I know you already love, and Mr. Osborne is not likely to be forgotten for any new suitor."

"I should hope not."

"We must trust to time which generally in the end sets all things even."

"Time will never see me alter in my sentiments towards Henry Osborn—never !"

Her friend made no reply to these observations, but stood contemplating her as she sat ruminating in her chair.

The conversation was abrubtly cut short by the entrance of Mr. Langford himself, and Miss Staunton made some trifling excuse to leave the drawing-room, so that father and daughter might be left alone.

The former gently bent over his daughter and imprinted a kiss upon her fair cheek.

"Father," said Honora, "I have been wishing to see you, as I have had something to say to you for some days past."

"Indeed, my sweetest, and why did you not do so ? I have been here or, at any rate, somewhere about the house. What is it, my love ?"

His daughter hesitated, and a heightened colour was observable on her features as she said, falteringly—

"Sir Richard Fleetwood seems to have avoided the house lately."

"Oh, he is busy with his own affairs, no doubt."

"Possibly so ; but I hope I have not offended him."

"Offended ! How can you have done that ? What an idea ! Offended, indeed ! My gentle Honora is not likely to offend any one wilfully, I am sure."

"I hope not, father."

"I am sure not."

"No, but the last time Sir Richard was here he made a declaration of his sentiments towards—towards myself."

"Indeed !" exclaimed Mr. Langford, in surprise, and then, after a pause, he said—

"And you—what said you ? How were they received."

Honora was silent for a moment or two, and then said, quietly—

"I told him the truth, father."

"Well, my child, I do not doubt that, but what was it ?"

"I told him I felt myself flattered by his preference, but—"

"Well, but what, Honora ?"

"My heart was already engaged."

She covered her face with her hands as she said this, and her father remained silent for a short time.

"My dearest daughter, you would not, I should suppose, think of slighting or refusing the attentions of a gentleman of Sir Richard's position ? It is a match of all others the most desirable."

"No match is to be coveted father, unless you feel you can give your heart as well as your hand."

"Psha ; you talk like a school girl. You can, and ought, to be able to give your heart to a man who is worthy of it. To institute a comparison between him and that Oxford student would be absurd—I mean a comparison as far as regards the man individually, apart from their worldly position, which, by the way, is a matter of some importance, however much young ladies may feel disposed to ignore it Honora, you must, as I have told you before, think no more of this Osborne. He is nothing after all but an adventurer."

"An adventurer, father ?" said his daughter, reproachfully. "You surely are not un-generous enough to call Mr. Osborne an adventurer ?"

"No, not exactly that—that which is generally understood by the term. He is, I dare say, a good meaning fellow enough, but he has to fight his way in the world, and if he even does attain anything like a position, which, after all, is problematical, it must be, of necessity, years hence."

"He has talents, and health, and honour for his guidance, and will be sure to succeed," she answered, proudly.

"My dear girl, you do not know the world, or you would not talk thus. It is not always the rarest talents and most indefatigable industry that always command success in our advancement in life. The dullards and rogues too often pass us on the road, and when you have lived as long as I have, you will be convinced of the truth of this. I know it is always an unpalatable truth for young people of either sex to believe, but it is a truth, nevertheless ; and as to imagining that you can or ought to wait for Henry Osborne, is an absurdity—more than an absurdity, as I have before told you. Now, do not think me harsh or prejudiced against the young man, for such is not the fact. On the contrary, I am disposed to view his character and actions in the most favourable light, but in our relative positions he is no match for you, Honora. If it be necessary, I will explain more fully my reasons for saying this, for I assure you, my dear girl, I do so advisably, believe me."

"I do not court a high position," said Honora, sadly; "I do not desire it."

"Psha! That's the way you all talk at your age, time, however, generally proves to you your mistake. Now, I charge you, Honora, not, at any rate, to treat this suit of Sir Richard Fleetwood's with contumely, for it is one of all others I myself should the most desire. He is a gentleman highly connected, a man of honour and general information, and would do credit to any one with whom he was connected."

"I do not deny his many good qualifications."

"And he, moreover, loves you, I suppose?"

"That I certainly believe he does—most sincerely."

"Well, then—why then treat him with coldness for this love-sick sentimental boy?"

"Had I seen and known him first it might have been different; as it is—"

"Well."

"As it is, my own sense of honour will not permit of my listening to his suit. It is of no use, father, giving a sacred promise at the altar of love, honour and obey, to one whom you feel it is impossible to say so to without committing perjury."

"Bah! You'll learn to love him in time, believe me."

"That is a matter upon which I must, and shall, be the best judge."

"You think so perhaps now, but hereafter you will be of a different opinion; but, however, we will let the matter drop for the present; I know how hard it is to reason with a girl upon a subject like this, only let me charge you, Honora, not to commit yourself any further with Mr. Osborne. He has had my answer, which, as far as I am concerned, is a final one. Let a little time pass over, Honora, and do nothing precipitate, and we will then recur to this subject again, for I should be sorry, my sweet girl, to cause you any unhappiness by too rigid a view of the question. There now, you know my opinion, and I wish it coincided with yours. As the case stands at present, I should wish it to remain, until I see or hear something of Sir Richard Fleetwood—which I shall do, no doubt, in due time, that is unless you have given him so decided an answer that he has taken umbrage and never intends to see us again."

"I should be sorry, indeed, if such were the case."

"I am happy to hear you say so. It is spoken like my gentle girl. Was he angry upon leaving?"

"He was very much excited, certainly," said Honora, thoughtfully, "and went away in great haste—I was sorry to see it, and certainly was not at all prepared for so great a proof of his attachment, which, to say the truth, I had hardly given him credit for."

"Well, we shall see—let matters rest as they are at present, and I think I would not offer any fresh encouragement to Mr. Osborne. As an honourable man he ought not, I think, to persist in pursuing his suit, for I have been very candid and explicit in my explanations and answer when he broached the subject to me. There now, don't fret and all will be well, I dare say, after all."

Mr. Langford stooped down, and kissed his daughter affectionately, and took his departure.

When he had gone, poor Honora burst into a flood of tears.

But what of Henry Osborne during this period?

His life at Oxford was anything but an agreeable one. He had felt convinced from the first that Mr. Langford's removal to London would in all probability cause an estrangement between his daughter and him, self, and, from the incidents already detailed, it appeared very probable that such would be the case.

Osborne found himself so wretched at Oxford, that the place had become hateful to him.

He could not bear to be wandering about the spots made familiar to him by the tender interviews he had frequently had with his dear Honora on the same ground. They put him in mind of the lost, or rather missing, enchantress.

Osborne felt himself perpetually wretched in Oxford since the departure of Miss Langford. He had but few acquaintances whom he esteemed, and indeed, to say the truth, he was treated as a poor student by the more aristocratic portion of college companions. His friends had advised him to seek for a living in the church—and this had been his original intention when he first commenced his course of studies at the university, but, lacking sufficient interest, perhaps, he had not, as yet, been able to succeed in obtaining an appointment.

Some time after the departure of Mr. Langford and his daughter from Oxford, Osborne had offered to him an appointment in a large mercantile firm in St. Mary Axe, trading under the name of Crasher, Baugham and Phipps. They did a large export trade, and Osborne was required as chief corresponding clerk—which his education eminently qualified him for.

Rather than remain in Oxford, and wait the possibility of a chance turning up in the church, he at once accepted this appointment, the more so as it afforded an opportunity of being in the town where Honora resided, and wrote off at once to the firm in question, and the terms were definitely settled, the required security was furnished by Osborne, and he bade adieu to Oxford, and started for the metropolis.

A new life awaited him, very different to the one he had been leading at Oxford. A commercial situation was quite at variance with the secluded and less active life of the student.

After he had been duly established in his situation, he took an early opportunity of waiting upon Miss Langford, upon arriving at whose domicile he was informed that the lady was out, but would in all probability return shortly.

"Would he see Mr. Langford?" inquired the officious flunkey.

Osborne did not like to refuse; indeed, in the absence of the daughter, he thought it best to see her father, and acquaint him with the fact of his residence in London. He was shown up in the drawing room, where he found two gentlemen. One was Mr. Langford himself, and the other was an austere, hearty-looking individual, in whose appearance he was not at all prepossessed.

Mr. Langford's manner was remarkably stiff and cool towards Osborne, who felt that he was not welcomed as a friend. Mr. Langford did shake hands, certainly, but it was in that peculiar icy manner which had been best left alone.

"Sir Richard Fleetwood," said Mr. Langford, introducing the baronet to Osborne. "Mr. Osborne," he continued, turning to the baronet, who gave one of his stiffest bows, and casting upon the young man a piercing look.

There was an awkward pause after this, and Osborne felt himself very ill at ease, and he regretted having sought the interview.

"I hope Miss Langford is well," he ventured to inquire, timidly.

"Yes, thank you," was the short answer.

Another pause; when Osborne, who felt himself in the way, and not treated with that courtesy he had expected or deserved, said—

"I fear I am intruding upon you, and will therefore with your permission take my departure."

"I will say a few words, if you please, before you go," said Mr. Langford, in a short manner, as he pointed for the party he was addressing to be seated. He then walked to the further end of the room, and leaning his elbow on the mantelpiece, conversed with Sir Richard Fleetwood in so low a voice, that Osborne neither could, nor indeed did he desire, to hear any portion of their conversation.

They continued to converse together for some time, leaving Osborne to himself, so he took up a book, which he quietly perused, without taking any notice of the two individuals who seemed to treat him with such indifference.

In a short time Sir Richard Fleetwood prepared to take his departure. His host saw him to the door, and the baronet, as he passed through the room, scarcely condescended to take any notice of him. He gave a sort of an apology for a bow and departed, followed by Mr. Langford.

As soon as he had seen his visitor to the outer door, he returned to the room in which he had left Henry Osborne seated. There was a grave or rather severe expression upon his countenance, which augured ill for the success of the young student's suit.

"So, Mr. Osborne," said Mr. Langford, "You have come to pay the metropolis a visit for a short time, I suppose. How long do you purpose staying?"

"I have settled in London," was the reply.

"Indeed! have you been appointed to a living, then?"

"No, sir; finding that it was doubtful when I might be favoured with one, I have accepted a mercantile appointment in a large house of business in St. Mary Axe."

"Oh!—I wish you success in your new avocation."

"Thank you, sir."

There was an awkward pause after this.

"It is, I hope, a tolerably lucrative one," said Mr. Langford, with an air of indifference, which did not escape the notice of his visitor.

"Pretty well to begin with. It is not, of course, all I could desire, but does well enough as a commencement, and may lead to better things hereafter."

"Ah, let us hope it will, you have my good wishes, I am sure, if they can be of any service."

Another "thank you," followed from Osborne, and then there was again a pause.

"I should have liked to have had the pleasure of paying my respects to Miss Langford," said Osborne, hesitatingly. "Do you think it will be long, sir, before she returns?"

"Yes, I believe it will," answered her father, abruptly.

Then, after a little consideration he said, more seriously—

"It is upon this point that I had wished to see you. I think, Mr. Osborne, it is as well to at once deal frankly with you. Upon the occasion of our last interview at Oxford, I think I was sufficiently explicit respecting my daughter. Since that time she has an accepted suitor—the gentleman whom you have but just now been introduced to—

Sir Richard Fleetwood. As a *friend*," continued the old gentleman, with a marked emphasis, "I shall be glad at all times to receive you ; but as a suitor for my daughter's hand, I must now once and for all distinctly inform you that I cannot receive you."

"Is this possible ?" exclaimed Osborne, as an expression of poignant anguish passed over his features.

"It is not only possible, but true, my friend."

"I thought Miss Langford—" he paused, suddenly.

"You thought what, sir?"

"I did not imagine Miss Langford would have accepted Sir Richard."

"Then you were mistaken, sir. I should hope my daughter knows her duty both to herself and me," he answered, with hauteur.

"At any rate I may beg to be allowed the melancholy satisfaction of hearing this from her own lips."

"I do not see, Mr. Osborne, what possible good that could do you. It would only distract my daughter's mind, and, I am afraid, render her very miserable ; and I think you had much better take an answer from me."

There was a cool, business-like tone assumed by the speaker which cut Osborne to the quick. He was so vexed and disappointed by his reception, and the unwelcome intelligence conveyed to him, that he scarcely knew how to comport himself. All his worst fears were then realised. Honora, his dear Honora, had then another suitor, who had not only found favour in the eyes of her father, but if he had heard aright, had actually been accepted by herself.

This last statement he could not nor would not believe. It was in direct contradiction to all the letters he had received from her, and he could not bring himself to imagine that she whom he almost worshipped could act with such duplicity. He repudiated such a thought as utterly unworthy of himself. He remained silent and crest-fallen for some time after the last speech of Mr. Langford's, and the old gentleman seemed to contemplate him with something like a feeling of pity, for he plainly perceived that his words had cut deep into the heart of Osborne.

"As a *friend*," he again repeated, "I need hardly say, Mr. Osborne, I shall be always glad to receive you."

"I thank you, sir," was the reply, "I am perfectly aware, Mr. Langford, that I have no right to persuade Miss Langford to forego another and more wealthy suitor in favour of myself. If she can be happy with him—if she says that she can give him her heart—it would be worse than selfish on my part to urge my own poor claims with that persistence which would be detrimental to her own

interests ; but, we have, I believe, learnt to love each other. At least, as far as regards myself, I can never love another. We have plighted our troth, and I am in hopes of still winning a position in the world which might warrant me in asking you to bestow her upon me at some future day."

"My dear young friend, you must at once dismiss such chimerical thoughts from your mind. In any case you must see that a gentleman, a baronet, holding the high status such as Sir Richard Fleetwood, is a much more eligible and well-suited match for my daughter than yourself. Your own sense must point this out to you, without my suggesting it. I do not say this in any disparagement of yourself, for whom, indeed, I entertain feelings of the most lively interest and friendship. That is all true enough ; but as a man of honour, you ought not to endeavour to press a suit which is objectionable to myself on the grounds of a serious injury to my daughter's prospects in life. There, now, be a sensible man ; let us be good friends, as we always have been, the which we shall certainly no longer be if you persist in running in direct opposition to my expressed wishes."

"I must receive my answer from Miss Langford herself first."

"Confound it, man, you will make me lose all temper with you, if you are thus obstinate," exclaimed Mr. Langford, in rising anger.

Osborne made no reply, as he saw the storm gathering on the brow of his companion.

"I say, sir, you will make me lose my temper, and say that which perhaps I may be sorry for," continued the other pettishly.

"I will not stay to offend you," said Osborne. "It is quite certain, Mr. Langford, that I shall never be able to persuade you to listen to me with patience upon this subject. If Miss Langford—"

"Still harping upon Miss Langford," exclaimed the old gentleman, with impatience. "Why persist in bringing my daughter's name forward in the matter. It is for you and I to settle the matter."

"You must pardon me, I think not," answered Osborne, firmly.

"But I say it is, sir," thundered forth the father. "What does a girl of her age know about the world ?"

"She knows her own heart, and that, Mr. Langford, is her world."

"Hang it, man, are you here to taunt me in my own house."

"I should hope not ; I would conciliate you."

"Then you never will, sir—never ! At least, not in the way you set about it."

"I regret that you should see cause for

anger. It has not been evoked by anything I have said, that is, I should hope not."

"Bah! you are mildly obstinate, if I may so term it, which is the very worst form of obstinacy, to my thinking. Pursue your own course, as you please. Only once and for all I have to inform you, that Miss Langford is engaged to Sir Richard Fleetwood."

"I am sorry to hear you speak thus, but hope we part good friends."

"That depends upon your own conduct. You have my answer; good-day," and with these words Mr. Langford turned and was about to leave the apartment.

Osborne did not wait till he did so, but took a hasty departure, and left the house, dispirited and sick at heart.

Upon his arrival in London he had taken apartments on the first floor in the aristocratic

locality of Goswell Street, and thither, in a most dejected mood, did he now wend his way—there to let himself in with his latch-key—there to eat his solitary meal—and there to brood over those sorrows which were too deep for human sympathy.

Now in the parlours of the house in which he lodged there dwelt a young man by the name of Squabshot, who was called by his more familiar companions Jack Squabshot, or sometimes Little Squabby. He had several times spoken to Osborne, and sought his acquaintance; but the latter, whose disposi-tio might be termed reserved towards strangers, had not been too forward to accept the invitation of his fellow lodger.

Mr. Squabshot was what might be termed a fast young man. He had mixed much in town life, knew a good deal about sporting

No. 11.

matters, had been up to a few dodges as he termed it, and was certainly fly to a move or to on life's chequered board.

When Osborne returned to his lodgings, after his unsatisfactory interview with Mr. Langford, silence and obscurity was what he courted ; but such, on the evening in question, was not what he was destined to enjoy. Squabshot's door was open, and he heard Osborne let himself in ; when no sooner had the half distracted lover entered the passage, when his fellow lodger presented himself, and catching Osborne by the collar of the coat, he dragged rather than asked him into his own apartment.

"Come, now, there's a good fellow. All alone, as the old maid said to her feline companion. Come, I want a pall to help me out with a bowl of punch."

"Thank you, I am rather dispirited, and you must excuse me to-night," said Osborne, endeavouring to get away.

"Nonsense, man," ejaculated the other, "if you are out of spirits that's the very reason you should imbibe some. Yes, imbibe's the word. Now sit down, and we'll have a little pleasant converse about mundane affairs."

The speaker shut the door of his apartment with a slam, and Osborne, who had but little energy left, was conducted to a seat by his host in passive obedience.

'You're down upon your luck, old boy," said Squabshot ; "you're down upon your luck, I can see it in your eye. You'll excuse my familiarity, it's a way I always had from my childhood. Now, what's the matter ? Nothing like a sympathising friend in the hour of misfortune. 'When angry clouds do lower o'er us,' &c., &c. ; you know the rest, I dare say. Now I suppose—if I may make so bold as to hazard a guess—it's a woman that's at the bottom of this, eh ?" and here Mr. Squabshot perked his head on one side, and looked so particularly comic, that Osborne, in spite of himself, could not refrain from smiling. "Ah, I see, that's enough ; been at the same game myself, my dear fellow. They are not worth a man's while to bother himself about. A woman, sir—bah, I would not fret, myself, about the finest one in the creation. I did so once, I am free to confess, but have lived long enough to see my folly. Now there was Seth Pocklington—lord bless you, I went distracted about her, swore I would hang myself, or something of the sort—didn't do it though ; catch Jack Squabshot at anything so green as that. But, you know, I was in love with that girl. Ah, desperately, cruelly, dreadfully, and distractedly in love "

Osborne saw at once that his new formed acquaintance was an original, and he felt a little amused at his free off-hand rattling manner. As he gazed round the apartment, which now for the first time he had entered, he saw pretty plainly all the evidences of fast life. There were fencing foils, boxing-gloves, rat-traps, a guitar, a masquerade suit, and a heterogenous mass of articles of a most incongruous description, distributed about the apartment in the utmost confusion.

"Here's to our better acquaintance," said Squabshot, as he tossed off a glass of stiff punch. "And if there's anything that Jack Squabshot can do to serve a fellow mortal who is in distress, name it, sir, name it, and—"

Here he placed his hand upon his breast, and bowed with mock gravity towards his visitor.

"I am much obliged to you, sir," said Osborne, whose quiet, unassuming, and grave manner was in direct opposition to that of his companion.

"I see how the case stands," continued the voluble Squabshot ; "she's proved inconstant, and all that sort of thing. What woman is not ?"

"You are mistaken in your surmise," said Osboone.

"Oh, well she's proud, or perhaps a little jealous—"

"Neither."

"Indeed ; then what has she been up to ? Jilted you ?"

"So I have been told," answered Osborne, who although from the first had not intended communicating the cause of his sorrows to his companion, had nevertheless been insensibly drawn into it in spite of himself.

"Well there are worse misfortunes than that, at least so my experience tells me. I have had them all. I have been in love, in debt, in liquor, in quod, and a host of other ins and outs, and I think I can safely say that being in love was the least evil of the lot."

"And which do you consider the worst ?" asked his visitor, who began to be much amused at the other's manner.

"Ah," said Squabshot, seriously, "in debt, that's the primary cause of a host of other troubles. Have you ever had the felicity of being dunned ?"

"Of being what ?"

"Dunned."

"No, not that I am aware of."

"Oh, you would be aware of it if you ever had."

"What is it ?" innocently asked Osborne.

"What is it ?" iterated the other ; "what is it not ? Torment on torment, of the most agonising description. Have you ever been in quod ?"

"No, never, I am happy to say as yet."

"My dear fellow, all your pleasures are to come then," said Squabshot, looking at his companion with eyes of curiosity. "Never been in debt—never been in quod!—why where have you been all your life then ?"

"Ah, I don't know. I've been in various parts of England, but the place I have last come from is Oxford."

"Ah, you are a man of note evidently—a remarkable man, no doubt. Indeed you must be, never to have been in debt; for in debt you certainly never could have been, seeing that you have never been dunned."

"Is it so pleasant ?" said Osborne, smiling.

"It has its comic and tragic phases," said Squabshot, reflectively. "I've had 'em of all sorts. The comic, the sentimental, the agonising, with thirteen children to keep—ah, that's the worst sort. I was once indebted to a fellow who haunted me like a bad spirit go wherever I would. He was a man, sir, of elephantine proportions, with a florid face and white hair. He would sit down upon the street door step, and pull out a pocket-handkerchief—a blue one with white spots — and actually cry, sir, because I couldn't pay him seventeen shillings and eightpence. Ah, he was a dreadful man—dreadful. Why, one day he came to me, and after I had given him what little silver I had, he went away. I went to a musical party, a soiree, in fact, and was ravishing the company with 'Sally in our Alley,' when the man-servant came and whispered to me that a gentleman in the passage wished to see me. I went down stairs, and to my horror, there was my plethoric seventeen-and-eightpenny friend. Yes, there he was true enough; he had followed me about from house to house, and with his usual apologetic manner—he always began in that manner—he informed me that his wife was dangerously ill with the cholera. What could I do—he had me at an advantage and that he knew well enough—I was forced to borrow a few shillings of one of the company, and get the fellow out of the house upon any terms. Well, sir, would you believe it, on the following night as my landlady's coals were coming in, I observed the tank at the back-door, and saw at the same time behind the sacks the stalwart form of a man loom in the distance. Sure enough it was my seventeen-and-eightpenny friend. His wife was worse, and he as usual was penniless."

"Ah, ah !" laughed Osborne, "you have indeed seen some life."

"Lord bless your soul, that's nothing," answered Squabshot, "nothing. I have had a woman sit the whole day upon the stairs waiting for me to come home—an ugly old woman, one of the ugliest it is possible to conceive— she brought her own grub with her, and also brought some tracts with her, or something of that sort, to amuse herself while waiting. Then comes the comic dun, who tells you that 'things are getting a little

sour, and so he's just come to see if you can let him have a little *sugar*,' which of course means his account. I don't care about this sort, so when the fellow tells me that his account has been standing a long time, I hand him a chair, and ask him to let it sit down. I then fire off a few jokes, and tell him to come in the cool of the evening, as the weather is too hot to pay money in the middle of the day."

"You are quite an adept at this sort of thing," said Osborne, who looked at his companion with some curiosity.

"A chap that's been knocked about as I have, soon get's used to it. Lord bless you, sir, its no use being down hearted. As to being miserable, that I distinctly declare I will not be. I've had my hundreds and thousands at one time, and done the thing in the right sort of style, I can tell you. No half-and-half business with me. Why, I won three thousand pounds upon the Emperor of Morocco."

"Dear me—what had you to do with that monarch ?"

"Monarch ! He wasn't a monarch," exclaimed Squabshot, with surprise; "he was a bird—a fighting cock !"

"Oh, indeed."

"Ah, to be sure, I bred him myself—at least, a chap by the name of Bill Dysen did for me, and a good thing I made of him—all gone now though. Did you ever see a cock fight ?"

"No."

"Must take you to one, then, when you have leisure."

"I am afraid it will not suit my taste sir."

"Won't it though. Suit any man's taste, I know—that is if he has any soul, and I'm sure you have."

"Thank you."

"By the way, do you do anything in this line ?" continued Squabshot, as he held up one of the boxing gloves.

"No," answered Osborn; "I never had an inclination for anything of the sort—I am but a quiet student, at least have been, I should say, rather."

"Oh, we'll show you a little life, then," said his companion, "study and myself have quarrelled long ago; indeed we never agreed very well at any time, but of late years we've chopped out altogether. I know I ought to have received a tolerable education, for my poor father paid plenty of money for it, but I never could get along with my books. Nature and mankind, sir, have been my study—I've gone to the fountain head at once. I've seen some of all sorts and know what a lot of duffers there are in this world. Ah, —and so Mr. Osborne you are in love !" exclaimed his host, suddenly recurring to the subject originally broached upon his entrance —"Ah, in love! When that is the case, a man has no relish for the pleasures of the world. No, indeed. His mind is absorbed in the object of his affectionate regard. He's a sort of human thermometer, whose spirits rise and are depressed as his mistress smiles or frowns upon him. Ah, never did the thermometer indicate the heat of the sun with greater correctness than does the human one under the influence of the saucy smiles of her who is his sun—his spirits rise and fall in proportion to her smiles. Ah, it is a sad thing, my friend, to give your happiness into another's keeping, be it man or woman," said Mr. Squabshot; "a sad thing, sir, believe me."

"Indeed it is," said Osborne, reflectively; "But then, you know, we can't always help ourselves in cases of this sort."

"I suppose not, but come you don't get on," said the goodnatured Squabshot—for goodnatured he certainly was with all his faults and eccentricities. "You don't get on, my friend ; believe me of the two deities Venus and Bacchus, the latter is by far the most worthy and constant—and mind you they are two deities which have slain more men, perhaps, than any other—brought them to ruin sometimes—driven them to madness and despair."

"That is true enough; without doubt, those two deities have caused more sorrow to man in one way and another than it is possible for the most fertile imagination to ever conceive."

"Now for yourself, for instance, you are suffering, or rather sacrificing, yourself at the shrine of Venus. I once, as I told you, was a martyr myself. I spent a heap of money over her—a heap, sir. Lost my time too—neglected to lay heavy on Lord Treddlefuddle's horse, which was third favourite for the Derby of that year, and the consequence was that I was clean mopped out, and, what is worse, I was, as usual, most confoundedly in debt. Have you ever been in a sponging house," inquired Mr. Squabshot.

"No, never."

"Dear me—dear me; what an extraordinary thing—ah, then, you have a great deal to see yet then. No man's education is complete till he has experienced that mysterious and talismanic tap on the shoulder which has a magnetic influence througout the whole human frame."

"Indeed—what is that?"

"Why, when you find a hand laid on your shoulder, and you turn round and behold an individual with an acquiline proboscis, redolent of dirt, finery and jewels, who informs you, as he presents a mysterious paper, that you are arrested at the suit of Messrs. Boggle and Shnapp, of Conduit Street, but he has no doubt you will be able to arrange the matter, as they are very honourable people. You inquire further, if you are a novice, and then you find that the individual with the acquiline proboscis is Mishter Bernard Solomons himself, and that the smouchy individual by his side, is his follower. You ascertain, also, that Mr. Solomon will accomodate you with a room in his hotel in Chancery Lane until the matter is arranged, which he hopes it soon will be. You find the room is a dark fusby hole indeed ; but miserable as it is you have to pay a guinea a day for it's use."

"A guinea a day ?"

"Yes, and put up with such board as the owner of the establishment chooses to provide you with—and what is worse they expect you to settle every night, or else you are nabbed off to Whitecross Street, the Fleet, the Compter, or the King's Bench. I have gone through it all, my friend."

"Indeed—how did it happen ?"

"After I was knocked off my legs by neglecting to back "Currant Dumpling," Lord Treddlefuddle's horse, I received an intimation from a gentleman with an acquiline proboscis, that a rascally tailor, whom I had done the honour of patronising, had been unreasonable enough to want a settlement of his account. You know, I was obliged to come out pretty strong while sticking up to the young lady whom I have before alluded to, and, of course, my tailor had a pretty stiffish order."

"Quite likely," said Osborne, with a smile.

"Well, when Currant Dumpling came in second, which he did, for Little Swivel rode him, why I found myself as I before told you, completely knocked out of time, and the consequence was that as the old gentleman would not advance me any more beyond my usual allowance, why Mr. Bernard Solomons collared me and took me under his protecting wing."

"Protecting wing !" exclaimed Osborne, in surprise.

"Exactly; I staid in Cursitor Street, Chancery Lane as long as I could, in the hope of settling the matter, but it was no go ; so to Whitecross Street I went, after spending all the ready cash I could muster at Mr. Solomon's hotel."

"And what did you do when you got there ?"

"Filed my petition and afterwards got whitewashed without opposition—so here's success to the righteous, which includes both you and me," said Mr. Squabshot as he filled up the two glasses of punch, and drained off his own.

Osborne merely put his lips to his glass, while his companion continued.

"Do you see, my friend, I have been led into difficulties by a woman myself, and that is not the only instance in which I have been a sufferer by a good many. Stake your cash upon a horse—upon a badger—upon a fighting cock, or anything but a woman—the chances are with the three former you may become a winner, or, at any rate, you may be able to edge, but, hang me, if you have the slightest chance with a woman, sir—not the slightest. Ah, you smile—you don't believe me—eh?"

"Oh, I don't say that, but I was smiling at the idea of staking your money upon horses and badgers."

"Well, sir, and why not?" exclaimed Squabshot, in perfect surprise at the question, "why not?"

"Oh, I don't know. Every man to his own particular fancy."

"There's been a rare lot of tin made by laying upon the right sort of breeds. I know that, from my Emperor of Morocco. Now, there's Bill Dyson, of the Cow and Cauliflower—now, look at him, he's done well," said Mr. Squabshot, holding out his hand as though appealing to his companion as to the truth of his statement. "He's done well."

"I don't know him."

"Oh, don't you? But of course not; I forgot you were not acquainted with the "fancy." Ah!—must put you up to a dodge or two as we become better acquainted. Like to live and let live."

Osborne, although amused with his companion, felt anxious to take his departure to his own rooms, but the other rattled on so fast, and seemed so well pleased with the society of his companion, that he did not wish him to leave.

In a short time, there was a knock at the outer door, and a gentleman inquired for Mr. Squabshot.

That gentleman, hearing the voice of some one with whom he was well acquainted, immediately rose, and opened the door of the apartment.

Osborne made a motion to retire, but Squabshot waived him imperiously to a seat, and would not hear of his departure for the present.

Politeness, therefore, dictated for Osborne to remain passive.

In a few seconds, the new comer was ushered into the apartment. He was a gentleman with peculiarly sharp features, which were close shaven. He wore a long waistcoat with sleeves to it, was bow-legged, long-backed, and did not appear to have an ounce of superfluous flesh upon his bones.

This gentleman rejoiced in the name of Dick Downey, at least, he was so called by his more familiar companions. He was what is termed one of the knowing ones in the sporting world. To see him in the zenith of his glory it would be necessary to pay a visit to the Horse and Jockey, where he was looked up to as the high priest, and treated as the oracle of all oracles.

As the company assemble, there are fifty knotty questions to be propounded to him. When a certain horse won the Derby, Oaks, or Doncaster race?—who were the winner's ancestors?—who fought the Belcher or Crib of that day, at what time and place?—what was the stake, and who were the backers?—Who was the owner of the celebrated pony, and what was the most he ever performed? What is the greatest leap on record, and the name of the horse that took it, with multifarious queries in the same categories, interspersed with questions relating to animals, birds, fish, reptiles, and insects. Their habits, uses, and mode of taking and training, together with an account of the diseases to which they are liable, and the *Materia Medica* as applicable to sporting animals.

Dick, in one particular, is a thorough bred John Bull. He either has or once had, the most superior animal of his kind in the country, and he knows, also, who is the owner of the fastest trotting horse, and is intimately acquainted with the pedestrian who is open to all England. He, too, caught the largest pike ever pulled out of British water, and at this moment possesses the highest couraged dog in the three kingdoms.

With all this varied and diversified information, he struck Mr. Osborne, at first sight, as being a quiet, unassuming man, but, in the course of conversation, he soon showed that he was not a greenhorn.

"Mr. Osborne, from Oxford," said Squabshot. "Mr. Downey sir," he added, turning to his visitor.

"Ah! I've had some good sport, sir, in the neighbourhood of Oxford and those parts," said Dick Downey, to Osborne. "A prime place—a rare place for your regular swell—your fast going card. It was only the other day I was over at Wheatly, where there was a badger that none of the dogs could draw. 'Stand out of the way,' says I and I let Grip join; and didn't he astonish the yokels as quickly as the twinkling of an eye. There was Lord John there, from Blenheim—I dare say you may know him, sir?"

"I have heard of him," said Osborne.

"Ah, so have most people. Well he offered fifty pounds for old Grip, but nobody knows the value of a good dog better than those who breed them, and it ain't money as'll always get the right sort, so I told him, and if he means to have Grip he must spring pretty considerably."

While Mr. Downey was talking, Squabshot

was pantomiming to Osborne to listen attentively to him, and he expressed, by motions, the superior judgment of his friend by pointing to his forehead, significantly.

"Did you happen to know a young fellow of the name of Golightly, sir, when you were at Oxford ?" said Dick to Osborne.

"Not that I remember."

"I am surprised at that—I thought almost everybody knew him."

"The gentleman doesn't mix in your sort society, Dick," said Squabshot.

"S'pose not ; then that accounts for it. Well this ere Golightly did the extensive to an alarming extent. He made the most random and extravagant wagers, and what was more surprising he was equally reckless in paying, as if he possessed unlimited funds. He was soon engaged in all sorts of parties, and as a matter of course was everybody's friend ; suddenly, however, there arrived in Oxford two persons, who took lodgings, and became acquainted with Golightly shortly afterwards, monopolising, as it were, the whole of his hours devoted to pleasure, and they were a few I can tell you; and didn't they pick him up and no mistake—and it turned out afterwards that they had so far fascinated him that he spent nearly the whole of his vacation in their society, emersed in the pursuits of metropolitan vices, until, in the end, poor Golightly found the depth of his purse with nothing remaining at the bottom of it."

A long conversation followed upon sporting matters, and Osborne was perfectly astonished at the revelations made.

In conversing upon some particular dog, whose qualities were supposed to be of a most extraordinary nature, Dick Downey happened to mention the name of Sir Richard Fleetwood. Osborne started and turned pale. Could it be the individual whom he had been introduced to in the earlier portion of that day ? There could be but little doubt about it, and prompted by an insatiable curiosity, he said to Downey—

"You mentioned the name of Sir Richard Fleetwood ; do you happen to know that baronet ?"

"Should just think I did," was the instant reply. "Lord bless you, know him—he and I have had many dealings together. Ah, his head is screwed on in the right way. No catching him on the grand hop, I can tell you."

"What sort of a man is he ?"

"Oh, a gentleman, certainly, but haughty to those beneath him. Ah, Sir Richard has been up to a few tricks, if all's true that's said about him."

"Indeed. Does he bear a good character ?"

"What for doing the square and regular ?" said Downey.

"Yes. Is he an honourable man ?" inquired Osborne.

"Well, now you bother me," said Downey "I suppose we are all honourable, according to our own thinking. Well, now, if I had a large property left me, I shouldn't care about Sir Richard being executor under the will—that's all."

"Why not ?"

"Because you see, the chances would be that I should be a long time before I came into my rights."

"Indeed ; then he can't be a particularly honest man."

"I should be sorry to say that. I have found him all right in his dealings with me ; but he has an old curmudgeon of a lawyer, a Mr. Sharpthorne, who isn't exactly a sort of gentleman who bears the sweetest odours in his profession ; and if he can draw the teeth out of your head, why, he's just the man as will do it, and no mistake."

"Did you know him at Oxford ?"

"Oh, no ; I've trained dogs and horses for him at his own estates. The one I mostly go to is at Acton."

"Oh, indeed, where is that ?"

"Some seven miles or so from London."

Osborne was lost for some time in reflection. It seemed to him singular that he should have tumbled over a person by the merest chance who seemed to know the history of an individual about whom he was naturally enough most interested.

It has been truly said that we don't know who may be useful to us in this world.

Mr. Osborne felt himself constrained to keep it up late in the apartments of his newly-formed acquaintance—for Squabshot was a gentleman who was not remarkable for good hours, and to use the hackneyed phrase which was often in his mouth, "time was made for slaves."

Osborne was glad enough to wish his two companions good night, with a promise to Squabshot that he would at another time do himself the pleasure of partaking of the hospitality of his host.

———

CHAPTER XIII.

THE CROOKED BILLET.—COLONEL JACK AT DULWICH. — THE HIGHWAYMAN'S GENE-ROSITY.

Safe in the possession of the box and papers —so adroitly rescued from the legal paw of Lord Mayor Gubbins—Colonel Jack kept himself tolerably quiet for some little time after his attack upon Gubbin's carriage.

The sanguinary struggle at Mr Baintree's house had been detailed to him ; indeed, as rumour generally magnifies and enlarges upon the real facts, the burglar's attack and gallant repulse seemed to the mind of the Colonel something fabulous.

He determined, therefore, to ride over to Dulwich at once, and pay a visit to Mr. Baintree himself, and learn from him the full particulars, and at the same time see if he had made an examination of the papers in question.

To the lawyer the colonel was only known as a respectable gentleman, and it was with no idea of following his usual calling that Colonel Jack turned his horses head towards Dulwich.

He was apparelled in the costume usually worn by gentlemen of the period, and Mr. Baintree, who had known him for many years, under his real name of Halford, entertained the highest esteem for him.

Perhaps one of the most painful facts of the colonel's career was the different manner he was treated under his own respectable appellation contrasted with that he was wont to receive when assuming the character of a highwayman.

Reckless, daring, and adventurous as was his nature, he possessed, nevertheless, in his inner man, a strong current of better feelings, which, had they been tutored to a different purpose, might have made him a hero instead of a highway robber.

It is a clear bright day, or rather the afternoon of the day, as Colonel Jack trots gently along the road leading to the village of Dulwich. The slanting rays of the sun cast fantastic shadows across the road, made by the tall trees on each side. Say what you will, the green leaves of old England possess in themselves an indefinable charm to the pedestrain or equestrian.

The colonel was in one of those reflective moods in which he often indulged when away from his companions and off duty. He had left the "shop" at home, to use an old phrase, and was now enacting the part of a quiet, respectable. English gentleman. He might have been such, he thought, as he journeyed along, if things had been different, and he had not been so self-willed and headstrong in his youth; for he came of a gentle stock, and might have been a respectable member of society.

"Bah!" he exclaimed, "where's the use of my thinking about that now? It's all past. I am what I am, no better and no worse; and if doomed to a hempen noose, why, we can die but once, I suppose. There, Ada—gently my girl, gently. So, ho, you've a gentleman on your back—so, gently's the word."

These last observations were addressed to his horse, or rather mare, as he kindly patted her sleek and arched neck.

"Gently, Ada, gently, girl."

The animal pricked up her ears, and shook her exquisitely formed head as though she thoroughly understood the meaning of the words which her master had been uttering, and she trotted along with a mincing pace. The rustics, as Colonel Jack passed, touched their hats, believing him to be some fine Lunnon gentleman; for at the time we write, Dulwich was very much further removed from the metropolis than it is in this our present day, and its inhabitants were yokels in every sense of the word.

No Crystal Palace then—no levelling down the beauties of nature, and cutting up her fine form into hard mathematical lines, and still harder and more arid gravel walks—painful for the eye in the summer's heat to dwell upon—no crowds of visitors packed in carriages so hot, that a fryingpan must be a luxury indeed compared to the swelling multitude.

When Colonel Jack arrived at Mr. Baintree's house, he eyed it with some curiosity; he had heard at the Badger's the point of attack chosen by the Nobbler, for whom, as a finished master of his art, in his own particular line, the colonel entertained a profound respect.

Ringing the bell the portly maid servant who had so unwittingly assisted the housebreaker, and afterwards so heroically saved her master's life opened the door.

The colonel gazed at her with admiration. He was a rare judge of the fair sex, and he doubted not but this young woman was the one who had listened to the advances of the man Dabbs, who was in the employ of the chief burglar.

Upon the colonel asking her if her master was at home, she replied in the affirmative. He sent in his card, with the name of Mr. Halford engraved thereon, and in a few minutes the cottage doors were thrown open and a groom held his horse, as our hero dismounted.

He was warmly greeted by Mr. Baintree, senior, and his better half, for Halford had been intimate with the family, and years before had often made one of their family circle.

The old gentleman was particularly loquacious in describing all those incidents of the burglary with which the reader is already acquainted.

He took the colonel to the room which lay at the rear of the house, and there showed him where the housebreakers had first entered, then conducting him through the adjoining rooms, he took the course which he supposed had been followed by the burglars. Then he came to the servants' room, and here he paused to expatiate upon the events which occurred there, calling up Anna, the servant, to give Mr. Halford her own version of the matter.

Then came the position of his son, and the recess. This excited the colonel's curiosity not a little, for deeds of daring always possessed a charm for him from early youth.

He examined the position occupied by young Mr. Baintree, and saw at once the possibility of his offering so desperate and obstinate a resistance.

In the course of a short time after this, young Mr. Baintree arrived home, and Colonel Jack eyed him with looks of considerable interest, for since the affair of the burglary, he had suddenly sprung up into a man. He was a quiet, mild, gentlemanly-looking young man, and did not seem from his personal appearance to possess any of those characteristics which would warrant the supposition that he was capable of sustaining so determined and obstinate a struggle as had taken place.

He was strong and athletic, it is true, but seemed rather of a mild and retiring disposition. Mr. Baintree entered into the particulars of the papers contained in the box, but he had made but a very cursory inspection of the same and was, therefore, unable to give so accurate a description of their contents as he had hoped, after a more careful examination, to have been able to have done. He, however, dropped enough for the colonel to make up his mind, at all risk, to retain them in his possession, and, at the same time, to felicitate himself that he had obtained them.

He did not, however, let the lawyer know that he had succeeded in regaining possession of them, and the old gentleman was deploring that they should have unfortunately have been now lost to the parties who were most concerned in their retention.

Our hero passed some very pleasant hours beneath the hospitable roof of Mr. Baintree after which he proceeded to take his departure.

The old gentleman and his son saw him to the outer gate ; and the colonel dropped a sovereign in the hand of the pretty servant before he left. Clapping spurs to the side of Ada, he trotted off, and soon was out of sight of the lawyer's residence.

"Such are the chances of life," exclaimed Colonel Jack, reflectively ; "these fellows will, no doubt, suffer the extreme penalty of the law for endeavouring to take that which I have twice obtained by force. Ah, after all, I'm glad I'm not a cracksman—the chances are against you—nothing like trusting to the back of my bonnie Ada."

Proceeding along towards London, he took a different road from the one by which he had entered. He was making his way towards an old-fashioned picturesque road-side inn, which the traveller may still see standing at the present day. It was called then, as indeed it is now, the "Crooked Billet," and it was situated on Penge Common. Its appearance both externally, as also in the interior, was particularly picturesque, and you are carried back to earlier days in England's history, as you contemplate this ancient and primitive hostelry, which possesses all those peculiar characteristics which were so often observable in old English Inns.

When our hero arrived at the Crooked Billet, he gave the reins of his horse to the stable boy, and hastily entered the house. A slight scream escaped the lips of the landlady as she recognised the colonel. She was serving behind the bar at the time, and a flush of excitement overspread her features. Quickly the little door which led into the private recesses of the bar and bar-parlours was opened, and our hero without a word entered.

"What, Frank!" exclaimed the landlady, all in a flutter as she spoke. Well, I declare, and whoever would have thought of seeing you?"

He entered the bar parlour, and she followed.

"Jane, my dear, how fare you?" said the colonel, as he put his arm round her waist, and kissed her. She did not appear at all loth to receive his embraces, nay more, she returned them.

"Well, and how goes it with you?" asked the colonel.

"Oh, middling—much the same as usual. And you?—I need not ask. You are the same handsome Frank as when I first knew you."

"There, no flattery," said the highwayman. "You are a married woman now, and should leave off that sort of thing."

"Married and unmarried," said the landlady. "You know poor Joe is gone?"

"Yes, so I heard some time ago."

"Ah, it was a sad trial," said the widow, endeavouring to look sentimental ; "a sad trial."

"We've all our trials in this world," said her companion, half seriously and half satirically.

"So we have, Frank, so we have; but I get on pretty well, considering. In fact, wonderfully well, taking all things into consideration. But what brings you down to this part—on business?"

"No, I should say it must be on pleasure, since I have come to see you."

"Psha—what a man it is," said the widow, pouting.

"Well, if you must know, I have been to pay Mr. Baintree a visit."

"Oh, indeed. Well, what a terrible escape the old gentleman and his family have had

to be sure. Of course you heard of the burglary?"

"Oh, yes; I heard all the particulars in London, and have had the whole affair fully explained to me this afternoon by the family."

"Ah, it's made quite a sensation here; indeed, so it has in London, and everywhere else I am told. I suppose they'll swing for it, Frank?"

"Not much doubt of it, I should think."

The widow looked grave. She knew the colonel's occupation, and the thought came across her that he might some day or other meet with a similar fate. He had been an old lover of hers, when she was a barmaid in a noted house in town. She was a fine woman, and good hearted withal. She could not be considered savagely virtuous as far as

men were concerned, but, she was a thorough good sort of woman, nevertheless; and if she had her likings and amours, that's her own business and no one else's

The colonel had always been her favoured man. His handsome features, dashing manner, and generous disposition fairly won her long before she knew Mr. Joseph Tapster, her deceased husband, and late landlord of the Crooked Billet.

"And so, Frank, you really have come to see a lone widow—"

"And an old sweetheart," said the colonel, in continuation.

"Well, yes," she said; "an old sweetheart —that's true enough. It's no use my denying it. And why should I?"

"Ah, why should you, indeed?" said the colonel, giving her another and more tender embrace. She hastily set things upon the table for supper, and the best viands which the establishment afforded, were placed on the board, and the colonel and the landlady sat down to a cosy meal and chat.

"Well, I declare," said the former, "and how's Hackett and Warrington, and all the rest of them ?"

"Oh, all right, Jane. Much the same as usual. We keep out of harm's way at present all of us, although we have had some narrow escapes."

"Ah, I suppose so. It's a desperate game, Frank—a desperate game, after all. Some steady business would be a good deal better."

"Business," he exclaimed, "pretty chaps we are for business any of us. Oh, no, we are on a road we shall never run off of till we run into another world," continued our hero reflectively. "Psha ! Jane, I am getting sentimental," he exclaimed, slapping his boot with his heavy riding-whip. "Come, one buss from your ruddy lips will restore my equilibrium," and he pressed the pouting lips of the hostess. "Here's to the health of the charming Jane," he said, as he tossed off a horn of liquor. "It's many a long day since we spent an hour or two together, for since you've been down in this out of the world sort of place we have missed sight of one another, and, by the Lord, it does one's heart good to meet an old friend and companion like yourself, Jane, for you are a good one, Jennie, and no mistake—a thorough out and out good one and nothing else."

"Oh, you always were such a flatterer," said Mrs. Tapster, reprovingly. "You know you always were, Frank. At least, ever since I have known you, and that's been a good many years."

"It's some time ago since I knew you, a pretty and, indeed, a lovely maiden. Time runs on with both of us, although he has left you untouched by his destroying hand. He's dealt kindly by you, Jennie, as, indeed, how could he do anything else, if there was an atom of gallantry in the old rascal's composition.

"There, go along with your flatteries, you foolish man. There's some one at the bar."

And up sprang the attentive landlady to see to her customer.

"Dear me," said the colonel, to himself; "she bears well, and is the same charming little creature as when I first knew her—and leads a happy life here, I'll be sworn—more happy than mine, that's quite certain—more happy than mine, I'll be bound. Well, well, so much the better, poor soul, for she is a good one, after all. It seems but yesterday since I gave her away at the altar to Joe Tapster, who wasn't exactly adapted for her ; but never mind that, he made her a tolerable husband, I suppose, at least a kind and in-

dulgent one, and that's been a great thing. Umph ! she's still young, and fresh, and amiable—that she always was though, and will continue so to the end of her life. Ah, Jane, you and I have seen a few merry hours together."

Mrs. Tapster now entered the bar-parlour again, and the colonel, after having passed a pleasant hour or two, directed his horse to be saddled, and reluctantly enough took leave of his fair and kind hostess.

The colonel struck across Penge Common, and intended to take the nearest road to town, for, by this time, the hour was late.

What with the pleasant company of the amiable Mrs. Tapster, and, before this, his kind reception at Mr. Baintree's, our highwayman found the hours had flown rapidly by, and very many miles had to be gone over before he reached his destination.

There were but few passengers on the road. Occasionally a pedestrian or equestrian would pass at long intervals, and now and then the rumbling wheels of a farmer's cart.

The colonel had ridden some three or four miles without any particular incident occurring to attract his notice.

He was arriving at the end of a lane from whence three roads diverged off. A large triangular patch of green sward was rudely fenced in where these three roads met, and one of those sign-posts, which are so common in our country, poised its three hands to inform the traveller which place these said roads led to. The hands of the post were twisted round, and each pointed to the wrong road, but this mischief was nutralised from the fact of the lettering on each being entirely illegible.

Across the green patch of grass Colonel Jack, whose eyes had been so well accustomed to detect every object at night from long practice in his calling, thought he observed the shadow of a figure thrown upon the open space by the fitful light of the moon, for several light, fleecy clouds were passing ever and anon over her disk and partially obscuring her light.

But it turned out that the colonel was not mistaken in his surmise, for as he approached the open space at the end of the lane, a figure on horseback suddenly sprung out, and presenting a pistol at his head, demanded his money upon pain of instant death.

The colonel was astonished as well he might be, and in the brief space of time which was consumed in his contemplation of the figure of the horseman, it is astonishing what a number of minute characteristics of the individual he observed.

He noticed that the hand which held the pistol was white and thin, and could not possibly belong to a man who had been accustomed to do much manual labour. Then again, the pistol trembled in the grasp of the holder, and there was a nervous twitching about the corners of the mouth and that part of the face which was left visible and unconcealed by the mask which he wore. The eyes, too, which peered through the mask were averted every now and then as the colonel fixed his own steadfast gaze upon the figure before him.

There was a pause for some time—the figure on horseback still presented his pistol at the head of the traveller—but it was evident enough that the latter was in no way intimidated thereby—for a smile passed over his features as he struck up the end of the other's pistol with his riding whip, and then burst into a short laugh.

"There, there—put up your barker," said our hero ; "you don't know the use of it at present—at least not as applied to this line of business. Why, man alive, we are both of the same trade, it appears—eh ?"

"I must have money !" exclaimed the horseman, "I must have some. Give me your purse at once, kind gentlemen," he continued, in broken accents. "If you knew how I needed money, you would not hesitate, I am sure."

"Oh," exclaimed the colonel, "he uses the persuasive—I never tried that dodge—not in my line I suppose," and our highwayman was highly tickled with the incident.

"So, my friend, like a good many more of us, you are greatly in want of the needful, money, eh ?"

"I do, indeed—and if you knew my necessities, you would say so yourself."

The pistol which the highwayman had presented at the traveller now hung down by his side, and the young man, for such he evidently was, did not attempt to offer any violence.

"You are not much used to your trade or profession, my friend or whatever else you may call it," said the colonel to the amateur highwayman—for such in reality he was. "Do you know who you are stopping ?"

"No."

"Colonel Jack!"

"Colonel Jack ?—amazement !"

"Yes Colonel Jack," said our hero, raising his hat, and slipping on a mask in the space of a few seconds ; he then pulled a pistol from his coat pocket and presented it at the other, who fell back in perfect amazement. "Yes, my friend," continued our hero, "you have chosen the wrong sort of customer in selecting me."

"I thought you were a gentleman," said the other.

"I was, but am now a highwayman—come two of a trade should not quarrel," continued the colonel, as he transferred the pistol to its place. "We must not rob one another,

after all—how long have you taken to this sort of business ?—not long, I'll be sworn, for you are an arrant bungler at it. If I had you for a short time I would teach you to manage the affair better."

"Alas," exclaimed the young man, sadly, "bungler, indeed—I have never, as heaven is my judge, either robbed or wronged man or woman, out of a farthing in the whole course of my life."

"Then this is your first attempt—better luck to you in your future efforts, my friend."

"I shall never more attempt such a thing —this is a lesson to me never to stray from the path of rectitude ; nothing but the most pressing necessity has caused me to thus disgrace a name which has been respected for generations past. But, oh, what will not poverty urge a man on to ? I have a widowed mother at home who is seriously ill, and I have not, believe me, sir, the means of providing her with the common necessaries of life—lean and hungry want stares us in the face. My poor sister is working at her needle for so small a pittance that it does not afford her a scanty sustenance. For myself, I have tried to obtain a situation in different capacities—for I have received a tolerable education—but all to no avail up to the present—what was I to do ?—what am I to do ? It is hard to starve, and see those who are dear to you starve, in a land of plenty. Oh," continued the young man, as he tore off his mask, "I have been driven to desperation, but never again will I lose sight of the right path."

Colonel Jack looked at the speaker, who still trembled as he passed his hand across his brow.

His features were small but prepossessing. Without being what might be called effeminate, they were delicately chiselled, and would lead a casual observer to imagine that their possessor was come of a gentle stock.

As our hero contemplated him there was an expression of poignant anguish and remorse visible upon his countenance which touched the highwayman.

"Young man," said Colonel Jack, in a serious tone, "it is indeed singular that in your first attempt you should choose me of all other persons in the world. Take my advice, keep within those bounds or limits which separate the more respectable portion of society from the lawless. Never again renew the attempt. Take my word for it— who has had enough experience surely, that we pay a dear penalty in pursuing this course of life."

"Thanks—a thousand thanks, for your advice, which you may rely upon being followed," said the young man, grasping the hand of Colonel Jack, and shaking it with warmth; "a thousand thanks, my friend, from you it is perhaps what might not be expected."

The colonel smiled, and turning his horse's head said :

"Come, you don't live far hence, I suppose. I have an hour or so to spare, and with your permission, will accompany you home."

The two turned their horses heads, and trotted off in the direction of the young man's abode.

It was about a mile and a half from the spot where the two had first met.

It was a small cottage standing in its own grounds, and appeared, although small, to be a respectable habitation.

The young man made the colonel promise that he would make no mention of the rencontre, as he purposed introducing his new acquaintance as a friend.

Upon Colonel Jack's entrance into the parlour of the house, he observed an elderly female seated in an arm chair beside the fireplace. She seemed, to judge from her appearance, to be very weak, and in declining health. Her features were much worn with care and illness, and a deep and settled melancholy was visible in every lineament of her countenance.

Immediately upon the entrance of the two, a young female, who was the daughter of the elderly one, rose from her seat, and came hastily forward to greet her brother. She started with some surprise when she observed the stranger who accompanied him.

Her brother introduced the colonel by his real name, Mr. Halford. She made a respectful obeisance, and our hero was struck with her general appearance and lady-like demeanour. She was exceedingly pretty and genteel, and seemed to be of a remarkably modest and retiring disposition, for a slight blush overspread her features upon the colonel's first entrance.

"I learn from your brother," said the latter, with that easy frank manner which he knew so well how to assume when it pleased him, "that he is at present swimming in troubled waters, Allow me, as a friend, to proffer what little assistance my circumstances enable me to do."

And he pulled from his pocket a well-filled purse, and placed it in the young girl's hand, whose astonishment at the generous act prevented her from either accepting or refusing the same.

Colonel Jack, however, did not wait till she had recovered from her first surprise, but left her standing in an attitude of doubt and uncertainty, as he strolled up to where the old lady was seated.

"Your son informs me, madame, that you have been in declining health for some time

past," he said, in a kind and considerate tone to the young man's mother.

"Alas, sir, yes," she said, in a weak and hollow voice. "My health and circumstances have both been in a depressed state of late, but we must all bow to the will of Providence."

"I have been telling your son that it is not at all improbable that I may hear of some situation which might suit him. Should I be fortunate enough to do so, you may rely upon my not forgetting to use my utmost endeavours to recommend him."

"You are kind, sir, and may the blessing of an old woman be upon you. My poor boy is a most deserving young man, and strictly conscientious. He will not disgrace any one who takes sufficient interest in him to interest themselves in his behalf. We have fallen, Mr. Halford, from a very good position in life, down to a very—very precarious state of existence. And troubles, when they come upon us in the autumn, or rather, winter of our existence, are indeed hard to bear."

"Let us hope, madam," said the colonel, soothingly, "that more prosperous days are in store for you. I have lived long enough in the world to feel that it is of no use giving way to despair at any period of our existence."

After some further conversation, in which the colonel endeavoured to cheer the occupants of the cottage in the best way he could, he took his departure, not, however, before the young female had made one or two efforts to return the purse which had been placed in her hand, which attempts were artfully parried by its donor.

The young man accompanied his new-found friend and benefactor some short distance on the road to London, and bid him farewell with many heartfelt thanks for his advice and assistance, at the same time promising to return the money as early as he possibly could.

CHAPTER XIV.

THE TRIAL OF THE BURGLARS.—THE DEFENCE.
—THE CONVICTION.—THEIR EXECUTION.

THE day arrived when the wretched men who had committed the burglary at Mr. Baintree's were to take their trial upon the capital charge.

The affair had attracted so much public attention, that the court was crowded to suffocation with eager and curious gazers, whose greedy appetite for the horrible led them to contemplate the visages of men who were supposed to be steeped so deeply in crime.

When the two men, therefore, were placed in the dock, every eye in the court was attracted towards them, and as their features were scanned, the spectators were surprised to find in their physiognomies nothing that would warrant them in supposing they were the ruffians they were said to be. One was a mild-looking young man, of not more than three and twenty. This was the young man who had been taken in custody with the cart after the Nobbler had alighted and concealed himself.

He was comparatively young in crime, and had originally been brought up respectably, and belonged to a respectable family. Evil associations, together with his persevering pursuit of the two deities, Venus and Bacchus, had brought him to his present unenviable situation. His friends, however, had got up a subscription to employ counsel on his behalf, and a gentleman of undoubted ability was engaged to defend him.

His companion was somewhat older in years as well as in moral turpitude; but even he did not look anything like the ruffian which might have been imagined.

Both the prisoners pleaded not guilty to the charge preferred against them, and the counsel for the prosecution commenced the proceedings in the usual way by his opening speech.

He expatiated upon the enormity of the crime of which the two prisoners stood charged—he dwelt upon the noiseless tread of the assassin in the dead of the night—and then he paid a flourishing compliment to the courage and determination of Mr. Baintree, jun.—so when that gentleman was summoned to appear in the witness box, he was the observed of all observers. He found himself risen into the position of a hero, and being of a retiring disposition, he was not at all well pleased at being placed in so prominent and conspicuous a place as the crowded and ill-ventilated court of Newgate.

His was the most natural evidence, and his examination was therefore somewhat lengthy.

He underwent a rigid cross examination by the counsel for the defence, but nothing was elicited which in any way shook his evidence.

The servant girl, who had behaved herself so heroically when her young master had been attacked after his endeavour to rescue her, attracted a large share of public attention.

The counsel for the defence, in his cross-examination, dwelt upon her amour with the man Dubbs; and by several unpleasant questions, he endeavoured to throw her off her guard, and treat her evidence lightly. After several unnecessary and not very pleasant questions had been put, the judge interposed, and ruled that such a course was irrevalent to the subject.

Altogether the evidence was of too clear a nature to admit of a shadow of a doubt as to the guilt of the prisoners, nevertheless the council for the defence rose to make a powerful appeal on behalf of the prisoner he was engaged to defend. He appeared for both prisoners, but was retained more especially for James Seabrook, the younger prisoner.

Mr. Sergeant Wiggins rose and said—

"Gentlemen of the jury, I am not about to address you to endeavour in any way to palliate in any way the horrible crime of burglary, which is in itself of sufficient enormity, and must cause a deep feeling against the perpetrators in the minds of all well disposed persons. The case before us more particularly, is attended with circumstances which must of necessity have attracted more than ordinary public attention, and I fear that a strong prejudice has been taken to the two prisoners at the bar—a prejudice, indeed, that you who are to try this case, may find it difficult to divest yourselves of. But I think I shall be able to prove to you that one, if not both the prisoners, who are here to day to stand their trial in a case of life and death, are men more sinned against than sinning. It unfortunately very often happens that the greatest culprit escapes while those of lesser guilt are brought to justice. Such is the case in the present instance. I shall be able to prove to you that the prisoner, James Seabrook, has been misled by the prime mover of this burglary —who, unfortunately, for the present has escaped justice. It appears that the origin of this sanguinary affair resulted from an engagement made by an individual known as the Nobbler, with the emissaries of a solicitor who was anxious to obtain possession of the box which was purloined from the house of Mr. Baintree. Who this individual is, we have not been able to ascertain; but one fact is quite certain, that the burglary would not have been committed at all had it not have been for the large reward offered for the abstraction of the box in question. In an evil hour, the young man before you was induced to join his more guilty companions to abstract it from Mr. Baintree's house. I am not here to tell you that he was not culpable for so doing, but I am here to tell you that his crime is not of such a nature, taking all the circumstances of the case into consideration, as to warrant you in condemning to an ignominious death. Persuaded by his more guilty accomplices to join them in their lawless work, he has really been but a dupe and tool in the hands of more designing men than himself, and taking a humane view of the question, I do think that in any case the capital punishment ought not to be inflicted;

and when you have heard all the evidence I shall place before you, I doubt not but that you will be of the same opinion. Gentlemen of the jury, the prisoner, James Seabrook, is a young man who has held a respectable position in society—he has a mother who, with perhaps the highest instinct of our common nature, maternal love, is watching with anxious eyes the result of this day's proceedings—he has a sister, possessed of many graces which adorn the softer sex, and she, too, is alike dependent upon your fiat this day for her future peace of mind and happiness—if I prove to you that the prisoner, James Seabrook, was a blind instrument in the hands of his guilty accomplices —if I prove to you that the thought of committing a burglary never would have entered his head, had it not have been for this and the large reward which had been offered and I have already named—I do think that the degree of moral turpitude is of a nature that, at any rate, would warrant you in finding for the lesser crime, if not acquitting him altogether. I shall be able to show, by a host of witnesses, that James Seabrook has borne a good character for some years past—in fact, since boyhood, for he is a very young man yet. I shall be able to show that, misguided young man as he certainly has been, he nevertheless is deserving of your sympathy. All the perpetrators of this outrage, save the two before you and the chief culprit, have paid the penalty of their guilt, and sleep the last sleep of death, having fallen by the avenging arm of the gallant Mr. Baintree. It is to be regretted that the chief culprit should have eluded the vigilance of the officers of justice; and it would appear hard that those who are the least culpable should be chosen as an example by the law. It appears that two individuals by the names of Grime and Flimby, were the parties who tempted the Nobbler to undertake this odious mission. Every effort has been made to arrest these persons; but they, too, have at present escaped, so that in reality the most culpable parties are not here to take their trial to-day. It now remains for me to enter into a minute detail of the circumstances attending this remarkable case."

The counsel here went over the whole of the evidence produced—gave a summary of all those particulars with which the reader is already acquainted—spoke of the subsequent robbery of the box from the mayor's carriage—called witnesses in favour of James Seabrook, as also his companion—and wound up by making a most powerful appeal in behalf of both prisoners.

Then came a reply from the counsel for the prosecution.

The judge summed up, which, by the way,

was dead against both the men at the bar, and the jury retired to consider their verdict.

They were absent for about half an hour, or rather more, and upon their return a deathlike silence prevailed, and the faces of the unfortunate men blanched, as the foreman was asked if they had agreed upon their verdict.

The answer was in the affirmative. They found both prisoners guilty upon the capital charge.

A faint scream was heard in the court. It proceeded from the sister of James Seabrook, who had fainted, and she was borne out of the court in an insensible state. The unhappy man trembled so visibly at the sight of his sisters despair that he had to be supported in the dock, and was eventually placed in a chair, at the order of the govenor of the prison.

The other prisoner although evidently affected, maintained a tolerably bold front. He had from the first fully made up his mind that a conviction would be the result, and was prepared to meet such an exigency.

The judge placed on his black cap, and proceeded to pronounce sentence in the usual form.

He then descanted upon the enormity of their crimes, and expatiated upon the awful result of their being the cause of having sent their companions into eternity, without there having an opportunity of repenting of their crimes—and at the same time he besought them to make the best use of their time in making their peace with their maker, and seek at his hands for that mercy which they could not expect to find here in this world.

The prisoners were then removed, and placed in the condemned cells.

According to the custom which prevailed until within the last few years, it was usual to only allow malefactors eight and forty hours after their conviction for a capital offence before the execution took place—and as Sunday was accounted a *dies non*, it was a common practice to try prisoners on a Saturday so that they might have the benefit of a Sunday intervening before the execution.

In accordance with this custom, the trial of the two burglars had taken place on the Saturday, and on the following day they were enabled to listen to the condemned sermon in the chapel of the prison.

Who shall describe the agonising hours passed by a criminal in his miserable cell previous to his execution?

That awful interregnum of time between the conviction and the last final ceremony in carrying out the law.

It was customary at the time of which we write, for those who were under sentence of death to be heavily ironed—and the two men were consequently put into fetters.

There were crowds of persons made application to the Governor of Newgate to obtain permission to see them—some of these applicants were prompted by curiosity only, whilst others were perhaps anxious to see the prisoners, and were actuated by a better feeling.

The chapel on the Sunday when the condemned sermon was preached was crowded to suffocation by well-dressed and respectable people—for it is astonishing, indeed, a morbid curiosity is, and always has been, evinced to catch a sight of any great criminal. The greedy appetite of the public must be appeased—alike its joy, whether its victim await the scaffold or the throne.

During the Sunday most of the clergymen besought the unfortunate men to make a full and ample confession, which they both did, detailing the incidents of their past lives—which was supposed to act as a warning to future generations.

The hawkers had already anticipated the wretched mens' confessions, and had it printed for the public's behoof, and were crying it in the streets of London and the suburbs.

All through the Sunday night a man with stentorian lungs was bawling lustily along Fleet Street and the Strand, whilst a crowd of persons of all denominations were following at his heels.

" Here you have the last dying speech, and full and true confession of the two unfortunate men who are now in Newgate under sentence of death, for the burglary at Mr. Baintree's house at Dulwich," said the man, as a gaping crowd listened attentively to what he was shouting forth so vociferously. "A true and particular account of the last parting of the younger prisoner with his mother and sister—most affecting to read—you have—"

" Give me one," said a tall austere looking man, who was passing. The speaker was no other than Colonel Jack.

" You have, also, the young man's life, and past career, and how he was first tempted to crime."

" Let's have one, guvn'r," said a shabbily dressed man.

" Sold again to a respectable gentleman," said the man ; " Here's the—"

"Let me have one," said a servant maid, rushing across the road, and, in her haste, forgetting to shut the door ; " here's the money—master and missus have been talking all day long of poor James Seabrook."

" Did they know him, then ?" asked a bystander.

" No, sir," answered the girl, who reddened as she observed a battery of eyes directed towards her.

" Oh, perhaps he was a lover," observed another.

The girl tripped off briskly at this latter observation, and hastened into her master's house, and then slammed the door in a pet.

" Poor young man ! It is a hard case, that it is," said an elderly female in the crowd, as she gave the man a penny and took one of his wares. " After all he was not so much to blame as his wretched, worthless, companions."

" Ah, the biggest rogues generally escape, missus," said a man in the crowd.

The night wore on apace, and on the following morn the unfortunate men were to be conveyed to Tyburn, there to pay the penalty for their crimes.

Before the morning's sun shone upon the old tower of St. Sepulchre's church, an immense crowd collected before the lodge at Newgate. It was quite dark when they commenced gathering to obtain good places for the forthcoming sight, but as some of the assemblage carried links they were enabled to see their way and choose a good spot to take up their station.

Before an hour had elapsed, since the fast gathering of the mob, the concourse had fearfully increased. The area in front of the gaol was completely blocked up.

It was a dull, foggy day, and the atmosphere was so thick and heavy that at eight o'clock the curious who arrived at the prison could scarcely distinguish the tower of St. Sepulchre's church.

By and bye the tramp of horses' feet were heard slowly ascending Snow Hill, and presently a troop of grenadier guards rode into the area facing Newgate. These were presently joined by a regiment of foot. A large body of the constables of Westminster next made their appearance, the chief of whom entered the lodge, where they were speedily joined by the civic authorities.

Meanwhile the stone hall was crowded by the inmates of the gaol, debtors, felons and turnkeys, together with those officers who could obtain permission to witness the ceremony of the prisoners' irons being struck off.

This was usually considered to be an interesting sight.

The man who was appointed to the office stood with a hammer in one hand and a punch in the other, near to the great stone block, ready to fulfil his duty. Close to him stood the figure of the executioner.

The apartment was lined with spectators who had been fortunate enough to obtain permission from the authorities to be present at this sad ceremony.

Presently the bell at Newgate began to toll, and was answered immediately by the bell of St. Sepulchre's. The great door of the stone hall was thrown open, and the sheriffs, in their full official costume, entered the room ; they were preceded by several javelin men.

Not a word was uttered by the assemblage, but a breathless state of suspense and expectation reigned throughout.

Another door was next opened, and preceded by the ordinary, with the sacred volume in his hand, the two prisoners entered the room.

James Seabrook was deathly pale, and he seemed to have aged in appearance by many years. Encumbered as he was with his heavy irons, he seemed to have considerable difficulty in making his way across the room.

His companion said something to him in a half whisper, which was meant to cheer him up, and he did certainly afterwards endeavour to put on a bolder and more dignified bearing. Seabrook's companion was the first to advance, with a firm step, to the stone block. He placed his left foot upon it, and then gazed round with curious eyes upon the assembly, who had done him the honour of seeing him act his last drama in this world.

The same ceremony was then gone through with Seabrook, after which the process of pinioning took place, and while this was going on, Seabrook trembled visibly and heaved several deep-drawn sighs.

While this was going on, every preparation had been made outside the prison. At the end of the long lines of foot guards stood the fatal cart, with a powerful black horse harnessed thereto. At the head of the cart was placed the coffin. Several mounted grenadiers, and a few javelin men guarded each side of the vehicle as it proceeded along.

Soldiers were stationed at different parts of the street to keep off the mob, and others were riding backwards and forwards to maintain an open space for the passage of the mournful procession.

To have viewed the scene outside the prison, one would have imagined that some glorious sight was about to take place—some joyous pageant, instead of two fellow creatures being led to an ignominious death. The crowds which had now collected seemed almost countless. Every house top, every window, every wall and projection, had its inhabitants. A sea of human heads was visible in every quarter. The walls of St. Sepulchre's Church were covered—likewise the tower. The concourse extended along Giltspur Street as far as Smithfield.

No one was allowed to pass along Newgate Street, which was barricaded and protected by a strong constabulary force.

The first person who attracted the notice of the eager and attentive crowd was the hangman, who, as he emerged from the prison, and took his seat upon the coffin, was saluted with a violent ebullition of disgust from the multitude, who saluted him with groans and hisses.

The hangman generally comes in for a large share of disgust, and is generally an object of peculiar detestation to the mob. At the appearance of the hangman, the mob became in a state of confusion, and staves and swords were required to preserve order.

A deep silence prevailed after this, broken only by the tolling of the bells. The mighty concourse became hushed.

Suddenly a cry was heard from some hundreds of throats as they exclaimed, " See, there they come ;" and the shout reached Smithfield, and told those who were gathered on Holborn Hill, that the malefactors and chief actors in the drama had made their appearance on the stage.

The two prisoners were led by officers laying hold of each of their two arms, and thousands of eyes were fixed upon them as they were led passively to the cart, where they had no sooner taken their place, than the ordinary seated himself between them, and opening his book of prayer, began to read aloud.

The cavalcade was now put in motion. It travelled at a very slow pace, as the horse soldiers wheeled round and cleared a path. After these came the javelin men, walking three abreast, and lastly a long line of constables marching in the same order.

When the procession reached the west end of the wall of St. Sepulchre's Church, in compliance with the ancient custom, it halted.

By the will of a merchant tailor, by the name of Mr. Robert Dowstines, appointed that the sexton of St. Sepulchre's should pronounce a solemn exhortation upon every criminal on his way to Tyburn, for which office he received a small stipend.

As soon as the procession stopped the sexton advanced, and ringing a small handbell, pronounced the following exhortation—

" All good people, pray heartily unto God for these poor sinners, who are now going to meet their death, and for whom this great bell doth toll. You, who are condemned to die, repent with lamentable tears. Ask mercy of the Lord for the salvation of your own souls, through the merits of the death and passion of Jesus Christ, who now sits at the right hand of God to make intercession for you, if you penitently return to Him. The Lord have mercy on you."

The two wretched men listened attentively to this exhortation, and seemed greatly affected by it, for the younger culprit was observed to shed tears.

This ceremony having been concluded, the cavalcade was again put in motion.

Slowly descending Snow Hill, the train passed on its way, attended by the same noisy vociferations, cheers, yells, and outcries, which had accompanied it on its starting from Newgate.

The guards had great difficulty in preserving a clear passage without resorting to severe measures; for the tide which pressed from behind, around, in front, and at all sides, was almost ungovernable.

The houses in Snow Hill were thronged like those in the Old Bailey. Every window, from the ground floor to the garret, had its occupants, and the roofs were crowded with spectators.

As the men glanced around, some few faces were discovered which were well known

to them. They waved an adieu to them as they proceeded along, and one or two endeavoured to reach the side of the cart to shake hands with the two unfortunate young men, but were kept back by the guards.

In this way they reached Holborn Bridge, which was then a bridge in reality. The passage here was so narrow, that there was only sufficient room for the cart to pass with a single line of soldiers on one side, and as the walls of the bridge were crowded with spectators, it was not deemed prudent to cross it till these persons were dislodged.

The entrance of Shoe Lane, and the whole line of the wall of St. Andrew's Church, the bell of which was tolling, was covered with spectators.

Upon the steps leading to the church the two men observed a number of their quondom companions and friends gathered in a cluster. They shouted to the occupants of the cart, and waved to them an encouraging adieu.

In the midst of this group, the stalwart form of the Bristol Badger was observed. He was dressed in his holliday suit, and had come to take a last look at his friends and customers. The Badger had grouped around him several other gentlemen who did him the honour of frequenting his house, and were most of them known to the wretched criminals. The Badger was in rather a melancholy mood, and was particularly reflective, for he did not like to see his customers cut off prematurely in the very flower of their youth.

While the procession paused opposite St. Andrew's Church, a serious interruption occurred. The advanced guard had endeavoured to disperse the mob in Field Lane, but were not prepared to meet with the resistance they encountered. The pavement had been hastily picked up and heaped across the street, and some doubts passed through the minds of the officers that a rescue was contemplated ; and, indeed, such had really been thought of and planned by the mens' companions in crime.

The Badger, although he had no hand in it, was aware such a scheme had been afloat ; and, indeed, the possibility of its being effected had been discussed over and over again at his house, both after and previous to the trial of the prisoners.

The arrival of the cart in its present place appeared to be the signal for this attempt being made, and it was surrounded by a lawless lot of individuals, who did not appear to have any concerted plan of operations, but were evidently bent upon creating a disturbance, and causing an obstruction ; when in the midst of the confusion, they were in hopes of releasing the two men from custody, and effecting their rescue.

The officers surrounding the cart, seeing the state of affairs, drew their swords and, by striking the rioters first with the blunt edge of their blades, and afterwards with the sharp points, succeeding in driving them back

Baffled in their attempt, the mob uttered a roar—or rather that portion of it which formed the more pugnacious party—and discharged a volley of missiles at the soldiery. Stones and brickbats were showered on all sides, and the hangman was almost dislodged from his seat on the coffin by the body of a dead cat, which was thrown with considerable force at him, and struck him on the face. A roar of derisive laughter followed this incident, which seemed to please the assembled multitude mightily.

At length, however, by dealing blows right and left with their swords, and even inflicting several severe cuts upon what were deemed the ringleaders, the soldiers managed to gain a clear passage, and drive back the assailants, who, as they retreated behind the barricades, shouted in tones of defiance—

"To the rescue !   On to Tyburn lads !"

The two unhappy men had sat all the while apparently unconcerned at the disturbance, until they recognised in the more riotous of the assailants some of their own companions, and a dawn of hope then passed through their minds of the possibility of escape ; but this, however, was soon doomed to be dispelled as they observed the crowd give way, and the cart once more proceed on its journey.

Such scenes as these were of frequent occurrence in the "good old days," as they were termed.

The reader may imagine, even in these more enlightened times, what an opening for disturbances would be given if malefactors had to be conveyed in an open cart from Newgate to the top of Oxford Street, just where the Marble Arch is now stationed, for there it was, or near that spot that Tyburn stood.

The procession now wound its way without further interruption along Holborn. Like a river swollen by many currents, it gathered force from the various avenues that poured their streams into it. Fetter Lane, on the left, Gray's-Inn, on the right, added their supplies.

At length the train approached St. Giles's. Here, according to another custom, a criminal taken to execution was allowed to halt at a tavern, called the Crown, and take a draught from St. Giles's bowl "as his last refreshment on earth."

These formed touching and pretty incidents for the public to dwell upon in the good old days when hanging was so much in fashion.

At the door of this tavern, which was situated on the left of the street, not more than a hundred yards distant from the church, the bell of which began to toll as soon as procession came in sight ; the cart drew up, and the whole cavalcade halted.

A wooden balcony on one of the adjoining houses was thronged with ladies, all of whom appeared to take a lively interest in the scene, so fashionable was villany at this time.

Every window of the public house was filled with guests, and, as in the case of St. Andrew's, the church-yard wall of St. Giles's was lined with spectators.

A scene now ensued highly characteristic of the age and the occasion—a scene, indeed, that the present generation will have, perhaps, some difficulty in believing, it is, nevertheless, strictly true, if history is to be relied on.

When the mournful procession halted at St. Giles's, it at once assumed a festive character. Many of the soldiers dismounted, and called for drink. Their example was followed by the javelin men and other attendants, and nothing was heard but jests and shouts of laughter—nothing seen but the passing of glasses and the emptying of foaming mugs.

The hangman, who had been so sadly discommoded on Holborn Hill, now picked himself up a little, and wore a more contented aspect.

He pulled from his pocket a short pipe, which he lighted, and commenced smoking very contentedly.

From the door of the Crown the robust figure of a man emerged with a tankard of ale. It was the Badger, who came to visit the two culprits in the cart, and spoke several encouraging words to them.

"Keep up your spirits, my boys," said the Badger. "I'm sorry things have run so cross with you, but it can't be helped, you know. We must all meet death at one time or another. Come, drink a last parting drain."

The two men hesitated, when Seabrook shook his head mournfully.

"Any request to leave for me to do?" said the Badger, kindly. "Anything you want done that an old acquaintance might undertake for you when you are gone, eh?"

"You may see my mother and sister," said Seabrook, "and say my last prayers were for them."

Tears slowly trickled down his face as he made the last observation.

"It shall be done, my boy, rely upon it," said the Badger, as he shook the speaker warmly by the hand; "it shall be done, or my name's not Bill Dyson; and, more than that, we have knocked up a bit of a subscription for them, and—"

"Thanks—a thousand thanks, Bill," said Seabrook. "You were always a good sort, Bill—always. Good bye, old boy—good bye."

"Good bye," said Mr. Dyson, who, with all his rough exterior, had some milk of human kindness in his disposition.

At this moment the landlord of the Crown, a jovial, stout-looking personage, with a clean white apron round his waist, issued from the house bearing a large wooden bowl filled with ale, which he offered the two unfortunate men.

"They have refused to drink with an old friend already, Joe," said Mr. Dyson, who was on intimate terms with the landlord of the Crown.

Seabrook's companion, however, took the bowl in his hands, and drank the health of his friend, and the younger culprit after this followed his example, mechanically as it would appear, for his thoughts were evidently upon other subjects, from his distracted manner and bearing.

Once more the cavalcade was put in motion, and winding its way by St. Giles's church, the bell of which continued to toll all the time, passed the pound and entered the Oxford Road, now called Oxford Street. It was, however, at this time, not unfrequently termed Tyburn Road. After passing Tottenham Court Road very few houses were to be seen on the right hand, and opposite Wardour Street it was quite open country.

The crowd now dispersed amongst the open fields, and thousands of persons were hurrying towards Tyburn as fast as possible, many leaping over hedges and breaking down every impediment in their course in their anxiety to be in at the death.

Besides those who behaved themselves more peaceably, the conductors of the procession noticed with considerable uneasiness large bands of men armed with staves, bludgeons and other weapons, who were flying across the fields in the same direction, and it was feared that some mischief would ensue, and one of the constables went with a small body of men, and rode forward to Tyburn to keep the ground clear till the arrival of the two prisoners.

The train in the mean time had passed Mary-le-bone Lane. Tyburn was now at hand. Over that dense sea of heads a black and dismal object appeared—this was the gallows.

The two unfortunate men whose backs were towards it did not see the painful object, but from the pitying exclamations of the crowd they became aware of its proximity and supposed it to be in view.

The wretched men gave a slight shudder when the exclamations of the dense populace reached their ears, and endeavoured to abstract their thoughts from all worldly objects by fervently praying themselves and listening to the prayers which the ordinary was reciting.

As the procession neared the fatal spot the executioner threw down his pipe and seemed to gather himself up for business.

A deep, dead calm, like unto that which precedes a thunder-storm, now prevailed amongst the assemblage. The thousand voices, which a few moments before had been so clamorous were now hushed—not a breath appeared to be drawn.

The troops had left a large space clear around the gallows—the galleries adjoining it were crowded with spectators—so was the roof of a large tavern there, the only house standing at the end of the Edgeware Road —so were the trees, the walls of Hyde Park, a neighbouring barn, a shed, in short, every available position.

The cart, meanwhile, had approached the fatal tree.

The guards, horse and foot, together with the constables, formed a wide circle round it to keep off the mob.

It was an awful moment—so awful that every other feeling except deep interest in the scene seemed suspended.

The unfortunate men comported themselves with tolerable composure as the cap was drawn over their eyes. The rope was then adjusted and the cart began to move—the next instant the two criminals were launched into eternity.

CHAPTER XV.

SCENE AT ACTON.—COLONEL JACK'S INTERVIEW WITH LADY BOSTOCK.—HER MACHINATIONS.

IT will be necessary to take a glance at the Fleetwood family, and once more to journey to the home of the baronet at Acton.

Some time has elapsed since the visit of Doctor Carruthers. Lady Fleetwood has recovered from her illness, and the child had become sufficiently old to be placed out, agreeable to the plans of the astute Mr. Sharpthorne and Sir Richard.

It was a hard pang when the time arrived for her to part with her infant. It is hardly possible to plumb the depths of a mother's love, and her ladyship's character was of that impregnable nature that she was deeply sensible of the loss she was about to sustain, but, in spite of all her struggles, she was overruled, and was a mere child in the hands of her designing keepers—for they could be called but little else.

Lady Fleetwood, at the time we are about to pay the mansion a visit, was walking in the gardens belonging thereto. These were very extensive, and beautifully laid out, as has been before observed.

As she strolls through verdant meadows beneath the shadow of some lofty beech and elm trees, she is accompanied by a lady of some few years, if not many years, older than herself.

There is a firmness and decision about the features of the elderly female which formed a complete contrast to those of the young widow herself, whose delicate face may be considered almost childlike in its expression.

There is also in the gait and bearing of her companion a certain air of imperiousness and hauteur which spoke of one who knew how to command.

Lady Fleetwood seemed very wan and pale, and wore a dejected air, as she listlessly sauntered through the grounds.—Her companion was the sister of Sir Richard Fleetwood, Lady Bostock by name, or rather title, in the fashionable world.

"It is of no use your repining, Beatrice," said Lady Bostock, "my brother has done everything for the best; I do not want to harrow up your feelings by alluding to past events—the marriage, in the first place, was imprudent enough—that is, had there been a marriage, which of course we know there never was."

"It is hardly worth while alluding to that now," said her companion, meekly, "I am willing, as I have shown by my actions, to do all that may seem best for the interest of the family, and whatever you or Sir Richard may have deemed best I have willingly complied with."

"Lady Fleetwood," said the other, haughtily, "it is well you take so sensible a view of the matter, and although the loss of your child may be a trial to you, rest assured that the course my brother has thought proper to adopt, is the best one under the circumstances, and is fully approved of and seconded by Mr. Sharpthorne."

"I suppose so," said the gentle young woman, as she gazed abstractedly on some buttercups and violets which lay jewelled on the green sward at her feet.

"Be not thus cast down—you have many *friends* still left who love you," said Lady Bostock.

"I know I have been to blame—very much to blame, for acting in direct opposition to the wishes of her who was more than a mother to me, and, alas, the kindest friend I have ever known," and here as the remembrance of her youthful and more happy days recurred to her, she sighed deeply; "I have paid a dear penalty for it in the end as most of us do, I suppose for disobedience and ingratitude."

"Tut—tut, child—you are so impressible in your character that you think too much upon those subjects which only serve to render you unhappy."

"It seems like a judgment after all, Lady Bostock, that poor Reginald should have been cut off so early in so shocking a manner—and that I should be left by his death and the death of Lady Reichbeck almost friendless in the world."

"Friendless! What can you be thinking of, child? Have you not me and my brother, Sir Richard?"

"True."

"Well, then, how can you consider yourself friendless?"

"I mean my earlier friends."

"Oh, that's a different reason—but you know, my dear, or will do so, some time or other, that we are doomed in our passage through life to lose our early associates one after another—It is the inevitable decree of providence that this should be so."

"Sir Richard has promised that I am to see the child as often as I please," said Lady Fleetwood, looking up into her companion's face with an inquiring look.

"Assuredly so," was the answer, "there cannot possibly be any objection to that. You must not imagine, my dear, that we have, any of us, the slightest wish to hurt your feelings, or act cruelly towards you or the little stranger; all that has been done has been prompted by an almost absolute necessity."

"I do not doubt that," said the meek young woman.

While the two ladies were thus conversing and walking in the garden, a footman was seen wending his way towards where they were situated, and Lady Bostock, as she caught sight of his approaching form, turned round and paused, while she waited his arrival.

Upon his coming up with the ladies he placed in the hands of the elder one a small card, which Lady Bostock looked at with considerable interest.

It had on it the name of Mr. Halford.

"Show the gentleman into my apartment," said Lady Bostock.

"Yes, ma'am," and the man retired the same way as he came.

"You must excuse me, love, for the present," said Lady Bostock to her companion, "a gentleman, a particular friend of mine, wishes to see me."

The young woman bowed, as her companion hastened into the interior of the house

Upon her entering her own apartment, she found Colonel Jack, alias Mr. Halford, seated on one of the ottomans, in a very easy and negligent attitude. He rose at her entrance, and warmly shook her hand with the familiarity of an old friend.

"So, Frank," said her ladyship, "you have really thought it worth while to come in person in answer to my note?"

"Am I not always a devoted slave of your ladyship's

"Psha, keep your pretty speeches for more attractive women."

"It is not possible to find one more attractive than your ladyship," he replied, with an air of gallantry.

"Come, a truce to your flatteries—I sent for you on more weighty matters. Frank," continued her ladyship, "my brother, Sir Richard, is in love!"

"Indeed! Poor fellow!"

"Yes; in love with a chit of a girl. By my faith! the Fleetwood family seem to be all losing their strength of character," said Lady Bostock.

"A mere petty amour, I suppose?" said Colonel Jack, as he caressed one of his long silken locks.

"No—not so. A deep and absorbing passion."

"So it is for a time with most of us."

"Ah, but this is serious; so serious, that I tremble, Frank; for he intends to marry her, and then—"

"I know the rest. With her the property is gone."

"For ever!" said her ladyship, in a hollow tone.

"Well, these things cannot be helped, I suppose?"

"They must be helped, Mr. Halford," said her ladyship.

"How?"

"Listen: this girl has another suitor, whom she herself prefers; my foolish brother is madly in love with her, of that I am well assured, nay, more poor man, I believe he thinks he cannot live without her. The father of the girl encourages the suit, whilst she herself is averse to it. Now, mind me. Frank, the match must never take place!"

"It will not, if you can help it."

"Nay it must not!—Do you understand me?"

"How is it to be prevented?"

"That remains for you and I to concoct between ourselves."

"What is the lady's name?"

"Honora Langford."

"The devil!"

"Ah, I dare say, she is a devil."

"Most women are at heart," said the colonel, smiling. "Honora Langford. Umph!"

"Yes Do you know her?"

"Certainly. She is a sweetheart of an old schoolfellow of mine, and I have promised that he shall have her," answered the colonel.

"What a good fellow," exclaimed her ladyship, placing her two hands affectionately on his shoulder.

The colonel gazed at her for a moment —for she was still a handsome woman, and he imprinted a kiss upon her lips which she returned.

"Have you discovered anything about those papers?" she inquired in a wheedling tone.

"Oh, yes. I have them in my own possession"

"Then keep them for the present, till we consult what had best be done. Now, Frank, how is this odious marriage to be stopped?"

"This Mr. Langford, the young lady's father, comes into a large property under the will of the late Lady Reichbeck—"

"Which he must never have," said her ladyship.

"I do not know that; I promised my young friend, Mr. Osborne—"

"Yes, that's the young man's name."

"I promised my friend that he should have the will to restore to Mr. Langford, and by doing this he no doubt would be able to claim the hand of the daughter."

"Ah, but the will must never be produced, Frank, never ! It would ruin all," said her ladyship.

"When I pass my word," said Colonel Jack, hastily, "I seldom break it. This young man is one of my oldest and dearest of friends."

"Well, as you please. Only some means must be adopted to prevent my foolish brother from marrying this girl. It's ruination to think of. No sooner is one obstacle disposed of, when a fresh alarm ensues. Do you know the contents of the papers left by the late Sir Reginald ?"

"In part I do."

"Much property under the Reichbeck will ?"

"A very great deal more than is usually supposed."

"Humph. You and I must arrange all these matters, hereafter, Frank," said her ladyship, as she sat down on the settee by his side, and placing her arm round his neck, tenderly embraced him. "It was to you, Frank," she continued, "that I gave up my virgin vows of love—it was to you that, years ago, I gave up my honour !"

She hid her face against his head and ample chest as she pronounced these latter words.

"We have each become a man and woman of the world since then," said the colonel; "and virgin vows and boyhood's love have long since been beaten out of us. And you owe allegiance now to Lord Bostock."

"Psha !" she exclaimed, contemptuously. "Frank," she continued, "a woman loves but once. You know what I would say—"

"I can guess."

"Well, you are my friend. Now, what is to be done about this odious, this detestable, this accursed marriage ?"

"Why, it is very clear that Sir Richard must never be allowed to marry Honora Langford ; that is quite certain, under any circumstances."

"It gives me joy to hear you say so."

"Why, first of all, Harry Osborne is madly in love with the girl, and she also is with him. I have promised, Harry these papers, but for the present, nay, indeed, for some months to come, they would be dangerous for him or any one else to produce. Lady Bostock," continued Colonel Jack, more seriously, "years ago, when we were little more than a boy and girl, and thought that we loved—"

"Thought, Frank ?"

"Yes, I say thought, my lady, for I am somewhat guarded in my expressions. Time has run on, and we have each become seared with—with the world's ways. We are no longer a dreaming boy and girl. Well, we have something left still in common, an interest in each other's welfare—"

"Yes, and if such is the case, Frank, this marriage must be stopped, no matter by what means. Even if the girl is to die—"

She fixed her eyes upon him with a basalisk gaze as she spoke the latter words, and scanned his features to see what effect her last observation had produced.

"If to die," he said, slowly fixing upon her in return a piercing look ; "she is not doomed to die, let us hope."

"Let us hope not," she replied.

There was a pause after this, each engaged in their own thoughts.

"Honora Langford," said Colonel Jack, "is a sweet, gentle, loveable young lady. Graceful, impressible in her disposition and character, and it is a matter of little surprise that your brother, or any other man, should love and admire her."

"Gracious me ! you are not smitten with her yourself, Frank ?" exclaimed Lady Bostock, in surprise.

"No, madam," he answered, "you may make your mind quite easy upon that point."

"Ah, that's as well. Now, what do you propose doing to break off this match ?"

"I shall see Osborne, and endeavour to persuade him to push on his suit as quickly as possible. That failing, I doubt not to hit upon some other scheme ; for I don't conceal from you that, apart from your own reasons that it should not take place, I have some of my own. I wish to befriend my old school-fellow, Harry Osborne, and am, in fact, pledged to do so."

"And the papers ?"

"They cannot be produced, as I have already informed you, for very weighty reasons. They have been forcibly taken from the Lord Mayor's carriage, and already, this very morning, two unfortunate men have met with an ignominious death for endeavouring to steal them ; besides this, some of their companions have fallen by the hand of young Mr. Baintree."

"Ah, you allude to the burglary at Dulwich. A shocking affair, indeed."

Colonel Jack was closetted with Lady Bostock for some hours, and a long conversation ensued as to that lady's schemes to retain the property of the family in her own right, after the death of her brother, Sir Richard.

Scheming, heartless man, as Sir Richard

was, he was as nothing compared to his unscrupulous sister, whose head was continually at work for her own aggrandizement. She had married Lord Bostock, who was a nobleman old enough to be her father, for position; but prior to this marriage, when in the full blush of her youth and beauty, she had had an attachment and amour with the colonel, who at that time was in a respectable position, and was a gay and fascinating young man, on excellent terms with both her brothers. In fact he had been, before his lawless career, a choice friend of the family; and even after he had taken to the road, was on tolerably good terms with Sir Richard, as the reader has already seen.

CHAPTER XVI.

HENRY OSBORNE IN THE CITY.—MEETING WITH COLONEL JACK.

HENRY OSBORNE, in his new capacity as clerk to Messrs. Crasher, Bangham, and Phipps, had several startling revelations made to him with regard to the way in which trade was conducted. In his unsophisticated innocence in the ways of the world, he was quite unprepared for the experience which was to follow his induction into the transactions of this respectable firm.

The first discovery he made was from a large purchase of goods from an individual who had them consigned to him from a Scotch house, at least, so he alleged. A sample of these goods were shown to Mr. Bangham, and Osborne knew perfectly well that the price asked for them was one third less than the cost price; for by this time he had become sufficiently aware of the prices of such commodities.

He ventured to suggest to Mr. Bangham that the goods were being sold at a ruinous cheap price, and his principal frowned and made some curt observation, which at once let Osborne know that his advice was not needed in the matter.

Later in the day the two partners, Messrs. Bangham and Phipps, sent for him into their private apartment.

"Mr. Osborne," said Mr. Phipps, "You are a young man in trade at present. I have wished to speak to you, to give you a word of caution as to your future conduct."

Osborne did not know what all this tended to, but he bowed to signify that he was all attention.

"When we make purchases, no matter from whom, and no matter at what price, you will do wisely to keep a still tongue in your head about the matter."

"I thought, sir—" began Osborne.

"No matter what you thought," said Mr. Bangham, "keep your thoughts to yourself."

"I will in future do so, you may rely upon it," said Osborne.

So saying, he retired, and closed the door of the counting-house.

"Ah," thought Osborne, "there is more in this than I imagined. I will take good care to see all, in future, and say nothing."

And ever afterwards he was as mute as a stock fish.

It turned out afterwards that the man who had sold the goods in question, had had them consigned to him by a Scotch house; in fact, he was agent for the same, in London, and keeping a large stock, by various manœuvres, he defrauded his principal, and in fact never paid for one quarter of the goods he received, and what was more, he never intended to pay. The realization of money was all he cared about, and hence it was that he offered the goods in question to Messrs. Crasher, Bangham, and Phipps, at a ridiculous low price. It was a fraudulent affair throughout, and there could be no doubt that Osborne's employers were fully cognizant of this, and were therefore as culpable as the man himself, who was afterwards prosecuted for felony and embezzlement, and eventually convicted on the latter charge.

This was the first discovery which Osborne made in ways of trade. The next was quite as bad, if not worse. His employers were in the habit of starting young men in shops, in our provincial towns, and giving them a certain amount of credit, that is, provided the credit at other wholesale houses. Bills of sale, and cognovits were generally extracted from these unfortunate dupes, for they seldom run more than two or three years' career, and when their affairs came to be wound up, Osborne's employers generally managed to get the lion's share out of what the stock realised. In fact, they were pretty well always paid, and overpaid in most of these transactions.

It would be a tedious task to trace all the various species of chicanery practised by the respectable house in which Osborne was employed. How bills were negociated, drawn, and accepted by the numerous individuals who never existed—how bills which were known to be forged were passed through their banker's hands; it will suffice to say, that Osborne's honest disposition was appalled at many of the transactions, and he felt himself by no means so comfortable in his new capacity as he had anticipated.

But by degrees—as soft water wears away the hardest stone—some of Osborne's scruples began to lose their intensity, and in the course of a short time he began to look upon all these things as a matter of course.

One evening, after business hours, Osborne

was returning from the warehouse at St. Mary's Axe to his lodgings in Goswell Street. The great bell of St. Paul's had struck eight some half hour as Osborne found himself in Cheapside, and was ruminating upon his prospects, which, to say the truth, as far as regards Honora Langford, were not very favourable at present.

He was so lost in his reflections that he did not notice the passers by, or the expressions of the countenances of each individual of that vast human tide which ebbed and flowed through the principal streets of London.

As he passed the end of Milk Street, he was saluted with a familiar slap on the shoulder, and turned round and beheld the well-known features of his old friend and companion Frank Halford.

"What Harry, my boy," said the latter; "the very man I was wanting to see of all persons in the world. So you are in London for good and for all? How fares it with—"

"Not much to boast of at present," answered Osborne. "I am in a mercantile house in St. Mary's Axe."

"And whither are you bound for now?"

"I am journeying home."

"That's all right. I'll go with you. Where do you hang out?"

"Eh?"

"Where do you live when you are at home?"

"In Goswell Street."

"All right. Lead the way, then."

And the speaker placed his arm in that of his companion, and the two proceeded along towards Osborne's lodgings.

Halford had not seen his friend since he parted with him at Oxford, and Osborne had a long history to detail to his companion, which he ran over as rapidly as possible during the walk home.

Colonel Jack, or rather Halford, accompanied Osborne into his own apartment, but previous to his doing so he was accosted in the passage by Squabshot, who had rushed out of his parlour to drag Osborne there for the remainder of the evening.

The latter was surprised to see Halford shake Squabshot warmly by the hand, and recognise him as an old acquaintance.

The two, however, excused themselves to Squabshot, as they had some private matters to discuss.

"So it appears you know my friend?" said Osborne.

"Yes, I've met with him before, certainly. Don't know much of him though."

"Ah! How singular."

"How long have you known him?"

"Since I have been here. He has been very solicitous of cultivating my acquaintance."

"He's fast rather, isn't he?"

"I should say so from his conversation—very much so."

"Well, Harry, and how do you get on with your love affair," said Halford, as he seated himself in a chair.

"Oh, miserably—most miserably. I am refused by the father and forbid the house. I have a rival."

"Yes, I know—Sir Richard Fleetwood."

"Ah, how did you know that?" asked Osborne.

"I know the gentleman himself."

"Indeed! Why, Frank, you know everybody."

"Well, a few, certainly. Well, Harry, it is a case of now or never with you. So don't lose time or it will be too late. You have the girl on your side—see her at once, and persuade her to make a runaway match of it."

"Oh, that I never could do. My honour would not permit it."

"Honour!—psha! In love, as in war, any stratagem is fair, unless you are lost, or rather, the girl is to you."

"But, Frank, I thought you were going to see if it were possible to obtain the missing papers?"

"Ah, I am sorry to say that for the present they cannot be obtained. I have done what I could, but some months must necessarily elapse before they will be produced, so it will never do to keep dilly-dallying till then, for Sir Richard will long before then have stolen a march upon you. No, Harry, that will never do—but I tell you what will. You must see Miss Langford, make desperate love —threaten to destroy yourself if you like— say you cannot live without her, and persuade her to fly with you."

"But my means will not warrant."

"Now, hold your tongue—never mind about that. You persuade her to fly with you. A desperate case requires a desperate remedy. When you have once succeeded in marrying her, trust to fortune for the rest. In the course of a few months I will let you have those papers, and you can then make your terms with the old gentleman for a reconciliation."

Osborne hesitated, and then said:

"My dear Frank, such a course appears to me a very dishonourable one."

"Bah! you are not half a man. It is perfectly justifiable. I should like to know if your rival would stickle at such a course?—I should think not indeed, or one twice or thrice as desperate. You don't know the cards you have to play with but I do—that's all the difference."

"But the money, and means, Frank—I am only—"

"There, hold your tongue. I will supply

you with whatever means you may require for this purpose—"

"You, Frank ?"

"Yes, me. Why, what's the man staring at ?"

"But I have not the means of supporting her in anything like the style she has been accustomed to."

"I will supply you with all the necessary cash for that purpose."

"My dear fellow, you are—"

"Yes, I know I am, a most generous benefactor. Now, never you mind about that ; it is my whim or pleasure to do so. You do as I tell you. See the girl at once, and persuade her to a clandestine marriage. You can do it if you like, and I'll help to carry her off, if you like."

"Dear me, Frank, I wish I had your bold-

No. 14.

ness. I will see Honora, but--" he hesitated.

"But what ?"

"Why, I am afraid she never would consent to run in direct opposition to her father's wishes. Ah, Frank, you don t know—no one can know, her gentle, kind, sweet, and unselfish disposition. I do believe she would sacrifice herself rather than do anything that she thought wrong towards her family."

The colonel smiled at the other's outbursts when he dwelt upon the virtues and good qualities of his enslaver.

"That is the very reason that you should adopt the course I am suggesting ; for Sir Richard Fleetwood is bent upon having her, and there can be but little doubt, that if she is of so self-sacrificing a nature, that her father will persuade her to accept his offer.

You love the girl, I suppose ?" he continued, with a slight amount of badinage.

"Love!" exclaimed Osborne, darting upon his companion a reproachful look. "Love! I—"

"There, that will do," said the colonel, smiling ; "you need say no more. You love her, Harry, that is quite certain, and as far as she is concerned, have won her. She is yours, in honour to her plighted troth. Why then hesitate ? You must understand, Harry, that I have certain reasons myself, that Sir Richard Fleetwood should not succeed with Honora Langford ; and consequently there's an additional reason, if any were wanting, my boy, why I am anxious that you should strike the iron while it is hot. There, go in and win, at once, and here's success to you," continued the colonel, as he tossed off a glass.

"I have not as yet been able to catch a sight of Honora, since I have been in London," said Osborne.

"Indeed ? Then you've been very neglectful."

"I called once, but her father received me very coldly."

"And so, like a simple chap as you are, you've not liked to call again, eh ?"

"I have written," said Osborne.

"And received any answer ?"

"Oh, yes, to all my letters."

"Then write again, and make an appointment. But stay, you may do better. Miss Langford goes to the masked ball at Ranelagh in a day or two. This I know for a fact, and I know that Sir Richard is to be there, also. I don't know if he accompanies her, but I rather fancy not ; at any rate, he will be there. That's your time to see her. Everybody is masked, and if you like we will go together. What say you ?"

"Oh, most decidedly—I should wish to do so by all means. I never was at a place of the sort."

"Then it's time you were. So we will consider that matter settled. I will ascertain before it takes place, what character Miss Langford intends to assume, as also her companion, Miss Staunton, for she is to be there also, I understand."

"Why you know everything, Frank. How do you obtain all your information ?"

The colonel smiled slightly at the latter observation, and said—

"No matter as to that. Let it suffice that I do know, and that is sufficient for our purpose."

"What characters are we to assume ?" asked Osborne, with a smile.

"It matters not. As it's a love affair, you had better be dressed as Don Giovanni, and I as Scaramouch."

"Ha, ha ! I should never be able to support the character with anything like credit," laughed Osborne.

"Very well ; we can procure two dominoes."

"That would be better, perhaps, and not appear so conspicuous."

"Then we will consider this matter arranged. I will make all the necessary preparations, and call for you here, where we can dress, and take a couple of chairs to the place of entertainment."

And after some further conversation, the two friends parted for that night.

CHAPTER XVII.

THE NOBBLER AGAIN.—THE OLD HOUSE IN WEST STREET.

WE left the Nobbler on the coal barge or lighter after his desperate encounter with the officers of Jonathan Wild, in which the reader will remember he came off victorious. He managed to ingratiate himself into the good graces of the man who had charge of the craft in question, and did not conceal from him that he had outraged the law, but he did not, however, deem it prudent to inform his newly found friend that he was the chief actor in the sanguinary drama at Mr. Baintree's house at Dulwich. The man who was in charge of the lighter was not himself of the most immaculate character, and there is a freemasonry amongst rogues which is easily recognisable.

The Nobbler was therefore concealed in the lower part of the vessel, and worn out as he was, and bruised and wounded in almost every part of his body, he was enabled, notwithstanding, to sink into a sound sleep. The vessel continued its course all through the night, undisturbed by any other attack, and the Nobbler was in the land of dreams until the man's wife woke him in the morning to announce breakfast.

The burglar rose, and found his limbs so stiff with his recent conflicts, that moving was a pain to him. He, however, managed to devour a hearty breakfast, after which he sat himself down to ruminate as to what his next course was to be. Hunted like a wolf, he sat panting and snorting like that lupine quadruped.

After turning over his affairs in his own mind, he came to the conclusion that it would be better for him to assume some disguise till the trial of his companions was over. He spoke to his newly found friend, and asked him if he thought it possible for him to obtain employment as a coal-whipper. The man said he did not think there would be any difficulty in his doing so by applying at any of the wharfs at London. This did not meet the burglar's views; they were in too close a proximity to the Thames police, and he thought, notwithstanding the disguise of a fantail hat and coalheaver's dress, that he might possibly be recognised by some of the city officers.

So this idea was given up as an impossibility for it to be carried out with anything like safety to his own sacred person.

He continued, therefore, on board the collier for some days, and having plenty of money about him, he paid the man handsomely for the accommodation.

At length, however, he got weary of being concealed in the dark cabin of the vessel, if such it could with justice be called; so one night, under cover of the darkness, he bid adieu to his kind protectors, and was landed near Wandsworth.

When he was placed on shore, he was still uncertain whither to take his course. As to going to his home, that was not to be thought of. He had, as we have already seen, an almost insurmountable objection to leave London, which feeling was still strong upon him. He thought of making for the Badger's, but the recollection of his recent encounter there deterred him from this course. Suddenly it crossed his mind that a Jew fence kept a celebrated house in the neighbourhood of Clerkenwell. Indeed, so celebrated was this house, that some few years since, when it was under the process of demolition, several thousands thronged to have a look at it; and we have no doubt that many of our readers remember the old house in West Street, which was destroyed some fifteen years ago.

At the time of which we write, this house was kept by an old Jew, of the name of Isaac Balasco, or Ike, as he was more familiarly termed by his associates. He was supposed to be immensely wealthy, as no doubt he really was, for he was regardless as to what means he adopted, not to turn an honest penny, as the saying is, but to gain a penny in any way.

This house was a famous resort for all the juvenile thieves in London, of whom he bought large quantities of goods. The Nobbler had had frequent dealings with him, and gentlemen who were under a cloud had frequently found an asylum in his house. Thither therefore the housebreaker wended his way.

He crept along the bye streets of the metropolis, like a guilty thing as he was; any passenger who might by chance honour him with a passing glance, was immediately set down as a detective, and the miserable man hurried on to be out of sight as quickly as possible.

Upon arriving at the old house in West Street, the housebreaker gave a significant tap against the dingy panes thereof, and the door was opened by a slender youth, known by the name of the "Chicken."

The Nobbler did not deign to ask any questions of this worthy, but pushed rudely by him, and proceeded to the rear of the house, to an apartment which was a sort of public reception room. He knew the Jew was within, for indeed he was seldom out, and he heard his voice addressing some juvenile pickpocket.

"Pinchbeck, my schild, ash I'm a sinner—nothing but pinchbeck. Not worth more than sheven shillings, and I should be loshing money if I were to give more. Take it shomwhere else, my schild. You know I wouldn't wrong you to shave my own life—you know that, my tear. There, take the monish, or leave it, just as you like."

"Very well," said the boy, who was addressed, "hand us over the brads, if that's all yer can give."

The money was counted out carefully in the boy's open palm, who flung up one of the half crowns in the air, making it spin round, when as he caught it again in his hand he spit upon it for luck, and pocketed the silver.

By this time the Nobbler had entered the apartment unobserved by Balasco, whose back happened to be towards the door. He became aware, however, of a new comer having made his appearance by the curious glances of those around. He turned suddenly, and fixed a pair of hawk-like eyes upon the burglar, and gave a sudden start of surprise.

"Mershy on me, Jem, if it ain't you. Why, I thought—"

"Thought what?" said the housebreaker, sharply.

"Why, my tear, I was afraid Jem, that you had fallen into the hands of the Philistines; but this ish goot, bear up, you are alive and well after all."

"Well be d—d!" said the burglar, as he shook his battered frame, and gave a grin, made still more hideous by the marks of a gash on his face, which was still visible

"Vell, sit down, my tear, sit down, Jem; you're with friends now—all friends here," he continued, in a wheedling tone, as he glanced round the assembly.

There were a number of young men and boys seated round at the various tables which were placed in the room. In the centre, from the ceiling, swung an oil lamp with three burners, and at the further end of the apartment was a large old-fashioned chimneypiece, with a grate adapted for culinary purposes. This was set round with Dutch tiles, and on the fire and the hobs of the grate were several dainties. Some fish was hissing in a pan over the fire, which Balasco ever and anon attended to and turned with a fork he held in his hand. Some of the company were playing at cards, others at pitch and toss, and most of them were enjoying themselves in one way or another; for it was a free and easy assembly, and the conventionalities of society were set at defiance.

"Tear me, I am sho shorry, Jem, to hear of that affair; sho very sorry—that I am—"

"Oh, yes, I dare say, gammon and all," said the housebreaker.

"Ash God ish my judge I am," said Balasco.

"Do you know when the trial comes off?" asked the Nobbler.

"It ash come off, my tear, haven't you heard?"

"No, how should I!"

"I ton't know, my friend; but it ash come off yesterday."

"Well?"

"Convicted."

"Both?"

"Yes, and sentenced to be hung. They are to be executed to-morrow."

"Ugh" said the burglar, as his strong frame underwent a visible shudder at the thought.

"It'sh a bad business, Jem. Poor fellows, it'sh a bad business, that it ish, and no mistake. What shall you do?"

The Nobbler made no reply to this question, but gazed round at the assembly, and as he did so, the Jew saw the meaning of his glance, and asked him into an inner apartment, and taking an old dirty blue bottle from a cupboard, he poured out a glass of brandy, and presented it to his visitor.

"Come, there's a good shap, sup that up, it will do you goot, and put you in better spirits."

The housebreaker did as he was desired, and then said to Balasco—

"Keeping dark's my game."

"Yesh, yesh, of course it ish," said the Jew, rubbing his hands together. "Vell, you know, Jem, you are all right here. I'll put you in a place that the tevil himself won't find you. You know, Jem, what short of a place this ish?"

"Yes," said the burglar; "all right. I shall remain here, then. But about these chaps?"

"They are all friends, my tear," said the Jew, emphatically.

"I know most on 'em," said the burglar; "but yer see there is a heavy reward offered for me, and—"

"Oh, they vould never do the dirty like that, never!" said Ike, indignantly, believing, or affecting to believe, in the high honour of all his customers.

"Maybe they may, and maybe they mayent," said his companion.

"Well, look here, Jem, we won't run any risksh. There ish no one besides myshelf and Levi shall know that you are in this plashe at all. When we go back to the public room you can wish me good night, and pretend to take your departure, and ihstead of doing that, when you get out I'll show you which way to turn. But oh," he continued, in another burst of confidence, "they would none of them think of peaching—none of them—or they would never more be friendsh of mine."

The housebreaker thought this was not a matter of such great importance, but he was nevertheless satisfied with the Jew's arrangement. He knew perfectly well that Isaac Balasco had subterraneous passages which led to intricate windings, that defied all attempts to capture any one once concealed therein. Indeed the house was so curiously built, that if faith were kept by the Jew, it was impossible for the most dexterous thieftaker, not even excepting Jonathan Wild himself, to take any one. There was one passage, which was entered from beneath the staircase, which led out to a court three streets off, and when once in this court, a labyrinth of streets ramified in all directions.

Isaac Balasco, although not nearly so considerate in his conduct as the Badger, generally kept faith with those who were under his protection, as he called it.

The Jew and the Nobbler now returned to the public room, and the former found a man waiting for him with a bag full of plate and valuables for sale. They had been all stolen from a gentleman's house on the night previous. The Nobbler at once recognised the man as one who belonged to his own craft, and spoke to him familiarly.

The man looked with some surprise at the sight of the Nobbler, as he said—

"Well, Jem, you have had a hard time of it, old boy. How the devil did you manage to escape? I heard you was drowned in the Thames."

"So I was almost; but I managed to get into a collier."

"Now then, Ike," said the man, turning to the Jew, "just run those over and see what they are worth to you. Now don't get putting the pot on, 'cause it won't do with me."

"I vill do vat ish honourable, s'help—"

"There, that'll do. Stow your gammon. See what they are worth."

The Jew examined the articles carefully.

"Ah, plated, I see," he exclaimed, as he took in his hand a handsome teapot.

"Plated be d—d," exclaimed the other, indignantly. "I know better than that."

"Vell, my tear, yer ought to be a better judge than me," said Ike, bowing with mock humility.

"Don't try yer nonsense with me. I know them to be all solid silver; see, here is the Hall mark."

"An imitation, my tear," said the Jew. "The gadroons are silver, so ish the handle and knob; the other part is plated."

"Well, then, take off the gadroons and knob, and weigh them, and I will keep the other parts myself. You know as well, and, indeed, better than I do, you old rascal, that every bit of them is silver."

The various articles were each put into the scales one after the other, and the Jew pretended to make a careful calculation of their worth, and then made an offer for them, declaring at the same time that in all probability he would be a loser by the transaction. After some haggling, a bargain was concluded, and the man took his departure.

After which, Balasco took the Nobbler into the secret part of his premises, and there concealed him from the myrmidoms of the law."

CHAPTER XVIII.

THE MASQUERADE AT RANELAGH.—THE DOINGS THERE.—COLONEL JACK AND OSBORNE.— THE DUEL.

THE masked ball at Ranelagh was to be on a grand scale. It was given on the occasion of the birthday of the king, and a variety of open air entertainments were to take place, in addition to the ball itself. So, young friend, whose eye may be wandering over the pages of the present work, it may be as well to observe, for your information, that the gardens of Ranelagh were, at the period of which we are writing, a fashionable place of resort for the nobility and gentry, as well as those parasites who generally follow in their train. These gardens were situated in that locality which is known now as Pimlico, but in the days when Ranelagh was in existence, the neighbourhood was guiltless of house or habitation, and the gardens were consequently quite in the country. The glories of Ranelagh are now past, as are also the days of Vauxhall, which was a species of entertainment very similar in its character to the former place.

Colonel Jack, agreeable to the promise he made to Henry Osborne, waited upon him at his own residence with the costumes required for this species of entertainment. Osborne was dressed in a simple domino and mask, while his friend the colonel chose for himself a dress similar to those worn by the cavaliers of Charles II. His fine figure and natural flowing locks were well suited for the character he had chosen.

When the colonel arrived at Osborne's residence, he found the latter in Squabshot's apartment, and to his infinite surprise he found little Squbby, as his friends termed him, encasing his dapper person in a rusty suit of black, to mimic the costume of the starved apothecary in Romeo and Juliet.

"Ah—ah, Halford, my boy," said Squabshot, as he inserted his dexter leg in the rusty smalls he was donning, "how fares it with you? All upon the same suit it appears—you and your friend are going to the gardens, so am I—generally in good things, you know."

"They don't seem to be particularly good things you are getting into now, at any rate," observed the colonel, smiling, as he pointed to some darnes and patches in the rusty suit in which Squabshot was encasing himself.

"Ah—very good," said the latter. "You are getting sharp, Halford—it's keeping my company, I suppose."

"Most likely. Well, Osborne, will you go to your room and dress," said the colonel, addressing his friend.

"Don't go without me," said Squabshot, as the two retired.

"Is he to go with us?" said the colonel, as he closed the door of Osborne's room. "It was hardly prudent to mention it to him, was it?"

"I did not mention a word to him about our going," said Osborne; "the fellow has been pestering me for some days past to go with him, and I have evaded the question as well as I could but all to no purpose, for, somehow or another, he got scent of our going, and since then I have had no peace. But what dresses have you got, Frank?"

"Oh, a simple domino for you, and a cavalier for myself."

The dresses were spread out upon the table for inspection, and the two friends began to array themselves in their respective costumes. When they had finished, Osborne contemplated the colonel with eyes of admiration. The dress of the cavalier was certainly a fine one—displaying a manly form, and well-proportioned figure—and Colonel Jack looked particularly well in the one he had chosen.

"I suppose we shall never be able to make our escape from the house without our friend noticing us?"

"That will be impossible. Do you not wish him to go with us?"

"Oh, I don't know—it would have been better avoided, perhaps."

As they proceeded down stairs, Squabshot emerged from the parlour and confronted them in the passage, and inquired if they were ready.

Having received an answer in the affirmative, he hastened off to procure three chairs —for in those days cabs were unknown—and ladies and gentlemen were accustomed to be conveyed by two stalwart fellows in a sedan chair, a luxury unknown to the fast youth of the present day.

"We can but cut him when we get to Ranelagh if we find his company troublesome," observed the colonel.

"Do you think it likely?"

"Oh, I don't know, only he is a fast man and knows all the fast men about town."

Squabshot returned in a state of great delight with the three chairs, and the parties placed themselves therein, and were soon on the road to Ranelagh.

It would be a tedious task to describe the number of visitors who took their way to the masquerade. Young ladies—many of them daughters of the aristocracy—went attired in the costume of cartermen—Hamlets, clowns, Turks, and dresses worn in every clime and age, were there.

In those days, when London streets were innocent of gas, the lights, which hung suspended from the trees in the gardens, formed—as the playbills of the present day would observe—a blaze of triumph, and the grounds themselves a galaxy of beauty.

When Colonel Jack and his companion arrived at the entrance, the former took Osborne's arm, and presenting the tickets which he had procured, the two strolled into the grounds followed by Squabshot, who rattled on, making a rapid commentary upon all that was passing. He pretended to know a number of persons whose names and position in society he told his companions.

Colonel Jack paid but little attention to the volubility of Squabshot, but his eyes were wandering about in search of Miss Langford and her party. He had ascertained that she would be present in the character of a French peasant girl, and her companion, Miss Staunton, was to be there disguised as her maid.

The colonel observed among the various groups many persons with whom he was well acquainted, but although he favoured them with a recognising glance he made no outward demonstration of acknowledging them.

In a short time they entered the gardens. Squabshot had been acosted by one or two of his more familiar pals, and whispering in the ear of Osborne that he would meet him and the colonel in the supper-room in half an hour, he took his departure, much to the satisfaction of both Osborne and Colonel Jack.

As they strolled through the grounds, a gaudily dressed female, attended by a cavalier, attired as a Spanish Don, addressed the colonel, and asked him how he had left his Majesty, King Charles.

The colonel made some suitable reply, endeavouring to keep up the character he was

assuming, and was about to leave, when the lady, who was desirous of showing off, offered some further observations, to which the colonel replied with one or two pointed remarks, but the lady was not to be abashed, and as her male companion seemed to amazingly enjoy the wit of his enamorato, the latter persisted in her sportive remarks to the colonel, who began to answer her in monosyllables.

"You are brusque, sir cavalier," said the lady, "your habiliments are fine enough, but your words, they do not ' rob the Hybla bees and leave them honeyless.' "

"The honey will be found on the lady's lips, I should suppose," said the colonel, turning to the Spanish Don, upon whose arm she was leaning.

The lady did not seem to relish this retort for she turned as if to move away, while the colonel continued:

"And as for her costume why ' fine feathers make fine birds,' as the old saying has it. Now you would suppose, that this same bird we have here was a denizen of the sunny East, as she rivals the cockatrice in her plumage, when, in reality, she is only a sparrow."

This last observation was made in such a sneering manner that the words told doubly from the tone in which they were uttered, for they seemed to produce a marked effect, as the lady turned suddenly away and dragged her companion hastily from the spot.

"You've managed to get rid of her at last, and somewhat suddenly too," said Osborne; "how was that?"

"I know her, and recognised her when she first addressed me—but, I suppose, she could not have been aware of this, or she never would have persisted in her observations. The fact is her name is Sparrow, and that chap with her is an admirer. In all probability she is here without her husband's knowledge, and by my last observation she was aware that she had been recognised."

"Ah, ah! that was a good ruse, certainly."

And after this little incident the two friends wandered about in search of Miss Langford's party, for it was not for the sake of the entertainment that either of them had betaken themselves to Ranelagh.

To give a description of this masquerade, with all the various incidents attendant upon it, would be a long and, perhaps tedious task. Then, as now, a masquerade in London, to speak an honest truth, is not a particularly edifying spectacle. There is certainly no perceptible or particular harm in some hundreds of persons of both sexes apparelled in various sorts of fantastic costumes, meeting together beneath several gigantic trees illuminated with many coloured lamps, and dancing to the music of a good band till three or four o'clock in the morning, but the place is not harmless, and this species of amusement is, after all, likely to provoke the visitors to acts of insubordination against public decency.

People go there to dissipate care, and unfortunately they but too often do dissipate to an alarming extent.

The *salle de danse* of a grand masquerade is the reunion of epicurean passions—an epitome of vice painted and spangled. Nevertheless it is still a very noticeable feature of London; but to the general public the *bal masque* is an expensive affair and a luxury not to be indulged without a plentiful supply of cash to pay the piper. It is so even at the present day, but it was still more so in the days of Vauxhall, and Ranelagh. First ticket a guinea, and if you take a lady which, of course, most gentlemen do, there's half a guinea more. Next, there's the costume for yourself, which is at least another guinea. Then there is the supper and the wine, for dancing makes you both hungry and thirsty, and the champagne, or rather what is sold as such, costs twelve or fifteen shillings a bottle, and a night at a masquerade makes a hole in a five pound note at the very least.

For this reason the persons belonging to the male sex who visit such gatherings must be divided into three classes : theatrical and literary nobodies, coming there for nothing, and not caring much about the place now they are come; young swells about town, with more money than wit, a class, and a very large one, too, who still exist in the present day.

Some saunter about with drooping tawny moustachois, and faultlessly made habiliaments, with irreproachable white neckcloths, with eyes half closed, with pendant arms and mirror-like patent boots.

These same swells saunter listlessly through the gardens with a quiet consciousness that all these pleasing and dazzling frivolities are provided for their own particular delectation.

And so indeed they are. As to the ladies who frequent these entertainments, the majority of them are what the late George Colman would call "fie fie ladies," for although there were, at the time we write, a good muster of the more respectable portion of society, the majority might be designated as daughters of folly.

In this said masquerade at Ranelagh, it would be difficult to enumerate how many sons and scions, or cousins, or nephews, or multitudinous and obscure offshoots of titled men who governed nowhere, there were ; or how many threads of connection were, in those gardens, between these butterflies and the ermine and lawn of the House of Peers.

Stand round the enchanting circle which run round the orchestra at Ranelagh in its fading days—see the festoons of lights in various wreaths of dazzling effulgence—devices of glass twinkle and radiate on every side—as a mere spectacle it must have been in those days brilliant and picturesque enough. But what can be said of the many living kaleidoscopes twinkling and corruscating in the vast area ?

There is, you may be sure, a considerable admixture of plain evening costume. After which comes paint, patches, spangles, and pearl powder—tawdry gold and silver, and sham point lace. Sham fox hunters, mostly of a Hebrew cast of countenance, in tarnished scarlet coats, creased buckskins, and boots with tops guiltless of oxalic acid, brandishing whips that oftener had been laid across their own shoulders than on the flanks of the horses they had ridden, and screening their mouths with palms covered by dubious white kid, shouting "yoicks !" and "hark away !" in strong nasal accents. Under graduates, in trencher caps and trailing gowns, who knew far more about Oxford Street than the University of Oxford—barristers, more likely to be pleaded for than to plead—Bartholomew Fair marshals, in costumes equal to him who rides on the lamentable white horse before the lord mayor's gingerbread coach and Bombastes Furioso, in the farce—Charles the Second's, with all the dissolute effrontery of that monarch, but of his wit or merriment none—Red Rovers—Williams in Black-eyed Susan—Conrad Corsicus—Red Indian chiefs —brawny Scotchmen, in kilt and tartans—a few Bedouin Arabs, a costume picturesque but inexpensive ; a couple of calico sheets for caftan and burnous, with the tassel of a red-worsted bellpull or so to finish off with, and you have an Arab chief complete, and done up in first-rate style—plenty of monks, who lead, we should opine, anything but a monkish life, with their robes of grey linen, a rope for a girdle, and a pennyworth of wooden beads for a rosary, and slippers cut down into sandals, they are cheap and effective—a knight in complete armour, (pasteboard with tinfoil thereon)—a Robinson Crusoe, with his goatskin (worsted) umbrella —a bear—a demon—a Romeo—a Chinese mandarin.

There are many who affect the cheap, but thoroughly masquerade, costume of the Pierrot, which is an easy and cheap disguise. A couple of shillings or so would suffice. Jerkin of long sleeves made of calico, galligaskins of the same snowy cheapness, scarlet slippers, any number of tawdry calico bows of any colour down the sides, a frill round the neck, the face thickly plastered with flour, so that there should be no room for the knave to blush even if the light hand of a transient conscience smote him on the cheek and bade him remember that he once had a mother, and was not always aide-de-camp in waiting to Beelzebub, a conical cap of pasteboard like an extinguisher snowed up, and there you have a *Pierrot*.

This character is generally assumed by foreigners. The Englishman sometimes attempts him, but generally fails in the assumption. In order to keep up the character well it is necessary to play an infinity of monkey tricks, to bear kicking with cheerful equanimity, to dance furiously, and to utter a succession of shrill screams at the end of every dance ; without these qualifications you are no true *Pierrot*, and these accomblishments are foreign to our phlegmatic manners.

As to the female costumes they were of of every conceivable variety. A beautiful woman, dress her as you may, will be beautiful still.

As the colonel and and Osborne took their way among the crowd, and peered curiously into the female portion, or rather that part of the face which the mask left uncovered, they observed a young lady in a riding-habit, who was so palpably unaccustomed to wear such a garment, and who was so piteously ill at ease in it, not knowing how to raise its folds with Amazonian grace, that she tripped up at every forth step or so, that she was more ridiculous than offensive.

There was also a ' middy,' with a pair of white trowsers, a turn-down collar, a round jacket, a cap, with a gold lace band ; she—for it was a female—sneaked about in a most woeful state of sheepishness ; now and then she burst out into delirious gymnastics which only ended in confusion and contumely.

What strange thoughts did this motley assembly suggest to the minds of one or two of the really thinking portion thereof—for be it known, that, strange as it may appear, there were a few thinkers among them, who came to scan the battered masks with ragged lace, snam orris, draggle-tailed feathers, tin-bladed rapiers, rabbit-skin and rat-skin ermine, cotton velvet, pricked stockings, frazed epaulettes, mended skirts, all suggesting thoughts of the the old clothes bag. Not without histories--some grave, some gay, some absurd, some terrible—must be these mended shreds of gaudy finery. Those dim brocades and Swiss shepherdess *corsages* have graced the forms of the fair-haired daughters of nobles at fancy balls. Great actresses or *cantarici* may have declaimed or sung in those satins before they were disdainfully cast by abandoned to the dresser, sold to the Jew costumer, cut down into tunics or page's shoulder cloaks, and furbished up with new tags and trimmings.

Real barristers, and gay young college lads have worn those wigs, and gowns, and trencher caps ; real captains have flaunted at reviews in those embroidered tunics and epaulettes ; swift horses have borne those scarlet coats and buckskins across country, but with real fox-hunters inside.

Where are the original possessors ?—Drowned, or shot to death, or peacefully mouldering insolvent or abroad, gone up to the Lord, or hanged, perhaps—who knows ? It may be that they are lounging here as swells, not recognising their old uniforms or academics, now worn by sham Abraham men—who can tell ? Where is the pinafore of our youth, and the first shooting jacket of adolescence ? Where are last winter's storms or last summer's blossoms ?

A grotesque dance was being performed in the gardens by professionals, for the edification of the visitors, while at another part there was a performance by mummers. The colonel and Osborne contemplated the antics of the former until they grew weary, when the former said—

" Come, what say you to a glass of champagne ?"

" As you please," answered Osborne.

" Ah, as I live there is—at least I think so—stay—no—come on," and the colonel dragged his companion towards the spot where a lady of meritricious charms was conversing with a youthful cavalier. The colonel passed once or twice and looked curiously into her face.

" Ah, ah, as I live, I do believe it is my friend, Mrs. Swansdown," he cried, to Osborne.

" What, Mrs. Swansdown of Headington, do you mean ?"

" Yes, sure enough, that is, if I am not mistaken ; but I shall soon ascertain by speaking to her. I shall know by her voice if it really be her."

He left the arm of Osborne, and sauntered leisurely up to where the two were conversing, and addressed some indifferent remark to the lady, who answered him rather quickly, and he at once knew the voice to be that of Mrs. Swansdown.

The colonel had spoken in a feigned voice, so that she was unable to recognise him. Being satisfied upon this point, he returned to Osborne and informed him of the important fact.

" Oh, perhaps you would like to join her," said Osborne ; " pray do not let me detain you."

" Not at all, my boy—I can join her at any time. She is a lady who is not at all likely to leave the gardens at a ridiculously early hour. Come, we will do this wine, first of all. You have heard of the groaning table, I suppose ?"

" The what ?" said Osborne, in some surprise.

" The groaning table."

"No. Indeed, I do not know what you mean.

"Well, then, you shall judge for yourself. Come this way," and he led his companion to a large refreshment saloon, handsomely decorated with lamps, and bearing the insignia of the royal arms, with the words "God save the king," in variegated lamps, and a transparent likeness of his Majesty in the centre. The two friends entered the refreshment saloon, where several beauteous Hebes were dispensing various species of viands.

"A bottle of champagne," said the colonel, to the most fascinating of these Houris; "and we will have it served on the groaning table, if you please."

"Have you tickets, sir?"

"No; will you oblige us with two?"

No. 15.

The priestess of the establishment handed two tickets to Osborne, for which she demanded a small gratuity, independent of the enormous sums which were charged for all refreshments served on the groaning table.

A numerous assembly were gathered round the table, and one old gentleman was expatiating upon the peculiar properties of this extraordinary piece of furniture. After he had entered into an explanation of the extraordinary phenomena, he shook the ashes of his pipe upon the top of the table, and as the incandescent refuse thereof began to burn the wood, deep groans were sent forth by the table, much to the astonishment and edification of the assembled visitors.

"You will observe, ladies and gentlemen, that there is no deception about this," said the old gentleman, addressing himself to those around. "If I cut the board which forms the top of the table, the same effect will be produced, which incontestibly proves that the wood of which the table is formed possesses feeling. I hope the hearts of our fair visitors are equally sensitive to the groaning and sighing swains who live only in their smiles. The discovery of groaning boards is not a new one. In the year 1682, an elm plank was exhibited to the king, and inhabitants of London, which being touched with a hot iron, invariably produced sounds resembling deep groans. This sensitive and very invaluable board received numbers of noble visitors ; and other boards, sympathising with their afflicted brother, demonstrated how much they were affected by similar means. The publicans in different parts of the city immediately employed ignited metal to all the woodwork of their houses, in the hope of finding some sensitive timber ; but I do not believe any were so successful as the landlord of the 'Bowman Tavern,' in Drury Lane, who had a mantle tree so extremely prompt and loud in its responses, that the sagacious observers were nearly unanimous in pronouncing it part of the same trunk which had furnished the original plank. The following paragraph, which I am about to read, ladies and gentlemen, appeared in the *Loyal London Mercury*, October 4th, 1682— 'Some persons being this week drinking at the Queen's Arms Tavern, in St. Martin's le Grand, in the kitchen, and having laid the firefork in the fire to light their pipes, accidentally made a discovery of a groaning board. One of the company having the fork in his hand to light his pipe, would need make a trial of the long dresser which stood there. Upon the first touch it made a great noise and groaning, more than the board ever did. They all having seen it, the house was filled with spectators day and night, and any company calling for a glass of wine was enabled to see it, which, in the judgment of all, was far louder, and made a greater groan, than the other ; which report, unless seen, seems incredible.' There can be no doubt but that this table was made from the same tree as the one referred to in the *Loyal London Mercury*."

And here the speaker, or lecturer, as he was termed, gave several other illustrations of the remarkable properties of the article he was expatiating upon.

While the companys' attention was engaged in observing the experiments, Colonel Jack nudged Osborne, and glanced towards a group at the further end of the room.

Osborne looked in that direction, and observed Miss Langford, her attendant, Miss Staunton, and by their side was a gentleman, in a Spanish cloak, which Osborne presumed was Sir Richard Fleetwood.

His heart leaped at the sight of this group, and he did not feel himself capable of any movement. The colonel, however, drew him gently towards that part of the room where they were standing.

"Engage her for the next dance," he whispered to Osborne.

"It would not be prudent to do so here."

"Ah, no, perhaps not. We can carelessly follow them when they go out, and then you will be able to find an opportunity."

"Good—that would be the better plan, without doubt."

The two friends stood watching the group, and in a short time an elderly gentleman joined them, whom they knew to be Mr. Langford himself.

After contemplating the experiments of the lecturer upon the groaning table, the Langford party began to move. Sir Richard escorted Miss Langford, while her father did the polite to Miss Staunton.

As they emerged from the refreshment saloon, Osborne and Colonel Jack followed at a respectful distance ; and when they had got out into the gardens, the dancing was at its height, and the company seemed to be getting into good spirits and warming to their work.

Entertainments of this character are generally flat at their commencement, and uproarious at their end.

Miss Langford joined in the merry throng, and, of course, had for her partner no other than Sir Richard himself.

As Osborne watched her he thought she went through the dance in a listless manner, and he thought, and indeed hoped, that she was not in good spirits. This thought was a selfish one, perhaps ; but he cared not to see her in a state of super-abundant mirth in the presence of his rival.

"Now," said the colonel, "we must each find a partner, and then, after one or two dances, you can ask the master of the ceremonies to introduce you to the lady in the amber-coloured silk dress. Ah, I see yonder my quondam friend, Mrs. Swansdown. Let us go and engage her for one of us."

They were soon at the side of the lady in question.

"Might I beg the favour of your hand as a partner for the next dance ?" said Colonel Jack, to Mrs. Swansdown.

The lady started at the sound of his well-known accents, for this time he spoke in his natural voice.

Her face and neck were suffused with a perceptible blush, and she did not for the moment reply,

"Even through this disguise and mask, the identity of this beateous face and form cannot be concealed from me. Were there nothing else to prove her name and quality the silvery voice of this enchantress would be sufficient," said Colonel Jack, aloud; while at the same time he bent over and whispered something still more soft and touching in her ear.

The lady made no reply, but gently placed her hand in his, and the two were about to take their places for a dance, when the colonel sidled up to Osborne, and directed him to meet him at the back of the orchestra should they miss sight of one another. Having made this arrangement, he and his fair partner betook themselves to the platform.

Osborne picked out one of the most modest looking females, and engaged her as a partner, and joined in the merry throng.

A stream of masquerading humanity are now gyrating round the well lighted and noisy orchestra.

After a while Miss Langford was tired—she has come here very much against her will, for it is not an entertainment at all suited to her taste.

On the left hand of the orchestra, at some short distance from the group of dancers, there is a large tent pitched. Outside this are chairs and tables—or a wooden platform some three feet from the ground—above this there is an awning. There ladies and gentlemen, who are not dancing, can sit on chairs provided for their accommodation, and partake of ices, jellies, or any other species of light refreshment suited to their taste. Sherry cobblers were not invented then, and it would, perhaps, have been no great loss to the world if they never had been; but chocolate was in vogue, and much patronised.

Sir Richard Fleetwood escorted Miss Langford to the platform and procured her refreshment.

She seemed to be more amused at sitting in one of the chairs and contemplating the motley assembly, than she had been while joining in its movements. Sir Richard is studiously attentive, and she is polite, certainly, but nothing more; nevertheless, he perseveres in his attentions. He believed that no woman could resist the continued attentions of a man, if persevered in a proper manner. In the main he was right, perhaps, in such a supposition, but not when she has favoured a prior attachment. Certainly time does much, and Sir Richard had been favoured with a clear stage, and consequently had it pretty well all his own way.

There was a sad expression upon the countenance of Miss Langford, and although she occasionally smiled at the sallies of wit in which the baronet indulged, her laughter was evidently forced, and did not come from the heart. Sir Richard saw this; he was too much a man of the world not to perceive that the young lady was but acting a part

out of politeness or complacency. In a short time Miss Staunton and Mr. Langford made their appearance on the platform, when after having partaken of some refreshment, the gentlemen left the two ladies to take a stroll round the grounds.

Colonel Jack and Osborne had both observed the motions of the Langford party, and when the former found the two ladies were left alone, he said to Osborne, as he passed him in figure—

"Now's your time, Frank, they are left alone; cut off as soon as you possibly can."

Osborne disengaged himself as soon as he possibly could from his partner, and instantly betook himself to the platform where Miss Staunton and his inamorata were seated, and indulging themselves in a running commentary upon the appearance of the various individuals who formed the assembly.

Osborne made his way up the short flight of steps, and quietly approached the two ladies in question. He stood contemplating them for some time before he could make up his mind what should be the precise nature of his proceedings. As, however, he began to reflect that by his hesitation he might be losing golden moments, as perhaps the gentlemen might return; he, therefore, said gaily, to Miss Langford, that he was in search of a lady for a partner for the next dance.

At the sound of his voice the crimson current rushed into her face, and then left it deathly pale, while her form trembled.

"Permit me to take the liberty," said Osborne, as he laid hold of her hand and motioned her to accompany him.

Upon the impulse of the moment she rose. He placed her arm in his, and was about to leave the platform, when Miss Staunton said—

"Are you going to leave, Honora? Where shall I find you? Pray don't leave me by myself."

"The lady is only going to honour me for one dance," said Osborne; "and after that I will bring her safely back hither—"

"With you, a stranger?" said Miss Staunton, in surprise.

"Not precisely a stranger," said Osborne, with a smile, as he moved quickly from the spot without further comment.

He led his companion to a retired part of the gardens, and then said—

"Honora, I have sought this interview—"

"Henry," exclaimed Miss Langford, as her frame trembled, "who would have thought of meeting you here?"

"I have been forbidden the house."

"Forbidden—by whom?"

"As a suitor, by your father"

"Indeed! I never heard of this."

"It seems you are engaged, Honora," said Osborne, reproachfully.

" I am tormented to death, Henry. Sir Richard Fleetwood has obtained the consent of my father, and is so persevering in his attentions that— Gracious me, I know not what to do. Never, surely, was unfortunate maiden so persecuted."

"Honora," said Osborne, " it is only from your own lips that I will consent to receive my discharge. If you love this Sir Richard Fleetwood, if you can be happy with him, I am not of so selfish a nature as to press an engagement which may be now annoying, perhaps, for you to reflect upon."

"Henry, can you doubt me," said Miss Langford.

"Doubt you—never. I know your worth and sincerity too well ever to doubt you. It is true that I love you so, Honora—I need not say how much, that were idle now ; but I feel that in my position I have no right to press a suit, which may be injurious to your future prospects. It may be that you see this, and although unwilling to acknowledge what you know to be an unpleasant truth to me, from feelings of consideration, it is nevertheless my duty to absolve you from an engagement which presses heavily on you."

"Henry, I have told Sir Richard Fleetwood that I am under an engagement to you —no, not you—I did not tell him the name of him to whom I had plighted my troth ; but I make no doubt that my father has mentioned it to him—and until you yourself absolve me from that engagement, I shall never break it, believe me."

This was said solemnly, and with greater firmness of tone than she usually assumed.

"I do not know Sir Richard Fleetwood," said Osborne, reflectively ; " but," he paused.

"But what ?" said Honora.

"Why, if you love him, Honora," he paused again.

"I do not, Henry. Let that suffice," she said, with energy.

"Then don't have him until I absolve you from the engagement."

A long conversation ensued, and eventually Osborne led the lady to the throng of dancers, and the two became partners in one or two of the next dances.

While this was taking place, a scene of great confusion occurred outside the refreshment platform or terrace, where Miss Staunton was seated.

A row ensued, how it commenced it would be difficult to say.

It appeared that a big fellow, dressed in the costume of a *Postillon de Longjumeau*, had been tormented and insulted several times by a Charles the Second cavalier. She, the cavalier—for it was a lady who was so attired, or rather a female—had incited a *Pierrot*, who was hopelessly gone in champagne, to knock the postilion down. He

hesitated at first to accomplish this interesting feat ; but gathering courage, and not liking perhaps to be humiliated in the eyes of a *debardeur* in claret coloured velvet, he kicked up wildly at the aggressor with his boots Then the cavalier scratched his face— then the claret coloured *debardeur* fainted— then an active member of the light-fingered gentry dexterously cut in and picked Lord Boodles pocket—then one of the constables struck an inoffensive fox hunter on the head with his staff—then four fast young men called out "fire," and sent forth several piercing screams—then a recruiting sergeant, who was also under the influence of several potent liquors, gave a loud roll on his drum, which he had forcibly taken from an unfortunate drummer-boy, who, was, however, a man of about fifty or thereabouts—then an inebriated vendor of gingerbread nuts, who had been treated to drink by some swells, challenged Lord Boodle to single combat— then somebody in the crowd knocked the aforesaid gingerbread nut vendor on the side of the head with his clenched fist—tables and chairs were upset, and a general *melee* ensued.

Miss Staunton and several of the ladies on the platform screamed, and endeavoured to make their escape, for the platform was now one wild scene of confusion and of war.

Miss Staunton was borne hither and thither by the disorderly crowd, out of which she found it impossible to make her escape.

A gentlemanly man amongst the mob stepped forward, and seeing her position, offered his arm and protection. He was a stranger to her, but she was too glad, under the circumstances, to avail herself of his protection, for his manners were evidently those of a finished gentleman, and she accepted his kind offer.

By main strength he managed to force a passage through the disorderly throng, and succeeded in escaping from the platform into the open part of the grounds.

" I presume, madam, that you have missed sight of your friends," said Miss Staunton's companion.

" Yes, sir," she answered ; " I suppose they found it impossible to return in consequence of the confusion which so suddenly ensued."

" We will endeavour to find them," said the gentleman

And with this they proceeded to the refreshment saloon, and sought in vain all over the gardens for Mr. Langford and Sir Richard Fleetwood.

Miss Staunton expressed her thanks to her protector, and at the same time begged he would not waste his time further, but leave her to find her friends as best she could. He, however, said he would not think of abandoning her to the mercy of so disorderly a multitude, for by this time several other fracas had ensued in various parts of the grounds.

There was one part, however, where they had not searched; this was the Pavilion, a small circular building, generally used for dramatic representations.

Miss Staunton's companion suggested that they should enter it, and see if her friends were there, and this proposition meeting with the lady's approval, the gentleman paid the price of entrance, and the two took their places in the front balcony.

Miss Staunton's companion treated her with marked respect, and comported himself in every way becoming a gentleman, and up to this period she fully believed him to be such. After they had taken their places, he in a short time requested her to keep his seat, as he was about to look round the house. She agreed to do so with pleasure, and observed him afterwards wandering about at the back of the boxes, and occasionally looking at the performance, which, however, was of a very mediocre character.

Presently she made a terrible discovery.

As her eyes wandered about in search of her friends, and in watching the movements of her protector, she observed the latter take from the person of a lady in the boxes a gold watch and chain. So dexterously had this been done, that she could hardly trust to her own sense of vision, and thought she must have been mistaken.

She, however, still directed her glance towards him, when she observed a necklace disappear from the fair throat of one of the females—then a broach from another lady—bracelets, pins, chatelains, and various other articles of value, mysteriously vanish in the like manner.

Miss Staunton trembled as she made this discovery, and so great was her fear, that she seemed spell bound to her seat, and incapable of motion.

She knew not how to act.

In a short time the gentleman, who had behaved with so much kindness, returned, and taking his place beside her, handed her some refreshments he had procured in the saloon, and was studiously polite in his attentions.

Poor Miss Staunton was so overwhelmed with the discovery she had made, that she found herself unable to speak, but she mechanically accepted of a portion offered to her.

There is no doubt that her male friend saw her state of trepidation, but he made no observation thereon.

After a short time had elapsed, he suggested their departure, as it did not appear likely that her friends would be found in the Pavilion.

The lady joyfully rose to depart, and was glad enough when she found herself again in the open grounds.

The gentleman offered his services to see her home, but this she politely declined; but as there did not appear much chance of her finding Mr. Langford, she allowed him to procure her a chair, when after having seen her safe therein, he gave instructions to the chairmen as to where they were to convey her, and as she was about to depart, he went to the window of the chair, and raising his hat, offered her his hand, which he gently squeezed. She thanked him again for all the trouble he had taken on her behalf, and he put his head in the window and said—

"I pray you do not mention it, madame. I have found it a pleasing duty, I assure you, and you may tell your friends," he said, in a still lower voice, "that you have spent some hours in the company of Brewster, the celebrated pickpocket. Adieu—good night," and with these words he again gracefully touched his hat, and immediately disappeared.

While this had been taking place, Sir Richard Fleetwood and Mr. Langford had returned to the balcony where they had left the two young ladies, and the row was then at its height. They in vain endeavoured to force a passage through the crowd, so waited until it had cleared away, but were then unable to find either Honora or Miss Staunton. They consequently made a hasty survey of the grounds, and upon a more close inspection of the group of dancers, Sir Richard observed Miss Langford dancing with Osborne.

A raging fire was at the baronet's heart, and the demon of jealousy clutched him in its invisible arms, as he observed Honora's beautiful form thread its way through the mazy dance. He did not know who was her partner, as Osborne's costume and mask served as a complete disguise; but nevertheless Sir Richard felt it could be no other than his rival.

At least that was the first thought which suggested itself to his imagination, as wild with fury, and speechless with rage, he contemplated the two dancers.

Mr. Langford's attention was called to the same direction, from the earnest gaze of the baronet.

"My daughter," said Mr. Langford, in unfeigned surprise.

"Yes," said Sir Richard. "She has obtained a cavalier in our absence. Do you know the gentleman?"

"I can't say I do, in his present costume," was the answer.

The two said no more, but continued to observe the motions of Osborne and Miss Langford.

Presently the dance finished, and Miss

Langford was escorted by her partner to one of the alcoves which were round the dancing platform. The two seated themselves, and some ices were ordered and brought by an assiduous waiter.

Sir Richard Fleetwood could contain himself no longer. He hastily strode towards the alcove where the pair were seated, and said, in rather a sharp manner—

"Miss Langford, both your father and myself have been seeking you everywhere ; but you are too well engaged perhaps, to need our services."

This was said in a sneering tone which, despite himself, he could not help assuming.

"I have been engaged with an old and valued friend, Sir Richard," said Honora, quietly.

The baronet hesitated, and then said, still with a perceptible sneer—

"I should be sorry to obtrude my presence where it was not needed."

Honora did not know what reply to make to this last speech, when Sir Richard again said hastily—

"When Miss Langford is disengaged, her father will be glad to see her in the refreshment saloon."

"I will conduct her thither presently, sir," said Osborne, who saw that Honora did not know what reply to make.

"I was directing my discourse to Miss Langford," said the baronet. "It is not my custom to either address strangers or receive from them answers."

"I will be with you very shortly, Sir Richard, believe me," said Honora, gently endeavouring to pacify the baronet.

By this time Mr. Langford himself had arrived at the spot.

"Your daughter appears to be engaged at present," said the baronet. "We had better leave them, perhaps, as she will join us presently in the refreshment saloon."

"Ah !" said Mr. Langford.

He was only able to utter this exclamation, as he was struck almost speechless by the presence of Osborne, whose form he had recognised. Knowing Sir Richard's irritable nature, Mr. Langford thought discretion was the better part of valour, and consequently he drew the baronet away, naturally dreading a collision between the rival suitors.

They waited in the refreshment saloon for some time. To Sir Richard it appeared an age—to Osborne but a few moments, so different does time fly with us, according to the position in which we find ourselves placed.

In a short time Osborne accompanied Honora into the refreshment saloon, and handed her to her father ; when gracefully and respectfully touching his hat, he was about to retire.

He had, however, hardly got to the door of the saloon, when he was accosted by Sir Richard, who said—

"A word with you, sir, before you depart."

"With pleasure," Osborne replied.

"Follow, if you please," said the baronet ; and the two went again into the grounds.

Honora had seated herself by her father's side, and the latter said, as Sir Richard was about to leave—

"Are we to wait here for you ?"

"Yes, if you please—do so by all means," was the reply.

The rivals walked on for a short time in silence.

"At present you are a stranger to me," said Sir Richard, to Osborne ; "I neither know your name or rank."

"We are strangers to each other," was the quiet answer.

"Pardon me, but I think that you doubtless know my rank and title !"

"Am I addressing Sir Richard Fleetwood ?"

"Yes, sir."

"I thought so ; nevertheless you are at present a stranger to me."

"And am I addressing Mr. Osborne," said Sir Richard, mimicing the tone of the other, for he found it difficult to keep in his pent-up passion.

"You are, sir."

"Good. Then learn, sir, that I do not allow any person to interfere with a lady who has placed herself under my protection."

"Yours ?"

"Yes, mine."

"Indeed !"

"I consider it an unwarrantable liberty you have taken in your interference with Miss Langford."

"Umph !—there we do not agree, it seems, for I am of a different opinion."

"Who values your opinion, sir," burst out the baronet, in a violent strain of passion.

"I do myself."

"You !—you are a conceited puppy, whom I shall know how to chastise."

"I thought I was being addressed by a gentleman," said Osborne, reproachfully. "Let this conversation end where it is. I do not desire to be insulted—neither will I by any man, peer, baronet, or commoner."

"Don't bully me, fellow," said the baronet, hoarse with rage, for he was unprepared for the high tone which Osborne had chosen to assume in this discourse. "Don't bully me. The Fleetwood's have always had a ready sword to punish braggadocias."

"I do not assume the bully," said Osborne, emphasising most painfully the nominative pronoun. "Neither have I sought this interview, nay, more, I wish it to end here."

"Coward," exclaimed Sir Richard Fleetwood.

"It would seem, then, that you have only followed me to offer insults."

"You can punish them, sir," said the baronet, with a sneer. "You wear a sword, I perceive. Not but that it is beneath me," he said, as though to himself, "to lower myself by fighting with a low adventurer."

"Adventurer!" exclaimed Osborne, now fairly incensed; "You lie. Mr. Richard Fleetwood, and more than that you forget the character of a gentleman."

"Draw, sir," said the baronet, as he unsheathed his own weapon and pointed it at the breast of his rival.

"I call you to witness," said Osborne, addressing one or two of the maskers who were by at the time, "that this combat is forced upon me."

Swords were crossed and some rapid passes were made in quick succession.

Sir Richard had made desperate lunges at his adversary, which he parried adroitly, and so infuriated was the baronet that he several times left himself unguarded, which, had Osborne chosen to take advantage of, the combat might have been brought to a speedy termination; but he had no wish to take Sir Richard's life, and, being an accomplished fencer—most collegians were at this time—he contented himself with acting on the defensive. By this time a dense crowd was formed round the combatants, who cheered alternately one and then the other, as is usual in such cases; the spectators had divided themselves in their opinion, one part backed Sir Richard and the other Osborne. Presently the combatants became wounded, and the partisans of each took them for a time under their charge much the same as the seconds at a prize fight of our present day.

Any species of combat seems to possess a charm for the multitude, and this one bid fair to eclipse all the other entertainments of the evening, for it was very evident that both parties were in earnest.

When the combat was again resumed Sir Richard pressed his adversary with renewed vigour. He had not counted upon finding so finished a swordsman, and was irritated beyond measure at the protracted nature of the fight in the presence of so vast a concourse of spectators, for he was not at all desirous of making a public exhibition of himself.

Osborne, at the renewed assault, had some difficulty in keeping his infuriated adversary at bay.

In the interchange of parry and thrust, Sir Richard received a severe wound in the thick part of the left arm.

A shout was sent forth from the partisans of Osborne, and the baronet was immediately attended to by several of the spectators, one or two of whom promptly bound up his wound.

"Let this dispute end here," said Osborne, "It has not been my seeking."

"Wretched imposter!" exclaimed Sir Richard, as he again placed himself in fighting attitude. "This quarrel can only end in your life or mine."

"Bravo! bravo!" shouted out several voices, and the two combatants were again busily occupied in a dubious contest.

The circle which had been made around them by the crowd entirely precluded the possibility of the other occupants of the gardens obtaining a sight of the duellists.

Sir Richard's patience was now getting entirely exhausted, and he fought with an energy which, considering his wound and loss of blood, was perfectly surprising. The swords of the two combatants became entangled, and the baronet grasped his adversary by the throat until he endeavoured to withdraw his own weapon from the hilt of Osborne's weapon. In his struggle to accomplish this, Osborne's sword broke off about half way.

"Yield!" said Sir Richard, as he flourished his own weapon. "On your knees miscreant, and beg your worthless life—"

"I scorn to beg any favour of Sir Richard Fleetwood," was Osborne's answer.

"Sir Richard Fleetwood!" exclaimed several of the bystanders, who now, for the first time, became aware of the rank of one of the combatants.

The baronet made several determined lunges at his adversary, which Osborne found the greatest difficulty in guarding with his broken sword. It is probable that in a short time he would have received his death at the hands of Sir Richard; but, at this juncture of affairs, a tall man found his way through the crowd, and, just as the baronet's sword was about to find a passage in the body of Osborne, it was struck up violently by the new comer, who exclaimed in a furious voice—

"Hold! would you have the charge of murder on your head?"

So violent had been the force of the blow that Sir Richard's sword was almost forced out of his hand. When, however, he recovered his first surprise from this unlooked-for assault, he turned round upon the assailant, and, in a voice of ungovernable fury, bid him defend himself, and immediately commenced a violent attack upon him.

Colonel Jack—for the intruder was no other than our hero—managed to keep the baronet at bay.

"Forbear, Sir Richard!" said the colonel. "Forbear for your own sake if not for mine!"

"Insolent intruder; you shall answer for this impertinence with your life," was the only reply the baronet made to this speech; and he again attacked the colonel with his sword, who, by a dexterous movement, managed to dash it out of his hand, and send it flying some yards from the spot where its owner stood.

A burst of applause followed this feat, and Sir Richard Fleetwood stood abashed and entirely at the mercy of his new antagonist, who sheathed his own weapon, and, flinging his hand upon the baronet's shoulder, said—

"What should have been a private quarrel has become a public brawl, as unseemly as well as injudicious. A word with you in private," and he motioned the baronet to follow him, which he did in moody silence. When they had got through the crowd, Sir Richard said—

"So, sir, it seems you have the impertinence to dictate to me. Chance has given you an advantage, I admit; but at some other meeting—"

"Bah!" exclaimed the colonel, contemptuously; "you don't think I want your life, do you? Of what service can your death be to me?"

"Death; so you presume to threaten because—"

"Because your arm is of little service against that of a man who has made the use of offensive weapons the study of his life. First, man, what's the use of you and I quarrelling?"

"Who are you, Sir Stranger, that you presume to talk thus familiarly?"

Colonel Jack made no reply, but simply denuded himself of his mask, and stood with folded arms in front of the baronet.

"Colonel Jack," said the latter in almost a breathless whisper; "I might have guessed as much by the voice."

"You will agree with me, Sir Richard, that it will not do for you and I to quarrel, eh?" said our hero in a slow and serious tone.

"No," exclaimed the other; "no," he again uttered to himself. Then, addressing himself to his companion, he said—"But wherefore should you interfere with my just vengeance against yonder puppy?"

"Better language, Sir Richard, Mr. Osborne is a gentleman."

"Ah! do you know him?"

"Perfectly well."

"Umph! you call him your friend, perhaps?"

"One of my most esteemed of friends."

"No matter for that," said Sir Richard, angrily; "neither you or any other man shall stand between us, or interfere with the deadly feud we have. Indeed, Halford, I can ill brook your present interference."

"Sir Richard Fleetwood in earlier years," began the colonel—

"Hush! I know what you would say. Enough; you need not recur to the past," said the baronet with a shudder.

"Good! I am glad your memory is sufficiently retentive, and I need not, therefore, remind you of events which would, perhaps, be painful to you to listen to. For you there is wealth, high position, and society; for me —bah! no matter—the outcast, the despised;" he spoke these latter words with some bitterness, and then paused suddenly.

"There is no ill blood between us, I hope, Halford?" said the baronet, offering the other his hand.

"No, none, Sir Richard." The colonel shook the proffered hand, and abruptly left his companion.

Sir Richard immediately betook himself to the refreshment saloon, where he had left Honora and her father, both of whom he found there in a state of great anxiety in consequence of his protracted absence; but Mr. Langford did not deem it expedient to inquire too particularly as to the cause of the baronet's stay.

Honora was more than usually serious, indeed, from her manner the baronet very shrewdly guessed that her father had been having some grave conversation with her upon the subject of Osborne.

Sir Richard politely offered her his arm, which she very reluctantly accepted; she would have liked to refuse, but did not know very well how.

Mr. Langford's carriage was called, and the three took their way home in solemn silence, each being occupied with their own thoughts, but previous to their leaving the gardens they had instituted an active search for Miss Staunton, in which they were, of course, unsuccessful. Miss Langford was delighted, however, to find her female friend at home upon her return, and excusing herself upon the plea of a headache she retired to her own room, there to detail all that occurred to her on that eventful evening to her choice and valued companion, Miss Staunton.

"Ah, my dear Edith," said Honora when the two young ladies were left together; "I have met with such adventures."

"So I should imagine," answered her companion; "and I, too, have been equally fortunate, or unfortunate, as the case may be."

"Indeed, how so?"

Miss Staunton now entered into the full particulars of the confusion on the platform, and her rescue therefrom by the celebrated pickpocket Brewster.

"And, oh, my dear," said Miss Staunton, in conclusion, "I will never go again to a masquerade—nothing shall ever induce me."

"Perhaps you are right, Edith," answered her friend. "Did you guess, my dear, who the gentleman was who was with me when I left you?"

"I had my suspicions—Was it Mr. Osborne?"

"Yes."

"Oh, so I thought."

"And oh, Edith, dear, my father is so angry at my taking any notice of him."

"Where did he see you, then?"

"He and Sir Richard observed us on the dancing platform."

"Ah, did you dance with Mr. Osborne?"

"Of a certainty, and wherefore not?"

"And Sir Richard?"

"Ah, he is evidently madly jealous, and can hardly contain himself from showing his temper. Indeed, I am afraid he and Mr.

No. 16.

Osborne must have had some words, for they left the saloon together and were gone such a time; and I think Sir Richard seems to be in pain, for he winced as he entered the carriage with us."

"It was an unfortunate rencontre for two rivals to meet under such circumstances; you cannot hold on with both, that's very certain."

"It would be the height of injustice to do so," said Honora; "I have told my father this—I have pointed out to him the folly, or worse than folly, in encouraging the addresses of Sir Richard Fleetwood, but with a mad infatuation and an almost fatal purpose he persists in using every species of sophistry it is possible for the fertile imagination of man to suggest to persuade me to abandon my engagement with Henry, which once and for all I have peremptorily refused."

"And Mr. Langford, I suppose, was very angry ?" inquired Miss Staunton.

"So angry that I have never seen him anything like it before. Oh, Edith, I am driven almost to distraction. Never surely was there an unfortunate maiden so persecuted. What am I to do, Edith ?"

"Consult your own heart and obey its promptings. No man has a right to come between you and your choice."

"And I never will break faith with him to whom I have plighted my troth," said Honora with unusual energy."

After a long discussion upon the subject, the two young ladies returned to their rooms for the night.

We left Osborne standing in the midst of the crowd after Colonel Jack had rescued him from the murderous attack of the baronet.

Several of the most officious among the spectators surrounded him, and offered their congratulations at his escape, while one proffered his own sword in lieu of the broken one which Osborne held in his hand.

He was politely declining this and several other offers which were thrust upon him, when a noise as of military music was heard, and a party of recruits, dressed as countrymen in smock-frocks and heavy hobnailed boots, forced their way through the crowd. They were headed by a recruiting sergeant with various coloured ribbons streaming from his hat, and several drummers and fifers were playing the loudest and most discordant music it was possible to conceive.

As they forced a passage through the crowd Osborne observed Squabshot by their side addressing the recruiting party in a sort of mock harangue. He caught sight of Osborne and immediately rushed forward—

"My dear boy, where have you been hiding yourself ? I have been hunting for you all over the gardens. Why, you seem hot and vexed, what's been the matter—a row or scrimmage, eh ?"

"Something like it," said one of the bystanders.

"Ah," said Squabshot, "as I live its Biffins, by the voice ?"

"That it certainly is," answered the individual addressed.

"It's Biffins, and no other."

"Well, to be sure ; why, all the world and his wife are here, it appears."

By this time Colonel Jack came to the spot, and immediately drew Osborne away from the crowd of curious gazers. When they had got some distance from the spot where the affray had taken place, Osborne said—

"My thanks, Frank, for your intervention,

without which I should in all probability have been, by this time, in the other world. You know Sir Richard, it appears ?"

"Yes."

"For long ?"

"Oh, for many years ; what was the cause of this dispute ?"

"I saw Miss Langford, as you know ; accosted her, and, eventually, after a great deal of explanations on both sides, she consented to dance with me. While we were thus engaged the father and Sir Richard Fleetwood returned. It appears they had been watching our movements, at least so I judge, for after the dance was over I took Miss Langford to one of the alcoves, and there it was that Sir Richard came to us, and said her father wished to see her in the refreshment saloon. He was very grand and would not deign to speak to me. After he had left for some time I escorted Miss Langford to the refreshment saloon, when Sir Richard followed me out, and by every insulting epithet sought a quarrel, which, in spite of my efforts to avoid, ended in a desperate conflict, the end of which you are already acquainted with."

"And the lady herself ?" inquired the colonel.

"She is as true as ever."

"Good ! then you must carry her off, my boy—and that as speedily as possible. Did you broach the question ?"

"No, she is of too gentle and delightful a nature to agree to such a course."

"Bah ! you don't understand women, Harry, so well as I do, or you would never hesitate thus. You must consider this over. So far you have sped pretty well. Where are you off to now ?"

"I propose going home—and you ?"

"I have a fair enchantress to see whom I have left in one of the alcoves."

"Very good, then, I will wish you good night."

"What ? You are not going so soon."

"I have no disposition to remain any longer. My object in coming here has been attained."

"Well, as you please. I know you are not sportive ; make the best of your way home, then, and I will give you a call in a day or two. Good night, Harry, and keep up your spirits," said the colonel, as he shook his friend warmly by the hand, and so the two parted, and Osborne immediately left the gardens, being in no humour to enjoy the wild orgies which had now ensued. Colonel Jack then sought for the fair Mrs. Swansdown, whom he found in the dark alcove where he had left her. She was in no amiable humour at his protracted absence, and evinced a considerable amount of ill temper.

"Fairest of women kind," said the colonel,

in his most winning tones; nature never formed that lovely face to be distorted by frowns. A devoted admirer kneels at your feet; you cannot, I am sure, find it in your heart to treat him with unkindness. It is a long time, dearest, since we met; to me it appears an age. If you knew how I have treasured your dear image in the innermost recesses of my heart. If you knew what uneasy days and sleepless nights I have endured since our last meeting, you would pity me."

"Mr. Halford," said the lady, "this must not be listened to—I have a husband—"

"Yes, one who is insensible to all your varied charms and graces."

"Go to, flatterer," said Mrs. Swansdown, endeavouring to put on an angry look, but it was evident enough to the colonel, notwithstanding the attempt, that she drank in all his flatteries. "I must endeavour to find my cousin," added Mrs. Swansdown, pretending to rise.

"Nay, my fairest charmer, have you not a protection in me; let that suffice for the present, and I have a friend who will in the meanwhile seek your cousin without the grounds."

"Where is he? Your friend I mean."

"I have sent him on the mission," was the colonel's ready answer. He had done no such thing, but he deemed it advisable to pacify the lady, by what he considered to be a white lie, and quite justifiable under the circumstances.

"And where is he to meet us if he succeeds?"

"At the back of the orchestra."

"Now are you sure you are not deceiving me, Mr. Halford," said the lady doubtingly.

"I would scorn to do so," was the reply. "Come, let us see what sports are going on," and the colonel led his enamorato from the alcove into the open ground, in a part of which there appeared to be a scene of uproarious confusion, the cause of which the colonel was at first quite at a loss to divine. As Mrs. Swansdown seemed desirous of ascertaining the origin of the disturbance, her companion led her towards the spot. Shouts, screams, and loud laughter resounded on all sides. There was a wide circle of spectators, who were in a state of delirious delight at the proceedings which were going on in the centre. The colonel and his fair companion pushed their way in amongst the spectators and endeavoured to catch a sight of the entertainment which seemed to afford so much satisfaction to the multitude. As they did so they heard shouts of—

"Bravo, Squabby! Keep it up, old boy! This beats cockfighting;" &c., &c.

Our hero and his companion were soon made acquainted with the state of affairs

In the centre of the charmed circle, the eccentric Mr. Squabshot was standing on his head, and around him were a group of danseuse who were indulging in the most grotesque and ridiculous evolutions it is possible for the most fertile imagination to conceive. It was, perhaps, one of the wildest scenes of revelry that ever was seen, even in unlicensed entertainments of this description. Squabshot's pals, the recruiting party, were among the chief actors in this ridiculous drama, and the drums and fifes were being played in so loud a manner as to completely drown the orchestra.

"Keep it up, old boy; capital;" shouted out several of Squabshot's ardent admirers; and the party addressed who was the chief actor still kept on his head with a determination which suggested to the mind of one the probability of apoplexy ensuing, but in spite of himself, the colonel and his companion could not resist laughing at the absurd scene.

"That will do," said the former. "There, that's enough, Squabshot."

"No, no," called out the spectators, "leave them alone; this is the best scene we have had to-night."

"Order—order in the grounds," said two or three officials, who had been attracted to the spot, and then became aware of the cause of the uproar. "Order—order; leave off, gentlemen. Where's the master of the ceremonies?"

"Ah, where is he?" said some of the spectators. "Squabby want's a partner; what lady will volunteer?"

Another burst of merriment accompanied this sally.

One of the men whose duty it was to keep order in the gardens, forced his way into the ring, and endeavoured to remove Squabshot from his undignified position; but before he could effect his purpose he found himself jostled among the crowd, who tossed him about in a most unmerciful manner.

"Order, gentlemen—help!" shouted the man, and two or three more of the officials made their way into the centre to assist their companion.

"This cannot be permitted," said one of them; "it is against the rules of the gardens."

"You be d—d," said a man, dressed as a *Postillon de Longjumeau*, while at the same time he smacked the long whip which he carried in his hand round the body of the party he addressed, who immediately collared him, upon which a struggle ensued between the two, in which they both fell to the ground, the *postillon* undermost. Several of the dancers then pulled the officer by the legs, and dragged him along the grass towards the outer circle.

Screams of merriment accompanied this feat, and a *debardeur* challenged the man, upon his recovering his legs, to single combat. In spite of his endeavours to preserve his gravity, the official could not help laughing at the scene ; when one of the dancers, seeing him smile, slapped him on the back, and swearing he was a first rate chap, invited him to partake of some champagne.

"Who says champagne?" said Squabshot, as he turned a somersault, and stood in attitude once more upon his legs.

"I do," said the colonel. "This way, Squabshot."

"It is the mellifluous tones of my worthy friend " said Squadshot, as he by a series of eccentric steps, which would have done honour to a pantomimist, approached the colonel.

The revellers made way for him.

"A good Samaritan in the hour of need—manna in the wilderness," said Sqabshot, as he came by the side of our hero.

Then seeing the lady who was with the colonel, he took off his hat, if such an eccentric head-dress could be conscientiously called one, and made her a low obeisance.

"I am always charmed, madam, to bask in the eyes of beauty," said the gallant Squabshot. "But by my faith, Halford, I am parched. The wine—oh—oh, wine—wine, that cheers the heart, and drives away dull care."

He had partaken of enough to have floated a moderately-sized four-oared cutter already, and was consequently in a state of exhuberant mirth.

"We will adjourn to the sutling house, Squabshot."

"But stay," said the latter, "I've one or two fellows of the right sort who will go with us—hate to drink alone, you know. Here, Phil, Potter! where are you ?"

"All right," said the two worthies addressed, as they presented themselves before their friend, little Squabby.

"Come along, my boys—going to imbibe—all right. Mr. Halford—Phil. Lovegrove, Jem Potter—now you know each other."

The colonel bowed to the two individuals, who were evidently of the nondescript order of humanity.

"Now, I tell you what it is, Squab," said the colonel, in a whisper, "you must keep yourself quiet, old boy, or we shall get into a scrape; besides which, I have a respectable lady under my charge, who is not likely to appreciate the capers of you fast chaps."

"I'm as discreet as a churchwarden," said Squabshot, whose equilibrium, however, was not of the most perfect order.

They all betook themselves to the refreshment saloon.

Colonel Jack seated himself with Mrs. Swansdown, at one of the tables at the further end of the room, calling for some champagne. He directed Squabshot to regale his companions and himself at another table, as the lady did not care about the company of strangers.

While the colonel was conversing with Mrs. Swansdown, he observed two eyes peering curiously from under a mask at himself and his female companion. Every movement made by himself or Mrs. Swansdown, was watched intently by the owner of the aforesaid eyes.

The colonel felt uncomfortable, and was cautious in his conduct. Visions of police officers and Jonathan Wild rushed past him. Was he recognised? This was not a pleasing thought, and it rendered him very fidgetty, for in the disguise assumed by all the visitors to Ranelagh, it was impossible to tell who might be there.

Our hero made up his mind to cut his visit as short as possible, and as Squabshot came to his table to pledge the lady in a glass of wine, he said to him—

"Do you see that individual, dressed in a suit of black, silk stockings, knee breeches, and buckles in his shoes ?"

"Where ?"

"Hush—don't look round suddenly. On the other side of the room near the door."

"What, he of the portly form ?" asked Squabshot.

"Exactly."

"Yes, I see him. Who is he ?"

"That's just what I want to know. He has been looking curiously here for some time past."

"Has he though ?"

"Suppose you go over and pretend to know him. You may perhaps recognise him by the sound of his voice."

"All right, I'm on—leave it to me," and away went Squabshot.

Leaning over the table, and looking into the eyes of the individual in question, Squabshot said naturally enough, as though he recognised an old friend—

"What, Slider, who would have thought of seeing you."

"You're mistaken, sir—I am a stranger to you," said the gentleman, in not a very amiable tone of voice.

"Ah, ah, it's of no use endeavouring to come the mysterious," said Squabshot, nothing abashed. "We know each other very well."

"Indeed, sir, you are mistaken, I assure you."

"Won't do, you sly old card," said the other, wagging his head knowingly.

"I tell you, sir, I do not know you," again persisted the individual addressed. "What may be your name, sir ?"

"Squabshot, or more properly speaking little S—Swabby," for by this time his articulation was being affected from the juice of Hungary's grape—or rather doctored wine.

"Then, sir, I do not know you; but I should be greatly obliged if you could tell me who the gentleman and lady are who are sitting opposite?—I mean the gentleman in the dress of a cavalier. I observed you spoke to them just now."

"Oh, oh," thought Squabshot, who, although a little on, had his wits about him; "that's his game, is it."

Then nodding his head towards Halford, he said—

"Do you mean those two?"

"Yes."

"Oh, I don't know the lady."

"Ah, you don't, eh?'

"No.'

"Well, the gentleman. Do you know him?"

"Yes"

"What's his name?"

"Ah," said Squabshot, "now you've done it for me."

"What do you mean?"

"Why, you see, he is here on the quiet, and wouldn't like it to be known."

"I should think not," said, or rather grunted forth, the portly gentleman. "Then you won't tell me?"

"I ought not," said Squabshot; "but yet I don't know that there can be any particular harm in it. Only, you know—you appear a gentleman—and you don't mind promising not to mention the circumstance, as you might com—pro—mishe me."

"Oh, I pledge my word. Pray be seated," and the gentleman made room for Squabshot.

"Well," said the latter, "you musn't mention it again, but that gentleman in the cavalier dress is no other than the Lord Mayor himself—Squire Gubbins."

"Dear me—you don't say so," exclaimed the gentleman.

"Fact, 'pon honour. Now don't say anything about it."

Squabshot rose and left his companion in a state of bewilderment. He strolled to where the colonel was seated, and then said to him—

"Don't know the old buffer—tried to persuade him that I did, but found it no go."

"What did he say?"

"Asked who you were."

"Did he though? What did you tell him?"

"Said you were the Lord Mayor in disguise?"

"Ah, ah, capital. Does he believe it?"

"Yes, most implicitly."

"Is he a police officer?" inquired the colonel, in a whisper.

"Lord bless you, my dear boy, no! What could make you think of such a thing? Oh, no, he's a quiet old card, evidently."

The eyes of the quiet old card, were, however, still engaged in a steadfast gaze at the colonel.

"I tell you what I wish you'd do, Squabshot," said the colonel.

"All right; what is it?"

"I wish you would take this lady out in the gardens, and meet me at the back of the orchestra."

"My dear boy, I shall be charmed," answered Squabshot, "perfectly charmed."

"What for?" asked Swansdown.

"I shall be with you in a few minutes," said the colonel; "but I have to see a friend in the gardens, after which I am your devoted slave."

"If any one asks you who the lady is, she's your wife—do you understand."

"Perfectly."

"Stay, I will retire first," said the colonel, and he rose and stalked majestically out of the saloon.

The individual with the inquiring eyes favoured him with a scrutinising glance, in which wonder and indignation were blended.

Soon after the colonel had made a safe exit, Squabshot, offering his arm to Mrs. Swansdown, was about to conduct her out, followed by his two friends, Potter and Phil Lovegrove. As he was about to pass through the door, the gentleman with whom he had been previously conversing with rose from his seat, and in an abrupt manner laid hold of his arm and said—

"May I ask who the lady is that you are escorting about?"

"My wife," said Squabshot, with admirable coolness.

"Sir," said the other, "it is but a few minutes ago that you said you did not know the lady. How do you reconcile that assertion, sir, with the one you are now making?'

"Ah, I see, you want to know too much," said Squabshot, shaking his head knowingly.

"Your conduct is most unaccountable," said the portly gentleman.

"Why, the fact is, old boy," said Squabshot, in a mysterious whisper, "if you had a wife yourself, and brought her to these gardens, you would not wish every tomfool to know it, would you?"

"Perhaps not—perhaps not."

"Well, then, you might have some consideration for me. I'm sure I have been civil enough to you."

"Are you sure this lady's your wife?"

"Well, that's a good one. What do you think of that, Phil?"

"Never heard of such a thing. The idea of a man not knowing his own wife," answered the individual addressed. "All I know is, that we were both at the wedding," continued Phil, turning to Potter for a corroboration of his assertion.

"That we were," said Potter, who, like most of Squabshot's companions, was always ready to back up the statements of his friends.

"Umph," growled the gentlemen in black smalls, "I suppose I am bound to believe them, and yet I could have sworn—that I certainly could—I could have almost sworn that—"

"Sworn what ?"

"That she was my wife, sir !" said the gentleman.

A slight scream issued from the throat of the lady, and Squabshot turned to her and said—

"Sarah, my dear, don't alarm yourself. Mistakes of this sort will occur in the best regulated families."

"I suppose I am bound to take your word, sir," said the individual in black; "but I know my wife is in these gardens, in much the same costume as this lady. Perhaps she will oblige me by taking off her mask ?"

"Dear me, no, my dear, don't do anything of the sort," said Squabshot, pretending to imagine that she was about to comply with his request, when, in reality, nothing was further from her thoughts.

"You really are asking too much sir," said Potter, reprovingly, "a great deal too much. It is not the custom, on occasions of this sort, for any gentleman or lady to unmask."

"It would set the matter at rest, sir," said the party addressed.

"What matter ?"

"My suspicions."

"Psha, what have we to do with your suspicions ? Every gentleman who comes into these gardens is not bound to unmask his wife because some blundering person chooses to imagine her his. It s perfectly preposterous."

While Squabshot's two friends were arguing with the corpulent gentleman, the former sheered off with Mrs. Swansdown without further parley. He immediately sought the colonel at the back of the orchestra, whither he conveyed Mrs. Swansdown according to agreement.

"Well," inquired our hero, "you got clear off, it seems."

"Here we are," replied Squabshot; "but as to getting clear off, why, I never met with such an obstinate buffer in the whole course of my life."

"How so ?"

"Oh," exclaimed Mrs. Swansdown, who was trembling like an aspen leaf, "oh, dear, dear, what shall I do ?—I am ruined—lost—irretrievably lost !"

"What's the matter, my dearest lady ?" inquired the colonel, endeavouring to pacify her.

"That gentleman was my husband, and I am certain he has recognised me."

"Your husband ?"

"Yes," said Squabshot, "so he said himself, and what is more, obstinately persisted in it."

"Where shall I go to, and what am to do ?" said Mrs. Swansdown. "I am a ruined woman, and my peace of mind is for ever destroyed. Who would have thought of Mr. Swansdown coming here ?"

"Never mind, my dear madam, leave it to me ; I will take care you are not compromised."

"He believes implicitly that you are the Lord Mayor," said Squabshot; "so keep it up, old boy."

The colonel was about to leave the spot, when he again observed the same pair of eyes peering through the mask. The owner of the aforesaid eyes touched the colonel on the elbow and said—

"A word with you, sir, if you please."

"Certainly," said the colonel, as he left the lady's arm, and handed her over to Squabshot.

"You must pardon me," said the gentleman, "but I believe I am addressing the Lord Mayor ?"

"How did you know that ?"

"Your friend—"

"Ah, that was very wrong of him."

"It will go no further, believe me. I have passed my word."

"What is your object in addressing me ?" inquired the colonel, hastily.

"That lady, whom your friend has on his arm, I believe, nay, I may say I almost know to be, no other than my wife. Your friend has the effrontery to pass her off for his."

"Oh, matters are easily explained," said the colonel, confidentially. "The fact is, that you know, I suppose, there has in the course of the evening been a terrible row in these gardens. That lady was in imminent danger from several ruffians, and I had the satisfaction of being instrumental in rescuing her from her unpleasant situation."

"It was very kind of you, I am sure."

"Yes ; well, when this had taken place, I escorted her about the gardens, where I met with that little individual, who is an eccentric sort of a character. He claimed her as his wife. I knew, or rather judged, such was not the case ; but in an entertainment of this sort, why, you know, full latitude is allowed ; and as I had other engagements, why of course I was glad to avail myself of his services, to afford the lady protection. May I ask your name, sir ?"

"Swansdown, of Headington, near Oxford," said the gentleman.

"Then without doubt the lady is your wife. What, ho! Squabshot!" shouted out the colonel. "I pray you resign this lady to better keeping."

"What, my wife!" indignantly remonstrated the party addressed.

"Come, let there be an end of this. Mrs. Swansdown, your husband," continued the colonel, as he laid hold of the lady's hand, and presented her to her liege lord. "I am happy, sir, to have been able to afford your good lady protection when most needed," he added, bowing politely to the gentleman, "and esteem it fortunate that circumstances have turned out as they have."

This was said with so much grace and dignity, that Mr. Swansdown was fairly taken in, and was profuse in his thanks, and at the same time invited the colonel to spend a short time with him at his estate in Headington.

"And I am to lose my wife, it appears, amongst the lot of you," said Squabshot, pretending to pull a most rueful visage.

"Go along with you," said the colonel; "a truce to that now. A joke is all very well in its place."

Then speaking in a lower tone, he said to the lady—

"Your husband will inform you, madam, that you have had no less a person than the Lord Mayor, himself, to afford you protection."

"Is it possible, sir?" said the lady, with well feigned surprise.

"Yes, my dear," said her husband, "it is true enough. There's an adventure."

"What made you come here, Joseph?" said the lady.

"To seek for you, my dear—to seek for you."

"Ah, how did you know I was here?"

"Alfred told me."

"Oh, did he?"

Alfred was the page, and Mrs. Swansdown determined that his career in her establishment should be of short duration. Poor Alfred's doom was sealed.

So admirably had the colonel and the lady acted their respective parts, that dust was thrown into the eyes of the too confiding Swansdown, who went away with the full impression that he owed our hero a deep debt of gratitude, and he left the gardens perfectly contented.

Colonel Jack, however, had ascertained from the lady that their stay in London would be protracted for some weeks, and he had extracted from her another appointment for a future day.

As to Squabshot, it would be useless to follow him through all his adventures after the departure of the Swansdown pair. There was scarcely any conceivable trick but what

he was up to, and, of course, he was the very last individual to leave the grounds.

———

CHAPTER XIX.

THE MISER.—THE MIDNIGHT MURDER.— OSBORNE'S PREDICAMENT.

IN that neighbourhood now known as Cow Cross, lying at the back or rather at the side of Hick's Hall, or what is now termed the Clerkenwell Session's House, there resided an old miser, who was supposed to be immensely rich.

Year after year had this man been seen about by the inhabitants of Clerkenwell, that the fact of his existence had become a tradition of the neighbourhood Year after year had this man been gathering grist and storing up grain.

In miserable rags he wandered about, buying and selling anything and everything, it mattered not what, so long as he could reap a profit.

He was alone in the world, and lived but to hoard up wealth. For what? We shall see.

One night, Jaber Crudge, that was the miser's name, was returning home to his miserable domicile; the streets were comparatively deserted, for it was near midnight, and the night was a dark one, but Jaber Crudge could find his way to his home blindfolded, so well had he been accustomed to tread the narrow, crooked, and dirty courts and streets.

He had passed down that beautiful spot, now known as Mutton Hill, and was turning round into Cow Cross by the celebrated Session's House, when, from one of the courts, the figure of a man emerged:

"Here he is, Jem," the man exclaimed, evidently to a companion in ambush.

The miser paused as he heard the latter words, and, feeling in his breast, placed his hand upon the handle of his knife. In another minute he found himself firmly grasped in the arms of some desperate assailant.

The miser drew from beneath his garments a long knife, with which he was about to wound his adversary, who, however, grasped his upraised arm firmly by the wrist, and said in a hoarse voice:

"Your keys, you old wretch—or, by the Lord, you will be made food for worms if you refuse."

"Help—help!" shouted the old man; but his cries were stopped by his assailant's hand, placed over his mouth.

"Now, Jem," said one of the men, "the keys."

"Where are they?" inquired the one addressed as Jem.

"He keeps his keys in his right hand pocket. Look sharp."

The man then thrust his hand hastily into the pockets of the miser, who, nevertheless, old as he was, made desperate struggles to release himself from the grasp of the robber. He succeeded in releasing the hand which grasped the knife, and with it inflicted a severe wound upon his adversary.

"D——n," shouted the man, "take that, you old miscreant," and he dealt the old miser a fearful wound in the chest, from which the crimson tide flowed in torrents. The unfortunate man sent forth a deep groan, and struck out madly with the knife he still held in his hand.

"Who would have thought the old rascal had so much fight in him?" said one of the assailants to the other.

A still more determined search was instituted for the keys, which appeared to be the sole object of the attack, but in this they were unsuccessful.

Jaber Crudge again called out for assistance—a distant watchman sprung his rattle incessantly as he heard the cries and then relapsed into somnolency—and the figure of a man was observed by the robbers making towards them.

"Queered, by ——," exclaimed the men, who, in their rage, gave the miser another and more desperate wound, and immediately took to their heels.

The unfortunate object of this murderous attack presented a most ghastly appearance; his aged and lined features were of an ashy hue, and he staggered and would have fallen had he not caught hold of some railings which run in front of one of the houses.

The young man who was hastening to the spot now arrived by the side of the wounded miser.

He started back in horror as he observed the dark pool of blood which had streamed on to the pavement.

"Mercy on me, but this is horrible," exclaimed Osborne, for the new-comer was no other than he.

"Help—help," said the miser, in a faint voice.

"Merciful Heaven! but this is a crime of a most horrible nature. Lean on me, my friend—where do you live? You had better go to the nearest surgeon's."

"No—no," exclaimed Jaber, "home—oh, Heavens, I faint."

"Where is your residence, my friend?" inquired Osborne.

"But a hundred yards from here—lead me thither."

Osborne supported the miser as well as he could, holding a handkerchief to his wounds to staunch the blood, which continued to flow in one continuous stream, perfectly horrible to behold.

"Who was it that attacked you?" inquired Osborne.

"Don't know them—they sprang upon me in the dark. Have mercy on me. I feel so weak and faint, and all—all—" he paused abruptly.

With considerable difficulty the old man succeeded in reaching a wretched domicile, which, he informed his companion, was his home.

Having arrived at the door, he felt for the keys, which he had secreted in his boots—no wonder, therefore, that the robbers did not succeed in finding them in any of his pockets.

He was too weak to turn the wards of the lock, so Osborne, when the miser had selected the key which fitted the outer door, opened it for him, and found himself in a dark passage—so dark, indeed, was it, that he could not see his way in.

The wounded man, however, managed to stagger into an apartment on the ground floor, and placing a tinder-box before Osborne the latter hastily struck a light and illumed the apartment by lighting a miserable candle.

The room was wretched to the last degree. There was scarcely any furniture, and what there was was covered with dust and dirt, which seemed to be the accumulation of ages. Luckily, in the cupboard, there was a bottle with some brandy in it, this Osborne procured at the direction of its owner, and poured some of its contents down the throat of the fainting man who recovered somewhat under its influence.

"Thanks," said the old man, feebly, "I am better now."

Osborne inquired if there was any other occupant in the house; the answer was in the negative. He then tore into strips a piece of calico, which happened to be in the apartment, and bound up the other's wounds as well as he could under the circumstances, but they were, evidently, of such a nature as to give rise to the supposition in Osborne's mind that the miserable man's hours were numbered—indeed, it seemed surprising to him how he had survived so long—having performed this task, Osborne suggested to his companion the propriety of immediately sending for surgical assistance.

The old man clasped the arm of his friend as though it were in a vice, and begged him to remain where he was.

Osborne was so bewildered by the new and extraordinary situation in which he found himself that he knew not how to act, and what to do, for the best under the circumstances.

"Take me up stairs," said the miser, feebly, but yet with an evident degree of anxiety; "take me up stairs—oh, pray take me up stairs!"

"You cannot possibly walk up—I must carry you."

"Can you do so?"

"Certainly. Do you think you are strong enough to hold the light?"

"Yes—certainly."

With this Osborne gently lifted the aged man in his arms as though he were a child —indeed, he was light enough. He was conveyed up to a room on the first floor, and having arrived at the door, an impediment was offered to their entrance.

The door was fastened firmly with a spring lock, and the right key had to be selected before it could be opened, nevertheless, Osborne

No. 17.

held the wounded man in his arms until he had selected the right one, and then managed to open the door; when this was done, there was found another, an inner door—this was also firmly locked, and had to undergo a similar process. When this was done, Osborne found himself in a spacious apartment, which from the character of the ceiling, walls, and fire-place, he should suppose to have belonged to a building of great antiquity, which was in reality the case.

There was a large, old-fashioned, massive, bedstead in the room, upon the bed of which the miser desired to be laid. When Osborne had complied with his request he took a rapid survey of the apartment.

It was filled with an heterogeneous mass of furniture, articles of vertu and jewels of various descriptions. Heaps of oil paintings lay about, boxes, massive carved oak chests, China, statuary, tapestry, oak carvings, in fact, a mass of materials of different descriptions, too numerous and of too mixed a character to comprehend at one glance. A handsome Swiss clock ticked on the elaborately carved mantle-place—it told the hour it was—forty minutes past midnight. Osborne observed this and referred to his watch and found the dial of the clock correct in its indication.

The wounded man now breathed heavily, and was evidently suffering great pain.

"I will now go for a doctor," said Osborne, soothingly.

"No—no," answered the miser, " I pray you do not."

"But I must, my friend, you will be sure to die else."

"Die !"

"Come, let me go, I beseech you," said Osborne.

"No—no ; give me—"

"What ?"

"My keys."

Osborne searched for the required keys, which having found, he presented them to the sinking man, who eagerly clutched them, and selecting one from the bunch, gave it to Osborne, and desired him to open a large chest which was placed by the side of the room.

Osborne opened it, agreeable to the request of the miser.

It was filled with gold coins, and must have contained an immense amount of wealth.

Osborne stood wonderstruck at the vast amount of money displayed to his gaze.

The miser gloated over the open chest, and prayed of Osborne to drag it to the bedside. This was a task which the latter found some difficulty in accomplishing. It was prodigiously heavy, and seemed to defy all efforts to move it ; but the miser urged him to persevere, when by superhuman exertion, Osborne succeeded in bringing the chest to the bedside of the suffering man, who immediately hung over his wealth with fond ecstacy.

He took up a handful of pieces, and run them through his hand, letting them fall into the open chest again ; and the chinking of the falling pieces seemed to be music to the ears of the prostrate man.

Even in this, the last hour of his existence, the ruling passion was strong in death.

For this he had lived and toiled, denying himself all but the common necessaries of life, and even of these he had allowed himself but a very insignificant share, barely enough to keep life and soul together.

Osborne contemplated the figure of the prostrate man with eyes of strange curiosity.

Was it possible, he thought, that the wretched emaciated object before him had passed a life of self denial to amass so much dross, which never could be of any use to him, and which he could never live to enjoy ?

Presently the miser desired Osborne to seek in the cupboard, at the further end of the room, for some cordial, as an increased pallor overspread his features.

"There, in the left hand corner," said the miser, with difficulty, for articulation seemed to be visibly affected, and he spoke with evident pain.

Osborne hunted in the cupboard, taking out one article after another to get at the required object, which after a search carried on for some time in silence, he succeeded in obtaining what appeared to be the object desired by the fainting man.

By this time Osborne became aware that the miserable candle which he held in his hand had burnt down nearly to the socket. Osborne turned round with the flaring candle in his hand, and gazed upon the bed where the form of the miser lay stretched.

He neither moved or groaned, which he had unceasingly done hitherto.

By the feeble, uncertain, and fitful light, Osborne could see that the old man slept the last long sleep of death.

The rigid features, the stark form, the glazed eyes, all told unmistakeably that life was no longer there.

The young man approached the bedside, and looked upon the wan and emaciated features of the deceased man, which now presented a frightful appearance to his fascinated gaze.

As his looks were rivetted upon the ghastly object, his flesh began to creep, as he became cognisant of some strange unaccountable noise in the apartment. He cast a furtive and hasty glance around the room, but could distinguish no living object to account for the strange sound.

He was not a superstitious man, nevertheless he felt himself in an awful situation in this chamber of death, and fears of no common order took possession of his soul.

Turning his glance again upon the bed, he became aware that there was something slowly moving upon its surface. An undefined horror crept over him, and his knees actually knocked together, and his hand trembled.

As he gazed upon the bed, he felt a strange looking pair of eyes meet his own. So appalled was he at this discovery, that for the moment he looked only at the strange eyes which were looking into his. Pesently, however, he observed that they belonged to a large black cat, who had crept up on the bed, and was now stretching herself out, and putting up her back, as though she were inquiring who the new comer was in her master's apartment.

This incident, trifling as it was in itself, lent an additional horror to the scene—at least, such was Osborne's impression; and he hastily went forward, upon the impulse of the moment, to drive the animal from its present position.

In his endeavour to do this, the candle which he held in his hand flared suddenly up, illumining for a moment the whole apartment with a fitful and sudden glare, and then with a sudden spluttering it went completely out.

Darkness now enshrouded the whole scene, darkness most horrible; but through that gloom, however—owing to the partial light which found its way through the dingy lattice windows—Osborne could trace the outline of the drapery of the bed furniture, the rigid lineaments of the dead man, and the strange and lurid eyes of the black cat.

Cold drops of perspiration stood upon his brow—a dead weight seemed at his heart—fire was in his brain—and an accumulation of horrors presented themselves to his heated and fevered imagination.

The clock on the mantelpiece chimed the hour, which reminded him of his first entrance into that strange apartment, and the circumstances which had led to his present unenviable position.

He bitterly cursed his folly for not insisting upon going for a doctor in the first instance, and began to have very natural fears as to what might be the result to himself; as there was no evidence but his own as to the cause of the wretched man's death.

As these thoughts presented themselves to his imagination, a fresh alarm for his own future safety made itself manifest. Hesitating how to act, he still kept his gaze fixed upon the eyes of the cat. He had not the courage to move and drive her from the spot, but eventually turned round and instituted a search for a candle or matches. He luckily found a few of the latter beside a tinder box, with which he immediately struck a light, and ignited one of the matches. With this he searched about for a candle, but was unable to meet with one before the match burnt itself out.

Osborne then struck another match, and commenced another search, but with no better success.

During the time each of the matches burnt, Osborne found himself surrounded with a lesser shade of horrors; but as darkness again ensued, the same deadening sense of oppression took possession of him.

What was to be done?

Match after match was being consumed in the fruitless endeavour to find a candle,

which he now began to think was an impossibility.

Upon igniting another match, he looked in the fire place to see if there was any fuel to light a fire. There was a mass of waste paper in the grate, and in the cupboard a few faggots of wood.

Arranging some paper at the bottom of the grate, and putting some wood on the top, he hastily set fire to the same, and had the satisfaction of producing a good blaze in the apartment; but he could not tell how long this would last, for coals there were none.

However, it relieved it for a time from the oppressive and horrible darkness which seemed to be driving him into madness.

While the fire was burning, he hastily sought for the door by which he had entered.

It was fastened!

He remembered then that both the doors had shut to with a slam, and he soon became aware that the inner one at any rate was fastened with a spring lock, which defied all his efforts to open.

A shudder passed through his frame as the thought came across him that he was a prisoner in this chamber of death, with no other companions but the black cat and the stark and rigid figure of the corpse.

This thought was indeed a horrible one, and made his cheek blanch with fear.

His first thought was to seek for the keys. Upon turning round, he observed them still in the grasp of the miser, who must have taken them out of the lock of the oak chest upon his wheeling it to the bedside.

Osborne could not find courage enough to try to wrest the bunch of keys from the dead man's hand; yet his necessity was such—his danger so imminent—that repugnant as was the act, he felt that it must be accomplished.

The fire by this time began to burn low, and gave symptoms of going out. Osborne sought in the closet for some more faggots of wood. There were but a few left, nevertheless he put them on, and in a few moments they crackled and emitted a bright blaze.

While they were yet burning, Osborne nerved himself up, as best he could, to undertake the hideous task of obtaining possession of the keys.

He approached the bedside of the corpse, which was appalling to look upon

It was the first time Osborne had looked upon a dead body, which with most of us, under the most favourable circumstances, generally produces a painful impression upon the senses; but in the present case the contemplation was horrible to the last degree. The ghastly face—the blood-stained clothes—the distorted features—all served to lend an accumulation of horrors to the mind of Osborne, who however now had but one thought, the possession of the keys, which he at once seized, and endeavoured to wrest from the dead man's grasp ; but so tightly did the emaciated and icy fingers clutch them, that Osborne found it impossible to remove them from the hand of the deceased man, which closed over them as though they were in a vice.

In vain he endeavoured to remove one finger after the other, they defied all his efforts, and he grew so nervous over his task, that his arms and hands seemed to have lost their natural muscular strength. He felt the perspiration pour down his face and body as he made repeated but ineffectual efforts to dislodge the keys.

While engaged in this task, the black cat came towards him, and rubbed her sides and head against his hands, and began purring with satisfaction, at finding a living being as a companion. Osborne gently put her from him as he again essayed to obtain possession of the keys.

Turning the hand of the deceased man back with a violent effort, he at length succeeded in detaching the bunch of keys.

It was well he had succeeded as he did, for by the time he had done so, the fire began to burn low, so low indeed, that it was all but out.

Alarmed at the prospect of darkness again, Osborne rushed wildly about the apartment in search of more fuel. Alas, there was no more wood to be found, but he threw on whatever papers lay handy, regardless of their importance.

Again a bright flame was the consequence, which, however, was but of a fugitive character, and would soon burn itself out. He strove wildly to obtain something of a more enduring character wherewith to sustain a fire, but his search was in vain.

To be left in darkness again, in that apartment, had in it, to his mind, something dreadful.

He rushed to the door and tried several of the keys without success—they none fitted the lock. He made frantic efforts to find the right one before the light of the fire departed.

In his alarm he became so confused, that he lost his presence of mind, and was unable to act with that clearness and care he would have been able to do under less painful circumstances.

At length he fancied he had the key belonging to the lock. He turned it with considerable force, but there seemed to be some impediment to its action.

As the light of the fire waned, he used force—horrible !—the key, which was an old one and much eaten away with rust, snapped short off at the end of the tube, and left a portion of it sticking in the lock.

Poor Osborne's situation was now, indeed, a dreadful one.

To turn the lock was now an impossibility, and he found himself a prisoner, alone, in a strange apartment, with a murdered man lying prostrate upon his bed.

By this time darkness had again ensued, and the situation of the city clerk was of a nature which a man possessed of the most iron nerves would shudder at the very contemplation of. Groping about in that lonely and desolate apartment, Osborne succeeded in finding a seat, and burying his face in his hands, he sought to shut out the horrible phantasmagoria which oppressed his imagination.

How he prayed for the light of day !

How many more hours of horrible suspense were in store for him ? What new events would the morrow bring ?

Truthful in his nature, he was determined to tell his own unvarnished tale to the first person whom he might see—but then, how would his present situation be known ? There did not appear to be any other tenant of the old and delapidated building in which he found himself a prisoner. Unless he could find some means of communication with the outer world, he might be there for days without a single human being coming to his assistance.

This thought oppressed him still more.

He presently became aware of the presence of a companion—the cat was climbing upon his knee ; and although he had at first been so intimidated by her appearance, he felt some little relief in any living companion, and he caressed her as she coiled herself up on his knee.

The clock struck four !

When would morning break ?—Minutes seemed hours in his present situation, and hours days.—And when morning did pale in the horizon, what then ?

A man was murdered, and he had been with him in his last hour. The natural inquiry would be—why did he not seek for surgical assistance in a case of such immediate and imminent danger? Who committed the murder ? Some unknown person in the street. What proof was there of that fact ? Osborne's own testimony, uncorroborated by any other evidence.

As he reflected upon all these facts, a cold shudder ran through his frame, and he felt his teeth chatter. Who would believe him ? Nevertheless, strong in the consciousness of his own innocence, he determined to brave the worst ; but then the night of horror he had to pass through ! Sleep was out of the question, nay, even a calm state was not to be thought of, such in fact, under the circumstances, was an impossibility.

The clock struck five !

Was there a dawn of light in the horizon? Yes, the room was evidently lighter—he could see more distinctly—the furniture in the apartment—the heterogenous heap of articles on the floor—the heavy hangings of the bed—the lattice windows assumed a less opaque appearance—yes, without doubt, the dawn was coming.

Oh, how he prayed for the blessed light of day. It would be some comfort to know that the world without was peopled with human beings, and that endless tide of humanity was passing through the streets once more, each busy with his own particular errand.

As this thought occurred to him, he rose and approached the window of the apartment. He had to pass close by the bed where the corpse lay, but nevertheless he was anxious to see if it commanded a view of the street. It was a lattice window, as has been before observed. He had some difficulty in opening it at first, but he did succeed notwithstanding, and flung back one of the windows, and thrust his head through the opening; he then had a view of the street. No one was at present visible, indeed it was not as yet sufficiently light to discern any passenger had there been any passing, and the house being one of those old fashioned ones, the sides of which abounded in several large projections, he could not conveniently obtain a view of the pavement upon that side where the house itself stood, even supposing it were sufficiently light for him to observe the passengers.

Osborne found some consolation in looking out upon the now deserted street. Anything was better than being immured in that gloomy apartment with all its unpleasant associations. So he continued to gaze out upon the miserable locality and found some comfort even in that—anything was better than the sight within.

In the course of a short time the day began to dawn visibly, and the light of morning was hailed with delight by the wretched occupant of the chamber of death—for it told of hope and succour, or at any rate a speedy release from his present miserable position of suspense and anxiety.

As yet the day was young, and no pedestrians were visible—still Osborne watched anxiously, and did not withdraw from the window.

Now at the time of which we write it was the duty of the watchman to call the hours —a duty in the present instance "more honoured in the breach than the observance;" for no voice of any vigilant "Charlie" had as yet saluted the ears of Osborne, however, as he gazed out upon the street, he was charmed to observe in the distance, as the first streak of morning appeared, the form of one of these watchful guardians of the silent night. He was calling in a cracked voice:

"Past five 'clock, and a fine morning."

Osborne anxiously awaited his approach beneath his window—for he had the satisfaction to observe that the man was coming that way.

As he came within call Osborne shouted out in a loud voice to attract his attention, but he took no heed of it, but continued to shout out the hour apparently with great satisfaction to himself.

"Help!—murder!" shouted out Osborne, as he saw that the only occupant of the street was passing without taking the slightest notice of him.

In an earlier number of this work we informed the reader that, amongst other fancies, we had a theory that waggoners were proverbially deaf—that is the old country waggoners; we have the same theory with regard to the old London watchmen, whom we believe, from the chronicles that have reached us of these worthies, make it a point of being deaf.

It would appear to be so in the present instance, for, however loudly Osborne called, his efforts seemed to be quite unavailing, for the man went on complacently enough, and did not condescend to take the slightest notice of the misirable prisoner in the chamber of death.

In vain Osborne called, the watchman had passed and was soon out of sight, indeed he had never been within hearing, so it appeared.

Osborne's hopes were again dashed; nevertheless he continued to watch for any other passengers.

The first persons who made their appearance after the watchman were the costermongers and purveyors of fish, who emerged from the various courts and alleys which run from the aristocratic neighbourhood of Cow Cross.

They came, several of these together, and commenced laying out their wares in the most tempting manner upon their trucks or barrows—hope again dawned upon Osborne as he observed these worthies busily at work some two or three courts off.

"Murder—help!" shouted out Osborne, once more.

A retail purveyor of the finny tribe heard the cry for help, and paused in his occupation of displaying his piscatorial dainties, and then listened with his head perked on one side.

"Hallo! help!" shouted Osborne again, in a still louder tone.

The man of fish looked round on all sides, but did not, for a moment, catch sight of Osborne, whose head, though out of window, was hidden from the other's gaze by a thick buttress which run up the side of the old building.

"Strike me lucky, Bill," said the retailer of fish to an itinerant purveyor of vegetables; "strike me lucky, if there ain't a cove in distress somewhere."

"No !" said the man of carrots and turnips, who seemed to infer that such a thing was an imposibility in so respectable a locality.

"There is then, and no flies," retorted the fishman."

"Nonsense !"

"Don't you hear ?—there."

"Ah, sure enough—I wonder what it is?" asked the respectably inclined vendor of vegetables.

"Can't be far off, that's quite certain."

"Hark ! There it is again."

"It's a man's voice."

"Yes ; that's quite certain. Well, I'm blest, if this ain't a go. Come, let us go and see."

And the two men left their trucks and proceeded towards the direction from whence the sounds emanated.

"Hallo, Bill, there's somebody looking out of the old miser's house. I s'pose he's had company and then bin and half starved one of 'em."

"Company ! Not he, unless it's his old cat."

However they looked up in the direction, and then observed the head of Osborne thrust through the open window.

"Now then, guvn'r what's the row ?" said the man of fish.

"Most horrible," exclaimed Osborne, " a fearful murder has been committed—help, I pray you."

"Murder ?"

"Yes ; pray let me out. I entreat of you to force an entrance into the house and release me."

The fishman looked at the green man, and the latter scratched his head.

"Release me, my good fellows, if you have any humanity in your composition. I have been shut up all night with a murdered man. Help—help."

"Well, but who murdered him ?—and how came you shut up with him ?" said the green man, who did not appear at all to comprehend the case.

"I will explain all satisfactorily," said Osborne, "only release me ; I am shut up in this house without a living soul in it besides myself."

"Can't you come down stairs ?" said the man.

"No ; the door of the room is closed with a spring lock, and the key is broken in it," said Osborne.

"The devil ! Well, this is a go, surely,' exclaimed the green man.

"I ain't going to break open the old chap's place to please anybody," said the purveyor of fish.

"It wouldn't be healthy," answered the vegetable seller.

"Don't see it, myself," put in the man of fish.

"The door must be forced by some one," said Osborne.

"Maybe they must, and maybe they musn't," said the man answering to the name of Bill.

This was a very guarded sentence, which no doubt the reader will duly appreciate.

"If you won't force an entrance into the house, will you go to the proper authorities and tell them of my position ? I will pay you for it."

This had an instant effect upon the two worthies who immediately consulted together.

"Where are we to go ?"

"To the nearest magistrate's office," said Osborne.

"Clerkenwell ? Oh, it ain't open yet."

"There is always some one there—or go to the watch-house if you like."

"Ah, that will be better," said Bill ; "what are we to say ?"

"I will write you a few lines, if you like," said Osborne.

"Well, do so, if you please ; me and my companion will wait while you do so. Now, Nick, keep her off the pavement."

This last observation was addressed to his son, who was allowing the donkey in the truck to stray upon the pathway.

Osborne took out his pocket-book and hastily scribbled a few lines stating the particulars of his present situation, then calling to the two men, he said :

"I have written on a piece of paper what is necessary, which perhaps you will take to the nearest watchman for me, and I have wrapped up some silver which you may keep for your trouble. Take out the money when I throw it down, and pray do not fail to convey my paper to the right quarter."

"All right, master," was the immediate answer to the last request.

Osborne threw the paper and money contained therein to one of the men, who dexteriously caught it ere it reached the ground. Upon opening it he divided its contents with his companion, after which they repaired to the watchhouse which then stood on Clerkenwell Green.

Neither of the costermongers could read, so they were utterly ignorant of the contents of Osborne's brief note. They were, however, true to their promise, and faithfully conveyed it to the watchman, agreeable to their promise.

They were ushered into the presence of the chief-officer, who sat in a commodious box, surrounded by books and papers, and with a mighty folio of loose leaves open before him —a book of fate, in fact.

There sat this Rhadamanthine man, buttoned up in a great coat—for be it blazing July, or frezing December, it is always cold at some part of the night.

Not a pleasant duty his, sitting through the long night before that folio—smoking and drinking being prohibited, the tobacco and warm alcoholic liquids only, we opine, surrepticiously indulged in ; sitting—only occasionally diversified by a sally into the night air to visit the somnolent Charlies on their beats, and learn from them what wicked deeds were being enacted during the night, or towards morning, a deputy taking his place meanwhile.

Painful duty this—almost as onerous as the Speaker of the House of Commons, but, ah, not half so weirisome, for the Rhadamanthine man in the great coat has sometimes to listen to tales of awful murders, of desperate burglaries, of harrowing suicides, of poverty and misery, that make you shudder, and your heart grow sick, and sometimes to more jocund narratives, harum-scarum escapades, drunken freaks, impudent tricks, ingenious swindles, absurd jealousy—for all jealousy is absurd, quarrels and the like—but they all, be the case murder, or be it mousetrap stealing, are entered on that loose folio which is, in fact, the charge sheet, much the same as that used in our police courts of the present day.

"Well," said the Rhadamanthine man, as the two costeromngers presented themselves before him.

"Please, sir," began Bill.

"What are you here for ?" interrupted the chief constable.

"Please, sir," replied Bill, now taking off his hat, for he felt himself in the presence of a representative of the law, and was mindful of the respect due to the same ; "please, sir, a gentleman's in trouble."

"That is nothing new. What is it about, my man ?"

The crumpled and now dirty piece of paper was presented for inspection. The officer read it carefully and then surveyed the two men.

"How did you become possessed of this, my man ?"

Bill, who was the spokesman, then explained the circumstance of their meeting with Osborne at Cow Cross.

"Murder, eh ? It's a queer story. Wait a-bit and I will go with you."

The officer left his desk, and shortly returned with two other individuals.

"Now, my men, just show us where this took place, will you ?" said the senior officer to the costermongers.

They all proceeded towards Cow Cross, the three officers, and the two costermongers leading the way.

As they went along, Bill, in reply to the questions of the officers, entered into fuller details of their meeting with Osborne. He did not, however, say anything about the silver which the latter had given him and his companion—perhaps he forgot it.

Upon their arriving at the Jew's house the head of Osborne was still visible through the open window, and an expression of satisfaction passed over his features as he beheld the four individuals making towards the spot. His features were, however, dreadfully haggard. The sight of misery which he had undergone had told upon him to a frightful extent.

"What is all this disturbance about ?" said the chief officer, calling up to Osborne at the window.

"There has been murder committed," was the reply.

"So it would seem by your note. You wrote it, I suppose ?"

"Yes."

"Break open the door," called out the chief officer.

The men at once proceeded to carry out his orders. The outer door soon yielded to their efforts, and they then found themselves in the passage of the Jew's house.

"Now we must find out the door belonging to the room in which the man says he is confined," said Mr. Blockett, for that was the name of the chief constable. "Just call up to him and ask which way it lays."

This was done, and a description of the premises given by Osborne.

"Shall we be wanted any more, sir, if you please ?" said Bill touching his hat to the chief officer.

"No ; you may go. But, stay, give me your names and addresses."

This was done, and Blockett put them down in his pocket-book as the men went off glad enough to be rid of so unpleasant a business.

They had hardly emerged through the door when they were suddenly called back by Mr. Blockett, who seemed to have taken a second thought in the matter.

"Stop a bit, my man, you had better stay till we force an entrance into the room. Your evidence may be wanted, and you will be witnesses, at all events."

They did not at all relish this last command, but dared not murmur, so they passively awaited the result.

The officer endeavoured to force the outer door of the apartment which led into the room where Osborne was confined. This was a task, however, which they found much more difficult than had at first been anticipated. The lock was so strong, that it defied all their efforts to open it. Mr. Blockett seeing that, in all probability, their efforts would not be attended with success, sent off one of the officers in quest of a locksmith, who resided in the immediate neighbourhood. In a short time they returned with the smith, who, after some time succeeded in opening the outer door.

They were all of them much surprised at finding an inner one even more strong than that upon which they had been operating, besides which, the key Osborne had broken in the lock entirely precluded the possibility of its being picked.

The smith was, therefore, under the necessity of boring several holes in the door with a centre bit, and then, with a fine saw, cutting the lock out.

This operation occupied some time, and the costermongers were in great trouble at being detained so long from their daily avocations.

When at length the inner door was forced, Mr. Blockett and his companions entered the miser's apartment, and, accustomed as they were to scenes of this description, they stood appalled at the shocking spectacle which the old man presented as he lay in the close embrace of death. The ghastly features distorted with pain in the last death agony—the emaciated hands firmly clenched, the enensanguined cloth, all lent a horror to make up a picture of terrible reality, now shown clear and distinct in the morning's light.

Blockett regarded Osborne with a scrutinising and suspicious glance, the latter's features were so haggard and wan in their appearance that, to the eyes of the officer, he looked a guilty man.

"Umph!" said Blockett, turning to Osborne. "Here has been murder, sure enough, but by whom, that's the next question."

"That I am unable to say," said Osborne.

"You will have to give an account of it, seeing that you were the only person present. How came you here? Do you know the man?"

"No, sir, I never saw him before in my life."

"Then how came you here?"

Osborne explained the particulars of the affray in the street on the previous night, and his arriving up at the moment the miser was staggering from the wounds he had received. He then informed the officer that, at the earnest request of the miser he conducted him home to his own residence, explaining at the same time all that occurred after he had entered the house with its owner.

"The circumstances are altogether singular and mysterious," said Blockett, "and I tell you what it is, young man: you have

acted in any case very imprudently—very much so indeed. It ain't, of course, for me to say, but you'll have a hard job to clear yourself of suspicion, leastways, if we don't find the two men who are supposed to have committed this crime."

"Good heavens," said Osborne, "you do not surely blame me for doing an act of kindness to a suffering fellow creature?"

"It is not any business of mine," said Blockett, "and it is not to me that you will have to give any answer. It is only my duty to take you into custody."

"Custody!" exclaimed Osborne, in affright. I shall be a ruined man. My character will be blasted. Merciful powers! this is horrible!"

"It can't be helped," said Mr. Blockett. "I must do my duty. It isn't because you are called upon to give an explanation to the proper authorities that you should be deemed a guilty man."

"Guilty! I should hope not."

"You see," said Blockett, "you ought at once to have given notice to the watch of this murder, not have remained here with the dying man."

"How could I when I found myself locked in?"

"Ah—no. That was very awkward, certainly."

"Besides, I did call out to a watchman who was passing."

"Well, and what did he say?"

"He did not appear to hear me, for he walked on without taking any notice."

Oh, indeed!"

"Please, sir," inquired Bill, the costermonger, "shall we be wanted any longer? Me and my mate want to go our rounds."

"No, my men, I believe there is nothing more required of you. I have got both your addresses, and you will be obliged to come and give your evidence to-morrow."

"Thank you, sir," said Bill, then turning to his companion, he said, "we had better hook it then," and so the two departed, very glad to get leave of absence.

"My eye," said Bill, when he had got out into the street, "this here is a go. I wonder if that cove with the pale face has settled the old buffer's hash?"

"Seems like it to me," was the other's rejoinder—"deuced like it, and no gammon."

"Do you believe about the attack in the street?"

"Seems a queer start to me."

"I hope as how we shan't be lugged into the affair."

"I'm precious sorry we had any hand in it."

"So am I."

That vigilant and efficient officer Mr. Blockett locked up the house of the miser as

well as he could, and left two of his brother officers to watch the premises while he proceeded with Osborne to the watch-house.

"And now, young man," said Blockett, "you will please to just show me, as we go along, where this affair took place when you first came up."

Osborne, as they went along, showed the officer the traces of blood upon the pavement, which were distinctly visible. As they arrived at the spot where the attack had first taken place, a dark pool of blood was observed by Blockett, together with several spots upon the adjacent houses.

"And which course did the men take?" said the officer.

Osborne pointed out the way they had taken, but said it was so dark at the time that he could not be certain.

No. 18.

"Should you know them again?" was the next inquiry.

"No, I did not catch sight of their features," he answered. "Indeed they had taken themselves off before I arrived at the spot."

"Umph! that's unfortunate."

They now proceeded to the watchhouse, where Osborne was detained while Blockett proceeded to the nearest magistrate's office to give a detail of the events of the previous night.

An order was given for Osborne to appear at the magistrate's office to undergo his first examination, and notice was issued to the coroner to sit upon the dead body of the miser.

CHAPTER XX.

OSBORNE'S DIFFICULTY.—INTRODUCTION TO MR. SHARPTHORNE.—EXAMINATION BEFORE THE MAGISTRATE.

OSBORNE, in his present hour of misfortune, found himself completely borne down. He had never been in custody before, for either debt, or upon the most trifling or insignificant charge, and he now felt that he was surrounded by a host of suspicious circumstances which gave rise to his worst fears. The very fact of being imprisoned, and the necessity of having to undergo an examination was, to his sensitive mind, most repugnant.

What would the world say ?—and, alas ! worse than all, what would Honora Langford think ? He felt that the very fact of his being mixed up in so unfortunate a transaction would, in all probability, be the means of digging a deep gulf between himself and Honora. This thought was agony to him, more than all the rest, for he doubted not but his rival would avail himself of the circumstance to prejudice him in the eyes of Honora and her father.

Osborne had but few friends in London, in fact, he was but little known in the metropolis, for being a man of steady and retiring habits, he was not likely to form new acquaintances ; and beyond his employers, fellow clerks, Squabshot and Halford, he did not know whose advice to seek in his present difficulty, for he was utterly inefficient to act for himself, and the chief officer kept pressing upon him the necessity of employing a lawyer to defend him.

Osborne hardly knew what course to pursue. To send to Mr. Langford or his employers was out of the question, and so he wrote a note to Halford detailing all the particulars, and at the same time sent a messenger to Squabshot, who would, at any rate, be able to answer for his respectability, and attest to his lodging in Goswell Street, and being habitually a steady quiet man in his general habits.

Osborne was conveyed to the Clerkenwell Police Court to undergo his first examination, we say first, as it was not at all probable that he would be discharged there and then.

While awaiting his turn in the outer office he was informed by one of the officials that Mr. Squabshot and another gentleman desired to see him.

They were at once admitted, and for Osborne's accommodation, they were all three shown into a private room leading out from one of the passages.

"My dear Osborne," said Squabshot, who was really a good hearted little man, with all his eccentricities. "I am sorry you've got yourself into this scrape. It is indeed a sad affair, and so, my boy, you must excuse the liberty I have taken, but the officer thought you were foolish in not at once having legal advice, and so I thought myself; and as this gentleman, who is a lawyer, happened to be at my place at the time your note came, I thought it advisable to bring him to see you at once. Mr. Sharpthorne," he continued, turning to the lawyer, whom the reader already knows, "my friend, Mr. Osborne, of whom I have already spoken."

The lawyer called upon his parchment features one of his most confidential grins, and bowing obsequiously to Osborne, said—

"So you have had the misfortune to be present at a murder, I understand ?"

"Yes," answered Osborne, who had some faint recollection of Mr. Sharpthorne's name being familiar to him, and at the same time, if he remembered rightly, the impression that remained on his mind was not a favourable one towards Sharpthorne.

He did not exactly remember where he had heard the name of the lawyer mentioned, but that he had somewhere or other he was fully convinced.

"If you want any one to help you over the stile," said Squabshot, in a whisper to Osborne, as the lawyer pretended to be busily engaged in the inspection of a paper at the further end of the room ; "if you want anybody to pull you through, why, Sharpthorne's the man. There's no mistake about that—keen as a hawk, and fly to every move."

"You think I had better employ him, then ?" asked Osborne, who now began to be fully impressed with the necessity there was for legal advice, since this had been dinned into his head ever since he had been taken prisoner.

"Yes, yes, certainly, I've brought him on purpose. Shall I speak to him ?"

"If you please."

"Mr. Sharpthorne."

"Sir," said that individual, turning suddenly round as though he had been so absorbed in the paper he was contemplating that he had not been aware of the other's presence.

"My friend, Mr. Osborne, wants to consult you respecting his defence," said Squabshot.

"I shall have much pleasure in doing my best in the matter," said Sharpthorne, "very great pleasure," he continued, puckering up his mouth into a smile ; "and I only hope it may be brought to a satisfactory issue."

Osborne then entered into the full particulars of the case, disclosing all the circumstances with that truthfulness for which he was remarkable.

The old lawyer considered for some time, and then said :

"Umph! you have no collatoral evidence to offer, that is unfortunate."

"I have nothing but the simple truth to state, which, I should hope, any reasonable person would at once understand," said Osborne.

"Ah, yes ; let us hope so."

"Do you doubt it then ?"

"No—no ; but circumstances are awkward. There is nothing but your bare testimony to offer."

"Which, I should hope, will obtain credence."

"Let us hope so too."

"I should suppose there would be no doubt of it."

"Well, you see, my young friend, judge, magistrate and juries are apt to look upon all testimony with a more suspicious eye than we ourselves."

"You think, then, the case is likely to get my friend into trouble ?" said Squabshot with some anxiety.

"It is hardly possible at present to know what turn it may take," answered the lawyer, "it will go right enough if the two men who are supposed to have committed the deed are found."

"Supposed ?" said Osborne, indignantly ; "there is no supposition in the matter ; they, and no one else, are culpable—that must be obvious to the most obtuse understanding."

"Clearly so."

"Well, then, assuming that they are not found ?"

"Which is not very improbable," said Sharpthorne.

"Even then I do not see what I am to be blamed for ; certainly not for doing an act of common humanity."

"No," answered Mr. Sharpthorn, interjectionally.

A recapitulation of the circumstances now took place, and Orborne engaged the astute Mr. Sharpthorne as his legal adviser, which after all was about the worst thing he could have done—not from any want of professional skill or tact on the part of the lawyer, but on account of his being closely connected with one of Osborne's most bitter enemies—to-wit, the unscrupulous Sir Richard Fleetwood.

The night charges had to be disposed of before Osborne's case came on, and Squabshot left his friend and the lawyer consulting together, while he took his way into the body of the court, there to await the more serious case.

Some of the cases brought before the magistrate were grave, and some of them of a comic character.

Miserably paid women, earning scanty subsistences, were there for pledging the goods entrusted them to make up—one or two swells were fined for knocking about some venerable "Charlie"—then came an irish row, which had taken place in one of the courts in the immediate neighbourhood of the office.

It was a pugnacious sort of court this, or rather, more properly speaking, the inhabitants thereof were pugnacious in their characters, for scarcely a week passed but one or two police cases occurred.

It appeared, from the watchman's account, that in going his rounds he was alarmed by hearing screams and cheers proceed from a house in the court, and he at once entered the dwelling, in the parlour of which the disturbance was taking place. Two women were on the floor, their hands entwined in each other's hair, fighting, struggling, and scratching at each other in a most determined manner. The husbands of these two women were smoking their pipes by the chimney corner, and were cheering them on in the contest, and there were several other occupants in the room who were friends of both the parties. It could not be called a fair stand up fight, seeing that both the amazons were laying down, and kicking and scratching to their heart's delight. The watchman said that he at once endeavoured to separate them, whereupon they both set upon him, and commenced a furious assault, in which they were assisted by their husbands and several of their friends present. He endeavoured to spring his rattle for assistance, when it was wrested out of his hand, and he himself was thrown violently to the ground, when the two women jumped upon him, and beat him on the head and face with his rattle. He felt convinced that he should have been murdered had not another party of Irish (the watchman himself had a strong Hibernian accent) rushed into the room and rescued him. A general battle ensued, during which he managed to get to the door and spring his rattle, when several of the watch came and took the parties in custody who were then at the bar of the court.

The man's statement was denied by the two amazons, but the truth of it, as far as their own contest was concerned, was but too apparent upon their scarred and bleeding faces. They were fined, or otherwise subject to a short imprisonment, and were taken from the court to be again looked up, as the fine was not forthcoming.

Eventually, as the cases of lesser import were disposed of, Osborne was placed in the witness-box.

"What's this case ?" said the magistrate.

"It's about the murder of last night, sir," said the chief clerk

"Oh—ah—yes I know—at Cow Cross?"

"Yes, sir."

"Are the parties in custody?"

"We have not as yet been able to find the actual murderers," said Mr. Blockett.

"Oh—who is this young man?"

"He was with the murdered man at the time of his death."

"Ah, I see. Well, we'll hear his statement. Very little can be done in it till after the coroner's inquest, but let him proceed with his account of the matter. What is your name, sir?"

This was addressed to the party about to be examined.

"Henry Osborne."

"What is your profession or calling?"

"I am at present a clerk in a wholesale mercantile house."

"Yes, exactly. Now what do you know of this affair, and how is it you have managed to get yourself locked up in a lonely and almost untenanted house with a dying man? Imprudent was it not?"

Osborne told his tale, the particulars of which the reader is already acquainted with.

"Were there no other persons in the street besides yourself?" asked the magistrate, looking over and then under his spectacles at the witness.

"No, sir, none that I saw."

"Nor no one at the windows of the adjoining houses?"

"I did not see any one."

"That's singular, isn't it? There must have been a great noise, seeing that there had evidently been a struggle for life on the part of the miser."

"I did not see any one," said Osborne, again.

"Were there no watch about?"

"No, sir."

"Still more singular. How about the watch, Mr. Blockett? You know the exact time when this took place, where would the watchman be at that time of the night?"

"Well, your worship, he ought not to have been far off, that is quite certain."

"Would he have been within hearing, assuming the murdered man called out or uttered any cry of pain?"

"Most certainly."

"Where is the watchman who was on the beat at the time this is supposed to have occurred?"

"He is outside, your worship."

"Let him be called."

In a few seconds the man in question made his appearance.

"Well, my man," said the magistrate, sternly. "So it appears murder is committed in the public street, while you are, God knows where."

"I went my regular rounds, your worship, I assure you most solemnly," answered the watchman."

"Explain to him the time at which this affair is supposed to have occurred," said the magistrate, to the usher of the court.

The usher did as he was requested.

"Now, how is it," said the magistrate, "that you saw nothing of it? Where were you at that time?"

"Close on the spot," said the watchman, firmly.

"Then how is it you didn't see what was going on?"

"I don't know, your worship; but I am certain I was close on the spot at that very time."

"You swear that?"

"Yes, sir, most positively."

"Now, consider what you are saying; you are quite certain upon this point?"

"Quite, your worship—I swear it, most positively."

Mr. Sharpthorne now rose, and said to the watchman—

"And pray, sir, what were you about when you were in the neighbourhood of Cow Cross at the time you state?"

"Walking my rounds and calling the hour," was the answer.

"Oh, you are sure of that?"

"Yes."

"What is the length of your beat?"

"About a quarter of a mile."

"Only a quarter of a mile. Is that a fact, Mr. Blockett?"

The latter answered in the affirmative.

"Ah, only a quarter of a mile," continued Sharpthorne, addressing the witness. "Are you allowed refreshment during the night, my man?"

"We get a cup of coffee sometimes towards the morning."

"Oh, nothing else?"

"No."

"How do you get that coffee—do you go into any house?"

"No, sir, we generally take it in the watchbox."

"Or any other refreshment you may happen to have, I suppose?"

The man hesitated, and then said—

"Some of my mates prefer chocolate."

"Ah, so I suppose; and some prefer a little gin perhaps, eh—or purl, perhaps?"

"Really, Mr. Sharpthorne," said the magistrate, "I do not see that this has any bearing on the case. The man was not intoxicated that night, as Mr. Blockett will be able to prove."

"No, your worship," said Blockett, "he was quite sober."

"I should be sorry to charge him with drunkenness," said Mr. Sharpthorne, assuming his usually mild manner. Then turning to the watchman again he said, somewhat sharply—

"Pray, my man, are you not a somnambulist?"

"A what, and please you sir?"

"A somnambulist?"

There was a general titter ran through the court at this question.

"No, sir, I ain't no dissenter at all, I belong to the church," replied the man, indignantly, thinking Sharpthorne meant some unknown religious sect.

There was a general laugh throughout the court at this reply, in which the lawyer, witnesses, and even the magistrate himself, joined.

"You misunderstand me, my friend," said Mr. Sharpthorne; "I mean, do you walk in your sleep?"

"No, sir, I should think not, nor nobody else either," said the watchman, still more indignantly. For he thought the audience were laughing at him, and the lawyer was holding him up to ridicule.

"Ah, I am glad of that. You do not walk in your sleep."

"No, sir."

"Not that you know of, I suppose?"

"I know I don't," said the other.

"Does your missus say so?"

"I ain't got no missus," said the witness, in a loud voice.

"Lucky man," chuckled the lawyer, at which there was another titter.

"Don't bother him, Mr. Sharpthorne," said the magistrate. "We must take his evidence for what it is worth. The probability is, that he was, at any rate, not far from the spot, and ought to have heard the noise of this affray."

"He is evidently deaf," said Mr. Sharpthorne.

"I do not perceive it." said the magistrate.

"Oh, but he is, though, I am sure of it."

"Indeed."

"Yes."

"He seemed to hear me very well."

"I say, my man," said Sharpthorne, "are you not a little deaf?"

This was said so low that the witness did not hear it. Sharpthorne had done this purposely.

"I am a little hard of hearing," was the reply.

I never knew a man who was deaf acknowledge the fact directly. It is always a little hard of hearing.

"Ah, I thought so. You see I was not mistaken, your worship."

"No—so it appears. Still he is quite capable of hearing any great noise, such as must have occurred on the night of this murder, and if not hear, he surely could see the struggle."

"If he was near enough."

"That will do, my man, you may go," said the magistrate. "We have done with you for the present. How is it," he added, addressing himself to Osborne, "that you did not attempt to catch either of the men who had committed the assault upon the deceased?"

"They ran off, as I before said, previous to my arriving at the spot."

"Did you not call out for assistance?"

"No, sir."

"Why not?"

"I was so completely overcome by the sight of the wounded man that, at the time I lost my presence of mind."

"Ah, so it would appear."

"Besides it would have been useless as there was no one in the street."

"It does appear strange conduct to go and shut yourself in a lonely house with a dying man, without making any effort to procure surgical assistance."

"We can hardly tell, sir," said Mr. Sharpthorne, "what effect fear or any sudden fright may have upon an individual. My client is a most respectable young man moving in good society, highly educated, being in fact a recent student at one of the universities of Oxford, where he has, I believe taken a degree. I should suppose, therefore, that bail will be accepted for his appearance after the verdict of the coroner's jury."

"I don't see how I can accept bail in the present stage of the proceedings."

"Not accept bail! Surely you would not inflict so serious an injury upon an innocent man as to incarcerate him, and prevent his following his usual avocations. He is in a situation, and if prevented by imprisonment from attending to his duties, the consequences will be most serious. Surely you will not refuse bail.

"I am afraid I must," was the firm answer.

"I am sorry to hear you say so, sir, and do trust that you will reconsider the matter."

"It would be better to await the result of the coroner's jury, and let us hope that our officers may be fortunate enough to capture the two men who committed this crime. Should you know them again if you were to see them?" he said, addressing himself to Osborne.

"No, sir; I did not catch even a hasty glance of their features."

"Dear me! How very unfortunate. Did the deceased man say if either of them were known to him?"

"He did not say?"

"But did you not ask him?"

"No, sir."

"Why not?'

"I did not think of it?"

"Why, bless me, I should have thought that would have been your first inquiry."

"I was too much taken up in waiting upon and attending to the dying man."

"Umph! you really have been very imprudent, I must say. The whole case is enveloped in complete mystery." Then turning to Blockett, he said. "Was there much property in the house?"

"Yes, sir, a great deal."

"Consisting of what?"

"Goods of various sorts, and a very large amount in gold."

"Has any been removed?"

"I should suppose not."

"How did you find the place?"

"The gold was in a large chest or trunk, which was open."

"Open?"

"Yes, sir," said Mr. Sharpthorne. "My client unlocked this trunk at the request of the deceased man."

"Ah, I remember—so he stated."

"The trunk itself had been drawn up to the bedside of the dying man."

"Were there no other inhabitants in the house?"

"No, sir—none that we could find."

"What, did this man live alone, without a servant or an attendant of any sort?"

"It would appear so. His habits were of a very eccentric nature; so the neighbours informed me."

"He has been reputed rich, I suppose?"

"Yes, your worship—fabulously, rich so the neighbours would infer."

"Has he any relations?"

"None that we know of at present," was the reply.

"Upon my word, Mr. Sharpthorne," said the magistrate, "this is really a sad affair for your client, but I do not see what can be done. The story is so singular, so wrapt in mystery that he must await the result of further evidence turning up in his favour, and let us trust some such will be forthcoming."

"But surely, sir," said the lawyer, "you don't imagine that there is anything transpired to throw suspicion upon my client?"

"I should be very sorry," answered the magistrate, "to prejudice any man's case—this, as you know, is only a preliminary inquiry, and, in the absence of further proof, we must detain the only individual who appears to have been with the deceased man in his last moments."

"But you do not mean to infer, I hope, that my client, Mr. Osborne, has any complicity in compassing the unfortunate man's death."

"Certainly not; I should be sory to cast such an unjust aspersion upon a respectable gentleman's character."

"What, then, are your intentions?" asked the lawyer.

"To serve the ends of justice it will be, I am afraid, necessary for him to undergo a temporary imprisonment during the inquiry; but if you think it policy to press the question of bail, you can do so in a superior court."

"At great cost?"

"Yes; it will be attended with cost, certainly, and if you take my advice you will not do so—however, that is for your own consideration and his."

After some further discussion poor Osborne was taken to the Compter prison, there to await the result of the coroner's inquest and and his next examination.

CHAPTER XXI.

OSBORNE IN THE COUNTER.—SIR RICHARD FLEETWOOD AND THE ASTUTE MR. SHARPTHORNE.

HENRY Osborne, the noble-minded simple-hearted and unsophisticated Osborne, is in the Compter prison, with the circumstances of a murder hanging over him in an unpleasant manner.

As yet he had not been accused of having any hand in the hideous crime.

Messrs. Crasher, Basham and Phipps have by necessity been communicated with. The particulars of the case have been fully explained to them by Mr. Sharpthorne, and they have behaved with kindness and consideration towards their confidential clerk, for they have throughout Osborn's engagement with them entertained the highest opinion of him.

His old and valiant friend, Frank Halford, had been several times to visit him in the hour of his trial and misfortune—although the colonel did not relish the atmosphere of a prison—he did violence to his feelings in the cause of friendship, as, perhaps, no one could enlist the sympathy of the colonel equal to Osborne.

The history of the murder in Cow Cross was detailed in the paper and became food for public discussion. As is usual in such cases, opinions were divided on the subject.

As yet no clue had been found to the real perpetrators of the tragedy. The law generally demands a victim, and, in the absence of any other, Osborne was held as a sort of hostage.

Sir Richard Fleetwood was felicitating himself upon the chance of events. Since his duel at the masquerade with Osborne, he had pressed his suit more strongly with Miss Langford, and he found, much to his chagrin, that she was firmer than ever in her determination to abide by her original engagement with his rival; indeed, he had received distinct answers to this effect from the lips of Honora, who, as she found herself hardly pressed, mustered up courage enough to speak so very plainly upon the subject that the baronet was for the moment completely nonplushed.

Home he rushed again to Acton; there to feed upon the most fearful thoughts—Honora's words had cut deep into the heart of the baronet. This was the one grand object of his life—to be thwarted in which was more than he knew how to bear up against. It was a dark day in Sir Richard's existence when he found that there where he had garnered up his heart was to him a desert—an arid, scorching, desert.

It has been said by an acute and observant writer, that the love of a man of maturer years is much more deep, lasting and passionate than that which generally takes possession of youth, and without doubt the observation is pregnant with truth.

For a man who has grown to a ripe and lusty manhood there is no second spring.

I have said that Sir Richard Fleetwood was a hard, callous, remorseless man; so indeed he was, and as the tale progresses this will be fully developed and appreciated by the reader. Nevertheless, callous as was his nature in a worldly point of view, he loved—"not wisely, perhaps, but too well."

He loved and worshipped Honora Langford and all the better qualities of his nature were poured out upon this pure font. To find this love flung back in his face—to find her whose very touch and presence was supreme happiness to him—whose very breath was perfume and whose very glance was intoxicating to his senses—to find that the form, the which to clasp would be ecstacy and a foretaste of heavenly bliss—was destined for other hands and for other lips was agony insupportable.

Ah, I pray that you and I, reader—be you male or female, whose eye is wandering over these pages, I pray that neither you nor I may ever know the mighty but unspoken grief consequent upon unrequited love, than which, in the whole category of human ills, there is no greater. I pray that neither you nor I are destined to endure those long and sleepless nights.

Better to have to contend with the world, fighting your way manfully as best you may, rather than have to undertake the hopeless task to patch up a broken spirit or a bruised heart.

Bad as was Osborne's present position, it was as nothing compared to that to Sir Richard Fleetwood.

It seems strange to assert this, seeing that the baronet, of all men, was the least likely to pine over the loss of a pretty or fascinating girl. So anybody would have thought; so indeed everybody did think. But, a word in your ear, my friends: we never know ourselves; how, then, can we plumb the depths of another's character with any degree of certainty.

There are mysteries in the human heart which are far beyond mortal ken. It is well, perhaps, that it is so. It is well that the inner life of us mortals is not made palpable and manifest to even ourselves.

Who can account for the fact of the hold that one particular woman has, more than another, over us. It is not always that she is the most beautiful of Eve's daughters,—it is not that she may be the most amiable—neither is it that she has greater wit or talents than her less favoured sisters—what is it? We call it love. What is love?—who can tell?

Its meaning is comprehensive, but very obscure.

I dare say you have, as well as myself, seen a beautiful and accomplished, and, it may be, a brilliant woman, in society, and yet when by chance you touched accidentally her form, it sent no thrill of delight through your frame equal to that which you experienced with comparatively a much more ordinary mortal.

There is some unknown attractive and resisting power, for which we in vain endeavour to account.

Man is a strange paradox, and so is woman—the more so of the two, perhaps—but they are paradoxes both.

I have said that the love of which Sir Richard Fleetwood was possessed, was the one grand passion of his life—I suppose you young ladies, who scan these pages, will laugh and say that love is always a grand passion—so to a certain extent it is, the master one; but after all, its consequences are not nearly so severe to the ductile and elastic mind of youth, than to one of a more advanced manhood.

In his lonely room at Acton, Sir Richard was a prey to an agony almost insupportable. His schemes of aggrandisement and own personal advancement, were all abandoned. There was but one dominant thought in his own mind, and that was, how he was to win the love of Honora Langford. His love for her was intense, scorching, and fiery in its character. It incorporated itself into its very existence—it fermented through his whole being—and now that he found himself foiled, it drove him into madness.

He had shut himself up for some days, and taken little or no notice of his sister or brother's wife, or any of the visitors who had chanced to call. In fact, he had given notice to his servants to deny him, save to a favoured few.

While in this moody and dejected state, his lawyer, Mr. Sharpthorne, was announced. Sir Richard was seldom or never denied to this worthy, for he was his head man in the management of those affairs for the transaction of which secrecy and discretion were needed.

As Mr. Sharpthorne entered the library, with that peculiar cat-like step which was habitual to him, Sir Richard saw, by the expression of his countenance, that he had something more than ordinary information to communicate.

When the old lawyer was seated, he said, quietly, as he pulled a newspaper from his pocket.

"You have heard the account of this murder, I suppose, Sir Richard ?"

"No," said the baronet, sententiously, for he was in no very pleasant humour. "No," he repeated, "I do not trouble myself about murders, burglaries, or things of that sort."

"Unless they concern you," said Sharpthorne, looking under his spectacles at the baronet.

"Concern me, Mr. Sharpthorne ; that's a very different matter."

"Rather, I must say."

"What mean you ? In what way can I be interested in the matter ?"

"Well, but I suppose you have seen the account of it in the public newspapers, Sir Richard ?"

"Indeed, no. In fact, I have not looked at a newspaper for some days," said the baronet, with a deep drawn sigh.

He looked very pale and haggard, and his countenance gave indications of that inward struggle which he had been undergoing.

"And have none of your friends mentioned the subject to you," said the lawyer. "The matter has become one of great public interest.

And he placed in the hands of the baronet the paper containing the account of Osborne's first examination.

Sir Richard's eye eagerly devoured the account of the Cow Cross murder. And oh ! what a fine sketch for a painting might have been made of the countenances of those two men.

Mr. Sharpthorne contemplated his client with a fox-like expression of countenance, and as the baronet's eyes wandered over the paper, the lawyer watched their changing expression, and every twitch and movement of the nervous features. Wonder was expressed thereon—wonder and surprise of no ordinary character.

The baronet having finished his perusal, handed back the paper, and gazed inquiringly into the countenance of the lawyer.

"So," he observed, "you defend this man Osborne, it appears ?'

Sharpthorne nodded, and began to knead his hands, making the knuckles thereof crack till it was quite painful to hear—that is, assuming that every individual is as nervous as myself.

"How came you to know him ?" said the baronet.

"Was introduced by a friend," answered Sharpthorne.

"Oh ! He is innocent of the charge—eh ?"

"Perfectly."

"And will be acquitted ?"

"He ought to be."

"And will, I suppose ?"

"If the real culprits are found."

"And if not ?'

"I cannot answer that question at present," said the lawyer.

"But you surely know ?" interrogated the baronet.

"Circumstances are much against him, and the case assumes an unpleasant appearance."

"Will he be committed ?"

"I am afraid so."

"Afraid ?"

"Yes, I fear he will have to stand a trial."

"What have you to fear if he does ?"

"His reputation will suffer. A stigma will always attach itself to a man who stands a trial upon the charge of murder, however innocent he may be. The world is generally verry censorious, not to say unjust, at times," answered the lawyer, looking up at the ceiling in a placid manner.

"Sharpthorne," said the baronet, in a hoarse whisper, "this Osborne must be found guilty."

"Indeed ! And wherefore ?"

"He stands in my way—between me and —Psha ! No matter ; he is in my way most confoundedly."

"Ah !"

"Yes, Sharpthorne ; what can be done to get rid of him ?"

The lawyer made no reply, but continued to gaze at the questioner apparently in a abstracted manner.

"Do you understand me Sharpthorne ?"

"Perfectly ; your meaning is clear enough, Sir Richard ; nothing, I should say, could be clearer.'

"Well, there is then enough evidence to lead you to believe that there is a probability of a conviction ?'

"At present, no."

"There is not ?"

"Decidedly not."

"Then more must be forthcoming," said Sir Richard.

"And pray how ?"

"That you can manage, I suppose?"

"Indeed I cannot."

"Why not?"

"In my professional avocation I have never as yet produced false testimony to compass the death of an innocent man."

"Psha! innocent, indeed! I believe the fellow guilty enough," said the baronet.

"Every one is at liberty to enjoy their own opinion," answered the lawyer, calmly. "It is well for mankind that no ruler has at present been able to forge chains to fetter thought."

"Sharpthorne," said Sir Richard, with an intense bitterness, "I would give anything to be rid of this man. He is a puppy—an adventurer—a scoundrel!"

"He does not appear to me to be such. But again I say that is a matter of opinion."

"What do you mean?" answered the other, in a fury. "Do you espouse his cause, then, because he is a client of yours? I tell you the fellow is not worth a shilling. Not a farthing, sir—not a farthing. He is a beggar, and a mere adventurer, travelling upon his good looks and soft insinuating manner. Bah! I have no patience to even think of him."

"What has he done to you?" said the lawyer, in that peculiar quiet manner which he knew so well how to assume when occasion required it.

The baronet started and changed colour at this very plain and natural question.

"What has he done, sir? what has he not done?"

"I do not know."

"But I do."

"Possibly."

"Well then?"

"Why, I don't, that is all."

"He has come between me and my fondest hopes," thundered forth the baronet. "He has usurped and poisoned the mind of as innocent, guileless, and fair a lady as ever God created. That is one thing he has done, sir. Now do you understand?"

"Perfectly; and that is quite enough to raise your indignation against him."

"Indignation, sir; I should think it was: hate—intense, absorbing hate—would be the better term."

"All that may be true enough," said Sharpthorne; "but that is hardly a sufficient reason for him to be led to an ignominious and violent death. At least the world would not deem it such.

"D—n the world," yelled out the baronet, as he strode along the apartment in excitement.

The lawyer remained quiet and passive in his chair. He was accustomed to these ebullitions from his client, and took them all as a matter of business.

"What am I to understand?" at length inquired the baronet, as he came to a halt, and, turning round, faced his legal adviser.

"About what, Sir Richard?" the other inquired mildly.

"Your own proceedings in this matter."

"Oh, I am retained for the defence, and should he have to stand his trial, must employ efficient counsel."

"Oh, indeed, you are then going to strain every nerve to get him off."

"I did not say that."

"You seemed to say something very like it."

"Did I? I had no intention of doing so I'm sure."

"Now let us understand one another, Sharpthorne: you are not going to humbug me by pretending to have scruples in this business. We know too much of one another to endeavour to hang over our actions such a flimsy blind as that. It is a simple question: are you my agent or his?"

"You know, Sir Richard, that I am always bound to you—our interests are identical."

"Good! so I should suppose. Spoken like a discreet man. Well then, you will—"

"Throw his case in as much confusion as possible," answered Sharpthorne.

"I am bound to you more than ever," said Sir Richard, with unfeigned delight, as he grasped the attorney by the hand, and shook it with warmth. "For ever bound to you," he continued with emphasis.

The lawyer puckered up his mouth into a sardonic smile, and fidgetted in his chair as though he felt overwhelmed with the other's protestation of friendship. He well knew its value, nevertheless; no man better.

"My feud with this man, Osborne, is of no common order," said Sir Richard Fleetwood. "If he can be hurled from his position, no matter how, I shall be content. Strive, my friend, to oblige me in this particular. Let a foul stigma attach itself to his name; even if he escapes see that some implied doubt exists of his innocence, and that will be enough."

"He will have a job as it is to come out of the inquiry free from suspicion."

"Ah, you think so?"

The lawyer nodded assent.

"'Tis then as I wished. What a fortunate occurrence this murder," exclaimed the baronet, with delight.

"To him?"

"No; of course not."

"To the miser?"

"No."

"Who to then?"

There was a pause.

"To yourself, perhaps?"

"Very likely."

"We view each other's misfortunes with different eyes," said Sharpthorne, with a grim smile.

"I want this man Osborne to be so cast out of his position that he may be for ever afterwards unable to reinstate himself. The fellow is a worthless hound, I believe; and would endeavour to lead a young girl to ally herself to him. To him, forsooth! A pretty husband, truly. Ah! we shall see; we shall see what events take place, Mr. Sharpthorne, eh?" chuckled the baronet.

"Yes, Sir Richard, we shall see all in good time."

Wine and refreshments were ordered, and the pair of worthies sat down thereto in a cozy, friendly manner; laying out the future fate of poor Osborne with the utmost degree of complacency and satisfaction to themselves.

———

CHAPTER XXII.

OSBORNE'S HOUR OF PERIL.—SCENE AT MR. LANGFORD'S.

IN the darkest hour of man's existence, and at a time when his spirit is crushed and his mind bids fair to break down under an accumulation of adverse circumstances, who so true and faithful as woman. Well may the poet say—

"Oh woman, in our hours of ease,
Uncertain, coy, and hard to please,
And variable as is the shade,
By the quivers of the light aspen made;
But when pain and anguish wring the brow,
A ministering angel thou."

Osborne was hemmed in by a series of disastrous and untoward circumstances. His case began to assume a much more serious complexion than it had done upon the first inquiry before the magistrates. Doubts were entertained by many respecting the truth of his original statement; from which, however, he had not deviated one iota. His house, or rather lodgings, were in the hands of the police. The whole of his effects therein underwent a most rigid search, and hints were given that something had been found which excited suspicion. Upon the coroner's inquiry a very important fact was brought against him. In the body of the deceased man there was found the blade of a knife, or rather the greater portion of the blade, sticking in one of the ghastly wounds. This wound penetrated between the third and fourth ribs, and the knife had apparently broken by coming in contact with the ribs, or else through the unfortunate man's recoil from the blow: be this as it may, there was the blade. The detectives were very active in searching for evidence, and near to the spot where the first attack had been made, they discovered the handle of the knife, with the other portion of the blade attached thereto. The two were compared, and they were found to fit exactly, consequently there could not possibly be any doubt but that the blade belonged to the handle found near the sanguinary spot; besides which, it was itself covered with coagulated blood. This might prove some clue to the perpetrators of the crime; and so indeed it did. So they supposed. The knife bore the maker's name, with his address, Sheffield; besides this, there were two initial letters engraved on a piece of silver inserted in the handle. These were carefully examined. They were "H. O," in old English, and answered to the first letters of Henry Osborne's name. A murmur of surprise ran through the court at this discovery, and the height of suspicion seemed now to be redoubled against the unfortunate Osborne. Upon his second examination the magistrate asked him if the knife in question belonged to him, or was ever in his possession. Osborne was about to reply to this when Mr. Sharpthorne immediately stopped him, and said he had better decline answering the question. Osborne paused, when the magistrate said he was not bound to criminate himself, and the question was withdrawn. A detective was sent down to Sheffield, and had an interview with the foreman of the works who made the knife. He said it had been manufactured at their establishment, but as to whom it was sold he was unable to say. However the matter was not permitted to rest here. Handbills were posted and advertisements published offering a reward for any one who could prove the sale of the knife. Eventually a cutler residing at Highstreet Oxford, came forward and distinctly stated that he sold the knife in question to Mr. Osborne, when a student there, and at his request he had his initials engraved thereon. By a reference to his books, it appeared that the purchase was effected some three years, or rather more, than the date of the murder. Here was one most damnatory fact against the prisoner, and the magistrate was felicitating himself at having refused bail for his future appearance. The finger of suspicion now pointed more directly to the prisoner, and strong doubts were entertained as to the truth of his statement, uncorroborated as it was by one tittle of evidence beyond his own bare testimony. Poor Osborne felt himself environed by a concentration of circumstances which seemed closing around him every day more closely. He was conscious of his own innocence, which was indeed the only consolation he had in all his misfortunes. Would Honora believe his guilt of so foul a crime? He spurned such a suggestion as it presented itself to his mind. Ah, no! Honora Langford, with a woman's undying faith in the virtue and integrity of him upon whom her heart was set, did not for a moment doubt his truthfulness. All the world might be against him, a jury might convict him—a dozen juries—but Honora never would admit the foul breath of suspicion to cross her doors. Henry Osborne, her own Henry, harm any living thing, it was impossible. Most cheerfully would she have exchanged places with him, and most gladly would she have undergone the inquiry to have spared him whom she knew was distraught in mind and broken down in spirits. She wanted to go to the compter, but Mr. Langford for the present overruled it. She would go in spite of her father's interdiction, if he needed her services. As it was she sent Miss Staunton to him, with the kindest of notes to Osborne, whom she most delicately offered whatever pecuniary assistance might be needed for lawyer's and counsel's fees. Osborne told her messenger that he did not need any, as he had sufficient funds of his own. Nevertheless he was overwhelmed with her kindness.

Sir Richard Fleetwood continued to pay occasional visits to the house of Mr. Langford. After Honora's declaration of her firm attachment to Osborne, the baronet's pride came to the rescue, and he discontinued his visits: he however found it impossible to keep away from the goddess of his idolatry. It was some comfort to be near her, if only as a friend; some comfort to inhale the same atmosphere she was breathing; some comfort, and not a small one either, to gaze at her form and beauties, and pay that respectful attention—I had almost said adoration, for it would be the truest word of the two as applied to his case—adoration or attention, which you please, and which the baronet knew so well how to do ; for withal, he could be the finished gentleman when he chose..

It was not Sir Richard's policy to take side with those who were against Osborne. On the contrary, he affected to believe in his innocence, and pretended to deeply sympathise with him for all his misfortunes. He knew this would please Honora, and consequently he assumed quite a commiserating tone, leading her to infer that, although they had been rivals, and Osborne the most successful candidate for her hand, he did not carry his animosity so far as to wish him any harm ; on the contrary, he had every reason to regret his unfortunate situation. The guileless Honora fully believed in the protestations of Sir Richard, and warmed visibly towards him for what she supposed to be his generous conduct ; for when her father would imply any doubt about the innocence of her lover, Sir Richard would evince much anger, and argue the matter warmly in his favour. In any way, to eat his own words, forswear his own creed if he had any ; in short he would do anything, he cared not what, so long as he could be permitted to be in the presence of Honora, so deeply and madly did he love this girl. Ah, Sir Richard, subtle master as you are in the art of duplicity, there are secret keys to the human heart, which are not to be turned by your hands.

"There has been a fact elicited during the coroner's inquiry which turns terribly against Mr. Osborne," said Honora's father as he entered the apartment, newspaper in hand, where his daughter and Sir Richard were seated.

Honora became ashy pale, and made no reply—the question was always a painful one when discussed by herself and parent.

"What is that?" inquired Sir Richard, sharply.

Mr. Langford placed the newspaper in the baronet's hands, and pointed out to him the evidence respecting the knife which the latter read in silence.

Honora sat watching the countenance of the baronet, but could not detect any visible change therein.

The truth of it was that Sir Richard was already acquainted with the fact before it appeared in the public journals, and, as the reader will no doubt surmise, he obtained his information from the lawyer Sharpthorne. When he had read the report of the inquest, he gently gave it back to Mr. Langford, and, with a deprecating gesture, he pointed to his daughter as though he would beg of him to spare her feelings.

Honora saw his motion to her parent, and became deeply sensibly of his delicate consideration for her, at the same time she wished for the full possession of the facts respecting the coroner's inquiry. Honora glanced towards Sir Richard Fleetwood, and then said, gently—

"Is there any fresh news about—respecting this sad affair?"

"Yes something ;—which, after all, may be only a chance circumstance of no importance."

"What is it?"

"It is respecting a knife supposed to have been used in the committal of the murder," said Sir Richard.

"That has been found?"

"Yes—now don't alarm yourself unnecessarily, my dear young lady," said the baronet, kindly.

"Who did it belong to?"

"To Mr. Henry Osborne, my dear," replied her father.

"Henry," exclaimed Honora, feebly ; and she nearly fainted.

The baronet was by her side in an instant, and sought to appease and reassure her. She looked dreadfully pale and wan, and her lips were bloodless.

"Have mercy on me !" exclaimed Honora, "some designing persons must have sought to fix the guilt of this dreadful deed upon poor Henry — heaven help him !—heaven help him!"

"As it always does to the righteous, let us hope," said the baronet.

"Circumstances certainly are against him, my dear child," observed Mr. Langford, in a peculiar tone.

"Pray heaven he has nought to charge his soul with," said Honora ; "you do not imply a doubt?"

"I do not say anything one way or the other," was the cautious reply.

"Then you ought. You ought at once to declare the impossibility of Mr. Osborne injuring man or woman. You know him to be the very soul of honour. Murder ! my very mind sickens at the thought—he is as innocent as the best and purest in his Majesty's dominions—he would not harm or wrong a child. You know this, father, as well as I do."

"I may think so."

"Think !—you know. Do not say think ! Where all the world is against a dear friend, such as him, is it fitting, is it seemly, think you, to use such cold and cautious expressions. On my life—on my very life, I dare be sworn, that Herny knows no more of this murder, beyond what he himself stated, than you do yourself. Is this a time to indulge in doubts and—" she was unable to complete her sentence, but burst out in an agony of tears.

Sir Richard bent over and pressed her temples, and appeared to feel deeply her present trouble.

"This is no time to offer cold comfort to the afflicted," said Sir Richard, turning to Mr. Langford, "this is no time to falter—rather let us see what may be done to assist this unfortunate gentleman; either you or I might be placed in a similar position by the same untoward circumstances—think of that, Mr. Langford, and have compassion on him who at this moment is in his dark hour of affliction."

His voice trembled as he spoke these words, and Honora regarded him with an admiring look.

Honora thought them noble words, especially when speaking of a rival. She pressed his hand warmly in acknowledgment of his generosity.

"Thanks, Sir Richard—a thousand thanks, sir," said Honora."

"Do not thank me, my dearest young lady—I share your sorrows as—" he paused here, and heaved a deep sigh, "as I would have done your joys—but, believe me, however, that your wishes and aspirations are mine—your sorrows are mine—and your very lightest word is with me a law indissoluble. If I could in any way alter the matter; if I could even be placed in the position of Mr. Osborne, so that he might be free, so that it might afford you comfort, I would cheerfully, gladly, do so, and reverse our situations."

"Oh, Sir Richard, this is more than you ought to say."

"It is no more than I feel," said the baronet, "not one word more than I feel, as heaven is my judge."

"You are of a kind hearted, generous nature," said Honora.

"More than you have given me credit for, perhaps," was the reply.

"Perhaps so. I may, probably have been unjust."

"That is impossible; it is not in your noble nature."

"We are all liable to errors of judgement," replied Honora.

The baronet reflected for some time after this last observation, and there was a pause for some minutes, during which Miss Staunton came by the side of Sir Richard, and, whispering in his ear, asked to see the paper containing an account of the coroner's inquiry. The baronet pointed to Honora, and went with Miss Staunton to the other end of the room.

"I would not show it to her at present," he said, in a whisper to his companion; "it would be hardly prudent; indeed, to speak the truth, I would have kept it from her knowledge altogether, if it had been possible."

"Does the evidence go much against Mr. Osborne, then?" inquired Miss Staunton, quickly.

The baronet shook his head sadly.

"Poor dear gentleman—what will he do?" asked Miss Staunton.

"Let us hope for the best."

"What new features are there in the case?" she asked.

Sir Richard as briefly as he could detailed all the salient points of the evidence. An expression of poignant anguish passed over the features of Miss Staunton as she heard the particulars.

"Oh, Sir Richard Fleetwood, what will be the end of this disastrous affair?" asked Miss Staunton.

"Hush!"

"What do you think will be the end of it?" she continued, in a lower tone.

"It is hard to say, my dear young lady—let us hope for the best."

"Oh, if you could see poor Mr. Osborne, you would, indeed, pity him—such a dreadful place too."

This was in allusion to the prison, and she gave a shudder as the recollection of the interior of the Compter came across her.

"You have seen him, then?"

"Yes; I went to the pri—, that is, the Compter."

"Ah?"

"Yes."

"With a message, I suppose?" said the baronet, carelessly.

"Wh-y, ye-s," answered Miss Staunton, stammering, "from our mutual friend, Miss Langford."

"Ah, just like her, always kind and considerate. Ah, Miss Staunton, what a heart she has—what a treasure!" and here he heaved a profound sigh.

"She has indeed; few know her worth—very few, I can assure you."

"It is written in every act of her blameless life," answered the baronet.

As the two were conversing Miss Langford rose and walked towards them, and placing her hand upon the arm of Sir Richard, she said:

"'Tis worse than we anticipated, and I know out of kindness and consideration for me you are keeping something from my knowledge."

"No, I assure you."

"Whence this whispering, then?"

"I was merely conversing with our friend, Miss Staunton."

"Upon what subject, Sir Richard?"

"Not upon indifferent or trifling subjects, I assure you."

"No, certainly not—what then?"

"Partly about yourself, if I must be candid."

"Sir Richard Fleetwood, this case assumes

a serious aspect. Tell me what has occurred, I pray you."

"Nothing but what you already know, my dear Miss Langford."

"I am bound to believe you, I suppose?" said Honora.

"I should hope so."

"Where is the paper then?"

"Oh—what the one which your father brought?"

"Yes."

"Oh, Miss Staunton has it, I think—have you not, Miss Staunton?"

"I had it," was the reply.

"Then give it me."

"No, my dear; we'll read the account, by-and-bye."

"Why not now?"

"When you are a little more composed, dear."

"Sir Richard," said Honora, "your lawyer is Mr. Osborne's lawyer; what does he say?"

"I—that is—" stammered the baronet, "I have not seen him since the inquest."

"But won't you?"

"Most certainly. I shall make it my business to do so."

"Thanks—and ascertain from him how he thinks the case is likely to go. Ah, Sir Richard, if money could purchase his release—"

"He would not stand in need of it, be assured," replied the baronet, "whilst I had any at my command."

Tears rose to the eyes of Miss Langford, and she grasped the hand of the baronet and kissed it.

Miss Staunton, like a discreet girl as she was, deemed it expedient to retire, which Mr. Langford himself had done some time previous.

The baronet led her into the inner apartment, and handed her to a seat; she passively, or rather mechanically, followed his guidance, without knowing why or wherefore, for her heart was too full to take any particular notice of either her own or his actions.

"You've a kind generous nature, Sir Richard, as I before observed," said Honora; "believe me, your conduct, your kindness, in fact, can never be erased from my memory."

"Miss Langford, this is not the time for me to arrogate to myself any qualities beyond my fellow men—and perhaps you will say that this is not a time for me to refer to that which, out of consideration towards yourself, I have studiously avoided mentioning or renewing. You certainly have to thank me for nothing beyond what every man situated as I am, and feeling as I do, would act according to his own natural promptings. I have told you that our interest is identical—nay, pardon me, I may not, perhaps, say this much—I mean that your interest is mine;

at least, I know it is—I find it impossible that it should be otherwise. In our relative positions you may think it strange that I should affect an interest in Mr. Osborne, of all men in the world. It seems strange almost to myself, but, alas, young lady, my love for you is stronger than anything else in my whole composition. It is hard to make such a sacrifice to a rival, but if as I think, and indeed, from your own words now know, if your happiness depends upon his, why then I say, at any cost, at all cost, the sacrifice of my own life, I would endeavour to make you happy. Psha! what am I saying? —my own life will be sacrificed!" he continued, as he turned suddenly away, and paced the apartment with hurried and excited steps.

She turned and regarded him with an inquiring and almost stupefied gaze, but made no observation.

He continued to pace the apartment for some time, and then coming suddenly to her side, looked tenderly at her, and heaved a deep sigh.

"It appears to me, Miss Langford, that an evil destiny is ruling all our fates."

"It would appear so in Mr. Osborne's case," she answered.

"And in mine," he said.

"I hope not."

"Yes, most certainly in mine. Young lady, let me ask you how was it that I was ever permitted to see you?—how was it that fate, or chance, or destiny, or whatever else you call it, should have drawn me towards you? For what?—good heavens, for what? To poison the whole current of my existence," he whispered to himself; "ay, poison, too surely, a deadly, insidious, but fatal poison."

"Sir Richard?"

"Alas, you do not know what I suffer—you cannot know—may you never know. Young woman, shall I tell you that which I dare not hardly confess to myself?—shall I tell you that if my hopes of happiness hereafter were placed in one scale, and your love in the other, that I should embrace the latter?"

"Sir Richard, this is surely wicked?" she said, deprecatingly.

"I know it. It shows what hard resolves, what terrible and dread alternatives we mortals are driven to. Oh, Miss Langford," he continued, now more tenderly in a broken voice, as tears almost rose to his eyes. "Oh, Miss Langford, I am shamed to think of this sad sad story—I grieve to reflect upon that future which is in store for me. One long and dreary night is all that I may ever know; and I envy Osborne—ay, envy him even now in his affliction—and would cheerfully change places with him, for he has your sympathy, your thoughts are for him—a happiness that I may never know."

He fell upon the sofa, his face downwards, and sobbed audibly.

"Sir Richard Fleetwood," said Honora, advancing towards him, " this is dreadful to see you thus. Pray do not be so afflicted. Good heavens," she continued, "what an unhappy fate is mine."

"And mine—just heaven, and mine !" exclaimed the baronet. " What have I done, to be persecuted thus ?"

" Have pity on me, Sir Richard," exclaimed Honora, as she kindly placed her hand upon his shoulder, and gently shook him. "Have pity on me, I do beseech you. My heart is sufficiently wrung with conflicting emotions, without, at this hour of affliction, adding to my weight of woe."

" Have pity on me, for I need it, my dear young lady, as surely as ever man did in this world."

" I sympathise with you, Sir Richard," answered Honora ; "and trust me when I say, that I fully appreciate your feelings and position, and believe in the sincerity of your expressions ; but—"

" But what, Miss Langford ?" said the baronet.

" I may perhaps be spared the discussion of this subject at the present moment."

" I would spare your feelings, Miss Langford, in this, as on all other subjects. I am not so selfish as to obtrude my own private woes upon your already distressed mind. No, I hope I am not selfish enough to do this. I must learn to suffer in silence."

He rose up from the sofa and walked to the other end of the apartment. A degree of suffering and deep woe was observable upon his features. Presently he came towards her and respectfully took her hand.

" Impressible as is my nature," he said, quietly, " I will not attempt now to renew a subject which, at the present time may, no doubt, be unpalatable and distasteful to you. I will, therefore, content myself by assuring you, as I before observed, that your happiness is mine. Anything that I can do, anything that my means can purchase to assist Mr. Henry Osborne, in this the hour of his misfortune, I shall feel a pleasure in rendering him, to assist him out of his present difficulty."

"This is generous and noble, Sir Richard ; and believe me, I appreciate it much more than I can find words to express."

He raised her hand to his lips, kissed it respectfully, when, wishing her a fond adieu, he took his departure.

———

CHAPTER XXIII.

COLONEL JACK AT HOME.—THE SHADOW OVER HIS HOUSE.

WE have before mentioned that our hero, Colonel Jack, had two sides to his character. So, indeed, have many of us, in a more respectable position in society.

To a vast number of his acquaintance the colonel was known only as Mr. Halford, and esteemed as a very respectable member of society.

We are about now to make his acquaintance at his own house.

The colonel was a married man, and had one child, a daughter.

Some years before he had followed the occupation of a highwayman, the colonel, or, rather, Mr. Halford, had become acquainted with a young lady of great personal attractions, with gentle, amiable manners.

It has been often said that we admire in others what we do not possess ourselves, and as a general rule this may be said to prove correct ; at least it was so in this case. The young lady was the very opposite in her nature to her admirer. Nevertheless, she did become deeply enamoured of our hero, and eventually, in opposition to the wishes of her friends and relatives, she married him.

Mr. and Mrs. Halford, since that time, had resided at a small house at Hornsey, which at that time was quite a primitive place, and was considered to be, which it in reality was, quite in the country.

Here they lived a comfortable, happy, and domestic life for a long period. Halford really loved his wife, and she, poor thing, was devotedly attached to him in return, and as far as his conduct went towards her, there had been nothing to complain of.

Time went on, as the sands run out from the hour-glass of our common enemy.

The long and continued periods of absence of Mr. Halford from his home, gave rise to sad reflections to his wife. She did not know, nor could she possibly devise, the cause of his frequent and mysterious disappearances. But so gentle was her nature, so uncomplaining her disposition, that she never upbraided him, or even ventured to inquire more than he chose voluntarily to make her acquainted with.

She was an extraordinary woman, you will say. Perhaps so ; but there are many such in the world, many self-sacrificing creatures of flesh and blood, who form, however, the exception, perhaps, to Eve's daughters, and not the rule.

When the colonel was at home, there was that in his bearing which could hardly fail to show to a most superficial observer that there was something lurking behind all this mystery which weighed upon the mind of Colonel Jack, and made his domestic hours anything but happy ones.

His confiding and self-sacrificing little wife, and pretty daughter, he felt almost as a reproach to him ; and often, in his more quiet hours, he would ruminate in an abstracted state by the chimney corner, as to altering the course of his life.

Then would he build castles in the air, which the first puff of wind would ruthlessly blow down.

The habit was too strong upon him now, and had become too confirmed for him to ever alter his course.

The colonel had returned to his abode at the time at which we are about to take a glance at him.

He had gone up-stairs to change his mud-bespattered clothes, after which he would perhaps betake himself to his own cozy parlour, where was Mrs. Halford, all smiles, and his only daughter.

Slott was in the hall, stretching out his legs, and contemplating the establishment as though he were lord of the domain. This quadruped had at all times a haughty bearing, but although he took a hasty glance at the place, he did not seem to be so well up in spirits as upon most other occasions when he returned with his master. After he had remained in the hall for a few minutes, looking up the staircase where his master had disappeared, he limped off, and took his way to the stable, where he ensconced himself under the manger upon some clean straw.

Mrs. Halford observed the changed manner of the dog, and upon looking along the passage where he had been, she observed spots of blood. She kept this fact to herself, as she had done so many others ; at what cost, my friend, neither you or I know.

She, however, rang the bell, when an elderly and faithful domestic appeared, who had been in the family of Mrs. Halford since the latter was an infant.

"Curson," said Mrs. Halford, "what is the matter with Slott ?"

"I don't know, mum."

"Why I thought he appeared lame when he came in."

"Did he, mum ?—I am sure I don't know. But I saw him in the passage just now."

"He has gone away, then ?"

"He generally takes up his place in the hall when he comes home with master—"

"Yes, but Curson," and here her mistress beckoned her old servant to come nearer ; "Curson, there are spots of blood in the passage."

"Spots of blood !" exclaimed the domestic, in a whisper.

"Yes, don't say anything about it to Sarah, but there certainly are, that is quite certain. I tell you what, I wish you could make some excuse to go out in the yard and grounds and see if you can find where Slott is gone to ?"

"Yes, mum," and off trotted Curson.

She returned shortly, and said that Slott was laying down in the stable, and seemed to be panting as though he were either over-fatigued or in great pain.

"Is he wounded ?"

"I think one of his legs appear to be broken. I tried to have a closer look, by removing the straw upon which he was lying, when he growled, and seemed disposed to snap at me ; so I thought it best to leave him alone."

"You did quite right. That is quite enough. He is wounded, without a doubt. Tell your master dinner is ready."

"Yes, mum," and away the old domestic went.

In a short time after this, Colonel Jack entered the parlour. He regarded his wife with a loving look, and she sprang forward and entwined her arms around him, upon which he gave her a kiss upon her forehead. Halford was more than usually pale and moody, and his wife tried to cheer him by simulating a liveliness which she was far from feeling.

"I thought you would be home to-night, Frank," said Mrs. Halford. "Indeed I expected you last night, but this one I made sure of."

"What made you so sure, my dear ?" said Halford, with a faint smile.

"Something told me so ; I can hardly tell you what it was, but I certainly did feel sure about your return ; and then you know you—"

"Have been a long time away, eh ?"

"Well, yes."

"So I have ; but many things have occurred which have detained me, and in spite of my anxiety to return, I have been compelled to stop longer than I had anticipated."

"Ah, I suppose so. You stay at home to-morrow, I hope ?" said Mrs. Halford, timidly, and hardly daring to look up into her husband's face as she made the inquiry.

"Yes, dearest—why ?" asked the colonel, in some surprise at this unusual question.

"Because it is the anniversary of our wedding-day."

Her countenance assumed a heightened colour as she said this.

"Ah, I forgot."

"But I did not, Frank—I did not forget."

She rose from her seat, and throwing her arms round his neck, gave him several kisses.

He felt happy in the love of so kind and gentle a creature, but a cloud came across this

sunshine of his home—a cloud, no bigger than a man's hand, but might it not gather in size and intensity?

"You look more charming than when I first knew you, Kate," said the colonel, now indulging in that species of flattery which had become habitual to him; "time but adds to your charms and graces instead of diminishing them."

"Oh, Frank, we are not lovers now," said Mrs. Halford, "I am not used to such flattery."

"By my faith," said the colonel, "but it is no flattery, you really look charming. What have you been doing, dearest, to make yourself look so fascinating? Ah, I see you have that dress on which I always so much admired."

"Yes, I put it on, dearest, because I heard
No. 20.

you say the other day that I looked better in it than any other."

"There's an obedient little wife," said the colonel, approvingly, "ever mindful of her husband's wishes."

Dinner being over, the colonel sat down in the chimney corner, and lit his pipe, while his wife went on working on the opposite side of the fireplace.

"Have you heard any more about poor Henry?" inquired Mrs. Halford.

She had known Osborne before her marriage with her present husband, but had not seen him since, as he did not know of her marriage with our hero.

"No," said the colonel, "there has nothing transpired; but, generally, the circumstances seem to be taking an unpleasant turn."

"Have you seen him again?"

"Yes."

"How does he seem ?"

"Very low and dejected—enough to make him, poor fellow."

"Is he much altered, Frank ?"

"In what way ?"

"In his character since I knew him."

"Not at all ; he is the same generous, simple-hearted fellow that he ever was."

"Ah."

"Why?"

"Nothing ; only time alters so many "

"So it does, but it has not altered my charming Kate."

She smiled at the compliment, but for all this there was something forced in the manner of both husband and wife.

"Henry will be acquitted, I should hope," said the latter.

"I hope so."

"Is it not certain, then ?"

"I should think not quite."

"But he is innocent—Henry is surely innocent?"

"Innocent, my good girl," exclaimed her companion ; "do you suppose, Henry Osborne capable of murder ?'

"No, no—of course not."

"Then why do you ask me such a question, my dear ?'

"I don't know ; only because I am a silly thing ; I don't know why I asked it. Poor Osborne! what a sad thing for him to be imprisoned when he is an innocent man. What is more dreadful than a gaol, and the possibility of being found guilty of some dark crime ?" said Mrs. Halford, while her husband winced under the observation—which in his situation of life seemed to point directly at him.

Such, however, was not Mrs. Halford's intention, for they were made without a thought perhaps.

After this the two sat for a long time in silence. The colonel was occupied in reading, and his wife in making some articles of dress for his infant daughter, who was now about two years and a half old.

After an hour or two more had flown by, the colonel arose, and took his way to the stable—it had always been his custom of an evening to look after his horse, and see that he was properly groomed and fed.

While he was gone Mrs. Halford undressed her daughter, and, upon the return of the colonel, she was presented to him for his customary kiss before the child was put to bed. The colonel embraced her affectionately, and the woman-servant, Sarah, took her to her cot.

It might have been about half an hour after this that an occurrence took place which it will be necessary to record in another chapter.

CHAPTER XXIV.

THE SUDDEN SURPRISE.—CAPTAIN RIGNOLD'S GENEROSITY.

AFTER Mabel Halford, for that was the child's name, was taken to bed by Sarah, the maid, Halford and his wife sat for half-an-hour or so, and indulged in a social chat, which was suddenly interrupted by their becoming aware of voices proceeding from the outer entrance, or gateway of the house.

The colonel changed colour and started ; his wife observed the sudden alteration in his manner and appearance, and an undefined fear took possession of her.

The voices were now heard approaching the house, and the colonel rose suddenly from his seat and regarded his wife with a look of anxiety.

"What is the matter ?" exclaimed the latter, in despairing accents, "what is the matter, Frank ?"

He made no reply, but looked anxiously about the room, and naturally felt for his pistol, which was usually in his belt, but, in his present costume, none was there.

"Deny me ; say that I am not at home ; I have not come home ; anything you like—I do not want to see these people."

As he said this he hurried from the apartment, and flew up stairs into the sleeping apartment as noiselessly as he could. By the time he had got there, three persons were in the hall with the man-servant, who appeared to be showing them in.

One of these entered the apartment where Mrs. Halford was. She started, and uttered a slight scream as he presented himself before her.

"Captain Rignold !" exclaimed the lady, as her cheek blushed and her form trembled.

The party so addressed gently shut the door of the room, and said :

"I am sorry for this, Mrs. Halford, very sorry, that I, of all other persons, should have been chosen for this unpleasant task."

"Unpleasant ! What do you mean, Edmund—that is, Captain Rignold I should have said ?"

"Is Mr. Halford here ?" he asked.

"No—he—is—I—has not come home as yet."

She said this as firmly as her shaken nerves would permit, but her looks and manner belied her words.

Captain Rignold understood the state of the case.

"I say, Kate, or rather, I should say, Mrs. Halford, I am sorry for this, truly sorry, believe me, but as the chief of the constabulary force, I have a duty to perform, although—"

and here he sighed, "although, of a surety, a painful one."

"Mercy, sir—mercy, I implore! What is the meaning of this? I beseech you to keep me no longer in suspense."

"Madam," said the captain, with a sadness in his manner which was not feigned, "your husband, Mr. Halford, is wanted."

"For what?"

He made no reply.

"For what?" she again inquired.

"I would spare your feelings, but my orders are to take him into custody."

"In custody! Oh, surely, Captain Rignold, you of all men should be—"

"Should be the last chosen for this purpose. I feel that, madam, believe me, as poignantly as yourself."

She stared at him in stupified surprise. So sudden, so terrible had been the blow, that she seemed as immovable and as petrified as a marble statue; indeed, she might have been almost taken for such as she stood contemplating the speaker.

He approached her and laid his hand gently on her arm.

"Mrs. Halford," he said, "painful as this is to me I have deemed it advisable to do this unpleasant duty myself foreseeing as I did that in all probability I should be more mindful of your feelings than any of my junior officers."

"Thank you," she said mechanically—"I thank you."

"You must be aware, however, that I am not alone, and it will be necessary for me to search the house."

A shudder passed through her frame at this intimation.

"Can you not leave?" she said.

"Madam, it may not be—nay more, it cannot be. I wish it were otherwise."

"Edmund," she said, "you would never surely do aught harm me or mine. You—you—oh—"

She covered her face with her hands, and appeared as though about to burst into a flood of tears.

Had she done so, she might have been relieved thereby, but such was not the case. Her brain seemed to be on fire. The captain contemplated her for some time with an expression of countenance in which pity and perhaps love were the chief elements.

"Madam," he said again, "I must, as I before told you search the house."

He then opened the door and called out the names of "Dash," and "Buckle," upon which the two individuals entered the parlour.

"Escaped," said Captain Rignold.

"Indeed?" exclaimed the men, simultaneously.

"Yes; you go immediately and search the garden in the rear of the house, whilst I will go over these premises. Do you hear? Mind, and look in every nook and cranny."

This was said in his usual sharp authoritative tone, and the two men were instantly off.

"And now, madam," he said, in a more gentle voice, "you will, perhaps, kindly accompany me over your establishment?"

She took the candle in her hand and proceeded into the hall, and from thence up the staircase like one walking in her sleep. The captain followed her. She was quite unaware as to where her husband had secreted himself, if he had done so; but she proceeded into the bed-room adjoining her own, where the little Mabel lay sleeping in her cot.

Captain Rignold paused and contemplated the infant sleeper.

"Yours, madam," he said, sadly, "yours, by the likeness. I remember— Well, no matter," and here he sighed again.

He bent down and kissed the child's cheeks several times, and seemed loth to leave the side of the cot.

"It's a pity for her sake," he said, contemplatively; and, then, turning to the mother, he added, "and a pity for yours."

She made no reply, but regarded the captain with a look which he, at the time, did not know very well how to interpret.

"We will proceed to the other apartments," said the captain.

But he still seemed to linger, and it would have appeared as though he were anxious to loiter away as much time as possible. However, he leisurely turned and went towards the bed-room occupied by Mr. and Mrs. Halford, where he made another pause, as he glanced round the room, as though unwilling to make a strict search. The lady thought that in all probability her husband had made for this room, and was surprised that he had not locked the door of the apartment, and doubtless he would have done so had it not so happened that the key was not in the lock.

Now it was that Mrs. Halford began to find that gift of speech which makes woman so eloquent when pleading for any loved object.

"Mr. Rignold," she now said, in moving accents, "Edmund, as at one time I used to call you—have mercy upon my poor husband, if there be anything against him. I know not, neither will I inquire what, but if there be anything against him, by the memory of our past love—by the memory of those days when you used to fondle me so as a child—by the holy friendship of bygone years—I implore of you to have mercy, and not to desolate a home and hearth which—which is, and has been, a happy one—"

She paused here.

"I would spare him, madam, for your sake, but my duty is paramount."

As he said this he strolled up to a large press which stood on one side of the room, and suddenly flung one of the doors open. As he did so, Mrs. Halford observed her husband concealed therein, and thought it was all over with him ; but it was not so.

The eyes of Captain Rignold met those of the colonel, but the former took no notice, and slammed the door of the press to, and walked away towards the window of the apartment as though he had been unconscious of our hero's presence.

Mrs. Halford now went on her knees before the captain.

"Oh, Edmund," she exclaimed, "have mercy on me—have mercy, I implore you. I know better than any one else in the world the kindness of your disposition—I know better than any one else in the world the generosity of your noble nature—I know that deep love you once bore towards me—that love, Edmund, which—"

She paused again.

"Which met with no return. Is that what you would say, madam ?" he inquired.

"No, no, you are not ungenerous enough to charge me with being insensible to your many and varied good qualities. You know —there—do not refer to that now ; but, oh, Captain Rignold, you once loved me—"

"I did, indeed, madam," he said, solemnly. "That is a fact, I should suppose, it were impossible for you to doubt ; but it is somewhat idle to recur to the past—"

"Oh, yes, it may be so, I know—yes, it is, perhaps— Forgive me, I know not what I am saying, but, Edward, I grieve now to think of the past. You cannot—you surely will not do that which may embitter the remainder of my days,—you do not bear him such deep animosity as that ?"

Here she pointed to the press where the colonel was concealed.

"Animosity, madam !" he exclaimed, indignantly, as he receded back a step or two ; "you do not suppose me capable of coming here to gratify any feeling of revenge on my own part ?"

"No, no, I do not mean that. Oh, pray forgive me, Edmund. Have mercy, for my child's sake !"

"I am here but for the fulfilment of my duty, as an officer of the crown ; and although I might be glad if your husband were not here—when I know he is—I should be playing a double game to connive at his escape ; and I hope Miss— I mean Mrs. Halford, that you will do me the justice to say, that when you knew me more intimately, that it was not my custom to play a double game with anybody or for anybody."

He emphasised the latter words most pain-fully, and they jarred upon the ears of Mrs Halford.

"I know," she said, with fresh fears rising in her breast, "I know you would scorn to do a dishonourable action. Alas ! I of all persons in the world ought to say this much of you—I who, from childhood, knew your upright and manly nature ; but for my sake, for the sake of that little dear one," she pointed towards where the child was sleeping, "for her sake, as well as mine, do not do aught that may harm Frank—ah—Mr. Halford."

"It is not me alone ; I have men. And even if he were to try and make his escape, I scarcely know how he would accomplish it. No, I hardly know how he would accomplish it. Confound those men ! No, he could never jump from this window."

And here the captain strolled up to the open casement, followed by Mrs. Halford.

"You see," he observed, "he could never jump from this window. To be sure he might ease himself down by the stem of the vine. Yes, he might do that, certainly ; but then you see, there are my men, Dash and Buckle—and I don't see them either."

He looked out of the open window to the grounds at the rear of the house, and eventually succeeded in catching sight of his active subordinates. After this he took a pistol from his belt, and set it at full cock. Mrs. Halford watched his actions with an unwonted degree of interest. Captain Rignold grasped the pistol in his right hand, and aiming at a shrubbery lying on the left hand of the garden, he flung the weapon with all his force towards this spot.

As it fell to the ground it went off with a loud report, and he observed his two men hastening in the direction of the fallen pistol.

"Ah, he might have a chance now," said the captain. "If he only knew the coast was clear, he might make his escape through the right hand gate, or even through the hedge, if needs must be. Yes, now would be his time ; and really, madam, I wish he could avail himself of it, for to tell you the truth, which perhaps I need hardly tell you, I do not want to have any hand in taking your husband. By-the-bye, I did not search the cupboard in the other."

The instant he made this last observation, he rushed immediately into the room where the child was sleeping.

Mrs. Halford opened the door of the press, and our hero stepped out without any further invitation.

"Oh, Frank," exclaimed Mrs. Halford, all in a tremble, "I know not what this may be all about, but make your escape—fly, at all events. Captain Rignold will not attempt to molest you. Fly, while there is yet time."

"Do not despair," said our hero, although

his own spirits were sadly dashed. "You shall hear from me shortly. This will all blow over."

"Do not waste words!—fly, Frank!" exclaimed his wife.

She assisted him to get through the window. He held on for a second or so to take a last look at her before he descended.

"Bless you, Kate," he said: "you do not deserve to be thus treated, and are worthy a better fate. No matter, we shall be happy in future. Tell Rignold he will not go unrewarded for this act of generosity."

He kissed his wife affectionately several times, and then began to descend from his position, and eventually she had the satisfaction of seeing him alight on the ground in safety, upon which she closed the window, and turned towards the door of the bed-room through which Captain Rignold now entered. They neither spoke for a minute or so, but at length the captain said—

"I do not think, madam, that Mr. Halford would do well to come home again for some time."

She silently nodded her approval of this advice.

"I hope he will be shortly far away from the neighbourhood," continued the captain, after a pause.

"I thank you, Captain Rignold," said the lady, in her own sweet dulcet voice, which had years before so charmed the captain to listen to. "I thank you for this, and also the very many other acts of kindness so cheerfully and gracefully rendered to myself."

The captain waved his hand deprecatingly.

"It is what you deserve," said the lady; "but cold thanks are a poor recompense for all you have suffered for my sake—suffered, Edward, uncomplainingly."

"We will not recur to past events now, Kate," said the captain, sadly. "We may remember them—at least I may. It would be well, perhaps, if my memory were not so retentive."

"Ah, Edmund, it would be as well if we could both ignore the past."

"We have only the future to look to now," was his reply.

"Yes, the future," she sighed. "What of that?"

"Madam," he said, as he approached her, and gently took her hand, "if in the future Captain Rignold can be of any service to you as a friend, or to save you from any forthcoming trouble, I need not say that you may command him. I am not a man who ever indulged in honied speeches," he emphasised the last sentence, "neither is it my habit to make protestations I—I do not feel."

"I know it—I well know that, Captain Rignold."

"Good. Then remember you can always count upon me as your friend in years to come."

She squeezed his hand in acknowledgment of her gratitude, and he said, as he turned away—

"And may you never need them for your own sake."

With this he went through the half-open door, and was in another minute in the lower apartment of the house. She stood for a minute watching his receding figure, then pressed her hands against her temples to collect her scattered thoughts, and then proceeding into the next room, she went to the side of her sleeping child, bent over it, and wept copiously.

Captain Rignold upon getting down into the parlour assumed that rough commanding manner which was habitual to him. He was generally accounted brusque in his bearing, but when addressing Mrs. Halford his voice was low and tender to the last degree.

He now took his way into the servants' apartments, and pretended to make a search therein, and the servants were overawed by his austere manner.

Presently Messrs. Dash and Buckle returned from their search in the grounds. Their officer regarded them with a look of unspeakable anger.

"Well,' he said, "what have you done? As I expected, he has escaped."

"Yes, sir," said Mr. Dash, submissively. "We saw him run through the grounds, and gave chase, but he was too far ahead for us to overtake him."

"Whose pistol was that which I heard go off?"

"I fired at him without success."

"You?"

"Yes, sir, and you please.'

The captain knew this to be a lie, for there had been but one report, the which he was well able to account for; he, however, took no notice. The fact was, that neither Dash or Buckle had seen Colonel Jack at all, but they had heard the report of Captain Rignold's pistol, and ran towards the spot without succeeding in catching a passing glance of the fugitive.

"Umph!" exclaimed the captain, "you seem to have managed to make a muddle of this business between you."

"I am very sorry, sir," said Dash; "I am sure it was through no neglect on the part of either myself or Buckle."

"There, that will do. I don't want apologies, all I should have liked would have been the man, but it can't be helped. Now you must stay here, and keep guard all night, for we are not certain, mind you, that the individual you say you saw,"—he emphasised these words, which made Mr. Dash very uncomfortable—"I say that we are not certain

—at any rate, I am not—that the person you saw running away was in reality the one we were in search of. So you must sit up all night here and keep strict watch. Do you understand ?'

"Yes, captain."

"And see that you have got your eye-teeth about you. Do you mind ?"

" Yes, sir," said both of the men.

"For it is not at all unlikely that the bird may fly home to roost before the night is over ; so mind you are not caught napping yourselves. You can take up your quarters in the kitchen, for Mrs. Halford is a lady, and I should wish you to spare her feelings in this matter as much as possible. Now you need not make any oration about this matter among the servants."

"Oh, no, captain," said both the men, simultaneously, and with that they took their way to the kitchen.

Captain Rignold then called out, in a loud voice, to Mrs. Halford, who was in the up-stairs room. She answered immediately and came down, drying her red and swolen eyes. The captain observed her distressed visage, and, perhaps, no sight could have caused him more pain.

"My dear madam," he said, "I am sorry to see that you have been fretting yourself thus. You need not give way to grief now, for as far as this matter is concerned, I think we may say that your troubles are over. At another time I will explain myself more fully, but for the present I deem it prudent to be silent."

"What is the cause of this ? What is Mr. Halford charged with ?"

"We will talk about that hereafter. I am compelled to leave the two officers in possession of the house—they will stay all night— sit up, in fact, but I have directed them to conduct themselves with discretion."

"You are very kind."

"Mr. Halford is not likely to return—to come home ?" asked the captain.

"I hope not."

"And so do I."

"Do you stay, sir ?"

"No, madam ; I shall pay you another visit in the morning to see if any event has taken place during the night."

"Oh—ah—I see! Thank you."

"Good night, Kate—I mean Mrs. Halford," said the captain, as he took her hand and raised it to his lips.

"Good night."

Captain Rignold mounted his horse, which stood ready outside the gate, and trotted off in the bright moonlight.

CHAPTER XXV.

THE TWO REPRESENTATIVES OF THE LAW.— ESCAPE OF THE DOG.

THERE was no sleep for poor Mrs. Halford that night. After the departure of Captain Rignold, she rang for her faithful servant Curson, who came into the parlour with a distracted visage.

"Oh, missus! Whatever has been the matter ?" exclaimed Curson.

"That is more than I can tell you," she answered.

"Is it for debt ?" inquired the domestic, for she was on sufficiently familiar terms with her mistress to warrant her in asking such a question.

"I suppose so."

"Oh, I am glad of that. Theodore thought it might be for something worse."

Theodore was the man servant, a sort of half footman and half butler.

"He is mistaken," said Mrs. Halford, sadly, "but he had much better mind his own business."

"So I say, mum, only Theodore always would talk and be so knowing."

"Ah ; I know."

"But you must not fret yourself, my dear lady," said the kindhearted Curson ; "you must keep up your spirits ; we have all our troubles in this world."

While Curson was endeavouring to console her mistress in the parlour, Messrs. Dash and Buckle were engaged in the kitchen dis-cussing some substantial viands, which had been placed before them agreeable to the orders of Mrs. Halford.

Those acute officers felt and knew that, in that establishment they were considered to be the representatives of the law, and conse-quently they thought proper to assume an oracular tone. They felt, also, that the law required sustenance, and thought it advisable to lay in a good stock when the viands were placed before them.

Sarah felt herself very uncomfortable in their presence, and contemplated them eating as though they were two ogres.

As to Theodore, he lounged leisurely against one article in the room and then another, ever and anon contemplating his calves with evident satisfaction, as the work of gastronomy went on with Dash and Buckle.

After the law had finished his meal, he, like any other animal, seemed in a measure to be appeased, and was not near so sharp as he was previous to his repast—After all there is nothing like a full stomach for inducing placidity.

"You are very tall, sir," said Mr. Dash to Theodore.

"Pretty well."

"I should say you were a tall man, nay a fine man," he added.

"That is a matter of opinion, you know," answered the footman, who was, however, pleased at the remark. "It is not the general custom of the law to indulge in compliments."

"Precisely," said Mr. Dash, "why what must you be now—six feet?"

"No; five feet seven."

"A good height. Why you look taller to me than many of the men in the guards," said Mr. Buckle.

"I am," answered Theodore, drawing himself up.

"I thought so."

"Please, gentlemen," said Sarah, "my mistress says what will you take?"

"We have had supper, my dear," answered Mr. Buckle.

"I mean to drink."

"Oh," exclaimed the representatives of the law.

"What shall it be, gentlemen?"

"Anything you may happen to have handy, my dear."

"Would you like some grog or beer?"

"I don't care; what say you, Dash?"

"A little grog, if it makes no difference," said that worthy.

Bottles, glasses, and hot-water were placed before the men of the law, who contemplated them with loving eyes.

"Would there be any objection to smoke, my dear?"

"Not in the least," answered the maid.

With this the law proceeded to indulge in a pipe. Mr. Dash offered one to Theodore, saying:

"Do you do anything in this line?"

"No; I do not."

"We should have been glad if you would have joined us."

Here was condescension on the part of the law! Theodore felt himself elevated in the social scale, and felt emboldened by their complaisance, so much so that he said, assuming quite a confidential tone:

"Is it anything particularly heavy against the guv'nor?"

Mr. Dash took his pipe out of his mouth and contemplated the speaker in mute surprise—the majesty of the law was outraged by such a question from such a man—a mere flunkey. Mr. Dash looked at Theodore so fixedly that the patagonian footman blushed visibly.

"No," said Mr. Dash, "it ain't heavy, my man, and if it were—" he paused, and emitted a large puff of smoke from his mouth, "and if it were? Now I have got a whisper for you, young man. Do you know or guess what it is?"

"No."

"Well, it is just this, my friend—mind your own business!"

"Oh, I see, exactly."

"Yes, exactly, as you say, exactly, that's it," and here the law nodded approvingly towards the speaker.

Theodore did not feel himself on quite such easy terms with the two gentlemen as he had done a few minutes previous to the last observation, so he deemed it expedient to leave the apartment a few seconds afterwards.

"A man of an inquiring turn of mind," said Mr. Buckle.

"Must be repressed, kept down in their proper place—every man to his own particular sphere," said Dash.

Shortly after this, Curson entered the kitchen.

"I hope you are making yourself comfortable, gentlemen."

"Well, thank you, ma'am; we can't very well be doing better."

"My mistress desires me to say that I am to see you want for nothing."

"I am sure we are much obliged to you—very much obliged."

"Oh not at all."

"Seems a very nice lady."

"Ah, that she is—a better never breathed in this world."

"So I should say—pipe offensive ma'am?"

"Oh dear, no; I rather like it."

Mr. Dash nodded to his companion to signify that they had got hold of a sensible woman. So she was, for she did not venture any observation upon the cause of either of the officers being present in the house, but sitting herself down in an old oak chair beside the fireplace—a place of honour always reserved for her in the kitchen, she, in a short time, sunk into a light sleep.

The law took care of itself during this time, and Mr. Dash and his companion had managed to make themselves pretty comfortable during these lonely hours of their watch in the domicile of Colonel Jack.

"This is the way the world runs," said Mr. Dash. "A cove gets his leg into a trap, and the hounds are upon him."

"Such is life," said Buckle. "Some folks take the straight road, and others cut along through all the bye-pathways. But he has hooked it cleverly enough, though."

"Wonder if he was in the house when we came?" said Dash.

"Hush!" said Buckle; and here the speaker pointed to Curson.

As he did this, his companion's eyes seemed fixed upon some object under the table.

"Why, what's the row, Dash?"

The gentleman addressed made no answer, but still kept his eyes fixed upon the same spot.

"What the deuce can it be? Looks like a pocket-book."

"Where?"

"Why, here under the table."

As he spoke these words he moved his foot, and there came immediately a low growl.

Mr. Buckle looked at his companion for an elucidation of the mystery.

"Why, curse me if it ain't the dog," said Dash.

"What dog?"

"Why his, of course."

"Where?"

"Here, right under the table," replied the officer.

"Come out!"

Another sharp growl followed. Mr. Buckle rose from his seat with the intention of coming to the side of his companion to look at the quadruped under the table, but Mr. Buckle found, upon rising from his chair, that his legs were not capable of performing their duty so well as they might have done an hour or so before.

The law was becoming oblivious.

"Hold up, old chap," said Mr. Dash, as he lent his companion a helping hand.

"Where is he?" asked Buckle.

"There; don't you see his eyes?"

Mr. Buckle did see his eyes, and teeth, too, for underneath the table, upon which the supper had been served, was the dog Slott. His face was smeared with blood, his eyes were red and bloodshot, his mouth was open, disclosing a set of teeth which caused a cold shudder to run through the officer, and suggest thoughts of hydrophobia.

"By the Lord, but it's the dog, sure enough," said Dash, in a hoarse whisper. Only think of his concealing himself here, under our very nose. Here, Carlo—Carlo! Neptune, or whatever may be your name. Come dog—poor fellow—come," and Mr. Dash thought it expedient to try the wheedling.

"Must make a captive of him, if possible," said Dash.

"Try him with a bit of meat," said his companion.

"He ain't to be had at that game. Come, boy—come."

But Slott did not seem at all disposed to come, but he stood, with his legs as usual wide apart, and regarded the two men with a most unamiable expression of countenance.

"My word," said Buckle, "but he is an ugly brute, and no mistakes."

Stoop down, and see if you can catch hold of him, Dash."

"Oh, yes, I dare say. I should like to catch myself at that game."

"Well, we must have him by fair means or foul."

"I ain't going to make a grab at him," said Dash.

And to look at the animal, it did not appear at all healthy for any one to attempt such a course.

The two officers sat down and endeavoured to collect their thoughts, that they might light upon some plan to capture the dog.

"What has he got under him?" asked Dash.

"A pocket-book, I think," answered the other.

"And so it is. Here, boy—here—good dog," and again the officer began to try the wheedling, with the same amount of success as heretofore. Slott was quite impervious to flattery of any sort.

"Confound the brute, how are we to get at him?" said Buckle.

Mr. Dash scratched his head, when, by this time Curson awoke, and glanced at the two officers.

The candle had burnt down nearly to the socket.

"What is the matter, gentlemen? Dear me, I've been fast asleep," said Curson.

"The dog, ma'am," said Buckle.

"Oh, Slott? Where is he, then?"

"Under the table."

"Do you want him?"

"Well, yes, ma'am, we do rather, please," said Buckle.

"Here, Slott—Slott," said Curson.

The animal gave a slight wag of his short stumpy tail to indicate that he knew who it was calling him; but he did not feel disposed to move from his hiding place.

"He don't feel disposed to come," said Curson.

"That he certainly does not, ma'am," said the officer.

"Do you want him particularly, gentlemen?" inquired Curson again, as her eyes caught sight of the pocket-book.

"Well, we must take him prisoner—leastways," said Buckle, correcting himself, "we should like to keep him till the captain comes in the morning."

"Ah, I see. Here, Slott," said Curson, again.

As she was endeavouring to propitiate the dog, Mr. Buckle went to the other side of the table, and thought he would try a *coup d'etat*. While the dog's attention was engaged with Curson, Mr. Buckle from the other side of the table inserted his right hand, and by a sudden movement sought to lay hold of him by the neck. A sharp angry growl followed this movement, and before the officer had time to withdraw his hand, the animal made a snap at it, and inflicted so severe a wound, that the man roared with rage and pain,

as the blood flowed copiously from the laceration.

"D—n!" exclaimed the officer, as he tried to staunch the blood with his handkerchief, "curses on the brute."

"Oh, mercy on me," exclaimed Curson, "I am so sorry; he always was a savage animal, and never will allow any one to come near him."

A cessation of hostilities now ensued, and the man's hand was bathed in luke-warm water, after which it was carefully strapped and bound up by the kind, good-natured Curson.

"We must have him by some means or other," said Dash.

"I really would not attempt to go near him, sir; you don't know what a fierce animal he is.

No. 21.

"My mate does," thought Dash.

"If you like I will consult missus, sir," said Curson.

"Perhaps she has gone to bed?"

"No; I think not as yet," answered Curson.

Curson then went into the parlour where she had left Mrs. Halford, to whom she narrated the foregoing incidents, telling her at the same time that the officers were desirous of making a capture of Slott.

"Indeed!" said Mrs. Halford, "I am quite sure that his master would be sorry if any harm were to befal him. What is to be done, Curson?"

"Well, perhaps, you had better come and see, ma'am."

"Very well."

Mrs. Halford followed Curson into the

kitchen. The two men rose upon her entering, and bowed respectfully.

"You want the dog, Slott, it appears?" said Mrs. Halford.

"We should like to have him tied up till the morning, if you please, ma'am," said Mr. Dash.

"I am afraid of him myself, especially in his unamiable moods," said Mrs. Halford.

"He knows you, ma'am, I suppose?"

"Oh, yes; but he won't always allow me to touch him—but if you wish it I will try, of course."

"I should be sorry if he should harm you, ma'am."

"I don,t think he will do that."

Mrs. Halford looked under the table, and at the dog, who regarded her with a suspicious look. She observed that the animal had a pocket-book immediately underneath his fore paw and chest, and from his manner it would appear as though he were guarding the same.

"Here, Slott, Slott," said Mrs. Halford.

The dog wagged his tail, and seemed better pleased since his mistress had spoke to him.

"If you can manage to slip this round his neck," said Mr. Buckle, producing at the same time a pocket handkerchief, "and then fasten him to the leg of the table, he would be safe till the morning."

Mrs. Halford took the handkerchief, and by coaxing managed to get Slott to submit to her fastening it round his neck; this done, she tied the other end of the handkerchief to the leg of the table.

Mr. Buckle thanked her for the trouble she had been at.

Mrs. Halford wished them good night, and then took her departure followed by her old servant, Curson.

"Well, she's done more than you or I could do," said Mr. Buckle to his companion. "Let us have a look at him."

Mr. Dash lifted up the table-cover and peered under the table. The dog gave another low growl, and showed his fangs in a most unpleasant and ferocious manner.

Mr. Buckle, who had become somewhat sobered by the exciting incidents, knelt down and made a close inspection of the animal—who, as the officer advanced his hand, made a snap at it; Mr. Buckle withdrew his hand so quickly that he struck his elbow against the chair upon which he had been seated that he yelled with pain.

"Confound the brute!" he exclaimed; "it appears that we are all to suffer from him in one way or the other."

The officers again cast a furtive glance under the table—Slott contemplated them with an eye of flame. They thought descretion was, in this instance, the better part of valour, and withdrew to their chairs, and

then they indulged in one or two more social pipes.

Night wore apace, and in the due course of time the two watchful representatives of the law became wrapped in a profound slumber.

Mrs. Halford was too much troubled in her mind by the incidents of the evening to be able to sleep. Curson sat up with her to keep her company and cheer her spirits as best she could.

"I wonder what they want with Slott?" said Curson.

"I don't know," replied Mrs. Halford, "but I wish he was safe away, out of the house—the poor animal seems to be severely wounded."

"Shall I go and see how affairs are going on in the kitchen?"

"You must be very cautious, then."

"Trust me, ma'am."

"If you can make some excuse for returning to the kitchen it would be as well," said Mrs. Halford.

"Leave that to me," said Curson; and away she went into the apartment where the two officers were now fast asleep.

They were slumbering audibly when Curson entered. She watched their slumbering forms, and then cautiously proceeded towards the table where Slott lay concealed. He did not give any indication of discontent as she approached. On the contrary, he seemed to be aware that her intentions were of a friendly nature—she at once proceeded to undo the end of the handkerchief which was fastened to the table; directly this was done the dog trotted out of the kitchen with the pocket-book in his mouth.

Curson followed the dog, closing the door of the kitchen noiselessly as she emerged therefrom, and went again into the parlour, into which she called Slott. He followed her, not in his usual bold manner, but in a quiet sneaking style of movement, very different to his habitual bearing.

"Here, Slott," said Mrs. Halford, as she held out her hand.

The hound came to her side, dropped the pocket-book at her feet, and licked her outstretched hand, which was a condescension that he did not often indulge in. He then glanced round the apartment, and then towards the street door, upon which he uttered a slight whine.

"What's the matter with him, ma'am?" asked Curson.

"He wants to go out," replied Mrs. Halford, who knew what these demonstrations indicated.

"He shall not want long, then," said Curson, and she noiselessly and cautiously undid the fastenings of the outer door, and eventually opened it.

No sooner was this done than the hound

rushed through, and trotted off at full speed, and was soon out of sight.

Curson then closed the door again, muttering to herself as she did so :

"Good Slott—sensible dog—ah, you are a faithful brute !"

They then returned to the parlour, without making the slightest noise in their movements, fearing that they might awaken the officers of the law who still slept soundly in the kitchen.

"Slott's off, safe enough ma'am," continued Curson, "but where I know not, but I'll wager that he won't be found on these premises in the morning."

"Thanks, thanks, good Curson. I am glad he has gone, at any rate."

"Never fear, ma'am, you might trust Slott as well or better than many Christians ; he is the most sensible animal that I ever saw in my life."

"He is indeed, Curson—his master values him very much."

"What's to be done now, ma'am ?" inquired Curson.

"We had better conceal the pocket-book, for it belongs to no inmate of this establishment."

When the morning's light found its way into the apartments of Colonel Jack's domicile, the law thought it expedient to wake from its slumbers.

Mr. Buckle was the first to be aroused from a state of somnolency, and he at once proceeded to arouse his companion.

"Dash !" he exclaimed, shouting to his brother officer, "wake up, old fellow, you've had a tightish snore."

"Ugh," growled Dash.

"Wake up."

"What's the row ?"

"Why, you have been fast asleep all the night."

"And you?"

"Been following your example, I've an idea."

"Then you haven't heard any noise during the night ?"

"Nothing but your snoring."

"Psha ! I never snore."

"Gammon and all."

"Where's the dog ?"

"Blest if I know."

The two worthies now made a strict search under the table and throughout the kitchen, but no Slott was to be seen.

"Gone !" said Buckle with a look of amazement.

"To a certainty," added Dash, looking at his brother officer, and rubbing his eyes, as if he was not thoroughly convinced that he was not dreaming.

Slott by this time was far away, despite his wounded leg.

Curson shortly afterwards came into the kitchen.

"I am afraid, gentlemen," she said that you must be quite worn out with sitting up all night ; shall I make you a strong cup of tea or coffee with a dash of brandy in it— I dare say it will be acceptable after this tedious watch ?"

"Thank you," said Buckle, "thank you— you are very obliging."

"Don't name it, sir."

"By the way, we can't make out what has become of the dog—have you seen anything of him ?" said Dash.

"No," said Curson, with well-feigned surprise.

"We can't find him anywhere," said Mr. Buckle.

"Is he not here ?" said Curson, looking under the table.

"Don't appear to be."

"Well, that's singular ; Mrs. Halford, I know, fastened him to the leg of the table— perhaps he has managed to get loose somehow or the other ?"

The two men scratched their heads and looked perplexed.

Breakfast was served, and Buckle said to Curson, as she came in with the coffee, that he would like to say a word or two to Mrs. Halford. He was immediately ushered into the parlour, where sat the mistress of the establishment.

"I beg your pardon, madam," said Mr. Buckle, "but it is respecting the dog that I wished to speak."

"Yes, sir."

"Well, you see, ma'am he is nowhere to be found."

"Indeed ! I fastened him up last night, agreeable to your request," said Mrs. Halford, assuming an air of astonishment at this announcement.

"He's managed to hook it—I beg you pardon, I mean he's escaped—got away," said Mr. Buckle.

"How can that be ?"

"I don't know, ma'am, but it is so," said Mr. Buckle.

"Well, I cannot possibly help it,' replied Mrs. Halford.

"Oh, no, of course not; only, you see, ma'am it is particularly unfortunate, and may be the means of getting me and my mate into trouble."

"I am very sorry for that.

"Yes, ma'am, but it is—now, you see, I've been thinking—leastways if you have no objection—I've been thinking that if you— you, would not mind saying nothing about —about it."

"About what ?"

"Why, about his being here at all," said Mr. Buckle.

"Oh, I have no desire to do so, believe me —it is not all likely that I should talk about it, or allow any of my servants to do so ; I detest gossiping."

"Do you think you can rely upon your servants ?"

"I could trust my life in their hands," said Mrs. Halford, with an expression of warmth that was indeed sincere, and showed the trust she reposed in them.

Mr. Buckle did not seem quite satisfied, and, after a pause of a few minutes he said, pointedly—

"But I mean you will not mention the affair to Captain Rignold ?"

"Mr. Buckle I am sure you have no cause to mistrust me."

"But," added the officer, "he will be here to-day, and if he thought we let the dog escape out of the apartment in which we were watching I am sure he would be very angry with us."

"You are quite safe as far as I am concerned."

"I am sure my mate and I am very much beholden to you."

"Not at all, Mr. Buckle ; I should, I am sure, be very sorry to get you into trouble." She could hardly restrain herself from smiling as she said this, but continued however with becoming gravity, "I should be very sorry if either you or your companion get into trouble on this account."

"Thank you, ma'am."

"Not one member of this establishment knew of the presence of Slott but Curson and myself."

"The tall servant, then—Theodore, I think you call him, who by the way, is of rather an inquisitive turn of mind—was ignorant of the presence of the dog in the kitchen ?"

"Yes."

Mr. Dash now knocked at the door, and was requested to come in by Mrs. Halford.

"Whatever has kept you so long ?' said Dash to Buckle, in a low whisper, which was however loud enough for the quick ears of Mrs. Halford.

Mrs. Halford then related to the officer the nature of the conversation which had taken place between herself and his companion.

Mr. Dash felt himself very much indebted to her and was about to pour forth a volume of thanks, when Mrs. Halford interrupted him, saying—

"From me, Captain Rignold will never learn anything of this circumstance, and I can rely on Curson if I caution her—she will never breath a word of it, rest assured, if I forbid her."

"We are extremely obliged to you, ma'am, I can assure you," said Mr. Buckle, rising from the chair on which he had been seated during the dialogue which had taken place in the parlour.

Mr. Dash bowed and scraped his thanks in silence, and in a few minutes they took their way towards the kitchen, where they patiently awaited the arrival of their superior officer.

When Captain Rignold came, which he did some two or three hours after this he was informed that all had been quiet in the establishment during the night, and he withdrew his two officers, much to the relief and joy of Mrs. Halford and Curson.

CHAPTER XXVI.

FLIGHT OF COLONEL JACK.

WE must now follow the footsteps of our hero.

The colonel, as the reader already knows, dropped from the window of his sleeping apartment, and alighted on the ground in perfect safety.

To run through the shrubbery of his own grounds, and dash through the hedge that enclosed them, was the work of but a moment.

Once having emerged from his own grounds he felt himself safe—for from what he had heard he knew that two of Captain Rignold's men were searching for him in the garden. The colonel paused for a few seconds, and reflected upon the course best for him to pursue. As he did so an expression of fear passed over his features.

What would his wife say? was his first thought. The blow would indeed be a severe one for her. She who had not the slightest notion of his occupation. His house at Hornsey was no longer a home for him—indeed, since this affair had become blown, as he termed it, there was no other alternative than leaving the neighbourhood for good and for all.

The colonel walked on in a dejected mood ; the incidents which had just taken place awoke him to a painful sense of his own reckless course of life—perhaps he had never before been so impressed with this. However, shaking off the temporary depression, he had recourse to what was usual with him, namely—action.

He hastened onwards towards a shed down a lane, which was, in fact, used as a blacksmith's forge when at work. A small cottage was attached to this, and here it was that the colonel was making for.

He proceeded to the back of the cottage, and gave, at the door, two or three mysterious raps. The casement was instantly opened, and a head thrust out

A low whistle was given by the colonel, when the window closed quietly, and the door opened.

"What's the matter, colonel?" said Crawley, for it was no other than that individual, whom, the reader may remember, was introduced in the second chapter of our story.

"On my lay," said his superior.

"The devil!"

"Yes—my horse; quick!"

"Yes. Will you come in while I get her ready?"

"To be sure; of course I will."

The colonel then entered the cottage, while Crawley set to work to saddle and bridle the colonel's horse which was sheltered in a stable contiguous to the habitation.

"On his lay; well, I'm blest. How has that occured? Well, I'm blest, but this ere's a go—it's all up in Hornsey for him, and, yes, I suppose, for me too—on his lay. Well, I never!"

In a few minutes the horse stood at the door of the house, and the colonel, with his usual agility, sprung into the saddle, and wishing his companion a hasty good night, was off.

Once upon the back of his noble steed, he felt himself once more safe from any coming harm.

As a key to the foregoing incidents, it will be necessary to put the reader in possession of the circumstances which gave rise to Captain Rignold's visit to his house.

In earlier years Captain Rignold had been a devoted admirer of Mrs. Halford. He was many years her senior, yet, nevertheless, she regarded him with feelings of deep esteem and friendship, if not love; the probability was she would have accepted Captain Rignold had not the colonel, or rather Mr. Halford, presented himself to her notice, and by persevering attentions he eventually won her for his wife.

It has often been said that women choose the crooked stick, and it proved true in the present instance.

Nevertheless, the colonel loved his pretty little devoted wife, and treated her with uniform kindness.

After they had been married for some time, Captain Rignold became aware of our hero's occupation, and the fact of Mr. Halford and Colonel Jack being one and the same person. He had carefully avoided dropping any hints on this subject to any one who might convey the painful intelligence to Mrs. Halford; for although Captain Rignold did not view the colonel with favourable eyes, the deep and endearing love he still bore for Mrs. Halford, made him mindful of him to whom she owed allegiance.

Chivalrous this, you will say. Yes, and rare; the more to be prized, my friend. At any rate it proved of essential service to Colonel Jack, who would have been safely locked up had it not been for the instrumentality of Captain Rignold.

The colonel, Hackett and Warrington had, it appeared stopped the carriage of a pig-headed country squire, a Mr. Greathead by name.

This gentleman, upon Hackett presenting his pistol at the open window of the carriage, struck it up, and discharged his own, without doing any serious mischief to the highwayman. He, however, sprang from his carriage, and called upon his attendants to resist the attack of the highwaymen.

The consequence of all this was that a general melee took place, and as the colonel heard the noise of coming horsemen, he deemed it prudent to beat a retreat.

The horsemen proved to be some of the parish constabulary, who, upon Mr. Greathead's informing them of what had taken place, at once proceeded to give chase to the highwaymen.

Mr. Greathead was so bent upon catching them, that he had one of the horses in his carriage taken out, and, upon this animal, he followed himself in pursuit.

Seeing how matters turned out, the highwaymen had recourse to their old ruse, namely, taking each of them separate roads, but unfortunately for our hero, he it was that the officers and Mr. Greathead chose to follow, and so persevering were they, that they were at his heels for some five or six and twenty miles. But they managed to get separated; one, however, happened to observe the colonel dismount from his horse, in a by-lane, and throw the reins to Crawley, after which he watched him towards his own house.

He did not feel quite confident that the colonel was the same person, for he had missed sight of them two or three hours, and in the darkness of the night it was not easy to be sure of his identity. However, he was sufficiently assured to make his way immediately to the head quarters of Captain Rignold, and there make him acquainted with the particulars of the attack on the carriage of Mr. Greathead.

The captain tried to persuade the man that he must have been mistaken, the more so as Mr. Halford, the owner of the house in question was a most respectable man, and not at all likely to be concerned in any robbery.

The man, however, was resolute, and persevered in his statement, and so Captain Rignold had no other alternative than proceeding at once to the house of Mr. Halford with two of his men, with what result the reader has already seen.

Colonel Jack, after he had parted with Crawley, hastened away from the neighbourhood where he had been respected and esteemed as an honest man. He felt that the dream was now for ever dispelled.

To return to his own domicile again he knew was an impossibility, and it was in no very pleasant mood that the colonel trotted along the road on the night of Captain Rignold's attempt, or rather pretence of capture.

He had ridden many miles from his own home without meeting with anything particular to attract his attention, when a surprise awaited him which he did not at all expect.

As he was passing the end of a lane which ran at right angles from the road he was traversing, his horse started, and at first gave an indication of his intention to rear. The colonel hastened to see what was the matter, when to his joy he observed Slott, panting and out of breath, his tongue hanging out of his mouth, and his sides reeking with perspiration. He had evidently travelled many miles at a rapid pace, and was well nigh exhausted; notwithstanding which he jumped up at his master, and evinced great joy at again finding him.

Indeed, he was so demonstrative that the colonel hardly knew what to make of the animal, as such evolutions were not usual with him.

As the colonel was about to turn the head of his horse towards the lane from which Slott had emerged, the dog whined and gave a low bark, while, at the same time, he jumped up in front of the horse and evinced a disposition to stop the progress of the horse.

The colonel halted for a moment, as he could not comprehend the meaning of these demonstrations on the part of Slott, who, as he reined up his horse, stood still in front, and appeared more satisfied.

His master was still at a loss to understand these signs, and he again gently urged on his horse. The moment he did so, Slott jumped up again in front and actually began to snap at the chest of the horse.

The colonel now began to have serious misgivings as to the dog's being afflicted with hydrophobia, which was anything but a pleasant reflection. As he endeavoured to take his way down the lane Slott again jumped up, and evinced the same demonstrations as before.

The colonel leant down by the side of his horse to make a more minute inspection of his dog, when, in doing so, one of the reins was considerably lowered, and Slott immediately sprung up to it, and caught it in his mouth, upon which he immediately dragged it back, and succeeded in turning the horse's head away from the course he was taking.

All these manifestations were so new in their character, that the colonel was fairly puzzled; he, however, passively permitted

the horse to be turned from his course, and raising himself up in his stirrups he took a survey along the lane, down which he was about to proceed. Some moving object was visible in the distance—it was the figure of a man on horseback. Who was he? Was it for this that Slott had been so anxious to turn the horse from his course?

The colonel watched the approaching horseman. He came nearer, and there could be no doubt about it now : the approaching figure was no other than one of the night patrols, and there could now be no mistake about the meaning of Slott's demonstrations.

He must have passed this man, and, by a wondrous instinct which may be said to be closely allied to reasoning powers, Slott had comprehended that danger was near, and hence it was that he had so pertinaciously persisted in his endeavours to make his master alter his course.

The colonel, when he perceived who the approaching horseman was, immediately turned his horse's head, and quietly trotted back to the road from whence he had diverged, and took a different course to the one he had originally intended to pursue.

Pondering, as he did so, upon the wonderful sagacity of his dog—singular, in the first place, that he should have been able to make his escape and find out the road he had taken, but still more singular that he should be enabled to discover that danger was at hand should his master take that particular road. As the colonel reflected upon these circumstances, his eye glanced towards Slott, who was now quietly trotting beside the horse.

He appeared so exhausted that it was with difficulty he could get along. His wounded leg was evidently very painful, as every now and then he stopped to lick his wound, and then trotted on again towards his master.

The colonel whistled him to his side, and catching him by the neck he deposited him safely on the pommel of the saddle, and then urged his steed into a faster trot than heretofore.

He did not know the fate of his companions, whether any of them had been overtaken or captured, and as there usual place of rendezvous was the Badgers, our hero was now taking his way towards the Cow and Cauliflower.

When Colonel Jack arrived at the Badgers he found Hackett, Goldie, and Warrington already assembled there. They had fairly given their pursuers the slip, after a chase of many miles. They were in solemn conclave in the landlord's bar-parlour, but upon the entrance of the colonel they repaired to the up stairs room, where they usually held their meetings.

"So," exclaimed Hackett, "you are safe, then, colonel. The Lord be praised! By my faith, but it was a smartish run, though."

"Safe, indeed," replied our hero. "They chased me home, and I was all but taken, and escaped by the merest chance."

"Followed you home ?—The devil !"

"Yes, and effected an entrance into my house."

"Indeed ?"

"Yes ; and by a most fortunate circumstance I did manage to get clear off ; but for my home at Hornsey—"

He paused, and heaved a deep sigh.

"What ?"

"Why, that is now a dream of the past."

"The whole affair is blown, then ?"

"Most completely. I can never return to those quarters again."

"How did they manage to find out your house ?"

"Oh, that is more than I can tell, but they did, that's certain."

"What one of those who were in pursuit of us ?"

"No ; I thought I had got fairly away, and, judge of my astonishment, after I had changed my dress and was smoking my pipe by our chimney corner, I say, judge of my astonishment, when my house was entered by Captain Rignold and two of his men, and—but you may judge the rest," said the colonel.

"Yes ; you stopped, I suppose, eh ?" said Hackett.

"I rushed up stairs and the captain himself soon followed. I hid myself in a press in my bed room."

"And were you discovered ?"

"Yes ; the captain opened the door, suddenly, and for a second or two we stood face to face."

"And you made a rush for it I suppose ?" said Hackett.

"No ; I remained passive."

"And what was the consequence ?"

"Why the captain would not see me. Do you understand ?"

"Ah, he was one of the right sort then—a wise man."

"Hackett," said the colonel, solemnly, "Captain Rignold is a noble fellow. In earlier years he was a suitor, as I have before told you, for the hand of—"

"Yes—I know, you told me that," said Hackett.

"Well, mindful of her feelings, he chose to spare the husband to favour the wife, and so—" he paused here, and sighed deeply.

His companion made no further observation, but saw plainly that the colonel was extremely moved.

"And so," said the colonel, in continuation, "he walked himself into the other room under the pretext that he was going to institute a search therein, whilst I, taking advantage of his absence, managed to make my escape from the window of my bed room and got clear off. I had left my horse with Crawley, who saddled it quickly and off I trotted, and you know the rest. And, now, here I am."

"The Lord be praised, say I," exclaimed Warrington.

"That thick-headed squire will not rest until he has raised heaven and earth to find us out," said the colonel.

"Let him ! It's all over now," said Hackett, "but the worst part of the affair is, that the colonel's home is blown. Curse the obstinate old fool !"

"It's no use repining over misfortunes," said the colonel, suddenly, rising and ringing the bell. "Come, let's have a bowl of punch to drown our cares."

The Badger appeared in answer to the summons—for when such distinguished customers as the colonel and his companions did him the honour of using his house he generally waited upon them himself.

"Your servant, gentlemen," said Mr. Dyson, "hope as how all matters are squared." This was his usual way of asking if anything was going wrong—and from the few hints dropped by the colonel's companions he judged that there had been some little difficulty.

"Oh, pretty well, Bill," said the colonel ; "what say you to come and join us in a bowl of punch ?"

"Why, thank you, colonel, thank you, I am not the man to refuse a good thing, I can tell you."

In a few minutes Dyson entered with a steaming bowl of punch, which he placed before the highwaymen, and then turned the key in the lock.

There was another door in this apartment, through which the highwaymen could make their escape in the event of a surprise, which was very improbable ; still Mr. Dyson was generally pretty well prepared in his well-conducted establishment for an emergency of any kind.

"Good health, gentlemen, and my respects to you !" said the Badger, as he tossed off a glass of punch which Colonel Jack had handed to him.

"Thank you—thank you," responded the highwaymen.

"Success to trade !" continued the Badger —this was Mr. Dyson's way of designating the profession of a highwayman.

"We've been obliged to cut and run, Bill," said the colonel to the landlord of the Cow and Cauliflower.

"Umph! All our friends seem to be getting in a mess," answered Mr. Dyson ; "now, there's the Nobbler, he's obliged to be up a tree for the Lord knows how long, while all his companions have already met with their death; ah, things go hard with a good many of us, that's certain."

Mr. Dyson, having delivered himself of this remarkable piece of philosophy, washed it down with another draught from the punch bowl.

"How gets on the Cow Cross murder?" asked Hackett.

The colonel made a movement of impatience, and dashed his hand heavily upon the table.

"Things don't look very promising with Osborne," he said, "in fact, they get worse and worse."

"He had no hand in it, I suppose, colonel, had he?" said Mr. Dyson.

"Lord bless you, no more than you have yourself," was the immediate reply of the colonel.

"Then how about the knife. That looked suspicious?"

"Ah," sighed the colonel, "that is the most fatal part of the affair; how that knife ever made its appearance, and where it came from, and how it should have turned up at such an unfortunate time as this, is more than I can tell?"

"But it was Mr. Osborne's knife it seems, colonel?"

"Oh, yes—most assuredly."

"Well, then, it looks smokey against him," said Mr. Dyson.

"Not at all. He has no more to do with the knife being there than you have yourself. The fact is, as far as I can remember, Mr. Osborne lent me that knife for some trifling purpose about two or three years ago. Mind, this is only as I think, I can't be quite certain of it. but the impression upon my mind is, that I had it in my possession about that period. Be this as it may, I am certain of one thing, that I had it in my possession, but where it went to, or what became of it, I am at present unable to tell. Whether it was lost or stolen from me I am equally at a loss about, but I do not remember to have ever returned it to Mr. Osborne."

"That's an awkward fix, colonel," said Mr. Dyson; "very awkward, seeing as how you can't put in an appearance, and give your evidence in the matter."

"Oh, that's an impossibility, and I don't see what good would result from it, even supposing I were to do so."

"Why, if the knife was proved to be in your possession, by your own acknowledgment, you would, of course, be instantly suspected as being one of the men who were concerned in the murder."

"I wish I could find out who the chaps were. I suppose you have heard nothing whispered on the subject?" said the colonel, addressing himself to the Badger, who, in reply, merely shook his head significantly.

If he did know, the colonel saw at once that he intended to keep dark upon the subject.

"Very strange affair, take it altogether," said Hackett, in a ruminating manner.

"Ah," said Mr. Dyson, "we all meet with strange adventures in our time. Now, there's our friend Warrington. He was telling me the other day, some incidents of his early life, which were positively quite romantic. I like anything of a romantic or sentimental turn—I was always inclined very much that way myself."

Shouts of laughter followed this declaration, as it was perhaps impossible to conceive a more unromantic person than Mr. Dyson.

Warrington sighed and looked up at the ceiling.

"Why, what are you thinking about, old boy?" said the colonel, slapping him on the back. "Your wits are wool gathering."

"I am thinking of the light of bye-gone years," said Warrington, sadly; "the light which was once shed upon my path from there—above," and he pointed upwards as he spoke. "A light which made a sunshine of my life—a light which is obscured by darkness now."

"Why, what do you mean, Warrington? You speak in enigmas," said the colonel.

"Oh, it was before I knew you—when quite in the spring time of my youth—before I was quite so care-hardened as I am at present, or supposed to be, which is, perhaps much the same thing."

"Well, tell us all about it," said the colonel; "let us know the story of your early life before you took to sinning."

"Oh, its hardly worth while to recur to incidents which, after all, had better be forgotten."

"Oh, nonsense, man; the story—come," said the colonel.

"He began telling me," said Mr. Dyson, "but something came and interrupted him in his story."

After some more pressing on the part of his companions, Warrington cleared his throat, and related the adventures which are recorded in the following chapter.

CHAPTER XXVII.

THE HIGHWAYMAN'S STORY.

"I DARE say," said Warrington, "that you will think I am romancing, when I tell you that I was born of respectable parents, who moved in the best society."

"Not at all; we know no reason to doubt your word."

"Well, then, my father was a man who had been originally in a large way of business,

HONORA LANFORD.

but finding the ground giving way beneath his feet, and having, moreover, but little confidence in his partners, he had the prudence to retire with what money he had already made, which, although not a princely fortune, was enough to suffice for his moderate requirements. I was an only child, and I need hardly tell you how I was spoilt by both my parents. My father did not live long after his retirement; whether he had some recent grief I am unable to say, but about a year and a half after he had given up business he was seized suddenly with some malady and in a few days he expired. I was very young at this time, and although I remember to have been grieved at the loss of my father, my sorrow was of but short duration. After his death we had a second cousin of mine on my mother's side come to reside with us;

she was a little girl of about my own age, and I understood it was my mother's intention to adopt her as her own daughter; her name was Mabel Ashford, and as children we were playmates and inseparable companions. Soon after her becoming an inmate of my mother's establishment she had the misfortune to meet with so serious an accident that the effects of it were visible to the latest days of her existence. I had erected a swing in our garden from two tall trees; in this both Mabel and myself had been accustomed to amuse ourselves by swinging each other alternately. On one occasion the rope broke suddenly while Mabel was being swung by myself, and she was precipitated to the ground with so great a force that I thought she was killed upon the spot. I screamed with fright but found myself quite incapable of moving

The servant and my mother rushed to the spot, and Mabel was taken into the house in an insensible state. A surgeon was sent for, and it was feared that Mabel's back was broken, which happily proved not to be the case, but in consequence of this accident her right shoulder grew out and gave her the appearance of being slightly hunchbacked.

"Well, but it was no fault of yours; it was only an accident, after all, which every one of us is liable to," said Mr. Dyson.

"No, I do not say it was; I wish I had nothing more to charge myself with than that. Alas, poor soul, she had a narrow escape of having her back broke, but she endured worse than that—ah, much worse! a broken heart. As we grew up a little older, we had, as is usual in such cases, much bickering, and I need not tell you that I had many young ladies who deigned to smile upon me, and offer every encouragement to my advances.

"No doubt of that," said Hackett, laughing, "Nat was always a very devil among the girls."

"But there were none who made so deep and lasting an impression upon me equal to my cousin Mabel. She received my attentions with a sort of biting irony, which was not only perplexing but piqued my vanity and self esteem, and I was fully convinced that she was listening to the attentions of some more favoured suitor. This idea drove me to distraction, and I became more and more persevering in my attentions to her, and when I gave utterance to some pretty complimentary speech, she would indulge in some reflection upon my own beauty. She was a riddle—an enigma, and I was at a loss in any way to account for her tone, and the conduct she generally chose to assume towards me. I suppose we have, all of us, a certain amount of vanity in our composition, at any rate, I know that at that time I was not entirely free from the charge. One day, after I had left my boon companions who had been rallying me upon my want of success with my cousin, I determined upon a bold stroke, a *coup d'etat* in fact. I went down upon my knees before my cousin, and said that I would no longer live without her, and in fact without her love my life was one round of endless misery. As I poured forth my love in what I deemed passionate and eloquent language, I felicitated myself upon the hopes that I was making an impression on her, and continued in the same rapturous strain. She listened to me without moving a muscle of her fine countenance, for she had features which were surpassingly beautiful. She heard me patiently to the end, and then gazed upon me, not with looks of love, but rather with an inquiring and curious glance,

while a kind of satirical smile played around her beauteous features.

"'Umph,' she exclaimed, 'you are eloquent, Nathanial, more than I should have given you credit for. You believe what you are saying, I suppose?'

"I started back at her tone, as well as the question, asked in such a cold and indifferent manner.

"'Believe,' I exclaimed; 'you surely do not doubt my sincerity, Mabel? Shall I lay bare my heart before you? Believe! You are jesting—I love you as no other man did before.'

"'Ah! or will do again, perhaps.'

"'Are you mocking me, Mabel? Do you doubt the truth of my attachment?'

"'Yes,' she cried, coldly. I started as though an adder had stung me; I felt humiliated, and abashed to the last degree, and gazed upon her with looks of undisguised anger.

"'I thank you Nat, for your admiration of myself, but am free to confess that I believe you are deceiving yourself—and,' she added still more coldly, although I must do her the justice to say that there was at the same time an evident sadness in her tone. And at the same time I may say that however you may deceive yourself, you are not able to deceive me.'

"'Mercy on me. Is it your intention to offer me a studied insult.?'

"'No,' she cried, quietly. "Only do not deceive yourself, cousin. There is too much vanity and self-love in your own disposition to admit of your sparing any for another. At present you are wilfully capricious, and in my opinion, not at all likely to entertain any lasting affection for any female at present; and until you alter very much, you are not likely to do so.'

"What do you mean?' I said, as I felt completely stupified by her words and manner, and bitterly regretted having been so hasty in declaring my passion.

"'Simply this, Nat, that you have been a spoilt child, and think that everything is to give way to you. As you get older you will find this is not likely to be the case. Reflect, therefore, and learn to endure—to bear and forbear—which is a maxim I am thinking that is not known in your vocabulary at present.'

"'I am not going to stay here and be preached to by a silly girl,' I said, as I took up my hat and rushed from the apartment in a towering passion. I did not stay to see my mother, but avoided entering the room where I knew she was; but I instantly betook myself to my companions and there, fool like, I explained to them the particulars of my interview with my cousin; for I was always of a disposition which would not admit of my keeping my troubles to myself, and to say the truth, I had been urged on to make my declaration to my cousin by one or two of my more particular friends. They all declared that she must be both selfish and hardhearted sentiments that even at that time I would not endorse ; for I had a better opinion of Mabel, notwithstanding her rejection of me. I inwardly resolved then, sooner or later to make her pay a dear penalty for what I deemed her cruelty towards me ; and well I kept my resolve—too well !" exclaimed Warrington, with a deep drawn sigh.

"What, did you not give her up after this, then ?" said the colonel.

"No, you shall hear. Upon my return home I assumed an injured tone, was more than usually reserved, and in the course of a few days I feigned illness. A doctor was called in, and I began to rave as though under the delirium of fever. I called upon the name of Mabel, and wept—yes, actually wept, and then burst out in a paroxysm of fury. My mother watched by my bedside occasionally, and in her attendance upon me was relieved frequently by Mabel, who was unremitting in her attention towards me. How I laughed to myself at the part I was playing ! How I hugged to myself the pleasing thought that my cousin was being completely deceived. At times, when I pretended to doze, I heard several discussions in the antiroom as to the cause of my malady. Our medical adviser told my parent and my cousin that I was under the influence of the master passion, and that this was the sole cause of my shattered health. I heard my mother converse in a low voice with Mabel, and from what few words I could catch, I could readily understand that she was making my mother acquainted with the particulars of my declaration and her rejection of the same. When Mabel again returned to my room I feigned to be in a deep sleep, and she watched me with eyes of pity. I knew this by an occasional sigh which she heaved as she trod noiselessly about the room. All works well, thought I; just as I could wish. The farce will soon be over, and I must begin to gradually recover. When I had played the part sufficiently long I did so. By degrees I made it appear that my malady was leaving me, and in a short time I was sufficiently convalescent to be able to take a walk in the garden. Mabel gave me her arm on these occasions, and watched my gradual recovery with the greatest interest. Days went on thus, and I had so far recovered as to be in no longer need of medical advice, and the doctor therefore took his departure. I need not tell you that he had been of little use during the whole drama, unless it were to keep up the delusion more effectually. One day, as Mabel and myself were walking in the shrubbery, we sat down upon a rustic seat beneath a large stone vase, which contained several choice plants. As we sat there side by side, I looked up into my cousin's face with tenderness, and she returned my glance with looks of pity and remorse for her unkindness. Poor girl, she was pale enough herself, and ought to have made me turn from my resolve ; but I was inflexible, and was determined to play out the drama. As I gazed into her face I said to her, as my eyes became averted before I spoke.

"'Mabel, how long is this to last ?'

"'What do you mean, Nat ?' she said in a low voice—so low, indeed, that she was hardly audible, close as we were together.

"'How long is this to last ?' I again inquired, still looking on the ground. 'Are we to be friends, or are we——' I paused here as though quite overcome by my feelings.

"She placed her hand gently on mine, and said in her own soft, gentle accents—

"'If it is my love you want, Nat, be assured, my dear boy, you have it already.'

"I started up and looked at her with eyes of fire.

"'Your love!' I said. 'The love of a miserable little hunchback. Bah !' and I turned upon my heel and abruptly left the spot. I shall never forget the flying glance I had of her as I left the garden. There was in her countenance an expression of such an unutterable amount of woe that I felt at that time the pangs of remorse for my cruel and heartless conduct. I left the house, however, and sought my companions, and there detailed to them the success of my ruse, and how I had brought my cousin to grief, and what a terrible revenge I had taken upon her."

"Ah, it was cruel—too cruel, Warrington," said Hackett ; "almost inhuman."

"I acknowledge it ; and many bitter hours has it since occasioned me—many hours which are dark spots in my existence. Would that I could recall the past—that I could have my time over again."

"What became of her after all ?" inquired the Badger, who began to evince a deep interest in the highwayman's narrative.

"I kept away from the house for some days, telling my mother that the doctor had ordered me change of air."

"And the lady ?"

"My mother found her in the garden perfectly senseless. She had swooned, and it was some time before she gave signs of returning consciousness. When she did recover her senses, she burst into a flood of tears, which were succeeded by hysterical sobs which continued for some hours, and the end of it was that she was laid upon a bed of sickness—not simulated as mine was but real, caused by a grief which was too deep seated for mortal utterance."

"Did she die, poor soul?" asked Mr. Dyson, who seemed to evince a more than wonted interest in the fate of Mabel.

"No, she survived the shock, I am happy to say," answered Warrington. "Although it could hardly be said she held up her head afterwards."

"And you?"

"Oh, I stayed away for some time and ran through a lot of money, I am sorry to say; for you see I was young, foolish, and reckless. I wished to travel, and my mother indulged me in my whim, as she had been in the habit of doing in all my caprices from my earliest childhood."

"And so I suppose you impoverished the old lady?"

"I should have done so, perhaps, and it is more than probable that in her old age she would have been brought to poverty, for she was defrauded of a great portion of the property which my father had left her, through the rascality of a stock-broker. But she died suddenly, while I was on the Continent; and upon my return to England I found the cottage in which she had resided shut up, and the old domestic of our family, who had been with my mother ever since I was born, located in an almshouse in the neighbourhood. From her I learnt all the news. My cousin had left some time before my mother's death, but whither she had gone, my mother's servant was unable to say. The residue of my mother's property was placed in trust for me with our family lawyer, and my mother had left in charge of the servant several papers for me; one was her will, another a long letter of advice for my future conduct."

"And did you get the property?" asked Hackett.

"Yes, what there was left of it after the lawyer had laid his unholy and rapacious paw upon some of it to liquidate his expenses."

"And you—"

"Exactly—spent it, you've just hit it."

"You did not feel much trouble in doing that, I dare say," said Colonel Jack, smiling.

"No, by industry I managed to run through it all, as other men have done before me and will do again, I suppose.'

"Did you hear any more of your cousin?" asked Mr. Dyson.

"Not for a very long time; and then under the most extraordinary circumstances it is possible to conceive, perhaps."

"Indeed. How so?"

"Well, you see I found my funds running short, and it became necessary that I should replenish them by some means or other, and——"

"I suppose you took the shortest and most efficacious mode, eh, Warrington," said the colonel."

"Precisely. At that time there flourished one Tom Spiggot. We all know him by repute. He's dead now, poor chap. Well, his business was generally transacted on the road, but he was not altogether too particular, and if a crib was to be cracked, he occasionally condescended to do it—to oblige his friends."

"One of which you happened to be, I suppose."

"Yes, I generally accompanied Captain Spiggot, as we used to call him, upon most occasions when he levied black mail. Well, one night the captain and his companions had a put up job, the precise nature of which I did not at the time know; only one fact, and which was this, that there was a heavy swag expected, and lots of plate. We started off early in the evening and trotted on in the direction of Enfield, which was where the crib was situated. We stalled our horses at the Old Bell at Tottenham, as the landlord was a particular friend of the captain's. There we partook of a little refreshment to keep up our spirits, and waited until we thought it the right time to commence our operations. It appeared that one of our men knew the housemaid in the establishment, and, consequently, our captain was possessed of all the necessary information to mature his plan of operations. We soon arrived at an old-fashioned detached house, standing in its own ground, and surrounded by a high wall which it was our duty and pleasure to surmount. I will not weary you with all the incidents of our entrance into Mr. Fortescue's house—for that was the owner's name. It will suffice for my purpose to say that we did effect an entrance in the same without detection. The lower rooms were ransacked, and then we proceeded to the next storey, as noiselessly as a lot of cats. Now the bed rooms required more caution in going through, and we took our way separately, that is, one or two of us for each apartment. I had a companion who accompanied me into the room I entered, which turned out to belong to the master and mistress of the establishment. My companion entered first, being my senior by many years. There was some one sleeping in the bed. The figure was evidently that of a female, but I could not see her face, as her back was towards us. My companion held a pistol to her head, and motioned me to ransack a bureau which stood at the side of the room. I proceeded in the fulfilment of the task, and transferred into my bag several valuables. As I opened one of the drawers, you may judge of my surprise when my eye lighted upon a locket of gold containing a portrait of myself. You must understand that as I reached the bureau my back was towards the bed. I held in my hand the dark lanthorn, with which I was attentively examining the ivory miniature of myself, which was in my mother's possession when I last saw it. I heard my companion say in a suppressed voice—"

"'Look sharp, Nat!'

"And then I was alarmed by a piercing scream. I turned round and beheld the woman in the bed struggling in the arms of my companion.

"'By the Lord that made me I'll scatter your brains against yonder wall if you are not quiet,' he said to the female. I rushed to the side of the bed miniature in hand.

"One glance at the disturbed features of the female told me at once who she was. I was rivetted and spell bound to the spot by a species of fascination, such as the rattle-snake is supposed to possess, and involuntarily exclaimed 'Mabel!' upon the impulse of the moment without due reflection. That single word acted as a luminary to light up all her recollections of the past, and she at once knew who I was, for placing her hand against her temple, she exclaimed—

"'Nat! and to meet thus. Oh, 'tis horrible—too horrible,' and here she indulged in a series of piercing screams.

"My companion grasped her rudely, and, as I heard him cock his pistol, I really thought he meant to carry his threat into execution. I rushed forward and seized hold of his arm; as I did so, my cousin made a snatch at the locket I held in my hand, and Captain Spiggot hearing the noise entered the room to see the cause of the disturbance. By the time he had arrived in the apartment, my cousin was senseless—she had swooned. What my feelings were at that time I can hardly tell you; they were of a mixed nature, but they were such as to almost overpower me. As I gazed upon the inanimate form of my cousin, I discovered that an infant lay beside her, apparently about two years old.

"'All right,' said Captain Spiggot, 'look sharp—have you cleared the room of the valuables?'

"'Nat's got pretty well all,' said the man who had been in the room with me.

"'Then come along.'

"'I cannot leave her thus,' I exclaimed, in passionate accents, 'I cannot leave her thus,' and I flung myself across the bed and kissed her parched lips.

"'Is the man mad?' exclaimed Spiggot; 'what's the meaning of this? Come, Nat, we are about to beat a retreat.'

"I hastened to the side of Captain Spiggot and said—

"'Pardon me, captain, but yonder female is my cousin, nay, more, was—'

"'Oh, I understand—your mistress very likely.'

"'No, sir, she was my sweetheart, and—and she loved me.'

"'Very romantic, but particularly inconvenient at the present moment.'

"He was a bit of a satirest was Spiggot, and did not entertain a very high notion of human affections.

"'I cannot leave her thus,' I exclaimed, as I gazed upon her marble and frigid features; 'I cannot leave her thus—I will not leave her.'

"'Her husband will be home shortly, and will have the satisfaction of being introduced to you under the most pleasant of circumstances.'

"'Her husband?' I exclaimed. 'Is she married then?'

"'Of course she is. Can you not see her child?'

"'Yes; that is true.'

"'Well, what is there astonishing in that? Come, don't be crazy, but let's be off. We've got the swag, and a pretty good booty it is. Come;' and Spiggot shook me violently by the shoulder to arouse me to a sense of my position. I took a hasty embrace of my cousin who still continued in a state of insensibility, and then hastily followed my companions. We all got safe off and repaired to the Bell at Tottenham. When there I inquired who the owner of the house which we had entered was. Spiggot informed me that Mr. Fortescue my cousin's husband was a gentleman of considerable property, and that he had married my cousin about three years previously, and that they had one child. Spiggot was acquainted with the whole particulars of the family as it appeared that the maid servant was a relative of one of our men."

"Ah, well," exclaimed the colonel, "she got over your cruel conduct, and solaced herself with a husband, which, under the circumstances was about the best thing she could do. Did you see any more of her."

"No," exclaimed Warrington with a sigh. "That was my last glance of her in this world."

"Ah, she's dead, then?"

"Yes, she did not live more than ten months after our entry into her husband's house. Indeed, I could see from the alteration in her features that she was slipping down into the other world. The seeds of consumption had even at that time made their appearance, and no doubt her malady was hastened by the troubles she had gone through, for there were many besides that which had been caused by my conduct."

"Did you never seek to have an interview with her?" inquired Mr. Dyson

"No, I never had the courage, but she

tried everywhere to find me out, so I ascertained from the servant; and eventually wrote me a long letter, and left it in charge of our lawyer, in the hope that I might call upon him and it would come into my hands. I did call, having learnt through the servant that a letter was entrusted to the lawyer's care for me. In it she expressed her horror at finding me leagued with such a lawless set of men, and at the same time she offered me assistance by forwarding me any sum of money which I might require for my immediate necessities, or a sufficient amount to set me up in some way of business."

"Well, and did you accept her kind offer?" asked Hackett.

"No! Even suppose I had needed it, she was the last person in the world of whom I should choose to accept of a favour."

"You are too thick-skinned, Warrington," said the colonel.

"I am not without some grains of self-respect, I hope, still in my composition," said Warrington, seriously.

"And so she died soon after that, eh"

"Yes, and the rest of my history, such as it is, you already know."

"Spiggot's end we all know."

"Yes, a cheer from the crowd below, and a leap from the leafless tree."

"Psha! a short life and a merry one," the colonel, as he tossed off a bumper. "My turn to-day, and to-morrow your's, as the old saying has it."

"Don't be down-hearted, colonel," said Mr. Dyson, "or you'll make me think there is no virtue in my liquors, which should drive dull care away. Has anything gone wrong with you?"

"Yes, more than one thing. I grieve for the fate of my friend Osborne; for, by my faith, but I'm afraid things look precious queer against him. Now, hear me, Bill; of course I don't want you to commit any of your pranks. Shouldn't do so myself; but *do* you know anything about the parties connected with the Cow Cross murder?"

"Of course not," replied Mr. Dyson; but there was that in his manner of saying this which led the colonel to have some doubts about the truth of the statement.

"You don't?"

"Of course not," replied Mr. Dyson once more.

"You think it's Osborne himself, perhaps, eh?"

"I've not said so."

"No; that's certain. I don't say you have, but you do know who the parties are; now, don't you?"

"No, I tell you, once more; and just look here, colonel, even supposing I did, you don't suppose I'm going to split, now, do you?"

"I am sure you wouldn't, neither would I myself, but that isn't to the question. You must admit that it is a horrible thing for an innocent man to be hung?"

"Of course I do; but it isn't the first time such a thing has been done by a good many."

"Perhaps not; but that does not render poor Osborne's case any better, or a bit more pleasant."

"No; that it don't—but it isn't no sort of business of mine."

"Can you not make it your business?" said the colonel.

"No. How can I?"

"Why, if you are on these chaps' lay, I suppose we could give in a message, eh, Dyson?"

"But I ain't on their lay, and don't know nothing at all about the matter—there now, that's the way to say it."

"What an obstinate animal you are, Bill," said the colonel; "you might do me an essential service in this matter if you liked—but you won't, confound you."

The Badger smiled, and turned the straw in his mouth, but made no reply for some minutes. Presently he said, reflecting—

"You seem to think I am bound to know everything."

"You know a deuced sight more than you choose to tell, old fellow, I am certain of that."

"Well I ain't fly to this affair, so stow all gammon."

"Perhaps you might be if you were to try."

"No; I ain't got such a thing as a scent of the matter."

"Well, look here, Dyson," said the colonel, confidentially, "I don't want you to peach or blow the gaff upon any one—it's not regular, and against both our principles, but, you see, Osborne's one of my oldest and most particular of friends. I esteem him more than my own brother."

"Well, I am sorry for the chap—as sorry as you are," said Mr. Dyson, "I can't say more, can I?"

"No, no—I dare say you are, nay, more, I am certain that you are, but that's nothing to the purpose; what I mean is this, that in consequence of the unfortunate circumstance of the knife, which is a most damnatory fact against him—he is placed in a most perilous position. As I told you before, that knife was in my possession, and I do really believe that I left it here, in this very house, some months ago."

"Here!" exclaimed Mr. Dyson. "I never saw it—upon my word and honour—I'll take my solemn oath."

"I don't say you did, but some one else did, that is quite certain, and it is equally certain, moreover, that that sombody else collared it."

"Can't help that, it is no fault of mine' I can't have my eyes everywhere, you know, colonel."

"I know that; I am not blaming you. Don't imagine that for one moment. All I say is this, that the probability is that you could, if you liked, find out who boned the knife."

"Oh, I dare say."

"I don't say you can do so, only you might if you like."

"I don't think it is at all likely, colonel," said the Badger.

"Will you try ?"

The Badger was silent.

"Come, Dyson, why don't you answer— will you try, old boy!"

"Well," said the Badger, "this 'ere beats cockfighting."

"What mean you ?"

"Do you wish me to place a chap's neck in a hempen noose? Much obliged to you for the offer. I tell you what it is, colonel, you are pressing me too much in this matter —too hardly. You wouldn't like me to peach against you or any of your companions, would you now ?"

"The Lord forbid !" exclaimed Hackett. "Better stow it now, colonel, or Bill will be riled."

"I'll say no more upon the subject then," said our hero, "only as a last observation, I may say, that if you can pick up anything that may be of service to Osborne without compromising any one else, I hope you are the man to do it. Now do you understand me, Mr. Dyson ?"

"Perfectly—that's all fair and square, and if I can, you may rely upon my doing so— there's my hand upon it."

The colonel shook hands with the Badger, and the subject, as far as Mr. Dyson was concerned, was then dropped, for in a few minutes afterwards the landlord of the Cow and Cauliflower left the room to attend to some customers below.

"He knows something about the matter," said the colonel, firmly, addressing himself to Hackett.

"You mean Dyson ?"

"Yes ; I feel convinced he does," said the colonel.

"I think so too," was the reply.

"But he is close as an oyster."

"That's his usual game. Catch Bill Dyson seeing more than is necessary," said Hackett.

"Umph ! I am afraid wild horses would never tear the secret from him," answered the colonel.

"Well, he's not to be blamed after all."

"No, certainly not, but—"

"Ah, but you would rather he'd be more communicative."

"In this instance, yes."

"Confound it, I wish I knew who these fellows were. It surely can't be the Nobbler who has any hand in the affair."

"Oh no ; the Nobbler hasn't shone head here for a long time."

"He's one of Bill's particulars though."

"Yes, always was ; but he's under the harrow just now, and has been ever since the Dulwich affair."

"Has he left London ?"

"I don't know, but I rather fancy not. That was never his game."

"Does Bill know where he is ?"

"I think not, but if he does, he keeps dark upon the subject."

"Well, finish up, we'll have another bowl of punch in at any rate," said the colonel, as he proceeded to ladle out the remains of the liquor into his companions' glasses."

"Here, Slott," and in an instant the highwayman's dog who had been sleeping under the table was by his master's side.

"Here, old boy, take a sup at that," and the highwayman poured some of the punch into a saucer and placed it down towards the animal, who lapped up the liquor with evident gusto.

"His leg seems queer," said Hackett, looking down towards the animal.

"Yes, precious queer ; looks as if it were broken." The colonel took the animal on his lap and examined the wound. A pistol ball had entered the shoulder and passed out laterally, inflicting a severe bled wound, but not one of either a mortal or serious nature.

"Umph !" exclaimed Colonel Jack. "Poor brute, he has been punished for his master's misdoings. You shouldn't follow the fortunes of such a scapegrace, Slott."

The dog looked up into his master's face as though he were fully cognizant of the meaning of the words which were addressed to him, for he wagged his tail and pricked up his ears, and gave a look full of intelligence.

"You'll hook it from Hornsey now, colonel, for good and for all, I suppose," said Warrington.

"I shall hook it most certainly, whether it will be for good or ill time alone will prove," answered our hero, sadly, for the storm which had broken over his home and household had brought upon him a deeper sorrow than he had known for very many years. Leaving the highwaymen at their carouse, we must hasten to take a glance at Henry Osborne.

CHAPTER XXVIII.

OSBORNE'S PERIL—FORESHADOWINGS—EVENTS
THICKEN—THE MISER'S WILL.

In taking a retrospective glance of our passage through life, how frequently many and most of us have been struck with certain periods which may be considered turning points of our existence. Few of us are without some such landmarks, which might have altered the whole fortunes of our lives. As the poet of all time says, "There is a tide in the affairs of man which taken at the flood leads on to fortune; withal all their life is spent in shoals and shallows." You, unhappy mortal, who treads a rough and troubled path, has at one time or another passed some narrow turning, which had you taken, would, perhaps, have led you to delightful vistas—prosperous gales of sunny fortune—cool grottos, and verdant sward—but you neglected it, and have, perhaps, to take your course along the hard and flinty road—smooth enough beneath the carriage wheels of the rich and great, but rough and jagged beneath the naked feet of the poor. Osborne may be said to have arrived at a turning point in his existence—not one that promised to lead him to future happiness, for it was but too evident that a dark and portentous cloud loomed in the future. Osborne had undergone several examinations before the magistrate; the meshes of the web which encircled him seemed to be strengthened, and every day seemed to add to the weight of evidence against him. The coroner's jury had returned an open verdict, as it is called, viz., that of "Wilful Murder against some person or persons unknown."

As yet the police had been unable to find anything which might lead to the slightest trace of the two men who were said to have committed the murder. At the time of which we write, juries were not so particular in finding a prisoner guilty for a capital offence as they are in the present day, for to speak the truth, they may be said now to go to the other extreme. Upon the last one or two examinations of Osborne, his counsel had pressed the magistrate to take bail, which was at once peremptorily refused, and, in fact, from the tone assumed by the magistrate, it was evident that he viewed the case in a much more serious light than he had done at first. After a brief examination, in which the main facts of the case were rapidly run through, Osborne was fully committed to Newgate to take his trial upon the charge of murder. Although his lawyer had throughout told him that it was no more than he might expect, he found himself completely prostrated when he entered the precincts of that gloomy prison. On one of the walls of the present building some unhappy prisoner had scratched the words "He who enters here leaves hope behind." Osborne, as he looked at these words which were forcibly scratched on one of the stones of the ward in which he was confined, thought them almost prophetic in his own case.

Every nook and corner of the miser's house was searched; every chair, box, and piece of furniture was ransacked by the police in charge of the premises. So, also, had Osborne's own lodgings, much to the annoyance of Squabshot, who declared the liberty of the subject was outraged, and that in future no man was safe in his own home. It is astonishing what a pitch of rage Squabshot had been driven to as the officer came to and from Osborne's apartments. When at home, little Squabby generally followed them up to his friend's room, and there rated at them in good set terms. They ordered him out when he became too troublesome, but this had no effect upon him. Eventually, however, a compromise was effected. One of the officers joined Squabby in a bottle of brandy in his own rooms, and the former declared his companion to be one of the right sort. He amused Squabshot with an account of many persons whom he had captured, and entered into a long account of their antecedents. Squabshot, who was really a good-hearted fellow, was anxious to know what the ultimate fate of Osborne would be, and he confidentially inquired the officer's opinion as to how matters were likely to turn out, either for or against him. The officer gave our little friend no very flattering account of Osborne's prospects, and as time went on he gave a less favourable account.

"Why you see, Mr. Squabshot," said the officer, in answer to his queries, "there is no one else to charge with the crime, and the law must be satisfied one way or another."

"The law! Why you do not mean to say that there is any satisfaction in execting an innocent man."

"Well—no—certainly not, only——"

"Only—what?"

"Why, it is better to execute some one than none at all."

"Gracious goodness, you think it's better to murder an innocent person in cold blood, because some miscreant or miscreants have committed a heinous crime."

The officer did not know what reply to make to this. According to his code, it would be far better to have a man found guilty, whether he was so or not, rather than have it said that the force was at fault in finding out the real malefactor. A condemnation and execution was supposed to satisfy the public—that hydra headed monster, whose opinions and wishes are so often mis-

quoted, and at the same time so misunder-stood.

Henry Osborne either was, or supposed to be, an orphan. He had been brought up by an elderly maiden lady, who declared her-self to be his aunt, and there was no reason to doubt her word, for she was a person of undoubted veracity. She was supposed to have received some small allowance for the support of Osborne, while under her care ; after which he was sent to Oxford, and his aunt granted him sufficient funds for his requirements at the university.

Osborne had not been committed to New-gate many hours when he received the fol-lowing letter :—

" DEAR HARRY,—I am sorry that, for the the present, I shall be unable to see you from causes which I will hereafter explain ; but

as an old friend, perhaps one of your oldest, I may take the liberty of advising you, without fear of giving offence. I would, therefore, caution you, to be particularly cau-tious of Mr. Sharpsthorne, *verbum sapientum.* I have every reason to warn you upon the subject for your own good. Be cautious ! I hear that you are about to trust him to get up your defence. Do no such thing— or, at any rate, if you are so committed with him, or he was so identified with the cir-cumstances as to render it impossible for you to discharge him—employ some one else in conjunction with him, so that his baneful influence may thereby be neutra-lised. Now don't you forget this—or depend upon it, my dear boy, if you do, you will see good cause to regret it, believe me. Adieu. I need not say that you have my best wishes, and heaven send that you may come clear out of the affair,

"And believe me to be,
"Yours ever respectfully,
"FRANK."

Osborne pondered over and over again. What could be the meaning of the epistle ? Mr. Sharpthorne seemed to take deep interest in his case, and he had the highest opinion of his trust, as well as his good intentions towards him. Osborne was quite at a loss to account for the foregoing missive ; but it was quite certain, that Halford would not have troubled himself in the matter, or have been so positive, had he not been fully impressed with the necessity of his so doing. While he was lost in doubts and fears from the contents of Halford's letter, Mr. Sharpthorne himself made his appearance, and the lawyer and his client retired to the further end of the large room, in which were many other prisoners besides Osborne. They seated themselves at the extremity of one of the large tables, when Mr. Sharpthorne placed his hands upon his knees, and looked at Osborne with an inquiring glance.

"We've our work to do now, and no mistake," said the little lawyer.

"Ah, I suppose so," said Osborne, dejectedly. "It's hard for an innocent man to be herded with such a set as these," and he pointed over his shoulder in the direction of the other prisoners.

"Umph, yes," said the lawyer, caressing his chin, "yes, it is hard certainly, but how is it possible for the legislature to tell the innocent from the guilty until the evidence is gone through ?"

"I am innocent," said Osborne sadly, "and any one might tell that."

"Ah, so you think, because you know it yourself—that's all very well, but other persons have to be convinced. Prisoners will always take an unilateral view of the question. It has been well said, that no man is a competent judge of his own case."

The lawyer looked more than usually grave, and Osborne's heart sank within him as he observed the bearing of Mr. Sharpthorne.

"It appear," said the latter, "that there has been a will found."

"A will," exclaimed Osborne, "a will of whose ?"

"The miser's ?"

"Well, what has that to do with me ?"

The lawyer shrugged his shoulders, and made no reply.

"What can that possibly have to do with me ?" again inquired the prisoner.

"Well, now, don't alarm yourself, my dear young friend," said Mr. Sharpthorne, as he gently patted his client on the shoulder. "Pray don't alarm yourself unnecessarily, but the fact is that it appears to me and everyone else that this document affects your cause very materially, so much so that—"

He paused here, and Osborne looked at him with evident surprise.

"That what ?" he inquired hastily.

"That it behoves us to go into the matter as fully and completely as possible."

"But the will of the miser has nothing to do with my case, I should presume" said Osborne. "It concerns only those who are the legatees, with which I have nothing to do."

"Pardon me," said Mr. Sharpthorne, "but it appears you have, my friend. If I understand it right, the deceased man Jabez Crudge was a relative of your's, and you are one of the heirs at law, perhaps, but be that as it may, you are so under the will—that is, assuming that we are right in your being the individual in question."

"A relative !" exclaimed Osborne, as he started back in perfect astonishment. "This is not to be believed. Good God, what next fact is to be added to those already brought forward. A relative ! Why, Mr. Sharpthorne, I never heard of such a man as Jabez Crudge, and no member of my family either on my mother's or my father's side ever bore such a name."

"Not that you know of," said the lawyer, quietly, as he proceeded to untie a bundle of papers smiling to himself the while. "I had the hardest job in the world, Mr. Osborne to procure a sight of the document or to be allowed to make a copy of it—the hardest job in the world, I do assure you, and had it not have been that I had a friend at court I think it problematical if I should have been able to obtain it at all. And yet," continued the lawyer, "it is of the utmost importance that we should be in possession of all the facts. Now tell me Mr. Osborne—your parents you did not know I believe ?"

"I do not recollect them. I have heard my aunt say that my father died in India, or in one of the West India islands, I forget which."

"And your mother ?"

"She died on her passage over to this country when I was but an infant."

"Umph ! Do you know the names of either or both of your parents, Mr. Osborne ?" said the lawyer, looking over the paper he held in his hand.

"I have heard my aunt say that my father's name was James."

"Ah, James—ah—that's right enough, as I expected ; and your mother's ?"

"I think was Frances."

"Indeed, then it is as I expected, you are the individual in question. Have you communicated with your aunt ?"

"No, sir, I have not liked to do so, for I have been in hopes that each examination would prove the last one, and that I should be discharged. My aunt lives a long distance in the country and I have been mindful of her feelings and did not like to wound them by letting her know that her nephew was charged, or suspected, of being guilty of so terrible a crime."

"You will be obliged to let her know," said the lawyer, quietly, "and it would be as well to do so as speedily as possible."

"Very well, sir, I will write at once; will it be necessary for her to appear as evidence on the trial?"

"I think so—but that is a matter to determine after we have had a consultation with our counsel."

"I am going to employ another legal gentleman besides yourself to assist you in my case," said Osborne, who, mindful of the custom of the colonel, and driven desperate from the fact of so many adverse circumstances presenting themselves, was determined at once to break the ice to Sharpthorne, as to his future intention."

"My dear sir," exclaimed the attorney, in evident surprise, "there surely will be no occasion for that; I require no assistance. Myself and Mr. Baggs, I trust, are sufficient for the requirements of your case, and we have given it our strictest attention. I hope you are not dissatisfied with the manner in which we have conducted the case."

"I do not see any reason for complaint," said Osborne, "only, when one's life is at stake, we may be excused if we evince a more than wonted interest."

"Precisely, my dear sir," said the lawyer, "I can readily imagine your anxiety. It is not for me to dictate to you upon such a subject, indeed it would come with bad grace either from me or my colleague. You must, of course, use your own judgment in the matter; but allow me to proceed with the information which I was about to convey to you. As I before observed, Jabez Crudge has left a will. He has died immensely rich, much more so than even the fabulous reports of his wealth would have led us to believe. By his will he has left the bulk of his property to the issue of James and Frances Osborne."

"Is this possible?" exclaimed the prisoner.

"A fact, my dear sir, an undisputed and well-established fact, which it would be utterly useless to deny. Had you, or have you, any brothers or sisters?"

"No, I always understood that I was an only child."

"Umph! then you are really the heir to the bulk of the property left by the deceased man, Jabez Crudge?"

"This cannot be possible," exclaimed Osborne, in unfeigned suspense. "It is perfectly incredible."

"Your father left England when quite a young man?"

"I have heard so."

"And went over to one of the West India islands. Antigua, as I understand?"

"Very possible."

"And there he became a merchant?"

"It may be so."

"Was for a time prosperous?" The lawyer was running his eye over some papers he held in his hand when he indulged in the foregoing observations.

"After some few years of prosperity, the tide of fortune turned against him, and he became comparatively a poor man; at any rate, if he was not actually poor, he was not nearly so well off as he had been in the early part of his career."

"All this is quite new to me," said Osborne.

"Very likely; but I believe I am not mistating facts. Just before the tide of fortune had turned against him, he married an English lady, Frances Minchaul by name. She had emigrated from England for some cause or other, it is supposed she had been sent over in some capacity by her parents, whether true or not, I am unable to say; but that she did emigrate to Antigua is quite certain, and thence marry your father James Osborne."

"What has all this to do with the case?" inquired Osborne.

"If you will have a little patience you shall hear," answered the attorney, somewhat testily. "In stating facts, which have been eluminated during the inquiry, it is necessary to turn back to the balance which contains the records of the past, and discourse of events which have taken place many years anterior to those which are more immediately before us."

Osborne bowed his head in acquiescence of this statement.

"It would appear," said Mr. Sharpthorne, leaning his elbow upon the table, and placing his hands together, after his usual fashion, when coming to some important point of his communication.

"It would appear, that in early life, before your father knew her, that Jabez Crudge loved your mother, when she was yet in her teens."

Osborne gave a start of surprise.

"Yes, young man, strange as it may seem to you, that the emaciated and wretched object you conveyed home, there to die, actually succombed to the tender passion, and even now his voice cries out from the grave of the truth and sincerity of that first, and, perhaps, only passion of a higher nature than the accumulation of wealth. Even now it is heard, for mindful of her who awoke in his breast the first dawn of love, he leaves the bulk of his property to the issue of James and Frances Osborne."

The unhappy prisoner was benumbed and stupified, as the lawyer brought his harangue to a conclusion, and the latter contemplated his client with his usual lynx-like gaze.

"What an extraordinary circumstance," said Osborne.

"Say rather scenes of extraordinary circumstances. The counsel for the crown felicitates himself from now being able to point out the motive."

"What motive?" asked Osborne, quite innocently—

"The motive which has actuated some one in compassing the unfortunate man's death," said the attorney, with a mysterious look.

"Who does the man mean who could have any such motive."

"The party or parties most interested," said Mr. Sharpthorne, significantly.

"Good God! Mr. Sharpthorne!" exclaimed Osborne "you do not mean to say that he points to me as having a motive in taking the life of a fellow-creature?" said Osborne, as his features were indicative of the utmost horror and abhorrence at such an accusation.

"That is his inference,' said his companion, gently.

A phosphoric light seemed to flash across the eyes of the prisoner—a light which showed him distinctly enough the lawyer's meaning in all its terrible force. From the tenor of his observations there was an implied guilt on the part of Osborne, and he almost felt convinced that his own lawyer began to waver in his opinion of the case. Osborne was so completely overcome that he buried his face in his hands, and did not speak for some minutes.

"Do not give way to despair," said Mr. Sharpthorne, "although circumstances have turned out particularly unfortunate throughout the whole of this affair, we shall be able to rebut the testimony and gain a verdict, let us hope."

He said this feebly, however, so much so, that his manner almost belied his words. The fact is that, independently of the influence used by Sir Richard Fleetwood, the acute lawyer had himself but a very indifferent opinion of Osborne's chances of getting off.

"I do not care about an acquittal," said Osborne. "My reputation is to me dearer than my life, and that is now for ever blasted. Oh, that for one act of kindness that a man should be punished thus. It's cruel—!"

The lawyer took no notice of this ebullition of feeling, but began again to proceed to business.

"You see, Mr. Osborne, that the fact of this will strengthen the case for the coroner. It is of no use our endeavouring to conceal that fact from ourselves. There has been not the slightest trace or clue obtained to the

men who are supposed to have committed the murder."

"Supposed, sir!" said Osborne, indignantly. "There is no supposition in the matter."

"No—no, of course not," said the lawyer, correcting himself. "No, there is no trace to the real perpetrators of the crime. The law, of course, assumes, as well as every reasonable man, that some one committed the outrage or murder, which you will ; and as you are the only person in custody—"

"Why, for want of any one else, I am to be sacrificed. Is that what you mean?"

"No, I do not say that ; God forbid!" said Sharpthorne, slowly. "Only, you see, there are awkward circumstances. Now, you know, there's that knife."

"Ah!" exclaimed Osborne, sadly. "Yes, that is indeed an unaccountable circumstance."

"Have you recollected anything more about it?" who you lent it to—if you lent it at all ; or if you lost or mislaid it ; and if so, where?"

"Alas!" said the prisoner, "I cannot remember where I missed sight of it, and still less how. Indeed, as I told you before, I believed it to be still in my own possession. I know I have not used it for a long time, but my impression is that it was in one of my drawers."

"It won't do to state that in your defence."

"Oh, indeed."

"No, certainly not. That would never do. Really, it does seem singular that you can't remember anything about the knife—very singular."

"I was not in the habit of using it at my office, and, indeed, I don't think that I once used it since I left Oxford."

"Do you think that you left it there?"

"No, I think not ; to the best of my belief I had it since I came to London."

"Surely it cannot be any acquaintances of yours that have been concerned in this murder."

"Oh, dear no. It's not at all likely that should be the case."

"Well," continued Mr. Sharpthorne, "I did not finish telling you about this will. I learnt from the magistrate's clerk, who is a particular friend of mine, that some such document was found ; at least, so he believed. At first, I did not deem it was of very great importance, only you know in dealing with detective officers, it is necessary to have your eye teeth about you. One of these worthies I know well, and so I called upon him at his private residence, and asked him respecting the will. He pretended at first to know nothing about it ; when after a good deal of prevarication, he admitted that some such documents had been found. I told him that

I would stand something handsome to have a look at it, but this he refused, saying that it was more than he dare do to show it me, even if it were in his possession, which it did not happen to be. I then inquired who had it, and he said that it had been placed in the hands of the counsel for the crown. I then wrote to the counsel for the crown, demanding a copy of the document for the purpose of preparing your defence—but I should have mentioned that I had ascertained from the detective, that the bill was supposed to be made in your favour. Of course, that made me still more anxious to have a copy of it. Well, the crown counsel refused me either a sight or a copy of it, saying that he did not feel himself justified in doing so, till the brief was prepared, and the counsel for the prisoner was retained. I luckily am intimately acquainted with the lord mayor, and I went to him and stated the case, and as he was and always has been friendly towards me he granted me an order for the opposing counsel to appear and show cause why he refused. This order I took myself, and had an interview with the attorney-general myself. After a good deal of discussion, he eventually allowed my clerk to go to his chambers and make a draft of the document in question. You would, perhaps, like to hear it read?" said Sharpthorne.

" Yes ; it would be as well."

The lawyer adjusted his spectacles, and laying the draft carefully out upon the table, commenced reading. It was as follows :—

"The last will and testament of Jabez Crudge of Cow Cross, Clerkenwell (money scrivener).

"I, Jabez Crudge, of No. 22, Cow Cross, Clerkenwell, in the County of Middlesex, and formerly of Clement's Lane, Strand, do will and bequeath the whole of my real and personal property to the issue of James and Frances Osborne, of Antigua, who are now deceased. And I, Jabez Crudge, do hereby will and devise that the real property be divided amongst the children of the said James and Frances Osborne, share and share alike ; but in the event of there being only one surviving child of the said James and Frances Osborne, I hereby will that such property should be his or her's entirely, save and except such bequests and legacies as are hereinafter mentioned."

"Then follows" said Sharpthorne, "a list of several sums, some left to individuals, and others to the various charities of London. This forms a numerous list, but it is insignificant when all added together, when compared to the balance of the property, which is left to you and for your use entirely. It is hardly worth while reading you the remaining portion."

" Oh, dear no," replied Osborne. " I am not interested in hearing it now, at all events if, indeed, I ever shall be, which is more than probable. But does the counsel for the crown know that I am the person named in the will?" inquired Osborne.

" Oh, yes, he is fully cognizant of that, you may be certain. In fact, I believe he is from private sources, and what is more, he intends to make use of it in proving the motive for the murder."

" He's very kind, I'm sure—very kind,' said Osborne.

" Well, you must not take it as unkind. You know that in all cases of this sort, each party avails himself of every fact to make out a case, and it is our duty to do all in our power to rebut the testimony or facts as they present themselves. I do not conceal from you that I wish this cursed will had been at the bottom of the sea before it had been brought up against us."

" What an impossibility the whole affair seems to me," said Osborne. " To think that a man should be living a few streets from me, who had left me an amount of money which might have made me happy for life, not from the fact of my being the possessor of riches, for beyond a moderate income sufficient for my wants I despise wealth. No, it is not that, but it would have enabled me to possess that which I prize beyond worldly wealth. And all this has almost been within my grasp—would have been, in fact, had it not have been for the unfortunate circumstance of being so near the unhappy man who chose me for his heir. It seems like a dream—a sort of hideous nightmare."

" It's a sad thing, most certainly," said Mr. Sharpthorne. Had the miser died, you would, unquestionably, have come into a large amount of property, but now—" He paused and seemed lost in reflection.

" But now," said Osborne, " My future prospects are for ever blighted, my fair name gone. Oh, that thought to me is worse than the most grinding poverty. That thought is in itself actual destruction."

" Do not, I pray, give way to despair," said Mr. Sharpthorne. All that legal skill can accomplish shall be done, believe me; and if you deem it necessary to have further assistance, why, do not hesitate out of any delicate scruple towards myself and partner, in acting according to the dictates of your own wishes in this matter."

" I shall feel more satisfied in having further advice," said Osborne, quietly.

Sharpthorne chafed inwardly at this resolution, but his command over his features was so habitual to him that he gave no outward demonstration of discontent, but smiled blandly at his client.

Shortly after this, the lawyer took leave of his client, and left the prison with many protestations of friendship and solicitude for Osborne.

———

CHAPTER XXIX.

SCENE AT THE COCK-PIT IN WESTMINSTER.

THE days are happily past when it was the custom to indulge in cock fighting, badger and bull baiting, in England. The march of intellect, as it is termed, has swept such brutal exhibitions from our fair island, and in describing a cock-pit and the scenes there enacted, in this our present chapter, we are but recording the barbarities of a past age. The cock-pit at Westminster was the very model of an amphitheatre of the ancients, the cocks fighting in the arena as the beasts did formerly among the Romans, and round the circle above sat the spectators on their several rows. Many of our readers have, no doubt, seen Hogarth's print of a cock-pit, which is a faithful representation of the one at Westminster. All classes of the community were frequent visitors at this species of sport or entertainment, from the lowest cadger to the peer of the realm. It was a marvel to see the courage of these trained feathered combatants, who in most instances always held fighting on, till one or both of them dropped down dead. A graphic writer of the period says, " I have been to numbers of these matches, and never saw a cock run away under any circumstances. I must, however, own it to be one of the barbarous customs of the island, and far too cruel for any entertainment of Christianised or civilised men. There is always a constant move amongst the spectators, fluctuating backwards and forwards, during each battle, which is a great amusement, and I believe abundance of people get money by taking odds on each stroke, and fund their account at the end of the battle, but these are people who must nicely understand it."

If a Frenchman or a German should by any chance come into one of these cock-pits, he would conclude the assembly to be all mad, by their continual cries of " six to four," " ten pounds to a crown," which is always repeated here, and with great earnestness, every spectator taking part with his favorite cock, as if it were a party cause. At the time at which we are about to pay the cock-pit a visit, the excitement was likely to run high, as two very celebrated birds were to be pitted against each other. One was the property of Mr. Richard Fleetwood, by name " The Lord of the Isles," and the other was of the Japanese breed, and was known as " The Westminster Pet." The whole arena of the cock-pit was crowded with anxious spectators. Fashionably dressed gentlemen were observed stationed around, intermingled with men of very questionable reputations. Neverthelesss, it was hail fellow, well met, with most of them. Our acquaintance, Bill Dyson, was there as well as Squabshot, as also Sir Richard, himself, and last, not least, our hero, with several of his companions. The proceedings were not opened with the two chief heroes of the day, as the birds who were first placed in the ring were as yet unknown to fame, except through their genealogy, which was generally stated much the same as the horses which run for the Derby in the present day. The owners, or rather the trainers and seconds of the birds brought them under their arms to place them in position for the battle. A cheer from the partisans of each was sent forth as the men and birds made their appearance. When the latter were placed on the ground opposite to each other, the heads of each were depressed, and the feathers of the neck were struck out, and then, for a minute or so, they stood surveying each other without the slightest movement. Presently, the two leaped up simultaneously, and the spurs of one entered the neck of the other. A cheer arose from the backers of the most successful of the birds, who were now encouraged to further hostilities by their respective backers. Bets were offered and accepted, and the excitement of the day's sport began in real earnest.

Sir Richard was lounging at the back part of the boxes, taking but little interest in the contest that was going on. He was waiting for the " Lord of the Isles " to make his appearance.

Colonel Jack took up his position by the side of the baronet, who was, at first, not aware of his presence. The colonel spoke to him, upon which the baronet turned, and offered his hand, rather stiffly—so our hero thought.

" Waiting for his lordship to make his appearance on the stage, I suppose ?" asked the colonel.

" Yes," was the reply. " They are the next on the list."

" Are they pretty well matched ?"

" About the same size and weight, I believe. Ah, Dyson, how are you ?" said the baronet, as he caught sight of the Badger making towards him.

" Amongst the middlings, Sir Richard— pretty well for an old 'un," said Mr. Dyson. " What's the Lord of the Isles going to accomplish ?"

" Win, I hope."

" So do I, for I am rather heavy on him, Sir Richard."

" That's a good sign, for you are a good judge. Dyson."

" Well, Sir Richard, I ought to be, but the

best are mistaken at times—the best of us you know."

The Badger having thus delivered his, by no means clear, opinion, made a respectful obeisance, and took his way to another part of the amphitheatre.

"Your friend has got himself into a pretty scrape," said the baronet to Colonel Jack. "A very pretty scrape, truly. I am thinking that he will have a difficulty in convincing a jury of his innocence."

"He is innocent, nevertheless," said the colonel, seriously.

"Umph !"

"As guiltless as either I or yourself !"

"I hope he is."

"I know he is—that's more."

"So much the better. No doubt his innocence will be able to support him through his present overwhelming difficulties," said the baronet, with a sneer.

"He has not acted wisely in his choice of a legal adviser," said the colonel, with a marked emphasis.

"And wherefore not ?" asked Sir Richard, with feigned surprise.

"Well, you see—that—"

"Mr. Sharpthorne is a very talented gentleman," interrupted the baronet.

"So he may be, and is, for aught I know ; nevertheless, he is not the man for Osborne to employ."

"Why not ?"

"You may possibly guess without any of my prompting."

"Indeed, I cannot."

"Well, I can, that's all, Sir Richard Fleetwood !" said the colonel.

The baronet bit his lips, and was silent for some minutes.

"We have all our game to play in this world," said the colonel, quietly, "each for himself, and—you know the old adage, Sir Richard."

The baronet nodded, but vouchsafed no other reply.

"Fortune's wheel is for ever turning," continued the colonel, "and Osborne is as low as he possibly can be just now ; whether he is to be lifted up again it is for time alone to show. We have seen some ups and downs ourselves."

The baronet winced at the manner in which he was coupled with the highwayman, but he did not dare say anything, for although his manner was constrained towards our hero at times, he was always mindful of exhibiting any ebullition of temper, and it would appear that Colonel Jack exercised some mysterious influence over him.

"This man Osborne's in your way, Sir Richard," the colonel said, in continuation ; "it is the fashion sometimes with great people to have such removed."

The baronet started, and visibly changed colour.

"What do you mean, Halford ?" he inquired, hastily, and with some warmth. "You do not, I hope, allude to me ?"

"It is not my wont to indulge in personalities," was the prompt reply. "I was speaking in a general sense ; nevertheless, Sir Richard, we know each other !"

"What of that ?"

"Henry Osborne is one of my dearest and best of friends."

"So you have told me before ; and again I say, what of that ?"

"Let Mr. Sharpthorne deal justly with him."

"Halford, you are driving at something ; I cannot divine what—I have nothing to do with Mr. Sharpthorne any further than my own private affairs are concerned."

"I am very glad to hear you say so," said the colonel, "and am, of course, bound to take your word."

"Take my word ? You do not surely—"

"Oh, dear, no—I do not make any implications, believe me ; only we know each other, I should hope—at least we ought to do so by this time."

A loud shout from the assembly now told that one of the two combatants was dead ; and a still louder crow from the successful champion heralded the supposed fact, which, however, soon proved to be a mistake, for the cock which lay bleeding, and without any signs of life, directly he heard the war clarion of his antagonist, rose once more upon his feet, and flew at the other, when, striking him with one of the steel spurs which were attached to his feet, he struck the other through the head, penetrating the brain, and was pronounced the victor.

A scene of riotous confusion ensued, and those who had betted largely on the vanquished bird were terribly chapfallen at the unexpected termination of the contest. The owner of the deceased bird took him up and found that life had departed.

"Clear away for the next pair !" said the master of the ceremonies ; "clear away—the contest has ended."

"Is it all over ?" inquired one of the spectators.

"No, gentlemen," said the director, in continuation, "the next contest will be between perhaps two of the most remarkable birds in this country."

"Oh, Walker !" shouted a voice in the crowd.

"How do you know that ?" bawled out several others.

"I said *perhaps*," was the reply of the director.

"Oh ! oh !"

"One is a celebrated fighting cock—the

Lord of the Isles, and the other is the Westminster Pet, bred from the celebrated cock, Tapho Mahoak."

"Hen—hen!" shouted out several voices; "out with them, and let's see what they are made of."

"Ten to five on the Lord of the Isles," said a voice.

"Thank you, sir—taken."

"Three to six on the Westminster Pet—any takers. Come, now's your time, before the birds make their appearance."

"I'm on," said the Badger, as he took out his book and entered the last therein.

"Which is the favourite?" inquired the colonel of the baronet.

"My bird, I believe," said the baronet, "at least he was."

"Now, gentlemen, complete your bets, before the birds come," said the director of the day's sport.

A confused clatter of voices was heard on all sides, and the degree of interest in the previous contest was nothing as compared to this.

Sir Richard left the side of the colonel, and proceeded to the private portion of the building, devoted to those who were engaged professionally in attending upon the belligerent birds.

Immediately after his departure Squabshot made his way to the colonel's side.

"Ah, Halford, my boy, how are you by this time?"

"What, Squabby, my boy, is it you—what brought you here?"

"The same as you, I suppose, to see the great contest between the two renowned champions. Always in where there's anything like good sport going on. I've only just left Osborne, poor chap."

"How does he seem?"

"Oh quite broken down in spirits. Things are likely to go hard with him, I am afraid —very hard."

"Ah, so I fear; circumstances are really most disastrous."

"Who was that talking to you just now? Was it not Sir Richard Fleetwood?"

"Yes."

"So I thought. He is a friend of yours, then?"

"Certainly; I have known him for some years."

The conversation was interrupted by the appearance of the two fighting cocks on the stage—a loud shout announced their entrance—and the voices of the assembled multitude were heard offering and taking various bets.

For some time nothing was heard but a confused babel of sounds, and many anxious spectators thrust forth their heads to catch sight of the belligerents.

Presently the fight began, quietly enough at first, but in a few minutes it waxed more furious, and the ground became dyed with blood from the wounds of the combatants.

Sir Richard again made his way in front of the amphitheatre. As he placed himself in his old position, his bird, the Lord of the Isles, received from his antagonist a desperate wound in the neck, and lay without motion.

Loud cheers arose from the opposing party, who began to believe that the contest had terminated; but when the Westminster Pet set up a loud and taunting crow up rose the Lord of the Isles, bleeding and staggering as he was, and flew at his opponent and fairly knocked him over.

A cry of derision arose as the Westminster Pet lay stretched without any signs of life; the Lord of the Isles now indulged in a loud crow, which immediately aroused the prostrate Pet, who again jumped up upon his legs and renewed the contest.

A long and determined battle again ensued, and it was difficult for the most experienced to say how it was likely to terminate. Both birds appeared to be about the same weight, and were, evidently, well matched. At each alteration in the fortune of the day, bets were offered on all sides, and the people present seemed to be almost beside themselves with excitement. Sir Richard bet largely upon his own bird, as did the colonel and the badger, for the latter had still the utmost faith in the Lord of the Isles coming off the winner. Several times after this did each bird in his turn lay without motion, but was aroused to further action by the war clarion of his antagonist. Sir Richard was, evidently, getting very anxious, for the contest had been prolonged beyond the usual limits of such exhibitions, and it seemed impossible that the two combatants could continue much longer without dying from sheer exhaustion. However, it did continue, with every now and then a pause of longer or smaller continuance. As the saying is, the fight was anybody's at present, and until a final stroke was given by one or the other of the combatants, it was impossible to say what would be its termination.

As to giving the reader any notion of the noise and confusion which pervaded the whole assembly, that would be an impossibility; but, amidst this noise and confusion, there came upon the ear of Colonel Jack a few sentences in a low voice which rivetted his attention, and completely took off his interest in the proceedings before him, and upon which most eyes of those present were anxiously turned. The words which reached his ear came from two men in close and private conversation.

"The matter is going on just as we could

wish it," said one of the two speakers, addressing his companion.

"Yes," said the other. "The young spark who came up so boldly, will pay the penalty of his interference. He'll get scragged, and no mistake. Serve him right, too, for interfering with business."

"The old man might have died quietly, without kicking up such a dust."

As these words reached the ears of the colonel, his attention became more and more wrapt. He did not doubt for one moment but that the two speakers were no other than the men who were engaged in the murder of Jabez Crudge. The colonel turned round and looked in the direction from whence the sounds proceeded; as he did so, Squabshot caught sight of the expression of our hero's countenance.

No. 24.

"What's the matter?" inquired Squabshot.

"Hush!" ejaculated the colonel, in a whisper. "Hush! I've heard words which have brought some hope to my mind in elucidating this mystery."

"What do you mean?"

"Hush,—Osborne," said the colonel.

"Ah."

"Listen."

The two bent their heads down and endeavoured to catch amidst the confusion the same voices which the colonel had first heard.

"Are you sure Moll is to be trusted?" said the first speaker.

"Oh, she is as true as steel," replied the other.

"Well, when once the chap is scragged, we can laugh in good earnest. Lord bless us, what a beautiful institution is the law of

England. So certain, eh! and so convenient and just. Ha! Ha!"

"Wery just. And only to think of that ere blessed bribe."

"Ah, what a fortunate circumstance."

"Do you know whose knife that was?"

"Why, Osborne's, of course.

"Yes, it was his, but I prigged from the colonel."

"Did you though?"

"Of course, I did."

Colonel Jack did not doubt now as to what the men were speaking about. He caught Squabshot by the arm, and gently led him from the spot. It was evident that the voices proceeded from some one who was beneath the boxes where the colonel and Squabshot were standing. The former led his companion down the staircase, and took his way among the spectators immediately beneath the position he had occupied above. He then listened attentively, but no further sounds reached his ears issuing from the mouths of the two men, whose voices he had heard so distinctly a few minutes before. In vain he listened; all that could be heard was the noise of the assembled multitude, which now seemed at its height, for both birds were down without showing any signs of life.

"Curse it," said the colonel to Squabshot, in a suppressed whisper. "The rascals very probably know me and most likely have caught sight of both of us, and are, consequently silent."

"If they know you, it is more than likely that you may also be able to recognise them," was Squabshot's reply.

"I don't see any one with whom I am familiar," said the colonel, as he took a searching glance at those present.

"Perhaps they have hooked it," said Squabshot.

"That's very probable, but don't look round again, pretend to be interested in the fight."

"Both birds seem to have had enough of it. See, they are down, and without motion. Ah, no, one is up. It is the Lord of the Isles."

A clarion note rang through the arena, the Westminster Pet made a feeble effort to rise, but fell again on his side, apparently quite exhausted and unable to rise.

Another crow was sent forth by the Lord of the Isles; when shouts of victory! victory! proceeded from those who had backed the latter bird, but the injured feelings of the Westminster Pet appeared to be too much wounded to admit of his any longer remaining passive; with a delusive effort he again rose to his feet, and flew at his opponent.

The fight was renewed, but in a short time the Westminster Pet was again stretched senseless, and the renewed crowing of his opponent failed to arouse him to further action or hostilities.

"Hurrah! Hurrah!" shouted out several of the spectators. "Three cheers for the Lord of the Isles. Hurrah! Where's the Westminster pet, now?"

"Order, order," shouted out several of the other party.

"He aint a dead stone yet. See, he moves."

But he did no such thing. The Lord of the Isles continued to crow vociferously, but the prostrate bird did not move. The man who officiated as director of the sports, and umpire, took him up in his hands; he was dead. The owner of the Pet rushed upon the stage, and the dead bird was placed in his hands. So great was the mortification of the master of the pet, that he was nearly shedding tears at the loss of his favourite, and as his distressed appearance was observed by the opposing party, he was greeted with derisive cheers.

"You that have won," said the umpire, "needn't be so cheeky about a chap's losses. Keep your tongues to yourselves. Do you hear?"

"Oh, yes—I dare say, Greenwood. Let them laugh who win, old boy. You mind your own business."

"It is part of my business to endeavour to preserve order."

"Oh, oh! Here's a lark; Greenwood has turned preacher. How much did you lay on the Pet?"

Mr. Greenwood did not condescend to return any answer to the latter query, but proceeded with the Lord of the Isles and his seconds behind the stage.

It was a curious sight to observe the different expressions on the countenances of the successful and unsuccessful betters. The latter's denoted the chagrin at the termination of the contest; some had staked their all in the excitement of the moment, and now a reaction had taken place in their minds. Colonel Jack had been pretty successful as he had backed the Lord of the Isles to a large extent, and had the pleasure of receiving several weighty gold pieces from various sporting gentlemen around.

Squabshot was also a considerable winner, and was most anxious to stand a bottle to his companion the colonel.

While the two were conversing together, the Badger was seen making his way towards them.

"Well, Bill," said the colonel; "your judgment was right, old boy—I suppose you have done the trick, eh?"

"Pretty well—amongst the middlings," said Mr. Dyson.

"I say, Bill, did you hear two men talking as you were coming down here some half an hour ago?"

"I heard a good many on 'em. What of that?"

"But, I mean, did you see or hear two fellows who were concerned in the—" he sunk his voice to a whisper—"the Clerkenwell murder?"

"No," said Mr. Dyson, in considerable surprise.

"They were somewhere about here nevertheless."

"Never—surely!"

"A fact, upon my honour."

"How do you know?"

"I heard it from above."

"Can't be—you must be mistaken, colonel, surely."

"Never was so certain in the whole course of my life. Ask him," he said, pointing to Squabshot.

"Oh, it is certain—sure," said that individual.

"Well, I never."

"Now I tell you what it is, Dyson. D—n the winnings, you may have all mine, in welcome, if you can only find out where these chaps are."

"And mine into the bargain as well," said Squabshot.

"Did you hear 'em?" inquired Mr. Dyson.

"No; for the moment Squabshot and myself made our appearance they were instantly silent."

"Know you, perhaps?"

"I am pretty certain of that," replied the colonel.

"How?"

"Why, one of them mentioned my name, and said that he had taken the knife with which the murder was committed from no other than myself."

"The devil he did!"

"Yes; I heard that distinctly."

"And did you not look about to catch sight of the worthies?"

"I was up stairs at the time, and presume that they were underneath."

"I understand, and so you could not catch sight of them."

"No."

"Oh, indeed."

Mr. Dyson inserted a straw in his mouth, and began to ruminate seriously for several minutes.

"Umph! this is a rum start."

"Can you help me to run down the game? If any man can, you are he."

"You are complimentary," said Mr. Dyson, sarcastically.

"Not at all, my dear Dyson," returned the colonel.

Dyson then pulled the colonel by the sleeve towards the door which led into the cock-pit, through which the colonel and Squabshot followed.

Having emerged from the building, the Badger looked remarkably mysterious, and, after a pause, he said, in a whisper, scarcely audible—

"Sir Richard Fleetwood was talking to you, was he not, when I came up?"

"Yes; for some time."

"What about?"

"Why, respecting the Clerkenwell business, and Osborne."

"That is all?"

"Yes; nothing else of any importance, that I can remember."

"Ah, he's a downy card."

"I do not want you or any one else to tell me that. I have known him before to-day. What has all this to do with the case in question?"

"More than you think. I saw Sir Richard talking to two fellows some time after he left you."

"What of that? He was making up his book, I suppose—he isn't too particular who he bets with."

"Perhaps not; but I do not think it was about betting that he was talking, for you know, colonel, that I really believe that those two men were the same that you overheard conversing."

"What makes you think that?"

"Never mind—that is my business."

"Do you know them?"

"I have seen them before."

"Oh, you have?"

"In course, and I think they were in the swing in the Cow Cross business—mind I am not sure on this point, but that is my impression, and if so, Sir Richard is fly to the whole proceeding."

"The devil! He is a blacker hearted scoundrel than I gave him credit for—that's all."

"Oh, you may give him a good long rope before he'll come to the end of the tether, I can tell you," said Mr. Dyson, in a mysterious manner.

"But what can he have to do with these men or their proceedings?"

"That is more than I can tell you," was the reply.

"He must have known them, then, I suppose?"

"There is no doubt about that," said Mr. Dyson; "but, stay—here comes Sir Richard. I will leave you, and then you can take an opportunity of questioning him upon the subject."

Upon this the Badger and Squabshot left the company of the colonel, who immediately followed the footsteps of Sir Richard, who shortly afterwards emerged from the precincts of the cock-pit.

He had only got a short distance, when he was overtaken and accosted by Colonel Jack.

"Sir Richard, a word with you," said the latter, in a hasty manner.

The baronet paused, and looked at the speaker.

"A word with you in private," continued the colonel.

"I am all attention, sir," answered the baronet.

The colonel walked gently on, followed by Sir Richard, who did not appear to exactly understand or like the present interception.

"Sir Richard Fleetwood," said the colonel, suddenly, and with marked emphasis, "you know the real murderer or murderers of Jabez Crudge!"

"Me!" said the baronet, haughtily; "Mr. Halford, what is your meaning?"

"It is plain enough, Sir Richard."

"It is rude enough, sir "

"And true enough, eh?"

"Sir, this is insolence," said the baronet, assuming an injured and dignified tone. "What has put this in your head, Halford, and how is it you presume to address me thus?"

"Sir Richard, you were conversing with two men some half hour ago who were known to me."

"Known to you—what of that?"

"And known also to be a pair of rascals who have been concerned in the murder at Clerkenwell."

"The cock-pit could doubtless furnish more than a pair of rascals," said the baronet, with a sneer.

"True," said the colonel; "two, perhaps. I appreciate the remark in its due force, but, nevertheless, it is not to the present purpose. These men must be brought to justice, or if not that, they must not be permitted to escape, scot free, while an innocent man is made to suffer for their crime."

"Have you followed me to preach morality, sir?' said the baronet, still carrying out the bantering tone he had at first assumed. "What have I to do with the punishment of criminals? Let each man take care of himself as best he may."

"Sir Richard Fleetwood," said the colonel, laying his hand upon the shoulder of the baronet, "you would not inflict so great a wrong upon an honourable young man as to see him die an ignominious death for a crime of which he is as innocent as yourself."

"That is the business of the law, not mine, besides, what can I do to assist Mr. Osborne? —for of course it is to him you are alluding, Mr. Halford."

"Act nobly, and do justice."

"Bah! justice, forsooth. I am thinking we should have enough to do in this world if we were quixotic enough to take up other men's business."

"Sir Richard, you know the real murderer or murderers of Jabez Crudge!" said the colonel.

"It is false, sir. I know no more about them than yourself—perhaps not so much," said the baronet.

"What were the names of those two men with whom you were conversing in the amphitheatre?"

"Who do you allude to? I have been conversing with some score or two, whom I only know by sight."

"Umph! I feel and know, now, that the fate of poor Henry Osborne rests entirely in your hands!"

"And I know that I have nothing to do with him or his fate—and there's the difference, sir!"

"Then you refuse to accede to my request —is that it?"

"I do not, at present, know what your request is."

"To give me the names of those two men —mind you, I shall have them sooner or later, I have no doubt; but an infinite deal of trouble might be saved by your serving me in this matter. Do you agree?" asked the colonel.

"I cannot, from sheer inability."

The colonel regarded the baronet with a meaning look, and paused for a minute or so as he regarded his companion—he then said, quickly—

"Are we to be friends or enemies hereafter?"

"Friends, I hope!" said the baronet.

"As you please. You make the election— abide by the consequences."

There was something so cold and sarcastic in the manner of the colonel as he uttered these last words that the baronet in spite of his usual self command started.

"Let us be friends for the future as we have been in the past!" said the baronet, in a more conciliatory tone than he had previously used.

The colonel could hardly repress a smile as this observation fell from the baronet.

"I understand your meaning. You do not care to have this question—or the contingent ones which must of necessity spring from it, discussed here. Perhaps you are right; at least I will assume that you are for the sake of argument. But I must remind you that time presses; and—"

"Well, you know where you can see me!" said the baronet.

"True! And when?"

"Whenever you please."

"To-morrow?"

"If you wish it."

"At Acton?"

"Of course—or anywhere else you please to appoint."

"At Acton be it then!"

"At any time to-morrow that suits you," said the baronet.

"I will do myself the pleasure of waiting upon you," said Colonel Jack, bowing. "Good day."

"Good day."

And the two parted somewhat abruptly.

"Curses on him!" said the baronet, as soon as his companion was out of earshot; "curses on him. I dare not openly quarrel with him, and that he well knows, as well as I do myself. Oh, that he were out of my path—out of the world—anywhere but here to cross and threaten me. What can he know about these fellows? The fellow has such secret information upon all subjects, that I dread him—yes, dread him, more, perhaps, than any man living. I know he holds those papers still—I feel assured of that—although he is as close as the grave upon the subject. Curses on him, but he is a bitter thorn in my side of a surety!"

Thus muttering, in no very enviable mood or temper, the baronet took his way to the residence of Mr. Langford.

Colonel Jack retraced his steps towards the cock-pit, followed by his faithful Slott.

"Well," said Mr. Dyson, as he came up to the colonel, upon the latter entering the cock-pit; "has he told you anything about them?"

"No," answered the colonel.

"Oh, he has not; he's in the swim, then, you may depend upon it."

"Have you seen anything more of them?" asked the colonel.

"I ain't set eyes upon them at all as yet," said the Badger.

"Nor you?"

This last observation was addressed to Squabshot.

"Not a smell on 'em," said the latter individual.

"We are queered, colonel in this 'ere business for the present," said the Badger.

"So it seems: but I am not going to let the matter rest here."

"Oh, you are not; what's your next game, then?"

"Going to the baronet."

"Oh!" and Mr. Dyson twirled the straw he held in his mouth, and peered out upon vacancy.

"He tried to ride the horse," said the highwayman.

"Did he though? And how did he succeed?"

"It was not much of a go with me, I can tell you."

"'Spose not."

"Oh, that's an old game of his," said Squabshot.

"He's mighty grand at times, so I've heard," observed Mr. Dyson, though he's generally pretty civil to me, I must say— generally pretty civil."

After diligent search in all parts for the two men whose voices had met the ears of the colonel, the three companions left the cock-pit, and repaired to the hospitable parlour of the Cow and Cauliflower.

CHAPTER XXX.

THE COLONEL'S INTERVIEW WITH SIR RICHARD FLEETWOOD.—STARTLING REVELATIONS.

ON the following day after the incidents had occurred described in our last chapter, Colonel Jack mounted his faithful mare, and proceeded to the residence of Sir Richard Fleetwood, at Acton.

The colonel was more than usually thoughtful. He was ruminating over a variety of subjects, which were of so mixed a character, and formed the key to such a multitude of important events, that it would be difficult for us to chronicle them here, and must content ourselves therefore with letting them appear in due course in the project of our tale.

He felt convinced that Sir Richard Fleetwood was fully cognisant of the real perpetrators of the murder of Jabez Crudge, and he knew moreover, from the character of the man with whom he had to deal, that nothing but the most pressing necessity would prevail upon the baronet to disclose their names or conditions, for his opinion of Sir Richard was by no means flattering to the baronet. He knew perfectly well, or guessed shrewdly enough, that Sir Richard would have no more compunction in sacrificing Henry Osborne, than he would have in drowning a blind kitten.

Where his own interest was concerned, Sir Richard was a remorseless man. In fact, he was guided in most of his actions by self-interest.

His love for Honora Langford was the leading principle of his life.

The colonel did not know, or clearly realise, this to its full extent. He knew Sir Richard was deeply enamoured with her, but he thought it one of those transient flames which, in the course of time, would burn itself out. He never gave the baronet the credit for a virtuous love. In fact, to use an old saying, he did not believe it was in him.

There he was mistaken.

We are apt most of us to view the actions and motives of men through a pair of spectacles of our own manufacture, and afterwards draw erroneous conclusions therefrom. The colonel did so in the present instance.

At the bottom of every man's heart there is some well-spring of affection, which gushes out upon a woman, or child, perhaps, and is that purer essence sent by the creator, and which most mortals, however hardened, possess, however it may lay concealed. None, we believe, are without human love and sympathy for their kind. Some are selfish in their love, some self-sacrificing; but the germs of that divine essence came in with our first parents, and will last as long as the world does.

Sir Richard Fleetwood was not an exception to the rule. He was a bad man—indeed, a very bad man, without a doubt—still his love for Honora Langford was the brightest and, perhaps, the only luminous portion of his character; and he cannot, I fear, afford to be defrauded of that. It may appear surprising that he could entertain so pure and devoted an attachment, but so it was, and Colonel Jack, who was no insignificant interpreter of the human character, was nevertheless unable to discern the master passion in the breast of Sir Richard Fleetwood.

Trotting his horse gently along the Bayswater road, our hero weighed in his own mind his own and the baronet's position in life. "Of a surety," thought the colonel, "my occupation has not the most dainty odour in the nostrils of righteous men, and Sir Richard Fleetwood is not a thought the honester man of the two, perhaps not so honest if the truth were told. No, not so honest, but he stands better in the eyes of the world—much better." Again did our hero become lost in deep reflection, from which he was hardly awakened until he reached the entrance to the mansion of Sir Richard Fleetwood.

The bell was rung, and leisurely and with a formal step the porter of the establishment proceeded to open the gate. He was a study—this man. He was of such elephantine proportions, that locomotion seemed to be a trouble to him. His duties were not very onerous. He lived in a small cottage within a few yards of the outer gate of the establishment, and all his duty consisted in opening this small gate, for which he was housed, clothed, and fed upon the best of the land. He had grown sleek in the service of the Fleetwood family, for he had been in it for one or two generations, and from his appearance you would have supposed the whole dignity of the family was centered in his corpulent person. His head was carried erect, his cheeks puffed out, and his silver whiskers were stuck out with a most agravating curl. Plethory seemed to have marked him for his own.

"Oh," thought the colonel to himself, " you have a hard time of it, my friend."

"Is Sir Richard at home," was the colonel's first inquiry, as a matter of course.

"He is," was the reply.

Descending from his horse the colonel was shewn into the library, where he found Sir Richard Fleetwood, not alone, for Mr. Sharpthorne was just taking his leave as the colonel entered. The lawyer bowed scornfully to the highwayman, and took his departure.

"So," exclaimed Sir Richard, handing his visitor a seat. "So you have come according to your appointment, it seems; there, be seated, my friend—and what will you take a glass of wine—or lunch."

"It is, as yet, too early for either," said the colonel, "thank you all the same. "That was Mr. Sharpthorne whom I met upon my entrance, was it not?"

"Yes; did you not recognise him again?'

"I judged it was him. Indeed, when you have seen his features once, you are not likely to forget them."

" I suppose not."

There was an awkward restraint between the two, which induced a stiffness on both their parts, neither of them likely to plunge into the subject which had occasioned the present interview.

"Well, Sir Richard," said Colonel Jack, determined at length to break the ice. " You know the object of this visit."

"Not precisely," said the baronet, calmly.

"Well, then, I will be at once explicit. Yesterday, there were two men conversing together and imprudently enough they let drop in the course of their conversation, quite enough to let me know that they were concerned in the Clerkenwell murder."

"Well, Halford, what of that?"

"Hear me out, if you please."

The baronet bowed, for it suited his purpose to be on his stilts, those useful articles which noblemen will at times don to suit their purpose.

"These two men, as I was observing were the principals in the Clerkenwell murder. They were conversing with you, Sir Richard. They were seen to pass through the entrance with yourself, and they were observed in close converse with you. Now, let us understand each other. You know who murdered Jabez Crudge," said the colonel, ringing out this last sentence in a voice of thunder. I do not want you to hand the murderers over to justice, but I want you to save Henry Osborne. Nay, more, you must do so."

"Must!" exclaimed the baronet. "So you come here to threaten, then,"

" I come here for justice," replied the colonel.

"Bah! you talk of justice, forsooth," replied the baronet, contemptuously.

"Well, we will put it in another shape. I desire Henry Osborne's release; he is my most devoted friend. I desire his release, and you can save him if you like."

"You take a marvellous interest in this young man."

"No matter for that. I want the names of those two men, and mind, I promise you that they shall not be delivered over to justice; but little would be required of them to exculpate poor Osborne. They might leave the country, for in the event of Osborne's acquittal, he would be enabled to furnish them with ample means to do so."

"Umph!—you are opening theories, my friend, which to carry out appears to be utterly impracticable. You see, Halford, you have come here upon a foolish errand, at least, so it strikes me. In the first place you are wrong in supposing that I know the real murderers of Jabez Crudge; and as to Mr. Henry Osborne, I do not entertain any such exalted opinion of his character as you appear to have formed of him. I tell you frankly, for once and for all, that you have come upon a fruitless errand in this instance, and that I positively refuse to interfere in any way in this matter."

"Thank you, sir, for so much candour," said the colonel, who, despite his mastery over himself was pale with rage. "Thank you, sir, for thus much. You have forgotten the incidents of your past life—you have forgotten—bah! Why should I repeat that which is indellibly written in this heart. You talk of justice—you, Sir Richard Fleetwood. By the Lord! such a word sounds well bandied about from our lips."

"Why this ebullition, Halford?" said the baronet, who saw and dreaded the gathering storm. Why this sudden rage? What can possess you to take so much interest in that smooth-tongued, spooney-faced puppy Henry Osborne?"

"Puppy!" exclaimed the colonel.

"Ah, surely. He's a conceited coxcomb."

"He is an honourable, upright young man, Sir Richard, which is more than can be said for either of us."

"Thank you for your compliments, sir," said the baronet. "You have come, it seems for no other purpose but to insult me."

The colonel strode backwards and forwards several times, taking no heed of the baronet's latter observation, and neither further spoke to each other for some minutes, after which he came to a halt, and said, as though speaking to himself.

"Sir Richard Fleetwood, baronet, came into his title and estates how? Let me see! Ah, by the demise of his brother. He, the present baronet, and the late Sir Reignald, were the issue or rather supposed issue of Sir Reginald, senior."

"Supposed!" exclaimed Sir Richard.

"Yes, supposed!" said the colonel, still speaking to himself and not condescending to cast a glance at the last speaker.

"I say supposed, or reputed, which you will," continued the colonel, "for neither of them were really the sons of the late Sir Reginald, for the real heir is still in existence."

"Liar and traducer you shall answer for this. I will at once hand you over to to justice," exclaimed Sir Richard Fleetwood, as he leant against the mantel-piece and was about to touch the bell.

Colonel Jack pulled out a pistol from his breast, cocked it, and presented the barrel thereof directly pointed towards the baronet, who started back in surprise and horror.

"Attempt to give the slightest alarm and I will stretch you dead at my feet!" exclaimed the colonel.

"Halford! Would you commit murder?" said the baronet, in unfeigned alarm.

"Not willingly—not unless driven to it by the exigency of the case, which may require it, and if it does—"

"Well."

"I shall not hesitate to take your life, Sir Richard!"

"Insolent miscreant."

"We will not bandy compliments, Sir Richard. Are you for peace or war—come, decide?"

"You speak in enigmas. Am I to listen to your unfounded insults, and pass them with impunity?"

"What I am saying may be unpalatable truths."

"They are falsehoods!"

"Sir Richard, I have not deviated one iota from the truth I say, the real heir to the Fleetwood baronetcy is still in existence, although—" and here he sighed deeply, "although the probability is that he will never endeavour to establish his claim to them."

Sir Richard was stupified with surprise at this speech.

"Ah," exclaimed the colonel, bitterly, "it is in vain now to recal the past. Need I remind you of our early days? Need I remind you of Frank Halford, whom you when a young man patronised so kindly—patronised forsooth! Who has made me what I am? Who first undermined my principles? Who taught me extravagant habits, and lured me into dissipation, until—God!—until I was forced to retrieve my fortunes by—you know how. You were my senior by many years, and," he added, bitterly, "I think that I have been made a sufficient scape-goat of already!"

"Hush! Do not recur to events we would both of us wish to forget," said the baronet, trembling.

"I can never forget them!" exclaimed

Colonel Jack; "you and yours have been my curse."

"Your curse, Halford, and wherefore?"

"You have made me—or, at any rate, mainly contributed to make me—what I am. The name of Fleetwood has been the evil star of our house."

There was a settled look of determination upon the features of the colonel at which the baronet quailed.

"This story of yours about an existing heir to the baronetcy is but a chimera of your own brain," said the baronet in a subdued tone.

"It is the truth I have told you," exclaimed our hero."

"And who is the claimant?"

"Colonel Jack!"

The highwayman drew himself up to his full height as he uttered this, and surveyed the questioner haughtily.

"Yes, Sir Richard, Colonel Jack, and no other. It would be a tedious tale for me to enter into now, but let it suffice that I hold the proofs in my possession—indisputable proofs, which places it out of the power of any one to dispute my statement, or doubt my claim."

Sir Richard was silent and abashed. He had heard whisperings of this fact for years before but paid little attention to it—but he had not the slightest idea that the colonel himself was the claimant to the Fleetwood estates.

Presently he said, in a more conciliating strain—

"And what am I to understand by this, Halford? Are you going to have the question tried upon the production of these—these proofs, that you say are in your possession?"

"That depends upon circumstances," was the answer.

"How so?"

"Well, frankly, I have no wish to thrust myself forward as a litigant in this case, provided you give me some compensation in return."

"What?"

First and foremost I must have your solemn promise—your oath, that you will cease from persecuting Henry Osborne; and next, I must have the names of the men who were the real perpetrators of the Clerkenwell tragedy."

"I never have persecuted Mr. Osborne," replied the baronet.

"Psha! Don't use subterfuge, Sir Richard," exclaimed the colonel.

"What is it that makes you take so deep an interest in this man?" inquired the baronet.

"That is my business."

"He appears to be one of your greatest friends, and, alas, he is one of my most bitter enemies."

"What has he done to you?"

"He has stood between me and one I prize beyond all else in this world."

"Bah! a woman," exclaimed the highwayman, contemptuously.

"Well, what of that. She is a woman who to me is my very existence."

A sarcastic smile played over the features of the highwayman as he said "I should fancy you were not a likely man to lose your heart—entirely out of your own keeping."

"But I have—Great God, I have!"

"Whose fault is that?—not mine," said the colonel.

"Nor mine," exclaimed the baronet.

"Miss Langford's then, I suppose?"

"You have no right to come between me and her at any rate," said the baronet.

"Nor have you any right to hurl Osborne from his position."

"Neither have I done so. It is the fault of circumstances alone."

"Sir Richard Fleetwood, this young man must not, nay, shall not be sacrificed. You know the real perpetrators of the crime, Mr. Sharpthorne knows them also; and both he and yourself are keeping them in the back ground. This may not be."

"Pray may I ask," said the baronet, "how you came possessed of these documents you speak of?"

"That is my business."

"And I suppose it is also mine."

"You may take my word that I am in the possession of such, and that is enough for our present purpose."

"Will you produce them?"

"If you compel me, I will in court."

"Umph! It is hardly worth while our quarrelling. Anything that is reasonable, I will willingly do. I need hardly tell you this. What is it you require?"

"I have already told you. In the first place, I want the names and addresses of those two men."

"I do not know them, and if I did, you do not think me villain enough to hand them over to the law. You would not do so yourself—now, would you?"

"I am here to gain the desired information, and for no other purpose. If you refuse, I shall know how to act."

"Again, I ask what can make you take such a deep interest in the fate of this man, Osborne?" said the baronet.

"Is it not enough, Sir Richard, that you have made me what I am, defrauded me of my birthright, without adding to that the curse of Cain upon me.'"

"The curse of Cain?"

"Yes, Henry Osborne is my brother," said the colonel.

"Your brother !" exclaimed the baronet, in unfeigned surprise.

"Yes, my half brother—whom I love and admire. He knows not of the relation between us, and I do not choose that he ever should. Some day or other the terrible truth will be made manifest to him that his dearest friend is no other than Colonel Jack; for at present he is ignorant of that fact."

"Your brother ! Well, I never dreamt of that. Ah, that accounts for your consideration in his behalf."

"Come," exclaimed the colonel, "time presses. The names of these two men, and I will promise to requite you with as good a gift at a future period."

"Really, Halford, you ask of me more than I am justified in granting; for as to your claim to the estates and title of Fleetwood,
No. 25.

I can contest it, and I am thinking you would have but little chance—very little chance in a court of law."

"But your own brother would, Sir Richard," said the colonel.

"If he were in existence, of course he would."

"He is in existence, Sir Richard," said the colonel, quietly.

These words fell like a thunderbolt upon Sir Richard. He staggered back some paces —his iron frame trembled—and he fell into a chair.

"My own brother alive ! Why, man, are you possessed, or have you sold yourself to the devil ?"

"Your brother, Sir Reginald, still lives."

"Nonsense ; you are mad to make such an assertion."

" I never was more sane or serious in my life."

"Why, he died on the continent, as you and every one else knows."

"He still lives," again said our hero. "Be advised by me. Make use of your time before the ground slips from under your feet. It will go hard with me if I don't hurl you from your present position ; ay, and will, as surely as there is a God above, if you refuse to act fairly by Henry Osborne."

The baronet was appalled. He had always stood in dread of Colonel Jack, but was quite unprepared for these startling revelations.

"You see," said the latter, "that I hold the master key wherewith I can unlock all your secrets. It is hardly policy to quarrel with me. You are too good a judge for that, if I read you rightly. When once Henry Osborne is free from the hands of the law, I promise you to stand your friend for the future ; but unless he is freed from his present position, I swear to be your bitterest enemy. Now you understand my course of action, and can make your own election in the matter."

"I will do all I can, believe me," said the baronet, now fairly intimidated, "all I possibly can."

"Then who were those parties with whom you were conversing yesterday?"

"I don't know that they were the murderers."

"But I do, which is much the same thing, and answers the purpose equally as well, perhaps better."

"Their names were James Parker and Ralph Slimcoe," said the baronet, in a half whisper.

"Good."

And the colonel immediately entered their names in his pocket-book.

"Now, where do they live ?"

"You must promise me, Halford," said the baronet, "you must promise me most faithfully that neither of these men will be handed over to justice. God forbid that I should cause the death of a fellow creature."

The highwayman smiled.

"I promise," he said, "they shall be dealt fairly with. All I shall want will be their attestation—that is all."

"Had you not better let Mr. Sharpthorne manage this business?"

"I think not."

"Wherefore? Sharpthorne is entrusted with Osborne's defence, and he appears to me to be the most fitting person to settle the affair amicably to all parties."

"Time presses," said the colonel. "Their address, if you please."

"Well, but, Halford, why not let Sharpthorne see to it? You must not be seen in it yourself, it would not be prudent."

"Of that you will allow me to be the best judge," said the colonel. "Come, the addresses, if you please."

"I don't know their address—" said the baronet.

"Psha !" exclaimed his companion.

"But I know where they are concealed," continued the baronet.

"Well, that is all I require now. Where is it ?"

"At one, Isaac Balasco's, a Jew, in West Street."

"I know it ; that is sufficient," said the colonel, "that is quite sufficient."

The baronet looked particularly uncomfortable when he had given up the names and whereabouts of the two men, and looked as if he had signed his own death warrant.

"I really think you had better consult Mr. Sharpthorne in the matter, before you leave," said the baronet.

"Before I leave ! Mr. Sharpthorne has gone, hasn't he ?"

"No, he has not left the house as yet, I believe."

"Oh, indeed. Well, there is no harm in seeing him."

"Ah, you think not ?"

And with great alacrity Sir Richard rose and rang the bell.

"Tell Mr. Sharpthorne I wish to see him," he said, to the domestic who made his appearance.

"Yes, sir," and exit domestic.

Mr. Sharpthorne soon made his appearance in his usual obsequious manner, rubbing his hands, and puckering up his features.

"Your servant, gentlemen," said the lawyer, as he bowed to Colonel Jack. "Ah!" he exclaimed, as he caught sight of Slott, eyeing him with no friendly glance.

"Come here, Slott," said the colonel ; "here, boy, lay down."

And the animal went immediately under the table, in obedience to his master's commands."

"Mr. Halford is interested in Mr. Osborne's case," said Sir Richard Fleetwood, with a flourish of his hand in the direction of the highwayman.

"Indeed, Sir Richard, indeed. So am I ; in fact, I am preparing the defence, as you already know. Ah, poor young man, I do hope we shall be able to get him off—I certainly do hope, although at present things look very black against him."

"The way to get him off, as you term it," said Colonel Jack, "is to produce the real perpetrators of the crime."

"Ah, true, of a surety—of a surety," said the little lawyer, rubbing his hands in his old manner ; "of a surety."

"And I am about to do so," said the colonel. "That is, if I do not produce the men themselves, I shall get sufficient from them to exculpate my friend, Henry Osborne."

"Do you know the real perpetrators of this—ahem—terrible crime?" inquired the lawyer.

"Sir Richard Fleetwood does."

"Sir Richard!" and Sharpthorne cast his ferret-eyes towards the baronet.

"I am in hopes, Mr. Sharpthorne," said the baronet, "of being able to put my friend, Mr. Halford, on their track."

"Oh, indeed. I am quite overjoyed at this unlooked for intelligence," said the lawyer. "Can I be of any service in this matter?" he inquired, as he gave another meaning glance towards his employer.

"We think we have, or rather are likely to get hold of the right parties," said the baronet; "and I think I am echoing the sentiments of my friend Halford when I say that we have no wish for them to be handed over to justice; for, in a measure, I know their names—only in confidence—only in confidence, you understand."

"Which must not be abused," said the lawyer.

"Of course not. I do not know what course Mr. Halford intends to pursue."

"That which will exculpate my friend," returned our hero.

"Ah, yes—very natural—certainly," said Mr. Sharpthorne. "Well."

"I shall see the parties, for they are known to me, and then—"

"Yes."

"And then I will call at your chambers and consult with you upon our future actions."

"Oh, indeed! Thank you for the interest you are taking. I shall be most proud to consult with you, and need hardly say that all my ingenuity suggests in this matter will be most gladly and cheerfully given."

"No doubt, Mr. Sharpthorne," said our hero. "I am much obliged to you, sir—very much obliged, as well as to Sir Richard himself."

And with these words he rose to take his departure.

"There is nothing else, then?" said the lawyer, who was rather in a fog at this new aspect of the case.

"No, nothing for the present," said the colonel. "Good day, sir—Sir Richard, I wish you good day, and will see you shortly and let you know how I have got on."

"Thank you," said the baronet, as he walked towards the door, with some uneasiness of manner.

"Do you leave so abruptly, then?" he said to the colonel.

"I have pressing business just now," was the answer to this interrogatory.

"Then I will not seek to detain you."

The baronet bowed politely, and his visitor departed.

"What is the meaning of all this?" said Sharpthorne, when the colonel had left.

"Hush!—curse him!" said Sir Richard, in a hoarse whisper.

"What's the matter?"

"I've been obliged to give him those names."

"Confound it, Sir Richard, it will spoil all. That was very imprudent."

"It has been forced from me."

"Forced?"

"Yes."

"How?"

"By threats."

"Why not, sir, have given the rascal in custody?"

"I dare not."

"Why?"

"I am in his power, and the scoundrel knows it."

"In his power?"

"Yes, most confoundedly."

"In what way?"

"Oh, in many ways—more than I can tell you."

"Hang it, that is unfortunate. He's a most unscrupulous rascal, that we all know."

"Yes; no doubt of that."

"But you must defy him. He's under the ban of the law. Why you could hang him if you liked."

"Perhaps so; but, Sharpthorne, the rascal holds papers—"

"What are they?"

"That is more than I can tell you."

"Why are you so afraid?"

It was evident the baronet was afraid, for he trembled in every limb, much to the lawyer's surprise.

"Ah," thought Mr. Sharpthorne, "there is more in this than meets the eye."

"Sharpthorne, that man appears to know everybody's secrets," said Sir Richard.

"And a pretty use he is likely to make of the knowledge."

"What is to be done now?"

"About what? I am utterly in the dark at present," said the lawyer.

"About these two men, Parker and Slimcoe."

"What address have you given him?"

"Balasco's, the Jew's."

"And he will go there at once, no doubt."

"Of course—that is his intention."

"It will ruin all."

"I am afraid so."

"Confound it. How could you have been so—so weak? You must excuse my saying so."

"There don't upbraid me. I was compelled. That is a sufficient answer. The only question is, what are we to do now?"

"Why, of course, give them notice."

"What for ?"

"That they may effect their escape."

"Ah, true ; I never thought of that. But there won't be time, and how is it to be effected ?"

"I will go at once myself, or else send Grime—"

"Oh, no ; go yourself, there's a good fellow," said the baronet, rising, and laying his hand upon the lawyer's shoulder. " Go at once, but you must be secret."

"Trust me for that."

"I will have a horse saddled at once, and you can gallop to London by a different road to the one he has taken."

"Do you know which way he goes?"

"Yes, the Shepherd's Bush and Bayswater Road."

"Then I will take the Hammersmith one."

"But you will never be before him."

"Never mind, I will try, that is all."

The baronet rang the bell.

"Bristow, saddle Dutch Sam for Mr. Sharpthorne ; he must ride to London upon pressing business," he said to the domestic who answered the summons.

"Yes, sir," and the man disappeared.

He, however, put his head in again at the door, and said—

"I beg your pardon, sir, but did you say Sam ?"

"Yes !" thundered forth his master.

The man disappeared on the instant.

"You can ride pretty well, I believe ?" inquired the baronet of his legal adviser.

"Oh, yes."

"For I have ordered you a fast horse, and he may be restive."

"Never mind that, the faster the better," was the reply.

"You must use discretion in this matter, Sharpthorne," said the baronet.

"I generally do, Sir Richard, I hope. What power has this man over you ?"

"You know those papers respecting the Reichbeck property ?"

"Of course I do; we've had trouble enough about them."

"Well, I am convinced he has them."

"I always thought so ; indeed, I felt assured of it."

"And they contain documents we little dream of."

"How do you know this ?"

"I only think so."

"Oh."

"But am pretty certain. What do you think he says ?"

"I have no idea—how can I."

"That he can prove my illegitimacy."

"That is possible."

"You think so ?"

"I do."

"And he says more than this, he can prove his own legitimacy."

"To what ?"

"To the title and estates of Fleetwood."

"Psha, I don't believe it."

"I am glad to hear you say so."

"I don't believe it."

"He positively asserts it as a fact."

"Who will believe him ?—how is he to make his appearance in court ? He can't come in with clean hands, that's quite certain. Has he the effrontery to say that he intends to try ?"

"No, he did not mean to say that he would press his claim."

"His claim !—he has none, you may depend on it. I wish you had called me in at first. He has evidently been bullying you."

"Sharpthorne, it is not our policy to quarrel with him."

"Perhaps not, at present. We must lay a trap for him."

"I wish we could."

"Leave that to me."

"Ah, that man, I wish he were out of my way. The fellow is so determined."

"But he can and will be overmatched by cunning."

"Yes, but don't quarrel with him at present."

"I don't intend to quarrel with him at all," said the lawyer, with a sinister and fox-like look.

"No, not at present, at any rate."

"Not at all, my friend—not at all ; all we want is to see him safely hung at Tyburn ; that is all," said the lawyer, with admirable coolness, as he took a pinch of snuff.

"The horse is ready, if you please, sir," said Bristow, as he put his head once more in the apartment.

"That's all right," said the baronet, " then I will not detain you, Mr. Sharpthorne ; make what speed you can, and God send you may be in time !"

"I hope so, most sincerely," was the immediate reply.

"You will let me know the result," asked the baronet.

"You may rely upon my doing so," answered the lawyer, as he proceeded down stairs into the court yard, and mounted the horse known as Dutch Sam, who happened to be a quadruped so remarkably dexterious in the use of his fore legs that he had been named after a celebrated prize-fighter.

The groom had some difficulty in holding him to allow the lawyer to mount, who, however, did manage to succeed in doing so, upon which the fine animal galloped off at lightning's speed.

"I shouldn't wonder if old parchment don't break his neck," said one of the stable men.

"If he wants to ride to the devil he has just got the horse for the purpose," added the groom.

"Oh, he'll go there some day without the trouble of riding," suggested the stable man, who had no very exalted opinion of Mr. Sharpthorne.

"I wonder what made the governor send him off in such a tremendous hurry?" asked the groom.

"To get rid of him, I suppose."

"He seems remarkably fond of his company, in a measure of speaking," continued the groom.

"Ah, he's up to snuff, you see."

"I should rather say he was, but he must be up to his work as a rider as well, or he'll come to his mother earth."

The two worthies now betook themselves to the stables again to regail themselves with a can of ale.

Sir Richard returned to his library, a prey to the most horrible thoughts.

"Curse that man!" he exclaimed, as he threw himself once more into the library chair; "curses on him; he is my evil genius. My brother alive! How does he know that? How—how?"

The baronet shuddered.

"He will snatch this prize from my hands, I do verily believe. Oh—oh!" and at the thought of losing Honora Langford the baronet sobbed aloud. "Curse the money, and the estates. What care I. If I could only obtain the love of Miss Langford I would go on the Continent, or some place far away, and lead a happy life for the remainder of my days. What care I for wealth or title without her I love? I would gladly lead a peasant's life for evermore, in obscurity, if I could get her to share my lot. God! how I love that girl! so much, that—"

He sighed deeply, and broke off abruptly in his reflections.

"So much," he continued, "that I would give up all for her sake—yes all—and yet I must be a fool to think thus; for, ah, I shall never have her—no, never—that thought drives me to distraction. If I could only get Osborne out of the way! But then the fellow will come into a large property himself if he is acquitted, and will be a more formidable rival than ever. Oh, that I could be fairly rid of that man, and his champion, Halford!"

As he reflected on this he sunk into moody silence, and was entirely wrapt in his own thoughts.

Mr. Sharpthorne, when he got on the main road, found that Dutch Sam intended going whether he would or no. The lawyer was bumped and jolted in a manner that he had little calculated, but he kept his seat, which was more than the grooms had anticipated.

It was a perverse animal he was riding, and he had some difficulty in making him turn down the road which led to Hammersmith. In fact, Mr. Sharpthorne was nearly thrown when he came to this part of his journey, indeed, it is a wonder how he did manage to persuade Sam to take the road he was desirous of going; however, after several determined efforts, Sharpthorne had his way, and the brute galloped off with him at a furious rate.

The lawyer did not cut a very picturesque figure upon his steed, but he cared little for that.

To reach in safety the Old House in West Street was his only desire, and at the pace he was going, he felt that consummation would soon be attained.

The idea of Sharpthorne being matched against a highwayman was in itself comic enough, but he had perseverance, and was determined if possible to steal a march upon our hero.

Away he went along the Hammersmith Road like a second Johnny Gilpin.

Kensington was soon reached by the lawyer, after which he threaded the narrow streets of London which led to that locality where Balasco, the Jew, dwelt.

Mr. Sharpthorne, before his arrival at the Old House in West Street, put up his horse at a livery stables in Liquorpond Street. and proceeded to West Street on foot. Arrived there, he inquired hastily for Isaac Balasco. The lad who answered the door knew Sharpthorne, and at once admitted him into the private apartment of that respectable establishment.

"Mishter Sharpthorne?" exclaimed the Jew, in some surprise, at the lawyer's sudden and unexpected appearance.

"Hush! Are we alone?" said the party addressed.

"Yesh. There ish no one to hear us, my shild."

"Has Colonel Jack been here? exclaimed the lawyer, in evident anxiety, looking carefully around.

"No," replied the Jew.

"That is all right. You are quite sure upon this head!"

"Do you think I vould deceive you?" exclaimed the Jew, with an attempt at an indignant look.

"No; I do not doubt your word for one moment, only he will be here in a minute or so, that's certain—Heaven be praised that I am before him!"

"Vy, my shild, vat ish the matter? vat do you mean?"

"The two men concerned in the Clerkenwell business—"

"Vell?"

"They must be off at once!" he said.

"Off—why ?"

"The colonel has their names, and knows moreover that they were concerned in the murder."

"Bless us and save us. You don't say so?"

"But I do say so, and what is more, the whole affair will be discovered if they are not removed at once. Now, do you understand ?"

"But how did the colonel know about this business? I thought the whole affair was kept dark ?"

"No matter how it came about; it is enough to know that these men must get out of the way, and that at once, or I will not answer for their safety."

"Lord preserve us, but this is bad hearings, Mishter Sharpthorne—very bad—very bad hearings."

"Are they in the house ?"

"Yesh."

"Let me see them at once."

"Not here—not here. It would not be safe."

"Why not ?"

"Oh, that would never do. You must come down stairs where they are at present concealed. Margott."

This was addressed to the boy who had opened the door to the lawyer, and in obedience to the summons the boy made his appearance.

"If any one should come for me show them into the public room, and say I will be there in the course of a few minutes. Do you understand ?"

The boy gave a nod of assent, and the lawyer accompanied Balasco into the realms below.

They were dark and numerous passages through which the two went, so dark and sombre that the lawyer shuddered, and began to doubt if he should ever come out of it alive.

In a dark and damp vault he observed the two murderers of the unfortunate Jabez Crudge.

They were playing at cards on the head of a tub, and seemed tolerably happy under the circumstances.

They glanced up in some alarm at the presence of the two new comers but were reassured when the Jew said—

"Don't be alarmed, it'sh only me and a friend."

Mr. Sharpthorne and the speaker advanced nearer to them and the Jew continued in a low tone—

"The colonel's fly, and you must hook it at once."

"Hook it! The devil!" they both exclaimed, now fearfully alarmed ; "and where to ?"

"That we must see about ; it will not do to remain here."

"Why not ? We are quite safe in these vaults."

"My tear, I tell you it wont do to stay here ; the colonel knows all about my secret places, and it would be dangerous to run any risks ; besides, how can I say consciously that you are not under my protection. Would you have me tell a lie ?"

"Lie be —" exclaimed one of the men, indignantly.

"Well, whether or no the colonel would not be satisfied with my bare word, and to stay here would therefore be an impossibility, you see."

The two men rose and threw down the cards, and without uttering another word gathered up a few of their things which were laying about, and proceeded at once to leave the establishment of Mr. Balasco, who showed them the way out with considerable alacrity.

The two men conversed apart for a few minutes with the Jew, and then hastily made their exit by the rear of the house.

Joy beamed in the countenance of the lawyer as he saw the two murderers clear of the premises, after which he and his companion returned to the rooms which they had but left a minute or so previous.

The two had hardly entered into this apartment when the lad made his appearance there, and informed his master that Colonel Jack was in the public room.

Mr. Sharpthorne made a hasty exit, and Balasco repaired to the room where the colonel awaited his presence.

The latter's first inquiry was for the two men who had so precipitately left the house.

"They are not here, colonel, as Heaven is my judge," said the Jew.

"Don't call Heaven to judge any of your actions, you old sinner," answered the colonel. "They are here, and I must see them ; nay, more, I will. Now do you understand me ?"

"How can you, my tear ?—how can you, when I declare that they have made their escape ?"

"Escape ! Get out you old blackguard, I know better than that. Come, no nonsense, Balasco. You've known me before, and therefore I needn't tell you that I'm not to be trifled with, so stow gammon."

"But, colonel, now do listen to reason. They were here, my child, I don't disguise that—they were here, but have left, indeed they have."

"When ?"

"Yesterday," was the Jew' immediate answer.

"Humbug ! You lie, you old rascal !"

"May I be—"

"There, that will do; I don't want any of your oaths—I know pretty well their value. Now look here, Balasco; I don't mean the fellows any harm, only I must and will see them; but mind, my visit is only a friendly one."

"I do not doubt it, colonel—I do not for one moment doubt it; but I swear most solemnly that they are gone."

"Gone where?"

The Jew shrugged his shoulders, and said—

"I don't know at present."

"Bah! that won't do for me. You have them safely secreted below. Why, it is not many hours since I saw one of their best friends and protectors, and he told me so."

"Who was that, my tear?" inquired the Jew.

"Sir Richard Fleetwood."

"Ah, then Sir Richard is mistaken. I dare say he thought so, but he is mistaken nevertheless. The fact is, colonel, they got scent that some one was on their trail, and so they hooked it. Lord—Lord—they were obstinate, surely. I told them that they were mistaken, but all I could do was of no avail, and so they stepped it."

The colonel fixed his gaze upon the features of the Jew, as though he would read his very thoughts.

"It'sh a fact, colonel, upon my word it ish."

"I'll go down below and judge for myself," answered Colonel Jack, still disbelieving the Jew's statement.

"You are welcome, my son—quite welcome to search every nook and cranny."

"Thank you," answered the colonel, sharply.

A light was procured, and the two took their way down to that mysterious locality where the two murderers had laid concealed. The colonel glanced all around, but of course did not succeed in catching a glimpse of the objects of his search.

"There, now are you satisfied?" asked Balasco.

"They are not here, that's clear enough," replied the colonel.

Then suddenly turning round upon his companion, he said, angrily, as he caught the Jew by the collar of his coat—

"But where are they? Come, no paltering—where are they? You have them concealed somewhere—where is it?"

"I swear to you, colonel, that they are gone," answered the Jew, as he began to tremble at the sight of the gathering storm upon the brow of Colonel Jack, who grasped the Jew by the throat, and shook him like a reed.

"By the Lord! but I've a great mind to twist your old neck, you shuffling rascal!"

said the colonel, as he tightened his grasp upon his companion's throat.

"Colonel!—mershy!" exclaimed Balasco, struggling to release himself. "Mershy, colonel! Would you murder me!"

"I should be doing no great harm if I did," was the reply; "and I swear too, that I will, if you play me false."

"But I am not, indeed I am not, my tear!" said the Jew, in his most wheedling accents.

"Get along with you," said the colonel, as he flung him from him.

The Jew staggered some yards, and looked most terribly frightened, as indeed he really was.

"Mershy on me! you are so violent, that I am afraid to speak or move for fear of offending you."

"Now mind me, Ike," said Colonel Jack, seriously. "You can't, and what's more, you shan't, humbug me. Where have these chaps gone to, if they are really gone?"

"I don't know, upon my word I don't, at present."

"When shall you?"

"In a day or two, I dare say."

The colonel hesitated, and then reflected for some moments, as he stood the while between the entrance of the vault and the Jew.

"Somebody's been here!" he exclaimed, suddenly.

"What do you mean, colonel? Of course, a good many persons have been here."

"Ah, yes, I dare say; but to-day—within an hour or so."

"Who?"

"That you best know. Somebody from Sir Richard Fleetwood."

"From Sir Richard who?"

"Oh, you need not pretend ignorance—from Sir Richard Fleetwood. I know your game—and his. Now, Ike, deal fairly by me, or—" and here the colonel pulled out a pistol and cocked it. "Or by the Lord that made me, you have not many minutes to live."

"Oh, mershy! Father of Abraham, have mershy!" exclaimed the Jew, now fairly beside himself with fear, as he threw himself on his knees before Colonel Jack, and held up his hands imploringly.

He was an arrant coward, and an arrant rogue, Mr. Isaac Balasco, besides his many other qualifications.

The colonel lowered his pistol, and pointed it downwards towards the head of the Jew, who recoiled back, and averted his gaze, as he placed one hand before his face, as though he would ward off the intended bullet.

"Now understand me, once and for all," said Colonel Jack; "somebody's been here from Sir Richard Fleetwood. It is, as I expected—a double game is being played.

Now, if you don't deal fairly by me, why, you shan't live to deceive any one else. You hear my determination, and you know also that I am not a man to promise and not perform."

"Oh, mershy! I will deal fairly by you—I swear I will," said the Jew, trembling with fright.

"Prove it, then, by speaking the truth. Who was it that came here—for I know some one did—to give notice to those men."

"Mr—r. Sh—arp—thorne," answered Balasco, as his teeth chattered together with fright.

"Ah! how long since?"

"About half an hour ago."

"Curses on it! foiled by that rascally old thief of an attorney," exclaimed Colonel Jack, in a paroxysm of rage. "Done by half an hour! Who would have dreamt that the old raven could have flown hither so fast? The hypocritical old rascal must have stolen a march upon me. And where are they now?"

"Who?"

"The two men."

"I don't know—I declare I don't, upon my life and soul."

"Neither of them are worth much. Unless you behave better, I shall take the first, and the devil will of course grab the latter—that is, if a Jew has a soul."

"Oh, colonel, do not talk thus," exclaimed Balasco. "I never deceived you, no one can say that of me."

"Go along, you contemptible old driveller, no one is likely to believe a word you say."

"Oh, colonel, I swear to you that I am speaking the truth—indeed I am."

"In this instance you may, under great pressure, but it is not your usual practice. Now, tell me, where are these men to be found?"

"I don't know."

"You know where they live I suppose?"

"I swear I do not!"

"When did they leave?"

The Jew did not reply. The question was repeated in a still more imperative tone, and the pistol again pointed at his head, menacingly.

"About half an hour since," said the Jew.

"Ah, as I expected—sold!" exclaimed the colonel. "Now, mark me, Ike, I don't know if it be true about your knowledge respecting their whereabouts, but one thing is quite certain, you can find it out for me if you like."

"I am not certain of that," answered the Israelite.

"But I am, and what is more, you must find it out in a day or two or I'll raise such a clatter about your ears that you shall not easily forget."

"I will do my best, I swear to you most solemnly."

"See that you do or it will be the worst for you."

The colonel put up his pistol, and he and Balasco betook themselves to the up-stairs room, there the former repeated his request, and, in no very contented mood, left the old house in West Street.

CHAPTER XXXI.

THE COLONEL AND SIR RICHARD FLEETWOOD AGAIN.

IRRITATED beyond measure at the perfidy of Sir Richard Fleetwood, Colonel Jack determined upon riding over to Acton on the following day after his unsuccessful visit to Balasco.

He knew very well that the baronet was a slippery, unscrupulous customer, but had not supposed that he would have had recourse to such a stratagem as that made manifest by the fact of Sharpthorne's visit to the old house in West Street.

The colonel chafed and fumed as he reflected upon this feint, and was irritated at the thought of being forstalled by a lawyer for whom he had a most profound contempt.

The baronet was not, strange to say, denied to our hero when he presented himself at the gate of mansion, but the colonel was immediately shown into his presence. The fact is that Sir Richard had not the slightest idea that Mr. Sharpthorne's visit would be made known to him; indeed, in his hurry and excitement, the baronet had quite overlooked the possibility of such an occurrence.

"So, Sir Richard Fleetwood," said Colonel Jack, as he entered the library, "so, Sir Richard Fleetwood, you have played me false it seems."

"What do you mean, sir?" said the baronet, hastily, drawing himself up to his full height.

"You know as well, and perhaps better than myself."

"I do not understand you, sir?"

"A truce to these heroics, between you and me they are simply absurd. Mr. Sharpthorne gave notice to the Jew, Balasco that these two men were in danger of being trapped, and with the discretion which always characterises that amiable individual he thought it prudent for the men to retire from the old house in West Street."

"Indeed, sir!"

"Yes, indeed," said the colonel, "and this was done at your instigation. Do not imagine you can deceive me in the matter."

The baronet coloured slightly, and bit his lips, while the colonel regarded him with a stern and fixed look of determination and anger.

"You are playing a double game, as is your wont."

"Sir!"

"As is your custom where your own self interest is concerned."

Sir Richard would have looked the speaker down, but the highwayman was more than his master in this respect.

"I do not understand the tone you are assuming," said Sir Richard Fleetwood, indignantly.

Our hero took no notice of the latter observation, but calmly proceeded to recal past events to the mind of his companion.

"Your brother, Sir Reginald Fleetwood,
No. 26.

was supposed to be cut short in his career by an untoward event."

"Supposed?"

"Yes, he fell with his horse over a precipice on the Continent."

"Well, we know that, and died therefrom."

"No," said the colonel, "he did not die."

"Not."

"No. You know that as well as I do. He was taken up senseless, and the world supposed him to be dead; nay, more, his wife attended his funeral."

"I believe not," said the baronet.

"No, you are right; Lady Fleetwood did not attend the funeral of her husband. She left for England before it took place, but mourned him as dead, and believes him to be so to this day."

"And so he is."

"He is dead to the world, Sir Richard," said Colonel Jack, solemnly. "He is dead to the world, poor man, dead to hope, perhaps—the last poor consolation us mortals have in the hour of our affliction—but, I digress, Sir Reginald was taken to a convent hard by where he had met with the accident. A raging fever ensued, and for a long time he was delirious. No doubt the brain had been injured, but he was not mad, Sir Richard, although he has had enough to make him so since, but he is no more mad than either you or I. After he was taken to the convent, he was attended to under the care of an efficient nurse provided by the lady abbess, and, in the due course of time, there is no doubt but that he would have sufficiently recovered to be at the present time in the enjoyment of his own rights in this country, but a *kind* relation—a near relation—his brother, in fact, thought proper to take him under his care. He procured a doctor's certificate to the effect that his elder brother, Sir Reginald Fleetwood, was mad—hopelessly and permanently mad. Well, Sir Reginald was really conveyed to England, not to enjoy his just rights, but to be immured in a private madhouse, where he is at present, and where I fear me he is likely to remain for an indefinite period."

The features of Sir Richard were of an ashy hue as he listened to this appalling recital. There could be no mistake about the truth of the colonel's statement, for the impress of guilt was upon the countenance of the baronet. He was so panic struck at Colonel Jack's knowledge of these facts, which he had narrated with such faithfulness, that he was not able to find words for a reply, or denial of the same.

"You will see, Sir Richard Fleetwood, that it is useless your endeavouring to deceive me. I hold in my possession sufficient evidence to unseat you from your present position. I have documentary as well as oral evidence to produce at any time such may be needed. Those who take their way over a powder magazine which may blow them to atoms, should be careful how they throw missiles at their neighbours."

The baronet was still silent.

"Poor Sir Reginald after all is not the real heir, but let that pass, he is the recognised one—he would be if he made his appearance to claim his rights."

"This story you have told sounds very well—to those who are credulous enough to believe it," said the baronet. "Impossible as the circumstances are, there are, doubtless, some persons who have an appetite for the marvellous—who might give it credence, but among that number I am not one."

"You know it to be true, Sir Richard Fleetwood," said Colonel Jack, quietly.

Your own conscience tells you so, without my prompting you. That is nothing, perhaps, but the fact of my being in possession of these facts is something, and an important something, too. Come, where are these two murderers gone?"

"I do not know."

"Yes, you do."

"As heaven is my judge, I do not," exclaimed Sir Richard.

"Then you must find out," said the colonel, turning upon his heel.

"I cannot."

"Ah, but you must, and what is more, you shall, or else—"

"What?"

"I shall be compelled in the first place to procure your brother's release, and in the next—ah, well, I don't know what else I may be obliged to do—that is, if you drive me to extremities."

"What is it you want of me?" said the baronet, in a much more humble tone than he had hitherto assumed.

"You know as well as I do, myself. I want and must have my friend Osborne exculpated from the heinous crime with which he is charged."

"How?"

"By the testimony of the two real murderers. Why go over the ground again? It is trifling. You know my wishes. These men's address, as speedily as possible; and see that you do not trifle with me again, for it is the last chance I shall give you, so look to it.

"I will do as you desire," said the baronet, quite humbled; for haughty and overbearing as he was to most persons, he found it difficult to assume this lofty bearing towards our hero.

While this conversation was taking place, an ear was being applied to the keyhole of the door which led into the library, and the whole of the conversation which took place between the baronet and our hero became known to a third party.

Who that was we shall presently see.

The baronet still paced up and down the library in a dejected and gloomy mood.

"Yes," he said, "I will see Sharpthorne, and make it all right with him; no doubt, he will be able to ferret out the desired information."

"He'll not have to ferret much," said the colonel, contemptuously. "He knows it now!"

"I do not think so."

"But I am sure of it, which is much more to the purpose—I am quite sure of it!" continued the colonel.

"Well, then, I will send off for him at once, Frank," answered Sir Richard.

He generally said Frank when he wished

to be on friendly terms, as to his being so, that was out of the question; his was too selfish a disposition to entertain any friendship of a lasting nature.

The colonel came to an amicable arrangement with the baronet, and eventually took his departure from the library. As he proceeded down the stone staircase, which led to the hall, he found his arm grasped firmly, and he was pulled towards an open doorway, which led to another part of the mansion.

He turned round to see who it was who grasped him so rudely, and he beheld Lady Bostock.

"Silence!" said her ladyship; "this way—that's it—good," and she handed him into her own private apartment—where he had before seen her on more than one occasion.

Lady Bostock handed him to a chair, and sat in one herself immediately opposite to him. She fixed her snake-like eyes upon him with a basilisk glance.

The colonel was at a loss to interpret her meaning; he was fully aware, however, that she had something of more than an ordinary nature to communicate.

"So," said Lady Bostock, in a hissing whisper, "so you know the history of the Fleetwood family by heart it seems?"

"Your ladyship knows that I am pretty well acquainted with it," answered the colonel, quietly. "Why this surprise?"

"I should say that there was good cause for surprise of no ordinary nature. So it appears that Sir Reginald Fleeetwood still lives," said her ladyship, in a sort of sepulchral whisper.

The colonel shrugged his shoulders.

"He lives!" she again itterated.

"And how came you to know that?" inquired our hero.

"And you, pray," was her rejoinder, "how came you to know it, my friend? and, still more, with the knowledge of it, how is it, that you did not put me in possession of the facts?"

"I suppose it is not necessary for me to let your ladyship know all the facts I am acquainted with?" said our hero, in a half-bantering tone.

"Frank, this is hardly right," she said, endeavouring to pout.

The day was gone by for her to do so prettily, but, nevertheless, she made the attempt.

"It is hardly fair," she continued, "to keep me in the dark upon the subject. Great heavens! where will the mysteries of the Fleetwood family end?"

"But how came your ladyship acquainted with this fact?"

"Ah, that is my business. It seems you can be secret, Frank—so can I keep my own counsel."

"It matters little to me," he answered, carelessly.

"Is it possible that my brother, Sir Richard, can do so great a wrong to poor Sir Reginald. I stand appalled, and my senses seem to shudder at the contemplation of his injustice and enormities."

The colonel smiled.

"The Fleetwood family, madam, are, methinks, like many other aristocratic ones, prone to overreach and cavil one against another."

"Thank you for the compliment, Frank," said Lady Bostock, endeavouring to smile satirically.

"Oh, of course, I do not include your ladyship. You are an honourable exception," said the colonel, with a half mocking sort of bow.

"Frank, when we were last here together, we were discussing how it was possible to break off this connection—I mean the one between Sir Richard and that milksop of a girl, Honora Langford."

"She is not a milksop of a girl, as your ladyship chooses to term her—but no matter for that; you and I do not wish her to marry him—"

"We did not."

"And do not, I suppose, at least, as far as I am concerned."

"Well," said Lady Bostock, "as Sir Reginald is now alive, my feelings upon the subject are altered. In fact I am indifferent about the matter."

"Let events take their course, then," said the colonel.

"Frank," said Lady Bostock, "you are cold and reserved to me—nay, indifferent. Have you forgotten our early love?"

"No," answered our hero. "There is nothing half so sweet in life as young love's charm. I have not forgotten it, believe me, but my way of life does not allow me now to indulge in aristocratic amours—and—" he hesitated for a moment, "and I have given up affairs of the heart, as also has your ladyship, I should suppose."

"Indeed not," she answered, as she placed her arm round his neck, and laid her head upon his shoulder. "A woman never forgets her first attachment. Never."

"Ah," said the colonel. "Ah, I suppose not."

He did not, however, respond very warmly to her embraces.

"Do you know where Sir Reginald is confined?" she inquired.

"No, indeed, I do not," he answered.

"Are you sure of that?" she asked, coaxingly.

"Yes, quite sure, madam."

"Or at any rate, if you know, you do not chose to tell me. Is that it?

"Madam, I do not know, as I have already said."

"Very well. Now, then, don't be angry."

"I am not at present disposed to be so. I have no reason for anger, I am sure, particularly with so charming a lady as yourself. Do you wish Sir Reginald to be restored to his rights, then?"

"Umph. No, certainly not."

"So I should imagine."

Colonel Jack could not help smiling to himself as he reflected upon the various feelings which actuated each member of the Fleetwood family. The wife or widow as she supposed herself of Sir Reginald, was the only member of the Acton household who was unselfish in her conduct and actions. The colonel cut short his interview with Lady Bostock, and left Acton once more for town.

CHAPTER XXXII.

THE LAST DAYS OF MR. LANGFORD.

WHILE the events recorded in the preceding chapter had been taking place, a cloud had come over the house in Mount Street, Grosvenor Square. Mr. Langford was seized with a violent fever. The best physicians were called in, and all that medical skill could suggest was done to combat the symptoms, but the disease seemed gradually, but surely, to gain head, and the friends of the sufferer had their worst fears aroused. Poor Honora was unremitting in her attentions by the bedside of the patient, in which she was assisted by Miss Staunton. These two young girls would not consent to leave the old gentleman in any other hands but their own, and Honora saw too plainly that alteration in the appearance of her father which brought her to the conclusion that a change was taking place which presaged death. Still she would not let him see that she was depressed, or that her fears were aroused, but endeavoured to cheer him up as best she could.

Mr. Langford had an old acquaintance, Doctor Carruthers, to attend upon him. The doctor had almost forgotten the eventful night upon which he was forcibly conveyed to Acton, to attend upon the accouchment of Lady Fleetwood. With all Sir Richard's care he had pretty well guessed the name and quality of the lady upon whom he had been attending, but like a prudent man he kept the secret closely locked up in his own breast, and endeavoured to dismiss the whole affair from his mind, for the doctor was mindful of the terrible threat which Sir Richard had enunciated when he was closeted with him in the library.

Mr. Carruthers found that Mr. Langford's symptoms were of so serious a character that he thought it advisable to tell his daughter and Miss Staunton that it was doubtful about his ultimate recovery, unless a favourable change took place. Mr. Langford, himself, after the fever had somewhat abated, felt so prostrated that he despaired of ever getting over the attack. One day when the doctor was by his bedside, Mr. Langford said.

"Doctor Carruthers, I charge you to deal plainly with me. I need not ask you if there is danger, for I feel and know that there is and has been throughout the whole course of my malady, and from my own sensations I feel that my days are numbered."

The doctor looked grave as most doctors do under such circumstances.

"You must not despair, Mr. Langford. You must not despair, my dear sir. Let us hope for the best; while there is life there is hope."

"Ah, that's the last consolation you medical gentlemen offer, I know that," said the patient. "But," and here Mr. Langford gazed earnestly at his medical adviser, "if I am to pass away—and something tells me that such will shortly be the case. I have several arrangements to make before I quit this world. My daughter. I am anxious about her."

The doctor bowed an affirmative to this proposition.

"She has a suitor for her hand, a gentleman of high birth and position, and before I depart I should like to have her consent to her union with the same."

"Does she object to grant this?" inquired the doctor.

"Hitherto she has."

"Indeed?"

"Yes, she has unfortunately a prior attachment for a Mr. Osborne."

"Why, not the man who—"

"Yes, who is now confined in Newgate upon the charge of murder."

"Dear, dear, what a sad thing."

"It has caused me a great deal of anxiety, Doctor Carruthers, more than most people can imagine."

"But, my dear sir, I think that any one would readily imagine that this is a subject of great trouble to you."

"It is, and has been for some time past. I have been pondering this matter over, for you know she is a dutiful, good girl, but I have not been able to persuade her to give way to me in this matter."

"Oh, girls are obstinate upon these points," replied the doctor.

"But I have been thinking, doctor—shut the door, if you please—yes, that's it, thank you. Well, as I was about to say, I was thinking that if she felt assured I was likely to die, that she would in all probability consent to my last wishes.''

"She might, and most likely would do so, but I hope, my dear sir, in extracting this promise from her, that you are not doing anything which might make her after life wretched."

"Oh dear, no. God forbid I should do such a thing. It is for her own good only. Girls do not know their own minds, and she is too young to be a competent judge of what is likely to make her happy."

"Ah," said the doctor, " perhaps so.''

" Yes, and perhaps not, you would say."

"That remains for time alone to prove. Is it asking too much of you to mention the name of the other suitor."

"Oh dear, no, not at all. It is no secret. Sir Richard Fleetwood."

"Sir Richard Fleetwood !" exclaimed the doctor, and his exclamation and look of astonishment were so apparent that the sick man was quite unable to account for the effect his words had had on the doctor.

" Yes, why do you seem so surprised, Mr. Carruthers ? Do you know the baronet ?"

"Ahem—ye-s," stammered out the doctor, " that is, I have heard of him, and, in fact, I may say, know him—not much though—I only saw him once."

" Ah, then, you have met him in society, perhaps ?"

" Ah,—ye-s," said the doctor.

" This was a white lie, which did not seem to fall very glibly from him, and like Macbeth's amen, it stuck in his throat.

The invalid gazed at him with curious eyes. He saw plainly enough that there was something lurking behind which Doctor Carruthers did not feel disposed to communicate.

" You know, I suppose, or, at least, you can readily imagine, that it is a very eligible match for my daughter ; Sir Richard is in every respect a gentleman, and actually doats upon my daughter ; no man could possibly love a girl more.''

" That is a great thing, Mr. Langford ; a great thing," said Mr. Carruthers. " Love lights up our path through life, from the cradle to the grave."

He said this as a general maxim, and did not seem to apply it to the present case in particular.

" Do you know anything of Sir Richard ?" inquired the invalid, who was still anxious to get from the doctor some information on the subject.

" No—no, my dear sir. No, I know but little of him," was the answer, given in a hesitating manner.

"Ah, he is a gentleman of a kindly disposition," said Mr. Langford.

" Yes, I dare say he is, my friend—no doubt.''

This was not spoken in too confident a manner though. The doctor was ill at ease after Sir Richard's name had been mentioned. He had not found the baronet of a particularly mild or kindly nature.

" And so, doctor, I am confident that I have not long to live. Now do not buoy me up with false and delusive hopes—my hours are numbered."

He sighed deeply as he spoke these words and moved uneasily upon his pillow.

" I will not conceal from you—indeed it would be wrong for me to do so—that you are in a very precarious position—I do not say that you cannot nor will not recover, but—''

" But, the probability is that I shall not— that is what you would say, and thanks for your candour."

"No, I do not go so far as to assert that, but your state is such that I should advise you to settle your worldly affairs."

"Thank—thanks, my friend," said the invalid, as he feebly took hold of the doctor's hand ; '' thanks for your plain speaking ; I could and did divine this fact without your assertion of it.''

" We have, all of us, a certain time allotted for our sojourn on this sphere."

" If I could see my daughter happy is all I care about, and then I should be resigned. Alas, this fated attachment !"

" What ?"

" Why, her love for Osborne.'

" Well, that must come to an end, for the unfortunate young man is, I hear, in a fair way of conviction."

" You think so ?"

" I don't know, but so I am told. I hope he is innocent, but certainly appearances are very much against him."

" My daughter fully believes in his innocence.''

" It is a dreadful crime to be charged with, particularly with such a weight of evidence against him," said the doctor.

" Well, now, tell me, Mr. Carruthers, do you not think, under all these circumstances, that it would be prudent for me, before I leave the world, to get my daughter to promise to espouse Sir Richard Fleetwood after my death. That is, if she will promise—if she will, which, after all is very doubtful,'' sighed forth Mr. Langford.

" Is Sir Richard Fleetwood a widower ?" asked the doctor.

" Oh, dear, no ; he has never been married. Why do you ask ?"

" For no particular purpose ; I thought he had been married, but I am mistaken. The fact is, I know nothing of him myself, only by report." The doctor found himself touching upon dangerous ground, so he drew back precipitately ; nevertheless, from his manner, Mr. Langford concluded that there was something lurking behind respecting Sir Richard Fleetwood, and it somewhat dashed him in his opinion of the baronet.

After Dr. Carruthers had left, the invalid sent for his daughter, who was at his bed side in a few seconds.

"My dearest child," said Mr. Langford, "Now do not fret yourself, but I know and feel that it is impossible for me to recover."

"Does Dr. Carruthers say so ?" inquired Honora, in undisguised alarm.

"I do not need his assurance upon this head," said her father, as a fervent smile passed over his emaciated features.

"Say not so, father—say not so," said Honora, as she bent over her parent and affectionately kissed him.

"Now, my child, before I take my departure from this world, I would wish to see to your happiness."

"Never mind me, father," said Honora, whose heart misgave her, and guessing what all this was tending to. "Never mind me, consider yourself, dear father. Do not despair. You will recover, let us hope by the blessing of God."

The old man sadly shook his head.

"Now, Honora, dear," he said in a half whisper, "I have been thinking, and, in fact, I have consulted Dr. Carruthers thereon. I have been thinking that as matters stand at present, that—that—it—" he hesitated, and scarcely knew how to come to the point. "Of course it is impossible to think any more of Henry Osborne now. I mean in the way of a suitor." She did not make any reply to this, although her father paused again at this point of the discourse. "And I have been thinking, before I leave the world, that I should see you have a protector ; and so, Honora—so—is it asking you too much, to plight your troth to Sir Richard Fleetwood."

"Father," said Honora, gently—"I suppose you would not ask of me to do anything that was likely to cause me future unhappiness ?"

"No, my child, surely not."

"That would," she said gently.

He was silent for some time, and lay tossing about on his pillow, apparently very uneasy, and in great pain.

"If you wish me to do this," said Honora, who thought that he was troubling and vexing himself at her refusal. "If you wish me to do this, to give this promise to Sir Richard Fleetwood, I—" her father's eyes were rivetted on the door which led into the bedroom. Honora turned round and gave utterance to a slight scream. Sir Richard himself was about to close the door, but seeing Miss Langford, he opened it and said—

"Pardon me, Miss Langford. I was about to come in to see how your father was ; but seeing you here, and hearing my own name mentioned, I was about to return, as in all probability you were in some private conversation."

"Oh pray come in Sir Richard," said Mr. Langford. "It will not be many times more you will have to call and see your old friend."

"My dear Mr. Langford, do not talk thus. Let us hope to see you up and about again," said the baronet, as he gently pressed the other's hand. "I hope I am not intruding upon any private conversation, but I knocked twice at the door, and, not receiving any answer, I took the liberty of an old friend and opened it, when I heard my own name mentioned."

"Oh, indeed! Was it ? Let me see. Oh, yes, we were talking about—the old subject Sir Richard," continued Mr. Langford.

"Ah, indeed, what was that ?" said the baronet, quite innocently. He had heard every word of the conversation, and opined from Honora's tone that she would never willingly consent to plight her troth to him—he therefore had made up his mind how to act, and that was to assume a generous bearing.

"Yes," said Mr. Langford, "I feel and know that I am soon to leave Honora, and I was anxious to get her consent to accept you as her affianced husband."

"My dear Mr. Langford, although this is the hope of my existence, I would not have your daughter controlled in this matter. Let her make her own election. Alas, in affairs of the heart we have but ourselves to consult, and fondly as I wish it, would not have you use your parental control in making Miss Langford do aught that might cause her pain hereafter."

Honora felt grateful to him for this generous speech, and upon her going down stairs again she told Miss Staunton of the baronet's conduct.

"Noble, generous-hearted man," exclaimed the latter. "You cannot but admire him, and his fine nature and disposition—you cannot but admire him."

"I do," said Honora, "and were it not for my previous engagement I should perhaps respond to his deep and devoted love ; but alas!" and here she abruptly ceased, and walked to the further end of the apartment, and became lost in thought for a considerable time, which her friend Miss Staunton did not deem it prudent to interrupt.

Some few hours after this the nurse who attended upon Mr. Langford, in conjunction with his daughter and Miss Staunton, came into the room, her face expressive of the utmost alarm.

"What is the matter ? " inquired Honora, with the utmost anxiety.

"Oh, miss, your poor father ! " exclaimed the nurse.

"What ? " said Honora, trembling, and turning of a death-like hue.

"He is insensible, and—"

"Merciful heavens ! " exclaimed both the young ladies simultaneously, and they immediately took their way into the apartment of the invalid. Honora uttered a suppressed scream ; her father lay like one dead, without life or motion, and a visible alteration had taken place in his features, which were set, and painfully rigid.

Doctor Carruthers was immediately sent for, and hastened back with the messenger who had been despatched to his residence. One glance told him the state of the case. The patient was in a state of syncope. The doctor shook his head, and Miss Langford watched his looks with all the solicitude and anxiety of a loving and affectionate daughter.

"Any hope," asked Miss Staunton, in a whisper.

"Alas, I fear not," said Doctor Carruthers. "We will see if he can be aroused from his present state."

And the worthy doctor essayed to do so by all the skill he was master of, but alas, the prostrated man was calmly and unconsciously slipping down to the other world, and in about three hours afterwards he breathed his last without a sigh or a groan.

CHAPTER XXIII.

THE HIGHWAYMAN ON THE ROAD ONCE MORE.

COLONEL JACK had not dared visit his house at Hornsey since his escape through the instrumentality of Captain Rignold. As he had observed to his companions, Hornsey was no longer a home for him, so he commissioned Knapp and Warrington to remove his effects, shut up the domicile, and bring his wife and child to town.

This his two companions effected with sufficient promptitude and secrecy. The accounts were paid and discharged, and it was with a sorrowful and sinking heart that the highwayman's wife left that abode where she had passed so many pleasant hours. Latterly, it is true, she had found reason for anxiety, and guessed too truly that her husband was engaged in some lawless pursuits. These suspicions were now confirmed, and poor Mrs. Halford awoke to the terrible consciousness that she was indeed the wife of one of the most remarkable highwaymen of his day.

It was a sad hour for her when she made this discovery, but with a woman's truthfulness to the man she loved and had given up her maiden vows to, she made up her mind never to upbraid the colonel for following his present course of life, but where would it end, she thought.

She, however, allowed herself passively to be conducted to London by Knapp and Warrington, who were scrupulously polite and attentive to her.

The colonel had taken fashionable lodgings for the present at the west end of the town, and here for the time his wife took up her quarters.

When she was comfortably disposed of there, Knapp and Warrington took their way to the Old Cromwell Posting House at Knightsbridge, which our hero called at in our opening chapter. The colonel was there anxiously awaiting their return.

"Has all gone on smoothly ?" inquired Colonel Jack of his two companions, when they made their appearance in the parlour of the aforesaid nouse.

"Yes," answered Knapp, "the goods are safely housed at old Paddicks, and the missus is at the lodgings."

"How did she bear it ?" inquired the colonel.

"Oh, much better than I should have given her credit for, under all the circumstances—like a heroine, in fact," answered Warrington.

"Ah, that is well," said the colonel, with a sigh, "poor girl, she little knew who she had allied her fate and fortunes to—well, no matter! It is useless repining. We have some business on hand to-night, and require some pluck in us, therefore it is no use being down-hearted."

"If you are, I shall be getting spoonyfied myself," said Warrington, "when I reflect upon the much wronged—"

"Psha, it is no use our ripping open old sores."

The colonel rang the bell, and called for a plentiful supply of liquor, and the three highwaymen proceeded to drown their cares in several deep potations.

After which they mounted their horses and trotted off, making their way to the top of Oxford Street, or Oxford Road as it was then called.

Having arrived there, they took that road which went through Paddington and led to Edgeware.

Once more upon the back of his sleek mare, the colonel's spirits began to be elated, and the thought of being again on active duty was a pleasurable reflection.

The three highwaymen were met on the road by Hackett, after which they gallopped along the ill-lighted road leading to Edgeware. For some time they were not fortunate enough to meet with any vehicle or equestrian worthy of notice—for our highwaymen did not usually content themselves with small game. After an hour of two's ride Hackett began to lose patience.

"By the Lord, colonel, I believe every one seems to have made up his mind to stay within doors to night, for we have met with nothing—positively nothing as yet," grumbled that individual.

"Patience, my friend. Wait awhile and we shall soon find something to take. Hark! What is that? I hear the sound of wheels —hark!"

"Very slow ones, then. Yes, though, there is surely something coming along the road and no mistake."

"It's a waggon, I do believe."

"Waggon or not we must have a turn at it," said the colonel.

"Hush! Let us ensconce ourselves here," said Hackett.

This was a high wall which ran at right angles with the road; and here our highwaymen hid themselves from the sight of those who were driving the vehicle.

The tinkling bells gave indication of its approach, as it came lazily along, conducted by a still more azy-looking driver.

The stage coaches in those days were, at times, slow enough, but as to the waggons, their tediousness was beyond description, and near enough to try the patience of the most lethargic.

There was one thing, however, the occupants had the luxury afforded them of, a snooze, which they seldom failed to avail themselves of.

The driver was walking by the side of his hooded vehicle—for it was toiling up hill, towards the spot where the highwaymen lay concealed.

When it arrived at the corner of the lane, Colonel Jack, himself, emerged therefrom, and shouted out—

"Halloa, my friend; stop your lumbering drag—do you hear?"

"What for?" said the man addressed. "Don't it go slow enough for you?"

The man was of a surly nature, and would have been a satirist had he the wit to have indulged his fancy.

"Slow or fast you must stop your team," said the colonel.

"Shan't for you or any other man," replied the driver, sullenly.

"Oh, yes, you will though," said our hero, as he trotted up to the man's side, and presented a pistol towards him.

For a wonder, a waggoner for once was active; whether it was a sudden fright that acted upon his nerves, it would be difficult to say, but before the colonel had time for reflection he found the pistol dashed out of his hand, and received at the same time a severe and painful blow on the arm.

The waggoner had seized his whip by the thin part, and struck the highwayman a severe blow with the butt-end thereof. It was a wonder it did not break the colonel's arm, and had it been a point blank blow the probability is that it would have done so."

"Curse the fellow," exclaimed our hero, who was suffering great pain in his arm from the effects of the sudden blow.

By this time Slott came to the rescue, and sprang at the waggoner, who shifted ground at the sight of his new assailant, and the dog was only able to seize hold of the end of his smock frock.

The waggoner defended himself with his whip, and a very pretty struggle took place. As to Slott leaving go, that was not to be thought of.

Seeing how matters stood, Knapp, Hackett and Warrington came out of their place of concealment, and stopped the further progress of the vehicle.

"Murder! thieves! highwaymen," called out the waggoner, as he saw for the first time the whole of his assailants.

"Silence!" exclaimed the colonel, threatening him.

"Murder!—captain!—highwaymen!" he continued to shout.

"Will you hold your tongue, you fool?" said Hackett; "what are you kicking up this row for? Hold your tongue or I'll blow your brains out!"

A report of firearms was heard, and some slugs came whistling among the highwaymen. They proceeded from a blunderbuss carried by a man who was sitting in front of the waggon, and Warrington was slightly wounded in the shoulder thereby. The rest escaped unhurt.

"My word," said Hackett, "this won't do. They want to have it all their own way. You sir, you may thank your lucky stars that you have to deal with merciful people, or you would be food for worms in a minute or two."

"Halloa!" shouted out a passenger in the inside of the vehicle, as he dropped from the end thereof to the ground; "what is the row? Highwaymen! by my faith, but they have come to the wrong shop. Surrender!" he exclaimed, now more authoritively, as he put himself in a warlike attitude and flourished a broad sabre.

He was dressed in a blue suit, turned up with red; long leather boots, a bag wig, and a cocked hat, and altogether cut a most warlike figure. In fact, he was an officer of marines.

"Surrender!" he exclaimed, " and, ahem! trust to our mercy."

At these words he arranged the frill of his

shirt, which stuck out a foot or so from his chest.

"You will get shot down like a dog if you are not better behaved, my friend," said Knapp.

"Oh, help—murder—assistance!" called out the marine officer to those inside, "highwaymen!"

A female voice was now heard.

"Get up—get up; here are highwaymen," said the female, who was addressing her husband, so it afterwards seemed.

A prolonged snore was her only answer.

"Get up—do you hear what I say? We shall be all robbed and murdered! Oh, mercy on me, was ever woman so plagued with such a coward of a husband? Get up, I say."

But as her liege lord would not stir, she
No. 27.

took off one of her shoes, with which she belaboured him, using the heel, of course.

While this was taking place, the highwaymen were surprised to find a new figure present himself on the scene.

This was a little man, dressed in the most fantastic manner.

He did not appear to be more than four feet high, which in reality he was not.

He was a German dwarf, who was travelling to join a caravan which attended country fairs.

He called himself Baron Luftentoft, and on the top of his head he wore a bunch of feathers, nearly as big as himself, and was presenting a pistol towards the highwaymen of gigantic proportions.

The latter burst out in a fit of laughter at his grotesque appearance, which seemed to irritate the little man amazingly, and Hackett thought it was quite time to knock his pistol out of his hand, which he accordingly did without further parley.

"Sacr—r—a!" exclaimed the diminutive individual. "Br—r—i—gand!—monstre!— you shall pay one dear penalty for dis same conduct, Mistare Highwayman!"

Warrington was busily engaged at cut and thrust with the captain of marines, and our hero had closed with the waggoner, with whom he was having a desperate and determined struggle.

The countryman was as strong as a rustic Hercules, and had it not have been for the colonel's superior skill, it is probable he would have got the worst of the conflict, for his arm was seriously injured by the blow from his antagonist's whip.

The colonel however, at length succeeded in fairly lifting the countryman off his legs, and treating him with a back fall.

He came to the earth with such a terrific and heavy weight, that the breath was pretty well beaten out of his body.

Our hero whistled to Slott, and pointed to the prostrate man. The dog was at his throat on the instant, and pinned him to the earth.

"Hold on, boy," said the colonel, to the hound; at the same time he took out of his pocket a coil of rope, with which he bound his antagonist hand and foot, who shouted and roared ten thousand murders the while.

"So," exclaimed our hero, breathless with his prodigious exertions, "it seems we've got our work to do. But there's one quiet for awhile, at any rate."

He then turned to the other actors in the scene.

The valorous Baron Luftentoft had sprung at Hackett, and endeavoured to pull him off his horse, and indeed had succeeded in climbing up the side of the animal, and was digging his long, talon-like fingers in the throat of Hackett, who endeavoured to beat off his assailant with his riding whip; but the little man was as active as a cat, and, it would appear, as ferocious as a tiger, for he fought with tooth and nail.

"Off, you little brute," exclaimed Hackett, "off, I say, or I will show you no mercy."

But the little man did not appear inclined to be off; and his gigantic feathers kept waving about with his exertions.

The colonel, seeing how Hackett was situated, and knowing his aversion to fire his pistol except at the last emergency, seized the dwarf by one of his legs, and by main force pulled him from the neck of his companion's horse, and held him suspended by the leg, head downwards.

Then the noise and screaming made by the baron was something fearful to listen to.

To keep him quiet, the colonel gave him several smart blows with his riding whip, on that part which is supposed to be the seat of honour; this only exasperated the little man more, and he endeavoured to bite the colonel's leg with his teeth. He was little, it was true, but he was very mischievous.

"D—n the little vagabond," said Colonel Jack, "I do believe he's Beelzebub himself. Quiet, you little imp, or, as sure as fate, I'll put a bullet through your brain."

"Help! murder! sacr—r—a!" exclaimed the dwarf, grinding his teeth with rage, and actually snapping once more at the colonel's legs.

"Here, Slott."

The animal trotted up to his master's side, who let fall the baron, and the dog pinned him to the earth.

The little baron fought with the hound as well as he could, but he found it impossible to rise, and began to feel exhausted, and, it is probable, somewhat frightened at his canine antagonist.

Knapp was hardly pressed by the officer of the marines, and had a hard job to defend himself from the other's furious attack.

"By my faith," said our hero, "we shall earn all we get to night, and no mistake."

And watching his opportunity, he sprang behind the marine officer, and pinioned him, who was then entirely at the mercy of his antagonist Knapp, who said, taking off his hat, as he spoke—

"I scorn to take advantage of a brave man."

"Thank you, sir," said the officer, thus addressed. "I would take off my hat to you, but your friend here has me too fast to admit of such a thing."

Hackett now rode up to the back of the waggon, and drawing the canvass on one side, he presented his pistol to the occupants. A scream from several voices was given, and the same woman spoke to her husband.

"Peter, are you a man, to allow us to be robbed and murdered in this way? Get up, and knock this fellow down. Oh—oh! what shall we do? Be merciful, good Mr. Highwayman."

"I hope we are always merciful and considerate to the ladies," he said; "but you see, we've had a hard time of it outside, and have now come for our reward. Now then, look sharp—your cash, without further parley, for me and my palls are getting a little impatient. Your money, at once."

A chorus of screams was his answer, and the unfortunate Peter was fairly ejected by main force from the waggon, and tumbled to the ground, where he cut a most rueful appearance at the feet of the highwayman's horse.

"You've been enjoying a nice nap, sir, it

seems," said Hackett, smiling at the man's rueful visage.

"Mercy, Mr. Highwayman. Where are my friends?"

"Oh, they are all right."

Peter managed to regain his legs, and regarded Hackett with a stupid stare.

Colonel Jack and Knapp, who had now mounted their horses, trotted up to the tail of the waggon, and demanded the money and valuables from the passengers.

The captain of the marines accompanied them, who, when he caught sight of the miserable Peter, exclaimed indignantly—

"Well, you are a poltroon. Psha, I hav'nt patience with you. What have you been doing there, hiding yourself, like a cur, as you are."

"You are quite right," said his wife, "he is a cur, and no mistake."

"Yes, and I fancy there are more like him inside," answered the captain, "and be d—d to them."

It was true enough. There were three other male travellers, who, if they had but evinced as much courage as the captain and the dwarf, might have turned the fortunes of the day, or rather night.

One of these worthies was hiding himself behind a stout female, who turned out to be his grandmother.

"Now, then, time presses," said Colonel Jack. "Your money, if you please."

Another chorus of screams ensued.

"More cry than wool, it appears," said our hero, smiling, and turning to the captain.

"Now, then, ladies and gentlemen," said the captain. "These people have more than earnt their money. Out with your cash."

Three or four well filled purses were handed to Colonel Jack.

These came from the ladies.

"Your trinkets," said Hackett. "We have all got sweethearts, and they will be useful."

"Oh, goodness gracious!" exclaimed a female. "Only to think that a highwayman's mistress should wear our jewellery."

However, several watches, brooches, and other articles were passed from one to the other, and then placed in the colonel's hand.

"Thank you. I will keep them in remembrance of the ladies; and now, then, gentlemen, we will trouble you to alight, if you please."

"Oh!" they exclaimed, simultaneously.

"Yes, or else we drag you out by main force."

They did not wait for this, but the three male occupants of the waggon crawled from their hiding-place, and alighted on the ground.

"So," exclaimed Colonel Jack, "a brave lot. Now, then, shell out, for we don't let you keep anything."

And without more ado the colonel seized one by the collar of the coat, and began unceremoniously to rifle his pockets. Knapp and Hackett served the other two in a similar manner, as each of them trembled with affright when they found themselves in the grasp of highwayman.

As for the marine captain, he rather enjoyed the scene than otherwise; he had already given up his property, and Colonel Jack had courteously presented him back his watch and a miniature set in gold and precious stones, saying, at the same time, that he was sorry to be compelled to rob a brave man.

After this had been accomplished, the valiant Peter was served in a similar manner. The man who had been sitting in front of the waggon when it was first stopped and whom it will be remembered fired the blunderbuss was now brought forward.

"Thee be'st woundy clever," said this individual, "but I knows who 'ee be—'ee be Colonel Jack."

"Colonel Jack!" exclaimed a dozen voices inside the waggon.

"Ees," said the man, "that's who he be, and he'll swing for it."

"Fool and liar!" exclaimed Hackett, as he struck the man several severe blows with his riding-whip—"fool and liar! I have a great mind to beat the brains out of your thick headed sconce."

"He be's Colonel Jack. I know'd his voice in a moment."

"Well," said the marine captain, "the greater honour to us for being robbed by the prince of highwaymen."

"I thought there was something very gentlemanly and aristocratic in his appearance and manner," said one of the females in the waggon.

"Colonel Jack or not," said Hackett, "you shell out, my friend, and no mistake," and he twisted him round by the nape of the neck and drew both his watch and purse.

"Oh, ye know your business, certain sure," said the countryman, "ye've been used to it loike."

"I have a great mind to give you another good drubbing," said Hackett, who was highly incensed with the man for both his folly and obstinacy, "that I certainly have, for you richly deserve it."

"You're a bright lot to whack a chap and rob him, too," said the countryman rubbing his already bruised shoulders. "All I can say is, that when Colonel Jack is scragged, which he will be some day or other, why, I'll come to Lunnun on purpose to see him turned off."

"Thank you," said our hero, "I am much obliged to you for your good wishes and friendship. I really think I ought to blow out your brains to save you the trouble of so long and profitless a journey."

The acute ears of the highwayman caught the sounds of horses' feet in the distance, and our hero thought it no longer prudent to prolong their stay, as there was no telling who they might be. He gave then the requisite signal to his companions, who instantly proceeded to beat a retreat.

They had got a little ahead of the colonel, who was stopped by the captain of marines, who called after him, as he was about to leave. The colonel halted as the captain ran up to the side of his horse.

A wave of our hero's hand told his companions to continue on their course.

"It is true, I suppose," said the captain, "you are the renowned Colonel Jack."

"Well and what if it is?" said the party so questioned.

"Oh, only I am happy to make your acquaintance," said the captain, "or the acquaintance of any such brave and generous man. I have heard of your exploits before this."

"Indeed," said the colonel.

"Yes, sir, and allow me to say that I am Captain Boodle. Was a smuggler myself at one time," he said to our hero in a half whisper.

"Glad to make your acquaintance captain, and hope we shall have an opportunity of meeting again."

"If you ever come to Portsmouth, inquire for Captain Boodle, and I need hardly say that he will be glad to see you and discuss a good glass of wine. Mind it's all mum about this—you know."

"Yes, thanks. I understand," said our hero; and if ever I do you may rely upon my seeking you out, Captain Boodle. Adieu, till we meet again."

For by this time the noise of the coming horsemen were painfully distinct to the colonel's ears, and also to the occupants of the waggon, who caught sight of the party from the brow of the hill.

Our hero felt that not a moment was to be lost. He called his dog Slott, who left go of the dwarf and was about to follow his master, who was now anxious to make good his retreat, but a new and unexpected incident arose.

There seemed to be no termination to the trouble occasioned by the savage and determined Baron Luftentoft, for no sooner had that individual found himself released from the fangs of Slott, than he sprang up to his feet, and as the colonel paused the baron leapt up in the air, and clutching his arms round the neck of the horse, he swung his body to and fro, and nearly brought the highwayman's horse on his knees. As it was the animal could not move, and it was in

vain its master dug the rowls of his spurs into its side.

Baron Luftentoft regularly pinioned the poor beast in spite of all its efforts.

"Let go you infernal imp—let go, or I'll fire," said our hero, but the baron was pertinaceous, and situated as the colonel was, it was with difficulty that he could manage to aim with anything like certainty without running the risk of wounding his own steed, in which case it would have been all up with him ; for his companions had departed, and he must have soon been overpowered.

"Let go, and be d—d to you," said our hero, who saw now that his danger was imminent, and he lashed and cut at the dwarf with his riding whip endeavouring to beat him off, but in vain. The party of yeomanry cavalry, for such in reality they were, now came up.

"Oh, gentlemen! Here bee'st a highwayman here," said the man who had recognized Colonel Jack. "Here bee'st one of them," he continued, pointing to our hero, who now felt his situation indeed critical.

"Where, where!" shouted out their captain, as he came up, but luckily could not for the moment discover our hero, as the waggon intercepted the sight. The colonel heard this colloquy, and, calling to Slott, directed his attention to the dwarf's legs, which were depended in the air, and with one bound Slott flew at the assailant, and fixed his fangs in the dwarf's right leg. He screamed and roared with pain and agony, and dropped to the ground almost swooning from fright and pain. The colonel lost not a moment, but put spurs to his horse, and galloped off at headlong speed, but not unaccompanied, for the party of yeomanry immediately gave chase, and were soon in hot pursuit.

CHAPTER XXIV.

FLIGHT AND CHASE OF COLONEL JACK.

COLONEL JACK heard the clattering of the horses' hoofs of those behind him, and gently stroking the neck of the mare, he said—

"Now, Ada, girl, you've got your work to do. Easy lass, easy, for a moment."

The colonel slackened the speed of the mare slightly, and whistled his dog ; Slott sprang up on to the shoulder of Ada, and the colonel caught the dog by the neck, and placed him safely in the saddle bag, which hung suspended from the side of the horse. Then striking his spurs into her sides, he urged her on.

The noble beast seemed to almost fly through the air, and sparks were emitted from her iron shod hoofs, every now and then striking against the flint stones on the road.

The colonel dashed on the road leading to Stanmore, a place celebrated of latter years for being the residence of Queen Adelaide. He heard the shouts of the men in his rear, but had full confidence in the powers of his own matchless steed. He was surprised, however, to find that his friends in the rear were by no means so far off as he had expected they would be after the first quarter of an hour's ride. The fact is, that they were very well mounted, and Ada had been wounded and alarmed in her struggle with the dwarf.

This Colonel Jack soon found out.

"Curse that dwarf," he exclaimed, "he has all but spoilt my mare. She's not half her usual metal to-night."

It was true enough. Ada was nervous and shaky, and seemed to be out of sorts. Nevertheless, she did her work bravely, and Stanmore was soon reached. The colonel was dashing through the chief street when a well known voice called out—

"Hold!"

The voice was Hackett's, and the colonel for a moment held the check rein of Ada, and then beheld his companions all drawn up under the gateway of an old-fashioned road-side inn.

"We thought you lost," said Hackett, "and it's by the merest chance we met, for the chances were that we should have made our way to town. Indeed we should have done so in a few minutes."

"Town be—" exclaimed the colonel. "We are pursued man—hark! Do you hear those sounds?"

"Horses' hoofs, by God!" exclaimed Hackett.

The colonel did not say another word, but put spurs to his horse, and desired his companions to follow.

"Who and what are they?" asked Knapp.

"Who do you mean?" said the colonel.

"Those behind us."

"Yeomanry cavalry—so I guess from their dress and appearance."

"Ah, then they ride heavy. We can distance them."

"Don't appear like it," said our hero. "They are probably on hunters, who've got some pluck in them."

"What detained you, colonel?" asked Warrington.

"That cursed dwarf, whom I should like to have the pleasure of strangling."

And he then gave his companions the full particulars of Baron Luftentoft's attack upon Ada.

"Confound the old lumbery waggon," exclaimed Knapp, "we had almost have better had nothing to do with it"

"It's too late talk about that now," answered the colonel. "Put your horses along, gentlemen, or by God we shall be captured," said our hero, as he raised himself up in his stirrups, and looking behind, beheld his pursuers at no great distance off. They saw his action, and sat up a shout of triumph.

"Hurrah! hurrah! gentlemen. Three cheers for him who captures the celebrated Colonel Jack."

And at the sight of the highwaymen they renewed their efforts. Several shots came whistling by the colonel and his companions, and matters were really growing uncomfortably serious.

I believe it is a fact, or was then, at any rate, that no yeomanry could ever hit anything smaller than a haystack; and it was lucky for our highwaymen that those in pursuit were not an exception to the rule, or it would have, in all probability, gone hard with them.

Stanmore was soon left behind; and our highwaymen galloped over Stanmore heath and then branched off on the road leading to Watford.

All the while their pursuers were close upon their heels, and Colonel Jack found that his companions were not nearly so well mounted as himself. Ada had somewhat recovered herself, and the colonel felt that she was not put out to her full speed, nevertheless the colonel did not like to part company with his companions.

As they were proceeding along the road leading to Watford, they came within sight of a turnpike—the man at the gate being unknown to them.

"Shut the gate—shut the gate—highwaymen!" shouted out the yeomanry. "Shut the gate—do you hear?"

The turnpike man did hear, and knew also the voice of the officer who was addressing him.

Running hastily up to the gate, he swung it to with a loud slam.

"Hurrah!" shouted out the same voice, "We have them now. On, gentlemen, the game is ours."

The highwaymen now found themselves in a complete fix.

"We must clear it, or we are lost," said Colonel Jack. "We are no match for these yeomanry butchers."

"It's impossible to clear it," said Warrington; "at least, as far as I am concerned it is an utter impossibility. Good heavens, what is to be done?"

"Take to the hedge," said Colonel Jack. "There is no time for hesitation. You that cannot clear the gate, take the hedge. They haven't got us yet."

A loud cracking of branches, and a fall of horses' hoofs on the soft grass, told that one of the party had alighted with safety on the other side of the hedge.

This was Hackett.

Warrington and Knapp then followed his example, but the latter's horse, who was not so well up to work, came down upon his knees, and nearly threw its rider.

While this was taking place, the colonel, who had measured with his eye the height of the gate, and carefully calculated the chances of clearing it, made up his mind to make the attempt, rather than take the open country, knowing pretty well that there Ada would have been had at an advantage, for the probability was that all of his pursuers were mounted upon experienced hunters, in which case they would be more than a match for him on the heavy soil.

"Now, Ada, girl, you've your work to do," said our hero, patting her neck.

In a minute or two more, she made one terrific bound, and cleared the gate gallantly.

"Bravo!" shouted out the turnpike man; "the finest leap I ever saw in my life. It bangs all I ever heard of, and she is a right down good 'un, and no mistake."

"Stop him!—stop him!" called out the pursuers.

The pike man made a faint effort to snatch hold of the reins of Ada but the noble animal tossed up her head indignantly, and cantered off merily with her master.

The gentlemen of the yeomanry now divided, some leapt over the hedge and followed Hackett and his companions, while others gave chase to Colonel Jack.

Poor Warrington found his horse to be sadly shaken with the leap and fall, and he was considerably in the rear of Knapp and Hackett, who were at least two fields off.

His pursuers pressed hard upon him, and to escape from the field in which he found himself, it was necessary to leap another hedge, or else ford a brook.

Jaded as his horse was, he chose the latter alternative, thinking the cold water might brace up the injured limbs of his beast.

He consequently made at once for the brook in question, but his heart sank within him, and he was possessed with the impression that his race was nearly run.

But life was sweet, and on he dashed towards the brook.

Again the pursuing party separated, or rather that portion who had followed in the meadows. Some went after Hackett and Knapp, and three or four branched off towards poor Warrington.

"We shall have this chap to begin with," said one of them; "but he's not Colonel Jack, I think."

Warrington plunged into the brook, the water of which rose up to his horse's flanks. His pursuers darted on and came within pistol range. One of them called out for him to surrender. A mocking laugh was the only reply to this question, and the man who had spoken discharged his piece without effect. Warrington returned the fire with a like effect, but the bullet passed within a few inches of its mark.

One of the others who was a more practical marksman, so it seemed, and who evidently could hit something less than a haystack, now took deliberate aim at Warrington, and fired. A flash, a loud report, and poor Warrington had a bullet lodged in his chest. He reeled from the effects of the wound, but although the life blood gushed out in a dark stream down his body he endeavoured to make good his escape.

More pieces were fired, one after the other, in quick succession, and the highwayman's horse was wounded in more than one place. Weak as he was, he did manage, however, to get on the other side of the brook. The poor animal then staggered, and made several faint efforts to continue on its course, but it was evidently a vain attempt, and in a minute or two more it fell on the green sward, with its rider, who, disengaging his feet from the stirrups, did manage to gain his legs.

The countenance of Warrington was now pale and ghastly to behold, and as his pursuers rode up they regarded him with a look of something like pity, for he was a handsome, gentlemanly looking young man, and from his appearance, one would have judged had been destined for a better fate.

The highwayman threw down his pistol to the earth, and casting a glance at those approaching, said—

"Which is the man who shot me?"

They none of them answered this question.

"Oh," said Warrington, "do not fear; I bear no animosty, hostilities are all over—my last hour has come," and seeing him reel one of the attacking party dismounted from his horse and caught the sinking highwayman in his arms.

"I thank you, sir," said the latter, faintly.

"Are you mortally wounded?" asked his companion, who endeavoured, as he spoke, to stanch the flow of blood with his handkerchief.

"I knew it would be thus," said Warrington. "Lay me down on the grass. I cannot stand."

The men did as he desired. By this time the other two came up, and peered anxiously into his face. Now that the excitement of the chase and conflict was over they deeply regretted the termination of the proceedings. Warrington observed their inquiring looks, and said—

"You are looking upon a dying man gentlemen," then turning to the men who had shot him, he continued—"You handle your weapon better than your companions. Your hand." It was presented, and the highwayman grasped it. His articulation after this became affected, and he found himself almost unable to speak. Several convulsive efforts were made by the fast sinking man. A stream of blood rushed into his throat, and he endeavoured to rise.

"Mabel, thou art avenged," said Warrington, and in another minute he yielded up soul to his Maker.

"He's done for poor fellow," said the party, who had inflicted the death wound. "His troubles are all over in this world. He'll never stop coach or drag again."

A pleasant smile was observable on the features of the dead man, and the lips actually curled round, much the same as they had done in life.

The peculiar relaxation which marks a death by a gun-shot wound may not be known to the reader.

Unlike most other modes of violent death, the victim's countenance assumes a placid tranquillity; every passion seems at rest, and the face, if of pleasant expression during life, seems as of one who dreams happily. Such did appear in Warrington's case

Poor fellow, he deserved a happier fate. The creature of impulse, the sport of circumstances, education and early parental indulgence, he had not known, poor man, that first duty, the art of governing himself.

It will now be necessary to see how our hero, Colonel Jack, fared.

His pursuers were determined upon a capture, and were, perhaps, the best mounted of the whole party. Their horses had great powers of endurance, and they dashed after the colonel, up Clay Hill, in a manner that rather surprised him, but Ada strained every nerve, and did not, as yet, show the slightest symptoms of distress.

The colonel did not know how many there were at his heels, but he shrewdly guessed that they were too strong for him to turn and offer them battle single-handed. When it came to the worst, he might be compelled to do so, and, in that case, he made up his mind to let down Slott to pinion one or two of the pursuers to begin with.

At present that respectable quadruped was ensconsed in the saddle-bag, his nose peeping out therefrom, and his eye ever and anon directed to his master to see how matters were going on with him.

Watford was in sight, and our hero pushed on for the main street. He thought that, in all probability, his friends behind would call out to any chance passenger in the town to stop him, and, consequently, he thought it prudent to push a-head, and clear the high street as soon as possible, not that it was probable that there would be many persons about, nevertheless, his situation was of two critical a nature to admit of his throwing a chance away.

And so he did manage to get clear of Watford, and pushed on by the side of Easherbury Park towards King's Langley—not that the place was a park at that time.

Over hill and dale, through nodding trees, by the side of quickset hedges and broken walls, the highwayman tore along at a pace which matched the antelope in speed, and which to any less determined men as pursuers would have been enough to have made them give up the chase as hopeless, but those at his heels were pertinacious and obstinate, and the thoughts of capturing so distinguished a knight of the road as our hero, urged them on in their endeavours. The reputation of our hero did him an ill service. He was not aware, also, that the sheriff of the neighbouring county was at his heels, the same sheriff who had formed one of the party of fox-hunters who followed him and his companions at the commencement of our tale.

"It will go hard," said this individual—Sheriff Underwood by name—"it will go hard if he gives us the slip and makes a fool of us again. I was at his heels for many hours, a long time ago, and he managed to elude us some how or other, but we'll manage matters better this time, or my name's not Underwood. A set of cut-throat scoundrels."

"He's well mounted," said one of his companions.

"Well mounted or not, we will wear him out, if it's for fifty miles longer run."

"Fifty miles, Mr. Underwood! I hope you don't think of running our horses to death?"

"I hope not; but I do not care if we do his. I tell you, I for one will not give in while my steed has a leg to stand on. We must have him, I tell you—we must have him, sooner or later—and so come along, with the best speed you may."

King's Langley was now gained, and Colonel Jack had got considerably ahead of his pursuers, whose horses were beginning to look jaded.

"I'd give the world if we could venture to stop for a minute or so, and give our horses a bait," said one of the party, as they neared Langley; "but I suppose we dare not venture?"

"If we do, we shall surely miss sight of him."

"It is not at all probable that his highness will stop to bait," said another.

"I should think not—he knows a trick worth two of that."

Colonel Jack felt himself very awkwardly situated, from the fact of his not knowing any house where he could stop at nearer than the Swan, at St. Albans, and to get there he must diverge from the high road, into a series of turnings with which he was but very slightly acquainted.

The Swan was kept by a widow, with whom our hero was on very excellent terms, and at all risks he determined to branch off, and take his chance in finding his way to St. Albans.

He turned round somewhat suddenly to the right, much to the surprise of Sheriff Underwood and party. Indeed they nearly lost sight of him, but eventually dashed down the bridle road after him in full pursuit.

Many more miles were accomplished, when Colonel Jack overtook an equestrian on the road, who turned round as he heard the clattering of our hero's horse's hoofs, and seemed anxious to take stock of him.

"Halloa! my friend, what's all this about?" said the horseman. "A! a highwayman, eh!"

Colonel Jack knew the voice. The individual in question was one who had bet with our hero in the cock-pit at Westminster.

The colonel thought it best to propitiate his new discovered friend, and take him into his confidence.

"I am pursued," said the colonel, "and most hotly too."

"Don't stop then," said his companion.

"I don't intend," was the quick reply.

The fellow put spurs to his horse, and said—

"I will endeavour to keep up with you as long as I can, and we can talk as we go along."

"Thank you," said the highwayman. "You don't intend to make a capture of me then?"

"I should think not—should be sorry to try; besides, I always endeavour to help a chap that's in distress. My word, but I shall never be able to keep up long with your mare, although my horse is somewhat higher than yours. Whither are you bound for my friend?"

"St. Albans, if I live to reach there."

"I live but a few miles from there myself. If the worst comes to the worst you can stall your horse in my stable, and conceal yourself in my house; only you see I have a wife," he said in a lower tone.

"Ah!" exclaimed the colonel, who saw which way the cat jumped.

"And you see," continued the horseman, "she might split."

"I am sure I am deeply indebted to you for the offer or thought of such a thing," said the colonel, "to offer shelter to such a lawless individual as myself. You know me, I suppose?"

"Yes, I know you when at the cock-pit

in Westminster. You are Colonel Jack, and all I can say, that if I can afford you assistance you shall have it. But I fear about the policy of taking you home."

"Your horse keeps up pretty well," said the colonel. "Hark! Do you hear our friends behind?"

"Hear them. I should think so, but they are some distance in the rear."

"I wish they would give up the chase, for it is beginning to be distressful."

"Now, I tell you what you shall do," said the colonel's companion.

"What?"

"Why, just this. When I get home we'll change horses. They know your's, I suppose?"

"I am afraid so."

"Well, what do you say to changing horses?"

"An excellent thought, but my dear sir, I am trespassing upon your kindness to an unwarrantable extent."

"I should be sorry to see you taken," was the answer; and, d—n me if you shall if I can help it," said the stranger, slapping his leg. "Where do you intend to go to when you do get to St. Alban's?"

"To the Swan."

"Ah, to the widow Morley's, eh?"

"Yes."

"Do you know her?"

"I should think I did."

"Oh, then, you are all right there, I suppose?"

"I should hope so."

The two horsemen, the colonel and his companion, continued on their course bravely, still pursued by the yeomanry, with an abstract determination, although they were now left considerably in the rear. In the due course of time, Mr. Parker's house was reached, for that was the name of the colonel's companion—or friend, we may now call him.

When they came within sight of Mr. Parker's domicile, its owner said—

"Now, I tell you what we will do, colonel, we'll ride into the stable, dismount, and rush into the house at all risks."

"Where I am afraid I shall be caught in a trap," was the answer.

"Never fear, I'll keep them some time at bay."

"I doubt it, for they are evidently determined."

"We'll try it any rate. You do as I tell you."

"I am in your hands," said the colonel, "and am hardly prepared just now."

"You are, my boy, but we'll do them yet, or my name's not Parker."

When the two arrived at Mr. Parker's mansion, they found the ostler waiting at the

gate for the return of his master, whom he expected.

"Open the gate, Jem, and door of the stable. Look sharp, man.

Both gate and door were instantly thrown open, and the two horsemen trotted into the stable.

"Now, Jem, take this steed to the rear of the house," said Parker.

"Which, sir ?"

"Mine."

"Yes, sir."

The two then entered the house of Mr. Parker. A shrewish-looking lady, who turned out to be Mrs. Parker, came forward as the pair entered the parlour.

"How late you are, Mr. P.," said the lady.

"Yes, my dear, I've been unavoidably detained."

"You generally are."

"Not always, my dear—not always, I hope."

"You do not introduce me to your friend," said Mrs. Parker.

"Ah, true, Co—ahem—Mr. Halford," said Parker.

"Halloa, there, open the gate—highwaymen—highwaymen!" shouted out four or five voices. "Open the gate."

Parker went through the kitchen to the rear of the house.

"Jem," he said, "leave them alone ; don't open the gate just yet. Pretend to be very deaf."

"All right, master," said Jem, who pretty well guessed how the case stood.

"Open the gate some of you, or we'll pretty soon break it down."

And several loud blows were heard against the woodwork.

"What is it, gentlemen?" said Jem, who began to fear that they would keep their word, and forcibly enter the premises.

"You've got a highwayman in these premises," said the sheriff, in a towering passion, "and unless your master gives him up, he will have to answer for the consequences. Tell him that, do you hear? Open the gate, man."

"I'm rather hard of hearing—curse the dog," said Jem.

The yard dog belonging to the premises now set up a loud and continuous barking.

"Will you open the gate?" said those outside.

"The gate, man," yelled forth one of the party, with stentorian lungs.

"What's all this about?" said Mr. Parker, now coming out of his domicile.

"You've got a highwayman here," said the sheriff.

"Oh, dear, is that you, Mr. Underwood?" exclaimed Parker. "Well, you have chosen a late hour to pay me a visit ; but you are well attended, it seems."

"You've got a highwayman here," said Underwood. "I don't know whether you are aware of it—I hope for your own credit's sake you are *not* aware of it—but you have, and that's all about it."

"Highwayman!" exclaimed Mrs. Parker, from the parlour window. "Goodness gracious! there is a gentleman come home with Mr. P.—leastways, I supposed him to be such."

"He's no such thing—he's a highwayman," said the sheriff. "Think of that, madam—think of that."

"Jem, open the gate," said the lady ; but her husband anticipated the command, and undid the fastening thereof himself.

"Well, gentlemen, I hope you have made noise enough," said Mr. Parker. "Now, what is your business, pray?"

"Mr. Parker," said the sheriff, "you have ridden home with one of the most notorious highwaymen of his day—to wit, the renowned Colonel Jack."

"I rode home with a gentleman whom I met on the road," said the party addressed ; "and certainly he was much more courteous in his behaviour than any of you appear to be."

"Search the premises," said the sheriff.

"Not without my permission," answered Parker. "I thought, Mr. Underwood, that an Englishman's house was his castle."

This was said in a mocking tone.

"Not when he harbours disreputable characters."

"Who do you mean?" inquired Parker, turning round and looking at those who accompanied the sheriff. "You don't allude to your friends here, I suppose?"

"There, that will do," answered the sheriff, "further parley is useless—worse than useless. We want Colonel Jack, and what's more, must and will have him."

"Will you?" said Parker, with a smile of derision. "You must first catch your hare before you skin him."

By this time Mrs. Parker emerged from the premises, and set up a series of, not screams, exactly, but exclamations of surprise, rather.

"Oh, dear, good gentlemen, what is the matter? Our house is regularly stormed tonight. What is the matter?"

"Robbery is the matter, madam, and the thief is concealed somewhere about these premises."

They did not wait for further parley, but dismounting from their horses, took several directions about the house and grounds, in their endeavours to discover the hiding-place of Colonel Jack, who, while all this had been going on, took his way to the rear of the house, and mounting Mr. Parker's horse, he walked him to the back gate, and got into a bye lane. This he traversed, and he found himself, at the end of it, some two or three hundred yards down the same road he had originally come by.

The colonel lost no time in making good his retreat, and hastily but cautiously galloped off towards St. Albans.

Our party of yeomen were of course unsuccessful in their search. Every nook and corner was inspected, but no highwayman. They went into the stable, and there, sure enough, they found Ada, comfortably stalled, and nibbling away at some fodder.

In his haste, Colonel Jack had forgotten Slott ; but it appeared his faithful hound had not forgotten him, for when he found the saddle was being taken off Ada, he took the liberty of emerging from his place of concealment, and going in quest of his master, whom he found mounting Mr. Parker's horse, which he followed down the lane.

"This is Colonel Jack's horse, or rather mare," said the sheriff ; "I should know her out of a thousand."

Then turning to Mr. Parker, with an angry look, he said—

"And so, sir, it seems you are on friendly terms with one of the greatest rascals in existence."

"What do you mean, sir, by this language?" inquired Parker.

"Simply this, that Colonel Jack, the notorious highwayman, has ridden home you, and here is his horse."

"The gent'emen who rode home with me is Mr. Halford, whom I have known in the sporting world."

"And pray, sir, where is he now?" asked

the sheriff. "He must be about these pro-mises somewhere."

"I pledge you my word he is not," said Mr. Parker.

"Where is he, then ?"

"I am not bound to tell you, am I ?"

"I should say so."

"I don't see it. Neither will I, if you ask in this authoritative manner."

"Well, well," said the sheriff, "I meant no offence. I know we've had one or two disputes before now ; but I mean no offence, Mr. Parker, only you must admit that it is exceedingly annoying, after chasing a high-wayman in two county's, to find him riding side by side with you, and his horse stalled in your stable, with no traces of its owner. It looks suspicious."

"I will deal with you candidly," said Mr. Parker. "The fact is, I met an individual on the road, who overtook me, and whom I at once recognised as a Mr. Halford, whom I had met previously on more than one occa-sion."

"Yes, precisely. Well ?"

"He informed me that he was in some little difficulty—in fact, he was being pur-sued by sheriff's officers, who were endea-vouring to arrest him for debt," said Mr. Parker, laying a strong emphasis upon the last word ; "for debt," he again repeated. "Well, I generally commisserate with any one so situated, and I offered him the pri-vilege of getting out of your way by riding into my stable. I leant him another and fresher horse than his own, and he has by this time trotted part of the way back to London."

"Not London," said Mrs. Parker, who would put her word in the matter ; "not London, but St. Albans."

"No, no, London, my dear."

"I tell you he has gone to St. Albans," continued the pertinacious Mrs. Parker.

"Well, gentlemen," said the sheriff, "if we wait all night here, I suppose we shall never be any the nearer in finding Colonel Jack. We'll be off at once."

And so saying, Mr. Underwood made to-wards his horse, which he had fastened up to the rails which run round the garden. The others followed his example, and hastily wishing Mr. Parker good night, or rather morning—for such it was by this time—they left the premises, uttering several inward anathemas against the owner thereof.

"Is there any truth about his having gone back to London, think you ?" inquired one the party of the sheriff.

"Oh, no, I should say not ; the woman was most likely to be right. He's gone to St. Albans, you may depend upon it. At any rate, it will be of no use our endeavouring to chase him back to London, seeing that

he's got a fresh horse, and ours are all jaded and pretty well done up."

"I am all but done up myself," said an-other of the party.

"Well, what shall we do, gentlemen ?" said another.

"We had better make for St. Albans, at any rate, and there put up for the night," answered the sheriff. "And if this beauty be in the town, which I verily believe he is, depend upon it he'll not be able to escape us."

The party put spurs to their horses, and trotted towards St. Albans.

CHAPTER XXXV.

THE SWAN AT ST. ALBANS.—STRANGE ADVENTURES.

AGREEABLE to his first resolution, Colonel Jack, when he had fairly given his friends the double, proceeded with as much haste as he could towards St. Albans.

Felicitating himself upon the stroke of fortune which he had met with in lighting upon such a good friend as Mr. Parker, our hero pondered upon the probable fate of his brother highwaymen. If they had been so hard pressed as himself the probability was that they were captured, and this thought was anything but a pleasing one to the colo-nel, who now deeply regretted having parted with them ; but it was too late to retreat now, and only necessary, therefore, under the existing circumstances for him to take what care he could of himself.

From the brief and hasty conversation he had with Mr. Parker at the back of the house, previous to his departure, the colonel opined that his friend would endeavour to persuade the yeomen that he was gone to London, but it was very doubtful—so our hero thought—if he could get them to be-lieve this, and he therefore wisely judged that they would make for the nearest town, which would bring them in unpleasant prox-imity with him.

What should he do ? He knew the ostler at the Swan, and he knew the landlady, both of whom he thought he could rely on. It would be better to get in before his friends entered the town—that is if they came to it at all.

Mr. Parker had agreed to detain them as long as possible. Colonel Jack therefore hastened on towards the Swan, which was at that time one of the most noted houses, and, indeed, the best, in St. Albans.

Our hero trotted into the yard as quietly as he could, for the hour was late, or rather early now, being about half-past one. Not a soul was visible in the yard, but the colonel knew where the ostler slept, and, instead of ringing the yard bell, he dismounted from his horse and taking some grains of gravel in his hand threw them against the window of the room where he knew the ostler slept. After one or two more efforts of this kind the window was suddenly thrown open, and the inquiry of—

"Who's there?" spoken in a male voice.

"Hush, Sam! It's me. Come down," said the colonel.

"Why, as I live, if it ain't the —"

He said no more but closed the casement, and in a minute or two more was by the colonel's side.

"Why, colonel," exclaimed Sam, "who would have thought of you coming at this time of night ?"

"I don't pursue my avocations in broad daylight."

"True ; I forgot that."

"Well, now stable the horse—I'm chased, Sam."

"The devil you are?"

"Yes."

"And have you managed to give them the slip ?"

"Yes, for the present; but I expect them in the town in the course of a few minutes, Sam."

"What's to be done ? I had better go and tell missus."

"Is she up ?"

"Yes ; I should say so."

"Well, put up the horse first, and make as little fuss or noise about it as possible."

With this our hero followed the ostler into the stable to continue his conversation ; and as the latter was grooming his horse, the colonel said—

"I say, Sam, it is more than probable that my enemies will be here."

"We must find you some place of concealment, then."

"Oh, if they suspected that I had come to this house, I am afraid, seeing there is a sheriff among them, that they would stand at nothing, and insist upon instituting a search everywhere."

"A sheriff, eh?" said Sam, who stood in great awe of any municipal authority.

"So," said the colonel, "I must brave it out. Now, I'll tell you what I wish you'd do, and that is, to go to your mistress and say I am here, and at the same time tell her the particulars of my being chased and how I am situated."

"Yes ; that I'll do immediately," said the ostler.

"But, stop a bit, I've not done ; you ask your mistress if she happens to have any sort of clothes which will afford me the means of disguising myse'f."

"All right," said Sam, with a knowing wink, "all right, colonel; I'm fly to your move."

"Very good. I will wait here till you return."

"Wait here ?"

"Certainly; you don't suppose I would venture in the house habited as I am ?"

"Of course not ; I forgot."

"I will wait here till you return, and should she be fortunate enough to have a disguise for me, why I'll even brave it out and meet Mr. Sheriff and his companions face to face."

"Ah—ah! bravo, colonel," said Sam, in admiration of our hero ; "you are a plucky one."

"But mind, Sam, you must not say a word to any one."

"Oh, I am as dumb as a stock-post," said Sam.

"Good. Now be off."

The ostler did as he was desired, for he was at all times willing to serve the colonel, who was an especial favourite with him.

There was a degree of romance about a highwayman in those days that generally enlisted the sympathy of a vast number of persons.

Besides this the colonel was generally very liberal and good to those who rendered him a service, which Sam had done on more than one occasion.

It is remarkable what a number of persons these knights of the road found to screen and protect them, and very often from persons moving in a respectable sphere.

Colonel Jack awaited the return of the ostler with some degree of impatience, for he seemed to him to be gone an inordinate time, which indeed he was, and the colonel was in a state of trepidation as to the probability of Mr. Underwood and party making their appearance before he was dressed to receive them in a fit and becoming manner.

In a short time more, however the faithful Sam did return, and, from his appearance, any one would have surmised that he had opened an old clothes shop, for he bore a mass of garments of different sorts in his arms.

"Why what have you brought ?" said the colonel, smiling.

"You shall soon see, master. Missus did not know what would suit you, for there is size and fit to be considered. Then there's the disguise—I mean the complete change in your appearance. Then—"

"Oh, never mind," said our hero, "let's have a look at them."

"This is a countryman's suit," said Sam.

"Oh, that won't do."

"No, but here is a better."

"Ah, what's that ?"

"It is a snuff brown suit, such as is worn

by elderly gentlemen, and here's the wig to match."

"That's the thing. Will it fit, I wonder," said the colonel.

"Better try," said Sam.

The colonel tried on the coat and it answered admirably. Then he had a try at the waistcoat and breeches. They were a tolerable good fit, and so he proceeded at once to ensconce himself in the garments. After which he tied up his own chestnut locks, and put on a white wig, with a quene attached thereto. Then fitting on a pair of tortoise-shell spectacles, his metamorphosis was complete, and it would have been an utter impossibility for his most intimate friend to recognise him, for being something of an actor, his whole bearing and manner were in accordance with the part he had chosen.

"Now, Sam," said the colonel, "take up my own clothes into the room I am to rest in for the night, and late as it is, I will go into the public room and have a glass of brandy and water. There is nothing like braving it out if these worthies do come."

"Lord, lord, what a good joke," exclaimed the ostler. "Well, this ere beats all I ever saw or heard on. Ha! Ha! Oh, do let missus see you."

"All right. I'll go and speak to your mistress first.

Colonel Jack now made his way into the interior of the tavern, and the mistress of the establishment was at first quite unable to recognise our hero, with whom she was well acquainted. She laughed immoderately at his metamorphosis. The colonel restored her equillibrium by putting his arm round her waist (he was always a gallant man) and indulging in several tender demonstrations, which were taken in good part by the landlady.

"Why, colonel," said the latter, "What is the meaning of this late visit, and the necessity of assuming this disguise?"

"You can readily guess, I should suppose," was his answer. "I have been pursued, and by my faith, my friends, who are so anxious to make my acquaintance, will in all probability be here soon."

"What will you do?"

"Meet them?"

"Indeed, won't that be dangerous, Frank?"

"It will be less dangerous than endeavouring to attempt concealment—better to face it out."

"You know best, or ought to do," was her answer.

"Where can I sleep?" asked our hero.

"You can have the blue room, from which as you know it will be easy to make your escape if necessary into the yard."

"That will do admirably. Now I will betake myself to the public room. But re-

member, I am Mr. Treman of the firm of Treman and Rettegree, Drysalters, of Tower-hill."

"But is there such a firm?"

"Certainly, and I am the principal. I shall ask you if those last hams I sold turned out satisfactory."

"Ah, very well. Shall I find fault?"

"If you like. It will appear more natural, perhaps. Your sex generally do like to find fault."

"There, go along. I don't know what you men would do without us."

"Nor do I, my angel," exclaimed our hero, putting his arms once more round her waist, and giving her a kiss. "A friend in the hour of need—a solace under afflictions—and a joy at all times—"

"What?"

"A woman."

"There, go to, flatterer."

The sound of many voices was now heard on the outside of the house, and the ostler's bell was rung violently, as Mr. Underwood was heard calling out—

"What ho—ho, ostler! Are you all asleep, or dead, or what?"

That worthy lazily emerged from his habitation as though he had been fast asleep and suddenly woke up, and proceeded to attend upon the new comers, who were of course no other than Colonel Jack's pursuers.

Our hero immediately took his way to the traveller's room, and lighting his pipe and calling for his glass of brandy and water, he was busily engaged in spelling over the "Public Ledger."

Mr Underwood and party were very full of inquiries to Sam, the ostler, as to who had been there that night.

"Had any gentleman arrived within the last hour?"

Sam put on a stupid look, and shook his head.

"Who was the last comer?"

"A commercial gentleman—didn't know his name."

"Where was he?"

"Gone to bed."

"Was no one up?"

"Yes, missus."

"Ah, no traveller?"

"Yes, he believed Mr. Treman was in the commercial room."

"Who was he?"

"A drysalter, of the firm of Treman and Rettegree, Tower-hill."

"How long had he arrived?"

"Some hours."

"What made him up so late?"

"Didn't know; he always was late when he came there. A queer old gentleman," answered Sam.

"Ah. He's not come here then, I suppose," said the sheriff, in a whisper to one of his companions.

"I suppose not."

"Shall we go into the public-room?"

"Certainly," said the other ; "I don't feel inclined to sleep without some refreshment."

The party were then shown into the coffee room by an obsequious waiter—that is, as obsequious as he could be, considering that the drowsy god had already got him half in his embrace.

When the party entered, they stared curiously at Mr. Treman, but made no observation upon their entrance, as that individual seemed to be too much absorbed in the perusal of the "Public Ledger," to take any notice of the new comers. Chops and refreshments were ordered and consumed, for most of them were hungry after their long ride.

When the inner man had been a little satisfied, our party of travellers began to be more loquacious.

"I wouldn't have minded giving one of my best fields of wheat," said a Mr. Stokes, who was a farmer on a large scale, "that I wouldn't, if we had succeeded in running down this highwayman."

"Highwayman!" exclaimed Mr. Treman, laying down the paper, and regarding the speaker with a look of intense surprise and alarm ; "have you been unfortunate enough to meet with a highwayman."

"I should think we had," said Stokes, "and what is more, we have given chase to him through three counties, I do believe."

"Two at any rate," said the sheriff.

"Umph, that's quite enough," said our hero ; "and with what success?"

"None at all, sir. The fellow has been betriended by a man who calls himself a respectable member of society."

"You don't say so? Has he robbed you of much, gentlemen?" said Mr. Treman, who purposely assumed a slow, mild way of speaking, the better to carry out the delusion.

"Oh, he has not robbed us at all—catch the scoundrel at that. We were too strong for him."

"Ah, of course. You are military gentlemen, I see."

"Volunteers."

"Ah, so I suppose. And you have lost sight of him, then?"

"Yes, but he's not far afield,' said Stokes, with a knowing jerk of the head.

The colonel felt uncomfortable for the moment, fearing lest his incognito had been penetrated. He soon saw, however, by the other's manner, that such was not the case.

"Then he's robbed some friends of yours, I presume?" said the stranger.

"He and his companions stopped a waggon, and stripped the passengers of everything they possessed," was the reply to this question.

The landlady now entered the room, and informed the guests that she was about to retire to bed, as the hour was late, or rather, early, and inquired if her customers desired anything else before she retired. A relay of glasses were ordered and served, when as the hostess was about to retire, Mr. Treman inquired if the last batch of hams proved satisfactory.

"Well, they were not all that could be desired," was the answer.

"Indeed," said our hero, with evident chagrin ; "I am sorry to hear that, my dear madam, very sorry. What was the matter with them?"

"They were hard, and rather too salt," she answered, as she with difficulty managed to keep her countenance.

"The weather, my dear madam—look at the weather. Our house find it difficult to hit the happy medium to please everybody. If they are not salt they are likely to go."

"Ah, they have all gone," she answered, with a smile.

"I am glad of it," he answered ; "but I mean they are likely to turn rusty, which you know is a greater fault than being a trifling degree too salt. Tastes differ."

"Yes, I know that. Oh, mind you, I don't say that they were so very bad, only for my customers I should like them a little more mild."

"It shall be attended to, believe me," said Mr. Treman.

And he took out his order-book, adjusted his spectacles, and proceeded to make a note therein in a business like manner.

"Anything else to complain of?" asked Mr. Treman, glancing over his spectacles.

"I should rather they were not quite so fat."

"Good," he answered. "You will find this shall be attended to in those we are going to send you this time."

"Thank you. Good night, gentlemen."

And the landlady then disappeared for the night.

"There's no pleasing everybody," said Mr. Treman, as he clasped his order-book and put it in his pocket. "It is astonishing what a man has to put up with in the way of business. Nevertheless, she's a reasonable woman enough generally."

"Oh, yes, and a very nice woman," said the sheriff. "Fair and honourable, and strictly conscientious in all her dealings."

"You know her then?" said Mr. Treman, to the sheriff.

"Oh, yes, and I knew her late husband. Oh, dear, I have known her for years."

"Ah, a very nice woman, I have always found her," was the reply.

"Where can that scoundrel have gone?" said another of the party.

This was, of course, in allusion to Colonel Jack.

"Gone on to town, I suppose," said another of the party.

"You must have followed him for many miles, gentlemen?" said our hero, inquiringly.

"Oh, dear me, yes; I can hardly say to a certainty how far," answered the sheriff. "But I know we've knocked up our steeds, and pretty well done the same with ourselves."

"Was he known to you?"

"By report. Why, my good sir," said Mr. Underwood, "it is no less a personage than the renowned Colonel Jack whom we have been chasing."

"Indeed! I should liked to have seen him taken."

"So should I," answered the sheriff, "for this is the second time I have been at his heels. I'll wager a hundred golden guineas that when I next catch sight of him, I'll take him dead or alive as sure as I am born."

"Ah, you are joking," said Mr. Treman, with a quiet smile, which seemed to aggravate the last speaker not a little.

"Joking, am I? I was never more serious in my life, and I'll bet any one a hundred guineas that I'll take the scoundrel when next I see him, be he wherever he may."

"That's a bold assertion," said Mr. Treman, "and one that I should not like to make."

"Why not, sir?" Why not I pray?"

"Well, I don't know, he is rather too desperate a character to make sure of, from what I have heard."

"A coward, sir," said the sheriff, who, under the influence of brandy and water disappointment and contradiction, was becoming wrathful. "Ah, these fellows are cowards when they meet an honest man face to face. I'll venture to say that I would capture him single handed if I came within range of him."

"May be so," said Mr. Treman, gently, who saw how matters were likely to go on, "but again I say, I should be sorry to make an assertion so positively."

"Why so?"

"Because I have a dread of highwaymen," said Mr. Treman.

"Oh, there you and I differ, that is as far as a fear of them goes. Why, the rascal cut off the moment he saw us coming"

"Ah, ah, that's not surprising," said the stranger, "seeing that there were so many of you all around."

"But he had several companions," said Mr. Underwood.

"Oh, had he, that makes a difference certainly."

"I tell you," said the sheriff, "all these men are cowards. I know it for a fact, and I know that I could take him single-handed, and what is more, I will if I ever meet him again and have a chance, an impudent, cutthroat, braggadocia."

The old gentleman smiled benignantly, but still incredulously.

"Well, you seem to doubt what I am saying, sir," said the sheriff, irritated by the quiet tone of sarcasm of the other. "Will you bet?"

"What?'

"A hundred guineas that I don't take Colonel Jack if I chance to meet him again."

"I don't mind," said the colonel, drawling out his words as though he were a very cautious man who was, however, being drawn into something which at first his prudence objected to. "I don't mind, but you are a stranger to me."

"My name is Underwood. Mr. Sheriff Underwood," said his opponent. "Pretty well everybody knows me in my own county."

"I have heard of you, sir. That is quite sufficient. I will bet you a hundred guineas that you never take Colonel Jack. Come."

"Good, shall we stake the money, or will you oblige me with your name?"

"My name is Treman, of the firm of Treman and Rettegree, of Tower Hill. The landlady of this house knows me, and will answer for my respectability."

"I don't for a moment doubt it, sir."

"But I will if you like, stake the money with her. Not but what she would pay it without any such precaution."

"That is quite sufficient, I will enter your name in my pocket-book."

"Yes, and the terms of the wager."

"Very good. Let me see. Mr. Underwood bets Mr. Treman one hundred guineas that he will capture Colonel Jack the very next time he gets within arm's length of him. Will that do?"

"That was not exactly the bet, but that is sufficient," said Mr. Treman, gently.

"Which were they, then, sir?"

"Well, the next time you see him."

"I will alter it then, if you ask it."

"Oh, no," said our hero. "He might be on his mare three fields off, and then, you know, I think there would certainly be a chance of your losing. No, let it stand as it is. At arm's length. So be it. I will enter the same in my book; and your name is—"

"Underwood."

"Aye, precisely. I really have to do with such a multiplicity of persons, that I am sadly at a loss to remember names. Ah, that's it, Underwood."

"And for the good of the world at large, I dare say you won't mind loosing, to see such a miscreant captured," said Stokes.

The old gentleman indulged in another quiet smile, and said. "No man likes to lose his money, my friend."

"No, but for the benefit of society."

"I am afraid I am not patriotic enough for that."

"Well, then, I am," said Stokes, glumpily. "Perhaps you have not been robbed by a highwayman."

"Have you, sir?"

"No."

"No, but I have been robbed in business, by the defalcations of those who have been in my employ, and I consider, myself, that secret and insidious plunder like that is worse than being stopped on the highway, for in that case you do know what you lose, but in the other, it may be going on for years without your knowledge, and you find yourself, perhaps suddenly, a ruined man. Mind, I am not defending highway robbers or dishonesty of any sort. God forbid !" said our hero, casting his eyes up to the ceiling in a most sanctimonious manner.

"I should hope not, sir," said the sheriff, with a severe look.

"I am sure not," answered our hero.

"But this Colonel Jack is a pest to society," continued the sheriff, "and sooner or later, he is bound like all such miscreants to pay the penalty of his crimes by expiating his offences on the scaffold.

This conversation was rather distasteful to our hero, who did not respond to this last remark, but took up the "Public Ledger again, and pretended to be perusing its pages once more in a quiet, reflective manner, while his companions indulged in further converse about their arduous labours in following the highwayman. Some time afterwards, one of them made a motion to retire to bed. The bell was rung, chamber candlesticks were called for, and the party were soon on the move.

"We shall sleep without rocking, I am thinking," said one. "At least I know I shall."

"And I," said another.

"And I," said our hero. "Good night, gentlemen."

"Good night, sir," said the sheriff. "You'll not forget your bet."

"Oh, no. Pleasant dreams. Adieu !' And the gentlemen were shown their respective rooms. The colonel whispered something to the chambermaid, who gave a meaning nod, and the sheriff and his companions took their way up stairs.

"You've put him in No. 9 room," said our hero to the chambermaid.

"Yes, colonel," was the ready reply.

"Good girl. Ah, Anna, you are a sweet creature," said our hero, chucking her under the chin.

"Oh, don't, pray don't," said Anna, as she struggled in the grasp of the colonel, who would insist, however, in snatching one or two kisses.

"You don't look like yourself in this dress," said the maid.

"Don't I, my charmer? You like me in my own costume the best ?"

"Yes."

"Well, you shall see me in my natural character by-and-bye."

"Not to night.'

"No, dearest, to-morrow, perhaps. Oh, you are a love, and that's the truth, Anna."

"There that will do. You must now want rest. See, this is your room. Good night."

"Thank you. Good night. And pleasant dreams."

And the colonel entered the room appropriated for his use.

CHAPTER XXXVI.

A NIGHT OF ADVENTURE. THE TABLES ARE TURNED.

SILENCE soon reigned in the interior of the Old Swan Hotel, and most of its occupants were wrapt in deep slumber soon after they had retired to their separate apartments. The sheriff and his companions were so worn out with fatigue, that they slept the sleep of the weary, and, let us hope, the just. Not but some one or two of them had their own backslidings to answer for, as most of us have I fear in this world, the good, bad, and indifferent. Man is not a perfect animal that is quite certain, at any rate, morally speaking. We don't know if the colonel's conscience was the most heavily burthened in this respectable hostelry, but, certainly upon his retiring into his chamber, he did not immediately seek his downy couch with that alacrity that one would have supposed, considering all that he had gone through within the last few hours. Let us take a glance at him. Upon retiring to his chamber, he drew a chair towards the window which looked out into the stable yard, and, opening the casement, he sat himself down in a ruminating mood. He continued thus for some minutes, apparently lost in reflection.

"Tyburn's tree," he exclaimed. "That's the end, Mr. Sheriff, is it ? Faugh ! Why dwell upon that cursed subject ? Fortune has divers ways of sending a man out of the world. I wonder how Hackett and the rest got on with their pertinacious pursuers. I have had a long ride enough that's certain. Ah ! What was that ?"

Some grains of sand or gravel were thrown against the window-pane, but so slightly, that the colonel thought they might have been thrown up by the air or wind.

"Was it my fancy, or did I hear a rattling against the pane?'

He had scarcely given expression to these thoughts, when the noise was repeated, and some few grains of gravel entered the casement which he had thrown open. There was no mistake about it this time, and our hero at once proceeded to thrust his head out of the open window.

"Hist!" said a voice. "Colonel!"

Our hero looked everywhere around, but could not catch sight of a human being. A light was burning in the other room and he thought at first the words he had heard proceeded from Sam, but that could hardly be

No 29.

the case, as the windows of Sam's bedroom appeared to be fast closed.

"Colonel," was again repeated in a subdued voice.

"I am here," said our hero, in a low whisper.

"That's his voice," said a figure, which now emerged from the buttress against the wall whither he had been secreting himself.

"Who is it?" said our hero. The man said nothing, but came out in the moonlight, and much to our hero's surprise and delight, he observed that it was Crawley, who, when he caught sight of the white wig, spectacles, and snuff-brown coat donned by his master, was lost in stupid wonderment, and stood with his mouth gaping, and his eyes dilated with unfeigned surprise.

"Hush, hush—silence! Crawley; it's me

Make no noise, as you value your own life and mine."

" Is any one up ?" asked Crawley.

" I think not.   What do you want ?"

" I can't tell you down here."

" No, of course not.   Can you climb up and get in at the window ?"

" There's nothing to lay hold by.'

" Is the stable door open ?"

" I don't know.   I ll see," and thereupon he tried the door, and found it padlocked.

" It is locked," said Crawley.

" Well, is there nothing in the yard you can get hold of to climb up with ?"

" I don't know."

" Look.   See, there, under the shed."

Crawley gently took his way to the shed, and luckily found a short ladder.

" Capital.   That will do," said the colonel.

In another minute it was placed against the wall, and Crawley ascended noiselessly into Colonel Jack's apartment, who closed the window the moment his companion got safely into the room.

" Why, Crawley," said the colonel, as soon as his companion had entered.   " What on earth brings you here ?"

" My horse," said that individual.

" So I suppose, old boy.   But how did you hear I was in the house ?'

" Sam."

" Oh, he told you, of course.   But what made you make for St. Albans."

" You shall hear.   You know we all on us went across them cursed fields."

" Yes.   And how about Hackett, Warrington, and the others ?"

" Don't ask me."

" What—are they taken ?"

" No ; none on em, as I know."

" Then what do you mean by that look ?"

" Poor Warrington's gone."

" Where, man ?"

" To the other world."

The colonel fell into a chair, and covered his face with his hands.

" Yes ; this is how it was ; you see, Warrington was badly mounted."

" I know he was."

" Well, some on 'em seeing this, pushed after him, for Warrington found it no use following us ; I don't know whatever induced him, but he struck off towards a brook."

" Well ?"

" And arter trying to ford it—leastways, while he was a trying to ford it, he was shot."

" Was his death instantaneous ?"

" Pretty nearly so, as far as we could judge, for of course we couldn't stop to see the last of him, poor chap ; but we saw him and his horse fall, and I heard afterwards as how he had gone."

" Poor Warrington !   Well, better that than the other fate ; his troubles are all over now."

" That is just what I say."

" They split up and took different directions, and from what I could judge the last time I caught sight of them I should say that they had got clear off—at least, I hope so."

" The same here—and yourself ?"

" Oh, I got on all right.   Arter I had galloped over several fields I took a circumbendibus sort of a lane, which I knew would lead me to the main road.   You see, I was anxious to follow you."

" Yes ; go on."

" Well, I did manage to come into the road you were taking, but no traces could I find of either you or them—downy chaps—so I galloped on, and I learnt from a turnpike man that a highwayman had been chased and that his pursuers were after him, but the man told me as how they had not past through the turnpike gate, but a gentleman on the road told him the news, so it appeared ; and, thinks I, it won't do to go back to London, for I shall stand a chance of meeting them."

" Yes, I see ; a wise precaution."

" So, knowing as how Sam would always let me in here and keep all snug and dark, I made for this direction."

" How is it we did not meet ?"

" Oh, you must have come much out of your way, by what I can judge, for I was a long way a-head of you when I asked the turnpike man."

" Yes, I did not know the direct road."

" Ah, that accounts for it ; I know every inch of the ground, and consequently I arrived here long before you."

" Have you been here long ?"

" Lord bless you, colonel, I stalled my horse some hour and a half before you arrived."

" The deuce you did.   Then how was it Sam said nothing about it to me."

" Sam was not here when I came."

" Oh, I see."

" So, the other chap put up the horse, and I thought it best to hook it for a time." said Crawley.

" And is the other chap here now ?"

" No ; he is only an odd sort of man who attends to the duty when Sam is out of the way, and it happened that Sam had gone out with a fly."

" Well, then, you did not know that I was here ?"

" Yes.   Arter I had hooked it for an hour or two, I comes back and sees Sam, who tells me you were in the coffee room with them 'ere yeomanry chaps ; oh, thinks I, that's cheek and no mistake.   It's more than I should like to do."

"Yes; but I am disguised," said Colonel Jack.

"That you are," said Crawley, looking at the speaker with surprise and admiration, "shouldn't have known you myself. Well, Sam said that you were going to sleep in the blue room, which was the only one as looked into the yard, and, thinks I, it will be best for me to keep dark and wait till all on 'em are gone to bed, and then just give you a signal, and so here I is."

"You have acted with great prudence and discernment, Crawley, that's all I can say, and you have come just in the nick of time, for I have more work to do to-night."

"More, master? What's your game now, then?"

"You shall soon learn; but, first of all, about our horses."

"Oh, they are all right."

"I do not mean that; but the stable door is locked and we may want to get at them all of a hurry. Sam should have given you the key."

"That's true; but, you see, he agreed to let me sleep in his place after I had seen you, and is sitting up now, most likely. Yes, there is his light; but, you see, he has given me the key of that place, and I can go in when I like."

"Oh, that is enough."

"Do you want anything more of me before we part?"

"Of course, I do—I've business on hand; I told you."

"Oh,"

"One of our pursuers is a rascally sheriff, who has had the effrontary to say that he will take me the next time he sees me dead or alive—I shall give him an opportunity of putting his threat into execution!"

"No—never."

"Yes, I shall, though. First of all help me on with these things. There, that's it." And in a few minutes the snuff-brown suit was exchanged for our hero's own attire; and Colonel Jack stood once more in his own proper character.

"There you are, sir," said Crawley, when he had finished assisting the colonel with his dress.

"Now, my mask."

"Here she is."

"The dark-lantern."

"Yes."

"And my barkers—that's well. Now, Mr. Sheriff Underwood, I'll show you some sport, such as you little dream of. Now, Crawley. I have promised this gentleman to meet him alone and so I will, but you had better keep guard at the door in case of accidents."

"Very good, master."

"Are your barkers in right trim?"

"Yes, colonel."

"I shall want a rope—ah! here it is—and, I suppose, a gag. Yes, that's all right."

"What are you going to do, then?"

"Bind him."

"Ah!"

The colonel lighted his dark lantern, and put out the chamber candle, and then waited for a considerable period to be quite certain that the inmates of the hotel were asleep.

Both himself and his companion were masked, and sat in silence now. After some time had elapsed, our hero rose, and cautiously opened his room door, and looked out into the passage, which was a large one. Indeed the house itself was of great antiquity, and was spacious and rambling, as is usually the case with buildings of this character. Not a sound met the ear of the highwaymen, who listened intently for a considerable time —all was quiet as the grave.

"It is time now," said Colonel Jack, to his companion, in a low whisper, and the two immediately went out into the passage.

Shading the rays of the dark lantern with his hand, the highwayman sought about for the door of No. 9 room, which was situated on the same side of the passage as his own. In fact these were the only two rooms on that side. Our hero cautiously opened the door of Mr. Underwood's room and peered in. All was quiet save the heavy and regular breathing of the sleeper who was evidently wrapt in a profound slumber.

"Wait where you are," said the colonel to Crawley. "Do not attempt to enter unless I call or give the well-known whistle. If you see or hear anybody stirring let me know.

"All right, colonel," was the immediate reply to these orders; and Crawley took up his position by the door of Mr. Underwood's bed-room, and applying his ear thereto listened for his commander's proceedings.

Colonel Jack trod softly on the well carpetted room, and pistol in hand for immediate use if required, he flashed the rays of his lantern across the face of the sheriff, who, however, did not stir or give any signs of waking. The highwayman strode to the bedside and contemplated the slumbering form of Mr. Underwood with a satisfactory smile. What would be his surprise when he awoke and found the veritable and much feared Colonel Jack by his bed-side, now armed cap-a-pie and dressed in his full professional costume.

The thought was pleasing to our hero, and he paused gazing at the sleeper. After awhile he said, in a clear distinct voice—

"Mr. Underwood."

The party so addressed moved slightly in his bed, but did not wake. The name was again repeated, and this time accompanied by a slight shake of the shoulder, after which

Colonel Jack placed his pistol at the head of the sheriff, and cast the rays of his lantern full upon his face.

He awoke! To attempt to give any description of his look of horror and amazement would be utterly hopeless. The tall and commanding figure of the highwayman stood revealed to his astonished vision, and with dilated eyeballs and open mouth he recoiled speechless with astonishment. There is no doubt, at first, that he thought it was a spectre, but he was soon undeceived upon this point.

"Colonel Jack!" he exclaimed, in a subdued whisper of intense surprise.

"Yes," said our hero, "he and no other. You have been seeking me. Here I am. Now what would you? Speak man."

"Villain!" said the sheriff somewhat recovering his first surprise. "You shall be captured now."

He was about to jump out of bed, and, no doubt, ring the bell or else seek for his pistols, but his strange visitant anticipated his intention, and seizing him firmly by the throat pinned him to his bed.

"Mur—" he endeavoured to shout, but the highwayman's grasp was tightened upon his throat and utterance denied him.

"Endeavour to raise the slightest alarm, and you are a dead man. Colonel Jack generally keeps his word, which is more than can be said for sheriffs."

"Would you murder me, wretch?" said the sheriff

"Not unless compelled to do so."

"Good heavens! Compelled?—what mean you?"

"Do as I command, and I will be merciful."

"What mean you!"

"First and foremost," said Colonel Jack, slipping the rope out of his pocket, "this."

And he rapidly bound the man's arms before he was clearly aware of what our hero was doing, so expert was he in his manipulations.

"Now I should advise you to behave yourself as a gentlemen should do under such distressing circumstances," said the highwayman.

The sheriff was speechless with surprise once more, and all his courage seemed to have forsaken him.

"And now, Mr. Underwood," said our hero. "I should not, perhaps, have troubled you, but the fact is, in escaping yesterday from your too pertinacious pursuit, I have spent all my cash, and just now run short of ready money to defray my expenses to London. You will oblige me with some. Oh, don't move I can help myself. Here are your things. What garment do you keep your pocket-book and purse in?"

"Insolence!" exclaimed Mr. Underwood.

"You do not feel disposed to answer Well, then, I must see for myself."

The pockets were soon ransacked, and their contents taken charge of by the highwayman.

"You'll hang for this, some day," said the sheriff.

"I hope not," said our hero, "I sincerely hope not. I am only going to borrow this money, you see, until I find it convenient to return it."

"Take it, sir, I am in your power, but tell me whose bed you sprung from, and how you managed to get into this house? Are you sleeping here?"

"No," was the reply to this query.

"Have you forced an entrance into the establishment?"

"Yes, but you seek to know too much, Mr. Underwood. Now, there is an old gentleman in the next room who has taken matters much more reasonably. He handed me his cash, made no inquiries, and has, I dare say, by this time gone off to sleep again like a wise man."

"Mr. Treman, I'll be bound," said the sheriff.

"I did not ask his name, not being a curious man, you see, but he told me that you had sworn to take me dead or alive the next time you saw me.'

"Did he?"

"Yes, and I thought this would be a good opportunity for you to accomplish your purpose. We are one to one only."

"Do you call overpowering a sleeping man fair, sir," said the sheriff; "and unarmed to—"

"Ah, true, you are had at an advantage, but where are your barkers. They may be serviceable to me. Do they carry well. Umph, not a bad make."

"I'll not lay here to be taunted and insulted by a robber and scoundrel like you," said Mr. Underwood, evincing a disposition to rise.

The colonel levelled his pistol, and said "Now don't you be a foolish man, or most assuredly you will lose what little brains you've got. It is dangerous work playing with a man who sees a halter in the distance, and the best thing you can do is to lay still and submit to that which is now inevitable. You are a valiant man, I believe. Now I tell you what I will do. I will make a bargain with you."

"What is it, sir?"

"You have said that dead or alive you would take me the first time we met."

"Do you call this a meeting, stealing like a cat to the bedside of a man in the dead of the night?'

"We will not quarrel about that now. I tell you what I will do. I will meet you anywhere you choose to name, so that you may capture me; but you must give me your word that you will come alone, and you may come armed as you please. We shall then see who is the better man of the two."

"Do you suppose I accept challenges from a lawless ruffian like yourself."

"Oh, I thought you were desirous of having the honour of capturing Colonel Jack."

"Honour indeed!"

"Yes, certainly, an honour I don't think you are likely to ever have."

"Your day will come, sir," said the sheriff. "The law will be too strong for you."

"Do you accept my offer?"

"What?"

"To meet me at a given place to try the issue out. Not in a court of justice, but on the open heath."

"Yes, to be stabbed and murdered, perhaps, by you and your lawless companions."

"I pledge my word that I will in the first place be alone, and if you can capture me, I will call no other assistance but this right arm of my own, and I pledge also, that you shall not be robbed of a sixpence."

"No, sir, this is an honourable challenge, and I would scorn to take advantage of you."

"I have wasted time and trouble enough about you already," answered Mr. Underwood, whose throat was still aching from Colonel Jack's grasp, and he did not feel altogether anxious to have another personal encounter with him.

"Oh, you are not game, I see," said the colonel; "well, you are the wiser man. Now, before I leave I must trouble you with something else."

"What is it?" asked the sheriff, who all this while had been lying so passively on his bed contemplating our hero.

"Why it will be necessary for me to get a good half-hour's ride before you raise any alarm."

"Well, sir."

"I must, therefore, take measures to do so."

"How?"

"Why, simply, by putting a gag in your mouth."

"Horrible! You surely do not contemplate such a thing?"

"I am compelled. I would not willingly do so—but what is to be done? The moment I am gone you will use that humourous voice of yours, and I shall not be able to get so nicely off as I could wish. No, I must trouble you with a gag."

"I'll not submit to such an indignity." said the sheriff.

"But you must," said the colonel, levelling his pistol—or rather one of the sheriff's own weapons. "I wonder whether they will carry well?

"Oh, don't—I submit," said Mr. Underwood.

"Good; that is enough."

Without further ado the highwayman thrust a gag in the mouth of the sheriff and left him to his reflections, which were anything but of a pleasing nature.

Colonel Jack took the key out of the door and locked it on the outside, he then put the key into his pocket, and went into his own room followed by the faithful Crawley who was in a state of ecstacy at the success of his captain.

"All is well, so far," said our hero, when he had regained his apartment; "now, you take the swag and be off as soon as you like."

"I am going to have an hour or two's rest in Sam's house," said Crawley.

"Very well; only be off before they are up in the morning."

"Shall I go on to town?"

"Yes, as fast as your horse will carry you. There will be a pretty shine here in the morning."

"What shall you do?"

"Stay and see the fun out."

"How?"

"I play the part of a drysalter when I get up—an unfortunate gentleman who has been robbed."

"Oh, I see."

"Now, hook it. Good night."

"Good night, colonel."

Crawley descended the ladder, and once more found himself in the stable yard. He returned the ladder to where he had taken it from, and went into Sam's domicile.

<hr>

CHAPTER XXXVII.

SCENE IN THE MORNING.—CONSTERNATION OF EVERYBODY.

COLONEL JACK, or rather Mr. Treman, slept soundly till the boots at the Swan Inn knocked at his door to call him.

He arose, and put on the garments he had worn on the previous night, and was the first down in the coffee room discussing a hearty breakfast.

He had previously made the landlady acquainted with his operations during that eventful night, and the good lady thought it advisable to say that the highwayman had paid her a visit and robbed her of a considerable amount, to keep up appearances.

The colonel had thrown down the key of Mr. Underwood's room in the passage previous to his coming down stairs.

Stokes and his companions were the next to make their appearance in the public room, and Mr. Treman, after the usual salutations had been gone through, said that a terrible scene had taken place during the night, and inquired if they had been robbed.

They answered in the negative.

"Then I have to a considerable amount," said Mr. Tremam, with evident chagrin, "and so has our worthy landlady."

"Dear me—how? and by whom?" they all inquired.

"Colonel Jack!"

"Impossible !"

"It is true enough, as far as I am concerned. I wish you had not troubled yourself to follow the rascal for it's only driven him further to rob and frighten innocent people."

"I am petrified with astonishment," said Stokes. "Where is the fellow we captured?"

"Pshaw. No," exclaimed Treman. "Captured, indeed; he's too slippery a customer for that ; and I tell you it would have been better to have left it alone. Confound the fellow. He has taken my order book, my cheques, and all my gold. It's positive vexation."

"Bless my soul," said Stokes. "Why did you not give an alarm?"

"A very likely thing with a pistol thrust in my mouth. Alarm, indeed. I am glad I escaped with my life, and think it wonderful I have."

"And Mr. Underwood ?"

"Oh, I know nothing of him."

"How is it he's not down? I hope nothing has happened to him."

It's very strange he is not down," said another.

Mr. Treman rang the bell—enter waiter.

"Has any one called Mr. Sheriff Underwood," said another.

"Yes, sir."

"Who?"

"Boots, I believe, sir ; but I'll inquire."

"Send boots here."

"Yes, sir." Exit waiter. Enter boots.

"Have you knocked at Mr. Underwood's door?" said Treman.

"Yees, sir, harf an hour agone or moore."

"Did he answer?"

"Noa, sir."

"The deuce he didn't! Why, gentlemen, we had better go to his room."

"E'es locked un door," said boots.

"Locked his door. What could that be for?"

"Oh, perhaps he heard thieves," said Stokes, " and tried to lock them out."

"He was anxious to capture the hero of the road," said Mr. Treman. "Well, we had better some of us go up, gentlemen."

"We'll all go," they said.

"Very good. So be it. Lead on," said Treman

"Oh, dear, gentlemen," exclaimed the landlady, who now came out of her bar parlour. "I am ruined—I'm undone. The character of the house too. We've had thieves here—burglars—I am lost—Such a thing never happened since I've been in business ; and now, when I'm a lone widow, and unprotected. Oh—Oh !" and here she relapsed into a series of sobs and shrieks.

"My dear lady," said one of the party, who appeared the kindest and most tender hearted. "My dear, good lady. You cannot help it. It's no fault of yours, of course, and cannot be in any way to blame in the matter. Pray don't give way in this manner."

"Oh, but I can't help it—I cannot. Have you seen anything of dear Mr. Underwood?"

"No, my dear madam. We are about to go up into his room and see after him."

"Oh, do, there's good souls—oh. I shall never get over this—in the dead of the night too—it's dreadful—and no notice."

"My good madam," said the same speaker, "housebreakers generally do come in the dead of the night ; and as to giving notice of their appearance, why your own sense must tell you that such a course would be positively ridiculous. These things must be borne with resignation. It's the Lord's will."

He distributed tracts, this man, in the neighbourhood where he came from, and the habit of calling upon the Lord was confirmed with him—a habit, by the way, that is " much more honoured in the breach than the observance."

The party now took their way up to the apartment of Mr. Underwood.

They knocked at the door, but received no answer—only some thumps against the wood work in reply.

"What is the meaning of this?" said Stokes. "Somebody's in the room, but does not speak. It's strange—very."

The door was tried, but was found to be locked. The key was searched for, and was eventually found in the passage, where the colonel had thrown it.

Mr. Stokes opened the door, and the whole party paused for a moment, as though they were afraid to venture in, lest some horrible sight might meet their gaze.

After a minute or so they entered in a body, to keep up each other's spirits.

Mr. Sheriff Underwood was sitting on the side of his bed, his arms firmly bound behind him, and the gag in his mouth.

"Goodness me, what is the matter?" exclaimed Treman, regarding the sheriff with a look of surprise and concern through his horn spectacles. "What is the matter?"

Of course there was no reply to this question, and Treman instantly began to unfasten the rope which bound the arms of Mr. Underwood.

"He's gagged," said Stokes, looking at the mouth of his friend.

"Yes," said Mr. Underwood, as he quickly pulled out the gag from his mouth. "That unmitigated scoundrel has been here—that audacious scoundrel, unmatched for his crimes and impertinence,' said Mr. Underwood. "Oh, what a night I've passed."

"Ah, Colonel Jack!" said Mr. Treman. "The fellow has stripped me of all I had"

"He has, eh?"

"Yes; and likewise our worthy landlady."

"How did he manage to get into the house bothers me?" said Stokes.

"He came in at my window," said Mr. Treman.

"Didn't you fasten it?"

"Yes, such a fastening as it is. But he managed to force it, and without my hearing him."

"Well, you've won your hundred guineas," said one of the party.

"Oh, bother the hundred guineas," said Mr. Treman, "that's not the consideration—it's our losses. My order-book—here I shall have to go over the ground again—look at the loss of time, and—dear me, what a disastrous circumstance."

"Is the poor gentleman all right?" inquired the landlady, from the bottom of the stairs.

"Yes, my dear madam, he is, the Lord be praised," said our tract distributing friend. "He's all right, with the exception of the loss of his property."

"Well, we will leave you to dress," said Stokes, "and proceed to get our breakfast. We must fortify the inner man under all ills."

And so away they went again into the public-room.

In a few minutes the sheriff made his appearance, very irrate, and in a marvellous ill temper with everybody and everything. Nothing was right on the breakfast-table—the eggs were not done—the ham salt—(this was Mr. Treman's fault)—the butter rancid.

"But, however, there is one satisfaction," said the sheriff, "I can't pay for it, for the rascal has not left me a coin."

"Oh, we can square the reckoning," said Stokes; "you need not trouble yourself about that."

After the party had finished their breakfast, the landlady made her appearance, her handkerchief to her eyes, as though she had been weeping. She did try to squeeze out a few tears, and, to her credit be it spoken, she succeeded; but it was an effort, and a smile played around the corner of her mouth soon afterwards.

"Oh, Mr. Underwood," exclaimed the hostess, "to think that it should come to this! My reputation is at stake—my house is robbed—"

"Not your house, madam," said the sheriff, "the people in it."

"Yes, precisely, that is what I mean; but I hardly know what I am saying, and that's a fact."

"You have been robbed yourself, madam, I am given to understand," said Mr Underwood.

"Yes, sir, my cash box has been carried off. My watch and jewellery—and—I don't know what else besides."

"How is it you did not raise an alarm. There were plenty of us in the house."

"I was not awake, Mr. Underwood."

"What did the rascal take these things from your bed room without disturbing you?" asked the sheriff.

"It appears so, for I knew nothing of my loss till this morning. My cash-box was in the bar parlour, but my watch and jewels together with several other articles, were in my bed room."

"Then he must have entered there."

"Yes, there is not the slightest doubt of it."

"Dear me, it is very extraordinary that a man should have managed to run through the house in this manner, and get clear off without a soul endeavouring to cap—"

Capture, he was going to say, but he bethought himself that, perhaps, it was not a very happy word to be used.

"Stop him,' he remarked, instead.

"Very unfortunate," said Stokes. "I don't see that it is so extraordinary."

"Nor I," said another.

"I only wish he may be tried in my county when he is caught," said the sheriff, "and that he may be handed over to me and my colleagues to see executed."

"Do you think you should know him again?" inquired Stokes, of the sheriff.

"Oh, yes, I think so. He's rather a remarkable man—I could not see his features, as they were completely concealed by the mask he wore—but he appeared to be a tall handsome man, with long ringlets of a chesnut colour, at least, so they appeared to me, by the light he carried with him."

"Was he with you long?"

"Oh, dear, yes. The fellow had the audacity to offer to meet me at any appointed place, to afford me an opportunity of—ahem—of capturing him."

"Ah—ah!" laughed his companions, "that's a good joke. Well, certainly, that is a joke, and no mistake. What did you say?"

"What do you suppose I should say?"

"Don't know."

"Why, treated it with the contempt it deserved."

"Ah, I see, didn't want to run your head into danger."

"Not with such a ruffian as that."

"Madam," said Mr. Treman, to the land-lady, "I much regret that it is quite out of my power to pay for my reckoning. I am in the same situation as our friend here—but of course you know that—"

"Oh, don't mention it," said the landlady, "pray don't mention it, Mr. Treman. I have money to pay you, but I am not sure that I have enough ready cash in the house ; but I can give you a cheque, if that will do."

"Not if it's inconvenient : I have several accounts to receive in the next town, but the worst of it is the fellow has taken my order book, which cannot be of any possible use to him, and is most important to me."

"Dear me, how vexatious," exclaimed the landlady, most "terribly vexatious," and she left the apartment to attend to the duties of her establishment.

After some further desultory conversation the party of yeomanry and the sheriff made up their minds to take their departure, and the horses were ordered to be got in readiness as the gentlemen returned to their rooms to finish their toilettes.

Colonel Jack was left alone in the parlour, and as he was ruminating upon past oc- currences, the door was slightly opened, and a head thrust in the corner thereof which regarded the occupant with rather a curious and inquiring look.

The colonel felt uncomfortable ; he knew the man well enough. He was one of the Bow Street runners, and the thought crossed our hero's mind that, be his appearance acci- dental or otherwise, it boded no good ; and he was, moreover, not so sure of deceiving this individual in his present disguise as he was with those of his yeomanry friends.

His uneasiness was increased when the man made another feint at the door and popped his head in ; not content with this, he entered the apartment and quietly seated himself.

"Fine morning, sir," he said, to our hero.

"Ye-es, it is," said the colonel, in a drawl, and a feigned voice.

The man gave another look at him, and took up the paper—not that he was engaged in its perusal, he did it as a blind to regard the occupant of the coffee room still more closely.

The colonel hastily left the room and went into the stable-yard.

"Saddle my horse at once, Sam," he said to the ostler.

"All right, sir."

"I must be off at once, Sam."

"What's up ?" asked the ostler.

"There's a queer customer in the parlour, and I am not quite certain but what he sus- pects me."

"Whew ! colonel," said Sam ; "missus will be vexed if this little job is found out."

"She sha'nt be found out if I can work it to rights, which, as far as she's concerned, I will, mind you. Listen. There's a beershop through the town called the 'Jolly Gardeners.'

"I know it."

"Yes. You send your lad on with the horse, then, and I will wait till he comes. Do you understand ?"

"Yes."

"I musn't go in these togs ; but will up in my bedroom and change them."

"What, put on your own ?"

"There's no alternative. I will leave by the back gate, and cut across the fields to the 'Jolly Gardeners.' They know me there. Now, on with the saddle, and don't keep me waiting."

Almost as quick as a pantomimic change, the colonel had donned his own attire, and stood again in his own natural character. He knew he was now running a great risk, but it was for the sake of his landlady's repu-tation that he did this. For even assuming he were caught outside the premises, no complicity could be traced to the landlady, and with dropping his snuff brown suit and horn spectacles, he dropped his identity.

His greatest difficulty was getting down the stairs without being seen, and fortunately for him he heard the chambermaid in the passage. He called to her and asked if the coast was clear.

She gave a slight scream at first, as she observed the alteration in his dress, but told him that there was no one about. The colonel did not waste another moment, but went down the stairs, then through the kitchen, and thus out into the private garden of the house, where none of the customers were ever admitted.

The gate of this garden led into a bye lane, which our hero gained without any difficulty, and cut across the fields to the "Jolly Gardeners," with perfect safety. Here he found his horse, and tipping the boy half a guinea for his trouble, off he trotted.

So far, so well, but, unfortunately, when he had got a few hundred yards down the road, he was confronted to his great horror by the dwarf, who had proved himself so determined an assailant upon him on the night previous.

The little man's eyes dilated at the sight of the colonel, and he uttered a yell that could be scarcely considered human.

"Murder—thieves—highwaymen !" now shouted out the little man. "Help—help !"

And he instantly sprang at the horse as before.

The animal reared, and was very nearly throwing its rider ; indeed it was with the greatest difficulty that he retained his seat.

The little man continued to shout so loudly, that there was every probability of his getting

a crowd of village rustics round him in the course of a few minutes.

"Curse you!" exclaimed Colonel Jack. "Leave go, or I'll—"

He did not finish his sentence, but proceeded to belabour the dwarf with all his might, who was, however, as obstinate, if not more so, than he had been on the previous occasion. Several individuals now came out from the Jolly Gardeners, attracted by the noise, and they cried shame upon our hero.

"Help," said the dwarf; "he's a robber—a highwayman! Gentlemen, assistance."

Two or three of the yokels now came forward, and stood staring in mute surprise. Colonel Jack saw that his danger was imminent, and by a sudden effort sought to shake off his tormentor. Some time necessarily elapsed from this rencontre, and our hero

No. 30.

heard the sound of horses' feet coming along the road.

He turned round, and in the distance beheld the sheriff and his party.

A thought came across his mind of shooting the dwarf there and then, so irritated was he with his interference; but with his natural repugnance to shed blood, which he always had, he tried a different course. He struck the dwarf several several severe blows in the face with his clenched fist. After a repitition of these, he did manage to so punish his antagonist as to cause him to leave go and drop to the earth. The instant this was effected, our hero set spurs to his horse, and galloped off amidst the shouts of the rustics, who did not, however, endeavour to offer him any obstruction; but the dwarf continued to scream and shout as loud as his little lungs would let him, and to judge from the noise he made, were not by any means of a contemptible character.

By this time the sheriff and his party made their appearance on the scene.

"What's all this about?" inquired the sheriff.

"Oh, I am nearly murdered," exclaimed the dwarf, whose face was covered with blood from the severe punishment he had received.

"Who by?"

"A highwayman," said a grinning rustic.

"Where and when?"

"Just now He's gone full tear down the road."

"The devil!" said Stokes.

"No, he be's a highwayman," said the aforesaid rustic.

"Then no time's to be lost. On, gentlemen," said Mr. Underwood, who was now aroused to a state of excitement, "on, gentlemen, at once. No time's to be lost."

The party now put spurs to their horses, and went off after our hero once more.

"By my faith, it seems we are doomed to be at this man's heels for the remainder of our natural lives," said the sheriff.

"Do you think it's him?" inquired Stokes.

"Not the slightest doubt of it. The fellow has been in the neighbourhood since the burglary, and no doubt has slept at that road side house."

"What, the Jolly Gardeners?"

"Yes, most likely. I'll make a note of that, and see who keeps it. The place is the resort of disreputable characters, that's certain, and it must be looked to."

"See, there he goes," said Stokes, as he caught sight of Colonel Jack's head above the quickset hedge, going along a circuitous bridle road which turned out of the one in which they were.

"It's him, and no mistake," said the sheriff. "Push on, gentlemen. This time he cannot escape us."

And now they urged on their steeds to their utmost.

"We'll have him," said the Bow Street runner, who had joined the party in pursuit. "We'll have him, unless he's mounted on his mare."

"He is not," said the sheriff, "that I know for a fact, for he left his mare at the house of one who calls himself a respectable gentleman."

"Oh, then, if he's not on his mare there's every chance for us," said the officer.

Colonel Jack had observed his pursuers, and found that the animal he was riding was by no means so fleet a one as his own Ada, and he made this discovery at a time when it was the most painful to himself. He felt that unless some ruse were adopted, the probability was that those in pursuit would run

him down sooner or later, and our hero felt like a hare with a pack of hounds at his heels. The horse he bestrode was evidently ill-pleased at being urged on at such an unwarrantable a pace—he was a quiet, country-fed quadruped, who did not seem at all to comprehend the necessity of putting out his powers to such an extent—and he certainly never had such a rider on his back before, for the colonel was a man who would make any horse go, that is, if he had any go in him; but the one he was riding appeared a discontented, sulky animal, and it required all our hero's tact and industry to keep him at all up to the mark. Certainly the colonel found himself in an awkward predicament. Inwardly cursing his unlucky stars at meeting with the dwarf, who, to say the truth, appeared his evil genius, he cast furtive glances ever and anon towards his pursuers. It became painfully evident that they were gaining on him, and it became still more evident that if matters went on in this way that Mr. Sheriff Underwood would have at last the felicity of capturing his enemy and taunter. What was to be done? The colonel's position was critical to the last degree, the more especially as he saw the Bow Street officer now at his heels, as well as the others, who of course were sufficiently irritated with him. The colonel felt that there was an absolute necessity for him to do something in this emergency—but what? When a man is riding at full speed, with a pack of bloodhounds at his heels, it is not the time for thought, at least not for calm reflection, to say the least of it. Still something must be done, for sooner or later they would be on him. While debating with himself as to what had best be done under the circumstances, Colonel Jack, to his great astonishment, heard a voice cry—

"Hist!"

"Hilloa," answered our hero.

"It's me master," said Crawley, from behind a hedge which run by the side of the bridle road along which he was galloping.

"What, Crawley?"

"Yes. Don't stop. But at the end of this lane is a narrow turning to the left. It's no thoroughfare. Go down that, and you will see a large barn. Jem Banks is in there."

"Well, what of that?"

"He knows me, and is a friend. If you get in there, Jem will bolt the door."

"What would be the good of that?" They would force an entrance, and be d—d to them."

"Can't you change things with him, and go out the other way?"

"If you think this could be done?"

"Try it, master, there's no help for it."

"And my horse?"

"Leave it with him."

This conversation was as hastily as possible, while Crawley galloped on the other side of the hedge.

"I shall be about to see how you get on, master." said the latter. "Do as I tell you."

"All right."

And the colonel urged on his steed to the utmost, and shortly gained the turning his companion had mentioned. He lost not a moment in making for the barn. The door was open, and a man in a smock frock, who was in the interior of the barn, instantly closed it.

"Thee bee'st pursued," said the countryman.

"Yes," answered the colonel. "They will be here directly," and he dismounted from his mare, and took off his hat and coat.

"You are a friend, I believe," said the colonel.

"Ay, sure, Master Crawley told me as how you were chased."

"Will thee change things with me. Look sharp, there's a good fellow."

In a few seconds Colonel Jack had on the countryman's smock frock and hat, taking the precaution, however, to put his pistols under the latter, in case of an emergency.

"Now, is there a back door to this barn, my friend?"

"Ees, sir."

"Now, you put on my clothes, and keep these fellows at the door as long as you can. If they take you for a highwayman, so much the better."

"But I bean't one," said the man. "Perhaps they'll keep un in the cage."

"Oh, no fear of that. If they do, you can get damages."

"Woand if I care, whether un do or not," said Jem Banks.

"Ah, you are one of the right sort, I see," said his companion, "and shan't go unrewarded. There's five guineas for you to begin with."

The man opened his eyes in perfect astonishment at this munificent sum.

"But, stay, we must change boots," said the colonel.

This was soon accomplished, and our hero taking a pitchfork in his hand, went out of the barn by the other door, taking his way across the fields, with the usual gait of a countryman. He heard the sound of his pursuers, but did not dare to turn round, but pursued his way as fast as possible, without attracting attention by too much precipitancy. He had not got the length of two fields off, before the door of the barn was assailed with a most violent series of knocks.

"Open the door," said the sheriff." It's no use your attempting to conceal yourself. Open the door, and surrender at once."

No answer was returned by the occupant of the barn, true to his word, he caused as much delay as possible.

"Open the door," shouted out the sheriff, "or else we'll force through it."

Jem Banks only stood grinning on the other side of it; but he made no noise, neither did he choose to speak.

"Batter the old ramshackling structure down," said Stokes.

"Fire in," said another, and agreeable to the suggestion, several shots were discharged at the door, and Jem Banks would have been in danger of receiving the contents of these, had he not taken the precaution of removing his respectable body out of the way.

"Oh, mercy. I'm a murdered man," said Banks, in a voice of pain and anguish. "It's all over with me."

"Our shots have taken effects," said Stokes, turning pale.

"Was it the Colonel Jack's voice," asked the sheriff.

"I don't know," was the reply of his companion Stokes.

"Nor I," said another.

"Will you open the door, before you are blown to pieces?" said the sheriff.

A low moaning noise was his only answer.

"By the Lord, but the fellow is mortally wounded, perhaps," said Stokes.

"Batter down the cursed old door," said another of the party, as he dismounted from his horse.

And seizing what had once served for a gate post, and which happened to be handy, he commenced a violent assault upon the barn door, without further parley. After two or three efforts, the wood work was splintered, and the assailant tore strip after strip off with his hands, until a sufficient space was made for a man to enter.

"Now, gentlemen," he said, "who's to be first?"

They did not any of them seem disposed to volunteer.

"I shall shoot the first man that dares to enter," said Jem. "My life's nearly gone, but I'll have my revenge."

"The scoundrel will fire, I dare say," said Stokes.

"It won't be particularly healthy to go on. Perhaps you'll go first, Mr. Underwood," he said, in continuation.

But the sheriff hesitated.

He did not seem to much relish the task, however, as he had been so valiant at the Swan, in words, he was compelled to lead the van, and therefore made a virtue of necessity, and entered the broken doorway. Instead of being saluted with a volley from Colonel Jack's pistol, he found what he supposed to be that individual in the barn, upon the broad grin.

"Oh—oh," thought the sheriff, that's it, my friend, making a jest of the matter," and he immediately pounced upon the occupant of the barn, and believing him to be wounded he did not deem that he could offer much resistance, in this, however, he was mistaken, for Jem Banks took the sheriff up in his arms as though he were a child and threw him over his head without more ado. "You infernal scoundrel," continued Underwood. "Help—help ! Stokes, or some of you, come, will you ?"

Two or three more of the party now entered and were surprised to find an athletic man, habited as a highwayman, grinning in a most undignified manner.

"Seize him," said the sheriff, "seize the scoundrel, thank heaven we have got him at last."

"Ye bees a bright lot surely," said Banks ; "I wonder who's to pay for Muster Newton's barn ?"

The voice and dialect of the man rather staggered his assailants, and they looked inquiringly into his face for some solution to the mystery, for by this time Banks was in their hands and offered no further resistance.

"Why this can't be he," said Stokes.

The sheriff rose upon his legs, and stood rubbing his shoulders and limbs which were sorely bruised by the fall.

"What is the meaning of this ?" he inquired, looking stupidly at his companions.

"There is his horse," said one of the men.

"And here—well this can't be Colonel Jack," said Stokes, looking at the bronzed face of the countrymen.

"Now, look here, sirrah," said the sheriff. "We shall take you to gaol for robbery on the highway."

"Will ee ?" said the man, with a grin, "then damme if I don't bring an action agin ee."

"Where is this scoundrel ?" asked the sheriff.

"Which" asked the countryman, looking first at one and then at another.

One or two of the party could not help laughing at the man's *naive* manner.

"We havn't got the real Simon Pure, that's quite certain," said one.

The sheriff rose, positively wild with fury. He stamped upon the ground, and, we are sorry to be obliged to record it, he indulged in several unseemly oaths, which were very wrong for a gentleman in his position.

"The fellow is a necromancer, a magician, a wizard," said Stokes ; "where can he have got to. Ah, there is another door, he has escaped through that, no doubt."

"Look here, sir ; I'll have you flogged at the cart's tail if you do not explain the whole of this affair—now, mind that," said the sheriff.

"Ees, sir."

"Yes, and you shall feel too, and smart pretty severely if you play us any tricks. What has become of the highwayman who came into this barn ?"

"I thought he beed a play actor chap," said Banks.

"A what ?"

"A play actor chap."

"Why ?"

"Because he said so."

"He did, the lying rascal," said the sheriff.

"Ees, and asked I to lend un my smock-frock and hat."

"And left you these in exchange ?" .

"Ees."

"The fellow is an idiot," said Stokes. "Clearly an idiot."

"I'm a ploughman," said Banks, with a grin.

"Well, after he changed clothes with you, my man, what then ?" inquired the sheriff.

"Oh, ee be coming back again."

"Coming back, is he ?"

"Ees."

"When ?"

"After the performance."

"What ?"

"The play. Ee be going to play a countryman on the stage."

"Where ?"

"At the St. Alban's Theatre."

"Oh, nonsense ; he's been playing you a trick."

"Ee left his horse"

"Ah, that's true," said the sheriff, who really believed the man's story, being under the impression that he was simply a fool.

"Well, gentlemen," said Stokes, "we are sold again, as clean as any one was in this world."

"It is no use waiting here," said the sheriff. "Nothing is to be got out of this zany. Let us be off, we may overtake him."

"Ah, true. Let us be off at once, gentlemen."

"Which way did he go ?" inquired the sheriff.

The countryman pointed in the opposite direction to the one taken by our hero, and the party mounted their horses, and were soon once more in pursuit.

Colonel Jack had by this time got some distance off—sufficiently far to be under no very immediate apprehension of being discovered and overtaken. After he had travelled some distance, he luckily fell in with an encampment of gipsies. He was pretty well acquainted with most of this fraternity, who were generally very ready to afford him assistance in the hour of need.

As he saw their encampment on an adjacent common, he at once made up his mind to see their chief, and make him acquainted with his present position. Taking his way into the midst of them, the colonel accosted an old man who seemed to be the patrician of his tribe. A few words explained the colonel's occupation and the dangers he had recently passed through.

The old man consulted with his companions, and the colonel was invited into one of their tents, where the wife and family of the old gipsy were busily occupied in discussing their morning's meal. The old man's wife, Zara by name, showed our hero the utmost degree of hospitality and kindness, and an excellent disguise was soon provided for the colonel to ensconce himself in.

This he readily availed himself of, for to travel to London in Jem Banks' costume was not to be thought of. Knowing well the habits of these people, he did not deem it prudent to refuse partaking of their hospitality. After he had completed his toilette for a third time that day, he sat down and partook of some refreshment.

"You had better stop here for the remainder of the day," said the old gipsy, and move on towards London when darkness sets in."

"I do not think it at all possible that I shall be recognised now," said the colonel, with a smile, "and I am anxious about my companions."

"Ah, true," he replied, "but I would not run too great a risk. You will have every protection we can afford you."

"Thanks, my friend. I feel assured of that," said the colonel, kindly. "I am indebted to you for these garments," and he took out his purse, with the intention of paying for the same.

The old man looked indignant, and put up one of his hard bronzed hands deprecatingly.

"No, my friend," he said, with a dignity that surprised his guest. "No. If we cannot serve each other in the hour of misfortune, without being paid for it by money, we are not fit to live in the world."

"Pardon me, I did not mean to insult you," said the colonel.

"A good action meets with its own reward," said the gipsy, "and is registered up above, far beyond our power to erase the register of it."

The colonel bowed assent to this very convenient doctrine. He put on the clothes, and that was the chief matter in his present emergency. Taking a grateful farewell of his kind friends, he was about to take his departure, when he observed the head of Crawley peering over the palings which enclosed one side of the common. He hastened towards him, and as he did so, gave the well known whistle which was the signal of his gang.

Crawley's face brightened up at this, and still more so when he discovered that it was his master who was making towards him.

"Why, colonel," he exclaimed, "how many more disguises are you going to put on."

"Hush!" said his superior. "Have you seen anything of our friends?"

"Yes."

"Where are they?"

"I do not know now, but they are not likely to be here."

"Why not?"

"Oh, Lord, oh, Lord—why not? Because Joe Banks has sent them upon a fool's errand."

"How so?"

"He has gammoned them to believe you were a play actor, and were going to act at the St. Alban's Theatre to night."

"That fellow is worth his weight in gold. Without him I should have been lost."

"I knew he would do the trick to rights."

"Have they gone to St. Alban's, then?"

"I don't know, but they've gone a contrary road to this. My word, wasn't the sheriff in a way?"

"Well, it won't do to be talking here. I must make the best of my way to London."

"How will you get there?"

"Must take the stage, I suppose."

"Hadn't you better mount my nag?"

"What will you do?"

"Oh, I can hang about somewhere, and towards evening fetch your's from Banks."

"No; I am afraid that would be dangerous, Crawley."

"Oh, leave that to me, master; you take my nag. I ain't so much sought after as you; and if they do catch me, it ain't of so much consequence."

The colonel smiled at the generosity of his companion, who would sooner be taken at any time rather than his commander.

"Take it, master," said Crawley.

"Very well, you won't be satisfied, I suppose, if I refuse. Now, mind, don't you be too venturesome, or get running any risks. We must see about the other horses, hereafter. You know the one Banks has got in the barn, belongs to Mr. Parker."

"Very well, but he's got Ada."

"Yes, but I don't intend him to keep her, you understand. She's worth all the horses he has got in his stables."

"I should just think she was," said Crawley.

The colonel mounted Crawley's horse, and took his way to London by a different road to that he had come on the previous night.

He would have liked to call upon Mr. Parker, but he dared not risk doing so at present, more especially as his better half seemed in no way disposed to stand his friend. He was most anxious to know how Hackett, Knapp, and the others had fared, and before proceeding to his own lodgings, he took his way to the memorable hotel kept by the Badger.

CHAPTER XXXVIII.

COLONEL JACK AT THE "COW AND CAULI- FLOWER"—SCENE AT LAWKER'S LANE.

WHEN Colonel Jack arrived at Bill Dyson's, that individual came forward to the bar and motioned our hero into the small parlour behind. Dyson occasionally assumed the mysterious, and it was generally his custom to do so when he thought there had been any difficulty ahead.

"Well," said the Badger, when they had got into his sanctum, "you have been in for it, I hear. Poor Warrington."

"It is all over with him, Bill," said the colonel; "all over. And our other friends—have you seen anything of them?"

"They are all safe and sound, and are in their old quarters. My stars, won't they be right glad to see you?"

"Where are they?"

"Up stairs."

"Oh, that's all right. I'll go up, then."

"Wait a bit, Colonel," said Mr. Dyson. "Wait a bit."

"What for, Bill?"

Mr. Dyson turned the straw in his mouth.

"Have you found out the name of them chaps?" he inquired, in an under tone.

"Who do you mean?"

"The Clerkenwell business," said the Badger.

"Oh, ah, well thought of. There is no time to be lost about this business."

"No, Osborne will be tried in a few days."

"Yes; I have ascertained their names," said the colonel. "One is Slimcoe and the other Parker."

"Slimcoe. Ah, I thought so," said the Badger, ruminating. "I thought so."

"Do you know where he lives?" inquired the colonel.

"Don't you?"

"Not at present."

"But you will know, I suppose?"

"I shall be able to find out; but time is of consequence. If you know, Dyson, which I feel convinced you do, pray do not hesitate in telling me."

"Umph," ejaculated the Badger.

"Why hesitate?"

"Well, we'll talk about this by and bye," said Mr. Dyson. "You are for up stairs now, I suppose?"

"Yes; I'll see you again presently."

And Colonel Jack at once took his way to the up stairs room, which was devoted to him and his companions' use. At his entrance he was cheered and hailed with unfeigned delight.

"Hurrah!" shouted out Hackett; "returned once more to our old quarters. Why, colonel, this is a sight. How have you fared?"

"I've had a briskish time of it, I warrant you, and have been all but taken two or three times. And you?"

"We've had our work to do; but here we are."

"All safe?"

"All but Warrington."

"Ah, he's gone I hear."

"How did you hear that—from Dyson?"

"Yes; but Crawley had previously told me."

"Oh, you've seen Crawley. Come, then, he's all right," said Hackett, turning to his fellow highwaymen.

"Yes, he's all right; at least, he was so when I left him."

The colonel now sat down and recounted all his adventures; after which he inquired the particulars of how his brothers in misfortune had fared.

"Well, I needn't tell you that we were pressed hardly enough," said Hackett.

"Yes, worse than me, if possible."

"You know the history of Warrington, in that confounded field?"

"Yes."

"You know, perhaps, or at least you would judge so, that I deemed it expedient to separate?"

"Of course the best thing always to do, where there is no use combining to offer resistance."

"Precisely. So we did separate; and it appears that by hook or by crook, in one way or another, our friends here managed to give them the go by."

"And you?"

"I came off the worst."

"How so—you are here."

"Ah, but wait a bit. Three of the best mounted of the party took it in their heads to follow me. Field after field was traversed, and I found that they were gaining upon me. The fact is, my horse was not up to the heavy soil so well as their's were."

"No, nor your heavy weight," said the colonel, smiling.

His brother highwaymen laughed at this observation.

"I am not so heavy—under twelve stone," said Hackett, reprovingly.

"Well, go on, old boy," said the colonel. "They were gaining on you—"

"Yes and two of them were unpleasantly near. A couple of shots came whistling about my ears, and I thought that there would be a chance of my sharing the same fate as poor Warrington. I turned round to have a look at my assailants—there were three of them—then measuring my distance from the hedge which skirted the bridle road for which I was making, for I was quite sick of the heavy soil I had been travelling on— I found that the probability was that my pursuers would be upon me before I got clear of the field—there was no time for hesitation—I turned round, took deliberate aim at the horse's chest of the foremost of my pursuers, and fired. The poor animal had received its death wound—he stumbled and fell, throwing his rider heavily to the earth. The others came rushing on, and I succeeded in breaking one of the forelegs of another of the horses, who kicked and plunged so much, that the man who rode him was also thrown, and received so many severe injuries from his wounded steed that he was left senseless."

" And the third one ?" inquired the colonel.

" Luckily for me he hesitated. I suppose he was debating with himself about seeing after his companions or following me. By his so doing I was enabled to gain the narrow road in safety."

" Did he not follow then ?"

" Yes, after taking a glance at his friends. I heard the one, whose horse had been killed, say to him, that he would see to the man who was senseless, and he urged him to follow in pursuit of me. He did so ; but the delay enabled me to get a little ahead, and after a canter of a few minutes, I espied our friend Knapp a short distance off. I called to him, and we succeeded in joining each other."

" Wasn't Knapp pursued then ?'

" No, he had given his friends the slip, and was making his way clear off. When the yeomanry chap saw that there were two of us, he hooked it, and turned his horse's head, and quietly trotted back to the two companions he had left behind."

" You have had a lucky escape," said Colonel Jack, " and with the exception of the loss of Warrington, we have fared better than we could have expected, all things considered. Have any of you been to Brook Street," said the colonel, sadly, as the remembrance of his wife came across him, and whom he had not seen since her removal from Hornsey.

" Yes, I have," said Hackett.

" How was she ?"

" Pretty well, all things considering," said Hackett.

" Inquire why I had not been there, eh ?"

" Yes."

" What did you say ?"

" Said you had been fiercely engaged."

" Ah, did not tell her that—"

" We had been pursued. ?"

" Ah."

" Oh, no, colonel, I should hardly do that."

" That's well."

Several more bumpers were drained off, and the party broke up, the colonel taking his way down stairs into Mr. Dyson's back parlour.

" Now, Bill," said our hero, after he had set himself down, " you know the Slimcoe's address, so out with it old boy at once."

Mr. Dyson became ruminative once more.

" Come, don't stand hesitating, man. I shall know it sooner or later."

" I don't like to peach, colonel. It's against my principal ; but as you say you are sure to know, why I suppose I may just tell you his address at once, to save trouble."

" That's just it."

" Only you must understand that you are not going to have him taken into custody."

" I don't want it any more than you do yourself. Dyson, all I require, is an exculpation of Osborne. Let him confess, and, as there are ample means to be found, he can be furnished with sufficient to go abroad."

" Umph. A pretty beauty he'd be abroad."

" No worse than he is here."

" Perhaps not. I warn't agoing to say that the fellow is worth a bunch of cabbage-stalks. He's a bad un—a rank bad un, and no mistake. That may be true enough ; but it's no reason that I should turn round and hand him over to justice."

" I tell you he won't be."

" Very well. I can take your word, that I know."

" I should hope so."

" Nat Slimcoe lives in Lawker's Lane,"

" Where is that ?"

" Seven Dials."

" Oh, I know.'

" It's named after old Lawker, what's dead. Him as kept the pop shop at the corner."

" And the other one ?"

" I don't know where he hangs out.

" Do you know the number in Lawker's Lane ?"

" No ; but it is on the right-hand going from the pop shop, and is as nearly as possible in about the middle."

" Is it at a shop ?"

" Yes."

" Of what description ?"

" Oh, handkerchiefs and shawls are hanging out. It's a fence."

" Oh, I am very much obliged to you, Dyson," said our hero, offering the Badger his hand.

" You'll do the thing that's right," said the Badger, as he shook the hand of the colonel, and so the two parted.

It was true enough that in a few more days Henry Osborne would have to stand his trial for wilful murder at the bar of the Old Bailey

Before he returned to his own home,

Colonel Jack proceeded to Lawker's Lane to see Nat Slimcoe. He had ascertained from the Badger, that the former lived on the second floor of the house in question in Lawker's Lane.

"The probability is, that you will, perhaps, find the passage door open, and, in that case, walk straight up into my gentleman's room," said the Badger.

Colonel Jack made up his mind to do this, if possible, and, after a smart walk from Westminster, the locality in question was reached. Lawker's Lane, at the period of which we write, was full of shops of almost every description. Fish, pickles, sweetmeats, old clothes, herbalists, barbers, receivers of stolen goods of every description, were all to be found in Lawker's Lane. Furniture shops, butchers, bakers, cooks shops, they were all there. Perhaps in all London at this time, there never was seen such a rookery. The colonel pretty well knew the place he was going to, and to say the truth, it was not altogether healthy for even he to venture upon such a mission alone, for Slimcoe was, perhaps, one of the greatest ruffians and scoundrels at that time in existence. However, Colonel Jack was bent upon doing all in his power to serve his friend Henry Osborne, and with a bold front he took his way down the lane in question. As he got to the house where Slimcoe resided, he luckily found a child just going into the door with a pint of beer. Patting her gently on the head, he inquired if Mr. Slimcoe was in his room up stairs. The child stared at the question, but made no answer, then going into the passage, she called out—"Carry."

No answer was returned to this, and the little girl then called out still louder—

"Carry. A gentleman for the second floor."

A dirty looking girl with her dress hanging loosely on her, with her hair unkempt, now made her way up the kitchen stairs.

"Never mind," said the colonel. "Don't you trouble yourself. I can go up to Mr. Slimcoe's room, and see if he be at home."

"I know he ain't," said the girl, who the colonel now noticed had a horrible squint.

"I'll go and see."

"But I know he ain't in, cause I see him go out about two hours ago."

"His missus is in perhaps," said the colonel.

"Yes." She thought Mrs. Slimcoe was in.

The colonel made no more ado, but ascended the dirty, ricketty staircase, and upon reaching the second floor, he knocked at the door of the room. No answer was made to this, when he knocked again, still louder.

Presently a miserable, pale-faced looking woman opened the door, and with a frightened look regarded our hero. Wretched as was her appearance, she had evidently at one time possessed a considerable share of beauty, although trouble and privation had robbed her of the greater portion of it.

"I wish to see Mr. Slimcoe—is he in the way?" asked the colonel.

"No, sir."

"When do you expect him?"

The woman hesitated.

"When do you think he will return?"

"He is seldom or ever here; in fact, he is not likely to be back at present," she answered.

"Indeed; how so?"

"He is in—the country."

"Might I inquire where?"

"I do not know."

"You are his wife, are you not?"

The woman slightly coloured at this question, and answered in the affirmative.

"May I have a word or two with you?" said the colonel.

She hesitated still.

"I am a friend," said our hero.

"Oh, perhaps you will walk in."

He did as she desired, and the woman handed him a seat.

It was a miserably furnished apartment, if it could be called furniture at all.

"It is a matter of considerable importance upon which I have called to see your husband—a matter of great importance. Now, understand me, I know he is at present under a cloud, and if he likes to accept of my terms he may be furnished with a munificent sum of money to suffice for a considerable period."

The woman bowed her assent to the proposition, and seemed much pleased, as well she might.

"I do not know what you may require him to do," she said in meek and humble accents, "but I know that he is at present in trouble enough as well as myself—ah, indeed, as well as myself," she said bitterly, and with a look of such utter dejection that spoke more forcibly than the words she had been uttering; then continuing, she said—"But it is not for me to say either one way or the other—he is wilful enough."

"No doubt; but you see, my good woman, I am disposed to make him a friendly offer. He can do me an infinite service if he likes without injury to himself—do you understand, without injury to himself."

"Yes, sir."

"Well, now I have said sufficient to let you see that it would be prudent and to his interest to make an appointment with me," said the colonel.

"Oh, certainly."

"Will you explain to him what I say, and at the same time tell him that I come from Sir Richard Fleetwood?"

"From Sir Richard Fleetwood!" exclaimed

the woman, with much surprise. She had never heard of the baronet although her husband had, and moreover had received several sums from him through his lawyer, Mr. Sharpthorne.

"When will you be here again, sir?"

"What time is it likely I can see your husband?"

"To-morrow morning early."

"What time does he generally go out?"

"Seldom or ever before eight."

"Good! I will be here before that hour then."

"Very well, sir."

And the colonel then took his departure.

———

CHAPTER XXXIX.

THE HIGHWAYMAN AT HOME.—SCENE IN LAWKER'S LANE.

MRS. HALFORD had, as we have already seen, been taken to her new lodgings by her husband's two trusty companions. Whatever her feelings were since the melancholy fact of her husband's occupation had come to her knowledge she kept to herself, and by a strong resolution endeavoured, and indeed succeeded, in comporting herself with calmness and resignation.

In the society of her child she of course found a considerable share of pleasure—for what mother does not? But, as yet, the colonel had not made his appearance at their new lodgings.

It was the most painful part of his duty to return home now and meet his wife for the first time since the discovery made by the sudden entrance of Captain Rignold and his subordinates in his pretty cottage at Hornsey.

However, after his interview with Mrs. Slimcoe he took his way to Brook Street.

Mrs. Halford had kept her place in the greatest order, hourly expecting her husband home. She sat up till a late hour from the first night but of course no Mr. Halford appeared.

Our hero was too busily engaged with his friends at the Swan.

Brook Street was soon reached, and in a few minutes the colonel stood in the drawing-room, on the first-floor.

"Frank!" exclaimed Mrs. Halford, and she rushed into his arms, laying her head upon his chest without another word.

Her husband embraced her fondly, more so, perhaps, than he had done for a considerable time past. Not but what he was generally kind enough to her on most occasions. Tears stood in the eyes of his wife, occasioned partly perhaps from joy and partly from unstrung nerves consequent upon her long vigils during his absence.

"Oh, Frank," she exclaimed, her countenance brightening up as she spoke, and a faint smile playing about her mouth; "oh, Frank, how I have been watching for your return. Hour after hour did I count last night."

"I could not come, my dear, —"

"I know that," she answered, quickly, "or at least I judged so, Frank—I judged so. I knew you had—business—and—that is, you would of course come home—"

The colonel bit his lip.

"I am not complaining, dear—do not imagine that I am complaining—far from it. Come—"

She was about to add something else, but was interrupted by their little girl running into the room, and rushing into her father's arms.

"How do you like the apartments?" said the colonel, as he seated himself, hardly knowing what to begin the conversation with.

"Oh, very well, very well indeed I've brought Curson with me."

"Ah, that's right; I am glad you did so."

"Yes, she's true and faithful, and can be trusted," said his wife.

"Of course; we've had sufficient proofs of that."

Colonel Jack looked over the rooms, which were the very pink of neatness, owing to the care bestowed upon them by his wife, and expressed himself well pleased with them.

"It's a change," he said, somewhat seriously, "a change from the place you have left, my dear; but you would not mind that were it not brought about by a still greater change in your own feelings."

"In my own feelings, Frank?" said his wife, in surprise. "How so?"

"I mean with regard to the prospects—our future prospects. The veil has been let fall, and you have learnt to view me in a new character. Not a pleasing one, perhaps," he said, sadly.

He did not like to enter into this subject, but now he had done so, he was determined to go on.

She made no reply, but turned pale.

"I do not ask you, dearest," he said, in continuation, "I have no right to ask of you to be now the sharer of my fate."

"Frank!" she exclaimed, deprecatingly.

"Nay, hear me out. When you plighted your troth to me, my own sweet girl—when you gave up your maiden vows at the altar—it was not with any idea that you were linking yourself with a lawless character. You will say, perhaps, or at any rate you have a right to, that to you my whole life has been one of unpardonable deceit."

"Gracious, no!" she exclaimed, with energy.

"But you have a right to say this," continued our hero. "You have a most perfect right to do so. It is not worth while now to enter into all the circumstances of our early life; let it suffice to say that you might of course have made a much more respectable match had you been dealt with fairly by me."

"Frank," said Mrs. Halford, "what means all this? Are you tired of me?"

"No, my love; were I to live the longest term allotted to mortality, I should never be tired of you."

A pleasant smile crept over her face at this latter observation.

"No, I am not tired of *you*," he again repeated; "but that is nothing to the purpose. You have every reason to be tired of *me*. I am not so exacting or unreasonable in my nature as to imagine, after the late exposure, that you can view me with the same eyes that you did of yore."

"While you are the same to me," she answered; "*I* do not intend to alter."

Now he smiled with evident satisfaction.

"My dear girl," he said, placing his hands round her temples, "my dear sweet girl!"

His lips trembled slightly as he began this. It was the first time she had ever seen him thus. He went on now, apparently to himself—

"A pretty household deity—trusting, self-sacrificing, an ornament and a joy in any household. Was it well to snatch this treasure, to keep it for one who—Faugh! who does not deserve it?—whose very life, existence, is and has been such as this same child in the world's ways must shudder at, abhor, and contemn? Was it fair to snatch so bright a treasure—for what—to bring it to years of untimely grief, and bitter remorse? Was this well?"

"Do not talk thus, Frank!" she said.

"Nay, but I must talk thus. The whole current of your life must be poisoned."

"Why?"

"By your fatal connection with me. I feel and know this fact, and every hour I become more impressed with it. Every day I feel acutely the great wrong I have done towards you."

"Do not talk thus," said his wife. "To me you have been ever kind and true."

"That may be, dearest; but still the melancholy fact remains the same. You have allied your fate and fortunes to an outcast and a lawless man, and I know that one of your gentle, trusting nature, must stand appalled at the circumstance. You might have been—— Psha, what is the use of talking about what you might have been! We cannot recal the past."

"And therefore let us make the best of the future," said Mrs. Halford, hopefully. "Let us make the best of that future which is in store for us—a future, let us hope, that may have many happy years in store for us."

"It may not be," said Colonel Jack; "I feel that I have no right to insist upon your sharing my fortunes now."

"Are you then tired of me?" said Mrs. Halford, as the tears stood in her eyes.

"Nay, dearest, not so," he answered, as he gently drew her form towards his, "I should never be tired of you, believe me. It is for yourself I am now speaking."

"To you I have rendered up my future life, be it for good or for ill, and I see no cause to regret it. Frank," she said, with considerable warmth, "I see no cause for regrets."

"Generous, noble-minded girl," said Colonel Jack, kissing the speaker affectionately; "it shall be my task to see that your self-sacrificing nature is rewarded for your devotion to so unworthy an object as myself."

CHAPTER XXXIX.

COLONEL JACK'S VISIT TO SLINCOE.

On the following morning our hero rose early, being mindful of his appointment with Slincoe, and took his way towards the lodgings of the murderer.

Now it so happened that Ralph Slincoe had not returned home to his lodgings till

nearly three o'clock in the morning, and then he was considerably the worse for liquor, and in so fierce and angry a mood, that his mistress—for she was not his wife—dared not speak to him, or mention the circumstance of her interview with the colonel. He was so incorrigible a scoundrel, that he did not stop at words, but in his violent moods, which, to speak the truth, were frequent enough, he would inflict blows upon the unfortunate woman who had been silly enough to become his partner.

Colonel Jack, however, in obedience to his agreement with the woman, proceeded to Lawker's Lane.

Now, at the time of his arrival, that classic locality happened to be in a state of considerable uproar.

How the row began, it would puzzle a more learned head than our's to say, or, indeed, what it was about; but when Colonel Jack arrived upon the spot, two women were rolling upon the ground, in close and terrific combat. They were clawing at each other to their heart's content, as they wound their hands in each other's hair.

Several men were inciting them on to further hostilities whenever there was any pause or flagging in the conflict.

"Go it, Moll," said a broad-shouldered man, in a fustian jacket, with a short pipe in his mouth. "Go it, she ain't got no friends."

"You hold your jaw," said a patron of the other belligerent, "and mind your own business."

"It's as much my business as your'n," said he of the fustian jacket. "You ain't everybody I suppose?"

"No more ain't you," retorted the other.

"You ought to be ashamed of yourselves, two great hulking men encouraging women to fight," said Colonel Jack, as he managed to elbow his way through the crowd; "you ought to be ashamed of yourselves. Why don't you separate them?"

"Oh, let them have it out, master. Fair play's a jewel."

At this point of the conversation the two women had risen to their feet, and the one who appeared to have the worst of it had escaped from her antagonist's grasp, leaving her, however, in the possession of a handful of her hair.

Colonel Jack stepped between the two, and interposed his body to separate them.

"You leave us alone," said one of the amazons, putting her arms akimbo, and thrusting her nose in the face of the colonel. "What business is it of your'n?"

"Be quiet, woman," said the colonel. "Is this feminine or decent, women fighting in the street like this?"

"What right had she to call me a hyena?" asked the woman.

"So you are, a grinning savage hyena," said the other belligerent.

"I don't run arter other chaps," said her antagonist.

"Perhaps not, marm, because you have enough of your own," said the other, assuming a quiet, mocking tone, as she arranged her hair, and wiped the blood off her face behind Colonel Jack.

"You are a pretty baggage to talk, I'm sure," said amazon number one.

"As good as you any day of the week," said number two.

"Come now," said the other, argumentatively, "barring that I'm a thief and fond of the men, what have you got to say against me?"

"Silence!" said the colonel; "go to your own homes, and let there be an end of this."

A violent altercation now took place with several others that came up who appeared to be friends of the two women, and our hero, finding that it would, in all probability, be a long job, ending in a series of vituperations and recriminations for an hour or two at the very least, was glad to take his way from the scene of action towards the abode of Ralph Slimcoe.

Upon his knocking at the outer door, it was answered by the same slatternly girl who had presented herself in the passage upon the occasion of his first visit.

Upon his inquiring for Slimcoe, the girl looked surprised and alarmed.

"Never mind," said the colonel, "I know he is in for I have an appointment with him—there, that will do."

And he ran up stairs without any further observations.

Knocking at Slimcoe's door, he received no answer; he knocked again, louder, still no answer; again, another knock, this time in so loud a tone that the inmates of the room must have thought the door was likely to be battered down.

The woman opened it, her features indicative of the utmost fright.

"Is he in?" inquired the colonel.

"Hush!" said the woman, in an under tone, "hush! I hardly know what to say to you, sir."

"Why?"

"Because I have not been able to tell him of your coming."

"Indeed; how's that?"

"He did not come home till three this morning, and then—"

"Well?"

"He had a drop in."

The colonel knew the speaker was a native of the Emerald Isle from the last expression.

"It matters not about your having mentioned the subject to him, seeing that you know but very little about the purport of my visit. Tell him that there is some one wishes to see him."

"Would you mind calling again?"

"No time like the present," said the colonel.

"But, sir—"

"Now, you go and say I am here. Where is he?"

"In the inner room."

"Asleep?"

"Yes, sir."

"What, did not my loud knocking awaken him?"

"No, sir, he was too soundly asleep."

"Well, go in, there's a good woman, and wake him."

She hesitated, and said—

"It's almost more than I dare do."

"Wherefore?"

"He is of such a violent nature when once put out."

"Umph! I cannot spare time to come again."

"Very well, sir. Will you wait here, sir?" said the woman.

"Certainly."

She went into the inner room, where the man lay upon a wretched truckle bedstead, in a deep sleep.

The woman shook him several times before she succeeded in awakening him to consciousness.

"Ralph—Ralph!" she cried, "there's a gentleman—"

"What?" exclaimed the man, in evident alarm, "who—what?" he repeated, as he rubbed his eyes, and stared at the woman with alarm and fear depicted on his unprepossessing features, "what do you mean?"

"A gentleman, Ralph," said the woman, mildly.

"Confound you; you've not said I was at home or in the way."

"Ye-es," stammered out the woman.

"You fool; you dolt, I'll—"

"Hush! don't, he is outside."

The man leapt out of bed, hurried on his things, and looked to see if there was any mode of escape.

"Where is he?" asked the man, in a hoarse voice.

"Outside, in the passage."

"Curse you; why did you not say I was out?"

"I could not, Ralph—indeed, I could not. The gentleman came here by appointment."

"By appointment! What, has he been here before?"

"Yes; he was here yesterday."

"Why did you not tell me then?" said Slimcoe, fixing upon her a malevolent look.

"I should have done so, only—"

"Only what, you fool?"

"You were not in a humour to hear anything last night."

"Oh, indeed; what a pity."

"Do not be alarmed," said Colonel Jack, stepping into the outer room—for he had overheard the foregoing conversation. "Do not be alarmed; I am a friend."

"Oh," exclaimed Slimcoe, sullenly, who saw it was now impossible for him to avoid his visitor, "I will be with you directly," and in a minute or two more he emerged from his bedroom into the one where our hero stood. Slimcoe regarded his visitor with a look of inquiry, and gave a sort of rough recognition of him.

"Your name is Ralph Slimcoe, I believe," said the colonel; and perceiving the man gave a look of alarm, and did not seem disposed to give an immediate reply, he said in continuation—"Oh, do not be alarmed. I am no officer of justice."

The man turned pale at this, and our hero observed his lips slightly trembled.

"Do not be alarmed. I am a friend," said the colonel.

"Oh, yes," said Slimcoe, "I understand—a friend—ah! ah! I have not got too many of them."

"No, I suppose not. Few of us have in this world. Still you see I want a few minutes private conversation with you."

"Oh, indeed," said Slimcoe, regarding the speaker with another dubious look.

"Yes," and here he glanced towards the woman. "And I suppose we had better adjourn to some—"

"Oh, I see; not here—exactly—of course."

He put on his hat mechanically, and stood before his visitor.

The colonel rose and proceeded towards the door. Slimcoe followed him, telling the woman that he would be back in half an hour or so.

Down the creaking and rotten stairs they proceeded, and shortly left the house. They then repaired to the parlour of a neighbouring public-house which was well known to the colonel.

A morning draught was called for by way of a cooler to the parched throat of Slimcoe, when our hero proceeded to open the business—which he thought it desirable to do in a roundabout way, like other diplomatists.

"You know Sir Richard Fleetwood," said the colonel.

The man stared and answered in the affirmative.

"Ah, so I thought."

"Are you a friend of his?" inquired Slimcoe.

"Well, yes, I may say so, seeing that I have known him since I was a stripling."

"Oh—ah—I see; then of course you are."

"Ahem! yes; but I am not exactly in the same suit upon the subject that brings me to you."

"Umph!" said Slimcoe, who was still in the dark.

"I am a friend of Henry Osborne's," said the colonel.

Had a thunderbolt fallen at his feet, or a gloomy chasm opened before him, he could not possibly have been more frightened than he was at the words just uttered by our hero. He trembled and shook like an aspen bough agitated by the passing breeze.

"Now do not be alarmed," said the colonel, "for that is quite unnecessary. As I have just now observed, I am a friend of Mr. Osborne's, and am anxious to get him off. The more so as he is an innocent man."

"Innocent, is he?" said Slimcoe.

"Certainly, you know that as well and better than I do."

"I?"

"Yes."

"What do you mean?"

"You know who committed the—the murder."

"Indeed. You are clever, you are," said Slimcoe, trying to assume a bantering and defiant tone.

"Now do not let us misunderstand each other," said the colonel seriously. "You know, undoubtedly, all about this Cow Cross murder, and of course there is no difficulty in ensuring your conviction."

"My conviction," said Slimcoe; the nervous twitching of his mouth giving unmistakeable evidence of his anxiety and trepidation."

"Certainly. You know me, I suppose?"

"Yes—Colonel Jack," answered Slimcoe, glumply.

"Well, that knife found near the spot originally belonged to me. You know that also."

"Not I. I do not know anything of the sort."

"Well, I do, and that's more important. Now look here, Slimcoe. I am the last man in the world, I hope, to peach; still I cannot allow my friend Osborne to be executed for a crime of which he is perfectly guiltless. What I want of you is a written confession."

The man rose from his seat and threw it from him with disdain, as his features became distorted with rage and a most diabolical expression passed over them.

"Confession," he iterated; "Confession—ah—well, that is a good one, indeed. Is that the fool's errand you have come upon? By the Lord, but you had better look to yourself."

"Now, it is no use your going on in this way, Slimcoe. Listen to me for a minute or so. Hear my proposition, and you can, of course, please yourself about accepting the terms. Should you refuse, I promise you that there shall be no information given against you by me."

"Umph. Well, go on," said Slimcoe, a little wrathful—"Go on."

"Henry Osborne's an innocent man."

His listener seemed to nod his assent to this proposition.

"All I want is, to prove his innocence, without compromising you."

He gave another nod at this second proposition.

"And I have been ransacking my brains how this was to be accomplished. You know, I suppose, through Mr. Sharpthorne, that in the event of Osborne's acquittal, an enormous amount of wealth, bequeathed by the old miser, Jabez Cudge, will fall to his share."

"Yes, I've heard that."

"Very well. That being the case, Osborne can well afford to give you a handsome sum, to live abroad for the remainder of your life."

"Oh, he's very kind, I'm sure," said Slimcoe, with an ill disguised sneer.

"Not at all so. He won't do so without some consideration."

"Ah, I see, without one on us swing instead of him."

"No, no. I don't want either you or Parker to be brought into any difficulties, far from it. You can both go abroad, but, previous to your doing so, leave a written paper, stating that Henry Osborne is guiltless of the crime. I don't know that there is any occasion for you to confess yourselves as being connected with it, but that will be for us to determine when we can settle the bargain."

"I don't see myself how you can expect me to sign a paper, which will only be putting my head in a noose. It's all very well to talk about going abroad, but talking's one thing, and getting clear off is another. Even supposing my mate were disposed to make the trial."

"Well, you can ask him. Consider the matter over, and I'll see you to-morrow."

Slimcoe hesitated.

"What say you? A handsome sum shall be provided for you, and you'll have no cause to regret leaving the country, for I can tell you that you are already suspected."

"Ah!" exclaimed Slimcoe, turning sharp round upon the speaker. "Suspected! Have you—"

"No," answered Colonel Jack, "you need be under no apprehension of my giving any information against you. I believe I may say, with truth, that I am the last man to do that."

"I don't say you would," he answered.

"Well, now consider my proposition over, and I will see you again to-morrow. Will that do?"

"If you like."

"I would rather not drive it off too long, for time runs short."

"To-morrow be it, then," said Slimcoe, gruffly.

"About this time?" inquired the colonel.

"Yes. That will do very well."

"Then I will be here to-morrow morning about the same time."

"So be it."

The two then parted, and our hero took his way towards Goswell Street, there to see the redoubtable Squabshot, who was his only, or, rather, chief means of communication with Henry Osborne.

When he arrived at the latter's lodgings at Goswell Street, he found little Squabby out. The fact was, he had gone to Newgate to see Osborne.

The colonel left word that he would be there again in the after part of the day, or towards evening.

Now, it so turned out since Osborne's incarceration, that Squabshot had proved himself a most sincere friend to his ci devant fellow lodger, and there was scarcely any office but which he was willing to undertake to assist Osborne, indeed, he was indefatigable in his exertions. Not that they were of much service in conducting his case, rather the contrary, for he would insist upon thrusting his evidence upon both the lawyers, for, agreeable to his resolutions, Osborne had employed another solicitor as well as Mr. Sharpthorne.

This gentleman had been recommended by Squabshot, and was working indefatigably for the defence.

As a line of argument to be used by the counsel, the lawyer was preparing a series of cases, to show the doubt and fallacy of circumstantial evidence.

By a singular circumstance, Squabshot himself happened to tumble over one that he thought bore upon the case, and, indeed, there is no doubt but what it did.

Squabshot, after his visit to Osborne, returned home to his lodgings in Goswell Street, and there learned that Colonel Jack had called in the early part of day, upon this he determined to wait in until the colonel came for the second time.

It was evening before he did so, and our hero informed Squabshot of the fact of his interview with Ralph Slimcoe, and wrote a long account of the same, to be given to Osborne upon the occasion of Squabshot's next visit to Newgate.

Upon the colonel leaving Goswell Street, Squabshot rose to accompany the colonel on his way home. They strolled on towards Islington, which, at this time was a suburban village. In the distance they observed Canonbury House, which was a well known place of entertainment, and most frequented by parties of pleasure, for it had large grounds and gardens attached to it.

Colonel Jack and Squabshot went their way towards Canonbury House, and entered the parlour thereof, which contained a large bay window. Several individuals were there, and in one of the capacious arm-chairs sat a stout individual, dressed in a suit of black, with a white neckcloth. He seemed to be the oracle of the room, for he said in an oracular tone of voice, as he laid down the paper which he had been reading—

"Say what you please, Master Knippins, but circumstantial evidence is at all times a most doubtful thing—very doubtful; and this case of Osborne, is, after all, a very doubtful one."

"I don't see it, Mr. Fubbles," said he, who had been addressed as Knippins.

"Ah, that's because you want experience," said the latter. "Now, I will just relate one story, at least, it's not a story, but a fact, the whole particulars of which I have in my possession at the present moment."

"Were they in relation to any crime?" inquired Colonel Jack.

"Yes, sir," said Mr. Fubbles, casting his eyes up to the ceiling.

"I should be glad to hear them, sir," said Squabshot.

Mr. Fubbles cleared his throat, and related that which is detailed in the next chapter.

CHAPTER XL.

CURIOUS CASE OF CIRCUMSTANTIAL EVIDENCE.

"THE history I am about to give you," said Fubbles, "occurred in this very room at the time of the wars between the cavaliers and roundheads."

The company gave a start of surprise.

"Sir John Barnard was a cavalier, who happened, at the time of which I speak, to be staying at this very house. He was acquainted with one, Sir George Hampton, a roundhead. In former years they had been good friends, and hearing that Sir George was in the neighbourhood, Sir John Barnard, out of old feelings of friendship, sent a note inviting his quondam friend to dinner in this very room. It was accepted, and on the evening in question the two knights were seated in this room.

"It might be eight o'clock; the bay window, which as you see almost touched the ground, was open, and the twilight began to draw in.

"Country gentlemen had stronger heads and better constitutions than they have now, and hard drinking was then in its full vogue. Both the knights carefully avoided mention-ing the name of Lucy, for it appeared that they had been suitors for the hand of a maiden of that name.

"The conversation ran upon those all-absorbing topics of politics and religion, that were then inseparably interwoven together, and the effect of the good Rhine wine soon began to be apparent.

"A violent altercation ensued, which was wound up by these words—

"'It is well thou art, George Hampton,' said Sir John. 'Thou hast many virtues. There, give me thine hand.'

"'Take it; but listen to my warning voice. You hasten on to your own destruction—precipices yawn around you on every side. Listen to me for the last time; renounce thine evil ways, thine outworn creed—return to thy duties in Westminster—and if thou must needs raise thine arm, let it not be against thy country, or thy dearest friend may become thy deadliest foe.'

"In this strain ran on the dialogue, and flask after flask of Rhenish wine was emptied of its contents, till the two knights scarcely retained the exercise of their reason.

"If the Roman adage respecting anger be true, it is equally so of intoxication—a no less brief frenzy.

"Harsh words, accompanied by loud vituperations and menacing gestures, passed on both sides, and so violent was the dispute, that the landlord of the inn, apprehensive of some ill effects from the quarrel, under the pretence of having heard them call, twice made his appearance in the room.

"They protracted their revels till a late hour of the night, and Sir John, who was anxious to lose no time in joining the King's parliament at York, seemed as though he would be in no fit state to commence his journey at daybreak, as he had designed.

"After the excitement occasioned by their ample potations, and the heat of the argument, and overcome by that of the weather, the disputants, however, fell into a profound sleep.

"At what precise hour it commenced, and how long it lasted, is doubtful, but to Sir John it appeared drawn out to an eternity by an appalling dream. He fancied that the floor was covered with a pool of blood—that his feet were dabbling in the hot gore—that he heard a stream of blood, first plashing, and then big gouts dropping into it from the hilt of a rapier, and that rapier—as in the case of an animal magnetist the veil is sometimes only partially withdrawn, so, though all else was dark about him, that rapier and its clotted blade gleamed with a crimson lustre. Like Macbeth's dagger, or Cassandra's axe, it appeared to him in form so palpable that he could not mistake its identity. He knew it by the peculiar character of the basket-work of the hilt, and by a tassel or wristband. which was of azure, the favourite colour of Lucy, supposed to have been knotted by her own hand, but whether in love or friendship, or a mere unmeaning piece of *galanterie*, I will not presume to say. You have heard of the death watch by the bed of some departing man—know, that one of the ingenious tortures of old was the filtering of water from a height on the head of a criminal, till it wore his life away in agony—may have read, in the works of the greatest of modern poets, a grim love scene of his with misery, where he says that—

" Her tears burnt like points of frozen lead :"

but no living anatomization, no dissection of the body nerve by nerve, could equal or compare with that drop, drop, drop, from his own rapier, in regularly repeated intervals, that tortured his brain to frenzy. So horridly vivid was this vision, that it dissipated all the fumes of intoxication, and roused him from his heavy and deathlike trance. The cold, white, sickly light of morning broke in upon the scene of the lasts night's debauch. His sight as well as his senses were awhile imperfect. The objects on the table, the fragments of the feast, the empty flasks and broken glasses, swam indistinctly before him. At last his filmly eyes fixed themselves on the sheath of a rapier lying on his left—the sheath only !

" A dreadful thought crossed his mind ; there was a dire conviction in it; a flash that precedes the tempest. He started—raised himself erect on his chair—turned his bewildered gaze on the opposite one. How shall I paint his consternation—his despair, when he perceived his friend—his eyes lustreless and wide open, his mouth fallen ; with a look—it could not be mistaken—and the rapier, his own rapier, buried deep in his side. With a countenance hardly less wan than that of the dead, and a fixed, stony stare, like that of one who had seen Medusa, and as incapable of motion he regarded him.

" Cases have occurred in which drunkards have committed crimes under the effect of inebriation, of which they were unconscious on the return of reason, and even in dreams, so vivid is the impression of the sensorium of the brain, that sleep-walkers have acted what the imagination presented.

" Did the possibility of such an occurence suggest itself to Sir John Barnard, or was his horror too overwhelming for all reflection ? Without attempting to dive into his thoughts, that seem to defy analysis, I shall only say that he was found as I have described him by a waiter of the inn, who had been desired to call him an hour after day-break, and who came to announce that his horse was ready caparisoned for his journey. Sir John

Barnard, in seizing this moment, might have escaped ; but had he been sufficiently master of himself to calculate his danger, he would have spurned all idea of flight, and by it for ever sullying his good name ; for flight would have converted suspicion, however strong, into the certainty of guilt.

" An alarm was soon given : the report of the murder roused all that the inn contained from their beds. Nor them alone ; but the rumour, spreading with the rapidity of wild fire through London brought numbers of its inhabitants to the spot.

" The Puritans mustered in great strength : they flocked together, uttering loud imprecations against the king's party, and denounced this murder as only the outbreak of a conspiracy to extirpate all godly persons in the kingdom. They could scarcely be constrained from wreaking their vengeance on Sir John Barnard by summary justice—an exercise of Lynch law.

" But the more wary, though not the more moderate, of the parliamentarians, who hailed this as a most fortunate event for the propagation of the good cause, and the means of irritating a general feeling against the Royalists, as well as stimulated by the desire of seeing a cavalier perish on the scaffold, saved him from the fury of the mob, and tumultuously dragged him along to the castle, where, for the present, we shall leave him.

" The news of the murder of Sir George Hampton quickly reached parliament. He had been well acquainted with Cromwell, who, from his intimacy with Walter and connection with Ireton, was not destitute of interest in the House. Notwithstanding its mighty preparations for the ensuing struggle, it found time to occupy itself with an accusation against one of its own members, when that member was a royalist. A parliamentary commission—which may probably be discovered among the discarded papers of the Record Office, that are now fetching such large prices at auction—was issued, and three commissioners dispatched with a considerable force to inquire into the circumstances : the selection of this trio of course fell on men devoted to the interest of the good cause, and one of them having smarted under the ridicule of Sir John Barnard, was animated with no common share of hostility against him. In less than a month after these events, this inquisition opened its proceedings. It is not my intention to make a legal report of all that passed at that tribunal, or do more than to recapitulate the facts already in possession of the reader.

" Certainly, never was circumstantial evidence so convincingly strong as against the prisoner at the bar. The letter written the day before the meeting, and found in the pocket of the murdered knight, though it

might well have borne a different interpretation, was construed into a premeditated design to entrap him into a net—a plot to pick a quarrel with him—in order that a rival might thus free himself from a rival; and if he did not take advantage of the means planned and offered him for escape, it was attributed to an interposition of Providence, who, as he struck dead Ananias, chose in this case to visit him with a no less fatal paralysis. Self-sacrifice and disinterestedness were virtues for which none gave him credit. The radicals of those times knew too well their own hearts. The two knights were also known to entertain widely different opinions in politics and religion—sufficient grounds, even between the nearest relatives, for the commission of any crime. That these topics had led to a violent dispute was proved by the landlord of the inn, a witness to the quarrel, and who was anxious by the conviction of the accused to wipe off any stigma that might attach itself to his house. None such, indeed, could fall on him or his; for the pockets of the deceased were unrifled; and, as an unanswerable and damning proof of guilt, there was the unsheathed rapier, that required no name engraved on its hilt to sum up the long catalogue of proofs against the ill-fated cavalier.

"Executions are now-a-days become a drug among novelists. There is no favourite work of fiction published but describes one in all its minutiæ; for me to do so would be a work of supererogation. I shall not even say whether the headsman or the hangman did his office on the occasion. I shall not describe the tolling of the deathbell from the cathedral ; or picture the city alive with all its population, at an hour when they had better have been quietly slumbering in their beds, and thronging the market-place, the roofs of the houses, the tops of the churches, —waiting with a savage delight to witness that degrading and disgusting exhibition— a headless trunk, or a swinging corpse. All I shall tell you is, that the noble and accomplished Cavalier prepared himself to die with all the firmness of a martyr—that a puritanical preacher endeavoured to extort from him a confession, finding which fail, he tried to shake the serenity of his soul, but equally in vain, by his denunciations of the eternal punishment ; and I shall add, that Sir John Barnard maintained his innocence to the last, and that his last words were, ' God save the king.'

" It is now time to rescue from ignominy the memory of an innocent man, and clear up the mystery of this horrible murder.

" There was a certain Covenanter, one of those If-Christ-had-not-died-to-save-thee-thou-hadst-been-*damned* Bareboneses (whose baptismal name was rightly abridged of all but the two final syllables), who, during Charles's visit to Scotland had migrated to Edinburgh from the barren highlands, with no other property than his kilt. He was endowed, like many of these mountaineers, with a certain rude eloquence—for the word will follow the spirit—that made some impression in that capital. The theme of this zealot's long prayers, and still longer sermons, was, popery, worldly pomps and vanities and the wailing and gnashing of teeth, to which were predestined in the next world all who differed from him in opinion in this. Elated by the success he met with from his new flock, this Highland shepherd, like the apostles of old, looked upon himself as chosen by the Lord for a divine mission—a crusade among the infidel English.

" Through the contributions of the godly, and collections made here and there on the road, he had contrived to reach Newcastle, which, being full of royalists, for some seditious language he was thrown into prison, where he continued for some months.

" On his liberation, atter being put in the pillory, and then publicly whipped out of the city, his heart, swelling with the pride of having suffered for conscience' sake, and burning with a thirst of revenge, he made his way to London, which he entered the day before that fixed for the meeting of our two knights. Then he held forth in Tomb-land ; but at his barbarous dialect (though I am aware that it is considered the only pure English) brought him only ridicule instead of pence, the wounds of his soul became still more exacerbated.

" On that eventful evening, then, behold him wandering through the streets in search of some shelter for the night. Chance—and an evil one it was—led him, in his peregrinations, into the Market-place, and past the Canonbury House ; and then the missionary, turning his eyes towards the open window, perceived the two friends partaking of their somewhat sumptuous repast. The table, covered with choice viands and flasks of wine, and the splendid dress of the Cavalier, and his plumed hat and rapier, inflamed the Scot with a more than common jealousy cf worldly distinction, and hatred of their possessors.

" Ragged and hungry, he looked upon all this luxury as an insult to his poverty and destitution, and he was half angry with his own spirit when he could not help confessing to himself a longing desire to allay his hunger with some of the knight's supper, and assuage his thirst with the Rhenish wine that sparkled in the goblets, as the bottles were continually handed from one to the other of the carousers. He was too proud to beg ; and had twice approached close to the window, in the hope that the sight of his wretchedness would have extorted, from pity or charity, a single glass of wine, or perhaps a portion of the repast. But Sir George beckoned him away as an intruder ; and the heat of the controversy, and the coming on of night, were the cause of his being unobserved the second time he stood leaning on the window-frame, and looking daggers at the unconscious pair. He for some hours paced the Market-place backwards and forwards ; every time he passed the open window at Canonbury House, worked up to a higher pitch of fury.

" St. Peter's Church, also, its façade ornamented with the heads and figures of saints —an abomination in the eyes of the Covenanters—and which were afterwards mutilated by the brutal and Vandalic spirit of the ignorant and besotted Puritans, still more inflamed his zeal and fanaticism.

" As the shades of evening advanced, he sate himself down under the window ; and though he could not follow their argument, could distinguish the voices of the two disputants, and the word conventiclers, and other contemptuous expressions applied to his countrymen, fell on his ear.

" At length the voices ceased ; the two knights had sunk into a profound slumber ; and he then formed the diabolical project of murder.

" Everything combined to favour the project.

" The candles had long since burnt out ; the hotel was still ; not a soul stirring.

" He raised himself up ; threw his leg over the low window frame ; and found himself in the room—so bright the moonlight, that it was sufficiently illuminated to perceive the sleeping knights.

"Should he kill both, or only one?—and which?

"The insults he had received decided *this* question.

"But a new and rapturous idea here flashed across his mind: he could, by one stroke, make two offerings to the Lord. Suffice it for *him* to sacrifice one victim, and the law would do justice on the other. He therefore put his hand on the rapier, and drawing it, replaced the sheath. He then moved, with bare and noiseless feet, towards Sir George, who was lying with coat unbuttoned, and shirt open, and taking a deliberate aim at his breast, plunged the weapon once, and yet again, in his heart.

"There he left it; a single groan, and all was over, and the assassin in the square as before.

"Having now brought this very remarkable cause to an end, a few comments are indispensable. And, first, as to circumstantial evidence in general.

"The chain of circumstances against the murdered Sir John Barnard—for a murder it must be called—though sanctioned by official forms, was strong and intricately interwoven in his case; and I shall not have sundered the links in vain, should future juries, through my means, be made more cautious how they found their verdicts on such evidence alone

"If historians are allowed to attribute certain events to certain causes, selecting from among conflicting ones such as are likely to have had the most influence—perhaps looking through the vista of two centuries at an obscure and isolated occurrence—I shall not be blamed for filling up, in my own way, the skeleton.

"I have, however, adhered to the main facts, as they were detailed to me by a friend, who received them from a clergyman, now holding one of the family livings of the Barnards.

"One thing more: I should be wanting in my character of a reporter if I omitted to state, that among the archives of that house has been carefully preserved an affidavit, containing the substance of what I have thrown into narrative, sworn before a magistrate by the tramper in his last moments. He died in the same year with Cromwell, and had, for a considerable time before his death, obtained great weight in the Scotch presbytery, and, by his cant and fanaticism, established a great reputation for sanctity.

"I have only to add, that the confiscation of the estates of Sir John Barnard was reversed at the Restoration, and that, together with this noble mansion, they are still enjoyed—and long may they be enjoyed—by those of his name—a name as bright and unsullied as any in the annals of England."

The narrator ceased, and gazed round the room at his astonished auditory.

"You have related a case, sir," said Colonel Jack, "that bears directly upon the one before us in to-day's paper—I am alluding to the Cow Cross murder."

"Ah," said Mr. Fubbles, "precisely. There is the knife traced to this young man, and upon my soul I believe he is as innocent as any of us in this room." ·

"I am sure of it," said Squabshot; "I feel quite convinced of it."

"Would it be asking you too much, sir, for a written narrative of this case of Sir John Barnard?" asked the colonel.

"Not at all, sir—I should be happy to furnish you with the particulars. I am in the legal profession."

And the speaker handed his card to Colonel Jack, who placed it carefully in his pocketbook, and said that he would do himself the pleasure of waiting upon him at his chambers on the following day. After this, he and Squabshot took their departure from Canonbury House.

CHAPTER XLI.

SCENE IN THE OLD HOUSE IN WEST STREET.—
JONATHAN WILD ON THE TRACK.

WHEN Ralph Slimcoe returned to his lodgings in Lawker's Lane, he glared at the miserable woman with whom he cohabited, and fixed upon her a look of the utmost ferocity.

"So," he exclaimed, "you'd turn traitress, would you?"

"No, Ralph," answered the woman.

"Liar!" exclaimed Slimcoe. "Have you not brought this man here, who knows—who—"

"I did not cause him to come here, believe me."

"Psha!—who made the appointment but you?"

"I did it for the best, Ralph. The gentleman told me that he would make you a handsome allowance for some service which you were to render him. I did it for the best."

"Ugh! the best, indeed. You'd play me false—that's what you'd do—play me false. How else could he have known where to find me?"

"Not from me—not from me, I swear," answered the woman. "Until he came here I never either saw or heard of him before."

Slimcoe thrust the woman from him, and struck her a severe blow as he did so; after which he hastily left the house.

Slimcoe was quite at a loss to divine how Colonel Jack had become acquainted with his present abode.

He proceeded to Balasco's, the Jew's, at the Old House at West Street, believing that he should there be able to find out something about the causse of Colonel Jack's unexpected visit.

"Mershy on me, my son," said Isaac Balasco, "vat could have brought you here? Vere is Parker?"

"In the country—up a tree—or whatever else you like to term it. He's mizzled—out of the way."

"Ah, itsh wishe of him to do so—very wishe," said Balasco. "And you?"

"Has any one been here for me?"

"No."

"Not any one?"

"Not a soul."

"Are you sure?"

"Oh, yesh. Do you think I would deceive you?"

"I should hope not."

"Vy do you ask?" said the Jew.

"Because Colonel Jack has been to Lawker's Lane," said Slimcoe.

"Colonel Jack!" exclaimed the Jew.

"Yes."

"When?"

"To-day—the first thing this morning—and he is coming again to-morrow."

"What for?"

"To make terms with me for a confession."

"A confession of what?"

"The Cow Cross affair."

"Ah, he's kind."

"Oh, he offers me a good reward."

"To put your neck in a halter—eh?"

"No, to go abroad."

"Ah, if you can escape and get clear off."

"Precisely, that is assuming I am able to do so."

While this conversation was taking place, a lad of about sixteen suddenly made his appearance into the presence of the Jew and Slimcoe, with terror depicted on his countenance.

"Hilloa, vat ish the matter, Nat?" said Belasco.

The boy was almost breathless, but managed to gasp out a few sentences which were significant enough.

"Jonathan Wild—Coming this way."

"What for? asked Slimcoe, as he turned deadly pale.

"For you," said the lad.

"How do you know?"

"Heard all about it," said Nat; "been to your house and seen Moll."

"Ah!" exclaimed Slimcoe.

"Yes, seen Moll, and—"

"Well?"

"She said as how you might have come on here."

"She did," exclaimed Slimcoe, striking his forehead. "Curse her, I knew she was treacherous—curse her. Parker always had his doubts."

"How came you to hear this?' asked Slimcoe.

"I was in the top room, and hearing the voice of Moll, I looked over the banisters and listened."

"And what did you hear?"

"I heard Moll in conversation with—"

"Jonathan Wild?"

"No, not with him, but with one of his men."

"Gracious heavens, can this be true?" exclaimed Slimcoe, now fully believing in the perfidy of the woman. "She shall—"

"What, Ralph?" asked the Jew.

"Die for it, as sure as I am a living man."

"And so," continued the boy, "as I heard she say as how you were gone on to West Street, most likely, I thought they would soon be on your lay, and thinks I, it would be best to cut off and let you know how matters stood."

The murderer was so panic struck that he hardly seemed capable of moving.

"It is no use standing here," said the lad, "for I have only headed them by a few minutes, and they will be here directly."

"This vay—thish vay," said the Jew.

"Where?"

"To the cellars below"

"Suppose they search there?" said the affrighted man.

"There is a way out to Coriander street."

"Is there?"

"Certainly. Come—follow me."

The Jew led the way towards the rear of the house, and opened a trap door in a dark passage, and pointed to the gloomy vault below for Slimcoe to descend. While this was taking place, a noise was heard in the passage, and Jonathan Wild made his entrance into the house. Slimcoe had scarcely time left him to descend into the vault, and Balasco hastily closed the trap door, when he immediately took his way back to the room used for his own particular purpose. Jonathan Wild and his followers were already there.

"Ralph Slimcoe," said the thieftaker, in a gruff voice.

"He ish not here, Mishter Wild," said the Jew.

"None of your nonsense, Ike," said Wild. "Produce him."

"I swear to you he is not here."

"I know he is not *here*," said Wild. "That is, not in this room nor in the next, for the matter of that, but he is on the premises, and is wanted. That is enough."

"Ash I hope to be shaved, Mishter Wild,

Ralph Slimcoe is not on these premises. Nowheres."

"Bah! You lie, you old canting hypocrite ; you know you lie."

"I shwear it ish true."

The thieftaker stamped his foot in a violent rage. "Search the place," he said to his men, as he proceeded from the room, and went up stairs accompanied by his companions. When he got into the passage he conversed in a whisper to one or two of them, and three of them left the house while Wild and the remaining officers went up stairs and instituted a rigid search in every nook and corner of each apartment, but no Slimcoe was visible.

"Umph !" exclaimed Wild. "The bird has flown, so it would appear—and whither ? This rascally Jew has secret places in this respectable establishment of his that would puzzle the wisest man in the world to find out. Let us go down stairs ;" and with this Wild took his way back to the Jew's apartment.

"Look here, you old rascal. You have got a lot of rat holes in these premises of yours ; and it is in one of these that Slimcoe is concealed. This fellow is charged with murder, and unless you give him up you will be indicted as an accomplice, and I shall take you into custody."

"Mershy, " said the Jew. " You would never harm an innocent man, Mr. Wild. As I am a sinner, I shwear to you that I am guiltless of any knowledge about Ralph Slimcoe. I swear it.'?

"Of what value is your oath ?"

"I would not lay the charge of perjury upon my soul—not the charge of perjury," said the Jew.

"Bah !" You would be very particular about that or anything else, to serve your purpose. Come, none of your gammon upon me, because it will not do. Where is this man ? Produce him, or else you shall away in his stead."

"Mishter Wild, have some consideration. Some mershy. I know nothing at all about him."

"Why, you lying old rascal, he was here not half an hour since. What am I saying, he was here not ten minutes since."

"Oh, Father Abraham, what will people say ?" said the Jew, holding up his hands in astonishment.

"What will you not say to serve your purpose ?"

"He ish not here, Mr. Wild, or I would produce him at once. But I shwear to you that he ish not here,"

"Do you deny that he was here some quarter of an hour since ?"

Balasco hesitated, and then said—

"Well, I scorn to tell a falsehood. He was here about half an hour ago, but he has left now.'

"How long since ?"

"A few minutes before you came in."

"And, pray, what made him leave ?"

"I did not ask him."

"Which way did he go ? Not by the front entrance, that is very certain."

The Jew hesitated again as Jonathan Wild scanned his features.

"I did not notice which way he went," said Balasco. "I only know that he left this room, and said he was sorry, but he did not shay for what, neither did I inquire, for I don't upon my customer's private affairs."

"You are monstrously particular. A considerate man, no doubt. Now, it so happens, that I know he's not left at all. What say you to that ?"

"I do not know what you wish me to say. I dare not open my mouth, without fear of giving offence."

"I don't want you to say anything, for my experience tells me that your word is not worth a bunch of cabbage stalks. All I want of you is, to produce this man, the murderer, Ralph Slimcoe."

"Murderer !" exclaimed the Jew, holding up his hands. "Ish it possible."

"Yes,' said Wild, "and you know all about it as well as I do, you old hypocrite."

"I declare I do not."

"Where is the man, Slimcoe?"

"I don't know."

"And where are your secret passages ?"

"I have none."

"Where are they ?" said Wild, stamping his foot, in a rage.

"I declare most positively that I have none."

"Impudent liar—do you thus seek to deceive me. Seize him."

Two of the officers laid hold of the Jew, who trembled in every limb.

"Vat ish this for—vat am I to be seized hold of for in this way ? I have not committed any offence."

"Take care of him till my return," said Wild; "and if this man is not found or forthcoming, we will find means to rouse his recollection a little."

Jonathan Wild now proceeded towards Coriander Street, which was the centre of a labyrinth of streets and courts, that it would be a task, almost amounting to an impossibility, for anyone to catch a flying thief in such a locality.

Jonathan Wild had heard that, from a secret passage in the rear of Balasco's house, there was a possibility of any one concealed therein making their escape. Where the termination of this passage was he could not tell, but he believed it to be near the neighbourhood of Coriander Street. In this he was right. The subterranean passage led into the vaults of a house in a low court, running out of the street in question. This court was arched over, and the upper stories of the houses went over the archway, which was of a pitch-like darkness, having no lights to dissipate the gloom.

Ralph Slimcoe, who had found himself in the vaults beneath the Jew's house, did not feel disposed to run the risk of staying there, as he was fearful that Jonathan Wild would find out his hiding place; he, therefore, made his way as fast as he could towards Coriander Street.

The passage which led to the court out of this street, was entered by means of a grating. Ralph Slimcoe hastened along the gloomy vaults, then through the passage leading therefrom, until he reached the grating in question, when in a minute or two more he found himself in the vaulted passage which led into Coriander Street. Indeed there was no other entrance from it.

When Ralph Slimcoe got into the court, he heard the sound of voices in Coriander Street. He paused and listened.

"It should be somewhere hereabouts," said one of the speakers; "at least from what I have heard."

"Ah, gammon and all, Jem," said another voice. "Neither you or any one else knows the back way from Isaac Balasco's crib."

"No, that's true enough," answered the other speaker; "but it's somewhere hereabouts, that's certain. Did the guv'ner say how long we were to wait?"

"Until he comes, I believe."

Ralph Slimcoe stood trembling in the passage as he listened to the forgoing conversation. It was clear enough to him that they were officers of justice, who were lying in wait, expecting his appearance in the neighbourhood of Coriander Street.

The passage in which Slimcoe stood was of a pitch-like darkness, consequently it was quite impossible for any one to see him. He therefore waited and listened attentively to hear if there was anything more to be gathered from the speakers' conversation. Presently he heard a new voice say—

"Well, have you seen anything of him?"

"No, sir, nor any one else. Not a soul has passed."

"I cannot make out where this passage can be," said the new comer. "It seems such a monstrous distance from the Jew's house. Let me see, that's the back of his house, is it not?"

"Yes, the further one."

"Hang me if I can make out where there can be any means of escape, then. We must surely be mistaken."

"No, sir, this is the way, I am quite positive."

"We must search the different alleys and avenues, then."

Slimcoe became alarmed at this observation. He dared not run the risk of rushing out from his place of concealment, lest he should fall into his enemies' hands.

The officer's went to the various courts, and Slimcoe felt that the one he occupied must soon undergo a search in its turn. He trembled with affright.

Presently the voices of the men were no longer heard, and he judged that they were engaged in taking a survey of the different localites in the neighbourhood.

"What should he do?" now became the next question.

While he was hesitating how to act, he again heard the voices of the officers.

"See yonder dark passage?" said Jonathan Wild, "we've not searched there."

He made no doubt but this alluded to the one he occupied. If they were to enter there, escape would be out of the question. In the height of his alarm, he rushed frantically out, and as luck would have it, Jonathan Wild and his men did not at the moment catch sight of him as he emerged from the passage.

He had not, however, got many yards before a wild cry was raised, and the officers were at his heels.

He had, however, managed to get a start, and terror lent him wings, and he fled at the top of his speed.

Away he rushed through the intricate windings of that densely populated locality.

"Stop him!—stop him!" shouted the officers in pursuit; "stop thief!"

But although there were several individuals who heard the cry, and could easily have captured Slimcoe, no one offered to make the least attempt. It was a spot where many of the most lawless individuals lived, and none of these were likely to have any hand in affording assistance to the officers in pursuit. After a determined chase, Slimcoe managed to elude the officers, and got clear off, dashing down so many different turnings, that they missed sight of him.

"We're done," said Jonathan Wild, "done as surely as ever men or officers were in this world. Hang the fellow, he's escaped."

"He'd be sure to be hung if he had not escaped," said one of Wild's companions.

"We'll go back to Balasco's," said Wild, glumpily, "and try if we can squeeze anything from him."

They then returned to the Old House in West Street.

The Jew was still in the custody of Jonathan Wild's men.

"So, you rascally old humbug, you've concealed a murderer in some of your secret passages."

"No, indeed, Mishter Wild. What can you say such a thing for? I have no one concealed here, I shwear."

"We'll soon see about that. You'll find yourself behind the bars of a prison in less than an hour or so."

"Oh, mershy, mershy," exclaimed Balasco. "You will never be so cruel to an innocent man, never, surely."

"The man's escaped at the rear of your house, and you'll have to answer for his disappearance. Do you hear that, you old vagabond?"

"Oh, Mishter Wild, have pity upon a poor old man, who strives his hardest to get an honest living."

"Honest, indeed" exclaimed the thief-taker, contemptuously; "honest! your whole life is one round of chichanery and dishonesty."

"No, no, Mishter Wild, I have been traduced and belied. I try my hardest to earn an honest penny."

"You canting old rascal, I believe if you had the choice of a shilling by honesty, and a penny by the other thing, you would prefer the penny, I do believe."

"No, indeed; I try to be honest, and surely you would not take a poor old man who never did you any harm? You would never take him away from his business, and bring him to ruin? Have some pity on me, Mishter Wild."

"Take him away," said the thieftaker, "to the Compter."

"Oh, Father of Abraham, have mershy on me," said the Jew, falling on his knees before Wild, and appealing to him in the most abject accents. "You might have pity on me, Mishter Wild—you might have some pity on me."

"Psha!" exclaimed Wild. "Bring him along." and, without another word, he left the old house near West Street. The prisoner and officers following in the rear.

CHAPTER XLII.

THE MURDER IN LAWKER'S LANE.

SLIMCOE, when he had run down one turning after another, sought refuge in an old iron shop, or, rather, a dealer in marine stores. Now, he remained concealed for some time, until he felt quite assured that his pursuers had taken their departure. When he felt satisfied that such was the case, he cautiously emerged from the place which had afforded him temporary concealment.

A demonical expression was on his counte-nance, so horrible, indeed, that it was enough to frighten any beholder.

Slimcoe did not feel disposed to return home for the remainder of that day, but went from one place to another, drinking heavily, and rendering himself still more fearful in appearance. Dreadful thoughts were passing in the mind of the man. He had met with the lad who had informed him of what had taken place at his own residence with the followers of Wild, and Slimcoe brooded over this, and a settled look of determination and ferocity was observable on his features.

The unfortunate woman who lived with him was at once deemed treacherous, and a terrible revenge was meditated by the murderer.

As night came on, Ralph Slimcoe took his way home to his own lodgings. His teeth were set, and his lips were compressed with ungovernable rage, and his features were of a death-like paleness. The rising devil in his breast was dominant, and held him in complete mastery.

Hastily ascending the stairs, he opened the door of his front room, and entered—

"Ralph!" exclaimed the female occupant of the apartment. "Is it you?"

"Yes," he exclaimed, hoarsely—so hoarse, indeed, and so different to his natural voice, that the woman could hardly recognise it.

"What is the matter?" exclaimed the woman, as by the indistinct light, she saw the expression of Slimcoe's face, and shuddered at its appearance. "What is the matter, Ralph? Shall I get a light?"

"Eugh—no!" exclaimed the ruffian. "There's light enough for my purpose."

"Ralph!" shouted out the woman— "Ralph—you—what would you do?"

"Daughter of the devil!" yelled the man, springing towards her, and catching her by the throat. "Accursed woman. You'd sell your own mother to the hangman."

"Me—what—mercy—Ralph. What is the meaning of this? You're not yourself. Have mercy on me!"

"Oh, heaven, have mercy, indeed, for I shall have none."

"Oh, heavens!" she screamed out, as she observed the man draw a clasped knife from his pocket.

"Oh, Ralph, you would not—surely you would not, after all my sufferings—murder me."

"Aye," exclaimed the man, "that's it—murder—if you like. Let go of my arms—let go. Do you hear?"

"Ralph—Ralph. Have pity. What is the cause of this? Oh!" and here she shuddered, and endeavoured to release herself from his grasp, he, however, tightened his hold on her throat, and nearly strangled her.

While thus engaged, he was compelled to

use both hands, placing the knife in his mouth to enable him to do so. As she was by this time fully aware of his fell purpose, she now made desperate efforts to release herself from his grasp, and had just succeeded in doing so, when he dealt her a blow upon the side of the head, which sent her staggering for some paces, and nearly stunned her. Seeing the determination of the man, she flew round the room in a distracted state, appealing for mercy from her heartless tormentor. He rushed after her, and followed her from place to place, she intervening one piece of furniture after the other between herself and her would be murderer.

Like an infuriated tiger or panther, he chased the miserable object of his rage.

"Ralph!" exclaimed the woman. "You are not yourself. Have mercy—listen to me—for the sake of past years—for the sake of—" she stopped short, and burst into tears.

"Curse you," exclaimed her brutal husband. "Curse you. Your last day has come. Never more shall you betray me."

"I have not betrayed you. As heaven is my judge. I have not. Listen to me."

"Psha! I'm in no mood to listen to your prating. Come here. It's of no use your endeavouring to escape me, for by the Lord I'll have you."

He sprang forward, and she pushed the table between herself and the assassin. He caught it up and wrested it from her grasp, but she still dragged it towards her once more. He stooped over it, and endeavoured to stab her with the clasp knife he held in his hand. She stooped down behind the table, and avoided the intended blow.

With a fearful oath he knocked it over, and endeavoured to clasp hold of her, she interposed one chair after another, running about like a mad thing ; indeed, she was little else at this particular moment.

He flung one of the chairs at her, the back of it struck her in the chest. She gave a faint scream, and flew from him once more.

"Ralph—Ralph—oh—mercy!" she exclaimed, in piteous accents, so piteous, that the agonising tones might have moved one whose head was inebriated, but they had no effect upon her brutal paramour, who, snorting and panting like some wild and infuriated animal, still persisted in his merciless attack.

"Heaven, have mercy on me," exclaimed the wretched woman. "Heaven, have mercy on me. I have but little to live for in this world."

She was nearly exhausted, but still endeavoured to escape, for to the most wretched of us mortals, life is sweet, even when there are but a few grains of sand in the hour glass of time for us. Her sands had well nigh run out, and her last hour was drawing nigh.

He succeeded in catching hold of her. As he did so, she uttered a piercing scream, which was unheeded by any of those who were in the house. They were used to deeds of violence, and wife beating was of daily occurrence.

He made a desperate stab at her with the knife. She put up her hand to ward off the blow, her fingers were cut fearfully thereby. With a horrid oath he again struck at her. The knife entered her neck, and a jet of blood spurted out from the wound. The wretched woman put up both her hands to stop the bleeding, but her murderer stabbed her again and again in the chest and neck. She fixed upon him one agonising look of reproach, and with a deep groan fell to the floor, striking her head against the fender as she fell. After which she did not move, or give any signs of life or animation, and in another second or two, the vital spark had fled.

Slimcoe gazed stupidly upon her prostrate form, now set in the rigidity of death. He was generally pale, and fetched his breath uneasily.

What was working in that man's mind we dare not hint at.

The only woman who had been at all faithful to him, and in the earlier portion of his acquaintance with her, no doubt loved him, now lay dead at his feet, slain by his own hand.

A fitful and feeble glare from the oil lamp in the street found its way into the room.

This was the only light that found its way into that miserable apartment.

Slimcoe, as he gazed upon the dead body of her, who, in the life, had been his companion and helpmate, and had borne his brutal taunts, and still more brutal blows, with patience. She was now a ghastly and fearful object to look upon, and would never more suffer from man's ingratitude, or cruelty.

Slimcoe, as he gazed upon her, might have had some few qualms of conscience left, which pricked him, for his great crime.

We may say might, as, for the credit of human nature, we are in the hopes that he had.

The man was hardened and callous enough, and had sunk into the very lowest depths of crime.

What was he to do now? To stay in London? To rush out into the country? Where?—ah, where? Parker had gone to his native place, away from his old haunts. Should he follow him? Yes, that would be the best course. Hark! What was that?—the dripping of something. Was it blood? Heavens! Should the ensanguined flood be finding its way through the boards into the room below? It might. Gracious powers! What would be the consequence? The

gallows. The expectant crowd of up-turned faces. The hangman, and the ordinary, all flashed across the mind of the murderer. But, he'd fly—yes, he'd fly. He would not wait here to be taken. Hark—what was that?

A knock at the door was now heard by the sinful man—a gentle knock. He had not the courage to return any answer to it. He actually meditated dropping from the window. Absurd as was the idea, for the house was on the fourth story, and such an attempt would have been only attendant with immediate and instant death, so that was out of the question.

"What could be the knocking for?" asked Slimcoe of himself.

There was certainly nothing remarkable in it, considering the lodgers in the house were

constantly sending to borrow something, and children were frequently in the habit of coming to the door for some trifling request. What wonder was it then that there should be a tap at the door?

Under any other circumstances, Slimcoe would have not been so surprised or alarmed; but now, when the wretched form of the murdered woman lay at his feet, his reason was not sufficiently calm to see things in a very clear light.

The knock was repeated. If not answered they might enter the room.

As this thought presented itself to the mind of the guilty man, he sprang towards the door, opened it, and with a haggard and guilty look.

A child was at the door of about eleven years of age

No. 33.

She wanted to see Mrs. Slimcoe; but as she gazed upon the features of the man, she became so frightened, that she hardly had the courage to inquire for the deceased woman. She did manage, however, to stammer out that much.

"She was not at home," said Slimcoe.

His voice was so strange, that the child retreated down stairs, and, as she did so, she turned round ever and anon, to gaze upon the murderer, with strange and curious glances.

"Hang you," said Slimcoe. "What are you staring at you hussy? Be off!"

There was no need of a second request of this sort.

The child retreated down the creaking stairs, as though a pack of demons were at her heels.

Slimcoe slammed the door to, and locked it, and when he had done this he trembled still more. To be locked in the room with that ghastly object, with the fitful light of the oil lamp coming through the dingy window panes, was horrible to the last degree. As he returned into the room he dare not trust himself to look at that dreadful object near the fireplace.

He went towards the window and looked out. Lawker's Lane was full of people of one sort and another, and Slimcoe, as he looked out upon the passing throng, envied them each their own particular feelings, which he thought were, at any rate, better than his. He stood at the window looking out, till his eyes ached. Then the thought came upon him, that, perhaps Jonathan Wild was on his track; as this occurred to him, he made a still more curious survey of Lawker's Lane, to see if the thief taker, or any of his followers, were lurking about, but none of them met his eye, and Slimcoe hastily left the window, and turned his gaze towards that, which, in viewing, a cold shudder passed through his frame.

Great Heavens—was it fancy, or did his eyes deceive him, He thought the figure moved. But no, it was a fallacy. Upon a second glance, he observed a stray lock belonging to the wretched woman, agitated by the passing breeze which came in through the open window.

As Slimcoe looked upon the stark figure on the floor—as he observed the thick pool of blood which stained the floor, his limbs trembled, and his lips quivered. Hastily snatching a sheet from the bed in the inner room, the guilty wretch threw it over the dead body, and gathering up a few things, he hastily left the house like another Cain, and locking the door of the apartment on the outside, and putting the key in his pocket, he fled precipitately down the creaking staircase. Whither, he knew not, but any-

where to be out of the sight of the scene of his heinous crime. Anywhere—no matter—anywhere, to be away from that frightful and agonising room.

It was about ten o'clock when Slimcoe took his way from the house.

The stars were shining from that immeasurable space above, and the night was calm, but a storm of no common order reigned in the breast of the murderer. He started at shadows like a guilty thing as he was. He appeared to think somebody was on his track, although there was not the least indication of anybody following him. A butcher ran up against him, he turned pale, and trembled in every limb. This was quite accidental, but the sight of this butcher had a marvellous effect upon him.

This man stared in some surprise at Slimcoe, whose manner appeared so strange. He knew him very well, and was on excellent terms with him.

What could be the cause of this sudden demonstration of fear? The butcher gazed after Slimcoe as he hurried from the spot, which only made the murderer still more alarmed—hastened from the spot, despair was at his heart, and fire was in his brain. Whither should he bend his footsteps? He did not know, but took his way towards Drury Lane, not with any definite idea of the particular course he was to pursue, for he looked strangely at the horses, and the streets he was passing through, as though he had lost his way, and was in some unknown region. Finding himself in Drury Lane, he paused for a moment, and seemed lost in reflection—if the many-winged thoughts which were rushing through his brain could be called reflection. He paused, however, and for the first time now that he stood still, seemed surprised to find that his limbs shook; he could not keep himself still. He had not noticed this when on the move, but it became painfully perceptible now that he remained stationary. What should he do? The passengers might notice this. It was very probable they would, and then he might be suspected of being a—faugh!—that thought; he now trembled more. Seeing a public-house opposite he rushed into it, and called for brandy. His demand was so sudden that the barman stared at him for a moment, and then served him with what he desired. Slimcoe drained off the brandy at one draught, and called for more. The man behind the bar seemed aghast, but served him; he was used to all kinds of characters in that locality.

Slimcoe, when he had finished his second draught, left the establishment, and hurried down Drury Lane, soon finding himself in the Strand. Passing through Temple Bar he proceeded along Fleet Street, still uncertain which way to take; but he must leave London. Jonathan Wild, he thought, would soon be on his track. As this thought crossed his mind he pushed along at a more rapid pace. Bridge Street, Blackfriars met his glance. Ah! he would go across the bridge, and take his way into the country—somewhere. Yes, that is what he would do. Hastening down the street, he soon found himself on the bridge. The moon was up, and her rays were reflected upon the dark waters of the Thames. Slimcoe saw her light dancing upon the mimic waves, which seemed to play with it in spirit.

He leant over the ballustrades of the bridge, and looked at the river beneath. The breeze therefrom cooled his throbbing and feverish temples. Dark thoughts found their way into the brain of that wretched man as he contemplated the rushing river. One plunge, and there would be an end. Ah! but he dare not. Guilty wretch that he was, what of the hereafter? He dare not; his knees smote together as he thought of this; his lips quivered; his chest heaved. A murderer! doubly dyed in guilt.

Some passenger brushed accidentally against him as he passed. Slimcoe turned round, his features assumed a death-like hue, and he trembled so much, that the passer, who had accidentally pushed him, was struck with his ghastly appearance, and apologised, but taking a second look at him, and scanning his pale features, which the moon's light showed clear and distinct, some thought seem to pass through the man's mind.

He believed Slimcoe was contemplating suicide, and instead of walking quickly on his course, he turned towards the murderer, who now became still more alarmed.

"You are in trouble, my friend," said the passenger, in a good natural voice.

"Umph—yes," said Slimcoe.

"Well, don't give way to grief. What is the matter; business affairs?"

"No," answered Slimcoe, mechanically.

"Ah, lost a relative, perhaps."

"Yes."

"Well, don't be down-hearted. We have all a certain amount of trouble in this world. Don't be down-hearted. Good night."

"Good night," said Slimcoe, and the man left him, not, however, without taking one or two glances as he went along.

Slimcoe followed slowly. He wanted the other to go on ahead, which, in a short time, he did, and was soon lost to sight.

A deep drawn sigh escaped from the chest of Slimcoe when he found the man had fairly gone away.

"He seemed happy and merry enough," so Slimcoe thought, "and he—"

It was, indeed, a strange contrast.

Slimcoe took his course down the Blackfriars Road, through an ill-lighted thoroughfare, with nothing but the old-fashioned oil lamps at long intervals, but he cared not for this. He courted darkness, and the garish eye of day he dreaded. To be found in London in the morning's light would be to him horrible. He wandered on, and soon found himself at the Obelisk, at the other end of Blackfriars Road.

Here he paused again. Which turning should he take?

He believed Parker was at some place near Shirley; but how to find his way there he did not know. He had, however, an indistinct notion that he was to pass through Brixton and Streatham.

He went down the London Road, and halted again opposite the Elephant and Castle, which was a famous place for stage coaches. Two or three were there as Slimcoe stood in front of the Elephant. He contemplated them as well as their outside passengers. They, too, seemed happy and merry enough. Their mirth and lively conversations jarred upon his feelings, and he turned hastily round to the road which led to Brixton.

Onwards across Kennington Common, which at this time was pitch dark, for the moon had now become obscured by clouds, and a storm seemed to be threatening.

Presently big drops of rain came down at intervals—heavy drops, that chattered upon the hard ground and neighbouring roofs. Slimcoe heeded them not, but he had got about one third across the common when the rain came down in torrents; the clouds seemed to have opened and discharged their contents in one sheet of water. He hesitated for a moment, doubtful if it were not the most prudent course for him to turn back, but upon second thoughts he preferred continuing on his course.

"What was a little rain to him?" he thought. "Of no material consequence—none."

However, before he had reached the other side of the common he was literally drenched to the skin, and as wet as though he had been dragged through a horse pond. As he came to the further end of Kennington Common he was met by some one on horseback. By the indistinct light, which now found its way from the lamp in the road, he could make out that the person on horseback was no other than our hero, Colonel Jack. When Slimcoe became aware of this fact, he was so alarmed, and completely overcome, that he was hardly capable of moving. Self preservation was, however, dominant in his mind, and anything rather than meet the colonel, or be seen by him, as he would then know which way he had taken.

There was no bush or gorse for Slimcoe to hide in, and Colonel Jack was making towards him.

Slimcoe rushed on one side, quickly, for about thirty yards or so, and then, wet as he was, he laid down on the grass, face downwards, for concealment. He had the satisfaction of hearing the horse's feet grow less distinct, and soon not audible at all. He waited a few minutes more, and rose from his prostrate position, and took his way along one more, when he had the satisfaction of being in the road direct to Brixton, although when he got there he did not well know what to do.

By this time he felt thoroughly chilled, and shivered as his teeth chattered together. He felt ill but was afraid to go into any house in the neighbourhood now, in case he should be seen by some one who knew him, and his course be traced thereby. No! He would hurry on.

After he had gone about half a mile down the road, however, he felt so dispirited and unwell that he availed himself of a roadside house to get another drop of brandy, which he took this time with hot water, which he swallowed hastily at the bar.

CHAPTER XLIII.

RALPH SLIMCOE CONTINUES HIS WANDERINGS.

THE miserable man, drenched as he was, did not dare to stay at any house for fear of detection, and, consequently, he continued on his course although it still pelted with rain. There was one thing, however, he could not possibly be more wet than he was, but it would be impossible for him to continue on thus all night ; nature would become exhausted.

It was already very late, and Slimcoe would have given the world to get near a fire and dry his things, which dragged against his shivering limbs and body with an unpleasant sensation.

He hurried on, however, and as he did so had serious thoughts of endeavouring to seek accomodation for the night at some roadside public-houese, but he reflected that such a course would be attended with considerable danger ; and so he still hurried on.

The rain had ceased for some time, when Slimcoe found himself at Brixton Causeway. There he made another halt, for he felt so tired, so low, dispirited, and altogether so very miserable, that he hardly knew what course to adopt for the best.

As he stood reflecting, he observed in the distance a thin vapour arise. It had the appearance of smoke, and every now and then a fitful flame shot up in the sky, which in this part appeared tinged with red.

Slimcoe was at a loss to divine what this was, and as there was a lane opposite which led in the direction, he immediately took his way down this.

The turning was a short one, and Slimcoe found himself in the open fields, which were devoted to brickmaking.

The smoke and flame came from a large kiln of bricks, which were now plainly visible through the fissures of the bricks, Slimcoe could see the lurid light, which appeared to be like liquid fire, so intense was its glare. The warmth emitted from the brick kiln had a pleasing effect upon the senses of the murderer, and he surveyed it with eyes of considerable satisfaction. At some distance off he observed a shed, and a rude hut, put together with bricks which were guiltless of mortar or cement of any kind.

Slimcoe went up to the kiln, and spreading out his hands, he warmed himself. The heat was intense, and a dense vapour was steaming from his clothes.

When he had turned round once or twice, taken off his coat, and aired it by the heat of the kiln, Slimcoe felt a little more comfortable, that is corporeally, his mind was troubled enough.

Having found such comfortable quarters, Slimcoe was not disposed to leave them, and so, gathering some straw together which lay about the four sides of the kiln, he placed it on one side, and stretched himself thereon to sleep.

Now so distracted was his mind, that the probability is that he, under any other circumstances, would have found it quite impossible to propitiate the drowsy god ; but the heat of the furnace or kiln, with that peculiar mefetic or gaseous exhalation, which was emitted therefrom, could not fail to draw him to sleep, which it did in the course of half an hour or so.

Slimcoe's position was not unattended with danger, and indeed it somewhat surprising that he did not lose his life as it was, for the heat was intense, and the sulphurous vapour was inhaled by the sleeper in large quantities.

All through that night, Slimcoe slept soundly.

In the morning the brickmakers came to their work.

A little girl, the daughter of the foreman, was the first to observe the sleeping man besides the kiln.

The child uttered an exclamation of surprise, and ran to her father, who was at work in the field. She acquainted him with the discovery she had made, and the latter followed the guidance of his daughter.

Upon his seeing Slimcoe, he shook him, and shouted out—

"Hilloa, mate; are you alive or dead? Wake up."

Slimcoe turned round, rubbed his eyes, opened them, and stared stupidly at the questioner.

"How long have you been here? and what brought you to this spot?" said the brickmaker.

"I have been caught in the storm," said Slimcoe.

"When?"

"Last night."

"Have you slept here, then?"

"Yes."

"What are you?" a tramp?"

"A traveller," said Slimcoe.

"You might have found a better roosting place for the night I should think," said the brickmaker.

"I am not well," said Slimcoe.

"Well, get up and shake your feathers, old boy," said the brickmaker, good-naturedly. "You haven't got no money, I suppose?"

"Not much."

"Ah!"

Slimcoe by this time had risen to his feet; his appearance was anything but prepossessing at any time, but it was especially miserable and disordered in its character at the present moment. Arranging his toilet as hastily as possible, he thanked the brickmaker for the shelter which had been afforded him, and precipitately left the spot.

"Umph!" exclaimed the latter; "a queer fish and no mistake."

The murderer now took his way again into the high Burton road, which he travelled for some time, until he reached the "Crown and Sceptre," at Streatham. Opposite the doorway of this hostelry he paused; he was hungry, and hesitated about going in to procure some refreshment, but his necessities got the better of his judgment, and he forthwith entered the parlour of that hostelry. Ringing the bell, a little girl of about eleven years of age entered. She seemed alarmed at the haggard appearance of the sole occupant of the room, for it was yet early, and he was the only customer.

"A mug of ale and some bread and cheese," said Slimcoe, in a hoarse voice, made doubly hoarse now from the cold he had caught on the previous night.

The child looked frightened, and went to the bar where her mother was, and told her what the gentleman in the parlour desired. The ale was drawn, the bread and cheese cut, and the child was directed to take it into the parlour. She, however, hesitated.

"What are you waiting for, Alice?" said her mother.

"I—I don't like to take it into the parlour," the child answered.

"Why not, my dear?"

"Why, he is such a strange-looking man."

"What of that; he won't eat you."

The little girl still hesitated. Seeing which the mother emerged from the bar and went into the parlour herself.

When she entered, Slimcoe was leaning his head upon both his hands and sighing deeply.

The landlady regarded him with a curious look of inquiry and placed the beer and viands before him. Slimcoe dived into his pocket for the wherewithal to pay the score.

"What road am I to take for Croydon?" asked Slimcoe, wishing to say something to break the unnatural stillness which oppressed him with a leaden weight.

"Straight on, sir, till you come to the church, then turn round to the left."

"Thank you," said Slimcoe, as he paid her the reckoning.

The bread and cheese was greedily devoured, the ale drank and Slimcoe proceeded down the road towards Croydon. The landlady and her daughter looked curiously after him as he took his way along.

CHAPTER XLIV.

THE DISCOVERY OF THE MURDER IN LAWKER'S LANE.

EARLY on the following morning Colonel Jack, true to his appointment, sought an interview with Slimcoe at his lodgings in Lawker's Lane.

As he was about to enter the house he caught sight of Jonathan Wild and his myrmidoms at the farther end of the lane, making their way to the spot.

Our hero had no desire to fall in with the thief-taker, and therefore deemed it prudent to fall back out of his way. Consequently he retreated to a distance, and watched the thief-taker's proceedings.

Jonathan Wild entered the dwelling of Slimcoe, and without deigning to make any inquiry, he rushed up stairs followed by the officers. The keen-eyed girl who had opened the street-door fled precipitately, in the utmost state of alarm at the sight of Wild, who, when he had got up to the landing, knocked loudly at the apartment occupied by Slimcoe. No answer was returned to this, and the knocking was repeated still more vociferously. Still no answer. Wild called out to those below. The girl made her appearance in the passage. Wild saw her over the bannisters.

"You stupid wench! Where is Mr. Slimcoe?" said Wild.

"He ain't at home, sir," said the girl, in a half scream.

"Oh, nonsense; that will not do for me, said Wild. "Come up stairs."

"Yes, sir."

The girl ascended.

"How long has Slimcoe been out," inquired Wild, fixing upon the girl a severe look.

"He ain't been at home since last night."

"Not slept at home?"

"No, sir."

"Are you sure? Now, don't tell me any of your crammers."

"I am quite certain, sir, that he went out last night and has not returned since."

"And his—wife—Mrs. Slimcoe?"

"I think she is at home, sir."

"Why don't she answer, then?"

"Have you knocked, sir?"

"Yes, you might have heard me, I should think."

The girl knocked at the door and called out "Mrs. Slimcoe" in a shrill voice. Of course, no answer was returned to this, any more than to Jonathan Wild's furious summons.

"Burst open the door," said Wild to his men.

They proceeded to make a forcible entrance into the room, which was the work but of a few minutes. The door was dashed open and Wild and his men entered. The thieftaker run his eyes over the apartment, and at first did not observe the dead body of the unfortunate woman. The first thing that attracted his attention was the ensanguined pool of blood which deluged the floor. Upon noticing this the body of the woman was seen covered over with the sheet. Jonathan Wild stooped down and tore the sheet from the body. A ghastly sight met his gaze. There lay the body of the woman, her wounds gaping fearfully open, and her rigid form presenting a most fearful appearance. Even the hardened and callous Wild started back in horror at the fearful sight which met his gaze.

"Murder, by all that's horrible," exclaimed Wild, as he contemplated the miserable object on the floor.

"Oh, goodness gracious," exclaimed the blear-eyed girl, wringing her hands. Oh, goodness. Oh—oh;" and here she relapsed into a series of sobs.

"Hold your noise, you fool," said Wild. "Do you think your blubbering will do any good?"

"Oh, poor, dear Mrs. Slimcoe, she is murdered," exclaimed the girl. "Oh, how shocking."

"Hold your tongue, I say," exclaimed Wild. "Do you think all that noise will do any good? Silence."

Then turning to his men, he said—

"There is another room beyond this. Let us see if there is any one concealed therein."

The thieftaker and his men now entered the room beyond, and made a search there, but of course there was no one there.

"This fellow has murdered his wife, or mistress, that's quite certain," said Wild, "and has now made his escape."

"She is dead, I suppose?" suggested one of his men.

The thieftaker now bent over the body, and looked at it attentively. There could not be much mistake about the unfortunate woman being "past all surgery."

"What is to be done with the body?" inquired one of Wild's men.

"Let it remain where it is," said the thieftaker. "I must give notice to the coroner. What time did this Slimcoe go out?"

This was addressed to the blear-eyed girl.

"About nine o'clock, sir," said the girl.

"Did you hear any noise?"

"No, sir."

"But I did," said a stout copper-faced woman, who was a fellow lodger in the house, "I did, and knew it was that nasty Slimcoe beating his wife."

"Beating, indeed," exclaimed Wild.

"Ah, mercy on me—if—why what—"

"He's murdered the woman, or somebody else has," exclaimed Wild.

"Oh, the monster!" exclaimed the copper-faced woman. "The nasty, brutal, detestable monster!"

The woman, coarse as was her nature, evinced a considerable amount of feeling as she contemplated the deceased woman, who to say the truth, had been a favourite with most of the occupants of the house.

Death is at all times a sad spectacle, but one of a violent nature, such as this, was fearful to the last degree.

Even death by natural causes is sad enough.

Who that has watched beside the sick, the dying couch of a beloved being, does not remember the dreary, desolate blank that succeeds the moment of dissolution? While life remains, hope will linger.

From the ark of its affections the heart still sends forth the dove over the wide waste of affliction, fondly dreaming of her return with the olive branch of hope and joy.

The mind, too fully occupied with the duties of the sick chamber, has scarcely leisure to dwell upon ought beside. To smooth the pillow—to watch over the unquiet slumber—to sweeten the bitter draught with affection's hand—to read the languid eye, and anticipate the broken wish, these and a thousand other kindly officers, till up the weary hours, and twine the loved one in its helplessness closer and close round the hearts. But when the last hour has closed upon the being we have so loved and tended—when the warm heart can no longer feel, nor the beaming eye smile its thanks—then it is that the weary frame and harassed spirit, sink together, in utter helpless hopelessness.

Beyond that silent chamber, the wide world appears one trackless waste; and as we gaze on the still cold features of the departed, we long for the wings of the dove to flee away and be at rest.

All this is sad enough; but what amount of remorse, bitterness, and despair, must find its way into the innermost recesses of the heart of the miserable and guilty Slimcoe?

"Well, it's no use looking upon this scene of horror," exclaimed Wild. "If any man ever did deserve scragging, Ralph Slimcoe's the man, and no mistake. I wonder whether the scoundrel will have the hardihood to return to this place?"

"I should think not, sir," said one of the men.

Wild now prepared to take his departure, but, previous to his doing this, he sent one of his men to the nearest locksmith, with instructions for the smith to return with the officer, and place a strong padlock on the door of Slimcoe's room.

In the course of about a quarter of an hour the smith made his appearance, and screwed on a strong fastening to the door, which being padlocked, Wild placed the key in his pocket, and descended the stairs. As he was doing so, the copper-faced woman said—

"Oh, do try and find out the wretch, Mr. Wild."

"All right, ma'am," said the thief taker. "You mind your own business, and I'll mind mine."

When he had got into the passage, he found it choked up with gaping people.

The news of the murder had spread rapidly round the neighbourhood, and a throng of anxious people were around the house, and in the passage.

"Get along with you," said Wild, gruffly—"Get away with you."

The people gave way and many of them—the doubtful ones—made off as fast as possible at the sight of the celebrated thief-taker.

Jonathan Wild now took his way to the Compter, where the Jew, Isaac Balasco, was confined. Of course, very little information could be extracted from Balasco, who, as the reader no doubt guesses, knew but little of the movements of Slimcoe. He judged that he had got safe off from the premises of the Old House in West Street, and beyond

this he knew literally nothing. When Wild arrived at the Compter, he had an interview with the governor of the prison, and acquainted him with the murder in Lawkers Lane.

"I am going to the proper authorities," said Wild, "but have thought it as well to see the Jew first, to try if I can obtain any scrap of information from him, as to the probable course taken by Slimcoe. I feel assured that the Israelite knows more than he chooses to divulge."

"Better have him in, then," said the governor.

"If you please."

Balasco was sent for and made his appearance in the governor's room, accompanied by a turnkey.

"Now, look here, you unworthy son of a despicable race," said Wild to the Jew; "do you know that this scoundrel, Slimcoe, has committed another murder."

"Mershy. Father have mershy on me," exclaimed the Jew, tossing up his hands in affected horror. "It ish horrible."

"Yes, we know that without your telling us," said the thieftaker. "But that is nothing to the purpose. You know his haunts better than anyone else."

"As heaven is my judge, I do not know his haunts," said Balasco.

"Now, don't interrupt me," said Wild, angrily. "It is very probable that you may know where he has gone to. Now, hear me, if you can be of any service to me in this respect you shall not only be set free, but no doubt the authorities will give you some reward."

"Oh, thanks, goot Mishter Wild," said the Jew, clasping his hands together in an imploring manner. "Ten thousand thanks."

"You have nothing to thank me for at present," said the thieftaker. "It depends upon your own conduct."

"I will tell all I know, Mishter Wild, I shwear to you that I will tell all I know," whined the Jew.

"Good—so much the better—see that you do so. Now, in the first place, where do you think it likely Slimcoe has gone?" asked Wild.

"I cannot tell."

"Do you know where this man Parker has escaped to?"

The Jew considered, as Wild watched him with the eyes of a hawk.

"Parker went to a relative's, at some place near—"

"Where?"

"Near Shirley."

"What, in Surrey?"

"Yesh."

"Are you sure?"

"Quite."

"Ah," and Wild noted down the address in his pocket book. "Do you think Slimcoe would join him there?"

"It'sh very possible."

"Do you not recollect the name of the place?"

"No, only it'sh a little village near Shirley. That ish all I know."

"Is he with a relative?"

"Yesh, so I was told."

"By the name of Slimcoe?"

"Yesh."

"Is there any other place you think it likely Slimcoe would go to?"

The Jew hesitated again.

"He might call at—"

"Well, where?"

"At the Badger's."

"Ah—in Westminster?"

"Yesh, at the Cow and Cauliflower."

"Ah, that is likely enough," said Wild. "Now is there any other place you can think of?"

"I do not know at present."

"Well, think by the time I come back, which will be in the after part of the day," said Wild.

"I will try and recollect, Mishter Wild, I assure you that I will," mumbled forth old Balasco.

"See that you do. And, as an earnest of good faith, I will procure your discharge," said the thieftaker.

The Jew clasped his hands, and uttered a series of thanks to the thieftaker, who then took his departure.

Wild was a man usually prompt in all his actions, and he forthwith took his way to the respectable establishment of Mr. Dyson, in Westminster.

That immaculate individual was at home, as usual, with the straw in his mouth, in one of his ruminating moods.

"Your servant, sir," he said to Wild, as the thieftaker presented himself. I hope as how all things are going on square with you."

"I tell you what it is, Dyson," said Wild. "This establishment of yours ought long since to have been shut up, because why? It is the resort of the most desperate characters in all London."

"Goodness me, Mr. Wild," exclaimed the Badger, deprecatingly. You are jesting surely".

"Indeed, I was never more serious in all my life," said the thieftaker. "But it is no good talking about that now. What I have come about is respecting a man you know, named Slimcoe."

"Who?'

"Ralph Slimcoe."

"Ah, I am afraid he is a bad lot," said Dyson

"I am not only afraid, but I am sure of it," said the thieftaker.

"Really?"

"Yes."

"No, you don't say so."

"Yes, he has been and done another murder."

"Can't think it."

"Yes,"

"No, never."

"But he has I tell you."

"Never."

"It's a fact?"

"Who is it?"

"The unfortunate woman he was living with."

"What her?"

"Yes?"

"Law," said Mr. Dyson, twirling his straw."

"Has he been here?" inquired Jonathan Wild.

"No.'

"Come now."

Wild fixed his penetrating eyes upon Dyson's face.

"No, that he certainly has not," was the reply.

"Now no shuffling. Are you certain, Dyson?"

"Quite positive."

"Have you any idea where he has gone to?"

"No, indeed."

"And if you had you wouldn't tell me, I suppose?"

"Hist! I swear I would," said the Badger.

"Oh, you are wonderous kind, you are," said Wild.

"Not at all," said the Badger, quite innocently.

"Now, look here, Mr. Dyson," said the thieftaker.

"Yes, I am looking."

The Badger looked straight at the door of the apartment.

"Yes, but listen."

"Well, arn't I listening, Mr. Wild?" said the Badger.

The Badger appeared to be all attention to what his visitor was about to say.

"Not very attentively."

"Yes, I am."

"Right," said Wild.

"All attention," replied the Badger, turning the straw in his mouth.

"Well, then—"

"Go on," said Dyson."

"Well, should this fellow come here, which is more than likely, you must find out where he is making for. Now do you understand?"

"Eh?"

"Do you understand?" said Wild impatiently.

The Badger nodded.

"And I will make it worth your while," added Wild.

Mr. Dyson promised to acquaint the thief-taker with any information he might chance to pick up. Indeed, the Badger was so disgusted with Slimcoe for the double murder, that he made up his mind, come what would, that he was determined no longer to screen him. It is true Slimcoe had been a customer of Dyson, and the Badger had endeavoured to screen the murderer, as he generally did with most of those who frequented his house, but as he himself observed, he would rather wash his hands of it, for the crime of murder was one that rather stag-

gered Mr. Dyson. Burglary, highway robbery, petty larceny of every description, he considered venial offences, and even an accidental murder as he called it in self-defence, he did not so much mind; but a deliberate murder with malice propense was a crime at which Mr. Dyson revolted, and really would have felt no kind of compunction in handing over the miscreant Slimcoe to justice and condign punishment. Jonathan Wild therefore took leave of the Badger with a good understanding with the latter.

———

CHAPTER XLV.

SQUABSHOT'S INTERVIEW WITH JONATHAN WILD.

It will be remembered that Colonel Jack, when he observed Wild and his men make an entrance in the house of Ralph Slimcoe, our hero fell back out of their way, and concealed himself from observation. The colonel watched until the thieftaker had left the premises, and then joined the crowd which was gathered round the door of the murderer's house.

Inquiring of one of these the cause of the confusion, the colonel was informed of the death of the unfortunate woman. At this information he stood appalled, as well he might, for he had seen her on the previous day in good health, although very much borne down with grief, and depressed in spirits. Colonel Jack did not wait, in case of any sudden return of Wild's party, consequently he took his way hastily from the spot; he had promised to call at the office of Mr. Fubbles to obtain from him the particulars of the case of Sir John Barnard, but as he concluded that Slimcoe would sooner or later be brought to justice, he abstained from waiting upon the lawyer for the present, and bent his steps in the direction of Goswell Street, there to seek an interview with the redoubtable Squabshot. That individual was at home, and hailed our hero as he usually did, for the colonel was an especial favourite with him.

"More news," said Squabshot, "and of terrible importance too?"

"What is it?" inquired his visitor.

"Jonathan Wild is even with us; he's on the scent."

"How so?"

"After Slimcoe," said Squabshot. "The fellow has committed another murder."

"You have heard of it then?"

"Certainly. I have had a chap here just now who told me all about it."

Squabshot, during this brief dialogue, was performing his toilette hastily.

"Where are you off to?" inquired the colonel. "You seem in a monstrous hurry."

"I am off to Jonathan Wild. That is if I can find him," said Squabshot.

"Indeed, and what for pray?"

Mr. Squabshot looked mysterious, and assumed an air of importance, so much so that our hero saw at once that something was up.

"This fellow" said Squabshot, in continuation.

"Who?"

"Slimcoe."

"Yes—precisely—I understand."

"This fellow has hooked it."

"So I understand."

"And has taken his way—"

"The Lord knows where," continued the colonel.

"Ah, that we shall see. Now it so happens that I have had a chap here who has put me upon the scent with regard to Parker."

"Indeed?"

"Yes, and I think that it is more than probable that Slimcoe has made his way to his old pal and fellow criminal. A pair of beauties they are and no mistake."

"Well, and what are you going to do, then?"

"As I said just now, I am off to Jonathan Wild."

"For what purpose?"

"To give him all the information I am possessed of. Things now assume a different aspect. Wild knows, or at any rate has every reason to believe, that these pair of worthies are the real murderers of Jabez Crudge, and it would be absurd now to offer them any terms for a confession."

"If that's the case it would be, of course."

"Wild has given notice that he is on the track of these men, and Osborne's lawyers have moved for the trial to be postponed in consequence.

"And were they successful in their application?"

"Yes, the recorder granted the request without any hesitation."

"So far it is well."

"But now the only question is how we are to succeed in capturing them."

"We? You are very active in this business, Squabshot," said the colonel. "Have you turned thieftaker?"

"I would turn anything to serve Henry Osborne."

The colonel held out his hand and shook that of Squabshot warmly.

"I would go with you," said our hero, "but I cannot be seen in the business."

"There is no occasion for it, my boy," returned Squabshot. "Not the slightest occasion, believe me."

"I am sure I am bound to you as well as Osborne for all your kindness," said our hero.

"Psha!" Nonsense. We are not worth living in the world at all, if we cannot serve one another," answered the colonel's companion.

Squabshot soon completed his toilette, and proceeded to leave the house. The colonel accompanied him on the road for some distance, and inquired whither he was bound for in the first instance.

"To Jonathan Wild's house," said Squabshot.

This was situated in Green Arbour Court, close to the Old Bailey.

"And if he is not there?"

"Oh, I dare say they will be able to tell me where he has gone to."

"Most likely."

As they viewed this spot, Colonel Jack bade his companion good morning, and left him to fulfil his mission.

Squabshot knocked loudly at the thieftaker's house. The door was answered by one of his men.

"Mr. Wild in," said Squabshot.

"No," was the answer in a gruff tone. "He arn't in. What do you want. Anything I can do for you?"

"Umph—I'm afraid not," said Squabshot. "It isn't a sort of business you are up to, my man"

This was said in a half patronising and a half deprecating tone, for Squabshot did not like this man's manner.

"Eugh!" grunted forth the officer. "It is something so very clever, then."

This was said in a glumpy, sneery tone.

"It isn't that it's altogether so very clever," said Squabshot. "Only you see, you hadn't better to be up to it."

"What is it you want, then?" inquired the man, hastily.

"Mr. Jonathan Wild," said Squabshot, in oily and bland accents this time.

"Well, so you said before; but he arn't in I tell you."

"Can you tell me where he is gone to?" asked Squabshot.

"Oh, he's gone to several places for the matter of that," said the man.

"How long has he been gone out, my friend?"

"Umph—it may be an hour, or it might be more. Is your business of such great importance?"

"That it just is, seeing that it's about murder," said Squabshot.

"Oh, you have got some information to give him, then?"

"That I just have."

"Beg pardon, sir," said the man in quite a different tone. "Mr. Wild's gone to the compter."

"Why didn't you say so before?" exclaimed Squabshot, in anger.

"Didn't know what you had come about," answered the man.

Squabshot did not wait for any further observation, but went direct to the compter. When he arrived there, he found the Jew Balasco in the governor's room, between two turnkeys, while the thieftaker was interrogating him. Wild turned round and regarded Squabshot with a look of inquiry upon his entrance; he was a perfect stranger to him.

"Your servant. Mr. Wild," said Squabshot, making one of his most graceful bows."

"Same to you, sir," said Wild, as he came to the side of the new comer, in a professional or business-like air.

"I'm glad I have been fortunate enough to meet with you, Mr. Wild."

The thieftaker gave a nod.

"For my business is, or rather, may, prove to be important. It is respecting the Cow Cross affair."

"Oh, indeed," ejaculated Wild.

"Yes. Have you any information respecting the miscreant Slimcoe?"

"No. Only I judge that he may have taken himself off to Parker, his companion in crime."

"That is my supposition," said Squabshot, with a knowing look.

"Are you—are you in the force, sir," inquired Wild.

"Umph—no." said Squabshot, "I am a friend of Mr. Osborne."

"Oh—ah! The unfortunate young man who stands charged with the murder."

"Exactly. And I believe from private information I have received, that I shall be able to find out where this Parker is concealed."

"Oh," exclaimed the thieftaker, "if you can do that my friend, it will be indeed a service."

"Well, I can't promise, but I have a clue."

"How did you obtain this information?"

Squabshot drew himself up, and assumed an imperturbable attitude.

"Oh," said Wild, "I don't wish to inquire about what, perhaps, I have no right to ask about. Let it suffice that you are willing to render me all the information you can."

"For the sake of Mr. Osborne."

"Precisely, for the sake of the unfortunate young man."

"Who is as innocent as either you or I," said Squabshot.

"Let us hope so. I fully believe it, from what information I have received."

"I know it," said Squabshot.

"Where do you suppose this Parker is?" inquired the thieftaker.

"At a village near Shirley."

"That agrees with the information I have received. Do you know the name of the village?"

"No, but I have a rough draft of the road. It is not more than a mile on the other side of Shirley."

Squabshot now produced from his pocket a drawing, or, rather, ground plan of the road in which the principal street in the village was marked out, as also the house where Parker was supposed to be located He directed the thieftaker's attention to the same.

"What is this place in red ink ?" inquired Wild.

"That is the house. It is a small beer and huckster's shop."

"Oh, I see."

"And I don't think we can make much mistake in the matter, that is, assuming that my information is correct which I do not doubt."

"I hope it may be, I am sure," said the thieftaker.

"Oh, I do not for a moment doubt it," added Squabshot.

"You will spare me this, then ?"

"As you please."

"It will not be possible to do without it."

"When do you purpose going down there ?"

"Immediately, my dear sir—immediately," said Wild.

"Oh—ah—yes, of course. Well, had I not better go with you ?"

"Would you mind doing so ?"

"Not at all. I have come for the express purpose."

"I am, indeed, much obliged to you for the trouble you are taking in the matter," said Wild.

"No, it's a pleasure," said Squabshot, " to succour the innocent"

"It shall not go unrewarded," said the thieftaker.

Squabshot put up his hand in a deprecating manner.

The fellow has escaped me already in a most extraordinary manner," said Wild.

"Has he, sir ?" exclaimed Squabshot.

"Yes, we all but had him at this Jew's house."

"Indeed—where ?"

"In West Street."

"Oh, I heard of that," said Squabshot. "How do you propose going down to Shirley."

"Drive there," said Wild," and if you will accompany me round to the stable you will find a trap already waiting for us."

"Oh, did you anticipate going there, then ?" inquired Squabshot.

"Yes, I should have gone upon the chance, even if you had not come."

The two now took their way round to the stable, where they found the horses already put to in a double bodied chaise, capable of holding four passengers. The back seat was occupied by two of Wild's followers, while the front held the thieftaker and Squabshot, the former driving. In the course of a few minutes the whole party were driving merrily off towards the place of their destination

---

CHAPTER XLVI.

SLIMCOE'S VISIT TO BAWKHAM.

RALPH SLIMCOE, after he had left the Crown and Sceptre at Streatham, proceeded along the road until he came to the Church, as directed by the landlady. He then turned off to the left, and took the road leading to Streatham Common—then a common in all its pristine rudeness. After walking some distance, he came to Broad Green, Croydon ; here he deemed it advisable to inquire again, and seeing a traveller some little distance ahead of him, he pushed on to overtake him and make the necessary inquiries. The individual in question was dressed in a velveteen shooting jacket, with drab leggings. He had something of the appearance of a tramp, and seemed a sort of individual of whom Slimcoe would have no compunction in addressing. As he neared him he called out—

' Is this right for Shirley ?"

The man turned suddenly and disclosed to the astonished gaze of the murderer the features of the Nobbler, whom the reader no doubt will remember as being connected, or rather chief character, in the burglary at the house of Mr. Brewster, at Dulwich. The Nobbler stared at the questioner, as well he might, for he knew Slimcoe perfectly well.

"Shirley ?" he exclaimed. "Humph, you are rusticating, Ralph, eh ?"

"Well, I declare if it ain't—"

"Yes, the Nobbler, said that worthy.

"Well to be sure, and who would have thought of seeing you ?" said Slimcoe.

"I might return the compliment," said the Nobbler.

"Why, what are you up to ?" said Slimcoe.

"Doing the honest," was the reply.

"Ugh ! find it profitable ?'

"Not particularly so. And you, what's your little game ?" said the Nobbler.

Slimcoe shuddered.

"Well, you don't look particularly healthy or happy over it, be it whatever it may.'

"I am hunted like a wild beast," said Slimcoe.

"What's up then ?"

"The Cow Cross affair," said Slimcoe.

"Oh, that was your handywork, was it ?"

"Partly.'

"Umph. Anyone on your track ?"

"Yes, Jonathan Wild."

"The devil !" exclaimed the Nobbler, with a start. "We are no company for each other then."

"Why not."

"Because he is just as anxious to see me as he is to make the acquaintance of yourself. We had better part company."

"Oh, you need not be under any fear,' said Slimcoe; "he has forgotten all about you. And in any case, he's not likely to come this road, for he has not the slightest idea that I have come this way."

"That's more than you can tell."

"Ah, but I'm sure of it," said Slimcoe, in a confident tone.

The Nobbler now directed his companion towards the place he was desirious of arriving at. After which, the two walked along the road, conversing upon various topics, chiefly relative to their own exploits and escapades. After which they parted company, as the Nobbler had to go in a different direction to his companion.

Slimcoe then proceeded on alone once more. Now that he had left London behind some miles, he began to pick up a little in spirits.

He thought after all that he had been doing a cunning trick in the course he was now pursuing.

He had the fullest confidence that not a soul knew of the whereabonts of his companion in guilt, Parker, and little deemed of the proceedings of Jonathan Wild and our mercurial friend, Squabshot.

Many more miles were traversed by the fugitive man—many many miles, and he was anxious to push on to the place of his destination without halting for any further refreshments; but he found this impossible, for he began to feel quite exhausted, and was compelled to go into a roadside house and call for some ale, and again inquired his way.

He had taken the longest route, so he found out; but that mattered little, he thought, as long as he did succeed in reaching the place at last.

Having finished his ale, he again trudged on in a little better spirit.

But still as he went along, the face and ghastly form of her whom he had so brutally murdered was presented to his imagination, and the wretched man shuddered, and would have given worlds to have her now alive; but it was all too late to express such a wish, or dream of such a thing now.

In due course of time he arrived at Shirley, and inquired for the village of Bawkham, where Parker's maiden aunt resided.

It was with this dame that her unworthy nephew had sought refuge.

Slimcoe had but little difficulty in finding out the village, and taking his way through what might by courtesy be termed the main street, the hucksters shop was soon found, for he observed through the dingy panes of this, Parker himself, serving therein.

Slimcoe entered the shop, and Parker was so surprised at his sudden appearance, that he hastily dropped the scales he held in his hand, and turned suddenly deathly pale, as he exclaimed—

"Ralph!"

"Ah, it's me, and no mistake," said that individual.

"Anything—wrong?"

"Everything."

"Come in," said Parker, opening the flap of the counter.

And motioning the new comer to enter the back parlour, Slimcoe entered, and as soon as the customers were served, Parker went in also.

"Well, what news?" said Parker, anxiously. "You look as though the hangman were at your elbow."

Slimcoe shuddered and trembled visibly.

"What is the matter?" said Parker, more vehemently.

"It's all with Moll."

"Ah, how so?"

"She split upon us."

"Never—ah, I always had my suspicion."

"And you were right."

"What's become of her, then? Have you—?"

The wretch nodded.

"Great heavens—and discovered?"

"Will be, of course. Jonathan Wild's been to Lawker's Lane."

"The devil. Why we shall be ruined. What brought you here?"

"Umph—what do you suppose? To get out of the way, of course."

"Well, but it will excite suspicion. Your being here, a stranger too."

"What of that?'

"Why, the people are so curious, of course they'll want to know who you are."

"Let them—what do I care—where am I to go—what am I to do?"

"Confonnd it," exclaimed Parker, who felt mightily annoyed at his pal's presence. He was snug enough himself in his present quarters, and naturally felt fearful that the presence of Slimcoe would compromise him, and bring him into trouble; but he knew it would not do to quarrel with him "

"Where's your servant?" inquired Slimcoe.

"Out at present; but she won't be long. Well, what do you purpose doing," said Parker, in continuation.

"What can I do? Wait here, if you've room for me."

Parker bit his nails with vexation.

"Room for you," he itterated.

"Yes, that's it, I suppose, if you'll have me, that's the way to say it."

"By the lord, but this is an unfortunate affair. Gracious goodness. What could induce you to lay violent hands upon—upon Moll?"

"Haven't I told you?" said Slimcoe.

"Yes, of course you have, but—"

"Well, then, why are you surprised. You have done the same thing yourself."

Parker made no reply to this. He certainly was the lesser villain of the two, and looked at his companion as almost too deeply dyed in guilt to have as an inmate of his establishment. He need not have troub'ed himself, however, upon this head, as we shall presently see.

"Confound it, man, but this is unfortunate," said Parker, after a pause. "cursedly unfortunate. This new affair will raise a regular clatter about our ears, just as the other was dying out. Why. Osborne's trial was to come on in a day or two ?"

"I know that."

"Well, when he was once condemned, we were safe, and he's sure to be found guilty, everybody says so down here."

"Everybody must be right," said Slimcoe. "In course there can't be no manner of doubt about that."

"Arn't you got no other place to go to?" inquired Slimcoe.

His companion fixed upon him a malevolent look.

"Well, that's a good 'un. In course I arn't. Oh, I see how it is you don't want me here. That's the way the cat jumps is it? Well, there is one thing, I suppose, that we shan't swing separately. The same rope as is used for one will serve the other."

"Now, don't you be for lost, Slimcoe," said Parker, getting alarmed "Of course we have been rowing in the same boat, and I thought as how matters were going on all right."

"Well, they arn't" said Slimcoe, tartly, "and that's all about it—they arn't."

"No, so it appears," answered his companion. "Was Wild fly to our having any hand in it before—ahem—this last go?"

"Yes, and Colonel Jack to."

"Colonel Jack," said Bawkham, in some surprise.

"What had he to do with it ?"

"He has been to Lawker's Lane."

"What for?"

"Why, to see me to be sure, and Nell made an appointment with him, curse her," he exclaimed, all his bad feelings now being called forth at the recollection of this circumstance.

"To see you, and what for, for goodness sake?"

Slimcoe now entered into all those particulars with which the reader is already acquainted.

"Umph," ejaculated Parker. "I wish you had accepted the offer."

"So do I now," said his companion. "But it was too late."

"How was that?"

"Why, because Jonathan Wild came full tear after me at Balasco's, and it was only by the merest chance or good luck that I escaped as I did. Nell sent her there."

"Ah," sighed forth Parker. "What it is to put your trust in women."

"She will betray no man more," said Slimcoe, with an hideous and malicious grin.

Parker's aunt now entered, and Slimcoe was introduced to her as a particular friend of her nephew's.

The old lady regarded the particular friend with a look of curiosity, blended with suspicion. To say the truth, this man's appearance was decidedly against him. Nevertheless, Miss Parker welcomed the friend of her nephew as best she could under the circumstances of the case.

———

CHAPTER XLVII.

SUDDEN APPEARANCE OF JONATHAN WILD.

THE vehicle containing Squabshot, the thieftaker, and his two companions, went merrily on its road. Wild was in excellent spirits, as he generally was when there was a chance of a capture of any notorious criminal, and he fully expected to be successful in his present attempt. When he and his party reached Shirley, Squabshot got out his plan, and the chaise was driven slowly towards Bawkham. They none of them knew the name of the village, but there could be no mistake when following the chart held by Squabshot. Presently the village appeared in sight.

"That's the place," said Squabshot, "I'll bet my life that's it, depend upon it."

"If you think so" said Wild, "we had better get out."

"Why so?" inquired Squabshot.

"Because you see, my friend, the fact of four persons driving in a chaise covered with dust will tell everybody that we have come some distance, most likely from London, and the attention of all the passengers will be attracted to us. I know what these yokels are. News spreads like wildfire in such a part as this, and the birds may be shy."

"Ah, I see," said Squabshot, laying his finger on the side of his nose. "An admirable precaution—Discernment is the word."

"That's just it," observed Wild. "You and I will stroll leisurely down the street, while my two chaps drive the trap into this lane, and there wait further orders."

This course was adopted, and Wild and his companion did as the former had suggested. As they went along, they observed a milkman in the street.

"Now," said Wild, "you ask this fellow if he knows the men."

"All right," answered Squabshot; "I'm on."

"Umph!" said Wild to himself. "A sharp fellow that; I have many worse than him under me in the force."

Squabshot crossed on the other side of the way, and said confidentially—his manner was usually confidential on all occasions.

"I say, my friend, you don't happen to know my cousin's shop about here?"

"Noa, I don't know who your cousin be; is it a he or a she?"

"A she," said Squabshot. "A Miss Parker—keeps an everything shop."

"Oh, Miss Parker," exclaimed the man. "I should just think that I did now—her—"

"Ah, indeed, then you are just the chap for my money," said Squabshot.

This was a London phrase which the countryman was at a loss to comprehend.

"Well, then, just show me where my cousin lives," said Squabshot, still confidentially. "Keep dark, for I don't want to put her into hysterics."

This the countryman did not understand either; he stared again at our friend Squabshot, and said, as he indulged in a broad grin—so broad, indeed, that Squabshot thought his face was coming in two.

"Well, thee bee'st a rummun," said the milkman.

"How are you off for chalk my friend?" said Squabshot, in a whisper.

This the man did not understand, but he grinned, nevertheless, believing it to be something funny.

"Do'e you want me to show un the house?" said the purveyor of the lacteal fluic.

"Ah, sure; if you have no objection."

"Well, you ain't altogether a bad sort," said the man. "Come this way"

Squabshot followed his friend with the cans, telegraphing to Wild to keep behind.

"There be Miss Parker's shop," said the milkman, as they had got by this time nearly opposite to the shop in question.

"Oh, ah, I see," said Squabshot. "I am much obliged;" and here he took off his hat gracefully to the milkman, who went away laughing, as he muttered to himself—

"He be from London, with his fine airs; there ain't no manner of doubt about that."

Squabshot then crossed over to where Wild stood awaiting the result of his inquiries,

"Well?" said the thieftaker.

"All as clear as the sun at noon day," said Squabshot. "That is, when the sun does happen to shine."

"Does he know where the shop is?"

"Yes, about a dozen doors down on this side of the way."

The thieftaker rubbed his hands in a state of ecstacy.

"Don't begin to crow before you know whether your friend is here or not," said Squabshot.

"Parker is here, at any rate," said the thieftaker.

"Ah, you know that?'

"Yes. Now what shall we do? You had better go in and inquire for Parker. Do you know Slimcoe?"

"No, never saw him to my knowledge," said Squabshot.

"Well, never mind, you go in and inquire for Parker. Try and pump Miss Parker, if she's in the shop."

"And if she's not?"

"You must act as you think fit—you don't want me to tell you. While you are in conversation, me and my chaps will come in. Only you had better go first, as you don't look like a—ahem!—a thieftaker," said Wild.

Squabshot pulled up the collar of his shirt at this observation, and adjusted his hair with a graceful twirl.

"If you see anything that may lead you to imgine that it would be advisable to communicate with us, come out, we shall be round the corner in the lane."

"And if I don't see anything?" said Squabshot.

"Well, then, stay and keep whoever may happen to be there in conversation. I will give you five minutes—not more. If I don't find you come out at the end of that time, I'll—"

"What?"

"Make my appearance on the scene," answered Wild.

"But suppose I see neither of them—that is Parker himself, or Slimcoe—what then?" asked Squabshot.

"Ah,' said Wild, "a good thought. You must say something."

"Yes, what is it to be? I can't inquire if Mr. Jobson lives there."

"No," said Wild, hesitatingly. "But if you are sure it's there, buy some tea, or sugar—"

"Ah, I see, or candles—that's it," said Squabshot.

"Anything you like—I leave that to your own discretion."

Squabshot now took his way to the shop of Miss Parker.

Upon entering it, he found a man behind the counter.

This individual was Parker himself, although the new comer did not know it for a certainty.

He guessed, however, that he was either

Parker or Slimcoe, and consequently was on his guard.

"Morning, sir," said Squabshot, with his usual easy jaunty air.

"Good morning, sir," said Parker, eyeing the new comer with a glance of inquiry.

He seemed to be more satisfied when he had taken stock of Squabshot.

He certainly did not look like a thieftaker, neither did there appear to be any mischief lurking about him.

To say the truth, he looked more like a light comedian than anything else.

Parker, however, saw plainly enough that he was not a native or resident in those parts, and that rendered him a little nervous and fidgetty.

"From London, I suppose, sir?" inquired Parker.

"Umph—no—not exactly," said Squabshot.

This was fencing with the question, but he was at a loss to know how to answer this plain interrogatory.

"What can I do for you, sir?" said Parker.

"I want half a pound of tea, if you please," was the answer.

"Black or mixed?"

"Black, if you please—green tea makes a man nervous," said Squabshot, pulling at his wristbands, and walking to the door, and stealing a furtive glance out into the street.

He was not altogether so comfortable in playing the part as he could have desired to be, and felt a little fidgetty at the forthcoming storm.

The tea was weighed and packed up, not with the same rapidity as our London grocers use, and consequently some time elapsed before it was ready. Still the time was not yet up, and no Jonathan Wild had made his appearance upon the scene.

Squabshot did not know very well how to eke out the time, but catching sight of some prunes in the window, he asked permission to taste one or two. This was granted, and he then ordered a pound of these to be weighed up.

"Psha," he exclaimed, to himself. "It isn't a nice part I'm playing, after all, though the fellow is a murderer."

There was, however, no help for it, and it was too late to recede. How slowly the minutes seem to pass. Squabshot thought the time must have expired over and over again. He looked at his watch, it still wanted a minute to the time.

"Oh," thought he, "it must be past the time now." Nevertheless he began to feel hot, and in a state of incipient perspiration.

The prunes were weighed, and placed before him, and Parker stood with his hands on the counter, waiting for the cash.

Squabshot pulled out his purse, and began to search for silver.

He laid several pieces on the counter and received his change, still no Wild appeared. "Surely the time must be up," he thought, but he did not like to pull out his watch again, for the eye of Parker was fixed upon him.

"You don't happen to know of good lodgings in this neighbourhood," said Squabshot, not knowing what to say to wile away the time. He now hesitated."

"No," he said slowly. "There is Mrs Leescome in Ewin's Lane. She has several rooms to let, I believe, but they are small and perhaps might—"

He did not complete his sentence, for an expression past over his face that Squabshot said he should never forget to his dying day. His features became almost convulsed. So painful was this expression. He had caught sight of Jonathan Wild through the window of the shop door. He trembled in every limb. Guilt was stamped upon every feature.

"Good heavens," thought Squabshot, as he gazed at him, "the man is punished enough."

Wild entered the shop, followed by his two myrmidoms. As he did so, Parker retreated to his back parlour, where sat Slimcoe, who, by the expression of his companion's features, saw at once that something had occurred. Slimcoe was near the door which led into the passage of the house; he slipped quietly through this, and heedless of his companion he shut it, and locked it on the outside. Wild, who was always prompt and ready for any emergency, leaped over the counter, followed by his two men, and rushed into the back parlour after Parker, who, finding the door locked, rushed towards the window, and throwing it open, he leaped into the yard. At the further end of this there was a sort of shed—or warehouse. It had originally been used as a workshop by a carpenter, who had formally occupied the premises. Parker made for this place, and rushing into it he hastily slammed to the door, and bolted it on the inside.

Wild and his two confederates had rushed through the window into the yard, and observed the actions of Parker, although they were not in time to catch him before he got under shelter of the workhshop. To spring at the door, and throw his shoulder against it with all his force, was but the work of a few seconds for Wild, but it resisted his efforts.

"Surrender!" exclaimed the thieftaker, calling out to Parker, who was on the inside. "Surrender—it is useless your endeavouring to escape."

"No answer was vouchsafed to this.

Miss Parker by this time came into the yard, and uttered several piercing screams. Wild took no notice of her, although she rushed about the yard in a demented state.

Wild pushed violently with his foot against the door, and splintered the bottom panel of it. One of his men got hold of a large billet of wood, and commenced battering away at the door, which was soon smashed to atoms, and the thieftaker entered.

With one bound, and a yell like a wild animal, he sprang at the throat of Parker, and forced his fingers in his neckcloth. The murderer positively screamed with fright, and his limbs shook, as though he were stricken with a sudden palsy.

"Oh, dear, kind gentlemen," exclaimed Miss Parker, "please say what is the matter. Oh, do have pity on my poor nephew. What

No. 35.

has he done? Is it for debt that you are arresting him?"

"Debt, ma'am," said Wild, in his usually rough, brusque manner. "It's a rum sort of debt, I'm thinking."

"What is it then?" inquired Miss Parker.

"Oh, only murder," exclaimed the thieftaker.

"Murder!" shrieked out Miss Parker, who really had not the slightest idea of the moral turpitude of her nephew.

"Murder! Oh, gracious heavens!" and she tottered some paces, and, no doubt, would have fallen, had not a new actress come upon the scene. This was an old domestic, who had found her way up from the kitchen.

"Dear heart!" exclaimed this individual. "Don't take on so. It's a false charge, depend upon it."

At this the murderer's aunt cheered up a bit, but she became again reduced to a state of despair as she observed Wild and one of his men pinioning her nephew, and tying his hands firmly behind him.

Wild conveyed him into the back parlour, and placed him in charge of one of the men, while he and the other went in search of Slimcoe.

By the time the aunt, nephew, and thief-taker had returned to the back parlour, Mr. Squabshot had also ensconced himself there. He had been keeping an eye upon Wild's proceedings, and, at the same time, kept the other eye open to watch the shop and front door, to see if he could discover any signs of Slimcoe, either making his appearance, or attempting his escape.

Miss Parker entered the parlour wringing her hands, and looking the very picture of woe, and, as to her nephew, Squabshot thought that he never saw such an alteration in any man in the course of a few minutes in all his life. He could hardly believe it possible that he was the same individual who had served him with the tea and prunes a few minutes previous.

Miss Parker stared at Squabshot as she entered, and Wild's man said, with glee—

"Netted one friend, guv'nor."

"Ah, so I see," said Squabshot, who then turned to Miss Parker, to whom he took off his hat, and said, kindly—

"I am sorry for you—truly sorry, believe me ; but these things will happen in the best regulated families."

"Oh dear, dear me," exclaimed the elderly maiden lady, "is it true, sir, that they charge my nephew with—oh—murder."

Mr. Squabshot shrugged his shoulders, and felt bound to declare that it was, indeed, too true.

"But, my dear madam, do not worry yourself, I pray," he said, in continuation. "After all, the case has to be proved, and—"

"Oh, sir, what shall I do. My good name is destroyed for ever. The credit of our family is gone. Oh, dear—dear," and here she burst into a violent flood of tears.

While this was taking place, Wild had sought in every room in the house above stairs.

Simcoe had flown from one to the other, and finally, as he heard the footsteps of his pursuers, he had arrived at the top landing, and sprang up at the trap door, which led on to the roof.

"There he is," said Wild. "Look sharp after him, and this time he won't escape us."

Slimcoe, was, however, too active, he was through the trap door in an instant, and before his pursuers had time to effect a capture ; he closed the trap with a loud slam, and was in the loft alone.

Wild drew a pistol, and fired it at the flying man. The report was heard below, but the shot did no other damage than penetrating the trap door itself.

"Curses on him ; but we will have him yet," said Wild.

He flew into an adjacent bedroom, and procured a chair. Upon this he mounted and endeavoured to open the trap door ; but Slimcoe was already standing on it, besides which, he had fastened it with the bolt on the inside of it.

Desperate efforts were now made by the two thieftakers, to effect an entrance into the loft above. Taking the handle of a broom which they happened to find on the landing, they inserted the end of it in the side of the trap door, and endeavoured thereby to force it open.

Slimcoe found that it gave way, and hastily leaving it, he hurried on through the loft door, which led on to the tiles. Opening this, he passed through, and gained the roof. While so doing, Wild had succeeded in forcing open the lower trap. He and his companion lost no time in passing through this, and entering the loft, when they observed the flying man getting through the other trap, Wild discharged his other pistol again without effect. With a terrible oath he followed, and he and his subordinate were soon on the tiles. They gazed round, but no Slimcoe was to be seen.

"Where can he have got to ?" said Wild, in evident surprise.

"Surely he has never had the temerity to drop from the roof?"

"I should think not," answered Wild's companion ; "such a course would be attended with certain and immediate death."

They looked down into the street below, as also at the side of the house, but Slimcoe was nowhere to be seen.

Suddenly Wild's quick eye caught sight of a small window in an adjacent house. It immediately occurred to him that the murderer had in all probability made an entrance through this, and he communicated his suspicions to his companion who, with the thieftaker, made for the window in question.

When they arrived at it, they found that it was fastened on the inside, but Wild was not a man to stick at trifles, he dashed his fist through it, breaking therewith several panes of glass, as well as sashes which enclosed them ; tearing these away, Wild effected an entrance, followed by his companion.

They found themselves in an empty room, at least, empty so far as any human inhabitant was concerned ; it was, however, furnished as a bed-room. Proceeding along this, they took their way into another apartment, similarly furnished, with a solitary occupant—an old woman.

"Hilloa!" exclaimed Wild, "what's gone of the man?"

He wisely assumed that such had been there.

The old dame uttered a faint scream.

"What has gone of him?" exclaimed Wild, still more vociferously.

"Down stairs, good kind gentlemen," she answered, in a tremulous voice.

"All right," exclaimed Wild, "come on."

And then they hastily descended.

When they arrived at the basement story, a man came out of the back parlour, and seemed almost as frightened as the woman had been above.

"Dear—dear," he exclaimed, "what is the matter gentlemen?"

"Where's the man?" said Wild.

"I don't know where he is, I assure you."

"Most likely not—we don't say you do; but where has he gone to?"

"A man, a perfect stranger, rushed down stairs into—"

"Ah, where, that's the question?"

"I don't know."

"Show us the way he went."

The inmate of the parlour preceded the two thieftakers down the stairs which led into the kitchens. Wild and his companion followed.

They made a hasty inspection of the front kitchen, then the back, or washhouse, as it was called, but no Slimcoe appeared visible.

"Have you any cellars to this house?" inquired Wild.

"Yes, sir."

"Show us them, then."

The man hastily obeyed, and the door of one of these was found open.

"Get us a light," said Wild, to the owner of the house; "do you hear? Be quick, man."

A candle was brought, and Wild made a minute inspection of the cellar; but no Slimcoe could be discovered.

While he was doing this, his companion heard some grating sound.

"Ah, what's that?" he exclaimed, as he rushed from the cellar out into the passage.

The noise ceased.

"There is another cellar, gentlemen," said the man who occupied the house.

"Where?" said Wild's companion.

The man showed him the door of this. It was fastened.

"Ay, Mister Wild!"

"Hilloa!" said the thieftaker. "What's up?"

"This way, master."

Wild was by his side in a second or two. The man pointed to the fastened door.

"Ah," exclaimed Wild, "that's it, is it?

Look here, my friend, have you locked this door?"

This was addressed to the landlord.

"No, sir."

A violent push was now made by the thieftaker against the door in question. It did not however yield to his efforts.

"Have you the key of this door?" he inquired of the man, who stood staring and trembling at these proceedings.

"The key was in the door," he answered.

"Oh, it was, eh?" said Wild, giving a meaning look at his companion. "Have you got a hammer or hatchet, my friend?" he continued, to the man, who immediately went into the kitchen or washhouse, and returned with a large hammer.

"Ah, that's the sort of thing. Now then."

A series of well-directed and heavy blows were now showered against the door, which soon yielded, and eventually Wild was able to burst it open.

Taking the light in his hand, he placed it above his head, and peered into the cellar.

As he did this, two flashing eyes, like those of some wild animal, met his gaze.

"Ah," said the thieftaker, "well and good. We have my gentleman, now, I believe."

An inward chuckle followed this speech.

True enough, Slimcoe was in the darkest part of the cellar, crouching like a wild cat. Jonathan Wild cocked his pistol, and then said—

"Hilloa, sir, yield. Do you hear?"

No answer was returned to this.

"Yield, or I will shoot you down like a dog as you are."

Still no answer.

"Hold the light, Jem," said the thieftaker. "Hold it high up, that I may see my way."

The man did as he was desired, and Wild entered, pistol in hand. There was a flash and a loud report—but not from Wild's pistol. It came from Slimcoe, and wounded Wild in the left shoulder.

"Curses on him," said the thieftaker, now aroused to a perfect fury. "Hold the light still."

Wild had scarcely uttered these words, when another report was heard, and a sort of smothered groan, and an indescribable noise followed. Wild had aimed at the man's head, but had caught the lower jaw, a portion of which it had carried away in its passage.

Wounded as he was, the thieftaker rushed now upon the murderer, and grappled with him. The wretch endeavoured to draw his knife from his breast, but even in the little light which now found its way into the cellar, Wild discerned the man's intention. He struck him a fearful blow with the butt end of the pistol on the head. So fearful and sickening was the sound, that it appeared as though an ox had been felled. All this was the work of only a few seconds, and scarcely had this occurred before the murderer was in the grasp of Wild's companions. He was soon dragged out into the passage, which was soon deluged with his blood, and his appearance was so hideous that the owner of the house staggered back a few paces, and appeared as though about to swoon.

CHAPTER XLVIII.

THE PRISONERS ARE CONVEYED TO LONDON. THE SUICIDE.

RALPH SLIMCOE could hardly be said to be conscious when in the grasp of Jonathan Wild's follower. The blow which the thieftaker had dealt upon his head had well nigh stunned him, and he was just capable of being guided into the house of Parker by his captor, and nothing more. Wild followed the two; a dark stream of blood was also flowing from his shoulder, and he was then in great pain, but held up however, and appeared comparatively cheerful. This was induced by the fact of the capture he had just made.

When the two made an entrance into the back parlour of Miss Parker's house, the fearful appearance of Slimcoe made every inmate turn pale, as a cold shudder run through their frames. A frightful and ghastly wound was on his temple, and a portion of the lower jaw had been carried away with the pistol ball. Altogether he presented a most fearful appearance. Parker gazed upon him in perfect horror, but he said nothing, but sat bound as he was in the chair where he had been placed by the officer who had brought him in from the yard. As to Miss Parker, her wits seemed to have entirely left her. The scenes she had witnessed had completely scared her understanding clear away.

"Ugh!" exclaimed Wild, as he endeavoured to staunch his wound with his pocket handkerchief. "Must have a doctor."

"My dear sir," said Squabshot, "you appear to be badly wounded, and as to—"

"The other beauty," said the thieftaker; "he has got it worth his money, but we mnch have a doctor—cannot go to London as it is."

"Shall I go out and see after one?" inquired Squabshot.

"Aye, if you will."

Squabshot was off in a minute, and very shortly returned with a little individual, with a pale face and a white cravat. This gentleman had luckily brought his case of instruments with him, as Squabshot had informed him how matters stood. The first person he examined was Wild. The pistol ball had passed through the muscle and flesh, and had lodged in the scapula or shoulder blade. The wound was probed, and, eventually, the pistol ball was extracted; the wound was then dressed and strapped up, and the thieftaker found himself much more easy, although rather faint from loss of blood. The doctor then proceeded to make an examination of Slimcoe, who by this time had recovered his consciousness, and was suffering intense agony. The wound on the forehead was strapped up, and the splinters of the jaw put together as well as they could be, but the wound was a fearful one, and seemed very painful. While this was taking place, Parker managed to pull his aunt by the gown, and as she leaned over, he whispered something in her ear. She did not appear to comprehend what he said, but he whispered again, and then Miss Parker disappeared up stairs, and after an absence of a few minutes she returned and again leant over to her nephew.

All this took place while the attention of the other persons in the room was taken up with the wounded men, so that the action of Miss Parker was hardly noticed at all, or if so. they thought she was but exchanging a few parting words with her nephew.

"Now, about conveying the prisoners to London?" said one of Wild's men to his master.

"We can't take them in our own vehicle," said Wild.

"What's to be done, then?"

"You must go, Bradley, to the chief of the district constabulary; but stay, I will go myself."

Agreeable to this resolution, Wild set off with Squabshot to the nearest magistrate, leaving the two prisoners in charge of his men.

He had an interview with the county magistrate, who gave him an order upon the chief of the rural police, and eventually succeeded in getting a prison van to convey the two murderers to London.

By the time this vehicle had driven up in front of Miss Parker's shop, a crowd of persons had assembled to catch sight of the two men who were to be conveyed thence to London; for by this time the affair had become noised about the whole neighbourhood. The two prisoners were conveyed into the van, and one of the rural police sat at the door behind, while the two other officers kept guard over the prisoners inside the gloomy vehicle.

Wild and Squabshot drove ahead in the double-backed chaise, the prison van following in the rear. In this way they proceeded to London.

It was Wild's intention to lodge them in Newgate, and on arriving at that prison, upon the two murderers being desired to alight, Parker was found to be lying in the corner of the van, and made no reply or movement to the request of the officer who desired him to get out. The latter shook him—still no reply. An odour, as of almonds, found its way into the nostrils of the officer. He shook the prisoner gently at first, then violently—still no answer.

" Good heavens, Jem," exclaimed the officer, " the man's dead."

" Dead—impossible."

" He's either dead or else in a swoon."

They carried him out, and took him up the steps of Newgate, and placed him in a chair.

The prison surgeon was sent for, who immediately declared the wretched man to be dead.

He had fallen by his own hand, having swallowed prussic acid.

It was a small phial containing this poison which his aunt had procured for him out of one of the drawers in his bed-room; she did not know, however, at the time, what it contained.

" He's gone," said the doctor, as the odour of bitter almonds impregnated the air.

Slimcoe was conveyed into one of the wards of the prison, there to await his trial. In a few days this came on, and the jury returned a verdict of guilty, in both cases, namely, for the murder of Jabez Crudge, as well as that of his mistress.

The case was sufficiently clear against him in the former case, and in the latter also, for the wretched man, Parker, had left a written confession of the whole particulars of the Cow Cross murder.

CHAPTER XLVIII.

THE CONDEMNATION AND EXECUTION.

HENRY OSBORNE was discharged from custody without a stain upon his character. The case against Slimcoe was so fully and substantially proved, that there could not be a shadow of doubt about the whole transaction.

In addition to this, the murderer made a full and ample confession.

He was obstinate at first, but from the exhortations of the ordinary he was brought to a sense of his awful position.

In the days of which we write it was not customary to give malefactors the same amount of time for repentance that is vouchsafed to them in this our more humane and considerate age. The wretched man underwent his trial on the Saturday, and on the following Monday he was doomed to suffer for his henious crimes, which were of that nature as to leave little room for sympathy in his behalf.

He was to suffer the extreme penalty of the law at the new drop in front of Newgate.

As Squabshot had been mixed up in the whole affair, he was determined to see the final act of the law carried out.

As Squabshot was to rise at three o'clock in the morning, he went to bed at ten, thinking that five hours sleep would be amply sufficient to brace him against the fatigues of the day.

He had determined to mingle with the crowd on foot, not having the advantage of a sheriff's order to admit him in the walls of the prison.

As might be expected, upon his retiring to rest, the event of the morrow was dominant in his mind; he heard all the clocks in the neighbourhood chime the hours in succession —a dog from some distant court kept up a pitiful howling. At one o'clock a cock set up a melancholy feeble crowing—shortly after two o'clock daylight came peeping in at the shutters, for Squabshot was sleeping at a lodging in the immediate neighbourhood of the prison. By this time a friend of his arrived who had agreed to witness the awful ceremony with him. A jovial friend on most occasions, but this was a scene that rather depressed his spirits. They had neither of them ever seen an execution before in all their lives, perhaps they would never again. We shall see. This friend had kept merry company all night, and made appropriate jokes upon the coming event. Many like to have their laugh and fling about it—there is a certain grim pleasure in the circumstance, a perpetual jingling antithesis between life and death that is sure of its effect.

In mansion or garret, on down or straw, surrounded by weeping friends and solemn oily doctors, or tossing unheeded upon scanty hospital beds, there were many people in this great city to whom that Sunday night was to be the last of any that they should pass on earth here. In the course of half-a-dozen dark wakeful hours, one had leisure to think of these (and a little, too, of that certain supreme night that shall come one time or other, when he who writes shall be stretched upon the last bed, prostrate in the last struggle, taking the last look of dear faces that have cheered us here, and lingering—one moment more—ere we part for the tremendous journey. But Squabshot could not help thinking, as each clock sounded, what Slimcoe was doing now with his wounded and shattered face, and still more shattered heart.

Has he heard it in his little room in Newgate yonder ? Eleven o'clock. He has been writing until now. The gaoler says he is a pleasant man enough to be with, but he can hold out no longer, and is very weary.

"Wake me at four," says he, "for I have still much to put down."

From eleven to twelve the gaoler hears how he is grinding his teeth in his sleep. At twelve he is up in his bed, and inquires of his gaoler—

"Is it the time ?"

He has plenty more time yet for sleep ; and he sleeps, and the bells go on tolling. Seven hours more—five hours more. Many a carriage is clattering through the streets, bringing ladies away from evening parties ; many bachelors are reeling home after a jolly night ; Covent Garden is alive ; and the light coming through the cell-window turns the gaoler's candle pale.

Four hours more !

"Slimcoe," says the gaoler, shaking him, "it's four o'clock, and I've woke you as you desired, but there's no call for you to get up."

The poor wretch leaves his bed, however, and performs his last toilette, and then falls to writing, to tell the world how he did the crime for which he has suffered. This time he will tell the truth the whole truth. They bring him his breakfast from the coffee-shop opposite—tea, coffee, and thin bread and butter.

He will take nothing, however, but goes on writing ; he has to write to his mother— the pious mother far away in his own country—who reared him and loved him ; and even now has sent him her forgiveness and her blessing. He finishes his memorials and letters, and makes his will, disposing of his little miserable property of books and tracts that pious people have furnished him with. Then he has a token for his dear friend the gaoler ; another for his dear friend the under-sheriff.

As the day of the convict's death draws nigh, it is painful to see how he fastens upon everybody who approaches him, how pitifully he clings to them and loves them.

While these things which are sad enough are going on in the prison, a carriage is about to convey a party of aristocratic young swells to the scene. The owners and occupiers thereof shortly debate whether it is better—when it is needful to get up so early in the morning—if it be not better to have an hour or two's sleep, or wait until the day's work be done, and then go to bed. The gentlemen have some brandy and soda water before they set out, as it clears the brain wonderfully. Thus primed, the party set out. The coachman drops asleep on the box, and wakes up wildly as the hall door opens. It is just four o'clock ; about the time they are making the—pshaw ! "Who is for a cigar ?"

The owner of the carriage does not smoke himself, but bows and protests in the kindest way in the world, that he does not care for the new drab linings of his carriage. One of the party who smokes mounts, however, the box.

"Drive to Snow Hill," says the owner of the chariot. The city officers, who are the only persons in the street, look knowing— they know what it means well enough. How cool and clear the streets look as the carriage startles the echoes that have been asleep in the corners all night.

Somebody must have been sweeping the pavement clean in the night time ; surely they would not soil a lady's white satin shoes, they are so dry and neat. There is not a cloud, or breath of air except from the cigar of the gentleman on the box, which whiffs off and soars straight upwards in balloons of pure white smoke. The trees in the squares look bright and green. He who keeps late hours do not know the beauty of London air and verdure in the early morning ; they are delightful, the freshest and most lively companions possible, but they cannot bear the crowd and bustle of midday. You don't know them, they are no longer the same things. The carriage has come to Grays Inn. There is actually dew upon the grass, and the windows of the stout, red houses are all in a flame.

As the party enter Holborn, the town grows more animated, and there are already twice as many people in the streets as you see at midday in an English provincial town.

The gin shop keepers have, many of them, taken their shutters down, and many persons are issuing therefrom pipe in hand. Down they go along the broad street, their blue shadows marching after them, for they are all bound the same way, and are bent upon seeing the man hanged.

At twenty minutes past four the carriage passes St. Sepulchres. By this time many hundreds of people are coming down Snow Hill. Before the man who is smoking a cigar, and the coachman, lies Newgate prison ; but something more awful still, which seizes the eye at once, and makes the heart beat quickly, is the black and awful gallows. There it stands ready jutting out from a little door in the prison. As you see it you feel a kind of dumb electric shock, which causes one to start a little, and give a sort of gasp for breath. The shock is one in a second ; and presently you examine the object before you with a certain feeling of complacent curiosity. At least, such was the effect that the gallows first produced upon the writer, who is trying to set down all his feelings as they occurred, and not to exaggerate them at all. After the gallows shock, the party in the carriage went down into the crowd, which was very numerous, but not dense as yet. It was evident that the day's business had not begun.

People sauntered up, and formed groups, and talked, asking those who seemed *habitues* of the place about former executions; and did the victim hang with his face towards the clock or towards Ludgate Hill? and had he the rope round his neck when he came on the scaffold, or was it put on by Jack Ketch afterwards? and had Lord W— taken a window, and which was he? A pseudo W— was pointed out at the opposite window.

A great number of coarse phrases are used, but the morals of the men are good and hearty. A ragamuffin in the crowd (a powdery baker in a white sheep's wool cap) uses some radiant expression to a woman near; there is an instant cry of shame which silences the man, and a dozen people are ready to give the woman protection.

The crowd has grown very dense by this time, it is six o'clock, and there is a great heaving and pushing, and swaying to and fro; but round the women the men have formed a circle, and keep them, as much as possible, out of the rush and trample. In one of the houses near to the scene, a gallery has been formed on the roof. Seats were here let, and a number of persons of various degrees were occupying them.

Several tipsy, dissolute looking young men were in this gallery; one was lolling over the sun-shining tiles, with a fierce sodden face, out of which came a pipe, and which was shaded by long matted hair, and a hat cocked very much on one side. This gentleman was one of a party who had evidently not been to bed on Sunday night, but had passed it in one of the delectable night houses in the neighbourhood of Covent Garden. The debauch was not yet over, and the women of the party were giggling, drinking, and romping, as is the wont of those delicate creatures, sprawling here and there, and falling upon the knees of one or the other of the males. Their scarfs were off their shoulders, and the sun was shining upon their bare white flesh.

The people about the gallows were very indignant at some of the proceedings of the debauched crew, and at last raised up such a yell as frightened them into shame, and they were more orderly for the rest of the day.

The windows of the shops opposite began to fill apace, and a man with ragged elbows pointed out a celebrated fashionable character who occupied one of them, and much to the surprise of those who had occupied the carriage, he seemed to be well acquainted with his history. The people about him took up the conversation, and carried it on bravely much to the surprise of the carriage occupants.

The character of the crowd was as yet, however, quite festive. Jokes bandying about here and there, and jolly laughs breaking out. Some men were endeavouring to climb up a leaden pipe on one of the houses. The landlord came out and endeavoured, with might and main, to pull them down. Many thousand eyes turned upon this contest immediately. All sorts of voices issued from the crowd and uttered choice expressions of slang.

When one of the men was pulled down by the leg, the waves of this black mob-ocean laughed innumerably; when one fellow slipped away, scrambled up the pipe, and made good his lodgment on the shelf, they were all made happy, and encouraged him by loud shouts of admiration. What is there so particularly delightful in the spectacle of a man clambering up a gas-pipe? Why were the inspectors kept for a quarter of an hour in deep interest gazing upon this remarkable scene? Indeed it is hard to say; a man does not know what a fool he is until he tries; or, at least, what mean follies will amuse him. The other day I went to Astley's and saw a clown come in with a foolscap and pinafore, and six small boys who represented his school-fellows. To them enters schoolmaster; horses clown, and flogs him hugely on the back part of his pinafore.

I never read anything in Swift, Boz, Rabelais, Fielding, Paul de Kock, which delighted me so much as this sight, and caused me to laugh so profoundly. And why? What is there so ridiculous in the sight of one miserably rouged man beating another on the breech? Tell us where the fun lies, in this and the before-mentioned episode of the gas-pipe? Vast, indeed, are the capacities and ingenuities of the human soul that can find, in incidents so wonderfully small, means of contemplation and amusement.

Really the time passed away with extraordinary quickness. A thousand things of the sort related here came to amuse us. First, the workmen knocking and hammering at the scaffold, mysterious clattering of blows was heard within it, and a ladder, painted black, was carried round, and into the interior of the edifice by a small side door.

We all looked at this little ladder and at each other—things began to be very interesting.

Soon came a squad of policemen—stalwart, rosy-looking men, saying much for city feeding—well-dressed, well-limbed, and of admirable good humour. They paced about the open space between the prison and the barriers which kept in the crowd from the scaffold.

The front line, as far as I could see, was chiefly occupied by blackguards and boys—professional persons, no doubt, who saluted the officers on their appearance with a volley of jokes and ribaldry.

As far as I could judge from faces, there were more blackguards of sixteen or seventeen, than of any maturer age ; stunted, sallow, ill-grown lads, in rugged fustian, scowling about.

There were a considerable number of girls, too, of the same age ; one that Cruikshank and Boz might have taken as a study for Nancy.

The girl was a young thief's mistress evidently ; if attacked, ready to reply without a particle of modesty ; could give as good ribaldry as she got ; made no secret (and there were several inquiries) as to her profession and means of livelihood.

But with all this, there was something good about the girl ; a sort of devil-may-care candour and simplicity that one could not fail to see.

Her answers to some of the coarse questions put to her, were very ready and good-humoured.

She had a friend with her of the same age and class, of whom she seemed to be very fond, and who looked up to her for protection.

Both of these women had beautiful eyes.

Devil-may-care's were extraordinarily bright and blue, an admirably fair complexion, and a large red mouth full of white teeth. *Au reste*, ugly, stunted, thick-limbed, and by no means a beauty.

Her friend could not be more than fifteen.

They were not in rags, but had greasy cotton shawls, and old, faded, rag-shop bonnets.

I was curious to look at them, having, in late fashionable novels, read many accounts of such personages.

Bah ! what figments these novelists tell us !

Boz, who knows life well, knows that his Miss Nancy is the most unreal fantastical personage possible ; no more like a thief's mistress, than one of Gesner's shepherdesses resembles a real country wench. He dare not tell the truth concerning such young ladies.

They have, no doubt, virtues like other human creatures ; nay, their position engenders virtues that are not called into exercise among other women.

But on these an honest painter of human nature has no right to dwell ; not being able to paint the whole portrait, he has no right to present one or two favourable points as characterising the whole ; and therefore, in fact, had better leave the picture alone altogether.

The new French literature is essentially false and worthless from this very error—the writers giving us favourable pictures of monsters (and, to say nothing of decency or morality), pictures quite untrue to nature.

But yonder, glittering through the crowd in Newgate Street, see the sheriffs' carriages are slowly making their way. The crowd have been here three hours. Is it possible that they can have passed so soon ? Close to the barriers the mob has become so dense that it is with difficulty a man can retain his footing. Each man, however, is very careful in protecting the women, and all are full of jokes and good-humour.

The windows of the shops opposite are now pretty nearly filled by the persons who hired them. Many young dandies are there with moustachios and cigars ; some quiet, fat, family parties, of simple honest tradesmen and their wives, who are looking on with the greatest imaginable calmness, and sipping their tea.

Yonder is the sham lord, who is flinging various articles among the crowd ; one of his companions, a tall, burly man with large moustachios, has provided himself with a squirt, and is aspersing the mob with brandy and water. Honest gentleman ! high-bred aristocrat ! genuine lover of humour and wit !

The crowd tried to get up a hiss against these ruffians, but only had a trifling success. They did not seem to think their offence very heinous ; and a philosopher in ragged elbows was not inspired with any such savage disgust at the proceedings of certain notorious young gentlemen ; he only said—

" So-and-so is a lord, and they'll let him off."

And then discoursed about Lord Ferrers being hanged. The philosopher knew the history pretty well, and so did most of the little group of persons about him, and it must be a gratifying thing for young gentlemen to find that their actions are made the subject of this sort of conversation.

Scarcely a word had been said about Slimcoe all this time. The crowd appeared to be in that state of mind as men are when squeezing at the pit door of a theatre, or pushing for a review, or a Lord Mayor's show.

Some asked those who were near them, whether they had seen many executions ? Most of them had, the philosopher especially ; whether the sight of them did any good ? " For the matter of that, no ; people did not care about them at all ; nobody ever thought of it after a bit."

A countryman, who had left his drove in Smithfield, said the same thing ; he had seen a man hanged at York, and spoke of the ceremony with perfect good sense, and in a quiet, sagacious way.

J. S—, the famous wit, now dead, had, I recollect, a good story upon the subject of executing, and of the terror which the punishment inspires. After Thistlewood and his companions were hanged, their heads were taken off according to the sentence; and the executioner, as he severed each, held it up to the crowd in the proper orthodox way, saying, "Here is the head of a traitor." At the sight of the first ghastly head the people were struck with terror, and a general expression of disgust and fear broke from them. The second head was looked at also with much interest, but the excitement regarding the third head diminished. When the executioner had come to the last of the heads, he lifted it; but, by some clumsiness, allowed it to drop. At this the crowd yelled out "Ah; butter-fingers!"—the excitement had passed entirely away. The punishment had grown to be a joke—butter-fingers was the word—a pretty commentary, indeed, upon the august nature of public executions, and the awful majesty of the law.

It was past seven now; the quarters rang and passed away; the crowd began to grow very ager and more quiet. Squabshot turned back very now and then and looked at St. Sepulchre's clock. Half an hour, twenty-five minutes. What is he doing now. Squabshot and his friend held their breath in suspense as they thought of this.

"He has his irons off by this time," said Squabshot—at a quarter—"he is in the press-room now, no doubt."

"What for?" inquired his friend.

"To be pinioned," resumed Squabshot. A shudder passed through the frame of the other.

How slowly the clock crept over the last quarter of an hour. Those who were able to turn round and see (for the crowd was now fearfully dense—and Squabshot found his chest being pressed almost flat) chronicled the time ; five minutes—at last—ding dong—ding dong—the bell is knelling the chimes of eight.

*   *   *   *

Between the writing of this line and the last, the pen has been put down, as the reader may suppose, and the person who is addressing him gone through a series of no very pleasant thoughts and recollections. The whole of the sickening, ghastly scene passes before the eyes again, and indeed, it an awful one to see, and very hard and painful to describe.

As the clock began to strike, an immense sway and movement swept over the whole of that vast crowd. They were all uncovered directly, and a great murmur arose, more awful, *bizarre*, and indescribable than it is possible to describe with any degree of accuracy. Women and children begun to shriek horridly, a dreadful, quick, feverish kind of jangling noise mingled with the murmur of the people, lasting for about two minutes. The scaffold stood tenantless, and the black chain was hanging down ready from the beam. Nobody came.

" He has been respited," said one.

" Oh never,' said Squabshot.

" Then he has killed himself in prison—destroyed himself like his fellow criminal, Parker," said another.

There was a breathless pause.

Just then, from under the prison door a pale head peered out. It was shockingly bright and distinct. It rose up directly, and a man in black appeared on the scaffold who was silently followed by about four more dark figures. The first was a tall, grave man. Everybody knew who that was. The second was Slimcoe, for his face was bandaged up, and his appearance was frightful.

" That is him—that is him," the people exclaimed, as a deep groan arose from the multitude. at which the wretched man turned still more pale, if possible.

His shirt was open ; his arms were tied in front of him ; he opened his hands in a, helpless kind of way, and clasped them once or twice together. He turned his head here and there, and looked about him for an instant, with a wild, imploring kind of a look.

His mouth was contracted into a sort of pitiful and unnatural smile ; he went and placed himself at once under the beam, with his face towards St. Sepulchre's.

The tall, grave man in black twisted him round swiftly in the other direction, and drawing from his pocket a nightcap, pulled it tight over the wretched man's face, hiding it from the gaze of that curious and anxious multitude.

Another minute, and Slimcoe was suspended in the air, as the gaze of thousands of upturned faces were rivetted upon the ghastly object which swayed to and fro in its death agony.

So ended the career of as great a villain as it was possible to conceive.

———

CHAPTER XLIX.

THE REUNION AT MR. SQUABSHOT'S SALONS.

HENRY OSBORNE, upon his being discharged from custody, took his way to his lodgings in Goswell Street, where the renowned Squabshot awaited his appearance with the utmost degree of anxiety. This last named individual deemed it not only expedient, but an absolute necessity, that some demonstration should be made upon the occasion of Osborne's being again a free man, not only free as far as his incarceration was concerned, but free from any stain upon his character, which to him was a matter of still greater satisfaction.

The ovation which Osborne received from Squabshot upon his appearance at his old lodgings, was something astounding. Osborne was not at all anxious for any display, but Squabshot insisted upon having a supper and an evening's entertainment on the first night of Osborne's return, consequently, a few friends had been invited, amongst whom was, of course, our hero. Squabshot had deemed it necessary also to fortify himself during the day with sundry potations to enable him to meet the coming affairs with fitting spirit ; he was, therefore, in a state of hilarious enjoyment when the party assembled. Congratulatory speeches and vows of friendship were the order of the evening, and, as was usual with Mr. Squabshot and his friends, the hours were beguiled with harmony from the assembled guests.

After supper had been demolished, and sundry potations had been swallowed, Mr. Squabshot rose upon his legs, as he termed it, and commenced as follows : —

" Gentlemen—I rise to propose the health of an individual who is known to most of you, and I am sure, my friends, that you will cordially respond to me, not only with your voices, but in your hearts—hearts that sympathise with ill-used and suffering men," said the speaker, emphasizing the last sentence, and glancing round upon the assembly, like a member of the bar who thought he had made a point. "Yes, gentlemen," he continued, "hearts that sympathise with those who are under the arrow, or have had the black ox tread upon their toe; and I am sure we may say that most of us have done so in the present instance. My esteemed and valued friend, Mr. Henry Osborne, has been, as I need hardly inform you, the victim of a foul conspiracy and untoward circumstances, he has, however, passed through the fire and come off scathless; he has been assailed with the slanderous tongues of malicious individuals—he has been cruelly libelled by a paltry press, but he has passed through all and triumphs over his enemies, and now shines again in his own natural effulgence."

At this period of his discourse the speaker again cast a glance round the assembly, one or two of whom uttered suppressed murmurs of admiration and approval.

"Gentlemen," continued Squabshot, "we have all our troubles and trials in this world, but I think I am speaking within bounds when I say that none more so than this gentleman, whose health I have now the honour of proposing. Of gentle, quiet, and unobtrusive manners, you behold in him the political scholar and finished gentleman; one whom I may say with truth, it is a pleasure to know, and knowing as well as I do, it is impossible to do otherwise than admire and esteem. (Hear, hear, from the assembled guests.) I am sure I am not indulging in hyperbole, or fulsome adulation, when I say thus much. I feel strongly, and although I may be at a loss for words to express the sentiments of my heart, I nevertheless hope you will take the will for the deed. I need not tell you that I have been mixed up with this affair—I allude to the Cow Cross murder—and it is my pride that I have been so identified with it in the way I have. I do not mean with the murder itself, but in being instrumental in bringing the real culprits to justice. For the first time in my life I witnessed with a friend, who is here amongst us this evening, that horrible sight—a public execution. I say horrible, for such I must ever consider it, although the victim richly deserved his fate. I will not expatiate upon the scene of carrying out the final act of the law. Slimcoe has gone to his account, and I believe in this great city there is hardly to be found one single individual who will have the hardihood to say that he did not merit the ignominious death he met with before the upturned faces of assembled thousands. But let that pass—Mr. Osborne is with us—that is he stands before us unsullied by the foul and pestilential breath of scandal. He is here once again, and will take his position in the social scale, which

his talents and high sense of moral rectitude must of necessity command."

The speaker paused to take breath, and swallow a little enlivening fluid. The colonel and Osborne were quite unprepared for this unexpected and sudden flight of their friend Squabshot. As to Osborne, although he could hardly repress a smile, he really felt uncomfortable at the flattering encomiums passed upon him.

"I cannot tell you, how rejoiced I am," continued Squabshot. "I cannot express to you the pleasure it has afforded me to have been fortunate enough to have been of service in this affair. To say that it is the proudest act of my life would be saying little, for I have very little to be proud of."

"Yes, yes, you have," said several voices.

"Indeed, gentlemen, I have not, I assure you; the only thing I can remember, is doing a rascally assassin jew money lender, and that I certainly was proud of at the time, but after all, it is not much to boast of, not certainly anything like so good an act as rescuing the just and righteous from the slough of despair. But I digress, gentlemen, the toast I am about to propose is "health, wealth, and long life to our friend, Mr. Henry Osborne."

It is needless to say that this toast was drank amidst the jingling of glasses and vociferous plaudits. When the clamour had ceased, Osborne was of course compelled to rise for his reply. He would have much rather have been excused from being a participator in the scene altogether, but nevertheless he felt deeply grateful to Squabshot, who had his own way of demonstrating his friendship.

"Gentlemen," said Osborne, "individually and collectively, permit me to express my most sincere and unfeigned thanks for the expressions and sympathy you have evinced in my behalf. To my excellent and sincere friend, Mr. Squabshot, I have especially to direct my thanks. I am sure if he had been my own brother, he could not have evinced greater consideration for me in the hour of my misfortune, nor worked harder to bring about an elucidation of that dark mystery which so weighed me down, and oppressed me with a deadening weight—which was oppressive to the last degree. It is useless endeavouring to conceal the fact that the whole framework of society is kept together by the dependence class has upon class, and one individual has upon another, and it is therefore impossible to say at any time who may be useful or serviceable to us. I have had this demonstrated to me in the present instance. I thank Mr. Squabshot for the flattering enconiums he has passed upon me, and I may say with truth, that I was not aware until to-night that he was gifted with so much eloquence in addition to his many other excellent qualifications of both hand and heart—"

"Oh, pray don't be too flowery, because I can't stand it, you know," ejaculated Squabshot, with mock pathos, as he affected a deprecatory gesture.

"I have, however, to express myself fully sensible of all his kindnesses towards me, which I shall never forget to the latest period of my existence. Gentlemen, again thanking you for the good wishes you have expressed this night, to each and all I return my best thanks."

The speaker than sat down amidst vociferous plaudits.

"I am sure I was not aware that we had so much eloquence in the company," said Colonel Jack, with a smile.

"My dear fellow," answered Squabshot, "it is the subject which inspires us. Who would not be eloquent after so great an escape, and so narrow a one, as our friend has experienced?"

While Squabshot was uttering these words, a knock was heard at the outer door, and a voice inquiring for Mr. Squabshot.

Colonel Jack knew the voice well enough, too well, indeed—it was the well-remembered tones of Jonathan Wild.

"Hush," said our hero, laying his hand upon the arm of Squabshot, to detain him from opening the door and emerging into the passage, as was his practice when he heard any one inquiring for himself.

"Hush, that is Wild's voice—I don't want to see him."

"Oh, don't you?" said Squabshot, biting his finger nails.

"No, old boy, and what's more, I must not see him. Where can I go?"

"Into the next room," said Squabshot, opening the door which led into the back parlour, which was Squabshot's bed-room. Colonel Jack did not wait for a second appeal, but hastily entered the back parlour, and secreted himself therein, closing the door after him, and locking it on the inside.

In all probability the quick ear of Jonathan Wild detected the noise occasioned by this movement, for he hastened towards the room door which led into the front parlour occupied by Mr. Squabshot.

He inquired loudly again for the latter individual, Squabby emerged from his room, and grasped the thieftaker by the hand.

It never took our friend long to become familiar with any new friend, and he had become on particularly good terms with Wild since his journey down to Bawkham.

"Come in, come in, my dear fellow," said Squabshot, jumping about like a parched pea in a fryingpan. "Do come in. Got a few friends to nights—choice spirits."

"Ah," said Wild, "'spose so—a sort of jollification."

"Yes, that's just it. Come in, and drink the health of an innocent and injured man."

This was of course in reference to Osborne who, when seen by the thieftaker, was immediately greeted by the latter most cordially.

"I am very glad to see you, Mr. Osborne," said Wild. "Glad to see you, sir, once more restored to your freedom, and am at the same time sorry for all that you have passed through."

"Thank you, Mr. Wild. It is chiefly owing to your own energy, and the kindness also of my friend Squabshot," said Osborne, as he shook hands with the thieftaker.

"We are drowning our sorrows in a bowl of capital punch," said Squabshot, as he proceeded to fill glasses round, and offer one to Wild, who accepted the same, and drank the health of the company present.

"There's been a reward, you know," said the thieftaker, glancing at Squabshot.

"Eh?" said that individual.

"A reward, you know."

"Ah, yes, of course, I forgot."

"For the apprehension and conviction of—"

"Yes, precisely, of the murderer."

"That's it. Now, you know, I generally like to do things upon the square. We are obliged to do them on the cross sometimes; but I prefer the square, when it's to be managed."

"Yes, quite right, Mr. Wild; so I do myself."

"Well, you see, Mr. Squabshot, you are entitled to your regulars in this affair."

Mr. Squabshot made a deprecating gesture, and said—

"No, my friend, I do not accept any blood money for my share in the transaction."

"Ah, that's all very well; but fair is fair, and you must have half at any rate."

"No halves for me. Whatever I have done has been purely from a wish to see the guilty punished and the innocent acquitted."

"No matter for that, you are entitled to your share, and, what's more, must have it. Indeed, I have brought it with me, for it's an old adage, that short reckonings make long friendships."

"Now, Mr. Wild," said Squabshot, "I do not desire anything of the kind, and you will greatly oblige me by dropping this matter."

"Psha," exclaimed the thieftaker. "Take what you have justly earned. I'm not sure if you are not entitled to the whole of the reward, but in any case we must whack it; there, now, that's all about it."

Squabshot hesitated as the thieftaker proceeded to count out several Bank of England notes upon the table. As he was doing this, one or two of Squabshot's friends expressed

LIFE OF A HIGHWAYMAN. 285

by pantomime their wish, that the latter would accept of the money proffered by Wild. Osborne took the same means of intimating his wishes upon the subject.

Squabshot, however, still hesitated.

Wild handed the notes to him, counting them up as he did so.

"Well, as you are so pressing," said Squabshot, "why, I don't know that I can refuse; but bear in mind, Mr. Wild, that I do not desire the money, neither have I had any hand in the late transaction, with any idea of gaining by it, in a pecuniary sense."

"Business is business, and fair is fair," said Wild; a sentiment, which no one could think of denying. "They are gains, sir, and fairly earned, that is all I have to say," said Wild, in continuation.

Mr. Squabshot placed the notes in a desk which stood upon a side table; he was certainly not too well off in the world, and the money was acceptable enough. Although he would have preferred obtaining the same sum by any other means; however, as all present seemed to think it was proper for him to accept it, he, like a wise man as he was, gave way to general opinion.

"I am much obliged to you, I'm sure, for your fairness and liberality," he said, addressing himself to Wild.

"You've nothing to thank me for, sir, believe me," answered the latter person. "I hope this will not be our last transaction."

"Oh, thank you," said Squabshot, laughing, "I don't think I shall be likely to have any hand in a similar case, at least, I hope not."

"Then, I hope you may," said Wild. "Because we work well together, and you are well up to the business."

A roar of laughter followed this speech from those present.

"Squably in a new character," they shouted, "Ah—ah."

Wild set himself down, and commeced smoking a pipe, which had been offered him by Squabshot.

The conversation waxed merry; and all this while our hero was listening to it in the dark bedroom at the back.

"I thought you had Mr. Halford here this evening," said Wild, turning sharp round upon Squabshot.

"Ahem—yes," said the latter, in some little confusion, for the question was put so suddenly and so unexpectedly, that the party addressed was a little flustered. "Yes, he was here," he answered; "but—ah—he has left."

"He's gone early," said Wild, puffing out a thick volume of smoke from his pipe.

"Yes, he was obliged to go to get an appointment," said Squabshot, inventing a lie upon the spot.

"Oh, an appointment, eh?"

"Yes," said Squabshot. "Did you wish to see him then?"

"Yes, I did."

"Particularly?"

"Rather so; he won't be back here this evening, I suppose?"

"Well, no, I'm afraid not," said Squabshot. "I did not know that you were acquainted with him."

"Oh, yes, but I am," said Wild, with a sinister smile.

There was a pause after this, when Squabshot whispered to Wild confidently—

"Nothing—ahem—nothing upon business, eh?"

"What?"

"With regard to Halford."

"Oh, no, no mischief, if that's what you mean."

"Because Halford is a good fellow," said Squabshot, aloud, "and one of my particulars."

"Ah, yes, precisely."

Now, all this while, our hero was, of course, in the next room, he applied his ear to the door which divided the two rooms, and heard sufficient of the foregoing conversation to know that he was wanted.

There was another door in Mr. Squabshot's bedroom, which led into the passage; through this one Colonel Jack had thought of making his escape, but upon his endeavouring to do so, he found that it was unfortunately locked on the inside; he might have picked the lock under more favourable circumstances, but that was now an impossibility. In the first place, any such attempt would be distinctly heard by Wild, and, in the next place, he was entirely in the dark; he next tried the window, which looked from the bedroom into the back yard, in the rear of the premises; but to his great mortification he found that this window had iron bars on the outside, that prevented any chance of escape in that quarter. What to do he knew not.

Wild seemed to have joined the company, and appeared as though bent upon making a night of it.

There was no other alternative than to wait patiently in his present quarters. Colonel Jack, however, did not feel at all comfortable in doing so, for he knew the habits of the men he had to deal with; he knew perfectly well that if Wild suspected he was concealed in the bedroom, he would be very likely, as the evening advanced, to choose a fitting opportunity to effect a sudden entrance into the bedroom upon some feigned excuse, and then all would be lost, that is, assuming he was after the colonel, which the latter did not for a moment doubt. What rendered him still more uncomfortable, was the reflection that Squabshot thought the door in the passage was, in all probability, open, and in that case he would feel assured that our hero had availed himself of that to effect his escape ; he felt more convinced of this from Squabshot's easy manner in the next apartment. After walking about the room, he was fortunate enough to meet with a small taper on the mantle shelf, which he ignited. It threw a feeble light in the room, and our hero was enabled to examine the interior thereof with greater care.

In the course of a short time Squabshot himself came into the bedroom.

When the colonel heard his hand upon the door he blew out the taper, and secreted himself.

Squabshot entered, and had the precaution to close the door after him.

"Hush," said the colonel, in a whisper.

"You here ?" said his friend.

"Yes, where else should I be ?"

"Why not have made your escape ?"

"How could I? The door leading into the passage is locked."

"Confound it, I remember the key is on the outside. I locked it myself preparatory to going out, but forgot to take out the key."

"What is to be done ?"

"Must manage to unlock it, that is very certain."

"I know Wild suspects I am here."

"You think so ?"

"I am sure of it from his manner."

"I must manage to get round to the door."

"I am afraid he will hear you, for depend upon it he is on the watch."

Squabshot once more entered the front parlour, closing the door after him. Wild regarded him with a look of suspicion, but that mattered not ; hastily making his way into the passage, he turned the key of the door which led into the back room, and again entered the front one, talking loudly all the time. In all probability the thieftaker suspected that something was going on, but he was at a loss how to act, and as Squabshot entered the front parlour again, he commenced recounting some racy anecdote to those assembled there ; he made as much noise as he possibly could, and gave renewed imitations of the parties of whom he was relating the anecdote.

While this was taking place, Colonel Jack was making good his retreat through the bedroom door into the passage, and having succeeded in gaining this without observation, he opened the front door with the utmost caution, and got into the street. He did not think it prudent to shut the latter door, as he found it impossible to do so without doing so with a slam ; he, therefore, left it ajar, and got clear off.

After our hero had left, Jonathan Wild stayed with a determination that surprised Squabshot. In fact, he found it impossible to get rid of him. The thieftaker was under the full impression that our hero was in the next room, and he was determined as the saying is, to stay it out. One by one the guests departed, and still Wild made no motion to go ; he discoursed upon various topics—his own adventures the number of culprits he had taken—how he had captured them—and a vast amount of matter which under any other circumstances might, and no doubt would have answered those present. Still there was no attempt or thought of going, and at last every one else had departed but the thieftaker and his host. When they were left alone, Wild said—

"We ought to understand each other, Mr. Squabshot."

"I should hope so," said the party addressed.

"And I should also hope it," replied the thieftaker.

"Well, I suppose we do," answered Squabshot.

"Yes, certainly ; but about this Mr. Halford ?"

"Well, what about him ?"

"Why, he is here, I suppose."

"Here? Goodness me, no !" he exclaimed, with a tragic start.

The thieftaker smiled a sardonic smile. Squabshot regarded him with a look of surprise.

"Now look you, Mr. Squabshot, I do not say that Mr. Halford, or rather Colonel Jack, is wanted, only you see I want to see him—that is all."

"You," said Squabshot. "I do not suppose it would be particularly healthy for him to see you ; at least I should hardly suppose he would think so."

"Oh, nonsense ; I mean no harm I swear to you"

He then pointed mysteriously to the door which led into the bedroom.

"What do you mean ?" said Squabshot. "Do you want to sleep here, or what ? At any rate you do not seem disposed to go."

"Oh, you want me gone," said Wild.

"Oh, no ; I am too glad of your company," was the reply.

Wild now made another gesture, and said—

"He is there, my friend. Come, now, do not endeavour to deceive an old friend."

"Umph, not very old," said Squabshot, with a smile.

"Well, a sincere one ; we will not quarrel about terms. Come, now, let me see the gentleman without further ado."

"I tell you once for all that Mr. Halford has left some hours since. If you doubt me, convince yourself," said Squabshot, opening the door of the bedroom at all hazards.

Jonathan Wild immediately availed himself of the offer, and hastily entered the apartment. Of course, no Colonel Jack was there, and the room was empty.

The thieftaker examined the room in every part, and was satisfied that our hero had effected his escape. After this he took his departure.

CHAPTER L.

SIR RICHARD FLEETWOOD IS DETERMINED UPON A DESPERATE EXPEDIENT.

SIR RICHARD FLEETWOOD, in his mansion, at Acton, was well nigh driven to distraction, when he learned how affairs were going on with Osborne. Honora Langford now appeared to be at a further distance from him than ever; he was a constant attendant at her house since the death of her father; he persevered in his attentions, sought her at all hours, begged of her in the most abject manner to listen to his suit. It was, however, all in vain.

Honora persisted in her attachment to Osborne, and Sir Richard left her upon the occasion of his last visit, in a despairing state. Again he returned in a disconsolate state to his home.

Mr. Sharpthorne had been continually at the baronet's house, and explained to him every variation in the fortune of Osborne. The wily lawyer knew pretty well long before the capture of Slimcoe, that Osborne was in a fair way of being cleared of the charge of murder.

Infuriated beyond all measure at the turn affairs had taken, Sir Richard was determined upon a desperate expedient.

We have before stated, that the baronet's love for Honora was the moving passion of his life; indeed, it was hardly credible to what an extent this passion was carried; he would dare anything and everything for her. When, therefore, he found that his hated rival was about to be discharged from custody, he determined upon a desperate expedient; he knew, or very shrewdly guessed, that he would have but little chance in gaining the affections of Honora, when Osborne was in the daily habit of seeing her, such, indeed, would be utterly hopeless.

Mr. Sharpthorne pointed out to him the fact of Osborne's inheriting the wealth of the murdered miser, Jabez Crudge, consequently, his rival would be equal with him in worldly wealth, and even supposing Mr. Langford himself were alive, the baronet felt that his case now would be almost a hopeless one.

Mr. Sharpthorne kneaded his hands, as he observed the baronet's chagrin, and regarded him in his library with a sinister look.

"Very hard case," said the lawyer—"very hard. When everything was going on so nicely too."

"Umph," exclaimed the baronet. "Sharpthorne, it appears to me that my life has always been a mistake. Never have I set my heart upon any particular thing, but so sure have I been doomed to disappointment. This cursed puppy—this smooth-faced, whining sycophant is now my evil genius. Years ago, there was—well, no matter. Then I was a victim to—"

"The tender passion," said Sharpthorne, running his hand playfully over his chin.

"No, not the tender passion that time," said the baronet—"No, not that time, but I was a victim—bah! Why recal the past? or, at least, that portion of it, which is already too painfully impressed upon me."

"We can't always bear to reflect upon our past actions," said the lawyer. "Indeed, to say the truth, they won't always bear the light of day."

"What do you mean, Sharpthorne," asked the baronet, strangely.

"Oh, nothing, Sir Richard, only a passing reflection, that is all, I was not referring to you in any way."

"Oh, indeed, that is well, my friend."

"I hope so," answered Sharpthorne, and then in continuation, he said—"By the way, Sir Richard, the Reichback affair stands where it did."

"Yes, and that puts me in mind of the threats of that—ahem—that fellow, Colonel Jack—curse him."

"Ah, an arrant scoundrel," said the lawyer, rubbing the knees of his small clothes, in the endeavour to clear it of some spot of grease.

"Sharpthorne," said Sir Richard, "that man is another of my evil geniuses."

"Who?"

"Colonel Jack."

"Ah, what is to be done with him?"

"He must be silenced."

"Ah, that is easily enough, but, how?"

"By a rope," said Mr. Sharpthorne, still scratching the spot on his knee."

"Or by money," said the baronet.

"Yes, or by money," answered the lawyer. "If you prefer this course, I must confess, however, that I should prefer the former alternative. It is much the cheapest, and by far the most efficacious."

"You think so?"

"Most assuredly," answered the lawyer, with the utmost coolness.

"We will talk about this hereafter, Sharpthorne," said Sir Richard, as he rose from his seat, and paced his apartment hurriedly, with considerable emotion. "Psha!" he exclaimed, "a rope—death—money or death the old story, to hide, or seek to hide the grim phantoms which haunt us throughout our life—who spring up at almost every turn in our existence. Money! bah! can that bring happiness—can it ease the overcharged heart? Can it give freshness to the wrinkled brow of age—or make light the overcharged conscience? Can it win woman's love?"

"It very often goes a long way towards it," said Sharpthorne.

"But what sort of love?"

"Ah, that I don't say; but it is sometimes such as satisfies us mortals," answered Sharpthorne, crossing his hands and looking up to the ceiling. "It satisfies some—many, perhaps."

"But not such as me."

"Perhaps not, Sir Richard, perhaps not."

The baronet cast a sudden glance at the shrivelled form of the attorney.

"Psha!" he exclaimed, "why am I talking thus to you? To you, indeed, who has no passion in your whole composition."

"All men are not formed alike," said Sharpthorne.

"No, I suppose not."

"And luckily so," said the lawyer, casting a sort of pitying or contemptive glance at his companion. "Perhaps so," he answered.

And then his mind run off again in a different course.

For some time he continued silent, and then he turned to business matters which more immediately concerned his temporal welfare.

After these had been entered into, the lawyer took his departure. To say the truth, his visits to the mansion at Acton were of a most feline character, he entered the house with the stealthiness of a cat, and left it in much the same way. When he was gone, Sir Richard paced up and down his library in his usual manner when excited—which to say the truth he was frequently enough.

The reader has no doubt seen at the Zoological Gardens the wolves in their eyries, how they pace backward and forwards—how continually and ceaselessly they are on the move. They are not a bad type of Sir Richard Fleetwood, who had no belief in the sincerity of any one, if we except Miss Langford. In her he had the fullest belief, but he knew perfectly well that Sharpthorne was not to be trusted, and yet he was, perhaps, one in whom he was by necessity compelled to put most faith in, and made him the recipient of those dark secrets which weighed heavy enough upon his own mind.

The lawyer, to use a strong expression, looked upon the baronet as simply a fool, as far as his passion for Honora Langford was concerned. In fact, to use his own words, he did not believe so great an amount of folly was in him. Sir Richard, in fact, saw this, and felt to a certain extent humiliated thereby.

"Oh," he exclaimed, as soon as Sharpthorne had departed, "that man is to be excused after all; he never knew what it was to have any passion or sentiment in his whole composition. A happy man — supremely happy without a doubt—a dried up, shrivelled old ninny. Honora Langford! Ah, there is my trouble—that name. Morning, noon, and night, it is all the same, for ever haunted by that vision—that *ignus fatus*—that dream—that delusion—that hopeless and eternal torment. Would that I had never seen her, but having seen her—" he paused and his features became fearfully convulsed. "But I will not stand this—I cannot," he said, in continuation. "I shall be driven mad. Already I feel my reason begin to totter. That bitter, that accursed puppy, will be with her, whose very touch to me is ecstacy, whose very breath is the perfumed air wafted to my intoxicated senses fresh from Partadise, I cannot, I will not stand it. It must be as I said."

He paused suddenly, and taking his coat and hat, abruptly left the house.

His carriage was already in readiness, and the baronet was driven rapidly to town.

While he is journeying thither, we will take a glance at the house of the late Mr. Langford, for we have not had occasion to pay it a visit since that gentleman's death."

Honora is seated in the drawing room. She is, of course, in deep mourning. Her face is much paler than when I last saw her, for she has grieved long and silently from the loss of her parent; but the sombre hue of her garments make her features appear still more pale. She has for her companion her faithful and attached friend.

Miss Staunton, Honora has been in the country since the death of her father, and has only recently returned to her town house. After the funeral, upon her return, she became so completely borne down that Mr. Littleton told Miss Staunton, confidentially, that he should soon have another patient if Honora was not permitted to have a change of scene. In her present abode there were so many things to remind her daily of the loss she had sustained, that it became a necessity that she should, for a time at all events, be rescued from a place which was fraught with the most fearful recollections and reminiscences. Honora complied, therefore with the advice of the doctor, and left London for some time, after which she returned to that house of misery, where we are at present about to pay her another visit. She had, however, determined upon leaving her present abode as soon as the notice was up, which she had deemed it prudent to give to her landlord.

"Miss Staunton is seated by the side of Honora. She has been reading aloud a newspaper.

"Discharged without a stain upon his character," exclaimed Miss Staunton. "Without a stain upon his character. I knew it would be so. Something told me so. Heaven be praised."

"Heaven be praised indeed," exclaimed Honora fervently. "What a deal of trouble we have to pass through in this world?" she exclaimed, as the reflection of Osborne's pursecution flashed across her mind.

"And he will soon be a rich man," said Miss Stanton, equal in wealth to Sir Richard Fleetwood.

"I never desired riches," answered Honora, readily. "My poor dear father thought a great deal of wealth and position, but as for

No. 37

myself I never desired riches. It does not bring happiness although many persons think otherwise."

"Money is useful enough," exclaimed Miss Staunton."

"True dear, we know that, and indeed to speak the truth, I had no idea that my poor father's affairs were in such a state ; no wonder why he was so solicitous for me to wed Sir Richard."

"Who after all would make an excellent husband," said Miss Staunton, "I am sure he doted upon you, if any man ever did love a woman."

"I do not doubt it dear ; in fact I never doubted it—but what of that ?"

"Oh, nothing."

"I'ts useless going over the same ground again and again—Sir Richard Fleetwood I esteem, and to a certain extent admire, but there is an end ; I cannot love two persons at once, you know."

"I should suppose not," answered Miss Staunton with a smile.

"Hark ! what was that ?" exclaimed Honora, suddenly, as a loud knock was heard at the outer door; and she heard a man's voice inquiring for herself. Presently the footman returned and informed his mistress that a stranger wished to see her.

"Ask him up," said Miss Langford.

"If you please, madam, he said he could not come up, he had somebody waiting for him."

"Did he give his name."

"No madam, I think he said something about a message from Mr. Osborne."

"Oh," exclaimed Honora," I will go down and see him." And she proceeded down stairs on the instant, leaving Miss Staunton in the drawing room. When she got to the doorway she observed a strange man awaiting her coming ; and before she had time to even utter one syllable she was caught up in his arms and forcibly conveyed to a chariot which was waiting at the entrance to her house. The assault and attack had been so sudden that Honora had only time to utter one or two screams when she found herself in the carriage by the side of the strangers, and the carriage was driven off at full speed.

"What is the meaning of this outrage ?" said Honora to her two captors.

"You will learn all in good time, madam," said the man who had conveyed her into the carriage. "For the present let it suffice that no harm is intended you: on the contrary this course has been taken for your good."

"Such conduct is most unwarrantable, and shall not go unpunished," answered Honora.

The speaker was silent, but the carriage still rolled on. Honora had some thoughts of endeavouring to open the carriage window and call for assistance, but she had not the courage to make the attempt, as her two male companions seemed from their appearance men of determination and desperate resolution ; and so the three took their way after this in silence. It appeared to Honora that they must have travelled many miles, and that they had long since been out of the Metropolitan district, for the road they where now taking was entirely guiltless of lights of any description, and was consequently enshrouded in dense gloom, which rendered her situation the more unpleasant.

"Where are you going to, sir?" inquired Honora of the individual who had condescended to speak on the previous occasion when she made any inquiries.

"To the house of a friend," he answered sententiously.

"No friend of mine."

"Yes, you will see an old and attached friend.

"What name ?" asked Miss Langford.

"I am not at liberty to mention, but you will learn all in good time ; have patience, my dear madam, and trust me you will have no reason to regret this journey.

Honora was again silent. She really began to think that it was Osborne she was about to meet. The means of her conveyance was strange, and certainly anything but promising or satisfactory, but it was impossible for her to come to any rational conclusion at present; and she therefore made up her mind as there was no help for it, to remain passive and await calmly the result of this adventure.

Nine miles were traversed, but Honora had not the slightest idea which road out of London they were taking, but that it was out of London she now felt convinced by the distance they had travelled. Her companions were civil enough, and did not offer any rudeness. Indeed they seemed to treat her with studied distance and coolness. She had occasion, she thought, to felicitate herself upon the fact, and, after a while, was surprised at the cool manner she had taken the whole of this painful proceeding. In any case, she thought the dictum must be passive obedience, which, after all, was a wise resolution on her part.

In the course of another half hour the vehicle stopped, and her two companions conversed in whispers. Presently one of them alighted, and then there was a pause of some minutes duration, which to Honora seemed an age. After this the man returned and said something to his companion, who, addressing Honora, said, in a respectful manner—

"Now, Miss Langford, I must trouble you to alight, if you please."

He got out of the chariot, himself, and then politely offered his arm to the lady who alighted, and found herself in what appeared to her to be a barren heath. She trembled as she looked round, and the sight struck upon her senses with an unpleasant sensation of chilliness.

"All right, Bill," said the man to the coachman, and the vehicle was turned round as Miss Langford was conducted by her two male companions towards a small cottage which stood about a couple of hundred yards from where they stood. This habitation stood completely alone, for from what Honora could make out of the surrounding country, there did not appear to be house or habitation of any description near.

"Ah," exclaimed Honora. "Whither are we going now !"

"We have just arrived at our journey's end. I dare say, madam, that your patience is well nigh exhausted, but I must do you the justice to say that you have comported yourself under these trying circumstances in a manner worthy of a heroine."

"I do not seek or desire to be a heroine," answered Honora; "and consider this to be nothing more than an unwarrantable breach of the liberty of the subject."

Her companion said no more, but led her gently to the cottage, unresistingly, arrived at which place, an old woman with a light in her hand presented herself at the entrance of the cottage, and smiled as Miss Langford was led up to the habitation.

"Miss Langford," said the men to the old dame. "The lady whom you have been expecting."

The old lady extended her hand to the young one, and led her into the front parlour of the habitation. This was furnished with neatness and simplicity, and altogether there was an air of comfort about the apartment, which a person would hardly have supposed from a cursory glance at the entrance of the habitation.

The old woman motioned her young charge to a seat by the fire, which was burning brightly.

Honora obeyed in silence, and in a few minutes she found herself alone with her female companion.

"Where am I?" she inquired, "and what is the meaning of all this? You are a stranger to me."

"At present, my dear, I am so, but I hope to soon be good friends with you; at least it shall not be my fault if we are not."

"What am I brought to this place for against my will?" inquired Honora. "You surely do not suppose for one moment that I am likely to entertain any friendly feelings to one who can have had any hand in this foul plot to deprive me of my liberty? And to what does it all tend?"

"Patience, child, and you will soon learn," said the old woman.

"For what purpose am I brought to this place? Answer me that," said Honora.

The old woman fidgetted about the room, but returned no answer to her visitor's interrogatory. Presently she left the apartment abruptly, and Miss Langford heard her conversing in an adjacent room with some other individual, and from the sound of the latter's voice she judged it to be a man, possibly one of those who had conveyed her to the cottage.

CHAPTER LI.

THE MYSTERY IS EXPLAINED.

HONORA LANGFORD sat reflecting for some time upon her strange position. Now that she found herself quite alone, she had leisure to view her position with greater calmness. She could not conceal from herself that she was entirely in the power of strangers, but at the same time there did not appear to be any disposition on their parts to treat her with any degree of harshness. Nevertheless, her situation gave rise to grave doubts and fears as to her safety. While thus occupied with her own thoughts, she became aware of the door of the apartment being opened partly, and turned round in the full expectation of seeing the elderly female. What was her astonishment, however, when she beheld the face and features of Sir Richard Fleetwood, who was unusually pale she thought. A half-slipped scream escaped her lips; in another moment the baronet was kneeling at her feet.

"Miss Langford—Honora, if I may be permitted to call you so—pardon me, have pity on me, for I need it—good girl, I do, indeed need it—as Heaven is my judge."

"Sir Richard!" exclaimed Honora, "and here! What can all this mean? Is it at your instigation that this outrage has been committed? I never will believe it."

"Have pity upon a humble, miserable suppliant, whose reason has well nigh flown from him. Oh, Honora, I cannot endure life upon the terms I hold it at present—I love you so, that—the thought— Psha! why dwell upon that which has driven me mad?—mad! young woman! Do you hear that?"

"Sir Richard, is this the way you deem it expedient to show your—ah, your love."

"What am I to do? You hold my destiny in your own hands. I cannot and will not pass the agonising hours I have endured of late. Miss Langford, you must, you shall be mine."

"Shall be, sir? I suppose you will admit that I am a free agent, to do as I think proper in this matter? You do not, I should suppose, after all your protestations, intend to use coercion?"

"I cannot live without you," he answered.

"But you must, if I so will it."

"I cannot—nay, I will not."

"Sir Richard, this language ill becomes a gentleman of your rank and position, not to say, education."

"I am no longer the same Sir Richard Fleetwood you knew on the outset of this—ah—unfortunate attachment—I cannot call it anything else, seeing that it has embittered my whole existence. Oh, Miss Langford," he now continued, more tenderly, "if you only knew—if you could only guess, or dream of the miserable and wretched life I lead—now living upon your slightest word—a look that would, or may, have given me some faint hope—if you knew what perfect thraldom I am held in by one of the fairest and gentlest of God's creatures—you could not, I am sure your kind and tender nature would never consent to let you treat me thus!"

"I have never, I believe, since we have known each other, treated you but as a friend—a kind and esteemed friend. What more can I do?"

"Friendship is too cold a term to be used as applied to me. I want your love, young lady—I yearn for it—I live but for that, and without it, I must perforce die."

"It appears to me," answered Honora, "that we are but going over the same ground again. Surely, enough has been said upon this subject. Am I to understand that you have had me forcibly taken from my own residence, merely to pour into my ear the same protestations, which you have thought fit to repeat on so very many occasions in my father's lifetime? If so, I think you have not adopted a manly or noble course of action, and can hardly expect to gain much by such conduct. I pardon it, of course," she said, as she observed an expression of anger pass over the features of the baronet. "I pardon it, on account of the great love I truly believe you bear towards me."

A smile of satisfaction passed over the countenance of Sir Richard, as she uttered the last observation.

"If you believe this—if you know and feel that my love is sincere—why hesitate, why doom me to be on tenter hooks, for day after day, week after week? Listen to me, Miss Langford—Mr. Henry Osborne has escaped."

"He is acquitted and exonerated from all blame, and his character stands as unblemished as your own," answered Honora, sharply.

"We will not quarrel about terms—he is free, that is sufficient. Now let me proceed. I say I love you. To say this is not, perhaps, admitting much. It is the same phrase which has been used by hundreds of thousands of my own sex as applied to yours; it's the same phrase which us men have thought fit to utter ever since our first parents learnt what love is; therefore it may sound cold, and possessed of no great weight; but when I tell you that my love is of that nature, that it is incorporated with my very existence—it is an atmosphere from which I draw the breath of life—it is the amulet upon which I live. Deprived of your love, I am what? A ship without a rudder—a world

without a sun—a man without a heart. Spare me! have pity on me! It goes hard with a man when he is obliged to beg thus abjectly of a woman, as though he were pleading for his life."

"I charge you, Sir Richard, not to kneel thus to me. It is unseemly, and quite needless. If I were free to dispose of my hand and heart I would, as I have before told you, listen to your suit without all these demonstrations—"

"If!" shouted out the baronet; "if, free! Is it so, then? Do you still persist in your same style of argument and treatment of this matter? If! Have a care, madam, have a care, or you will turn that love I bear you into—what? Into hate, deep, bitter, deadly hate! Once poison the channel through which this pure passion flows—once turn all the sweets to bitterness—and then, madam, look to it."

"I know not what you mean," answered Honora. "Cannot possibly guess. This is the first time, Sir Richard Fleetwood, that you have assumed a threatening tone, the more surprising, since you have thought fit throughout our acquaintance to assume one directly opposite."

Miss Langford, circumstances have, I hear, been changed, so much so, that I feel our acquaintance must now be brought to a happy close—a close, indeed, which will make me the happiest of men, or else doom me to perpetual despair."

"I am at a loss still to understand your reason for having been the principal in this outrage upon my liberty, for that you are, I feel convinced."

"Miss Langford," commenced the baronet, as he drew a chair by the side of hers, and seated himself thereon—"Miss Langford, I have already told you that I love you, I know not how often. The time, however, has arrived for me to tell you something more than this I have examined my own heart, plundered the depths of this unfortunate passion, for I can call it nothing else; and find that, however difficult I might find it to live without you, and that it might be probable that I should not be able to do so for long—I say, however difficult this might be. To see you in the possession of another would be unendurable—to tell you this, I have had you conveyed hither—a course, you will say, that does not redound to my honour, but one, however, that I have seen fit to adopt, under the circumstances of the case, which oppress and weigh them down "

"You have brought me here merely to tell me this, Sir Richard Fleetwood," exclaimed Honora, as she gazed on the baronet, and began really to believe that he had for the nonce taken leave of his wits altogether —"you have brought me here merely for this purpose ; why, surely, you do not mean to say that this was your only motive."

"Nothing more," answered Sir Richard—"nothing more, believe me. I have told you that it will be death to me for you to be in the possession of another."

"Well, sir, I cannot help that," she answered.

"I say death, madam," said Sir Richard, shouting out his words as though he veritably were a madman. "Can you, will you, doom me to so sad a fate?"

"I really do not understand you," said Honora.

"Miss Langford, you are perverse and wilful, or you would not misunderstand my meaning. Do you still persist in asserting that you love Mr. Osborne?"

"Assuredly. You know that, sir. I have not had anything to alter or change my sentiments towards him."

A shade of uncontrolable anger passed over the features of the baronet at this declaration ; he gronnd his teeth with rage and mortification.

"Miss Langford, I swear to you, that you shall never be Mr. Osborne's."

"Sir—Sir Richard !" exclaimed Honora.

"I swear it most solemnly. I pledge myself to it. You shall never become the wife of Henry Osborne, while I have a voice or an arm to prevent it."

As the baronet spoke these words, his features were so disturbed with rage, that they were something fearful to look upon.

"Yes, madam, I swear it. I have tried all in my power to prevent this state of affairs from coming to pass. I have laid my heart bare before you ; and had you been possessed of anything like pity for a man, whom you yourself had driven to distraction—"

"I cannot help it, sir. It's a pity we ever met," said Honora, as she, with some difficulty, retrained her tears, which were fast filling her eyes—"a thousand pities we ever met, for both our sakes."

"Amen, to that," answered the baronet, in a hollow voice, deep and sepulchral. "It is a pity. Had we never met, I should never have loved so blindly, and a world of trouble might have been spared me—aye, a world of trouble ; and, who knows what more lies hid in the womb of time. One thing is, however, quite certain, you shall never be the wife of Henry Osborne ; that I have already sworn."

"Gracious heavens," exclaimed Honora, "what is the meaning of this? You would never have recourse to violence—you would never dare."

"I would and will dare anything and everything," answered the baronet. "There is no bounds to my determination upon this point. His wife you shall never be, not if it be at the cost of my own life, his, or yours, to prevent this."

"Mercy on me. Do not talk thus," said Honora.

"I have said it," he answered, with a degree of determination in his tone and manner, which appalled poor Honora, who could bear up no longer, but burst into an agony of tears.

"What have I done?—good heavens—what have I done to be punished thus?" exclaimed Honora. "Is this kind? Is it just to thus make unholy vows? Sir Richard, by the love you profess to bear towards me, I conjure you to permit me to return to my own home."

He shook his head, and said—

"It may not—it must not be. I have willed it otherwise."

"Am I then a prisoner?" she inquired.

"Until you give me a solemn promise to renounce Osborne, you are," he replied.

"This conduct is unpardonable," said Honora. "I would never have believed you capable of such conduct."

"You have driven me to adopt this course, maiden," he replied, coldly. "I have no alternative now left. Let us still be friends. I will give you till to-morrow to consider the matter over, and then I will see you again, and, in the meantime, you will have leisure to calmly reflect upon your future line of action, till then, farewell," and with these words he strode heavily from the apartment, leaving his victim a prey to the most poignant sorrow.

CHAPTER LII.

COLONEL JACK MEETS WITH A TINKER.

WHEN the Colonel had succeeded in getting clear from Jonathan Wild, whom, it will be remembered, he had met with so unexpectedly at Squabshot's lodgings ; he did not deem it advisable to return to his own residence at the west end ; he therefore took up his quarters for the night at the Badgers, deeming that to be the safest place of the two ; he was wise in adopting this course, not, however, that Wild knew where he resided.

Wild, however, had spoken the truth when he informed Squabshot that he did not intend to capture the highwayman ; he was actuated by another motive, and was after all but an agent of the astute Mr. Sharpthorne. That worthy had been, as the reader already knows, most particular anxious to gain possession of the papers and documents respecting the Reichbeck property ; once in his possession the lawyer thought he would have Sir Richard

Fleetwood completely in his power, of which there would be but little doubt but what he would. As yet the wily lawyer had been behind on more than one occasion in the fulfilment of his most ardent wish upon this head. He had worked hard, and had left no stone unturned to accomplish his purpose, but had found all in vain. He felt fully confirmed that Colonel Jack had the papers in his possession ; and as he reflected upon this he cogitated in those musty old chambers of his, in the Temple, as how it was possible for him to wrest them from the beginning. After mature consideration, he came to the determination of employing Jonathen Wild in the affair, and explain to the thief taker how the Colonel had got the papers, which he the lawyer was most anxious to get out of his hands by any means, legal or illegal. He did not exactly make use of those two words, but sufficient fell from his lips in the course of conversation to leave the thief taker no other alternative than to come to that conclusion. The consequence of all this was, that Wild had determined to see our hero and threaten to convey him to prison, unless he agreed to give up the required documents ; hence it was that he had sought him at Squabshot's ; where however he was baffled in his purpose as we have already seen. After this failure he proceeded on the following day to the temple, where sat in his desk room the redoubtable Sharpthorne himself, whose lynx like eyes lighted up with an enlivened expression, when he caught sight of the thief taker.

"Umph, queerish," said the thief taker, "queerish, most confoundedly. The fellow was in Goswell Street, of that I am convinced ; but he contrived to slip through my fingers somehow or other."

"Confound it, that is unfortunate," exclaimed Sharpthorne, with ill concealed chagrin. "What are you going to do now ?"

"Drat him," answered Wild, "must take my chance of tumbling in with him on a future occasion."

"But can't you—can't you waylay him ?"

"I told you before I have not got anything particular against him, and I don't know as the case stands, that I should be justified in detaining or arresting him."

"Well but you know him to be a highwayman !" answered Sharpthorne.

"Oh, that is all very well ; I may know it, but I must have some distinct case against him, or else have a warrant in my possession for his apprehension, neither of which I happen to have."

"Well, what would you have done if you had seen him at Squabshot's then ?" inquired the attorney, smoothing his chin, and regarding the thief taker with his cat like eyes.

"He is not bound to know that I have no warrant, is he?" said Wild, sullenly.

"Oh, no of course not—I see."

"I should very likely have frightened him into finding out the papers ; at any rate I would have tried it on."

"Ah, yes, good excellent tactics, capital tactics Mr. Wild," said the lawyer approveingly. "But now of course—

"Why of course I can't do it."

"Don't you know his haunts ?"

"Some of them I do certainly ; but he is not so easy to catch, I can tell you, far from it."

"Ah, no, I suppose not. But what do you say to putting a watch upon him—eh ?"

"I have not time and it would not pay," said Wild.

"Well, but I can have a watch put upon him," said the lawyer.

"That is a horse of a different colour," answered Wild. "If you can do the business yourself, you do not want me."

"Oh, I do not mean that, Mr Wild. You must pardon me there ; of course I rely upon your better judgment. My only object in suggesting this course was this, that I have one or two men whom I sometimes employ in legal matters, and who from their very occupations, are willing to act the parts of—"

"Spies" said Wild.

"Precisely. They have been used to that sort of business, and it occurred to me that, perhaps, their services might be enlisted in this affair with, let us hope, some good result. They might ascertain something about the movements of Colonel Jack or—ahem—Mr. Halford—and then you know I could communicate with you. My only object in proposing this, is, of course, only to save you trouble."

"Please yourself ; you know best," answered the thieftaker. "If you can let me know at any time where I can pitch upon the colonel, why, I will be ready to either go by myself, or else with one of my chaps, and see what can be done. Only I must tell you this, that I do not want to bring him to justice as you term it."

"Oh you do not."

"No," answered Wild.

"And wherefore not—if it is a fair question," inquired the lawyer.

"That is my business," answered Wild. "He is not in my black books, that is all, and I shall not arrest him for any one until I am compelled, and that is all about it. But I will do as I have promised the moment an opportunity occurs, but as to racing after him, why I have other fish to fry, as the saying is."

"Leave that to me," answered the lawyer, "and I will communicate with you again, and let us hope it will not be long first, Mr. Wild."

So saying, the lawyer shook his visitor

warmly by the hand, and forced him out of his office with great ceremony.

Leaving the attorney and Wild to pursue their own schemes as best pleases them, we will now take a glance once more at our hero.

Some days have elapsed since he was at his friend Squabshot's reunion; he is now that we are about to take a glance at him, on the bowling green of a roadside inn—to wit, the Woodman, at Highgate, which was then a rustic and picturesque old-fashioned roadside house. Indeed, it still retains many of its pleasing characteristics, or did when we last visited it some dozen years ago.

Colonel Jack and Hackett are on the green of this establishment, they are playing at bowls with several of the company, and have been engaged in this sport for perhaps an hour or so, or it may be more. The wooden summer houses round the green itself are pretty well filled with visitors, for the house itself, besides being a place of call for chance passengers on the road, was frequented by various pleasure parties.

"Both in," exclaimed Hackett, "as he followed the ball he had thrown up. "That makes us four. Come, follow your go, gentlemen."

The colonel strolled up to the side of his friend.

"Hackett, he said, in a whisper, "finish this game as soon as possible, for do you know, I do not feel quite so secure as I could desire."

"Indeed! Why so, colonel?" exclaimed Hackett, in some surprise.

"Look yonder."

"Where?"

"Carry your eye to the third box on the left hand side of the green. There, don't stare, man, or we shall be observed."

"Well," said Hackett, "I've done so, but see nothing to be afraid of. There are people seated there, but what of that?"

"If I am not much mistaken, that fellow dressed in black is Mr. Underwood."

"Well, who is he?"

"Why, the sheriff who followed us to St. Albans."

"No—never. Oh, we had best cut it at once."

"We can't do that now. It will excite suspicion, and it is probable that he does not recognise us, for he must have been there for the last half hour or more."

"Well, we had better go after this game, then."

"Yes, but we can't, if we win, as of course they will have another for the conqueror. Lose, therefore, as quickly as possible."

"Now, gentlemen, the stage waits," called out the colonel's opponent.

"Oh, I beg pardon," said our hero. "I'm

very remiss," and with this he took up his position and resumed his game.

The probability is that even if he had tried to win he would not have been able, for his attention was too much occupied in stealing every now and then furtive glances at the box where sat the supposed Mr. Underwood. Whether this person was watching his movements or not, Colonel Jack was unable to say, for he was in the further part of the box in which he was seated, and consequently was too much in the shade for the highwayman to catch a sufficiently clear sight of his features. From what he did see, however, he was strengthened in his conclusion that it was really Mr. Underwood that was there.

A waiter made his way across the lawn, with a tray full of jugs and glasses.

Colonel Jack waylaid him, and whispered in his ear a few words. These were, to tell the man to have his horse saddled and bridled, as well as Hackett's.

"Nothing lik getting all ready, and taking time by the forelock," said the colonel to himself. "I have got Ada this time."

He thought the game would never conclude. Merrily as he had passed the previous hour or so, these last few minutes seemed to drag their way along with a leaden weight. Thus do we wear the course of time, according to the circumstances in which we find ourselves placed.

While our hero was throwing up the balls for the last time, he hoped, he became aware of the presence of Crawley, whom he observed at the further end of the green.

There was a degree of anxiety upon the countenance of Crawley, which at once rendered his master uneasy, for he judged by his follower's manner that something was going on likely to turn out wrong.

As soon as the colonel had delivered his balls, he hastened up to the side of his faithful and attached follower.

"Hist!" said Crawley, in his usual whisper. "To horse, master, as quickly as possible."

"What's the matter?" inquired our hero.

"Grimes has been watching your actions the best part of the day, and he's now at the bar; and Mr. Sharpthorne is not far distant."

"Mr. Sharpthorne—what of that? They are not upon that suit?"

"What?" inquired Crawley.

"After me or Hackett?"

"I don't know that, master. I've seen many things I don't like the look of. You get to horse as soon as possible, or you may find yourself in the wrong box."

"There's some fellow in yonder box whose appearance I don't like at all."

"Where?" said Crawley.

"Yonder; but don't look, or he'll think we are watching him; but I suspect he's watching us."

"Who is it?"

"Mr. Underwood, if I'm not mistaken, and I seldom am, when I've seen a man once; but, stay, I don't see him now," said our hero, in continuation, as he, for the first time discovered that the said box which had been occupied by the individual in question, was now vacant. "No, I certainly can't see him now."

"What's the matter," inquired Hackett, who now came up to the side of Colonel Jack.

"Why, our friend is gone."

"I don't see him in his old place," said Hackett."

"No, nor anywhere else," observed the colonel."

"Most likely, after all, it was only a false alarm."

"Sharpthorne and Grimes are at the bar, so Crawley says," observed Colonel Jack. "Let us lose no time, but mount our horses forthwith."

While he was making this latter observation, he observed the ferret eyes of Sharpthorne peering through the glass door which led from the bar into the grounds at the back of the house.

Colonel Jack waited no longer, but bent his course to the stables, closely followed by Hackett.

The two sauntered down the yard, but no horses were outside the stables as the highwayman had anticipated.

Muttering to himself some anathemas against the ostler for his neglect, he went into the stable to seek for that worthy.

The horses were in their stalls, saddled all right enough; but our hero had scarcely crossed the door of the stable when he found it slammed to and locked, and ere he could recover his surprise at this sudden action, he found himself firmly pinioned by some one who emerged from behind, and a low, chuckling laugh reached his ears, as a voice said, with a tone of satisfaction—

"My prisoner at last—ha! ha!"

The colonel knew by the tone of his voice that the speaker was no other than Mr. Underwood.

"Unhand me," said the colonel, making a desperate struggle to free himself.

"All your struggles are useless, and must only end in your own discomfiture and exposure. You are my prisoner, Colonel Jack, and I've won the wager."

"Not as yet," exclaimed the colonel, who, although had at a disadvantage, was determined to make a desperate effort; by striking out with his legs, he continued to punish his antagonist sufficiently so as to make him relax his hold in a slight degree, then the colonel suddenly let himself down, and by an expert movement he threw the sheriff off, who, however, shouted out for assistance, and again sprung upon our hero. A short, desperate, and decisive struggle ensued, for Mr. Underwood finding that he was no match for his more athletic antagonist, began to shout out lustily for assistance. The colonel found that he would arouse several to his assistance, and infuriated beyond measure at the course the sheriff was pursuing, he struck him a terrific blow full in the face with his clenched fist, which felled him like an ox; he was sent sprawling on the floor of the stable, and in falling struck his head against the woodwork, and he lay senseless and without motion. The colonel now sought to open the door, but found it locked. Mr. Underwood had done this upon our hero's first entrance, and had thrown the key among the straw.

"Open the door," said Hackett, "or we shall be lost."

"It is locked, is the key on the outside?" inquired the Colonel."

"No," answered Hackett.

"Where can it be than?" said our hero; and he looked about in vain for it on the floor of the stable.

"Confound it, we must get the door open." exclaimed Hackett, with considerable impatience, for he was expecting every minute to see Mr. Sharpthorne with his officer.

Crawley who had originally been a housebreaker, now made an effort to pick the lock, which luckily was successful. The door was opened, having yielded to his efforts, and the two horses were had out; while the colonel and his companion were mounting them Mr. Sharpthorne came into the yard followed by Jonathen Wild, who was on horseback. The thief taker put spurs to his horse and galloped up to the side of our hero.

"Yield," exclaimed the thief taker. There is no harm meant, but I have business to transact with you, but I am going to clap you in the stone jug colonel; but not if it can be avoided."

"Thank you," said Colonel Jack. "I do not intend to let you, my friend."

"You had better come along with me, gently, colonel," said Wild, in what for him must have been considered a friendly tone.

"You know your business, Wild, and I mine" said the colonel, laughing. "Catch me who can."

He was about to start when the thieftaker laid hold of his reign, and the suddenness of the act nearly threw the rider. In fact, with any other steed, the probability is that the highwayman would have been grassed; but Ada knew her business as well as her master.

"Unhand the mare," exclaimed the colo-

nel, "or by the Lord that made me I'll fire, Wild!"

He presented the muzzle of his pistol full in the face of Wild as he said these words.

"You've no call to be riled—no harm is meant."

"Leave go of the reins, or we shall quarrel," exclaimed Colonel Jack.

"You're an obstinate fool," exclaimed the party addressed, "and don't know your friends from your enemies."

"Hold him fast," exclaimed Sharpthorne, who, while he listened to this parley, was under the impression, that Wild was about to face the highwayman.

"I shall remember you, Mr. Sharpthorne," said our hero, turning round with a look of rage upon the attorney. "I'll give you one for this."

No. 38.

"Will you be advised by me," said Wild, who, throughout, had shown an evident disposition to treat the highwayman with consideration.

"Leave go of my reins, and I'll then talk to you," said the colonel; but Wild would not let go; and before he had time to catch sight of the highwayman's dexterous movements, the colonel had whipped out his knife, and cut the rein, leaving that portion of it which was held by Wild in his hand, and off he gallopped at headlong speed.

"They're off—they're off!" exclaimed Sharpthorne, in perfect horror. "Follow them—give chase!"

Wild set spurs to his horse, and dashed after the fugitives.

By this time the sheriff had recovered from his fall, and ran out into the yard.

When he saw the two highwaymen making off, he mounted his own horse and followed after them, the attorney did the same. His horse was in front of the house, indulging in some hay and water.

By this time a throng of pursuers had found their way outside the Woodman, and set up a yell and shout, that added not a little to the excitement of the scene.

A chase of highwayman, even in broad daylight, was a sight worth looking at, and when one of the pursuing party was Jonathan Wild, and another a sheriff, the excitement was still greater.

"Hurrah—hurrah!" exclaimed several voices. "I hope these fellows will give them the slip."

"Same here," said another voice.

The evening was, indeed, a beautiful one. The rays of the fast setting sun lighted up mead, hill, and dale, with a golden tint, under any other circumstances, a ride, on such an evening, would have been a delightful one, but, with such a pack at his heels, Colonel Jack and Hackett felt anything but comfortable. As to Crawley, he was unknown to any of the pursuers, and consequently he gazed at the throng outside the Woodman, and watched after his master with anxious eyes.

"The Lord be praised that the colonel's on Ada. I'll forgive them, if they overtake him," thought Crawley; "and yet Wild is, of course, well mounted, trust him for that."

"What's the matter?" exclaimed a corpulent individual, who had been playing at bowls with our hero and Hackett in the earlier part of the afternoon.

"Giving chase to a highwayman," answered one of the bystanders.

"Aye, to be sure," said another. "Those two gentlemen were playing with Mr. Bramble."

"Why, they appeared to me to be perfect gentlemen," said Bramble, in unfeigned astonishment.

"They were highwaymen, nevertheless," answered his companion.

"Dear, dear me; how one may be taken in to be sure."

"Never trust to appearances," exclaimed another.

"Well, all I can say," said a burly individual—"all I can say is, that I hope they mayn't get cotched."

"Bravo!" shouted out several of the assembled party. "So say I."

The sun's rays no longer lighted up the forms of the flying party, for to those outside the Woodman, they did appear actually to fly, but still the eyes of all were strained to catch a glance of even Colonel Jack, as our reader already knows, was on the back of his favourite mare, Ada.

She was young, fresh, and fleet as the winds.

Under ordinary circumstances the colonel knew well enough that she would baffle pursuit, as there was no horse in the three kingdoms who could come up to him. Nevertheless, her master knew well enough that he had a pack of determined men at his heels. And Wild was in all probability well mounted, for he knew what business he had come upon, and had the picking of some of the best government horses; and he was a man, moreover, who was not likely to be baulked in any undertaking upon which he had set his mind. All this the colonel ran over in his mind, as he calculated the chances of his getting off, while he galloped the first half mile or so.

Both he and his companion Hackett, fully distanced their pursuers on the first start. They rattled through Highgate, and took there course on towards Finchley. Nevertheless, Wild, Sharpthorne, and Mr. Underwood, followed at their heels, with a determination of overtaking them.

As to the sheriff he was positively wound up to a perfect pitch of fury, and was utterly regardless of the life or limbs of his steed.

"He ain't mounted on a bad bit of horse flesh, " said Wild. "Ada is second to none."

"No matter," answered the sheriff. "There never was horse or man yet in this world, but what his match was to be found."

"Ah, that may be all very well," said the thieftaker, ruminating, "but none of our beasts are a match for Ada, I can tell you that, so it's no use your endeavouring to deceive yourself."

"Zounds," exclaimed Mr. Underwood passionately, "you don't mean to say that it's impossible for us to overtake him?"

"I think that there is not much chance of it, if we are to have a fair run, and have only the speed of our horses to rely on," said Wild, coldly.

"Confound it man, you mean to say we had better give up the chase at once. Is that your meaning? If so, I beg to declare that I for one do not intend so easily to be stalled off."

"I ain't a man likely to give up this ere business in such a hurry as all that," replied Wild. "What I was a saying, was simply this, that it won't do to rely entirely upon the speed of our horses."

"What then pray?"

"Why we must circumvent him, that is all," answered Wild.

"Ah!" exclaimed the sheriff, who did not clearly understand how this was to be accomplished.

"Yes," said Wild, "unless we can succeed in circumventing him, I do not see very clearly how we shall ever be able to effect a capture. However, we must put our horses out to their utmost, and trust to circumstances."

By this time they were passing through Findley, and had barely lost sight of the colonel, and Hackett, Wild, began to be fidgetty, believing that our hero had given him the slip. Uttering fierce invectives, he pui spurs to his horse and dashed on at still greater speed. A man in a market-cart was coming by, and Wild hailed him—

"Hilloa, you sir," said the thieftaker. "Have you seen any horsemen pass as you came along."

"Yes," answered the man, "two gentlemen galloping away as though they would save their lives."

"Which way did they go?"

The man pointed out the road they had taken.

"All right, thank you, sir," said Wild, and then he muttered to himself—"galloping away for their lives; ah, indeed, they were, and no mistake."

While this conversation was taking place between those in pursuit, Colonel Jack and Hackett were urging on their steeds also. As to the former, there could be but little doubt that he would have fairly bid his friends behind good bye, but he did not like to part company with Hackett, mindful as he was of the death of poor Warington, upon the last occasion when they adopted a similar course. Unfortunately, Hackett was not nearly so well mounted as his companion, and the consequence was that the colonel was compelled to slacken his speed; notwithstanding this, they were still some distance ahead of those in pursuit, as we have already seen.

"Don't you stop, colonel," said Hackett. "Leave me to take my chance. You get clear off while you can."

"No, no," answered the colonel, "we must both escape, or neither. I have had enough of that; remember poor Warrington."

"Oh, let us hope I shall be more fortunate than him," answered Hackett.

"We won't run the risk of it, at all events, besides, Wild does not wish to take me, that I know."

"Do you think not. Why is he pursuing, then?"

"Urged on by some one or other, I suppose, but you could see from his manner in the stable yard that it went against the grain with him, besides he is too sharp a man to have let me cut the rein, if he had not wished to have favoured me. So in the event of our being overtaken, it is just possible that I may make some terms with him, where you would not. Do you see that my friend?"

"Of course I see it when you tell me, but I have not such faith in Wild, myself."

"Nor I; but I know that I am not in his bad books. At any rate I was not; but of course there is no telling what may have happened since then."

"Aye—hoi! there they are!" shouted Mr. Underwood, as he and his two companions caught sight of the highwaymen in a turn of the road. "There they are—hurrah!"

"Curse you, don't kick up such a row," muttered the colonel, between his teeth. "They have caught sight of us again, Hackett, and it inspires fresh courage into them."

"Never you mind, colonel," said his companion, "don't you be foolish and wait any longer for me. I shall manage for myself, I dare say. Now be off at once."

The colonel shook his head; he appeared obstinate upon this point.

"If you don't go, colonel, the chances are that you'll be taken; so take my advice, and be off at once."

"Oh, no, I shan't be taken, I dare say," answered his companion; "and if I am, it will be in good company," he said, with a smile.

CHAPTER LIII.

THE STUGGLE.—THE CAPTURE.

VERY little incidents occurred in the pursuit. After this, Hackett and Colonel Jack managed to push on so far ahead, that they were enabled thereby to pass through each turnpike without any impediment, Wild and his companions being too far behind to give notice to the pikemen for them to close the gates.

Thus affairs continued, until our highwaymen had nearly reached Barnet, and in all probability they would have got clear off, for they had distanced their pursuers; but Wild, who was as crafty as a fox, seeing that in all probability the fugitives would elude his grasp, had recourse to stratagem.

From the high road in which they found themselves, there was a bye lane which led by a short cut into the one which the thieftaker knew the highwaymen must of necessity take. To gallop down this lane, and reach the other road, was but the work of a few minutes.

Having arrived here, Wild said with a chuckle—

"Now we shall have them. Keep quiet, and leave it to me."

And so saying, he drew back his companions behind a hedge, and quietly awaited the issue. In a short time he had the satisfaction of hearing the tramp of the high-waymens' horses.

"They are coming," he said, in a hoarse whisper. "Now for it."

"Ah, ah," said the sheriff, "now I shall have the satisfaction of taking this miscreant."

Wild only indulged in a quiet laugh at this observation.

Colonel Jack and Hackett came on in complete ignorance of the close proximity of those who were in wait for them, and as they came to the end of the lane, they found themselves suddenly confronted by their three pursuers.

"The game's up," exclaimed Wild, "you are outwitted. Yield!"

So sudden had been this surprise, that Colonel Jack and Hackett, were well nigh running clean into their opponents. They did, however, manage to turn their horses heads in time to prevent a collison ; and would fain have endeavoured to pass, but the road was too narrow to admit of their doing so, taken up as it was by their three adversaries. Mr. Underwood sprang forward and caught hold of the head of Colonel Jack's horse.

"Mine this time," he said, with an air of satisfaction, as he levelled his pistol at the chest of the highwayman. The colonel was generally pretty prompt in all his actions, and before the sheriff had time to see his motive, he dealt him a heavy blow on the wrist, with his riding whip. The pistol was dashed out of his hand, and discharged itself into the air, happily without doing any harm. Underwood was wild with rage and pain, and grasped the highwayman by the throat, and endeavoured to pull him off his horse.

"Curse you," exclaimed the colonel, "curse you."

"I'll stick to you now while I have life, you scoundrel, for my own personal revenge, as well as upon public grounds ;" and he hugged away at the colonel, and was nearly bringing him to the ground.

"Hold on," exclaimed Sharpthorne, "hold on, Mr. Underwood, but the attorney did not however, deem it advisable to come to such close quarters himself. The sheriff then received a terrific blow upon the face from his antagonist, which staggered him not a little, but he still retained his grasp, for he was pale with rage.

"Once more I charge you to leave go ; or by heaven I will have your life," said Colonel Jack who's temper was now getting the mastery of him.

"I'll never leave go of you, you scoundrel, you thief, and—"

He did not complete his sentence, for a crushing blow upon his forehead, from the colonel's riding whip, rendered him senseless,

and he fell forward upon his horse's neck, perfectly helpless. Sharpthorne believed he was killed.

"Good God," he exclaimed, "Mr. Wild, see, Mr. Underwood is murdered. The colonel will escape—haste."

Wild had been engaged with Hackett, while this was taking place, but finding that in all probability the colonel would make good his retreat, he left his brother highwayman in charge of Sharpthorne, who had strolled up to his side, and grasped hold of the rein of Hackett's horse. Wild then went forward and succeeded in pinning Colonel Jack from behind. A desperate and fearful struggle now took place between these two.

"You have brought this upon yourself," said Wild, holding him with the firmness of a vice. "If you had taken my advice, affairs would not have come to this pass."

He then whispered into the colonels ear.

"I didn't want to take you prisoner, you ought to have known that, had you acted as you ought to have done. I could have nabbed you scores of times. If you had taken my advice and listened to me when at the Woodman, I should not have been compelled to bring natters to this pass. You have been a fool for once."

"Fool or no fool," answered the colonel, "I'll prove myself more than a match for you. Leave go or by the Lord that made me I won't spare you, Wild.

"Psha," exclaimed the thieftaker, contemptuously, "you know me, I ain't to be frightened, never was."

"Nor am I," answered Colonel Jack, now struggling still more desperately to release himself. Although his arms were held firmly behind by Jonathan Wild, he might have discharged the pistol he held in his hand no doubt with effect, but he hesitated at having recourse to this alternative, which he felt was but a desperate one, the more so, as he could not possibly see his enemy, and would therefore be compelled to fire at random; and would in all probability deal a death wound.

"I tell you colonel, it ain't of no manner of use," said Wild, as he resisted the fierce efforts of the highwayman. "So you had better be quiet, and give up at once, for depend upon it, now that you have brought matters to this issue, I am not going to give you up for my credit's sake.

The colonel made no reply to this, but by a desperate effort succeeded in lifting Wild off his horse, fairly out of his stirrups. So great was this feat of strength, that even the thieftaker himself, who had been in all sorts of frays, was fairly astonished ; he however retained his hold of the highwayman, and dragged him to the earth as he fell, and so the two were struggling desperately on the ground, beneath the body of Ada, Colonel Jack's mare, and the probability is that they would have been both kicked to death.

There is no doubt that Hacket could have easily managed to have got away from Mr. Sharpthorne, but he refrained from doing so, as he was anxious to see how matters where going with our hero. When he saw him and the thieftaker fall heavily to the ground, he endeavoured to shake off Sharpthorne, who having become suddenly pugnacious, being wild with the fear that the colonel might probably escape. The lawyer presented the muzzle of his pistol to Hackett, and assumed a defiant and warlike attitude.

"You miserable anatomy of a man," exclaimed the highwayman, contemptuously, as he grasped the pistol by the barrel, and flung it some yards from the spot.

Mr. Sharpthorne had but little physical strength, but his mind was set upon the capture of Colonel Jack, and he feared Hackett's interference with the two on the ground, so the attorney sprang at Hackett, and grasped him by the throat. The latter was perfectly astonished at the lawyer's temerity, and for the moment became almost speechless with surprise; however, when this was over, he caught Shapthorne by what he supposed to be the hair of the head, which he found out to be only a wig, for it came off its owner's head in his hand, disclosing the bald pate of the attorney.

It was not a time for indulging in laughter, but under any other circumstances, the risibility of Hackett would have been excited in no ordinary degree.

Finding that the head of Mr. Sharpthorne eluded his grasp, he thought he would try the feet, one of which he grasped firmly, and lifted the attorney off his horse, head downwards.

Then it was that this limb of the law began to howl and shout in a most piteous manner for mercy.

The highwayman let him gently upon the ground, inflicting upon him several cuts with his riding whip on that part which is supposed to be the seat of honour.

"Oh—oh!" roared out Sharpthorne, who began to think that an affray with highwaymen was a much more serious thing than he had anticipated, and he heartily wished himself once more in his chambers in the Temple.

Hackett was now about to see what could be done to rescue his comrade, when Wild, who observed his movements, fired his pistol, and wounded Hackett in the right shoulder.

The sound of horses' feet were now heard, and a party of horsemen were observed on the brow of the hill, making towards the spot where the affray was taking place.

"Fly, Ned!" said Colonel Jack; "fly, my boy, while there's yet time."

"No, no," answered his brother highwayman, as an expression of poignant anguish passed over his features, at the sight of the colonel in the grasp of so determined a man as Jonathan Wild

"Fly, Hackett!" said the colonel, now more authoritatively; "I command you to fly, as you value your own life or mine. I can't explain, now," he said, as he rose up, still closely grasped by Wild.

Hackett hesitated for a minute or so, and then, as he observed the approaching horsemen near the spot, he reluctantly did as his superior commanded.

Mr. Sharpthorne, when he saw that he was fairly rid of his antagonist, now rose to his feet, and said to Wild—

"Have you got him all right?—hold him fast!"

But Wild found it almost more than he could do, to retain his hold of Colonel Jack, and he declared afterwards that he never, in the whole course of his career, met with so determined and desperate a man.

The probability is, that the colonel would have managed to have got away, if the horsemen had not come up as they did.

Mr. Wild immediately accosted them, and took upon himself to explain the situation of affairs, and solicit their assistance, which they immediately gave.

Two of them dismounted, and assisted Wild to bind Colonel Jack, who was then placed upon the back of his own horse, which was led by Wild, who had mounted his own.

Sharpthorne then instituted a search for his wig, which he found in a ditch beside the road.

It was so saturated with muddy water, that he thought it hardly worth while to take it with him, and therefore left it where it was.

He also mounted his steed, and consoled himself with the reflection that after all he had the gratification of travelling by the side of Colonel Jack, who was bound, and a safe prisoner. And the party wheeled, or rather trotted off.

"This wasn't my fault," said Wild to our hero, in so low a tone, that none of the others could hear. "It's been all brought about by your own obstinacy."

"How do you mean, not your fault?" inquired the highwayman. "You're a good one to talk, Wild. I should like to know which of the lot would have taken me if you had not."

"Oh, I don't mean that," answered the thieftaker.

"What the devil do you mean, then. You are confoundedly mysterious."

"You know, I don't want you to swing, you know that well enough."

"Oh, that's it, is it ; but others do, eh ?"

The thieftaker nodded, and said—

"But, I can't help myself now. I might have done, but not now."

"Curse me if I can understand you," answered our hero.

"You've not gone the right way to do so."

"Why not ?"

"By not listening to me at the Woodman, when I told you I wished to speak with you."

"Wish to speak to me, indeed, I like that, Wild. Everybody knows what you mean, when you wish to speak to them. They are spoken to for a journey to the other world."

"You must listen to reason," said Wild, as he trotted gently ahead of the party. "And there's where you've lost yourself. All I wanted of you was simply this—you hold some papers."

"Well, what of that—what's that to you ?"

"Psha ! Nothing to me, man, nothing to me, individually ; only they are wanted, and not you."

"Well, you've got me, but you have not got the papers, and, what is more, I'll take d—n good care that you don't have them, and that's all about it. Who has put you up to that—Sir Richard Fleetwood ?"

"No, his lawyer."

"Oh, no doubt at his instigation."

"That I can't say."

"Sir Richard Fleetwood had better mind how he plays with edged tools. I know that which would bring him into not a little trouble."

"You'd better have given up those papers, colonel," said Wild.

"That's my business," answered the highwayman.

"Well, if you are obstinate, you must take your own course."

Mr. Sharpthorne now trotted up near the two ; he was anxious to learn what they were conversing about, but was afraid to come close to them, for he stood in some awe of the highwayman, and, singular to relate, just at this time, Slott, the highwayman's dog, came trotting up.

The reader will no doubt be surprised that this canine quadruped had not played his part in the drama, but this is easily accounted for.

The animal had been shut in the stable at the Woodman, by accident ; and when he heard that his master had left, he set up such a continued howling, that the landlord of the Woodman was constrained to go himself to let him out. This did not, however, take place till some time after the highwayman's departure, and the consequence was, that Slott could not overtake him, although he followed at a respectful distance ; indeed, had he started at the same time, he would have found it quite impossible to have kept up with his master, at the pace he was going.

As Mr. Sharpthorne neared Wild and Colonel Jack, he became aware of the close proximity of the dog to him, of whom he had always had a great horror.

"Hang the hound," exclaimed the attorney. "Why, here's the dog."

"What dog ?" inquired Wild.

"Colonel Jack's," answered the attorney.

At this observation our hero turned round, and observed Slott.

It would be utterly impossible to convey to the reader, any faint notion of the expression upon the face of the dog, when he beheld his master bound, and a prisoner. One glance seemed to tell him the state of the case, and, for the first time, he sent forth a low and plaintive whine.

From a motion made to him by the colonel, Slott trotted away from the party ; his master was afraid that they might endeavour to capture the dog. It would not, however, have been a very easy task to have captured him, as we have seen on a previous occasion.

When the animal was out of sight, which he soon was, Mr. Sharpthorne, on his grey horse, hovered about the colonel and Wild, like a harpy, as he was.

The former turned round, and fixed his eye upon the lawyer with a settled look.

"So," he exclaimed, "this is partly your business, eh, Mr. Sharpthorne. Partly—what am I saying it is wholly yours."

"Ahem—I but do my duty to my clients," answered Sharpthorne. "Sorry to see you in this position, I am sure."

"Humbug ! sorry, indeed !" exclaimed the colonel. "I am only sorry that I have not got my hands free to tan that old hide of yours, you shrivelled up anatomy of a man."

"Mr. Wild will bear me witness that I am as sorry as yourself for this."

"Psha," exclaimed our hero, indignantly. "Wolves and tigers are sorry when they devour their prey, I suppose."

"Ahem—I hope I am not a wolf or tiger," said the lawyer, deprecatingly.

"You are not much better, if as good," answered Colonel Jack.

Mr. Sharpthorne pulled back his roman nosed grey horse at this observation, and fell into the rear without another word ; he had always been afraid of the colonel, and would not have ventured to have come in such close proximity to him unless he had been firmly bound.

———

CHAPTER LIV.

THE LODGMENT IN BARNET—CAGE THE ESCAPE.

In our description of the capture of Colonel Jack in the preceding chapter, we omitted to give the reader an account of how it passed with Mr. Underwood.

Upon the party of horsemen coming up at the time of the struggle between the colonel and Wild, the attention of one or two was attracted to the unfortunate sheriff, who was lying prostrate on the earth. One of the party happened to be a surgeon, and he at once made an examination of the sheriff's wounds. He certainly had an ugly crack on the crown, which had effectually sent him into oblivion for some time, but luckily the skull was not fractured, although the sight which the wounded man presented was something frightful. What with two black eyes and a bloody nose from his assailant's fist, and a large protrubrance and a sickly wound from the butt end of the whip.

Mr. Underwood was, however, carefully attended to by the gentleman who had dismounted from his horse for the purpose of examining him. Mr. Underwood was conveyed to the nearest cottage and there bled. After awhile, he recovered his consciousness, and the first question was—"whether that scoundrel had escaped?"

He was informed that the colonel had been made prisoner by Jonathan Wild. At this intelligence, a smile of satisfaction passed over his features, and he would fain have gone off at once to have had the gratification of seeing our hero, but his medical adviser forbade his removal, and he was compelled to remain in bed until the following morning.

Jonathan Wild in the meantime was conveying the colonel to Barnet cage. This was a small square building, into which it was the custom to convey offenders, for a short time, previous to their removal to either London or the county gaol. Wild had other business on hand, and consequently deemed it advisable to place the highwayman in the cage, who, in the morning, he proposed taking up to London. The cage itself had but one door as an entrance, which was strongly studded with iron nails. Above the door were some fetters, tending by way of ornament it is to be supposed, or else as an indication of the nature of the building. Outside, in front of the side where the entrance was, there had been placed a small wooden box for a turnkey to keep guard. Sometimes two of those worthies were placed here.

"Ah," said Sharpthorne, "you are going to lock him up in the cage, are you?"

"Yes," said Wild, who was glumpy, and not at all pleased at the part he had been playing.

"Don't you think that it would be better to convey him at once to London?" inquired Sharpthorne.

"No, I have not time and cannot, so that is all about it," replied Wild.

"Oh, you know best," answered Sharpthorne. "Of course you know best, Mr. Wild, only I should be sorry if—ahem—he were to escape."

"He is a great deal more likely to get away by our taking him to London to night."

"Indeed, how so?"

"Because we shall very likely meet with some of his companions."

"Well."

"Well, you say; I do not think it well. There would be rescue most likely, or an attempt at it, and we are not strong enough for another fray with desperate and well armed men.—Though to be sure there is yourself." This was of course said in derision, which Sharpthorne well understood.

By this time they had arrived at the cage, but the man who kept the keys, and should have been at his post, did not happen to be there. He had found the night rather cold, and had consequently adjourned to a public-house, rejoicing in the sign of the "Robin Red Legs." Wild knew his habits, and his usual haunts, consequently he dispatched one of his companions to the said hostelry, and in a few minutes the man returned, much the better in the inner man for one or two pots of purl. The door was opened, and the colonel was thrust in, bound as he was. Wild whispered in his ear to remain quiet till the morning, when he would himself fetch him, and if possible, see and square matters. He meant by this that the colonel would be suffered to escape, provided he gave up the papers, or promised to do so on the following day. The colonel said nothing, but entered the domicile provided for him. The massive lock was turned, the door bolted, and for the first time our hero found himself behind iron bars, and enclosed in stone walls. Now the sensation occasioned by this is seldom a pleasant one under any circumstances, even for some rediculous small debt, but when the party is caged knows that his life is concerned the reflection is anything but a pleasing one. Wild, after he had left strict injunctions for the man to keep careful watch and ward throughout the night, then left for London, accompanied by the attorney Sharpthorne and the gentlemen who had assisted in the capture remained some time conversing with the man, after which they too left. Nevertheless, the place was not quite deserted, for several rustics who had heard a highwayman had been captured, came ever and anon, and gazed earnestly at the building which had the honour of enclosing one of the most celebrated highwaymen of his day. While several of these yokels were inspecting the building from all points of the compass, a new comer appeared who was unknown to any of them.

"What's been the row?" said the man, who was attired as a country farmer.

"There be a highwayman," said one of the yokels around.

"Where my friend?"

"In soide there," pointing to the cage.

"Ah, indeed, been there long?"

"No, about an hour or so."

"What's is name?"

"Colonel Jack," said another of the group.

"Oh, that's a good job," said the new comer. "It's a celebrated man, so I have heard."

"You are right," answered a rustic.

After their curiosity had been gratified, and it took more than two hours to do this, they one by one departed, and Barnet cage was left once more under the watchful guardianship of the janissary who usually took charge of it.

The moon was now up, and the night clear, and, although an old-fashioned structure, Barnet cage, as it was termed, was a picturesque object enough.

It had been originally termed the round house, for what reason it would be difficult to determine, with any degree of accuracy. Most probable it was from the appearance of its roof, which was of a circular form, and run up to a point, surmounted by a gilt vane, fashioned like a key.

It had in its day—for it was very old—lodged some hundreds of disorderly personages.

The man who had inquired, respecting the prisoner, from the gaping crowd, slowly departed, as he found the others go, and after he had travelled for some quarter of a mile or more, he was joined by a companion, who had one of his arms in a sling.

"Well," said this individual, "it is as we expected, I suppose."

"Yes, poor chap, he's safely lodged in the cage," and the speaker's tones were so melancholy when he made this observation, that his companion regarded him with a look of surprise, blended with commisseration.

"Then he must be got out by hook or by crook," answered the other, who was no other than our friend Hackett, who had followed Wild's party at a respectful distance; he presumed that Colonel Jack was being conveyed prisoner, but could not be positive upon this head, as he dared not come sufficiently close to observe with a sufficient degree of certainty. The other individual was

Mullins, whom the reader will, perhaps, remember, in the opening chapters of this tale.

"He must be saved," said Hackett, "if we blow the brains of the man out who is in charge of the round house."

"But, then, how are we to get him out?" asked Mullins.

"Possess ourselves of the keys which he has in his pocket."

"Oh, I see," and here Mullins ruminated for some time.

"Do you know the man in charge of the cage?" inquired Hackett.

"No," answered Mullins; "but I tell you what, captain," (he always called Hackett captain) "I tell you what, my humble opinion is, that we shall find it a hard task to get the keys from this ere chap."

"Well, what else is to done?"

"Why, a brilliant thought has occurred to me. I know a woman in this neighbourhood who was—"

He hesitated.

"Well, what? Go on, man. An old sweetheart of yours—is that it?"

"Well, something like it, captain."

"What's that to do with the matter?"

"Why, you see, she knew this man, also. In fact, she knows him now, I believe."

"Which man?"

"He that's in charge of the cage."

"Ah, then she may be of essential service."

"What I was thinking of is just this. You must know that this beautiful cage has two small gratings near the top. One of these is in the front, and the other on the back part. I suppose they were made to give air—"

"Most likely."

"Well, if we could get this man's attention engaged by any means, I might possibly be able to speak to the colonel."

"How so?"

"Why by climbing up the back part of the cage to the grating."

"Oh, I see; but how is that to be managed, Mullins?"

"That we'll see. We have all the night to work the oracle, and it must go hard if we don't manage it somehow or other. Now follow me, captain."

Hackett did as his companion suggested, for he was anxious to see what could be done to save Colonel Jack, although his wound from Wild's shot was very painful.

Mullins led the way down a lane, then across two fields by a narrow footpath, then through another and still narrower lane, where he eventually stopped before a little low, white-fronted cottage, built of what is termed rubble.

Mullins opened the door, as Hackett re-

mained outside leaning against the low palings which run in front of the habitation.

"Jane," said Mullins, in a low voice.

A woman appeared from out the parlour, if it could be dignified by such an appellation.

"Joe,' she exclaimed, "I thought you'd left for London. Coom in lad."

"I've a friend outside, Jane."

"Can't he coom in?"

Mullins beckoned to Hackett, who then entered the passage, and after this the parlour.

"One of our pals has got into trouble, Jane," said Mullins.

"Oh, dear, but that's a bad job," said the woman.

"Yes, and is at present lodged in the cage."

No. 39.

"What, Barnet Round House?" she inquired.

"Yes. Now I tell you how you can be of service to me," said Mullins.

"Well, you know, Joe, that I shall be too glad; but sit down, and your friend too."

"Thank you, marm," said Hackett, "I shall be but too glad to avail myself of your offer."

And he seated himself forthwith.

The woman, with that hospitality which we believe generally characterises the rural population of England, placed supper on the table, and drawing a jug of ale, she offered a glass first to Hackett, he being a stranger.

"I've been thinking, if I ain't incorrect," said Mullins, "that you know this ere cove who has charge of vagrants and such like persons who are generally lodged there."

Hackett observed the woman colour slightly at this observation of his companion, and she turned away to get something from a corner cupboard.

"Law," she exclaimed, "what made you think of that, Joe."

"Just because I thought it would be useful," he answered.

"Selfish, like the rest of the world," said Hackett, with a smile.

"Yes, I know him, certainly," she answered.

"What's his name ?"

"Luke Driscoll."

"Well, now look here, Jane," said Mullins, as he sat himself confidentially by her side ; "I told you that you might be useful. Me and my friend," and here he nodded towards Hackett, "me and my friend want to have a little bit of a chat with him as is in this cage."

The woman nodded, expressive of her perfect understanding of this proposition.

"Well, you see, we don't know how that's to be worked."

"And you want me, then, to ask Luke to let you inside. Is that it ?" said the woman.

"No, no, my sweet girl," said Mullins, giving her a kiss. "It ain't exactly that, for you must understand that I somehow don't think he would consent. No, you must not say a word about our being friends of his, or we shall be in a mess ourselves."

A prolonged "oh," was the woman's answer to this.

"No, what I meant is just this—"

He paused and reflected for a minute or two.

"Couldn't you manage to engage him in conversation, whilst I go at the back of the cage and peep through the grating ?"

"I'll try if you like," answered the woman, "only I should be sorry to get Luke into a scrape."

"Oh, you need not be under any fear of that," answered Mullins. "You know, my dearest Jane, that nothing in the world would induce me to get you into trouble."

The woman smiled, and after a short time consumed in desultory conversation, Mullins, Hackett, and the woman Jane, proceeded to the round-house, where Colonel Jack was confined.

"Now," observed Mullins, as they proceeded along, "what I want you to do, my dear, is just this—which I think a girl of your natural abilities won't have much difficulty in managing for me—just go and indulge your friend Luke with some of your fascinating patter. Give him a glance or two from those ere brilliant eyes of your own—and of course he will be taken off his legs, as the saying is. There ain't no call for to say anything about such a miserable

individual as myself—'cause why, he might be jealous. So, while you are giving him the treat of your company for a while, I shall be able to go round upon the quiet to the back part of the cage, or whatever else you may choose to term it."

"I will do as you wish," said the woman, quietly.

"Ah, that's a good girl, spoken like your own self, when we were boy and girl together. Ah, those days, Jane, eh ?"

And at this part of his speech, Mr. Mullins indulged the lady with a kiss of tenderness and affection.

While all this was taking place, Colonel Jack was an inmate of that miserable place where he had been left by Jonathan Wild.

A prison at all times is bad enough, even under the improved regulations of our own days ; but at the period of which we write, the authorities deemed it not only expedient, but a positive necessity, to render those places as uncomfortable and wretched as it was possible for them to do.

Colonel Jack gazed round upon the gloomy walls, as the thought of escape first enlivened his mind, but the place was so dark, that he had some difficulty in making out its distinctive features.

There was certainly one small oil lamp, set against the wall out of his reach, and it was surprising that he was treated with this comfort, although its feeble rays hardly served to dissipate the gloom for two or three yards round where it had been placed.

The walls had originally been whitewashed, but this had long since worn off, and given way to an incrustation of mildew.

There were several staples and hooks in the walls, where refractory malefactors had been tied to.

As the colonel caught sight of these, a smile passed over his countenance. They might, he thought, be of service to him ; but then he remembered, sadly enough, that his arms were firmly bound.

After some time lost in reflection, of not a very pleasing character, he tried to reach his waistcoat pocket with his right hand, but this attempt proved a failure ; he did manage however to get with an inch or two of the same.

"Confound it," exclaimed our hero, "if I could only get my knife out, all would be well, as far as the cords are concerned, and then, when they open the door, I could but make a fight of it, which after all would be better than Tyburn."

He made another attempt to reach his pocket, but without success. When he had been bound, he had managed to so place his arms as to give himself some little room to move them, but it would appear not enough for the purpose of getting at his knife.

After repeated attempts, he was forced to give it up as a hopeless case, and he sat himself down upon one of the stones, and began to ramble off into thoughts which were anything but pleasurable ones.

For nearly half an hour he sat thus disconsolate and dejected.

Presently, to his infinite surprise, he heard his own name called, by a voice which was well known to him, although the speaker gave utterance to it in a whisper.

"Colonel—master—'tis I," said Mullins, through the grating on the back part of the prison house.

"Hist!—who's that?" said Colonel Jack, not knowing whence the voice proceeded from.

"'Tis I—Mullins," said that individual. "Don't speak loud, colonel, or you may spoil all. How fares it with you in this cursed hole?"

"Oh, badly enough, Mullins: but that's nothing—it's what is to come after."

"We must manage to get you out, master, before the night's over," said Mullins.

"What brought you here?" inquired the colonel.

"I met with Hackett."

"Ah, indeed! And is he all right."

"Yes, only he's wounded."

"Ah, that I know; but nothing serious, I hope."

"Oh, no, only a flesh wound."

"Have you got a knife in your pocket?" asked the colonel.

"Yes, master."

"Will it go through the grating?"

"I think so."

"Well, then, let's have it, for I am bound, and if I once manage to cut these cursed cords, half the work is done."

Mullens dropped the knife through the grating, and in another second or so it was in the possession of Colonel Jack, who had to lay flat down on the ground and pick it up with his mouth, for he found it was impossible for him to do so with his hands bound as he was.

Having possessed himself of this, his next care was to transfer the same into his hand, and see if he could contrive to cut the cords which so firmly bound him. After one or two unsuccessful attempts, he contrived to do this, and when he once more freed himself—free as far as his own bodily movements were concerned, he felt his spirits elated when he found this, and called to Mullins in a low whisper—

"I am here, master," said that worthy, "but I don't know how long it may be for. So just let's arrange matters, and say what we have got to say at once."

"Have you got your dark lantern with you?" inquired the colonel.

"Yes," answered Mullins.

"Then just send its rays in here for a minute or so, that I may see something about this abominable hole, for it is more than I can do now."

"Will it shine on to the other grating," inquired Mullins.

"I don't know, but I should say not, if you manage matters properly."

Mullins held the bull's eye of his lantern against the grating, casting its rays low down so as to avoid the opposite grating.

"Will that do, colonel?" he inquired.

"Yes, all right; now turn it to the left."

This was done, and then to the right, and so on, until the colonel was enabled to make an inspection of the whole interior of his prison house.

"Hold hard, Mullins, that will do. Now, then, have you a rope, for I've cut mine pretty well to pieces."

"No, that I've not," said Mullins, "but I dare say Hackett has, and if he's not, why, I'll get one some how or other."

"Very well, do so, and if you can manage to get a chisel, all the better, or else a screwdriver."

"Won't a pick do?" asked Mullins.

"Ah, to be sure."

"Well, then, I have one with me."

"Throw it down then. The ground is soft and it won't make much noise, but stay, I'll catch it, for fear of accidents."

Mullins did as he was desired, and the colonel caught the pick without any difficulty; he then said—

"Now, Mullins, get me the rope as soon as you can, and then—"

"What?" said his companion, in some anxiety.

"Then I'll see if it be possible to make my escape."

"How, colonel?" inquired Mullins.

"Through the roof if it's to be managed. How about the man on guard?"

"Oh, I have managed to engage his attention by—ahem—a feminine female," said Mullins.

"Well, then, let's have a rope as soon as possible," answered the colonel.

Mullins disappeared, and in a few minutes more returned with a rope which he had procured from Hackett. This he threw down to the colonel, who then desired him to retire and watch the movements of the man, Driscoll.

While this had been going on, the woman, Jane, had been engaged in conversation with Driscoll, who was quite innocent of the knowledge of the close contiguity of Hackett or Mullins. The former had been watching at a respectful distance the motions of both. Mullins then proceeded to a little road side house near to the cage, and procuring a steaming jug of hot spiced ale, he took his way up to Jane and Driscoll, and pretending to recognise the former for the first time, he greeted her as an old friend; he then offered some ale to Driscoll, who was a man too fond of creature comforts to refuse the proffered draught.

"An old friend of mine," said Jane, introducing Mullins, although studiously avoiding, at the same time, mentioning his name.

The man nodded, and Mullins said to him—

"I understand, master, that you've got a celebrated highwayman inside."

The man nodded, and Mullins went on—

"Well, I never did see a highwayman, and I 'spose it's more than you dare do to let's have a peep at him."

Now Mullins had not the slightest idea that the request would be granted; he merely made it to throw the man off his guard, and as he knew, that in all probability, by this time, that our hero was about to climb up to the roof, it would have been one of the most imprudent things possible for him to have sought an interview with him.

Driscoll said that it was quite impossible for him to let anyone see the prisoner, as the thieftaker had left strict orders for him not to open the door upon any pretence whatever, and—he did not say so—but he felt too glad that such instructions had been left with him, for, to say the truth, Mr. Driscoll had rather a horror of highwaymen, and was not at all anxious to have an encounter with them.

The can of hot spiced ale rapidly disappeared, or, rather, the contents of the can, whereupon Mr. Mullins kindly consented to get another.

Upon his return with this he heard a scratching noise, as though the colonel was at work with the pick, which was, in reality, the case.

"Confound it," thought Mullins. I wonder he don't hear it," and he glared anxiously at Driscoll, who, however, did not appear to be at all conscious of any strange noise. To say the truth, the jailor had imbibed a pretty good quantity in the course of that eventful evening, and although he had his wits sufficiently about him to be on his ground and attend to his duty, he could not be said to have the finer senses in their full powers. Malt and hops does have a soporific effect upon the human frame and constitution.

Still Mullins thought that he must hear the sounds, so he commenced talking as loud as he possibly could, to drown the noise.

His eyes were ever and anon directed towards the roof, and, in a short time, he observed a hand appear and remove a tile, then another, and another. Mullins' heart beat violently against his ribs Now was the critical time.

Presently the colonel's head appeared through the opening, then his shoulders, and then the whole of his body.

Just as Mullins observed this, his fears were awakened by the report of a pistol or gun, he could not tell which, and a voice calling out in loud tones—

"Luke! Luke! He's escaping."

Driscoll heard his own name, and gazed suddenly round in all quarters. Then it was that he observed the colonel on the roof of the cage, in the very act of dropping to the ground. Its height was considerable, but the colonel did not hesitate, and jumped down at all risks.

Upon his alighting, he found himself in the grasp of a strange man, the one who had fired the pistol, as it afterwards appeared.

A desperate struggle now took place with these two; however, with one well directed blow, the colonel was able to send his assailant staggering for some yards, and before he had time to recover himself, he made off at headlong speed.

Driscoll's fears were now awakened to such an extent that he grew desperate, and immediately gave chase, as well as the man who had been struggling with the highwayman.

"Follow," said Driscoll to Mullins—"Follow, my friend. He has escaped, and we may want assistance."

Mullins did follow, to see how matters were likely to go, and was soon up by the side of Driscoll.

Colonel Jack darted down a dark lane, where he met with Hackett.

"Hilloa," exclaimed the latter, as the colonel neared him.

"Out of the way," said the latter. "It's me, Hackett," exclaimed that individual·

"The Lord be praised, that you are once more free, colonel. This way."

The two run on side by side, for several yards.

"You are badly wounded, Ned," said the colonel.

"Nothing of such great importance. Only let us get clear of these fellows, for I can hear that they are following us."

"Where's Mullins?" asked the colonel.

"I left him outside the cage talking to the man its charge."

CHAPTER LVI.

THE HIGHWAYMAN MEETS WITH A FRIEND IN NEED.

COLONEL JACK, now that he found himself

once more at liberty, was determined to make a fight of it, and, in the event of his being overtaken, not to be taken alive.

He did not know who the man was who had grappled with him when he had fallen from the roof of the prison house; but one thing was quite evident, and that was, the latter's determination to capture him, if possible; but, however, the free use of his limbs, and the fact of his no longer being in confinement, gave our hero some better spirits to meet anything which might befal him.

As he took his way along with Hackett, he heard the sounds of his pursuers, like a pack of insatiate hounds at his heels.

"We shall never be able to outrun them, I fear," said Hackett.

As he made this observation, his pursuers voices showed that they were nearer. Pushing on as fast as they could, they came to the end of a lane which appeared to have no outlet, for it evidently led to a large mansion —at least, so it appeared to be, for the colonel observed the massive wrought-iron gates and carriage road to the mansion itself.

"What's to be done now?" inquired Hackett; "we can go no further."

"Over the gate as quickly as you can and trust to providence," said the colonel. "It would be an act of madness to think of turning back."

Hackett, wounded as he was, did not feel himself quite up to the mark in clearing the gate, so his companion gave him a lift up, and Hackett dropped quickly on the other side.

No sooner had he accomplished this feat than the colonel followed his example, and the two highwaymen found themselves in the grounds of a stately mansion.

Taking their way by the side of some evergreens, which effectually concealed them, they proceeded to the rear of the premises. As they went along they were surprised to see a light in an outhouse at that time in the morning.

"Hilloa!" exclaimed the colonel, "what have we here?"

"Better retire," said Hackett.

"It's impossible now," answered colonel Jack. "It would be only making matters worse. Oh, no, we must face it out."

With this last observation the colonel walked boldly up to the building where the light was observed.

It proved to be a stable, and a man was inside, so he judged by the voice, but before he had entered, he heard words spoken in the voice of a woman.

The colonel hesitated.

"What's up, I wonder? There's a woman's voice," he said, in a low whisper to Hackett.

The two highwaymen listened for a second or so, and while doing so, the stable-door was suddenly opened, and the figure of a man presented itself.

His astonishment at the sight of the two highwaymen can hardly be described; he was speechless with horror.

Colonel Jack was the first to speak.

"You are up late, my friend," he said, glancing at the man, who was evidently a servant.

"Yes; and what is that to you? What do you do on these premises? Burglars, I suppose."

"No," answered our hero; "we've missed our way, that's all."

"Umph! A pretty story. How did you get in?'

The colonel walked coolly up to the man and laid hold of him.

"See here, my friend, we're in difficulties just now, and—Well, no matter. Are we to look upon you as a friend or an enemy? If the latter, we shall know how to treat you," and here he pulled out his pistol. "If the former, stand by us, and we'll make it worth your while. Now do you understand?"

"Not exactly. Who and what are you?"

"Gentlemen in difficulties."

The man stared, as well he might, at this indefinite and vague account.

Hackett then went up to his side, and as he did so the man favoured him with a scrutinising glance.

"Why, if it ain't Ned," said the man.

"Ah, Ned it is, and no mistake, Charley. Come, let us go in, for it isn't exactly healthy to be staying out here."

The man hesitated.

"You'd better come in," he said, after a pause.

The three then entered the stable. Passing through this, they were led into a room beyond, which, it appeared, belonged to a small habitation built by side of the stable for the groom to live in.

Colonel Jack was surprised to find a female of no inconsiderable attractions seated at a table in this room, upon which said table there was the remains of a steaming bowl of punch, and a half empty tobacco pipe beside this.

The woman coloured up and looked confused as the two highwaymen entered, but the colonel, who was ever mindful of the fair sex, took off his hat gracefully, and bowed to her with some show of respect.

A smile played about the features of the colonel's companion.

"You've been enjoying yourself, Charley," he said, turning to the groom, for such he in reality was

"Ah—yes—an old friend of mine," he said, pointing to the woman, who made a curtsey and left the apartment without another word.

The three men were then left alone.

"Charley," said Hackett, "you must find some place to conceal us, for we have been pursued, and I am uncertain if our enemies are not already in these premises."

"You know, Ned, I don't mind doing what I can, but I'm only a servant here," answered the groom.

"I suppose not. Whose house is this?"

"Mr. Underwood's."

"Mr. Underwood's!" exclaimed the colonel, unable to conceal his astonishment.

"Yes," said the man. "What of that?"

"Oh, nothing; only he's not one of our most particular friends, that's all," said Ned, with a smile.

The groom appeared to be, for a moment or so, lost in reflection.

"I suppose you ain't going to turn round upon an old friend?" said Ned, now somewhat seriously, for he began to think Charley as he called him was beginning to falter.

"Oh, no," answered that individual. "Let me know what you want, and if you can work the matter, you may rely upon my doing all that man can do. I can't say more than that, can I?"

"No," answered Ned. "Well, the case stands thus. My friend has just escaped from Barnet cage, where he was lodged after a hot pursuit by Jonathan Wild and others."

"Who is your friend?" inquired the groom.

"Colonel Jack," was the reply.

To give anything like a description of the groom's surprise at this declaration would be a vain attempt.

He turned his gaze towards our hero as though he were in the presence of one of the most extraordinary men in the three kingdoms.

"Colonel Jack!" he muttered, "The same whom my master has sworn to capture dead or alive."

"Precisely that's him," said Hackett, "and now, Charley, we are here, that's quite certain, and being here, it is impossible for us to leave at present, and I charge you, by our old friendship, when you and I were boys together, and after then—Well, no matter, we won't run over the old ground now, but you must stand by us."

There was now heard a violent ringing at the bell of the outer gate, and the sounds of voices were heard calling out loudly for admittance.

"Hark!" exclaimed the groom. "What was that?"

"Our friends," said Hackett, "without a doubt."

"What is to be done?" said the groom.

"You must conceal us first, and then I suppose you must let them in ; but, stay, we may as well douse the glim, for it don't look well for me to be up at this hour in the night, or, rather, morning."

With this he blew out the candle, and the two highwaymen and the groom found themselves in darkness, with the exception of a feeble light emitted from the dying embers of the fire in the grate.

"I don't know where else I can put you, but in my bedroom above this," said the groom.

"That will do," said Hackett.

"But then—" and the man hesitated.

"Then what, my friend?" inquired Hackett.

"Why, Becky's there."

"Well, what of that? The more the merrier."

The groom did not seem to approve of this logic.

"Better let her come down here, I suppose," said the man, reflecting.

"Oh, dear, no," answered Hackett. Never put trust in a woman. She may never tell, but when frightened, as she is pretty sure to be, why, you know the consequence."

The groom made no reply to this, but led the way to the upstairs room, which served as her bedroom.

Hackett, who appeared to know his customer, approved of the arrangement accordingly, for he judged that Becky, as he termed her, was paying the groom a nocturnal visit, without the knowledge of Mr. Underwood, his master ; and he urged, therefore, that for his own sake, his friend Charley would not be at all anxious for anyone to invade the privacy of his sleeping apartment, while the woman was there. Hackett felt, therefore, that he had additional security, from this circumstance.

The two highwaymen were shown up into the groom's bedroom, where was seated the woman Becky.

A loud ringing at the bell now took place, of a much louder and longer peal than the previous summons.

"Open the gate some of you. Are you all dead? Highwaymen—thieves—murder!" shouted out those who sought admission into the mansion

It was not the groom's business to open the gate under ordinary circumstances ; but as all the inmates of this establishment were by this time all asleep, Charley, the groom, thought it expedient to make a pretence of arousing himself, and opening the gate, which he forthwith proceeded to do.

"Is that you, sir?" he said, as he neared the gate, pretending to believe that it was his master returning home.

"No, it's me," said Luke Driscoll. "A highwayman has escaped from the cage, and he must have entered your grounds."

"Is Mr. Underwood at home?"

"No, he's not," answered the groom.

"Nor your mistress?"

"Yes, she's abed."

"Well, don't disturb or alarm her, my man, only let us in, that we may institute a search."

"Who are you?" inquired the groom.

"Driscoll. You know me. Keeps the door of the round-house."

"Ah, yes, to be sure. I know you now that you speak in your natural voice."

"And you know me," said another voice.

"It's Mr. Hambler, is it not?" inquired the groom.

"The same, my man, at your service," answered the speaker, who was the man who had seized hold of our hero when he had fallen from the roof of the round-house. This individual was one of the county constabulary, and the cause of his attack upon the colonel can be easily explained. After the departure of Jonathan Wild from the round-house, Mr. Sharpthorne, who may be likened to a vulture hovering round his prey, could not bear to leave the neighbourhood where the colonel was confined; he, therefore, made some excuse to Wild for not accompanying him to London, and when the thieftaker had fairly departed, Mr. Sharpthorne took his way to a neighbouring house, where he put up his horse, and indulged in some refreshment. As luck would have it, this did not happen to be the "Robin Red Legs," or the consequences would most likely have been fatal to the highwayman, for thither it will be remembered Mullins had betaken himself to procure some spiced ale. But in the parlour of the house where the lawyer had put up, there happened to be one of the district constabulary.

To explain the whole particulars of Colonel Jack's capture was the first business of Sharpthorne, and after some time had elapsed, he could not content himself with quietly retiring to bed, but must needs go and have another glance at the cage, or round-house, sending on the officer first, who arrived just as our hero was making his escape. Had Sharpthorne and this worthy been but a few minutes earlier, the probability is, that the colonel would not have succeeded so well as he did. Of course the lawyer gave chase along with the others, and as they took their way along, Mullins would have given something to have been allowed to "ornament his frontispiece," as he termed it.

Charley, the groom, opened the outer gate, and the party entered.

"Now, gentlemen, your pleasure, if you please," said Charley.

"Two rascals have escaped justice, and have secreted themselves somewhere here, either in the grounds or premises," said Sharpthorne. "Have you heard any noise, my man?"

The man had not—so he said, but the violent ringing of the bell.

"Well, then, we must trouble you for a lantern," said the parish constable.

"Certainly, gentlemen," answered the groom; "with pleasure, if you'll step this way, but I suppose I ain't doing wrong in the absence of master?"

This was addressed to Driscoll, with whom he was better acquainted than any of the others.

"Oh, dear, no," answered that individual. "Right or wrong, we must search these premises, and I am sure, Mr. Underwood would wish you to offer every facility to the officers of the law."

"Is this Mr. Underwood's house, then?" inquired Mr. Sharpthorne, in evident surprise.

"Yes," answered Driscoll. "Do you know him?"

"Know him," exclaimed the attorney. "Why, it was Mr. Underwood, himself, who accompanied us when we followed these rascals this very evening, and poor, dear gentleman, he is dangerously, if not fatally wounded by Colonel Jack, himself."

Charley, the groom, opened his ears wide at this information.

"Oh," thought he, "and I am affording them shelter. I shan't catch it much if I'm found out."

But he said nothing, and proceeded in silence towards the stable, where he procured a lantern, and handed it to the party, who immediately made an inspection of the grounds.

Mullins was the most energetic of the whole party in this search, and peered into every nook and corner—out-houses, cow-houses, even piggeries—were examined, but no highwaymen were discovered.

Meanwhile, the colonel and his companion were quietly and snugly ensconced in the groom's bedroom. When he had departed, the colonel said to his companion—

"He means fair, I suppose, Ned?"

"Oh, dear, yes. I would trust him with my life. Why, I've been acquainted with him from boyhood. We courted the same lass. Ah, you may stare, marm," this was addressed to the woman called Becky, "we were a great deal younger than we are, I assure you."

"No doubt you were, sir," said the woman, smiling.

"He had always a good taste for the fair sex," said Ned, chucking her under the chin, "as is proved in your own case, my dear."

"Oh, don't—be quiet."

"Well, I've no wish to make any noise, I can assure you," answered Ned; "on the contrary, just to be as silent as possible. Some other time, my dear."

"Yes, yes, some other time," answered the woman.

The colonel strode up to the door of the apartment, and turning the key, locked the door, and placed the key in his pocket.

"Are you going to lock us in?" inquired Becky, in some alarm.

"I have done so, my dear, for security sake," answered our hero.

He then glanced out of the window which he had opened, to obtain a better view. The sound of voices met his ear, and the lantern was seen in the distance, between the evergreens which surrounded the house. He turned his face and drew in.

"They are searching the premises," he said to Hackett.

"Ah, and will insist upon coming up here, you may depend upon it," answered the latter. "What's to be done then?"

"Then will come the tug of war," answered our hero.

"Oh, dear, I hope there's to be no fighting," exclaimed Becky.

"Silence, madam, if you please," answered the colonel. "'Sufficient for the day is the evil thereof.'"

Colonel Jack again applied his head to the window. The voices of the men were much nearer, and he heard the opening and slamming to of doors, which he judged were those belonging to the outhouses of the premises, and he judged rightly.

"What place is that?" said Mr. Sharpthorne, pointing to the stable.

The groom informed him what it was.

"Ah, then we'll search there at once," said the attorney.

"Hang me if that isn't Sharpthorn's voice," exclaimed the colonel. "I thought he was off to London, long ago."

"Ah, he is a carrion crow, who will hover about wherever a carcase is," answered his companion.

The voices of the party were now heard in the stable, which was immediately beneath the room in which were the highwaymen.

As the officers entered here, a low whistle was heard.

It proceeded from Mullins, to warn the highwaymen.

He did not know where they had concealed themselves, or even if they were in the premises at all, but as he came to each outhouse, he gave vent to the signal which would warn them of the coming danger.

"There is a room above this," said Luke Driscoll, who knew the premises.

"Yes, my bed-room," answered the groom.

"We must search there, then," said Mr. Sharpthorne, eyeing Charley.

"But I know they are not there," an-swered the groom, but his manner was hesitating, which did not escape the lawyer's notice.

"No matter," answered Sharpthorne, "we must search there, or we shall not be doing our duty—at least, we shall be only doing it by halves."

"But," remonstrated the groom, "really, gentlemen, you must take my word upon this subject. I swear to you that there is no highwaymen concealed in my room. I hope you don't think so badly of me as to suppose me capable of harbouring dishonest characters."

"Dishonest characters may be there my friend," said Sharpthorne, placing his hand upon the groom's shoulder confidentially, "without your khowledge—do you see that? The law supposes every man innocent till he is found guilty, and an innocent person generally courts inquiry."

Colonel Jack and Hackett heard every word of the foregoing conversation, for the lawyer's voice, although by no means one of a stentorian description, was harsh and grating, and found its way into the upstairs apartment."

Colonel Jack looked at Hackett, and the latter returned his glance of inquiry.

"What's to done now?" he said. "Up they will come, without a doubt. Is it possible to drop from the window?"

"Not without making a noise," answered the colonel.

"Have you got a rope," continued Ned.

"No, the one you sent by Mullins I was compelled to leave in the round-house; had no time to bring it with me in the confusion."

"Confound it, that's unfortunate."

"Madam," said the colonel, bowing to the woman, "I am afraid we shall be constrained to borrow your shawl."

The woman hesitated, and looked alarmed. Indeed, the turn affairs were taking had pretty well scared her wits, which to say the truth were never of the highest order. Seeing her hesitate, and knowing that there was but little time to lose, the colonel took her shawl off her shoulders without another word, and proceeded to roll it up. He then fastened one end to the window frame, and let it dangle down outside.

"Now, you go first—look sharp," said the colonel to his companion. "This ought to have been done in the first instance, but every moment is of consequence."

Wounded as he was, Ned found some difficulty in dropping from the window. His companion, however, helped him out, and fortunately he succeeded in alighting upon a flower-bed beneath the bedroom, and immediately made off. The colonel followed, with similar success, as far as dropping from

the window was concerned, but not with similar results afterwards, for Hackett succeeded in getting clear off the premises without the slightest obstruction in his passage; but the colonel was not so fortunate.

Thinking to make a short cut, he ran across the grass plat which led to the back entrance of Mr. Underwood's mansion, the back door of which was open, for by this time one or two of the domestics had become aroused by the noise and confusion, and had opened the back door to see what was the matter.

As the housemaid of the establishment was looking out at the lantern dancing about in the hands of Luke Driscoll, she caught sight of the colonel crossing the grass plat, and she uttered a faint scream.

"Silence, my dear," said Colonel Jack,
No. 40.

placing his hand over her mouth. "Your indiscretion will ruin all. Don't be alarmed —we are only seeking for highwaymen, who we think are concealed in or about your premises. I am an officer, one of the London police, and will take care to protect you and your mistress from all harm. Mr. Underwood is not in, so Charley informs me."

"No, sir," said the girl, now pacified, for she most likely believed what was told her. "No, he's not in, and missus can't think what has detained him."

"Well, I must be off now," said Colonel Jack.

"Oh, pray don't go, sir," said the girl. "Do come in and search the house, to see if the horrid highwaymen have got in."

Here was a mess; he had been telling the girl lies for a pretty purpose.

"No, no, my dear; you go in, and shut the back door, like a good girl."

But the good girl had hold of our hero, and she did not seem at all disposed to let go of him. She had been awakened suddenly out of her sleep, and hardly knew what she was about.

"Pray leave go of me," said the colonel, as the housemaid endeavoured to draw him into the passage, clinging to him from very fear, and glancing out at the laurels and various other shrubs as though she thought them peopled with highwaymen.

The gleam of the lantern was now seen on the other side of the house, and the colonel beheld the party were making for the gate. In that case, his retreat would be cut off.

He hesitated. What should be done? Upon the impulse of the moment, and fully believing that the party in search of him would very likely make their appearance upon the spot, he obeyed the girl's mandate, and entering the passage closed the door after him as gently as he could, to avoid attracting the attention of his pursuers.

CHAPTER LVII.

WHAT BEFEL COLONEL JACK IN THE SHERIFF'S HOUSE.—OUR HERO IS FORTUNATE ONCE MORE.

WHEN Colonel Jack found himself in the entrance of Mr. Sheriff Underwood's house he wondered at his own temerity, but he was ready enough on most occasions to meet the exigency of circumstances, but certainly in this instance it appeared to be bearding the lion in his own den, but then he had only a choice of evils left him.

The girl led him mechanically through the whole suite of rooms which were on the basement of the premises.

Apartment after apartment was examined with the utmost care, but, of course, no horrid miscreant was discovered.

At the girl's request he then proceeded up stairs, and he was surprised to find that the premises were much more extensive than he had at first supposed.

Searching for the robbers or highwaymen seemed to be a longer job than he had bargained for, and he was on tenter hooks, all the while fully expecting that the pursuing party might take it into their heads to come in, for it was impossible for him to tell whether they had heard the girl's scream when she had first observed him crossing the lawn.

Presently a loud knocking at the front door was heard, and loud voices called out for admittance.

The girl was about to open it, when the colonel suddenly stopped her. Here was a situation! He was fairly entrapped. The pursuing party were evidently bent on effecting an entrance. Most likely they suspected his being in the interior of the sheriff's mansion. What should he do now? Upon the impulse of the moment he said to the girl.

"They are the officers in search of the highwaymen, but I should be sorry for them to disturb your mistress, and the rest of the household. You can open the door, and tell them that Mr. Parsloe, of the London police, has made a strict search over the premises, and all is right. Do you understand?"

"Yes, sir,"

"Mr. Parsloe," said our hero, again. "You won't forget?"

"No, sir," said the girl.

The colonel then went to the back entrance of the house with the intention of making his escape thereby, while the others were entering the front way. To his horror he found it fastened, and so securely as to defy all his efforts to undo the lock, which had flown to with a spring. He heard the bolts of the outer door being withdrawn, as also the voices of those outside.

What was to be done? Clearly no time was to be lost. In another minute they would be in the passage and see him.

The colonel seeing the exigency of the case, rushed up the grand staircase, and trusted to fate and his own good luck for something to turn up.

He crept quietly up to the first floor, and he had hardly arrived at the landing of this when he heard the voice of Mr. Sharpthorne interrogating the girl. Question after question was asked, and he heard her say that Mr. Parsloe, of the London police, had made a careful search of the premises.

Mr. Parsloe was well known to the lawyer and the two other officials, and they believed the girl's statement, and still thought it strange that the officer should have come in that mysterious manner.

"Most likely Mr. Underwood himself has sent him," suggested Driscoll.

"Does your master know him, my dear?" inquired Sharpthorne.

"Yes, I believe so, sir," answered the girl.

She knew nothing of the sort, but in her confusion hardly knew what she was saying.

Where is he now, was the next question.

The girl looked round the passage, and said that he was there but a few minutes ago.

"We must search the premises," said Sharpthorne, who could not clearly understand the state of the case. "We must search the premises in spite of all the Mr. Parsloe's in the world."

Colonel Jack stayed to hear no more. He crept softly up to the next story, and tried each window as he passed, but they were all fastened. He found himself in the very centre of a suite of rooms, which he judged rightly enough to be sleeping apartments. From one of these, through the crevice of the door, there came a light; some one was either up or else burning a candle during the night; he hesitated which room to enter. The probability was he thought that the light was burning in one of the servants' rooms, and after some little reflection he was determined to enter this one at all hazards. Colonel Jack opened the door, and he paused for a moment on the threshold and looked in.

Beside the fireplace, before which a table was placed, a lady sat reading in a loose wrapper. The colonel did not for a moment doubt who she was—it was evidently the mistress of the establishment. She was conning the contents of some volume by the light of a Cambridge reading lamp. As the colonel stood on the entrance into the apartment, she turned round and said, in a sweet gentle voice—

"Is that you, Alice?"

Colonel Jack closed the door, locked it, and put the key in his pocket.

"No, madam," said our hero, "it is I, a stranger to you, but one who is at present in trouble, and is constrained thus precipitately to throw himself upon your protection."

"Sir!" exclaimed Mrs. Underwood, rising, and uttering a slight scream. "A stranger, and a man, in my sleeping apartment—you—What is the meaning of this?"

She came forward with greater presence of mind than the intruder could have given her credit for under the circumstances, and gazed curiously upon the features of her visitor.

"What is the cause of this intrusion, sir, upon my privacy? I charge you to leave this room, and these premises at once."

"Madam," said the colonel, in his most winning tones, while at the same time he knelt at her feet, "behold a humble suitor kneels before you. It is seldom that man, in hours of distress, has to appeal in vain to woman. Listen to me. I am pursued by enemies who would seek my life. Nay more, they have already done so. Have pity on me, madam—have pity, I implore you."

"Who and what are you, sir, and wherefore this intrusion and entreaties?" said Mrs. Underwood, who was evidently prepossessed in favour of our hero, both from his appearance and the earnest manner in which he pleaded his own cause."

"Alas, madam, I am proscribed by the law, and have only your protection from meeting perhaps death. You cannot feel it in your heart to hand me over to the myrmidons of the law? Something tells me so. I am sure you cannot feel in your heart to turn upon me thus."

"Sir, I do not understand you," said Mrs Underwood. "My husband, in his official capacity, is bound to see the law carried out."

"But, madam," it is not to your husband that I am appealing. It is to lovely woman. Indeed, so lovely, that when she smiles, it is like the sun in my path."

"I charge you go, sir," said Mrs. Underwood. "I would not willingly do you any harm, but this sudden intrusion into the house—at this hour, too—what am I to think? How did you obtain admittance?"

"Madam, to escape from my pursuers I upon the impulse of the moment was compelled by necessity to jump over the palings which ran round your garden. To conceal myself in one of the outhouses was my next course, for I heard my pursuers ring the bell, together with the sound of their voices calling upon the domestics to open the gate. This noise I presume awoke one of the inmates of your house, for I found the back door open, while my pursuers were knocking at the other door for admittance. I rushed up stairs, and seeing a light was in this apartment, presumed that some one was up; then like a deer bayed by a pack of hounds, I rushed anywhere for succour and protection. And I feel convinced, madam, from that benign expression which pervades your countenance, that my appeal will not be made in vain. Hark! they come," said our hero, as he heard the tramp of feet, and the voices of Mr. Sharpthorne and party.

"Open the door, sir," said Mrs. Underwood, as she endeavoured to open it herself, and found it locked. "Open the door. What means this insolence? Have you presumed—have you dared to make me a prisoner in my own room? Insolence—unparalleled insolence. I desire you will open the door."

"Madam, you doom me to fall into the hands of my enemies by such a course. Say, do you wish this?"

Mrs. Underwood hesitated. She did not seem disposed to give up Colonel Jack, nevertheless her situation was a strange one, and had come upon her in such a sudden manner, that she hardly knew how to act in the case.

"I have no right to harbour you here, sir," she said hastily. "You may be a robber of the very worst description, and what right have I, the wife of a sheriff, to give you protection? Besides," she said, in continuation, now more herself, "what will the world think—my domestics—for me to have a man concealed in my sleeping apartment?"

"Madam, the exigency of my case compels me to have recourse to any alternative however desperate. It is not my wont to threaten any of your sex, more especially one who is so charming as yourself; but what am I to do? I cannot, nor will not consent to leave this apartment," and here he just drew his pistol, to intimate that he did not intend to be trifled with.

The lady gave a slight scream, upon which the highwayman said reprovingly—

"Nay, madam, I must command your silence, or all will be lost. It is necessary to keep perfectly quiet. These people, who no doubt are now making a careful inspection of the other apartments for your humble servant, will doubtless endeavour to effect an entrance into this one, in which they must not be allowed to succeed. It is for you to answer them as I dictate."

"Do you dare to threaten me?" said Mrs. Underwood.

"You leave me no alternative, madam. Admirer as I am of your sex, and mindful also of their very many gentle qualities, I must perforce demand that which I had hoped your own generosity would have given of your own free will."

"What is that, sir?"

"Merely your protection for the space of a few minutes. This room is sacred, and if you answer these bloodhounds as I desire, they will not dare to enter the sleeping apartment of the mistress of this princely mansion. Under your protecting wing, therefore, I shall escape unhurt. This is all that I desire. Is it so great a favour then to ask, that you thus hesitate, and force me to have recourse to measures which, to say the truth, my better nature revolts at? Come, madam, you cannot, nay, you will not, I am sure, refuse me this one favour."

"It seems I have no alternative—at least you leave me none, sir. What can a weak, woman do against an armed man?"

"I do not wish to offer you any violence," said the colonel; "nothing is further from my thoughts, only when a man is driven to desperation, which to say the truth is my own case, what is he to do? It surely is not asking so very much of you, to permit me to remain concealed here for a few minutes. When once the party have left the house, I swear to you that I will not seek to intrude upon your kindness, but will take my departure with as much secrecy as possible."

"And pray, sir, what construction will the servants of the establishment put upon this conduct?"

"What can they or any one else say to it? Suppose I had secreted myself in your room without your knowledge?—I might have done so. Let them imagine that I have really done so, and that you, hearing the noise in the house, very naturally locked the door, there could be nothing very extraordinary in that. Well, then, supposing these two events have occurred, you can

refuse to open the door, and say that there is no one concealed here. Come, madam, woman's wit, tact, and address, in the hour of peril, has oftentimes been superior to those of the sterner sex."

"Missus—missus—are you awake?" said Alice, the maid, now knocking at the room door.

"What is it?" said Mrs. Underwood.

Colonel Jack gently laid his hand upon her wrist, and drew her to the farther end of the room, where the fire was. He then motioned her to a seat, which she mechanically took.

"Say after me—repeat what I dictate," said the colonel.

The lady nodded.

"Please missus will you open the door? It's locked, I think, and here's a lot of gentlemen as have come to see after some wicked men who has been running all over the premises, and has now come into the house. Dear me, my heart's in my mouth."

"There's no one here," said our hero, which was instantly repeated by Mrs. Underwood."

"Madam," said Mr. Sharpthorne, "we have traced a man over the premises, and he has sought refuge in the house; will you kindly permit us to make an inspection of your apartment?"

"I am in bed, but previous to my retiring I locked the door, as I heard the noise at the outer gate. There is no one here, and I pray you to go away, as I feel assured you may do so with perfect satisfaction to yourself; and I must most decidedly decline opening the door of my bedroom upon any pretext whatever."

All this the lady repeated after Colonel Jack, who had leant over and whispered it in her ear.

Mr. Sharpthorne felt himself bound to take this answer, and turned away very discontented at the issue of the night's proceedings.

"He's hooked it, that's quite clear," said Driscoll. "I'faith, but he's a slippery customer and no mistake."

"D—n the fellow," said the lawyer, "he has the devil's luck and his own too."

"I shall get nicely in for it," said Driscoll, ruefully. "I dread to see Jonathan Wild in the morning."

"You've done all that man could do under the circumstances," said the parish constable. "What more could possibly be required of you by any reasonable person?"

With this the party descended the stairs, and after some further conversation, and loitering about the premises, they were compelled to take their departure, however reluctantly.

When they were supposed to be gone,

Colonel Jack spoke to his companion in his natural voice.

"Madam," he said, "I owe you a deep debt of gratitude, which believe, I shall remember to the latest period of my existence. The name of Mrs. Underwood will be cherished as one of the few good angels who have shone on my path, and made what otherwise would have been a gloomy track, ever and anon lightened up with golden sunshine."

"You know my name, then, sir?" said the lady, in some surprise.

"Yes, madam. Only by the merest accident have I been made acquainted with the name of her who has this night been my protector—or, in fact, saviour."

"You have placed me, sir, in one of the most awkward positions I ever remember to have been in during the whole course of my life," said Mrs. Underwood. "Mindful as I am and I hope always have been for any one in distress or difficulty, I nevertheless have no right to compromise myself thus, for I feel and know that I have compromised myself—and for whom? A perfect stranger, and one too, who, may be— There, I don't want to hurt your feelings; but you know, sir, it's impossible to tell who and what you are, and it is now in your power to say anything that the wicked imagination is possible for man to suggest."

"Madam, I hope you will do me sufficient justice to imagine and believe that I should not make so bad a requital for your kindness by speaking ill of you, or making that very kindness a handle whereby your feelings might upon some future occasion be hurt or wounded," said the colonel.

"I hope not, sir—I trust not," said Mrs. Underwood, and there was that gentle, soft bearing in the demeanour and countenance of the sheriff's wife which must of necessity win upon most persons who became acquainted with her, for Mrs. Underwood was of a kind and philanthropic disposition—the very reverse of her husband, who was a sort of "Dogberry," in his way, and a tyrant to his wife and his whole household. "And now, sir," continued Mrs Underwood, "as you have made me tell a falsehood, which is a sin I cannot accuse myself of using frequently, at any rate; but as you have compelled me to have recourse to subterfuge and prevarication, to cover your own purpose, it would be well if you could go hence without any of the domestic knowing of your presence here."

"I desire to do so, madam, for your reputation, as well as my own safety. I hope you will do me the justice to believe me when I declare that you are dealing with an honourable man, at least, honourable as far as you yourself are concerned."

"I hope so, sir—most sincerely hope so. And now let me hope, also, that after this you will alter your course of life," said Mrs. Underwood, laying her hand gently on his arm, and looking up beseechingly in his face. "I know not what it may be, but presume it to have been a lawless one. Let a weak woman persuade you to alter your ways. Nay, turn not from me—it is now for me to plead. I see in you something above the ordinary stamp of lawless men. One glance told me that upon your first entrance into this apartment, or the probability is, that I should have been more alarmed than I was. Use your energies to a better purpose, and believe me, my friend, sooner or later you will find out and be impressed with the truth of the old adage, 'that honesty is the best policy.' It is an old axiom, but not the less true for all that. Come, now, it is a woman who pleads to you," said Mrs. Underwood, in that sweet gentle voice of her own, so silvery and mellifluous in its tones, that it found its way direct to the heart of our hero.

Say what you will, there is that in the voice of some women, that carries with it an eloquence which the first of our orators would find it difficult to evoke.

Colonel Jack was quite unprepared for this appeal from the woman who had so recently stood his friend, and he hardly knew what reply to make to it. At length, however, he said—

"Madam, too many men are the sport and are at the caprice of fortune. We are, the very best of us, but the creatures of circumstances."

"Yes," she answered, "that is true enough. I have had sufficient proofs of that in my own experience; but still we can always command a certain amount of selfwill in all our actions. We can and ought to guard against doing wrong, and be to a great extent free agents. Perhaps you have a wife and little ones, who look to you for support; consider what their feelings must be to see their father brought to disgrace, and perhaps— There, I don't want to hurt your feelings, by indulging in any harrowing description, but take my advice, ere it be too late, and turn from your present course of life."

Colonel Jack stood for some moments contemplating the speaker with eyes of admiration, for he felt and knew that she was sincere in her expressions.

"In all my future wanderings," said the highwayman, "I shall remember the kind feelings which have prompted you to make this appeal to my better nature; and believe me, madam, that your advice shall not be thrown away."

"I shall esteem it fortunate that we have

met this night, if my words have not fallen upon an unattentive ear," said Mrs. Underwood, seriously. "And now, my friend, we must see how it be possible for you to make your escape without attracting the notice of any of the domestics. See here—" and she went to the end of the apartment and opened a French window, which led on to a balcony, beyond which was the grass plot at the rear of the house. "Will it be possible think you to drop with safety from this balcony?"

Colonel Jack followed the lady, and made a careful inspection of the place.

"I doubt not but I shall be able to alight upon the ground with safety," he answered.

"And without noise?" inquired the sheriff's wife.

"Doubtless, madam," answered the colonel, and he went through the open window on to the balcony. Its height was considerable, and Mrs. Underwood observing him hesitate, besought our hero not to make the attempt, if it was likely to be attended with any risk. The colonel assured her, however, that he was quite safe, and before dropping from the balcony, he approached the lady, and, taking her hand in his, respectfully raised it to his lips.

"I shall not be forgetful or unmindful of all your kindness," he said, as he wished her good night.

He laid his hands upon the rail of the balcony, when Mrs. Underwood approached him, and said, in her own gentle voice—

"What is the name of him who has this night sought my protection?"

"Colonel Jack," said our hero, and, in another second, he alighted on the grass-plat in safety.

Mrs. Underwood staggered back several paces when she heard the name of Colonel Jack, and, pressing her hands against her temples, she was a prey to anything but pleasing thoughts.

In a minute or two more, our hero was clear from the premises of Mr. Sheriff Underwood.

———

CHAPTER LVIII.

THE COLONEL MEETS WITH ANOTHER ADVENTURE.

WHEN Colonel Jack had got clear of Mr. Underwood's premises, he took his way up the lane which led him and Hackett into their recent difficulties; he had got about half way up the lane, when he was surprised by a figure emerging from the hedge, which ran by its side.

"All right, colonel; don't be alarmed," exclaimed the well known voice of Hackett, who had been lying concealed since his escape, anxiously awaiting the appearance of his comrade.

"Umph—it's you," said the colonel. "You somewhat startled me. Who would have dreamt of finding you here? Is the coast clear?"

"Yes, our friends are all gone grumbling like the very devil," answered Ned Hackett.

"I should not have stayed here so long as I have done, only I overheard part of their conversation, and from what I was able to catch, I learned that you had not been either discovered or taken."

Hackett joined the colonel, and the two proceeded up the lane cautiously enough, lest they might attract the attention of any of the pursuing party, who might possibly be lurking about.

They proceeded to the house of the woman Jane, whither Hackett had promised Mullins to betake himself. Upon their arriving there, they found the latter worthy awaiting the appearance of one or both of them, with considerable anxiety.

While they were all there conversing in the interior of the cottage, the colonel's quick eye detected some noise, like a low whining.

"What is that?" he inquired, looking at Mullins. "Have you a dog here?"

"No," answered the woman. "But it sounds something like a dog. Shall I open the door; the noise appears to come from the outside."

The woman opened the front door, and in a second or two Slott came frisking into the kitchen, where his master and brother highwaymen were stationed.

Slott was more than usually demonstrative. He jumped up to his master and capered about in a manner which was not a common practice with him. In fact he expressed himself as eloquently as it was possible for any canine quadruped who was not gifted with the power of expressing his thoughts in speech.

When these demonstrations had somewhat subsided, Colonel Jack consulted with Hackett as to how they had best get to town. It will be remembered that our hero was conveyed to the round house on the back of his own mare, Ada. Mullins informed him that Ada had been turned out in a field near the cage.

The highwayman soon managed to catch Ada—Hackett, of course, had his own horse —and in a short time he and our hero were once more trotting gently along the road which led to London. They had travelled some four or five miles, when they beheld at some distance ahead of them a figure on horseback.

"Who is that, I wonder," said Hackett, who had first caught sight of the individual in question.

Colonel Jack looked in the direction pointed out by his companion, and has he did so, he exclaimed—

"If I'm not very much mistaken, that same individual is no other than our friend Mr. Sharpthorne."

"Sharpthorne," exclaimed Hackett. "If it be as you suspect, now's our time for a summary vengeance upon him."

The colonel smiled, and trotted a little faster on the road, lessening the distance between himself and the horseman.

As he neared the latter, he found out that his first impression was a correct one. It was, of a surety, no other than the lawyer himself, who was seated on his roman-nosed grey horse.

Altogether he cut a comic figure, for his face was scratched in several places, and he was without his wig, displaying his bald head, which was utterly devoid of hair.

"It's Sharpthorne, and no mistake," said our hero. "A plague upon the rascal. He has no one with him, that I can see."

"No," answered Hackett, "Wild is in London long since."

The two highwaymen trotted up to the attorney—the colonel on one side, Hackett on the other.

Without uttering one word Mr. Sharpthorne found himself in the iron grasp of Colonel Jack. When he found this, he screamed and yelled in a state of abject fear. His surprise was so great at this sudden and unexpected assault that the miserable attorney was well nigh beside himself with fear.

"Hold your noise," said the colonel, "or I will silence you in a way you least expect, or at any rate, such as you will hardly admire."

"Oh, mercy, mercy, gentlemen," said Mr. Sharpthorne, trembling and shaking like an aspen bough.

"You have been at some trouble, sir, to seek me," said the colonel, sarcastically. "I hope you are now gratified since you have your wish. Here I am, and I suppose you have business with me, or surely you would never have taken the trouble or been at the pains you have to obtain an interview."

"Oh, dear no, I have no wish—that is, I have no business, I assure you; on the contrary."

"Then I have with you," said the highwayman, solemnly.

"Oh, dear! What is it? Call at the office in the morning," said Mr. Sharpthorne.

"Oh, dear, no," said his tormentor. "I'm not so fond of dancing attendance at the old musty fusty chambers of an attorney. First and foremost, you have been the means of having me incarcerated—of having me bound. I shall adopt a similar course with you. Halt!"

"Oh, colonel—Mr. Halford—what would you do? Would you murder me?"

"If I were to do so it's no more than you deserve. However, as I am a merciful man, I shall have recourse to what is called in the law secondary punishment."

While he was uttering these words, the colonel had slipped a cord out of his pocket and proceeded to bind Mr. Sharpthorne's arms.

The attorney set up a sort of shout or cry, and Colonel Jack dealt him a blow beside his left ear that flashed lightning in his eyes, and sent his ears singing for the next hour or so.

"Hold you row," said Hackett, "or as sure as you are a living man I will twist that confounded old neck of yours."

Mr. Sharpthorne was silent, and quietly submitted to the manipulations of the highwaymen.

"Now, what shall we do with him?" said Hackett. "He made an attempt upon my life, and I vote for hanging him on the next tree."

"Hanging!" exclaimed Sharpthorne, his teeth chattering like castanets. "You would never surely—"

"Oh, yes, we will though," answered Hackett. "We ain't at all particular in our courts of law."

"He's not fit to die till he repents," said the colonel, "and I'm afraid that will take a long time."

"Oh, dear, kind gentlemen, have pity on me,' said Mr. Sharpthorne, in the whining, voice of a broken down old man.

All his courage had forsaken him, that is assuming he ever had any physical courage, which is problematical.

"Now answer me truly," said the colonel. "Did Sir Richard think proper, or believe it expedient to have this search made for me, or was it your own doing?"

The lawyer hesitated.

"Why don't you answer, you old fool?" said Hackett, striking Sharpthorne, a blow across the shoulders with his riding whip.

"Sir Richard Fleetwood," said the attorney.

"Well," answered the colonel. "Yes, Sir Richard. What of him? Did he commission you or Wild to—to seek me out?"

"No."

"Who then?"

"I don't know."

"You lie, you old rascal?" said the colonel, giving him another clout on the ear.

"I—oh! Mr. Halford," said the lawyer, "this is cruel. I only wanted to see you—"

"Why, just now you said that you had no business with me. What do you mean by that?"

"I only wanted to come to an amicable

arrangement about the Reichbeck papers, that is all."

"And very amicably you set about it," said the colonel.

"This has not been my seeking—" began Sharpthorne.

"No, not this interview, clearly. Look here, you unworthy limb of the law. The next time you endeavour to circumvent Colonel Jack, look to it; for as sure as your name's Sharpthorne, you will either swing or have your throat cut if you make the attempt. These words are wasted upon him —turn him round."

This latter observation was addressed to Hackett, who understood its meaning, for he lifted up Sharpthorne as though he were but a child, and placing his legs across the horse, he reversed his position, making him ride with his face to the animal's tail, and his back towards its head.

"You'd better tie him on, or he will perhaps fall off before he reaches London," said the colonel.

"Very well," answered Hackett.

He immediately jumped down from his own steed, and tied the legs of the attorney to the girth of the saddle.

"Anything else?" he said, with difficulty restraining his laughter.

"Oh, only a ticket, so that he may be known."

A large card was produced, and on it was written, or rather printed, in large letters, the word "thief." This was fastened on the back of Sharpthorne.

"Now I think he may travel to London," said the colonel.

"Good bye, Mr. Sharpthorne. You will remember me, I dare say," said Hackett, as he gave the roman-nosed horse a cut across the haunches with his riding whip, which sent on the animal at full gallop.

Jolt—jolt! bump—bump!—Mr. Sharpthorne was well nigh shaken to pieces, and nearly dead with fright.

In his passage his hat had come off, and his head, now as bare as an egg-shell, was disclosed, and subject to every passing breeze.

The miserable little attorney thought he should never reach town alive.

Colonel Jack and Hackett followed at a respectful distance, and ever and anon indulged in explosive and sudden fits of laughter.

The colonel, seeing that the roman-nosed quadruped which the attorney was bestriding had began to slacken his speed, called to Slott.

"After him, boy—send him along!" said the colonel, to his dog.

Slott required no second command. He tore after Sharpthorne, barking loudly.

The roman-nosed horse increased his speed—so did Slott, who in a short time was jumping up every now and then and having a snap at the attorney's legs, who was possessed of such an innate horror of the dog, that he almost swooned as he felt his fangs against his legs.

"Oh, have mercy upon me!" exclaimed Sharpthorne. "What shall I do? It's the hound. Heaven have mercy upon me, I'm a miserable sinner."

He then endeavoured to mutter some long forgotten prayer—then he took the opposite course, and fell to cursing.

This fitted his mouth much better than the other.

"Hell and furies!" exclaimed Sharpthorne; "but I'll be revenged for this, that is, if I ever survive it," he put in as a sort of rider, for he felt the point of Slott's teeth uncomfortably close to the calf of his dexter leg. "That is, if I ever survive it, and if I do, I'll have an action for assault and battery. Let me see; lay the venne in Middlesex, and have the case tried—Oh!—mercy! The hound—I swoon and faint! No, I never shall survive it, that's clear. I wonder where I am? Strange that there should be no passengers, either equestrian or pedestrian. But the hour is late. In all probability I shall not meet with any one until I reach London, and how far that is I really don't know. This is a disastrous business; I ought to have followed Wild, and never attempted to come along the road by myself. Ah, what was that?"

The horse stumbled, and threw its rider forward, or rather backward, nearly dislocating his spine.

The animal, however, luckily for the attorney, managed to pick himself up again, and proceeded on his journey once more.

Colonel Jack ran the attorney within half a mile of the Oxford road, upon which they left him to his fate, the colonel whistling to Slott, who followed his master, and left the attorney to his fate.

Mr. Sharpthorne's horse trotted past Tyburn turnpike, the man at the gate happening to be asleep. The lawyer called to him loudly as he passed, but failed in waking him.

Every bone in the body of Sharpthorne seemed to be dislocated, and he was bruised from head to foot, so he said, and believed. Certainly he was sadly used, and had he been a man of anything like integrity, he might have enlisted our pity on his behalf. but as it was, we are disposed to record a verdict similar to one of our country juries, namely, "Sarved him right."

Mr. Sharpthorne, or rather his horse, for he had no control in the matter, got into the Oxford Road, now called Oxford Street.

Some few hundred yards on the town side of Tyburn turnpike there stood a stall for the sale of a refreshing and invigorating fluid called coffee. This was dispensed to the various early travellers at so much per cup.

It would have been a matter of interest to the present generation if any chemist of the day had taken the trouble to have analyzed the delicious compound, for we opine that the "fragrant berry" formed but an infinitesimal portion of the said composition.

However, the man who kept the early coffee stall drove a prosperous trade, and the drivers of market carts generally patronised him.

Several persons were round the stall in question, for by the time Sharpthorne arrived near the spot it was daybreak, or nearly so, and he had the felicity of seeing

London streets in a new aspect; for the lamps were still burning, although the east was streaked with the rays of the golden sun, making those miserable luminaries sing very small, and look particularly foolish in their appearance.

A market cart also stood close by the coffee stall, the driver of which was indulging in a cup of "hot," and three or four slices of bread and butter, of about the thickness of a moderately-sized paving stone.

It was this heavy handed individual who first caught sight of the lawyer.

The piece of bread and butter which he was about to convey to his mouth was stayed in its progress—nevertheless the mouth itself was wide enough open to have taken a decent sized cricket ball.

The man's eyes were also rather wide open

and he stood the very picture of wonder and unmixed astonishment.

"Well, I'm blest!" said the rustic, for such indeed he was.

"What's the matter, Jem?" said one of the throng; "you seem to be struck comical all of a sudden."

"Why, lookee there!" said the man, pointing with his hand which contained the knife and bread and butter, "If ever I seed the loikes of that ere!"

Every eye was now turned towards the large roman-nosed grey horse, who was picking his way along most deliberately, while Mr. Sharpthorne, with his bald head, his rueful visage, was nodding like a Chinese mandarin towards the horse's tail.

The attorney looked, of course, more like a madman than anything else, and, indeed, the whole of those who were around the coffee stall believed him to be so in reality.

They set up a shout, and then indulged in an immoderate fit of laughter.

There were not many of them who could read or write, for in those days this was considered to be, as indeed it was, a rare accomplishment.

The coffee-stall man, however, who happened to be above his fellows in this respect, espied the ticket affixed to the attorney's back, and he cried out in a loud voice—

"Umph!—thief!"

"What—who bees a thief?" said the man belonging to the cart.

"Why, can't you see that ticket?" exclaimed the coffee-stall keeper.

And he pointed out and explained the meaning of the same to his customers.

Now Mr. Sharpthorne himself had not seen this group of early breakfast consumers—not, certainly, till he had passed them, for from the very nature of his position on the back of his grey quadruped, he had his back towards them, and consequently he only knew of some one being near by the shouts and laughter, which smote his ears with painful distinctness, and he then became aware that he must be a ridiculous object, which in truth he was.

When he had passed, he observed the gaping crowd, and he made a most touching appeal to them.

"Gentlemen, will you kindly assist me? I have been most barbarously treated by highwaymen, and am nearly killed. Will some one assist me off my horse?"

"What does he say?" said a man, in the group, who was rather hard of hearing.

"Been stopped and robbed by highwaymen," answered the coffee-stall keeper.

"Poor chap, he looks as if he couldn't help it," said another.

By this time Mr. Sharpthorne's entreaties became still more urgent.

"Some of you go and stop the horse, and see what's the matter with the old gentleman, can't you?" said the purveyor of Mocha, who was disgusted with their apathy.

Away started three or four of the party at full tear, which was the most imprudent thing they could do, for two of them belonged to a hackney coach stand—mere watermen, in fact—and these worthies had on thick wooden shoes, which, with their running, kicked up such a clatter that the stately roman-nosed animal, which bore upon his back the lawyer, became alarmed at the sudden rush and noise, and he set off into a brisk trot.

He had been taking his way along, after the departure of Slott and his master, in a manner very satisfactory to himself, but when he found this sudden and unexpected noise and clatter at his heels, he thought it advisable to put his best leg foremost, as the saying is, and away he went.

The men in pursuit seeing this, shouted and followed through the quiet and deserted streets as fast as their legs would carry them. The faster they went, the faster went Sharpthorne's horse, for what, perhaps, rendered the quadruped still more hasty in his movements, was a piece of rope dangling by his side, which, as he went along, kept beating against him, and the animal naturally enough thought his owner was applying the whip.

This rope had not struck him as he went at a slow pace, but now that he began to put out his speed its vibration chafed him. It was part of the rope which Hackett had wound round the back and arms of Mr. Sharpthorne, who, when he found how matters were going, actually screamed with affright, which, of course, only added to the horse's pace, for the animal happened to be of a nervous temperament, and naturally enough became alarmed at his rider's sharp and discordant voice, and so away he went helter skelter.

Now it is just possible that those in pursuit might have overtaken the lawyer and his steed, say in the course of the first fifty yards—it is just possible, though very improbable, as affairs turned out, for as they were pursuing, the lawyer's face was towards them, and his appearance was so strange and exquisitely comic, that it would have disturbed the gravity of a judge or a bishop—for what with Mr. Sharpthorne's bald head, his rusty suit of black, and as he took his way along, by the motions of his horse he was jerked backwards and forwards, which gave him the appearance of nodding to his pursuers, in a most grotesque and ridiculous manner possible. So comic was the effect produced, that it set the men in pursuit in one continued and uncontrollable fit of laughter.

Now, we dare say, many of our readers have experienced the difficulty of keeping up at their wonted speed when their risible faculties were excited to any great extent.

The action of laughter consumes a considerable amount of air, and our party in pursuit of Mr. Sharpthorne found themselves winded much sooner than they otherwise would have done had their bearing been marked with greater and more becoming gravity.

One by one they fell into the rear, distanced and fairly beaten by the grey horse.

Sharpthorne groaned deeply when he observed this. He shouted also, he screamed, he yelled like a maniac, indeed, so much so that his last remaining friend in wooden shoes really thought he was one, and paused on the kerb-stone, and said—

"Drat the man! I don't believe he has been stopped by highwaymen or anything of the sort; he's only doing this for a lark."

For a lark! The suggestion was a cruel one. Poor Sharpthorne! It was no lark to him, indeed. It was very nearly death.

However, his wooden shod pursuer gave up the chase, and leant, panting and well nigh breathless, against the nearest lamp-post gazing curiously after the lawyer.

Many of our readers have, no doubt, heard of West's celebrated painting of "Death on the pale horse." Mr. Sharpthorne might be considered to embody a comic version of that celebrated subject, for by this time he looked more like death than any living denizen of this sphere.

As he took his way along the Oxford Road one or two "Charlies" emerged from their wooden habitations and endeavoured to give chase, for Sharpthorne had besought them to stop the animal. Of course, encumbered with their capes, thick coat, and enormous rattles, and being withal old worn out men whose powers of locomotion had long since departed, it was perfectly preposterous to imagine that they could have any chance in the chase.

However, two of them did make an effort—a feeble one, it is true—but still the attempt was creditable to them, and when they found the impossibility there was of their being any use, they, as was usual with that fraternity, had recourse to their rattles, and shouted out to some imaginary person to "Stop him!" spoken in a strong Hibernian accent.

This, of course, only added a fresh impetus to the gallant steed, who set his ears back as though he meant mischief this time, and rattled through the streets in a manner that was perfectly appalling to its rider, who now began to feel that sickening sensation which precedes faintness. A dizziness came across his forehead—the oil lamps danced and waved about as though they were torches borne by an excited multitude. The very houses seemed to topple over and nod to each other. Mr. Sharpthorne's throat and lips were parched, dry and feverish, and his limbs were painful, almost beyond endurance.

He passed St. George's Church, which then stood in the fields, and his grey horse proceeded along what is now Broad Street, St. Giles's.

By this time the pathway was sprinkled here and there with a chance passenger. One looked at the lawyer, and laughed, exclaiming that "He supposed the lawyer was riding for a wager."

Another considered him a madman, and one or two did make a futile attempt to stop the horse, who only went on the faster for this.

By this time the early morning sun lit up the pathway of the strange and grotesque traveller, who shuddered as he found the utter uselessness all attempts had been to stay the course of his grey Bucephalus. As he got into the city the passengers became more frequent, and it happened to be Smithfield market day. A drove of oxen were coming down Snow Hill with the drover at their heels. As Mr. Sharpthorne neared these, he cried out still louder, his back being to the drover he could not see that worthy till he had passed him, but when he did catch sight of the man he besought him in the most abject tones to stop the horse.

The man glanced at his bullocks, and hesitated.

"I'll pay you handsomely—anything you may demand," said the lawyer, "if you will get me off this cursed animal. I'm dying."

The drover left his oxen in charge of a lad, and then he and his dog gave determined chase to the much injured Mr. Sharpthorne.

Away went the lawyer, and away went the drover shouting to the roman nosed quadruped as though he thought the animal was possessed of the gift of reason.

By this time a number of chance passengers joined in the chase, but it is probable that the animal would never have been stopped had it not have been for a circumstance which occurred in Cheapside. A brewer's dray happened to be in the road, and was about to discharge its contents of casks at a neighbouring public-house. The drover, when he caught sight of this vehicle, called out to the driver to draw it across the road.

The man promptly obeyed, and the grey horse finding it impossible to proceed, and deeming that a charge at the dray might be attended with danger to himself, like a wise quadruped, came to a sudden halt, whereupon the drover sprang forward, and laid hold of his head. Panting, snorting, and almost breathless, the crowd that had been pursuing gathered round the horse and its rider, many of whom found it impossible to resist a smile at the appearance of the unfortunate lawyer, whose cords were unbound and who was eventually lifted off his horse and placed safely in a hackney coach.

As Colonel Jack had not taken any property belonging to the lawyer, that worthy had his purse in his pocket, and he pulled out the same and rewarded the drover for the trouble he had taken in his behalf, and the man of sheep and beeves walked away well satisfied with his day's work.

Mr. Sharpthorne, who had the appearance of a shaved lunatic being conveyed to Bethlehem, ordered the coachman to drive to the Temple. In the deep recesses of which place he intended to hide his head and concoct future plans to be signally revenged upon the perfidious Colonel Jack.

CHAPTER LIX.

INTERVIEW WITH JONATHAN WILD.—VISIT TO THE MADHOUSE.

HACKETT and the colonel, after they had left Mr. Sharpthorne, took their way to the Badger's. When they arrived there, our hero found that Jonathan Wild had been to that respectable hostelry upon his return to town, and had acquainted Mr. Dyson with the safe lodgment of the highwayman in Barnet cage.

He was there, also, on the following day after the incidents described in our last chapter. Wild informed the Badger that he had no animosity against the colonel, on the contrary, but he desired most particularly to see him upon important business, saying at the same time that if the colonel would grant him an interview he would guarantee his safety from any harm befalling him.

"And so you see," said Mr. Dyson, when he informed our hero of this, "I should almost think it advisable, colonel, between ourselves, for you to see Mr. Wild, leastways that's my own candid opinion of the matter."

"Yes, and suppose it should be a trap," said the colonel.

"Oh, I am quite certain upon that point," answered Dyson. "Wild isn't a man who passes his word upon such a subject as this without intending to keep it, of that I am convinced."

"Then I'll take your advice and risk it," said the colonel.

"Good! And you may be sure I wouldn't advise you without I felt that all was square."

In consequence of this an appointment was made to meet the thieftaker on the following day, and in the afternoon both parties repaired to the Cow and Cauliflower.

A satirical smile played over the features of Wild as he caught sight of our hero, as he was ushered into the parlour of Mr. Dyson's where Colonel Jack was ensconced waiting his coming.

"Give you good day, Halford," said Wild. "Glad to see you once more at liberty."

"Umph! You were at some pains to place me under lock and key," answered the highwayman. "It is not often Mr. Wild is glad to see people at liberty, so the compliment is the greater, I suppose."

"You ought to have known, Halford," said Wild, and this time without any lurking smile upon his countenance—"you ought to have known that it was no wish of mine that prompted or caused your capture. I told you at the time that nothing but the utmost necessity would have caused me to serve you as I did. You ought to have known this and put more trust in me for the sake of her who has now passed away," said Wild, uttering a short snort like a rampant steed, and wiping his forehead with his large pocket handkerchief.

"Yes, if it were only for the sake of her," he repeated, and then lapsed into silence.

The colonel made no reply. The Badger had prudently withdrawn to the public-room.

"You see," continued Wild, taking a chair and seating himself thereon, "that there's been a precious shine about some papers you hold. They are not yours, and I should suppose cannot be of any use to you. More than this, two chaps have already swung for them, and if you'd take my advice you'd get shot of them as soon as possible. At least, that is my opinion of the matter."

"I'm much obliged to you for your advice, Wild," said the colonel, "but that is a subject upon which you will allow me to be the best judge. At present the papers are out of my possession, more than this, they relate to matters which it will be necessary to have seen into by an efficient lawyer—not Mr. Sharpthorne, certainly who only wants them for his own particular use and purpose."

"Well, they ain't yours, colonel," said Wild.

"I am not quite so certain of that," said the colonel. "I am not certain, whose they are at present."

"Sir Richard Fleetwood's I should presume," said Wild.

"Maybe they are, and maybe they ain't, as the saying is."

"May they belong to the Fleetwood family."

"So do I," said the highwayman, sententiously.

"You," exclaimed Wild, in perfect wonderment. "Why, Halford, you jest."

"It is not my wont to do so," he exclaimed, "and least of all where serious subjects are concerned. It's too long a tale to enter into now, Wild, and would by its repetition be only ripping open old sores, which I wish had been better healed. Let it suffice, then, for our purpose to declare this much: Those papers are as much my property as they are Sir Richard Fleetwood's. Their contents interest other persons as well as that immaculate baronet, and more than this they were come quite as honestly by as the title and estates Sir Richard himself holds with so much hauteur and grace."

"Umph!" exclaimed Wild, between his teeth.

"All this is new to me," continued the thieftaker, after a pause.

"No doubt," answered Colonel Jack, "but it's very old to me; and you will please to do me the justice to believe that I am speaking the truth, when I say that Sir Richard Fleetwood is not a whit more a honest man than myself."

"Oh, as to honesty," exclaimed Wild, "that is but a term, and we ain't a going to quarrel about the name of a thing. I know nothing about the history of Sir Richard, but this I do know, a certain sum has been offered by his lawyer—a handsome sum, in fact, and I should have thought it best for you to accept of this, and settle the matter amicably."

"Whatever is to be done in this matter must be negociated between Sir Richard and myself," answered Colonel Jack. "As to Mr. Sharpthorne, I distinctly decline listening to any proposals from him."

Wild laughed outright at this observation, at which his companion stared.

"You are merry, my friend," said the colonel.

"Enough to make one so," was the reply, "when you reflect upon the manner you and your companion served the attorney. Ah—ah!"

The highwayman laughed also.

"Have you seen anything of him since—since his pleasant ride."

Wild nodded.

"How fared he?"

Wild entered into the particulars of the stoppage of the grey horse, and the return of Sharpthorne to his chambers.

"And he is vowing vengeance against you," said the thieftaker, shaking his head ominously.

"Let him. I care not for his threats," answered Colonel Jack. "In fact, I despise the miserable attorney."

"You had a hard job to get clear off from Barnet?" said Wild.

The thieftaker fixed upon the colonel a searching look.

"Rather so," answered the colonel. "How is Underwood?"

"Ah, poor man, he is very bad," replied Wild.

"Not seriously so, I hope?" said Colonel Jack

"Well, he can't leave his bed at present. Why, you took refuge in his house, I have heard."

"Was forced to do so; there was no choice about the matter."

Again Wild laughed.

"And, by the way," said Colonel Jack, "I hope you won't be hard upon that man Driscoll, for he really was not to blame in the affair."

"Oh, dear, no. I am quite aware of that. Only discipline must be observed," answered Wild.

Some further conversation ensued, all of which tended to show that the thieftaker was not hostile to our hero; in fact, he was rather the contrary. There was, perhaps, no one whom Wild would have been more sorry to capture than the highwayman, and he had only done so, in the recent instance, in consequence of the presence of Sharpthorne and Mr. Underwood.

Wild took his departure from the Cow and Cauliflower, extracting a promise that the colonel would take an early opportunity of seeing Sir Richard, and observing at the same time that, after then he, Wild, would wash his hands of the affair altogether.

The colonel ruminated for some time, in Mr. Dyson's back parlour, upon the thieftaker's departure.

"Sir Richard Fleetwood—ah!—well, the name sounds bravely in the ears of the world. Sir Richard, forsooth! To hold the title, and for how long?—while the real heir to it is still alive. So, Sir Richard, this is your game, is it? You have yours to play, and I mine. Pull devil, pull baker, as the saying is. We shall see. Wandsworth—Hardy's establishment, Wandsworth—that's it."

And here the colonel took out his pocketbook, and carefully inspected a leaf of the same containing some address, which he conned over with considerable curiosity.

He had not been engaged thus for a very long time, when Mr. Dyson put his head in the bar parlour, straw in mouth as usual, and said—

"What's the game?"

"Oh, the papers, that's all," answered the colonel; "which I don't intend to give up."

"Oh, that's the size of it, eh? Well, there's no harm done, I suppose?"

"No, all square and right."

"That's well."

Colonel Jack then took his departure from

the cozy parlour of the Cow and Cauliflower, and proceeded towards Wandsworth.

It was here that the establishment of Mr. Hardy, for the charge of lunatics, was situated, and it was to see one of these that our hero was about to visit the place where those of our miserably afflicted brethren were confined.

Perhaps there is no place which awakes our sympathy for suffering mortality more than that which is set apart for those whose minds are in sad darkness, and miserable chaos. The light of reason once fled—the divinest gift of a wise and beneficent Creator —what remains but the empty shell or husk ?

But Mr. Hardy's establishment was of that peculiar description, that took charge of those who were likely to be afflicted with the loss of their reason. In other words, persons were put away, as it was termed, upon the plea of madness, when it was well known that many of its inmates were as sane as the reader of this work.

However, the reader will see the nature of the establishment by the scenes which are about to be sketched for his behoof.

Colonel Jack mounted his mare, and trotted on towards Wandsworth.

He had in his possession an order to see an individual by the name of Sabine, and armed with this paper, he rang boldly at the bell, the handle of which depended by the side of the outer gate.

The house itself was gloomy enough—iron bars were against the windows in front, as well as the back part of the premises—and the front garden was thickly studded with large and melancholy looking trees—two in particular, they were cedars.

A man unbarred the gate, and stared at the highwayman.

"What was his pleasure ?" inquired the man.

The idea of pleasure in that establishment was preposterous.

However, the colonel said he wished to see an inmate of the establishment by the name of Sabine.

At this the man hesitated.

"Can I see him ?" inquired the colonel.

"Ah, I don't know. Have you got an order ?"

"Yes," was the rejoinder.

"Then you had better walk in and see the master," said the man, as he opened the gate and admitted the highwayman, who walked his horse into the front garden.

Dismounting, he handed the reins to the man, and was conducted into an apartment on the ground floor of the premises.

Here he was introduced to a man of wiry and unprepossessing appearance, who regarded him with looks of mistrust, and

almost fear. He, however, handed him a seat.

"I have an order to see one of your patients, Mr. Hardy.

"What name, sir ?"

"Sabine."

And he then produced his order from one of the doctor's of the establishment.

The man, or rather Mr. Hardy, contemplated this for some time, and ran his eye over its contents, reading the words written on the paper over and over again. It was not for the purpose of inspecting its contents that he did this, but while so engaged he was considering if he could frame any excuse to prevent the colonel from seeing the unfortunate individual who had the misfortune to be incarcerated in those gloomy walls.

"Are you a relative of Mr. Sabine's ?" inquired Mr. Hardy.

"No," answered the colonel.

"Ah—a friend, I suppose ?"

"Yes, a friend of his and his family's."

"It is not usual to allow strangers to see patients in my establishment," said Mr. Hardy.

"Am I to understand you refuse?" said the colonel.

"Umph !—I hardly know what to say—I don't like to be uncourteous."

"I understood this order was sufficient; but if not, why I must of necessity have recourse to a magistrate's order."

"Oh !" ejaculated Mr. Hardy.

This threat seemed to bring him a little to his senses.

"Oh, I should hope there will be no necessity for that," he answered, in a milder tone of voice, which was evidently assumed for the occasion, for the fellow was perhaps one of the greatest ruffians of his day.

"Well, only let me know how you intend to act," said the colonel, "for time presses, and I am particularly anxious to get this interview over, for I need hardly tell you these scenes are painful ones at all times."

A nod in the affirmative was the only reply vouchsafed to this speech.

"And, therefore, the sooner its over the better," said the colonel, drawing a long breath.

"Ye—es," said the keeper of the house. "Only you see—"

"What ?" inquired the colonel.

"He might not be in a fit state to see any one."

"Indeed – why not ?"

"He might be in one of his paroxysms."

"Is he violent, then ?"

"At times," was the cautious answer. "They are all so, occasionally. But allow me to offer you some refreshment."

"Indeed I do not need any, thank you,' said his visitor.

"Oh, but you must; and in the meanwhile I will go up to the ward where your friend is, and return in a few minutes."

The bell was rang, and wine and cakes were placed on the table by a domestic.

Colonel Jack, who knew his man by report, was particularly cautious in partaking of either of them, and Mr. Hardy took himself off, and left his visitor alone.

He appeared to be gone a long time, an unnecessary long time, so the colonel thought, and he began to think that he should not be able to get a sight of the inmate whom he had come to see.

At length, however, Mr. Hardy returned, not with a smile on his countenance, it is true, for he did not at all like granting an interview to the visitor.

"Well," said the colonel, "am I to see him or not, that's the simple question?"

"He's low and desponding now," said Mr. Hardy, "and it would be advisable for him not to be interfered with; but if you insist upon it—ahem!—that is, if you have any particular business with him, why, of course, I will show you up. But I cannot help saying, that I think it would be better if you took another and more favourable opportunity."

"I would much rather see him now," answered the colonel; "as I have come a long distance, and I know not when I may have time to come again."

"Is your visit on business?" again inquired Mr. Hardy, eyeing the speaker with a sinister look.

"Oh, dear no. It's hardly possible to have business with one who is so sadly afflicted as I should suppose my unfortunate friend is. I merely wanted to see how he was—how he fared—and, of course, report his present state to his relations."

"Oh, you know his relations, then?" said Mr. Hardy, eyeing his visitor with another sinister look.

"Yes, one or two of them."

"Ah! Oh, you will find, sir, that he has every attention paid to his comforts. I may say this much, without coming under the charge of egotism, or unnecessarily boasting or vaunting my establishment."

The colonel bowed.

"It will be necessary for you to have a keeper with you during the interview," said Mr. Hardy.

"I do not fear for myself, if that's what you mean," answered Colonel Jack; "and would rather be alone with my friend."

"I should not advise you to do so," said the owner of the establishment, with a grave shake of the head. "And, indeed, our usual custom is to adopt that course; for you see, it is hardly possible to tell what ebullition may suddenly take place, and it is always necessary to use caution in the treatment of those unfortunate individuals who may happen to be placed under our charge."

"Who placed him with you?" asked the colonel, so suddenly, that the man started, and seemed a thought paler.

"A relative," he answered sharply, after a pause.

"So I should suppose. What was his name, if it's a fair question?"

Mr. Hardy evidently did not consider this a fair question, for he did not make any immediate reply.

Presently he said—

"We do not usually give up the name of our employers."

"Oh, it's a matter of no great importance," answered the colonel. "I hardly knew why I made the inquiry. It is of not the slightest importance believe me."

But Mr. Hardy did not believe him, but he prudently said nothing about the matter, like a wise man.

He rose from his seat, and proceeded to conduct Colonel Jack up to the room where was confined the supposed Mr. Sabine.

CHAPTER LX.

COLONEL JACK'S INTERVIEW WITH THE HEIR OF FLEETWOOD.

COLONEL JACK ascended the stairs of the lunatic establishment, conducted by the owner thereof, who, when they had got to the second flight said, in a mild voice—

"If you wish to see your friend alone, without the presence of a keeper, I do not wish to thwart you in any way, and you shall have your wish gratified, that is, assuming you have the courage to do so."

"I am much obliged to you," answered our hero. "I should prefer doing so, if it makes no difference to you."

"So be it, then—we will consider that matter settled," said Mr. Hardy, as he inserted the key of the door in the massive lock.

The door was opened, and Colonel Jack found himself in a large room, at the further end of which a man was seated, with his head resting on hands.

He did not appear to take the slightest notice of those who stood on the threshold of his apartment. In fact, he seemed listless, and utterly regardless of everything around.

"I must lock you in," said Mr. Hardy, in a whisper. "When you want to get out kick at the door.

The colonel nodded.

Hardy retired, closing the door after him, and turning the key.

For a minute or two the colonel stood contemplating the form of him whose mind was supposed to be distraught, and whose spirits were evidently broken.

The colonel contemplated him with eyes of pity for some considerable time, and his gaze then ranged over the wretched apartment.

There were two windows in it, along which strong iron bars run on the outside. At one end of the room, on the opposite to where the man was seated, there was also a strong iron grating, which ran from the ceiling some length down the wall.

The colonel remembered afterwards to have noticed this.

After looking round, he approached the spot, or rather table, where the inmate of this room sat in moody silence.

As he neared him, he was struck with his appearance. He was fearfully thin and emaciated, and long and deep furrows were on his countenance, not caused by the scythe of time, but eaten away by corroding care.

"Mr. Sabine," said the colonel, in his gentlest accents—and his voice was tuneful and harmonious enough when he chose to make it so—"Mr. Sabine, it is a friend who speaks to you."

The man looked up. The tone of voice—the manner and bearing—was so different to what he had of late been used to, that he stared with perfect astonishment.

He passed his hand across his brow twice or thrice, and then gazed curiously into the face of the speaker.

"You do not know me, Mr. Sabine, or—Sir Reginald Fleetwood," he continued, in a much lower voice, indeed, almost in a faint whisper.

As this name was uttered, the wretched occupant of that apartment started up in perfect astonishment.

"Hush!" he exclaimed, laying his hand upon the colonel's shoulder. "Hush, for mercy's sake, or you will ruin all. Sir Re—"

He paused suddenly, as a shudder ran through his frame.

"Heaven above! that name has been my curse. It has haunted me throughout my life. Breathe it not—bury it in oblivion. Would that I had never owned it."

"You do not remember me?" asked the colonel. "It is so many years since we have met."

"I know your features," answered the supposed lunatic. "Why, it's Frank Halford!"

A smile passed over his features as he uttered this name—a sickly one, it is true, but nevertheless it was a smile of sweetness, for he felt himself in the presence of a friend.

"You thought me dead, I suppose, like the rest of the world? And ah, Frank, often and often have I prayed for death in this gloomy and desolate chamber, where hope never enters. Is it not horrible—truly horrible, to be thus immured—to be buried alive, in fact?"

"What is the cause of this inceration?" inquired the colonel.

Sir Reginald Fleetwood, for it was, indeed, that unfortunate baronet, placed his mouth to the ear of his visitor, and said—

"My brother."

"Ah," exclaimed his companion, "I asked you, it is true, but that I already knew."

"You did?"

"Yes, and have done so for a long time, but have never been able to ascertain where you were confined, till by the merest chance in the world I was enabled to find it out, and therefore lost no time in coming to see you after I had ascertained where you were to be found."

"Kind, generous, noble, Frank—just like you."

"And more than this, Sir Reginald, now that I have found you, it will go hard with me if I don't release you from your present captivity."

A sunny smile this time passed over the features of the imprisoned man. Hope dawned again upon him. The words that Colonel Jack had uttered gave him hope of succour. A new life seemed to be infused into that emaciated frame."

"You will not desert me," he said, laying his hand beseechingly upon his companion's arm, "I am sure you will not desert me, for you are the only person who knows of my existence besides my brother and—"

"And who?" inquired the colonel.

"These people and Mr. Sharpthorne."

"Curse him! I suspect it was at his suggestion that you were made an inmate of these walls."

"Do you see my brother?"

"Sometimes. Not lately, it is true, for we are not the best friends."

"And my poor wife?" exclaimed the baronet, clasping his hands. "I shall never see her more, in this world."

"Why not?"

"She has passed away," he answered, in a solemn voice.

"No such thing," answered the colonel. "Your wife lives, of that rest assured."

"Lives!" exclaimed the prisoner. "Oh, Frank, if I thought this were true—"

"I know it to be so, for I have seen her."

"Then where is she?"

"At Acton, under the care or your brother. Oh, I have a long story to tell you,

but it must not be now—not now. Let us only think how it is possible to get you outside these cursed walls. I'll burn the whole place down but what I will accomplish it, for your sake as well as my own. And then, Sir Richard Fleetwood, Sir Richard only by courtesy, we will see who pulls the strongest, the devil or the baker. Out of this place you must be got, that is quite certain; and what is more, be restored to your rights."

"But how?" inquired Sir Reginald.

"I will set a lawyer to work, and see how it is to be accomplished. I know who and what you are, and how you are incarcerated here at the instigation of your vile and worthless brother."

An exclamation from somewhere found its way in the room as the highwayman uttered the last observation.

No. 42.

The colonel glanced round the apartment, and his eye fell upon the grating at its further end. He saw a pair of eyes peering through the grating, and a thought crossed him—it might be an erroneous one—that they belonged to Sir Richard Fleetwood himself. Like a mist on the mountain, they disappeared, and vanished away, and nothing remained but the cold and remorseless bars.

"It was strange," so thought the colonel, "that some one's face peered through the grating."

And he paused suddenly in his conversation.

He was not long kept in suspense, for before he had time to reflect, two men entered the apartment, and coming up to where he and Sir Reginald were conversing, without saying a word, waited till they had come by the side of our hero, and suddenly seized him from behind, before he had time to be either aware of their intentions or offer any resistance.

When he found himself in their grasp, he made a desperate struggle to release himself, but in vain. A straight waistcoat was round him before he was aware of it, and he, too, was a prisoner.

Mr. Hardy now made his appearance in the room. An immobile expression was on his countenance, and he scarcely condescended to favour our hero with a single glance.

"Take the patient to number five room," he said to the two men who held Colonel Jack.

They conveyed him to an apartment at the further end of the ward.

The colonel was hastily thrust into this room by his two keepers, as we must call them, for they were literally nothing else. The door was closed with a slam, the massive lock turned, and Colonel Jack was left alone to his reflections, which were anything but of a pleasant nature.

The apartment in which he found himself was much the same in its character as the one in which Sir Reginald Fleetwood was confined.

All the horrors of a confinement in a madhouse, kept by a man of the worst description, flashed across the mind of the colonel. For some time he was left to himself. He went to the window of his apartment, and gazed through the grating, at what he supposed to be the garden in the rear of the establishment.

He had not been occupied thus very long, when he heard the door of his room unlocked, and a keeper presented himself, who was, however, neither of the two who had so unceremoniously conveyed him hither.

"Umph !" exclaimed that individual ; "trying to see if you can make your escape, eh ? You're clever, too clever by half, I should say ; but you are under bolt and bar, you see, for all your cleverness."

"Scoundrel," exclaimed our hero ; "what is the meaning of this ?"

"Why you are now under proper control, that is all," was the cool rejoinder.

"What for ?"

"As a lunatic. Now do you understand ?"

A sickening sensation came over the highwayman as these ominous words were uttered, but seeing that he had been deprived of his pistols, and being without weapon of any kind, he thought it best to remain quiet, to see what would be the termination of the affair.

The man paused, and appeared to have a wish to be communicative.

He was a ruffian to look at certainly, but not of the moody sort ; on the contrary, there appeared to be a lurking demoniacal sneer on his countenance.

"We ain't hard here to patients," he said, "that is, if they conduct themselves properly. Perhaps you don't like being stowed up in this room ?"

"I should think not, indeed," answered the colonel ; "and what is more, I won't be for long."

"Oh, won't you, my hearty, we shall see. But as I told you, we are not hard upon our patients, and you shall have every indulgence. Remember, we did not send for you. It was your own pleasure to come here, and it's our pleasure to keep you now you have paid us a visit."

"Give me my liberty," said the colonel.

"That will extend to the grated door at the end of the passage. There, now, you ought to be grateful, for you will have the whole extent of the corridor to walk about in ; and that I consider extraordinary indulgence."

"Indulgence !" exclaimed the colonel ; "why am I confined at all ? By heaven, when I regain my freedom, you, and all of you who have so villanously deprived me of it, shall pay a dear penalty for it."

"No doubt we shall when——" and here the scoundrel paused. "Ay, when you regain your freedom. Perhaps you would like to ascertain exactly when that is likely to take place ?"

The colonel nodded assent.

"Ah," exclaimed the man, "my failing is being too tender-hearted. I cannot keep people in suspense. You entered the corridor of your own free will, when you leave, it will be at my master's pleasure. You came here in full health and spirits, when you depart it will be—not on horseback."

The scoundrel paused.

"Go on, fellow," said Colonel Jack.

"You will be carried out."

"How ?—what mean you ?"

"In a coffin," he answered in a low muttering voice that froze the very current of our hero's blood.

"Good God ! Am I to be murdered ?" exclaimed the colonel.

"Well, no—murder is an ugly phrase. No, if that were to be the case, I need not be at the trouble of taking charge of you, and the governor need not be put to the expense of keeping you. In this house we kindly take care of people who, like yourself, have not the wit to take care of themselves. Now and then from other parts of this place we do return patients to the world, but you are honoured with what we call the state apartments, and I never knew any occupant to leave it but with life,"

"Cold-blooded, cruel, heartless murderer !"

exclaimed the colonel. " Can such things be in a Christian country ?"

The man only indulged in a hideous grin.

" Surely you do not object to such distinguished hospitality as you are about to receive from us ? Some people are never contented, not even with a comfortable home when its provided for them. It is quite a little—secluded, I admit ; but then no one here will trouble you for rent or taxes. You are boarded gratuitously—no washing charged for, in short nothing, and still, I dare say, you are selfish and unreasonable enough to wish to escape. Well, I will point the means out to you."

" You would be conferring an inestimable favour upon me if you would."

" Oh, I am always ready to oblige," and here the fellow grinned sartirically. " The mode is simple enough. You see that holdfast ?"

The highwayman looked in the direction to which the fellow pointed, and close to the ceiling he observed a nail driven into the wall.

The cord which laces your bedstead may be turned to an excellent purpose. You need not fear the holdfast, it has been tested before now, and has borne a heavier burden. And now farewell. The door remains unlocked and the whole corridor is open to you, should that extent of liberty be insufficient, you can enlarge it at your own discretion."

And looking carelessly from the nail to the bedstead, the ruffian took up his lamp, quitted the room, and went away, singing along the passage. Colonel Jack heard him secure the door at its extremity with bolts and chain, and the next moment he was left in hopeless solitude.

———

CHAPTER LXI.

MORE REVELATIONS OF A MADHOUSE..

FOR a considerable time Colonel Jack remained in a state of stupified astonishment. He was incarcerated for life, that was quite certain, and no doubt at the instigation of Sir Richard Fleetwood. He felt assured of this the more he reflected upon the events of the last hour or so. It was the baronet's features he had seen looking through the grating of the apartment occupied by the unfortunate Sir Reginald. He should not, perhaps, be assassinated, they would only drive him to commit suicide, and supply him with the means, and the demon who had charge of him had hinted at the mode of death. He looked at the holdfast in the wall, and the bed containing the cord. The bolt had been tested, it had sustained a

human burden. He was in a death room Horrible thought ! Worse than a den of murderers, for here the victim was obliged to be his own executioner. Good God ! from that iron bar, wretches driven to despair have ventured to unholy means to free themselves from never ending misery. He fancied he saw the suicide suspended—the tortuous movements of departing life were pictured to his imagination—the limbs convulsed— the blackened countenance—the last struggle—a breathless body hanging against the wall—the keeper entering, looking at the dead man with a feverish smile, and retiring to announce to his employer that the unholy shrine of murder had another victim.

This hideous dream soon passed, and then his thoughts ran into another course. His days were numbered—his death foredoomed —the grave was yawning to receive him— the end unavoidable—and poor Sir Reginald in hope of succour—would now find its way into his heart. The only individual who could possibly afford him any assistance was in as bad a plight, if not worse, than he was himself.

Lost in these melancholy reflections the night wore away, as nights all do with all of us, be our pleasures or troubles ever so great.

After being quite worn out with his own miserable thoughts, Colonel Jack threw himself upon his bed, and slept till morning.

When daylight came he arose and made another inspection of his room, and in moving about, he became aware of some heavy substance in his coat. He felt to ascertain the cause, and to his infinite joy he found a small pistol which had slipped down between the lining of his coat and the exterior portion of the cloth.

This had evidently escaped the notice of those who had conveyed him into his present prison-house.

The mariner who drifts upon the boundless ocean, with nought but a frail plank between himself and eternity, viewed not the vessel bounding before the breeze to his deliverence with livelier joy than did our hero at the sight of this small pistol which was indeed one that he had taken from Mr. Sharpthorne, and forgotten all about.

He examined the weapon carefully, but, alas, he had neither powder or shot. As he remembered this, his hopes vanished once more.

To guard against discovery, he hid the weapon in the mattress and then strolled up and down the corridor, while the keeper entered it, bringing with him a scanty breakfast.

" I have got into a row, and all about you," he said, as he entered the colonel's apartment.

" What for?' inquired Colonel Jack.

" For allowing you to walk up and down this corridor. I told you I was tender-hearted, and it's always got me into scrapes."

Colonel Jack thought it best to be civil to the man, as possibly he might be useful to him, at any rate, he had it in his power to make matters still more uncomfortable to our hero.

" I am sorry for that," answered the latter. " If you are likely to get into trouble on my account, the matter is soon settled, and I will not avail myself of the privilege you have proffered and permitted."

" Oh, as to that, it's all over now. Come, here's your breakfast, I suppose your hungry ? mad people generally are."

" But I'm not mad, and that you are aware of as well as I am," said the colonel.

" Ah, that's the old story. They all say that. Never see a madman yet but insisted upon it that he was the sanest person in the world.

" You know I am not mad," said the colonel.

" Well, we won't dispute," said the man, as he placed down the breakfast things and retired.

The colonel partook of the morning's meal, such as it was, and once more strolled into the corridor.

He found that it contained three deserted rooms beside his own, each with a latticed window looking into the vegetable garden, which he judged was at the rear of the house.

From the central chamber the iron bars had been removed, and a wall-flower and a few dead plants stood on the sill, and showed that not long since the desolate chamber had been tenanted.

A female had been in all probability its occupant, for the walls and wood work were covered with pencillings of fruit and flowers, roughly but ably executed. Many sentences in small but beautiful characters, were loosely interspersed among these drawings, all expressive of a mind whose intellect was overturned.

While still gazing at these melancholy records of hopeless and confirmed insanity, the keeper entered the corridor.

" So," he exclaimed, " you have found your way into a fair one's chamber, who just a month ago exchanged it for another."

" Ah, poor thing," said the colonel. " I hope she recovered her reason."

" Humph ! She never complains now, at any rate. She made a pretty row one time, but she is quiet now."

" I hope you have removed her," said the colonel, to another part of the building, preparatory to restoring her to society once more ?"

" I have already told you, my friend, that from these chambers there is but one exchange. Look," he said, pointing with his finger to a clump of evergreens. " What see you beyond those bushes?"

" Four or five hillocks," replied the colonel.

" They are graves That one on the right is the last resting-place of the lady whom you seem to take such an interest in."

" Merciful heaven ! then she has passed away from this world, and can no longer be a victim to man's cruelty."

The keeper smiled one of his sarcastic grins. He paused for a moment and reflected.

" Dead !" he exclaimed. " Aye, she is, in truth, dead enough. And yet had it not have been for her own folly, she might have been alive and well. Merry and happy, perhaps."

" How so ?"

" Well, you must know, she was very pretty, and her father was exceedingly poor. A bad state of things for a young girl to commence the world with. Now, it so happened that an old gentleman returned from India, he was immensely rich, and took a monstrous fancy to the young girl, and would have married her; and she, like a little fool as she was, actually refused to have him, when, of course, it would have given her happiness and her father comfort as well, but no, she must needs fall in love upon her own account, and, of course, with a miserable, sickly youth who was a struggling artist. She preferred poverty to wealth; her head was crammed with fantastical notions about love in a cottage. Now, her father did not happen to be so deeply impressed with these notions, and after remonstrance and argument had failed, he thought that medical treatment and a little wholesome restraint might bring her to her senses. Our governor was sent for, a sporting fee was given, he examined the lady, and, of course, pronounced her mad."

" Unnatural scoundrel," exclaimed the colonel.

" And mad she must have been," continued the keeper, " and consequently she was brought here, and—" here the monster laughed—" the thing altogether is so funny, that I cannot help laughing," he said, in continuation, " for you must know, that in less than two months she was as mad as any one could desire. I've seen a good deal in my time, but I never saw anything so violent as she was at times. Her screams rang through the building, and were even heard beyond the walls, and to prevent exciting attention out of doors, we were obliged to remove her here. Well, her insanity became confirmed, and under the violence of the disease, her strength sank rapidly. At times she had an interval of mental repose, when nature had become exhausted, and then she sketched those drawings on the walls, or talked for hours to that wallflower, which she had persuaded herself was her lover in disguise. She died, and I came in just as life had departed, and would you believe it, the last words which passed from her lips was a blessing on the curate."

While this man was describing the treatment of the unfortunate girl, and her ultimate death, our hero had with difficulty restrained himself from an outburst of passion, but when the man had concluded, he could restrain himself no longer.

"Infamous villain !" he exclaimed, " murderer is too mild a term to describe such a monster by ! I have read terrible accounts of monkish barbarity—of the atrocities of the inquisition—but the horrible cruelties practised in an English madhouse surpasses all. Go out into the world, beg upon the highway, rob, murder, do anything—"

"Ha, ha !" laughed the ruffian, " a goodly harangue, truly—very fine advice. Go out into the world indeed ? Thank you for your good advice—much obliged, I'm sure I ought to be ; but you see, I am not quite certain what sort of a reception I should meet with outside these walls."

"Ah," exclaimed the colonel, " you are already stained with crime?"

The fellow laughed.

"You're a pretty fellow to talk," he said. "You haven't been on the road yourself, I suppose—and are not one of the most celebrated highwaymen of your day ?"

"Have you been on the road?" inquired the colonel, with a considerable amount of interest.

"No," answered the man, " but your first guess was right. I have done something that would make my return to the world rather dangerous. It appears that you take an interest in me now, so I will just give you a few reasons why I prefer retirement to society. Of course, this communication is strictly confidential, and when you get out you won't abuse it."

The marked emphasis the fellow laid upon his words did not escape our hero. He was doomed to die, then, that was evident from the man's manner and observation.

The man drew a chair up by the side of the table in the apartment and said—

"So you would like to hear my history, eh ?"

The colonel nodded his acquiescence to this proposition.

The man began—

"I was brought up for an apothecary, and soon after I had completed my apprenticeship, my master died. He had left some little money to his widow, who determined to carry on the business for her own livelihood, consequently she engaged me to take the management of it. I did so. Mrs. Brady, that was the widow's name, was old enough to be my mother, but as she did not consider me too young to be her husband, she lost no time in letting me know her opinion upon that subject. She had a house, business, and more than a thousand pounds, and so, seeing that she over head and ears in love, to prevent her dying of a broken heart, I foolishly married her."

"Foolishly ?" exclaimed our hero. " There could not be much folly in the matter, considering that you had a business, and a good round sum in the bargain."

"Oh, you must hear me to the end," he answered. " The wedding was rather precipitate, as the old chemist had not been buried three months before it was solemnised, and it seemed that the neighbours thought so, for they abandoned the shop, and left us to make love at our leisure. I need not tell you that our honeymoon was short, and that I obtained beauty elsewhere, and very soon fancied that a wife of half the age and size would suit me a great deal better. I began to prefer the parlour of the Goat and Boots, to my own—and my stout spouse, in my absence, had recourse to the brandy bottle by way of solacing herself for my neglect. The course we both pursued was not calculated to remove the prejudice against us occasioned by what the villagers called the indelicacy of our marriage. Not a soul would allow me to drench or blister him—a rival chemist opened a shop, and as a natural consequence, very soon closed mine. I believe it is generally admitted that we are never so ridiculous as when love sick—not that I was love sick—but Mrs. Brady was, and on the evening I had made her mine, the amorous relict of the defunct doctor transferred to me his cash box, containing all his savings for years before.

"Within a twelvemonth, the contents had marvellously disappeared.

"The parlour of the Goat and Boots, the cock-pit in the rear, and a race course in the neighbourhood, having pretty well equally divided the chemist's cash.

"As I put the last five guineas in my pocket, I began to think it time to look about me.

"I had nothing left but a house I seldom inhabited, a shop that no one entered, and a wife who would outweigh every woman in the parish by a stone."

"And about whom you cared nothing, I suppose ?" said the colonel.

"Precisely—you have guessed it—I did care nothing about her. But you must understand, that there was somebody else whom I did really love. This was one, Ruth Sandford, and with her I was desperately enamoured. She was the prettiest girl in the parish.

"I lavished presents on her—she received them, and as I afterwards learnt, laughed at me for my folly.

"If I talked of love, she reminded me that I had a wife—and when I praised her beauty, she told me that I had a cart load of it at home, at the same time she seemed to say that, had I have been unmarried, that I should not have sighed in vain. And I may confess the truth at once, I wished my wife was with her former husband, the departed doctor."

"Where she soon was, I suppose?" said the colonel.

"You are right again in your guess," answered the man. "I returned home one evening, more enamoured than ever with the sweet Ruth, as I termed her, and found that my fat helpmate was indisposed, which she generally was after an over dose of brandy. She asked for some corrective from the surgery, some simple medicine, to restore the tone of her ill-used stomach.

"I made a slight mistake between the bottles—I administered a mineral poison instead of ether, and in about an hour after this I was informed, at the Goat and Boots, that the draught had proved effectual, and my wife was dead.

"People said I had poisoned her, and a stupid jury called the accident wilful murder.

"I was imprisoned, arraigned, and tried. A crotchety judge discovered a point which favoured my escape—one juryman agreed in the same opinion—and I was acquitted.

"I returned to my home. Every face was averted from me with abhorrence. I wrote to Ruth, told her that I was single now, and offered her my hand. She flung the letter in the bearer's face, and told him that if I ever dared to approach the house, she would have me ducked in her father's pond.

"The boys broke my windows.

"I was sitting in my lonely back parlour, for it was lonely now—it is true that I had never loved my wife, still she had been my companion, and I missed her more than I could possibly have imagined—well, I was sitting in my parlour, with my last guinea in my hand, and wondering when it was gone where I should get another, for the next morning I was to give up possession of my house, which I had been obliged to dispose of to defray the expenses of my trial—and, between ourselves, bribe the juryman through whose means I had escaped the gallows—some one knocked at the street door.

"I went up stairs, and looked out of one of the windows.

"A man was standing on my doorstep, wrapped in a riding coat, closely buttoned.

"After some hesitation, I mustered courage, lighted a candle, and went and let him in.

"My visitor was a perfect stranger to me, but when he had inquired my name, he threw off his riding coat, took a chair, and signified that he wished me to be seated also. I obeyed; and the conversation then began.

"'You were tried last assizes for murder, were you not?" inquired my visitor.

"'Yes,' I answered.

"'And had a narrow escape?' says he.

"'Rather,' I answered, a little glumpily; for you must understand that I did not like this unceremonious commencement.

"'Well,' said he, "you are the very person I have been wanting. Let us understand one another, and proceed to business at once. I presume the late affair has not increased your practice?'

"'It has ruined it altogether,' I answered, although, to tell the truth, the cock-pit and race course had done that effectually before the trial.

"'Then I suppose a lucrative patient would not solicit your advice in vain?'

"'Assuredly not,' I answered.

"'Do you know Natchly Hall?' he inquired, 'or anything of its proprietor?'

"'I have heard of the place, but do not know aught of its proprietor.'

"'Come there to-morrow evening, and inquire for Major ——.'

"And he handed me his card.

"'But stay, you had better take another name, for your own does not smell very savoury in the nostrils of a discerning public.

"'What do you require me to do?' I asked.

"'You will learn that all in good time,' he answered.

"And then pulling a purse out of his pocket, he counted out twenty pieces, and handed me the gold.

"'This,' he continued, 'is your retaining fee. Be useful, and it shall be made a hundred when you have completed the expected cure.'

"'Twenty guineas!' I muttered.

"'Mind you do not fail in coming at the appointed time; be punctual, and I shall be ready to receive you.'

"He resumed his riding coat, and buttoned it closely, so that his features were effectually concealed. We settled on the fictitious name I was to assume, and the stranger took his departure, leaving me richer by twenty guineas, and overwhelmed with curiosity and surprise.

"'What could this strange and mysterious visitor want with me? What were the services required from a reputed murderer?'

"Well, no matter what the business was,

it made little difference to me. I was ready to do his bidding, be it for good or for ill.

"The place he desired me to repair to on the following evening, was distant about six miles from my own home. It was nearly twilight when I reached the neighboured where Natchly Hall was situated, and entered the inn called the Robin Red Legs."

"What, at Barnet ?" inquired Colonel Jack.

"Yes, do you know it ?"

"I am acquainted with Barnet," answered our hero.

"I seated myself in the parlour, called for some refreshment, and entered into conversation with a man who was the parish clerk, who was communicative enough.

"I learned from him that the owner of the mansion, whither I was going, was a gentleman of sottish habits, and a secluded disposition. Nothing could be duller than his mode of life ; and, if rumour was correct, nothing could be less happy than his domestic relations.

"His lady was young enough to be his daughter, and possessed of great personal attractions united to an ardent taste for pleasure, and impatience of restraint.

"It was said, that this ill-assorted union produced the fruits that might have been expected.

"His sottish habits were confirmed, and her original indifference turned to hatred and disgust.

"'The squire,' continued the clerk, 'has a step brother, twenty years younger than himself. He has returned six months ago from the Indies, and since he has resided at the hall, things have gone smoother. He pays great attention to the lady, and his civility compensates for his brother's neglect. No relations can be more affectionate—people do say—but Lord, it's all scandal, and the captain's is only brotherly civility, after all.'

"When I paid the reckoning, and set out for Natchly Hall, I reflected upon the clerk's communication. No doubt the unknown visitor was the younger brother of the squire, and a hundred nameless suspicions crossed my mind.

"Upon arriving at the hall, I found a man awaiting to conduct me to the house, and leaving the great avenue, he led me by a private path to the postern, opened the door, showed me to a parlour, lighted candles, and retired, telling me—

"'That his master would be with me in a few minutes.'

"In a short time after my entrance, the stranger, with whom I had conversed on the previous evening, entered the room.

"A hurried greeting was exchanged; he drew a chair, and seating himself thereon, immediately proceeded to turn the conversation on business.

"'You are punctual,' he said. 'This is well. I promised you, last night, a patient. Treat him skilfully, and he'll prove a profitable customer—or, at any rate, I will, It matters little to you which it is, I suppose ?'

"'I will do my best, but possibly it may be some secret disease, a malady not to be detected, and possibly baffle all my professional skill.'

"'No, no, my friend ; in a day or two I will undertake that you shall understand the case, and then you will know how to treat it. In the East Indies I was attacked with a malignant fever, and a hospital assistant of the same name as the one you have assumed watched me with unremitting care ; with that name my brother is familiar, and I have told him that I expected my preserver on a visit, consequently he will be thrown off his guard. You must personate that man, and as I owe life to one doctor and expect much from the other, I add ten guineas to his fee.'

"He placed the money in my hand, gave some directions for my conduct, and when he thought me perfect in the part I was to act, conducted me down stairs, and introduced me to the lord and lady of the mansion. No doubt he had prepared the parties for my visit, for the squire received me as an expected guest, and the lady welcomed me with a gracious smile.

"The squire was a man of about fifty, with a stupid, stolid expression of countenance, nevertheless, he possessed a frame of great strength.

"He was a sensualist who slumbers life away in never ending inebriety.

"I don't know that I ever saw him absolutely drunk, but he was always muddled. From the time he rose in the morning until he retired for the night the bottle was always at his elbow, and from which he indulged in frequent libations. He lived for no other purpose apparently, nor had he a care beyond that regarding the quality of the liquors he indulged in.

"Nature had given him an iron constitution, or he never would have been able to have led the life he did with impunity, and so little inroad had sensual indulgence and sedentary habits made on the owner of Natchly Hall that he bade fair to reach the extreme age of existence, which men of more temperate habits did not always succeed in arriving at.

"His lady had not reached her thirtieth year, and to features of beautiful regularity united a faultless figure. The animation of her dark and lustrous eyes formed a striking contrast to the dull, unintellectual heaviness of her leige lord.

"At first sight of her you would perhaps have been greatly predisposed in her favour, but upon a closer inspection your opinion of her character would not have been so favourable, for there was pride upon her lip, and haughty impatience on the brow, while the whole expression of the face, for which nature had done so much, was passionate impulse, too violent to be controlled, and freely permitted to run riot.

"The major, who, as I before told you, was my employer, was in the pride of manly vigour, he had every advantage that a fashionable exterior and military air could present. Although his features were regular and his figure manly, his haughty manner took from the favourable impression they would have secured.

"When I retired for the night, and reflected upon my singular introduction to Natchly Hall, I felt convinced that some dark deed was contemplated.

"From what I saw it was evident enough that a criminal attachment existed between the lady and the major.

"I saw quite enough to convince me of this, even in the presence of the unfortunate husband.

"Glances were passed, and blandishments were interchanged, while at other times so little did they study appearances that they were seldom or ever on their guard.

"On the second day after I had been located at Natchly Hall, the major followed me, after supper, to the apartment I occupied, and although we had both drank pretty freely of wine his servant opened another bottle and then left us to ourselves.

"I saw something was coming, that whatever the major required of me was now about to be made manifest, and a few minutes more proved that I was right in my conjecture.

"'Dawson,' he said, calling me by the name I had assumed, 'I think I have already seen enough of your character to warrant my reposing implicit confidence in you. We have both of us been used hardly enough by an ungrateful world. You have been hunted from society like a mad dog, while I have been thwarted in the dearest wish of my heart. Because I came later in existence than my brutal brother my life has been rendered miserable, while he passes his time in one scene of debauchery. I with talent and spirit to take a bold position among my fellow men have not the means to open the path to fortune, but hang upon the bounty of a besotted and capricious sensualist for the bounty which enables me to hold the position of a private gentleman, to which birth and profession have adapted me to. Would you do aught to better your condition, and win the lasting gratitude of those whose powerful aid might help you to independence?"

"I did not altogether fancy the commencement of the proceedings, and looked at him with considerable feeling of mistrust.

"'Speak,' he said, suddenly. 'I have put the question to you fairly, and like a plain answer? What say you?'

"I am here, sir, to do your bidding. It is not for me to inquire into your private affairs. It is sufficient for me that some service is required of me, when I know what that is I shall be better able to answer you."

"'Good,' he replied. 'Wisely spoken—so be it.'

"The major hesitated; there was a silence for a few minutes or so. There was evidently a passing struggle through the mind of the major, some few qualms of conscience, perhaps, still left.

"Preeeently he mastered them, and continued—

"I must disclose my purpose, and leave nothing to be guessed at. Well, be it so, and yet for one saved by a mere quibble of the law you seem marvellously punctilous, but— I will speak out, and, I doubt not, with sufficient purpose. You have been accused of murder. Your victim by every sacrifice had earned your gratitude. You *drugged her.* Psha! why mince matters? Eleven out of the twelve men declared you guilty. Now, there is a stranger useless to his relations, useless to the world, and I would fain see him quit it as quickly as may be. His removal can be of no consequence —he's better out of the world than in it.'

"'For you, perhaps,' I answered.

"'Yes, and for every one else. He must die!' he exclaimed, in a hissing whisper. 'For by his living two beings are rendered supremely wretched—so wretched, in fact, that life is robbed of all its charms."

He paused, and our eyes met A glance of fearful meaning passed between us. I perfectly understood what he was driving at.

"'Am I to proceed?' he said.

"'If you please,' I replied. 'I am all attention.'

"'Good! I thought we should understand each other.'

"'I am not dull of comprehension,' I replied.

He filled his own glass and mine also, and both were drained off.

"'I shall deal frankly with you,' he said, in continuation. 'I shall now repose implicit confidence in your discretion, and also in your faithfulness.'

"I bowed my assent.

"'Even if you betrayed me no one would believe you, for your character is already too blackened. You see, I am candid.'

" ' Most particularly so. Pray go on.'

" ' To me your crimes and necessities are full security. And now listen to me. At supper you sat at table with three companions. To secure the happiness of two one must be removed.'

" ' Now, do you understand my meaning ?'

" ' I should be a dunce not to read the riddle,' I replied, draining off another glass of wine.'

" ' Ah, I am right in my man—you are no dunce, my friend.'

" ' No ; but why accuse me of a crime which a jury of my countrymen have declared me guiltless. If I make an unfortunate mistake ?'

" ' You will have the less objection to commit another. Listen to my proposal, and accept or decline it as you please.'

No. 43.

" ' I need not trouble you with anything but the result of one half-hour's conversation. The major and I understood each other perfectly well, and I agreed to remove him—"

" To murder him," exclaimed Colonel Jack, with an expression of horror on his face. " I anticipate the result of your fatal interview. The man, or monster, whichever you please to term him, offered you blank money, and you accepted it for the fulfilment of the unholy office assigned to you."

" That's just it. You could not have hit it more, surely, only you are wrong in one important part. I did not agree to murder him myself—I only consented to prepare the dose, and the major himself was to administer it."

" A nice distinction, truly."

"An important one, as you will presently see," answered the man.

"Good heavens! Did he consent to murder his own brother?" exclaimed Colonel Jack.

The miscreant nodded.

"Well, I havn't much time to waste with you longer," he said sharply, "and so let me hasten to a conclusion—that is, if you are interested."

"Certainly—pray proceed."

"The object to be obtained was to avoid suspicion, and seek life's foundation by slow but certain means—and make the removal of the victim appear to be only natural decay."

"For a time our work proceeded well—daily the patient became weaker, and it was bruited about the neighbourhood by myself and several emissaries, that the squire was daily destroying himself by his confirmed habits of intemperance. As the doomed man showed symptoms of approaching death, his wife and her guilty paramour became still less guarded in their conduct; and had it not been for this, I do believe all would have been kept dark. But in spite of all my remonstrances, they would not put a guard upon their conduct, and the servants of the establishment were fully cognizant of their billing and cooing under the very nose of the fast dying man.

"The declining health of the husband and the profligacy of the wife reached the ears of a kinsman ; and we heard, with considerable fear, that he was about to pay a visit to Natchly Hall, and, what we dreaded more, bring an experienced physician with with him. A secret consultation took place, and I urged postponement, but the major and the lady overruled the objections I made. The death of the patient was decided on—and, in a few mornings after this, the tenants were informed that the squire had been found dead in his bed—from apoplexy, produced by intemperance.

"Even the rash precipitancy with which the death had been accomplished might probably have escaped suspicion, had there not have been an indecent and unusual haste in committing the unhappy man to the grave. The funeral took place by torchlight on the second evening, and none of the gentry in the vicinity of the Hall were invited to attend. At this many of them took umbrage, and, consequently, they were numbered among the enemies of the two guilty survivors.

"Ah! it was a badly managed affair; but it would have been very different if I had been allowed to manage it.

"Whisperings and doubts, and shaking of men's heads, was succeeded by a burst of public indignation. Encouraged by this popular display of digust, the inmates of the Hall made revelations that led the world to believe that one foul crime had been succeeded by another ; that adultery had paved the way to murder. The consequence of all this was, that we were arrested upon the charge of murder. The body of the dead man was exhumed—and ample evidence, from a post-mortem examination was obtained as to how the squire had come by his death. The result may be told in a few words. A link in the chain of evidence was wanted—and I supplied it.'"

"You became approver, and turned king's evidence," exclaimed Colonel Jack, with difficulty restraining his disgust at the villain's perfidy.

"Right again," exclaimed the man.—"Spoken like a book. Ah! I see you are up to a move or two yourself. Been upon the same dodge yourself, perhaps?"

"God forbid!" said Colonel Jack.

"Well, to cut the matter short, I brought the major to the gallows; but the lady managed to escape. And now, when you counsel me to return to the world, will you undertake to guarantee me a gracious reception? But, hark! the bell tolls—the supper hour is ready. Observe, I trust you with an open window—and you might escape. Could you surmount the solid masonry without?"

Saying this he hurried down the corridor, bolted the door by which he had entered, and left our hero once more to himself.

When the last sounds of his retreating footsteps had died away, Colonel Jack felt relieved from the presence of a malignant being in the shape of a man, whose nature appeared to be more akin to that of a demon than anything human. He had been listening to the confessions of a wretch who had poisoned the life's current of the very being whom at the altar of his God he swore to cherish and protect in sickness and health ; and, at the bidding of an adulteress, he had remorselessly removed an unsuspecting husband.

Crime has its gradations; and of all the guilty, the insidious and remorseless poisoner is perhaps the worst.

Colonel Jack's reflections were of a most unpleasant character. His life was hanging on a thread—he felt and knew this perfectly well; he knew also that Sir Richard Fleetwood would now use every endeavour to prevent his ever appearing again in this world. He had every reason for doing so. In the first place, it was quite certain that Sir Reginald would possess an active and determined friend in the highwayman, if he was once permitted to appear again in the world. The story of the unfortunate baronet's incarceration at the instigation of his remorseless brother, would become a matter of public scandal, to say the least of it. More than this, Sir Richard knew perfectly well that the colonel could not rest content until he had rescued his elder and much-injured brother from his present position.

Colonel Jack felt that he was at the mercy of the wretch who already, by his own confession, declared himself to be a double murderer. What was he to do? and how was he to effect his deliverance? He felt that open violence was not likely to succeed, and he must therefore meet villainy by cunning; and so, while he was considering what should be his future course of action, he endeavoured to mask his design by effectually assuming in his bearing towards his keeper a semblance of hopeless despondency.

For two or three days, he maintained a moody silence—listened with indifference to the jailor's remarks, and scarcely spoke to him in return. He thought that the scoundrel observed his increasing melancholy. As he believed it with eyes of satisfaction, and by a steady perseverance in deception, he succeeded in blinding his jailor to his heart's content. He evidently looked upon the Colonel as a despairing wretch, who was only anxious to wear a miserable existence away, without sufficient energy to even contemplate any exertion, or scheme to achieve his deliverance.

Even the most artful villains may be deceived at times, and such appeared to be the case in the present instance, for, without doubt, the jailor had quite mistaken his man.

When the jailor entered the cell in the evening, the colonel feigned to be asleep. The man cast an indifferent and careless glance at him, and muttered to himself—

"Another week or so, and Sir——will receive some intelligence that will be welcome to him, and I the promised reward, Good! So be it!"

"By my faith," muttered the colonel, in an under tone, "but you were never more mistaken in your life, my honest and worthy friend; I have not the most remote intention of destroying myself to oblige you or your worthless employer."

"How strangely is the human mind constructed? Colonel Jack in a madhouse, and in a room where some unhappy wretch had ended his miserable existence—hopelessly situated as any of the victims who had preceded him.

He nevertheless would not give way to despair, but clung to hope, the only last resource left to the wretched.

The night was starry and bright, and the colonel remained standing at the open window which looked upon the deserted garden. It was a dreary and heart-sickening prospect, for the graves which his scoundrel keeper had pointed out, lay just below. The colonel was to fill the next.

He laughed—it was a bitter mocking laugh—for he felt a full determination that, come what would, his intended murderer should precede him to the tomb.

While he gazed vacantly from the window, the moon rose suddenly, escaping from a cloud which had hitherto concealed her. The stream of light was startling, and every shrub and object visible in the broad daylight, was now revealed distinctly.

The soft moonbeams fell upon the graves, and the colonel reckoned them.

"So," he muttered to himself, "four victims have gone to their account, offered up as sacrifices to injustice, and cruelty of man. A fifth is wanting—and I have been selected. Well, if I am fated to fill a grave beside those already there, it shall, at least, be a bloody one. Ah, how soundly sleep the dead—free from all wordly troubles—the shrieks of despair—the furious outbursts of insanity; all is hushed and quiet."

He stood with folded arms contemplating the scene he looked upon, conjecturing who might have been the tenants of those nameless tombs, and under what circumstances each spirit had quitted its tenement of clay.

In the profound stillness of the night, the rustling of a falling leaf would strike the ear.

The colonel heard a movement in the shrubs, and a figure, which seemed to have risen from the earth, stood in the centre of the grassy mounds, motionless as a statue.

Had the dead arisen?—was the form living clay?—a denizen of this sphere, or a discontented spirit, walking its nightly rounds?

The colonel was not a superstitious man, far from it—his was a practical nature—nevertheless, his heart beat, and he held his breath in terror and surprise, when the figure suddenly glided from the spot it occupied, approached the window where the colonel stood, and sat down on a rustic bench beneath it.

Before a minute had passed, he ascertained that the midnight visitor was no "spirit from the other world," for a sigh escaped from him, so deep and melancholy, such as only escapes from bosoms overloaded with hopeless sorrow, reached the colonel's ear, and a furtive glance from his open casement assured him that it proceeded from a sickly-looking pale young man.

———

CHAPTER LXII.

THE COLONEL IS MISSED BY HIS BROTHER HIGHWAYMEN.

As days went on, Hackett, Knapp, and Galdie were at a loss to account for the non-appearance of their leader, Colonel Jack.

Some thoughts crossed their mind that he had been captured and clapped into gaol by Jonathan Wild, and this was perhaps a very natural conclusion to come to, seeing that the thieftaker had so recently made an appointment with him at the Badger's.

Their first inquiries were consequently made of that individual.

Mr. Dyson informed them that the colonel had parted with Jonathan Wild upon the very best terms imaginable, and in fact he would wager his existence that no harm had befallen him at the hands of " Jonathan the Great," as he was sometimes termed.

Hackett then remembered that the colonel had told him that he was going to pay a visit to some house for the detention of lunatics at Wandsworth, but he did not remember to have heard the name of the individual who kept it.

The fact is that our hero generally kept his own counsel with regard to the Fleetwood affairs, as they had nothing to do with his fellows on the road, and although he had accidentally mentioned that he was about to proceed to Wandsworth upon the occasion of his last parting with Hackett, he did not say one word to him as to who he was about to pay a visit.

However, no colonel made his appearance, and as time went on, his companions began to be seriously alarmed.

Knapp suggested their calling at every house for the reception of lunatics in Wandsworth.

Now it so happened, at the period of which we write, that this suburban district was famous for houses of this description, consequently it would have been a long job for the highwaymen to have inquired at all, more especially as they did not know very well how to set about it, seeing that they could not say, with any degree of certainty, as to whom it was that our hero had intended to visit.

After several discussions, Knapp said that he would call upon Mrs. Halford, and see if she knew anything about her husband's movements; and after all, he might be ill at home, confined to his bed, so Knapp suggested.

This was negatived by the others. They knew their leader too well to believe that he would remain away of his own free will without giving them some intimation as to the cause. He had never done such a thing before, during their connection together.

Knapp, therefore, after this declaration of his companions, undertook to wait upon Mrs. Halford, and see if she knew aught about the colonel's movements.

It was only as a last resource that the highwaymen had determined to adopt this course, for it was seldom, and, indeed, hardly ever, that any of them ever ventured to intrude upon their leader's domestic privacy; however, there appeared to be now no other course left for them.

When Knapp arrived at the colonel's domicile, he inquired for Mrs. Halford, and was immediately shown up into the first floor front room.

After waiting for a minute or two, Mrs. Halford herself made her appearance. A death-like paleness overspread her features, and in spite of her endeavouring to conceal her agitation, her visitor saw that she was trembling.

For a moment neither seemed to be able to find the power of speech, but stood gazing at each other in mute surprise.

" Has anything happened to—to my husband ?" said Mrs. Halford, with difficulty staggering to a chair.

" Do not be alarmed, madam," said Knapp, " I should hope he is quite safe—only we have not seen anything of him for some days. And—"

" Not seen him !" exclaimed Mrs. Halford; " then something has indeed happened to him. My worst fears are realized."

" Home—that is, has he not been home ?" inquired Knapp.

" No," answered the unfortunate wife of the highwayman. " Indeed, no; and I fully thought he was engaged—ah! with his companions."

" I wish he had been," said Knapp, who felt for the evident grief of the lady before him.

Where was he when you saw him last ?" inquired Mrs. Halford.

Knapp explained to her that Colonel Jack had parted with Hacket with the intention of visiting some house at Wandsworth for the retention of lunatics. After which they had seen nothing of the colonel. Promising the lady that every means should be taken to find out the missing highwayman, Knapp took his departure, with the assurance that he would call and let Mrs. Halford know the result of these inquiries.

He informed Hackett and his brother highwaymen of the unsuccessful nature of his visit to Mrs. Halford, and they altogether eventually determined to journey to Wandsworth, and inquire at the various houses for the reception of lunatics. But previous to their doing so, they made inquiries of the Badger.

Mr. Dyson informed them that he had heard the colonel repeat the name of Mr. Hardy; but whether that name related to the establishment the colonel was about to proceed to was more than Mr. Dyson could say.

At all events, Hackett took note of the circumstance and the name and proceeded with Knapp forthwith to Wandsworth.

They inquired at several houses for a person of the colonel's description, but with no other result than disappointment.

Stopping at a roadside house, they inquired for a person of the name of Hardy.

A man in the parlour, a sort of groom, informed them that a person of that name kept a lunatic asylum about a mile distant from where they were. Upon this they started off, accompanied by Slott, who had been with them throughout the whole of their journey.

This animal had been in a state of despair in consequence of the loss of his master. He had been to the colonel's house, to the Badger's, and a host of other places in search of the colonel; he had even taken to the road and squatted himself on his hind quarters, and watched the night through, but all to no effect, and Slott could not make up his mind to rest anywhere. Indeed, so distraught was he, that at one time it was supposed that he contemplated hydrophobia.

Never, surely, was a canine quadruped in such a state.

He was not a handsome dog at any time, and never had been known to pay much attention to his toilette, but since the departure of his master he wore a most miserable and neglected aspect, and was positively hideous to look upon.

He followed at the heels of the two highwaymen in a moody, discontented, and almost snarlish state.

Upon arriving within sight of Mr. Hardy's respectable establishment, Hackett paused, to call a council of war.

After some deliberation, it was determined that only one of them should ring at the bell, and make the necessary inquiries, and Knapp was chosen for this purpose, being supposed to be the most innocent looking of the two.

The same man answered the gate that had appeared to the colonel's summons.

Knapp described the personal appearance of the colonel, and inquired if an individual answering the description, had called at their establishment?

The answer was in the negative. and the porter assumed an imperturbable look.

Notwithstanding this, there was that in the man's manner which led Knapp to come to the conclusion that the man was not speaking the truth.

He was, however, compelled to take the answer, and returned to Hackett, informing him of his non success.

"Now what's to be done?" said Hackett; "I am fully convinced that this is the establishment, but how to ascertain; they are evidently on their guard."

"Let us go to the rear of the premises, and see if we can catch a sight of the back windows," said Knapp.

At this suggestion the two highwaymen went to the back part of the house, and Hackett, climbing up the garden wall, in which he was assisted by his companion, took a hasty view of the gloomy building.

While this was taking place, Slott pricked up his ears, and sniffed, as though he were conscious of the presence of his master.

"Look at the dog," said Knapp; "he's awake to something, depend upon it."

No doubt the hound was fully cognisant of the close proximity of his master to the spot, for he wagged his tail, appeared to be very fidgetty, and altogether evinced signs of impatience and anxiety.

"Depend upon it the colonel is confined here," said Knapp, who was now more than ever struck with the demonstrations of Slott. "There cannot be the slightest mistake in the matter. Look at the dog, sniffing about like a mad thing."

"Shall we put him over the wall, and let him drop into the garden?" inquired Hackett.

"Oh, no, he will only be caught up by some of the keepers, and the Lord knows what his fate may be then."

"Hilloa, there!" shouted a man, who was crossing the back yard. "What's your business?"

Hackett immediately dropped from his elevated position at the sound of the man's voice, not deeming it prudent to remain any longer. He and his companion Knapp took a hasty departure from the spot, determined to revisit it upon a future and more favourable occasion, for they felt convinced now, beyond a doubt, that Colonel Jack had been unfairly dealt with by those belonging to the establishment.

CHAPTER LXIII.

SCENE WITH THE UNKNOWN.

WE left Colonel Jack, in our preceding chapter, gazing out of the window in his apartment upon the strange figure which had so suddenly come before him. The young man sat moody and dejected in the garden chair, occasionally heaving deep sighs, and muttering words to himself, the precise meaning of which the colonel could not hear. His appeared a melancholy species of madness, if it was madness at all.

"Heavens, what a sad thing is a dethroned mind!" exclaimed the colonel. "How supremely wretched he seems—and yet not more so than myself, perhaps—it may be not so much."

Colonel Jack remained for several minutes silent and indecisive, while the unknown individual was quite unconscious that any human being was near.

The colonel felt a more than ordinary curiosity to penetrate the mystery of the young man, but he feared that any effort to announce his proximity might seem a trespass upon sorrows which, perhaps, admitted of no alleviation.

He at length determined, however to make the attempt, and called out in a mild and gentle voice.

"Ah!" exclaimed the young man, "a strange voice! Who is that?"

"Fear nothing," said the colonel, as he observed the young man's countenance express alarm. "It is a friend."

"Who are you?" inquired the stranger, looking up.

"One as wretched as yourself," was the answer.

"Are you an officer belonging to this hateful establishment?"

"No, I am a prisoner like yourself, I should suppose. A man, whose hope of deliverance is as desperate."

"You are unwillingly detained here, then?"

"I am."

"And with no immediate prospect of escape?"

"Yes, one is left me."

"What is that?"

"The grave."

"Alas, such is my own case, and the sooner the better, say I."

"Our fates are similar," said the colonel, who saw at once, from the young man's answer, that his mind was unimpaired. "Do you know much about the interior of this place?"

"I am allowed to walk in the garden for air and exercise, and only know what I see," answered the young man.

"Hush!" exclaimed the colonel. "You and I must consult together—our fates are similar—and we—"

"What?"

"Not now—to-morrow evening—and we will plan some scheme. Shall you be here again to-morrow?"

"Yes, in the evening. Can you leave your room?" inquired the young man.

"I am allowed to walk in the corridor."

"Ask to be permitted to do so in the garden," said the stranger.

With this the unknown waved his hand in signification that the keepers were about, and walked away, and thus closed the conversation for that evening.

On the following morning the keeper made his appearance as usual with our hero's breakfast.

The colonel was sleeping when he entered, and the man's sudden appearance caused him some alarm.

Had his conversation of the previous night been heard? If so, a more stringent imprisonment would be kept upon him.

"You are early my friend," said Colonel Jack.

"Friend!" returned the scoundrel. "That is a convenient phrase, and generally applied to a person one hates or despises. It was always the term by which my old patron, the major, at Natchly Hall, addressed me, and I believe that he would have drugged me as well as the squire. Well, friend, if such must be the term, I am thus early because the governor bid me say that you must want some change of linen, and you see, as you cannot conveniently send home for this, the governor, with his usual kindness, will provide you with the same. I am sure you ought to be grateful for all the kindness shown to you. Now this might be considered a dangerous tool," he said, as he took up a razor which had been placed in the colonel's apartment, "but I may indulge you with every luxury—and as I have left you a rope, I suppose I may entrust you with a razor. You know, I do this on my own account, because I told you before, that I was always soft hearted. It's been my failing through life. The governor and myself had a row last night, for a gentleman who, like yourself, required temporary retirement and medical advice, contrived, heaven knows how, to conceal a knife—and—"

"Committed suicide!" exclaimed Colonel Jack.

"Lord, no," responded the villain. "We might have overlooked that; it would have been only taking a personal liberty with himself. No, faith! the fool fancied he might escape—made a rush from his cell, and stabbed a couple of our people before he received a cracked skull from me. He'll give us no further trouble now."

"And did you murder the unhappy wretch for merely attempting to regain his freedom?"

"I wish you would drop that phrase, 'murder.' It sounds so oddly."

The colonel thought that of all the cold-blooded scoundrels he had ever heard or fancied to exist, this poisoner was certainly the most superlative. If ever a tiger's heart lurked in a human bosom, it did in his. To increase the agony of despair—rouse moody madness into frenzy—add mockery to suffering,—these seemed the only objects for which the villain clung to an infamous existence.

From close associations the natural dispositions of men undergo an involuntary change, and catch an impulse foreign to earlier feeling. The colonel felt this in himself. He who was to have been our hero's murderer, the colonel was assured would in all probability himself be the victim.

On wore the day—and long and heavily it passed. The evening meal was brought; and the keeper, after his customary manner, secured the doors and left the prisoner.

Colonel Jack knew but little of the place beyond what he was able to observe from his own window. Morning, noon, and night his whole thoughts were upon but one object—namely, how to make his escape. Some gleam of hope seemed to find its way into his bosom when he caught sight of the unknown in the garden. Doubtless he had been an inmate of the establishment for a much longer period than the colonel had, and consequently might be acquainted with the interior of the building.

When alone, Colonel Jack examined the garden attentively, for it was his determination to seek a closer interview with the unknown than that of the preceding night. He found that the means of descent were not so very difficult.

An old fruit tree, nailed against the wall beneath the window would, with management, afford him the means of alighting in the garden at the rear of the premises. By attaching the cord to the old fruit tree, he could reach the bench below, and re-ascend at his pleasure. The colonel soon completed his simple operations, and waited with no small impatience for the promised interview with the stranger.

Every sound was hushed—and two or three lights which had twinkled over the trees, gradually disappeared. Having ascertained that the cord was securely fixed, the colonel made his descent with safety into the garden.

In a few moments a footstep was heard approaching, and the figure of a young man issued from the clump of evergreens.

"How is this, sir?" he said. "As total strangers, are we justified in meeting thus at midnight?"

"We are bound together by the ties of misfortune," answered Colonel Jack. "We are both wretched—both ill—at least, I know I am."

"And, I also," answered the young man

"Well, then, in seeking this interview, I am anxious only to know if we can be of service to one another. In my anxiety to escape myself, I may possibly be the humble instrument of assisting you in a similar object. United by the bond of misery, if we cannot succeed, we can at least make the attempt—and, even in this infernal den, render my name memorable to its ruffian inmates. Young man, dare I trust you?"

The stranger scanned the features of the highwayman for a minute or two, and then said, slowly—

"You may. There is that in your countenance which tells me that you are to be relied on as a friend. I have the facility vouchsafed to me of reading the characters of most men at first sight."

"Ah!" thought Colonel Jack. "A dreamer evidently;" for there was that in the young man's manner which immediately led him to such a supposition. The colonel paused, and then said—

"Are you sure that we are free from interruption? You know more of this place than I do, I should suppose. Do you think it likely any one may overhear us?"

"I think not, as the keeper restricts his visits to the day."

"As for me," he continued, "I am regarded as nearly dead, and too heart-broken to ever dream of leaving this place with life. But they little know me, nor dreamed that a spark of latent hope remained within this withered bosom—and though it smouldered unperceived, the flame that kindles unexpectedly, will not be the less dangerous. Would that my power were equal to my will—weak though I am, I would attempt escape, no matter how desperate the chance, and reckless of what consequences would follow an attempt at a failure."

"Young man, you seem to have suffered the cup of sorrow to the brim. Has your imprisonment been long?"

"Long—long, indeed," he said, with a deep drawn sigh. "Six years have rolled away since I was stolen from the world and buried in this living tomb."

"Was there any cause to warrant or even afford a pretext for such an outrage? for you are evidently sane enough."

"No, indeed; but I have had more than enough to drive me mad."

"Then who has caused your present imprisonment?" inquired the colonel.

"One who ought to have protected me—my father's brother. By getting me out of the way, he comes into a large property, which by right is mine."

"This, then, is the curse of wrongs," said the colonel.

"Wrongs!" exclaimed the stranger. "Mine are worse than wrongs. Fancy every injury that villain offers to man—and from one, too, who ought to have been my protector.

Beggared—ruined! Deprived of my just rights, and, lastly, robbed of liberty itself. To this tale of wrongs, could aught be added?"

"And your uncle, what has become of him?"

"He lives in splendid infamy upon his ill-gotten wealth. The villain occupies a lordly hall—while his victim drags on a miserable existence in that worst of gaols—a madhouse!"

"We will not indulge in a recital of all our individual woes," said the colonel; for he saw that the topic was a favourite one with the injured young man by his side. "Let us, therefore, make the best use of our time by concocting some scheme for our deliverance."

"Ah!" exclaimed the stranger. "How is that to be effected?"

"Have you courage?' inquired the colonel.

"Desperate men, situated as I am, usually have," was the prompt reply.

"Good! Then we must take our enemies by surprise.'

"But, how?"

"That remains to be seen."

"It is impossible to scale this wall,' said the stranger.

"Possibly so; but there may be other means—we shall see. You know not what may be accomplished yet."

The young man shook his head despairingly.

A sudden alarm recalled the two prisoners to their present situation. It was the sound of several voices, proceeding from men who were apparently engaged in some drunken revelry.

"We must part instantly," said the young man, in a suppressed whisper. "The villains are carousing, and there would be danger in remaining longer here. In drunken moments they sometimes ramble through the building; and, I believe, for no purpose beside disturbing the wretched prisoners—and rousing them to consciousness of the misery which they are doomed to undergo. To-morrow night we meet again—and then to think of freedom. Heavens! how that word awakes my soul to hope. Farewell—be prudent, and desperate as our fates appear, some kinder future than we have yet met with, may restore us to liberty."

He offered the colonel his hand, which the latter grasped and shook warmly; and the stranger immediately disappeared among the trees.

Colonel Jack regained his chamber, undressed, and threw himself upon his bed, and slept soundly enough, dreaming of his attempts at liberty and conflicts with his catiff jailors.

CHAPTER LXIV.

SIR RICHARD VISITS HIS VICTIM.

COLONEL JACK was aroused from his slumbers by the opening of the door of his apartment. Lights flushed upon his eyes—he looked up—three men were standing in the room. One he recognized as the person who regularly attended upon him; the other was Mr. Hardy himself, the master of the establishment; and the third was a tall figure, hidden in a long riding cloak, while his features were concealed with a mask. The keeper, who seemed half intoxicated, held down the lanthorn, as the colonel sat upright on the bed, throwing its light upon his face, while he sneeringly observed to his companion,

"Look, sir—what think you of the patient? Has not a change of air and cool regimen improved him marvellously? He's calm now—the fever has subsided. We have patched him up well. And should he not be thankful for all the kindness we have been at? But would you credit it, the fellow grumbles after all. Ah, the ingratitude of man!"

"Pshaw! I cannot believe it," returned Mr. Hardy. "The gentleman's too happy, could he be in his sound reason to understand and appreciate the kindness received from us."

And then both the scoundrels, master and man, indulged in a hideous grin.

The colonel's blood boiled, and it was with difficulty that he could restrain himself. He clutched the pistol he had taken from Mr. Sharpthorne, beneath the bed clothes, but, alas, he had neither powder or ball. Nevertheless the thought crossed his mind—it was a desperate one—of using it as an offensive weapon and suddenly rushing upon the three men; but his better judgment forbade his making the attempt. It was lucky he obeyed its dictates.

He could not, however, retain his calmness and self-possession to remain passive. The sight of Mr. Hardy awoke all his pent-up passion to an outburst.

"Cowardly villains!" he exclaimed, "I fling defiance at you both. What are you? —the lowest scoundrels in the scale of infamy. That outcast wretch," painting with his finger scornfully at the keeper, "a poisoner by trade, and there," he said, addressing Mr. Hardy, "a wretched agent to worthless and guilty men."

The unexpected boldness of this address was not lost upon the midnight visitors. The cheeks of the man in cloak assumed a still paler hue, and the colonel saw, notwith-

standing his disguise, that it was Sir Richard Fleetwood who stood before him.

"You may well turn pale, Sir Richard Fleetwood, baronet only by fraud, deceit, and crime. Go, unworthy scion of an ancient house—go, hide your head from the sight of all good men. Live, accursed by your ill-gotten title and wealth. We have known each other of yore. You have me at an advantage now—your turn to-day, to-morrow mine. For as surely as I see you now, triumphing in your short-lived advantage, so surely will I make you rue the hour that you ever trifled with Colonel Jack. Double dealing monster as you are, you have at last thrown off the mask."

Sir Richard was visibly affected—his limbs seemed quivering with rage—and through the mask the colonel heard his teeth grind.

No. 44.

"Go," continued the colonel, "and hug to yourself the thought that you have done the trick cleverly, aided by two such mis-creants as these worthy tools, in the hands of a worthy employer. Learn this fact, that although you have confined the body, you cannot bind the spirit of your victim. Let your conscience whisper in your ear, that a day of retribution must and will come, that your brother, whom you have persecuted for years, must be restored to his just rights after an imprisonment which has nearly dethroned his reason. Psha! monster of iniquity! I heap curses on your felon head—on you, worse than murderer!"

While fulminating this defiance, the keeper and Mr. Hardy looked at each other as though surprised at the boldness of a wretch whom, no doubt, they had expected to find a subdued and drooping figure—one whose hopes and spirits were equally extinguished; but on the masked figure the effect was astounding—his agitation was sufficiently apparent, and produced a burst of rage beyond control.

The colonel heard a muttered "Damnation!" and a click of a pistol cock distinctly followed; but Mr. Hardy flung himself between the baronet and the prisoner, and in a low hurried voice exclaimed—

"Not by your hand, Sir — For Heaven's sake have patience, and all will be well"

The remonstrance was effective, and the baronet strode from the room, followed by his two worthless companions, who grinned sarcastically, and seemed but little disturbed by the scene which had taken place.

They were used to such in the course of their extensive practice, and took it all as a matter of course in the way of business.

Not so the baronet; he was evidently overcome by the suddenness of the threats and taunts hurled at him, and would, perhaps, not have stopped at murder under the curses of our hero, had he not have been restrained by the more prudent Mr. Hardy.

The keeper returned to secure the cell after the other two had departed.

For a moment he silently regarded the prisoner, and as he did so, there was a quiet devilry in his look which was altogether inexpressible.

"I thank you," he said, "for the flattering character you have given me. You describe me as an able druggist. Well, probably, lest I forgt my art, I shall endeavour to keep my hand in practice. A week or two will tell. And now, to bed. Sleep soundly, you shall not be disturbed again, believe me, for fear it might ruffle your temper—ah, ah!—and cause you to perhaps curse me, which would be, indeed, a pity. Oh, no, you shall not be disturbed again," said the wretch, with hypocritical calmness, and he shut the door to, and walked slowly away down the passage.

The colonel heard the bolt drawn, and was once more left to himself.

He was in a state of feverish irritation at the scene which had passed.

The horrible threats of the gaoler, suggestive of slow poisoning, were enough of themselves, situated as he was, to turn the brain of an ordinary man, for it would be impossible for him to avoid being the victim of the wretch's vile arts, did he choose to practise them.

The footsteps of his gaoler had died away, when in about ten minutes or so afterwards, he was startled by a slight noise, as though sand was flung against the window of his apartment.

Again and again the sound was repeated,

and springing from his bed, he hastened to the window.

Beneath, the stranger was standing, and to a hasty inquiry, he replied by requesting the colonel to dress himself, and descend instantly.

In a few seconds he was clothed, and beside his companion in the garden.

The stranger's looks and manners were unusually excited.

"Listen," he said, in a whisper; "collect yourself—the crisis of our fate is at hand. This night decides the destiny of both of us, and success or failure will be attended with freedom or a grave."

"I am prepared in either case," said our hero. "To remain here now is certain death."

"How so?"

"They have paid a visit to my room, not a quarter of an hour since, and I have threatened them."

"Well?"

"And in turn, the rascally keeper has threatened me with the most appalling death—namely, by slow poisoning; and I doubt not but the miscreant will practise his hellish arts upon me."

"Ugh!—horrible!" exclaimed the young man, with a shudder. "Remain passive for the present," he said, in continuation.

And the two prisoners stood, straining their ears, to catch the slightest sound.

CHAPTER LXV.

SCENE IN THE GARDEN.—THE FIENDISH PLOT.

WITH every nerve strung to the utmost degree of tensure, Colonel Jack and his newly found friend remained pensive in the garden for several minutes. The highwayman was at a loss to know what was to follow, for the two hardly dare converse even in a few hurried whispers.

"Now," exclaimed the young man, "Now for a bold heart and ready hand, and let us hope all will be well. Follow me, and step on the grass and avoid the gravel. Observe, do as I do. Breathe not on your life.—Come on."

"Have you any arms?" inquired the colonel, making a pause.

"No; and you—"

"Have only a small pistol, without either powder or shot. It can't be helped. We must not falter. We must trust to Providence!"

Now the colonel, to say the truth, had always greater confidence in a well-primed pair of pistols than he had in Providence;

but it was no use repining his lot — his barkers "were gone"—and "gone was his mare"—and gone also his faithful Slott. Unarmed as he was, his indomitable spirit did not desert him in this trying hour, and, come what would, he made up his mind to fight with nature's weapons, in lieu of any others which the ingenuity of men manufacture for the destruction of his fellow-men, therein being superior to the lower animals.

The colonel committed himself to the guidance of his companion, who evidently was much better acquainted with the place than he was. No wonder since he had had six years' experience in the same. The two crossed silently the wilderness of a neglected garden. Clump after clump was passed—through evergreens which, from their height and closeness, appeared for many a year to have escaped the visitatious of the pruning-knife—the light which the colonel had indistinctly observed from his window, beamed from a ground-floor lattice ; steadily, and directed by his companion, the two reached and ensconced themselves in a patch of bushes grown into a bold exhuberence of branch and leaf directly in front, and within two or three paces of a lighted chamber.

Within this four men were standing, and they were talking earnestly in low voices.— From the position of the owner of the establishment, and another enveloped in a railway cloak, at once told the colonel who they were

Sir Richard held his mask in his hand, although as his back was turned towards the window, his features were not disclosed. The third individual was a short ill looking man, dressed in black ; and the fourth was the poisoner.

Sir Richard's air was haughty and commanding, as was usual with him—his companions were marked with a servility of manner which men of a lower grade assume in the presence of superiors. He seemed impatient of the undertone in which the other three conversed, for, raising his voice to a pitch which rendered it audible to the two listeners, he exclaimed—

"What a vile atmosphere !—stale liquor and villainous tobacco ! Up with the window ! An ill-ventilated room is an abomination to me."

The baronet was evidently out of temper, he was chafing and fuming at the bitter denunciations which had fallen so recently from the lips of the highwayman.

As he spoke, he pointed with his arm to the window.

The order was instantly obeyed.

"No eavesdroppers, I hope, doctor," he said, addressing the ill-looking man dressed in black.

"None within pistol shot," was the reply.

"No, no, Sir Richard, fear nothing. This establishment, although it may appear a boast of mine, is conducted with the secrecy of the grave."

"But, by Heaven, I do fear," exclaimed the baronet, passionately. "You know not the man you have to deal with—Colonel Jack, the notorious highwayman."

"Who ?" exclaimed Mr. Hardy, who for the first time became acquainted with our hero.

"Why he that we have seen to night, and who dared to threaten me with retribution, and—bah! I know not what! Curse him—he's been a bitter thorn in my side for years past. You know not the man you have to deal with."

A sardonic grin passed over the features of Mr. Hardy.

"We've tamed worse than him," he said, with a chuckle.

"Insulting scoundrel !" exclaimed the baronet ; "but for you, I really think that I should have inflicted summary punishment on him, and sent him to another world. I would speak a few words to you alone—'tis nearly time we were moving. I must be home ere daybreak. A visit of mine to this house would, were it known, create more conversation than we might desire."

"Nay, Sir Richard," answered Mr. Hardy. "I will not delay you more than a short half-hour—supper is now prepared, and 'tis long since you have dined."

"Go," said he, turning to the poisoner, "and hasten the meal."

"And you may as well," said Sir Richard, "tell my man to bring the gig to the door, within fifty yards down the lane, and under the same hedge we stopped at. We cannot be too cautious, for there may be treachery in this establishment."

"Oh, dear no, Sir Richard," answered Mr. Hardy, "Be not under any fear of that—all who are in this establishment are bound to me by some tie or other. The man who has just left dare not be false to me,—did he venture outside these walls, the very pavement in the street would rise up and stone him."

"A good security," returned the baronet ; "and yet not the worst a man may depend upon. Are we alone ?—secret ?—none to interrupt ?—none to overhear ?"

"This secures our privacy," said Mr. Hardy, as he and Sir Richard passed through the door, and the former locked it.

"There," he said in continuation, pointing to the garden, "for fifteen years the bat has been the sole proprietor. Speak freely, we are without living witnesses in this direction. Did you believe in ghosts, I might not be so confident. A few departed patients whom we did not wish to expose to the ordeal of a coroner's inquest or Christian burial, are here interred. As a matter of course, they may probably perambulate the garden. Well, they have it to themselves—no living foot has passed the doorway since the last fool who hung himself was put in clay."

Colonel Jack smiled at the confidence of the villain. The very man whom the scoundrel dreaded more than any other on earth, was at the present moment watching every look and hearing every whisper.

The colloquy which ensued was interesting both to speakers and listeners, and the colonel and his companion held their breath in suspense as they listened to catch every word which fell from the two villains, for such in reality they both were.

"Hardy," said Sir Richard, " I saved you from transportation."

The party so addressed bowed.

"I enabled you to take this place."

Another assenting movement admitted this fact.

"Directly and indirectly I have been your best protector since. Have I a claim upon your gratitude?"

"Sir Richard, indeed you have the deepest," answered Mr. Hardy, with a bow of servility.

"Then hear me, and mark me, too. On your life, be careful with the prisoner whom we have so recently paid a visit to. If he once escapes, all is lost. Heaven only knows now he has managed to obtain information respecting this—ahem—Mr. Sabine. It must have been through some treachery on the part of your subordinates. There are traitors in this establishment. Nay, start not, that fellow, whom I dread beyond all others in the world, must have obtained his information here. How else could the man have known of the existence of my brother, whom the world supposes to be dead long since? There is treachery in your house, Hardy, of that I am fully convinced."

"Impossible, Sir Richard,. I have used every precaution, and can place implicit confidence upon all in my establishment."

"Well, the discovery is made somehow. I suppose it is useless to inquire how, although I have my own opinion on the matter. Now hear, and mark me well. If this Colonel Jack manages by any means to make his escape—"

"Oh, fear not that, Sir Richard, such an event is most improbable, nay more, almost impossible, I was about to say."

"Well, I say, supposing," answered the baronet. "The escape of my brother will shortly follow, for the fellow is determined, and is not likely to let the matter rest in peace where it is. Exposure is sure to follow, and at that, ruination."

"Clearly so," answered Mr. Hardy,

"How long people seem to live in madhouses," said the baronet, and he directed a sidelong look towards his companion.

"Indeed, Sir Richard," said Hardy, with the appearance of perfect simplicity, "I have often thought the same. Quiet—abstraction from worldly care—a judicious regimen, and no annoyance."

"Psha! man. No more cant, I am in no mood for such nonsense. In a word, how is it that Mr. Sabine has lived so long? and why does this serpent in my path, which bids fair to bring me to ruin, encumber the earth. Hardy, let us understand each other perfectly."

A dead pause ensued.

The baronet had spoken plainly out, a direct answer was required, and the keeper of the madhouse hesitated to give one.

Colonel Jack stood appalled and spellbound at the horrible suggestion. His own life as well as that of Sir Reginald's would, in all probability, be forfeited.

"Sir Richard," said Mr. Hardy, "the ablest physiologists can only assign to general causes the duration of human existence. The best probably may be good constitution, a quiet life, and temperate habits. The former your brother has, the latter advantages the inmates of this house enjoy abundantly."

The baronet, with marked impatience, listened to the evasive answer of his companion, and seemed to have some difficulty in curbing an angry outbreak.

Hardy," said the baronet, with a determined coolness not to be misunderstood, " reserve your foolery for a fitting opportunity. While my brother lives I feel myself insecure, for he is absolutely dangerous. Were he once at liberty—"

Mr. Hardy gave a significant nod.

"Nay, this is quite probable, and it causes me to feel like a man who is sitting over a powder magazine. Gaols have been broken—madhouses evaded. I tell you that a sword hangs over me supported by a single thread, a hair. Much is already suspected, and were a little more known correctly, the finger of scorn would be pointed at me, and I should be driven from my native clime adisgraced and beggared criminal. My very existence depends upon my maintenance of my position in society. That secured, the storm may be weathered—but lost, poverty and exile follow. Have I not spoken plainly?"

His companion bowed assent.

"Hardy, no flattery. I saved you once—fail me now, and your ruin will follow mine."

The desperate calmness of the baronet's manner was not to be mistaken. The paleness of his minion's countenance proved that he understood his patron's threat.

"Sir Richard," he answered, "you do me

an injustice in supposing that I am not ever obedient to your will, instead of being indifferent to your welfare. You ask me why those you wish removed are living? I will tell you. It is only because I expected they would themselves do that which would have saved us the trouble of effecting the end described. I have used every means to drive this man desperate, and how reason has withstood the ordeal it has been subjected to is a mystery to me. More active means shall be resorted to. Be at ease, Sir Richard. Before a week expect a letter with two black seals, and then both shall be resting yonder," and the wretch pointed with his finger to the mounds in the garden.

"Enough," said the baronet. "Give me your hand. I shall not forget the obligation, but one will suffice."

"Very well, so be it," answered the wretch.

A tap was now heard at the door. Hardy opened it with the key he had thrust in his pocket, and the poisoner announced that supper was served.

"Will you take off your cloak, Sir Richard?" inquired Mr. Hardy; business is now settled, and you really must have some refreshment. Go see how the night is," said Hardy to the poisoner. "You may leave the door unfastened, as Sir Richard will be leaving the house presently."

CHAPTER LXVI.

THE ATTEMPTED ESCAPE.—THE CONFLICT.

OBEDIENT to the orders of his employer the poisoner unclosed a door on another side of the apartment in which the midnight council had been held. It opened on a passage directly opposite to the spot where Colonel Jack and his companions stood—and as the corridor was lighted by a lamp, they could see distinctly that another door formed its termination. They observed the keeper undo the fastenings and look out upon a moonlit space before it, and Colonel Jack felt his companion press his arm.

Our hero understood the meaning of the pressure. There lay the chance—the only desperate chance from a house of slaughter! They saw the villain close the door carefully, come up the passage—enter the room—and announce that the night was fine, and that the moon had risen. Sir Richard laid his railway cloak on one side. Mr. Hardy led the way through a side entrance to the supper room, while the poisoner's attendance was required to wait upon his master and his worthless and guilty visitor.

As the villain quitted the room and closed the door, the young man who had hold of the colonel's arm trembled with excess of emotion.

"Escape now depends upon ourselves," said Colonel Jack. "If we hesitate or falter we are lost, dare you venture.

"Fear not," answered the young man. "My frame is weak by long suffering, and my nerves shaken, but my heart is as determined as your own."

"Then follow me and we will stand by each other to the last."

"And may Heaven assist us," exclaimed his companion. The two stepped easily from the garden into the deserted apartment, and in the supper room heard three voices in loud and careless conversation, flinging the baronet's cloak around him, Colonel Jack wrapped his companion in a loose coat which opportunely enough had been left on a chair, and then opening the door leading to the lighted corridor, the two threaded their way upon tip-toe—but found the fastenings numerous and intricate, entirely removed, and lifting the latch was all that was needed to ensure liberty. Next moment the two fugitives were standing on the sward outside of the infernal building—the door was softly closed, and the two deemed that their escape had been effected without hindrance or alarm.

"Time passes" exclaimed the colonel in a whisper—as his heart beat high at the prospect of his release from captivity—luckily he had been able to snatch up a rapier, which lay against the corner of the hall and armed with this weapon he felt more confidence.

"One trial more," exclaimed our hero, and Sir Richard Fleetwood I defy thee!"

"And what is that?" inquired his companion—

His gig is waiting—and this pathway leads to the lane, for in the moonlight I mark a line on the hedge."

"But is there not a man there?"

"Yes, and he must be disposed of. Advance silently. He must be taken by surprise."

The colonel was unwilling to slay the scoundrel, if it could possibly be avoided.

For a moment the true direction where the vehicle waited its owner's coming, was rather doubtful, but the humming of an air from some Italian Opera announced the locality of Sir Richard's valet. Deceived by the cloaked figure which approached, the valet fancied that the colonel was his master, and a shattering blow from the buttend of the pistol taken from Mr. Sharpthorne was the first intimation he had of his mistake. This stretched him senseless on the sward.

Never was blow given with better will, and never did one prove more effective. Without a sign of life the scoundrel remained prostrate, while "to render assurance doubly sure," the colonel bound him with his own handkerchief hand and foot.

While thus engaged, a cry of alarm proceeded from the young man—and in another second, the colonel found himself surrounded by five or six persons, who roared with rage at discovering him. These men consisted of Mr. Hardy, Sir Richard, and keepers belonging to the establishment.

Springing with the agility of a cat into an upright position, the colonel faced about and held his assailants at bay at the point of his sword.

Sir Richard drew his weapon, set his teeth, and eventually made up his mind to capture the colonel or fall in the attempt. Their swords crossed, and without a word being exchanged on either side, several thrusts and feints were made. Seeing the numbers against him, the colonel placed his back against the buttress of a wall which enclosed the garden, and determined to sell his life as dearly as he could.

While this was taking place, it would appear that the party had not taken any notice of the young man who had escaped with our hero, for he had been suffered to retire to some distance off.

"Fly," exclaimed the colonel, as he observed him hesitate. "Fly, on your life, I charge you."

His companion hesitated, and regarded the speaker with a look of terror and pity ; but upon a threat to the same effect, he made good his retreat, which had one good effect, namely, drawing off two or three engaged with the colonel, who was still hotly pressed by Sir Richard Fleetwood.

The baronet was a skilful swordsman, so indeed was Colonel Jack, but he found that he had pretty well got his match.

"Surrender !" exclaimed Mr. Hardy, who was doubtful of the issue of the contest. "Surrender ! It is madness to endeavour to compete with such odds."

"Curses on you all !" exclaimed Colonel Jack. "Curses on you! I surrender only with my life. Better die by the sword than be the victim to the hellish plot which you and your worthless employer have concocted. So, two victims were to be offered up at your unholy shrine ?"

"I'll shoot you down like a dog !" exclaimed Hardy, drawing a pistol.

"Help ! Murder !" exclaimed Colonel Jack, in vain calling for assistance, while, at the same time, he assumed the offensive, and pressed his opponent hard.

It was now Sir Richard's turn to be on his guard, and his unworthy minions rushed round like a pack of wolves, striking at the colonel with their sticks.

Wild with fury, he made one lunge at Hardy, and ran him through the body. He fell with a deep groan, and his assistants pressed round, and Colonel Jack must have eventually fallen, either mortally, by his opponent's sword, or else knocked senseless by the sticks of the keepers, had not an unlooked-for succour arrived.

The first intimation the colonel received of this was a cry of pain from Sir Richard himself, as he turned round to see what had assailed him.

As he did this, Slott sprang up to his throat, and dug his fangs in the baronet's thorax.

Yelling with agony and fright, Sir Richard dropped his weapon, and caught the hound with both hands, and endeavoured to throttle him.

Slott turned his head, and bit the baronet so severely in the right hand, that he let go, and the dog fell to the ground once more ; but in the next minute he was again at the baronet's throat.

Bleeding profusely, panting, and half dead with fright, Sir Richard, upon the impulse of the moment, drew a clasped knife, and, in all probability, Slott's career would have come to an end, had not timely succour arrived.

By this time Hackett, Knapp, and Mullins, were on the spot, together with the young man, who had made his escape at the commencement of the affray.

As the baronet was about to plunge the knife in the dog's body, Mullins caught him by the arm, and spun him round with such force, that he stumbled and fell with considerable force to the earth, where he lay for some minutes, exhausted with loss of blood, and the concussion of the fall.

Hackett, Knapp, and the colonel, made but short work of the madhouse keepers, who thought it prudent to offer but little resistance, and retreated, after a slight skirmish, to a respectful distance.

It was hardly possible, late as it was, for all this disturbance to take place without attracting the attention of some one.

What with the cries, the oaths, the clashing of swords—the quiet echoes of the neighbourhood were awoke, and several constables made their appearance.

Sir Richard's valet had recovered from the blow he had received, and screamed and shouted as though he were being murdered.

"What's all this row about?" exclaimed the first constable who came up.

"Lunatics endeavouring to escape, and worse than that, they have been committing murder," exclaimed the poisoner, "ungrateful miscreants as they are. We want your assistance to take them back to their rooms, in Mr. Hardy's establishment."

"Stand off!" said Colonel Jack. "I am no more a lunatic than you are yourselves.

Falsely imprisoned in that cursed asylum, at the instigation of a man deeply steeped in crime, I have luckily succeeded in making my escape; and, by the Lord above, neither you nor a hundred such, shall convey me back to that vile hole, where wretched creatures are imprisoned at the instigation of guilty and designing men."

"Don't listen to what he says," said Mr. Hardy. "Mad people always talk in that incoherent strain, and imagine their best friends and protectors are their bitter enemies. Don't heed what he says, but seize him. He has already committed murder; and even if he was a sane man, you know, as officers of the law, that he is amenable to justice."

"That's true enough," said one of the officers, who seemed to be the chief of the party. "Come, yield, before you have your head broken."

This was addressed to Colonel Jack.

"If so be as he is to be taken, why taken he must be," drawled out one of the men; "but for my part, it is difficult to understand who is wrong, and who is right, in cases of this sort; and my maxim is, to let every man fight his own battles. I ain't at all sweet upon you madhouse coves, and that's all about it, and no flies."

Having delivered this speech, the speaker looked round at his brother officers for approval.

"Curse me if I know what to do," said his superior officer, looking hard at Mr. Hardy. "What's your name, pray?"

This latter question was addressed to the owner of the madhouse.

"Hardy, at your service, keeper of one of the best establishments for persons of weak intellect, in the three kingdoms."

"Humph! Hardy, is it?" said the officer. "Oh—ah—I see—Hardy—that's it."

"Yes, Hardy," exclaimed that individual, not liking the manner of the man. "What have you to say to that? Do your duty?"

"Don't you be so fast. I must first learn what is my duty."

"Why, to assist me in mine, and recapture the prisoner or prisoners."

"Maybe it is, and maybe it ain't."

"I shall report you if you neglect it," said Hardy.

"Oh, no you won't."

"But I will!" said the madhouse keeper, snappishly.

"But I say you won't."

"Insolence! Why not pray?"

"Because you dare not, Mr. Hardy. Do you see that?"

Mr. Hardy did see it, and thought it advisable to drop the bullying tone, and come the persuasive; he could do each by turns, as it suited his purpose.

"Well, you know, I am the last man to get any one into trouble, and all I want of you is, to afford me and my servants protection in carrying out the law."

"Insolent liar!" exclaimed Colonel Jack. "If you have the effrontery to stand there and utter such falsehoods, I'll knock your worthless skull against this wall. Begone—out of the way, and let me pass, for I am weary of this scene."

"Sieze hold of him!" exclaimed Mr. Hardy.

But the officers did not seem inclined to obey this order.

Seeing how matters stood, the poisoner made a rush at our hero. Knapp darted forward, and caught the miscreant by the throat.

A desperate struggle then ensued, and as the two closed with each other, Knapp called out to the colonel to make good his retreat, but the latter hesitated.

By this time the poisoner was thrown violently to the earth, and Knapp held him forcibly down.

Galdie besought the colonel to be off, and leave himself and his companions to shift for themselves.

Under the circumstances our hero availed himself of the opportunity thus afforded him, and flew off, no one endeavouring to follow him, for he still carried his drawn sword in his hand, and was unquestionably a dangerous and desperate customer to cope with.

When he had got fairly out of sight, the highwayman released the poisoner, and the officers interposed to prevent further hostilities.

"Well," said he who had appeared to be their chief, "how is it to be? Is any one to be given in charge? Who are these men?"

This was said in allusion to Mullins, Galdie and Knapp.

"I don't know them," answered Mr. Hardy.

"Well, do you give them in charge?"

"Of course I do."

"You had better not, Mr. Hardy, for we know one or two little affairs that may get your neck into a hempen noose."

This was a random shot, but it hit the mark, and Mr. Hardy contented himself with spluttering out something about robbers, cut-throat hounds, and similar chosen epithets from his own matchless vocabulary, and so eventually he and his assistants were fain to go back to the house, whither they conveyed the wounded man, whom it will be remembered had been struck down by Colonel Jack with Sharpthorne's pistol, and thither also did Sir Richard Fleetwood betake himself to have his wounds received from Slott dressed by the surgeon.

The baronet was perfectly wild with fury. Bleeding and pale with rage, he submitted himself to the surgeon with the best grace he could.

A sickening sensation came over him from loss of blood, consequent upon the wounds he had received, which were, however, of not a dangerous or mortal character, so the doctor asserted—that is, he put in as a proviso, that the dog was not afflicted with hydrophobia.

At this observation the baronet became still more pale, and the sickening sensation so increased, that he fairly fainted right off.

The doctor darted a look of inquiry towards Mr. Hardy.

"Well," said the latter. "He ain't dead, is he?"

"No, but he's swooned," replied the doctor.

"What's to be done, then?"

"Oh, I'll bring him to. Open the door," said the doctor.

This was done.

"And the window."

This order was also immediately obeyed.

"The baronet will not be able to go home to-night," said the doctor.

"Eh?—what?" said Sir Richard, suddenly coming to as the fresh air found its way through his lungs.

"You had best not think of going home to-night, Sir Richard," answered the doctor, shaking his head dubiously.

"But I must—I will. Zounds! to be incarcerated in a madhouse—"

"For your own safety, I should advise you to go to bed and court sleep, which, from your loss of blood, will be quite sure to follow."

"Ah!" said the wounded man, closing his eyes in horror. "What a night this has been."

"We must make the best of it, Sir Richard," answered Hardy." "Let me beseech you to look to yourself, and, after a night's rest, we shall be able to look at the matter a little more in the morning."

To say the truth, Sir Richard did not feel himself capable of a journey to Acton, and was therefore accommodated with the best bed-room the establishment afforded, and in a few minutes after his retiring, he was in a sound and peaceful slumber.

CHAPTER LXVII.

THE COLONEL'S FUTURE PLANS.—HIS VISIT TO OSBORNE.

HAVING got safe from the respectable establishment of Mr. Hardy, our hero immediately repaired to his own home, to reassure his wife by his presence that he was safe, for Galdie had informed him of his interview with Mrs. Halford.

After this, he deemed it advisable to proceed forthwith to Osborne's, in Goswell-street; for as yet he was uncertain which course to pursue, to procure the release of the unfortunate and illused Sir Reginald Fleetwood.

An order from a magistrate might be obtained to examine into the state of the unfortunate gentleman's health and mind, but the colonel knew perfectly well that it would be attended with considerable difficulty for him to go forward and make the necessary application for this purpose. Under these circumstances, he deemed it expedient to to see Osborne

Upon his arriving at his friend's lodgings, the first person he met with was his precious friend Squabshot, who hailed the appearance of our hero with many expressions of true delight.

"It's as good as gold to clap eyes upon you again. Hang me, if it a'nt," said Squabshot. "Come in. Want to see Osse?" This was his abbreviation of Osborne's name.

"Yes. Is he in?"

"No, but he's out," said Squabshot.

"So I should suppose, if he's not in," said the colonel with a smile. "Really Squabby; you are too sharp—"

"Sorry for that. I'm generally considered a plain blunt chap, though there's very little *blunt* about me. Ah, ah!"

"When do you expect Harry in?"

"Oh, he wont be long; but you know he's going to hook it from here. Lord bless you, this place wont do at all for him now."

"No, I suppose not."

"Oh, dear no. But he's coming into his property shortly, and then I'll show him how to do the thing up brown."

"Oh, go along; don't you trouble yourself to do anything of the sort."

"But, Lord bless me, where have you been hiding yourself?" said Mr. Squabshot, suddenly mindful of the colonel's absence.

"I have had a series of adventures, not of a very agreeable character," was the reply to this question. "In fact, I have been a prisoner in a madhouse."

"No, you don't mean that?"

"I have."

Mr. Squabshot indulged in a loud and prolonged fit of laughter.

"Well, that is good. Why, it's worse than a sponging house?"

"I should think it was," answered the colonel.

"Why, you don't mean to say that they took you for a madman?"

"They imprisoned me as one."

"Well, I never."

Mr. Squabshot produced refreshments, and offered his companion, or rather forced him into a seat.

"Well, this beats cockfighting," said Squabby, "all into fits."

"I have a great wish to see Harry," said the colonel.

"Is he likely to come into his property, then? I mean that which was left by the late Jabez Crudge."

"Yes, not a doubt about it, I should say," was the answer.

"But law bless you, Osse is as miserable as a man with an overdue and unpaid bill in his possession."

"How's that?"

Mr. Squabshot applied his forefinger to the side of his nose.

"Love!" he said, significantly.

"Well, he will be able to prosecute his suit with success now."

"He'd be clever to do that."

"How so?"

"The lady's non est."

"What do you mean?"

"Sloped—mizzled—hooked it."

"You are speaking in enigmas. Miss Langford has not left her house; and if she had, Osborne would have received notice of her whereabouts."

"Ah, but she has left, and he has not received notice. On the contrary, he is moving heaven and earth to find her out. Oh, he's mad, I tell you. Ah, colonel, the man who sets his hopes upon a woman, is no longer a man; he's a chameleon, and feeds upon air. from air he takes his colours, holds his very life, and changes, poor wretch, with every wind ; grows lean or fat, buoyant with hope, and then becomes green with jealousy, or pale and distracted with speechless despair—just as the gale varies from one point of the compass to the other. Woman, sir—bah !—she is the author of such a book of follies in man, that it would take all the tears in the world to blot them out."

"You are eloquent, my friend," said the colonel, with a smile.

"Of what use is advice ?" said Squabshot. "He's taken the bit in his mouth, and runs his own course as best pleases him ; or rather it don't please him at all, for he looks worn and unhappy."

"Where is Miss Langford, then ?" inquired the colonel.

"Don't know—nobody knows. She's spirited away by some evil genius."

"But this is strange. Has Sir Richard Fleetwood—"

"I believe so—you have just hit it—as good as a conjuror, I declare."

Mr. Squabshot then entered into the particulars of Miss Langford's sudden disappearance from her own home.

"It can be no other than Sir Richard, d—n him. He has that to answer for amongst the rest. Ah, Sir Richard, we are now deep and deadly enemies. You have been playing a bold game—see that it don't turn against yourself."

"He's a queer lot," said Squabshot, draining off a glass of brandy, "a very queer lot ; that was always my opinion."

"He's an unmatched scoundrel—a ruffian—a villain— Psha! I know not why I waste such passion over him."

"What, has he been up to some new caper ?"

"Psha! you know nothing of this man's perfidy and wickedness," exclaimed the colonel, striding hastily through the apartment.

"Whew !" said Squabshot, to himself ; "some new game's afoot."

Then addressing his companion, he said—

"Never mind, Halford, we can defy him now. If he has run off with Miss Langford, it will carry its own punishment with it."

"Oh, it is not of that I would speak," said the colonel ; "although that is bad enough, for I know not what may the fate of Miss Langford."

"Oh, as to that," said Squabshot, "I've always found that a woman was more than a match for a man ; and let us hope that the young lady may be able to take care of herself."

"But have you no clue to any of those who so suddenly abstracted her from her house ?"

"No, all we learn is from Miss Staunton. Ah, there is a girl !" ejaculated Mr. Squabshot, clasping his hands in ecstacy ; "there is a girl, if you please."

"I thought you sneered at women in general ?"

"So I do ; but you will not find such another as Miss Stanuton in a hurry. Sensible, discreet, practical, with no fal-lal nonsense about her."

"I am glad you admit some women are possessed of good qualities."

After some further desultory conversation, Mr. Henry Osborne made his appearance upon the scene.

"Frank !" he exclaimed, in joyous accents, as he shook the hand of our hero with both his ; "this is a joyful sight. Where have you been ? I thought you had cut your old friends."

Colonel Jack indulged in a sickly smile, and shook his head somewhat mournfully.

"That's not likely my boy," he answered.

"Where have you been then ?"

"In a madhouse."

"What for ? Not as an inmate ?"

"Ah, but I have, and terrible revelations have been vouchsafed to me."

"Indeed ?"

"Yes. Sir Richard Fleetwood—"

"What of him ?"

"Is a villain, unmatched in atrocity. But sit down, and I will tell you all."

Osborne did as his friend suggested.

"First and foremost you must know that Sir Richard had, nay, has an elder brother."

"I know he had, but he died abroad, so I understood."

"No such thing ; he lives, lives to be immured in a wretched dungeon, at the instigation of his unworthy and cruel relative."

"Can such things be ?"

"It is true. Hear my tale. I learnt that the unfortunate Sir Reginald Fleetwood lived, and more than this, I ascertained, from sources it is not worth while detailing now, that the unfortunate baronet was in a madhouse. After some time I succeeded, by stratagem, in obtaining an order to see the wretched prisoner. Armed with this, I presented myself at Mr. Hardy's establishment—for that is the name of its worthless proprietor."

"Well, did you succeed in obtaining admittance ?"

"After considerable difficulty I did, and saw Sir Reginald. While conversing with him, Sir Richard peeped into the room, and I was suddenly made a prisoner."

"Upon what plea."

"The one they usually adopt—insanity."

"Such a tale appears absolutely incredible," said Squabshot.

"It is as true as I am here before you. I was imprisoned for many days, and luckily by the most unforseen circumstances, I was eventually able to make my escape."

Colonel Jack then related all those particulars with which the reader is already acquainted.

"And now," he continued, after he had concluded the narrative. "Now I am in sad trouble respecting the unfortunate baronet who is incarcerated in these accursed walls. I feel and know that he has not many days to live."

"Is he so bad, then?"

"Harry! unless he is rescued, he is doomed to die by the means of slow poisoning," answered Colonel Jack, in a hollow whisper.

"His brother never would——"

"He would not hesitate to become a murderer."

"What! poison his own brother?"

"Without the slightest remorse," said the colonel.

"Ah, I cannot believe it possible."

"But I know it. It is useless to blink the question. The fate of Sir Reginald Fleetwood is sealed, unless something is done to rescue him, and it is for this purpose that I have come to consult you."

"How can I assist him?"

"Why, you must know that relief can be afforded to this unfortunate gentleman by obtaining a magistrate's order to see him and examine into his case."

"Well, and how is that to be set about?"

"By an affidavit."

"You will have no difficulty in making one."

"Pardon me, but I have. There are reasons, my dear Harry, why I can not appear in the matter. It is hardly worth while entering into these, but, unfortunately, I myself am not able to make the required affidavit."

"Umph! that is unfortunate. Can I see Sir Reginald?"

"I don't suppose any one in the world will be admitted now. He is as completely shut out from the world, as though he were in the dungeons of the Inquisition."

"Then how will you proceed?"

"Why, I have been thinking, Harry, that if you would not mind making an application before a magistrate, the matter could be easily managed; but you see, time is of the utmost importance."

"But how can I, Frank? I have not seen this unfortunate gentleman."

"But I have. You can relate all I have told you, which would do as well."

"Why not go forward yourself. That would be the best inquiry."

"Say I am abroad—in the country—anywhere, for an excuse."

Osborne hesitated. He was such a stickler for the truth, that he did not like to go forward with a false tale.

"Can't I do as well," said Squabshot. "I am not so remarkably particular where a good end is to be obtained."

"You might," said the colonel, reflecting.

"Yes, no doubt, your testimony would answer the purpose."

"I don't carry such an appearance of honesty and integrity as our friend Osse, but I shall be able to cheek it out."

"Have you any objection to make the attempt?"

"My dear boy, I shall be delighted. But I tell you what we had better do. You know that lawyer we met at Canonbury House?"

"What, he that related the case of circumstantial evidence?"

"The very same."

"Yes, I remember him, but I never called at his chambers."

"Well, what do you think of our consulting him in this matter?"

"Oh, as to that, I have a legal adviser upon whom I can rely, and who has known me for years."

"Well, go to him. What's his name?"

"Mr. Baintree."

"What, the one who lives at Dulwich, and had a burglary committed on his premises some time ago?"

"Yes, that is the gentleman."

"Has he an office in town?"

"Yes; but he is very seldom there now, for the elder Mr. Baintree is getting well advanced in years. We can see the son, however, and if you have no objection, we will proceed thither at once."

"I'm your man," said Squabshot, who was ever ready and prompt on most occasions, as we have already seen in more than one instance.

Colonel Jack, accompanied by Squabshot, started off towards Bedford-row, leaving Osborne with a promise to return shortly and let him know how they had succeeded.

Mr. Baintree, senior, was not at the office, but the two were introduced to the son, who received the colonel with his usual courtesy. He had not seen our hero for many months, and had been surprised that he had not waited upon either himself or his father respecting the great Reichbeck will case, which had been standing in abeyance, and very naturally come to the conclusion that it was upon this very subject that the colonel had called.

"My father has been expecting to see or hear from you, Mr. Halford, for some months past. Indeed, he began to think that you had honoured some one else with the management of your legal affairs."

"He wronged me there, Mr. Baintree," observed Colonel Jack. "After our acquaintance of years, and the trouble I have unworthily occasioned him, it is not likely I should seek other legal advice."

The young man smiled.

"He has leisure to go into that matter now, when you are disposed to intrust him with the papers."

"I shall shortly do so—for time presses, and I have already been too tardy in having the matter seen into. But it is not relating to that which has induced me to pay you this visit."

"Ah! some other matter, eh!"

"Yes. Have you leisure for an hour or two?"

"I am entirely at your service."

"You have heard of Sir Richard Fleetwood."

"Most certainly, on many occasions."

"He has a brother alive—an elder one, who is defrauded out of his rights and title."

"Indeed!"

"Yes."

"Upon what grounds?"

"He is immured in a house for the reception of lunatics."

"Is he not of sound mind, then?"

"As sane as either you or I."

"Who placed him there?"

"His brother, Sir Richard."

"Ah! such things are done," said Mr. Baintree, sadly. "People will not believe it, but I know such acts of cruelty are of frequent occurrence. Has any one seen the unfortunate gentleman?"

"Yes, I have."

Colonel Jack then put the lawyer in the full possession of all that had transpired. After he had concluded, Mr. Baintree said—

"Your affidavit would enable us to procure an order from a magistrate to visit the baronet."

"Ahem! Yes, I suppose so; but, you see, I have reasons for not wishing to appear in the business, and thought that possibly my friend, Mr. Squabshot, as he is well acquainted with the affair, might make the required affidavit."

"Has he seen Sir Reginald?"

"Humph, no! but he can rely on my statement."

"It ought to be the party who has visited the prisoner. What one man tells another is not evidence—at least, not direct evidence. It may come in to strengthen the other testimony as collateral evidence, nothing more. I am almost afraid that we shall not be able to ensure getting an order without your own testimony."

"You think not."

"I don't say that with any degree of certainty, only it is doubtful, that is all, I mean. And if you are particularly interested in procuring this unfortunate gentle-

man's release, I should advise you by all means to endeavour to step forward yourself."

"I am afraid I should not be able to do so. Is there no other course?"

"Oh, we can try if this gentleman's testimony will do. Will you favour me with his name."

"Squabshot," said that individual, suddenly. "Squabshot—at your service."

The lawyer smiled, and said, "In this instance you will be at the service of my friend Halford, or Sir Reginald—which you please."

"I care not which so long as justice is obtained," answered Squabshot.

"What reason are we to assign for the person who visited the imprisoned man? What reason are we to assign for his not making the affidavit?" said Mr. Baintree.

"I am going abroad," he said, quickly.

"Oh! well you see, Mr. Halford, I should advise you to institute proceedings against this Mr. Hardy for false imprisonment. You would be sure to get heavy damages."

"It's hardly worth while."

"Well, he richly deserves it."

"So he does ; but let that be an after question. All I want to compass now is the release of poor Sir Reginald. But unless that is done, I am convinced he will be murdered, as sure as I have a head on my shoulders."

"Sir Richard must indeed be a bold, bad man."

"So you would say, if you knew him half as well as I do. He is a bad man, without a doubt."

"We will see what can be done. These cases are generally difficult ones to deal with, but we will lose no time in seeing what can be done."

"As speedily as possible," said Colonel Jack. "For every hour, nay, every minute, is of consequence."

"Without a doubt. Can your friend make it convenient to come here to-morrow morning?"

"Yes," said Squabshot, "my time's my own."

"Oh, I forgot!—what is your profession?"

"I have not any," was the reply.

"Oh, we must put you down gentleman, then, I suppose."

"I wish some kind maiden aunt would supply me with the means of supporting the character. You may put me down what you please—but I am a very poor gentleman, if I am one at all."

"You must be a gentleman, since you have the honour of Mr. Halford's acquaintance and friendship, I should say."

Mr. Baintree saw that Squabshot was an original. He had an original name—had an original appearance—had original manners.

"I have been in the Bench, and in a lock-up house, and have lost money over sporting animals and birds of various descriptions, and am rather a loose fish myself," said Squabshot.

"We shall not insert that in our affidavit," said the lawyer, with a smile.

"No; it would hardly be worth while," observed the colonel.

"Very well. I shall require your attendance here to-morrow—say at eleven, or half-past."

"Very good. You will see I am a man of my word. I will be here, without fail," answered Squabshot.

"And by that time I will have all prepared. When shall I tell my father that he will have the pleasure of seeing you?"

This was addressed to Colonel Jack.

"It cannot possibly be deferred much longer," said the colonel. "Indeed, it is highly important that these papers should be seen into now as early as possible. I thank you for the trouble you have taken, and will be here to morrow morning with my friend Squabshot."

Wishing the lawyer good day, the two returned to Osborne's lodgings in Goswell Street.

"How have you succeeded?" was Osborne's first question.

"Oh, admirably," exclaimed Squabshot. "Nothing could be better. I have to make an affidavit, which, of course, I shall have no difficulty in doing, and the matter will be settled. Sir Reginald will gain his liberty, and come here and have a tripe supper, I have no doubt, and wind up with a bowl or two of punch."

"Ah, ha! You lay it all down very agreeable to yourself," said Colonel Jack.

"I can see it all in my mind's eye," said Squabshot.

"Harry," said the colonel, "you look disappointed. I need not ask what is the matter."

"Honora," exclaimed Osborne; "poor Honora! No one knws what has become of her."

"We can make a shrewd guess," said the colonel. "Sir Richard Fleetwood, that unnatural villain—that miscreant, is the cause of her removal. I can never believe that he is possessed of any pure passion for a woman. Oh, Harry, if you knew all about that man."

"I know quite enough," answered Henry Osborne.

"My dear fellow, you don't know half, a quarter of this man's rascality. From my earliest boyhood I have known him. It was his example and companionship that first taught me to stray from the paths of rectitude."

Osborne stared. He was not at all aware

that Colonel Jack and Mr. Halford were one and the same person.

"Yes, Harry, you may stare, as well you may, but I tell you it was no other than Sir Richard Fleetwood who caused me to become what I am."

"As far as I know, you have nothing to blush for Frank."

The colonel smiled, when, after a pause, he said. somewhat suddenly—

"No more of this just now. We will talk of it hereafter. I have been long wishing to have a little private conversation with you. For the present farewell."

And shaking hands with his companions, the colonel took a somewhat hasty departure.

CHAPTER LXVIII.

THE AFFIDAVIT.—SHARPTHORNE'S COUNTER DECLARATION.

On the following morning our hero waited upon Mr. Baintree, and Squabshot was conducted by the lawyer to the nearest magistrate's, and then and there sworn to all those particulars concerning the imprisonment of the unfortunate and ill-used Sir Reginald Fleetwood, with which the reader is already acquainted.

After some consultation with Mr. Baintree the magistrate informed that gentleman what he had already surmised, namely, that Squabshot's affidavit was not evidence.

Under these circumstances, Colonel Jack, by the advice of Mr. Baintree, was induced to step into the witness-box, and disclose all that had come to his knowledge from his own personal observation.

This was all that could possibly be required, and an order was forwarded to Mr. Hardy for him to permit the unfortunate Mr. Sabine, as he was called, to be seen by proper persons to examine his state of health both bodily and mentally.

Thus far all seemed in a fair way, but when the colonel called again at the office of Mr. Baintree, he was shown a counter affidavit, made by Mr. Sharpthorne, in which that individual swore that the whole of the story told by our hero was a false one. Moreover, that he was a person not worthy of credence, being, in fact, no other than the notorious Colonel Jack. That no such person as he described was incarcerated in the establishment kept by Mr. Hardy, least of all any relation of Sir Richard Fleetwood.

Mr. Sharpthorne, moreover, asserted that the colonel had merely had recourse to this stratagem for the purpose of extorting money from his client, Sir Richard Fleetwood.

Here was an exposition to Mr. Baintree, who had not the slightest knowledge of our hero's calling

The colonel was wild with rage, and, upon the impulse of the moment, told the lawyer that he himself would answer the calumnies of Sharpthorne.

"You had better be cautious how you deal with him," said Baintree, "for he is a litigious fellow, a rotten limb of the law."

"I know him better than you do, sir," said the colonel, chafing.

And without further ado, he set off, accompanied by Squabshot for the Temple.

"Now, don't lose your temper, old boy," said Mr. Squabshot, as they took their way along. "Don't lose your temper. It will only make matters worse."

"A scoundrel!" exclaimed the colonel. "He's in the plot. I tell you, Squabshot, that they intend to murder poor Sir Reginald, as sure as you are a living man."

"You don't mean that?"

"Don't I?—but I certainly do. Now I tell you how we will manage. You shall send in your name to Sharpthorne. He won't admit me, I dare say, if he knew I had come with you. But he don't know you, does he?"

"'Not as I knows on,' as the girl said."

"Very well—his clerks don't know me. So that's settled."

"All right."

Arrived at Sharpthorne's chambers, Mr. Squabshot presented himself to the chief clerk, and informed that musty individual that he most particularly wished to see Mr. Sharpthorne.

Mr. Sharpthorne was engaged just then; but could he, the clerk, do as well?

"Oh, dear no, not at all," said Squabshot. "Me and my friend can wait, we are patient men."

"What name, sir?" quoth the clerk.

"Squabshot, of Goswell Street—friend of Mr. Wild's."

"Oh!" said the clerk, who regarded the name of Wild as a passport into the penetralia of his principal.

He ducked his iron grey head into the private room of the lawyer, and returned and informed the two gentlemen that Mr. Sharpthorne would be disengaged in a very few minutes.

"So much the better," said Squabshot, taking a seat, sans ceremony.

All this while the colonel had been seated behind some cloaks and hats, and an umbrella stand.

In a few more minutes the two were ushered into the interior room, where sat the lawyer.

Squabshot entered first, and the colonel immediately after.

The moment the lawyer's eye rested upon our hero, he turned unusually pale, and a slight tremor was observable in his frame.

"Well met, sir!" said the colonel. "So, in addition to chicanary, robbery, and contemplated murder, you have thought proper to add perjury to your list of crimes!"

"Mr.—ahem!—Halford, this language to a respectable solicitor, is uncalled for, unjust, and—ah—actionable."

"Miserable, contemptible reptile!" exclaimed Colonel Jack; "if you don't unsay what you have already asserted upon oath, I'll strangle you, as sure as you are a living man!"

"What is the meaning of all this?" inquired Sharpthorne.

"Listen to me," said our hero. "You know as well, if not better than I do, that Sir Richard Fleetwood, as he is called, is playing a game that will ultimately end in his own destruction—and yours as well, unless you mind what you are about. Sir Reginald is incarcerated in a madhouse—his worthless brother has cheated him out of his just rights, and worse than all this, contemplates murder. Ah, you may stare, but I know more than you imagine—enough to hang both you and Sir Richard."

"And yourself," chimed in Sharpthorne, with a malicious grin.

"Ay, and myself—I don't conceal that; but mark me, it will not be alone that I shall suffer. I hold proofs enough to convict both you and your worthless employer. And by the Lord that made me, I shall not go down to my grave without having the satisfaction of being revenged upon those whose crimes have made me what I am."

The lawyer was somewhat alarmed.

"You know as well as I do—or at least you ought to do so—that I have no wish that we should be enemies. On the contrary, I told you on a recent occasion that I had rather we should come to an amicable arrangement—at the time you so maltreated me," said Sharpthorne, with a shudder, at the recollection of his "gallant grey."

"Your actions are strangely at variance with your words, Mr. Sharpthorne," said Colonel Jack.

"Not at all so, my friend—not at all so. You don't make any allowance for professional men, who are compelled to do their duty by their clients. I'm sure I have endeavoured to do mine to Sir Richard."

"Canting hypocrite!" said the colonel, in unfeigned disgust; "is lying doing your duty?"

"What I have asserted on affidavit is true," said Sharpthorne, with the utmost effrontery.

The colonel sprang forward and seized him by the throat, pressing him against the wall of his own room, while at the same time he shook his fist menacingly in his face.

"Insolent, contemptible scoundrel!" exclaimed Colonel Jack, shaking him. "If you dare to repeat such a statement in my presence, I will anticipate the last act of the law, and throttle you here where you stand."

"Help—mer—" the lawyer endeavoured to call out; but his utterance was stopped by the highwayman tightening his grip.

"Now then, old parchment," said Squabshot. "You'd better behave yourself, and not tell any more of your lies. We've had enough of them for a week or so."

"Mr.—Hal— Col— Pray—oh! mercy!" gasped out the attorney, who was now completely overwhelmed with fright, that he hardly knew what he was saying.

"Deny your abominable calumnies!" said the colonel; "or, by God, I'll not release you!"

"I do—I do!" said Sharpthorne, "It was not true; but I was compelled to obey the orders of Sir Richard—I assure you I was. Upon my soul it is not my fault—indeed it is not."

The colonel flung the lawyer from him.

"Mr. Halford, really, I am half killed," said Sharpthorne, endeavouring to recover himself. "I tell you that I have no wish that we should be enemies."

"Every one is an enemy of mine, who is a friend of Sir Richard Fleetwood," said the colonel.

"I am not his friend—I'm only his lawyer," said Mr. Sharpthorne, in a meaning manner.

"You do his dirty work, it seems," said the colonel.

"I have been compelled to do that at which my better nature revolts," said Sharpthorne, with a hypocritical manner. "But if we could understand each other," said the lawyer, now emphasising his words in a meaning way, and kneading his hands most carefully. "If we could understand each other, why, a fig for Sir Richard—a fig for Sir Richard. Do you see?"

The colonel did not see, and said so, in his usually blunt manner.

"Well, sit down, gentlemen," said Mr. Sharpthorne.

He now for the first time handed his visitors a chair each.

"Why, you hold papers, about which there has been already enough disputation and unpleasantness," continued Sharpthorne. "What the contents of those are, it is impossible for me to say; but if I might suggest—"

He paused.

"Well go on," said Colonel Jack

"If I might suggest you know—it would be just this—make me your lawyer, and then

I'll do all I can for you, and a fig for Sir Richard. I'm sick of him," said Mr. Sharpthorne, actually snapping his fingers, by way of defiance.

"Not a bad suggestion," said Squabshot, "Not at all."

"You think not?"

"Most certainly I do."

"I cannot listen to any proposition from you, Mr. Sharpthorne, until your affidavit is taken off the file. First and foremost I must inform you that it is not days, but hours, that are of consequence to the unfortunate baronet, who is confined in Mr. Hardy's establishment. He is to be murdered as speedily as possible."

"Impossible!" exclaimed Sharpthorne.

"It is true," answered his visitor. "I don't know if you may be aware of it, but, it is as true as Heaven is my judge."

"That is enough my dear sir—I will withdraw the affidavit at once. Do not for a moment doubt me it shall be withdrawn—believe me as an earnest of good faith."

"Very well," said the colonel. "Do that and I shall have a better opinion of you, and after then, I will see you again, and perhaps we may come to an amicable arrangement."

He rose to depart.

"I shall be most delighted," said the lawyer, seeing his two visitors to the door.

"I shall see you in a day or two, I suppose, Mr. Halford," said Sharpthorne, as he and Squabshot emerged from the room into the outer office.

"Yes certainly," said our hero, and with this he departed.

"Capital, you've managed first rate," said Squabshot; "better to promise as you did—but I don't suppose you intend to keep it."

"That depends," said Colonel Jack.

CHAPTER LXIX.

HACKETT'S STORY FOR CHRISTMAS.

WHILE the events were taking place described in our previous chapters—Hackett and Galdie were pursuing their avocations without their principal. It was on the eve of Christmas, and the two highwaymen after a sharp ride of some miles, stalled their horses at the Bell at Edmonton, and betook themselves to the parlour of that comfortable hostelry. Toast and ale and several bowls of punch had been served at the expense of the liberal landlord, who knew our highwayman remarkably well.

Jest, song, and story, went round, and after several of the company had told anecdotes in their own lives, Hackett was called upon to relate something.

"Gentlemen," said Hackett, "I am not much of a spokesman—"

"Yes—yes, you are," said several voices. "Whet your whistle, and begin."

"Well, what I am about to relate, may be applicable to this time of the year. It is singular, and appears almost improbable; but the circumstances which form the basis of my narrative are, I assure you, strictly true."

"Hear, hear!"

"I am not aware of their having been related before, except in a brief, contemporaneous report, which may have appeared at the time of their occurrence. One or two cases are on record in the criminal annals of this and other countries, in which similar motives induced similar conduct, but infinitely less mysterious, systematic and atrocious than that which I am now about to relate to you; and as one of the chief actors was a relative of mine, I am able to vouch for the authenticity of the narrative."

Chairs were shifted, and everybody in the large room of the Bell tavern were on the tip-toe of expectation, as Hackett's preface had aroused their curiosity.

The speaker cleared his throat, and began his story thus:—

"Shrewsbury clock was tolling the hour of twelve, on a fine, frosty night, ushering in the Christmas of 1760, as a waggoner, with a snow white smock frock on, and a half emptied jug of ale in his hand, sallied out of the 'Huntsman Inn,' one of the cheapest in Shrewsbury. His waggon was standing before the door, the covering encrusted with hoar frost, and a noble team of horses, attached to the well laden vehicle, were refreshing themselves with hay and water, quietly submitting the while to the sibilatory civilities of the ostler.

"The waggoner watched them with complacency, as he drained his jug, and then lifting up his smock, he extracted a few halfpence from his pocket, and gave them to the ostler.

"'And do you go into the tap, ostler,' said he, "and see whether these two parties are a stirring themselves. Hang me, an' I don't think they will sit there till this time tomorrow.'

"He was interrupted by shouts of boisterous laughter from the tap room, for, you see gentlemen, they were enjoying themselves even as we may be now."

"I say, within there!—Bill!—Thomas!" cried the waggoner.

"'What be you doing there, sitting? Come—come, ye know as well as I that it is near starting time! Do you hear, it has just struck twelve by the church clock?'

"'Then 'tis to-morrow,' quoth one of the wags he was addressing.

"'Come, come now!' continued the waggoner. "We've a weary week's drive before us—and you know it as well as I. Are you moving, eh?'

"'Ah, ha, Dick! Isn't this Christmas morning? Come, don't ye be sulking on the beginning of this blessed day; but sit ye down a little longer, and drink a merry Christmas to one another!'"

"'No, I won't,' replied the waggoner, resolutely.

"Well, then, an' you must start, do ye drive the waggon slowly, and we'll both be after you before you reach the baker's pond. There's some ale a-spicing for us, Dick," replied Thomas, smacking his lips enticingly.

"'No, no—I know my duty, and I'm off,' grumbled the waggoner, quitting the room. He went out, cast his careful eye over the trim of his horses, and had just reached down his whip from the waggon-head, when one of his companions touched him upon the elbow, and proffered him a cup of warm spice-scented ale.

"'Come, Dick—come, drink it off,' said Bill, coaxingly, a good-natured lad of one or two-and-twenty, that could say fair things as well as many of his betters. "Come, you won't refuse to drink us a merry Christmas? This ale is special, man! Won't ye drive on slowly for half an hour, or so—and we'll be with you, as sure as death, by when you reach the baker's pond? Come—come, Dick—we'll do, maybe, more for you at a pinch!'

"The good-natured waggoner was not proof against fair words and spiced ale. He yielded, took the cup, drained it in a twinkling, shook Bill heartily by the hand, wished him a merry Christmas and added—

"'Now, don't ye be long a following; for drive slowly as I will, you'll have two or three miles to run for it, I know.'

"'We'll look to that, Dick—good-bye,' replied Bill, hurrying inwards, while Dick betook himself to his horses' heads, cracked and smacked his whip; his horses pricked up their ears and away they went.

The ponderous waggon rolled over the stones of silent Shrewsbury, accompanied by the clattering of twelve pairs of horses' hoofs, and the occasional 'Gee—a—whoop! Come up! On Smiler!' of the driver, who was soon out of sight of the jovial Huntsman, and fairly started on the broad London road.

He walked slowly by the horses' heads for some time, whistling and humming to himself, and every three or four minutes turning his head towards Shrewsbury, to see whether his companions were yet on the road.

"He had proceeded, however, at his very slowest pace for more than an hour without their appearing.

"'Now this is unkind,' quoth the wag-

goner to himself, as he trudged along; 'but did I not say it would be so? Here are Bill and Tom sitting snugly by the fire, drinking till they be drunken. What shall I do? I must go on. Lord, lord, how bitter cold it is!'

" He laid his whip across the shafts of the waggon, and stood still, slapping his hands against his sides for warmth. By the time he had done, his waggon had proceeded thirty or forty paces a-head of him. Just as he was overtaking it, he passed a milestone, and with alarm and surprise caught a glimpse of the figure of a brawny sailor-looking man, sitting beside it, with a little basket by his side.

"'Good morning!—A merry Christmas to you, master waggoner! How are you, eh?' inquired the stranger.

No. 46.

"'Pretty well, but desperate late—desperate!' replied the flurried waggoner, passing by the speaker.

"'Stop, just stop a minute,' said he, 'have you got any body in your waggon?—Can you make room for me, eh?'

"'Lord, sir, no, I'se got three men sleeping there already,' replied the poor fellow, his heart beating fast—thinking he had hit upon a good device for terrifying one whom he took to be a highwayman. 'They're all soldiers—all three of them, and I am giving them a lift for ten miles or so. They've all got their muskets.'

"'Eh! What? soldiers, did you say?' inquired the man, evidently disconcerted.

"'May I die if I havn't!' replied the waggoner, stoutly,

"'What in the world brings soldiers into these parts, eh?'

"'O sir, I don't know. You had better ask them, for they're calling to me. Good morrow, good morrow sir,' said the waggoner, and running up to his waggon, he affected to be walking in conversation with some one inside of it. He was very much alarmed at the slight accident just recounted, and was growing more and more uneasy at the prolonged absence of his companions. His head was filled with fears of murder and robbery. Could he doubt that the person he had been speaking to was a highwayman? Often did he look over his shoulder, to see whether the man who had addressed him was following; but he saw nothing moving on the long line of high road he had passed, and his fears began to abate.

"It was not far from two o'clock, and the morning continued bright and frosty. Like the eye of beauty, the moon shone forth radiantly and cheeringly from the unclouded blue. No sound interrupted the solemn silence, except the drowsy tinkling of a few bells above the horses' heads, the clattering of their hoofs, and the monotonous rumbling of the waggon-wheels. For an hour and half the waggoner had met nothing moving on the road, except the mail, which had thundered past him about twenty minutes before. He seemed to have forgotten the occurrence which had so alarmed him. Even the prolonged absence of his two companions seemed to have ceased disturbing him; for he made up his mind to continue at his next putting-up place till they arrived. Recollecting suddenly that it was Christmas, he clambered up a little holly-hedge on the left hand side of the road, to pluck a conspicuous piece of glistening miseltoe. While in the act of cropping it, he thought he saw, in a cross-road at some little distance, the figure of some one, running very fast. But what was there alarming in that? he thought as he leaped down, and overtook his waggon. He stuck his miseltoe in the brim of his great white hat, resumed his whip, and went on, cherily singing the verses of a Christmas carol:—

The holly's berry is not so red
As the blessed blood that Jesus shed;
Nor pretty miseltoe,
Though it be white as snow,
So white as—

The words were still on his lips, when, arrived at an abrupt turn of the road, he was suddenly seized by several men in sailors' dresses, and thrown down on the ground. In spite of all his strugglings his arms were fastened to his sides, his legs tied together, his eyes were bandaged, and a gag was forced into his mouth. He was pressed down by the knees of his ruffianly assailants, flat into the road; and a voice addressed him, in hurried but distinct tones—

"''Tis no use to struggle. If you are not immediately quiet, your brains will be dashed out directly. Only be easy, and you will not have a hair of you head hurt; but if you attempt to make a noise, there is a pistol always loaded and cocked within a few inches of your head—see!' and the bandage was slipped from his eyes for a moment, that they might look at a large horse-pistol in close contiguity with his forehead.

"Short and fearful as was the glance which the waggoner gave at the formidable weapon, he did not fail to observe that the hand holding the pistol was the fair white hand of a gentleman, and that there was a sparkling ring on his finger. After what he had seen and heard, the waggoner perceived the folly of attempting to disturb or resist his captors. Perfectly passive, he was elevated on the back of one of the men, who carried him about twenty yards backwards and forwards, and then round-abouts, evidently to mislead him as to the direction in which they were about to take him He was then placed in a vehicle, whether post-chaise or a carriage he could not tell; some one entered with him, the door was shut, and a voice called out to the driver,

"'Ready!—drive on!' and away they went, rapidly.

"The agony occasioned by the gag in his mouth, the aching of the teeth, and straining of the jaws, became soon intolerable; and, quite careless of consequences, he groaned and gasped piteously, and strove to articulate. The choking sounds he uttered, seemed to alarm one of the persons sitting beside him; for the gag was presently removed, and he was asked, in a kind tone, whether the gag hurt him. The poor fellow's jaws fell together the instant the gag was removed, and for some time he could not separate them so as to utter a single syllable. He seemed pitied by the persons beside him; for he was told that if he would but be silent, the gag should not be applied again; but that the moment he attempted to make any disturbance, it would be replaced, even if it tortured him to death. He was told further, that wherever he might be taken, it would be useless to call for assistance; for he would be taken to a place were no living being would be near him, but those who had him in their custody. All this was said in a mild expostulating tone and manner, though with evident attempts to disguise the voice.

"Putting all things together, hasty as was his attempt to reason upon his situation, the waggoner's terror began to give place to sheer amazement. He could not conjecture what could be the motive of those who seized him.

He could scarcely think plunder their object, till he suddenly adverted to his waggon, fully laden,—ah! the thing was feafully probable! How did he know but it contained, unknown to himself, yet known to those who had seized him, articles of very great value—money or plate? Horrid thought! was he conveyed by highwaymen to their secret place of rendezvous, there to despatched, that he might tell no tales?

"He was trembling with terror occasioned by these surmises when the vehicle stopped; the cords which bound his legs were untied; and he was told to step out. With the shivering reluctance of a sheep being urged into the slaughter-house, the waggoner obeyed screaming.

"'Mercy, mercy, mercy, gentlemen!' and he dropped upon his knees.

"He was suddenly plucked up, however.

"'Silence, sir!' whispered the voice of one who firmly grasped his right arm. 'Remember!'

And the waggoner felt the muzzle of a pistol touching his ear.

"His limbs could scarcely support him; so he was rather dragged and pushed than anything else, along a paved place. He heard the sound of a wooden gate being unbarred; and presently the scent of cattle and stables that met his nostrils, led him to conclude that he was in a farm-yard. He was stopped a moment by his conductors, and one of them whispered, in low, earnest tones—

"'Now, step very lightly, hold your tongue, and make haste; or I, who shall follow close behind, with a loaded pistol almost touching the back of your head, will, without hesitation, fire at you. All this mystery and fright will be over in half-an-hour. Now, sir.'

"'O I will obey, sirs, I will,' quivered the captive, and went whither he was urged. He ascended some narrow steps, creaking and shaking under him. Then he was led through a passage and a door into a room with a fire heard crackling in the grate. Then he was conducted out again into another passage by a different door, and down a long flight of stone steps; these brought him to another passage, at the end of which another door was unlocked, unbarred, opened —and he felt himself once more in the open air. He had scarcely walked a few steps, however, before he was conducted through another door, which, unlike any of those through which he had previously passed, was carefully closed and locked after them. He was then turned round till he was quite giddy, in which state he was snatched up in some one's arms, carried a few steps, and set down in a very close warm room. He heard another door closed on them, and several

voices speaking in low whispers. A chair was placed behind him, and he was told to sit down in it.

"'You are now in the presence,' said a voice, in a low determined tone, 'of those who can murder you, and bury you, so that none shall ever find you, or hear of you again. We can despatch you this instant; our hands are filled with weapons, and our hearts have no fear. We shall do no harm to you, however, unless you are frolish and obstinate enough to refuse what we shall require of you, which will be easy and reasonable. Quick, decide!' continued the voice, with sudden and startling sternness. "Will you seize a chance for life?'

"For some seconds the waggoner was too overpowered with agitation to speak; he moved his hands as far as he was able, his hands being tied, imploringly.

"'Tell un, masters, tell un what I am to do,' he groaned.

"There was a pause, and then a hurried whispering.'

"'First, swear by the great Dispenser of all goodness that made and can destroy you, that if you should leave this place alive, you will never in any way make known what has been, and shall yet be done to you, or attempt to find us out, or try to come again to this place to which you may hereafter fancy yourself to have been taken. Swear, I say.'

"The waggoner paused.

"'Come, you hold life cheap,' whispered a voice—and he heard the sound of a pistol cocking.

"'I swear—I swear—I swear!' he faltered.

"'On your knees, kissing the Bible.'

"The waggoner dropped on his knees, and kissed a book which was held to his lips.

"'Again,' resumed the terrible speaker, 'say you wish your soul may perish for ever, if you break your oath.'

"'I do,' gasped the waggoner. 'And now, dear gentlemen, what am I to do? What do you want? I will do all I can.'

"There was a pause. The waggoner sobbed, and the tears were seen trickling down from under the bandage which was over his eyes.

"'What ails you?' inquired some one, sternly.

"'I am thinking of my poor old mother —and that my employers will call me a thief and a villain,' he replied, crying bitterly.

"'You may soon be free, perhaps, if you will do your duty.'

"'And what is that?' he inquired, faintly. He received no answer.

"'Remove the bandage from his eyes,' said

an authoritative voice; and the bandage was instantly taken off

He found himself in a small room, lit by one candle, and the walls covered with what appeared sheets and blankets hung on them, as if to prevent the chamber being recognised. The first fearful object, however, that met his eyes was a pistol held closely before him, and by the very same white hand, with the ring on, that he had noticed when he was first seized. The person who thus menaced him was sitting closely fronting him on a table, wore a white coat buttoned up to the chin, and a white nightcap was drawn over his face down to his mouth, as when a man is hanged, evidently to conceal his features. Then there were three others in the room, all effectually, and indeed similarly disguised.

"'What is your name?' inquired the person who held the pistol in his hand.

"'Why, Forster,' replied the waggoner, promptly.

"'Forster,' echoed several voices, in tones of consternation.

"'Is it really so?' inquired the person opposite to him, agitatedly, and lowering the pistol he held, till it touched the waggoner's bosom—'is it so, in the presence of God, on your oath?'

"'It is!' replied the waggoner, firmly; 'the only name I was ever called by,—Richard Forster.'

"'I will send you perjured into hell, if you speak false—is it Forster?' was again demanded.

"'Yes—yes—yes!' repeated the waggoner, solemnly, looking upwards.

"The pistol was removed; the person who held it suddenly struck down the candle from the table, and the room was left in darkness.

"'Pho!' exclaimed the voice that had all along been speaking, in a low fierce tone; 'we are wrong after all.'

"There was a pause, and a hurried consultation in whispers for a second or two.

"'What shall we do with him?' the affrighted waggoner heard asked, but could not catch the reply.

"'My poor fellow,' said the voice now familiar to him, 'we have unfortunately mistaken our man. We have frightened you nearly out of your senses, and all in mistake. You are not the man we want—you cannot do what we wish. Here is a trifle by way of making you some amends,'—and several pieces, apparently guineas, were put into his hand. 'And if you will tell us the name of the place where you live, you shall have twenty pounds before the new year. We shall not hurt a hair of your head, but shall put the bandage round your eyes once more, and lead you safely where we found you.

Don't be afraid; only remember—remember your oath.'

"'What!' inquired the waggoner, 'are you going to release me?'

"'Yes, directly.'

"The waggoner fell on the floor in a swoon. When he recovered possession of his senses, he found himself seated in a vehicle driving on rapidly, situated exactly as he was before. The first words he heard were—

"'You dropped four guineas out of your hand in the chapel. We have put them in your pocket, where you will find them when we leave you.'

"This was spoken in a very kindly manner; and much more was said by the same speaker, expressive of sorrow for having so needlessly frightened him, and assuring him that he had been mistaken for some one else.

"He was told again that he would receive twenty pounds before New Year's Day, but that, if ever he opened his lips to any one breathing about what had happened to him, or gave information about it to magistrates, or did anything to lead to inquiry, he would, as surely as he was now about to be released, be shot within twelve hours of his doing so, wherever he might be, in whatever part of England, now manysoever guards and constables he might get about him.

"'We have got a man,' continued the voice, 'who will, unknown to you, watch you for months after this, to see if you break your oath. You will never find him out, and yet he will be always near you to do our wish. He is a kind of devil, and he is charged to kill you, if you dare do contrary to what you have sworn. Remember all this, Richard Forster, and be but honest and true, and it shall be well with you for the rest of your life.'

"After an hour's driving, the vehicle stopped. The waggoner was again addressed.

"'You are now within about fifty yards of the place from which we took you. We shall set you on the hedge side, with this bandage still on your eyes, but shall remove the cords from your arms, and so leave you. You must neither stir, nor remove the bandage from your eyes for an hour, as near as you can guess. If you do, you will be shot, for we shall leave a man sentinel over you for an hour.'

"The bewildered waggoner was then led out of the vehicle, his arms were unbound, and he was placed by the hedge side, as he had been told.'

"'Now, remember,' said the voice, and the hands of the speaker shook those of the waggoner. 'Break your oath, and the grave will yawn for you the next moment. Farewell!'

"The waggoner heard the sound of retreating footsteps—then the door of a vehicle closing, and it drove fast away, but in an opposite direction from what he had expected.

"The waggoner sat still as a mouse, scarce daring even to breathe, much less shift his posture, lest it should be construed into an intention of rising before his time. It might be all a farce about the man left to watch him; but what if it were not!

"Overcome with fear, fatigue, cold, he fell fast asleep. He was woke up by some one suddenly pulling off the bandage from his eyes, and shouting in his ears, at the same time shaking him violently by the shoulder.

"'Why, Dick—Dick—Dick! where hast thou been, Dick Forster—hey, hem—stare at me. I will do thee no hurt, heaven knows; but where hast thou been? why, and how here?' said Bill Fowler, one of the two whom Foster had left drinking at the Huntsman Inn, and who now, after a long and terrified search stood scrutinizing his companion's features by the help of a lantern.

"The waggon had arrived safe, though unattended, at its nearest point of destination, followed shortly by the arrival of the two waggoners who had been left at Shrewsbury—and then the startling question was—

"'Where is Dick Forster?'

"Unable to answer the question, they, with several others, instantly set out in search of the missing waggoner.

"'Why, man, where have you been?—what have you been doing?—what has come to you—who has put this bandage before your eyes?—how long have you been here?' were questions asked in a breath, without time given for answers, even if Forster had been able or so disposed.

"He stared stupidly at the man who addressed him, and muttered some such incoherent words as—

"'Don't—don't shoot me, kind sir, for heaven's sake—it was not I that took off the bandage. For mercy's sake don't murder me—I'll never tell!'

"His companion recoiled from him as he uttered these affrighted exclamations, and stared at him with unspeakable concern and wonder.

"'Why, Dick,—Dick!' said he, again shaking him by the shoulder, 'don't 'ee know un?—don't 'ee know where thou art? where the waggon is? Agad! art mad, or drunk, or devil-struck?'

"Dick made no answer, but stretched out his arms and legs, and groaned, as through exhaustion.

"His companion began to get alarmed, and his own apprehensions were aggravated on seeing, owing to a sudden change in Dick's posture, that there rolled out of his pocket several guineas.

"'Why, Dick Forster! why—why—why,' he stammered, turning pale, and holding his lantern down towards the golden coins.—'Who gave thee these? Where didst thou get them? Hast thou been out a—a—a—robbing? or—hast—tell me, Dick Forster, or I'll go and fetch some one that shall make thee!' and he shook him violently.

"Dick began to come a little to his senses on being so roughly handled, and was answering some questions rather angrily put to him, when there was heard a faint rustling by the other side of the hedge.

"Dick suddenly clasped his arms around his companion, his eyes glared on him with wildness, and he gasped—

"'Save me!—save—save me! he'll shoot me—he'll murder me.'

"His companion stared at him first with an alarmed and then a distrustful air, folded his arms on his breast, and with a resolute air, said to him,—

"'Now, Dick, may I die here this blessed Christmas morning, if I do not think thou hast done ill since we met.'

"He paused with agitation.

"'Speak, man!' he resumed, 'this money—where didst get it? for what? for whom? Is all this thy frighted manner but a-deceiving of me? Come, come, Dick! thou shalt tell thy tale to a magistrate, or my name is not Bill Fowler.'

"Dick slowly lifted himself up, and clasped his companion's hand, whispering faintly, 'Bill Fowler, let us but leave this lonely place—help me to the high road—then to some house or other, and I will tell thee all—it will make thy hair stand like a hedgehog's.'

"Well, come now — that is reasonable enough—let us away, and as for any one shooting thee, I would not run from old Nick himself, with a pistol in each hand. Come—I long to hear thy story, for I much dread me it will be a black one. But come.'

"At that instant a pistol was discharged from the other side of the hedge, and the bullet whizzed close past the astounded waggoners.

"Fowler fell down with the suddenness of the shock, but found his feet again in a trice, and made desperate but fruitless efforts to get through the high and thick hedge. All the while he heard the sounds of one running as it were for his life across the frozen furrows of a plowed field; and though tantalised and irritated almost to frenzy, he was obliged at length to give up the pursuit, and hastened his companion to the high road.

" Half dragging and half carrying him, he succeeded in bringing Forster to a small farm-house, about a quarter of a mile down the road, where they were both of them known. Though it was five o'clock, and a Christmas morning, they found the good people stirring. Each of them got a little ale, the good effects of which were soon visible on Forster, for he began to look about him with some composure.

" ' Where is the waggon gone ?' was the first sensible question he asked.

" ' 'Tis now standing at Job Winton's,' was the reply.

" ' And where is Thomas ?'

" ' He is, I warrant him, out searching for thee now.'

" ' And what is the hour ?'

" ' A trifle past five. And now, Dick,' said his companion, no longer able to conceal his impatience, ' tell us all that hath happened to thee.'

" ' No,' replied Dick, firmly, ' I will not tell thee a word now, and here ; but take me before a magistrate, and I will tell thee and him all. I have sworn before heaven, it is true, that I would not tell a word, and may be shot for doing so ; but I care not—I will ease my soul, and put my life into heaven's hands. O Will, Will ! when we parted last evening at the Huntsman Inn, how small thought had I of what would befall me.'

" Bill made no answer, but grew visibly paler, and wiped the perspiration from his forehead ; he rose from his seat, and stepped to and fro across the small room in which they were sitting, with great agitation in his manner.

" ' Well, Dick,' he muttered, ' I don't know what the ending of all this will be ; but I fear for thee ! I dread me the devil hath been at thee ! 'Tis said he walks these parts on Christmas morn.'

" He presently resumed his seat, and tried again to extract his companion's secret from him ; but in vain. Dick was inflexible : he took the four guineas out of his pocket, and gave them into Bill's hand saying—

" ' I don't value this gold. It may be gotten ill by those who gave it me. Do thou keep it, and see what the magistrate will say about it ; for to one we will go this day, or my name is not Richard Forster.'

" By two o'clock that afternoon the two waggoners found their way to the house of a country magistrate, to whom Dick gave a full account of what had befallen him. His words were taken down ; but there was such an air of exaggeration—of blank improbability about the whole, that it was evident the magistrate did not attach overmuch

credit to it. What could he do in the matter ?—The waggoner swore that, if his life depended on it, he could not tell by which of the four cross-roads he had gone or come ; he had never seen the faces of those who had so mysteriously seized him, and could not describe the voices of any one that spoke to him.

" ' So they were surprised to hear that your name was Forster, eh ?'

" ' Yes, your worship.'

" ' They said you were mistaken for some one else ?'

" ' Yes, your worship.'

" ' Now, do you know any one among your associates that has a name any thing like your own ?' inquired the magistrate, as if a sudden thought had struck him.

" ' Think a little, my man,' he continued, seeing the waggoner very thoughtful, and rubbing his forehead with a puzzled air.

" ' No, no,' replied the waggoner, at length, ' I don't know any one of my name, nor any one like it.'

" ' O, please your worship,' said the other, ' I hope your worship's honour will forgive me—but *my* name is Fowler, but that, again, as your worship knows, is not Forster.'

" ' So I should suppose,' drawled the magistrate with a smile, looking at his watch, and then taking down the name.

" ' How do you spell it, my man ?'

" Fowler repeated the letters of his name separately.

" ' And are you a waggoner, like your unfortunate friend here ?'

" ' Yes, your worship—and go the same road, and serve the same master.'

" ' You neither of you know any one that is likely to have ill blood against you ?'

" ' O, love your worship—no, your worship !' replied both in a breath.

" I hope you are an honest, sober fellow, my friend,' inquired the magistrate of Fowler, amused by his *naivete* and eagerness.

" Fowler hung down his head and blushed,

" ' Why, please your worship, as for the matter of honesty, I am as honest (as one might reverently say) as your worship yourself ; but I own—I humbly say—" he continued, with an embarrassed air.

" ' Ha, ha !' exclaimed the magistrate, quite tickled ; ' you like your glass, eh ? a friendly glass ?'

" ' Not exactly, your worship ; give me a plain jug ; a plain jug, with ale in it.'

" His worship and his clerk laughed heartily.

" ' And, pray, who are your father and mother ? Where do they live ?'

" ' Both dead, your worship, long ago.'

" ' Richard Forster,' said the magistrate, ' a word or two more with you about this strange story of yours. Do you think you could recognise the room in which you were, or the yard, doors, and passages through which you were led, if you were to be taken to them again ?'

" 'No, your worship, on the oath of a true man. Your worship will recollect that I was not only blindfolded, but turned round and round like a cockchafer ; besides being all the while nearly dead with fright.'

" 'Why, can't you say whether you went towards the north, south, east, or west ?'

" 'No, your worship !'

" 'Did you hear any bleating of sheep—any snorting or neighing of horses—any lowing of cows, when you passed through what you took to be a farm-yard ?'

" 'No, your worship—nothing like it.'

" 'Did it seem a large or a small house—or what sort of place ?'

" 'Please your worship, I know about as much of it as a dead man knows of the shape of his grave !'

" 'Humph !' exclaimed the magistrate. completely nonplussed, rubbing his hand over his forehead.

" 'Oh, please your worship !' said Dick, suddenly, 'I forgot one thing. I saw the hand of one man twice ; first when he seized me by my waggon, and then when he held the pistol to my breast in the little room—and marked especially that it was fair and white, like a gentleman's, and had a shining ring upon one finger.'

" 'Ay !—ay !—ay !—are you sure of that ?' inquired the magistrate, with much interest ; 'a gentleman's hand, with a bright ring on ? One might make something of that !'

" He paused.

" 'And yet—pho ! What is such a trifle as that, to lead to discovery ? There must be something strange behind all this, I am confident !'

" The simple fact was, that the magistrate was completely at a loss. What, indeed, could be done, in the matter ? What great harm had been done, after all ? To be sure, there were some symptoms of threatened outrage on another of his Majesty's subjects, when he could be found ; but, as for the present complaint, he had been clearly much more frightened than hurt. Here he was, sound and whole, richer by four guineas than he was before, unable to give a spark of available information about his seizure, capture, or journey.

" What could be done in the affair ? The magistrate knew not.

" However, he decided on sending a memorial of the whole affair to the Secretary of State's office, and so throwing the business on the shoulder's of Government.

" He directed the waggoner, in the meanwhile, to return to his ordinary work, and granted him the services of two constables, to ride all the way inside his waggon to London, and back again, with fire-arms, which they were authorised in using without hesitation, in case of emergency.

" His worship also directed Forster to keep the four guineas, and gave Bill Fowler half-a-crown, to enable him to get a plain jug of good ale.

" And so the affair ended, as far as the waggoner was concerned.

" The result of the application to the Secretary of State, was an order to advertise the affair over the whole county, offering a reward, on the part of the Government, of a hundred and eighty pounds for the discovery of the perpetrator of so extraordinary an outrage : which was done, but in vain. Not a tittle, not a glimpse of evidence was obtained, by which to trace or fasten the occurrence anywhere ; and after a fortnight, or so, the affair was forgotten by the public, in spite of the stimulating paragraphs that, as in our day, ran the round of the papers, *vires acquirentes eundo.*

" The waggoner, Richard Forster himself, resumed his ordinary business without interruption, and gradually dropped his fear, treating the whole affair, when it was mentioned to him, rather as a joke than otherwise.

" One word, in passing, concerning the magistrate. The first thing he did, after dismissing the waggoner, as has been described, and entering his library, was to take off his gloves, hastily pluck off a ring from his little finger and fling it into the fire grate. That is the full particulars of the story as it was narrated to me many years ago by Dick Forster himself," said Hackett. " Dick was a distant relative of mine, and many a time and oft he used to take me, when a lad, in his waggon. He's dead now, poor chap, simple-hearted honest creature as he was. He lived to see a good many Christmases after that, but he was eventually called away, and no longer drives a waggon in this world at any rate."

" Then you suppose that the magistrate had some hand in the business ?"

" That's more than either you or I can tell," said Hackett ; " I never like to come to any hasty conclusion upon such slender evidence. The mystery was never cleared up, and I know that Dick Forster himself had always a great objection to recur to the subject. Why, I know not, any more than I should suppose that the recollection of that Christmas was not a pleasing one, seeing that he had suffered considerably from the fright ; for as I told you before, he was a simple-hearted creature, and mystery of any sort would be sure to cause him great mental excitement. A plain, straight-forward danger he would not mind meeting, but anything that was wrapt in gloom and mystery he shrank from with horror."

"Well, gentlemen," said the landlord of the Bell, "you don't get on. There's more punch brewed, and only waits to be drunk."

"We must take care that we keep within the rules of sobriety ourselves," said a sanctified individual in the corner of the parlour.

"Christmas eve, gentlemen," said the landlord, "think of that. It's a poor heart that never rejoices."

CHAPTER LXX.

THE CLERK'S STORY.

"The story you have been relating, sir," said a respectable looking middle aged man, who formed one of the company assembled in the parlour of the Bell, "puts me in mind of a circumstance which occurred when I was a banker's clerk at Aylesbury."

"Indeed," said Hackett; "I thought my tale of the waggoner had no parallel. I never heard of a similar one, or indeed anything like it."

"Neither has it, I should say, sir," said the first speaker, whose name, by the way, was Bridgeman; "neither has it. The only resemblance is in the ring."

"Well, narrate it—tell it us, Mr. Bridgeman," said several voices; "don't keep the audience waiting—tell it us."

"I don't know that there's much in it that will amuse you," said the party addressed. "The only interest it may possess is from the fact that it is true, and as, with our friend here, the facts came under my own personal observation.

"Very many years ago, I was clerk in the Aylesbury Bank, Challis and Co., bankers. The old gentleman is since dead, and the bank is now carried on in another name. Well, you must know, that one Christmas eve the governor, as we used to call him, was being driven in his own carriage along the road leading to Wimbledon. Mr. Challis had come to London to spend the Christmas with his relations, and was proceeding to his brother's house, at Wimbledon, when the incident I am about to relate occurred. I was with him in the carriage at the time, for I was to sleep at his brother's, and in the morning take the coach to Aylesbury, to attend to the business transactions of the house.

"It was a bright moonlight night, with a clear bracing air. The road we were going was a lonely one, but we were in excellent spirits, and never dreamt of robbers or footpads, who had frequently committed depredations and robberies in that neighbourhood.

Suddenly the carriage was brought to a stand still, and I was about to thrust my head out of the window which I had opened, when to my infinite astonishment, the barrel of a pistol was suddenly presented at the window, and I beheld a masked figure on horseback. I drew back, and exclaimed in a voice of surprise—

"'Highwaymen, sir.'

"Mr. Challis leant forward, and regarded with looks of horror the apparition at his carriage window.

"'Your money! Quick!' said the highwayman. 'Come, time presses.'

"From what we could see of the figure, we presumed him to be a young man, from his evidently slight, although tall figure.

"'Do you hear? Are you asleep, deaf, or what?' said the masked figure.

"'Young man,' said Mr. Challis, severely. 'Hast thou no other means of obtaining the necessaries of life but by having recourse to robbery, which is sure to end in an ignominious death? Repent, and turn from your present calling. You do not appear to be a ruffian.'

"'Make haste,' said the highwayman—'make haste. I am in no mood to listen to homilies. Money I must and, by God, will have to-night, or else—but you know the consequence of your refusal.'

"The pistol was presented at Mr. Challis's head significantly.

"'You'll regret this,' said Mr. Challis, as he felt for his pocket-book in the breast pocket of his coat.

"As he did so, both he and I observed a diamond ring on the second finger of the highwayman's hand. There was also the mark of a large uncured wound on the ball of the thumb of the right hand, in which he held the pistol. We also noticed that the hand trembled. For a moment I thought of offering resistance, but the governor, who from my sudden movement, anticipating my intention restrained me.

"'No, Bridgeman—no violence, if you please. It would be worse than useless.'

"He then proceeded to count out several notes, and placed them in a bag of sovereigns which he carried in one of his other pockets.

"'The pocket-book,' exclaimed the highwayman, 'and that will save all trouble.'

"'I have given you all its contents,' said Mr. Challis, 'or at least any that can possibly be of any service to you. The rest it contains are only private memorandums.'

"He then handed the leather bag to the robber, who thrust his hand in the window of the carriage to secure it. We both observed that it was a small white hand, almost as delicate as a woman's. From his bearing and general appearance we judged him to have been originally a gentleman—in all

probability a broken down one, who had most likely lost his substance at the gaming table, and sought to repair his fortune on the road. He had no sooner received the bag containing the notes and money, than he galloped off without another word.

"Mr. Challis then thrust his head out, and told the coachman to drive on, and inquired the reason of his sudden stoppage, seeing that there was only one man who had managed to rob three? The coachman, however, informed us that there had been two, and that while one went to the window of the carriage, his companion kept guard over the driver of the vehicle.

"The vehicle then once more proceeded on its journey.

"'Now that young man, if I am not much mistaken, belongs to a respectable family,'

No. 47.

said Mr. Challis. 'His manner was evidently that of a novice, and his appearance was really almost aristocratic. I wonder who and what he is?'

"I should have mentioned," said the narrator, "that when Mr. Challis put his hand forward to give the bag of notes and money, that an involuntary exclamation escaped from the lips of the highwayman. What it meant, we could not understand, but we judged that the governor's features were not unknown to him.

"I agreed with my employer, that the highwayman was an amateur, and that the probability was, that this affair was his first attempt.

"When we arrived at Wimbledon, of course, all that had occurred on the road formed the chief topic of conversation for that night, and Mr. Challis said that he had been robbed of nearly a hundred and fifty pounds.

"Of course he had taken the number of the notes, in fact, we never had any pass through our hands without doing so. The first thing the governor did was to have handbills printed, offering a reward to anyone who would give information as to who it was who had committed the robbery. Bills were also issued containing the list of stolen notes, which were given to all the London bankers; and the London police officers were also put into full possession of all the particulars concerning the robbery.

"Whether the governor had any suspicion as to who it was, is more than I can tell you; if he had, he kept it to himself, but of course he charged me to keep a sharp look out for any of the notes, and I need not tell you that I did not fail to do as he had requested. However, time went on, but no notes came. Whether they were in circulation or not, we could not tell; but one fact was quite certain, they had none of them been either paid in to the Bank of England, or any of the London or country bankers.

"I should suppose it must have been between two or three years after this, that I attended the annual ball at our assembly rooms, at Aylesbury. I had taken a young lady there, my present wife, in fact, for you know we all of us do these foolish things sometimes before marriage," said the speaker, with a laugh, in which his companions all joined. "Well, we had a merry time of it—there was a vast assemblage of all the elite of the town and the neighbouring districts. From the grand room there were two smaller ones, used as refreshment rooms, and while I was talking with my partner, whom I had handed to a seat, a voice struck upon my ears, the tones of which appeared to be familiar to me.

"Where I had heard the voice before, I was totally at a loss to understand. My eye glanced in the direction from whence it had proceeded, looking through the opening into the refreshment room, I was struck with the reflection of a figure in one of the large looking glasses, which were in the sides of the refreshment room.

"The face of the figure I could not see, only part of his back and one of his hands, distinctly reflected in the glass.

"The ring was on the second finger of his right hand, and the mark on the ball of the thumb, precisely the same as when I had seen it on the occasion of his stopping the carriage.

"Well, gentlemen, I assure you that I was so thunderstruck at this apparition, or rather the reflection of an apparition, that I hardly knew what I was about. I posi-

tively had not the courage to move from the spot where I was seated.

"An exclamation of surprise escaped me when I first caught sight of the figure in the glass, and upon second consideration, I rose and proceeded into the refreshment room. When I arrived there, the figure, for such I supposed it to be, was proceeding through the door which led into the passage. His back was still towards me, and he was conversing with some other gentleman as he left the room.

"Of course, had I been possessed of sufficient presence of mind, I ought, and no doubt should, have hastened after him; but I know not what power or influence it was that stayed me, but so it was.

"I did not then make up my mind at once, but after a minute or two's reflection, I did hasten out into the passage, and had the satisfaction of observing the man, whose reflection I had seen in the glass, go down the grand staircase accompanied by his friend.

"Even then I could not catch sight of his features, and he left the establishment without my doing so; but I felt convinced in my own mind that the individual who was now making such a hasty retreat, was no other than he who had stopped Mr. Challis on his road to Wimbledon.

"I felt convinced of this, and I felt quite ashamed of my own want of energy in neglecting to follow him earlier, and catch sight of his features.

"When I returned to business, I told Mr. Challis of the circumstance, and he, naturally enough, was much annoyed at my failing to find out who the individual happened to be.

"We made several efforts after this to do so, by inquiring of the people who kept the assembly rooms; but these were futile. I believe myself that the owner of the rooms knew who the person was, but from some cause or other he did not choose to disclose his name."

"And did you never find him out?" said Hackett.

"You shall hear. Years passed over, and the circumstance had become forgotten. None of the stolen notes had found their way into any bank, at any rate, none that we could ever trace.

"Mr. Challis himself had become an old man, and contemplated retiring from the business.

"One afternoon a stranger entered the bank, and upon my inquiring what his business was, he informed me that he had come to pay in some cash and notes to the account of Sir Edgar Bramley.

"He gave me a canvass bag containing fifty pounds in gold, together with a roll of notes, amounting in all to something above a hundred pounds.

"Upon my proceeding to make an entry of them in the book, you may judge of my surprise, when I found that two of these were notes which had been stolen years before from the governor.

"I hesitated, and looked hard at the bearer of the notes, and as he observed my glance of inquiry, I saw him suddenly draw his hand from the counter; but quick as was his movement, I had time enough to perceive that there was a mark upon the ball of the thumb precisely similar to that which I had observed on the highwayman's hand. This time I was determined not to lose sight of him, although I hesitated for a moment, and debated with myself whether I should go into the interior office and tell Mr. Challis of the circumstance.

"I said, addressing the individual who stood in front of the counter—

"'Pray may I inquire where these notes came from, sir?'

"'What do you mean?' said the stranger, haughtily.

"'Simply this, that they are stolen notes,' I answered.

"'Impossible! he said, turning a thought paler. 'Sir Edgar Bramley is not likely to have stolen notes in his possession.'

"'We are all liable to do so, however cautious we may be,' I replied. 'But I will speak to my principal. Will you be kind enough to step this way?'

"'Certainly not,' he said, in a most haughty and imperious manner. 'I will not stay here to be insulted. You had better settle this matter with Sir Edgar Bramley himself.'

"And with these words he opened the swing door which led into the banking-house, and left in dudgeon, before I had either time to detain him, or communicate with the governor.

"Well, you must know, that in the morning of the following day, who should present himself at the bank but Sir Edgar Bramley himself, accompanied by a friend, a Major Smithers.

"'I wish to speak to Mr. Challis,' said Sir Edgar.

"He was shown into the governor's private apartment, and as I was about to retire, Mr. Challis bid me stay; but turning towards Sir Edgar, he said—

"'That is, unless your business is of a private nature?'

"'Oh, dear no, not at all; I only wish to know what balance you have in hand of mine?'

"Mr. Challis immediately turned to his books and said, as he reckoned it carefully up—

"'Seven thousand, four hundred and thirty pounds.'

"'Good,' said Sir Edgar. 'Then, Mr. Challis, I will withdraw the same, if you please.'

"'To-day, Sir Edgar!' exclaimed Mr. Challis, in some astonishment.

"'Yes, this very hour.'

"I was ordered to go into the banking department and fetch the amount; in a minute or so I returned with the same, and the money was counted out by Mr. Challis.

"'I do not want Aylesbury notes,' said Sir Edgar, tossing a roll contemptuously back.

"'What would you like, then?' said Mr. Challis; 'gold!'

"'No, Bank of England notes will do.'

"I was desired to fetch these, to make up the required sum, which was handed to Sir Edgar.

"When this had been done, Major Smithers, with even a more haughty manner than Sir Edgar, said—

"'I will thank you to inform me what you have to my credit.'

"Mr. Challis again looked at his books, and informed the major that the balance in his favour was something over four thousand pounds.

"'Then I shall also withdraw my balance,' said the major.

"'As you please,' said Mr. Challis, who, nevertheless was perfectly astonished at the proceeding altogether.

"The amount was placed before him, and he, too, insisted upon having Bank of England notes. Of course, the natural supposition was, that they were under the impression that our bank was not in a state of solvency. Some such thought as this must have crossed the mind of Mr. Challis, for he said with a faint smile—

"'I suppose you have lost confidence in me, gentlemen?'

"The baronet stared at his companion, and then looked hard at Mr. Challis.

"'Not at all, sir,' said Major Smithers.

"'Well, then, whence this hasty withdrawal of your principal?' inquired the banker.

"'Simply this, sir, that we are not, and never have been disposed to submit tamely to insults.'

"'Insults!' exclaimed Mr. Challis, in surprise; 'I should hope, after the years I have had the honour of being connected with both of you gentlemen, that I have not given either of you cause to complain of any want of courtesy; but as to insults, that would be most unwarrantable, and should hope, also, an impossibility. There must be some misunderstanding.'

"'Not at all so,' answered the baronet.

'A friend of Major Smithers was paying me a visit, and as he was passing this way, I begged of him to pay in some cash and notes yesterday, and your clerk thought proper to insult him.'

"'Most grossly insulted him,' said the major; 'so much so, that nothing would induce me to continue banking at your establishment.'

"I was in the room when this observation was made, and the governor turned an inquiring glance towards me.

"'You hear what the gentleman says?' he observed.

"'I am quite certain I did not offer any insult to the gentleman who came with the cash and notes from Sir Edgar Bramley,' I answered, indignantly. 'Of that I am quite certain. As I told you, sir, there were two of the notes paid into the bank which were stolen ones.'

"'Stolen!' exclaimed Sir Edgar. 'I will not stay here to listen to a repetition of these insults!'

"And without another word, both he and the major bounced out of the office, and left the bank in a state of rage and anger such as I had seldom observed before.

"'Strange!' said Mr. Challis, when they were gone. 'There must be something more than the mere fact of your saying the notes were stolen ones, that has offended the irate Sir Edgar. And yet he is a highly respectable man—in fact, has always been considered to be a gentleman of the most unsullied and spotless character.'

"Well, to cut the matter short, gentlemen," said the narrator of the tale, "it turned out in after years—at least we had every reason to believe—that the highwayman who stopped the governor was no other than Sir Edgar's own son."

A murmur of surprise escaped from the assembled guests in the parlour of the Bell at this declaration, while Hackett and his companion exchanged significant glances. After an hour or two's more hilarity, Hackett and Galdie took their departure.

CHAPTER LXXI.

THE COLONEL AND MR. SHARPTHORNE.

AGREEABLE to his promise, Colonel Jack waited upon the astute Sharpthorne, not, however, with any intention of placing in his hands the papers relating to the Reichbeck property. This was the bait which our hero thought it advisable to hold out, to induce the lawyer to aid him in procuring the liberation of Sir Reginald.

Immediately upon the colonel's appearance in the outer office, in the Temple, he was ushered into the presence of Sharpthorne, who rose and greeted him with what he intended to be a patronising and supercilious smile—the latter it certainly was.

"I have withdrawn the affidavit," said Sharpthorne, handing our hero a seat. "And now, my friend, let us understand each other. You see," and here he began to knead his hands as of yore—,'you see. I cannot serve both you and Sir Richard. That, my dear sir, is impossible."

"So I should suppose," answered our hero. "But you have served Sir Richard long enough."

"Quite long enough, believe me—too long, in fact. And—ah—let me see—you are an especial friend of Sir Reginald's, I believe?"

"Yes, I have known him for very many years."

"Precisely. And in the event of his release—ahem! I am merely throwing this out as a suggestion—in the event of his release, that is, supposing I do all in my power to serve him, I suppose, now, there would be some consideration, eh?"

"What do you mean?" inquired his visitor.

"Why, simply this. Of course I am talking to you like a man of business, and you know in this world that it is not usual for either a man of business, or indeed anyone else, to work without being paid."

"No one wishes you to do so," said the colonel.

"No, my dear sir, I do not say you do. But you see, I should like to know, in the event of my consenting to overturn Sir Richard—for we shall overturn him, without a doubt, both you and I together—I say, in the event of our overturning him, I suppose Sir Reginald would, in all probability, retain me as the family lawyer; else otherwise I should be losing—it is of no use endeavouring to mince matters—I should be losing a good customer, and like the dog in the fable, should be snapping at the shadow and losing the substance."

"I cannot answer for what Sir Reginald will do," was Colonel Jack's reply.

"No, you may perhaps not be able to answer, but you might tell me what you think is likely—what you would advise, in fact?"

"Oh, I should certainly advise him to make you some recompense," said our hero; "and the probability is that he would retain you as his legal adviser. This is my opinion, but I cannot answer for it."

"You have still the Reichbeck papers in your possession, I suppose," said Mr. Sharpthorne.

"Yes, and am not likely to part with them."

"Ah! indeed, I thought that you had intended to place them in my hands."

"We will talk about this hereafter; for the present, it is sufficient for my purpose that Sir Reginald Fleetwood is safely restored to his liberty."

"I have withdrawn the objectionable affidavit, but you are aware, my dear sir, that you have a wily enemy to deal with. Even with your magistrate's order, I am afraid you will find some difficulty in obtaining the liberation of the unfortunate and ill-used Sir Reginald, for Mr. Hardy is a man up to every move, and will not easily give up his prisoner."

"He cannot help himself," answered the colonel.

"It's not unlikely that he will deny having such an individual in his establishment. You don't know what manoeuvres these sort of people are capable of practising. I hope most sincerely that you may succeed in emancipating the unfortunate baronet from his present position."

"If Sir Reginald Fleetwood be still alive," answered our hero, in a menacing manner, "I doubt not, by God's blessing, to obtain his release."

"And then farewell to Sir Richard," said Sharpthorne. "May the next heir of Fleetwood be as good a client as the late baronet. I am speaking already in the past tense, you will perceive," said the lawyer, with a sickly smile.

Colonel Jack then took his departure from the lawyer's office, to see and get the required order to visit the imprisoned baronet.

He had not been gone more than an hour or so when the carriage of Sir Richard Fleetwood drove into the Temple, and the baronet alighted therefrom, and entered Mr. Sharpthorne's office.

Rage and desperation sat upon the countenance of Sir Richard.

The wounds he had received from the fangs of Slott, had healed, but the animal had left his marks on the baronet's hand, as well as one or two small punctures in his throat.

Upon Sir Richard's arriving at the outer office of the lawyer, he did not wait to inquire of the clerks if their principal was at home, but strode majestically into the inner office, without deigning to exchange a word with the underlings.

Mr. Sharpthorne was at home, and more than that, quite alone, ruminating upon the interview he had had with our hero. The lawyer was carefully calculating the chance he might have upon the accession of Sir Reginald to his title and estates, supposing such an event to take place. His reverie was suddenly interrupted by the appearance of his client in his chambers.

"Ah, Sir Richard Fleetwood," said the lawyer, in his most oily accents, "how fares it with you?"

"Fare, indeed! Sharpthorne, I am driven nearly mad. That scoundrel—that viper—that serpent—Colonel Jack, has once more crossed my path. I tremble for the consequences. Already has he sought to release my brother."

"Indeed!" exclaimed the lawyer, with well-acted surprise.

"Yes, he has seen Sir Reginald—was plotting with him, in fact, discussing the means of his escape when I overheard him."

"I judged there was something of the sort, from the fact of receiving instructions from you to prepare that affidavit."

"Which I hope you did not fail to do?" said the baronet, sharply.

"It has been executed according to your instructions," answered Sharpthorne.

"That is well."

"But I regret to say that I have been compelled, upon reconsidering the matter, to withdraw it."

"Never, surely! Upon what grounds?"

"I should lay myself open to a prosecution for perjury."

"S'death, man, what matters that? The affidavit must stand as it is, or all will be lost. This fellow has procured a magistrate's order, which will of a surety be executed, without your statement stands to oppose it."

Sharpthorne shook his head.

"What do you mean?" inquired his client.

"I dare not let it stand," was the reply of Sharpthorne.

"Zounds! you would play me false, you hypocritical lying old sinner. If you dare to refuse me, you know the consequences."

"I dare not let the affidavit stand, and what is more, Sir Richard, I *will* not, either for you or any other man."

"Perdition!" exclaimed the baronet, striking his forehead with his clenched fist. "Everything seems to be going against me. You must serve me in this instance. Come, Sharpthorne, why this sudden quaver of conscience? You executed the affidavit, and wherefore seek to withdraw it? Having once made it, you stand in precisely the same position, as it can always be brought to bear against you."

"Oh, no," said Sharpthorne.

"Why not?"

"Because I have made a counter statement, wherein I declare that the former deed was sworn to under a series of false representations."

"Made by whom?" exclaimed the baronet, turning suddenly pale. "Made by whom?"

"Not by yourself, Sir Richard. I have not in any way compromised you."

"Ah," exclaimed the baronet. "So far, so well. Proceed." '

"I have only deemed it expedient to state that I have been misinformed, which was in reality the case," said Sharpthorne, glancing over his spectacles.

"What is to be done, Sharpthorne ?" said Sir Richard, drawing a chair in front of the fire, and seating himself.

The lawyer shrugged his shoulders, and contemplated the embers in the grate as well as his visitor.

"What is to be done ?" again inquired the baronet, after a pause.

"You see," said Sharpthorne, slowly, "you have so many irons in the fire that the chance is, sooner or later, one or the other of them will be tumbling out and burning your fingers."

"Confound you, what's the use of talking in that strain ?" said the baronet, turning sharp round upon the speaker.

"The thought suggested itself to me, and I have very naturally given expression to it," was the lawyer's answer.

"Umph ! and of a surety it's not a very pleasant thought," answered the baronet. "Again I ask you what is to be done ?"

"You'd like to get Colonel Jack out of the way."

"Like!—and will!"

"How, Sir Richard ?"

"By handing the scoundrel over to justice."

"Do you know where he is to be found ?"

"I don't know where he is supposed to live, but Wild knows his haunts."

"Very likely."

"Well, that is sufficient, I'll give the thief taker a five hundred pound note to lodge the highwayman in Newgate."

"An excellent device, upon my soul—excellent !"

"Nothing could be better," continued the lawyer, rubbing his hands. "Once get him behind the bars, and all will be well. We have then our most active and determined enemy removed.

"Will you see, Wild ?" inquired the colonel.

"Who?—me ?" said Sharpthorne, pretending not to comprehend the question.

"Aye, you. What are you surprised at ?"

"I would rather not."

"Why ?"

"Don't like him," said the lawyer, sententiously.

"What matters that. It won't be for the love you bear him that leads you to seek an interview. I don't like him. What of that ?"

"We have already tried to make a capture of the colonel, if you recollect, and perhaps you may also remember how the affair terminated. If you don't, *I do*," said Sharpthorne, significantly. "No, Sir Richard Fleetwood, "that, too, I must decline. I've had enough of following at the heels of highmen in more than one instance."

"Damn you !" exclaimed his visitor. "You seem disposed to decline everything that is likely to be of service in this emergency."

"I don't like to run into further difficulties."

"Psha !" exclaimed the baronet, indignantly rising from his seat. "You are an old dotard, and, I believe, are getting imbecile."

"Thank you," exclaimed Sharpthorne. "Thank you for the compliment."

The baronet regarded the speaker with a look of rage, and without another word strode from the apartment into the outer office, and from thence to his carriage, which was waiting for him in the broad carriage drive in the Temple.

———

CHAPTER LXXII.

THE VISIT TO THE MADHOUSE.—THE CAPTURE OF COLONEL JACK.

COLONEL JACK knew perfectly well that no time was to be lost in the case of the ill-used Sir Reginald. The probability was that his worthless brother was already driven to desperation, and the colonel trembled when he thought of the probable fate of him, whom he had known since his boyhood.

After his interview with Mr. Sharpthorne, he at once betook himself to Mr. Baintree's office, and had the satisfaction of seeing that gentleman, who was already aware of the fact of the affidavit of Sharpthorne having been withdrawn.

"Now, my dear sir, not an instant is to be lost," said the colonel, after the first usual greetings had been exchanged. "Sir Richard is no doubt on the alert, and unless we strike the iron while it is yet hot, all may be lost. What are to be our next proceedings ?"

"I have an order already in my possession from the presiding magistrate for competent persons to visit the unfortunate gentleman. Now who had we better employ for this purpose ?"

"It must be a medical man."

"Yes, one who is fully competent to judge of the case, but it would be as well to have, at least, two or three besides ourselves."

"Ourselves! Do you think it requisite for me to go ?"

"Assuredly, as it has been granted solely

upon your representations and statement. You have no objection?"

"No. I will go."

"As also will I myself. Now for the doctor. Who shall we take?"

Colonel Jack considered for a moment or so, and suddenly Mr. Carruthers occurred to him, whom the reader will doubtless remember in the opening chapters of our tale, when he was forcibly conveyed by our hero to the house of Sir Richard Fleetwood at Acton. He mentioned the name of this gentleman to Mr. Baintree.

"No one could be better adapted for our purpose. But do you think he will go?"

"I will pay him handsomely for his services," said the colonel.

"Very well; see him immediately, and let me know to day whether he is willing. I think I can furnish you with another party, who is a friend of my father's, and we will go to Wandsworth to-morrow the very first thing."

"Why not to-day?"

"If we can complete our arrangements in time. I don't know what the visiting hours are, but I should be rather afraid that we can hardly be ready to day. But, however, do you see Mr. Carruthers at once."

Colonel Jack lost no time, but immediately started off from the lawyer's office and took his way to Brook Street, Grosvenor Square.

The doctor was at home, and our hero, as briefly as may be, explained to him the particulars of the case.

The doctor hesitated. It was not a task he at all courted, for his practice was so extensive, and the demands upon his time so frequent, that he could hardly be spared.

However, he was naturally of a humane disposition, and was moreover fully cognisant of the numerous and frightful cases there were of innocent and sane persons being immured in private lunatic asylums; and, so mindful of this, and listening to the account given him by our hero, which, to say the truth, was graphic enough, he eventually consented to go, but it could not be, in any case, until the following morning.

No sooner had Colonel Jack obtained this promise, than he hastened back to the chambers of Mr. Baintree, and made that gentleman acquainted with the success of his application to the worthy doctor.

Arrangements were then made for the other medical gentleman to meet the colonel and Squabshot at the office of Mr. Baintree early on the following morning.

They were then to call for Mr. Caruthers in Broad-street, and from thence proceed to Wandsworth.

They did meet there and then, agreeable to their arrangements, the whole party were then conveyed in a carriage to the place of their destination; and as there was not room made for the five of them, and as Mr. Squabshot was desirous of puffing his fragrant weed, he rode with the driver of the vehicle on the box.

It was one of the most remarkable characteristics of this individual, that he made himself acquainted with those whom he might chance to fall in company with for the first time in the space of a few moments. He was very shortly in conversation with the coachman, who was driving the vehicle towards Chelsea, from which place it was the intention of the party to cross over Battersea Bridge.

"You don't happen to know what part of Wandsworth the house is situated in, do you, sir?" said the coachman to Squabshot.

"Can't say I do, my friend; but I know one of our inside passengers does know, because he has been there."

"Mr. Hardy keeps a madhouse there, does he not, sir?"

"He rents a house for the reception of lunatics," said Mr. Squabshot correctively, "and sometimes receives gentlemen who are not damaged in their upper storeys."

"More shame for him," says the coachman; "but I have heard of that afore now."

Battersea Bridge was crossed, and in a short time the coachman was stopped by our hero thrusting his head through the window of the carriage and directing him which way to go, and in the course of another quarter of an hour or so, the carriage drew up before the gate of Mr. Hardy's establishment.

Mr. Baintree alighted, accompanied by Mr. Caruthers.

The same porter answered the gate as had originally opened it to our hero. Upon the two visitors inquiring for the owner of the establishment, there appeared to be some hesitation on the part of the man.

"We bring a magistrate's order to see a patient," said Mr. Caruthers, handing in his card.

"Take that to your master, and tell him that I and my friend here have come to see Mr. Sabine."

The man closed the gate, leaving the two gentlemen on the outside, and, it was supposed, proceeded to the interior of the establishment. They awaited his return patiently enough, but were surprised at the time he was gone.

"Some screw loose," said Squabshot, from the box; "some screw loose, as I am a sinner."

"Looks very much like it," said our hero.

"We must give him a reasonable time," said Mr. Carruthers. "Have patience."

And it was found necessary to have a considerable amount of patience, for it was at least twenty minutes before the porter returned. When he did open the gate he was all smiles and affability.

"Sorry to keep you waiting, gentlemen, but the fact is, Mr. Sabine is in one of his paroxyms, and my master has had a deal of trouble with him. Will you be pleased to walk in?"

Upon this Mr. Baintree, the colonel, Squabshot, Mr. Carruthers and the other medical gentleman passed through the open gate into the broad walk which ran round the front of the house.

As our hero made his appearance, the porter regarded him with a sinister look, but said nothing.

There was, however, a sort of half satirical smile upon his ill favoured features.

"Well thought the colonel, "I think they must be clever if they manage to detain me now, and yet that fellow wears a smile as though he thought I was putting my foot in some trap."

The whole party then proceeded into Mr. Hardy's apartment used for the reception of visitors, doctors, and those who came to see patients.

Mr. Hardy came obsequiously forward, and smiled blandly at the two doctors. He did not condescend to take any notice of our hero, Squabshot, or Mr. Baintree, whose presence he seemed to ignore entirely.

"Mr. Sabine it is whom you want to see?" he said, in his usual hypocritical accents.

"If you please, sir," said Mr. Carruthers.

"You had perhaps better see the medical gentleman of my establishment, before proceeding to the patient's room."

"As you please," observed Mr. Carruthers. "I do not see the necessity of this, but if it is customary, neither myself or my colleague can possibly have the slightest objection."

"You have come to inquire as to the state of the unfortunate gentleman's health, I presume," said Mr. Hardy, with a degree of calmness that perfectly astonished our hero.

"Precisely," answered Mr. Carruthers. "We are strangers to each other, sir, and I may as well tell you at once, that I have come here to fulfil a solemn duty.'

Mr. Hardy bowed, and seemed to tick off the words of the doctor with his head.

"A solemn duty, Mr. Hardy," said Mr. Carruthers. "We are led to believe, upon credible testimony, that the unfortunate gentleman who is incarcerated in these gloomy walls, is in reality perfectly sane."

Mr. Hardy now laughed outright, at which his visitors stared in perfect astonishment, Colonel Jack, especially.

"You must really pardon my laughing," said Mr. Hardy, "for to say the truth, it is, after all, no laughing matter; but the fact is, rumour is such a very liar, that I do verily believe, and my experience bears it out, that there never was a lunatic confined in any asylum, and taken proper care of, but what some one person or the other, thinking himself, no doubt, wiser than his fellow man, has declared the said party to be sane. However, you will be able to judge for yourselves, and give the lie to this false and malicious report."

He glanced at Colonel Jack as he concluded this speech, and our hero had some difficulty in restraining himself from bursting out in a fit of rage, but he thought it best to keep calm.

"If you will permit me, I will call Mr. Craddick, the medical gentleman who has attended upon the inmates of this establishment for some years past."

With this he left the room, and was gone for some time. When he did return, he was accompanied by the same individual in rusty black, whom Colonel Jack had noticed in the garden on the memorable night of his escape.

Mr. Craddick was a fuzzy little gentleman, who proceeded at once to enter into the particulars of the unfortunate's gentleman's case.

The conversation was carried on with what our hero and Squabshot termed technical jargon, for they neither of them understood its purport, further than that Mr. Craddick was endeavouring to prove that the unfortunate Mr. Sabine was mad, north, east, west, and south.

The two doctors listened to him complacently enough. Medical men have a happy knack of doing so, with each other, although perhaps they don't believe a word each other may be saying.

The colloquy ended where it had began, namely, that the visitors would see the patient.

Mr. Hardy and Mr. Craddick opened the door of the room, and intimated that the two visiting doctors were to follow. They did so, as well as the colonel, Squabshot, and Mr. Baintree. As these three last named individuals presented themselves, the owner of the establishment gave a start, and said, he presumed that that they were not all going into the room of Mr. Sabine.

"Indeed, but we are," said Squabshot.

"I am afraid it would be hardly prudent," observed Mr. Hardy, turning towards Mr. Carruthers.

"Mr. Hardy," said the latter, mildly, but firmly, "I hope I come here unprejudiced; but as allegations have been made by a gentleman present, which seriously affects your character, I think it but just to both of you, that he should be present when we visit the unfortunate Mr. Sabine."

"Affect my character!" said Mr. Hardy. "False assertions from one who is a professional robber, is not likely to injure me."

"Insolent scoundrel!" exclaimed Colonel Jack. "Liar!—wretch!—monster as you are—"

"Hold—hold, my dear sir," exclaimed Mr. Carruthers. "We really must not have such language. Let us fulfil our errand, and leave personal quarrels for a future period."

"I was incarcerated in these very walls, and should have been murdered, had I not succeeded in making my escape."

"You will be incarcerated in other walls, in all probability," said Mr. Hardy, tauntingly.

Colonel Jack was about to spring upon the keeper of the madhouse, but was restrained by Mr. Baintree, and the whole party then

took their way up into the unfortunate gentleman's room.

Upon their arrival there, our hero stood perfectly appalled at the appearance of the unfortunate Sir Reginald Fleetwood. He sat in moody silence—his eyeballs seemed starting from their sockets—and there was that expression about the eyes themselves, which betokened madness of the worst form. He was foaming at the mouth, and appeared to be in a state of complete prostration, consequent upon a violent fit.

Colonel Jack had almost a difficulty in recognising him, and at first thought that the party had been led purposely into another patient's room.

Mr. Carruther's and Mr. Findley, the other doctor, who had been brought by Mr. Baintree, approached the patient. As they did so, he started up, and burst forth in a series of violent vituperations.

"Come, now, come," said Mr. Carruthers, soothingly. "We are your friends. Calm yourself. Believe me, we are your friends."

"I have none—none in the whole world," sighed forth the wretched man ; and falling into a chair, he relapsed into a series of half broken sobs, painful to listen to.

Mr. Craddick went softly on tiptoe, and placed his hand on Mr. Carruthers's elbow, and drew him and Mr. Findley from the patient.

"He has been fearfully violent," said the madhouse doctor, "and has only just recovered. At least he has not recovered, but the worst has passed for the present."

"Are these fits of frequent occurrence?" inquired Mr. Findly.

"Sometimes their occurrence is very frequent, and at other times he will remain in a passive and dejected state for weeks perhaps ; but, poor gentleman, his wits are, I am afraid, hopelessly gone."

"I should like to remain with him for half an hour or so," said Mr. Findley, looking hard at the doctor of the lunatic asylum.

The latter started, and said quickly.

"Well, do so if you please—do so, by all means—that is, if you think any good can accrue therefrom, which I much doubt."

"I can hardly judge—in fact we can neither of us judge of his state by a cursory glance. He may be under some influence."

Again Mr. Craddick started, and fidgetted about.

"I do not know what you mean," said Mr. Craddick.

Mr. Carruthers now stepped up to the side of the patient, and laying his hand on his shoulder, endeavoured to get him into conversation ; but the poor gentleman seemed past that—his intellects were evidently wandering—and he gazed about him like a man in a dream.

Mr. Carruthers placed his thumb and forefinger on the upper and lower lids of one of his eyes, and opening them, he carefully examined the pupil of the eye.

He was engaged thus for some time, and was joined by his coadjutor. A consultation took place between the two, and while they were contemplating the patient, a thick froth was suddenly emitted from his mouth, and a pungent odour found its way to the nostrils of the two examining doctors.

They exchanged significant glances.

The froth emitted from the patient's mouth was unlike that which they had observed upon their first entrance—this was yellow, whereas the first was quite white.

Mr. Carruthers pulled out his own handkerchief, and wiped the mouth of the sufferer.

Mr. Hardy then came officiously forward, and attended upon the patient. Colonel Jack also came to the side of the latter, and said, in a low tone—

"Sir Reginald."

A cry escaped the lips of the baronet. He started up in his chair, and looked stedfastly at the speaker, and then said—

"Frank!"

"Ay, it is indeed Frank," answered our hero. "What have they been doing with you since I left? Tell me."

"Eh?—you left?—what? Ah, yes, you were here—let me see— Oh, they have treated me so badly."

"You have no right to ask these questions, sir," said Mr. Craddick.

"I shall please myself about that," answered our hero. "You have been playing some of your d—d tricks with this poor gentleman, and you know it, you grey-headed old scoundrel."

"Hush—hush, sir, be careful," said Mr. Baintree. "You will subject yourself to an action for libel."

"What have they given him?" said the colonel, turning to Mr. Carruthers and his companion. "Something, I know; and I only pray to Heaven that the poor gentleman's not poisoned."

"Sir!" exclaimed Mr. Craddick, endeavouring to put on an indignant and injured look. "What do you mean by making such an assertion?"

"Hush, my dear sir," said Mr. Baintree. "You really must be a little careful, upon my word you must."

Colonel Jack was silent.

Mr. Hardy walked up to where the two doctors stood, and said, quietly enough—

"Well, gentlemen, what is your opinion of Mr. Sabine's state of health?"

The doctors shook their head, and Mr. Carruthers said—

"I do not see any indications of confirmed madness. From what I can judge, the unfortunate gentleman seems to be under some influence. The eyes are like those of a man suffering from apoplexy."

Then, turning round upon Mr. Hardy, he said, sharply—

"Has he been drugged?"

The question, and the manner in which it was put, coming so unexpected, made Mr. Hardy fairly start back several paces ; for a moment or so he was quite unable to answer this point blank question, put in such a significant manner.

"Drugged!" exclaimed Mr. Hardy, stupified.

"Ah, surely," said Mr. Carruthers, in a smooth, oily voice ; "narcotics and irritants."

"What do you mean, sir?" inquired Mr. Hardy, endeavouring to put an injured look.

"Listen," said Mr. Carruthers, coming

close up to the speaker. "There must be an end to this farce, which, to say the truth, is in reality more like a tragedy. Sir Reginald Fleetwood is not mad, believe me, any more than you or I am."

"Ah, ah, that's a good joke," exclaimed Mr. Hardy, endeavouring to force a laugh, "an excellent joke, forsooth."

Mr. Craddick then came forward, and leant his ear towards the two examining doctors.

"Drugged!" exclaimed Mr. Carruthers, turning from him.

The madhouse doctor then turned towards Mr. Findley.

"Drugged!" exclaimed that individual; and the two walked towards the door.

Mr. Hardy, finding himself unsuccessful in his conciliatory course, turned round and began to act the bully.

"You don't mean to say that Mr. Sabine, the occupant of this room, is of sound mind? You haven't the audacity to make such an assertion?—because, if you have, you are—" he paused, and then added—"uttering a foul and malicious falsehood."

"We have not as yet made any statement," they both answered; "and when we do, it will not be to you."

"You are d—d polite!" exclaimed Mr. Hardy; "very polite, sir. So, you think to come here, and try and spoil my reputation! You think, I suppose, for my own amusement, that I have got a sane man here? D—n it, what do you mean?" exclaimed Mr. Hardy, stamping his foot upon the floor, and bellowing out his words like a great bully as he was.

"I have no further answer to make to you," said Mr. Carruthers. "Both myself and my colleague have our own opinions upon the matter, which, for very special reasons, we deem it advisable to keep to ourselves. We have seen enough, and more, no doubt, remains to be disclosed."

"You come in pretty company—with a man who merits the gallows."

"Good words, if you please, sir," said Mr. Baintree.

"And who the devil are you?" exclaimed Mr. Hardy, who was now bent upon acting the ruffian; "and who are you, I should like to know? Some escaped convict, I suppose."

"You are an impertinent scoundrel!" said Mr. Baintree, "and were it not for the law, I would inflict summary punishment upon you at once."

"Oh, oh! your're a brave fellow to talk. Get out of my place. You are satisfied that the party you have come to visit is mad enough, and are only vexed at the failure of your visit. As to that fellow," he said, in continuation, pointing to our hero, "he would swear any man's life away for a guinea. Oh, you are a nice lot. Parkins, show these people out."

This was addressed to one of the attendants, who preceded the party along the corridor.

Both the doctors saw plainly enough that the ill-used baronet had been drugged, purposely to give him the appearance of a man of diseased mind, and a superficial observer would have been led to such a conclusion; but Mr. Carruthers and his coadjutor were not to be so easily deceived, and they saw clearly enough how the case stood.

The whole party then took their way along the corridor, and from thence to the rear of the premises, from whence Colonel Jack had managed to make his escape on that memorable night.

They were going along the walk which led to the back gate, when our hero found himself suddenly confronted by Jonathan Wild and two of his myrmidoms.

A cry of surprise and alarm was the first indication the party had of this sudden apparition. It proceeded from Colonel Jack, who found himself suddenly in the grasp of the thieftaker.

"Treacherous hounds!" exclaimed the colonel, "I am not to be entrapped thus."

And with a sudden movement, he threw Wild from him, and ran across the garden.

"Follow him—don't let him escape!" shouted out Wild, who had been thrown to the earth by the highwayman.

Colonel Jack gave once glance around. To gain the door would be an impossibility, and upon the impulse of the moment, he ran across the garden, and with an agility which appeared incredible, actually run up one of the buttresses which supported the wall. In another second he was on the top of this.

"Cut him down!—fire!—anything!" said Wild, who now saw that the probability was that the prisoner would make his escape.

His two men rushed forward, but were held at bay a moment, for the colonel, with his knees on the top of the wall, in a half-crouching attitude, presented a pistol at his two assailants, and dared them to come on at the peril of their lives.

Mr. Baintree, the two doctors, and our friend Squabshot, were stupified with astonishment at the suddenness of this encounter.

Wild by this time had gained his legs, and instantly made towards where the colonel was. He urged on his men, and one, more determined than his companion, rushed forward.

A sharp report was heard—a groan—and the man staggered back a few paces and fell, the ground being dyed with his blood.

"Hang you!" exclaimed Wild, who now made an attempt to scale the wall, and finding this impossible, he discharged his pistol at our hero.

The shot lodged in the thick part of his thigh, but he made no cry or demonstration of having received a wound, but quickly dropped on the other side of the wall.

"The gate!—the gate!" said Mr. Hardy. "Fly round to the gate, and you will yet have him."

Wild took no heed of this, but bidding the man who was not wounded to give him a back, he sprang up on the top of the wall, and in another instant he was on the other side.

"Follow, Bradley, as quickly as possible, follow!" shouted out Wild, from the other side of wall.

Squabshot had now come up to the scene of action, and Bradley, Wild's follower, begged of Squabby to give him a leg up. It so happened that this individual was the same who had accompanied the party who had took Slimcoe, the particulars of which the reader will doubtless remember.

"Give us a leg up, Mr. Squabshot. Help a lame dog over the stile," said Bradley.

"I'll see you hanged first, and then I won't do it," said Squabshot, indignantly.

The man turned round to the others, upon which Mr. Hardy rushed forward, and hoisted Wild's follower over the wall.

Colonel Jack, wounded as he was, had managed to run about fifty yards or more, but he grew weak from loss of blood, and a deathlike faintness came over him. Still life is sweet at all times, and he persevered in the endeavour to make good his retreat. Nature, however, was fast becoming exhausted, and our hero felt this—he felt, moreover, that the odds were against him.

In a few minutes Wild was by his side, his hand at the highwayman's throat, and the muzzle of his pistol against his temple.

"Yield!" shouted out the thieftaker "The game's up, colonel, and the darbies are ready."

"Curse it, Wild, but this is sneaking and cowardly."

"What?"

"Lying in wait like this, after all that has passed between us, and after all you have promised."

"It ain't my fault. I'm deuced sorry to be obliged to have any hand in this business."

"Oh, humbug!"

"You won't say so when you know all, but for the present"—and here the thieftaker slipped a pair of handcuffs out of his coat pocket, and slipped one on the wrist of the highwayman, doing the same office with the other immediately afterwards.

"One—two, and all told," said Wild, as he shut the gyves with a sharp snap.

"I'm deuced sorry things have come to this pass, but there warn't no help for it, as circumstances turned out. You've spoilt one of my best chaps, too."

"I'm pretty well done up myself," said Colonel Jack, his features assuming a ghastly hue."

Wild said nothing, but held up his hand to some one in the distance.

The sounds of revolving wheels were heard, and in a minute or two a horse and cart drove up to where the highwayman and his two captors stood.

"Jump up," said Wild. "We must make for the stone-jug this time."

"I can't move," said the colonel, "I seem to have lost the use of this limb. Your shot is buried here."

And he pointed to the spot where he was wounded.

"Whew!" exclaimed Wild, "that's it, eh? We must lift you into the cart."

By this time the whole of the party came to the spot. They had emerged through the back gate.

"Stay," said Mr. Carruthers "Whatever has happened to cause this affray I know not, but it would be cruel to take a man away so badly wounded as our friend appears to be without seeing what the injury is. The probability is that he might die before he arrives at the place of his destination."

"Perhaps you will be kind enough to see what can be done for him," said Wild. "It ain't my fault; he's brought it on himself."

"Psha! the old story," exclaimed the colonel, writhing with pain as the men attempted to move him.

"Ah! your servant, Mr. Squabshot," said Wild, turning round, and seeing the individual he so addressed for the first time."

"You're a nice lot, you are, and no mistake," said Squabshot.

"What's the matter?" said Wild.

"There, that will do. You know what's the matter as well as I do. Ain't you ashamed of yourself?"

"What! for doing my duty?" said the thieftaker.

"Hang your duty, and you to! If I only had a pistol I would have brought you down when on that wall, as sure as my name's Squabshot."

The colonel's wound was dressed by Mr. Carruthers, and when bound up was somewhat easier. The ball was lodged deep in the flesh, but Mr. Carruthers did not deem it advisable to attempt to extract it then, indeed it would have been impossible for him to have done so, as he had neither probes nor forceps with him.

"What about my chap?" said Wild. "I am afraid he's spoilt for life."

"Mr. Findley is attending to him."

"I am sorry to see this," said Mr. Baintree, grasping our hero's hand, and pressing it warmly. "If I had had the slightest idea that there was any likelihood of such a sad termination to our day's proceedings, I would never have advised this course."

"It's the fortune of war, and can't be helped," said Colonel Jack.

"I'm sorry for this," again exclaimed Wild, "very sorry, colonel; but it ain't been my fault. Howsomever, it can't be helped."

Colonel Jack was now placed in the cart, preparatory to being conveyed to prison. When seated therein, Mr. Baintree came to his side, and inquired if he would need his legal advice?—whereupon the colonel informed him that he was about to be conveyed to Newgate, and would be glad to see his solicitor on the following morning. Wild jumped into the cart, which was immediately driven off without further parley.

CHAPTER LXXIII.

THE HIGHWAYMAN IN PRISON.—THE CRIMINAL BROTHERS.

COLONEL JACK, for the first time, found himself in that gloomy abode, where so many poor wretches had awaited their fate with that sinking of the heart and depression of spirits which rendered existence hardly tolerable.

Our hero felt himself more miserable than he had ever felt in the whole course of his life. He felt fully convinced that the primary cause of his capture was no other than Sir Richard Fleetwood; indeed, Jonathan Wild had hinted as much, as he was conveying his prisoner to the Old Bailey.

As the colonel was so seriously wounded, he was conveyed to the infirmary, where the doctor, who usually attended the prisoners, extracted the bullet from the colonel's leg.

The first person who came on the following morning was Squabshot, who had been driven to a state of distraction by the incidents of the previous day.

When he arrived, the colonel was stretched on a couch, his leg bound up, and placed in a cradle.

"My dear fellow," exclaimed Squabshot, "this is a pretty termination to our day's proceedings. Confound that old Wild, I'll cut his acquaintance."

"Does Osborne know of this?" inquired the colonel.

"No, he's not at home—down at Oxford."

"Then don't say anything to him about it."

"Indeed!—why not?"

"Never you mind—only do as I tell you.

I may manage to pull through this, for to tell you the truth, I don't even know what I am brought here for at present."

"There's something against you, I suppose?" said Squabshot.

"Oh, no doubt of that; but what it is, I am not at present able to say."

"How's the wound?" inquired Squabshot.

"Oh, that will be all right in a few days. It is not that which troubles me, it's being caged up here that's preying upon my mind. Curse it, how could I have been caught in that trap—for I feel quite certain that it was a trap, laid by no other person but Sir Richard Fleetwood. Curse him! I hope to be even with him yet. Now, Squabshot, mind what I have to say—don't you tell Osborne a word about this affair."

"What am I to say? He'll be sure to inquire how we got on at the madhouse."

"Say what you please—anything; but pray keep this affair a secret, for I would not have Osborne know of it on any account. It would only cause him unnecessary anxiety, which, after all, would be sympathy thrown away, for he cannot possibly do me any good."

"He don't know that—he may be of service to you."

"In what way, pray?"

"That we don't know; but it surely cannot be wrong to let all your friends know of your misfortune, for you know, my dear fellow, there's no discredit in being in trouble. We all of us have our share of it in this world."

"Umph!" exclaimed the colonel, "I know I have."

This conversation was obliged to be carried on within the hearing of several other patients or prisoners, who were confined in the ward where our hero lay, consequently the two speakers were obliged to be cautious in their observations to each other.

Squabshot eventually took his departure, with a promise that he would not mention the circumstance of our hero's capture to Osborne.

In a day or two Colonel Jack was sufficiently convalescent to be removed from the infirmary, and he was then placed in the ward used for the reception of prisoners awaiting their trial.

It so happened that the sessions were on when the colonel was taken to Newgate, consequently the interior of the prison was in a state of bustle and confusion; added to this, it was more than usually full.

There is no doubt that a correct history of crime and criminals would be a desideratum, because much of the history of the times is ever involved in the prevalence of particular crimes, and the career of criminals.

In every age and country, since the foundation of society, events have been occuring of which, though too minute and figurative for the vast and rapid page of general history, it must be regretted that no record has been preserved.

Few that have written on crime and criminals have kept in view anything but the *crime* or *criminal,* and the holding up of both to the execration of mankind. They have seldom sought for those proximate or remote causes which may have led to the commission of crimes by individuals, and occasioned whole classes of criminals. Neither has there been at any time a disposition manifested to scan the criminal's character fairly, that is by comparison, connected with the environment of circumstances, and in reference to the conduct of prosecutors in general.

Investigation, by comparison, is the surest road to knowledge, the whole system of daily intercourse throughout the world is carried on by it.

The passing over all the circumstances connected with the exciting causes to the commission of crime, is the result of a nation of very general prevalence. It is thought that, in allowing crimes to be palliated by circumstancs, we lesson the effects of public examples ; but whenever it is proper to publish accounts of persons or events, it is always desirable that the truth should be spoken.

We have already stated that it was session time, at Newgate, and there was a very heavy calender of crimes for the consideration of the grand jury. The carriage way before the court-house was thickly strewed with new straw—the court-yard was thronged with an assemblage of persons of both sexes, whose habiliments, physiognomy, and general bearing, strongly marked them as the equivocal class of society.

These were dispersed in groups, discussing the peculiar conduct and character of prosecutors and witnesses in general, the majority, however, were emphatically descanting on the species of evidence usually given by public officers.

Many were contending which should have the priority in relating instances of their talent in buffing it strong (*i. e.,* committing perjury).

Numbers were asseverating the truth of their statements, and advanced such a mass of specious matter, that their auditors were dumbfounded at the atrocious conduct of our preservers of the peace.

" Poor fellows !" ejaculated a knot of females, thereby meaning the prisoners who were to be tried. " Nobody is safe from these police officers."

Just under the wall, in front of the prison, were other groups of surrounding females, who were wiping their tears away with their aprons, and relating tales of the reprobate conduct of a husband or son, then under the ban of the law. These persons consisted of mechanics' or labourers' wives, who had brought the money to pay a counsel to plead for those who had made their lives miserable. They were also there to watch the hour of trial, and to send some kind friend into court who might say a word in the prisoner's favour.

The longanimity of these children of sorrow however exhausts itself. None of those husbands or sons that were in trouble possessed a bad heart, or were naturally prone to evil courses. They were comparatively innocent themselves—it was others who had drawn them into bad company, and occasioned all these troubles.

They were, however, sure that the party for whom they were interested now saw his error, and if he should have a merciful judge and jury, would be sure to reform and make a good man.

The judge's carriage, on its way to the court, then passed, and was pointed out to them. Imploring looks were directed towards it, and prayers put up that he might be merciful.

Round the doorway of the prison there was assembled a number of women and young girls, all having bundles of some kind in their possession, and each contending for precedence in obtaining an entrance, being probably afraid that those they were going to visit should be called up for trial before the recently washed shirt or vest could be conveyed to them.

In the interior of the prison, the governor was inspecting the cells, which had been whitewashed and made clean for the reception of new comers. He was also ordering the doors to be kept open, that they might be well aired. The cellkeeper, attired in his best suit, was at his post, ready to receive the company that usually visited that compartment of Newgate at, and just after, session time.

The under-turnkey stood with keys in hand, ready to admit the first capitally convicted felon. The wardsman sat in the empty wardroom, gazing at the vacant seats, and conjuring up in his imagination the countenances of those whom he had seen leaving the place bound and ready for the hands of the hangman. He looked like the last man praying for a new creation, that he might enjoy once more social fellowship.

At the iron rails that enclose the prisoners within the several yards, discussions were going on as to the probable number of prisoners that would be sent to the cells during the session, and the number that would. out of the batch, ultimately suffer ; while others, having made bets on the two events, were continually inquiring whether any were yet gone to the cells.

Newly-appointed city functionaries were seen every half hour threading the winding passages, each with a friend under his arm, to inquire whether there had been any arrivals, and returning from the cell yard apparently disappointed at having received an answer in the negative.

When Colonel Jack was transferred to the north ward of the prison, after leaving the infirmary, he then met with a number of anxious faces of prisoners who were hourly expecting to be taken into the court-house to undergo the terrible ordeal of a trial—terrible in all cases, but when life or death depends upon the issue it was, of course, more especially so. Our hero had not been long in his new quarters, when he found himself suddenly grasped by the hand, and upon looking up, he observed two young men, who were brothers, looking with eyes of conciliative curiosity at him.

"What, Halford!" said the elder of the two, "who would have dreamt of meeting with you."

The colonel regarded the speaker with a glance of inquiry, for the moment he did not recognise him, but upon the speaker smiling, our hero became aware that the two young men before him were old acquaintances.

"Why. Richard!" said the colonel, "I might return you the compliment. Who would have thought of seeing you here, or indeed James either? What is it for?"

"Forgery!" said the elder brother, sadly.

"When are you to be tried—this session?"

"We are expecting to be called every minute. Indeed, had it not have been for a case which has occupied the court a more than usual amount of time we should have been put out of our misery before now."

"It's a case of life and death," said the colonel.

"O!" sighed both the young men simultaneously, "and we fear the worst."

This conversation was suddenly cut short by the officers of the prison conveying the two young men away to the court-house. They shook hands with the colonel, who whispered into their ears his good wishes for them, and the sincere hope that they might be acquitted; and once more he was left with the heterogenous throng of unknown prisoners. Our hero amused himself with contemplating the barren expressions of countenance of those who were pacing the yards like wild animals in a cage. While doing so Mr. Baintree entered the yard. He shook our hero warmly by the hand, and inquired for the two young men who had been conversing with the colonel a few minutes before. It appeared that he was engaged for their defence, and upon finding that they had

been taken to the court, he hastily excused himself, and left the colonel with a promise of seeing him again after their trial.

We will not enter into the whole of the evidence against the forgers. It is enough to know that they were both convicted. And about three o'clock in the afternoon there was a general movement along the iron rails. It was known that something of interest had occurred, and each prisoner was on the alert to obtain the first information.

Presently a buzz ran round the yard—

"Two gone to the cells, own brothers, they say, no hope for them in this world—hard lines—one out of a family ought to have been enough to satisfy a sheriff."

The capitally convicted brothers were indeed at that moment pacing the space under the north wall of the condemned yard. They seemed more agitated than depressed.

"Why do you so frequently refer to the past, James," said the elder one. "We cannot now retrace our steps, and if we could as we never intended a robbing we might fall into the same error—"

"No, Richard," said the other. "If you had followed my advice we should not have been here now, there was a time you know, but—"

"Hang your buts, I cannot endure to be upbraided with the past. It cannot be now recalled."

"And the future?" said the other, and they both sighed at this reflection.

Death hovered over them, an ignominious dreadful death, for at the time of which we write the law was not so merciful as at the present period.

Hanging was considered to be a panacea for all ills.

As this last sentence was uttered, the more agitated of the two brothers had to pause and lean against the wall. He was dreadfully convulsed, and his brother ran to the pump, which was hard by, to procure water.

The ordinary had entered the yard unnoticed, and his practised eye in a moment discovered the condition of the elder brother, who was at that moment under the influence of all the passions which tear and rend the soul of man. He trembled as does a kid when thrust into the cage of a boa constrictor for food. The fear of the future was then presented before him, and in his excited imagination the executioner was busy about his person. In the next moment the demon of rage triumphed, and rendered him furious for revenge.

He gnashed his teeth, his hands were clenched, every nerve was braced, each muscle was constrained, and his whole frame was gathered up like a tiger prepared to spring upon his prey. A pause, and the futility of his efforts were apparent to his mind, his head dropped on his chest, and tears of conscious weakness came to his relief.

Awaking in a measure from the paroxysm of conflicting passions which so strikingly exhibits the weakness of our nature, and seeing the sheriff and his friends, and the reverend ordinary around him, he drew himself up and said—

"Gentlemen, I am neither so guilty nor so weak as I appear at this moment in your eyes. I am, however, an injured human being, and cannot but feel my wrongs."

Then relapsing, he eagerly inquired if they had come to lead him to the place of execution.

Being desired to calm the perturbation of his mind, and hope for the best, he again reviled his prosecutors in unmeasured terms of reproach, while his younger brother seemed to have merged his own sorrows into those of his more agitated fellow prisoner.

Hopes of pardon for both—but, alas! fallacious hopes—were kindly held out by the witnesses of this scene. The brothers retired afterwards to their gloomy cell, there to meditate on their prospects of living the remainder of their lives in slavery, or of being in a short time cut off and put to death by the hands of the public executioner.

The following morning, as the cell doors were opened, the ordinary, in the faithful discharge of his duties, was there to minister to all the minds he should find diseased. The elder of the two brothers had passed a night of horrors. He appeared in the yard with a countenance as haggard as if the brunt of years, under an accumulated weight of woes, had passed over his head. A patch of hair on the right side of the head, perfectly circular in form, which the evening previously had certainly been of a dark brown colour, was now white as December's snow. His eyes, also had lost several shades in depth of colouring, while their action indicated excessive shyness and cunning ; they had also sunk deeper into their sockets, and appeared to be constantly peering round for a place where he might escape from his keepers, or where he might hide himself from those who proffered him words of consolation.

His case was, however, past cure. The night in the cells had done its work upon his mind; its possessor no longer spoke of injury inflicted on him, or talked of revenge. He was like a plant cut down in one night by a frost—the stalk or stem indeed remained, but the blossom and beauty had departed, and all the symbols of decay only remained.

The two brothers as they moved called to mind the remembrance of the story of the united twins—the one that remained alive carrying his fraternal dead load about with

him premonitory of his his own dissolution. They had had a sleepless night, and the stronger nerves of the younger had discovered from his brother's conversation the abberation of his mind long ere the scanty streak of light permitted to enter his cell enabled him to notice the havoc mental agony had made on his countenance.

The sufferer held his brother fast by the arm as if afraid of losing a protector, and he moved as from the same impulse.

The city authorities of that time took a lively interest in criminals—and in the space that elapsed from the period of their trial to the day of execution.

Collected from the younger brother the particulars of their previous life, we shall reserve this for our next chapter, and give the narrative *verbatim*, as it is actually a true story, related by a criminal who suffered the extreme penalty of the law, and shows forcibly the career of a section of the trading community, and many more strange stories might be eliminated from this great moving world of London.

———

CHAPTER LXXIV.

THE FORGERS' NARRATIVE—HOW TRADE WAS CARRIED ON.

"I WRITE the following history of my past career, to show to the world how a young man may be drawn into crime by evil communication and bad example. I may say with truth that I was almost educated by circumstances to become a forger, and as I am about to pass from this world. I hope that sufficient justice will be done me by those who read my last words, to believe that they are substantially true, seeing that I can have no motive to commit to paper a series of falsehoods—more especially as I cannot in any way be served thereby.

"Myself and my elder brother, Richard, were sons of a respectable person, who, like too many in this world, thought his own occupation the worst of all others.

"Possessed of this notion, he determined to apprentice us to some business in London. My brother was placed with a silversmith at the west end of the town, and I, twelve months after, was articled to a woollen draper. Our masters were known to each other, and had money transactions together. It also appeared that they were both similarly circumstanced, in respect to want of capital to carry on business, and give that credit which the nature of their trades required.

They had, however, both discount at the Bank of England, from which they drew

considerable sums weekly. The bank was in advance at the time I was old enough to be employed in cash transactions to my master, of whom I shall now particularly speak. About seven thousand pounds, the whole of which had been received out of that establishment on bills, the time of payment on which did not exceed two months after date. In order to work this capital and retain it in his trade, it was necessary that, as the bills became due, others should be sent in every week, on which cash might be obtained, and thus keep the current paper in the hands of the bank discount committee nearly up to the same in amount.

"It was my business every week to carry in these bills on one day, and go for an answer on the next and bring back the money. On what security the money was

advanced to my employer in the first instance, I have now no means of ascertaining; but when I became acquainted with the affairs of the house, more than one-third of the bills in the hands of the Bank, held as security for money advanced to him, were acceptances of mine—then a boy, the shopman and the porter of the house—and the remainder fictitious bills, made up every week; that is, pretended acceptances of unknown persons.

"The residences of master tailors, in a little way of business, to whom credit for a cut of cloth was oftentimes an accomodation, served as places in which they could make the bills payable, and give them an appearance of having been derived from various sources in the way of trade. Bills sent to be discounted at the Bank at that period were

ed in this particular instance, and that they would not willingly encourage such a system.

"My brother's master, however, and many other houses that I could name, of which I will if required, give a list drew their weekly money to carry on that business in the same description of paper. When any of our bills were thrown out by the committee and the same with other houses, with whom we are acquainted, are used to exchange them, and thus given the appearance of going again into the discount office in the regular course of negotiation.

"But to remove every doubt as to the cognisance of the Bank of England's committee of the nature of the paper they were discounting, and to set forth in a striking manner the school in which I was brought up, it will only be required that the following statement should be believed to be, as it really is, *true*.

"During my apprenticeship, a period arrived when the Bank of England Directors resolved on restricting their discounts to wholesale dealers only; this was a measure which at once threatened ruin to all retail houses dependant on the weekly discounts at the Bank for the support of their credit.

"I was called out of my bed by my master one night to be informed of this circumstance, and the resolution he had formed of going the following morning, when the discount committee were to meet, and informing its members of his then actual situation in trade, and also of the nature of the securities they held for the monies advanced to him. I was then desired to spend the remainder of the night in looking over the account-books, and prepare myself to accompany him as evidence of the truth of his intended statement.

"As, however, the committee met to decide only on the discounts to be granted, and not to hold conferences with parties sending in bills, a difficulty arose about obtaining admission. At length he addressed a note to the chairman, informing him that a loss would accrue to the Bank of many thousand pounds, if he had not immediate audience with the committee.

"In a short time he was admitted, followed by me with a blue bag, surcharged to the mouth with vouchers. He at once entered on his business, and addressed them thus—

"'Gentlemen, you see before you a retired trader, who has for a number of years carried on a large business, and brought up a numerous family with a capital borrowed from you. I have been a faithful steward. I have spent your money far and wide, and have been an active agent in giving circulation to your notes. I have been the means

to the treasury in the way of a direct tax, but for me and the money you have been so kind as to entrust into my hands, and for the use of which I have paid you considerable sums in discount, and have largely contributed to the revenue for stamps. But I will not name the amount of these sums. My only surprise is how I have surmounted it all.'

"Here the members of the committee looked each other in the face. They had been waiting for a declaration of insolvency. The speaker, taking the cue, proceeded—

"'Gentlemen, do not mistake me. I am not out of the worst yet. I only want your willing aid, and all will be right.'

"'Explain yourself,' called out one of the committee.

"'The case is succinctly this,' continued the speaker. 'I commenced business without a single shilling of capital but what I got from you. That capital is spent, as I said, far and wide—hundreds are living by it, and doing so well that it will all come back to me with good interest, and through me to you. But this will be a work of time. The debtors on these books (pointing to my bag) must be handled with much tenderness, for any attempt to extract the money out of them rashly must break them all up—for they gave long credit, and therefore I gave them the same. You have some of their acceptances which they cannot pay—neither do they expect to be called upon to do so. I have used them as my tools; their acceptances are mere accommodations to me, and I must have the candour to inform you further that all the paper you hold of mine is not, if you attempt to enforce payment on them, worth the stamp on which the bills are drawn. In fact, gentlemen, it is the same to you as if the acceptances never had existed.'

"Several members of the committee nodded their heads at each other as the last sentence was uttered, indicating that they each understood its meaning.

"The woollen draper, nothing abashed, continued—

"'Unless you enable me to pay them I am here to make a proposition which will meet the interests of all parties. Consider, gentlemen, that I am your debtor for nearly ten thousand pounds—that you have no available security for the debt but myself, and such is the peculiar nature of my trade, that if it be broken up you will not realise half a crown in the pound. On the other hand, if you leave me to manage my own affairs, and continue my trade, I will undertake in the ratio of fifty pounds. With this arrangement, I think, gentlemen, I shall save both my own credit and your money.'

"After my master had been requested to withdraw and went to the lobby, he had the satisfaction of seeing the chief clerk in a few minutes, who informed him that the committee had acceded to his proposal unconditionally; and I know that after this arrangement made with my master, so far from his lessening the discounts by fifty pounds a-week, that he was ever afterwards granted unlimited amounts of discount, all of which was obtained on paper, more valueless if possible than heretofore—such as acceptances of his own wife and daughter, dated in the country, and made payable in London.

"I am not stating these particulars with any idea of palliating my own crime, but it must be admitted that a youth who had been brought up for seven years in such a school could hardly be expected to think much of executing *a made-up bill*, as we used to designate them, especially as they were never intended to defraud others. The house in which my brother served his time ran a bill career much the same as the one I have described.

"But the Bank of England was not the only channel through which discount for these bills were obtained. Private bankers, during the bill mania, made advances on them, and I believe with a full knowledge of what they were. I have known more than one instance of a banker sending for his customer; then taking him into his private room, address him as follows:

"'Sir, as you are become very irregular in your account with us, and there are several returned bills remaining with us unpaid, I feel it to be my duty to inform you that I am well acquainted with the nature of the bills you have been in the habit of sending into our house. A hint, I suppose, will be sufficient. Let them be all paid. We shall not, however, offer any bar to your opening an account elsewhere. Only let me advise you to take care of yourself for the future. But let our bills be paid, or good, substantial, *bona fide* bills be substituted for them.'"

This is precisely the same language the late Sir William Curtis is said to have used on a similar occasion to Hunton who was executed on forgery, Hunton took the hint and paid him, afterwards relapsing into the same practice in another quarter. That the era to which this statement refers was an extraordinary one none will doubt Many persons, availing themselves of the indiscri-

the west end of the town at that period, remain unsettled to the present hour, the proprietor himself having been in prison for a long series of years. Then, also, parties of tradesmen united under a compact to raise money on cross acceptances, with which either to commence business or extend the range of their mercantile speculations.

The recollection of these days calls up a thousand associations connected with the moral changes which society has undergone, that cannot be understood by those who have only had a view of its modern phrases.

The forger brother had not long concluded his narrative and handed it to the ordinary, when his mother and sister were announced by the turnkey. When they were announced he flew to the bars.

The first visit a condemned man has from those who are dear to him is as painful a moment as any he has to pass through.

He is in one instant informed of the tainted isolation of his position, when the mind shudders and shrinks into itself at the thought of never again being permitted to press the hand or cheek of her who gave him birth, or to clasp in his arms those whom he loves and by whom he was loved.

There, separated even from the reach of his touch, stood those who had all their lives ministered to his comforts, and in whom all his affections were concentrated. Even an endearing word was polluted, and lost its efficacy, by the presence of the keeper, who stood between the double row of bars that kept them apart.

In the bound of joy that came with their names, a momentary forgetfulness of his situation had passed over the mind. The approach to the bars dispelled the happy delusion. The blood paused in its course, and left the countenance pale as the image of death. The expressions of delight at seeing those who were dear to him died on their passage to the lips; and the feelings of affection themselves seemed on the instant to have become defunct.

The mother and daughter were also under the influence of their situation, and were bathed in tears. It required no words to explain the intensity of their anguish; and as the cold damp gloom of the place chilled the heart and repressed warmth of expression, they all three for some minutes remained in silence, with heads hanging down like mourners over the remains of the now dead beloved.

During the pause, the elder brother was brought to the bars. His altered countenance broke the spell, for there was no mistaking his appearance. The portrait of his former self was gone; and the deplorable condition of his mind was written in legible characters in his eye. He gave his mother and sister a look, which must be seen to be understood. It was not the look of madness or of idiotcy, but a mixture of utter despair, affection, and fear. He was however, the first to speak, saying to his mother,

" What brought you here ?"

The mother replied by asking her other son, in almost choking accents, what had happened to Richard ? James remained still silent ; while it was becoming every moment more apparent that the females could not much longer, from agitation, maintain their position—each were grasping a bar of the iorn rails for support ; and the daughter, with her disengaged arm, was making a feeble effort to sustain her mother in a upright position.

"Go, go," said Richard, in a hurried manner : "you know not where you are. Make your escape—make your escape !"

James, whose feelings had mastered his reason and resolution, and who had the whole time, with heaving chest and rigid feature, indicating that his sufferings were too intense to be expressed in words, seemed to recover in a degree as his brother spoke, giving him a look of pitying interest, that said, " Hard as is the task of brooking our situation, and shameful as is our condition, I still possess a heart that can commiserate a brother stricken to the heart with grief.

It was now impossible for the mother and daughter to remain any longer at the bars, as other visitors pressed forward ; and, considering the purpose and occasion of their visit, ribald tongues were going. Pride, therefore, came and mingled itself with grief. The mother and daughter waved their hands and fell back, to give place to others who had been brought up in a less delicate school, and between whom and themselves there was not the slightest verisimilitude beyond that of being of the same sex.

" Jack," called out a female, elbowing her way to the grating, " it was that bluebottle that smashed you, the ——!" But the reader must imagine the language in which the most guilty and depraved of our species are capable of clothing their acrimonious feelings, and from which delicacy shrinks as from the touch of an adder.

" Poor fellows !" ejaculated the mother, as the ordinary, who had watched the interview drew them away, if possible, to assuage the anguish of their minds by soothing words, and holding out the hope that mitigating circumstances might yet be discovered to avert the execution of the extreme penalty of the law.

" God be merciful to them, and ' temper the wind to the shorn lamb !' " exclaimed James, breaking silence as he lost sight of his mother at the angle of the wall. The two brothers remained for some minutes gazing into each other's eyes, as if to penetrate the far-down workings of the soul.

"Are they coming ?" said Richard, his countenance changing as the dark thought of death passed over his mind.

"Come," replied his brother, taking his arm, " come let me urge you to reflection, and prepare for more manly conduct at our next interview'—and so the younger brother did all in his power to alleviate the sorrows of his more depressed companion in guilt or misfortune.'

The ordinary, in the course of his visits to the prisoners, elicited from the younger one those particulars which had led them into error.

They had been in partnership, and had commenced business without any capital, and had been consequently in the power of one wholesale dealer. To bolster up their credit they had made use of fictitious bills ; and eventually forged upon well known names. Being unable to meet their payments, they were prosecuted upon one of these last-named bills—hence their commitment, trial, and condemnation.

The effects of commerce in civilising a country are wonderful, but the good is greatly alloyed by the too frequent concomitant, the destruction of morality. It too often engenders a grasping spirit and a cupidity that freeze the warm springs of benevolence in the heart.

When, however, the work of gain is over, and a retrospection of the past awakens the conscience, many sad hours accompany the close of life. At the time this case occurred, the governor and company of the bank, merchants and bankers in general, looked on with perfect indifference, and without emotion, while rows of human beings were hung up for their benefit, as they actually thought and affirmed.

Nor is it improbable that the same state of things would have existed to this day, had not the same love of gain discovered that they were in error, and that to stop hanging for forgery was the most likely method to abate the crime.

The fate of the brothers appeared to excite interest ; such, however, was the state of feeling in the city at the same time on the question of forgery, that none came forward to pray that their lives might be spared ; yet, three years subsequently to their execution, the bankers were seen petitioning the government to repeal the capital part of the punishment, on the plea that it augmented the number of forgeries. The several interviews that were granted to the brothers with their mother and sister were of too painful a nature to be detailed at length ; they may be more readily imagined than described.

The most remarkable feature in the case was the condition to which Richard, the elder brother, was reduced immediately after his condemnation.

It has frequently been stated that, in cases were persons of superior station in society have been under orders for execution, they have, through interest, obtained narcotic drugs, by which their sufferings have been lulled, and their feelings sunk in forgetfulness; and that in that state they have been led to the scaffold, perfectly insensible of what was going on.

In this instance the elder brother, Richard, fell into a state of partial insenibility, through the intensity of his feelings. Mandragora could not more effectually have thrown him into a state of apparent forgetfulness—we say apparent, for, although his eyes spoke of terrible fearfulness, he could not be brought to give any answer when the subject of his speedy dissolution was reverted to.

He recognised, however, his brother, mother, and sister ; but could not, or would not, keep up a connected conversation with them.

It appeared as if in mercy to his weakness of resolution, the mind had been suddenly rendered too imbecile to entertain so weighty a subject as the contemplation of death. The brothers had been partners in business, they were partners in the crime for which they forfeited their lives—they died at the same time—on the same scaffold—and were interred in the same grave.

Colonel Jack, by permission of the governor, had been permitted to have several interviews with the unfortunate young men previous to their execution. He had known them from their boyhood, and their untimely end made a deep impression upon him, for he knew not how soon he himself might meet with a similar fate. It is true that his name was not down for trial that session, and, after all, he felt it might be a question whether his prosecutors could obtain a conviction, although there could be no doubt about his being a notorious highwayman, and having outraged and violated the law on numerous occasions ; nevertheless, legal evidence was requisite, and our hero hoped as men will hope under most adverse circumstances, that the glorious uncertainty of the law might possibly favour him.

During the first few days of his incarceration the colonel was an object of considerable interest. Hundreds of visitors to the prison had made excuses to obtain an entrance therein merely to be gratified with a sight of our hero, who was in sooth "the observed of all observers."

The sessions were over, the prisoners were drafted off as their various degrees of punishment suggested ; some to transportation—some to short terms of imprisonment, and a few, happily the smallest section, expiated their crimes on the scaffold.

CHAPTER LXXV.

WILD AND THE COLONEL.

It appeared, so Mr. Baintree informed our hero, that the solicitors for the crown were preparing a host of cases, upon which the colonel would have to take his trial. The first and foremost of these, however, was the robbery committed upon Mr. Underwood.

This was the first case upon which he would have to be tried. When Mr. Sheriff Underwood was informed of the safe capture of our hero he came post-haste up to London to gratify his optics with a view of the caged highwayman.

Mr. Underwood, when he arrived in London, waited upon the Lord Mayor. Mr. Gubbins had made him fully acquainted with the particulars of the robbery which had been committed upon him by the colonel at St. Albans. The sheriff obtained an order to enter the prison of Newgate for the purpose of satisfying himself with a view of the celebrated highwayman.

The colonel was pacing up and down the yard, and as he did so, he observed the sheriff gazing at him with eyes of curiosity through the bars which enclosed the yard. As our hero came near to these Mr. Underwood indulged in a satirical grin of satisfaction. Several persons were with him at the time, some of the aldermen of the city of London.

"So sir," said Mr. Underwood, addressing Colonel Jack, " you have run to the length of your tether now, and the world will soon be rid of such a troublesome customer as you have been for years past to honest folk."

"This is not seemly, Mr. Underwood," said Mr. Baintree, who happened to be walking with the colonel at this time. " You surely have not thought it worth while to come hither for the express purpose of taunting a man in misfortune ?"

" Misfortune, you call it, forsooth !" exclaimed the sheriff. " I should term it a great blessing that so notorious a malefactor had an end put to his lawless career, a very great blessing to the world."

" Every man is supposed to be innocent until declared guilty by a jury of his country, and is, or ought to be, protected from the vulgar gaze and taunts of prying visitors."

"I'll thank you to mind your own business, sir," said the sheriff, with an indignant toss of the head.

"And I will thank you to mind yours, sir," said Mr. Baintree, who was not to be overawed. "More than this, I rather fancy I am minding mine, by protecting my client from the interference of intruders."

"A fine office, truly," answered Mr. Underwood. "However, you will find some difficulty in protecting him from the tender mercies of the public executioner."

"Hush, hush, my dear sir!" said one of the aldermen, who stood by. "You really must not indulge in any such observations as these before the trial, and even then it is unkind to tread upon a fellow man."

Mr. Sheriff Underwood was silent, and looked rather glum at this last observation. He contented himself with muttering some half suppressed anathemas against malefactors in general, and Colonel Jack in particular, after which he took his way from the prison-yard, accompanied by the aldermen. What his object was in paying our hero a visit Mr. Baintree was at a loss to divine, unless it were to indulge in taunts at the imprisoned highwayman, who was glad enough to be rid of his disagreeable visitor. Mr. Baintree had not the slightest idea that Colonel Jack and Mr. Halford were one and the same person until our hero had been taken prisoner by Jonathan Wild, and been lodged in Newgate. When he had made this discovery, great as was the surprise, he, nevertheless, did his utmost to serve Colonel Jack, and was, in truth, as staunch a friend to him as heretofore. Notwithstanding, it was impossible for the lawyer to conceal from his client, that upon one or more of the cases which the counsel for the crown proposed bringing against him, that it was pretty certain that a conviction would be ensured.

Miserable as was his present situation, there was an elasticity about the mind and organisation of Colonel Jack which would not admit of his giving way to despair, and his thoughts were both by day and night occupied as to how he was to surmount his present difficulties, which, to say the truth, appeared insurmountable.

Soon after the sessions were over Jonathan Wild presented himself at the door of the passage which led to the ward where Colonel Jack was confined.

"Well, Muster Wild," said one of the turnkeys, "it's good seeings to clap eyes upon you."

"Never you mind about that, or anything else as don't concern you; and only thank your lucky stars that you are made turnkey of this respectable establishment, instead of being lagged as you deserved."

"Oh, don't be hard, Mr. Wild, upon a faithful servant of his Majesty's," said the man, with a grin.

"Where's Colonel Jack?" asked the thief-taker.

The man gave a nod with his head to that part of the prison where the highwayman was confined.

"Want to see him?" he inquired.

"Yes! Open the gate, will you, without more ado."

The turnkey did as he was desired, and upon Wild passing through, he unlocked the other iron gate which led into the yard. Wild passed through and ascended the stone steps which led up into the large blank and cheerless room in which Colonel Jack was seated, in moody silence.

"Humph! It's you," he exclaimed, as the thieftaker entered the apartment. "And what brings you here?"

"Simply to see you," said the thieftaker, taking a seat by the side of the large fire-place.

"Well, you are gratified—here I am," said the colonel glumpily.

"Now, look here," said Wild, "it ain't of any use you and I getting at loggerheads. I told you before, colonel, that this ain't been of my seeking."

"It's been your doing, though. If you had not have played the part of a traitor, I should not have been cooped up here. You've played your game, and a successful one its been. I know that to my cost."

"Well," said Wild, "I suppose you are not so green as to stay here upon the chance of an acquittal."

"Stay here! Well I like that! How can I help myself?"

"Don't know. It's not for me to suggest. Only you see, colonel, I should try and give the beaks the slip. I'm only saying what I should do, if it were my own case."

"Oh, you are too clever," said the colonel, half sadly, and half bitterly.

Wild regarded the speaker with a curious look of inquiry. And there was after this a pause for some minutes.

"I did think you were a more plain dealing man, Wild," said Colonel Jack. "After all that has passed years agone—after your solemn promise when I last saw you at Dyson's, and after the understanding we had there, I think you haven't acted fair and square—and that's all about it."

"How could I help myself? Sir Richard Fleetwood gave notice to the police at Bow-street that you were to be at that house at Wandsworth at a certain time. I had orders to be there also; and as two of our commoners were there with me, how could I help myself? Let me ask you that?" said the thieftaker.

"By giving me timely notice, of course."

"But I did not know where to find you. I went to Dyson, and left word there for you to be on your guard, and keep out of the way—ask the Badger if I didn't."

"Psha! How am I to ask a man whom in all probability I shall never see again?" exclaimed the highwayman, in a tone of indignation. "And if I did, what good would it do me? Let the past be the past. It's no use looking back now."

"Well, I swear to you, colonel, I'm sorry for this, as Heaven is my judge."

"Ah! I dare say."

"You don't believe me."

"It matters not, whether I do or not."

"For the sake of her who is dead and gone—for the sake of her, you might believe what I am saying," said Wild, in a tone of voice far different to his usual grating and harsh manner.

"Well, perhaps you do mean fair, after all. I know not which to think—for, to say the truth, for a man who means the honest thing, you have acted in a most extraordinary manner."

"Is there anything I can do to prove my sincerity—anything you want?" said Wild.

"I want to be out of this cursed place."

"Ah, yes! Of course you do."

"Well, then, I want a mason's hammer, a chisel, and a file," said Colonel Jack.

"You shall have them," said Wild, rising and clapping the speaker on the back. "Now we understand each other—and what do you intend to do with them?"

"That is my business," answered the colonel.

"Well, I won't inquire—perhaps it's best for me not to know any thing about the matter. Only I hope it's a safe game you're after."

"It isn't particularly safe, that you may depend upon."

"Well, all I can say is this, that in the morning you shall have the articles you have named," said the thieftaker, "and after that, I will give you a drop in to see how you are getting on."

"And poor Sir Reginald Fleetwood will be by this time, in all probability, murdered."

"Nay—not so. Let us hope not," said Wild. "The gentleman whom you took with you, a Mr. Carruthers, I believe, is determined not to let the matter drop, and is straining every nerve to get him out of that abominable hole where he is at present confined."

"And with any likelihood of success?" inquired our hero.

"I should suppose so, from all I hear."

"Then heaven will reward him for so good an act," said Colonel Jack; "and I do most sincerely hope he will be successful."

Wild took his departure, and agreeable to his promise, one of his men came with a message from him, and without making any observation placed the tools our hero had requested, before him. They were enclosed in a canvas bag, and the thieftaker's follower regarded our hero with a significant look as he placed them before him, and then silently took his departure.

"So he has kept his word in this instance," exclaimed Colonel Jack. "Perhaps, after all, he may mean fair—it looks like it. And now—ah! now I've got my work to do; and if I succeed—if! Ah! how my heart beats at that little word, so suggestive of doubt and uncertainty. If I succeed, Sir Richard Fleetwood, thou—and I have a long score to settle, which has been running for years and years, and increasing with the advance of time—a long—long arrear to settle."

CHAPTER LXXVI.

THE CONTEMPLATED ESCAPE.

THE room in which Colonel Jack was confined had but two other occupants. One of these was a man who had been committed on the charge of burglary, and the other was charged with body-snatching. They were both of them of a low class of criminals; but as it is an old adage that "misery acquaints us with strange bedfellows," the saying held good in the present instance, for within the walls of a prison a prisoner is generally herded with lawless companions.

The colonel, however, was a man who generally fraternised with all classes, gentle or simple; and he had not been many days in the walls of Newgate, before he and his chums were on the best possible terms.

In the evening they run over the narrative of their past career, and beguiled the weary hours with a tirade against the more respectable classes of society, pleasing themselves with the belief that they were injured beings, and generally illtreated by their fellow men.

From the first hour of our hero's incarceration thoughts of making his escape had taken possession of his mind, but to any one acquainted with the interior of Newgate, such an attempt must be looked upon as almost an impossibility. However, Colonel Jack had thought of it by day, and dreamt of it by night; in fact, it eventually became his only thought. How this was to be effected was the question, and as we are about to give the reader as plain a description of his proceedings as possible, we must direct his attention to the locality. It is hardly possible to convey to the mind precise particulars, unless the party so addressed had seen the interior of the building. Some of our readers may possibly have done so, by an order of one or more of the city corporation; and in this description of our hero's escape we are not indulging in any higher tale or romance—for very many years ago the writer of this work visited the prison, for the purpose of making drawings of that portion of it from which five prisoners had made their escape on the day previous. The room in which Colonel Jack and his other companions were confined was on the third storey, if such a term can be applied to such a building. At any rate, there were two other wards or set of rooms beneath. The windows of all these looked into the yards. There were three yards, namely, that belonging to what was termed the transport ward, which was on the left hand side of the one occupied by the colonel, which was called the schoolmaster's ward, the lower rooms being used for the reception of juvenile offenders, and the one on the right was used for the reception and selection of state prisoners, such as persons sent for a term of years to Newgate, either for libel, smuggling, high treason, piracy, or a host of other offences against the statute. Now all these wards were situated in that wing of the building which abutted against Newgate Street.

The reader must imagine, therefore, the situation of the colonel's room, on the third storey. Above this was what is termed the bread room, which was used solely for the purpose of the reception of bread, flour, and other stores which supplied the prison. The wall which faced these yards was built of solid brickwork faced with stone, and indeed, to a superficial observer, it looked precisely like a stone wall and nothing else. Now, there were three small windows in Colonel Jack's room—we call it his—as he at present occupies it. These windows looked into the yards below. Massive iron bars ran across these—so massive, indeed, that our hero knew it to be hopeless for him to attempt to remove these, besides this, such a course would have been attended with certain discovery, as it would attract the notice of the turnkeys. The roof of Newgate was a flat one, leaded, and all night long watchmen paced these leads to keep guard over the whole of the prison, besides this, the turnkeys, whose duty it was to open the iron gates which admitted persons into the yards, were also up all night, and were ensconced in little wooden boxes in the corner of the passage. The difficulties, therefore, which were in the way of the highwayman making his escape appeared to be almost insurmountable.

Colonel Jack had considered and reconsidered the matter over and over again. He had looked up from his yard towards the windows and wall of the apartment occupied by himself and his companions. He had then glanced around and noticed the position of the turnkeys in their wooden hutches. When coming from chapel on Sunday he passed by the places they occupied, and as he did so he noticed carefully the possibility of their seeing him, supposing he could effect a passage either through the wall or the window. It was a great stake he was playing for—life or death, and it required all his skill and determination, and it would not do to be lightly undertaken. When the colonel had mentioned to Wild respecting the tools, he had pretty well made up his mind what course to adopt with regard to the contemplated escape.

It was one evening that the colonel and his two companions were seated in the room where they were confined. They were locked in for the night, for the entrance to their room had two doors, about six or eight inches apart from each other. The outer one was of immense thickness, studded with nails, with bolts, catches, massive locks and fastenings of various descriptions, so as to defy all attempts to open it, besides this the inner door was almost as strong, and shut in against the solid stonework. From the inside it was customary for the wardsmen, accompanied by the turnkeys, to lock and bolt both these doors every evening at dusk, and open them the first thing on the following morning.

The colonel and his two companions, as we have before observed, were locked in.

"And so you think," said the highwayman, turning to the housebreaker. "You think that there is but a slender chance for you to escape a conviction, eh, Murdock?" said Colonel Jack.

"Dooced little chance of that 'ere," said the party so addressed.

"And you, Chitty?" said the colonel, turning to his other companion. "What say you?'

The man gave a groan, and shrugged his shoulders.

"Well," observed the burglar, "if so be as you are convicted it's only a lagging case."

"Don't make so sure as all that," said Chitty.

"Body-snatching ain't a capital offence," replied Murdock.

"If so be as the cove was a stiff 'un afore he was collared," said the other.

"Oh, that's it, eh? Why, you ain't been and dosed the poor crow?"

"*I* didn't," said Chitty.

"Oh, *you* didn't, but you know some one as did, which is much the same thing."

The man was silent.

"Well, gentlemen," observed the colonel, "we are all in the mire together; and such being the case, why, of course, it's best for us to stand by one another."

"Right you are, governor," said the housebreaker. "Spoken like a book; and it's as good as gold to hear you talk."

"There are but three of us here," said Colonel Jack, "and as I just now observed, we ought to stand by one another, seeing that no one will help us. I have a scheme. Are you two game to go hand and heart with me?"

"To the death!" exclaimed both of his companions.

"Good, I'll take you at your word, seeing that I cannot do otherwise. We must try and get out of this place."

No. 50.

"Ah," exclaimed both of the other prisoners, "but how?"

"Listen. Above this room is what is called the bread room. There's seldom any one there, except when they portion out our rations; so there isn't much danger in that quarter. Well, below us is the boys' ward, and I suppose the young rascals won't take much notice of what we do up here?"

"'Spose not; but what of that?" said Murdock.

"Why, just this. If we could manage to break an opening in this wall, we are within about a dozen or eighteen feet from the roof of this building."

"Well, and what then?" said Murdock.

"If we could manage to get through this opening by throwing something over the iron spikes which run round the roof, could we not climb up on to the roof itself?"

"And then be snatched up by the watchmen?"

"We must take our chance of that, my friends. There are three of us, and all our lives depend upon the success of our enterprise. We can't be worse off than we are at present, that's quite clear."

"Certainly not," exclaimed both of the men.

"Well, as we are all three of the same opinion upon that head, why, let us try our chance."

"There's my hand on it," said the housebreaker, rising from his seat, and presenting his horny palm to the colonel.

"But how are we to make an opening into this wall without the turnkeys in the yard seeing us?" said Chitty.

"We must work our way to the outer stonework, for you must understand that it is but bricks and mortar on this side. When we have worked our way to the outer facing, which is of stone, we must leave the removal of that to the last, and on the night of our escape, contrive to remove this as silently as possible, and then trust to providence."

All this was agreed upon, and after some further discussion, it was agreed that they were to commence operations on the following day.

As it turned out, it was lucky that they had not settled to do so that night, for early on the following morning, what was Colonel Jack's surprise to find a new prisoner added to the number who were already occupants of the north ward.

Our hero recognised him on the instant—he was no other than our old acquaintance, the Nobbler, whom Jonathan Wild had at last succeeded in capturing.

As soon as the turnkeys, who had conducted him into his present quarters, had departed, Colonel Jack at once presented himself to his notice.

The Nobbler was in a very surly mood, but as he had known our hero, he was a little more courteous to him than he might possibly have been to a stranger.

Of course the ground had to be all gone over again.

It would have been impossible for the original occupants of the room to attempt an escape without the concurrence of the new comer; but Colonel Jack surmised, naturally enough, that he was just the sort of person to fall in with the proposed scheme, and so, indeed, he was.

He was quite charmed with the idea, and entered most cordially into the discussions as to how it was to be effected.

On the following night, all the preliminaries were arranged.

Perhaps no man in the three kingdoms was so well adapted as the Nobbler to carry out the project which had been proposed by Colonel Jack.

Let us hear what he says upon the subject, as, in affairs of this sort, he was unquestionably an authority.

The Nobbler gazes at the wall of the apartment, and ruminates for some time, and then shakes his head.

"Won't do, colonel; we shall be clean licked if we attempt to do as you propose," said the housebreaker.

"Why so?" inquired our hero.

"It's just this 'ere. If we once begin to pick this wall to pieces—say even that we give ourselves only a day—how are we to be sure that some other cove may not be brought in here? And then, in course, the screwsman twigs our game, and darbies and the cells is our doom, till sich time as we are handed over to the bigwigs. Won't do, I tell you; we should be bowled out as clean as a whistle."

"Hang it, Jem," said Colonel Jack, "you haven't come into the stone-jug to throw cold water on our schemes?"

"Not I indeed, only you see it muzn't be done this ere way."

"How then?"

The Nobbler went towards the large chimney-place which was in the room occupied by Colonel Jack and his companions. He made a careful examination of this, which appeared satisfactory to himself.

"Ah, that's how it must be worked," said the Nobbler. "Above this apartment is the bread room."

"Yes."

"We must set to work as soon as the screwmen lock our door, and then—"

"Well, what?"

"One on us must turn climbing-boy, and get up the chimney, and work all night, if needs be, until we force a passage into the bread-room."

"And what then?"

"We must make an opening into the wall, and get on the roof."

Agreeable to this plan the Nobbler set that night to work; climbing up the chimney he supported himself by a portion of one of the bedsteads, and then, with the hammer and chisel furnished by Jonathan Wild to Colonel Jack, succeeded in forcing a passage into the chimney which run into the room. In this there was seldom any occupants, and the Nobbler had arranged matters so artistically, as to replace the brickwork, so that it was not at all probable that any one would see the effects of his his handywork, even supposing any curious eyes gazed into the chimney, or suspicion was in any way excited. The following day came, when, in the early portion of it, some of the officials took their way up into the bread-room. The Nobbler heard them descend, and in the afternoon thereof he, with the Colonel, gained a safe entrance into the room, and proceeded to make an aperture in the wall as near the ceiling as possible.

This was a work of considerable difficulty, for the brickwork was very strong, and at first resisted all their efforts; however, it eventually succumbed to the perseverence of the Nobbler and our hero. When they had removed a considerable portion they had the satisfaction of perceiving the entire coating of stone. This it was impossible for the prisoners to remove at present in consequence of the turnkeys in the yard. It was determined, therefore, to leave these few stones until the last thing, namely, on the night of their escape. It was usual for the men who had to portion out the victuals of the prison, to visit the bread-room sometimes twice, and at others three times a week, and the Nobbler and the Colonel calculated, therefore, that they would not do so on the following day—after their fissure in the wall. If they did, of course, their scheme would have been frustrated, as there was already well nigh a cart load of bricks on the floor of the apartment.

The colonel and his companion, when they had completed the work above descended by the chimney to their own apartment. What with the anxiety, the future, and the fear of discovery, they were fully well worn out, and the excitement produced by the attempt they were about to make forbade the possibility of any of the four sleeping, consequently they lay on their mattresses for the remainder of the night talking about the probability of their success. Colonel Jack knew the nature and disposition of the man with whom he had to deal. The Nobbler, as our readers have already seen, was a ruffian of no ordinary character, and in carrying out his views he would not be particular in sacrificing human life. He was quite certain that he did not stand the most remote chance of escaping capital punishment for his various crimes. Indeed, the burglary at Mr. Baintree's was not yet forgotten, and that in itself was quite enough to ensure his execution.

"Now, Jem," said Colonel Jack, as he lay tossing upon his bed, or rather mattress of straw. He was obliged to call him by the familiar name of "Jem," although he had a natural repulsion to the burglar—however, they were rowing in the same boat now, and were therefore by necessity considered palls for the nonce.

"Now, Jem, assuming that this affair turns out successful, and we gain the roof of the building—it is not at all probable that when we are there, that one of the watchmen may spring upon us—what's to be done then?"

"Why, just silence him," answered the Nobbler.

"Ah!—but how? There must be no murder," said Colonel Jack.

"Humph! Murder! I don't like the name—it ain't a purty term. Murder! I should first like to know this 'ere—'sposing you saw a man about to cut your throat, wouldn't you put a stopper on him? In course you would—murder indeed!"

"That's a different thing, Jem," said the colonel. "The watchmen are innocent persons, and in running their heads against us, are only fulfilling their duty."

"Well, we know that, and ain't we fulfilling ours, I should like to know?"

"Not by murder then?"

"Wouldn't the law murder us?"

"In course," chorussed the two other men, who evidently took the Nobbler's view of the question.

"Well, let it be distinctly understood," that I set my face against violence, or at least, such violence as sacrifices human life."

"Ah, as to that," answered the Nobbler, "it'll be one for his nob, whoever he may be, and that'll render my gentlemen insensible for a time."

"Yes, but one of your cracks on the crown are very likely to render insensible for ever."

"We must take the chance of that. It won't do to be nasty particular."

"Jem," said the colonel, "I wish you would leave the dealing of these men to me."

"Very good. So be it master—you're captain in this business, and colonel unto all, so that's all well and good."

The morning came, and the prisoners were constantly upon the listen to hear if any one was ascending the staircase to the bread-room. Luckily, none of the officials of the prison visited it that day, and Colonel Jack and the Nobbler were felicitating themselves that all was going on well.

Our hero paced up and down the yard, and every now and then his eye glanced up towards the spot where he and the Nobbler had chosen to operate on. He could only guess at the spot, for as yet the outer stonework had not been removed.

In the course of that day, which was an anxious one to our hero, as well as his companions, the renowned Jonathan Wild made his appearance in the prison yard.

Upon his catching sight of Colonel Jack, he at once hastened to his side, and entered into conversation with him.

"Make your mind easy, colonel, respecting Sir Reginald Fleetwood. He ain't dead, and, let us hope, not likely to be so for the present."

"And Mr. Carruthers?"

"Has acted like a brick. Although his time is so valuable, that he can't spare much to see into the business, nevertheless, he has obtained another order from a magistrate, and, I believe, is in a fair way of getting Sir Reginald Fleetwood released from his present captivity."

"I am, indeed, much pleased to hear you say so," said our hero.

"You got the tools all right?" asked Wild, with a meaning look.

"Yes, and many thanks for the same," said the colonel.

"You have a rare scoundrel among your crew."

"Who do you mean?"

"The Nobbler," answered Wild.

"Yes, that's true enough; came in the day before yesterday."

"You must be cautious in dealing with him."

"Oh, as to that, I've known the fellow before to-day."

"Don't let him into your scheme," said Wild, in a whisper.

"Oh, no, of course not," answered Colonel Jack, carelessly, and endeavouring to turn the conversation.

"Well, I won't inquire further," said Wild. "I don't want to know any of your secrets; indeed, I would rather not. Only I shall be glad to see you on the outside of these walls, and if there is anything more you want of me, send a message by Bradshaw, and it shall be attended to. There, I can't say more than that, can I?"

The thieftaker shook hands with the highwayman, and took a hasty departure.

He had not been gone long before Squab-shot made his appearance. Indeed, the latter individual had been constant in his attendance upon our hero, and scarcely a day passed without his visiting the prison.

"My dear fellow," exclaimed Squabshot, "how fares it with you."

"I live," exclaimed the colonel. "I find that trouble does not kill."

"And in good spirits?"

"Well, I can't say much as to that; but hope has not as yet quite deserted me."

"Do you think there is any chance of your obtaining an acquittal?"

"Not the slightest."

"What have you to hope for, then?"

"Hush!—breathe not a syllable—Squab-shot, I am about to make an attempt at an escape."

"Never, surely!" and Squabshot looked around at the strong stone walls which enclosed the prisoners.

"Listen, Squabshot. This very night myself and three other companions intend, if possible, to gain the roof of this building, and then, if possible, gain the street."

"Pray heaven that you may succeed, old boy," exclaimed Squabshot, grasping the highwayman by the hand. "I shall be all on tenter hooks until I learn the success of your project. To-night, say you?"

"Yes, this very night, or rather morning, most likely."

"I will be on the watch," said Squabshot, in great glee.

"Where?"

"In Newgate Street."

"Oh, don't do that, for it is quite uncertain at what time we may be able to make good our retreat."

"No matter, I shall be on the watch if it's all night," exclaimed Squabshot.

"You have not mentioned anything about my being here to Osborne?"

"Not a syllable, believe me."

"That is well. I am much beholden to you, Squabshot, for this, as for many other favours. Now look here, Squabshot, if you do really mean to be on the watch, bring with you a good long rope."

"What for?"

"Why, not to hang ourselves with," rejoined the colonel, with a laugh; "but it may be useful, in case of emergency, to let ourselves down into the street."

"It shall be done. By the Lord, but this will be glorious! Escaped from Newgate! What joyful words are those!"

Once more promising to be on the watch that night, Squabshot took his departure.

CHAPTER LXXVII.

THE ESCAPE.

LUCKILY for the prisoners, there was no other individual brought in as a prisoner to their ward, and when the time came for them to be locked in for the night, the turnkeys came round and fastened the door, little suspecting the plot which was hatching under their very nose.

The prisoners waited for two or three hours before they dreamt of making any attempt to reach the bread room.

They heard the shouts and noise of the juvenile delinquents in the room beneath. These same lads generally made a great noise after they were locked in for the night, and were, indeed, an uproarious set of young rascals.

"My heart goes pit a pat, as the time draws nigh," said Chitty, the body snatcher, "I wonder whether we shall succeed?"

"It's no use making wry faces when you've got to swallow medicine," answered the Nobbler. "We shall have to be up and doing, and the chief difficulty will be Hawkins, the turnkey. He commands a view of the spot where we have to break through, and if by chance he should have his peepers wide open, it will run awkward with us; but we must chance that."

"I think Hawkins won't have his eyes particularly wide open to-night," answered Colonel Jack.

"You think not—why?" exclaimed the Nobbler, fixing upon his companion a look of sudden surprise,

"Because, if all goes on as I expect it will, our friend Hawkins won't be at his post at all—at least, I hope not."

"You don't mean to say that, colonel? What makes you think that?"

"I have a friend who's invited him to a small tea party," answered the colonel, with a smile.

"Ah, ah! Hope he'll enjoy himself," laughed the Nobble. "How did you manage that?"

"A friend of mine to whom I just dropped a hint, said that he would manage to get Hawkins off his post to night for an hour or so."

"At what time?" eagerly inquired the Nobbler.

"At bout eleven or a little after was the reply.

"Excellent arrangement, then all will go well, I feel assured of that."

The four prisoners waited with patience till the bell of St. Sepulchre's struck the hour or eleven, upon which the one after the other ascended the chimney, taking with them a portion of their bedsteads, some rugs, and a small piece of rope, which, however, was not sufficiently strong to bear their weight with safety. They all gained the bread-room in safety. A flood of moonlight poured into this, which rendered a light unnecessary. The vast pile of bricks lay upon the floor precisely as they had left them the previous day. Now came the difficulty of removing the outer stonework from the inside without any portion of it falling on the pavement in the yard below. This was a task which required the greatest care and skill in accomplishing. Indeed, so much so, that it appeared to be almost an impossibility. Nothing daunted, however, the Nobbler, who was the most dexterous hand at this sort of business, commenced scraping away the cement which fastened the stones together. In a short time the prisoners had the satisfaction of seeing the vault of heaven through the fissure of the stones. Their heart beat quickly. In a few moments more the first stone was sufficiently loosened as to be capable of removal. The Nobbler, however, hesitated in taking it from its position. Suppose some watchful eyes were directed towards the spot. Strong nerved ruffian as

he unquestionably was, he nevertheless hesitated in the completion of his task.

"Just you go to the farther window one of you," said the Nobbler, "and have a squint at Hawkins's hutch, he may stag us arter all."

Murdock and the colonel intantly took their way to the window, and gazed out. No Hawkins met their anxious gaze.

"He ain't there I think," said Murdock, in a hoarse whisper. "Leastways, I cant see nothing on him."

"Sure? Look again," said the Nobbler.

"No, the hutch is empty," said Colonel Jack. "I knew it would be so, and he judged rightly. He had sent round to Wild in the after part of the day, telling him to contrive by some means to draw off the obnoxious Hawkins, and the thieftaker had kept his word.

"Then here goes for it," said the Nobbler.

By a great effort he began wriggling about the stone, but it did not become detached so soon as he had expected. It still held tenaciously to its brother stones, as though loth to part company with them.

"Hang it all! but the cursed thing won't come out. What holds it, I wonder!" exclaimed the Nobbler, the perspiration now pouring down in thick beads on his forehead.

"Why there's a piece of wrought iron running from one stone to another," exclaimed Colonel Jack.

The Nobbler staggered back a pace or two at this unwelcome discovery. More work lies to be done, but how was this difficulty to be got over? The housebreaker paused. "It's too thick to file," he said, "even if we had one."

"Try the next stone. You may be more fortunate with that," suggested the colonel.

No time was to be lost, so once more the Nobbler set to work. Again the mortar was gradually scraped away, and soon the moon's rays found their way through the narrow aperture. The four men shuddered, however, as they heard several pieces of mortar fall upon the stones below.

"Be careful, Jem. Good luck to you, be careful, or we shall be ruined. The other turnkey will hear the noise of the falling mortar in the silent and dead hour of the night."

"You'd better manage it yourself then," retorted the Nobbler, sulkily, "for I'm blest if I arn't getting sick of the job, and that's all about it."

"There, that will do, Jem, we don't want to be squabbling now," said the colonel.

"Who said we did? Not I," said the housebreaker.

"Well then, fire away. Out with the stones"

Once more the Nobbler commenced wriggling backwards and forwards the two stones. This time he was more successful, although these were fastened together by a piece of iron there was not much difficuly in removing them both together. By a sudden effort the burglar wrested them from their position, and threw them on the heap of bricks which strewed the floor of the apartment. A stream of light came into the room, and the cold night air fanned the hot and fevered cheeks of the four prisoners. So sudden had been the act of their operating mason, that they all four drew back as though subject to some sudden and undefined fear. After a moment the robber said—

"Now we can look out and see if there be any prying screwsman on the look out, and if there be, why—"

"It won't be healthy," said Murdock.

Colonel Jack crept to the opening, and peered out. It was a strange sight—below were the three yards, with their iron rails at the farther end of each—beyond these was the passage paced in the day time by the turnkeys, or screwsmen, as they were termed by the prisoners—and beyond that passage was the wall of another portion of the prison. Luckily, this was what is called a blank wall, having on it no windows or doors—besides the one which led into the vaulted corridor, through which the ordinary and officials were wont to take their way. Not a soul was stirring, at least, no one that the colonel could see. Of course, the watchmen were pacing their usual roads upon the roof, but none of them were in sight, had they have been so, it would have been all up with the four prisoners, for the alarm could have been given, and then good-bye to sweet liberty.

"All is as silent as the grave," said the colonel, withdrawing his hand from the aperture, and gazing at the Nobbler, who stood fainting and snorting like an old race-horse.

"It's of no use hesitating, and we ain't nice to creep through a hole like that 'ere," said the Nobbler, and he forthwith set about removing three or four more stones, and in a very short time after this the orifice in the wall was sufficiently large so as to admit of the body of a man passing through it.

When this had been effected, the Nobbler put his head and shoulders through, and looked up towards the roof, along which ran a chevaux-de-frise.

"Curse me if any on us shall be able to get upon the roof with this miserable bit of rope. What's to be done?" he inquired hastily, for by this time the whole party were well nigh beside themselves with excitement.

"Blow me, if I know," said Murdock, looking out.

"I have it," exclaimed Colonel Jack.

"Here's part of this bedstead; that will answer the purpose. Part of the head is on, and that will lodge on the spikes, and we can tie the other end inside."

The Nobbler took another survey, and without losing time in discussion, pushed out the bedstead, fixed the end firmly on the spikes, and in a minute or so more bound the other end with his cord.

"It's neck or nothing. May be it won't bear us, but it ain't of no use striking upon trifles. Whose the first man to mount?"

"I will, if you like," said the colonel.

"All right—so be it, then. On you goes."

Colonel Jack passed through the opening. A giddy and sickening sensation came over him, he as he glanced at the yards below, he was trusting himself to a ricketty, and wretchedly frail structure, which swayed with him as he lay hold of it.

Had he hesitated for only a second or so, the probability is that he would have become incapable of making the hazardous attempt —but he nerved himself up to his task, and knew that it was no time now to falter.

Life and death were the stakes, and so crawling cautiously along the rail which had served for the side of his bedstead, he succeeded in gaining the top of the wall.

When he got there, he found it impossible to get over the chevaux-de-frise; but he had been prepared for this, so grasping the spikes he got his knees on the wall, and succeeded in laying himself at full length on this, then rolling his body round the spikes, which were moveable, they turned with him and in another second he tumbled into the gutter which ran round the building.

All this had been preconcerted by himself and his companions.

The Nobbler, the moment he perceived the body of our hero disappear, adopted a similar course with a like success. He, also, dropped into the gutter.

"Lay still for the present," said Colonel Jack, in a low whisper. "The chaps on the roof can't see us where we are, as it's in shadow. Lay still till the other chaps get through."

The Nobbler did as our hero suggested, and the two waited for some time expecting to see one of their companions, who, however, did not make their appearance.

"What on earth can they be about?" said the colonel.

"Hush! They come," said the Nobbler, and the noise of a crawling figure was heard along the rail of the bedstead.

The two men in the gutter strained their ears to catch every sound, when a cry of piercing agony rent the air, and the dead and sickening sound of a falling body on the stones beneath came upon the senses of the two escaped prisoners.

Murdock had gained the wall, and in endeavouring to put himself under the chevaux-de-frise, he either turned giddy, or else his foot slipped, or from some cause or the other he missed his hold, and he fell with a fearful crash on the stones below.

"Merciful heaven, he has fallen," exclaimed Colonel Jack, as he looked over the wall of the prison, and saw the disfigured and shattered body of his companion in misfortune in the yard beneath.

"We must hook it at once, then," said the Nobbler, springing to his feet. "The game will be up in another minute or so."

And with these words he ran over the leads on the roof, the colonel falling. As he did so he found himself suddenly in the grasp of one of the watchmen.

"Help! murder!" shouted out the man.

"Hold your row!" said the Nobbler, striking the man with his clenched fist so terrible a blow that he was felled like an ox, and lay prostrate on the leads.

"Help!—help!" shouted out the watchman, and he endeavoured to spring his rattle—but in another second the Nobbler's knee was on his chest and his hand on his throat.

"Quick!—the rope!" said the Nobbler. "Now tie his arms—that's it—and his legs. Good. Now thrust your wipe in his tater-trap."

All this was but the work of a few seconds, and the man bound and gagged was left to his fate, while the colonel and his companion ran on towards the end of the prison which abutted on Newgate Street.

Before they had reached this point another of the watchmen caught the colonel by the throat, and screamed out much more lustily than his coadjutor.

This worthy was a son of the emerald isle.

"Och, I shall be kilt entirely—almost, I mane, but, murther—thieves! Bad luck to me, but you ain't a goin' to give us the slip intirely. Murther, I say, and treason."

A desperate struggle ensued between the man and the colonel, and it was hardly possible to tell how this would have terminated, for the man kept calling out, and would have soon had a host around him, but the Nobbler struck him a blow on the side of the head with the mason's hammer he carried in his pocket, and in another minute he fell prostrate and senseless with a fractured skull.

Upon this the colonel hastened to the other end of the building. When he arrived thither, he saw in the street below the figures of Squabshot, Hackett, Knapp, and Mullins.

"Throw up a rope, some on you'" shouted out the Nobbler.

"Hackett had a coil of rope already prepared, but to throw this to the top of a building like Newgate was a feat which would have puzzled the most experienced and practical mariner. Two ineffectual attempts were made—the coil of yarn fell down into the street.

"My God, we shall be lost," exclaimed the colonel. "I hear the sound of distant voices. They have discovered most likely the body of Murdock."

"I have it," said the Nobbler, as he hastily took a thin piece of rope, which he had cut from his own bedstead. "I'll drop this down and then they can fasten the other to it."

This was done, and in another minute the two prisoners had the gratification of hauling up the coil of rope which their friends and companions had brought with them.

When they obtained this, there was another difficulty which presented itself. There was nothing to which they could fasten it, but the Nobbler who had brought with him both the mason's chisel and hammer, at once proceeded to drive the former into the mortar of the stonework which ran round the building.

To fasten the rope to this was but the work of a few seconds, and the burglar then threw it over the parapet, and left it dangling into the street.

"Now then, colonel, look alive. You go first as before," said the Nobbler.

Colonel Jack had scarcely swung himself over the parapet, and began to descend by the rope, when he heard the sound of many voices. Several turnkeys and other officials were making towards the spot.

"Look sharp!" exclaimed the Nobbler. "The whole prison seems to have turned out upon the roof, and we shall be grabbed."

He did not wait for the colonel to descend, but swung himself over the parapet of the prison, and slid down the rope, his feet touching the shoulders of the colonel as he descended. It was a wonder that he had not thrown him off the rope by his sudden fall.

As luck would have it, the two alighted on the pavement in Newgate Street in perfect safety.

"Hurrah!" shouted out Hackett and Knapp.

"Fire!—fire upon them!" said the Old Bailey officials.

Two reports were heard from pistols, which were discharged at random, and did no harm to those in the street.

"You scoundrels! we'll have you yet!" exclaimed the deputy governor.

A shout of derisive laughter was the answer to this threat.

A rush was made into the street by several of the prison authorities, but when they arrived there, nobody was to be seen but a dosing old Charley, who shouted and sprang his rattle without any clear knowledge of what it was all about.

———

CHAPTER LXXVIII.

COLONEL JACK and the Nobbler had got clear off.

It will be necessary now to take a glance at the two other individuals who had formed part of the four prisoners who had attempted their escape.

Murdock, it seemed, had become nervous upon climbing through the aperture in the brickwork. It was this nervousness which had been the cause of his death.

Upon his falling upon the pavement beneath, Chitty, the body snatcher, became so completely prostrated with fear, that he found it impossible to make the attempt himself. He gazed stupidly upon the prostrate form of his companion below, and actually groaned with anguish.

The noise of the falling man aroused those whose duty it was to watch the interior of the prison during the night.

Several rushed towards the spot. The gate which led to the yard was opened, and the dead body of Murdock found upon the pavement.

He was quite dead. His skull was fractured, his back broken, as well as several smaller bones of the body. For a moment or so the awful appearance of the dead man, whose ghastly features were revealed by the moon's rays, rather staggered those who looked upon him. Indeed, the sight was enough to apall the stoutest heart.

The next thing that attracted the attention of those who had been aroused was the large opening in the brickwork.

Then it was that the particulars of the proceedings began to dawn upon them, and calling to those on the roof, they inquired if anyone had made their escape over the leads. No answer was returned to this interrogatory.

One man lay bound hand and foot, with his mouth gagged; and the other one was stretched senseless by the blow dealt by the Nobbler.

However, other persons were eventually aroused.

The deputy governor looked out from the window of his sleeping apartment, and inquired what was the matter?

Upon being informed, he aroused several sleeping turnkeys, and as there was a passage from his own room on to the roof, he and five or six others took their way across the leads.

Had they have done so but a few minutes earlier, the probability is, that our hero and his companion, the Nobbler, would have been captured, and led back ignominiously to " durance vile."

When the deputy governor and his party found that the escaped prisoners and their companions were nowhere to be seen, either in Newgate Street or its surrounding neighbourhood, they returned, disconsolate enough, to the prison once more, and aroused the governor. Not that there could be any possible use in their doing so, but it was considered a matter of duty.

The governor, as might be expected, was irritated at the state of affairs, and immediately proceeded to the spot from whence the colonel and his companions had made their escape.

Proceeding up stairs to the room where the prisoners had been confined, they observed its only occupant, Chitty, trembling in every limb.

One glance round the room showed the governor that all the birds had flown with the exception of the poor unfortunate body snatcher. One bird had tumbled to the earth as he had endeavoured to wing his flight through ether.

" So, sir," said the governor, to Chitty, " what's the meaning of all this murder, eh ?"

" Oh, oh !—please, sir, I haven't had no hand in it. I knew how it would be. 1 told them so, but they wouldn't listen to reason. Oh, dear, dear, poor Murdock—oh, oh !"

" There, that'll do—don't pitch us any of your gammon," said the wardsman. " We want to know—leastways, the guv'nor does —how all this has occurred ? One chap lies dead beneath, and two other coves have hooked it, and in course you know all about it."

" I'd nothing to do with it—I'd swear it," said Chitty.

" Now, look here, my man," said the governor, " it's impossible this foul and abominable scheme could have been concocted and carried right under your very nose, without your knowing all about it. If you refuse to tell, I shall order you to the press room, and there force you to tell all you know—force—do you understand?"

" Oh, yes, sir, please I'll tell all I know," answered Chitty, who well knew the tender mercies of the press-room; however, perhaps our readers, or, at any rate, a section of them do not.

It was customary, in the earlier days of the administration of the English law, to take prisoners into the press-room, to force from them a confession of their crimes. This was done by laying them between two large stones, and adding on to the top of

these two heavy weights, until the agony produced thereby became almost insupportable. Happily, this barbarous practice has become a remnant of the past, over which is drawn the curtain of time.

"Please, sir," says Chitty, "Colonel Jack and the Nobbler have hooked it."

"Well, we know that, my man, but how? They have not made their escape from this room it is quite clear."

"Humbly begs your pardon, sir, but they worked their way up the chimney."

The governor and his assistants stared with surprise, as well they might. Chitty took them to the fireplace, and showed them the aperture there made by the Nobbler.

"And they then got into the bread-room," said the body-snatcher.

No. 51.

The whole party then wheeled off up stairs, and entered the room in question. The first thing that met their gaze was the large pile of bricks on the floor of the room, and saw plainly enough the escape had been effected. This done, they returned again to their different stations in the prison. The governor immediately started off a messenger for Jonathan Wild, who came back with him, and went into the governor's house.

"Well, Mr. Wild, here has been a pretty affair taken place in the course of the night. We shall get into sad discredit with the corporation. Two prisoners have managed to make their escape."

"From what part of the prison, sir?" inquired Wild, "and who might they be?—if I may make so bold as to ask."

" Colonel Jack, and a ruffian called the Nobbler."

A smile played over the features of the thieftaker.

"And have they got clear off?" he inquired.

"Yes, I regret to say they have. You must hunt them down, Wild—they *must* be retaken, for my credit and—for your own."

" If they can be caught they shall be, that you may depend on," said Wild.

"If! There is no if in the matter—you, or some of your followers, know their haunts. They are marked men—notorious men, and cannot, must not be allowed to escape justice."

" Let us hope not, sir."

" Confound it! don't talk about hoping —there will be a pretty fuss about this matter when it gets known."

Wild promised to do all in his power to recapture the escaped prisoners, and then took his departure.

In the morning of the following day the Lord Mayor, the sheriffs, and some of the aldermen paid a visit to the city prison. Mr. Gubbins, the Lord Mayor elect, stalked pompously through the ward and passages of the gloomy prison, and the whole party pursued their way up into the bread-room. Of course, all they could see was a huge pile of bricks, and a large aperture in the wall.

We are not going to treat the reader with the number of stupid questions that were put by these sapient city authorities. Sapient at all times, but especially so at the time of which we write. One great man, an alderman, expressed his astonishment that any man could have had the temerity and hardihood to attempt such an escape, if it were only for feelings of consolation towards the governor and his family, " For," observed this worthy, " they must have been well aware that it would get you into disgrace, you who have always treated the occupants of this prison with such kindness, and forbearance." The idea of two men, who had the prospect of an ignominous death before their eyes having a chivalrous consideration for the governor and his family was too ridiculous, and some of the party could not help indulging in a quaint smile. It was Squire Gubbins's turn to speak—he was oracular, and attempted to be dignified—dignity did not sit easily upon him, nevertheless, he endeavoured to assume it.

"These things cannot be allowed," he said, turning to the governor. " In a Christian country, where the laws which protect the honest man from his dishonest fellow ought to be carried out—nay, more, they must be."

" Yes," interrupted a stout alderman, who was disposed to take a comic view of the question, and thought, perhaps, after all, that it was rather a clever business than otherwise. " But you see, Mr. Gubbins, it's impossible to carry out the law with these rascals—they are before us, they have carried themselves out. Ah! ah! it's a simple question of debit and credit."

Mr. Gubbins inflated his ponderous anatomy—he felt scandalised. Such jests upon such a grave subject were, in his opinion, quite out of place.

" I say these things must not be, and shall not be while I hold my present position. It's scandalous that we cannot build a prison sufficiently strong to hold those who have outraged the laws. It must be inquired into. I shall make it my business to see that this is done, or else I shall feel, if I neglect doing so, that I am not doing my duty to the corporation and city of London—to the livery of London, and—and," he paused, and then completed his sentence, by adding, " the world at large."

" The world in quod you mean, said the coarse alderman.

" Mr Boodle, sir!" exclaimed the mayor. " You really—upon my word, sir—I don't understand this liberty."

" I very deeply regret this circumstance," said the governor, parenthetically. " I'm sure that it has been from no want of care and watchfulness on the part of the officials of the prison. I very deeply regret this unfortunate occurrence, and all that can be done to recapture these daring offenders shall be, believe me."

" Recaptured they must be," exclaimed Mr. Gubbins. " The majesty of the law is outraged—the whole framework of society is broken down. Of what use are enactments, laws made for the protection of the honest class of the community, if they are not carried out. Escaped from Newgate !—it appears impossible."

" It appears to me, to be not only possible but very probable, and what is more, particularly certain," exclaimed the alderman who had taken a comic view of the case.

" Umph!" exclaimed the mayor, in unmitigated disgust. " I see no cause for jesting in this matter—one that must of necessity bring scandal upon the Corporation and City of London."

And with these words, the chief city magistrate stalked majestically through the yard, into the passage, followed by the rest of the assembled individuals, and shortly afterwards left the prison.

———

CHAPTER LXXIX.

A GLANCE AT SIR RICHARD FLEETWOOD.

It must not be supposed that Sir Richard Fleetwood, during this period, had remained in a passive state. On the contrary, that unworthy baronet was watching, with eyes of the utmost anxiety, all the circumstances connected with Colonel Jack.

The baronet had been the cause of the highwayman's capture.

When he had become acquainted with the time it was likely for our hero to be at the house kept by Mr. Hardy, in company with the visiting surgeons, Sir Richard had given notice to the police authorities, who, in consequence, sent Jonathan Wild and his followers, and hence the capture.

Sir Richard had a miserable time of it, however, for he trembled each day, as the news reached his ears, that Mr. Carruthers was making strenuous efforts to effect the release of his elder brother from the establishment of Mr. Hardy.

The baronet was perfectly appalled at these proceedings. He saw in them certain destruction to his hopes and present position. It was in vain for him to endeavour to conceal from himself that he would be hurled from the position he occupied, and obloquy and disgrace awaited him.

He still kept Honora Langford close prisoner in the cottage near to Barnes Common, whither his emissaries had originally consigned her.

In vain the baronet had used alternately threats and entreaties—in vain had he had recourse to violence. Honora Langford had resisted all his appeals, and although borne down with grief, that she had daily waxed thinner and thinner, nevertheless the baronet found her impenetrable to all his appeals.

It is probable that he might have had some chance with her if he had not adopted his present course of action; as it was, Miss Langford was naturally incensed at being made prisoner, and too much disgusted with the baronet to ever even respect him again.

In the cottage in which she found herself prisoner, Miss Langford had no other companion but the old woman, Dame Ludlow, who was kind enough to her, only continually pestering about the virtues and admirable character of Sir Richard, all of which was annoying enough to Honora, who several times had made an effort to so ingratiate herself in the graces of Dame Ludlow, as to win her over as a friend. She was, however, faithful to the trust of Sir Richard, and positively refused to convey any letters to the post office for Honora.

We must now take a glance at the baronet himself, as he is seated in his library at Acton.

Leaning back in his arm chair, and throwing the paper he had been reading on one side, Sir Richard Fleetwood becomes aware that there is another individual besides himself in the apartment in which he was seated.

This person had come into the room with noiseless footsteps. How he had managed to open the door so quietly, and present himself before his master, is a mystery known only to himself; but there he was, with a quiet, placid, impassible expression of countenance, grave in its character, humble, too. So humble and unobtrusive was this man's manners and movements, that he seemed to express thereby—

"Please, sir, may so unobtrusive an individual as myself be permitted to exist in the same room as yourself, to breathe the same atmosphere without contaminating it?"

In fact it would be almost impossible to convey to the reader's mind the humble bearing of this individual.

He was the confidential servant and valet of Sir Richard, and was in a good many of his secrets.

"Ah, it's you, Morgan?" said the baronet, raising his eyes.

"Yes, if you please, Sir Richard," said the man so addressed, who, like a pet spaniel, when his master addressed him, looked pleased, and wagged his tail.

Mr. Morgan looked pleased, and a sort of satisfactory tone came from him as he uttered these few words.

"Umph! Any news, Morgan?" said the baronet.

"Beg your pardon, Sir Richard, but in respect to what?" said Mr. Morgan, perking his head on one side, and glancing at his master with his dexter eye.

"Respecting anything—this absurd imposition that it has pleased some half crazy doctor to imagine, or pretend to imagine—ah—I allude to the madman whom this Mr. Carruthers chooses to suppose to be a relative of mine?"

"People will say such strange things in this world," said Mr. Morgan.

"You have heard no more of it, then?" said the baronet, who knew perfectly well, or guessed, that Mr. Morgan had come in for some purpose or other.

"I believe Mr. Carruthers has seen the gentleman," said the valet.

"How long since?"

"I think, yesterday."

"Alone?"

"I think not alone; but I cannot say as to that with a certainty."

"Ah, a meddling fool!" exclaimed the baronet, striking the table with his fist.

" I believe, sir, that Mr. Carruthers thinks he shall be able to effect his object, and get the release of this—ahem!—(a gentle cough behind his hand) unfortunate and misguided gentleman."

"How have you heard this?" inquired Sir Richard sharply.

"Oh, if you please sir," said Morgan, and then suddenly paused.

"Well, go on," said his master.

"Ahem!" (another cough, deprecatory this time), "I should be sorry to trouble you with servants' gossip, and begging your pardon, sir, it isn't exactly altogether my place to trouble you with any such tittle-tattle; but it so happens that I am acquainted with an individual who has the honour of belonging to Mr. Carruthers' establishment—least ways, sir, I am wrong in saying has the honour—"

"Never mind about that," said Sir Richard, impatiently. "You know one of the servants of Mr. Carruthers—well and good—so be it."

"And I understand from him that his master, the doctor, felt quite certain about getting the release of the unfortunate person—ah—about whom you have already heard enough."

"Is that all, Morgan?" said the baronet. "We knew as much as this more than a week ago."

"We did, Sir Richard—we certainly did," answered the valet.

His master looked curiously at him. He felt quite certain that the man had not come into the library for no other purpose than to utter that which he knew perfectly well could be no news to him.

The two stood silent for a minute or so, and then Mr. Morgan began to busy himself about the room, and arrange his master's library table.

The baronet took up a book, and carelessly turned over the leaves. This was done without any intention of reading it, for his mind was too distraught to admit of his entering into the interests of any work.

"Ahem!" said Mr. Morgan, with another cough (his throat seemed always dry and husky); "you have heard the news from town, I suppose, sir?"

"No—what? I have not heard anything in particular," answered his master.

"Why, the escape from Newgate," answered Mr. Morgan.

"Escape from Newgate!" exclaimed the baronet. "What—who—when did it occur?"

"Last night, if you please sir," said Mr. Morgan.

"Indeed!—how was it effected? But, stay, I mean, who escaped?"

"Two individuals, so I am told, sir," said the valet, in his usual slow, drawling tones.

"One of them was a person, I believe, who—ah—was a very bad man, a burglar—which I believe means a housebreaker—and the other—"

"Yes, the other."

"Was a highwayman, known to the world as the celebrated Colonel Jack."

"D——n!" exclaimed the baronet, turning deadly pale, and actually trembling with rage, or fear, or whatever the emotion might be, for it would have been difficult to say which.

"Colonel Jack escaped? Impossible! You must be mistaken—misinformed."

"Begs pardon, but I think not," said Mr. Morgan, with a shrug.

"How did you hear of this?"

"Snatcher, who comes from London every day with his cart told me so—he heard of it this morning in the market," said Morgan.

"Do you think there is any truth in this story?"

"Oh, dear yes, sir," said he, with a stronger emphasis on his words than he had hitherto indulged in—"Oh dear yes, sir, it is quite true."

The baronet leant his head upon his two hands, and looked at the table with a fixed and earnest gaze. There was that in his countenance which was really fearful to look upon, so disturbed was it with violent emotion or passions. He waved his hand to the valet, who suddenly, but noiselessly, left the room without another word.

When he had left Sir Richard rose and hurriedly paced the apartment.

"Escaped!" he exclaimed. "That man bears a charmed life. My evil genius—escaped! to torment me and make existence unendurable. Curses on him!—must leave the country. It will never do to risk staying longer here. No, I must fly to the continent—anywhere to be out of the way of a sneering and envious world."

The baronet rang the bell, and Mr. Morgan appeared in answer to his summons. The valet merely breathed gently, and looked at his master.

"The carriage," said Sir Richard.

"To be got ready, sir?" said Morgan.

"Yes, as quickly as possible."

The valet disappeared without another word, and in a few minutes the carriage was in readiness. Sir Richard drove to London, and had a long interview with Mr. Sharpthorne. He then went to his bankers, and there made a transfer of a considerable sum of money to be made payable at a French bankers in Paris.

All these proceedings were taken to make preparations for his starting for the continent, when he had completed these arrangements he drove to Barnes Common. Putting up his carriage at a livery stable, he walked on foot towards the cottage where Honora Langford was confined. Giving a well-known knock at the outer door—it was opened by Dame Ludlow.

"Oh, it's you, Sir Richard," said the old woman, dropping a curtsey as she led the way into her own private apartment, not the one occupied by Honora Langford herself.

"How does your charge, Mrs. Ludlow," inquired the baronet.

"Oh, much the same as usual, Sir Richard, much the same. I have talked to her, reasoned, done all I can in fact, but she is obstinate, Sir Richard, and I fear self-willed. Dear me, what it is to love! Now I remember myself, when Phil Slasher, of the 14th Buffs, first made up to me, why, Lord bless you, there wasn't a person in the whole world who had eloquence enough to make me turn from him. I was mad, Sir Richard, literally stark staring mad."

"Yes, yes, I dare say," answered the baronet. "No doubt—so are half your sex, madam."

"Well, as I was about to observe," said the dame, in continuation.

"Ah, never mind that just now," said Sir Richard. "I have come upon rather pressing business."

"Indeed! anything new, Sir Richard?"

"Well, your young charge must get herself in readiness to take her departure, for she leaves for the continent to-morrow."

"Indeed," exclaimed Mrs. Ludlow. "This is sudden."

"Yes, but it is so by necessity. There is no alternative—she must get herself in readiness, for go she must, whether she likes it or not."

"She will not like to leave here."

"Indeed, I thought she was most anxious to do so as soon as possible—she always said so."

"Perhaps you had better see her yourself, Sir Richard," said Dame Ludlow.

"Certainly—see your charge, and say I would speak to her."

Dame Ludlow left the apartment, and proceeded into the one occupied by Honora Langford

In a moment or so more Sir Richard himself entered the room occupied by Honora, who started as he made his appearance, and an expression of pain and discontent passed over her beauteous features.

"Miss Langford," said the baronet, quietly, "circumstances compel me to leave this country for awhile."

"Well, sir," said Miss Langford, "your movements have nought to do with me."

"Pardon me, madam, but they most materially affect yours. In fact, I cannot go without you, consequently, I bid you prepare to accompany me by to-morrow."

"Accompany you?—never!"

"It is useless your endeavouring to thwart me," answered Sir Richard. "I have had patience enough with you I'm thinking."

"What am I to think of this conduct?" answered Honora. "It is such that I can do nothing else but despise you for the part you are playing. Can it be possible that you who profess to be a gentleman should so far forget yourself as to use force towards one who has never injured you by word or deed?"

"I love you," he said firmly.

"I will never believe that a man regards me with any such feeling who has acted in the manner you have towards me. Oh, Sir Richard, have mercy on me! Have respect for yourself. Have some small share of humanity to one who is distraught in mind, and borne down by a weight of affliction too terrible to contemplate. You surely must have some spark of human pity left in your composition. If so, have mercy on me—cut off and isolated from my friends, I am here among strangers and without help."

"Miss Langford," said Sir Richard, "we will not go over the same ground which has already been trodden by both of us on so very many occasions. Prepare yourself for to-morrow. Mrs. Ludlow will attend to all your wishes, and will, to save appearances, or scandal, accompany us to Dover. After which you may choose your own ladies' maid or female attendant. Farewell for the present," and the baronet left the room without any further observation.

CHAPTER LXXX.

THE BELOVED IS UP AND DOING.

IT will be necessary now to return to Colonel Jack and his companion the Nobbler. It will be remembered that these two got clean off after they had alighted in Newgate Street. Taking their way up Giltspur Street, they crossed Smithfield, and threaded their way through a labyrinth of streets and courts which ran out from St. John Street. As this locality was well known to both of them, and had often times afforded a sure shelter for the lawless of London from thieftakers and Bow Street officers, the escaped prisoners felt themselves pretty secure from being recaptured. They betook themselves to a notorious house at that time known by the sign of the "Pickled Egg." Into this establishment they obtained an entrance, for they were most of them known to the landlord, who got up out of his bed to let them in.

They were shown into a large room at the rear of the house. The front door was bolted and locked, and a solitary candle was placed on the chimney-piece in the room in which they were seated, so that the back and front of the premises were guiltless of a light visible from any of the windows. This done the landlord awaited their orders.

"Brew us a bowl of punch, Charley," said Hackett, who was well known to boniface.

"Doesn't know as I can. I'm afraid the fire in the kitchen's gone out."

"Well, let's have something hot and strong. It don't much matter which it is," returned Hackett. The landlord disappeared to see what he could contrive to please the palates of his visitors. He was a complacent man the landlord of the Pickled Egg, and was used to being disturbed in the dead of the night.

When he had gone Colonel Jack shook hands with his companions, as he one more imbibed the free air.

"Now what will be our best course," said the colonel. "They will be sure to set the bloodhounds after us."

"We had better make ourselves as comfortable as we can here for awhile," said Knapp. "No one will suspect that we are here, and after the first hour or so has passed they will be off the scent, and seeking us most likely in other quarters. Any way, it will be better to remain concealed here."

"But how did you manage to effect your escape, colonel ?' said Galdie.

Our hero gave his companions a brief account of his adventures, and said that he should not have been able to effect his object without the assistance of the Nobbler, whose experience in matters of that description was undoubted.

Certainly, the Nobbler's physiognomy was unprepossessing to the last degree, nevertheless, the whole party shook hands and fraternised with him.

"Well, I wonder where this punch is," said Squabshot, who laid himself across one of the tables in a state of hilarious delight. "But, colonel, I've a bit to tell you, and you have only just got out in time, for, hang me if the world could have gone on much longer if you had been cooped up in that cursed prison."

"Ah, ah!" laughed the company. "The world could not have gone on!"

"Not the respectable portion of it," said our hero.

"Ah, clearly not," echoed all present.

"How is Osborn ?" said Colonel Jack.

"Patience !—mum at present ! He's all right, or rather will be," said Sqabshot.

"The missus is down," said Knapp, addressing the colonel in a half whisper.

"You have seen her then ?" inquired the other.

"Oh yes, several times, and have brought her up with the hope that you would get clear off."

"Thank you," said our hero, grasping his companion's hand.

There was a pause for some seconds after this, when the landlord entered with a steaming bowl of punch.

"That's the sort of thing," said Squabshot. "Now, then, who is to do the honours ?"

"Oh, you, of course."

"Very well," said Squabshot, who immediately began to serve out the beverage.

The party remained for an hour or so at the Pickled Egg, after which they took their departure by the rear of the premises.

Colonel Jack was persuaded by Squabshot to seek shelter for the remainder of the night at the latter's lodgings in Goswell Street, and parting with his companions, our hero went with his friend.

Osborne was at Oxford, and letting himself and his companion in with a latch key, the two entered the front parlour.

Squabshot in a few minutes lighted a fire, and he and the highwayman sat down before this, for Squabshot declared that he was in too excited a state to seek repose, besides he had a lot to tell his companion, so he said—

"First and foremost you must know, colonel," he said, "that we have, or at least, I have discovered where Miss Langford is concealed, or rather imprisoned."

"Indeed!' said our hero. "Who, then, has carried her off ?"

"Sir Richard Fleetwood."

"And where is she now, then ?'

"At Barnes Common, in a small cottage close by at any rate."

"Have you been there ?"

"No."

"Nor Osborne ?"

"He does not know of this. It's only since he has been at Oxford that I have found it out, and then only by the merest chance in the world."

"Hang him! I'll be even with him yet," exclaimed the colonel.

"What I propose is this," said Squabshot. "I have been most anxious for you to get out from durance vile for many reasons. What I propose is, that you and I should go down to the cottage, and see how the land lays. You know, I am pretty certain that Miss Langford is concealed there, in charge of some old woman, and when we once ascertain this we can make our arrangements to release her from her oppressor, and all this may be done before Osborne comes back from Oxford. There will be a surprise for him."

"Yes, if it's not attended with danger," said the colonel. "Wild will be sure to be on the alert."

"Oh, don't trouble yourself about that I have seen Wild, and I am in fact, on most excellent terms with him, and I know, moreover, that nothing is further from his thoughts than a recapture of yourself."

"Oh, I don't doubt that."

"Well, then, no one will suspect you of going down to such a quiet locality as that, and I think it must be done for more reasons than one. First, for our dear friend Osborne, and next—"

"To be revenged upon the miscreant, Sir Richard Fleetwood. It shall be as you say, Squabshot. "I'll go there in the morning with you."

"Then I am your man upon such an expedition as that," answered Squabshot. "So that matter is settled."

"And now it would be better to recruit our strength by snatching a few hours of repose," said the colonel, "for to say the truth I feel rather jaded."

It was now past three o'clock, and the two friends retired, and were soon both of them in a sound sleep.

They rose earlier than might have been expected, and looked remarkably fresh considering all the fatigue and anxiety they had been subject to.

Colonel Jack, after he had partaken of a hasty breakfast, said that he would first of all go home, and after that proceed with Squabshot to Barnes.

The latter was to meet the colonel at the corner of Oxford Street, and our hero then proceeded towards his own home.

We shall pass over the interview with his gentle and trusting wife, and accompany him to Barnes.

Obedient to his appointment, Squabshot was at the place before his time, and quietly awaited the appearance of our hero, who came mounted on his horse, and leading another animal for Squabshot.

The two friends then trotted off towards Barnes.

Having arrived there, Squabshot had some difficulty in finding out the cottage. Indeed the information he had received was so imperfect, that he had to inquire at numerous habitations, none of which turned out to be the right one.

"What is to be done now?" said Squabshot. "The hounds seems to be at fault."

The two walked their horses on to the common, where they observed a gipsys' encampment. As the colonel's eye ranged over their tents, he said to his companion—

"If anyone knows about this affair, those are the people."

"Do you think so?" said Squabshot, who did not half relish gipsies at any time.

"Most certainly—we had better inquire," said the colonel.

"Ah," said Squabshot, "'spose so."

"Will you dismount, or shall I?" inquired the colonel.

"Oh, I don't care," answered Squabshot, indifferently. "I will hold your horse, if you will go and make the necessary inquiries."

"So be it,' said Colonel Jack, who immediately dismounted, and handed the reins of his steed to his friend.

He then strolled towards the gipsy encampment.

A savoury smell of cookery found its way to his nostrils, and the blue smoke from their fires went curling upwards towards the sky.

As Colonel Jack came near to their tents, he observed the old gipsy who had stood his friend on a previous occasion, when he was making his escape from Mr. Underwood.

He recognised the highwayman immediately, and came forward and shook him warmly by the hand.

"You are the last person in the world I should have expected to see," said the old man.

"And why so, my friend?" inquired the colonel.

"I thought you were in trouble," said the man.

"So I am, and have been; but where can I come for assistance, but among my friends?'

The old man smiled, and said, quietly enough—

"I am glad you are able to do so."

"Ah, ah, you thought I was under lock and key, oh?"

The gipsy nodded an affirmative to this question.

"I am seeking for a small cottage which is inhabited by an old woman," said the colonel.

"There are many cottages occupied by old women," answered the gipsy.

"Yes; but you know these parts, I suppose?"

"I should think I did."

"And who are the inhabitants?"

"What is the name of the woman?"

"I don't know."

"Nor the name of the cottage?'

"No."

"Umph! You have come upon rather a doubtful errand."

"Listen. A young girl has been taken from her home by a worthless scion of the aristocracy."

"Ah—to be seduced?"

"I suppose so. Well, she has been placed in charge of an old woman, and for the life of me I cannot tell where she resides."

"Is she a relation of yours?"

"No."

"Ah—a friend, perhaps?"

"Yes."

The old man hesitated, and then, begging of our hero to wait a few moments, he went into one of the tents.

He had not been gone many minutes, when our hero observed him emerge from the tent, accompanied by a swarthy individual, with long black hair, who appeared to be a young man of about four or five and twenty.

The two came to the side of the highwayman, and the old man introduced his younger companion by the name of Black Hugh, who bowed respectfully to our hero.

"You want to know about the young woman, sir?" said Black Hugh.

"Yes; one who was carried off—"

"By Sir Richard Fleetwood," interrupted the man.

"Yes; do you know aught of her?" said the colonel.

"I have heard of the affair. She was confined at Dame Ludlow's."

"And where may that be my friend?"

"In a cottage not far from here," was the reply.

"The very same. Can you direct me to the cottage?"

The young man glanced at his elder companion, who nodded significantly.

"She ain't there now, sir," said Black Hugh.

"Not there? When did she leave, then?" said the colonel.

"This morning."

"Alone?"

"No, sir, she was taken away in the carriage of Sir Richard Fleetwood, accompanied by Dame Ludlow herself."

The colonel looked blank at this information, but upon again inquiring where the cottage was situated, Black Hugh offered to accompany him to the house in question.

Upon this our hero returned to Squabshot, who had been watching the interview in the distance.

The three then proceeded to the cottage of Dame Ludlow. After repeated knocks at the door an old woman opened it.

"Where is Mrs. Ludlow?" said Colonel Jack.

"Not at home," was the reply to this question, which had to be repeated twice or thrice, for the old woman was deaf.

"And the young lady, Miss Langford? is she out, also?"

"She's gone away," said the old woman, who eyed the new comers with suspicion, and she was about to shut the door, but the colonel placed his foot against it, and then pushing it back he quickly entered the passage.

"This won't do, my good woman," he said, authoritatively. "We are friends of Miss Langford's, and you must tell us where she has gone. Do you hear?'

The old woman either did not or would not hear, and did not deign to make any reply, any further than some half uttered anathemas against mankind in general, and Colonel Jack in particular.

The latter entered she parlour, accompanied by Squabshot, whereupon the old crone set up a scream.

"Silence!" said our hero in a voice that might have awakened one of the seven sleepers.

"Murder! thieves!" exclaimed the woman, who now began to be really alarmed.

"Hold your tongue, you fool, or we will soon make you," said the colonel. "We are officers of justice. Do you hear me?—officers of justice; and if you don't tell us where Sir Richard Fleetwood, Miss Langford and Mrs. Ludlow are gone, we shall take you into custody, and the probability is that then you will be burnt as a witch."

"Oh, mercy, mercy, gentlemen," said the woman, wringing her hands. "That I should ever live to see this day. A witch! mercy! mercy!"

"We will not only show you mercy, but reward you for your trouble," said Squabshot, "provided you tell the truth; but if you don't, woe betide you, for there will be no mercy shown. Now, where is Mrs. Ludlow gone to?"

"To—to—Dover," stammered out the old woman.

"How long since?"

"About an hour and a half ago."

"Confound it!" exclaimed the colonel; "we are too late"

"You are sure you are not prevaricating?" said Squabshot, looking hard at the woman.

She did not understand his meaning—the last word did not happen to be in her vocabulary.

"I doesn't know what you mean," she answered.

"Are you sure that you are speaking the truth?"

"Yes, as heaven is my judge."

"Enough. Now, how long do these people intend to stay at Dover?"

"I don't know."

"Are they coming back?"

"Mrs. Ludlow is."

"And the baronet and the young lady?"

"Are going to foreign parts, so I have heard."

"That is sufficient," said Colonel Jack. "They are going abroad. I suspected that would be his next move. We may be yet in time. Let us be off, we have got all the information we can. Now then, my good woman," he continued, turning to the old dame, "here is a guinea, if you will tell me

where the party are going to put up at Dover. What is the name of the hotel?"

"I heard Sir Richard say— But, Lord, I ought not to tell you—I am doing very wrong," she exclaimed, as she sunk into a large arm chair.

The colonel pulled a pistol from his pocket and placed it to the side of her head. The woman uttered a scream, and placed her hands up to protect herself from the point of the weapon.

"Now listen to me," said the colonel; "you may either have this guinea, if you tell us where the party are going to, or else have the contents of this weapon, if you refuse. Now, do you comprehend?"

"Oh, certainly, sir," said the woman.

"Ah, a sensible old dame, I perceive, after

all," said our hero. "Now, look sharp, and tell us all you know."

"I heard Sir Richard say that he was going to the Flying Dolphin."

"Thank you—that will suffice. Here's the guinea," said Colonel Jack.

He placed the same in the hand of the old woman, and then left the cottage with Squabshot. Black Hugh had, during this interview, remained outside.

"We have to thank you, my friend," said the colonel, to the gipsy.

So saying, he pulled out his purse, and offered the man a few pieces of silver therefrom, which he positively but respectfully refused to accept, and in spite of all the colonel's persuasions, he could not prevail of him to take them.

The three then returned to the gipsy encampment, and thanking the old man and Black Hugh for their kindness, they trotted off towards London.

CHAPTER LXXXI.

THE FUGITIVES.—SCENE AT DOVER.

COLONEL JACK, as he took his way along the road, accompanied by his companion Squabshot, discussed with him what was best to be done. It was quite clear that Sir Richard Fleetwood was about to fly to the continent, and it was equally certain to our hero that this would end in the destruction of Honora's peace of mind.

Colonel Jack was a man of prompt action, and, as the saying is, did not usually " let the grass grow under his feet."

He was irritated beyond measure with Sir Richard, and had sworn, in those lonely and miserable hours he had passed in Newgate, to be sooner or later revenged upon him.

His resolve was soon determined upon. He would go down to Dover with his companions, and intercept the flight of the baronet at all hazards.

Upon his return to town, therefore, he saw Knapp, Hackett, and Galdie, who were soon in readiness to start to Dover, or anywhere else that their commander led them.

Squabshot would insist in having a finger in the pie, as he termed it, and so, behold, in the afternoon of that day which had seen the two at Dame Ludlow's house, saw, also, the four highwaymen and Squabshot, galloping as hard as possible towards Dover.

It was a bright and beautiful afternoon— the sun lit up hill, dale, and woodland, with a golden glory.

Once more upon the back of his own Ada, our hero felt himself again.

A smart ride in the fresh air of the country, is very different to being immured in the cold and cheerless walls of a prison.

The colonel was in exuberant spirits—so was Squabshot—and so, indeed, were they all. They clattered along the road, and chaunted snatches of songs, in high glee. One would have supposed that the whole party were out merrymaking, instead of chasing a worthless baronet, and bent upon some deed of violence.

Strange are the contrasts of the human heart, mysterious in all its various emotions, inscrutable to the eye of imperfect and eratic man.

In the days of which we write, railroads were unknown, and there was consequently no other conveyance but the Dover stage, or posting it, as it was termed. The colonel

was not disposed to avail himself of either of these, but preferred riding down, although the distance was more than a horse ought to be expected to do in one day.

Upon the party arriving at Dover, their first inquiry was for the Flying Falcon. It was a well-known house, and Squabshot was directed to make the necessary inquiries. The whole five of the new comers had dismounted, and stalled their horses at a small establishment about half a mile out of the town, and here it was the four highwaymen waited till Squabshot had obtained all the necessary particulars respecting the baronet and Miss Langford.

Squabshot therefore sallied forth into the town, and jauntily taking his way up the principal street, he inquired for the house in question. Everyone knew it—it was the first in the town. Squabshot soon found himself opposite to it, and placing himself in one of his most aristocratic and graceful attitudes, he regarded it with eyes of curiosity. The principal waiter was lounging at the doorway, looking listlessly up and down the street at any new comer, and wondering whether he was a Londoner, a countryman, or from foreign parts ; the last-named were easily told in the days of which we write, for there was then a much more marked difference between the natives of our own isle, and those of our continental neighbours, than there is at the present day.

Squabshot was a sort of nondescript, and as the waiter's eye caught sight of him, it lingered in contemplating him.

Squabshot, who was naturally a kind man, thought he would give him an opportunity of indulging in a closer inspection, so he walked across the street, and in another second or so was under the doorway of the Flying Dolphin.

" Nice town this," said Squabshot.

" Yes, sir. Is it the first time you've been here ?"

" Ah—yes."

" From London, I suppose, sir ?"

" No," answered Squabshot, carelessly, " no, not from London—Glasgow."

" Indeed, sir."

" Good town this for business, eh ?" inquired Squabshot.

" I believe so, sir," said the waiter, who fancied he saw in Squabshot the commercial gent.

" Well, where's your coffee-room ?" said Squabshot.

" This way, sir."

The waiter obsequiously conducted the new comer into the room in question, in which two or three individuals were already seated.

The bell was rung, and a female waiter, or waitress, as it is the fashion now to term them, appeared in answer to the tintilatulary summons.

Squabshot regarded her with looks of admiration, and ordered some refreshment.

One of the individuals, an old gent, then left the room, leaving therein but two other occupants besides Squabshot.

The waitress returned with the refreshments which had been ordered, and Squabshot said, carelessly—

"Pretty full of visitors, now?"

"In the town, sir?" she inquired.

"No, in the hotel."

"Not particularly so," she answered, leaving the room.

"Oh!" exclaimed Squabshot, taking a deep draught.

"Been long in Dover, sir?" said one of the individuals, to the new comer.

"No, I only arrived to-day," was the answer.

"Ah—a stranger to the town, perhaps?"

"Yes, it is the first time I have been here," said Squabshot.

"It's not so full as I have seen it," said the gentleman.

"Indeed, sir."

The conversation then dropped for a few minutes.

Squabshot considered and reconsidered the matter, as to how it was possible to ascertain if Sir Richard Fleetwood was an inmate of the hotel. He dare not ask either of the two individuals in the coffee-room, and, indeed, he did not very well know how to ask any of the servants in the establishment, without exciting suspicion; for it would never do to let Sir Richard imagine that there was anyone in the town who was interested in his movements.

After considering some time, Squabshot strolled into the stable yard, thinking, perhaps, that he might be able to pick up some few scraps of information from those engaged therein.

The ostler, seeing him taking his way along the yard, inquired if he wished to see his horse fed, most likely taking him for some one else.

Squabshot's answer was in the negative.

"He had no horse there at present," he said, "but expected one to arrive with his trap in the course of a day or two."

He then inquired if there happened to be a loose box?

The ostler's answer to this was in the affirmative.

"Ah," said Squabshot, "you've nice stables in this establishment."

With these words he strolled into the first of them, followed by the ostler, who, like his brethren, was solicitous of showing the beauties of the establishment.

Squabshot was a connoisseur in horse-flesh, and made a rapid and running commentary upon those animals which happened to be in the stable.

After this he again emerged into the yard, and observing a plain chariot, he walked towards it, and inquired of the ostler, who owned it.

"A gentleman from London, I believe," answered the man.

"Been here long?" asked Squabshot.

"No, only arrived to-day," was the man's reply.

"With a lady?"

"Yes, a young and beautiful lady."

"Ah," exclaimed Squabshot, "a tall gentleman, rather haughty in his manner and bearing?"

"Yes, sir."

"Are they in the hotel?"

"They have private apartments to themselves—lovers, I suppose; but the lady seems very sad, so I heard Clara say."

Squabshot was at no loss to divine that the new comers were Sir Richard Fleetwood and Honora Langford.

He inquired the name of the gentleman; whereupon the man said that he did not know it.

Sir Richard, it appeared, had not chosen to give any name.

Having ascertained thus much, Squabshot returned to the coffee-room, and after sipping up the contents of his glass, he returned to the house where Colonel Jack and his friends had put up at.

They were anxiously awaiting his return.

"Any news?" said the colonel.

"Yes. I have seen the ostler, and ascertained from him that two persons, answering to the description of Sir Richard Fleetwood and Miss Langford, have taken private apartments at the Flying Dolphin."

"Umph! So far, so well," exclaimed the colonel. "Now what must be our next proceeding? Have you ascertained whether they stay there for the night?"

"There is no packet leaves for Calais before the morning."

"Then they must stay, by necessity," said the colonel.

"Yes."

"Then it is time we made up our minds what course to pursue."

"Precisely."

"Which is rather a difficult question to answer," said Galdie.

The colonel was lost in reflection for some minutes. After this, he turned to Hackett, and said—

"I have it. We must manage to get Sir Richard to come here. That done, the rest is easily managed. These people can be relied on?"

"Who?" said Hackett

"The landlord of the house?"

"Oh dear, yes."

"Good. Then I think the matter is easily settled."

"How so?"

"Who is the most expert at imitating the handwriting of an individual?" inquired the colonel.

"Galdie can manage that business," said Hackett.

"Or I will," said Squabshot. "I am rather an adept at that sort of thing."

"But you would not like to commit a forgery," said the colonel, with a smile.

"Forgery!—no," answered Squabshot. "What is it you want done?"

"Listen. I want a letter written to Sir Richard, as though it had come from our friend Sharpthorne, making an appointment here at ten o'clock to-night."

"But I don't know what sort of a hand Sharpthorne writes."

"I have one or two letters of his in my pocket," said the colonel, pulling forth the same.

Squabshot glanced over them, and at once declared his willingness to imitate the handwriting of the crafty lawyer.

The colonel then sat down, and dictated a brief epistle as follows:—

"*The Merry Mowers.*"

"DEAR SIR,—I most particularly wish to see you upon most pressing business. I have posted from London to Dover on purpose to see you. Delay not, but meet me here at ten o'clock to-night, as the subject upon which I wish to see you materially concerns yourself, and I cannot wait upon you at your hotel, for reasons which I will explain when we meet. Please not to fail coming at the appointed time, as I am compelled to go out now, but shall return at half past nine or ten to-night.

"Yours, truly,
"J. SHARPTHORNE."

Squabshot copied this epistle, imitating the lawyer's hand so well, that it would have been very difficult for those acquainted with his writing, to have detected the imposition.

When this had been done to the colonel's satisfaction, the next question was, who was to convey it?

Sir Richard knew Squabshot by sight, and consequently it would not do for him to convey the letter.

After some discussion, it was eventually determined to send the waiter of the Merry Mowers, with the missive in question.

The colonel paid him handsomely, and told him to say that an elderly gentleman had given him the letter to convey, and that the said individual would be back at the Merry Mowers, at the specified time, ten o'clock, that evening.

All this being satisfactorily arranged, the waiter set off on his errand.

CHAPTER LXXXII.

THE CAPTURE OF SIR RICHARD, AND RESCUE OF HONORA LANGFORD.

OBEDIENT to his instructions, the waiter of the Merry Mowers proceeded to the Flying Dolphin. Inquiring of the landlady if a gentleman and lady from London was staying there, he informed her that he had a letter for the gentleman.

The landlady did not know the name of either of her visitors, but sent up the waitress to the apartments occupied by Sir Richard and Honora.

After some time had elapsed, the female domestic returned to the bar, and showed the man up into Sir Richard's apartment.

The haughty bearing of the baronet for a moment overawed the colonel's messenger. He handed him the note, however, with several awkward bows and flourishes of his hat.

Sir Richard's eye glanced over the contents, afterwards he turned to the bearer of the missive.

"Who sent you with this, my man?"

"Please, sir, it was rather an elderly gentlemen as gave it me."

"When did he arrive at the—"

He glanced again at the colonel's letter.

"The Merry Mowers," continued the baronet.

"This afternoon, sir," said the man, again twisting round his hat awkwardly.

"Say I will be there at the time specified," said the baronet.

The man was about to take his departure, when Sir Richard called him back, and handed him some silver for his trouble. He then took his leave, and returning to the Merry Mowers informed Colonel Jack and his companions of the success of his mission. He got handsomely rewarded by them also, so that altogether he had not made such a bad job of his journey. He did not say anything to the colonel about the sum he had received from Sir Richard—he had forgotten it, perhaps.

"Now," said Colonel Jack; "now for a bold heart and a stout arm, and then, Sir Richard Fleetwood, it will be my turn to crow."

"What do you propose doing?" inquired Hackett.

"Tying him hand and foot, and gagging him," was the prompt reply.

"And if he resists?"

"I'll slay him, if needs be, rather than he

should escape; but there will be no need for that; he will be shown into this room."

"Yes."

"And instead of seeing Sharpthorne, as he expects, he will see either you or myself. While he is lost in surprise, yourself, Galdie and Knapp will come into the room and pinion him. The rest is easily managed."

"And the young lady?" inquired the other.

"Once master Sir Richard, we shall not have much difficulty in rescuing her."

The highwaymen watched the appearance of the baronet, and the hours seemed to roll slowly by till the appointed time, ten o'clock.

It should be noted that the house in question—the Merry Mowers—stood by itself on a moor. It was consequently well adapted for any deed of violence, and to say the truth was not held in very good repute in consequence of whisperings of several affrays having taken place in it.

Sir Richard, however, was not at all aware of its reputation, indeed he did not mention the circumstance of his intended visit to any one in the town, but kept himself secluded in his own apartment, while Honora and Mrs. Ludlow were in a room to themselves.

As it neared the hour of ten, Sir Richard, without saying a word to Mrs. Ludlow or her young charge, proceeded towards the Merry Mowers.

It was, as we have stated, some mile or so out of the town, nevertheless, Sir Richard was not long in reaching this respectable hostelry.

Colonel Jack had told the landlord to show anyone into the back parlour who inquired for Mr. Sharpthorne, and consequently when the baronet mentioned the name of the crafty lawyer he was conducted into the room where Colonel Jack stood awaiting his appearance with such anxiety and suspense.

Has Mr. Sharpthorne returned?" said Sir Richard, as he proceeded along the narrow passage.

"Yes, sir, will you please to walk this way," said the landlord. He has been expecting you for the last half-hour or so."

Colonel Jack heard this conversation in the back-room where he was stationed, and turning down the oil lamp which illumined the room, he placed it in semi darkness. Indeed, so obscure was the apartment, that a stranger upon first coming in would have some difficulty in recognising any of its inmates.

There was, however, but one there at this time, which was, of course, our hero.

The landlord opened the door and disappeared. As Sir Richard entered, his eye ran round the room in search of the lawyer's well known person, but he failed to discover him. He would have been a clever man if

he had, considering Sharpthorne was some fifty miles or so from the spot.

The room was so sombre that the baronet did not recognise the highwayman at first, but believed him to be some stranger. The truth, however, flashed upon him as he observed Slott, the colonel's dog, looking up towards him with his mischievous and blood-shot eyes. Sir Richard started, and then glanced towards the colonel.

"You here?" he said, turning deathly pale.

"Yes, Sir Richard Fleetwood—Sir Richard by fraud only—I am here, more free than welcome."

"Where is Sharpthorne?" exclaimed the baronet, hardly knowing what he was saying for the sudden surprise had well nigh scared away his wits."

"He will be here in good time," answered the highwayman

"What is the meaning of this?" said the baronet. How is it you have the effrontery to make your appearance here, having just escaped from Newgate, and cheated the law of its due. By the Lord, but I myself will arrest you if no one else will," said the baronet, drawing his sword, and presenting the point towards the highwayman, who on the instant drew his, and their weapons crossed, and for a moment the two stood eying each other with looks of hate.

"Miserable trickster, cheat, robber, assassin!" exclaimed Colonel Jack. "Dost thou think, thou wretched impostor, to act the bully as well as the shuffler and scoundrel!"

Sir Richard made no reply, but made a lunge with his weapon, which was dexterously parried by the colonel.

So fierce had been the baronet's onslaught, that his feet striking against a small stool which stood in front of him, he stumbled and fell. As he did so, Slott sprang to his throat, and held him down.

"Help!—murder!" shouted out the prostrate man; "help!—watch!"

Galdie, Hackett, and Knapp, now rushed into the room, locking the door after them as they entered. In a second or so, Hackett was on the chest of Sir Richard, pinning him down to the earth with one of his knees, While Knapp and Galdie held his legs and arms.

"Heavens! would you murder me, villains?" exclaimed the baronet, now becoming fairly alarmed.

"It would be a blessing to the world if we did," exclaimed the colonel.

Sir Richard began to shout out lustily for assistance, whereupon Hackett thrust his handkerchief to his mouth, and compressed his throat with a tighter grip.

The unfortunate Sir Richard now found

himself at the mercy of his ruthless assailants, and in spite of all his efforts to put as bold a face upon the matter as possible, he found his spirits sink within him, and he passively allowed himself to be bound hand and foot with cords, and a gag thrust into his mouth. This done, the highwaymen seated him upon one of the benches in the room.

Colonel Jack then turned up the lamp, and a bright light was suffused throughout the room, much to the astonishment of the prostrate baronet, who for a minute or so closed his eyes in agony.

The four highwaymen then gazed at each other, as though asking what had best next be done.

"We must take him to London, as speedily as possible," said the colonel.

"To-night?" inquired Hackett.

"Yes, this very night," replied our hero. "Delays are dangerous."

The baronet looked from one to the other, as this conversation took place, in a state of alarm, and motioned with his head as though he would speak.

"Well?" said Hackett; "you want to have a share in the discussion, eh?"

Another motion from Sir Richard was the only answer to this, the meaning of which it was impossible to interpret.

"Wants to speak," said Hackett.

"Yes, and kick up a row, I suppose," said Galdie.

The baronet shook his head violently at this observation.

"Oh, yes, I dare say," said Galdie. "You are very quiet now, my friend, and had better remain so—'cause why?—it's a deal more agreeable to me. Now do you understand me?"

"Will you promise to be peaceable if I take the gag out of your mouth?" said the colonel.

The baronet gave a nod in the affirmative. The gag was removed, and Sir Richard gasped for breath.

"Heavens! I faint!—I choke!" he exclaimed, now glad enough to respire a few cubic feet of fresh air. "What is the meaning of this outrage?" he continued, turning his eyes inquiringly towards our hero. "I will pay you handsomely, any sum, to be released. Give me my liberty, and name your own terms, Halford. Let bygones be bygones."

A derisive sneer passed over the features of the highwayman as Sir Richard made the foregoing observation.

"Never! Sir Richard Fleetwood!" exclaimed our hero; "never! The past cannot be cancelled. It would be well for you if it could, and, alas! well for both of us, if the curtains of the past were never removed; but this may not, cannot be. We are now avowed enemies. You have played your game, and 'tis now my turn. It's well to talk of bribes—bribes from you—psha! I scorn your ill-gotten wealth as I scorn and despise you."

"Listen to me, Halford," said the baronet, beseechingly. "I will make it worth your while to release me. It is better for both of us that we should be friends."

"Ah, ah—is it?' said the colonel. "Thank you for the information—I happen to think not, my friend. My very sincere and valued friend, between you and I a deep gulf is dug, made by yourself, Sir Richard Fleetwood; a gulf which will never be bridged over."

"Let us come to a better understanding," said the baronet, now fairly broken, and assuming an abject manner, which was quite unusual with him. "I will give you enough money for you to retire to the continent—abroad—anywhere out of danger from the law. Sooner or later you will be caught again in its meshes, and then—"

"Psha!" exclaimed the colonel, "I fear not for myself. The part I am to play in this world is already written down in the book of fate—a part which it is too late now for me to throw on one side. If this is all you have to say, let there be an end to this useless conversation. You are my prisoner, and until I have worked out my own ends, you must remain with me as a hostage."

"What would you do then?"

"That is my business, and it remains for time to develope. You are my prisoner—the tables are turned—and you must submit with the best grace you may."

The baronet hung down his head dejectedly, and Colonel Jack left the apartment, followed by Hackett, to whom he had made a motion for him to follow. The two highwaymen went into another room, where they could converse privately.

"What is to be done with the baronet?' was Hackett's first inquiry. "All has gone on right thus far."

"Convey him to town as speedily as possible," was the answer of Colonel Jack.

"But how? It will never do to take him on horseback, for he will be sure to call out to the passengers."

"That is quite certain," said the colonel, "so to obviate that we must hire a close vehicle somewhere in the town, and put in one of our horses, and drive the baronet to town. This is our only course."

"And the young lady?" inquired Ned Hackett.

"I will see to her."

"What before we start?"

There was a sudden pause as the two highwaymen heard the door of the apartment being opened by some one, and in another second or so Squabshot thrust his head in.

During the attack upon Sir Richard Fleetwood he had not made his appearance, considering wisely that it would be best to keep out of the way. Now, however, hearing the voices of the colonel and Hackett he ventured into the room.

"Ah, Squabshot," exclaimed the colonel, "the bird is caught."

"So I hear," answered Squabshot. "That is well. Now what cage is he to be put in?"

"We are going to convey him to London to-night."

"And I will go and release Miss Langford," said Squabshot, in great glee.

"Will you?"

"Yes, if you approve of the course."

"Nothing can be better. You are the very man adapted for the purpose."

"Then I am on," exclaimed Squabshot, in great glee.

It was eventually arranged that Squabshot should call at the Flying Dolphin, and take charge of Honora.

After the highwaymen had come to this conclusion, Colonel Jack, said—

"What think you of sending to the Dolphin and ordering Sir Richard's carriage?"

"They will not get it ready without an order from the baronet, I suppose?" said Hackett.

"We'll make him give the order if needs be."

"But I shall want it to convey Miss Langford to town," suggested Squabshot.

"You must post up to London, then," answered the colonel, as he left the apartment, and proceeded to the one occupied by Sir Richard Fleetwood.

The baronet looked inquiringly at him as he made his appearance.

"You must write an order for your carriage, Sir Richard," said Colonel Jack.

"For what purpose, and how can I possibly write, bound as I am."

"We will release your right arm for the purpose."

"But they don't know me by name at the hotel."

"No matter, when they see your signature and the crest on your carriage, that no doubt will be sufficient."

"I will not write unless you promise to release me when we arrive in London?"

The colonel smiled.

"I give no such promise, neither do I intend to commit myself by any pledge."

"Then I refuse to write."

"We will find means to make you," said the colonel, drawing a pistol. "Understand, Sir Richard Fleetwood, that you are dealing with a man who is not to be trifled with, but you know that of yore. I'll stretch

you lifeless on the floor if needs be rather than be baulked in my wishes or determination."

"I consent," stammered out the baronet, who thought it best for the present to adopt a concilliatory course. "Give me the necessary materials, and I will do as you desire."

Pen, ink, and paper were placed before the baronet; his right arm was released from the cords which bound it, and in a few minutes an order for his carriage to be got ready, and given to Squabshot, was placed in the hands of the colonel, who left the room and proceeded to where the redoubtable Squabshot awaited him.

"Here, take this to the Flying Dolphin, and get the ostler to put the horses to Sir Richard's carriage. If they make any inquiries, you can say that the baronet is suddenly called to town. Miss Langford will keep to the same story if you caution her, and then there will be no suspicion."

"I understand," said Squabshot. "You will wait here till my return?"

"Yes, but stay a moment," said the colonel, pulling out his purse, "you must pay the hotel bill. There is money for the purpose."

He handed several pieces of gold to his companion, who pocketted them, and started off on his mission.

CHAPTER LXXXIII.

THE RETURN TO LONDON.

SQUABSHOT felt himself elated with the success of Colonel Jack's ruse; he was also proud of the task assigned to him—that of ordering a baronet's carriage, and paying a baronet's bill.

He strutted into the yard of the Flying Dolphin, and calling out to the ostler in a loud tone, told him to put to the horses of Sir Richard Fleetwood's chariot.

The man did not know who it was he alluded to, but upon hearing Squabshot's explanation, he proceeded to do as he was desired.

Squabshot then went into the bar of the house, and speaking in his most winning and aristocratic tones, he showed the landlady Sir Richard's note, and asked for the bill.

"Does not the gentleman return, then?" said the landlady.

"No, madam. He has gone to meet his lawyer, who informs him that business of a most pressing nature requires his immediate attendance, and consequently he is compelled to drive up to London, to-night, to be at the judge's chamber the first thing to-morrow morning."

"Oh," said the landlady, looking rather disappointed at losing so distinguished a personage as a baronet. "And the lady goes as well. I presume?" she inquired.

"Yes," said Squabshot. "I am a cousin o Sir Richard's, and am to take the young lady back to London, after he has started; for his business is of such an urgent nature, that he will not be able to wait for Miss Langford. I am sorry we are compelled to take such an abrupt departure, for I have not had time to even have a look at the town."

"But you will return, I suppose, sir?" said the landlady.

"Oh, dear yes, as speedily as possible; as soon as my cousin, Sir Richard, has settled his business. And now, with your permission, I will go up stairs, and see Miss Langford."

With this, Squabshot was shown up into the apartments by the waitress, who knocked at the door, and announced the new visitor.

Both Mrs. Ludlow and Honora imagined that it was Sir Richard himself who had returned, and were consequently perfectly astonished as Squabshot entered the room, and presented himself, bowing gracefully as he did so.

"Miss Langford," said Squabshot, "you must pardon this intrusion; but I am directed by Sir Richard Fleetwood to escort you back to London."

"Ah!" exclaimed Honora, who was but too glad of this change in the baronet's proceedings; "I shall be but too happy to attend you sir."

"What is the reason that Sir Richard does not come himself?" inquired Mrs. Ludlow, in some alarm. "It's strange that he should so suddenly have altered his mind. Escort us back to London? Where is Sir Richard Fleetwood?"

"He has departed—left the town of Dover for the Metropolis," answered Squabshot.

"And what is the reason of this, sir?" said Mrs. Ludlow.

"Business, madam—most urgent business. Sir Richard is compelled to accompany his solicitor, Mr. Sharpthorne, immediately to London."

"I can hardly believe it possible. Have you his authority?"

"Certainly," answered Squabshot, showing the letter which the baronet had written.

"Ah, that is the handwriting of my respected master," said Mrs. Ludlow, after she had glanced at the well known caligraphy of the baronet. "Well, we must get ready, my dear."

"I am compelled to leave you for an hour or so," said Squabshot; "but upon my return you will, no doubt, be able to set off at once for town."

"Oh, certainly," said Honora, with unfeigned joy.

Squabshot then left the two ladies, and once more found his way into the stable-yard.

"Is the trap ready?" said Squabshot, with a swagger.

"Yes, sir," said the ostler, touching his hat, respectfully.

Upon this, Sir Richard's coachman, who had driven the vehicle from London, made his appearance, and was about to mount the box. At this, Squabshot was rather nonplussed.

"Ah, it's you?" he said, carelessly, as though he knew the man, who, by the way, he had never seen before.

"Yes, sir; where am I to call for master?"

"Well, you see," said Squabshot, hesitatingly, for he hardly knew how to get out of this difficulty. "Well, you must know that the governor is obliged to attend a trial in London, and as there are six persons to go besides myself, there is no other alternative than for one of these to drive, otherwise there will not be room. So Sir Richard thought it best for you and I to return with the ladies."

"Oh!" exclaimed the coachman, who was rather staggered at this information.

"And how are the ladies to go, sir?" he inquired.

"Well, that we will see about, my man," said Squabshot, laying hold of the reins and adjusting them to his satisfaction. "You wait here till I come back, and I will ask Sir Richard what he wishes to be done in the matter. Come, look sharp, ostler, I must be off, or Mr. Sharpthorne will be half crazy."

And so saying he jumped upon the box and drove off the chariot with the greatest coolness.

He soon reached the Merry Mowers, and found Colonel Jack and Hackett at the door anxiously awaiting his return.

A shout of joy arose from the two highwaymen, as Squabshot made his appearance. He jumped down, and explained to them the whole of his proceedings.

"Excellent!" exclaimed Colonel Jack. "Squabby my boy, you are worth your weight in gold."

"There's more brass than gold about me," said Squabshot, with a smile. "Now then, what's to be done about the coachman and the ladies?"

"They must be taken to town in a post-chaise, if one can be got. But it's getting rather late now."

"Never mind," said Squabshot, "I dare

say I shall manage that all right enough And the coachman ?"

"Ah, I don't know what to say about him. Can't you tell him to wait at the hotel till his master returns ?"

"I am afraid he won't tumble to that," said Squabshot.

"Well, then, I tell you what—send him to some other house in the town, and say that his master is waiting there for him."

"No, that won't do either, for I have already said that Sir Richard would be gone by the time I got back."

"You must bring him with you, then. But yet that's awkward ; he may kick up a dust when he arrives in London."

"I'll try and drive off without saying anything to him, and if that does not succeed, why I will tell him to take the first

coach in the morning for London. Now, do you want anything else of me ?"

"No, my boy, no ; only many thanks," said the colonel.

"Where shall I take Miss Langford to ?" inquired Squabshot.

"To her own house, to be sure," answered the colonel.

"Oh, not to Goswell Street ?" said Squabshot.

"Goswell Street ?—of course not ! It would not be seemly."

"Very well, to her own house be it then ; and so, fare thee well. I will see you in the morning, and good luck attend you with your charge."

Squabshot parted with the two highwaymen, and he then returned to the Flying Dolphin.

Miss Langford and Mrs. Ludlow were in readiness to start, and Squabshot went to the nearest posting-house, and after some discussion, succeeded in finding a man willing to post up to London.

In half an hour or so, the post-chaise was at the door, and the ladies were handed in obsequiously by their male companion and protector, *pro tem.*

Sir Richard's coachman then made his appearance, and eyed these proceedings suspiciously.

Squabshot turned to him, and said—

"I've seen your governor, and he says, my man, that you are to take the first stage to London, to-morrow morning, and then proceed to Acton. Here is money to pay for the same."

The man looked still more suspiciously at Squabshot, and very reluctantly received the pieces which were counted out to him. He did not half like Squabshot's manner, and most particularly objected to the familiar phrase "my man." However, he took the money, sulkily enough, and when he had got out of earshot of the party in the chaise, went muttering to himself down the yard.

"Umph!" he exclaimed, addressing himself to the ostler; "I don't half like that chap, and it wouldn't surprise me if he isn't up to some caper or other."

"What do you mean?" inquired the ostler.

"Why, just this—that he is tricking the governor in some way or other. It's a darned strange thing to me, that the governor should want to go to London in such a break-neck hurry."

"Well, that's no business of your's, or mine," said the ostler. "He does want to go, or else he wouldn't be at the expense of posting."

"The first coach in the morning, eh? Well, I won't miss it, you may depend upon that."

"The Endeavour goes at nine—will that do for you?"

"Yes, if there is none earlier."

"No, that's the first for London."

Squabshot seated himself between the two ladies, and began conversing upon different subjects for the first hour or so, after which he observed that Mrs. Ludlow was fast asleep. At first he thought she might be feigning, but after he became assured of the reality of her slumber, he whispered to Miss Langford a few words of consolation. They were these—

"Don't make any noise, my dear Miss Langford ; but you are now in the hands of your friends."

Honora stared in mute surprise.

"You are not travelling to London at the will of Sir Richard—you are about to return to your own home."

"To my own home !" exclaimed Honora, with difficulty suppressing a slight scream. "Can this joyful news be true !"

"Perfectly so, madam. I am a friend of Mr. Osborne's."

Honora pressed her soft white hand upon his, in mute acknowledgment of his kindness.

"Thanks—a thousand thanks, sir, for this news. Where is Sir Richard ?"

"Gone to London."

"With whom—and how has this been managed ?"

"With Colonel Jack. He it is whom you have to thank."

"Colonel Jack ?"

"Yes, madam, or Mr. Halford, as he is called in private life."

"Can it be possible, that the gentlemanly Mr. Halford is the celebrated highwayman known as Colonel Jack ?"

"It is not only possible but true," said Squabshot.

"I am perfectly astounded !" exclaimed Honora.

"Say no more upon that head at present. When you get to London, and free from eavesdroppers, I will explain all more fully to you."

"And Mrs. Ludlow ?"

"Oh, she must be sent to her own house."

"But she knows nothing of this ?"

"Not a word—pray be cautious.' '

"I will not breathe a syllable. Oh, how very kind of you to take all this trouble for me !"

"Madam, it is my pleasure," answered Squabshot, laying his hand upon his breast.

Soon after this the musical snore sent forth by Mrs. Ludlow, convinced the other two occupants of the carriage that the old lady was fast locked in the arms of Morpheus ; they could thus converse with greater security, as the post-chaise rattled on towards London.

"Miss Langford," said Squabshot, "you must have suffered much since you have been at the mercy of that scoundrel—I can call him nothing else."

"What, Sir Richard ?"

"Yes—you have been in his power ?"

"Alas, yes."

"And let us thank fortune that you are now released from his persecutions."

"Let me rather thank you," said Honora, with a winning smile, and her own sweet voice.

Squabshot blushed up to the roots of his hair at this speech.

"Ah—ah—as to that—it is not me you have to thank ; though, luckily, I was the first to find out where you were imprisoned."

"Ah, indeed ! Then you have been to Barnes !"

"Yes, on the morning of this very day."

"And Mr.—"

Honora hesitated.

"Osborne," said Squabshot, who was at no loss, from her confused manner, to interpret her meaning. "Oh, he is quite well—at Oxford now. When I say quite well, though, I am wrong, for he has not been the same man since you left your residence."

"Have you seen anything of my friend, Miss Staunton?"

"I made it my business to do so, on very many occasions. Ah, she is a young lady—every inch of her!" exclaimed Squabshot, with enthusiasm.

"Where is Sir Richard?" inquired Honora.

"He is in the hands of Colonel Jack," said Squabshot.

"How, as his prisoner?"

"Yes, madam."

"And what does he intend doing with him? I hope no violence will be used."

"Oh, dear no. Only you see, madam, there is a long history, a dark history, connected with the house of Fleetwood, and Sir Richard, in particular, which—ahem!—has been made manifest to—to the colonel, and which he, and he alone, can set right."

"Indeed!"

"Yes, madam. Sir Richard is, in fact, what I may term an impostor—in fact, he is not a baronet at all."

"Not a baronet!" exclaimed Miss Langford, in perfect astonishment. "Surely you must be mistaken?"

"I am quite sure I am not, and can speak positively upon this head. His elder brother, the real heir to the title, still lives."

Miss Langford said no more, but was lost for some minutes in reflection.

"Yes, he still lives," said Squabshot, after a pause, "although, at present, imprisoned in a madhouse at the instigation of his cruel and heartless brother."

"Sir Richard then is a bad man?" said Honora.

"Alas, madam, a very bad man, I am sorry to say."

Then there was another pause after this of a still longer duration.

"And where are you about to convey me, Mr. Squabshot?" inquired Honora.

"To your own residence, madam," was the prompt reply.

The postillions now drew up at a roadside house to change horses, and in a few more minutes the vehicle was rolling on at an accelerated pace towards its destination.

The road was by this time without any passengers, save an occasional market cart and now and then a patrol or two, and in a short time the streets of London were visible in the distance.

As Honora neared her own house her heart beat high with hope and expectation.

She knew how glad her own darling Edith would be once more to see her after so long an absence.

When the vehicle entered the streets of the metropolis, the somnolent Mrs. Ludlow awoke, no doubt, by the jolting of the stones which were at this period anything but agreeable to pass over.

"How far are we from Barnes now?" said Mrs. Ludlow. "This is London, is it not?"

"Most certainly," answered Squabshot; "but we are as yet some miles from Barnes."

"Ah, I suppose so."

"But that is of little consequence, as we do not propose going there."

Mrs. Ludlow uttered a slight scream.

"Oh, Lord, sir! Where then are we going?" said the old dame, in some alarm.

"Miss Langford." said Squabshot, emphasising his words; "Miss Langford is going to her own home."

"Impossible! She can't—she must not," exclaimed the old lady.

"But she is."

"And Sir Richard?"

"Oh, never mind about him, madam. He is safely lodged."

"What is the meaning of all this? There is some treachery!" exclaimed Mrs. Ludlow.

"There has been treachery," answered Squabshot, "but there is an end to it now. Understand, madam, that this lady is now no longer a prisoner of either yours or Sir Richard Fleetwood's, as he is unjustly called."

"Heavens! help! murder!" exclaimed Mrs. Ludlow.

"You will do well to hold your tongue, and conduct yourself like a discreet woman, or else it may be worse for you," said Squabshot.

"Oh, goodness gracious! I am in the hands of robbers, or—ahem—ruffians."

"No, madam, you are in the charge of a gentleman, who, when he has seen this young lady to her own residence, will willingly escort you to your pretty little rustic cottage at Barnes."

"Cottage! Have you ever been there?"

"Certainly; this morning."

"What for, pray?"

"Can you ask?" said Squabshot, with a smile. "Of course to see you."

He focussed his eyes upon the old lady, which were at all times of a comic expression, but now more especially so.

"To see you," he iterated, "and Miss Langford, who is a particular friend of mine."

"Oh, I did not know—"

"No, but I did," answered Squabshot, "with a scarcely perceptible sneer on his humoursome features.

The vehicle very shortly after this arrived at the door of Honora's residence.

Squabshot jumped down and gave a long, loud, and continuous rapping at the knocker thereof, but as it was by this time early morning, too early though for any one to be stirring, the knock remained unanswered.

It was repeated again in a still louder tone, and being eventually opened by the footman, Squabshot offered his arm to Honora and handed her out of the post-chaise.

As she alighted, she turned round and inquired of Mrs. Ludlow if she would sleep at her residence till morning?"

"It's morning now," replied that lady; "and I must see Sir Richard. Can't you tell the postillion to drive to Acton?"

"If they did you would not see Sir Richard, as you call him," answered Squabshot.

"Oh, Lord, Lord! what shall I do?" exclaimed the old dame, wringing her hands.

"Go home, madam, go to bed, and go to sleep; you need it," said Squabshot, with a smile.

However, after a little more discussion Mrs. Ludlow thought it advisable to accept of Honora's offer, and so the two ladies were handed into the hall by Squabshot, who finding that Miss Staunton was still in bed, and as in all probability she had not been aroused by the knocking, he took his departure, with a promise to call on the following day.

———

CHAPTER LXXXIV.

RELEASE OF SIR REGINALD.—HIS RETURN TO ACTON.

WHILE Colonel Jack had been engaged in making his escape from Newgate, and rescuing Honora from the clutches of Sir Richard, Mr. Carruthers had not been idle in respect to the confined baronet in the establishment of Mr. Hardy.

The worthy doctor had succeeded by lodging sundry affidavits, both of his own and his colleague, in getting the commissioners of lunacy to inquire into the case.

We all, or at least most of us, do know how difficult it is to put any of the government authorities to move in any case which demands inquiry. It was worse at the time of which we write.

However, by dint of indomitable courage and perseverance, Mr. Carruthers did eventually succeed in getting a day appointed by the said commissioners for proper persons to visit the unfortunate baronet in company with Mr. Carruthers and the other medical gentleman who had visited the patient in company with Colonel Jack on the occasion of his capture by Jonathan Wild.

Mr. Baintree had been indefatigable in his exertions to bring about this desired visit.

It is probable that Sir Reginald would have been let gently down to the other world by his ruthless keepers had not Mr. Hardy have become alarmed and awakened to the sense that his movements and proceedings would be carefully watched by men of skill and high repute.

"It would not do, therefore, to play any tricks with the baronet," he said to the doctor, who attended to the inmates of his establishment.

Consequently the death-knell of the baronet had not as yet been rung.

When the visiting commissioners and doctors paid their visit to the establishment of Mr. Hardy, they were fully convinced of the sanity of Sir Reginald Fleetwood, and a report of his case, together with a memorial of his state of health, was forwarded to the authorities, and in the due course of time an order was sent down for his release.

Mr. Hardy was therefore compelled, however reluctantly, to give up the patient, who was carried off from the house for the reception of lunatics, and was once more a free man.

It would be impossible to give any notion of the strange feelings which the sense of freedom evoked in the breast of the ill-used baronet.

He felt like a man standing upon some giddy height, and an undefinable fear crept over him when he found himself outside those walls which had so long formed his prison-house.

To be again in the outer world—whose jarring and antagonistic elements were so opposed to the painful and oppressive calm of the madhouse—had an unaccountable terror to him.

He felt like a man may be supposed to feel who had been resuscitated, or suddenly awoke from a trance.

The persons who had him in their charge, inquired if he desired to be conveyed to his own house?

The baronet hesitated, whereupon Mr. Carruthers, who shrewdly guessed the state of the unfortunate gentleman's mind, offered to convey him to his own residence.

Sir Reginald gladly accepted the invitation, and the doctor conveyed him to Brook Street, in his own carriage, and upon their arrival, the commissioners of lunacy took their departure.

Sir Reginald was shown into the doctor's study, and soon found himself seated in one of the easy chairs, while his host sat on the other side of the fire-place.

"I think it best, my dear, sir," said the worthy Mr. Carruthers. "I think it best, for your own sake, to remain here for awhile, and shake off the first surprise which a man, suddenly brought again into the world, after so long an incarceration, must of necessity feel."

"You are very kind," said Sir Reginald. "I can't tell you what my sensations are! Oh! that horrid place!"

"There, think no more of that," said the worthy doctor.

"I must have good friends to interest themselves on my behalf—not the least of whom is yourself, Doctor Carruthers, who is a stranger to me and mine."

"Not so great a stranger," answered the doctor.

"Indeed! We have never met before, that I can remember."

"I know your brother."

"I was not aware of that."

"Our acquaintance was a singular one," said Mr. Carruthers, as he entered into the particulars of the accouchment of Lady Fleetwood, which the reader will no doubt remember in the earlier portion of this work.

"And my child—what has become of it?" inquired the baronet, when the doctor had concluded his narrative.

"Still lives, I believe; but where it is, I am unable to inform you. You must understand, Sir Reginald Fleetwood, that I was bound by an oath to secrecy, never to divulge the particulars which I have been narrating, but as circumstances have so strangely come about since then, I do not feel myself compelled to respect a solemn adjuration, which was obtained by threats and force. Your brother has acted in so unnatural a manner towards you and your wife, that it is now time the law restore you to your rights, and punish those who have so cruelly persecuted you and yours; but more of this hereafter. For the present, you must endeavour to recover the tone of your mind, which must of necessity have been sadly shaken, from the amount of suffering and misery you have endured."

Sir Reginald Fleetwood stayed at the worthy doctor's house that day, and the day after, and began to materially alter in appearance.

Even the brief period of time that had elapsed since his escape from the thraldom of the lunatic asylum, had done wonders, and he felt great anxiety to have an interview with Lady Fleetwood.

At his urgent request, Doctor Carruthers consented to convey him in his own carriage to the house at Acton.

Although a mild man, Mr. Carruthers was a firm one, and not easily put aside in the fulfilment of his duty.

He communicated with Mr. Baintree, who in answer to his letter, consented to accompany Sir Reginald and the doctor to Acton; and on the following day the trio drove towards the baronet's house.

Lady Fleetwood fully believed her husband to be dead, and the doctor deemed it advisable for either Mr. Baintree or himself to see the lady before Sir Reginald entered that establishment, of which he was the lawful master.

As the doctor's carriage took its way along, Mr. Carruthers suggested, for the sake of security, the necessity of calling at the chief police office, and taking with them an officer, in case of any breach of the peace.

Mr. Baintree explained the whole of the particulars to the superintendent of the force, who immediately placed at the disposal of the party an officer of acknowledged experience and tact.

It must be understood by the reader, that in speaking of police, we do not allude to the force at present in existence, for at the time of which we write, no such an establishment was in vogue; those to whom we allude, were detectives or peace officers.

The whole party then took their way towards Acton.

Doctor Carruthers and Mr. Baintree had learnt from the domestics belonging to Sir Richard, that their master had gone for some weeks to the continent, consequently they were under no apprehension of ebullition of temper on his part.

When the doctor's carriage arrived at the old gateway of the baronet's mansion, the doctor alighted, rung the bell, and upon the gate being opened, inquired for Lady Fleetwood.

The porter hesitated—"he would see if her ladyship was in the way," and then departed upon his errand.

In a few minutes he returned, and desired Mr. Carruthers to walk in.

The doctor followed the domestic, pompous and ponderous in his livery suit, and was shown into a room into the rear of the house.

Its sole occupant was a middle-aged female of rather lofty bearing.

The doctor hesitated, and bowing low, said that he wished to speak to Lady Fleetwood.

"Her ladyship is rather indisposed, sir," said Lady Bostock, for it was no other than that person who was addressing the doctor. "Her ladyship is rather indisposed, but if you will acquaint me with the object of your visit I will communicate with her," said Lady Bostock.

"The intelligence I have to convey to Lady Fleetwood can only be done by a personal interview with her ladyship."

"Possibly so, sir; but I should presume

that you can have no objection to acquaint me with the nature of your visit?" said Lady Bostock, turning over the doctor's card, carelessly.

"No; I do not see that there can be any possible occasion for secrecy, for where there is secrecy there is always suspicion. It is of Sir Reginald Fleetwood I would speak," said the doctor, emphasising these last words, and looking full in the face of his companion.

"Sir Reginald!—the deceased Sir Reginald! It will be painful for Lady Fleetwood in her delicate state to discourse of her late lamented husband."

"Lady Bostock," said the doctor, "it is time that this fiction be dropped. Sir Reginald Fleetwood lives."

A pet scream from her ladyship—a gasp for breath—several hysterical sobs, and then she collapsed, and fell back into her chair as though she had fainted. But she hadn't though, and the doctor who was too well practised in this species of drama to be deceived, quietly sat upon his chair, regarding her ladyship with a benign and passionless countenance.

"Sir Reginald lives, madam," he iterated, "and the joyful news will, I hope, restore his gentle wife to her wonted spirits."

"It's impossible," said Lady Bostock, now assuming a defiant tone.

"Utterly impossible," she continued, after a pause. "Sir Reginald Fleetwood was consigned to the grave—his last resting-place—years and years ago."

The doctor shook his head dubiously.

"He not only lives," he answered, "but is at the outer gate of this mansion, in my own carriage, in company with his lawyer and a peace officer."

"Insolent! Peace officer, forsooth!" exclaimed Lady Bostock, rising and pacing the room in an uncontrollable passion. "Lives! It's false—false as dicers' oaths! Ah, ah! a pretty tale truly. Some wretched impostor!"

"Lady Fleetwood will know her own husband, and you, madam, I should presume, will be able to recognise your own brother."

Lady Bostock made no reply to this observation, and the doctor regarded her with a look of inquiry.

But she merely paced the apartment, apparently in great anger or emotion.

"My own brother," she iterated, with an expression of scorn on her lip. "Of a surety I should be able to do so were he my brother. But a truce to this folly, it is but trifling with our best, our holiest feelings. We have mourned my unfortunate relative as dead. Do you hear me, sir? And dead he most assuredly is."

"Lady Bostock," said Mr. Carruthers, calmly, "I do not know if you are aware of all those circumstances connected with your supposed deceased relative. I should hope you were not, but the unfortunate and ill-used Sir Reginald Fleetwood has been incarcerated as a lunatic at the instigation of one who ought by right to have protected and shielded him from the storms of fate. I allude to your second brother, Sir Richard, who has a fearful account to render both to man and his Maker."

"Psha!" exclaimed Lady Bostock. "Have you come here to preach me these homilies?"

"I wish to see Lady Fleetwood. Will you take up either my name or card to her ladyship?"

"For what purpose, sir?"

"I have already told you, madam."

While this conversation was taking place, Lady Fleetwood unexpectedly entered the apartment.

She was not aware that any person was there, but had been walking on the lawn, and had come in quite accidentally. She drew back in some surprise, as she observed the doctor, and was about to retire, believing him to be on a visit to Lady Bostock.

"Pardon me, madam," said Mr. Carruthers, rising from his seat, "but I presume that I have the pleasure of addressing Lady Fleetwood?"

Her ladyship bowed.

"Ah, my dear," said Lady Bostock. "This gentleman has come here upon really a most ridiculous errand."

"Madam," said the doctor, deprecatingly, "you ought to take a different view of the case. Pray spare the feelings of Lady Fleetwood, who I am permitted now for the first time to behold."

Then turning to the younger female, he said, in a gentle voice—

"You must prepare yourself, my dear madam, for a surprise—a very great surprise. Now do not be alarmed, but it is of your husband I am about to speak."

"My husband?" said Lady Fleetwood, turning suddenly pale, and staggering to a chair.

"Yes," said Lady Bostock, with a scornful laugh, "our worthy friend here has the effrontery to say that Sir Reginald Fleetwood still lives."

"And so he does, madam," said the doctor.

Lady Fleetwood made no reply. A death-like pallor overspread her features, an icy sensation crept over her, and she fainted.

Doctor Carruthers was by her side on the instant. He chafed her hands, opened both the French windows of the apartment, and applied some strong, pungent odour to her nostrils.

It was some time before the lady was restored, but when she did open her eyes, she fixed them steadfastly upon Doctor Carruthers, whose features she for the first time recognised.

She sent forth one deep-drawn sigh, and pressed her hand to her side.

"Calm yourself, my dear madam," said the doctor. "You are better now—much better. There—so—be not alarmed. I bring you good tidings."

"Ah, sir, pray heaven that you are not trifling with me. We have met before, I think.

"Yes, madam—yes. Upon another painful occasion. There do not be frightened, take my arm, and walk in the open air."

"She's too weak," said Lady Bostock, sharply.

"That you will allow me to be the best judge of," said Doctor Carruthers. "She is or rather was my patient. Come, madam."

The doctor offered her his arm, and the two strolled out on the velvety lawn at the rear of the premises. There was situated the park, teeming with beauty. The mansion of the Fleetwoods rejoiced in beautiful grounds. The sward was as green as emerald, and soft as a mole's back, and gigantic trees reared their heads, with centuries circulating in their gnarled massiveness.

The sky was sullen, and summer, like a fine froward wench, smiled now and then, and anon frowned the blacker for the passing brightness.

It seemed a very nest, this estate of the Fleetwood's—a nest warm and green, for human life, with the twilight haze of time about it almost consecrating it from the aching hopes and feverish expectations of the present.

The face of nature possesses an indescribable charm, and generally the contemplation of its beauty harmonises the mind almost imperceptibly.

Lady Fleetwood felt much relieved when she once more found herself in her old favourite walk, beneath some nodding chesnuts.

Perhaps she felt more satisfied at being away from the presence of Lady Bostock, of whom she stood in dread at all times

"My dear madam," said the doctor, "I told you to prepare yourself for a great surprise, and I fear me much that even with all my caution that your gentle frame and susceptible nature is hardly able to bear the shock which awaits you."

"What shock, sir?" said his companion.

"I told you that your husband, Sir Reginald, still lived!'

"Yes."

"I spoke the truth, and more than this, he is—ahem—not far from where we now are."

"Heavens! Can this be possible? Where?

—tell me where, that I may hasten to him. Lives! Impossible! Oh, Doctor Carruthers, this news is too good to be true."

"Lady Fleetwood, in a few minutes I will bring your long lost husband to your side," said Doctor Carruthers. "Come, madam, do not look so alarmed. Let me beg of you to seat yourself on this garden chair till my return, which, believe me, will be very soon."

Her ladyship reclined on a rustic seat in the garden, and the doctor took his way back to the outer gate, where the carriage awaited his return.

While the two were conversing in the garden, Mr. Morgan popped his head into the room the two had left, and where still sat Lady Bostock.

"Oh, I beg pardon, my lady, but—"

"Oh, come in," said her ladyship. "What is it!"

"Nothing particular; only there are strangers arrived. Are they sent by Sir Richard, if you please, madam?"

"No. Sent by Sir Richard indeed! I wish your master was at home."

"And so do I, if you please," said the valet.

"Why?"

"Because the place don't seem comfortable like without him, and—"

"And what?"

"And I'm afraid there's some mischief brewing."

"What makes you think that?" asked the lady.

"Sir Reginald, madam."

"Well, what of him?"

"Is alive, my lady."

"How did you know this, Morgan?—I mean, what could make you imagine such a thing?"

"He has been at a madhouse, my lady," answered the valet, in his most mellifluous tones.

To have heard the man speak, anyone would have supposed that he was uttering some charming piece of information to delight his auditor.

"Been at a madhouse—you are mistaken, Morgan."

"Beg pardon, my lady, but I am not at all misinformed. Oh, dear no—Sir Reginald has just been released from captivity."

Lady Bostock was perfectly thunderstruck at this revelation. She had not the most remote notion that the valet was aware of even the existence of Sir Reginald, still less that he had been imprisoned at Mr. Hardy's establishment. However, she bore the observations of the valet with surprising *sang froid*, and turned carelessly away, saying, as she did so—

"That will do, Morgan, for the present. I shall most likely want to see you shortly, upon this business; for, in the absence of my brother, you are my confidential man. Keep a still tongue, and—"

"Yes, my lady," said Mr. Morgan, as he suddenly, but quietly, left the apartment.

Doctor Carruthers, when he got to the outer gate, desired the three occupants of his carriage to alight, and enter the house. They did so, and the four gentlemen soon found themselves in the back room where Lady Bostock had been seated.

She was not there, however, when the party entered.

Mr. Baintree and the officer took chairs, offered them by Mr. Morgan, in an obsequious manner, while the doctor and Sir Reginald strolled into the garden. The latter looked deathly pale, and his form and features were so shrunk, that even his own relations would perhaps, at first, have failed to recognise him.

However, as he took his way along the gravel walk in the park, the quick eye of his wife caught sight of his figure; emaciated as it was, she did not fail to recognise him, and springing from her seat with the agility of a fawn, she rushed forward, and flung herself into his arms, uttering his name, "Reginald!" as she did so, and then burst into a passionate flood of tears.

The doctor, from notions of delicacy, left them, and returned into the parlour, where he found Lady Bostock, who now assumed quite a different bearing.

"Ah, Mr. Carruthers," said her ladyship, in bland accents, "you must pardon my incredulity, but of a verity it is indeed my own dear, long lost brother, you have brought to us."

"Have you seen Sir Reginald?" inquired Mr. Carruthers.

"I caught sight of him from my room up stairs, as he took his way along the garden walk with yourself," said Lady Bostock; "and from that cursory glance, I was able to recognise the features and form of my dear long lost brother—although, poor fellow, he is sadly wasted. Ah, the ways of providence are inscrutable," said the lady, with a deep-drawn sigh.

The doctor marvelled much at the alteration in her tone, as well he might.

"Can I offer you any refreshment, gentlemen?" continued her ladyship, in her most bland manner.

All the gentlemen declared that they did not stand in any need of refreshment.

Her ladyship then seated herself, and conversed upon indifferent subjects for a few minutes.

"I will not intrude upon my brother's first interview with his dear wife," she at length observed; "although, to say the truth, I am myself anxious enough to behold

once more his beloved form. Ah, Mr. Carruthers, how deeply indebted we are all to you for your pure kindness in this business; believe me, it is a debt of gratitude we shall never be able to pay. But a good action always meets with its reward. You will, I am sure, pardon my incredulity when you first entered."

"There is nothing to pardon, madam, believe me. This gentleman is Mr. Baintree, Sir Reginald's solicitor; he it is who has been mainly instrumental in procuring the release of the injured baronet, who will now be restored to his just rights."

"Oh, yes, of course."

"Sir Richard—or rather, Mr. Richard—is not in town, I believe?"

"No, sir, he is on the continent for the present."

At this point of the conversation, Sir Reginald and his wife were observed approaching the house.

Lady Bostock rose, went into the hall, and from thence into the grounds, and rushed into the arms of her brother.

She shed tears over him, rained tears in fact, and was so particularly demonstrative, that the whole party were fairly taken in by the power of her acting, for it was nothing else, seeing that she was fully cognisant of his incarceration in the house of Mr. Hardy, and the cruelty practised on him by her worthless brother. However, she showed the new comer, who had so suddenly and unexpectedly returned to his baronial home, every attention, and pretended to be greatly rejoiced at his return home. So much for the duplicity of woman.

Mr. Baintree took Sir Reginald on one side, and said to him, in an undertone—

"You do not think of stopping here, at present?"

The baronet hesitated.

"I suppose not," he answered, slowly.

"Not until you have a restitution of your rights, which will take some week or two before that can be done."

"Very well; for the present I had better take up my quarters in town."

"I think so," said Mr. Baintree.

And so, in the course of another half hour or so, the party wheeled off in the doctor's carriage.

CHAPTER LXXXV.

SIR RICHARD FLEETWOOD IS CONVEYED TO LONDON.

AFTER Squabshot had placed the baronet's carriage at the disposal of Colonel Jack, the latter, and his companions, conveyed their prisoner, bound as he was, into the interior

of the chariot, the Colonel, Hackett, and Galder took their places inside, while Knapp acted as coachman. All this had been done in gloomy silence, and the party had travelled for some half-hour on the road before a word had been exchanged, save a few hurried whispers which had passed between the highwaymen. Sir Richard at length spoke.

"What is to be the end of this, Halford?" he enquired, in a most abject manner.

"Time will show," was the brief rejoinder.

"Yes, time," iterated the baronet—"time shows all things if we have but patience. Time indeed! I want my liberty—at any cost Halford. Do you hear me?—at any cost."

"Liberty is sweet;" said the highwayman, "I have found that out."

"Name your terms, and whatever they may be, I accede to them unconditionally."

"I do not barter with you; that is long since past."

"What do you purpose doing with me. You certainly do not intend to—to commit murder?"

"Not if it can be avoided."

"Heavens! with what coolness you talk upon such a subject," exclaimed Sir Richard in alarm.

The vehicle still kept jolting over the hard road.

"You might have mercy, Halford—some touch of pity for him who has known you from boyhood. Do you remember those hours?"

"Remember!" exclaimed Colonel Jack, "think you I shall ever forget them. Who made me what I am? who blasted my prospects for life? you—you—no other but

51

you. Oh, no, Sir Richard, there is too long an arrear of injuries between us two to ever have the breach filled up. You are outwitted my prisoner—and, until I have fulfilled my trust, you must remain my prisoner. You see, Sir Richard, I can't afford to part with you, or perhaps I may be again confined in Newgate; for thanks to you, I have already made acquaintance with the interior of that prison."

"To me?"

"Yes, my worthy Sir Richard Fleetwood, it was at your instigation that Wild dogged my footsteps at the house of Mr. Hardy—at your suggestion. By the Lord! you must take me for an egregious fool, to imagine that I would let you off. No, not if you counted out untold wealth to me would I do it. There you know my determination."

The baronet hung his head upon his breast, and the next hour or so was found in gloomy silence.

When the carriage reached London, Knapp drove towards what is now called Whitefriars, but in the days of which we write it was better known as Alsatia—being the resort of the most lawless characters of the metropolis; so much, so indeed, that the neighbourhood defied the efforts of the peace authorities, and may be said to be out of the pale of the law or the law's instruments.

When Sir Richard became aware of the course the vehicle was taking he became more than ever alarmed.

"Heavens! we are in Alsatia," he exclaimed, with a shudder.

"We are taking one way to that classic locality," said Colonel Jack, with a sneer. "A fitting place for so trusty a baronet."

"Is this your haunt, Halford?" enquired the prisoner.

"No, Sir Richard, but it is going to be yours."

The party in the vehicle again lapsed into silence. Presently the chariot halted before a dilapidated-looking house of gigantic dimension. It was situated near to the water side, the waters of the river Thames dashed against the side basement. Knapp turned the vehicle round, and Colonel Jack hastily flung open the door and alighted. Taking a bunch of keys from his pocket, he selected one, and inserted it into a lock which fastened a small low door studded with nails. The creaking hinges sent forth a melancholy sound as the door was swung back, and the Colonel said—

"All right, bring him in!"

Upon this, Galder and Hackett descended the barouche to alight, as he did so. They each of them caught hold of his arms, and

conducted him into the passage of the gloomy abode—if abode it was. Sir Richard then found himself in a narrow passage; the door was slammed to, and the whole party were in utter darkness. In another second or so Colonel Jack had struck a light and ignited his dark lantern. He then hobbled forward and said to his companions:

"Follow me!"

They did as he desired, bringing with them the despairing and miserable Sir Richard Fleetwood. The baronet was conducted down a flight of stone steps; then turning round he descended some dozen or fifteen others, and eventually found himself in a dark, gloomy, and noisome vault, which was supported by a series of short thick columns, which were so thick and squatty that they seemed as though they had been destined for another building, but had been cut off either at the top or bottom to fit this one. The roof was of stone, and arched, and the noise of the footsteps of those who entered reverberated with a loud sound. Sir Richard actually shuddered as he found himself in this gloomy and filthy abode—for it was dirty to the last degree.

There were piles of goods—and wares of different descriptions strewed about the floor—in several recesses and niches in the walls. From out of one these niches a figure, clad almost in rags, emerged and confronted the new comers. He screened his eyes from the rays of the lamp which the colonel turned full upon him, and then, in a cracked and unusually shrill voice, exclaimed—

"Bless us and save us, if it ain't the colonel!"

"That it is, Reuben," said our hero. "How fares it with you—all quiet?"

"As silent as the grave! There ain't been a single soul a bothering on me."

"That is well. Now—look here—I want you to have an eye upon a piece of live-stock."

"I am your man," answered he who had been called Reuben. "Where is it?"

Colonel Jack pointed significantly to the baronet, who recoiled from the gaze of the filthy and dilapidated individual who favoured him with a glance of enquiry.

"What's his rig? Out of the way of the beaks—or an escaped convict?"

"Neither—he is my prisoner. See that he don't starve, if by chance I should neglect to call and see him."

"Ah! as to that, he shall have grub enough, of one sort or another," answered Reuben.

In one of the columns which supported the building there was inserted a staple, and from this a measured chain depended. Colonel Jack laid hold of Sir Richard, and conducted him to this. At the end of the chain there was attached a large clasp, which fitted to the size of an ordinary man's waist. This clasp closed with a spring, which could not be undone without a key. To place this round the baronet's body was the work but of a few minutes. As our hero did so, Sir Richard sent forth one wild cry of despair.

"Monster!" he exclaimed—"would you chain me up like a hound? Release me, or I will raise the whole neighbourhood by my cries!"

"You may spare your lungs, Sir Richard Fleetwood," said Colonel Jack. "You are in a part of London now the inhabitants of which are too used to noises of this sort to take heed of them: for the present this must be your prison-house. I regret that I have no better accommodation for you; but there is no help for it—this being the best I have. So you must make yourself as comfortable as circumstances will admit. I will bestir on the business I have in hand; and that done, you may rest assured that you shall be released."

"I possess no better accommodation for those whom I have under my charge. And mark me, Sir Richard—or rather Mr. Richard—such as it is you must make up your mind to submit to the place with the best grace you can."

The colonel did not condescend to say any more, but proceeded to take his leave with his companions. As he did so, the baronet indulged in a series of violent imprecations; but threats and vituperations were lost upon the highwayman, who left, after leaving a few hurried instructions to the ragged figure left in charge of the baronet.

"So," exclaimed Colonel Jack, when he had emerged from the building, "the bird is safely caged, and under lock and key. Much remains to be done."

CHAPTER LXXXVI.

THE HIGHWAYMAN'S HOME.

WE have taken but little heed of the wife of Colonel Jack, who, during the colonel's incarceration, had passed those lonely and wretched hours which were even more bitter than those endured by the highwayman when he found himself a prisoner in Newgate. Mrs. Halford had heard of our hero's capture—she had heard of his incarceration in Newgate—for he had sent several messages to her not to make her appearance at the prison upon any pretext whatever. Mrs.

Halford had felt annoyed and hurt at this, but she said nothing. When, however, the colonel made his escape from Newgate—for it was at this time quite the town talk, and therefore could not fail to reach the ears of the highwayman's wife—when he made his escape Mrs. Halford naturally had expected him to return to his home, but as we have already seen, our hero's attention had been sufficiently taken up with Sir Richard Fleetwood, and consequently he had not as yet returned home. During the colonel's absence Captain Rignold had frequently waited upon Mrs. Halford with the view of devising some scheme for her husband's liberation. As an old friend Captain Rignold was received with courtesy by Mrs. Halford. His visits had become frequent—he commiserated with her upon her misfortunes—ran over the incidents of their past life, and in her lonely hours was a solace to the unfortunate and neglected wife. When it was known that the colonel had made his escape, his partner in sorrow watched for his return. Her ear listened for his well-known footfall, but she heard it not. Her tearful eye watched for him, but she saw him not.

How long is the anxious vigil of love, when every minute groweth into an age, and expectation maketh the soul sick with its unfulfilled hope! Where is he, and what doeth he that he lingers so lon? And the eye of the fond wife droops with her sorrow. What will not that man have to answer for who crushes the faithful bosom with the cold hand of indifference? The murderer expiates his blow—perhaps the hasty blow of passion or madness—on the gibbet, the block, or the scaffold; he lieth under the ban of society, and the curse of his fellows; but is it nothing to slay by the slow poison of neglect?—to kill by instalments, to agonise the victim, and to make the path to the grave long and heavy? It is a hard thing for the hand of love to put forth its hand to the harvest of hope that it hath sown, and gather only the tares of disappointment and woe that have reared their evil forms in the field of the human heart. Where is he, and what doeth he? for he comes not yet. The straining eye and ear watch and listen for him, but he cometh not. Is the hand of sickness on him? Has he again been captured by the indefatigable Jonathan Wild? Is it his woe or his despair that hath borne him away? Is the voice of his vain repentance reaching his soul with its fierce rebukes, or scourging him with its futile agony? Where is he now, and what detains him? Weary question when there is no answer. What wonder is it that the cheek of Mrs. Halford hath grown paler, and her form wasted? It was an evil destiny, poor girl, that threw thy young heart away upon a highwayman.

The thin skin and firm flesh have worn down till the fair brow and sickly face look like the spirit of Death in a new and lovely form, for the intense loveliness of the large and lustrous eye flashes only more gloriously from the depths of sorrow and affliction. But the heart sickens with the mournful picture, till it were a relief for the tongue to upbraid him who hath brought it on her. But no! the trusting, gentle Mrs. Halford kept her woes locked up in the chamber of her own soul. Beautiful love! magnificent spirit of joy and sorrow, with the rainbow present, and the sable future!—when shall we cease to adore thee, though thou blast thy worshippers as they kneel before thy shrine?

A knock is heard at the door, a gentle knock—and a flush of expectation comes over the face of the young wife. She rises suddenly from her seat, and presses her hand to her side as she hastens towards the door and listens. Hark! It is a man's voice—but not his. Then comes the sinking of the heart again, and some footsteps are heard ascending the stairs; then a knock at the door, a "come in" from Mrs. Halford, and Captain Rignold entered the apartment.

"Oh!" exclaimed Mrs. Halford, "it's you! —I thought—"

"What, my dear madam?" enquired the captain.

"I thought it was my husband."

"Has he not yet returned?"

"No," said the wife with a deep sigh; "what can possibly detain him?"

"I have learnt indirectly that he has proceeded to Dover," answered the captain.

"To Dover!—Not to go on the continent —not to cross the channel surely without one last visit to his home—his wretched home!" said Mrs. Halford, now fairly broken down and bursting into tears which she could no longer restrain.

"I am sorry to see this," said Rignold, sadly, "it pains me to know that you have cause for so heavy a sorrow, and I cannot but think the colonel will be here soon; he surely would not be so unmindful of the duty he owes to one, who— Well, well, I will not proceed. There, calm yourself; and believe me, Mrs. Halford, if there were anything in this world which man could do to alleviate your sorrows, I need hardly say you might command me."

"I know it!—I know that, my ever elevated friend. But, oh! Captain Rignold——" she again sobbed convulsively, "this dear child, what is to become of her?" she exclaimed, turning towards her young daughter, who was sitting on the sofa crying in sympathy with her parent.

"Mrs. Halford," said Rignold, "you know how in my earlier youth—you know how I—loved you!"

A deprecating gesture from Mrs. Halford was the only reply vouchsafed to this question.

The captain continued:—

"I need not remind you of those days, they are past never to return. The curtain of time like a funeral pall hangs over them. Alas! there is indeed buried the hopes of a life. The sun of my existence went down, and I have been left in utter darkness ever since. But you know as well as myself to what I allude."

"Yes, yes," hastily answered the highwayman's wife, "it is useless to recur to the past now. If I have been unwise and indiscreet, I have at least paid a bitter penalty for it; and indeed am doing so now."

"I need not be reminded of that!" continued the captain, "for, to say the truth, it is self-evident enough—painfully evident; but from the ruins of this love, if I may so term it, there has sprung up a deep and enduring friendship, one that will only cease with my own life. And oh! Mrs. Halford, I do assure you," said the captain, his voice now assuming a tender tone—"I do assure you that to see you thus makes regret for the past still more heavy to bear, and sorrow more poignant; for I fear me much that a dark and dreary future lies before you. All evil to one, who——"

Mrs. Halford darted upon the speaker a reproachful look.

"There!" exclaimed Rignold, "I meant not to pain you, I will therefore be silent on that head."

"I have made my election and must abide by the consequences, Captain Rignold!" answered Mrs. Halford; "my path is chosen, be it for good or for evil; I owe a duty to my husband, be he whom or what he may."

The captain bowed: "What must be the feelings of the man who is blessed with so inestimable a wife?" he answered.

"I know, Captain Rignold, your generous nature," said Mrs. Halford, "time has already given me proof of that; and as an old friend I receive you, for I know that you are that in every sense of the word; and, alas! I have not many such!" she added sadly.

"It is not for me to suggest, but——"

"What?"

"But in the event of your husband neglecting you, deserting you for so long a period, you would surely be justified in seeking a separation."

"If I desired it," she answered, coldly.

"Oh, yes of course, if you desired it; if not——"

"Why I should remain as I am."

"Precisely."

"Well, then I do not desire it. No! it shall never be said by the world that I was coward enough to shrink from doing my duty to him who I have sworn to love and obey. He may treat me with indifference, with cruelty—although he has never done that—but even if he had I would cleave to him in foul as in fair weather; yes, though it be at the cost of a broken heart."

"I fear me much that it will break your heart," Mr. Halford said. "Good Heavens! is it not horrible to see one whom you have adored fall away before your eyes. Can there be anything more supremely bitter?"

"Let us hope," said Mrs. Halford—"let us put our trust in Him who sees and knows all hearts."

"Oh, Mrs. Halford," said Captain Rignold—"I will not remind you now—I need not remind you, how deep and devoted a love I have borne towards you. It may be unseemly in me to refer to it; but being past we may be pardoned, perhaps, for discoursing on the ruins of that passion, out of which has grown so strong a friendship. I wish to see your state of existence somewhat more happy. I would wish to see your husband following a less dangerous, and you must pardon me when I say a more honourable one than what he is at present following. For your sake I wish this: and possibly, if the suggestion came from yourself, and was backed by me, perhaps we might persuade him to alter his present course of life. If so, I will use my influence in putting him forward in the world. You know, or at least may guess, that I have interest in the government—through my relatives—and I do assure you that nothing should be neglected by me in endeavouring to bring about a more happy state of things for yourself, and I should hope at the same time for him. He has talents—great talents, and wonderful energy; which, were they applied to a different occupation, might make him honoured and respected. Now, think of this; and at the same time believe me that I am not saying thus much to pain your feelings, but my only motive is to see you more happily situated."

"I thank you, Captain Rignold," said Mrs. Halford, "for this as for the very many other acts of disinterested friendship, which you have on so many occasions gratuitously, and at the same time so gracefully rendered. Believe me I do thank you from my very heart."

"I do not need thanks," returned the captain. "The memory of those days, when we as almost children played together and shared each other's troubles, is a sufficient recompense for whatever poor services I may be able to do you or yours."

"Ah! those days, Captain Rignold, I often think—the thought may be a sinful one—but when sitting here alone one is apt to travel over things which in a more active state of existence would never perhaps been thought of. Do you know, I often think that it would be a happy thing for many of us, and myself in particular, if we had been called away to another sphere, ere our hearts had become callous and hardened by—ah! a wicked world: I mean before our first delightful impressions had passed away."

"Youth, madam," answered the captain—"is full of illusions, which our passage through life is pretty sure to dispel."

"Indeed I have found that out!" answered Mrs. Halford.

The two—the captain and Mrs. Halford—were seated side by side, and it may be pardonable for the former to gaze into the face of her who had been his life and light. They sat thus conversing upon old times for some hours, for the minutes flew swiftly by; and in her loneliness Mrs. Halford was but too glad to have a companion. While thus engaged in conversation a gentle knock was heard at the door which was opened by Becky, the maid, who had on more than one occasion cast sheep's eyes at the handsome highwayman. She, however, guessed something had occurred by hearing the frequent and repeated sobs of Mrs. Halford—for truth compels us to admit that Becky had an awkward knack of listening at the keyholes of doors, and consequently being rather of an inquiring mind, and her being a quickwitted individual, she had become acquainted with Mrs. Halford's deep-seated sorrow.

"Lord!—lord, if it arn't Mr. Halford!" exclaimed the maid.

"Is your mistress in?" enquired the colonel, who was in no mood to play up to the serving-woman.

"Yes, sir," said Becky, dropping a curtsey—"but she ain't alone." This was said in a mysterious whisper.

"Who is with her, then?" enquired Colonel Jack.

"Please, sir, a gentleman who is often with missus when you are away."

It was not so much the words that were uttered, but the tone and manner, which made an impression on Colonel Jack.

"A gentleman who comes often when I am away! What do you mean, wench?" exclaimed our hero.

"Oh! nothing, sir; only it's a Captain Rignold who is with missus."

"Captain Rignold!" said the colonel.

"Yes, sir; I believe he's some relation of missus. Ah! it's time you came home."

"Zounds, woman!—are you a fool, a knave, a serpent, or what?"

"I ain't no serpent!" said Becky, bridling up. "Leastways, not as I know on. I came from honest people: if they were poor, they were honest, which is more than everybody can say!"

There was something about the girl's manner which considerably annoyed our hero.

"Honest—who has doubted your honesty? You are half beside yourself, or something! Go!—"

"Somebody is beside of missus!" answered the maid, who began to be spiteful.

"Now, I tell you what it is," said Colonel Jack—"I shan't allow any one to take such liberties with me, or the name of my wife, as you have chosen to do to-night; and so, for the future, you will oblige me by being a little more discreet in your observations—or else you and I must part."

"Begs your parding, sir!" said Becky, now taking the end of her apron and applying it to both her eyes. "I am sure I did not mean to offend. I hopes as how I knows my place. Servants should be servants—but they've got their feelings, though some people think they haven't any. It's very cruel that a poor girl should be called a serpent—just as if I was a boa-constrictor, and hugged people to death!"

At this the colonel could not help smiling.

"And you would rather be hugged yourself—eh, Becky?" he said, with a laugh.

"Oh dear, yes, sir!" said the girl, dropping a low curtsey.

"Well, well—there, don't make yourself miserable! There's no harm done. Only, for the future, keep a guard upon your tongue. Is Captain Rignold upstairs now, then?"

"Yes, he has been with missus the whole of the evening."

"What do you call the whole of the evening, my most veracious informer?"

"Three or four hours, sir," answered the maid.

"Well, there's nothing remarkable in that."

"No, my missus in course likes to see her relations." Becky did not know whether Captain Rignold was in reality a relative of Mrs. Halford's, consequently she was what is termed fishing for information on that head.

The colonel heard no more, but gently ascended the stairs, and opened the door of the front room, first floor. A slight scream escaped Mrs. Halford upon his entrance, and in another second or so he was in the fond embrace of his wife.

"My own dear Frank returned once more!" exclaimed Mrs. Halford, "what weary hours have passed in your absence."

"Not without some solace, it would seem," returned the highwayman, glancing towards Captain Rignold.

"Frank!" exclaimed his wife, as the colour mounted to her face.

"I thank you for your attentions to Mrs. Halford during my unavoidable absence," said the highwayman, glancing at Rignold, who stammered out something, and it must be confessed looked somewhat confused. He however stood up to Colonel Jack, and was about to offer his hand, but there was that in the latter's countenance which forbade his doing so.

"Captain Rignold," said the Colonel, hastily, "I frankly confess that I hardly expected to see you here."

"And why not?" said Mrs. Halford, "he is our friend—one of our best friends; have we not had proofs of this upon more than one occasion?"

"He is your friend, without doubt," answered Colonel Jack.

"And yours," said Mrs. Halford, with an energy that somewhat surprised her husband.

"We will not discuss the question of friendship, madam, upon which subject we very possibly differ; I have lived long enough in the world to be mistrustful of the most promising of friends."

"Frank, this is unkind," said Mrs. Halford, turning away.

"I do not seek to force my presence on you, Halford," said Captain Rignold. "Possibly the sight of me may not be pleasing to you, but you do me an injustice if you imagine I have forced my way into your house and home for any other purpose than solacing your poor wife in the lonely hours of her misfortune."

"Solacing!—lonely hours! By the Lord, sir, I would have you know that Mrs. Halford does not stand in need of any solace from you or any other gentleman in Christendom."

"But I did—I did, and wished him to come. If anyone is to blame it is me," said Mrs. Halford, with the natural generosity of her nature. "Blame not Captain Rignold, for I am sure if he, or indeed if I, had thought his visits would be displeasing to you he would not have forced his way here. It was for your good he came."

"For my good!" exclaimed the colonel, with a mocking laugh. "Well, madam, you are playful."

"Mr. Halford, sir!" exclaimed his wife, "you surely do not impute any improper motive to Captain Regnold. You never would insult him—or insult me—by such an aspersion."

" Is this the way we meet after so long an absence?—this the welcome a loving wife gives to her truant husband?"

" Frank, forgive me," answered Mrs. Halford, rushing once more into his arms; all the tenderness of her woman's nature being once more aroused, " forgive me—let no broils mar our happiness now."

" Happiness!" exclaimed the highwayman, bitterly. " Happiness! It is a small share we either of us get of that."

" It is not my fault—is it, Frank?"

" No; it is mine, I suppose," answered the Colonel—" mine. Granted, whose else can it be?"

" Nay, do not reproach yourself, dearest."

Captain Rignold felt himself in the way. He stepped forward and said :—

" Mr. Halford, I will take my leave. From your manner and bearing I am naturally led to the conclusion that my visits here are distasteful. We cannot, perhaps, altogether ignore the past. Before I leave, allow me briefly to state the object of my visits. Hearing you were in Newgate, I naturally enough concluded that Mrs. Halford would be in a state of despair, and I have been here to devise some scheme to obtain your release."

" You are kind," said the colonel.

" I hope so," answered the captain; " at any rate, Halford, I endeavour to be so."

" Well, sir, that is past now, for I have made my escape, as you are no doubt aware of."

" And I am glad to see you once more in your own home."

" Thank you, sir," said the colonel; whereupon Captain Rignold took a somewhat hasty departure. When he had done so, Mrs. Halford burst into a passionate flood of tears. The husband looked upon her in silence for some minutes—" Indeed but she is strangely altered," he said to himself, as the truth flashed across him that this gentle being was withering beneath the rough blasts of the world. Mighty is the change that has come over her! Short is the space which sorrow takes to plough up the roses on the cheek of beauty! and Mrs. Halford's had been one of no common order. And as the highwayman gazed upon her, he noted how faded was the youthfulness of her fair form. The visitation hath been on her heart, and though it hath left the fragrance of the blossom, it hath crushed out the glorious colours that once flushed upon it. What evanescence is there in the tints of loveliness! How soon the rosy fingers of the morning quench in the yellow glare of day! How soon the virgin silver dims in the heated hand which clasps it! How soon the bloom brushes from the grape! How quickly the fair locks of childhood dull

and darken with age! And how rapidly doth the beauty of woman lose the fresh lustre which is to it what its untouched freshness is to the sunny peach!

Colonel Jack was touched for the moment: upon his first entrance he had given way to an unworthy suspicion—but, upon a second reflection, the better part of his nature asserted her supremacy, and he regretted his undue haste, and the harsh words which had fallen from him. " What an alteration there must be in the hopes and expectations of this woman!" he thought. " And who has caused it? Me!" And, then, as he thought of this, remorse taught him a better lesson; for he loved his wife, and at the bottom of his heart there was a tender chord, which, once struck, made him the gentlest of the human family. Alas! conscience—not of the gentle and mild strides across the downfallen spirit of the highwayman. What are his dreams of the future? He may hope—but what shall his hope be? Death—the threshold of a more fearful doom—eternity—begirt with horror, and pointed to by fear!

Yet doth he bear with him one alleviation—he hath one fond heart tied to his woes for ever—he shall not go unloved! But even this, at times like the present, must enchance his torture—to look upon the beauty his hand hath turned to sorrow—to gaze upon the lineaments so like the dying—to hear the reproach of lips that murmur not against him. There were times in the career of our hero when despair was almost too mighty for him. Let no man envy guilt; it may stand in the sunshine of greatness, and wear the jewelled robes of fortune, and bound in the haunts of pleasure—but its privacy is not looked upon; few see it in its hours of solitude in its loveliness—not of being but of soul, when the one mighty consciousness standeth alone like a giant in the desolation which it hath made. The colonel was touched; his iron and firmly built frame actually shook like a man stricken with a sudden fear. In another minute he was on his knees before his wife, his hands clasping hers, and his face looking up into her own.

" Forgive me, my own dear girl!" said Colonel Jack, tenderly, " I pray you forgive me! Alas! you have suffered much, and all for my sake. Have I not led thee forth from thine home and the happiness of thy youth? Have I not been the cloud on thy life, the spot that has stained thy pure existence, the canker worm which has fed upon thy very heart? and is it for me to complain, my ever true, trusting, and gentle wife? Forgive me!"

" Nay, Frank, I am nervous; and, perhaps, have been as much and more to blame than yourself. It is not for you to talk of forgiveness."

"Listen to me, dearest," said the colonel, still kneeling : "the loneliness of this place is wearisome to you; in my absence dark thoughts come across the brain, and the condemnation of a deceptive husband speaketh more fiercely in the depths of your solitude."

"Nay, nay—not so!" exclaimed Mrs. Halford.

"Excellent one, how shall I ever repay thee for all thou hast lavished on me ? How shall I pay thee kindness that hath heaped its warmth on so unfruitful a soil ?"

"Not unfruitful, Frank; say not so."

"How shall I pay thee?" continued the highwayman, "for all that care that hath watched over the darkest hours of my fate? the love that hath soothed the gentle hours of my sorrow? Never!—never can I do so!"

The tears of his wife dropped like rain on the head and brow of the highwayman, as he drew her gently towards him.

"You have little to thank me for, Frank," answered Mrs. Halford.

"I have everything : the gratitude of a life. Nay, dearest, do not smile. It is true, I owe the gratitude of a life! Has not yours been sacrificed to me ?—has it not been embittered ?"

"Not embittered, Frank. When you are with me I am content; but—"

"Ah! when I am away—which you know, dearest, has been so frequent of late—a sadness comes over your gentle spirit, and you curse the hour that ever saw you wed to one who has outraged the laws of his country—is under their ban—and your poor fluttering heart beats with an unwonted fear for the fate of him whose fortunes are so interwoven with your own. Is it not so ?"

"I — that is — of course I feel anxious about you, Frank. You cannot expect me to be otherwise."

"I have hurt your feelings, my own sweet wife! I have treated Rignold with contumely. I am very sorry for this. Forgive my too impetuous nature! I must make, or, rather, send an apology to him in the morning. There—don't make yourself uneasy upon that head : I will make an ample apology."

"Ah! as to that, it is hardly needed; but you know not how kind and considerate Captain Rignold has been. He has—you will not be angry with me, dearest ?"

"No, no, my own sweet one! Go on !"

"Well, the captain has offered to use his influence with his relations, who you know are grand people, and some of them in Parliament—the captain has offered to procure

you some situation, so that you may leave—" Mrs. Halford paused, and looked confused.

"Well, dearest, I know what you would say—that I may leave my present lawless calling. I know this is what you would say, although your delicacy forbids your doing so."

Mrs. Halford was silent.

"It is useless now to talk of the past, or to endeavour to alter my course of life. Such as it is, I must follow it to the end of my days in this world !"

"I do not complain, dearest," said Mrs. Halford. "I do not complain—only it is so attended with danger !"

"It may be so, but it is too late to alter my course now. Every man has his destiny, which it is in vain for him to endeavour to wrestle against; our lives are marked out for us, some for good, and others for evil. Had it not been for one who poisoned the whole current of my existence, I should have been in a different position; as it is—well, no matter."

Colonel Jack's little girl now came running into the room, and the discussion was then dropped.

CHAPTER LXXXVII.

THE RETURN OF OSBORNE.

MR. Squabshot returned to his lodgings in Goswell Street, in a state of high glee, after he had safely lodged Miss Langford at her own residence. On the following morning he wrote to Osborne, and acquainted him with the joyful intelligence, after which he waited upon Miss Langford at her residence. The first person he saw was Mrs. Ludlow, as neither Honora or Miss Staunton were up.

"Oh, dear—dear me, sir," exclaimed Mrs. Ludlow, "I am a ruined woman—lost, irretrievably lost. What will Sir Richard say? and to think that I should be entrusted with our dear young lady, and—oh, dear, dear."

"Now it's not worth your while troubling yourself about the matter," said Squabshot. "What's done can't be altered now; and it is quite certain it was no fault of yours. So you have no cause for regrets on that score."

"But Sir Richard Fleetwood—where is he ?" enquired Mrs. Ludlow.

"You will not be troubled with his presence for some time," answered Squabshot.

"Gracious goodness !—has anything happened to my master ?" said the dame, in alarm.

"You have no cause to be alarmed upon that head : only, for the present, he is out of the way—'up a tree,' as the saying is."

"'In prison?' inquired the old lady.

"Something very much like it—he is not at large."

"I am at a loss to comprehend you, sir," she said.

"It does not concern you. Sir Richard's private affairs require his absence, that is all. How is Miss Langford?"

"She is not strong as yet."

"Ah, fatigued, I suppose, by the journey and the late hours?"

"Precisely."

"I will wait, then."

"As you please, sir."

"Is Miss Staunton still a devotee to Morpheus?"

Mrs. Ludlow did not understand the question, but she answered by saying that Miss Staunton, she believed, was out.

No. 55.

"Ah!" said Squabshot. "I will wait, if you have no objection."

A gentle knock at the door was heard, and he steps of a female ascending the stairs.

In a minute or two afterwards, Miss Staunton entered the room.

Squabshot made his best bow, and advanced to meet the new comer.

"Oh, it's you, Mr. Squabshot," said Miss Staunton. "Permit me to thank you for all the kindness and consideration you have shown towards my dear friend and companion, Miss Langford. I am sure, sir, no one can possibly have been more anxious than yourself for the restoration of Honora; and no one could have been more indefatigable in your endeavours to find out the mystery of her sudden disappearance and detention."

"Miss Staunton," exclaimed Squabshot, laying his hand upon his heart. "Praise from you would fully recompense me for anything in the world; and, indeed, I may say that I would cheerfully risk my life over and over again, merely to listen to any commendation from yourself. But the little that I have done for Miss Langford hardly deserves a passing notice; still less such expressions as have fallen from yourself."

"I know not how you have accomplished it, Mr. Squabshot; but this I know, that your conduct throughout has been disinterested in the extreme."

"I am sure, it seems altogether a dream to me," said Mrs. Ludlow; "and I, for one, don't understand it; however, as soon as convenient, I shall be glad to go to Barnes. Poor Sir Richard! to think that he should be in prison. It is really sad to reflect on this—very sad."

"Poor Sir Richard, as you term him, madam," said Squabshot, "does not much deserve any one's sympathy. I am only surprised that a respectable female, as you appear to be, should have lent herself to so nefarious a scheme as the abduction and detention of a young lady against her own will."

"I only did as Sir Richard desired me," answered Mrs. Ludlow.

"But you had no right to do so—No right to do a great wrong at the instigation of any man or baronet in the world. Your own sense would have told you this; for we none of us do wrong without knowing when we do so. There, I do not want to upbraid you, but pray don't get up any sentimental or sympathetic tears for a man who is a disgrace to his species."

"Disgrace?" exclaimed Mrs. Ludlow.

"Yes, a disgrace! However, we will not pursue the subject further. You can go home to your own residence as soon as you please."

"Thank you, sir," said Mrs. Ludlow, putting her handkerchief to her eye, "thank you."

While this conversation was taking place, Miss Langford made her appearance in the room. Upon her entrance she stepped forward towards Squabshot, and warmly greeted him. At the same time expressing her sincere thanks for all the trouble he had been at in releasing her from the clutches of Sir Richard Fleetwood. When this was over, her next question was about Osborne.

Squabshot had received a letter from Oxford that very morning, and in it Osborne informed him that he would be home in the after part of the day.

"And I need not tell you, Miss Langford," said the speaker, "what joy awaits my friend Osborne."

Honora coloured slightly and smiled.

"Ah! when a man loves," continued Squabshot, "that sweet dream of our mundane existence. When he loves, who shall tell the rapture he experiences in meeting with the object of his choice, after so protracted and painful an absence."

"Really, Mr. Squabshot, you are quite eloquent," said Miss Langford, smiling. "I did not know that you had so keen an appreciation of the tender passion."

"Madam, we learn from experience," answered Squabshot, turning his eyes towards Miss Staunton, who could not resist a quiet smile.

"Poor Sir Richard!" exclaimed Mrs. Ludlow. "What must his feelings be?"

"You need not trouble yourself upon that head, ma'am," said Squabshot. "It is very doubtful to me if Sir Richard has any feelings."

"Goodness gracious!" answered Mrs. Ludlow. "We have all got our feelings; of course we have. I know I have."

"No doubt, ma'am; there can be no doubt of that, and if you will take my advice you will seek your own rural retreat at Barnes as speedily as possible."

"I want to go now," answered the lady, "but it is too far to walk for an old woman like me."

"I will procure a fly," answered Squabshot "I have not brought you to London to leave you unprotected and uncared for. It would not be prudent for a lady of your attractive appearance to parade the streets to the wicked city alone."

"Pshaw!" exclaimed Mrs. Ludlow, indignantly. "I don't want to be made game of."

"No, madam, but in a close fly you will be all right. Say when you wish to proceed towards your own home, and the affair can be arranged satisfactory, say in the course of half an hour or so."

"I want to go at once," answered Mrs. Ludlow.

"So be it. If you will excuse me, Miss Langford, I will seek for a vehicle to convey this good lady home to her residence."

And with these words, Squabshot took his departure, and in the course of half an hour or so, returned with a fly, into which he placed Mrs. Ludlow, directing the driver to convey her to Barnes, and call at his lodgings for the fare.

And thus the old dame took her departure, not however without sundry complaints as to the way in which she had been treated.

Squabshot then took leave of the two young ladies, and returned to his own lodgings, where he awaited the appearance of Osborne by the Oxford coach, which was due about half past four o'clock in the afternoon.

Strange to say, it actually did come in within an hour or so of the appointed time, and to the great joy of Mr. Squabshot, his friend and fellow lodger was seen through the parlour window of the house in Goswell Street, complacently seated in a hackney coach, the roof of which was piled up with luggage, for it is a singular fact that in the olden times travellers always thought it requisite to travel with enough garments to serve half a dozen ordinary individuals at the very least.

Well, the Oxford student, but now so no longer, did arrive, and Squabshot, with the alacrity of a waiter, was at the door in a second or so, and busily occupied himself in assisting the coachman to bring into the parlour his friend's trunks, &c., talking all the while with a volubility which was habitual to him.

"My dear fellow," exclaimed Squabshot, as soon as the coach had rolled lazily off, and Osborne was seated in an easy chair—"my dear fellow, how are you?" But I need not ask that question. You are looking first-rate, and would captivate any woman in the three kingdoms—that is, any woman who possessed a spark of taste or discernment."

"You are complimentary, Squabshot," said Osborne, laughing. "But a truce to these encomiums. I received a letter from you that has made a new man of me; and, my excellent friend, let me in the first place thank you for the share you have taken in this business. I shall never be able to repay you, Squabshot."

"Psha! nonsense, old boy. A good action always meets with its own reward, as we used to learn from the copyslips when we were two good little boys."

"Well, and how about this affair? Miss Langford is at last restored to her own home?"

"Yes. I saw her this morning—called there out of politeness; for you must know that it was late, or rather early in the morning, before we reached London from Dover."

"Dover?"

"Yes, the worthy Sir Richard was about to proceed with the fair young lady to the continent."

"The scoundrel!"

"Ah, that he is, and no mistake, every inch of him; but no matter for that, he is outwitted."

"For the present."

"Ah, and for good, or I am much mistaken. But we will talk this matter over presently. First of all, you refresh the inner man with some refreshment. 'Tilda! Confound that girl, where is she?" exclaimed Squabshot, as he opened the door of his room, and called out again.

"You must know," he said, turning to his visitor, "that our old duchess has got a new slavey—a slow, stupid, untidy wench, who requires a sledge hammer to drive anything into her thick sconce. Here, 'Tilda!—do you hear?—bring up some hot water and chocolate."

"Yes, sir," answered a voice from the regions below, and the landlady was heard upbraiding the girl for her want of attention to the lodgers, and her household duties in general.

"Ah, this is the pleasure of living in lodgings," said Squabshot. "You not only don't get attended to, but are perpetually annoyed by the servants being blown up by their mistress."

"I don't want anything," said Osborne. "I dined on the coach, I assure you that I did?"

"No consequence about that, some refreshment you must and shall have. You must allow me to have my own way—always would you know."

To satisfy his friend, more than his own appetite, Osborne partook of a portion of the viands set before him.

When he had done so, Squabshot brewed a bowl of punch, and the two were comfortably tiled in for the night.

After Osborne had listened to a discription of the proceedings connected with Sir Richard he turned to another subject, one, indeed, which had been weighing upon his mind for some time past. It was in reference to our hero.

"Squabshot," said Osborne, "you and I know as good a fellow as walks this town, but—"

And here the speaker paused, as his companion gave a significant nod.

"Go on, old boy—I guess what you would say."

"Well, it's just this, Squabby—Mr. Halford and Colonel Jack are one and the same individual!"

"I say nothing," answered Squabshot, with a wink.

"No matter what you say—they are the same. I am sorry for this, deeply grieved on many accounts. Look at the risks—look at the end of such a career. Heavens! I shudder at the contemplation!"

"It is not a pleasant one, to say the least of it; but we have all our destiny marked out for us."

"I am right in my conjecture?"

Squabshot gave him another nod of acquiescence,

"And you and I must put an end to this," said Osborne, firmly.

"How? old fellow—how?"

"Listen. By the will of the late Jabez Crudge, I have come into an amount of property beyond the dream of the most sanguine person. It is more than I desire, or want, and, indeed, to say the truth, a moderate competence, is all that a man requires in this world."

"I shouldn't complain if Dame Fortune were to shower her golden gifts upon me," answered Squabshot, turning his eyes up towards the ceiling.

"No, nor do I," said Osborne. "But now that I have become possessed of so much wealth, my first thought is to see what good I can do with it."

"A very noble thought," answered Squabshot.

"And such being the case, my desire is to place Halford in such a position as to remove him from his present course of life. I know he has been driven to it by circumstances, over which, perhaps, he had no control."

"Just so, that's it."

"Let him take a sufficiency for his desires, and then—"

"Ah, but he won't."

"Won't—why not?"

"There is a charm about his present calling. A charm—a fascination—which he will find it difficult to forego."

"What makes you think this?"

"I am sure of it."

"Why, it is only a few days since he escaped from Newgate."

"I know that, I was in the swim," said Squabshot.

"You?"

"Yes, me, my friend. You see I have been playing an active part in the world of late. A thieftaker, a visitor to a lunatic asylum, a knight errant, who saves beauteous damsels from wicked barons, and an assistant to a highwayman, when he makes his escape from Newgate—and oh, I forgot, a friend of the notorious Jonathan Wild."

"You are a wonderful man, Squabshot, and deserve the thanks of a grateful public."

"Which I shall never get, and what is more, never require. Well, no matter for that. And so, old boy, you really have come into the possession of all that vast wealth bequeathed by the late Jabez Crudge?"

"Yes, its all mine now, and I shall not forget my old friends, believe me. But, Lord, Squabshot, how strange a dream is human life. What a number of friends I have whom I never dreamt of. Why, half Oxford makes acquaintance with me. I, who, when a pale student in that classic town, could scarcely find one to recognise me, now have people inquiring for me from all quarters. What a thing it is to be a millionaire."

"Money makes the man. The old copyslips, which I have before quoted, say that 'manners make the man;' but I say diffently. It is money—nothing but money. You are now a man of note and mark, Harry, and can show them how a man of spirit can spend his fortune."

"First let me see how to make good use of it to assist my friends. Where is Halford now? Out of the way, I suppose?"

"No; I know where to find him."

"Good. Then I wish you would see him as soon as possible. Make an appointment for him to come here, and we can talk the matter over. I know his nature, and I know also that he will be grieved enough when he finds that I am acquainted with his identity. It would spare my feelings as well as his, if you would break the matter gently to him; you understand."

"Perfectly; only I must object to saying that I have told you."

"There can be no occasion for that, since you have not. I learnt it through various channels. Indeed, to say the truth, I have known this for a long time, but have deemed it prudent not to say anything on the subject for various reasons."

"Then you may rely upon my doing what you require," said Squabshot.

"We shall not be long together as we used to be. In fact, we are not so now. But hear me, Squabshot, I should be very sorry if this wealth I inherit should be the cause of digging a gulf between us. It too often happens that such is the case. Now, I do not pretend to be an exception to the general rule, or to be a better man than my fellows; but I do hope, that in the golden dream which is now realised, I shall not be unmindful or forgetful of those whom I have known when fortune was less favourable to me."

"I am sure you will not, and that is more," answered Squabshot.

"Don't be too certain on that head. We are none of us masters of ourselves. Prosperity is sometimes as hard to bear as adversity—indeed, in some cases harder; but I have endeavoured to school my mind to meet the case."

"Ah! you'll be married soon, I suppose?" said Squabshot, endeavouring to give a new current to the conversation.

"Osborne colonred and said—"that depends upon circumstances."

"Circumstances! Why, you don't mean to cast off the sweet and charming Honora Langford in the hour of your prosperity."

"Can you suppose such a thing?" answered Osborne, angrily.

"No, no; I was only joking, my boy. Of course, I don't suppose such a thing. Oh, no! Therefore I say you will soon be married. Soon keep your carriage, your town house, and your estate in the country; be returned member of—Bucks, or Westminster—and vote against the ministry—be a man of the people—the light of the age—the great reformer—"

"There, that will do," interrupted Osborne, smiling.

"Good ; I hope it will do ; nay, I am sure it will, and that is better."

Thus the two friends conversed upon various topics till past midnight ; for Osborne, who had been always an early and steady man in his habits, found himself so elated and pleased with the cheerful society of Squabshot, that he was not disposed to go to bed at his usual early hour.

We have seen him a pale Oxford student,—a merchant's clerk. We have now to see him in his future career, as the wealthy and favoured son of fortune.

Early on the following morning after his arrival in London, he paid a visit to Honora Langford.

But we must now return to the home of the highwayman.

CHAPTER LXV.

THE SHADOW OF DEATH FALLS UPON THE HOME OF COLONEL JACK.

It will be remembered by the reader that upon Colonel Jack's return he observed a visible alteration in the appearance of his wife. It is astonishing that he had not noticed this before; but it is a singular fact, which no doubt many of our readers have had come under their own observation, that one member of a family or household may be gradually changing or fading away, and this will perhaps never strike any of the inmates of the house. A stranger—a friend may come in and suddenly note the change, but those who are actually with the individual, herself or himself, remain in perfect ignorance of the fact that one of their little family had been "spoken with"

Mrs. Halford's was a gentle, trusting nature, sensitive to the last degree, and all unfit to bear the storms of life. Deep in her own breast she had kept the recent grief which was eating its way into her very heart, sapping and opening the very springs of life, and withering her in her prime.

Who shall tell what that woman suffered ?

She always endeavoured to put a cheerful face upon the matter, or, at any rate, as cheerful a face as it was possible under the circumstances; but, alas! at what cost! that of a broken heart.

Since the colonel's imprisonment in Newgate, Mrs. Halford had been constantly a prey to the most poignant grief ; and after

his escape, she really believed that he was not going to return to her.

The messages he had sent by Galdie and Hackett, for her not to make her appearance at the prison, all gave a colour to this supposition, and it hurt her more than anything she had yet endured, for with all our hero's faults, she loved him still.

Sublime passion, that teaches us to cleave to the one we have taken for "better or for worse," through bad and good repute, in sickness or in health.

Man is supposed to be a selfish animal. Unquestionably he is by nature, and more so than woman; he is too often unmindful of the great sacrifices that the latter often makes for him.

Not that Colonel Jack was more selfish than his fellows, perhaps not so much so, for his was a generous nature; but he did not, or could not see the tender flower which was withering on its stem under his very eyes. His nature was more impulsive than reasoning, and he of all men was perhaps the least adapted as a companion to a woman of Mrs. Halford's fine and delicate organization.

Strange, how many ill assorted matches there are in this world.

Some few days after the capture of Sir Richard Fleetwood, Colonel Jack returned home somewhat earlier in the evening than was his custom. Becky opened the door, and from the expression of the girl's countenance, he concluded that there was something amiss, for her eyes were red as though she had been weeping.

"Why, how now, what's the matter, Becky ?"

"Missus !—oh ! Mr. Halford."

"Your mistress !—what do you mean ?—has anything happened ? Speak ! for mercy's sake don't keep me in suspense."

"Oh, missus is so ill."

"Ill ? When was she taken then ? She complained a little of her head yesterday, but there was nothing serious. Was it to-day ?"

"Last night—"

"What ?"

"She swooned away and was senseless for nearly two hours."

"Merciful heavens !" exclaimed Colonel Jack; "and I not here ! But she will be better after a little rest and some medicine. Did you go for a doctor ?"

"Yes, sir."

"What said he ?"

"Gave her some medicines, and said she must be kept be kept very quiet," answered Becky.

"Well, then, she will be better soon, I have no doubt. Plague take the girl, how you alarmed me."

Becky pulled Colonel Jack by the sleeve,

and conducted him into a small room on the ground floor, which was seldom occupied. Having done this, she closed the door of the apartment, and without saying a word, placed her candlestick on the table, and motioned the colonel to a seat, who mechanically obeyed her, although he was at a loss to understand the meaning of all this.

When he had seated himself, and looked inquiringly into the face of the maid, she began thus—

"Oh, master, I hope you will forgive a poor, foolish, misguided girl."

"What for ?"

"For saying what I did about Captain Rignold. Missus is an angel upon earth, that's what she is."

"Well, I know that. I know her excellent qualities better than you do."

"I hope so, Mr. Halford. If you don't, you ought, that's all I have got to say."

"Well, what is the meaning of all this ? You surely have not brought me in here merely to tell me this ?"

"No, sir," said Becky, dropping a curtsey, "certainly not; but I thought it best to tell you all that has happened before you go up stairs."

"Ah!" said the colonel, with a heavy sigh, for he fully believed some new revelation was about to be made known to him.

"Well, sir, you must know that missus has been crying to herself for some time past; but I told you that when you came home after your long absence."

"Yes, I remember."

"And missus was taken so bad last night, poor dear lady, that I thought she would have never lived to see the morning's light. She's been wandering and delirious."

"Delirious!"

"Yes, and has been talking about such strange things."

"How did the attack first commence?"

"Why, missus fell down upon the floor, senseless, and her dear little girl came running down stairs to call me, or some one to her assistance. I rushed up on the instant, and found the poor lady stretched upon the floor, apparently without life. We put her to bed, and Andrew run for a doctor. But law, Mr. Halford, you won't have her very long."

"Won't have her long!" exclaimed the colonel. "What do you mean ? Won't have her long."

"No, sir, that's my humble opinion; certainly I have no right to say anything, perhaps, being only a humble servant, but my opinion is that missus is going."

"What in the name of heaven makes you imagine that?" inquired our hero.

"Haven't you seen it?" said the girl.

"Seen it—seen what?"

"Seen how the poor dear soul has been fading away ?"

"Not I, indeed."

"Ah, that's always the way; those most interested are the last to see these things, the very last."

"What has your mistress been talking about in her wanderings?"

"Oh, lots of things—about highwaymen, robbers, executioners, and all the most horrible things you can possibly imagine. I have heard of a good many things, but nothing like this. Poor soul, what could have put all this into her head?"

Colonel Jack looked greatly alarmed at these observations, as well he might. In fact, he had some difficulty in concealing his confusion.

"Is she better now ?"

"She was sleeping when I went up, about half an hour ago. Oh, master, I hope that my observations about Captain Rignold has not preyed upon her mind ?"

"Psha, no ! What makes you think that ? Has she mentioned the captain's name?"

"Yes, once or twice—in fact, several times—and it appears the captain is not a relation of hers."

"No. What made you imagine that he was?"

"I thought so."

"Well, I will go up."

"I am afraid that your sudden appearance might give a shock to missus, and the doctor said that no one was to see her without her being prepared to see them."

"Ah; then in that case do you go up and say I am returned. I will go into the front room and await your coming."

"Very well, sir, perhaps that would be the best course."

The colonel then followed Becky up into the first floor front room, and the maid crept noiselessly into her mistresses room. In a few minutes she returned, and beckoned the colonel to follow her. Our hero did so, and as they went along, Becky said in a hurried whisper—

"Missus couldn't be left, so we have got her a nurse. She's with her now."

"Quite right," answered the colonel.

The two then entered the bed room of the sick woman.

Mrs. Halford was asleep, and as she lay on her couch, Colonel Jack contemplated her features,

He then, perhaps for the first time, became seriously alarmed for his wife. There was that in her pinched and pale countenance, which struck the highwayman as something painful to look upon, as he had never noticed before how thin and wasted she now was; besides this, there was an expression of resignation upon her countenance, emaciated as it was, that had in it a sweet and touching melancholy.

"Indeed, but she is very ill," said our hero.

"She is not in so much pain, sir," answered Mrs. Santly, the nurse.

Mrs. Halford gently opened her eyes. As they rested upon her husband, a pleasant smile passed over her countenance, and he was at her side on the instant.

"Frank," she exclaimed, "I have been so bad."

"But you will be better dearest," he answered.

She made no reply to this, and Mrs. Santly and Becky left the apartment.

"Why, my own sweet wife, what has been the matter?" said Colonel Jack.

The sick woman made no reply, but her eyes filled with tears.

"Nay, my dearest, cheer up; you will be better."

"Do they think so?"

"Who?"

"The doctor."

"Yes, of course they do. It's debility—nothing but debility, and in a short time you will be restored to your usual health and strength."

"Frank," said Mrs. Halford, sadly, never. Do not deceive yourself, my ever kind and considerate husband, my hours are numbered."

"This is mere phantasy. Gracious goodness! for my sake, for your own, do not talk thus. Cheer up, you must make an effort." said our hero.

"I have, Frank, many. Ah, no! the time has come when all that is useless, quite useless now. Do not fret, Frank. We must part some time or other, and why not now. It is hard to leave those you love, but it must come, and—".

"And what, dearest?"

"I don't know that I have much to live for."

"Have you not your child, and—"

"You," said Mrs. Halford, again indulging in a sweet smile.

"Yes, you, that is true enough," she said, again.

"Well, then, many happy years are yet in store for us. I know this. I am sure such is the case. Nay, turn not thy head away. You will, you must be better."

"I hope so—let us hope."

These words almost sounded like a mockery coming as they did from lips which were almost colourless.

The flesh of Mrs. Halford had been so worn down that her fair brow and sickly face looked like the spirit of death in a new and lovely form, for the intense loveliness of the large and lustrous eyes flashed only the more gloriously from the depths of sorrow and affliction.

But this night there was surely some other change, for in spite of her haggard countenance and wasted form, she seemed lighter and more full of hope than before, and the colonel threw himself by her, to carress away her sorrow, the old times seemed to come once more and married his soul to happiness again.

And Mrs. Halford's look brightened, and her thin lips quivered till she leaned upon his bosom, and wept her woe away.

How rapidly a strong motive of action purges the heart of man of its doubts, its dreams, and its indecisions.

For some time Mrs. Halford lay in her husband's arms, until her increasing weight and unmoved silence awakened him to a feeling of alarm.

He looked at her features, and found them fixed and rigid. She lay motionless, and then the colonel, for the first time became aware that she was senseless. She had swooned away. At first her husband believed her to be dead, but upon a closer inspection, he observed that she breathed gently.

He hastily left the bedside of the patient, and called Mrs. Santly.

"How is the dear lady?" said the professional nurse.

"She has fainted," said Colonel Jack. "Send for the doctor. Does he live far?"

"No, sir," said Mrs. Santly, as she rang the bell for Becky.

"Poor thing, it has been too much for her. I was afraid of this. Indeed but she is very weak."

Becky was despatched for the doctor as Mrs. Santly busied herself in an endeavour to restore the poor sick woman to consciousness.

A sleek, solemn individual made his appearance shortly after this. He was dressed in a suit of black, and wore an habitual solemn look.

"Ah, a relapse," he said, softly, as he felt the patient's pulse. "Has she taken her medicine, Mrs. Santly?"

"Yes, sir, every four hours as you directed."

"And kept it on her stomach?" asked the doctor.

"Yes, sir."

"Has she slept?"

"Yes, occasionally, about half an hour at a time."

"In much pain?"

"No, sir; I have not heard her complain, but I left the room for a short time as Mr. Halford returned."

"Oh," said the man of drugs, turning towards the colonel, who he then, for the first time, observed.

"Is there any danger ?' was the latter's first question.

The disciple of Esculapius shook his head.

" Her situation is a critical one," he answered slowly and in solemn accents.

" But she is young—has in all probability an unimpaired constitution, and—and—let us hope for the best. While there is life there is hope."

" Good heavens ! is she so bad as all that," said Colonel Jack.

" She is very bad."

" What is her disease."

" Perverted nervous action, sir. We cannot call it anything else. No particular organ, as the frame has given way, at least, none that I have been able to discover. Nevertheless, her situation is a critical one. I fear she has been giving way to some recent grief."

" Oh dear, no ! I hope not," answered the colonel.

While this conversation was taking place, Mrs. Halford had remained in a state of collapse. Presently she opened her eyes once more, and breathed a deep sigh. The doctor bent over—

" Well, my dear madam, and how do you find yourself by this time, eh ? Very weak and dispirited. Come ! cheer up, you must not give way. You are better now ; the pulse is stronger and more regular."

" Have I been asleep ?" asked Mrs. Halford.

" Yes," said the doctor.

" Oh, I have been dreaming, I think. Where is Mr. Halford."

" I am here, my dear," said her husband.

" Oh ! it was not a dream, then ?' said the invalid, pressing her hands against her temples.

" What ?" inquired Mrs. Santly.

Oh, nothing—nothing," answered Mrs. Halford.

The doctor left the room, followed by Colonel Jack.

The two went into the drawing room, where the Colonel handed the medical man a chair.

" I have but just returned home, and find my wife as you see her. I need not say, sir, how anxious I am. What do you think of the case ?"

" It is, as I told you in the first instance, a serious one. Your good lady is so weak, and her nerves are so completely unstrung, that it is difficult to say, with any degree of certainty, what will be the result ; but, as I said before, let us hope for the best. It is at all times most difficult in cases of this sort to set a limit to the powers of the constitution."

" What is the cause of these fainting fits ?"

" Hysteria is the nearest term we can give them. She is of a fine and delicate organisation. and of a peculiarly sensitive temperament. I should be sorry to say that she would not recover ; but yet, I am bound to tell you that the chances are uncertain in either way ; in fact, almost evenly balanced."

" Good heavens ! how sudden this has been," exclaimed the colonel, hardly believing his senses.

" Not so sudden, my friend. It must have been coming on for some time. The disease is an insidious one of slow growth, and although it has not been made manifest at an earlier period, nevertheless it must have been gradually coming on for some time, although unperceived by either yourself or those who were around her."

" Can nothing be done ? Gracious heavens ! can nothing be done, my friend ?"

" All that my experience suggests has been and shall be," answered the leech. " If you wish for further advice, I shall be most happy to meet any one you may think fit to call in."

And with this the doctor took his departure. He had no sooner done so, than Becky, the maid, tapped gently at the drawing room door.

She held up her apron to her eyes, for she was weeping and sobbing every now and then hysterically.

" Oh, Mr. Halford," said the maid, " poor dear missus—she's very bad."

" There can be no doubt of that," answered the colonel, sadly. " Not a question about that."

" And I begs your pardon, sir—it ain't for a poor ignorant servant like me to suggest—only don't you think it would be better to have some further advice ?"

" I perfectly agree with you, Becky, and am about to go round to a gentleman in Brook Street."

" What's his name, if I may make so bold as to ask ?" inquired Becky.

" Mr. Carruthers."

" Oh, he's a very celebrated man. Do go for him."

" I am about to do so," answered the colonel, as he once more took his way to his wife's bed-room.

" She's much better now," said Mrs. Santly, turning towards the colonel. " The sudden shock was too much for her weak nerves."

" You are better, my dear, and, let us hope, will soon be well," said her husband.

The same sweet smile passed over her features at this observation, which the colonel noticed on several occasions.

" Where are you going ?" said Mrs. Halford, as she perceived that her husband had had his hat on.

" Only a little way, my dear,"

"A little way—where, Frank? Shall you be long?"

"No, my own sweet girl, not long," he answered.

"Ah, that is well."

"Do you not wish me to go, then?" he said.

"I would rather you stay at home while I am here—"

"While you are here! What do you mean?—here—"

"It may not be for long, you know, Frank—and I would fain look upon you before I take the long, long journey."

Colonel Jack turned away his head, tears were in his eyes, and his frame shook with emotion.

For some time there was a dead silence after this.

"I was but going for a friend of mine," said the colonel.

"A friend—what for—who?"

"A doctor—Mr. Carruthers."

"Ah, I want no more doctors. They can do me no good," answered Mrs. Halford.

"Ah, dear, it's wicked to say that," said Mrs. Santly. "Where should any of us be without them?"

"I do not need any other medical advice now."

"But my dear," said the nurse, who considered that the greater the number of doctors there were, the greater were the chances of the patient's recovery. "But, my dear, you must not be obstinate. You know that other persons are the best judges in this matter. It is impossible for a sick person to know what is best for them. Come now, master will bring some one who will be sure to do you good."

"As you like," said the patient, feebly; "I do not desire it, but if it is necessary—"

"It is only for my own satisfaction," said Colonel Jack. "You will then not refuse me this one favour?"

"Ah, no, if you desire it, certainly not."

Colonel Jack bent over his wife, and imprinting a kiss upon her wan cheeks, took his departure.

As luck would have it, Mr. Carruthers was at home, and his surprise at the sight of the highwayman may be readily imagined. He had heard of the escape from Newgate, but had not the most remote idea of the object of his present visit.

"Mr. Carruthers," said Colonel Jack, "I already owe you a deep debt of gratitude, and I doubt not but that you are vexed to see me cross your threshold—"

"Not at all—not at all," said the good-natured doctor.

"Permit me to briefly state the object of my present visit."

The doctor handed the speaker a chair, and the two sat down.

"You must know, Mr. Carruthers, that I am residing in this neighbourhood, and am known under my real name, that of Halford."

The doctor bowed.

"In the house I occupy, I pass as a respectable member of society, and consequently I need not say to a gentleman of your discretion and knowledge of the world, that I should be sorry if that illusion is dispelled."

"You have nothing to fear from me, sir," said Mr. Carruthers.

"Of that I feel confident. My wife, whom I love as few men love woman, is dangerously ill, and as I have no confidence in any gentleman equal to yourself, would it be asking too much for you to come and see her?"

"I will do so with the greatest pleasure," answered Mr. Carruthers. "We live in this world, my friend, to be useful to one another. Do you wish me to accompany you now?"

"If you can make it convenient," said the colonel.

"Certainly. It is not far, I presume?"

"No, less than half a mile."

"In that case I will walk."

Doctor Carruthers having got ready in a short time, proceeded in company with the colonel towards the latter's own residence, and crept softly up to Mrs. Halford's bed-room.

The invalid was in a deep slumber when the two entered. She was awoke, however, by the nurse, whereupon Mr. Carruthers went to her bedside, and carefully examined the patient, asking her a multiplicity of questions respecting her general state of health previous to her present attack.

The colonel had, during the interview, left the room, and after the doctor had sufficiently satisfied himself as to the state of the lady's case, he joined the colonel in the front drawing-room.

There was a seriousness on the countenance of Mr. Carruthers, which the colonel at the first glance noticed—a solemn gravity, more than usually observable upon the doctor's features.

"She is very ill—you find her so—eh?" exclaimed our hero, hurriedly.

"My friend, it would be wrong of me to say otherwise, she is very ill indeed; but by God's blessing, let us hope that we may see her better, although—"

"What?"

"Although she is in so precarious a position that it is really hard to say what may be the result."

"You consider her in immediate danger, then?" inquired the colonel.

"It is impossible to say, with any degree of certainty. The flame of life is fitful and flickers—now shooting up with a vivid but transient glow, and then a scarcely perceptible glow is seen in the dying embers. We all of us, the best and strongest, hold but a frail tenure of existence; but with one of such a delicate frame and susceptible a temperament as your good lady, this is more particularly felt.

The worthy doctor then entered into a general diagnosis of the patient's complaint, and the manner in which she was to be treated, and with a promise to come again in the morning, Doctor Carruthers took his departure.

The terrible truth then flashed more surely upon the mind of our hero, that she, who had been his companion, his uncomplaining, gentle companion, the loved one of his heart and bosom, was fading away—yes, gradually but surely fading away. He understood little of professional statement of the case; but he knew enough to be fully aware that she who had given up her maiden vows at the altar—who had linked her fate to his, for better or for worse—she who had been to him and faithful wife, was passing away as one of the bright and beautiful things of this earth, never more to glad the eyes of him for whom she had suffered so much, and suffered with a gentleness of manner, and uncomplaining, unrepining a spirit, which was all too good for this world.

"Too good!" exclaimed our hero, striking his clenched fist against his forehead. "Too good, much too good for this world."

He sat himself down in a massive leathern chair, leant his face upon his hands, and bit his fingers to the quick.

"Ah!" he sighed, as though some pent-up agony was inclosed in his breast. "Ah, my life, from first to last, as far as it's gone at present, seems to have been one grand mistake. Why was I ever allied to such a gentle trusting creature as this? whose very nature was perhaps the least adapted for my wife or companion. Why was she doomed to fall a victim to a love which has proved her curse, and bids fair to bring her to a premature grave? Bah! fatality!—the worst of fatality, for her and for me. I know the cause of her disease—I know why it is that her gentle spirit is broken. I am the cause of this—I alone. It is I that have crushed this gentle spirit in my too rough grasp. Fool, idiot that she was, to have listened to the suit of one who has, in truth, been her curse —her bitterest curse."

He leant forward on his hands, and actually groaned aloud with anguish, as these thoughts and a host of others, rushed through his excited brain.

He sat some time thus, racked with the deep anguish which had entered his soul. He was not a man much given "to the melting mood," not a man whom the world would understand by a refined sensibility. Nevertheless, rough, brusque, and commanding at times as was his manner, he was possessed of acute feelings when once touched; but the outer shell or incrustation which shielded this, was thick and indurated, but the feelings were there, although deeply seated.

Who shall plumb the depths of the human heart? Who shall map out its various phases?

The highwayman leant forward upon his hands and wept like a child. His strong frame shook, his hands trembled, and his lips quivered, as he consumed the grief which weighed his spirits down, in that chamber, alone, and in silence.

He had not the courage to move.

The day was declining, the grey twilight found its way feebly into the room, and after then, that disappeared, and all was darkness.

The colonel was suddenly awakened to the more immediate affairs of life, by a sudden flash of light finding its way into his apartment. It came from a lamp in the street, on the opposite side of the way, which had been just lit by a lamplighter who was going his usual rounds.

This slight incident recalled him to himself. He rose from his seat, and walking across the room, gazed out abstractedly into the street.

There was nothing remarkable there. The place looked dull enough, and, indeed, in the colonel's melancholy mood, it is probable that any place would have worn a dull aspect.

After watching for a short time the few passengers who were taking their way along the street, the colonel again returned to the interior of his apartment, and flung himself down into his arm chair.

A strange sadness was on him, which he in vain endeavoured to shake off—a sadness which was unusual to him.

He ran over the incidents of his past life—few of us can do this without seeing some cause for regrets—with him there were many—what he might have been, and what he was?

Sad reflection!

His eyes were bent upon the ground in an abstracted gaze, and while they wandered over the surface of the apartment, their glance fell upon another pair of eyes meeting his own.

These were Slott's, who had been crouched under the table, and had been watching the countenance and proceedings of his master, without the latter being in any way conscious of his presence; he started, therefore, at the sight of the dog, the more so as Slott's countenance was melancholy and dejected to the last degree.

The colonel contemplated the animal for some time in a ruminating manner, and the latter was evidently well aware that he formed the subject of his master's thoughts. We never will be brought to believe anything else, but that dogs are fully aware when you are talking or thinking about them, that is, of course, if they are present at the time.

"Ah," said the colonel, apostrophizing his canine friend, "you are the fittest companion for me. You are not possessed of a fine organization and a susceptible nature. The frowns and scorns of the world make but little difference to you. It matters but little if old friends treat you with contumely and contempt, it would never break your heart, Slott. What care you for the opinion of the world, you great practical philosopher? Nothing, absolutely nothing—you are above that. Happy animal!"

Slott looked up towards his master, although he was evidently in no happy frame of mind to judge from his expression—not a jot more happy, perhaps, than his master.

As the colonel sat contemplating the dog, he was too much engrossed with his own thoughts to notice that the door of the apartment was gently opened, and a little fairy-like being entered with noiseless footsteps, and taking her way towards Colonel Jack she laid her hand on his shoulder, and wound her little arms around him.

Our hero turned, and then, for the first time became aware that it was his daughter, Rosalie, who had found her way to his side, and took her on his lap, and tenderly embraced her.

Tears stood in the eyes of the child, who, as her father embraced her, sobbed convulsively as though her little heart would break.

At first our hero was at a loss to clearly comprehend the meaning of this demonstration on the part of his infant daughter.

"Rosalie, and crying. What is the matter, child?"

She returned no answer, but hid her little head in the breast of the highwayman.

"Speak, dear. What is the matter?"

"How is mamma?" said the child. "She is very, very ill, I know that. How is she? Mrs. Curson won't let me go into the room, because she says it will disturb her as she's asleep. She can't always be asleep. How is she, dear papa?"

The colonel did not know what reply to make to this speech, but he said to the child that her mother would be better.

"And is she not better now?" inquired Rosalie.

"Oh, yes, a little better, my dear."

The child laid her head upon the breast of her father once more, and seemed more satisfied, although she still sent forth several sobs.

The colonel felt his grief much enhanced by this demonstration, and he was glad enough when he was relieved by Curson entering the room.

This person, the reader will remember, was an old and faithful servant of the family.

"Ah, it's you, Curson! How is your mistress now?"

"Much the same, sir,' said Curson. "Come, Miss Rosalie, you are wanted."

The child kissed her father, and was taken down below by the domestic, and placed under the charge of Becky the maid, after which Curson herself returned once more to the drawing-room.

"Nurse wants to go home to-night," she said to the colonel, "and I am going to set up with missus."

"Oh, there is no occasion for that," said Colonel Jack; "not the slightest occasion, Curson. I will lay down in the next room, and if there be any occasion can call you. No, no, you go to bed, or you will be knocked up. Now, don't you attempt to set up again."

"I shouldn't be satisfied if I did not," answered the woman.

"Why not?" inquired the colonel, quickly. "Do you think your mistress is in such danger then?"

"I shouldn't feel satisfied to leave her," answered Curson.

Colonel Jack said no more, and the woman left the room.

"Not satisfied," he exclaimed; "ah, not satisfied—no, I suppose not; these people know by intuition the approach of that grim monster Death. There is a strange and serious way with Curson, she thinks more than she chooses to give utterance to. Oh, that I could know the end of this. And yet after all, she does not appear so bad—she's weak, nervous, but certainly not so bad as they would make out—not in immediate danger, I should say."

And Colonel Jack, with his hands crossed behind him, paced once more his apartment with uneasy and restless strides.

CHAPTER LXVI.

FADING AWAY.

READER, has it ever been your lot to watch by the bedside of a sick person? Has it ever been your task to count the weary, anxious hours throughout the long night, to note the various alternations of some terrible malady which shakes the frame, prostrates the human form, and renders the strong man in his pride and prime to the helplessness of an infant?

Perhaps the being you are thus watching may be a dear and loved relative who relies upon your attentions to minister to his comforts. It is a sad task, believe me—a task which demands a great stress upon the nervous system, it breaks down the stronger spirit of man than woman, who seems by nature better adapted for the task.

Colonel Jack once more took his way into the bedroom of the invalid. Mrs. Halford was awake, and her eyes brightened at the approach of her husband, who sat down by the bedside of the patient, and inquired kindly how she was.

"Much the same, Frank, much the same," she answered.

"Heaven be praised that you are no worse."

"Where is Rosalie?"

"With Becky."

"Ah, gone to bed?"

"Not yet I should imagine. Has she been in to wish you good night?"

"No," she answered feebly.

"Then of course she is not gone to bed," he said.

"I suppose not."

"Shall I ring for her?"

"If you like."

"Nay, dearest, it is as you like."

"Yes, ring, then."

The colonel did as she requested, and Becky made her appearance.

"Bring up Rosalie, and then she may go to bed."

The maid did as she was desired, and the child came into the room in a half frightened state.

Children do not always understand illness—they have sometimes a strange intuitive horror of the same.

Mrs. Halford tenderly embraced the girl, and seemed loath to part with her.

Strong is a mother's love for her offspring—one of the deepest and purest passions which moves the human soul.

For a long time Rosalie lay upon the bed locked in her mother's embrace, until Curson came into the room and gently took her away.

"You seem better, dearest," said the colonel, when the child and servants had left, "much better, I think."

His wife smiled another of those peculiar smiles of resignation and contentment it would have been difficult to have interpreted correctly.

"Don't you feel better?"

"Much the same," she answered in a feeble tone.

Curson came into the room and busied herself in making the invalid as comfortable as possible.

Colonel Jack supported her in a half-sitting position, as the faithful domestic arranged the bed more comfortably.

As our hero did this, he was appalled to find what a thin anatomy he was clasping, he said, however, nothing upon the subject.

"There, now you will be able to rest more comfortably," said Curson.

The invalid nodded, and by her looks expressed her thanks for what was being done for her.

Curson then left and went into an adjoining apartment.

Colonel Jack sat down in the chair by the side of his wife's bed. In a short time the invalid dozed off. She had been fatigued by even the slight exertions she had gone through.

The colonel watched her thin features as they were calm and passionless.

It might have been about an hour, or rather more, that the sick woman had slept; after which she awoke, and called her husband by name.

"I am here, dearest," he said.

"Frank," said Mrs. Halford, "when I am gone—"

"Gone," said the colonel, sadly, observing that the speaker paused suddenly.

"Yes, Frank," she continued, after a pause, during which time tears stood in her eyes. "Yes, dear Frank, when I am gone, be kind to Rosalie."

"Goodness me, yes, of course; am I not, have I not always been so?"

"Yes, yes, dear, I know that. Don't think

that I am going to upbraid you; but I want a promise from you."

"Well, you know you have but to name your wishes, and whatever they may be, they shall be respected."

A smile of ineffable sweetness passed over the wan features of the sick woman. She laid her thin white hand upon that of her husband, and turned her sweet face towards his.

"You will not be angry with me for what I am about to say, will you?" she asked.

"Lord no, be it what it may, I cannot find it in my heart to be angry with you, my own sweet wife. Angry, indeed, you who have—"

"There, that will do," said Mrs. Halford. "I know what you would say. Never mind that, but the promise, dear, the pledge—its the last favour I shall ask of you—the last. When I am gone, will you promise me that Rosalie shall be brought up in ignorance of—of—"

She paused here, and an expression of pain passed over her features.

"I know what you would say, dearest," answered our hero. "In ignorance of her father's calling."

"Yes," sighed forth the unhappy woman, as she half hid her face in the pillow. "You will promise me that?" she repeated.

"I swear it," answered her husband, in deep but broken accents. "Rosalie shall be with one—"

"My mother," said Mrs. Halford.

"If you wish it, yes."

There was no answer to this.

"And you do wish it, I suppose?"

A half suppressed "yes," was the answer to this inquiry.

Then there was a pause, which was broken by the colonel saying—

"But you talk as though you were about to leave me."

"And so I am, Frank," said the sick woman, pressing her hand on his, and then gently kissing his hand with her thin and colourless lips.

This was almost more than our hero could bear. He felt quite unmanned, and could not find words to make any reply. A choking sensation came over him, and he was for the time fairly broken down.

"It's no use deceiving ourselves, Frank," continued Mrs. Halford. "It's no use endeavouring to war against the decrees of providence. It is hard to part from those we love, hard to leave a world, be our lot never so sad in it; but such things are inevitable. We must all pass away at some time or other."

"Do not talk thus," said the colonel, in accents which were broken and painful to listen to. "Don't talk thus, Agnes."

"If it pains you I will not. I have said

enough. I have your promise. Remember your promise in after years. Remember the promise given to her who has never crossed you during the whole of our acquaintance. You will not forget, Frank?"

"Of course I will not, dearest; but let us hope—"

"What?"

"That there will be no occasion for it to be remembered. You will live—will recover —I am sure of it."

"Do not deceive yourself. Never! That inward monitor that is within me, tells too surely that I am passing away—yes, passing away—to—to—another world."

"Oh," exclaimed the colonel, sadly, "this is terrible!"

"Are you a man, and a bold one, that you cannot bear to hear the truth spoken?"

"I cannot bear to part with you," said our hero.

"But you must," she answered. "Pray heaven that you may have no heavier sorrow to bear."

The colonel sighed deeply but made no reply.

"No heavier sorrow," she iterated. "I would say something more to you, Frank."

"Proceed, Agnes; I am all attention."

"In one of those drawers you will find a parcel of papers addressed to Captain Rignold. Do not look angry, now. I swear to you, Frank, that the captain, while he has been to me and you a sincere friend—and a discarded lover of mine—has never offered me the slightest rudeness, or indulged in the slightest familiarity. I swear this. Respect him for it; and you will, I am sure, believe me when I say, that those papers do not contain any expressions of—of love."

"I do not suppose such a thing for a moment."

"Well, then, let him have them. Open them if you like before you give them to him."

"I should despise myself if I could be guilty of so mean an action," answered her husband.

"Enough—I do not suppose you would, my own dear husband. Let the captain have them, and say that I remembered all his kindnesses, even when I was on the threshold of another world, I remembered all the kindnesses I had received from him in this. And now, about my mother. You know we have not been good friends since—"

"Since your marriage with me—I know that."

"But she will do her duty by Rosalie, I know. She will do her duty, and I do not see that any other course is left for us but to place her under my mother's charge. She will be away from the metropolis, where there is so much temptation for a young girl, and

she will be well educated and taken care of. I feel convinced of this, and—you have no objection to this course, have you, Frank?"

"No," answered the colonel, sadly, "your wishes are mine."

"Well, then, let her go to my mother. Only you will not be able to see her often, eh?"

"No matter for that, I must do so as often as I can. She may come up to London in the holidays."

"Yes, certainly, that could very easily be arranged. You see, I am talking and arranging about these matters as though I were some duchess, who could command."

"No duchess in the world could command me like yourself, my own sweet Agnes," answered the colonel. "Your wishes are law."

"I feel easier, now that we have settled these points," said Mrs. Halford; "for you must know that they have been weighing upon my mind for some days past, and I did not know well how to broach the subject. I was afraid it would be a painful one to you, which I am sure it must be; but then what will you not bear for my sake?"

"What have you not borne for mine?" exclaimed our hero, bitterly. "What! are you not laid here upon a bed of sickness through me—all through me."

"Frank, pray don't imagine such a thing as that. What have you to do with my bodily ailments?"

"I fear me much that I have been the primary cause of them," answered Colonel Jack.

"Indeed, then, you are quite mistaken. Do not for a moment imagine that. You do yourself an injustice. We none of us can insure health or strength, and none of us know how soon one or both may be taken from us. Oh, no don't suppose you have aught to do with my state of health. I have not liked to say anything about it, but I have felt myself gradually getting worse long since, however, that is past now, I am quite resigned, Frank—quite, and, indeed, to say the truth, it's a troublesome world to get through, very troublesome to most of us. How is your friend Osborne and Miss Langford?"

"They are both quite well," said our hero with a sort of hesitation in his manner.

"Ah, Osborne has come into a large fortune, I suppose?"

"Yes; he will do so, if he has not already."

"Ah, a large fortune. Well, I wish him happiness, and her, too. I believe she deserves it."

"That she does," answered the colonel.

The invalid closed her eyes as though she were about to resign herself to sleep, nevertheless she continued to talk in a suppressed tone.

"Knapp has been very kind and attentive to me during your absence. Remember me to him and the others. Galdie and Hackett—they have been all kind—all. Do you hear me, Frank ?"

"Yes, dear, I hear you," said the colonel, who had refrained from speaking or making any reply believing his wife was about to doze off.

"Why don't you answer, then ?—don't be afraid of speaking. I like to hear your voice if it is only—only for the sake of listening to its tones, no matter what you say. I am too weak to talk much, you know—but—"

"Yes; don't you fatigue yourself, there's a dear. You have been talking already a great deal. Try and compose yourself."

"Yes, I will."

Curson came into the room with the invalid's medicine, but from a motion by our hero she retired, the latter then crept softly out of the room into an adjoining apartment.

"It's best not to disturb her now," he said.

"But it's time for her to take her medicine," said Curson, who was under the impression, like a good many other people, that life and death depended upon the patient taking her medicine to the very minute.

"It's best not to disturb her now," he said. "Doctor Carruthers said that sleep was better than drugs, and that we were on no account to disturb or worry her when she was disposed to sleep."

"Oh, very well, sir," answered Curson.

"You can give it her when she awakes."

"How does she seem ?"

"Not in any particular pain—although she insists upon it that she is going."

"So she is—so she is, master," said Curson.

"My girl! you think so. What makes you say that ?"

"I have seen it a long time," answered Curson.

"And did not mention it to me."

"Where was the use of it. You could not alter it. Even if you had known how bad missus was. Ah, Mr. Halford, she's had that upon her mind, which I hope may never fall to my lot to hear.

"I understand your meaning, Curson."

"Well, it is now two o'clock. You had better lay down upon this sofa, to snatch an hour or two's rest."

"No, I do not need it," answered the colonel.

"No matter, you had better do so, I will call you if it is required. Take my advice and do as I say.

"Very well," and so Colonel Jack stretched himself upon the couch in the room adjoining his wife's, and after listening for some time, and tossing about, he fell off into a sound slumber, nature being fairly worn out, not so much with fatigue as the anxiety he had been subject to.

Colonel Jack slept it is true, but his slumbers were haunted by frightful visions. How long he had remained thus it was impossible for him to guess, but he was awoke by a series of strange sounds, which came upon his senses in a confused manner—formed, in fact, part of his dreams. He heard the sound of strange voices, in hurried and suppressed whispers, and springing up from his couch, he listened. Several persons appeared to be in his wife's bedroom. The one in which he was in was in perfect darkness. As he sprang up from the sofa, Mrs. Curson made her appearance in his room.

"Oh, you are awake, sir."

"Yes; is anything the matter ?" asked the colonel.

"Missus—"

"What ? Is she worse ?"

The old woman shook her head.

"Great Heavens is she—What ? speak !"

"The day will soon break," said Curson sadly.

The colonel did not understand her meaning. He gazed at her in stupid astonishment.

"The day will break! What of that ?" he asked.

"There will not be another day for poor missus. "Oh, Mr. Halford !" said the faithful domestic. "Oh, Mr. Halford !"

The party so addressed was not aware of the fact so often asserted by nurses and those who attend upon dying persons, that the spirit often escapes from its earthly tenement at or near the break of day, that is assuming it has not departed at its decline.

Our own experience teaches us that there is some truth in this. Why, it is hard to say, nevertheless, it is a fact, we believe, that more deaths occur at that period, taking them in the aggregate than at any other in the four-and-twenty hours.

The colonel, as we have already seen in a number of instances, was a bold man. Nevertheless, he stood upon the threshold of his wife's room, and his knees actually smote each other, and he felt as though he had no strength to move. Indeed, the probability is, that he would have hardly screwed up courage to have done so, had he not have been called to himself by Curson placing her hand upon his elbow, and saying—

"Will you go in or not, sir? Perhaps you are better away."

"No, no," exclaimed the colonel, "away, indeed !"

And he opened the door, and entered the room.

Alas! we will not linger over this already too painful a scene.

When he entered, he found Becky, the maid, the doctor—not Mr. Carruthers—and the child, Rosalie. The latter was on the bed, clasped in the embrace of the now fast dying woman, whose face was pinched, whose features were drawn, and who was evidently in her last mortal struggle—who was, in fact, already in the clutch of death.

There can be no mistake about this, to those who have once seen it.

The colonel gave one glance at his wife, and was at her bedside on the instant, hanging over her, and kissing her colourless lips.

"Agnes, 'tis I—do you not know me?"

A slight movement on the part of the dying woman, told that his words did not fall upon a deaf ear; but she did not appear to be able to give utterance to her feelings.

"Agnes, my own, my dear wife—'tis I—Frank—your own Frank! Speak, oh, in mercy's sake, speak!"

"Do not torment her," said the doctor; "she is past that now."

He was, however, mistaken, as doctors often are. Mrs. Halford raised her right arm, and pointed with her hand upwards. It appeared a painful effort for her to speak, but she did articulate with difficulty—

"Up—above—there!—that name—Frank! Remember Ros—Rosalie!"

The arm fell, and the figure on the bed was motionless and silent.

The doctor came forward, after a minute or so, and looked at the two figures—mother and child. He gave a glance at Curson, who came forward.

"Remove the child," he said softly.

The arm of the mother was gently removed, and Rosalie was taken from the bed. Then the doctor gazed into the face of her who slept her last sleep in this world.

He turned away, and his eye lighted upon Colonel Jack, who had been watching every movement of those in the room.

The doctor said nothing. It was not necessary for him to do so. There was that in his face which declared, clearer than printed type, that the spirit of Mrs. Halford had passed away.

Hitherto the colonel had comported himself tolerably well, at all events, before those who had attended upon the sick woman; but now, when the sudden truth was made manifest to him, and he saw the rigid form of her whom he had loved beyond all else in the world, he knelt down by the side of the bed, covered his face with his hands, and wept like a child.

It was a sad scene, supremely sad, to see that man, in his strong agony, prostrated with a mighty grief. His chest heaved, his frame quivered, and there was that amount of utter and insupportable woe, so terrible, so overwhelming, that the spectators of the scene were moved to a sudden pity.

Curson was in the adjoining room, weeping bitterly, and the doctor, who it appeared had been sent for by Curson without waking the colonel, stood in that gloomy chamber of death, treading about softly, as though he was afraid of arousing her who now slept so well.

He, too, seemed to be in a nervous and fidgetty state. He went to the side table ann gathered up his instruments, placed each in its particular compartment, and then folded up his leathenr case, wrapping it round again and again. All this while he had taken but little notice of Colonel Jack, who was sobbing convulsively by the side of his wife's bed.

The doctor came forward and laid his hand upon the shoulder of the higwayman, who started as the other touched him.

"My friend," said the doctor, solemnly, "calm yourself. She whom we have watched thus carefully, has passed away. Now, the living demand our more immediate care. For your own sake, as well as your child's, I charge you to bear up against this great misfortune. A mighty grief is consuming you, but you must learn to meet it witn philosophy. Come away now, I would speak to you."

The colonel rose from his kneeling posture, as he did so, the doctor gently drew him from the room, and the two went into the front room first floor.

"Now let me charge of you to bear up against this," said the doctor, "for you have at any rate the satisfaction of knowing that all that could be done to save this poor dear lady was done. If unremitting attention and excellent nursing could have warded off the approach of death, I am sure she has had both. Independently of this the best advice has been had, when I say the best, I am, of course, not speaking of myself. I allude to Doctor Loftus Carruthers, than whom there is not a more eminent or talented man."

"Could nothing have been done to save her?" exclaimed the colonel.

"Nothing, my dear, sir—really nothing," said the doctor.

"What was the matter with her?" asked the colonel.

"Nature gave way?"

"Well, but what was the disease?" inquired the colonel, who was not satisfied with this vague and loose description.

"The tissues, my dear sir—the tissues. The whole of these were injured, the nervous tissues especially. Alas, there was

very little to be done in such a case—very little."

"Nothing, it would appear, since the patient has sunk under the disease, or whatever else you may term it."

"It may be termed a general prostration of the whole system. This lady, if I mistake not, has had something weighing heavily upon her mind, which has sapped the very springs of life. What could be done in such a case as this? Shakspeare says, it is not possible to 'minister to a mind diseased,' and we know of no drug to meet the exigency of such a case."

"Cruel, cruel fate, that all my dreams of happiness should end thus—I—oh—"

Again he fell into his chair, and seemed quite prostrated with the recollections of the gentle being whom he had lost.

No. 57.

"If I can be of any service," said the doctor, pausing, "I need not say that you may command me."

"Thank you, I will remember—yes, thank you, I will remember all your kindness."

He hardly knew what he was saying, but the doctor took the answer, wished him good morning, and took his departure.

It was, as we have already described, in the evening, that the colonel had occupied that room, when his daughter had made her appearance so suddenly on the scene. He remembered this now, for as his eye wandered towards the window which looked out upon the street, he noticed that the grey mists of morning had disappeared, and it was broad daylight.

What a change had come over his house and home since those few hours? What a wreck to his happiness in this world! It seemed an impossibility that so much should have taken place in so short a time. What should he do now? Go out—or stay, and let the corroding canker of grief eat its way into his soul? He thought it would be best to leave the place for awhile—and yet, it would not be seemly, so early, too; besides, he did not feel sufficiently firm in his nervous system to venture abroad immediately. He would have breakfast—yes, that is what he would do—breakfast—faugh—it was not a time to think of eating—he felt that the first mouthful would in all probability choke him—breakfast, indeed!—there was no need for that.

Ringing the bell, Beckey appeared in answer to the summons, whose eyes were red with weeping.

"Where is Curson?" inquired Colonel Jack; "up stairs or down."

"Up stairs, sir."

"Engaged?"

"No, sir."

"I would speak to her—say so—tell her to come down when convenient."

Becky disappeared, and returned with Curson, who entered the room, closed the door after her, and approached her master's side.

The two were silent for a minute or so—the colonel was the first to speak.

"There—ahem—there will be a good deal to be done, Curson, a good many arrangements to make."

"Yes, sir, a good many."

"First of all, while I think of it; it would be as well to attend to this at once. You will find in the chest of drawers in your mistresses bed-room, a roll of papers; they are in the top right hand drawer, I think, but here are the keys. Look till you find them, for to say the truth, Curson, I have not the courage to go up myself—it's more than I can bear."

"It would not be prudent for you to do so, sir."

"No. Well, that's one thing. Now, the next is, with regard to Rosalie—she will have to be taken into the country."

"Indeed, sir! Is she not going to stay—I mean, be at home?"

"No, Curson, no; your poor dear mistress wished Rosalie to be placed under the charge of her grandmother."

"Grandmother," said Curson; "why, I thought—"

"Precisely; we are not, or rather have not been on the best of terms. You must know that I am not consulting my own wishes in this matter. On the contrary, if I were to consult my own judgment, I should let you take the charge of her until she went to a boarding school."

Curson made a curtsey, and said that she was sure "she always tried to her best."

"Yes, I know that; but as it was your poor dear mistresses last wish, why, you know—"

"Ah, dear, that is quite enough," said Curson.

"And now, Curson, you have been with her more than I have, and have, in fact, been one of her most faithful and attached friends—"

"Have I not known her since she was this high?" said Curson, stretching forth her hand. "Attached friend—why, Mr. Halford, I would have willingly laid down my life for her at any time. Poor dear soul—"

"I know that, Curson, but it's useless to talk of that now; but as I was saying, you have been one of her most faithful and trustworthy of servants. Do you know the cause of her sudden decline and death?—for—psha!—I can make nothing out of this doctor's jargon, absolutely nothing."

"The poor dear lady had her troubles, Mr. Halford," said Curson, "troubles which have weighed her down, and I fear, brought her to a premature grave."

"Ah, I can guess what these were," sighed the colonel.

"You may, my dear master, as well and better than I do myself."

"Well, fetch me those papers," said the colonel.

Curson went up stairs into the gloomy chamber of death, and in a short time returned with the roll of papers, which was tied carefully up, and addressed to Captain Rignold.

The colonel took them from the faithful domestic, and thrust them into his coat pocket, without making any observation.

CHAPTER XC.

SIR RICHARD FLEETWOOD IN HIS PRISON-HOUSE.

WHILE the spirits of our hero were borne down by the terrible affliction which had come upon him—an affliction which had for a time quite prostrated him, and left him the victim of despair—Sir Richard Fleetwood remained in that gloomy prison-house where we left him, unheeded and unnoticed by the colonel or his companions.

The place in which Sir Richard found himself confined, was literally nothing better than a cellar; indeed, it was not half so good as many such, for it was wretchedly damp, dark and cold.

It was beneath the foundations of a house which had been originally in the occupation of some nobleman; but it had long since sunk into decay, and had become the resort of perhaps some of the most lawless characters in the metropolis.

Most of our readers are doubtless aware of the terrible character which Alsatia, as it was called, has received from the hands of historians at this period.

The whole neighbourhood, at this time, was beyond the pale of the civic and police authorities.

This cellar, if it could with propriety be so termed, was the resort of disreputable characters of all sorts. Here burglars would deposit their ill-gotten wealth, pickpockets, cutpurses, shoplifters, people who committed robberies at the docks, or on the River Thames, would put off in a boat at night, pull the same to the stairs which were at Whitefriars, and deposit their plunder beneath these arches.

The man Reuben, who has been already introduced to the reader, was high priest of this temple. He slept there—took charge of all the property—and was paid for the same, and liberally too, by those who deposited their goods.

He would undertake that they should be looked after, and it is but justice to this individual to say, that he was generally a faithful steward.

"Honour among thieves," is an old saying, and certainly, in Reuben's case, the aphorism was carried out.

We left Sir Richard Fleetwood chained up to a column of this inhospitable abode.

When our hero and his companions had departed, he was left to the tender care of Reuben, who was as jealous of his trust as though he had a valuable stock of gold and silver vases, or some heavy bags of gold. After the colonel had left, he took a careful survey of the baronet.

The man was half daft, as a Scotchman would say, and one of the most uncouth beings to look upon, it was well possible to conceive.

Sir Richard returned his glance in moody silence.

"Umph," said Reuben, "you're a fine gentleman, I guess."

"I'll pay you well, nay, handsomely, my friend, if you will release me, and give me my liberty."

"Ah, ah, not to be done at no price at all. Reuben Matchly knows a trick worth two of that. Now, what's been your game? You may as well tell me, for you see we shall be companions for a long time to come, I dare say—longer than you like I suppose—eh?"

The baronet made no reply; he was too much disgusted with the ragged and dirty creature, who was addressing him.

"Ah, you are happy, eh? Umph! just as you like—we can be friends or enemies, just as you please—I am not anxious to make your acquaintance. I live here with no other companions than the rats, and they suit me; they ain't proud."

"Rats!" exclaimed the baronet, in unmitigated disgust; "rats!"

"Yes, to be sure. Why, what is the man staring at? Do you suppose that I should like to live alone here?"

"Alone!"

"Yes, certainly. Oh, no, I like company, I do, when they know how to behave themselves. I don't like your proud upstarts. Oh, no, none of that kidney suit me—oh, oh, I'm 'ticular, I am."

"Am I to remain here chained up like a dog?" said the baronet.

"Maybe that you are a fierce one," said Reuben, looking marvellously cunning.

"Release me, my friend," answered the baronet; "I'll make it worth your while."

"Why they ain't left anything on you have they?"

"Yes, enough to reward you handsomely. Come, release me."

"More than I dare do. No; when Reuben Matchly passes his word he never breaks it. No, can't be done at the price, I tell you."

The baronet after this was silent for some time, and Reuben busied himself in arranging the various portions of the spoil which was under his charge. After then he made towards the door which led from the miserable apartment.

"I am going out upon business," said the man. "Make yourself as comfortable as you can till I come back. I needn't tell you not to run away, seeing as how that ain't to be done at no price."

He put the key into the massive lock, opened the door, went out, and shut it too with a loud slam, which reverberated through the vault like distant thunder.

Sir Richard Fleetwood was then alone.

The baronet shivered with cold, his teeth chattered, and a wretched feeling of despair came over him.

Alone in that wretched place, chained up like a prisoner in the Bastile, or Inquisition, Sir Richard Fleetwood felt like a condemned culprit—without hope, beyond human sympathy, worse than this he felt like a guilty wretch.

As his eye wandered over the place a swarm of rats came forth from their different runs or holes; they looked up at the new occupant of their chamber, and then began to pick up several crumbs and broken victuals which Reuben had left.

The baronet shuddered, the horrors of the place were now doubled; the baronet had an instinctive dread and dislike to rats, he rattled his chair and stamped his feet, whereupon the rats suddenly disappeared.

It was a relief to him when they took their departure.

For more than an hour he was left thus to commune with his own thoughts. He prayed for the return of his companion, miserable wretch as he was, anyone, rather than be left alone in such a place.

Shortly after this he had the satisfaction of hearing the lock turn, the door was opened, and Reuben appeared.

His first glance was directed towards the baronet.

"Ah, that is well. You're all right, then? Had any company?—s'pose not, people don't come where they can't be amused, entertained or feasted with the good things of this life. S'pose you're hungry now, eh?"

The baronet made no reply.

"Well, I've brought something in. Here's your health."

Reuben pulled a large stone bottle from his pocket, poured some of its contents into a drinking horn and drained it off.

He then proceeded to light a fire with which he cooked some victuals.

When this was done he placed some of the same in a platter, with a slice of bread, and walking up to the baronet handed it to him.

Sir Richard refused.

"What, quarrel with your bread and butter?—your like a spoilt child. Oh, you'll get over that, believe me—you'll get over that."

Sir Richard said he was not hungry.

"Oh, very well, we'll wait till you are," said Reuben. "S'pose you'll have no objection to my eating?"

The baronet replied in the negative, and Reuben seated himself in front of a small oak table, and began to partake of the food he had prepared.

If Sir Richard was not hungry it would appear that his companion was, for he devoured his repast with the voracity of a wolf. After he had partaken of part of this he rose from his seat and said—

"Oh, I forgot—maybe you are thirsty."

Sir Richard nodded.

"Then drink my health."

The speaker handed his companion the well-filled horn, which the latter drained off at once.

"So, that is well," said Reuben. "We are getting on, we are, and shall understand each other after a while. Here's to you."

He then drained off another draught himself, and once more sat down, and proceeded with his repast.

When he had finished he strewed a portion of the same on the floor.

"I ain't selfish you see. Live and let live is my motto. This is for our friends, the rats."

A cold shudder passed through the frame of the baronet, but he said nothing.

When night came on, Reuben glanced at his companion, and said—

"How are you going to sleep, eh?"

"Am I to be chained up like a prisoner in the dark and savage ages of man's existence, or are you going to release me?"

"Not to be done at the price," said the other.

"I pledge my word that I will take no undue advantage of this favour, I swear it most solemnly."

"Not to be done at the price," answered Reuben.

"Then rest is forbidden me, and in the course of a few days I must, of necessity, die of exhaustion."

"I tell you what I can do. I can lengthen your chain so that you will be able to lay down. Will that suit you?"

"It would be better than nothing," answered the baronet, "if that is all you can do."

"Can't do more than that—daresn't."

He then proceeded to unclose the chain which confined Sir Richard, to the extent of two or three yards.

This done, he fetched a matress from the store of goods which the place contained, and placed the same at the foot of the column to which the prisoner was chained. After this several rugs were placed on the matress, and a tolerably comfortable bed was made up therefrom.

"And now you may go to sleep whenever you like," said Reuben. "Don't mind me, I shan't disturb you, because I ain't a going to bed myself just yet, for I shall do a pipe."

"Thank you, I am not sleepy," said the baronet.

"Oh, ain't you? Well, you can lay down till you are, that's all," answered his companion.

The man then betook himself to his seat at the table once more, lighted his pipe, and warmed himself by the fire which he had lighted in the earlier portion of the day.

Sir Richard stretched himself on the pallet which had been prepared for him; after a bit he spoke again to his companion.

"Do you always live in this wretched abode?" he inquired.

"Oh, you ain't asleep? Yes, always. I like it."

"Do you?"

"Yes, business keeps me here. Sometimes I have a companion or two—sometimes a deal too many."

"Have you no relatives?"

"What?"

"Relatives."

"Lord! no. What could put that into your head? Relatives! no; I should think not."

"No father or mother?" asked Sir Richard Fleetwood.

"Why, no, of course not," answered his companion.

"You are a young man, and might have one or both parents alive in the ordinary course of things."

"I never had no parents," answered Reuben.

"Nonsense man, you must have had at some time."

"Tell you I haven't; never had, and that's all about it."

"You are a strange being."

"Always was. Now, there you are right."

"Who brought you up?"

"No one. I grew up."

"So I suppose; but who educated you?"

"No one; I ain't educated."

"But when a boy you must have had some protector—some one whose duty it was to take care of you."

"Oh, dear no, not at all. I grew up."

"How did you live?"

"By going up the sewers, and picking up whatever I could find. That's where I got so fond of the rats."

"Fond of rats! Horrible!"

"Would you like a smoke?" said Reuben, turning to the baronet, "because if you would, I've got a spare pipe. Now, would you?"

"Thank you; if you will oblige me with a light I will ignite one of my own cigars."

Reuben rose from his seat, and handed his companion a light.

Sir Richard thanked him, and enjoyed the luxury of a cigar.

"Well, we get on pretty well together," said Reuben, after a pause. "I didn't much fancy you at first, but you are better than I took you for. It only shows that we should not be prejudiced."

"Ah!" said the baronet, who could not resist a smile at the man's naive manner.

They conversed for some time, until both of them began to be drowsy and fell off into a deep sleep.

When Sir Richard awoke he found his companion stretched on a matress before the consumed embers of last night's fire.

He was still fast asleep, but in the course of half an hour awoke, shook himself, and rose to his feet.

He then proceeded to light the fire again and prepare the morning' meal. Of this the baronet partook, for by this time he felt hungry.

After this, in the space of an hour or two, several uncouth looking characters found their way into the vault.

They brought with them some casks which they rolled down the stairs, and deposited in the safe custody of Sir Richard's keeper.

One of them, a seaman, it would appear, by his dress turned to where the baronet was.

"Hilloa, Reuben, what hang dog have we here? A prisoner?"

"Yes; under my charge."

"Who is he?"

"Don't know."

"Who brought him here?"

"That's my business, Master Zeoman, and ain't yours. So mind your own business and let me mind mine."

"Oh, I don't care, so long as he don't run away with the stores. No fear of that though so it would seem. How now, my hearty? Do you like your new berth?"

This was addressed to the baronet, who did not condescend to make any reply.

"Umph!" exclaimed the man glumpily. "You won't answer, my gaol bird. Do you know what is done with a bird that can sing and won't?"

"I'll give you a good round sum—say a hundred sovereigns—if you'll take me from this accursed hole," answered Sir Richard Fleetwood.

"Not to be done at the price, Zeoman, is it?" said Reuben.

"Not if he doubled or trebled the sum," said the sailor.

The baronet once more hung down his head in despair.

There appeared to be no chance for him, so he thought—not the most remote chance.

The men took their departure.

That day passed over in much the same way as the preceding one, and the next, and the next.

No, Colonel Jack appeared, much to the surprise of Reuben.

Towards evening, when these two men were closed in for the night, Reuben had sat for some time without speaking, and the baronet had been a prey to his own gloomy thoughts, the former said suddenly—

"Your friends don't seem particularly anxious about you. They don't come to see how you get on, eh?"

"It appears not. I suppose I am left here to perish, to die by inches. Oh, horrible fate."

"You've no occasion to perish—you've plenty to eat and drink haven't you?"

"Yes," answered the prisoner.

"Well, then, you ought to be comfortable."

"Indeed."

"I should say so."

"In such a miserable place as this?"

"I ain't miserable," answered Reuben.

"Oh, you are fanciful."

Once more these two men laid themselves down to sleep, and even in that miserable abode their slumbers were sound.

CHAPTER XCI.

THE MYSTERIOUS VISITOR.—THE STRUGGLE AND CONFLICT.

On the following day Reuben went out for a longer period than he had done since the baronet's incarceration, and during his absence the latter felt doubly wretched. Even the companionship of his gaoler was to him some solace, some small source of comfort, and he anxiously awaited his return, for the loneliness of the place was well nigh insupportable, and he cheerfully hailed his reappearance when he brought in their midday meal.

This passed over as usual, when, later in the afternoon, Reuben once more took his departure.

He had been gone about an hour or so, as nearly as Sir Richard could guess, when he became alarmed at some noise proceeding from the bales of goods or casks which were in the vault. At first he thought it was the rats, and stamped and made as much noise as possible to drive them away, but the noise continued. Sir Richard shouted—it was all of no avail, the strange noise continued. It seemed to come from one particular cask, to which his glance was directed. A strange, new, and undefined fear crept over him. The day had declined, and the place was almost in utter darkness, except such light as came from the half extinguished fire, and the grey misty light which came creeping in from the gratings in front of him; this, however, could not be called light, for it was but semi darkness.

Sir Richard groaned in anguish, a superstitious fear fastened hold of him, and he actually trembled. Truly has it been said, that "conscience does make cowards of us all."

With his eye rivetted on the cask in question, the baronet drew his breath heavily—an oppressive weight seemed to be on his chest—but the climax of his fear had yet to come.

While he was watching the cask, what was his horror to observe the lid of it carefully and cautiously raised up, and a human head protrude.

The baronet, when he saw this, screamed with fright, and well nigh swooned. But there was a degree of fascination in the vision, and the prisoner, with distended eyeballs, could not take his glance from it.

The head was that of a man, dark, swarthy, with a grizzly beard, unkempt hair, which hung in matted locks, and piercing eyes.

He regarded the baronet with a curious and inquiring glance, but spoke not.

"Heavens!—mercy!" exclaimed the baronet. "Speak, for mercy's sake! Who art thou?"

The man muttered something in a language which the baronet did not understand.

"Speak, man, if such you are, what would you?"

The figure put his head, shoulders, and arms out of the cask, and pointed to where Reuben had been seated. Sir Richard then began to comprehend his meaning.

"He has gone out, if that's what you mean."

"Ah, true, that is what I do mean," said the figure.

It was a relief to the baronet to hear these words, although they were spoken in broken English, the party who uttered them evidently being a foreigner.

"Are we alone?" he next inquired.

"Yes, quite alone. Who and what are you?"

"I have come over in a grand ship," was the answer.

"And a pretty place you have come to," said the baronet; and he was going to say, a pretty fellow you are, but he restrained himself.

"Mynheer, I am a persecuted man," said the individual.

"So am I," answered the baronet.

"Ah, you are a prisoner?"

"Yes, a prisoner in this most wretched place."

"Ah, I have come across the sea, and have been concealed in this—bah!—tub, cask, or whatever you call it."

"Well, what made you come here in that way?"

"To escape death, mynheer. Bah! I have been nearly choked—suffocated."

"I can't help that, and what is worse, I can't assist you; for, as you see, I am chained up like a hound."

"Ah, that is dreadful—very dreadful."

"I am worse off than you."

"Can we not make our escape?" said the man.

"I don't see how that is possible—I wish I did."

"I will get out of this tub, and then I will tell you what I shall do—I will go to you, and give you your liberty. What say you to that?"

"It's impossible. I am too firmly fastened; besides this, the door is so secure, that it would resist all our efforts, even assuming it were possible to unchain me from this cursed pillar."

"Ah, but we are to be friends—are we not brothers in misfortune ?"

"I should hope so," answered the baronet, a gleam of hope falling upon him, as he saw the possibility of escape.

"Then I will get out of this barbarous tub," said the man, who drew himself up by his hands, and placing his knees on its side, emerged from his place of concealment. ·

When he had done so, the baronet had an opportunity, as far as the dim light would permit, of seeing this strange apparition more closely. He was a short, thick set man, apparently of not more than five feet in height. He was dressed in a jacket, with buttons down the front and on the sleeves, a close-fitting garment of cloth encircled his chest, a belt was round his waist, and loose, baggy breeches encircled his loins, reaching as far as his knees, round which they were fastened, tight-fitting grey stockings, and shoes with buckles, completed the costume of this nondescript.

"We are brothers in misfortune," said the small individual.

"Yes, and I should hope we are to be friends."

Upon this the man approached close to Sir Richard, and examined the fastenings with which he was firmly bound. He then shook his head.

"Ah, it is not possible to unloose you from these bonds," he said, sadly, "quite impossible. Now what is to be done ?"

"I know not, unless you spring upon our gaoler and overpower him."

"And then how am to unloose you ?"

"Most likely he has the key in his pocket which fastens this iron girdle round my waist."

"Ah, you think so?"

The baronet nodded.

"That is good, if he has that same."

"I have no doubt he has."

"Then I will overpower him," said the man.

His physical strength, however, did not appear equal to the task, for Reuben was of athletic proportions.

"When will he come back ?" inquired the stranger.

"I don't know."

"Well, say nothing about my appearance here. I will go back to my tub, and in the night, when he is asleep—"

"Oh, no, that won't do. We shall never find our way out of this place at night, never. Wait till morning's dawn, and then spring upon him unawares; taken at such an advantage, success is certain."

"Oh, yes, I have one pistol, that I can blow his brains out with. That is a good plan. Anything for life and liberty !—hurrah !"

The man snapped his fingers, and cut a caper.

"There is no occasion to sacrifice human life unless it is unavoidable. The fellow, to say the truth, has not behaved badly to me, and unless there be an absolute necessity for his death, I should say let him live."

"Well, as you please—as you please. Now I shall go back to my tub; but I am hungry—what is there to eat ?"

The colonel pointed to the provisions which Reuben had left upon the table, whereupon the stranger went up the same, and helped himself to a plentiful supply, taking some of them with him into his tub.

The two prisoners then conversed for some time which dialogue only ceased when Reuben Matchley came in.

The latter did not appear to be in the best of tempers when he returned, for he did not condescend to address himself to the baronet as had been his custom on previous occasions.

"Umph ! we'll see about that master Zoeman,—we'll see about that. Don't you think I'm going to work for nothing. Well paid indeed for my live-stock—that's all you know about the matter, and if I was, what business is it of yours—paid indeed, it's a lot of money I get for serving people—a lot."

"Ahem !" said the baronet.

"Ah, I was forgetting you," said Reuben, turning towards the prisoner. "That I was. Well how do you get on—dull without me, I suppose."

"Rather so," answered the party so addressed.

"Have anything."

"Well I should like something to drink, if it be only a draught of beer," answered Sir Richard.

"But would prefer wine I suppose."

"Most certainly."

"Ah, I thought so."

"What you haven't got I suppose."

"Oh haven't I ? There's enough to float a four oared cutter here, or a seventy four frigate for the matter of that—I don't say it's all paid duty—None on it to speak the truth, but it ain't none the worse for that, rather the better to my thinking."

"But is it yours ?"

"I can take as much of it as I like for myself and friends—and friends."

"Ah I see !"

Reuben then went in to what appeared to be a recess—but it was in reality an opening which led into a cellar beneath the vault in which the baronet was confined—beneath this flowed a dark pool of water which came from the river Thames.

"I should like a little wine," said the man in the tub. "I am so very dry."

"Hush !" said the baronet, " or you'll ruin all—Hush ?"

Reuben Matchley was gone much longer than the baronet had anticipated, he returned however with two capacious bottles, and placing them on the table eyed them lovingly.

"What do you prefer, white wine or red?" he inquired.

"Oh I am not particular, anything that's handy."

"They are both here."

"Then I'll take the red if you please."

"What am I to charge you for board, and lodging?" said Reuben with a smile.

"Any price if you'll give me my liberty afterwards."

"Ah! I've got so used to you now that really I don't think I should like to part with you—and I dare say you have the same feeling."

"Ahem! of course I should be sorry to loose so charming a companion, but fresh air and sweet liberty do possess charms."

"Ah, I suppose so. Well, there's your wine, and it ain't a bad sort, I can tell you."

The baronet tossed off a bumper, which was succeeded by another, and then another. He lighted his cigar, and Reuben lit his pipe.

"Hilloa! who's been wolfing all the grub?" said the latter, his eye for the first time lighting on the provisions on the table. He then looked up towards the baronet.

"The rats, I suppose," answered the latter.

"Rats, indeed. They don't usually cut ham with a knife, do they?" inquired the other.

"Certainly not."

"Well, then, who has been at this ham? You? Why, deuce take it, you ain't been clever enough to get unfastened, have you?"

"No, indeed; I wish I had."

"Do you?"

"That I do."

Reuben Matchly rose from his seat, and went direct up to the baronet, whose chains he carefully examined.

"Oh, that's all right. You are safe enough."

"I should say I was," said Sir Richard, shaking his manacles.

"Has anyone been here?"

"No, not a soul."

"Then who the devil has been collaring our grub?"

"I don't know."

"Don't know? But you must know if anybody has been here?"

"Not that I have seen"

"Why, man alive, they couldn't come and take the grub before your very eyes without your seeing them."

"I've been asleep," answered Sir Richard Fleetwood.

"Oh, you have?"

"Yes."

"Well, this queers me. They appear to have had a good appetite."

Reuben then sat down, and was lost in reflection for some time.

The little man in the tub was enduring an agony from the smell of the tobacco smoke, he was half strangled from suppressed coughing. He hardly knew how to check himself.

After some little time had elapsed the baronet heard a suppressed cough proceed from the recesses of the tub.

"Ah! What was that?" said Reuben.

"It was me," answered the baronet, endeavouring to imitate the strange cough.

"You, eh? Caught cold!"

"Yes, a slight one."

"Ah! First time I've heard you cough," said Reuben.

"I'm not usually susceptible of cold," said the baronet.

"That's a good thing, 'cause this place is a little damp."

"I should think it was."

"There again! Well, hang me if it ain't a rum cough that of yours."

To save his friend in the tub, Sir Richard abstained from smoking, upon the plea of having a headache, caused by the cold he had taken.

After some time had elapsed the baronet had the satisfaction of seeing Reuben stretch himself on his matress, and in a few more moments his heavy breathing told that he was asleep.

Sir Richard was so much excited by the incident we have described, that he found it quite impossible to compose himself.

His eyes were directed towards the cask, which he could faintly distinguish in the ruddy glare of the fire.

In a short time the head of the stranger protruded therefrom.

"Hist!" he exclaimed.

"Silence," said the baronet, in a whisper. "Be cautious, or all will be lost."

"Is the gentleman asleep?" said the figure in the tub.

"Yes; but our talking will wake him. Remain quiet till the morning, and you know the rest."

"Why not now?"

"No, no; in the morning, I tell you."

"Oh, well, as you please. Only I am tired of this tub—very tired."

In about an hour after this Sir Richard fell off to sleep. Not so his companion, whose cramped position in the tub precluded the possibility of his doing so with anything like comfort to himself. It is probable that he would have made an assault upon Reuben in the night, had not the fire gone

out, and left the place in utter darkness. He therefore watched for the first appearance of morning, and as the first faint streaks of light found their way into that gloomy prison-house, the man in the tub cautiously crept out of his hiding place, and looked around him.

Both his companions were fast asleep!

Creeping noiselessly, with a cat-like caution, he stole up to where Reuben was lying, pistol in hand. He then hesitated what to do.

Should he blow his brains out then and there, or should he endeavour to get the key which opened the door, and make off without any regard to Sir Richard Fleetwood ?

This he would have gladly done had it been possible, but to get the key from the

pocket of Reuben was not an easy task, and in all probability he would be awakened in the attempt.

At last he made up his mind as to his course of action.

Placing the muzzle of his pistol within an inch of Reuben's head, he began to feel in his pockets. As he did so, the sleeping man turned uneasily over, and then awoke. What was his surprise when he beheld an uncouth figure of a man, in strange attire, standing over him with a pistol within an inch of his temple.

Reuben rubbed his eyes, believing at first that he was dreaming, and he then gave his companion a look of inquiry.

" Who the devil are you ? ' said Reuben.

" Hush ! you must favour me with your

keys, or else I shall blow your brains out of your head. Do you understand ? I must go through that door. The keys at once—quick !"

Reuben made no reply to this, but with one sweep of his arm, sent the little man sprawling on the floor. The pistol was discharged without injuring any one present, but it had the effect of waking Sir Richard Fleetwood to a sense of his position. Reuben then rose to his feet, as also did the little man.

"Confound you, where did you spring from ?" said Reuben. "I'll twist your ugly head off your shoulders."

By this time the man had pulled another pistol from his pocket, but before he could level it, Reuben sprang upon him, and the two then closed in deadly strife.

As far as physical strength was concerned, the stranger was no match for his more athletic adversary, whose chief attention was taken up in his efforts to wrest the loaded weapon from his antagonist, who, however, held on with a pertinacity that appeared surprising.

As the two were struggling, the weapon was discharged, and Reuben received a severe wound in the right shoulder, and staggered for some paces. As he did so, the other, believing him to be mortally wounded, sprang forward, and clutched hold of him.

Now another desperate struggle ensued, in which the stranger was thrown to the earth several times.

He rose up, however, and grasping the barrel of the pistol, sought to disable his adversary by repeated blows with the butt-end of the weapon ; but Reuben grasped hold of it, and succeeded in wresting it out of his hand.

The stranger then drew a long dirk, and made a rush at Reuben. Several times he made plunges with this weapon, but his antagonist struck him with his clenched fist, and kept him at bay.

All this while Sir Richard Fleetwood had been watching the issue of the contest with the utmost anxiety.

Reuben received a deep flesh wound in the arm from his antagonist's weapon.

"Curses on you !" he exclaimed, as he dealt the stranger a fearful blow on the temple with the butt-end of the heavy pistol in his hand.

Wild with rage, the wounded man endeavoured to close with Reuben, but another blow was given with the same weapon, and the man was felled to the ground like an ox. He fell to the ground without motion.

Reuben stooped over him, and looked in his face. A dark pool of blood flowed from the ghastly wound—the skull was fractured and beaten in—the man was dead.

Reuben, panting, bleeding, and in a state of excitement, glared round the wretched apartment. His eye fell upon Sir Richard, who, silent and unmoved, looked at the two, the living and the dead.

"So," exclaimed Reuben, "is this some friend of yours ?"

"Mine !" ejaculated the baronet, "mine ! I know nothing of him—have never set eyes upon him until I found him engaged with you in sanguinary strife. Friend of mine, forsooth—I have to thank you for the compliment."

"He's dead, dead as herrings," answered Reuben. "How came the scoundrel here, I wonder ?"

He then proceeded to bind up his arm, and a faintness came over him from loss of blood, and the pain consequent on the wound in his shoulder from the bullet of his antagonist.

"How came this about—where did this fellow spring from ?" inquired the baronet. "I was fast asleep, until suddenly awoke by the noise of the conflict. Are you much hurt ?"

"Hurt, indeed !—the miscreant has got his deserts, be he whom he may—I am wounded both with dagger and bullet. Oh, but my shoulder is fearfully painful."

Reuben then went out to seek the advice of a doctor, and have his wounds dressed. In about half an hour he returned, with three or four individuals, among whom was the man who had been addressed as Zeoman.

"Look you here, Master Zeoman, there he lies, the blood-thirsty scoundrel ; and I've to thank my lucky stars that I am alive. I've nothing to thank you for, that's quite certain."

Zeoman looked at the prostrate form of the deceased man, and then turning to his companions, said—

"Vanderbent, by all that's horrible—yes, Vanderbent, and no mistake. How on earth could he have found his way here ?"

They examined the casks one by one, and the mystery was soon explained. They then proceeded to remove the dead body of the man in silence, Reuben going with them, and once more returning to the vault.

"How are you now ? Had your wounds dressed ?" inquired the baronet.

"Yes, and the bullet extracted. Ah, but that was a painful job."

"Anything very serious ?"

"No, so the doctor says—I shall soon get over it."

"Who was the individual ?"

"A notorious pirate, who had made his escape in this cask," said Reuben. "It appears he was condemned to death for I don't know how many murders, and he was within an ace of adding another to them."

CHAPTER XCII.

THE RISING OF THE TIDE.—THE ESCAPE.

THAT day passed over much the same as the preceding ones since Sir Richard Fleetwood had found himself a prisoner in the gloomy chamber.

Towards evening on the following day, Reuben left the prisoner to himself for some hours. The latter was miserable to the last degree. He now saw not the most remote chance of escape—his last hope was gone.

As Sir Richard lay upon his pallet, he observed numbers of rats come out from different parts of the building. He drove them away as before, but they soon returned. Once more he succeeded in driving them off, but they as quickly came again—in swarms—in shoals; not as heretofore, a dozen or so at a time, but in hundreds.

In vain the baronet sought to rid himself of these unwelcome visitors, his efforts were futile, and at last they did not condescend to take any notice of his motions.

Sir Richard yelled, and ground his teeth in agony.

Hark! what was that?

A new noise came upon his ear—a noise of rushing waters—a roaring torrent, boiling and bubbling! It still continued, and Sir Richard's ears were on the strain to catch these sounds.

In a short time he observed the floor of his prison house covered with water. Surprised at this phenomenon, his glance was fixed upon the same, and in the space of about quarter of an hour, as nearly as he could guess, the floor of the vault was filled with water, which was about an inch, or from that to an inch and a half in height, and the matress which formed his bed became saturated with wet.

The rats now flew about in all directions. Many made their escape through the grating at the back of the vault, and not a few climbed upon the casks and bales of goods which were piled up in various parts of the subterranean and noisome prison-house.

Sir Richard Fleetwood became seriously alarmed for his own safety. It was impossible for him to assign a cause for this strange phenomenon, and he shouted and yelled like one bereft of reason.

Every faculty was on the stretch to hear the footsteps of his gaoler descending the dark staircase, but as yet there was no indication of the man's reappearance, and the nerves of the baronet were stretched to the utmost degree of tension as his mind became impressed with a sense of his own imminent danger.

The water, as surely as sand falls through the hour-glass of time, was gradually rising higher and higher.

In the space of about another half hour, it was more than a foot in height, the matress and covering of the unfortunate prisoner was floating on its surface, and his feet, ancles, and part of his legs were immersed in the fluid.

Sir Richard's situation was now one of unmitigated horror. Slowly but gradually he felt the water rise, inch by inch it crept up his legs, immersed his knees, and seemed as though it would never cease. Bales of goods, pieces of wood, and various articles in the apartment, were floating about in admired confusion.

Aroused to his state of danger, driven to desperation therefrom, the baronet called loudly for assistance. He screamed out "Murder!—help!—fire!"—anything that he thought would be likely to attract the notice of such as might chance to hear him. Alas! no one appeared in answer to his summons. In vain he sought to release himself from the chain which confined him—in vain he cursed, and poured forth imprecations against our hero and his companions.

Slowly the water continued to rise. The whole place appeared one vast reservoir.

The baronet shivered with cold. His body had become immersed up to his waist—soon after this it reached his chest—horrible!—there seemed now to be a certainty of his being drowned—another foot of water, and it would be all over with him.

It is hardly possible to imagine a position more awful than the one in which the unfortunate prisoner found himself placed.

He screamed and yelled like some wild animal, and he felt his reason totter on its throne.

Oh, to die in that cold, awful place, alone and uncared for!—and such a death! What worse could fate have in store for him?

Hark! there are footsteps descending the stairs!

The baronet's heart leaped at the thought of assistance or human sympathy. The door was opened with difficulty, and the face of Reuben Matchly peered in.

"Help! mercy! help!—I'll pay you a princely sum—anything to be released," said the baronet.

Reuben was speechless with astonishment.

"Do you hear, my good friend—we have been friends—and you never can find it in your heart to leave a fellow creature to die thus," said Sir Richard, in moving accents.

"What can all this mean?—the place is flooded!" exclaimed Reuben.

"Flooded, yes, for the last two hours the water has been ceaselessly rushing in. Have pity on me! See, I am up to my neck in it, and well-nigh frozen to death. In a few minutes more I shall drown. My dear friend, name your own terms, and, as heaven is my judge, you shall be rewarded handsomely if you save me—save my life!"

"Bah! look at the property," answered Reuben. "What's your life worth, I should like to know? And then again, I have no other prison to convey you to. You'd like a drier one, I suppose?"

"Oh, do not make a jest of sufferings which have been almost unendurable, but release me."

"How can I?" inquired his gaoler. "You seem to have brought ill luck to this place since you've been here. First, one cove has been sent to his account—not but what he deserved it—and in the next place, the whole of the property under my charge is likely to be destroyed—all through you."

"Me!—what have I to do with it." said the baronet.

"You've brought ill luck, I tell you. Confound you, I wish you had never found your way into this place. It was a comfortable one before you come here—a very comfortable place."

"It's not been very comfortable since I have been here," answered the baronet, who was hardly able to articulate from his teeth chattering together.

"I didn't ask you to come," returned Reuben.

"Oh, but pray release me, or I shall surely drown."

"I can't, I tell you."

"Throw me the key of the girdle which encircles my waist, and I will unlock the padlock myself."

"Oh, yes, I dare say; and suppose you were not to catch it?"

"But I will, I will."

"Yes, and then you would make your escape?"

"Good God, man, you never surely would be inhuman enough to let me drown?"

"Umph! I suppose I must go and fetch a small boat, and then we will see what can be done."

"But in the mean time I shall perish. While we have been talking, the water has risen full an inch"

Reuben hesitated for a few seconds, and then, without saying a word, waded through the water to where the baronet was. He took the key from his girdle, and inserting it in the lock of the girdle which encircled the baronet's waist, unfastened it, and the baronet was free.

Oh, the joy of that moment! In his delirium of delight he rushed towards the entrance to that gloomy chamber, and he then became aware of his own weakness; for the first time he tottered and stumbled forward, as his foot struck against some object on the floor. for a moment or so he was under water, battling and contesting with the element—his head again reappeared above its surface, and he succeeded in reaching the foot of the staircase.

"Hold hard," shouted out Reuben, "I'll be with you directly. Hold hard, I tell you!"

"Very well," said Sir Richard, as he ascended the stairs, and seeing that the outer door was unfastened, rushed up the same, and in less than a minute he was in the street, slamming the door to as he made his hasty exit.

No sooner had he got safe out from his dark prison house, than he set off at headlong speed, which mocked and defied all pursuit.

Reuben, however, hearing the outer door shut, suspected the trick which the baronet had played him, and hastened as fast as possible after him.

When, however, he reached the street, no Sir Richard was visible. Fear, and the prospect of escape, lent wings to his speed, and he had threaded a series of intricate and narrow passages which run from the spot where he had been confined.

Reuben did not think it worth while to endeavour to overtake him, and gave it up as a hopeless case.

Sir Richard was of course wet through, and with his unshaven beard and dilapidated appearance, he cut but a sorry figure as he raced through the streets. The eyes of the passengers were ever and anon directed towards the fugitive, but as the inhabitants of the whole neighbourhood were used to scenes of violence and disturbances of various descriptions, it was but a passing notice that the baronet met with, who paused not until he had fully satisfied himself that he was out of danger from being overtaken.

When he did come to a halt, he was breathless with his exertions, and the excitement consequent upon his sudden and unexpected escape. As he paused, his eyes glanced round, and discovered that he was by the river side, in that part which is now called the Strand, which, at the period of which we write, was literally what its name indicated, the strand, or river side, with a house only here and there on it at irregular intervals.

Not caring to go into the town, Sir Richard hailed a boatman whom he espied lying off the shore in a wherry. The man rowed to the shore, and the baronet at once jumped into the boat.

"Where to, sir?" said the boatman.

"Lambeth," answered Sir Richard, which was the first place that came into his head.

Upon this the boatman pulled at his oars.

He glanced at his strange-looking fare for some time in silence, who had the appearance of a gentleman, but a most dilapidated one, it must be acknowledged.

"Met with an accident, sir?" said the man, glancing at the baronet, the dripping from whose garments gave a large supply of water to the bottom of the boat.

"Yes, fell into the water," answered Sir Richard.

"You'd better get somewhere as soon as possible where you can change your things," suggested the man.

"That is precisely what I wish to do," said Sir Richard. "You don't happen to know of a quiet house where I could—ahem —get a bed, for it is too late for me to find my way home to night."

"Yes, sir; there's a nice quiet house near the palace, where I think you would be treated well. It ain't a very aristocratic house, but they do the thing properly."

"Oh, never mind about its being a humble place, it's better suited to me at the present moment; for to say the truth, I don't cut a very aristocratic figure. What is the sign of the house you are speaking of?"

"The Pickled Gerkin," said the man.

"Then pull towards it. Is it far from the shore?"

"Only a few hundred yards."

"Good, that will do then. I'll take off my things and go to bed at once. They will be able to dry them by the morning, I dare say."

"Without a doubt, Sir Richard Fleetwood," said the man.

The baronet started, and said—

"Oh, then you know me?"

"Yes, Sir Richard."

"I should have hardly thought my most intimate acquaintance would have recognised me in my present dilapidated condition: for of a verity I am somewhat tarnished in my external appearance."

"In truth, Sir Richard, you are," answered the boatman; "but rest and a clean wash and a shave, will restore you to your wonted appearance."

There was a pause after this, when the baronet said—

"I've fallen into the hands of lawless characters, who have kept me close prisoner in Alsatia."

"Alsatia!" exclaimed the man. "Have you been there?"

"Yes, against my own will, as you may imagine," answered Sir Richard.

The boat had now arrived at Lambeth stairs.

The baronet landed, and pulling out his purse, was about to discharge the price of his fare, when the boatman asked him if he should accompany him to the Pickled Gerkin.

Sir Richard availed himself of the offer, and the two proceeded towards the house in question.

It was a small, low, old-fashioned hostelry, standing alone, in a low part of Lambeth.

Sir Richard was introduced to the landlady by his companion, and taking his way up to his bed-room, he undressed, and gave his clothes to the waiter, to take down stairs and dry at the kitchen fire. In a few minutes the baronet was fast asleep.

When he awoke in the morning, he found his things all placed ready for him, and having performed his toilette, he took his way into the public-room, breakfasted, and then sallied forth.

Crossing over Westminster Bridge, he hailed a hackney coach, and desired the man to drive to Acton.

Upon his arriving at the latter place, he alighted and rung the bell, which was answered by his own porter, who stared in stupid astonishment at the sight of his late master.

"Sir Richard!" he exclaimed, in an undertone.

"Well, what are you staring at?" inquired the baronet. "Is there anything so astonishing in my coming to my own residence?"

"I thought—"

"Thought what, sirrah?"

"That you were on the continent."

"Psha! you keep your thoughts to yourself," answered the baronet, as he strode up the garden walk, and entered the hall. The first person he met with here was his valet, who with his own peculiar soft voice said to his master—

"Beg pardon, Sir Richard, but—ahem!— you have returned—"

"Well, I know that—you see I have. What of that?"

"I don't think you were expected," said the man, in an oily voice.

"Expected?" exclaimed the baronet; "Expected? What does the man mean?"

"I suppose you know, sir?"

"Know what?"

"That Sir Reginald has returned?"

Sir Richard staggered back several paces. He was quite unprepared for this, and stood staring at the man in perfect astonishment and mute surprise.

"Returned!" he ejaculated, "returned! When?"

"Some time since."

"Is Lady Bostock here?"

"Yes, sir."

"Tell her I have arrived. I will wait in her own room."

"Yes, sir."

The man took his departure, as Sir Richard went into Lady Bostock's room. He was sadly dashed in spirits, and for the first time felt himself an intruder in his own, or what he considered his own house.

In the course of a few minutes, Lady Bostock made her appearance. She gave a tragic start of surprise as she entered the apartment, and then sprang forward and fell into her brother's arms. She did it well, as though she was perfectly overpowered with her feelings.

"Welcome, welcome, dear brother, welcome home once more. Alas, we have had a strange scene here, and strange changes," she said, in a whisper. "Reginald has returned."

"So I hear. Is he in the house now ?"

"Yes, up stairs."

"I do not wish to see him, and it would be better for me to leave this house as quickly as possible."

"My dear brother, you ought not to have left it as you did, and then all this would not have occurred. Now he has possession, and is reinstated in his rights."

"How so ?"

"Oh. it's all settled. I don't understand these law proceedings, but it appears Mr. Baintree, a solicitor, has obtained all the necessary documents, and—— In short, the whole affair is settled. You are no longer Sir Richard Fleetwood—the title reverts to your elder brother."

"How—how has he managed to make his escape ? Curse that Hardy—a bitter curse light on him !" said the baronet, as he paced up and down the room in a state of excitement. His frame shook, and his lips quivered with emotion.

His sister regarded him with a look which was calm and immoveable. For some time the two remained silent.

"To be cheated, duped, foiled at every point," said the baronet, striking his forehead with his clenched fist. "Oh, fool, fool, to lose all through a woman ! Bah !"

As the thought of Honora Langford rushed through his brain, he became frantic, and eventually fell into a chair, and covering his face with his hands, actually sobbed.

Had Lady Bostock had any pity in her composition, she would have had some compassion for her brother, who was evidently borne down and completely prostrated. He exclaimed, somewhat suddenly—

"The child—does he know aught of the child ?'

"No, how should he ?" she answered.

"Then he never shall—that will be one satisfaction," exclaimed the *ci devant* baronet.

While this conversation was taking place, Lady Fleetwood, Sir Reginald's wife, made her appearance in the room. She gave a start of surprise as she beheld the two occupants of the apartment. The colour came to her face, and then left it unusually pale.

"Oh, I beg your pardon, I did not know you—that is, anyone was here."

"My brother, my second brother," said Lady Bostock, "has returned to what is now no longer his home."

"I should be very sorry, and so would Sir Reginald, if his brother did not make this his home. Let the past be forgotten, forgiven ; and between relatives. and, let us hope, dear relatives, let no strife exist."

She went forward to where Mr. Richard Fleetwood sat, and held out her small thin white hand, to grasp his. For a moment he hesitated, but upon a second reflection, he shook hands with his sister-in-law.

"So, there now," said Lady Bostock. "let us be friends. I will tell Sir Reginald that you are here."

"No, no," exclaimed Richard Fleetwood, "no, I would not have it. I do not desire it—I do not desire any interview with my ill used brother."

"And wherefore not ?"

"I do not desire it."

Lady Fleetwood sat herself down, and looked at the haggard and careworn features of her brother-in-law. Since his last departure from Acton, ten years appeared to have been added to his life ; more than this, he looked thin and emaciated.

"No doubt." said Lady Bostock, who, after an awkward pause, came to the rescue, "no doubt it is repugnant to the feelings of my brother—ahem—Richard, to meet one whom it must be confessed, he has deeply injured, or supposed to have injured ; for after all, my dear, you know your husband was supposed to be out of his mind. When I say supposed, I am speaking with all due caution. The doctor's certificate confirmed and justified this conclusion."

"They were mistaken," said Lady Fleetwood, "greatly mistaken, there can be no doubt of that. My poor husband has suffered quite enough, and it is in vain to recur to that now. Let it pass. I am sure his own generous nature would not prompt him to bear any malice against those who have injured him. He is restored to his just rights, and therefore can have now no reason to complain, neither is he likely to do so. I am quite sure, therefore, he would not let the memory of his past sufferings dwell so much upon his mind as to place an irreparable gulph between himself and his younger brother."

"It's very kind, dear, really very kind of you to say this much," said Lady Bostock ; "I am sure it's much to your credit. But my brother Richard has also been a sufferer in more than one thing. It is not pleasant, you must acknowledge, to be thrust from a position, a lofty position, you have been holding. You must acknowledge this," she continued ; "indeed, it is useless to attempt to deny it."

" I do not attempt to deny it," answered Lady Fleetwood. " I know perfectly well that it is not a pleasant thing to be hurled from a position ; but that position was, to say the least of it, a false one."

" That is true, dear," said Lady Bostock, in a tone which was half patronising, and half sneering.

While this conversation was taking place, Sir Reginald entered the apartment. Both the brothers turned pale as the latter one made his appearance.

" Richard !" exclaimed Sir Reginald, " you here ?"

" Yes," answered the former, " I am here, but am here only as a visitor—as an intruder. I will not stay to offend you."

Richard Fleetwood rose, and was about to leave the apartment, upon which his brother intercepted his passage.

" Sit down, Richard," he said. " I am not now about to upbraid you for the past. Let that be forgotten."

" Psha !" exclaimed Richard Fleetwood ; " it never can be forgotten—never can be ignored. You have your rights—let that suffice you."

" Let there be no ill will between us, Richard," said Sir Reginald.

" I have no answer to make to you, sir," said Richard Fleetwood, haughtily, as he strode from the apartment, took his way along the passage, slammed to the hall door, and left the house.

CHAPTER XCIII.

THE MARRIAGE OF OSBORNE AND HONORA LANGFORD.

While these events were taking place, Henry Osborne was a constant attendant at the house of Miss Langford. He was unceasing in his attentions, and besought her to name an early day for their nuptials.

Miss Langford could not be prevailed upon to do so for some time, but eventually acceded to his request.

Henry Osborne had not seen anything of Colonel Jack, neither had Squabshot ; however, Osborne did not feel himself authorised in waiting for his appearance to be present at his marriage.

Osborne had taken a large house in Park Lane, which was to be his town residence, also a country villa on the banks of the Thames, near Twickenham. Both these residences were furnished with sumptuous magnificence, for, as the reader is already aware, their owner was a millionaire.

Mr. Squabshot, in his humble lodgings, at Goswell Street, was left solus ; his quandom companion having left ; nevertheless he was a constant visitor, and much to his credit, evinced no pride at his elevated position in the social scale.

Some ten days before the one appointed for the wedding, Squabshot was seated in his arm chair, conning over the incidents of his past life and his future prospects. A knock was heard at the door, a postman's knock, and the high priestess of that classic temple entered the room, and placed in the hand of Squabshot a letter, which from the handwriting of the superscription, he knew to be that of Colonel Jack.

Squabshot opened it, and read the following :—

"Dear Squabshot,—I have met with a sad bereavement. Poor Mrs. Halford has died suddenly, after a short illness, which was only of a few days' duration. I have not been able to come round to see either yourself or Osborne, for to say the truth, I am quite prostrated, and broken down in health and spirits. Remember me kindly to Osborne, and accept my best wishes yourself.

" Yours, ever—
" Frank Halford."

Squabshot turned the letter over and over again, and then sat down in his arm chair once more.

" Dead !" he exclaimed. " Poor creature. No wonder. One of her delicate and susceptible nature was but ill adapted to bear up against the storms of life."

He sat for some time ruminating over the contents of the colonel's note, and soon afterwards Osborne himself made his appearance in Squabshot's lodgings. The latter handed to his friend our hero's note—Osborne read it in silence."

" Did you know her ?" said Squabshot, when he had finished his perusal of the letter.

" Who ?"

" Mrs. Halford ?"

" Oh, dear yes—she was one of the gentlest of her sex. I am sorry to learn this, Squabshot, very sorry," said Osborne, " the more so as my marriage is to take place in ten days from this time, and I ought, perhaps, in consideration of the death of Mrs. Halford, to put it off."

" I don't see that, old boy. Oh, no, there's no occasion for that, I'm sure."

" I'll go and see Halford at once ; don't you think I had better? Where does he live ?"

" Brook Street. That's where the letter is dated from."

" Ah, then I certainly think it better to see him. I have never been to his present residence, but what matters ?"

"Oh, there won't be much difficulty in finding it out, if that's what you mean. I see you have your carriage at the door—suppose we both go?"

"Very good, so be it."

The two companions then entered the carriage, which was driven to Colonel Jack's residence.

When Osborne and Squabshot arrived there, they found our hero in the first floor room, moody and dejected. He brightened up, however, at the appearance of Osborne, and shook him warmly by both hands.

"Frank," exclaimed the latter, "I'm very sorry to hear of this. I need not tell you that though, for I knew and esteemed her who is now, let us hope, removed to a happier sphere."

"Let us hope so, Henry; her's was not a happy life, anything but a happy life. However, let us not discourse upon that. It's all over now. How fares it with you?"

"He was about to be married in a day or two," said Squabshot.

"Was?—and what has prevented this?"

"Oh, nothing—nothing," answered Osborne; "only now—"

"Oh, don't let that interfere with you—it would be perfectly absurd. No, no, Harry, neither you or myself can now recall her to life; and it would be unjust for me to expect you to let my private troubles interfere with your arrangements."

"I have wanted to speak to you, Frank," said Osborne, "for some time past."

"Indeed!—what about?"

"Well, I hardly know how to broach the subject now," said Osborne, turning towards Squabshot.

"The fact is," said the latter, "that our friend Osborne, as you already know, is a wealthy man, a very wealthy man, and he wishes to do as much good with his money as possible."

"A very laudable desire," said the colonel.

"Precisely. And so you see, he and I have been talking matters over, and, I think," continued Mr. Squabshot, assuming a ministerial manner, "I think I am justified in what I am about to say?"

"You are," said Osborne, giving him a nod of approval.

Mr. Squabshot went on—

"Well, in that case I will proceed. As I was observing, our friend Osborne is no miser who wishes to store or hoard up his wealth—quite the contrary, I assure you. Well, this being the case, he very naturally turns his thoughts to those few friends whom he esteems and admires."

"Yes."

"You are one of these, and he, of course, doesn't mean to offend you—nothing is further from his thoughts—but he wishes you

to accept of a certain sum annually, which will suffice to render you independent of the world. Now, do I make myself sufficiently understood?" said Mr. Squabshot, falling back in his chair, and regarding the colonel with a look of inquiry.

"You are perfectly intelligible," said the colonel, with a faint smile. "Perfectly so."

After this there was a pause.

"What say you to the proposition?" said Squabshot.

"I am much obliged, I am sure," answered Colonel Jack; "and I know, and always have known, your own generous nature, Harry," he said, turning to Osborne. "I did not require this test of it to be sufficiently impressed with your good feeling towards myself; but such things cannot be. Colonel Jack can never be beholden to anyone for the means of existence. Ah, no, never. We have all our own paths to choose or follow through life. You'll say mine is not a reputable one. I cannot help it—it is too late to alter now. I have been too long on the road, too long accustomed to the excitement consequent upon my calling, to alter now. Harry, my boy," said the colonel, solemnly, as his lips quivered, and he laid his hand on his friend's shoulder, "Harry, a glorious and happy future lies before you, a dream of human happiness, which has now turned suddenly to a reality, and is a dream no longer. You have been tested in that crucible, trouble, and have turned out 'current gold indeed.' You will not, in after years, think badly of one who, from the force of circumstances and an erratic disposition, turned to folly first, and guilt afterwards. An unworthy member of an ancient house—"

"Do not reproach yourself thus," said Osborne, who was visibly affected.

"I do not reproach myself, Harry, far from it; but I cannot conceal from you my own identity. Start not, but in your old friend, in the companion of your boyhood, you behold the celebrated highwayman, Colonel Jack."

"I knew this," said Osborne.

"You did—and never said anything about it?"

"It's only lately that it has come to my knowledge."

"Ah, only lately—I see. Well, Harry, lately or not, be this how it may, it is, as I have already said, too late for Colonel Jack to quit the course of life he has been following. Born for better things perhaps, destined for better things it may be; but, alas! a destiny which has been turned on one side by the wickedness and treachery of man! Bah! enough of this. Why refer to the past—the miserable past—the miserable present—and, it may be, the miserable future?"

The colonel leant on the table and covered his face with his hands. Osborne had never seen him thus moved. He placed his hand gently on his shoulder and said, in a kind voice—half in a whisper—

"For my sake as well as your own, Frank, accept of the offer I have made. I have almost unbounded wealth, at any rate, more than I desire or know what to do with."

"Harry," said our hero, "I've trotted on my road of life for many years now, and shall trot off into the other world only when I come to the end of it—for her sake," he continued nodding towards where the dead body of his wife lay, "for her sake I ought have altered my course—but that is past now—I have but little to care for—very little, and few to care for me—and so Colonel Jack will make his name remembered

No. 59.

by posterity, if not as of one of an unsullied reputation, still he will be remembered."

"I am sorry for this," said Osborne, sadly —"very sorry."

"Ah, as to that, Harry, your path and mine now lie widely apart, but for the rest we shall doubtless be as good friends as ever. The same blood flows in both our veins although the world knows nothing of this. It is as well that they never should. I do not wish to bring disgrace upon one whose character is pure and spotless—unsullied by a single stain, keep that character so, Harry, and I shall look towards you as some one who in his passage through life has done naught to raise the blush of shame—as for me I am past that now—past hope and past care," said Colonel Jack mournfully.

Osborne was sad, silent and dejected.

"I have not had the courage," said the colonel, "to look upon the features of her who, in life was the sun of my existence, a sun which has been obscured by a cloud shot across its surface by myself."

"Not by yourself, Frank," said Osborne, "but by the hand of providence or fate."

"By myself, Harry," said the colonel solemnly. "I cannot conceal from myself this fact—but its useless to talk of that now—and so you are a going to be married, eh!"

"Yes," answered Osborne, with a heightened colour.

"And when?"

"The day after to-morrow is to be the happy day," answered Squabshot.

"And Miss Langford. How is she?"

"Quite well."

"Ah, I forgot to ask you, Squabshot," said our hero. "You took her home all right from Dover?"

"Yes; and Sir Richard Fleetwood. What of him?" inquired Squabshot.

"Ah! Sir Richard," exclaimed the colonel suddenly.

"I had really quite forgot. Why I left him in Alsatia close prisoner. Indeed but I ought to have seen to him ere this—I had quite forgot him—I must send Hackett and see how he gets on."

"You know then Sir Reginald himself had his release and that he is restored to his just rights.

"No, indeed I was not aware of it."

"It's a fact then, I assure you."

"I am delighted to hear it. But Sir Richard—"

"Or rather Mr. Richard," said Squabshot.

"Precisely—well he must be seen to."

"I would again urge of you to accept of my offer, Frank," said Osborne. "Consider my dear fellow how many risks are run in your present course of life."

"Those many risks lend a charm to my calling Without them life would be dull and insipid and robbed of half its charms. Ah! Harry, you don't know—and happily for you perhaps can't conceive, what a supreme delight it is to surmount dangers and difficulties, to one of my nature especially."

While the colonel was speaking, Knapp made his appearance, but seeing two strangers in the room, he was about to retire. Colonel Jack however bid him remain.

"Knapp," said our hero, "I had quite forgotten Sir Richard, or rather Mr. Richard Fleetwood."

"He has made his escape," said Knapp.

"Escape! Impossible! How?"

Knapp then entered into those particulars with which the reader is already acquainted.

"Well, it matters little," said Squabshot. "Sir Reginald is restored to his rights, and the teeth of his savage brother are drawn."

"Not so," answered Colonel Jack. "He will be able to bite at me. But this is bad news. No matter, it cannot be helped now. Reuben was true to his trust, I suppose?"

"Oh, yes," said Knapp. "He is not to blame in the matter, of that you may rest assured."

After some further conversation, Colonel Jack's visitors took their departure.

It was in vain that Henry Osborne pressed upon our hero the annual settlement which he had so generously offered. Colonel Jack was inflexible, and could not entertain the proposition.

When they had gone, our hero went up stairs to have a last look of her who in the life had been so faithful and self-sacrificing a companion to him through all his troubles.

Mrs. Halford lay in her last sleep, the features were tranquil, and a pleasant expression was on the face of the dead woman.

Curson accompanied the colonel into the chamber of death; removing the lid of the coffin slightly, the face of the dead woman was disclosed.

The colonel gazed at it for a moment or so and then burst into tears. His grief was of no common order—it came from the heart.

How bitterly he repented of all his neglect to the sweet being who had been true to him in bad and good report. But we will not dwell upon this fearful scene. Most of us have had to go through similar trials in the course of our passage through life.

On the following day the funeral took place. Mrs Halford was buried with much ceremony—every respect it was possible to pay to her poor remains was shown by her husband and friends.

Doctor Carruthers was one of the mourners —he evinced great kindness towards the bereaved husband, and stayed with him after the other guests had departed, endeavouring to cheer him as best he could in this his lonely hour of affliction.

"It is no use giving way to grief, my dear sir," said Mr. Carruthers, when they were seated together in the evening. She could not possibly have lived much longer, and all that could be done to save her was done, and so you have that consolation, and believe me that it's not a slight one under the circumstances."

"No, I suppose not," answered the colonel, "her spirit was broken, poor thing, and she has succumbed to those corroding and consuming cares which wear the best of us out in the end. You have seen enough of this, I dare say, Doctor Carruthers, in your extensive practice?"

"Indeed I have," said the doctor. "I often think that what a history some of my brethren in the medical profession could tell were they to give to the world the benefit of their experience. Even my own would be interesting enough. I have attended upon some of the greatest men of the age in their last moments, and how deeply these have been regretted by their fellow men it is hard to say.

"The pen of the historian or the eulogist is, alas, doomed beyond that of all others, not only to spread regret and gloom over all who pursue his labours, but to self inflict a sadness when he, sifting and waking forth the Things that are with the Past, is called upon to record the untimely end of Genius—and when is the end of genius not untimely? Is man's life so long on the earth that, did he not die till twice three score and ten revolving years had sown their silver over his frame, would he not be mourned, missed, and lamented by the sorrowing friends he leaves behind? Would not the death of Genius be far, far more so, even did it usurp the honoured age of Methusaleh—is not its existence all too brief? But when it is snatched away from our tearful, our adoring eyes, clothed in all the strong-limbed vigour of maturity —the early manhood of its power—when we have dreamed with delight as we watched over its young promise, how great, how glorious would be that maturity—when we behold it suddenly withdraw from our gaze, and the once bright eye, whose flashings, so watched, so prized, spoke of the inner fire which in the Temple of the Mind was ever burning, is closed and dim—when the form of beauty that once breathed its divine images, lies stricken by the unerring shaft of Death, pulseless, inanimate, and cold— then, oh, then, do we not feel how deplorable, how irremediable is our loss, when the bright soul radiates in its orbit no longer, and the maturity of genius is gone—fled for ever.

"Indeed, that is true enough," answered the colonel. "The finer the organisation of the human frame, the more easily is it assailed by disease—at least, I suppose so."

"In most countries it is," replied the doctor. "I remember attending upon a young girl in the hospital—she gave me her history—and, indeed but it was a tearful one. I remember that it made a great impression on me at the time. There is, perhaps, no spot to open in the mind a train of more melancholy reflections than the interior of an hospital—that spacious chamber where death holds his court—the ante-room to the grave. The poor-house, with all its galling dependance—servile subjections—wearisome toil—with all its bitter associations of scattered hopes, vacillating fortunes, and humiliated pride—breathes not into the ear of the spectator so striking a lesson of patience and of gratitude. The church-yard alone takes a higher grade in the cause of instruction. In that great volume of morality where

every page speaks of the nothingness of time —the vastness, of eternity, the mind may be edified, and the soul comforted."

"Ah! who has not longed while treading its peaceful earth to lay down the burden of existence—all life's worthless enjoyments, idle disputations, and fatiguing cares beneath its verdant turf, and to enter at once into that blissful state where pain and sorrow are not known. Yet, though, to some it is redolent with hope and emulation, there are others to whom it is fraught with terror and despair, who enter its hallowed precincts encompassed in that net which guilt inevitably weaves for its victims, that net—the dark bondage of remorse, whose meshes they can never heal.

"Who among us can walk in a church-yard and not remember friends we have slighted —vows we have broken—hearts we have pierced—insults we have offered, or injuries we have designed for those who sleep beneath. The whispers of conscience may be stifled in the busy city, or the crowded street—aye, even in the silence of midnight solitude they may be hushed, but in the church-yard the stern reprover summons forth all his might and will be heard. The dead speak again, and the tomb hath its voice, and who is it that dares refuse to listen to the spirit of eternity?

"But I am indulging in a melancholy homily, Mr. Halford," said Mr. Caruthers, awakened perhaps by the present occasion.

"Oh! I esteem it a great favour that you have been kind enough to stay with me thus long," answered Colonel Jack, "but I fear me that I'm tresspassing already too much upon your valuable time."

"Not at all—not at all, my dear sir. I have nothing to do for this evening. At least nothing that I am aware of. I left word at home where I could be found, and if I am wanted they are to send for me."

"In that case," said the colonel, "I should like to hear the story you were mentioning."

"With all my heart," said Doctor Caruthers, who was pleased that he had imbued his companion to some degree of interest in the narrative.

CHAPTER XCIV.

THE DOCTOR'S STORY.

"A few years since" said Mr. Carruthers, "I was led in the absence of a friend to officiate in my professional capacity at the St. ——'s Hospital. It was somewhat late on the evening of a merry Christmas day, when I entered. How forcibly did the contrast strike me of the happy smiling faces I had just left, with the pale, haggard faces which everywhere met my view! of the blithe sounds of mirth and music without, and the groans of anguish within! I thought of the sumptuous boards of plenty where appetites was eagerly indulged in satiety, and saw the scanty overtempting nutriment of sickness offered to parched lips which could scarcely open to receive it, and deeply I felt how necessary to the miserable sufferer patience was, and yet how hard, how very hard it was to practice it. Every pallet was to me a homily. Those whom I saw before me had sung, and danced, and played on many a Christmas night, and where were they now? fettered, listless, and strengthless, yet many of them seemed cheerful, and I blessed the religion which alone could make them so.

"Some of the beds were unoccupied. They had been tenanted yesterday, but those tenants would never press them again—they were dead. One of these humble resting-places was preparing, as I learned, for the reception of a patient, who, through high influence, was to be admitted that evening, although it was not what is termed an open day.

"Having fulfilled my duties, I was about to retire, when my attention was suddenly arrested; the door of the ward opened, and a decent-looking middle-aged woman entered. supporting the almost lifeless form of a young female. Humanity naturally led me forward to proffer my assistance.

"The invalid, unable to endure the fatigue of undressing, was merely divested of her bonnet and shawl, and laid upon the bed. I had now an opportunity of contemplating the being before me; and though, perhaps, in the splendid drawing-rooms of the great I might have looked on faces of more dazzling beauty, never had I beheld a countenance of such touching and singular loveliness. The rosy hue of freshness bloomed not on her cheek: it was pale, and cold, and wan; save one vermillion streak, the last impress of receding health, which, lingering, shed its sweet but treacherous tint. The contour of her face was evidently foreign. There was the lofty forehead, the pencilled brow, the gently aquiline nose, the bewitching mouth, which we so often see and admire in the natives of the south.

"Had any doubt of her country existed, it was at once dispelled by the exquisitely melodious voice and slight Italian accent in which she pronounced the words—

"'Who is near me?'

"'I, your friend, Ellen Gordon! how do you feel, my child?' soothingly, replied the woman who had accompanied her.

"'Just as I should wish—dying. And am I, indeed, indeed, in a hospital?' continued she, as she opened her eyes and threw a quick glance around, but hastily shut them again, as though the scene was all too strange and painful to her view.

"After a short pause, during which the quivering of her lip, and the variations of her eloquent countenance, showed that gloomy thoughts were coursing each other through her mind, like dark clouds over the face of heaven, she burst into an hysteric sob, exclaiming—

"'Oh! my mother! my mother! could you behold me now; me, your pride, your boast, your darling, with none but strangers to listen to my last sigh, inquire my last wishes, and receive my last blessing! But 'tis well, 'tis meet, that I should suffer—all who love must suffer—and I have loved, oh, God, this breaking heart tells how deeply!'

"Apprehending that I might unintentionally have overheard confessions intended only for the licensed ear of friendship, I expressed to Mrs. Gordon my sincere wishes for the recovery of her interesting charge, and moved towards the door.

"She thanked me gratefully for the interest I had manifested, adding—

"'Ah, sir, did you know that beautiful young creature's history you would scarcely wish for her recovery; her feelings are too quick and too warm for her happiness. Mayhap, sir, you will come and talk to her, and comfort her, for she has so often wished to have the consolations that a friend could afford.'

"I observed that she was then too much exhausted to employ her mind in conversation but I willingly engaged my future services in her behalf. Accordingly, under the most powerful emotions of curiosity, not unmixed, I trust, with a worthier motive—the desire of smoothing the pillow of a dying fellow-creature—I repaired to the hospital early on the following morning.

"In answer to my inquiries of the nurse how her new patient had passed the night, she replied—

"'Why, very restlessly, sir. Poor thing, she seems but badly; the bed will soon be empty again, I guess. The doctor has just left her, and he says he thinks a few days will see the end of her. But you will go and see her yourself, sir! she has asked for you a great many times.'

"I approached the bed, When she learned who I was, a faint smile hovered on her lip, and gave a temporary brilliancy to her dark languishing eye, whose lustre struggled through the dimness of disease, like the expiring sun through the shadows of the evening,

"I conversed with her for a considerable time, and had the satisfaction of observing the agitation of her mind succeeded by tranquility. Although upbraidings of her own weakness and folly constantly escaped her, yet she started with horror from the imputation of guilt.

"'No, sir, I am not guilty; I would not live so. Yet it was very sinful in me to love as I did; but all Florence was in love with him, and how should I help it?'

"Conceiving that she evinced an anxiety to make me acquainted with her history, I requested that she would relate it to me; which she did in two subsequent interviews, and I committed it to paper for the benefit of my own family. To my daughters it appeared to offer an excellent illustration of the fatal consequences which may accrue from the indulgence of that morbid enthusiasm, which many a young female thoughtlessly revels in; and with my sons it might operate as a warning against that mean, unmanly trifling with the value of a woman's heart which uses every art to win her love only to slight it when it shall be won.

"I give the narrative in nearly the words in which it was delivered, fictitious names being substituted for the true ones. Should any one imagine that it has too much of the warm tinge of romance for reality, let him remember that it was uttered by a sanguine Italian girl,"

"With a fire in her heart, and a fire in her brain"

"'My name is Francesca Vitelli; alas, there yet lurks in this bosom too much of earthly pride, for I feel a repugnance to pronounce in a hospital that name, which only two short years since was a passport to the noblest saloons in Italy. Well, let it pass! but, oh! reveal it not again; I would not that every vulgar tongue should syllable its sound. I was born at Florence, where my father held a lucrative situation connected with the government. I was an only child, the treasured idol of parents who loved me to a blameable excess. Every gratification within the limits of their power to obtain for me was mine. They boasted of my beauty—oh, could they look upon me now! but I thank heaven the misery is spared them of seeing their beloved child a debtor to a strange country for a bed to die upon. My dear mother, how sanguine is maternal affection! fondly anticipated that my personal attractions would procure for me a settlement of high rank, and with that view I was educated in the most fashionable and expensive manner.

"'My accomplishments, with the natural vivacity of my disposition, afforded me incessant invitations from wealth and fashion; and the singing, dancing, and beauty—beauty of Francesca Vitelli!—were heard of in every circle in Florence.

"'Perhaps it is sinful, sir, to say, that all this gaiety and homage made me happy; yet I must be candid, and confess that I was happy—very happy. Vanity has its pleasures, and mine was abundantly fed, for I heard no voice save that of praise. Oh, how bright the world appeared then! Sorrow and suffering seemed to me as a fable: the sun above me, the waters before me, the flowers beneath me, were all bright and smiling; and why should human life alone be dark and gloomy? It was not natural—it was impossible. You smile, sir, at my folly; but recollect that I was at that time only seventeen—warm, confiding, enthusiastic, and visionary.

"'At that period a new ambassador from the English Court arrived at Florence. How little did I imagine, when my father recapitulated the titles of the most distinguished individuals in his suite, that my own destiny should be so closely linked with one of them! Instinctive nature, methinks, should have made him pause at the name of the murderer of his child; for, oh, he is the murderer! yet, it is sweeter to die for him than to live for all the world besides.

"'One morning—well do I recollect it—'twas the 13th of June—a gentleman called at our house with an official communication from the ambassador to my father. On learning that he was absent he requested permission to await his return, and employed the interval by strolling in the grounds. There, in an arbour to which I had retired from the burning rays of the sun, we first met.

"'Even now, sir, I could recall every word that was spoken at that blissful interview. Mutually pleased with each other, I assented to his earnest entreaty to see me on the following day, when he should repeat his visit to my father. He came, and came again and again, availing himself of the facilities which business ostensibly afforded him to come to the house daily. My parents deemed themselves flattered by his intimacy; and my proud heart, knowing whence it originated, became prouder still. Not even the ambassador himself was an object of such univeral attraction and interest as his handsome and fascinating cousin.

"'He was allied to one of the oldest families in the English peerage, and the heir to one of its noblest titles and estates. But these alone were not the distinctions of Frederick—no; I had nearly suffered that magic name to have escaped my lips; but no, I cannot tell it you; do not require me to repeat it; yet you have doubtless often heard it; for surely his splendid endowments, his persuasive oratory, have been well known to his fellow-countrymen.

"'At Florence he was the idol of all ranks; he possessed the rarest conversational powers; and to be anmitted to his society was coveted as an honour by every one. Think, then, how flattered I felt, to be selected from all Florence, the companion of his daily walks, hearkening to his voice so silver sweet—oh, 'twas too sweet for truth—as it poured the irresistible language of love into my ear, and, as I fondly believed, into no other ear than mine!

"'When I remind you that he was young and strikingly handsome, you will not imagine that those qualities tended to weaken the impression which his captivating manners had made upon me. I loved him with all the fervour and enthusiasm of my nature, and credulously thought that because he lavished on me idle compliments and the most devoted attention that I was beloved in return.

"'Frank and confiding, I concealed not my passion; abandoning myself to the delicious delusion, that the more I loved he was the more my debtor; that it lessened the disparity of rank between us, and would be the medium of equalising our state.

"'I tendered to him the unalloyed treasure of my heart's vintage, and received in return only the glittering counterfeit coinage of the lip! For awhile the dream lasted; I thought, nay, all expected, save himself, that I was to be his bride. Many a scheme of happiness and grandeur floated on my mind, when Frederick was hastily summoned to England by the death of a near relation. How did I long to accompany him to that land of liberty!

"'It was on a bright summer's evening that we parted. I shuddered as I looked on the setting sun, and knew that on the following night I should watch its decline alone. But little deemed I that my happiness had then expired! Why did he not tell me we were to part for ever? Why mock me with idle promises of a speedy return, and eternal fidelity and love and bliss and marriage? Oh, sir, there are men who would recoil with horror, if desired to point a pistol at the breast of the woman who has trusted in them, who yet will calmly and deliberately, with the weapons of perfidy and falsehood pierce her bosom through and through, and let out existence drop by drop!

"'And is that less murder, which occupies years in its completion than which is the deed of a moment? I am a young moralist, sir; but sorrow is a powerful instructor. It makes me soul-sick to retrace what I then endured.

Where was I? Had I told you that he sailed without me, done that which he had so often sworn he could never do? For some months the receipt of kind letters from him consoled me for his absence; yet, after awhile these became less frequent and less fond, until at length they ceased altogether.

I did not suppose I could have survived it, and yet I did; the heart is often long, too long in breaking.

"'About twelve months after his departure, I was separated from my beloved parents for ever in this world. An epidemic fever deprived me of them both in one short week. Yet though I never quitted their bedside, I could not imbibe the contagion. How earnestly did I wish that I might, so that one grave should hold us all. At their deaths I found myself compelled to look around to procure my own subsistence, for my father's income died with him; and, having always lived up to its full extent, I found myself, after discharging his debts, the mistress of but a trivial sum.

"True, indeed, I had relations who offered me an asylum; but my pride revolted from the servile dependence which is exacted from a poor relative.

"With spirits broken, and health impaired, what was I fitted for? Gladly did I accept the offer to become nursery governess in the family of an English countess.

"It is now exactly a year since I arrived with her in this country.

"As the countess was in a bad state of health, we resided entirely in the country, and thus the slight chance which an abode in London would have afforded me of meeting with Frederick, was frustrated.

"The caprice and tyranny of Lady Arlington was almost insupportable; but I was attached to her little girl, and bore with it. At length she grew tired of my perpetual apathy, as she termed my forbearance, under her insolence.

"Well knowing, however, that I had a spirit which, when once thoroughly roused, slumbered not easily, she reproached me with endeavouring to wean the affections of her husband—a poor fool, whom in my heart I scorned and despised—from herself. Vainly I asserted my innocence. She was determined to disbelieve me, and eventually made this pretence a reason for my dismissal.

"'I was advised to come to London, and almost felt grateful for any chance that made me an inhabitant of the same city with Frederick. It was something to inhale the same air with him, to tread the same streets. Once—once only—I thought of addressing one more letter to him; but, thank heaven! my native pride triumphed over my weakness, and spared me the mortification of proving that I still remembered, where I was forgotten. Finding my little stock of money rapidly diminishing, and no prospect of a situation presenting itself, I acceded to the suggestions of Mrs. Gordon, the kind-hearted woman in whose house I lodged, to offer myself as an assistant at a celebrated French artificial florist's. My application was successful, and in the course of a few days I became an inmate of the house. I continued in this employment with as much content as could be expected, broken-hearted as I was, without home, friends, or country. My mistress (long was it ere I could teach my lips to pronounce that word) was extremely kind, and strove by every method in her power to counteract the fatal effects of the vicissitudes I had undergone. Happily for me her efforts proved abortive. Each day I felt my strength fail more and more, and saw, with satisfaction, the grave—the long-wished for grave—opening before me. I might perhaps have lingered on through many tedious months, but heaven mercifully accelerated my fate by a circumstance which I am now about to mention.

"'About six weeks since, while engaged in waiting on some ladies in the show-room, of which, from the superiority of my manners, I was constituted superintendant, my ear caught the name of Frederick, as it was frequently pronounced in another part of the room. I never could listen to that name without endeavouring to discover if the individual who owned it was worthy to bear the same designation that he bore. I instinctively turned and beheld—oh, it will kill me if I go over that scene again!—you may guess who it was: it was my soul's idol! Yes, it was he, accompanied by a lady, whom he regarded with looks of the fondest affection. I did not shriek, for the sick and suffocating emotion I felt almost stifled me.

"'Wishing, yet fearing, to prove whether he would recognise me, I contrived to separate myself from the party I was attending, to offer my services to the lady who was his companion. 'What a beautiful girl!' exclaimed she, as I approached. What think you was his answer?'

"'Oh, God, it thrills through my frame now! 'Yes, has been—but looks so sickly.' Sickly! and who made me so? If his own brow was bright with the glow of health, why, so had mine been, ere he chased away its bloom for ever. What, then, he would spurn a wan cheek and attenuated form, even though his perfidy had caused them!

"'I struggled, and forced myself, by an act of desperation, to offer to him a bouquet of flowers, such as I knew he admired.

"'These were imported from Florence, sir,' said I, laying strong emphasis on the name of the city. 'Ha!' cried he, and I fancied I saw a slight variation in his countenance; when his fair companion made some remark, and, turning to reply, he carelessly threw the flowers out of his hand, even as he had flung away my love. I made no farther trial of his memory. How did I wish I had no memory myself—but over the ruins of health it still flung its fated light. No tears filled my eyes, but my heart wept. Were you, sir, one of my own sex, I should not be ashamed to tell you what burning envy fired my bosom, as I heard my lover bestowing on another the same epithets of affection which he had been accustomed to lavish upon me. I could not bear it, and I withdrew to an inner room to hate him : it was all the satisfaction there was left me—and I could not hate him in his presence.

"'In a few days afterwards I saw his marriage announced in the newspapers! From that hour I grew gradually worse. I remained in Albemarle-street as long as these thin fingers had power to wreathe the flowers together; but when even that light employment became fatiguing and painful to me, I insisted on resigning my situation and quitting the house, knowing that your blessed country provides alike for the stranger and native, a home for the sick and poor.

"'It was very reluctantly that Madame Rozea allowed me to depart; but finding me firm in my intention, she herself obtained from one of the governors of this establishment an order for my instant admission.'

"The third day after Francesca had terminated her narrative, on paying her my accustomed visit, I was shocked to observe the fatal alteration that had taken place in her appearance! It was too certain that the hour was near which to her would have no successor in this world. She exhibited every symptom of rapidly approaching dissolution. She had, to a singular degree, that distressing restlessness which is so frequently the forerunner of death, when the spirit seems, as it were, to be impatient to emancipate itself from the thraldom of the flesh, and wing its way to its eternal home! Yet she retained perception and speech, and conversed with me cheerfully and rationally on religious subjects. Her mind was perfectly tranquil and resigned ; and when she found conversation fatiguing to her, I read to her out of that sacred volume which, during her illness, had been her constant hope, companion, and friend.

"'While thus engaged, she suddenly uttered a piercing shriek, and, making a violent effort to raise herself in bed, exclaimed—

"'No, no. I cannot be deceived ; 'tis he, 'tis he! Let him come and see where he has laid me! Yet, no ; I would forgive all now, even thee—oh, Frederick!'

"She pronounced the last word in a tone so vehement and peculiar, that a gentleman who was standing near, but whom I had not before noticed, with one of the medical attendants, turned hastily round, and I recognised him to be one of the governors of the hospital with whom I was well acquainted. On perceiving me he came up to the bed of Francesca saying—'

"'Did you wish to speak to me, Mr. Carruthers? I thought I heard you mention my name?'

"'No, my lord,' I replied ; 'I did not see you till this moment— it was not I who called you ; this poor girl. Why, Francesca, my dear child, what means this dreadful agitation?'

" I gazed on the dying girl in astonishment, and never can I forget the extraordinary expression of her countenance! If I may be allowed to use the phrase, I would say that life seemed to hover only in her eyes, the rest of her features being rigid and fixed, while her large dark eyes, stretched widely open, glared with a frightful brilliancy on the person before her. I feared, from the wildness of her look, that reason had fled for ever ; but, as though she had read my thoughts, she said—'

"'I am not mad ; he has done all he could to make me ; but I am not though. Would to heaven my senses had left me, long, long ago ! Don't you see he is too proud to remember me in an hospital.'

"'Who remember you, my dear?'

"'He—he, who stands before you there— Frederick Mortimer!'

" This was the first time that she had mentioned her lover's surname. It was also the governor's title. An indistinct recollection floated on my mind that Lord Mortimer had invariably evaded the subject of his tour to Italy whenever I had by chance recurred to it. I fixed my stern gaze on him, and perceived that he was strongly agitated, while I said—

"'My lord, is this young female known to you'   .

" He answered not ; but, after scrutinising her face with intense anxiety, exclaimed—

"'Gracious heaven ! it cannot be ! Yet that voice ; those eyes ! You are not—you dare not be Francesca Vitelli !'

" He caught her cold, bloodless hands, which she released from his grasp, and drew from her bosom a little miniature that she had preserved close to her heart.

"'Frederick,' she murmured, 'when you gave me—yes, me, Francesca, this—you are not deceived—you bade me keep it till my dying hour ; that hour has now come—take it, I have no further need of it. Yet one more kiss—it has been a sweet solace to me ; it never altered when you deserted me ; and when you coldly adverted your face, this still smiled on me, fondly as ever. Oh, promise me—yet the request is selfish—never to give it to another !'

"'Never, never, on my soul !'

"'Enough ! Now speak no more Fre-

derick. I fain would love you in my dying moments, and when I hear that fatal voice, all your broken vows rush on my recollection. I do not believe that you designed to kill me, yet you well knew that I never could survive neglect. But I thank you for my fate ; death hath peace—and what hath life in it so good as that ? You have a wife —does she love you? She never can so much as I have done. Ah, where are you gone ? I cannot see you—my sight grows dim. Oh, do not leave me, I implore you, Frederick !'

" He groaned aloud in anguish, as he pressed her icy, bloodless hands to his bosom, saying—

"'Leave you, my beloved ! would that I had never left you ! But, Francesca, you have not forgiven me. But I deserve your curses.'

"'I never cursed you,' she cried. 'May heaven pardon you as freely as I do. He (pointing to me) he will relate to you all that has happened to me He has been the best friend I have met with since I lost my parents. Oh, I shall soon meet them now ! I have suffered much since we parted, Frederick ; sickness, and poverty, and scorn : you were wont to say your poor Francesca was only born to be happy.'

"'For mercy's sake, forbear !' exclaimed Lord Mortimer ; 'drive me not to madness ; 'tis I have done all this. I have revelled in luxury, while yon—oh, 'tis too much ! had I but kept the oaths I swore to you, you might have been—'

"'Not happier than I am now, Frederick. Think of me sometimes ; on your deathbed remember me. Oh, all is dark around me, and my heart is cold—quite cold !—Am I in your arms still, Frederick ? I cannot feel you — farewell — Oh, mercy, mercy, heaven !'

" Her head fell back on Mortimer's bosom ; one short groan, one convulsive sob, and the struggle was over ! The soul was free ; and Francesca Vitelli at peace for ever !"

" Now hers was an excitable and nervous temperament," said Dr. Carruthers, " easily moved, and capable of deep feeling, as you have already seen, from what I have related of her."

" Poor thing," said Colonel Jack ; " like many others of her sex, she paid a dear penalty for loving not too wisely, but too well."

The doctor had not concluded his story many minutes before he was sent for to attend a patient ; wishing Colonel Jack good night, Dr. Carruthers took a somewhat hasty departure.

———

CHAPTER XCV.

MR. RICHARD FLEETWOOD'S PROCEEDINGS.

WE left Mr. Richard Fleetwood as he took his way hastily from his brother's home—his brothers!—the thought was such poignant agony to the *ci devant* baronet that he actually foamed with rage. He was not a complaisant man Mr. Richard—never had been, and it was not likely he would be now; that he was goaded on to almost madness; his only thought, therefore, as he took his way along the broad Acton Road, was how he might be revenged upon his enemies, as he chose to term them.

As to Colonel Jack, he did not intend to

No. 60.

rest till he had brought him to the gallows, as he publicly expressed it.

As to his brother Sir Reginald, he had hardly made up his mind what he should do with him. One thing was quite clear, he would keep his child from him.

"Ah, ah!" chuckled Mr. Richard Fleetwood to himself, "they can't get that," and so he walked on with hasty steps towards town uncertain as to what course he should pursue.

He rented the upper part of a house in Harley Street, Cavendish Square, to this place he bent his way; but from Acton to Harley Street was a long way—so far, indeed, that Mr. Fleetwood did not feel disposed to walk. He was tired, and for the first time found out that he was not so strong as he could wish to be.

His imprisonment in Alsatia, together with the excitement and disappointment upon his return home, that he felt weak—positively weak—perhaps for the first time in his life. He was too glad, therefore, to avail himself of a roadside house near to Shepherd's Bush. He went into the front parlour of this and rested himself, gazing out of the bay window to the green in front of the house. Several market carts and a waggon were at the door, drivers of which were handing round the mug of ale as they discussed the markets, the crops, and the state of the weather. Their bronzed and shining features elimina-nating health and happiness.

Mr. Richard Fleetwood looked at them, he was envious of their happiness.

"Pshaw!" he exclaimed ; "after all these fellows have no care, whilst I—I—am worn and fretted until life is robbed of all its charms. Would that I were some country clown."

Once more he sat himself down, and then rung the bell and ordered more refreshment, and in the meanwhile took up the newspaper —he skimmed over the contents of this, tur-ning over page after page listlessly enough —none of the news interested him. He glanced at the births, deaths, and marriages.

"Perdition!" exclaimed the baronet, as he threw the paper down in an uncontrollable rage. "A curse light on him—my curse— the bitter curse — of — a— broken-hearted man."

He fell with his face forward on the table and covered it with his hands. It was the account of the marriage of Henry Osborne, with the young and beautiful Miss Langford which had so suddenly overcome Mr. Richard Fleetwood.

He was only aroused from his prostrate and wretched state by the appearance of the waiter bringing in refreshments. Mr. Rich-ard Fleetwood began to partake of them, and in the course of half-an-hour he was surprised to see a number of persons taking their way along the road towards London ; some were on foot, others in carts and vehicles of various descriptions; and there never was heard such a noisy throng; so Mr. Fleetwood thought.

In the course of a few minutes several persons entered the parlour where he was seated ; and Mr. Fleetwood was enabled to gather from their conversation that there had been a match come off between two celebrated pedestrians about two miles down the road ; and the motley throng consisted of backers, betters, and spectators. In the course of a few minutes a man entered the room who stared curiously for a moment or so at the ci devant baronet. Mr. Fleetwood at once recognised his features—he was our old friend the Badger.

"Sir Richard, as I live," said Mr. Dyson, coming up to Mr. Fleetwood and respect-fully saluting.

"Ah, Dyson, it's you, eh?" said the party so addressed. "What's all this about?"

"A match has come off to-day, Sir Rich-ard," said the badger, "between trundling Jem and the old 'un. Jem has won by three yards"

"And you've backed the winner I hope," said Mr. Fleetwood.

"Why, thankee, Sir Richard, I haven't done amiss, if they all come up to the scratch. Are you on at all?"

"No, I knew nothing about it. I have been on the continent."

"Ah, so I heerd, leastways he heerd that you were going there," said Mr. Dyson, cor-recting himself.

In the course of a few moments the whole party sallied forth, and Mr. Fleetwood was once more left to himself and his own reflec-tions which, to say the truth, were miserable enough. After a while he rang the bell for the waiter, who, when he made his appear-ance, the baronet inquired if a postchaise could be had.

"The governor lets out traps," answered the waiter, looking hard at the speaker.

"Send him in then, or stay, ask him if I can have a vehicle to convey me to London. Do you hear?"

"Yes, sir," and away went the waiter, re-turning in the space of a few minutes, he said that one could be had in almost a quarter of an hour.

"Very good," answered Mr. Fleetwood. "Get it ready then."

In less than the quarter of an hour the vehicle was at the door, and Mr. Fleetwood soon found himself at his town residence.

Upon his arrival there he changed his attire, and for some time seemed as though uncertain about what should be his next proceedings. At one time he thought of waiting upon Sharpthorne, but upon recent consideration changed his mind. He had a livery servant and a brougham in Harley Street, and ordering this to be got ready he jumped in and desired the man to drive to Brixton.

In a short time the vehicle was at the last-named place, and Fleetwood ordered the driver to pull up at the nearest house of accommodation for man and horse.

He left the brougham and his servant at the roadside house, and struck off on foot down one of the lanes which led from the left hand.

After about a quarter of an hour's walk he came in front of a small cottage : opening the gate of the little garden in front, he knocked at the green door, and an old woman made her appearance.

"Mrs. Parker within?" inquired Mr. Fleetwood.

The old woman had been washing, for soapsuds were on her hands and arms.

"Yes, sir," she answered, as she wiped off the same from her arms with her apron. "Did you wish to see her?"

"Yes, if you please."

Mrs. Parker, a gentleman wishes to speak to you, called out the old woman in a shrill voice.

Another woman of about the middle age now presented herself, and made a respectful curtsey to the baronet, as she supposed her master to be still.

"Ah, Mrs. Parker—that is well," said Mr. Fleetwood.

"Walk in, Sir Richard, pray walk in," said the lady so addressed.

The baronet, that had been, entered the front parlour and seated himself.

"Now, Mrs. Parker, how fares your young charge?" said Mr. Fleetwood.

"Quite well, Sir Richard—quite well. I will fetch her, if you will excuse me for a few minutes."

"No, not now. I have a word or two to say to you."

"Yes, Sir Richard, certainly—I am all attention."

"First and foremost, Mrs. Parker, I must inform you that circumstances are changed with me."

"Indeed!" exclaimed the widow, for such in reality she was.

"Yes; my elder brother, whom we all supposed to be dead, has returned alive and well. I am, therefore, no longer Sir Richard Fleetwood, only plain Mr. Fleetwood, and have no wish to be addressed by a title to which I have now no claim."

"Dear me, Sir— I beg pardon, Mr. Fleetwood, but I am sorry to hear this."

"Yes; well, no matter, it's of no use regretting the past, or that which is inevitable. I have had enemies, Mrs. Parker, as we all have in this world, the best and the worst of us."

"Certainly, Mr. Fleetwood, that is true enough. I myself, for instance, when poor dear Mr. Parker was alive—"

"Yes, I know," said her visitor, with a deprecating gesture. "Of course, I remember—you told me; but let us proceed to business. In the first place, I will pay you for the last quarter's board for Jessie Bryant, for I have come to take her away with me."

"Take her away," exclaimed Mrs. Parker, in unfeigned astonishment. "I hope that there is no dissatisfaction? I am sure—"

"My dear madam, quite the reverse. I am perfectly satisfied that you have been a mother to Jessie; but there are reasons, which it would be idle and superfluous to enter into now, which make it imperative for me to remove her. This is my only reason, and at the same time permit me to say, that I am fully sensible of your kindness to the child, and in after years I hope she will not forget it, but entertain a lively recollection of— her second mother, as I may with truth term you."

"Thank you, Sir—, I mean, Mr. Fleetwood; I am sure I am much flattered by your good opinion. It makes me feel proud when I hear you say this much."

Mr. Fleetwood counted out upon the table the amount due to the woman, and in addition to that sum, made her a present of a couple of guineas.

She then left the apartment, and returned with a little girl between three and four years old.

The child looked at Mr. Fleetwood with a degree of awe, with which he had at all times inspired her, whenever he had paid a visit to the widow's cottage.

"There, go to your uncle, like a good girl," said Mrs. Parker, "go to your uncle—do you hear, Jessie?"

The child did as the woman had requested, and Mr. Fleetwood took her on his knee. She turned her large lustrous eyes up to his in an inquiring glance, half of fear, and half of submission.

Parting her glossy ringlets, and patting her cheek, Mr. Fleetwood endeavoured to reassure her. He then said to her, kindly enough—

"So, my sweet Jessie, you are going to leave your kind friend and protector, Mrs. Parker."

At this the countenance of the child became sorrowful, but she said nothing, only hanging down her head dejectedly.

"Yes, you are going with your uncle, Jessie. Now don't look so sorrowful, my dear, for it is for your own good."

At this the child burst into tears, and it was some time before she could be pacified. Eventually she was taken away, dressed in her little bonnet and cloak, and in the course of another half hour was taken by her uncle to the house where he had left his servant with his brougham, and shortly afterwards she was on her road to London.

It will be hardly necessary to tell the reader that Jessie Bryant, as she was called, was no other than the daughter of Sir Reginald and Lady Fleetwood.

———

CHAPTER XCVI.

THE HIGHWAYMEN ON THE ROAD.—HENRY OSBORNE'S MARRIAGE.

MRS. HALFORD had been interred with much ceremony—days had passed over since this event, which were gloomy and sorrowful enough to Colonel Jack; but it has often been remarked that time, in the end, wears away the traces of grief, as it does with love, hate, or any other of the human passions—the colonel's daughter was placed under the charge of her grandmother, agreeable to the request of Mrs. Halford—Curson had taken her down to the old lady; who cheerfully undertook the charge of her. And, as Colonel Jack was not a man to let the rust of inactivity eat its way into his frame, he was soon once more afield, and at his vocation.

"Henry Osborne had during this time led the young and beauteous Honora Langford to the altar. It would be idle and unnecessary to describe all the particulars of the gorgeous wedding. Chronicles of this description are the same thing over and over again. The young and blushing bride—the handsome bridegroom—the beauteous bridesmaids—the throbbing hearts—the sumptuous repast—the distinguished guests—the sympathetic tears of the females—joy for the present, and hope for the future. All these are part and parcel of the attendants on a wedding.

With Honora and Osborne, there was, and had been throughout, a deep seated attachment—one that, it is to be hoped, will strengthen with time. Theirs was no mercenary match, but prompted by the purer springs of the human heart. But, even such a one as this does not always resist the destroying influence of time. Squabshot was, of course there. He was certainly not a sentimental, or indeed a dignified man; but as we have already seen, he was a thorough kind hearted though eccentric individual.

Miss Staunton, was also one of the party; and, indeed, it would be a long task to enumerate all the fashionable notabilities who honoured the nuptials of Osborne and Miss Langford with their presence. Wealth and position in society at all times finds its votaries; and, both of these Osborne now had. After his marriage he went with his bride to the continent to make the grand tour as it is termed, and Mr. Squabshot, was therefore left once more alone in his apartments in Goswell-street. He had never at any time been what is termed a marrying man; indeed, he had affected to sneer at the holy institution of matrimony as a state of elysium, which his position in the world and natural organisation had totally unfitted him for;

but since his introduction to Miss Staunton, he felt himself "knocked over," to use his own phraseology; and in the silence of his own apartments in Goswell-street, began to chew the cud of many a bitter fancy. Leaving him to pursue his own reflections, we must turn our thoughts to Colonel Jack, and his doings.

In the days of which we write, society was very different to what it is at the present time. The race of highwaymen have now passed away; and, it is only through their history handed down to us by writers of the time, that we are enabled to gather the particulars of their doings. Gas, steam, and a metropolitan police have been mainly instrumental in doing away with the race of highwaymen, and the consequence is, that what was done by bold daring, is now accomplished by chicanery and art. Believe me, there is no more honesty in the world at present than there was when the knights of the road levied contributions from the passing wayfarers. As a strange contrast to the doings of our hero, we subjoin the following account, extracted from a paper of the period, of how a robbery was effected in our own day:—

There are few more accomplished artists of any sort in great Britain, or anywhere else, than the proficient London thief. Living by his wits, ingeniously plotting a robbery with consummate ability, one of the very few who have eluded the unwearing toils in which the quick-eyed officers of justice have involved thousands upon thousands who have ventured on the same perilous career, he must live a life of at once intense excitement and painful apprehension We speak not of the burglar or street robber, but of the professional swindler and thief, who does two-thirds of his work with his head, and the other third with address. Let science take ever so wild a flight, and seem to leave him too far behind to follow, it is not long before he is abreast of his victim—his fellow-man. The giant, steam, shot off from him with the whole industrious race, leaving the lumbering mail-coach stripped of its hitherto delayed and exposed passengers. The London thief took as great a start as science. He stole the gentleman's ticket while he twirled it in his fingers; he robbed the "exquisite" while he stared at the passengers; he picked the lady's pocket ere she reached the train, and his right and left fellow-voyagers as soon as they took their places. Nay, more, he left the carriage while rushing onwards at a speed of sixty miles an hour, and robbed the post-office under the very eyes of half a dozen guards, where, if detected, escape was impossible, where a moment was an age in the measure of success, and a false step was death.

But it was the London thief on the old road

in 1822, that we professed to tell a tale about; and a tale true to the very letter; for one of the parties, who had nearly been the victim of a false suspicion, is still alive, and we dare say will peruse these particulars with some little interest.

A young man engaged as a traveller for a mercantile house, left York on a Friday evening inside the London, Stockton, and Newcastle mail—the night bleak and stormy, in December, 1822. It was his first journey as a commercial gent. There was not a single passenger in or out until they reached Easinwold, when an outside got up. The mail proceeded on to Thirsk, where the coachman and guard said to the stranger that, as the night was exceedingly wet and stormy, he might get inside if he wished. He did so without any remark, and when inside he wrapped himself up in his large dreadnought coat, and turned his back to the young traveller, who, despite sundry courteous endeavours to elicit his views on the condition of the country and the state of the weather, neither saw his face nor heard his voice. A grunt of acquiescence measured his loquacity, till these efforts at being pleasant died away. Nothing else transpired till the coach reached Stockton, where a young man approached, and inquired if there was room inside? The reply was, "plenty." The stranger in the dreadnought, by this time left, paying the coachee, but remarking that if he did not find a friend he expected to see, he would return before the coach started. He disappeared in the darkness of the night, but he only made a circuit round the coach, and stood couched like a tiger at the opposite door. He was a London thief, and a sharp one, who had laid his plans well. The young gentleman who asked about the room was a banker's confidential clerk, in charge of a very large sum of money, upwards of twenty thousand pounds, in gold and notes. Our young traveller also came out here, and was warming himself at the fire, when, as a kindness to the coachman and guard, the banker's clerk ordered some brandy, and while it was being brought he took out his case with his own hand and placed it securely under his seat, shutting carefully the door of the empty coach, but before he had left the coach six paces, the London thief had opened the opposite door, and was off with the treasure. The horn blew, the passengers were seated, the mail started, and nothing occurred between Stockton and Sunderland, except that an old woman got a lift of six miles, and left at Castle Eden, without incurring any observation. When the coach arrived at Sunderland, the young traveller's destination, he had his luggage carried to the principal inn.

The banker's clerk was now left alone, and was driven onward in fancied security, when, verging towards the conclusion of his journey, he took the liberty of looking that his box was safe, and to his astonishment and horror found it gone! There was an instant and eager search, and a consultation with coachee and guard led to the confident and apparently inevitable conclusion that the young traveller was the robber, and that the old woman was an accomplice, these being the only passengers after the banker took his seat.

The banker, who was an energetic person, instantly ordered a coach and four and drove back as fast as wheels could carry him. Here his suspicion was tenfold confirmed. The young traveller, finding Saturday market-day at Sunderland, could do no business; and like many young travellers, determined not to lose a day, he took a gig to Newcastle, where he found it market day also. Again foiled, he hired a horse and rode to Hexham, twenty-two miles, where he called upon some customers of the house he represented, and after a little business returned to Newcastle, jaded and fatigued in the extreme—had tea, and off to bed. Unwilling to lose the opportunity of seeing a friend he had at North Shields, he spent Sunday there.

By this time the banker was on his trail, and had magistrates and police out on various routes tracing him like a fox, while suspicion deepened at every turn and winding. The banker, with his party, reached Shields a few hours after him, and searched all the inns and many houses, but the young traveller's friend chanced to be far above suspicion, and the pursuers were quite at fault, for the gentleman drove the object of their pursuit past them next day in his own carriage to Sunderland.

Here the young gentleman transacted his business very much to his mind. He then started on the outside of the coach for Newcastle; but here he was soon discovered.

The stake rendered him of some importance. Two policemen in plain clothes were taken up on the coach beside him. Six expresses passed the coach on the road, summoning the magistrates and the police along the road, and making sure arrangements that escape should be impossible.

On the countenances of all it was plain that they knew their game was in view.

Four policemen were stationed at Gateshead, and as many on Newcastle-bridge, and a tolerable party waited the arrival of the coach at the Turf Hotel; but not a word or movement showed the young traveller that he was exciting any interest.

He was allowed to leave the coach and proceed to the Turk's Head, where he immediately ordered dinner, and retired. Before he got his coat off, however, the waiter gave him notice that he was wanted in the traveller's room. He said it was impossible, as he did not know a single individual in Newcastle; but on the waiter giving his name as that of the gentleman wanted, he proceeded to the other room, where Forsyth met him politely, locked the door, and expressed his regret at the necessity of leading him to prison.

It was some time before the young man could be made to understand Forsyth's interference, the charge and the suspicion against himself; and when he did, he staggered back and fainted.

He was taken before the magistrates of Newcastle, and the more the case was investigated, the more conclusive seemed the evidence, coupled with his flight, and the fact that in his declaration he forgot to mention the old woman, who could nowhere be traced, and who was now decidedly regarded as an accomplice.

Bail was consequently refused till the references he gave in Glasgow were applied to. But much to the wonderment of all ready to pronounce him guilty, the replies were all to the effect that the thing was next to impossible—that his character was unimpeachable—that respectable men pledged their existence for his innocence—and that the writers would bail him to any reasonable amount.

On this bonds were immediately executed, and the unfortunate youth was again at liberty; but till his dying day, if it has not arrived, and if so it must have been recently (for when we heard of him last he was a most respectable citizen of Glasgow) he could never forget the feeling of degredation and injured pride that rose within him as when liberated, he passed out, with tears in his eyes, through a crowd of spectators, eager to catch a glimpse of the clever robber; and one desperate character, more acutely cruel than his fellows, gave him a hurrah for his cleverness in baffling justice.

The suspicion, groundless as it was, gave him great uneasiness. Starting in life, it haunted him awake and asleep; and a joyful heart had he when he learned that the harpies of the criminal law, "harking back" over the false scent, had drawn remark upon the passenger with the dreadnought coat leaving the coach, and had ascertained that on the night in question a chaise and four had taken him from the next stage to London, without losing much time by the way, or leaving any trace behind.

Advertisements were immediately inserted in the London papers, offering a handsome reward for a box lost at Stockton on the night in question, containing a large sum of money (the amount mentioned), but no reply was made till a month elapsed after the bank had ceased advertising.

Then, however, came a letter from London saying that the writer had observed several advertisements regarding a box lost at Stockton; that the writer knew of a box lost there at the time mentioned, but it contained a larger sum than was named, and therefore, probably, was not the same; if it were, however, it would be returned for a draft for two thousand pounds, and seven hundred pounds more for expenses; but in the meantime there must be forwarded a bond of security for the fulfilment of the contract, and no questions were to be asked.

This looked like compounding a felony, so a compromise was attempted, but it was never answered.

The full terms were then concluded, and the bond of security despatched, and eight hours before the mail that carried it returned, a person with all the address of a gentleman, with an easy and confident air, walked into the bank with the identical box, and an open note, which told its own tale, simply soliciting an answer.

On opening the box the contents were found precisely as lost. The stranger was paid over two thousand seven hundred pounds, and left the bank with a bow to the manager, but without uttering a syllable, and posted back to London as he came, with four horses.

A few days afterwards the manager received from the same quarter a case of excellent wine, value about thirty pounds, thanking him for his good faith, complimenting him on his business habits, telling him that the expenses of his party in the transaction had been heavy, as they had made four attempts before they succeeded, and concluding by an offer of similar services.

The account of this artful robbery may be relied upon as an actual occurence. It is in direct opposition to the course pursued by Colonel Jack, and it is probable that our hero would have scorned to have any hand in such a transaction. Every man has his own code of honour, and no doubt this description of robbery would be against that of the one embraced by the colonel.

Once more on the back of his favourite Ada, Colonel Jack felt himself imbued with fresh life. Action to him was the very soul of his existence—without it, his spirit chafed and fretted in hopeless sorrow.

As he inhaled the fresh breeze, along the road which led to Lewisham, our hero felt his spirits elated with every motion of his matchless mare. He was accompanied by Galdie and Hackett.

"Hurrah!" exclaimed the colonel; "once more, my boys, we are on to our work—once more we have left smoky and gloomy London to take care of itself. So ho! Ada, lass, your fleet limbs are ready to bound at the first stroke of the spur. Woa, so ho! lass, gently, girl, gently."

The three highwaymen trotted gently along the road, conversing together upon past events. Presently they arrived at a sign post, which stood where three roads branched off in different directions, here they halted.

"Which road will he take, think you?" said the colonel to Hackett.

"One of these two," said the latter, pointing to those to which he alluded.

"Umph! then we'll e'en wait here till my gentleman makes his appearance. Here, Slott, lay down boy."

The dog did as his master requested, and crouched himself beneath the shadow of an adjacent hedge.

The highwaymen then drew their horses into a lane, and remained there quietly enough for some time. In the course of half an hour or so, the noise of carriage wheels was heard coming from the road which led from town. The vehicle appeared to be a lumbering one, for its progress was evidently slow enough.

"Hist!" exclaimed the colonel; "hist! What is that?"

"Sounds like a drag of some sort," said Hackett.

"Drag it is, and no mistake," said Galdie. "And more than that. It's a two horse trap, or I am much mistaken."

"It's his carriage," exclaimed Hackett, as he peered over the hedge, and caught sight of an old-fashioned heavy vehicle coming along the road.

"His carriage, by all that's lucky," said the colonel. "Now, gentlemen, each to his duty."

In a few minutes the carriage was in sight, and in a minute or so more it was within a few yards of the spot where the highwaymen were stationed. Slott, whose eyes had been watching those of his master's, came out from his hiding place.

"On to them, boy," said the colonel, and in another second the near side horse of the carriage was brought to the ground by the sudden onslaught of Slott.

The carriage came to a sudden halt—a cry of rage and fear rose from the antediluvian coachman—a shout issued from the interior of the vehicle—and then the coachman endeavoured to put his horses together. This, however, was a vain and futile effort, and as he was thus engaged, a head protruded from the window of the carriage, and the owner thereof said, in a querelous tone of voice—

"What is the matter, Theodore?—why are you stopping?"

"I don't know, Sir Peter," said the man, tugging at his reins. "I think it be a mad dog."

"Oh, goodness me!" exclaimed Sir Peter Primley, for that was the name of the elderly gentleman in the carriage. "Mad dog!"

And he shut up the window with a loud slam.

His man might be bitten by twenty mad dogs, but for a knight of the shire to be attacked by a delirious canine quadruped, it was not to be thought of for a moment.

"Dog ought to be muzzled—all dogs!" exclaimed Sir Peter; "and I'll never rest till I move Parliament to pass a bill to that effect."

"Don't shut the window, Sir Peter," said Hackett, trotting up to the side of the carriage, pistol in hand.

To have seen the countenance of the knight at that time, would have done your heart good. Surprise, consternation, terror, and half suppressed rage, were all depicted on his thin and pale features. He wore a black skull cap, from beneath which his thin grey hair came out on either side of his face; he had on also a pair of gold spectacles, and a white cravat.

Hackett quietly opened the door, and favoured the knight with a sight of his pistol. No sooner did he catch sight of this persuader, than he flew to the other side of the carriage, and hid himself behind a young and very pretty female.

"Assault and battery!—murder!—treason!" exclaimed the alarmed Sir Peter Primley. "Theodore, why don't you drive on? Gentlemen, what is it you want?"

This last observation was addressed to the highwaymen, not that he saw more than one at present, but he judged there was at least a dozen, so great was his fear.

"Now let us understand one another, Sir Peter Primley," said the colonel, who now opened the other window of the carriage.

"Gracious goodness! you know me!" said Sir Peter, in still greater alarm.

"Yes, Sir Peter, we do know you. You have a cash box in the carriage, I believe?"

"No, no, indeed I have not—no such thing—you are misinformed."

"Oh, yes, but you have, my dear sir. Shame of you to tell an untruth—you, a knight, too—shame, Sir Peter. Come, now, hand out this same cash box."

"I won't—I can't—I haven't got any, I tell you."

"But I say you have," said the colonel. "It's no use trying to deceive us—we know everything. In that box is the dower of your ward and niece."

"Dower!—goodness me, Isabel!" exclaimed the knight, popping his head out of the folds of his niece's dress, and gazing into her face.

"You will compel us to have recourse to harsh measures, Sir Peter," said our hero, "which will be painful to our feelings; time presses—hand out the box. My friend here is about to be married, and he only wants a little ready money to begin the world with."

"You would never rob a young lady of her marriage portion ?" said Sir Peter.

"Not if she were going to marry the man of her choice," said the colonel; "but as you are about to hand her over to a mercenary wretch, who is altogether unworthy of her, I have no compunction in taking that which is better in my hands than his."

"Mercenary wretch—it's false, sir—Mr. Slopperton is a gentleman, and a man of honour."

"Man of fiddlesticks!" exclaimed the colonel. "I appeal to Miss Isabel, if I am not speaking the truth ?"

"Oh, gentlemen, don't ask me," said the young lady. "I—that is—I do not like Mr. Slopperton—uncle knows I do not."

"You silly jade," exclaimed Sir Peter. "You ought to be ashamed of yourself to side with such highwaymen—ruffians—cut-throats—"

"I'm sure they seem very gentlemanly people," said the young lady. "More so than—"

"Hush, hush, child," said the knight.

"Again I say, time presses," said the colonel, as he inserted his pistol into the carriage, and pointed it at the knight.

"Oh. don't, pray don't, you'll hurt the young lady," said Sir Peter, "indeed you will. You can't fire without hitting her. Oh, don't, pray don't! Go away !"

"Ah, ah ! go away indeed; well that is too good a joke, but as we don't want to hurt the young lady, why, you see Sir Peter, we shall be compelled to drag you out and hand you over to the dog."

"Oh mercy, mercy, gentlemen ! here's the box," said the knight, now in a perfect frenzy : "take anything—take all."

"Your chain and watch," said Hackett.

They were both handed over to the highwayman, and the young lady handed her jewelery to the colonel at the same time.

"No, Miss Isabel," said Colonel Jack; "keep your trinkets, we do not rob one of the fairest of her sex."

"Oh, how kind—how generous of you !" said the young lady.

"Will you be pleased to step out of the carriage a minute or so," said the colonel.

"Who, me ?" inquired Miss Isabel.

"If you please."

"Certainly."

She did as the highwayman requested, and had a long conversation with Colonel Jack apart from his companions, from her smiles and affability she seemed well pleased

with her interview ; the colonel handed her into the carriage, took her hand in his, kissed it, and raising his hat to Sir Peter Primley, the three knights of the road galloped off at full speed ; for by this time the noise of horses hoofs were heard coming along the road. And the colonel and his companions thought it best to make good their retreat.

They galloped some four or five more miles on the road, put up at a well-known house of theirs, and betook themselves to the parlour thereof.

They were all in high spirits ; and as the hour was early there were several guests in the parlour of the public-house. Among them was a small individual who had been conversing, so it seemed, with the other inmates of the room, upon murders, robberies, and crimes of various descriptions.

Soon after our hero and his companions came in he entered into a narrative which he declared was a true one ; and as it is possessed of a considerable amount of interest we reserve it for our succeeding chapter.

CHAPTER XCVII.

THE MURDER DISCOVERED BY A DREAM.

"My grandfather," said the narrator, "had an elder brother a substantial manufacturer, of whom he ever spoke in the highest praise, and in a manner which showed that his esteem arose no less from a consciousness of his personal merits as a man than his feelings as a brother.

"It was the habit of my grandsire to visit us annually, or oftener, as his duties permitted him. On one of these occasions he was accompanied by his brother, who at that time lived at a distant part of the kingdom. He was an elderly man, partly and somewhat magisterial in his appearance, but of gentle manners. I can just remember his person—he wore a well-powdered wig, with three tiers of curls, a Lord Townley-cut coat, huge flaps to his waistcoat-pocket, and a pair of immense silver buckles in his shoes. As he sat after dinner in a cumbrous arm-chair, enjoying the soothing influence of his pipe and tobacco, he looked the very picture of honest old English luxury. I might, however, from lapse of time, when aided by no other *technica memoria*, have forgotten both him and his appendages of wig, flap-pockets, silver shoe-buckles, pipe and all, but for two circumstances : his having presented me with a handsome silver watch, and his recital of a tale, in which he was himself concerned when a young man, and which for years afterwards was deeply engraven on my mind,

on account of its mysterious development of a dark and diabolical transaction. Years, however, passed away, and my great uncle died, and even the tale itself began to fade from my memory, and made me sometimes fancy that as I was at the time it was related but a child, the whole might have been a mere fiction, and that I had jumbled it up with some other tale of mystery, of which among nurses and domestics there is no lack. It happened, however, the last visit my grandfather (who lived to the verge of extreme old age, but is now gathered to his fathers) paid us, the conversation taking a ghostly turn, I reverted to the story which my uncle had many years ago related whilst sitting after dinner in the very arm-chair then occupied by my reverend ancestor, and

No. 61.

requested the latter as far as his memory would permit, to give a circumstantial detail of the whole affair, which he did as follows—

" ' Although a period of some length has intervened since the adventure to which my brother alluded took place, yet it has ever since made an indellible impression on my memory. After the same manner in which your uncle related it to you, so he did to me when the matter had just transpired. I was then at college, and as often as I have had conversation with him as touching the singular adventure, he has never varied in the substantial part of his narrative. He was at that time the junior partner of an extensive manufactory, and in that capacity was appointed to travel a certain round every year. As he was recently married, his wife usually accompanied him on these occasions. It happened at the close of one summer's day, or rather towards nightfall, he arrived for the first time in his life at a small obscure town in the northern part of Suffolk, and alighted with his wife at the commercial inn, which happened to be just at the entrance of the place. As he was a stranger, and withal fatigued with his journey, he determined to betake himself to his supper and then to repose; accordingly, having given the necessary orders, which were promptly obeyed, he dispatched his meal and soon retired to rest—resolving, like a thrifty man of business, to spend the next morning amongst his customers. He was not long before he fell into a profound slumber; but during his sleep he had a dream, which, although by no means extraordinary in itself, yet from the events that followed, and its singular coincidence with those events, might be considered as one of those wonderful instances of a providential interposition in the affairs of men, for the purpose of revealing a series of crime which has long remained buried in oblivion to all but the criminals themselves. He fancied that he had just alighted at the very inn in the middle of the day, and instead of entering the house, he amused himself by walking up the town and observing, with the curious eye of a stranger, everything worthy of notice—he came to the end of the main-street, and turning the corner to go down another, which appeared to lead out of the village, the parish church came in sight. After pausing a minute or two to mark its structure, he went on following the track of the second street, until it led him into the high road, the opposite end of the town by which he entered. He continued his walk, however, till he reached a lane; feeling as if urged on by some strong impulse, he turned down its narrow winding till he reached a cottage of miserable and desolate appearance. He entered the garden, where nothing met his sight but a well—but on looking down, he saw to his horror the resemblance of a human skeleton. When he awoke, he endeavoured to shake off the disagreeable recollections of his dreams by calling to mind the various engagements of the day, and as it was high summer and a clear bright morning, he rose early for the purpose of taking an airing and enjoying the freshness of the cooling breeze. Being, as I said before, a man of business and activity, he did not suffer the unpleasant nature of his nightly slumbers to disturb the duties of his waking moments; accordingly, having dressed himself, he sallied forth on his morning ramble. The sun was mounting brightly in the clear blue firmament; the birds chirped merrily from the trees, and the lark soared high and gaily leaving a train of song behind

him, whilst the sweet air borne over fields of clover and meadows of newly-made hay brought freshness and hilarity to the waking world. It was now about seven o'clock, and as my brother strolled along, sniffing the morning air, and turning his eyes from one side to the other, scanning the busy apprentices opening their shops, and house-maids scouring the steps of the doors, or rubbing the brass knockers that glistened in the morning sun, something struck him that the shape and appearance of the street and houses were not altogether strange to him, and as he passed along an indistinct idea of something like the present scene floated across his brain. 'Surely,' said he to himself, 'there is something marvellous in all this; I cannot have seen this town before, and yet it somehow calls up an association of former ideas. He had now reached the end of the street, and as he turned down another at right angles, a church presented itself directly opposite him; he started, and for the first time his dream shot across his recollection. He stood gazing for a few seconds wondering at the strange coincidence, he then walked onwards, and every step brought something that bore a striking resemblance to the objects of his dream.

"'Am I dreaming now?' he inwardly exclaimed, with a slight degree of trepidation creeping over him, 'or is the whole scene to be realized?'

"He now felt himself as if spellbound, and giving way to the impulse, he hurried on till he reached the identical lane. Nature was pouring forth her richest beauties; but the sparkling field and feathered choruses were unheeded by my poor brother; he was not a superstitious man, and was too much a man of the world to enter deeply into the metaphysical doctrine of spiritual agency, yet, as he told me, he felt as if under the influence of enchantment.

"Although, as he expected, he found the hovel at some distance down the lane, in the same condition that he had seen it in his dream, yet when he beheld for the first time its dark and lonely aspect, he started from the loathsome spectacle, associated as it was in his dream with a deed of foul mystery. He essayed to reconnoitre the garden, which seemed cold, dark, and neglected, and expected every moment to behold the well, but was disappointed,—this one subject was wanting to perfect the prophetic vision.

"As he returned to the inn, a thousand strange thoughts came crowding upon him. He could not feel satisfied at the idea of abandoning the adventure so singularly commenced, and at last came to the conclusion of sifting the affair to the very bottom.

"While they were at breakfast, his wife, observing his unusual abstraction, eagerly inquired the cause, whereupon he related the whole of his mysterious adventure. At her suggestion he was induced to call in the landlord, that he might furnish them with what information he could respecting the house and its inhabitants.

"The host immediately attended the summons, and, after asking several unimportant questions, which were answered with a circumstantial detail in proportion to their insignificance, my brother came nearer the point by inquiring to whom the cottage belonged, which stood by itself in the narrow lane, and occupation of its tenants.

"The landlord looked rather surprised at the apparent interest which so wretched a hovel had excited in his guest ; and answered, that he believed it was inhabited by an old man and his daughter ; but such was their mode of life and unsocial habits, that few knew or cared about them, separated as they were, from all the town beside, by situation and unneighbourly feeling.

"This account rather stimulated than allayed my brother's curiosity ; and, having finished his breakfast, he resolved to call at once upon the magistrate, in order that he might obtain further advice upon the matter. He just reached the door as this official person was stepping into his carriage.

"My brother requested a few minutes audience, which the other, seeing perhaps from the earnestness of the demand that it must be upon a matter of some moment, politely assented to, hoping, however, the conference would be brief, as business of importance then demanded his attention.

"The other was not long in delivering his errand, for he had a peculiar habit of telling a tale in a straightforward manner, without a simile or metaphor. At the close, however, the magistrate seemed struck with its singularity, and regretted that he could not afford him his personal attendance at the investigation ; but, if it were his wish, he would allow a couple of constables to attend him in any search that he might be inclined to make.

"To this proposal my brother readily assented ; and, having thanked the magistrate for his politeness and attention, went, accompanied by the two officers, who had already received their instructions from their superior.

"The trio soon reached the cottage, and entered the patch of ground by which it was surrounded. Here they were met by the old man, who, in a surly forbidding manner (upon the constables making known their intention to search his house and premises), told them—

"'They might do as they pleased.'

"They entered the abode, where everything around wore the appearance of extreme misery ; they examined every place to no purpose, for they could find nothing of a suspicious nature, and every effort to discover the least signs of a well were unavailing.

"Having been engaged for some time in a fruitless labour, they were about to return, much to the disappointment of my brother ; when it so happened, that a number of people, whose curiosity had been moved at the appearance of the constables going on some official errand with a strange gentleman, followed them to the spot.

"By this time there were about a dozen collected, besides a proportionable complement of children. It soon became rumoured among the wondering group that the object of investigation was the discovery of a well.—

"'A well ? a well ?' exclaimed an old woman, pressing forward, 'why, what can they want with it—there has been none to my recollection for nearly forty years ? I remember it, however, as though 'twere yesterday, and many a time have I and Gaffer——'s daughter amused ourselves by throwing down stones to hear the rolling echo that sounded like thunder.

"This was sufficient to call up the feelings of my brother to a fresh state of excitement.—

"'Where was the spot ?' said he, eagerly.

"'Where ?' re-echoed the old woman— 'why, as near as I can guess, you are now standing over its mouth.'

"'It must be so,' he mentally answered.

"Upon this piece of information they went to work with renewed ardour, and by the assistance of the by-standers the earth was soon cleared away, till they came to some planks and brick-work closely cemented. A pick-axe, however, being procured, this obstruction was soon removed, and the aperture was distinctly seen.

"'I thought that must be the spot, or I was much mistaken,' said the old informant, as she moved away, thinking, doubtless, it was merely some caprice of the owner in having the well re-opened : 'he was a cursed old fool for blocking it up, and thus gave himself the trouble of trudging a quarter of a mile every day for fresh water.

"It was some considerable time before they could fix the apparatus for a decent ; but when the grappling irons were fastened, and the rope let down, there was a breathless silence in the interval ; the line was drawn up several times without anything but rubbish attached to it.

"At length, however, something heavier than usual was laid hold on by the grapplers —an uncouth box, or trunk, was drawn up, scarcely held together by reason of its damp and rotten state. They managed, notwithstanding, to land it ; but when it was broken open, a sight presented itself that filled the by-standers, who were not prepared for the spectacle, with horror—it proved to be the skeleton of a child !

" ' The sensation of my brother cannot be decribed.—' This is a foul deed, neighbours.' observed one of the constables—watch the body a few minutes' and we will return.'

They instantly darted into the cottage, secured the old man, who, although past eighty years of age, made an obstinate defence. They succeeded, however, in binding his hands, and leaving him to the charge of two men, recommenced their search in the apartment.

" In a little time they had removed a pile of fagots, and other lumber that lay heaped up against the wall, and here they found, crouching like a hunted cat, a woman about sixty, of wretched appearance, the daughter of the old prisoner. It seems that at first sight of the officers she had, from a consciousness of guilt, thus secreted herself. The whole village was by this time gathered round the house, each one having something to say, and withal declaring they always entertained a suspicion that all was not right. The prisoners were brought before the same magistrate whom my brother had met in the morning.

" On their examination, although the older culprit maintained a dogged silence, yet the woman, overcome by a sense of her situation, confessed the child to have been hers by her own father ; that shortly after its birth they conspired to destroy it; and, to prevent detection, secured it in a strong box, and threw it down the well—then, by way of further precaution against any accidental discovery, they closed its mouth with boards, and bricks, and garden earth. They had lived together ever since like two proscribed spirits, shut out from all intercourse with their fellow men. A crime so dark and revolting, accompanied by so many extraordinary circumstances which led to its disclosure, created a strong sensation at the time among the inhabitants of the little town, who looked up to it as a special instance of the finger of Providence, in appointing a stranger to become the discoverer of a crime that had been committed among them nearly forty years previous.

" It remains only to be said that the guilty parties were tried and executed at the county town shortly after ; the house was pulled down, and the well being filled up, the whole premises was laid out and made part of an adjoining field. My brother, who usually visited that town twice a year for a considerable time afterwards, always found a warm reception from the magistrate and the principal inhabitants of the place ; and it was through the interest of the former that I obtained the living, and have preached so long in that very church which formed so prominent an object in the landscape of my brother's strange adventure.'

———

CHAPTER XCVIII.

SCENE AT ILSCOMB COURT.—ISABEL'S INTERVIEW WITH COLONEL JACK.

SIR PETER PRIMLEY, after his encounter with Colonel Jack, proceeded in his carriage to Ilscomb Court, which was situated some few miles from where the affray with the highwaymen had taken place.

Enraged beyond measure at the robbery which had taken place, Sir Peter did what many weak-minded individuals would have done under similar circumstances—he commenced upbraiding his niece for the part she had chosen to take in the transaction.

It was mainly her fault, so Sir Peter said ; had it not have been for her patronage of the lawless freebooters, he would no doubt have been able to overawe them. It would perhaps have been difficult for him to have accounted how this would have been accomplished, but he chose to make the assertion, and having once done so, he persisted in it.

The money which the colonel and his companions had taken, was considerable, amounting to nearly three thousand pounds in gold and notes.

The latter Sir Peter stopped at the bank next day. But we all, or at any rate most of us, know what stopping notes are at our present time, and at the period of which we write, such a course was all but useless in detecting the practical robber or thief.

Of course, it is next to impossible to prevent the notes being circulated ; for instance, in the colonel's case, his friend the Badger was good to pass them to some of his continental friends, and then all traces would of necessity become lost.

Nevertheless, Sir Peter hugged to himself the pleasing solace that he had done a very clever thing, and one that would in all probability result in the total discomfiture of Colonel Jack.

Ilscomb Court was an old manorial building, surrounded by a large wall, which enclosed the grounds, which were in front and at the sides of the mansion, which was built of that peculiarly red brick, so frequently made use of in the erection of early English houses.

A thick row of chesnuts ran on either side of the wide gravel walk, or rather road, which led up to the principal entrance of the domain.

The garden in front was kept with scrupulous care. Not a stray pebble was allowed to be on the gravel walks—the mould of the flower-beds was carefully raked—the shrubs were well trimmed—and the velvetty lawn, soft as a mole's back, and green as emeralds, invited the beholder to stretch himself on its surface, and muse, like Jaques, upon the affairs of the outer world.

Sir Peter was a widower, without any children: but he had, however, a maiden sister, many years younger than himself, who officiated as housekeeper or mistress of the palatial establishment.

This virginal representative of the Primley line was a lady of starch principles, and rigid in her management of her brother's household. Occasionally a flirting, forward hussey, one of the domestics, would shock and scendalize the maiden lady, who was generally deaf to the appeals of her niece to look with a lenient eye upon the two susceptible damsel.

The carriage containing Sir Peter and his ward at length arrived at the outer gate of the mansion.

The deep-toned bell was rung, and in a minute or so the head of the groom appeared at the small gate. When he observed his master's carriage, the two large gates were thrown open, and the vehicle was driven in up the centre roadway, and stopped at the door of the house.

All this while the baying of the dog in the yard was heard.

A shudder passed through the frame of Sir Peter Primley, when he remembered the ferocious eyes and significant fangs of Slott, and he felicitated himself at having arrived safe home, which was at any rate some comfort, all circumstances considered.

Miss Dorcas Primley, Sir Peter's sister, made her appearance at the hall door when she heard the carriage stop. Handing her niece out, and taking charge of one or two small packages, she went into the front room with the latter, leaving her brother to follow at his leisure.

Sir Peter was a little man, as we have before observed—a very little man, it might be said: but he was, however, great in his own estimation, and his dignity had been sadly hurt in the affray with the highwaymen; this in itself was bad enough, but worse remained behind—he was the loser of nearly three thousand pounds.

As he alighted, he cast upon the coachman a look of anger and contempt.

"Now hark you, sirrah," said Sir Peter, "I think that in a few days the probability is that you will see your successor. Do you hear that?"

"I don't know that I have been negligent in my duty," said the man. "If you have

had any reason to complain of me, Sir Peter, I think you might have told me what it was, and I would have made it my business to have altered it."

"What do you mean, sir, by driving me into the mess you have done?"

"Beg pardon, sir, but I don't know what you are alluding to."

"What right had you to stop the carriage because those men, those cursed robbers, chose to tell you to do so?"

"I didn't stop the carriage, sir," answered the coachman. "It was a dog as brought my horses to a dead stop—a confounded brute, who pinned one on 'em."

"Oh, a dog, was it?" said Sir Peter; "a dog! Oh, if I catch hold of those miscreants, I'll dog them; and no doubt I shall catch hold of them sooner or later—no doubt of that—a set of rascals! Why didn't you fire the blunderbuss, Theodore?"

"Please, sir, I tried, but found that the power was damp, and it wouldn't go off."

"How was that?"

"Yesterday's rain, sir, if you please," said the man.

"Oh, ah, I forgot, it did rain, and Miss Dorcas had the carriage out in the afternoon?"

"Yes, sir."

"Oh; well, you ought to have driven on in spite of all the highwaymen and dogs in the world."

"So I would if it had been possible," answered the coachman. "Hope you won't blame me, Sir Peter. I'd lay down my life for you and Miss Isabel."

"Well, well, perhaps after all you are not so much to blame. I'll consider the matter over; and all I have to say to you is—do your best to find out these scoundrels. They may be heard of on the road, at some of the houses perhaps, and if you *do* find them out, I'll double your wages, that's all, Theodore—that's all. If we do find them out, we shall know how to treat them—'a short shrift and a leap from the leafless tree.'"

With these words Sir Peter Primley took his way into his own comfortable apartment, which was illumined with a large penumbra lamp, with a ground glass shade to it—moderators were not then in existence

The knight of the shire found a cheerful fire blazing in the grate—his easy chair wheeled into the chimney corner—a screen by the side of the same, to prevent the fire scorching the skin of his face—his slippers were placed all ready for him—and Aunt Dorcas, as she was termed, proceeded to unbuckle his shoes; for in those days, large lustrous buckles, occasionally set with brilliants or paste, were the fashion.

She was a prim old lady, Miss Dorcas, not so old, either, for she was some fifteen years younger than her brother, who was scarcely sixty, but she was stiff and prim in her bearing, and consequently had therefore the appearance of being much older than she in reality was.

Taking off her brother's shoes, she put on his slippers, and then sat herself down upon a chair beside him.

The knight was not in one of his best tempers, he was a fidgetty old gentleman, make the best of him, but his recent adventure had put him out, and ever and anon he cast a savage glance at Isabel from beneath his shaggy eyebrows.

"My niece informs me," said Miss Dorcas, placing her hands in front of her, something after the fashion of the Quakers of the present day. "My niece informs me, Sir Peter, (she always said Sir Peter) that you have met with a sad misfortune—have been the victim to wicked and lawless men, robbers, highwaymen, in fact."

"Yes," answered Sir Peter, "and worse than that, our niece thought proper to admire one of them."

"Isabel!" exclaimed Miss Dorcas.

"Aunt!" said the young lady.

"Worse than all," answered Sir Peter, "they have robbed me of Isabel's dowry—nearly three thousand pounds gone at one fell swoop."

"Horrible!" said Aunt Dorcas; "positively horrible! Can such things be in a Christian country?"

"It is quite certain that such atrocities do occur. What was the conversation, the confidential conversation, that you thought proper to favour the highwayman with?" said Sir Peter, turning to his niece.

"Confidential conversation, Sir Peter!" said Miss Dorcas, holding up her hands. "I should hope that our niece would never so far forget herself—to demean herself as to enter into converse with miscreants, wretches, wearing the garb of humanity—like that?"

"Law, aunt, do not be so bitter," exclaimed Isabel. "I am sure the highwayman conducted himself in a most gentlemanly manner."

"Oh, gracious!" exclaimed Miss Dorcas; "and this from our own niece!—it's monstrous! positively monstrous! Isabel, you are forgetting what is due to yourself, to your sex. Converse with a male creature you may happen to meet with on the road, and that creature a—ahem—a vile highwayman!"

"I am sure, aunt—"

"There, hold your tongue, I will not listen to such tales," said Miss Dorcas, putting her hands to both her ears to stop out the words which were about to fall from the lips of the fair Isabel. "Silence, girl, silence—I command it!"

"Yes, silence!" exclaimed Sir Peter, backing up his sister in her order. "Silence, Isabel."

"Very well, uncle; I do not wish to offend you by any observation, I am sure."

"Pray don't tell Mr. Slopperton," said Miss Dorcas; "for the credit of our family do not let him know of the—ah—conduct of our disobedient and self-willed niece."

"Ah, Mr. Slopperton, indeed—that is the worst part of the affair. Isabel's wedding is to take place the day after to-morrow, and now the dowry is gone. What will he say to that?—and, alas, what is to be done?"

The knight heaved a deep sigh as he gave utterance to the last words—so did Miss Dorcas—but not so Miss Isabel, she only smiled.

"You know, my dear sister," said the knight, in continuation, "that by the will of Isabel's father, a certain amount of money was to be settled upon her on the day of her wedding. I need hardly say that a suitable and and respectable match for my ward has been one of the dreams, if I may so term it, or rather, the most anxious wish of my life. I can see no better husband for her than my old and esteemed friend, Slopperton."

"Certainly not," chimed in his sister.

"He is in every way suited to her."

"As you think, uncle," said Isabel, mildly.

"As every one must think," answered the knight. "At least, every one who is at all reasonable, or got any judgement at all. Mr. Slopperton is a gentleman whom I am proud to call my friend."

"So you have said before, uncle," answered the girl. "What of that, I don't like him; but you, as my nearest relative and guardian, insist on my marrying him, and rather than act in direct opposition to your orders, I have consented, reluctantly enough, it must be admitted, to sacrifice myself at the altar of duty, if I may so term it."

"Sacrifice yourself!" exclaimed Aunt Dorcas. "Ungrateful girl."

"It's hardly worth while," said Isabel, "for us to go over the same subject again and again. I have given my consent, aunt, and there is an end of that matter. The least thing I am entitled to ask is, that I should not be troubled with a repetition of the numerous excellent qualities of my intended husband."

"Hoity toity!" said her aunt; "I always understood that young girls liked to hear their lover's spoken well of."

"I am in this instance an exception to the rule," said her niece.

"Oh, very well, miss, we'll drop the subject. I pray of you, Sir Peter, not to offend the ears of our niece by naming Mr. Slopperton."

"You had better go to bed, child," said

the knight, "as I do not choose to have a curb put upon my tongue by a parcel of girls."

Isabel rose, and proceeded to her own apartment, as it was the very thing she had desired.

When she had gone, Sir Peter turned to his sister, and said—

"She talks in the old strain—still obstinate and self-willed."

"It would appear so, Sir Peter. What about her marriage portion ?'

"The very thing I was about to name. It's gone—clean gone. I must acquaint Slopperton with the fact, and rely upon his generosity to dispense with it; or the worst comes to the worst, I can but make it good, for she shall have him, of that I am determined—she shall have him."

"A young girl is a great charge, Sir Peter."

"Oh, dear yes, a very great charge, especially a self-willed one like her. Not but she's a good child, take her altogether, a very good child; only upon this subject she appears to have run mad."

"Girls will do so, Sir Peter," said Miss Dorcas; "they will do so—always have. It's only towards the meridian of our existence that we have the powers of discernment given to us."

"True, true, my sister," said the knight; and in the course of another hour or so the sapient pair retired.

On the following morning, Isabel went out, as was her frequent custom, for her morning walk. She strolled down the green lanes for the distance of about half a mile; the morning was fine, the air balmy, and birds were carolling forth their morning song from every bough.

At the distance of about a mile from her uncle's residence was situated the village church, which was very old and primitive in its appearance, the tower being overgrown with ivy.

Towards this Isabel took her way. In the course of a few minutes she was in the lane which led to the building in question.

Arriving here, she paused, and leaning against a stile, looked carefully around.

She stood thus for some time, her young heart fluttering, and her form slightly trembling with a new and strange fear; presently she observed a figure coming along the road, he approached, and in a few minutes Colonel Jack was by her side.

"Sir—I—oh, you have kept your word," said Isabel, to the highwayman.

"Colonel Jack generally keeps his word in every appointment he may happen to make with a lady; and he would be unworthy of the name of man if he could so far forget himself as to disappoint one so fair and lovely as Miss Isabel Foster.

A heightened colour suffused the face of his companion as he gave utterance to this speech, and she turned her head away, half coquettishly.

"It is kind of you, certainly, to come, very kind," she said; "and, indeed, I hardly—"

"Expected it, I suppose—eh ?" said the colonel.

"To say the truth, I did not," answered the lady.

"Thanks, for your candour, many thanks; it's more than we expect from every young lady. Now listen to me—you are conversing with the notorious highwayman, Colonel Jack. Start not, he has never been unkind or inconsiderate towards your own sex. First of all, I must inform you that I am your friend. I knew you, as I said, upon the occasion of our last interview, I knew you when a girl, a child."

"How, and where?" said Isabel.

The highwayman made a deprecatory gesture.

"No matter," he said, "seek not to inquire into that. Enough for our own purpose that I am your friend. You would not wed this Mr. Slopperton ?"

"I have passed my word to my guardian and uncle."

"So you have already informed me; but you would not wed him if it could be avoided ?"

"Indeed not; I do not like him, and—"

"Therefore would not have him; I understand. That is sufficient. Now walk down this turning behind the church, or perhaps your character may be compromised."

"How so ?"

"By being seen with a strange gentleman, by some chance wayfarer."

The two then proceeded out of the highroad, if it could be so called, and were able to converse without any person either seeing or hearing them.

"Now, Miss Forster, when is this marriage to take place ?"

"The day after to-morrow."

"And where ?"

"At St. Jude's Church."

"I know it, about three miles from here, is it not ?"

"Yes, as nearly as I can guess."

"The marriage shall be prevented."

"How ?'

"That is my business," answered the colonel. "Only you must understand, Miss Foster, that I have your word that you do not wish to marry this man. '

"Indeed I do not; but there must be no violence—no deed of violence."

"I promise you that, also. You love another."

The young girl hung down her head.

Colonel Jack gazed into the countenance of the fair girl, whose face was suffused with blushes.

"I need no answer, Miss Foster," said the colonel. "Rely upon me, upon my discretion, upon my honour."

"I will," replied Miss Foster, extending her hand, which the colonel pressed in his own. "There is something in your manner which tells me that I can place confidence in your word—that you are too noble-minded to wantonly trifle with my feelings, or seek to make my love the sport of an idle hour."

"In truth, I am," replied our hero, "for I myself have loved deeply, fervently ; and though her on whom that love was centred, has passed from this world, yet the remembrance of it will always make me respect the same passion in others."

Leading his fair companion into the highroad, Colonel Jack wished her farewell, took his departure, and in the course of half an hour was on the back of his favourite mare, trotting on the high-road towards London. Isabel returned home to Ilscomb Court.

CHAPTER XCIX.

THE MARRIAGE INTERRUPTED.

MR. SLOPPERTON, the suitor of Isabel Foster, presented himself at the house to see his intended, who had gone out at the time to meet our hero.

The intended bridegroom was ushered into the studio, as he termed it, of Sir Peter Primley, who received him with his accustomed courtesy, for he was quite an especial favourite with the knight.

The first salutations over, the history of the highwayman's attack, and robbery of Isabel's dower, were detailed in full to the wonder-stricken Slopperton, who was speechless with astonishment ; so much so, in fact, that he was for the nonce utterly unable to make any reply.

At length, when he did manage to find the means of utterance, he stammered out the words—

"Three—thousand—pounds !"

"Very nearly, very nearly, my dear Slopperton ; but the notes are stopped, that's one comfort, and who knows but this may be the means of tracing out the perpetrators of this abominable outrage—who knows?"

"Ah, who indeed," said Mr. Slopperton. "He was quite certain that he did not."

"But, my dear sir," said the knight, "this will of course not prevent my niece from marrying you—or rather, more properly speaking, your marrying my niece at the appointed time."

"Ah—ahem—no—oh dear no," said the eager and anxious bridegroom, who, notwithstanding his manner, was evidently rather chopfallen at the loss of his bride's marriage portion.

"Because you know," said the knight, in continuation, "because, you know, Isabel shall not go to her husband without some settlement. I myself will cheerfully come forward with, let me see, what shall we say, a thousand—eh, friend Slopperton—will that do ?"

"My dear Sir Peter," said Mr. Slopperton, "you really must not be permitted to—to—be a loser. If the money bequeathed by her father is lost, irredeemably lost, it cannot really be considered any fault of yours. It might have happened to myself or any one else travelling on the road on that particular night."

"Precisely. Only I was saying, that my niece shall not go to her husband empty handed. I will settle upon her a thousand pounds."

Mr. Slopperton rose from his seat, grasped his friend's hand, made a deprecatory gesture, pantomimed a series of motions, the real meaning of which it was impossible to divine, and then sat himself once more down in his seat.

All this was doubtless very expressive, or at any rate intended to be so ; but it was not quite clear as to the precise meaning of the gentleman who was so demonstrative.

However, the two gentlemen hobbed and nobbed together, and the marriage was determined on at the time originally named between them.

Mr. Slopperton was certainly not a particularly young man, neither was he a very handsome one. Nature, in forming him, seemed to have made some mistake—his features were upon so large a scale, that they suggested to the mind of the spectator the idea of their having been originally cast for a much larger man, but had been put upon one whose body they did not exactly fit.

There was also a disagreeable expression about the mouth, and certainly a superabundance of eyebrow, enough to have served three ordinary men at the very least, so that we cannot blame Isabel Foster for not much liking the match.

Mr. Slopperton was an old friend of Sir Peter's, and he was supposed to be very rich.

In fact, he was so, being a retired indigo merchant.

When we say retired, the reader is led to imagine that he had been all his lifetime in business, and had been the architect of his own fortune; this was not, however, the case, his father had originally established the business.

The son, after his parent's death, had carried it on, without, however, taking any active part in the business, and he eventually sold it, and led a life of comparative retirement.

Sir Peter Primley, in the earlier portion of his life, had had large transactions with the house of Slopperton and Co., his acquaintance with the present Jasper Slopperton, Esq., who, if he had originally dealt in indigo, had not put any of that colour upon his own face, which, to say the truth, was as yellow as a duck's foot.

This may be accounted for from the fact of his having resided for many years in the earlier portion of his life in the East Indies.

The day arrived which was to see the young and beauteous Isabel Foster united by

the bonds of holy wedlock to Jasper Slopperton, Esq.

Ilscomb Court was the scene of considerable excitement on that eventful morning. The bride began by shedding tears, and was in a state of considerable flirtation—Aunt Dorcas affected a rigid and imperturbable gravity, during the preliminaries of dressing, &c.—in fact she set to work with what might be termed military precision.

When the toilet was completed, Isabel looked surpassingly lovely, although her countenance wore an anxious and at the same time, melancholy look.

Upon her appearance in the drawing-room, Sir Peter Primley came forward, and kissed her affectionately on the forehead.

Sir Peter, himself, was perfectly radiant.

No. 62.

He was attired in what might be termed full court dress, with a real sword girded round his waist, the hilt of which was studded with brilliants.

Sir Peter was in a state of great flustration, for there had not been a marriage in his family for very many years, not since he had led the late Lady Primley a young and blushing bride to the altar.

The family carriage was at the door, the driver and footman rejoicing in snow white favours; and in a short time the cortege was on its road to St. Jude's Church, where the marriage ceremony was appointed to take place.

That antique virgin, Miss Dorcas Primley, was one of the bridesmaids. There were, however three others, of radiant beauty, and as to poor Isabel, she looked more like a prisoner than a happy bride.

Few words were spoken during the journey to the sacred edifice. Having arrived at which place, the bridegroom and his party were there, and the chief actors in the scene were placed round the altar.

As Isabel took up her position, she glanced furtively round the church. Several of the pews were occupied, but she had no time to make a close inspection of their occupants—her heart sank within her.

Colonel Jack had promised that the marriage should never be allowed to take place. "Where was his promise now?" thought Isabel.

The first few words were uttered by the clergyman, and when he came to that part of the service in which he has to say—"If any man has reason to object to the nuptials," &c.—a voice from a neighbouring pew said, in loud tones, which ran through the building—

"Yes, I do."

Consternation sat upon the countenances of all present. Mr. Slopperton turned suddenly round, and beheld an elderly man who had risen to his feet in one of the adjacent pews.

Then there was a dead silence for a second or so, after which the person who had spoken came forward, leading a young woman, a creole.

"I forbid this marriage," said the man.

"Sir," exclaimed the priest, "what is the meaning of this unseemly interruption?"

"The marriage must not proceed?" answered the man.

"Insolence!" ejaculated Sir Peter Primley.

"Do not lose your temper, my friend," said the clergyman. "Permit me to make the necessary inquiries. Now, sir," he said, in continuation, turning towards the man who had so suddenly interrupted the marriage ceremony. "Your reasons, if you please?"

"Because Jasper Slopperton is *already married*," said the speaker. "Behold his wife!"

As he said this, he led forward a young woman by the hand—the creole already mentioned.

It would have been a fine picture for an artist to have sketched the look and manner of the intended bridegroom—consternation, rage, and disappointment sat upon his features, and his frame shook with emotion.

"Is this true?" inquired the parson.

"He dare not deny it," said the man.

"He cannot deny it; I have the marriage certificate with me."

"Sir, is this story true?" exclaimed the clergyman.

"No, it is false," ejaculated Mr. Slopperton.

"Nine years ago," said the other; "nine years ago, in Calcutta, you married this woman. Shame upon you!

"The marriage has been annulled—annulled," answered Slopperton. "I was young and foolish, forced into an odious and detestable ceremony, but since then it has been annulled."

"How?" inquired the clergyman.

"By mutual consent."

"That will not do," said the priest, closing his book, and laying it down upon the communion table. "There must be an end to this. Young lady, you are free."

This was addressed to Miss Foster.

"Curses on you!" exclaimed Slopperton. "Where did you come from? How is it that you and this creature have found your way here to-day?"

"That is my business," answered the man. "we are here, and this is your wife, and like a faithful husband, you ought and must take her home."

"Perdition!" exclaimed Slopperton, who, without more ado, rushed out of the church, sprang into his carriage, and bade his coachman drive off, which he did immediately.

Miss Dorcas Primley was appalled, so sudden had been this unlooked for interruption, that she, under the influence of so fearful a catastrophe to the day's proceedings, nearly fainted away; then it was that the other female attendants commenced a series of attentions to the unfortunate and susceptible maiden.

As to Sir Peter himself, he was agitated and speechless with surprise. He stood staring at one and the other in stupid astonishment.

The clergyman appeared to be the only party who was self possessed; he called Sir Peter Primley to himself by observing, in an under tone—

"Do not trouble yourself in the matter, Sir Peter Primley. After all, it is a happy release—a very happy release. It is better to make this discovery now than niece's marriage, much better."

Sir Peter thought the same—so he said—but he looked the very picture of misery, nevertheless. He could never have believed that his darling friend, Slopperton could have behaved so badly, and with so much duplicity he would never have any faith in the promises or word of man ever again.

It is needless to dwell upon this scene any more ; the wedding party had to dance back to Ilscomb Park, in the state carriage, in a state of despair, with the exception of the bride, who was felicitating herself upon the issue of the day's proceedings. It is needless to observe that this ecclaircissement was brought about by no other person than Colonel Jack.

Mr. Slopperton had fallen in love with the creole who had been presented in the church, this occurred years before the present ceremony. Slopperton had, so it appeared, seduced the young creole, and under pressure was compelled to marry her.

This took place in India, and when Slopperton returned to England he thought he had fairly got rid of his first wife, whom he had learned to detest most cordially.

Colonel Jack became acquainted with the creole and her companion, and had contrived the interruption to the marriage of Slopperton, as already described.

He took an opportunity of seeing Miss Foster after the scene in the church, and told her that whenever she thought fit to marry the man of her choice the dower was at his disposal.

———

CHAPTER C.

SCENE IN NEWGAEE.—THE CONDEMNED CELL THE FORGER.

AFTER the interruption to the marriage ceremony, Colonel Jack returned to London. He was not in the best spirits, for the sessions were over at Newgate, and one or two of his quandom companions were condemned to death.

The Colonel had waited upon Jonathan Wild and heard from him the particulars of the session list, always an interesting one to the lawless portion of London's occupants

The reader may gather interesting and truthful statements, which we subjoin, from the note book of the ordinary of Newgate, that individual who has the last sad duty appointed to him to bring the minds of the culprits to a sense of their awful condition :—

The ordinary's notes now refer to his second visit to the cells alone.

On the following day he entered the ward where they were all assembled to breakfast, when he commenced what he deemed to be his sacred duty, namely, the work of prepreparing their minds as dying men. As they were all condemned, he thought it right to treat them all as persons sure to suffer.

Noticing a man about thirty-five years of age, of respectable appearance, he commiserated his character and office, when the man rose and said—

" 'The newly elected ordinary, I presume.'

" He was then informed that the gentleman whom he addressed would be pleased to render him any assistance consistent with his duty ; to which he replied—

" ' Assist me in reaching the other side of these walls—you have no power to render me any other service ; and that will be but a common act of justice to an ill-used man. You will thereby snatch another victim from the ruthless hands of the accursed law.'

" 'This is not befitting language,' said the minister, 'for one in your situation. When I come here to visit men doomed by the law to suffer death, it is natural for me to expect that I shall find minds weighed down with a sense of guiltiness, in a contrite and broken spirit seeking for pardon from an offended God ; but you shock me with your state of feeling, and the example you offer to your fellow-sinners, who probably have not had the same advantages of education as yourself. As to the laws to which you have applied so coarse an epithet, if you were in a state of innocence, and a calm looker-on, instead of being a sufferer under them, it is probable you would come to the same conclusion I have come to, that they are just. As a preliminary to an improved state of feeling, I implore you to cast away rancorous and rebellious notions.'

" During this short rebuke, the reproved man was impatient to speak. The light of fire flashed from his eyes, his whole countenance became animated ; and as the reprover concluded with—

" ' However imperfect the institutions of a country may seem to be, they are commonly suited to the state of the people by whom they have been embraced,' he rose from his seat, and, striking the table violently, exclaimed—

" ' A fallacy ! a palpable fallacy !—so palpable that the merest surface creature in existence must see it.'

" Then, addressing the ordinary, said—

" ' Sir, you appear to be a gentleman, and I suppose you are a scholar ; permit me then, in the name of both, to entreat you not to lend yourself to bolster up such a system of laws as ours. In what nation on the globe have the *people* embraced the laws under which they live? Have not all laws had their origin in barbarous times, under the most despotic tyranny? And what is the history of the world from those early periods? What but one continuous effort of subsequent civilised ages to convince rulers that the laws—criminal, especially—of a barbarous age, are unsuited for an improved social condition of mankind? Have not the intelligent masses of the people, for centuries past, in every European country at least, expressed their disgust and abhorrence of the laws under which we live? Reflect on the thousands of pens which have been employed, and the waste of energy which has been expended, in endeavouring to convince rulers of the unfitness of the criminal laws to our state of civilisation. If you do, sir, reflect, you will cease, almost at the commencement of your coming into the prison, to attempt to justify the laws which doom us to die by the hands of man. Look at my case. Those very authorities that now refuse me merey are the persons who taught me to commit forgery. So did those who have sent you here to break down my spirit, and to justify all their legal murders. I mean, sir, the aldermen and sheriffs of this city. For them and the government I kept a forging shop, under the nose of your chief magistrate, not covertly, but openly. They were my customers. They paid me, and complimented me for the superior excellence of my performances. For the government authorities I forged foreign ship's papers, foreign edicts and proclamations, on which, false as they were, they might justify their own measures to the public, tax the people, and found pretexts to continue an unholy war. For your merchants, I have furnished their ships with six sets of forged papers for one voyage, for their skippers to shew as emergencies might render expedient. The public treasury and the ship-owner's money taught these fingers to commit forgery, enable me to live extravagantly, and tempted me to launch into expenses, which, while money flowed in so rapidly, I thought would have no end. When, however, peace came, my occupation was gone. I had made no provision for such an event; and in a moment of desperation, after the loss of my all at a gaming-table, I committed a forgery for myself, for which I am now to be hanged by the neck like—O Heavens! I feel the chocking sensation now!—the fall, the check, the spasm, the convulsive shudder, the flash of light in the eyes! Oh, that the last were over, and the soul had taken its flight, winged, as it will be, into my Maker's presence, not by his command, but by feathers plucked from statutes framed by demons and executed by furies. And you too, sir, will stand by, uttering the language of Christ, while this devil's work of public

murder is perpetrated. But you will take your morning-walk, with your usual serenity of demeanour, considered becoming to a minister of the church. You will bring the same appetite to dinner, drink the same quantity of wine, and chat with as much hilarity, as if no sin had been committed by choking a fellow-creature in the presence of a multitude. Depend on it, sir, till those who direct the moral machinery of government in a nation teach, by their own example, the high regard they have for the life which God alone can give, and who alone should take it away, laws will never deter others from holding the life of a fellow-creature in as light an estimation as they do.

"'If you must murder, sir, why do you not do so in the most merciful and in the least possible cruel way? Why not follow the example of some of the Eastern nations, and, as the sentence is passed, send the executioner behind the culprit with the bow-string? Why this torture in these horrible cold cells, under the specious pretext of preparation? Preparation indeed! Agonise the mind, deplete the system, place human beings alive in the tomb, immerse them for eighteen hours out of the twenty-four in mephitic air, reduce their physical and mental powers by torture, and then preach to them the punishment of the damned in another world. Alas, for your mercy and consistency as Christians! Heaven defend me from such Christian notions of charity! Every hour in the night do I wake with the fall of the drop, the choking of the throat, the flash of lightning in the eyes, the last convulsive struggle, to find myself in a deathly cold, clammy perspiration, every fibre of the body trembling and quivering. Then do I grasp my wind-pipe, to be assured that the rope is not there; then impulsively do I press it with all my strength, first to try the effects of the sensation, and next to ascertain whether I shall have, at the last extremity, power enough to hold on long enough to produce strangulation myself, and save the public from one demoralising example, in the hanging up of my body to be blown about by the passing winds. After these paroxysms, through nights lengthened to weeks by terror, I rise to view my body, wasting away by pounds-weight at a time. Yes! your merciful treatment effects the exhalation or evaporation of the body by torture, before you set the soul free.

"'For your patient hearing, sir, I will now promise to give you as little trouble as possible—that is upon one condition, namely, that you will endeavour to aid me in escaping from that worst of all tortures, the condemned sermon. I dread it more than the hangman, with his accursed vulgar instrument of murder. I look on that ceremony as one of the most horrible species of torture ever invented. In the name and under the guise of religion, a cruelty is inflicted on the feelings of the mind, far exceeding that of the body which the public is called to witness on the scaffold.

"'In this ward I shall be happy to listen to you, and give you an honest reply. In the chapel you have it all your own way. Now, as you are recently inducted into office, permit me, sir, to advise you to use your advantage over us with moderation. God alone knows the secrets of the heart, and He is the only competent judge of man's degrees of moral turpitude. The laws of man I have but once offended, and in that act, as it has turned out, I have not injured any human being. I have, it is true, like most others, had my indiscretions; still I hope the balance-sheet will not show such a heavy arrear, as you may feel it your duty or whim to make up against me in the harangue called a condemned sermon, which in your situation you are paid to deliver. In that capacity, armed as you are by the reigning authorities and long custom, you have a giant's strength; but 'tis tyrannous to use it like a giant. And, to be candid with you, I hate pulpitical oratory; there is so much assumption and dogmatism connected with it. I do not mean to give you any offence. I have spoken against the *system*, not against *you*. I have, like you, had the benefit of an education, and do not desire to be thought to abuse it. You said just now, that if I were a calm looker-on, I should probably think as you do. If you, as a calm looker on, were in my situation, environed with all the circumstances which have attended my history, and those which invest me at this moment, you would think as I do.'

"It may be imagined that this monstrous speech, made before thirty-two more or less illiterate condemned men, to whom the reverend divine had come to preach the word of salvation, considerably annoyed him, especially as it took him on the threshold of his probational duties. Respect, however, for himself, and the authority it was necessary to have over the others, was at stake, without which the benefits they might receive from his advice would be lost. He therefore replied:—

"'Neither you nor I have any power to alter the laws; and therefore, while I do not agree with you, whatever they are, it is our duty to obey them. You, at least, have not the ignorance of them to plead in your defence. You knew the law; and you knew that the penalty of death would be exacted for its violation. I cannot see that you have anything to complain of. You intended the appropriation of another man's property to your own uses. You may think lightly of

signing a slip of paper; but look at the motive—robbery. Robbery is robbery, however effected. These men,' pointing to the other malefactors, 'as you would call it, *only* committed robbery. The law, however, has overtaken you all; and it is not only now useless, but wicked and foolish, to waste the few valuable hours left you in railing at it. Whatever may be the state of your mind, you have no right to distract the attention and disturb the feelings of you fellow-sufferers. It is of little consequence to any of you what the law is; your lives are forfeited under it. You have now only to turn your fervent attention to the saving of the soul. Our Saviour died that sinners might be saved —a truth which it is my happiness to announce and explain to you from the Word of God.'

"Among the group that surrounded the minister were three malefactors, who had committed highway robbery, one of whom was continually making most horrible contortions of the features; his eyes rolled in vacancy; and as he had suddenly shifted his position near to the ordinary, he became uneasy, and removed from him to the opposite side of the table, when the man exclaimed, "I have now got you face to face; and, as I'm the Duke Marlborough, I'll fight you like a true soldier. Make ready! present! fire! Fire is the word of command. Obey your commander, you scoundrels!" turning to his fellowprisoners. "Fire! I say." He uttered these words as he placed himself in a commanding attitude.

"On hearing this, the man who had made the previous harangue hastened round to the chaplain, and in a low voice said, "Can'st thou not minister to a mind diseased? There, sir, there is a subject will give you full employment, and test your abilities. Yet it will be a sin to cure him. Poor fellow! he is now in a blessed state of unconsciousness as to his fate, and is comparatively happy. He neither feels the cold, clammy dampness, or gloom of his cell, nor fears the hangman, often singing the night through. If the mind be the soul, his fate is already settled both here and hereafter. But my own head!' placing his hand again with violence on his forehead; 'would it were really like his! Would that I were actually mad, and could fancy myself a judge, an ordinary, a gaoler, or even a hangman—any one or any thing, rather than what I am!'

"'Hangman!' vociferated the maniac, for such he really was; 'I'm Duke of Marlborough, and have the power to shoot or hang everybody.'

"'Humour him, humour him, sir; you had better humour him; call him Duke of Marlborough, and he will be quiet directly,' said an athletic, burly Irishman, standing near the chaplain's elbow, who had committed highway robbery.

" ' Why, what's the use a calling a man that's going to be hanged up by the neck a lord ? They don't hang lords, nor them sort of folks, you fool : it's only for such poor devils as us that topping law be made for,' replied another malefactor, who was under condemnation also for highway robbery. This man is described as the most ferocious looking culprit of the party ; his crimes, and readiness to repeat them, were deeply engraved in every line and feature of his face. Turning his eyes towards the minister, he added,—

" ' If the parson stays here till we are all rotten as a medlar, he'll never have to preach to a lord."

" The ordinary then addressed the man who had before said so much on the nature of the laws—

" ' See the mischiefs you have worked on these ignorant men. It appears to me that there is not one of them free from the taint of your unbecoming levity, and of the silly sophistry with which you lard your conversation. You have already enough to answer for ; and therefore let me entreat you not to increase your load of guilt, by standing in the way of these wretched men and the efforts I may make to effect a change in their minds.'

" ' Change in their minds !' he retorted ; ' that's good !'

" Whenever two men differ in opinion on matters in their nature wholy speculative, and the one succeeds in bringing the other over to his way of thinking, it is always designated a happy change of mind in the proselyte, when the odds are that they were both most egregiously in error before they commenced the disputation ; the difference between them being that each before had his own error, but now both have adopted a new and common error in addition.

" As for these men, I know they are ignorant, and for that they are to suffer death ; for had the state educated them, as is its duty, the chances are that they would not have committed crimes which generally lead to violence against the person ; or, at least, for which those who contemplated their commission, must be always prepared.

" ' My offence is of a different character. A false and perverted education placed me in a rank of society above my means ; plunged me into expenses, to meet which I was kept in a constant state of excitement, till at length, under a sudden deprivation of all my available means, the precipice was placed before my eyes, over which I was to be hurled from my false position, there to grapple with poverty among such beings as these,' pointing to the group who had by this time dis-

persed, and were parading the flagstone yard in company with the maniac, who appeared to afford them much amusement.'

" Unacquainted with the vast variety of character and cross-grained ethical notions with which he would have to complete in the course of his experience, the reader will not be surprised at the chaplain giving this man more laxity of speech than on other occasions might be justifiable.'

" ' Well,' said the minister, renewing the conversation, ' you were about, I believe, both to find excuses for these men's offences, and to exculpate or extenuate your own ?'

" ' Yet, sir,' he resumed ; ' I was last speaking of myself. I saw, as I said, that I was on the point of losing caste ; that is, being disgraced by poverty in the eyes of a few individuals called our circle of acquaintance. You will probable say I brought myself to that precipice by going to the gaming-table ; but it was to avoid that precipice, which I had previously had a glimpse of, that caused me to go there. Starched moralists only look to the proximate cause of an evil ; they cannot see that all proximate causes are but the last links in a vast series of causes, the remotest eluding the most acute minds, whether in the moral or physical world.

Habit had given me a facility in imitating the handwriting of others ; when, therefore the passions were excited, under the frenzy of disappointed hope, the suggestive principle readily turned my attention to the use of my fingers, the former success of which lulled every thought of being detected. I began with being a friend to my country : I served its government and its merchants. Now it will be said I am a disgrace to it. The extremes appear to be great, the progress from one to the other is, however, short and easy.

" ' With respect to those men,' turning towards the other prisoners, ' I know myself that all they have done has been done in ignorance ; and it is far better that they should die in ignorance.

" It is cruelty to teach at the eleventh hour that which you ought to have taught when they first commenced their career of crime.

" At the present moment, they see no further into the cause of their condemnation, than the judge and jury.

' If you open their minds, and dissipate their ignorance, they must walk to the scaffold execrating those who have neglected their duty towards them.

" It becomes the refinement of cruelty to inform them of their duplicated murder.

" ' What an impious mockery of religion is the sentence of the judge—' You are to be taken to the place from whence you came, and from thence to the place of execution, there to be hanged by the neck till you are dead ; and the Lord have mercy on your souls !'

" ' The Scripture says ' That the soul be without knowledge, it is not good ;' yet your employers, the rulers of the nation, keep millions without this corrective knowledge, and then have the effrontery to address the Deity, in the very act of preparing for the murder of His creatures, into whom He has breathed the breath of life, praying him to have mercy on their souls."

" As this sentence was concluded, the maniac was making towards the minister, followed by five or six others, who forced him forward for the purpose of creating some confusion and excitement—a plan frequently attempted by prisoners when congregated in a body ; to avoid which the ordinary made a sign to the turnkey to let him pass, and thus abruptly terminated his first regular visit to the cells of Newgate.

" Being anxious about the maniac, he immediately reported his case; when, to his astonishment, he was told that it was feigned in the vain hope of escaping death. The governor and the surgeon were both of this opinion, and observed that such artifices were of frequent occurrence : the ordinary, however, was however a dissentient, and felt very uneasy at having such a man to deal with, mixed as he was with so large a body of doomed malefactors ; all of whom were in imminent danger, both of body and soul. Still, notwithstanding this, he continued his visits several times each day ; till, on the third from the one on which he entered office, the report came down at eleven o'clock, at night, when it was his duty to attend at the unlocking of the cells, one after the other, with the other functionaries, and announce to each felon the determination of the council.

The imagination cannot picture to itself the awful gloominess of these passages, visited at such an hour, and on such an awful mission.

The condemned yard—or, as it was formerly called, the press yard, was once the Phoenix Inn, Newgate Street. This inn being near to the Newgate prison was pulled down for the purpose of enlarging it; and on its very site had been erected these tombs of the living.

" When it was first taken in, it was considered as a part of the governor's house, who derived a good income by exacting large sums of money from the prisoners he accommodated there. Those who desired the privilege of a few yards of space, to walk two or three abreast, were compelled to pay twenty guineas, besides a weekly payment of a pound or more for the accomodation of part of a filthy bed in a place where there

were fewer cubic feet of air than of human flesh.

" The press-yard took its name from the custom of conveying there such prisoners as refused to plead when placed at the bar, there to be pressed by having a board laid on their bodies, with a continual addition of weights, till they either consented to plead or died under the insupportable pressure.

" The cells of Newgate now comprise three rows of stone building, the front being in the press-yard adjoining the chaplain's house in Newgate Street.

" The cells are eight feet long by six wide, and formerly it was the custom to lodge three, and sometimes four, prisoners in each of these ; the accomodations for them consisted of a rope-mat, such as is used for wiping the feet on, and one common stable-rug, with an iron candlestick for the use of the inmates. The walls, floors, and roofs, are all of stone, with a hole through the front wall, three feet thick ; which hole is barred across, so as to be almost closed, leaving very little space for the admission of light.

" In these places the unhappy men remain confined from the dusk till day-light during winter ; and in summer, from dusk till eight o'clock the next morning. At the extremity of these cells are two large rooms for the use of the prisoners during the day, called wards.

" The entrance to these cells in a narrow dark staircase, with darker passages running at the back of each row of the cells, into which the strong door of each cell opens. The way to the press yard from the entrance of the prison is through narrow, devious passages, intersected with, and defended by, numerous doors of great strength, and an efficient number of turnkeys to open them for ingress and egress. The only communication prisoners have with their friends is across a passage, terminated by iron bars, between which is a turnkey, to see and hear all that passes.

Murderers, women, and very young boys, were not removed to these cells, immediately after a verdict of guilty was pronounced. Murderers are confined in a cell set apart for that purpose, and were heretofore executed in a few hours after sentence ; the law said within four and twenty, but now it remains with the judge to fix the period when the execution of the sentence shall take place. A separate place is also assigned for women under sentence of death.

Threading their way through the cold passages, preceded by two turnkeys, each carrying a lantern and a huge bunch of keys, accompanied also by the two sheriffs, the governor of the prison, and four or five strangers brought by the sheriffs, whose curiosity excited their desire to behold wretched men receive the messenger of certain death, they all arrived at the outer door of the cell staircase as St. Paul's great bell announced the hour of midnight.

There were twenty-seven to be informed of their release from the dread of death, and five to hear that the day was fixed for their execution. Among the latter was the maniac, who had every day since the sentence been gradually getting worse, and exhiting symptoms that his malady was not only real, but of a permanent character. His cell was the first opened, the turnkey having his list in hand, with the aid of the light in the lantern, called over the names of those he knew to be in it. Three naked, attenuated, pallid figures, rose before us.

"Wake up, A——n ; he's at his old tricks," called out the senior turnkey.

After some time he was forced from his mat on his knees, in which attitude he began to strike in every direction; the light, however, when thrust in his face by the turnkey, attracted his attention. He was the only one in that cell unrespited.

As might be expected, every effort was made to impress on his mind the awful communication which was about to be imparted to him; but all was no avail, he only contorted his countenance, and then huzzaed as loud as his feeble lungs enabled him. The other three, at the ordinary's bidding, placed themselves on their knees, and mechanically muttered after him a few words of thanks to the Lord for their deliverance from death. We may say mechanically ; for, during this, to them, awful crisis of their fate, one had his tongue thrust in his cheek ; while the other winked, and actually pinched his companion that was by his side.

Closing this door, they proceeded to the next cell, where there were two who were left for execution, and two respited. One of the latter, when he heard of his escape, exclaimed, "There, Jim, I have won that wager ! I thought the beggars couldn't hang me, be jiglered if I didn't." To this, as is supposed involuntary expression, one of the doomed malefactors answered with an oath, that 'they,' meaning the council, 'were a set of bloodthirsty murderers !' while his companion, who was to suffer with him, muttered, as he laid himself down, something about "that it was foolish to wake people up to bring bad news ; the morning, any how, might have been time enough for that."

The next cell entered contained the malefactor who had been condemned for forgery, and who had inveighed so loudly against the practice of hanging. He was one of the unhappy number doomed to suffer. He heard the news with more composure than was expected ; while, at the same time, he bit his lips, and clenched his hands, indicating signs of internal agony of mind.

The usual forms of commending the condemned to prayer and repentance, and the respited to thanksgiving, having been gone through in each cell, till the whole number of criminals had been seen, they were again securely locked up, and left to their own thoughts.

For all useful purposes of conveying an idea of this kind of scenes, that were so common at the time of which we write, the above short sketch may suffice. The feelings of too many would be shocked by repeating the language, or explaining the conduct, of prisoners who were ordered for execution, and who are the first to take offence at the anxiety of the chaplain and others to imbue them with religious sentiments,

The law, they think, is their natural enemy ; as well as every one connected with its administration. After such a visit as above described, passionate joy, wild despair, jealousy, envy, hatred, and the utmost brutal rage, all reign at one time in those dreary places.

Although a minister knows that not an instant should be lost in offering counsel to those who are soon to be led to the scaffold, yet the following morning is the most inappropriate time to carry such a design into practice.

"At the usual hour the cells are opened, they are all assembled in the yard, and an hour afterwards the doomed men are desired to stand on one side, the others being arranged in a row apart,

"Presently a turnkey makes his appearance, calling out, 'Respites to the north side !' (the transports' yard) ; and away they march through the press-yard gate to their destination, leaving those who are to be executed looking only at that moment, in consequence of their comparative situations, upon the others as liberated men, and internally cursing and profanely denouncing those who have made the distinction.

"This, it may be conceived, is not the moment for the minister to approach them. They have but just been aroused from a broken slumber, in which the hangman, like a huge spider, has been crawling about them.

"They now stand half awakened out of the hideous sense of what is to come. They are still dizzy with a dull head and heartache, the tongue is feverish and parched, a leaden weight hangs on their eyes, that overwhelms their frame with a sickness of soul only known to themselves.

"The eye takes a hasty glance at the walls, and *chevaux de frise* with which they are surrounded, in a vain resolution of the mo-

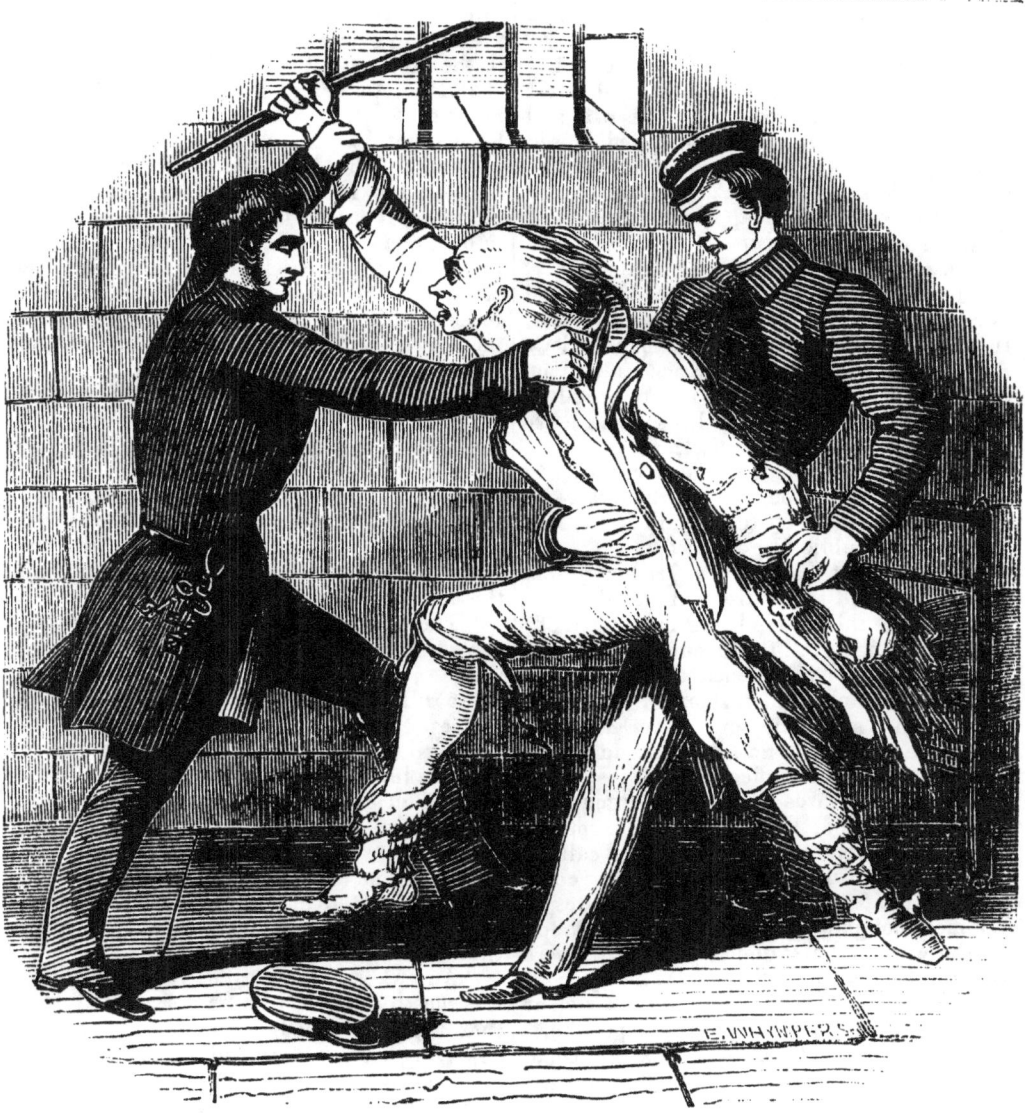

ment to effect an escape. The sickness of despair again overwhelms them, and their eyes look down wistfully on the pavement as if to implore the earth to open and swallow them up. Despair and desperation alternately seize the half-unconscious minds, rendering them unfit even for the mockery of sympathy.

"How shall an honest divine treat such a condition of humanity? His best course is to appeal to their manhood, and mildly reprove their cowardice. He ought at first only to attempt regularity and decency of behaviour; if he aim at too much at once, he will only make hypocrites of them. No one understood this better than the minister of whom we write.

"It will be unnecessary to dwell much longer on these particular cases; three of

the malefactors were stolidly ignorant and brutally obstinate, denying the right of the law to deprive them of life: a feeling their more educated companion had been mainly instrumental in bringing about. Another had been decidedly insane from the period of his condemnation; and though every attempt was made to bring him to a sense of his situation, all proved ineffectual.

"The ravings of this poor wretch were at times fearful. Upon one occasion, he tore from its sockets one of the bars which crossed the window of his cell, and caused the utmost confusion in the prison by the noise he made striking it against the door. Upon the keepers entering, they narrowly escaped being brained by the formidable weapon. They however succeeded in securing him. His dress was in great disorder, and he generally pulled the legs of his stockings down about his ankles.

"The fifth—the forger, as he styled himself by profession — after one of the most heart-rending interviews with his wife and three children, perhaps ever witnessed, lapsed into something like imbecility of mind, and occasionally sobbed like a child, and again at intervals rallied to apparent firmness—periods employed in vituperating those whom he considered to be the cause of his death.

"There can be no doubt that a long period of agonising suspense destroys, more or less, the powers of the mind, and hence little reliance can be placed on the accounts given to the world of the condition of mind in which those who suffer on the scaffold leave their sublunary state of existence.

"After four days' of anxious exertion to perform a most onerous and sacred duty, the ordinary was called on to officiate at the last scene of this public tragedy.

"At half-past seven the Irishman was brought forward to be disencumbered of his irons ; while these were being hammered off, a knife was inquired for to cut some part of the cordage which confined the irons ; on which the wretched man stooped, and, with superhuman strength, tore them asunder with an effort which nothing but an agony of feeling could have effected.

"The other three having undergone the same preparation, the maniac was brought out, when he commenced dancing and calling out, 'I'm the Duke of Marlborough!' clapping his hands and distorting his features in the most horrible manner. This he continued all the way to the scaffold ; and when there ran up the steps with great rapidity, continuing to dance and kick in the most violent manner, apparently to amuse the spectators, at no time ceasing to call out, 'I'm the Duke of Marlborough!' Two men were engaged holding him, while the remainder of the awful ceremony of adjusting the rope was performed. Scarcely had the platform fell, when, to the astonishment and awe of the people, he rebounded from the rope, and was seen dancing by the side of the ordinary, calling out loudly and apparently unhurt, 'What do you think of me now? Am I not the Duke of Marlborough?' The executioner then mounted the scaffold and pushed him off, and in this manner did he at length render up his soul.

"The reflections of the ordinary after witnessing this harrowing scene, the first of the kind he attended, appear to be of the following nature :—That whenever the law, in cases of death is chargeable with cruelty or carelessness in execution, the public will invariably decide in favour of the malefactors. When the malefactors themselves see the law about to be executed in the teeth of injustice, they triumphantly appeal to the public, and screw their resolution up to go to the drop with the courage of martyrs in the cause of a principle of justice. He also notes that, although twenty-seven evil-doers, loaded with equal, or a greater weight of guilt than the five ordered for execution, were spared in the name of the prerogative of mercy, it cannot but have the effect on the public and the sufferers, that an act of injustice in their cases is perpetrated. The council in no instance made public the reasons which actuated them in the selection, merely ordering for execution one out of eight or nine actually condemned.

"The impression on the public during these times of hanging appear to have been that the government dared not have the temerity to go beyond taking the life of a certain number of criminals. It then naturally follows, that all who were executed were looked on as sacrificed ; while those on whom the letter of the law was not executed felt all the effects of malice defeated.

"There can be little doubt that the will, according as it has occasion, or is disposed, has the power to dwell on any circumstances, or to blind itself to any contingencies it pleases. The majority of individuals when about to suffer always fastened their mind on some injury or injustice, real or supposed, which had been inflicted on themselves by prosecutors, witnesses, advocate, or judges, whom they would begin with imploring, and end with denouncing to all the pains of the damned, and ultimately persuading themselves that they were more sinned against than sinning.

"And where the culprit's life was forfeited, it is most probable, in nine cases out of ten, that the public thought so too, thus entirely depriving society of the advantage supposed to be derived from example in these cases. The example, certainly, of executing an insane malefactor, was not the way to produce any salutary impression on culprits.

"It may be remarked, that some malefactors possessed, in an extraordinary degree, the power of mind, when accumulated adverse circumstances surrounded them, of setting them at defiance ; and when inevitable, as in the case of being ordered for execution under the law, they have even courted them. This latter description of sufferers seldom complained of the prison treatment, or overtly repined at any thing that had befallen them. About one-fourth fell into a feebleness of mind, acknowledged the truth of any proposition propounded to them, and mechanically responded to the prayers they heard. Those who were suddenly brought to display a lively faith in the doctrines of Christianity, frequently ceased to think of their situation otherwise than as they looked forward to the approaching execution as the happiest moment of their lives.

" If, however. a reprieve came, truth compels us to say, that in too many instances penitence no longer remained; and, ere a few days had elapsed. they, like others, might be heard scoffing at religion.

" Those who were brought under the influence of Christianity when waiting for the day of execution. were generally in excellent health compared with the scoffers; the former retained their appetite and slept soundly— their pulses were regular. and they had moist skins. On the contrary, those who were contending with themselves in a rebellious spirit, generally had a variety of morbid appearances : an irregular pulse, a parched skin and a foul tongue, with all the symptoms of atrophy, or wasting away. It has often happened on the scaffold. that while the real penitent has almost blessed the executioner for assisting him to a state of salvation through faith in Him who died for the greatest sinners, a fellow-sufferer has been cursing and swearing at him. Let the religious community reflect on either or both of these conditions of mind, in which men were turned off from this world—the one reviling his God, cursing his fellow-men, and rejecting the helps religion afforded him in his state ; the other using every means of obtaining the help of mercy and pardon at that dread moment when he was about to enter into the presence of God.

" It was the ordinary's invariable practice to watch every case of committal for capital offences, and to visit the accused as early as possible after his actual entrance into the prison. His manner of addressing them was peculiarly original. He had always in view the object of leaving no impression that he had paid them a visit intentionally or designedly. This course he adopted that it might not be thought he anticipated a judgment of death, or appeared to prejudge their case, before they came as convicted malefactors in the regular way under his religious surveillance.

" Having read in the police reports of any examination for a heavy crime, he usually left word at the office that when the party was brought to the prison he should be informed of their arrival; so that the following morning at prayer, as the prisoners came in or went out of the chapel, he might be made acquainted with his person.

" Every day, immediately after service, it was the ordinary's custom to visit every yard and ward in the prison, so that his appearance on any more extraordinary occasion than usual should not excite particular notice.

" Having also previously ascertained the division of the prison in which the prisoner he wished to see was located, the better to effect his purpose he would go there the last, that it might not appear a direct visit ; and as his other visits were then made, he might have, if required, the more time to work out his object.

" Entering the yard in question, he would appear unconscious of any new arrivals, looking most frequently as he went into a ward at the shelves where the rugs were stowed away for the day, and round, to observe if cleanliness and order prevailed in each ; then remarking—

" 'Cold last night ; had you a sufficient allowance of rugs? Coals enough for the ward supplied you? if not, I will speak about it Don't be extravagant, but I will see you have enough. I suppose your friends have informed you that the session commences on the twentieth?—next Tuesday week, you know. Be prepared, have all ready, and be sure to urge your friends to attend in time. Any advice I can give you, you know, you may have. You, who do not employ attorneys must be more particular in impressing on your friends the necessity there will be to watch and keep together the witnesses who may come to speak to your characters. Courts won't have their time trifled with—mind that. They will receive no excuses, so many make them upon false grounds.' Then addressing a prisoner standing near the one he wishes to especially examine, ' Well, I have seen your brother, and have told him what is necessary to be done to prove the truth of your statement; and I sincerely wish it may turn out as you state it to be. Eh ! have I seen this face before in the ward?' Looking at his man, and then turning to the prisoners in general— " A stranger is it not among you?'

" The wardsman then steps forward and announces the prisoner's name, and the charge against him, which, in this case was murder.

" 'Indeed ! a heavy charge,' said the ordinary, eyeing the prisoner from head to foot. He then began the conversation by asking, 'Do you employ counsel? In charges of this nature, however false they may be, I always strongly recommend the prisoners to obtain the very best assistance they can command. Any man may be placed under circumstances of suspicion—strong suspicion —and yet after all he may be innocent. But in these cases it is one thing to be innocent and another to prove it—bear that in mind. The court will hear the evidence against you —if it be exaggerated or wholly false, remember, it remains with you to prove it so I presume you have friends who will see to these matters? I mention it in case you have not; and if so, rather than see a fellow-creature placed at the bar on such an awful charge without support, I will see what can be done for a defence. You shall not be lost, at any rate, for want of a fair trial. It is true, we all expect that ; but, on a charge where the inevitable consequence of a verdict of guilty is *death*, it behoves us all as Christians to see that nothing goes wrong, and that all causes of complaint in every quarter be removed. Don't for a moment imagine that I am presuming you to be guilty, or prejudging you ; as one who has had some experience, independently of my duty as a minister, I am now tendering my advice as a Christian friend to you, as I would do to all mankind, and I hope you will receive it as such. On the other hand, should your own conscience have already pronounced you guilty, which God in his mercy forbid !— I say, should your own heart, which will not—cannot hide secrets from yourself, spasmodically pulsate—"

" ' Spasmodically !—that's the very word, that explains all ?" vociferated the accused of murder. 'All ! it's all explained ! It's no fault of mine—none of mine—no none of mine !" sobbing aloud at every word he uttered in broken accents.'

" ' What do you mean ?' said the ordinary, in a manner so bland that a child, a stranger to him, might have been tempted to approach and unbosom itself. ' You appear to be suddenly affected—does your head pain you ?'

" A suspicion had crossed the reverend gentleman's mind that his remarks, intended as they were to be probing, although couched in language of advice, had, through the mental agony of feeling they produced, for a moment disordered the brain; no very uncommon case in the history of this prison and its inmates. Many extraordinary actions and expressions of prisoners can only be accounted for but by supposing that acute phrenitis supervenes at intervals after protracted mental agony. These momentary inflammatory attacks on the brain, often repeated, occasion an exsiccated condition of that organ, when the disease becomes chronic.

" ' I am liable to be suddenly affected,' exclaimed the man charged with murder ;' ' I'm spasmodical all over my frame; my whole life has been made the sport of the positive and negative powers, which produce all the phenomena of the natural—yea, and of the spiritual world, too.'

" ' Be calm, my good sir ; let me advise you to moderate your feelings, and endeavour to acquire a serenity of mind that may enable you to go through your trouble like a rational being,' said the ordinary, as he gently placed his hand on the shoulder of the accused. ' You appear to have had a good education, let it now be turned to useful

account at this crisis of your life. But, perhaps, I had better visit you again when you are more composed ; less excited, I mean.'

" ' Excited, did you say ?' answered the supposed temporarily disturbed in mind, in the most calm and placid tone, even for one in the most happy state of mental contemplation to assume. ' Do you not observe that I am now negative, as passive and as quiescent in my nature as a Brahmin ? Ah, that I could always remain so ! but now again I feel the electric burning fire, driving towards me from across this accursed yard. Ah, I smell it, coming in sulphurous flames, again to bring on those horrible spasms !'

" Then clapping his hands together, he exclaimed—

" ' There, now they enter !' contorting himself for some time ; then again becoming placid, he said, ' it's all over for the present.'

" Then walking up to the ordinary, he continued—

" ' Do not, sir, think I am dissembling; I have no desire to feign, or to be really mad ; but you know not what I suffer from certain changes of the atmosphere. I have notice much sooner than a spider of its proneness to vary. My nerves are more delicate than his —and then again, consider what a larger body there is for the elements to act on, and I am sure you will pity me.'

" ' I do pity you,' replied the ordinary, interjectionally.

" The prisoner went on to say—

" ' Would you believe it ? But it is as true as the most commonplace fact in natural philosophy, that sometimes I elicit from the air—I mean that I, as a negative body, take in as much electric matter in a few hours as the most powerful electrical machine could evolve and deposit in a battery in a whole day's working of it's plate.'

" ' Surprising !' ejaculated some of the hearers

" ' Surprising ! ay, it is surprising !" continued he ; " but what is that to my suffering in giving it out again ? I have to walk about for hours to meet with negative bodies ; and when I do meet with them, and lessen my positive condition, the internal concussions are awful. Bang ! bang ! bang ! they go off. Thunder, as it is heard and not felt, is nothing to it. And now, sir, about spasmodical action, that you spoke of ; it was that—that killed the man ; my arm, not me. Mind, my volition had nothing to do with it. I never willed an evil thought against any human being. Have you seen a man clench his hand in an expression of energetical feeling ? Say !'

" ' I have," replied the person addressed.

" ' And without intending to strike or injure any one ?'

" ' Certainly.'

" 'You have it—you know it all—that is the whole of my case. The unfortunate man was rude to me—threatened me with his fist. The knife lay before me—I siezed it only to prevent his approaching me—and, to avoid a collision with him, I even drew my arm away that I might not injure him. The muscles were tense. I saw a spark escape from the point of the knife, and felt my arm forced forward at the rate of lightning speed : no wonder—it was lightning, that is, electricity, that impelled it ; the sensorium had nothing to do with the act—it was never consulted. Yet you will call this an act *malum in se*, because it is act *malum prohibitum*. However, sir, I will say that I look upon it as a kind of quackery in government, involving a want of solid skill, to apply the same remedy for all diseases, however varied or modified in their character ; that is, to supply the *ultimum supplicium* in every case. You have now, sir, my confession ; make what use you you please of it. Mine has been a spasmodic life. I thank you for the word, sir. I have committed a spasmodic offence, and, I suppose, must die a spasmodic death.'

"He then retired to a corner, sat down, and taking a book out of his pocket, apparently commenced reading it.

"The ordinary goes on to say—

" 'I immediately applied to the medical attendant of the prison, who had him removed to the infirmary, in order that he might be watched, and the real state of his mind be the more determinately ascertained.'

"This man's subsequent demeanour and conduct was in keeping with his behaviour that morning. He did not hesitate to make the confession that he stabbed the deceased. The slightest change in the weather affected his nervous system, which made him alternately exhibit depression and excitement of spirits, attended with muscular contortions. Such evidence was adduced on the trial as induced the jury to bring in a verdict of unsoundness of mind ; alter which he was consigned to a proper asylum for the treatment of his malady.

"Many cases of insanity are related, but never one in which the patient could so clealy describe the state of his feelings and the working of his mind. After his trial, when again visited, he said, 'I understand it all. They suppose me mad ; but it is a mistake ; it is only a disease of the nerves—a preternatural sensitiveness to atmospheric changes. Still I think that it is proper I should be taken care of.'

CHAPTER CI.

THE ORDINARY'S NOTES

AMONG those who were condemned to suffer death was one Leonard Dalton, an Irishman. The ordinary had occasion to visit him amongst the rest of the unfortunate culprits, and he gathered from him the particulars of his past life. The history of which may be gathered from the following sketch, which forms a few pages of Life's volume.

In every large city there may be found the strangest and most bewildering diversities of human life. From the shivering pauper who must crawl for shelter to the public archway when the storm howls around him, and the cold rain saturates his rags, to the enervated votary of pleasure who wastes his faculties amid scenes of extravagant splendour and cloying voluptuousness, the varieties of men, through all degrees and differences of station, condition, and capacity, may there be scanned and studied..

To stand apart from the current for a few minutes, in a public thoroughfare, and survey the passing forms, or obtain even a glance of the expression that marks each countenance, speaking to the imagination of that which works within—to walk thence along the crowded street, or into the lonely alley—to loiter in the magnificent square, or hurry through the squalid lane — to note what is seen, and ponder on what has been noted ; to employ thus an hour of leisure, is useful to him who would know more of his kind than what he can learn in his closet from books, or in the country from the unobstructed view of nature, in her hours " of glory and of gloom."

All feeling that exist and fade away—all aspirings that conduct men to greatness, and all passions that hasten them to ruin—all occurrences that delight or sadden, that create or destroy, that surprise or alarm—all circumstances that illustrate human nature, or diversify human life, are found in extensive towns.

A city is hourly the grave of brightest hopes, and often the cradle of noblest fortunes ; the place where hearts that have been broken, " yet brokenly *lived* on," sink at last to rest, and where those that once were happy feel the blight upon their hopes come slowly or suddenly—where the light laugh of mirth falls like " a mocking echo" on the ear, that has just heard the low moan of misery, or the wild despairing cry of baffled crime—where contrast that startle or sadden the heart are continually presented to the eye.

Though the worst of passions are developed in the close and selfish contacts to which those in cities are exposed, there are some in whom the fount of early feeling is never sealed—in whom purity of mind lives unadulterated by the corruptions of their fellows — whose hearts continue to beat freshly, while others around them fall into rottenness. Thus is it, that in towns, virtue and vice have their illustrations in extremes, such as, in the absence of extraordinary trials and temptations, can scarcely ever be witnessed in the country.

Our Irish metropolis shares in these characteristics of cities, though in a greatly inferior degree to London ; but there are peculiarities mingled in the scenes that form " life in Dublin," for which it would be vain to search elsewhere. Every variation of Irish nature is here most distinctly brought into action. Preferring particular illustration to general description, we shall endeavour, in the course of our random chapters, to exhibit a few of those distinctive marks which belong to life in Dublin.

It was nearly the noon of a bright spring day—a sunny day in the early spring—one of those whose cheering influence floods young hearts with hope, and steals away a few depressing cares from even the old and sorrow-bent — when a well-dressed young man walked smartly among the crowds that jostled their way through Sackville Street. He was comparatively a stranger, and could not help noticing the eager and busy appearance which most people assume when passing through this noble street.

On went each, with as quick a pace and as intent an air as if some mighty result depended upon the rapid movement, though, if the truth were known, it would be found that the majority of these apparently busy people had not any useful occupation to follow.

Many, very man, of the multitudes who are attracted "upon town" by a bright day thus benefit the shoemakers, for no purpose except to escape from thought, and destroy hours too heavy to be borne in loneliness.

But the well-dressed, prepossessing young man whom we have mentioned, was not merely " taking a walk " He passed through several streets, and, turning from the hurrying crowds, reached that quarter of which a slight description has been given. Marvelling at its quietude, for he had never been in this street before, he passed along, looking at the doors on either side to ascertain the numbers. This was not an easy matter, for time and neglect had aided in defacing many of the figures. Very few of the windows were without labels, announcing " a furnished room," " unfurnished lodgings," or " lodgings for single gentlemen," to be let, thus preparing the landlord of these houses, should he have passed in that direction, for a pitiful story, instead of cash, whenever the

call for rent might be made. The young man had proceeded nearly the entire length of the street, when he stopped ; and after examining a massive door, ascended to it by a flight of three or four steps. Of what had once been a huge knocker, nothing remained but a melancholy resemblance of the human visage, against which he was obliged to tap smartly several times with a silver-headed cane, before the door was opened. As might have been expected, the woman who appeared bore marks of antiquity upon her person. Indeed, it is wonderful how large a number of the servants of Dublin consist of old women. Many of the feebler sex, whose childhood was laughed away by the banks of some merry stream, in some pleasant vale, are compelled in maturer years to "seek for service" in the metropolis ; and, if they escape the snares which surround them, live on till age unfits them for active servitude, when they are cheaply hired by families whose "heavy work" is performed by others. But it is strange that there are *so many* old female servants in Dublin. Where they obtain such a constant supply of venerable childless dames is a subject of puzzling inquiry. There are, also, multitudes of young, handsome, active girls, at service, through the city, but the appearance of one of these in the old streets would be exceedingly anomalous.

Most servants, like most people in other stations, become civil or saucy when asked a question. The wrinkled representative of her class, who answered the knock of Charles Keatinge—for such was the young gentleman's name—appeared inclined, it will be seen, to alternate, in her replies, between respect and wrath.

" Pray does Mr. Dalton lodge in this house ?" inquired Keatinge.

" *Well* you know he does, my gentleman !" replied the sharp-tongued dame ; didn't I see you with him ? Don't come over me that way, with your 'pray does he lodge here ;' *pray*, indeed ! oh, then, it's I pray, sure enough, that it's somewhere else he'll soon be lodgin'. Keepin' me up night after night, sometimes to let him in of a night that he wouldn't, maybe, come until mornin', and more times to wait till his company, and maybe they not the best, 'ud go away—for it's burn the house they would, if I didn't watch them—and you, that was with him, I'd a'most swear to you, the whole of last night, to come here with your jackeen pretending not to know anything f him. He's the quare young man, so he is !"

Charles allowed her to rattle on till she paused for breath for he had a secret and sad motive in learning from her whatever he could of Dalton's conduct.

" You mistake, my good woman, I was

never here before; but is this truly the manner in which Mr. Dalton spends his time?"

"Good woman! But maybe you're right, and maybe I'm wrong, an' if you don't share in his vagaries, an' if 'twasn't yourself was here, it's not like a gentleman to get so much out o' me about him—that I must tell you, for it's he that's good and off-handed, wid all his faults, an' if he'd come in reg'lar, it's he that would be the nate lodger."

"Is he at home, now?' was the next inquiry.

The woman paused and hesitated, like all persons who balance the counter reasons in favour of a true and false answer

"Why, then, I'm not sure, sir! An' maybe it ye'd call at another time it's more likely ye'd be to see him."

"No; I must see him now, if he's within. If he is out, I'll wait in his room for him," replied Keatinge, rendered suspicious by the woman's manner.

"But he'd be vexed if I let any one find him in bed this time o' the day, when he had only a few hour's sleep"

"Not up yet!" exclaimed the young man; "but show me his room, or I must find it myself.',

Grumbling something which Keatinge did not heed, she led the way up stairs, and pointing to a front room on the second floor, requested, if Mr. Dalton should be angry, "not to let him blame her."

Keatinge tapped at the door, but there was no response. Having tapped again, ineffectually, he opened the door, and entered a capacious apartment. which, however, was in darkness, except where two streaks of light struggled in between the closed shutters. The noise made in opening the door, aroused the sleeper, and made him inquire, in no gentle tone, "Who the h—ll is that."

Keatinge advanced, unclosed the shutters of one of the windows, and then stood by the bedside of his cousin, Leonard Dalton.

"Gracious heaven! Charles—how came you here?—oh, God!"

And the young man, who had raised himself in the bed, sunk back and covered his face with his hands, as if the countenance of his friend, or the light of day, was more than he could bear to see.

"No matter now how I found you; but Leonard, Leonard, you little know what suffering you have caused by your conduct. Since you stole away from me," continued Keatinge, his eyes softening as he witnessed the convulsive heavings of the other, "my mind has not known a tranquil thought—why, why did you act so?"

"Say nothing of it now, Charles; say nothing, for God's sake, say nothing now!—my brain, my heart, are burning. If i have

made others suffer, oh, I have been suffering too. When you hear of all my madness, you will know how deeply I am punished."

Keatinge looked round the apartment, having first unclosed the second shutter, and admitted full light. The merry beams of the sun shot into the room, revealing every object, and illumining the relics of a scene which created some surprise and sadness in the bosom of Keatinge.

The room was sufficiently large to answer the double purpose of a sitting or sleeping chamber. On a sofa bed lay Dalton; his face, strikingly handsome, bore traces of recent dissipation and passion.

Throughout the room were evidences of a debauch.

On a circular table in the centre were several glasses, some upset, and others containing the sediment of whisky punch or porter. Two or three were but half emptied, showing that those who had been using them "had drunk till they could drink no more." Scattered amongst them were fragments of tobacco pipes and cigars.

A pack of cards, some clean and some soiled with punch, ashes, and candle-snuff, were strewn in nearly equal portions on the table and the carpet.

The carpet itself, old. worn, all its bright colours faded into one disty drown, was more suitable to the place than one of less antiquity would have been. Three or four fresh spots on it, showed where porter had been recently spilled. and near them was a broken bottle, labelled "Guinness's XXX."

Clothes thrown negligently into a corner—a second table covered with books, gloves, stocks, a cap, brushes, a few surgical instruments, and other matters—the walls, on parts of which were old prints of some unknown subjects, and modern ones of less decorous nature - a violin with only two strings suspended over the mantle-piece—wooden pegs for clothes, without any clothes upon them — and, throughout, dust, dirt, confusion, waste, and negligence, were revealed to Keatinge.

Upon the mantel-piece was one stocking, the fellow of it being still on the left foot of Mr. Leonard Dalton, in attempting to remove it from which, he had tumbled on the floor some hours before.

He had sufficient sense left in his reeling brain not to make a second attempt. How he contrived to undress, with that exception and then stagger to bed, must puzz'e all who have not seen how often instinct guides those in whom reason has been temporarily extinguished.

But an enumeration of all that Keatinge saw would occupy, as the newspapers say, "more space than we can afford."

If the reader has a young tavern haunting

acquaintance, who resides alone in Dublin—has money to spend, and no absorbing occupation to follow—whose passions are an overmatch for his prudence, and whose companions are of the class emphatically known as " dangerous"—let him steal into his room some fine day, and he may be enabled to complete the picture which we leave unfinished.

Keatinge slowly surveyed the apartment, the two glistening and straining eyeballs of Dalton fixed intently on his countenance. They quailed, however, when Charles gazed with a look full of reproach and sorrow on his friend.

How strong a contrast is presented when the bright blaze of the noon-day sun rests upon the undisturbed relics of riot and revelry.

Abroad—light, and life, and cheerfulness—the world awake, and its myriads of animated beings fulfilling the designs of creation; within, the wearied reveller, surrounded by memorials of those noisy hours, which leave behind heaviness, remorse, the thoughts of wasted days and blighted hopes, the reactions of the heart, the weakness of body and overwhelming depression of spirit.

This contrast Keatinge felt as he looked round the room, and then turned to Dalton.

Charles Keatinge and Leonard Dalton were medical students, and, as we have already intimated, cousins

The former was about twenty-four, and the latter twenty-three years of age. Born and reared in the same pretty village, about one hundred miles distant from Dublin—educated at the same seminary, in boyhood and in youth together; they knew each other thoroughly, and loved each other well.

Boys, as well as men, of opposite tastes and tempers, sometimes contract the closest friendships; and such was the case with the cousins, in whom, perhaps, the intercourse of relationship tended to soften those points of character in which they differed.

Keatinge was serious and steady from his childhood, seldom excited to passion; kind, good-hearted, and prudent. He was one of those whom you frequently hear old people recommend for imitation, as " a patern to the neighbourhood."

Dalton, on the other hand, was passionate and imprudent—easily excited to good, or seduced into evil. Often, indeed, was it prophesied, by those who understood his temperament, that his ways through life would not be " ways of pleasantness." Yet he possessed some of the finest qualities of man, and, had circumstances favoured their growth, his fate might have been different from what it was. But the weeds grew apace, till the flowers were nearly choked. In person, too, the cousins differed.

Charles was, at the time of their leaving home, of middle height, stout, and fair; his features were both intelligent and handsome. Leonard was tall, and possessed almost faultless beauty of limb and feature. Dark flashing eye, dark complexion, hair " black as the raven's hue," and the other perfections of white hand and musical voice, which captivated young ladies in their teens, when their heads are " full of romance." and their hearts ready to yield to " soft persuasion," rendered Leonard the envy of many a dumpy, snub-nosed, school-fellow.

Keatinge was an only child, while Dalton had brothers and sisters. Their fathers were in comfortable circumstances, being what are known in Ireland as " gentlemen-farmers;" though at what point of affluence the right to gratify a weak ambition, by assuming a title above one's neighbours, commences, we cannot tell.

The cousins decided on adopting the medical profession; Keatinge with the design of practising in his native village; Dalton centering his professional hopes in being able to get an appointment in the army. In accordance with a customary and commendable system, they had first been placed with an apothecary.

By what is experienced in apothecaries' shops, many a noble-hearted boy is vitiated and ruined; but many also are preserved by prudence and carefulness.

The cousins, though exposed to much temptation, escaped; even Leonard resisted the evils of vicious example, but his strength lay chiefly in the counsels and watchfulness of Charles.

During their apprenticeship a circumstance had occurred, which, if known to those nuisances, the professed "gossips of the village," whose depreciating comments on human nature spring solely from a knowledge of self, would have afforded ground for the assertion that the friendship of the cousins would ultimately, if not immediately, give place to hostile feeling.

Within a mile of their village a wealthy farmer, named Rowan, resided, and with him dwelt his son and daughter, the survivors of many children.

The cousins had been from infancy intimate with the Rowans, and in the breast of of each, without either knowing it—for the first approach of love is seldom felt, he steals into the heart so softly until he has rifled it of peace—a deep and ineradicable passion for the beautiful Maria had been silently growing.

A short time before their departure to encounter the perils of the metropolis, the secret of Leonard was revealed.

It was at the close of a lovely sabbath evening, when the last golden tints of the

western sky were fading away, and solitude favoured the avowal of love—it was then, in her own summer-house, when no human eye was upon them, that Leonard first felt he loved, and first told his feelings.

There was, of course, the usual portion of blushes, diffidence, doubt, hesitation, tenderness, and protestation, before the struggle of terminated, and one swiftly-whispered feeling word made Leonard happy.

Their hearts rioted for awhile in a mutual ecstasy, which was unchecked even by the prospect of approaching separation. Imprinting the first kiss of love, pure and joyous love, upon her lips, he bade her good night, and sought out Charles Keatinge, to confide to him the secret of his happiness

Who has outlived youth, and all but the memory of youth's purest love, that does not,

No. 64.

in the gloom which so often overspreads the hopes of mankind, sometimes revive the recollection of the first kiss of love, and feel his spirit winging its transient flight, backward to that brief moment of enchanting happiness?

Whether youthful affection be darkened by the blight of disappointment, or rewarded by the fulfilment of hope, it hath periods of unalloyed rapture in its duration, which often and often afterwards touch the hidden springs of memory, and awaken sweet and tender emotions in breasts that time and toil had seemed to harden.

The memory of love's first kiss rises in hours of sorrow, to calm many a troubled soul by the reflection, that although suffering now, a time has been when it was blest. Some may sneer at such a sentiment, but they are only those who have never felt the kiss of pure and youthful affection.

It is easy to imagine the joy with which Leonard cofided the secret to his cousin, but it is not easy to imagine the chilling effect it produced on the feelings of poor Keatinge, for he became aware of the strength of his love only when made acquainted with its hopelessness.

However, Leonard was too much wrapped in his own feelings to perceive the momentary agitation of his cousin ; and the latter, loving like the few who love with perfect truth and purity, bore the tidings manfully, and determined to aid in bringing happiness to the two who were dearest to him.

Maria Rowan was one of those girls whose grace and goodness cast spells around the hearts of all that come within their witching influence.

There are some ladies who live in the unhealthy atmosphere of what is called "high life," and have never known the fresh and untainted air which braces the morals of the middle classes, who do not believe that *grace* —though they admit that *goodness*—can be found in an Irish farm-house.

But those who know better will acknowledge that amongst the wives and daughters of Irish farmers there is as much of beauty, of virtue, and of all the charms that strengthen the power of the softer sex upon the hearts of men, as in any other rank in the country.

Maria was such a girl, about twenty-one years of age, just ripening into womanhood, as the coldest heart could not help loving. Her soft blue eye and bright brown hair— her full rich lip, and delicate but healthy complexion — her well-formed figure and graceful air—her cheerful disposition and ever-ready kindness—had won the love of many besides Leonard. Unlike other women —not however the majority—she rather regretted than rejoiced at the homage of hearts whose affections she could not return.

A celebrated English lady mentioned, in one of her entertaining letters, that "the description of a face or figure is a needless thing. as it never conveys a true idea."

As our readers may be of a similar opinion, we shall not enter into a further description of the fair and gentle Maria.

The day arrived when the cousins were to leave home for Dublin. The advices, cautions, promises, and blessings, usual on such occasions, were lavishly bestowed.

"And, Charles, darling!" said the quiet and loving mother of Leonard, as she whispered to him, while her son was engaged with other members of the family ; "Charles, darling! won't you keep him from harm, for he has the wild drop in him? Ah, if he was as steady as you, Charles, dear, I would not have the heavy fear on me now ; but won't you mind him, and be my comfort when ye are far away ?"

There were tears in the poor woman's eyes, as Charles promised faithfully that neither he or his cousin should ever give her cause for sorrow. How unforseeing are men in ther promises—how feeble in their efforts to fulfil them !

It has been the lot of nearly all, from whom the sunny days of boyhood or girlhood have glided away, to know the sweets and bitterness of love ; therefore, imagination or memory will enable you, fair reader, to judge of the pang of the parting hour between Maria and Leonard.

She was pale—very pale ; and he—but we leave the reader the pleasure of imagining the scene—the half-uttered words of tenderness — the solemn pledges of fidelity, repeated for the thousandth time by Leonard, while *she* could scarcely speak—the extravagance of feeling which, at another time, would have been more than ridiculous—the last pressure of breast to breast—the faintly-murmured " Won't you take care of yourself, Leonard ?"—the " Good bye—God bless you, dear Maria !"—and the anguish which all who have experienced a similar scene of " mingled bliss and misery" can so well understand.

It was one of those " partings" which Lord Byron has finely described—

> " such as press
> The life from out young hearts."

Those who leave home generally find in novelty and excitement a healing for the grief that separation from beloved objects may have caused ; but those who remain on the spot hallowed by dearest associations find their grief kept alive by mute yet eloquent memorials of the absent. So it was with Maria and Leonard. The pang soon passed from his heart, though the love was faithful, while every object around Maria recalled his image and shaded her brow with the melancholy produced by those sad forebodings with which, in absence, lovers have a foolish fashion of tormenting themselves.

The cousins arrived in Dublin, and engaged lodgings together. When once before in the metropolis, their stay had been too limited to enable them to behold "the sights." Now, however, they resolved to devote a few days to the gratification of curiosity, before commencing their studies.

Having seen, as they considered, all that was worth seeing in the city, and visited the public places of amusement, the cousins were walking one day, arm-in-arm, amid the throng and gaiety of Grafton-street. Their attention was attracted by a line of five or six old and ragged men, walking closely after each other, the front and the back of each being protected from view by a large board, suspended from the neck. On each board was a placard, announcing in Patagonian type an exhibition of fire-works at the Rotunda Gardens.

The cousins had never before seen human machines used in moving advertisements; and having read the announcement, which from the size of the letters they easily did, notwithstanding the motion of the machines, resolved to witness the exhibition. Though we do not wish to repeat observations more worn-out than the only coat of a dandy long broken down, we cannot help saying—how often a man's fate is influenced by causes the most trivial. Had Leonard not seen that advertisement, how much of subsequent misery might he have been spared!

It was a fine night, and, as the weather favoured the exhibition, crowds of the fashionable, gay and idle, were in attendance. A military band performed at intervals, "and" —we must again borrow from the newspapers—"considerably enhanced the amusement of the evening."

During one of these intervals the cousins were led to observe a group standing quite close to them. It consisted of four persons, who, to the uninitiated in Dublin scenes, appeared but ill-assorted. The most remarkable figure in the group was a tall, beautifully-formed, and richly-dressed young woman. Her face seemed to Leonard to possess faultless loveliness; but in the free expression of the eye and lip there was that which would have checked admiration in experienced beholders. Another woman, neither tall, nor young, nor handsome, nor yet old, or ugly, or dwarfish, gaudily dressed, was standing with her. They were conversing, in tones sufficiently loud to be heard by the cousins, with two young men, who, as belonging to a numerous and noxious class, deserve but a brief description.

The countenance of the elder and taller was disfigured very much with pockmarks, which pleasing ornaments did not counteract the impression caused by his eyes, of which one was dark, restless, and piercing; the other was quite different—it was large, sightless, and bore a strong resemblance to a pickled oyster. He wore a broad-brimmed "Jerry," cocked knowingly on the oyster side, so as in some measure to conceal it, and was closely buttoned in a blue pilot great coat, into the side pockets of which his hands were thrust, without, however, entirely concealing an instrument patronised by persons of an *amiable and courageous* disposition, and known as a "skull cracker," one end of which peeped out above his elbow.

The companion of this prepossessing personage was of a different appearance; he evidently aimed at the enviable dignity of dandyism, but chiefly "after a fashion of his own." A hat, with a brim very narrow, and a crown very distant from the brim, lay on a mass of oiled and curled hair, sufficient to stuff one of those chairs in which gouty aldermen may repose. That hat did not cover the head, for between them was the cushion of hair. It was wonderful how well he balanced the hat, for although it appeared to totter at every move of the head, it did not fall. He was low-sized, and of very slender make—so low, that the hat and the head seemed as long as the remainder of his person, and so slender, that the little face and the enormous curls, measured together, were of vastly more bulk than any other portion of his body. He stood on two supporters, in the shape of legs, which, though nearly as slight as parlour tongs, were also as strong, else they must have yielded under the superincumbent weight of bear's grease and hair. Occasionally in his right hand he twirled a smart cane, with the air of Hercules playing with his club, for the smaller and weaker men are, the bigger and stouter they strive to look. His trowsers, coat, waistcoat, stock, shirt, and boots were neat miniatures of the prevailing "fashions for gentlemen." Little grey eyes, little cocked nose, and little mouth, from which was occasionally heard a little attempt at a manly laugh, completed the contrast between him and his worse-featured comrade. A little chain, imitative of silver, was glittering from his neck, and was attached to—nothing—in his waistcoat pocket. An eye-glass, supported by a yard of black ribbon, gave employment to his left hand. He was one of those who excite both alarm and wonder, as they passed along the street, seemingly about to be overturned every moment, yet managing to balance, and sometimes to swagger, as if reckless of danger, or ambitious of admiration. If the space which in other heads is filled with brain, contained anything of weight equal to one shining curl, they could not maintain their "centre of gravity" for five minutes.

Had the cousins been acquainted with the ways of town, they would have recognised two different specimens of a tribe whose varieties are infinite—that respectable division of the human race, known as "Dublin jackeens." The reader will find that one of those who have been partly introduced to him was of the *knavish*, the other *silly*, kind. There are a multitude of other varieties, some of whom look like other men; but, with any of the class, except our "unfavorable specimens," we have no present business.

While Charles and Leonard were listening to the music, or looking at the different objects around, this group were conversing.

"I say, Honeycomb," said the little fellow, 'I've, spotted the cove that made you scud yesterday from Grafton-street—aye, 'pon honna—and your fair acquaintance with him."

The *maneen* had raised the eye-glass, and was gazing at a distant group. The gentleman addressed as *Honeycomb* looked in the same direction, and then saying to his companion—

"By all that's handsome, and that's my own phiz, I believe, Jaff, you're right—stay here, till I see nearer"—the one-eyed personage walked away.

"Of whom *dee* ye speak?" asked the gaudily-dressed lady, whom we have not described.

"Oh, there was a nice *go* with me and Honeycomb—Frank, I mean—yesterday, he—he!" responded the little gentleman known as Jaff.

"Why do you call Frank, Honeycomb?" interrupted the tall girl.

"Didn't you know that, Amelia? he—he! That's *my* christening. Frank, you see, has a face so rough that it would require only a gentle rub on it, to light a lucifer match—he—hah !—it's very like a hard honeycomb, and, as he's always making game o'me, I call him that, and sometimes sponge phiz; but it's only when he says anything to provoke—he—heh ! It's a right good un ;" and the little man again sounded the little laugh. "But, I say, as I was telling you, we went yesterday, Frank and I, to nob it in Grafton-street ; he had on the green specs, to hide th' ugly ogle, and was in very stylish trim. When we wish particularly to do the heavy—only for fun you know, pure fun—we bow to the finest carriages that pass, and the coves that see us think—'pon honna—that we must be high gents, knowing so many ladies in carriages and all that, and before the spoonies can see whether the ladies bow to us in return, the carriage is gone by, you know—he—heh !—that's the way to nob it like lords—to do it *particularly* heavy—eh ? Good fun, isn't it ? Well, as I was saying, we walked up and down, at both sides, and into the green, for nearly two hours, and there was one carriage which we noticed go by six or seven times, and each time we bowed to a damn fine gal in it. 'Pon honna, Frank,' said I, as it turned into College-green, ' that gal noticed us, I think.' Before Honeycomb could reply, a genteel-looking young cove marches up, and says, 'I'd be obliged to you, if you'd inform me who owns that carriage just at the statue.' Frank suspected that the cove was up to the thing, and wanted to have a laugh at his gagging-go, but he was determined to gull him if possible—all for fun, you know. ' A very intimate friend of mine;' says Frank, 'Sir Malachy Mala-

chy'—(you know we have always a stock of names ready for use when necessary—he—heh !) Well, listen now, Amelia, it's d——d good. " Indeed,' says the stranger; 'and pray, who may the young lady be ?' ' O,' says Frank, determined as a bouncer, ' she's an officer's daughter that Sir Malachy seduced. But what right have you to question me ?' 'Because, you scoundrel,' says the other—*scoundrel*, think of that. Amelia—' *I'm the lady's brother !*' With that he made *a wipe* at Frank, with a cudgel that might floor an ox ; but Frank, you see, didn't wish to have the goggles smashed, and his tender eye exposed to the sun-light—he—heh !—so he cut to the College side. The blow fell on the basket of an old orange-women, and scattered a few of her oranges. ' Blaizes to yer ugly soul,' she cried, ' and sweet bad luck to you, every day you see a pavin' stone, and every day you don't.' The stranger threw her some money, and darted after Frank, but he was *luke* of catching him ; and, besides, was nearly run over by two cars—Frank escaped ; that's the stranger, there, beyond, and his sister—isn't she a foine gal—d——n foine, 'pon honna ?"

And the little man gazed admiringly when he had finished the recital of this instance of a practice, common amongst many frequenters of the Dublin *pavé*, whose heads and pockets are equally empty.

" There are so many leedies there," said the lesser female, " that I can't recognise her. But what did her brother say to yourself ?" she asked, surprised that he should have told a story not very flattering to himself or his friend ; but Jaff did so for the purpose of contrasting his own valiant with Honeycomb's cowardice.

"Oh, damn me, nothing—'pon honna; if he had, I was determined to slate him. O, no—he didn't mind, *me*—I stood my ground ; but he knew better than to attack me ;" and the miniature caricature of man endeavoured to " look big." "But, I say, here's Frank Well, buck-o, wasn't I right—eh? Did you speak to your *friend*—he—heh !" addressing the gentleman with the pickled-oyster eye, who had returned, the collar of his coat having been turned up so as to hide his features.

"Faith, yes, Jaff ; and, by G——, here they come, too ! You're in for a pounding, my customer—he can't know *me*. Look, Amelia ; look, Jane," he continued, with a laugh, addressing the females ; " see, how poor Jaff's weeny *crubeens* are trembling, as merrily as a fellow's hand after a batther."

Certainly, the little fellow's supporters became alarmingly insecure as he saw the stranger, in company with the fair occupant of the carriage, another lady, and a gentleman, approaching.

"Eh, now don't be always *at* me, Frank; as if I cared one damn—he—heh!" and there was heard the faintest imitation of a very faint laugh.

The strangers, however, though they came close, turned back, and the heart of Jaff expanded under the influence of indescribable relief.

"Blast the fellow," said Jaff. "I'd have leathered him, only he was wise enough to turn back;" and the little fellow spoke stoutly, as a cur will bark loudly at you, when well beyond the reach of stick or stone.

But he had been seen, and in a few minutes, to his horror, he perceived the stranger returning alone, as he had slipped away from his party. The truth is, that Jaff had also fled the day before, but in a different direction from Honeycomb, who was the particular object of the stranger's wrath. Now, however, the stranger—a tall, stout resolute-looking young man—was at his side, before he could escape. The same cudgel—a genuine south-country shillelah—which had terrified him the previous day, was in the stranger's right hand, and the sight of it transformed the knees of the little fellow into a pair of most melodious castanets.

"You, fellow," said the stranger, "were with the ruffian who fled from me yesterday in Grafton-street. Tell me, instantly, where I'll find him, or—look at this!" and he exhibited the cudgel, a gentle stroke of which would have caused the little soul of the poor jackeen to escape for ever from his minikin body.

Jaff was very pale—his heart had again diminished to the size of a withered daisy—his whole body shook, yet, positively, his hat did not fall off his hair.

"Sir," he replied, in a pitiable voice, "Si-r, —I'm not aware—"

"Neither lie, or delay," interrupted the stranger threateningly.

"It's not, I must say," whined Jaff, looking terrified, though striving to look offended, alternately at the stranger's cudgel and the stranger's countenance. "It's not like a-a-gentleman, to insult another—a-a-nother gentleman in the company of ladies."

Having thus ingeniously enlisted the sympathies of his female companions, Jaff lost a little—very little—of his fear.

"Gentlemen!—ladies!" exclaimed the stranger, with a sneer—"a contemptible thing like you, and these well-known reputable lasses! But, answer me, fellow!"

The tall girl's dark eyes flashed, but she did not speak, in reply to the insulting allusion. The other muttered—

"It's a sheeme, indeed so it is—a great sheeme, to show such conduct before leedies."

The stranger gave an angry glance at her, and then, seizing the jackeen by the collar with his left hand, partly raised the cudgel with his right—

"I tell you what," he said slowly and determinedly to her, "if this wretched little particle of an abortion does not instantly tell me where to find his companion, I'll mark on his body, with this good stick, a message for the other."

"If you breek the peace," said she, "we'll call the pelice,"

"Police be d——d!" cried the stranger —"come, sir, I can't delay—answer," and he shook Jaff violently; still the hat did not fall off.

Jaff dreaded annihilation too much to continue disobliging. A happy thought struck him, and the big fear was removed from his heart.

"Don't strike, sir," he cried.

"Pree doon't be violent, you rude fellow, you!" chimed in the old woman who had before spoken.

"Speak," said the stranger.

Honeycomb had remained during this dialogue highly amused at the predicament in which his companion was placed. He did not dread exposure, nor care much about it; he was not, therefore, prepared for Jaff's words, as he cried, pointing to him.

"There he is, sir."

A row was the consequence, and, in a few minutes nearly all the persons in the garden were congregated round the spot. The police were in prompt attendance, but not till Honeycomb had escaped amongst the crowd, having left a taste of the skull-cracker with the hot-headed stranger, in return for a few blows of the shillelah. Jaff, of course, had evaporated. In the jostle, crush, and confusion, the cousins were separated; Charles having withdrawn from the immediate scene of the row, while Leonard remained to witness "the fun."

When the crowd were again dispersing to resume the promenade of the gardens, Leonard looked around for his cousin, and his eyes encountered those of the tall and beautiful woman who had been addressed as "Amelia." She also had been looking for her companion; and now for a moment or two, there was a mutual gaze between her and Dalton.

"Sir," said she, advancing boldly, and speaking with a very sweet voice, "perhaps you'd be kind enough to accompany me to the gate, and call a car for me, for I cannot find my friends—this unpleasant occurrence has separated us."

Leonard hesitated, for he did not know whether his compliance might be right or wrong.

"Oh, sir!" said she, "I beg your pardon; you must think it strange of me to ask you to trouble yourself, but, really, I am *so* frightened;" and she looked around, as if in anxious search of her companions.

"No trouble, ma'am; I'm looking, too, for a friend," said Dalton, "but I'll be happy to accompany you to the gate."

"Oh, thank you, thank you," she exclaimed, and seized his arm.

"I wish I could see Charles," thought Leonard.

Very rarely, indeed, is there difficulty in procuring a car under such circumstances; for the carmen generally crowd the avenues leading to places of public amusement, where they are pretty sure of being engaged on the termination of the performances. Yet, when Leonard and his companion arrived at the entrance, they saw only two or three cars, and, on inquiry, these were found engaged. The result was, that Leonard was induced to "see her home."

Alas! that evening Leonard Dalton forgot his fair and faithful Maria. The acquaintance thus accidentally commenced was continued until vice had impaired the strength of love, and rendered the counsels of friendship distasteful.

Leonard Dalton became a constant attendant at the heels of the fair but frail Amelia. In a short time he was her acknowledged admirer and lover, and in a few months she became his mistress, and he her slave.

It is hardly possible to fathom the deep current which bears a man on, for good or for ill, throughout his probation on this sphere. A designing and immoral woman, having him in her toils, as firmly as Amelia had her lover, could either make or mar him. Alas! she became Leonard Dalton's bane, or curse.

Step by step he became lowered in the moral scale, and more than one forgery had been committed by the infatuated admirer. Maria was for ever lost to him, and, indeed, he did not dare present himself to her on even one occasion.

His cousin well knew how he was going on; he reasoned with him—besought him, with tears in his eyes, to become a reclaimed man—but his entreaties were in vain

Leonard had diverged from the straight path, had been shunted off from the right line, and he could not return. Ashamed of his conduct, he flew with his enslaver to the metropolis. Here he lived in a grand style, frequented places of fashionable resort, and became a man of fashion. How he obtained the means to live at the extravagant rate he chose to adopt, was a mystery to the uninitiated in the world's ways: but he did run an extravagant and reckless career.

All this while Charles Keatinge was a constant attendant at the house of Mr. Rowan; he endeavoured to palliate the conduct of his cousin, Leonard Dalton, by a series of specious tales. He told Maria that he was sure Leonard would come back an altered man as soon as he had sown his wild oats, as he expressed it; he had a good heart, so he said, and he felt that Leonard would, sooner or later, see the error of his ways. All this, Maria Rowan found it impossible to believe, but she concealed her feelings as best she could, and mourned in silence.

Poor Keatinge was madly in love with her himself; but he never gave expression to his feelings, but remained a staunch advocate for his rival—few men would have been so self-sacrificing in their nature.

Time went on, and it would be hardly worth while for us to follow Leonard Dalton throughout his career of crime—sooner or later it must come to an end.

It did so, and eventually placed Leonard Dalton where we found him, in one of the condemned cells of Newgate. She who had lured him into crime had already passed away from the things of this world.

When Jonathan Wild, with his followers, entered the house occupied by Leonard Dalton, the latter offered resistance, but after a short struggle was captured and conveyed to prison upon a capital charge.

The guilty Amelia was to have been taken at the same time, but she rushed up stairs into her bed-room at the first intimation that the officers were in the house, and swallowed prussic acid, and upon Wild's breaking open the door of her apartment, he found her stretched upon the floor a lifeless corpse.

There was no chance for Leonard Dalton now; he had too many charges brought against him, and his career was too well known to the authorities, for him to hope for a reprieve.

The news of his conviction fell like a thunderbolt upon the Rowan's: not so, however, Charles Keatinge, who had dreaded such an event. He had heard the particulars of the life his cousin had been leading, and had journied to London on more than one occasion to try and lure him back to the paths of rectitude, with what result we have already seen.

Maria Rowan fainted away when the intelligence reached her of Dalton's condemnation. Charles Keatinge did all in his power to reassure her. After the first shock was over, and she recovered her consciousness, he said that there might be a reprieve—he would journey to London and see what could be done—after all, things might not be so bad as was anticipated; and, agreeable to this resolution, off Charles started for the metropolis.

His heart sunk within him as he approached the city in which stood that gloomy pile, called Newgate.

He had journeyed from Dublin to Liverpool, taking with him a short, stiff-built shambling pony, upon whose back he had been accustomed to ride. Mounted on this animal, Charles Keatinge endeavoured to reach London by easy stages, for at the time of which we write, this was perhaps the quickest course for him to adopt.

He had succeeded in reaching Edgeware, and night had fallen over his path for some hour or so, when he was suddenly confronted by a masked figure on horseback, who presented a pistol towards him and demanded his money.

"My money!" said Charles Keatinge. "It is but little I have with me; only enough to suffice me while I stay in London. You would never rob a man who has come some hundreds of miles for the purpose of saving the life of a fellow creature. Alas! I have a dear relative condemned to death, and lies now in the cells of Newgate. Have pity on me, therefore—pity for the sake of him who needs comfort and succour in his last hour."

"What is your relative's name?" inquired Colonel Jack, for the highwayman was no other than he.

"Leonard Dalton," answered Keatinge.

"Ah!" said our hero, at once dropping his pistol. "Pass on, friend, I take nothing from you. In sooth, but you are in trouble enough. There is no chance for Leonard Dalton—he must die."

"Do you know him?" exclaimed Charles Keatinge.

"Yes," answered our hero, "perfectly well, and have known him for a long period. Foolish young fellow, I knew what all this would end in."

"He has run a reckless career, I suppose?" said Keatinge.

"Perfectly so. Pass on, my friend. When you see your relative, tell him that Colonel Jack inquired after him. He has my best wishes, not that they are of any use to him. Farewell."

And so saying, the highwayman clapped spurs to his horse, and gallopped off, leaving Keatinge in a state of surprise and wonder at the strange incident.

For a few minutes Keatinge paused, and then he trotted on towards London.

In about a couple of hours after this, he found himself in front of Newgate, and inquired for his cousin, Leonard Dalton.

It was late when he arrived, and beyond the time for strangers to be admitted within the walls of the prison, consequently Charles Keatinge was refused admittance. He appealed, however, in a most abject manner to be allowed an interview with the prisoner. The only answer to all this was a blank refusal. Keatinge, who knew but little of the prison regulations, said he would see the

governor of the prison. He was informed that such a course would be useless.

While he was conversing with the turnkey, the ordinary made his appearance at the outer lobby. He had been attending upon the prisoners, and was about to take his way from the prison.

Upon learning who the applicant for admission was, and why he had presented himself at the doors of the prison, he undertook, upon his own responsibility, to grant permission for Charles Keatinge to enter the prison, and he himself conducted the young man into the cell where Leonard Dalton was confined.

Who shall describe the meeting between the two cousins?

Leonard was by this time an altered man, and in answer to Charles's inquiries, he said, sadly, but with firmness—

"Nay, I do not wish to live, Charles. I see the error of my ways. It's too late now for me to reform. I am a lost man, and wish to die."

"Oh, Leonard, why talk thus? Wish to die! Surely if your life could be spared—"

"Hush!—do not keep up that ridiculous fiction. My life will not be spared—let that suffice. How is—is—Maria?"

He struck his clenched fist against his forehead, as he made this inquiry.

Keatinge gave as favourable an account of her as he could, so that he might spare the feelings of the unfortunate man as much as possible.

"Poor Maria," exclaimed Leonard. "She was too good for me, and after all, has had a lucky escape. She will find some solace in you, Charles—some little solace. Be kind to her for my sake—though I need not tell you that."

"How—what mean you?" said Keatinge, in unfeigned astonishment.

"You love her, Charles, deeply love her. I know that—have known it long, long ago. She loses nothing by my death—nay, she is a gainer."

"How is—"

"I know to whom you are alluding—she is dead."

"Dead?"

"Yes."

"How?"

"By poison."

Keatinge uttered an exclamation of surprise.

"Administered by her own hand," continued Dalton.

We will not dwell upon the painful parting of the two cousins; these scenes are terrible and appalling enough at all times, and with all his errors, Leonard Dalton was beloved by his cousin, Charles Keatinge, and the feeling he evinced, when taking his final leave of Leonard, moved the prison chaplain to tears.

Little remains to be told. Leonard Dalton expiated his crimes on the public scaffold. Time rolled on, and some two years after the execution of Leonard, Charles Keatinge and Maria were married.

This was one of the cases of which the chaplain was led to speak of in a feeling manner.

The situation of ordinary was not one of his own seeking, nor was he ever easy in it—the duties of the office being those of the most appalling nature. To be for the great part of his time in juxta position with criminals, and those, too, of the very worst description; to hear their imprecations, or to witness the agony of their feelings, and wasting away of human flesh occasioned by atrophy of mind as well as body, was as painful to him on the last day of his holding office as on the day he commenced it. A public execution shook his frame to the centre. On all such occasions, the reverend ordinary of whom we write suffered for days preceding the fatal morning, and could only recover with difficulty from the shock for days afterwards. When the order was given for an execution, he immediately instituted every inquiry into the malefactors' cases, with a hope of finding some mitigating points to urge in their favour, and to obtain a reprive. No distance deterred him from pursuing, and following up to the last, an inquiry which might turn the scale in favour of mercy, employing every hour either in seeking for evidence or in endeavouring to persuade some of the city authorities to interpose in the good work of saving human life. All other leisure moments were occupied in going to and from the office in the interior of the prison to make inquiries if anything had transpired in favour of those who were to suffer.

On some occasions he was in the office every half-hour, saying—

"Well; any news? No message? Heard nothing? oh! Nobody gone to the secretary—anybody talk of going? Has the sheriff been here again? Has the alderman quite given the case up as hopeless? I thought I had made an impression on him this morning. Did that inquiry about the witness end in nothing? I think it ought to be followed up; because, if it really be as the man says it is, it might turn the scale, even now, in his favour. You know," addressing the governor of the prison, " in how many instances we have succeeded in cases where the phases were blacker than this. Recollect how we saved those three men for burglary, even at the eleventh hour; and at last we proved their innocence, in spite of their unwillingness to receive the proof. You also recollect the case of the two unfortunate fellows for highway robbery?—that was peculiarly a case of my own—I effected that single-handed you know. What may we, then, not accomplish, if we all pull together? I could wish we always had sheriffs like Wilde. You remember what he did?"

Few equalled the ordinary in perseverance, which frequently occasioned him to be considered troublesome at the office, and to draw forth a remark that considerably annoyed him, namely—

"Well, if you take such a view of the man's case, I wonder you don't go down to the secretary yourself."

This observation cut him to the soul; as latterly he had received a rebuke which deprived him of the advantage of personally appearing in these cases, and of snatching the victims of the law out of the hands of the executioner. One day he received a command from the secretary of state to attend at his office, where he was addressed in the following manner:—" I have frequently had occasion to notice the zeal with which you take up the cases of malefactors, with a view of procuring a commutation of their sentences. You appear to have always something to urge why the extreme penalty of the law should not be carried into effect. I have no doubt, sir, that you act conscientiously, and may have the humane object in view of sparing life; but we, the government, have a stern duty to perform. You are one of our agents in carrying the law into effect. It is your province to impress on the mind of offenders that their crimes deserve the punishment awarded them; and that they should submissively bow to the majesty of the offended law, and repent of their sins before God. As a minister of Christ, I cannot see that you are called on to offer any opinion as to the nature of the law itself, or the manner in which it is administered. It is your duty to break down the obstinate and rebellious spirit of guilty men; and the better to effect this, you should hold out no hope to those who have had an impartial trial by an impartial jury. It devolves on you to prepare such unhappy beings for the sentence of the law. I have sent for you to give you my advice, and it is this. If there be any peculiarity in the cases of malefactors, I recommend that in future you leave it to others to make it known to the proper authorities; and that you strictly confine yourself to your clerical duties I have now only to request, that what I have said may be taken in good part, as I mean well towards you. I want no reply. Good morning, sir."

On this, he abruptly left the astonished ordinary to wend his way back into the city.

This reproof affected the ordinary most acutely; still he never relaxed in his efforts

to stimulate others to save life; and when the office of Secretary of State passed into other hands—being then treated with a little more ceremony and urbanity—he again felt his influence recognised, by the attention which was given to his opinions and judgment As, however, the major part of his official duties were exercised during the reign of a sovereign who conscientiously, though unfortunately, thought that political and social order could not be preserved without the frequent use of the gallows, his humane exertions were by no means so successful, on the whole, as he would have had them. Adverse to these exhibitions, from a conviction that they were unnecessary, not to say mischievous to society, and the repugnance he had to be made a party in them, occasioned him to be frequently involved in

controversies on the subject. This induced him to refresh his memory from time to time from a note-book, in which he entered the cases as they occurred in the course of his experience, and the impressions they made on his mind.

'Tis from this present memorandum book that we have been enabled to present the reader with a few interesting cases which at an earlier period would have perhaps been improper.

We have, however, now arrived at a new legislative era,—an hiatus has thrown a beam of light on the subject of legislation for the prevention of crime. Everything, therefore, which may tend to exemplify the good or ill effects of one line of legislation or the other cannot fail to be interesting, and act as a beacon to warn future rulers from relapsing again into the errors of those who, perhaps with the best of motives, held fast to a system which occasioned seventy-two thousand human beings to fall by the hands of the common executioner, in the course of one king's reign, for robberies alone, exclusive of religious murders, without leaving the country in the slightest degree morally improved,—averaging six executions a day, Sundays included. We state this fact on the authority of Hollinshed, who averages the executions in the reign of Henry VIII. at two thousand per annum: and Sir John Fortescue tells us, that in his day (the reign of Henry VI.) more persons were executed in England, for robberies, in one year, than in France for seven. "As the British nation has a long arrear of debt due to humanity," writes the ordinary, "let us hope that, the days are passed away, never again to return."

CHAPTER CII.

THE BURIED TREASURE.

Mr. SQUABSHOT, after the departure of his friend and companion, Henry Osborne, for the continent, chewed the cud of many a bitter fancy. He was meditative and contemplative. His affairs were in anything but a prosperous state. In fact, Mr. Squabshot was not only short of ready cash—not an unusual trouble with him—but he was over head and ears in debt ; and what was perhaps worse than this, he was over head and ears in love—in love with Miss Staunton. Squabshot cared little for worldly wealth, indeed he had never been what is termed a prudent man, as far as money matters were concerned ; but now his thoughts seemed to take a different complexion, and he considered over and over again how he might better his condition, for without worldly wealth it would be impossible for him to aspire to the hand of Miss Staunton.

Hour after hour did he consider and reconsider the ways and means of increasing his ways and means, but hitherto he had not been able to hit upon the desired scheme to repair his fortunes.

Osborne, before he had left the continent, had pressed upon Squabshot a considerable sum of money, at the same time declaring to his friend his willingness at all times to open his purse for the use of Squabshot ; but the latter would not listen to any such proposal, and consequently Osborne did not like to press the matter further. The consequence of this was, that Osborne departed for the continent, and Squabshot was left in very straightened circumstances. The former,

however, when he bade his friend good-bye, desired him to write immediately if he required any pecuniary assistance. Squabshot promised to do so if he needed any ; but he forbore doing so, for with all his random and uncertain ways, he had a code of honour, and was to a certain extent, peculiarly sensitive upon certain points. He, therefore, would rather make any shift, or be up to any dodge, than do so.

One evening Mr. Squabshot paid a visit to a friend of his, a young man by the name of Ubsdell ; he was a clerk in some office in the city, and Squabshot had known him since he was a lad of fifteen or sixteen years of age.

The evening was fine, and the two friends were seated in the summer-house at the rear of the house where Ubsdell lodged. This same house was in Leadenhall Street. Many of the houses in the city, at the time of which we write, were furnished with gardens ; a luxury which the domiciles in the suburbs seldom possess now.

The conversation between the two friends had embraced various topics, when Squabshot said—

"I tell you what it is, old fellow, we are both of us much in the same situation."

"How—what do you mean ?" inquired Ubsdell.

"Both hard up. It's always been my fate to be hard up, though."

"And mine also. Now there's the governor, he's as close as an oyster, a hard-fisted old card, and as to getting any rise from him. Why, lord bless you, it ain't to be thought of, and you know I can't go on in the way I have been, that is quite certain. It won't wash, as the saying is, but—"

Mr. Ubsdell paused suddenly, and looked mysteriously at his companion.

"Well ?" said Squabshot.

"But I hope to make an alteration."

"Ah ! leave your present berth ?" inquired his friend.

"Umph ! no," said the other, indulging in a short whistle.

"What then ?"

"A scheme, sir, a scheme," exclaimed Ubsdell.

"Ah, I am fond of a scheme—always was, provided it's a good one," said Squabshot.

Mr. Ubsdell was silent for a minute or so ; he kept puffing out the smoke from his pipe at regular intervals.

"Well, and your scheme," said Squabshot.

"Ah ?" said Mr. Ubsdell, looking remarkably cunning.

"You are very close, my friend," said Squabshot.

"Squabby, old boy," said his companion, "can you keep a secret ?"

"Yes, of course I can—why do you ask ?"

"Because that I have one that I dare not trust to everybody.

"May I trust you?"

"I should hope so."

"Listen then, and believe that wealth—enormous wealth—is within our grasp."

Squabshot stared, and looked at the speaker as though he thought he had taken leave of his senses.

"Yes, old boy; prodigious and enormous wealth."

"Nonsense."

"But it's no nonsense, I tell you, but an actual fact. You must know that a buried treasure—at least I believe so—lies buried within a few yards of where we are now seated."

"Impossible!"

"I tell you that such is the case, or at any rate I have every reason to believe so. You must understand, that at the farther end of the garden yonder, I commenced digging for some gravel. I had not proceeded more than three feet down, when my spade struck against some hard substance. Holloa, says I—what's up now? I removed the earth a little more; and then what do you think I discovered?"

"I can't possibly tell."

"Why, part of an old oak chest; so it appeared to be, from what little of it was disclosed. Well, when I found this, I shovelled in the earth again; and, of course, said nothing about the circumstance to any one."

"Very discreet, indeed," said his companion.

"Well, you must know," continued the narrator—"that I have not been able to rest in my bed in consequence of this discovery. Some days have elapsed now since I first met with this strange adventure. I have been ransacking my brains to hit upon some scheme to remove the chest without discovery. Of course, if my landlord had the slightest notion that there was any such concealed treasure on his premises, he would be after it immediately; and then, farewell to my dreams of wealth, and future happiness."

"Well, and did you succeed in falling upon any scheme?"

"No; I am as far off as ever. There lies the treasure!" said Mr. Ubsdell, pointing with the end of his pipe in the direction of the spot in question. "There it lies; but how to unearth it is as yet a puzzle. It is for this purpose, that I am led to consult you."

"Umph! your landlord is at home."

"Always. Confound him, he will not go out, and leave the house for a single day."

"It may be no treasure after all," suggested Squabshot.

"Oh, as to that—I have not the slightest doubt upon that head. You must know that I have every reason to believe that this house stands upon the walls of an ancient one before the great fire of London. In fact I don't believe there is the slightest doubt upon this point. You see the earth which forms the foundation of this and many other houses, is several feet higher than those buildings which stood before the great fire of London, and there are actually houses, or parts of houses under those at present occupied by tenants. Oh! it would be a curious history if we could know all this earth contains—" said the speaker, contemplatively.

"There is no doubt of that," answered his companion.

"Well, you must know," said Ubsdell in continuation—

"It is my opinion that this chest was buried by some occupant of these premises burned when the fire took place; and the party or parties who so deposited it, no doubt intended to return after the general conflagation, and claim it as their own."

"Then why did they not do so?"

"Who can tell? Not you or I. Possibly they were stricken down with the plague, or lost their lives—the Lord only knows how! Be that as it may, one fact is quite clear—there is the chest; and that it contains a considerable amount of treasure, I am fully convinced."

"Umph," exclaimed Squabshot; "but how is it to be obtained? There is the great difficulty."

"And at present it appears to be an insurmountable one."

"How many occupants are there in this house except yourself?"

"Old Morley himself, and his housekeeper, that's all."

"Don't he ever go into the country?"

"Very seldom; in fact scarcely ever."

"We must wait till he does—that's all."

"And then, there's the housekeeper?"

"Oh, she won't take any notice, it's Morley that's to be feared; he's as sharp as a needle."

"We must work it somehow or other. Can't it be managed at night?"

"Oh, an excellent thought! That would be the only way to work the oracle."

"Then let us try."

"Mind, Squabby, I promise you to go shares. Whatever we may find shall be divided between us. I can't manage the matter single-handed, and without a pal. You are just the sort; so let us strike a bargain at once."

Agreed! Now let us arrange how we are to carry out our project. Where does Morley sleep?"

"In the front top room."

"Then his window does not command a view of the back garden?"

"No."

"That's all right; and I don't after all see any such great difficulty in the matter. It's quite clear that it must be all managed in one night. The chest must be got out and removed."

"Ah, but how?"

"By means of a cart."

"Can you procure one?"

"Of course I can."

"But then there will be a third party in the transaction."

"Not at all; leave that to me. If it shall be necessary to bring a man with the horse and cart, it does not follow that he should know where the chest is, or what it contains. Say it's yours, and you are moving it away on the sly in consequence of a quarrel with your landlord. Now, do you understand?"

"Perfectly."

"And we will commence to-morrow night. How am I to get in?"

"That is easily managed. You won't find much difficulty in scaling the wall."

"And you?"

"Will, of course, be in the garden to receive you.

"Ah, what time?"

"Between eleven and twelve o'clock."

Squabshot then parted with his friend, and returned home to his own lodgings in Goswell Street. All night he ruminated upon the singular circumstance detailed to him by his young friend, whose nature he knew would, from its want of firmness, prevent him carrying out any such project alone. Mr. Squabshot felt, therefore, that destiny had made him the agent in this transaction, and his sleep was disturbed by wild visions of untold wealth.

————

CHAPTER CIII.

THE MIDNIGHT MEETING.—THE NIGHT SURPRISE.

IT was nearly midnight when Mr. Squabshot arrived at the low wall which encompassed the garden, in the rear of the old house in Leadenhall Street. All around was hushed and as still as the grave. Not a solitary individual was to be seen in the deserted streets, save occasionally one of the city watch pacing his lonely rounds. The deep-mouthed tongue of time struck the hour, and then chimed out three quarters past eleven. Squabshot took his way by the side wall. The moon lighted up with a flood of light the surrounding locality, when he arrived at that part of the wall which he had determined to scale; he sent forth a low whistle, which was immediately answered by his companion. Squabshot was about to

jump over, when he caught signs of the figure of a watchman in a neighbouring street. When he perceived this guardian of the night, he deemed it advisable to walk on, to throw the man off his guard. As he did so, the officer regarded him with a suspicious look; but Squabshot had a jovial look at him, wishing him good night, and went his way singing a bacchanalian song. In a short time the officer was far away from the spot, and Squabshot returned and vaulted over the wall with the agility of an acrobat. As he alighted on the other side, his friend, Ubsdall, appeared from the shadow of the house, and grasped his hand in silence. Squabshot could not help observing that his friend's hand trembled; but he took no notice of this circumstance to his companion

"Is old Morley in bed?" inquired Squabshot.

"Yes, and fast asleep; I heard him snoring a few minutes ago."

"The coast is clear, then?"

"Yes."

"Then we will to work."

"How about the cart?"

"It's to be here in about two hour's time."

"And then I don't know how we are to get the chest into the vehicle"

"Well see about that hereafter. Let's to work."

"Do you know, Squabby, I feel very nervous," said Ubsdall.

"Nonsense, man, you must not give way to idle and ridiculous fears. Here, take a draught from my brandy flask. There, that will put you in better spirits."

His companion did as he desired, and seemed in a little better courage. The two then proceeded to the spot where the buried treasure was concealed.

Squabshot commenced digging, and with as little noise as possible removed several spadesful of earth. In a short time he had the satisfaction of descrying the end of the chest which his companion had lighted upon some days previously, and covered up again.

Squabshot stooped down, and made a closer inspection of the object in question.

It appeared to be made of oak, studded with nails, and iron fastenings at the corners, which were of a grotesque character, and of an old-fashioned appearance; and from their form and manufacture, he was led to the inference that they were the work of the fifteenth or sixteenth century.

His eyes dilated, as he caught now, for the first time, a glimpse of the buried treasure, for he felt convinced that here indeed lay the garnered wealth of some son of Adam, who had long since passed away from this sphere.

His breath came heavy and thick, as he contemplated this memorial of a past age but it was not now a time for either himself or his companion to indulge in any dreaming fancies. Prompt action was his watchword, and he set to work with renewed energy to remove the superfluous earth.

In this task he was assisted by Ubsdell, who had gathered courage from his friend's determination.

Shortly after this, they had the satisfaction of seeing nearly half of the top part of the chest.

They surveyed it with hungry eyes; their curiosity as well as their cupidity was aroused, and the two continued to toss up heavy spadesful of the soil in silence. What with excitement, and the work, they became heated, and big drops of perspiration rolled down their features.

"Oh, dear me, we shall never be able to manage it in one night," said Ubsdell, "never."

"Pshaw!" exclaimed Squabshot, contemptuously. "We must manage it, my friend. It's no use faltering, now the business is once begun. On to your work like a man, and who knows but we may be both made for life—be millionaires. What say you to that? —be able to snap our fingers at Lady Fortune, who has treated us so scurvily."

The two friends again proceeded with their work. Inch by inch the large proportions of the chest became disclosed to their view, and it was evidently of much more gigantic proportions than they had at first anticipated. A thought crossed their minds, and a very natural one too, that there would be considerable difficulty for any two persons to remove it from its position, even after the surrounding earth was shovelled away.

In a short time the whole of the lid of the box was visible.

In the centre of this there was a large plate of wrought iron, very ornamental, and bearing some inscription, which was, however, for the present, perfectly illegible; from this centre plate several other pieces of wrought iron, of different devices, met that which fastened the corners. Besides this, it was, as we have before observed, studded with nails in almost every part.

Indeed, it looked as if it were the receptacle of some great treasure, and the two midnight workmen felt that such was indeed the case.

They were, however, now beginning once more to be exhausted with their exertions, and were fain to have recourse again to their brandy flask.

After some further labour, they succeeded in removing the earth sufficiently to get at the chest, at the sides of which there were two massive handles.

Squabshot jumped into the pit, and endeavoured to lift one side of the ponderous chest, but it resisted all his efforts to move it from its position.

Beads of perspiration poured down his face from exertion.

He gazed at his companion, who stood by the side of the pit, silently contemplating him.

"We are as far off as ever now," said Ubsdell.

"Umph! it seems so," exclaimed Squabshot.

"What is to be done?"

"Goodness me, but it is immensely heavy. What can it be filled with, I wonder?" said Squabshot.

"Bullion, you may depend on," answered Ubsdell. "Can't you manage to open the lid?"

"No, it's fastened by locks and bolts," was the answer.

"Force it open."

"We should make too much noise in doing so, even supposing it were possible," said Squabshot.

The two friends were so wound up to a pitch of excitement, that they were half beside themselves, and stood stupidly gazing at the supposed treasure which lay at their feet.

After a few more minutes had passed, they both jumped into the pit, and tried by their united efforts to raise one end of the chest. They did manage to succeed in raising this some few inches from the ground, but were compelled to leave go, and the ponderous chest fell down again with a dull heavy sound.

They stood some time wiping the perspiration from their foreheads and were irresolute how to act. The silver moonlight fell upon the yawning chasm they had made in the garden and the silence was as yet unbroken, presently they heard the sound of wheels and in a few moments a cart with two figures in it was seen above the low wall, which skirted the garden which was the scene of their operations. Squabshot turned his glance in the direction of the vehicle. He gave a look of recognition to its two occupants, and the cart drew up opposite to where he and his companion stood.

"Are you ready?" said one of those in the cart.

"Hang me if I know what's to be done," said Squabshot. "So you've come yourself, colonel."

"Yes," answered Colonel Jack, for it was none other than our hero. He alighted from the cart and jumped over the low wall and in a second or so was by the side of Squabshot.

"My friend Ubsdell," said the latter, introducing his companion to the highwayman.

"Well, this is the booty, eh?" inquired Colonel Jack.

"Yes, there it is, but how it's to be removed is more than I can tell."

"Why so?"

"It's so cursedly heavy."

"So much the better, it contains the greater treasure?"

Colonel Jack jumped down and laid hold of one of the handles of the box—he raised it with apparent ease.

"It is heavy of a surety," he exclaimed, "but it can be removed, I'll wager a thousand crowns. Where is the landlord of these premises?"

"In bed and asleep." answered Ubsdell.

"Ah, and his room, where is it situated?"

"In the front of the house, at the top."

"Good, then he must be our first care."

"What do you mean?"

"Simply this, that he must be safely fastened inside of his respectable dormitory."

"But he generally locks himself in, and the key is on the inside," answered Ubsdell.

"No matter for that, we carry fastenings with us," said Colonel Jack, taking out of his pocket a padlock, Then going to the side of the wall he told Mullins to drive on the horse and cart and return in half an hour. The vehicle slowly wheeled off, and once more the colonel turned to Ubsdell—

"Now then, sir, if you please, perhaps you will introduce me to the door of your landlord's bedroom."

Ubsdell hesitated and looked with some alarm at the highwayman.

"What's the man afraid," said the colonel, addressing himself to Squabshot. There could be no question but he was very much afraid, but he slowly took his way towards the house, followed by the colonel. When he arrived at the back door of the premises he paused.

"Suppose we should wake old Morley," he observed.

"We must run the risk of that. 'Safe bind,' is an old and excellent motto. We will, if you please proceed up stairs as quickly as may be, and then leave the rest to me."

"There must be no bloodshed," exclaimed Ubsdell.

"Oh, dear no. It's only bunglers who have recourse to such extremities. Leave it to me, young man. Lead the way."

Ubsdell ascended the stairs with the utmost caution, followed by the colonel. In a few seconds they were at the door of Mr. Morley's sleeping apartment.

They listened attentively, and the heavy breathing of its occupant gave unmistakeable evidence that he was fast asleep.

Colonel Jack managed to fasten the door on the outside without awaking the sleeper, after which he crept cautiously down stairs, followed by his companion. As they emerged again into the yard they closed the back door after them, and locked it on the outside, putting the key of this in the pocket of Ubsdell.

Once more they returned to the scene of operation.

The colonel contemplated the chest for a few minutes, and then glanced round the yard, or rather back garden, for it contained a grass-plot and was planted with shrubs.

"What are you looking for?" said Squabshot.

"Some billets of wood."

"There are some in yonder shed," said Ubsdell.

The colonel took his way thither, and returned with several strong pieces of wood. One of these was about five feet long, and appeared to be the thick branch of a tree which had been lopped off from its parent stem. He then sent Ubsdell for some shorter pieces. He formed a lever with the longer piece, and succeeded by this means in raising the chest on one end. He then propped it up with the shorter pieces, and with the aid of his two companions had the satisfaction, in the space of about a quarter of an hour of bringing it to the surface of the earth. His two companions had a difficulty in restraining themselves from giving forth a shout of joy as the box stood revealed to their gaze, tipped by the silver moonlight.

"Umph!" said Colonel Jack "It is without doubt confoundedly heavy, but if all goes on well, I think we shall be able to remove it without discovery."

"But it will attract the notice of the passers by," said Ubsdell, who was still oppressed by a strange and undefined fear.

"That I have arranged," said the colonel. "Now about getting the chest to the wall."

He then proceeded to place several of the most round pieces of wood, and with these he formed rollers, by the means of which he conveyed the trunk safely to the wall.

The next difficulty was how this heavy chest was to be conveyed into the cart. As to lifting it over the wall that would be an utter impossibility. However, the colonel who was generally ready to meet any emergency hit upon a scheme. He made an inclined plane of some wood which he found in the outhouse, and then putting roller after roller ready for immediate operation he placed one end of the chest in readiness to be rolled up the plane This last operation he left till Mullins returned with the cart. In about ten minutes more he made his appearance.

"Are you ready, governor?" inquired Mullins.

"Yes; hand over a rope."

Mullins threw a stout rope to his master, and the colonel then fastened one end of it round the box and threw the other end to Mullins.

"Now," said Colonel Jack, "when I give the word, you pull at the rope. Make as little noise as possible, for it would be a pity to disturb people out of their sleep."

"All right, master," answered Mullins.

"Now you two put your shoulders to the end of the chest while I work with the lever. Now, all act together. Are you ready?"

"Yes," was the reply of his companions, in a low whisper.

"Pull away, Mullins," said the colonel, as he gave the first impetus to the chest with the stake he was using as a lever.

The chest went up the inclined plane about six or seven inches, whereupon the colonel inserted a couple of wedges to keep it in its position. They all paused for a moment or so to recover breath, after which the same process was gone through, and a few more inches were gained in its ascent—and thus by degrees was it conveyed almost noiselessly into the cart.

When it was safely deposited there, Mr. Ubsdall seemed suddenly to awake to the knowledge of the unpleasant fact that his dream of wealth was vanishing before his eyes. Hitherto, surprise and excitement had caused him to be silent upon the subject; but now that he beheld the charmed box about to take its departure he began to be demonstrative.

"Squabshot," said Mr. Ubsdall, "but they are not going to march off with the chest in this sort of manner?"

"All right," said Squabshot, "leave it to the colonel; without his assistance we should never have succeeded this far."

"But I don't like it; and what is more—I won't have it," said Ubsdall, assuming for the nonce an authoritative tone. "Who is the colonel, as you call him? I thought that you said there was to be only one entrusted with this secret. Mind, I do not consent that he and his companion are to go shares."

"Of course not—who said they were?" answered Squabshot.

"Well, but where are they going to take it to? that's what I want to know."

"Hold your tongue I tell you, it's all right. I'll answer for that; the colonel is as true as steel—he's an old friend of mine."

"That may be, but I know nothing of him. I'll go with the box."

"As you please."

"Then I'll go; that's all about it."

"What's the matter, my friend?" said Colonel Jack, who could not help hearing a portion of the foregoing conversation.

"He don't like to part with his property," said Squabshot, with a smile.

"It's in safe keeping," said the colonel.

"I want no share in the contents of the trunk; I suppose you won't mind paying me for my trouble." This last observation was addressed to Ubsdell.

"Oh, dear no; I will pay you handsomely."

"If there is anything worth having in the chest?"

"Yes. Ah, precisely. Where are you going to take it to?"

"To a place of safety."

"To Squabshot's lodgings!"

"As you please."

"Oh, they would suspect, perhaps."

"What?"

"I don't know; but wouldn't it look strange for me to take an old-looking medieval chest like this into my apartments?"

"I know where to take it to, if you will trust it to my care," said the colonel. Then turning to Mullins, he said—

"Now, look sharp. Do as I have already told you."

Upon this Mullins covered over the chest with bunches of green, carrots, and various sorts of vegetables, so that it was completely concealed from view, and the vehicle in which it was deposited, presented the appearance of a market cart, so that no passenger could possibly suppose it contained the mysterious and ponderous chest.

When Mullins had performed this metamorphosis, he drove the vehicle gently on, and the colonel and his two companions jumped over the wall, and followed at about a hundred yards distance.

"I purpose taking your treasure—if treasure it in reality be—to Whitefriars; there it will be safely deposited in the charge of men whom I can trust. In the course of a few days you may have it at your own lodgings, but for the present I should think it advisable for it to remain where it will be impossible for any one to get at it besides ourselves."

"Ah!" ejaculated Upsdell, looking at Squabshot.

"Does that meet with your approval, gentlemen?—if not, say so."

"I think it the best course, decidedly," was Squabshot's answer.

By this time the three had arrived at the front part of the house in Leadenhall Street. They were surprised at beholding the head of Mr. Morley protruding from the window of his bed-room.

"Hist! fall back!" said Ubsdell. "There's old Morley, as I'm a sinner! What can cause him to be on the look out, I wonder?"

"Watch!—help!—thieves!" shouted out Mr. Morley, who had been aroused by the noise in the rear of the premises, and jumping out of bed, had found himself locked in his own room.

"Let him shout out to his heart's content," exclaimed Colonel Jack ; "the sooner we get clear off the better. Is there no other way besides that round the front of the house ?"

"Yes, let us cut down this street," said Ubsdell.

"Good, come on," answered the colonel. "No time is to be lost. He will arouse the city watch, and we shall have them at our heels."

They took their way down the bye street which Ubsdell had pointed out, and in a short time were in view of the cart, which was quietly making its way down Cheapside. They watched its progress, and saw it pass on without interruption.

Turning round St. Paul's Church Yard, Mullins arrived at Ludgate Hill. Here he paused, and looked round.

At a motion from the colonel, he continued his progress, and soon arrived at Fleet Street, whereupon he made for Whitefriars.

Colonel Jack had arranged that the property should be placed in charge of Reuben, whom the reader will no doubt remember as gaoler to Sir Richard Fleetwood.

It was by this time early morning, and day was contending with night for the mastery.

There was some difficulty in getting the heavy chest out of the cart, but not so much as there had been to get it in, and so, in a short time it was safely deposited in the cellar which had been the prison-house of Sir Richard Fleetwood.

When it had been safely lodged, the colonel and his two companions regained the street, and after some conversation, it was ultimately agreed that in the course of a few day's it should be conveyed to Mr. Spuabshot's residence; and so they separated, Squabshot and Ubsdell taking their way together.

"Now, old boy," said Mr. Squabshot, whose spirits were in an exuberant state, in consequence of the successful issue of that day's proceedings. "Now, then, what shall we do?"

"I am not going to return to Leadenhall Street."

"Not going to return to your lodgings ?" said Squabshot, staring at his friend, with surprise.

"No, I shall not go back again," was the answer.

"Why not ?"

"Oh, old Morley—"

"Well, what of him ?"

"He's a dragon."

Squabshot could not forbear smiling at this remark of Ubsdell's, who looked very serious.

After a few minutes pause, Squabshot said—

"Nonsense !—afraid of an old chap like that ?"

"I won't return," said Ubsdell, quite determinedly.

"Well, please yourself, my friend," said Squabshot.

"I have said it, and shall not alter my mind."

"Very well—so be it. What shall we do now ?"

"I am sure I don't know," Ubsdell answered.

The two friends walked on in silence for some short distance, both in a ruminating mood. At length, Squabshot, brightening up, said—

"Let's see, it's now about half-past four— I can't go into my own lodgings yet—I tell you what we will do. Suppose we take a boat on the river?—it will give us a cooler after our night's excitement."

"With all my heart—so be it."

Squabshot hailed a boat at the stairs at Whitefriars, and told the waterman to row them to Stepney. Having arrived at which place, the two friends landed, and Mr. Squabshot by this time felt the absolute necessity of refreshing the inner man.

"Now, I tell you what it is, Ubsdell, breakfast must be had, for I feel faint."

"So do I," said the other.

They strolled through the High Street, until they arrived in sight of an ancient hostelry, with a deeply projecting roof. The windows of this establishment were of the old Roman gothic, and latticed with the old description of lead crossings. A sort of wing of the building, if it could so be termed, sprang out in front of the building, nearly at the top of which, was suspended a sign board, upon which was painted a pig, with a contemplative countenance, and a curly tail. From this, the reader was to guess at the sign of the house, which was the "Hampshire Hog." There were several sailors, with their lasses, on the outside of the building. One was seated on one of the benches outside, with not a bad-looking girl by him, at whom he was gazing lovingly. Another man was seated on a form, raising a glass up, and pledging a companion's health.

Two young women were inquiring about their sweethearts of the sailor whose health was being drunk, he having, it would appear, from their conversation, spoken with them in some harbour abroad. At a short distance from the building a jolly tar, who had drank somewhat too much grog, was practising a hornpipe with his sweetheart, who, to humour his whim, was going through a few steps, much to the delight of those who formed the company in the balcony.

Beneath the balcony, and forming the entrance to the hostelry, were a crimp and a

sailor bargaining about some lodging the latter required.

"This seems a lively establishment," said Squabshot; "what say you to trying this?"

"As you please," remarked Ubsdell.

The two friends entered, and upon inquiring for the parlour, they were shown into a gloomy old-fashioned room at the back part of the house.

This apartment was filled with a motley and not a particularly discreet assembly, and although it was broad daylight, a two-wick'd oil lamp was suspended from the ceiling.

Several persons were seated at the table. One of these had something like the appearance of a dissipated clergyman. He held a quart pot in his hand, and was conversing with a rough-looking man of very questionable appearance; and on the opposite side

No. 66.

of the table there sat another doubtful-looking gentleman, who was leaning forward and listening to the conversation.

Several other figures, with pipes and glasses, made up the not very promising or pleasing occupants of the parlour.

Squabshot, when his eye glanced over this assembly, and the strong odour of tobacco smoke found its way to his nostrils, gave a gesture of impatience.

"Have you no other room besides this?" he inquired of the waiter.

"This is the parlour, gentlemen," said that worthy; "there is a private room, but that is occupied by a foreign gentleman. If you like, I'll ask missis."

"Do so, for I don't like this crib at all," said Squabshot, following the man to the bar.

After some slight hesitation, Squabshot

and his friend were shown into another room, where they found a stout, dark, elderly gentleman seated at breakfast. He had the appearance of being a German.

In a short time Squabshot got into conversation with him, and learnt that he was a foreigner, recently arrived in England. He spoke the English language with a strong accent, but nevertheless he had a tolerable flow of language ; and after a brief account of the various countries he had passed through, he gave the two friends the following singular history, which we shall reserve for another chapter.

CHAPTER CIV.

THE ENCHANTED CASTLE.

FOR the better understanding of our readers, we shall put the stranger's detached incidents into the form of a narrative.

Our first scene is in a royal palace. The Emperor Maximilian is seated at the festive board, surrounded by the principal noblemen of his court. He had for a time forgotten the monarch in becoming the jovial companion. Numerous libations had heated and inflamed the imagination of the revellers, and the health of the most celebrated beauties of the day had been drunk in succession. The intervals between these toasts were filled up with the history of their amours, and in many cases the narrators had drawn largely upon their imaginations. Even the empress herself had not escaped, to such an extent did the rich juice of Hungary's grapes encourage the audacity of the guests and the forbearance of the royal chief of the banquet.

Negligently lounging in his arm-chair, the monarch suffered one hand to play with the glossy ringlets of a youthful page, who happened to be standing nigh him, while, with a smile, he listened to the history of the youthful Baroness of Ebersdorf, who had been surprised at the sudden return of her husband, and who had so far retaind her presence of mind as to urge her lover to encase himself in a suit of ancient armour, which was stationed in the hall. All were anxiously awaiting the *denouement* of this perilous adventure, when a sudden and loud noise at the door of the room precipitantly brought the narrative to a close. A muscular and powerful arm thrust aside the two guards that were stationed at the entrance of the apartment, and a knight of tall stature, with a cloak, made of bear skin, hanging over his mailclad shoulders, advanced boldly towards the monarch.

"What means this insolence ?" exclaimed the emperor. "Have we no guards in the place, that we should be broken in upon thus abruptly ? What means this outrage, sirrah ? Knowest thou not who we are ?"

"I know," replied the stranger, abruptly, "that you are emperor, and it is that knowledge that makes me seek your presence now. It is my duty, my liege (and I never shrink from the performance of it), to obey implicitly your orders as the chief of this empire, and to serve you in your wars ; but in return I demand justice when I require it. Could I, therefore, have chosen a more fitting opportunity when no cause or business of the state engages your attention, and when you are passing your time in feasting and revelry ?"

Maximilian cast around angry glances, and exclaimed, somewhat fiercely—

"Can none of you inform me who this saucy wight is that dares to address us thus rudely ?"

An old general, who, in spite of his frequent libations, still preserved his self-possession answered, with much *sang froid,* as follows—

"Sire, even though the vesture of this knight did not declare his style and name at once, his demeanour and language, which are somewhat in keeping with his garb, would enable you to recognise him. He is the noble Hermann of Lueg, surnamed the Bear of Carniole."

"Say you so ?" exclaimed the emperor, sarcastically. "The Bear has doubtless left his native wilds, attracted by the savoury odour of our kitchens. Sir Knight of Lueg, your castle is far distant from Vienna, what inducement have you had to undertake so long and wearisome a journey ? Is it hunger, or cold ? or have you been surprised and assaulted by banditti, and need my assistance ?"

"In my castle," answered Hermann, haughtily, "we experience neither cold nor hunger. Did it please your Majesty to honour it with a visit, I would undertake to regale your suite, with the richest of viards, and to supply you with green vegetables and delicious fruits in this season, whereas I perceive that your table is covered only with dried figs and grapes. As to the idea that maurauding robbers could surprise my castle, or that I should need aid from your Majesty, I should not be afraid, with God's help, to defend it against your Majesty's self, did it suit your fancy to besiege it."

A loud and universal shout of laughter from all around followed this speech, and the emperor was compelled to join in the mirth. Hermann darted savage glances upon the whole assembly, and when he gazed at the emperor it was but too evident that respect alone compelled him to restrain his wrath. At length Maximilian perceived that the dignity of his rank suffered by this scene, and he adopted a more eligible measure to ascertain the object of the knight's visit.

"Great and mighty Knight of Lueg," said the monarch, "who are master of such vast riches, and a castle so well defended, what can you have to demand of our feeble means?"

"I have said it—justice!" quickly replied Hermann; "justice against one of your followers, who has grievously injured me."

The emperor's brow contracted.

"Always *justice*," he muttered to himself; "every one has that word upon his lips! It would almost seem, that when once seated upon throne of the Cæsars, a monarch has nothing else to do than listen to complaints and pronounce sentences. Hermann, could you not, as many others have done, avenge your own wrongs? and does it appear to you that you have chosen the most favourable and convenient hour to exercise the sagacity of our judgment?"

"The quality of the offender," answered Hermann, seriously, "did not permit me to take the law in my own hands, before I had recourse to your Majesty's justice. As for the time and place, they both seem to be favourable, since your Majesty can hear all parties, my adversary being now present."

"Here!" exclaimed the monarch; "you say that your enemy is here! Who is he?"

"Behold him!" cried Hermann, pointing to the nobleman who was nearest to the monarch at the banqueting table. "I demand justice against the Grand Marshal, the Count de Papenheim."

"Papenheim! do you hear?" demanded the emperor, in much surprise. "Look at this knight! What relations exist between you and the Bear of the Carniole?"

The Grand Marshal, according to custom, was the least sober of the whole company; and he was now in that soddened state, between slumber and wakefulness, when speaking—hearing—thinking—and talking, are almost a fatiguing task. But at the voice of his master he raised his eyes, and made a vain effort to fix them upon Hermann, observing, with a hiccup, "I know not this man—I never saw him. I have no dispute with him!"

"More than you think, my Lord of Papenheim!" ejaculated Hermann. "Perhaps you do not know *me*; but haply you recollect the young damsel whom you seduced from her monastery at Inspruck, and whom you abandoned at Saltzburg, when you had gratified your impure desires."

"A young girl debauched! Is it so, Papenheim?" demanded the emperor of his favourite. "Really, you are absolutely incorrigible!"

"At Saltzburg?" murmured the Grand Marshal. "Oh!—ah, I think I remember—yes—Ida, a beautiful girl!"

"That Ida," cried Hermann, in a terrible voice, "that Ida, whom a fatal beauty has precipitated into the abyss which you opened at her feet—that Ida is my daughter—my own blood—my child—the last scion of the house of Lueg!"

At these words a low murmur rang through the hall, and gaiety and mirth immediately disappeared; and many of the party were half sobered by the impassioned manner of Hermann.

"Lord of Lueg," said the emperor, in a kind tone of voice, "the accusation which you bring against the Count de Papenheim is indeed of a serious nature; the honour of the vassals of the Holy Empire is intrusted to me, and I must fulfil my duty as its defender. This affair shall be carefully looked into; but at the present moment you perceive that your adversary is in no fit condition to reply to me. To-morrow we will take measures to bring matters to a friendly issue."

"And how can your Majesty suppose that such an affair can terminate in reconciliation?" demanded Hermann.

"By proportioning the reparation to the extent of the outrage," answered the emperor.

"One mode of reparation is alone possible," replied the Knight of the Carnoile; "and, painful though it be for me to receive as my son-in-law an individual so debased by dissipation as the one I now see, still must honour triumph over every other consideration. Your Majesty has learnt from that wine-stained mouth the avowal of the crime and the proof of the injury. No further investigation is necessary; and your Majesty will now order Papenheim to espouse my daughter, whom he has dishonoured, seduced, and cruelly betrayed."

A moment of silence succeeded this speech. The Grand Marshal looked first at the emperor, then at the knight, and appeared to have understood the nature of the latter's demand, for he exclaimed, with a loud mocking laugh—

"I marry Ida! Ha! ha!"

The emperor darted a severe look at the Grand Marshal, and seemed for a moment embarrassed; but speedily assuming that air of dignity which he knew so well how to put on, he turned towards the knight, and addressed him as follows:—

"Lord of Lueg, even were it now demonstrated to our sovereign justice that your complaint is entirely well founded, that the Grand Marshal has been guilty of grievous wrongs on his part, and that your daughter is the victim of rape or seduction, I could not force him to contract the union which you desire, because he is married already!"

At these words the knight's countenance fell, and he gnashed his teeth fearfully together. A species of convulsion agitated his whole frame, and the bear's skin which he wore rose round his neck, so that he seemed but little different from the redoubtable animal the spoils of which he had converted into a garment. A species of moaning escaped his breast; and nearly every one present was affected. Even the ebriety of Papenheim disappeared at the ferocious aspect of his accuser. He raised himself on his chair, and returned the indignant glances of his enemy; while, at a sign from the emperor, the two guards stepped forward and placed themselves close by the Bear of the Carniole, who, almost suffocated with rage, at length gave vent to his wrath in the following words—

"Married, wretch! And my poor Ida is lost—irretrievably lost! No justice—no reparation can now be effectually sought at the hands of the emperor but blood—vengeance—death! Were you not protected, Papenheim, by the sacredness of this asylum your life should even now pay the forfeit of your crime. But I defy you, Count de Papenheim—I defy you to mortal combat, on foot or on horse-back, with lance or with sword. This is my challenge to a deadly feud—and may it be the presage of your defeat!"

Scarcely had these words escaped the lips of Hermann, when he detached the heavy iron gauntlet from his left hand, and hurled it with tremendous force at the face of Papenheim. So violent was the blow, that the Grand Marshal fell heavily upon the breast of the emperor, and deluged him with blood. One of his eyes was completely dashed out of its socket, and the left temple presented a frightful appearance, being fractured by the terrible gauntle.

For a few moments his members contracted, and then suddenly stiffened; a convulsion passed over his frame; and in another instant all that remained of the drunken *debauchee* was a disfigured corse in the arms of Maximilian! A cry of horror burst from the assembly, and every one rose to arrest the murderer, but Hermann had already disappeared. One of the guards who had been hurled to the ground, rose with much difficulty, and the other reeled back, stunned by the blow which the knight had dealt upon his head, to compel him to release the hold that he had taken of his garments. Some of the guests rushed out of the apartment to pursue and arrest the fugitive at the gates of the palace; but it was soon discovered that Hermann had penetrated into the imperial banqueting-rooms by a private door, which was usually closed, and which, on that account, was not guarded by sentinels. The knight was thus enabled to effect his escape through the same avenue of egress.

On the following morning heralds were dispersed about the different quarters of Vienna, declaring by sound of trumpet, that a reward of four hundred ducats of gold would be given to him who should deliver into the hands of justice, dead or alive, the knight Hermann of Lueg, the murderer of the Grand Marshal. Messengers were also despatched to all the governors and regents of the cities of the empire, to order them to adopt every possible measure to arrest the Bear of the Carniole. The funeral of Papenheim was then celebrated with the utmost pomp and ostentation; and a month passed away without the capture of the assassin.

At the end of that period, the authorities in Vienna received the following communication from the Captain of the canton of Laybach:—

"In pursuance of the orders of his Majesty I have endeavoured to obtain all possible information relative to the Knight Hermann of Lueg, a native of this part of the country, and usually resident in his castle, situate about five leagues hence, on the frontier of Italy. It appears that the knight passed through this town about three weeks ago, at day-break, having spent the night at the house of a poor widow in the faubourg Corinthia. He was accompanied by a young lady, who sate upon the croup of his saddle, and who, though very beautiful, seemed sorrowful and ill in health. Two of the inhabitants of Idria met them a few miles distant from hence, amongst the mountains. The horse, being overcome with fatigue, and unable to continue the journey, was abandoned by Hermann to its fate; and while the knight carried a trunk in one hand, with the other he supported the trembling steps of the young lady, whom the travellers all imagine to be his daughter. They were, however, both lost sight of in the narrow and steep defiles which lead to the castle of Lueg.

"Having obtained this information, I despatched a serjeant-at-arms, with ten soldiers, to seize the assassin in his strong hold, and conduct him to the prison of Laybach. The serjeant has never returned; and of his ten companions, only one has made his appearance to report to me the details of that unfortunate expedition.

"Although the distance hence to the castle of Lueg be scarcely twelve hours' march, the little squadron only reached the environs of the fortress at the end of the second day. The difficulty of traversing those snow-covered paths in this season of the year was partially the cause of the delay—but the chief impediment in the way of the detachment, was the necessity of waiting till a guide could be procured, as all the peasants in the neighbourhood of the castle fled so soon as they learnt that it was to be besieged.

"Their wives, moreover, declared that the fortress was inaccessible, and defended by supernatural powers. At length a young peasant was found, and induced to guide the detachment to the castle.

"Arrived at the base of the rock in the midst of which the castle stands, the soldiers began to scale the almost impervious road leading to the entrance; but they were soon stopped by a wall of terrible height, which completely barred their passage. They endeavoured to find means to overcome this obstacle, when a noise was heard above their heads, which rivetted their attention. They then saw, says the soldier, a number of bears, from whose mouths issued terrible sounds that seemed to defy the power of the assailants. At that moment the guide was so overcome by his terror that he took to flight. The sergeant ordered the soldier to pursue him, and this command was the cause of his safety; for scarcely had he succeeded in catching the peasant, when the wall of snow gave way behind him, and an avalanche as large as a mountain buried his unfortunate companions. He declares, at the same instant, he heard bears give vent to the most terrible cries, in token of victory, and that he saw them run towards the rocks like shades from the infernal regions. A profound silence then reigned around, and the two survivors of that deplorable expedition returned to report the catastrophe. The particulars of this adventure have been bruited about in every direction, and have only seemed to satisfy the prevailing belief, that the castle of Lueg is protected by spirits whose spells are favourable to him who inherits the fortress.

In consequence of this report, the Aulic Council directed the military governor of Carniole to invest the castle of Lueg—to take it by fire and sword, and to capture all those who might be harboured within its walls. But before this order reached the governor, a more singular circumstance than any which had yet occurred, appeared to corroborate the mysterious belief that prevailed throughout the Carniole with regard to the supernatural resources of the Knight of Lueg.

In the morning after the first expedition, the inhabitants of Wipach, a village situated in the most northern part of Italy, on the left hand from Udina to Laybach, and at a distance of about ten leagues from the castle of Lueg, found ten men asleep upon the public market place, at the gate of the church. By their uniform they were immediately recognised to be soldiers of his Imperial Majesty —but when they were awakened, it was imposssible to learn from them the motives of their visit to the territories of the most serene republic of Venice, at that time enjoying a profound peace with the emperor. As they seemed to be labouring under the effect of cold and weakness, the magistrates of Wipach supplied them with refreshments, and procured them a vehicle, which transported them on the following day to Adelsburg, an imperial city, where they were immediately conducted into the presence of the commandant of the castle. Upon being examined by that authority, it was ascertained that these individuals were the serjeant and nine soldiers whom every one had believed to have been buried in the sow at the bottom of the valley of Lueg.

No reasonable account of this strange adventure, could be furnished by the men. They were each questioned separately, and all declared that they had not the slightest notion of the manner by which they were conveyed into Italy. Having lost all knowledge of what was passing at the moment when the mountain of snow suddenly fell on them, they were as much surprised at the event as those who interrogated them. They, however, declared that they entertained a vague and distant impression, like the reminiscence of a painful dream, of having visited the infernal regions, and been carried by demons before a large fire, where boiling potations were forced down their throats. But they were all of one accord in asserting that they had been made the sport of evil spirits, who had most probably conducted them through the air to the market-place of Wipach.

Despising popular rumours, the governor of the Carniole determined upon executing the orders of his superiors, and accordingly placed himself at the head of a small detachment in order to lay siege to the Castle of Lueg.

He took with him two small pieces of artillery called falconets, which then began to be employed in warfare; and he adopted such measures that his camp was well provided with all kinds of provisions, so far as the rigour of the season and the sterility of the country permitted.

Having taken these precautions, he advanced with his troops to the vicinity of the fortress.

The Castle of Lueg was situated on the summit of a high rock. It had been built in an excavation hollowed by nature, and was completely embedded in the rock itself, being surrounded by it on all sides, save in the opening looking towards the sea. From the base of the rock, and even from the valley on which it looked, the castle could not be perceived; it was only visible from the adjacent heights, and even these were at too great a distance to enable any artillery that might be placed upon them to reach the fortress.

A road, cut out of the solid rock, meandering in every direction, and often winding back upon itself, led to the gate of the extraordinary castle; and it was in this path that the soldiers who were first despatched against Hermann were buried by the avalanche in the manner which we have before related.

Having made himself acquainted with these particulars relative to the situation of the castle, the governor of the Carniole judged it to be impregnable on any side, save through the medium of that eccentric road; and he announced his arrival by the discharge of his field pieces and a number of muskets.

The balls shattered a few fragments of the rock; but none of them reached the castle, which from that point could not be perceived by the artillerymen.

Sentinels were posted upon all the neighbouring heights, and as the snow and ice rendered the road of which we have spoken inaccessible, and a single man could in that strange path have consequently arrested the progress of an entire army, the governor deemed it prudent to convert the siege into a blockade, and vanquish by famine those whom nature had taken care to protect by so extraordinary a position.

It was at that period nearly the termination of December—the cold was piercing in the extreme—and the encampment of the besiegers was but a poor protection against the inclemency of the weather.

The provisions, which had been transported from a considerable distance, were nearly all frozen on the road.

A thick smoke, however, constantly emanated from the chimneys of the castle, and seemed to announce that the inmates of the fortress possessed everything that was necessary to conduce to the comfort and support of life.

The governor had endeavoured to intimidate the garrison by menaces and threats; but the soldiers of Hermann replied only by cries and exclamations of contempt and mockery.

Every evening the report of one of the falconets resounded throughout the valley, in order to arouse the attention of the sentinels; and at the same time, while a similar report emanated from the castle, the guard was also changed upon the platform of that fortress.

Matters continued in this state till the beginning of March; and the governor was then persuaded that the besieged could only hold out a few days longer, on account of the failure of their provisions, it having been whispered to him that at the period when Hermann shut himself up in his castle he had but a scanty supply within its walls.

The conjectures of the governor seemed to be verrified, when, after more than three months' siege, or rather blockade, he one morning espied a white standard hoisted upon the banner-staff at the extremity of the road leading to the castle, and several individuals, unarmed, near it agitating their kerchiefs.

Persuaded that the besieged were about to capitulate, the governor despatched two of his officers to receive the heralds and conduct them to the camp.

At that moment four men, accompanying a species of intendant, and carrying four enormous baskets amongst them, descended into the valley. Having deposited their burthens at the foot of the rock, the intendant presented to the two officers a despatch for the governor, and retired with his four followers.

The baskets and the despatch were carried to the camp.

The document consisted of a letter from Hermann, in which he counselled the governor to abandon an expedition which could only terminate in the death of himself and his army, through the severity of the cold, as he would never succeed in reducing a castle defended by a power more potent than the sovereign who had despatched him against it. He, moreover, deplored the privations to which he (the governor) and his troops must necessarily be subjected, and begged him to accept the little present which he had forwarded, promising to renew it, during the remainder of the bad season, as often as the governor would do him the honour to accept of fresh supplies.

This singular epistle being read the baskets were opened. The first was filled with Cyprus wines, Italian liquers, and excellent pastry; the second contained fish, which had evidently only been caught within a few hours; in the third were the finest oranges and lemons the eye would wish to behold; and the fourth was filled with green vegetable, salads just gathered, and strawberries and raspberries in the full maturity of ripeness.

The surprise which was occasioned by this extraordinary supply was soon succeeded throughout the encampment by a conviction that the Knight of Lueg was assisted by supernatural powers, and that all attempts to capture the castle would be in vain.

In the course of a few days the governor, having thought it prudent to accept the offer of Hermann relative to a farther supply of provisions, made known his desire; and in a short time the intendant and the men again appeared, with the four quarters of a bullock and twelve lambs, already roasted.

The soldiers again declared their belief that the castle was protected by unearthly agents; and a mutiny amongst the imperial troops was to be dreaded hourly, if the blockade were not raised.

The governor, however, did not agree with the army in their opinion concerning the secret powers which protected the castle; and, after a short and private conversation with the intendant, he wrote a despatch to Vienna, in which he stated his conviction of being shortly enabled to accomplish his purpose, and reduce the castle.

The weather had been bitter and piercing during this period; but the inclement season drew near its end. The snows still covered the whole region of the Julian Alps, amongst which the Castle of Lueg was situate—the streamlets and the lakes were still frozen there; but at the southern foot of the chain the soil of Italy began to array itself with verdure.

While the woodcutters of the Carniole remained still shut up in their smoky cabins, the farmers on the banks of the Italian rivers, at a little distance only, hastened to the fields, with the first rays of the sun of March, in order to resume their rustic labours

In the little town of Gorice, the principal place in that happy region, there had lived for a number of years a worthy disciple of Æsculapius, who, in the peaceable exercise of his art, had acquired the esteem and veneration of all around.

Doctor Belgarbo really merited the reputation which he had obtained. Beneath an exterior which was somewhat of the rudest, he concealed a heart filled with philanthropy and rectitude; he was not only a talented physician, he was also an excellent friend, and, in cases of emergency, a discreet and prudent adviser.

Towards the end of Lent, in the year which marked the events that form the subject of this narrative, a domestic in rich livery, mounted upon one horse and conducting another, magnificently caparisoned, stopped one morning at the gate of the doctor's abode. He was the bearer of a letter, written in the most pressing terms, and requesting Belgarbo to proceed immediately to a castle situate in the neighbourhood of Idria, to minister his aid to a young lady of distinction, who was grieviously indisposed.

Accustomed to such demands, Belgarbo enveloped himself in his cloak, put his little case of instruments into his pocket, gave some orders to an apprentice, who was used to supply his place during his absence, leapt upon the horse that waited for him, and took, with his guide, the road which led into Austria.

At the end of several hours they passed through the village of Wipach; and towards the evening they arrived at the extremity of the valley, at the foot of the high mountains which must be passed to reach the Carniole.

While the doctor was on the road, he remembered that the letter did not mention any name, and he forthwith questioned the domestic upon that subject; but the servant was either unable or unwilling to give Belgarbo any other information except that they would arrive at the end of their journey before night.

They were by this time at the entrance of a defile which was narrow and dark, and in the vicinity of a dismal torrent, over which travellers passed by means of a small bridge. The guide turned suddenly to the right, followed the course of the stream, and penetrated amongst the precipitous rocks, the foundations of which formed its bed. The doctor was astonished that such a path could lead to any human dwelling; and at the termination of a few yards, the road suddenly stopped at the foot of a perpendicular rock, from which a torrent descended and fell, at a little distance, with fearful din. The guide leapt from his horse, and desired the doctor to imitate his example, exclaiming, "The road which we have now to pursue must be followed on foot."

The doctor glanced around him with anxiety. The sun had just set; and immediately before him, amidst the obscurity of the evening, he perceived the entrance of a low cavern, whence in a few moments two men suddenly issued, advanced towards the horse, without uttering a word, and attached the reins to the roots which hung from the rocks. The aspect of their leathern gaiters, their caps made of the skins of wild boars, and their buff jerkins, led the doctor at first to imagine that they were miners who dwelt in the Carniole: but, besides this singularity of attire, they wore upon their shoulders cloaks formed of the hides of bears, which descended to their waists.

In the meantime the domestic struck a light; and the two men, having provided themselves with a couple of torches, desired Belgarbo to follow them into the subterranean cavern. The doctor was a man of courage; and without being at all intimidated by the strangeness of his situation, he said to the messenger who had conducted him from Gorice—

"I came to tender my professional aid to a young lady in a castle, and not to penetrate with strangers into a dreary cavern. I shall therefore at once return to mine own home, unless you will vouchsafe to explain the object for which my presence is desired—the place whither you are leading me—and the names of the individuals who demand my succour."

"You would be wrong," answered the guide, in a tone of politeness, "to yield to your fears. You are in no danger—the master whom I serve throws himself upon *your* mercy, since I have brought you without the slightest precaution into a place with which it is highly important for him that no stranger should be acquainted. My orders are to conduct you to his presence—but to use no violence. If you persist in refusing to follow me, I shall be under the painful necessity of leading you back to Gorice, upon the sole condition that you pledge yourself solemnly never to reveal to a soul the secret of this path. But, believe me, you would do much better to proceed on your journey, and you will not have to repent the confidence you repose in him whom I serve. My master is generous, and a liberal reward will remunerate your services, besides the duty which humanity entails upon you to succour a young and beautiful lady, who is at this moment in the greatest possible danger."

During this long harangue, the doctor, who attentively examined the calm features and the unruffled countenance of the individual who addressed him, felt his repugnance to continue the journey diminished by degrees; and these last words determined him to proceed. Although arrived at a mature age, the idea of a young and suffering female invariably excited in him the most lively interest, to which was now added a sentiment of curiosity. He accordingly informed his guides that he was ready to follow them.

Ascending four or five steps cut out of the solid rock, they entered the cavern. The two miners went first with torches, the doctor and guide following,

In the course of a few minutes the subterranean passage appeared to be terminated by a huge block of stone, which seemed to form a species of door. This the miners succeeded in turning round, after a great deal of difficulty; for the block of stone moved upon pivots concealed in the ground beneath and the arch above; and the opening revealed a small and narrow passage, along which the calvalcade was obliged to proceed upon hands and knees. At the conclusion of this path, which was about fifty yards in length, they arrived at an immense cavern, the walls of which were adorned with stalactites of a thousand variegated shapes, and by which the light of the torches was reflected in all directions. At the bottom of this cavern a river traversed a fissure in the rock, over which the travellers passed by the aid of the plank. The nets which hung from the banks showed that the stream abounded in fish. A little further on they arrived at a narrow path hanging over a dark precipice of inconceivable depth: thence they proceeded to a steep acclivity, which, having ascended, they reached a consecutive range of caverns of different sizes, where the variegated incrustations and transparent columns dazzled the sight. For a long time did they pursue that

vast labyrinth; the doctor admired those wonders of nature, and was frequently desirous of stopping to examine them closely; but his guides marched onward in silence, and the noise of their feet resounded throughout the immense excavations.

This subterranean road, however, seemed to have no end; and by the fatigue and hunger which the doctor experienced, he judged that he must have proceeded upon that humid and dangerous path for upwards of two or three hours. At length he and his companions arrived at the termination of the chain of dismal caverns, and entered a corridor, the walls of which were evidently smoothed and cut by the hand of human workmen. At the end of this passage was a large iron door, which, when opened, discovered a staircase. Here the two miners stopped; and the servant requested the doctor to follow him up the steps, on the top of which another door was thrown open. Belgarbo then found himself in a saloon magnificently furnished, well lighted, and warmed by a good fire; and a man of noble appearance hastened to receive him.

"By my troth," said the doctor, placing his glass upon the table, at which he and his host were seated, "the excellent young man, whom you sent to bring me hither, was right when he declared that I should not regret proceeding on the journey, since I have found an old acquaintance, and, I may say, a friend of my youth. But wherefore did you employ such precautions, and make me come by that infernal road. A word, signed by you, Lord Hermann, would have sufficed to have brought me by the direct path, which, if I do not mistake, passes at a little distance from the castle."

"I was not sure that the reminiscence of our former friendship would have sufficed to induce you to undertake this journey," said the Knight of Lueg; "and, in case you should have refused, prudence required the concealment of my name. As for the road, it was impossible to choose a better, the troops which besiege me having taken possession of the other avenue that leads to the fortress."

"Besieged!" exclaimed the doctor, with the most unfeigned surprise; "why—how—and by whom?"

Hermann answered all these questions by narrating to Belgarbo the events with which the reader is already acquainted. When he had terminated that portion of his narrative he informed his friend of all the circumstances connected with his flight and the blockade of Lueg, which had lasted upwards of three months.

"The ten soldiers, who were buried in the avalanch of snow," added Hermann, "which my followers had prepared for the purpose in

front of the terrace of the castle, were soon after extricated by my orders; they were insensible, and I had them brought into the very room in which we are now seated. They were speedily restored to animation, and every precaution was taken to prevent them from suspecting the place in which they found themselves. The moment their senses returned, a sleeping portion was administered to each; and when they were once more unconscious of all that was passing around them, they were transported, by the aid of the three men who brought you hither through the subterranean passages, to the frontiers of Italy. My faithful agent, with two covered vehicles, deposited them upon the public market-place of Wipach, before any one was awake in that town. By those means, and without having to re-

proach myself for another assassination, I was disencumbered of these unpleasant guests, and the most important mystery of my defence was not compromised; for, with the exception of yourself, of those three men who brought you hither, and whose fidelity has long been tried, and myself, no earthly being is acquainted with the secret passage by which you came, nor the existence of that little door which admitted you into this room."

"And now," said the doctor, after a moment's silence, "what plan do you intend to follow? You cannot hope to resist the force of his Imperial Majesty with a dozen or two of miners and peasants?"

"I am not so foolish," answered Hermann. "In less than a month, perhaps, the ice and snow, which now render this castle inaccessible, will have disappeared, and it will then only require the attack of a few hours to force an entrance. My project is to retire to Venice, to which city I have already consigned all that I have been enabled to save of my fortune."

"The sooner the better," cried the doctor; "and I am only surprised that, possessing so convenient a means of retreat, you have not, ere now, taken advantage of it."

"For the last week," returned Hermann, "I have been daily thinking of leaving the castle; but the illness of my daughter has prevented me. It is precisely to assist me to overcome this obstacle that your experience and knowledge are required. So soon as you shall have seen her," continued Hermann, ringing a bell, "you will be enabled to tell me the extent of her danger, and whether she can undertake the journey which you have this day performed."

The great door of the saloon opened, and a domestic appeared.

"Announce to my daughter," said the knight, "that the physician, whose arrival I awaited, is here; and ascertain if she be disposed to see him at present."

The servant scarcely seemed to hear the orders of his master; as soon as he saw the doctor in the room, he stood like one petrified with astonishment. Curiosity was also depicted upon his countenance; his eyes wandered round the room, and were then cast once more upon the doctor, who remarked the man's emotions, and in his turn began to examine his countenance with attention,

"Well," cried Hermann, "wherefore art thou staring about thee thus? Didst thou not hear the order which I but now gave thee?"

The domestic left the room without uttering a word; and Hermann was about to continue his observations, when Belgarbo interrupted him, took his arm with an air of serious importance, and said, "Tell me, who is this man? Do you know him well?"

"He is an old servant," returned the knight, "who has long filled the office of majordomo and intendant."

"Mistrust him," cried the doctor, hastily; "I examined his features with attention, and the lines of his physiognomy betoken nothing good."

"You will allow," said Hermann, with a partial smile, "that many years of faithful service should have more weight with me in reference to my opinions concerning that man, than all the rules of a science founded upon conjecture."

"Do not despise those rules which you do not understand," exclaimed Belgarbo. "I have seldom been deceived in their application. Mistrust that man, I repeat; I scrutinized his features well, and I see nothing but perfidy and treachery marked upon his countenance."

"I will not contest the point with you," said Hermann, "especially as I have nothing to fear from that man, whom I do not intend to take away with me in my suite. He does not know the secret of my subterranean avenue; and you yourself must have observed the astonishment with which he glanced upon you. He could not divine in what manner you obtained ingress to this castle."

Belgarbo made no reply, and Hermann took up the thread of the conversation, which had been interrupted as follows :—

"I was telling you that the illness of my daughter was the only obstacle to my immediate departure. However culpable she may have been, I am, nevertheless, her father, and I would rather perish myself than expose my only child to the slightest danger. The precipitation with which I was pursued when I came to take refuge in my castle, did not allow me the necessary time to bring a woman with me to minister unto my daughter, and the poor girl is confined in her chamber, with only myself to console and solace her. From the first day of her return she took to her bed, and refused all nourishment save a little milk and bread; the bloom of her countenance has disappeared, and her features are thin and care-worn. When I proposed to carry her away from the castle, she assured me that she could not support the journey, and begged me to leave her to die in peace. My dear Belgarbo, her condition is sufficient to break my heart; and never could I consent to abandon my dear child !"

"Her illness must be very severe," said the doctor, after a moment's reflection, "if she cannot support the removal from hence to Gorice, where she could find an asylum at my house."

"If you can do aught to aid me in this dilemma," said Hermann, pressing the doctor's hand with friendly warmth, "I shall owe you an eternal debt of gratitude. But you may now judge for yourself, relative to the situation of my daughter. The majordomo will conduct you to her presence."

The intendant entered the room at this moment with a torch; and the doctor endeavoured to pursue upon the ignoble countenance of the servant the phrenological examination he had commenced a short time previously; but the major-domo avoided this repetition of an unpleasant scrutiny by turning abruptly away, and led the doctor to the apartment of the young lady, with whom he left him.

When Belgarbo returned to the saloon, the knight exclaimed—

"What is your opinion? What do you advise relative to the state of my daughter?

Is it possible for us to prepare for our departure?"

"A week ago," answered the doctor in a serious tone of voice, "the scheme was practicable; but it is now too late! You should have summoned me ten days back."

"Great God!" ejaculated Hermann; "do you despair of my daughter's life?"

"I did not say those words," returned Belgarto, slightly embarrassed. "Thank heavens, very few women succomb to this malady; and I may safely say that after the interview I have had with the young lady, I confidently hope she will recover from the crisis which draws near."

"What is the nature of my daughter's malady?" demanded Hermann, turning deadly pale.

"By my troth." replied the doctor, after a moment's pause," you *must* learn the truth in the end. But your brow contracts, Lord Hermann—let us procrastinate the explanation till to-morrow. You will then be more calm, and can understand—"

' I have understood your meaning but too well already," interrupted the Bear of the Carniole. "All my suspicions are then well founded! Dishonoured! lost! debased daughter. Execrable Papenheim!"

It was in vain that the physician essayed to moderate the wrath of his friend. Like a fire which, after having been long smothered, suddenly bursts forth with terrible violence, the anger of Hermann increased every moment; and the only intelligible words which fell from his lips upon the ears of the doctor, were—

"Accursed daughter!" and "Execrable Papenheim!"

At that moment the clock of the castle proclaimed the hour; and that which the eloquence of the doctor could not accomplish was produced by the iron tongue of the monotonous bell. The ire of the Lord of Lueg suddenly ceased; and after a moment's silence he took the doctor's hand, and said to him in a sombre, but tranquil tone of voice—

"Eleven o'clock, my friend! This is the moment when my hand, although involuntarily, dealt death to the seducer of my daughter. He perished in the midst of a bacchanalian orgie, without being prepared to stand before the tribunal of his Maker! The irreparable misfortune was caused by my impetuosity, and every evening, at this hour, I endeavour to atone for it. Come, let us hasten and pray for the soul of Papenheim!"

The doctor followed in silence; his bosom divided between compassion and admiration. He, however, stopped suddenly, and addressed his friend.

"Will you not grant to your own daughter that pardon which you so generously bestow upon your enemy?"

The knight raised his eyes to heaven, and then turned them upon the doctor, with an expression of resignation and kindness.

"Let us pray for my daughter also!" said Hermann, pressing the doctor's hand tenderly.

As they issued from the saloon they met the intendant, who, with a torch in his hand, conducted them to the chapel, of which it is indispensably necessary to give an accurate description, in order that the events about to follow may be properly understood.

At the extremity of the platform or terrace of the castle, and on the side opposed to the entrance, was a vertical fissure in the rock, which was visible in the valley beneath, to the level of which it descended. At the bottom of this semicircular hollow there was, in former times, a reservoir of water, supplied by neighbouring springs; and as the Castle of Lueg at that period was deficient in water, its ancient possessors had availed themselves of this circumstance. On the summit of the fissure, on the edge of the terrace, a little projecting building had been erected, and in it were placed a block and a windlass. The middle of the floor of this little edifice was perforated with a large aperture; and thus the whole contrivance, with the aid of a bucket and a cord, performed the functions of an ordinary well.

The chapel belonging to the castle of Lueg, had been built over the yawning chasm. One end of it rested on the rock which formed the base or foundation for the castle itself. The other rested on a jutting piece of rock work. It will be seen, therefore, that the floor of the chapel ran over a deep pit of some three or four hundred feet from the building itself.

Hermann and the doctor entered the chapel, preceded by the intendant. As the latter approached the centre of the sacred edifice, there was that in the expression of his countenance which denoted fear, and according to the doctor's interpretation, a guilty conscience. He called the attention of Hermann to the violent trepidation of the major-domo. Hermann regarded the features of the latter with a searching gaze, before which scrutiny the man quailed.

"Treacherous—I'll dare be sworn," said the doctor, in a hurried whisper.

"Hark ye, sirrah," exclaimed Hermann, turning sharp round upon his supposed faithful domestic. "Hark ye, some secret prompter tells me that you are playing me false. Dost hear? false! and if it be so, your life shall pay the forfeit of your treachery. Here, on the instant, on this spot," continued the Lord of Lueg, drawing his sword, and grasping the man by the throat. The intendant trembled in every limb—which his mastter observing, he concluded that his surmises were correct.

"I swear, I am innocent," said the major-domo. "On my honour ; on my life, I swear to it."

"Kneel at the altar, and swear by your hopes hereafter, that you are free from this foul charge," said Hermann, endeavouring to force the major-domo towards the altar-piece.

"Oh, mercy ! mercy ! not true," said the affrighted man struggling with his superior.

Hermann observing the suddenly awakened fears of his servant, and his unwilllingness to be brought within the circle of the sacred spot, being under the impression that he had taken the man at an advantage. He dragged him forcibly before the altar-piece—the major-domo resisting with all his might, and crying out for mercy, in broken and suppli-cating accents. The more unwillingness he evinced, the more determined was Hermann ; and by a violent and sudden effort he drag-ged the trembling intendant in front of the altar-piece. The doctor was watching these proceedings ; and his horror may be ima-gined when he observed the floor give way—with a loud crash—and both the Lord of Lueg and his treacherous domestic disap-peared through an aperture in the boards of the floor. A stifled cry was heard for an instant, and then a dead and sickening sound, as the two bodies reached the bottom of the yawning pit. The doctor then cau-tiously crept up to the orifice in the broken floor, and endeavoured to gaze down into the yawning chasm ; but he could discern nothing. He then hastened to the other part of the castle, and in company with some of the domestics proceeded to make an inspec-tion of the base of the chasm. Here they found the dead bodies of the Lord of Lueg and the faithless intendant, both firmly locked in their last death embrace.

It appeared that the major-domo had cut away the boards of the chapel floor, for the express purpose of destroying his master, whom he expected would be at that precise spot when paying his evening devotions. Thus it was, that he had fallen into the very trap he had set for his master.

The sequel is easily told. The doctor fled with Hermann's daughter to England, where he placed her under the charge of a respect-able elderly female. When the narrator had told the foregoing narrative to Squabshot and his friend, the reader may judge of their surprise, when he informed them that he was was none other than the doctor himself.

———

CHAPTER CV.

THE CONCEALED TREASURE BROUGHT TO LIGHT.

Some three days after the incidents men-tioned in our last chapter, Colonel Jack caused the trunk which he had placed in charge of Reuben to be removed to the lodgings of Mr. Squabshot. This was done at night, and with as much secresy as pos-sible. With what eager hungry eyes did Mr. Ubsdell contemplate the large and promising proportions of the collossal trunk or oak chest. How did he hunger after its contents ? Now, that it was once more in his sight, he felt re-assured, and believed that he was in truth likely to have his share of the booty, about which he had had serious doubts when he saw it disappear in the vault under charge of Rueben. Mr. Squabshot, himself, was in a state of delirious delight when he saw its large proportions half filling the front room of his apartments.

Colonel Jack as soon as he had seen the chest safely deposited in the charge of Squab-shot and Ubsdell prepared to take his depar-ture, for he did not wish to intrude upon the privacy of the two friends, neither did he seek or desire to be present when the box was opened. Squabshot however, endea-voured to persuade him to stay and see if it was in reality the great prize they had anti-cipated ; but Colonel Jack made some excuse, and promising to look in on the following morning to learn the particulars respecting the contents of the trunk—he took his de-parture. Ubsdell and Squabshot were alone with their cherished prize. How like two greedy misers did their eyes wander over the goodly proportions of that ponderous trunk ? How they calculated what it was possible for it to contain, assuming that it was filled with treasure.

"And now," said Squabshot, " here we have it safe and sound ; now the next ques-tion is, how is it to be opened ?"

They both of them contemplated it for some time and observed that it was fastened by several catches besides the lock itself, diffi-cult as it might be to open the lid of the chest it was a task that must be accom-plished. There could be but little doubt upon one point. It was quite certain that neither Squabshot or his companion would rest content till this disederatum was accom-plished. The former had gathered together all the tools he had in his possession, and in anticipation of the coming prize he had pur-chased several others such as files, saws, centre-bits, &c,. &c. It would be necessary in conducting these operations to make as little noise as possible for fear of disturbing the household. Mr. Squabshot had never cared at any time what boisterous and uproarious mirth his bacchanalian companions indulged in at all hours of the night; but these were different sounds to the noise of file, screwdriver, and mallet and chisel; and as he stood contemplating the chest, his heart beat high with alternate hope and fears. His first proceeding was to try every key he had in the house to see if any would turn the lock. As might he supposed this was perfectly useless, there was not one that gave even a promise of turning it; in the first place the lock was very old, of a different fashion and make to those then in use, and moreover it was so much rusted by time and damp that it was all but next to an impossibility for it to be turned.

Leaving the lock to the last, Mr. Squabshot proceeded to file away the other fastenings which bound the lid of the box to its sides. Some of them he forced with a mallet and chisel, when at length, wearied with excitement and the labour he had been at, he paused, and pouring out a flagon of wine, drained off its contents. This gave him renewed strength and courage to persevere in his task, and it was past two o'clock in the morning when both Ubsdell and himself, breathless and faint, were compelled to give in, and throwing themselves into a couple of chairs, they wiped the perspiration from their brows. They then glanced at the trunk which had so obstinately resisted their efforts. It would appear that the fastenings were never ending.

"What's to be done?" inquired Ubsdell; "What *is* to be done? We shall never be able to open it to-night, or rather morning, and yet I do not like to desist."

"Oh, we must cut it now," said Squabshot, lighting his pipe. I'm fairly done up, and so we will renew our labours in the morning."

"Morning, indeed," said Ubsdell, as he heard the watchman calling out past two o'clock. It is morning now."

"Well, we must have a few hours rest first, and then we shall be better able to resume our labours, for to tell you the truth, I am pretty well done up."

"Oh dear, oh dear," said Mr. Ubsdell. "It's clear we shall not be able to see what the chest contains to-night—oh dear!'

It is of no use killing ourselves, and so let the affair remain in abeyance until the morning."

After another half hour or so had passed, Squabshot and his companion retired to rest, and slept soundly until morning. After breakfast, they again resumed their labours with renewed energy. Night, however, had come again before they had succeeded in opening the lid of the chest. When they did so, their eyes dilated with surprise and universal wonderment. The trunk was chiefly filled with old guineas of the time of Charles I. and the Commonwealth. On the top of these there were a number of choice pieces of plate, antique vases, gold cups, and candelabras.

When the full blaze of this treasure burst upon the senses of Squabshot and his companion, their delight knew no bounds, they danced and capered with joy. Their next act was to kneel down and carefully examine the contents of the chest. Ubsdell held a candle above his head, and stooped over the vast amount of wealth that was there revealed to his delightful gaze; a faint tremulousness crept over him—the tremulousness of delight. Here within his very grasp lay that precious metal—for which men sold their best and brightest virtues and inspirations. Mr. Ubsdell took a handful of the golden guineas, and let them fall through his half opened fingers like husks of corn or barley; the chink of the ringing metal was pleasing to his senses, and he continued to take up handful after handful, and play with them like a child with a toy. Squabshot took in his hand one of the antique vases; it was of exquisite workmanship, and appeared to be unusually heavy. It was solid gold—rare and antique in its ornamentation.

"We are made men for life," exclaimed Ubsdell. "No more work, no more black looks from your employer. Hurrah! No more boring over the confounded desk. Hurrah! and he snapped his fingers like castanets.

Mr. Squabshot sat himself down on the edge of the box, and said to his companion, deprecatingly—

"Don't make such a noise. Remember there are other persons in this house besides ourselves, and it behoves us to use caution."

"Oh, ah, true, I had forgot," answered Ubsdell; "true, caution is necessary. I wonder how much there is in the chest?"

"Oh, more than will suffice for thou and I; but stay, what is this?"

"Squabshot placed his hand upon a bundle of papers which were in the corner of the chest. They were tied up with red tape, and he proceeded to unfasten them, and found them to consist of several documents. He opened them one after another, and he could not at first understand their precise nature. One was a brief abstract of the wishes of one Gabriel Beechcroft, goldsmith. This was a sort of will. In it, the said Gabriel Beechcroft stated that the treasure contained in the oaken chest was buried by him during the great fire of London, and he stated, in the event of his decease, who the property was to revert to. It was to be divided among his relatives—people who had been dead for more than a century. Squabshot read this document aloud in a solemn voice, much after the style of a lawyer reading a will, which, in reality, the document was.

Well, it was quite clear that the relations were long since dead. and Mr. Squabshot and his friend agreed that they were the two residuary legatees, and consequently made no kind of scruple in taking possession of the property in their own right. There was no one to dispute their claim.

Another document contained a history of the Beechcroft family, and amongst the papers were a series of chronicles, legends, and tales—some about ancient London, others of Paris and the continental capitals, and others of the Court. In the course of our work, we shall have occasion to recur to these from time to time, and ever and anon give our readers a specimen of the chronicles left by the deceased goldsmith, whose industry and business-like habits had enabled him to hoard up so much gorgeous wealth. The first story we shall present to our readers, is a Jewish chronicle—doubtless written by some wealthy Israelite—and given by him to Gabriel Beechcroft.

While Mr. Squabshot and his companion are examining the contents of the box, we will give in our next chapter a tale of the Temple.

CHAPTER CVI.

MARIAMNE, A TALE OF THE TEMPLE.

THE fading rays of the sun had already cast their parting splendour on the proud city of David, gilding the pinnacles of her magnificent Temple, the crested towers of her battlements, and the lofty summit of Mount Olivet, with that rosy hue which alike marks his rising and setting beauty. A throng of the inhabitants were issuing from the eastern gate, eager to enjoy the delicious coolness of the approaching evening, which is no where more appreciated than in the arid climate of the east. The sage elder and the sacred Levite might be seen bending their steps in sober gravity, pausing alternately to return the salutes of reverence bestowed upon them by the passers-by, or to contemplate, with benevolent satisfaction, the various groups of lovely children, that, rejoicing in their freedom, from the restraint which the intense heat of the day necessarily imposed, frolicked, in innocent play, by the side of their watchful mothers. Occasionally, a stern Pharisee, the sanctimonious and scornful expression of whose countenance accorded with the exclusive and peculiar doctrines of his sect, hastily passed the cheerful parties in his

way towards the valley of Jehosaphat; the gloom of which, increased, rather than relieved, by the hoarse murmurs of the brook of Kedrem, harmonised with the unsocial complexion of his feelings. The golden beams of the fading luminary glanced yet more faintly from the horizon; the many stars, the gems upon the mantle of night, were beginning to sparkle in the heavens, when the curiosity of the Hebrews was excited by the singular appearance of two travellers, who, descending the mountain, where they had been detained by the involuntary admiration of the scene before them, guided their tired steeds towards Jerusalem. Both were in the garb of Israelites (probably from one of the cities of the Desert), but formed with an unusual richness of material. The elder was clad in a vest of deep saffron-coloured cloth, worked at the hem with threads of gold and purple, which descended to his sandalled feet ; a belt of the same device, but exceeding it in cunning work, confined it to the waist; his outer garment of Tyrian dye, ornamented with stripes from the skin of the fox, fell, in many folds, around his person, and fastened in front with clasps of goodly work. The turban of twisted white and scarlet linen, was adorned with a scroll, on which Hebrew characters were traced, signifying Aran, of the tribe of Benjamin, a chief of Israel. The face of the wearer was of that expressive character which at once impresses the beholder with an opinion of its shrewdness and determination—an intellectual eye, a well-arched brow, added to its spirit and vivacity—sobered, perhaps, by the sable beard which fell gracefully upon his breast; in place of arms, he wore, suspended from his side, a stilus, and materials for working. The features of the younger bore an almost womanish resemblance to the countenance of his brother, for such was the connexion between them. In lieu of the ample beard, the first down of manhood curled lightly round his lip, concealing its naturally scornful expression ; his head was cast from that mould of beauty in which the intellectual and voluptuous are equally predominant, and alike suited to the character of a Sardanapalus or Epicurus. Unlike the peaceful bearing of his brother, a light cuirass of gilded steel was girded upon his breast, and a sword depended in its silver scabbard from his thigh ; a bow, with a plentiful supply of arrows, fastened to the head of his saddle, but so lightly as to be ready for instant service, completed his military equipment ; in other respects the garb of the brothers was the same. The inscription upon the scroll of the younger being Eli, of the tribe of Benjamin, a captain in Israel. The two strangers had approached within hail of the gate of the Holy City, when as if by mutual consent, they reined their horses, and the younger of the two addressing a Hebrew, who for some time had been regarding them with a dissatisfied look, demanded if he could guide them to the house of some person of good repute, where they might be entertained for the night within the walls.

"Is thy servant a dog?" replied the Pharisee—for Eli had addressed one of that stern sect—"or a mule without a name, that he must answer the question of every idler, put without reverence? speed thy way!" he continued; "or ask of such as may feel bound to answer thee."

"Discourteous contemner of hospitality!" exclaimed the youthful horseman, his brow reddening with anger at the churlish reply he had received, "make me answer speedily, or I will smite thee like a helot;" and, raising his riding staff of cedar wood, he would have executed his threat had not his less irascible companion restrained him.

The astonished Pharisee, accustomed to receive from his followers the most respectful devotion, was vehement in his expressions of indignation at the threatened outrage, and soon attracted by his cries a number of the citizens around him.

"What new thing is this?" he began, when he found himself supported by his friends; "are the dwellers of Jerusalem to be questioned and beaten by every idle scorner? Shall a humble-minded Pharisee, who liveth not as other men live, but walketh in the fear of the Lord, be assailed within bow-shot of the Holy Walls?"

"Shame! shame!" exclaimed the easily excited Israelites, whom his artful speech had worked upon, "it shall not be permitted; let the evil-doers be delivered unto the judges: to prison with them!"

Vain were all attempts on the part of the two travellers to obtain a hearing; a dozen eager grasps secured the weapons of the younger, and rendered his exertions unavailing. Seeing him disarmed, even the more timid rushed upon them, and would have succeeded in tearing them from their horses, had not a loud voice commanded them to. desist. In an instant the tumult was hushed, the Jews recognising in the speaker the awful presence of the high priest.

"What idle disturbance is this?" he exclaimed, looking sternly around him; "is it thus the children of Israel receive their strange brethren? Is it not written that the wanderer is the guest of the Most High, and ye assail them as they were thieves and murderers!—give me answer—why have ye done the evil?"

"They have railed at and beaten a holy Pharisee," replied an opulent citizen, one of the most forward in the outrage.

'False witness," interrupted Aran, for the first time breaking silence, "no blow hath been struck but by thee and thy ungovernable companions Honoured of Judea," he continued, bowing in deep humility, "thy servants are from the desert, journeying to Jerusalem to worship in the temple, as is the custom of our people; my brother did but request yon Pharisee to guide us to some house of good resort, for we are strangers, when he replied, with most inhospitable scorn, which, with the intemperance of youth, his questioner retorted; these, his friends and followers, surrounded us: their violence thou hast witnessed; judge, then, between us.'

"Is this so?" said the indignant high priest, directing his glance towards the abashed hypocrite, "begone!—know that charity is a garb more sacred than the vestment of outward observance, and that the worst pride is that of the self-righteous. You," he continued to the rebuked Hebrews, "conduct these strangers to my dwelling; they are guests whom the Lord hath sent me;" and without waiting to receive their thanks, the holy man pursued his way.

Their guides now became as officious in their kindness as they had before been offensive in their hostility. Strangers who had quarrelled with a Pharisee, and the favoured guests of the high priest, were widely different persons in the estimation of the Jews, who vied with each other in attentions, and excuse for their former outrage. Arrived at the stately palace where fortune had so unexpectedly provided them with a home, they were first conducted to the bath, that indispensable article of eastern hospitality, and, after refreshing themselves, left by the obsequious attendants to repose.

"This is beyond my hope," exclaimed the elder, as soon as they were alone. "Belus prospers our design; the very house of our enemy is open to us. Not for another Babylon would I forego my triumph."

"And yet," replied Eli, musingly, the old man was kind to us; but for his aid we might have perished 'neath the violence of the people—it was the dotard's fate."

"But what," continued Aran, bending his brow, "is the meaning of this coldness? hast thou forgot thine oath to the mighty gods of Babylon, that the fairest maiden of Israel shall be their scorn, even the daughter of this hoary priest?"

"No,' replied the younger, firmly, "it is registered with thine. Beauty hath ever been my passion, my destiny; none ever yet escaped my arts, I will make vengeance a pleasure, and add this famed Mariamne to to the number; then, in our father's hall, will we mock at the virtue of Jerusalem."

"While I," resumed his brother, "profane their detested temple, the rival of our imperial city, enter its mysterious sanctuary, and erect upon its shrine this symbol of our worship,"

As he spoke, the disguised idolator drew from his vest a golden image of his deity, which, for the daring purpose he had avowed, he carried secreted upon his person. Learned beyond the spirit of their time, both the brothers were well calculated to sustain the characters they had assumed, that of travelling Israelites from one of the cities of the Desert.

The evening meal was prepared upon the house-top, as was the custom in the city, in order that the inhabitants might enjoy the only hours of coolness which the summer season afforded them. There did the virtuous Simeon and his fair and innocent child await the arrival of their guests. Accustomed even as the younger had been to the voluptuous beauties of his father's court, he was electrified by the superior loveliness of Mariamne, who, half reclining on a pile of cushions, by the side of her venerable parent, gently inclined her head at their approach. Her figure might have been termed fragile, but for the exquisite harmony of its proportions, which the folds of her white cymar could not entirely conceal; her face possessed all the characteristic regularity of the noble and high-born of her race—raven hair, arched brows, and black lustrous eyes, relieved by a complexion which even the daughters of the North might have envied for its fairness; but it was in her garden, or while attending upon her father, her veil cast freely aside, moving like a spirit more than a being of the earth, that the full splendour of her beauty was revealed.

Before commencing the repast, the high priest offered up his thanksgiving to the bounteous Creator of all things, a duty in which the strangers joined, the elder having first, unseen by any but his brother, spat upon the ground, as in abhorrence of the rite. Eli was too wary to startle his intended victim by open and intense admiration; gently and imperceptibly, like the approach of the poisonous adder, he endeavoured to beguile her into conversation, carefully choosing themes of beauty and virtue as more congenial to her retiring nature; while Aran, anxious to assist his brother's detestable design, engaged his unsuspecting host in deep discourse, who, charmed by the wisdom and seeming piety he displayed, congratulated himself on entertaining such an honourable guest. Time passed rapidly, and the high priest was surprised to find, on the first pause that ensued, that the shades of evening had already deepened into night; meanwhile, the gifted, but impious Eli, had made good use of his opportunity with the unsuspicious Mariamne.

"Time hath passed swiftly," observed her father; "the hour of rest to man is come; but first, child, thy lute; I would not to my couch without my accustomed hymn."

The maiden obeyed; but felt, in doing so, she knew not why, a tremour and hesitation, which subsided, however, as the sacred song burst in harmony from her lips:

"I have read the Lord's might in the fair
      evening star,
In the pure worlds of light He hath scattered
      afar;
Not more wondrous their orbs, as the proof of
      his power,
Than the insect whose home is the bright-
      tinted flower.

I have heard His stern voice in the deep
      thunder's sound,
In the roar of the tempest His wrath scatter'd
      round,
Yet His dread will is spoken, as plain as in
      these,
When borne on the delicate voice of the breeze.

Oh! there is not a thing, that hath being or
      life,
From the emmet's small form, to the ocean's
      wild strife,
The dew on the stem, or the life-giving shower,
But are pledges alike of His wisdom and
      power."

After receiving the benediction of their host, they parted for the night—Eli to indulge in intoxicating dreams of pleasure, and Mariamne, for the first time in her life, to an unquiet couch.

Who can read the human heart? Man? He is the slave of its devices. Woman, she is the victim of its weakness. It is a mystery even to the angels who stand before the throne of the Eternal. His wisdom who framed can alone unravel it. Mariamne's innocent and unsuspicious nature, guileless itself, suspected not guile in others; her heart was easily captivated by the gifted form and eloquent tongue of the idolator, who beneath the veil of seeming virtue, concealed the consummate art of the refined seducer.

By the most tender assiduity, by the most unremitting attention, he succeeded in possessing her affections so entirely, that her being became wrapped up in his. Had Eli escaped heart whole? No, the passion glowed in his own bosom with intense ardour; more than honour was now pledged for the success of his impious scheme—his happiness, his life—both he felt depended on the smile of Mariamne; his thoughts, his dreams were of her.

"How much longer is this irresolution to last?" impatiently demanded Aran, whom a

residence of several weeks in Jerusalem had rendered impatient : " ere this I might have performed my vow, had I not waited for thee, loiterer ! You boast that this paragon loves you—hath at your bidding concealed it from her father ; yet," he added, scornfully, " I see no proof of your success."

" You know not the purity I have to cope with," replied the lover.

" She is a woman,' answered his companion, with a sneer ; " one of a sex with whom till now Eli hath held his arts invincible."

" And they shall prove so," answered the youth, stung by the sarcastic manner of his brother. " This night both our designs shall be accomplished ! If I have the power to move her, this night shall she meet me in the temple."

No. 68.

" I will station our concealed followers near," added Aran ; " our triumph once secured, farewell Jerusalem !"

With this understanding they parted. To dwell upon the arts, the tears, and entreaties, by which Eli prevailed upon the confiding girl to grant him the required meeting, were to delay the interest of my readers—sufficient that his eloquence was successful, and Mariamne was pledged to meet her lover at midnight.

" What have I done," she exclaimed, when alone, and her feelings, which had been artfully excited, became more subdued ; " promised to quit my father's roof to hold a meeting with my suitor ! Alas ! it is not thus that Israel's daughter shall be wooed ! There must be wrong in this, and sin !" she added, as her naturally fine sense pictured the appointment in its proper light; a blush fell upon the maiden's cheek at the mere thought. "God of Abraham," she continued, sinking upon her knees, "I am motherless, be thou my guide; I am week, be thou my help, my counseller!" As she spoke her father entered the chamber. He had just returned from the mid-day service of the temple; the holy ephod shone resplendent upon his breast, and upon his brow the mitre blazed with the *ineffable name of* " God " His arrival at that moment seemed an answer to her prayer. She dared not resist the omen, but, casting herself at his feet, declared, with tears and blushes, her love for the young stranger, and the tumult the concealment had created in her soul. Anger was the first emotion of the high priest on hearing the strange, and to him unexpected, confession; a feeling which soon yielded to the natural benevolence of his heart, the tears of his daughter, and anxiety for her happiness.

"Rise, my child!" he exclaimed, "if thou lovest the youth, and he proves worthy of thee, my blessing shall not he wanting to thy union; meet him in the temple, since thy word is given; its holiness will be a safeguard against all idle thoughts, and there reveal unto Eli the secret of his happiness."

With a light heart, and beaming countenance, the now happy girl sank upon the breast of her parent.

It was midnight; an awful gloom obscured the heavens; not a ray of light, save from the ever-burning golden lamps, illumined the vast court of the Levites; two figures might be seen, by their mild beams, pacing the marble pavement—they were the idolators.

"The hour I have dreamed of is at hand!" exclaimed the elder, proudly drawing the golden image at the same time from his vest; " Belus, soon shalt thou be avenged!"

"Peace!" said his brother, eagerly, as he beheld a veiled figure approaching through the cloister: "she comes, my prize—the richest gem of Israel—away, to the fulfilment of your oath."

Aran, without replying, hastened to the accomplishment of his impious design, while Eli advanced to meet his intended victim.

"Mariamne," said the accomplished dissembler, taking her by the hand, "this is a lonely hour, but suited to our parting"—

"Parting!" reiterated the maiden, with a look of surprise.

"I cannot live," he continued, "so near heaven, and yet continue hopeless; this fever of my heart will end me; I fly, ere reason follows my wreck of happiness."

"And is that thy only grief?" demanded his happy mistress, with a smile.

"Can it be," exclaimed Eli, reproachfully,

"that you mock my misery! then, indeed, life hath lost its hope.

"Not so!" replied the blushing girl, "it never blossomed fairer, Eli, dear. Eli, restrain thy happiness; listen calmly while I tell thee that my father knows of our love, and sanctions it," she added, eagerly, alarmed at the expression of his countenance. Did I not tell you we had wronged his generous nature by unwise concealment?"

This was a blow little calculated upon by the concealed idolater. For a few moments he was speechless from surprise and disappointment. He had now no pretext for urging their flight, on which his hopes depended. After a struggle with the bitterness of his feelings, he seized the hand of the confiding virgin.

"Mariamne, dost thou love me? answer me, for I am frantic. Canst thou, for my sake, cast aside the prejudices of thy nation —of thy faith?" he added in a deep, low tone, fearful lest the marble columns should echo his impiety. Hear me! shrink not— stir not. I am no Israelite!"

Had a thunderbolt fallen at the feet of his astonished listener, she could not have been transfixed with greater horror. Shrinking from his side, she fell upon her knees, veiling her brow to hide the intenseness of its agony.

"Listen, fairest of earth," he continued; "it is no wandering outcast of the desert who hath devoted to thee his love, but the son of regal Babylon, the second of his race. His powerful brother, who even now is wandering in the temple, loves him. His father hath many realms ; a crown awaits thy royal brow."

Encouraged by her motionless silence, he ventured to take her hand. She shuddered, and withdrew it from him as from the embrace of a serpent. Rising gracefully, and unveiling her tearless countenance, in which, however, strong traces of mental agitation and outraged feeling were visible, the maiden calmly replied—

"Idolater, I have heard thee; and if I punish not thy insolence to the daughter of the high priest of Israel, it is that contempt is stronger than anger—farewell!"

"Mariamne!" he uttered, frantically, "thou hast never loved me!"

"Would I never had," she replied, mournfully; "I then had escaped this shame and sin; but thy venom is harmless; thou hast thyself, in revealing thy true character, performed the cure."

"Cold and insensible!" he muttered; "but I will not be baffled; one dear revenge is in my power."

Approaching her, he would have clasped her in his arms: but she, perceiving his design, retreated to an adjacent column.

"Advance one step," she exclaimed, flushed with virtuous indignation, "and I yield thee to thy fate! One blow," pointing to a silver gong suspended within her reach, "and a thousand Levites fill the court. One word from these lips consigns thee to the doom of sacrilege. Begone! and know Mariamne of Judea scorns, and pardons thee." With a heart overwhelmed with gall and disappointment, Eli rushed from her presence.

For some time the excited girl remained in humble prayer to that Being who had given her strength to struggle with the weakness of her passions, and resist the seducer's art. "Eternal father!" she exclaimed, as a sudden thought rushed upon her brain; "heathens are in the temple, and thy holy sanctuary unguarded. Must I then give him up to death? Be it," she added, choking with tears and agitation, "my atonement." With desperate resolution she struck the gong; the summons brought a crowd of priests and her father to her presence A few words revealed the real character of the strangers.

"To the sanctuary!" said the high priest, trembling with indignation; "Lord, let not this evil be accomplished!"

Rashly the terrified Levites rushed to the gates which led to its awful precincts—they were fastened.

"To the galleries!' they exclaimed, "there we may behold them,"

In pursuit of his impious purpose, Aran had reached the portal which led to the Holy of Holies, and to prevent surprise, fastened after him the ponderous door. His foot was upon the steps, at whose termination hung that mysterious veil which no human hand save the high priest's might raise, and then but on the feast of atonement for the sins of the people, when the thronging Hebrews appeared in the galleries above.

"Behold! ye priests of Israel," exclaimed the idolator, in scorn, waving at the same time the golden image over his head—the emblem of Great Belus; "that will I place within your sanctuary; to him will I re-dedicate your temple.'

He reached the topmost step as he spoke. The high priest and Levites bowed their heads in shame to avoid witnessing the fearful profanation; but scarcely had his daring hand touched the embroidered hem of the sacred veil, when the thunder pealed within the sanctuary, and a ray of light, more, intense than the concentrated brilliancy of a thousand suns, darted through the scarce perceptible opening, struck the worshipper of Belus to the ground, and burst assunder the strongly barred gates. Well was it for the Hebrews that they had veiled their sight; no mortal eyes could have endured the splen-dour of that blaze. The now sightless orbs of the idolator were melted in their sockets. He was instantly secured by the awe-stricken priests. At the same instant Eli, who had been found lurking in the temple, was led by a party of Levites before the high priest.

"Harm them not!" he exclaimed; "un-scathed by mortal hands, let them depart, the scoff of Israel—a warning to the heathen. The Eternal hath pronounced their punishment, and man's wrath may not efface the record of the living God!"

Unharmed, and in silence, the baffled and the blind together left the temple.

CHAPTER CVII.

MR. SQUABSHOT AND HIS FRIEND'S PROCEEDINGS.

WE left Mr. Squabshot and his friend Ubsdell bending over the treasure disclosed to their enraptured gaze. A golden sea of wealth lay before them—a yellow, glittering, golden sea—dazzling their eyes, and making their hearts leap with hope and expectation. Their dreams of wealth were realised.

You who perchance have followed the fortunes of our hero through many a prosy page—you who may have toiled and toiled for years past for bare existence, who may have been the sport and toy of fortune in this work-day world of ours, you may have known, perhaps like thousands of your brethren, how the world frowns upon poverty and what fulsome adulations, what blind worship and devotion is paid to the possessors of wealth, whilst cold indifference and cheer-less looks are given to poverty.

"The learned pate ducks to the golden fool," is a trite saying of the bard of all time.

You unwashed artizan I am addressing you! You can judge of the delight of our two adventurous friends, who have dug from the bowels of the earth a second time the dross that the world worships, judge then of their ineffable delight when they found themselves the possessors of so vast a treasure, one, indeed, which was far beyond their most sanguine expectations.

Mr. Squabshot took the papers carefully out of the chest, and placed them in a bureau of his own under safe lock and key.

These consisted of the will made by the deceased Gabriel Beechcroft, the tales and legends, one of which we have already given the reader in our previous chapter.

Having placed them on one side Mr. Squabshot reflected for a few minutes what had next best be done. He had before commencing his examination of the chest taken the precaution to double lock the door of his room, draw down the blinds of his windows, and fasten the shutters thereof.

Now he paused, and taking a pipe from his extensive collection he filled and lighted it, handing, at the same time, one to his companion. This done, the two sat down and puffed away at the fragrant weed for some minutes.

Ubsdell was the first to speak.

"This is all ours, Squabby—all, eh?"

"Of course—every stiver. Who says it's not?"

"Old Beechcroft is dead. Heaven rest his soul!" said Mr. Ubsdell. "He can't by any possibility come to this world again, that is quite clear."

"Of course not. Who says he can?"

"Not I."

"Nor I."

"Well, then, it's a question of share and share alike."

"That's just it. Nothing can be clearer."

"And," said Mr. Ubsdell, sinking his voice to a whisper, "I don't think it would be advisable to let our friend know what was in this."

Here he nodded significantly towards the open chest.

"Psha!" exclaimed Squabshot. "Nonsense, man. What reason is there for concealment?"

"Oh, I don't know. Only caution is always advisable. He may want a share."

"And suppose he does, there is plenty for all three."

Mr. Ubsdell started to his feet.

"Confound you!" he exclaimed in sudden anger. "You don't mean to say that he is to come in for his thirds?"

"I have said nothing of the kind," answered Squabshot, "so don't you be quite so fast, my friend. I know Colonel Jack too well to suppose for one moment that he would even accept of such, assuming that we were even to offer it to him."

"But we are not going to offer it,' said his companion, in some alarm—"we are not going to offer it him. Eh, eh!"

And he laughed hysterically.

Ubsdell, old boy, you're a fool," said Squabshot, puffing out a thick cloud of smoke; "take my word for it, you're a fool!"

"Perhaps I am, but I am not going to be chisselled out of my rights for all that."

"Now, do hold your tongue. I tell you that Colonel Jack will not accept of any share of this prize. All he will require will be to be paid for his services, and handsomely, too."

"Oh, yes, of course. That's all fair enough."

"Good; then now we understand each other upon that head. The next thing, and a very important one, too, is how we are to dispose of this property."

"Dispose of it?"

"Ay, certainly."

"You take one half and I take the other half"

"Yes, precisely."

"Well, then, where is the difficulty?"

"My most esteemed and valued friend has it never occurred to your fertile imagination that it is just possible that your old buffer of a landlord will find at the bottom of his garden a deep hole."

"Oh, don't!" exclaimed Mr. Ubsdell, in alarm.

"And when he discovers this," said the first speaker, in continuation, "has it never occurred to you that he will ask himself one or two questions."

"Oh, pray don't," supplicated Ubsdell.

"And asking himself one or two questions he will naturally inquire of himself the reason why his respectable and much esteemed lodger so suddenly evaporated—nay, more, it is not likely he will stop there, the probability is that he will inquire of the neighbours, of the city police, of the Lord Mayor, perhaps."

"Oh, oh, oh!" shouted or rather groaned Mr. Ubsdell.

"Then you will be advertised for—your name will be printed in that remarkable publication 'The Hue and Cry.' You will be entreated to return to your disconsolate friends, to the distracted Jemima, or Julia, as the case may be, and the pit or hole at the end of the garden will be examined and carefully searched, as the natural inference will be that you have made away with yourself, and like a prudent man, as you were always known to be you had the forethought to dig your own grave before you took your flight to that place where, to use the language of Scripture, 'the wicked cease from troubling and the weary are at rest.'"

"Oh, don't be too flowery. I can't stand it."

"Then again," continued Squabshot, casting his eyes reflectively up to the ceiling —"then again there's your employers. What will they think? Of course their first idea will be that you are behindhand with your accounts; after a day or so your desk will be broken open—your books examined."

"And if they are, what care I?"

"I don't know?"

"They will be found all right. I have not wronged them of a penny."

"So much the better. I don't say you have. Indeed, I am sure you have not, and that is more."

"Well, then, what have I to fear?"

"Now, don't you be in a hurry. Let us

hope that you have nothing to fear. Only, you see, the whole town will be in a state of anxiety about you, and such being the case you will be sought after. It is possible that they may come here."

"Who?"

"How should I know? The officers, perhaps."

"Officers? I have done nothing."

"No, no; we know that. But people are apt to suppose a missing man has been up to something, and in your case they will not be far from the mark. You know we ought to look things in the face and prepare for the worst, and so again I say how had we best dispose of that?"

Mr. Squabshot nodded once more towards the open chest.

"How dispose of it? Get it out of the way as soon as possible. Well, first of all we must ascertain how much it contains. You see, my friend, that these same coins are old guineas, and if we pay a number of them into any bankers, the very natural question will be where did you get them all from? Don't you see that?"

"No, I don't."

"Well, I do; but we won't dispute about that. You do as you please with your share and I with mine, the only question is, what are we to do with the coins as we count them out—what are we to put them in?"

"Canvas bags," suggested Ubsdell.

"Ah, we shall want a pretty lot of them, and of a good size, too. That may also look suspicious. I tell you what had best be done, buy the canvas and make our own bags."

This suggestion being approved of by Mr. Ubsdell, Squabshot at once proceeded to the nearest linendrapers, bought several yards of canvas, needles and thread, and in a few minutes after his return, both he and his companion sat down to make bags to contain the gold they had become so strangely possessed of.

In the course of an hour or so half-a-dozen bags were made. Mr. Squabshot then went to the side of the chest, and began to count out guinea after guinea into one of the canvas bags.

"I don't know that we need be particular to a coin or two," said Squabshot. "We might fill our bags, and then weigh them before dividing."

"Oh, it will be a long job to count all this gold," said Ubsdell, looking whistfully at the treasure disclosed to his enchanted and enraptured eyes.

"But for curiosity's sake we will see what this bag contains," answered Squabshot, as he counted the coins, while filling the bag with the same.

He found it held, when quite full, one thousand four hundred guineas, and there was apparently but a small diminution of quantity in the oaken chest.

The other five bags were filled, and this done. Mr. Squabshot said to his companion—

"You choose one, I'll choose the next, you the next, and so on to the end."

Ubsdell did as he was desired, and they were then possessed of three bags each. Mr. Squabshot marked his with his own initials, and desired Ubsdell to do the same, which he did promptly enough.

More bags were made and filled, and as nearly as they could calculate, the amount of money contained in the box must be between twenty-five or thirty thousand pounds, that is, inclusive of bank notes, &c.

While the two friends were engaged in these operations, they were startled by a knock at the door of their apartment. They both started like guilty things, and did not make any answer; but upon Squabshot hearing the words "It's only me," in the well-known voice of Colonel Jack, he ventured to unlock the door, whereupon the colonel entered without any further ceremony.

"Well, colonel," said Squabshot, "how fares it with you?"

"Excellent well, i'faith; but how fares it with you?"

"We've opened the treasure of a box."

"Well, and with what result?"

"Behold!' exclaimed Squabshot, opening the door of a large case, in which he had placed the bags of gold.

"What are these?"

"Guineas—all full of guineas, my boy," was the answer.

"You have had a good haul, then?" said the colonel.

"Yes, take it altogether, notes and all, we had upwards of twenty-five thousand pounds to divide between us."

"Why, Squabshot, you are a made man for life," exclaimed the colonel.

"But, oh, I forgot, there is the plate—the vases; I do not know what their value is."

"Three or four thousand more, at the very least," said the colonel.

"Do you think so?"

"I'm pretty sure of it."

"And now, colonel, what are we indebted to you?" inquired Squabshot.

"Oh," answered our hero, with a smile, "I shall leave it to your own generosity."

"A thousand or two, eh?" said Squabshot. "Will that do?"

"Yes, I should think it would."

Two thousand guineas were counted out upon the table in front of Colonel Jack.

The latter refused to accept of more than one thousand, but upon Squabshot pressing the matter, he laughingly pocketted the same.

This done, Squabshot brought out pipes, tobacco, spirits, hot water and sugar, and in a few minutes the trio were seated round the festive board, enjoying themselves amazingly. Mr. Squabshot never let any event pass in the whole course of his life without having a few friends to pass a convivial evening. His might be termed a genial nature, for quaint and curious a specimen of humanity as he was, he was not selfish; on the contrary, he did not like to partake of any of the good things of this life without having others to share it with him, and now that he had come into so vast a sum, he had serious thoughts of inviting every friend he knew, and having a regular jollification.

Upon his proposing the same to Colonel Jack, after they had been seated for a few minutes—

"Oh, there's plenty of time for that, Squabby," said our hero, with a smile; "plenty of time for that. You will not stay here, of course?"

"Oh dear no—most certainly not."

"Well, then, wait till you've got into your new quarters, and then give a housewarming. Myself and one or two of my comrades on the road of life will come and fumigate your new quarters."

"Done!" said Squabshot. "I shall keep you to your word, and if you fail me, I will never speak to you again—never, I swear it."

"Pshaw, man, you need not be so vociferous or demonstrative. We are all of us glad enough to come where good things are provided. You need be under no apprehension but that you will have a host of friends rally round you, friends that you little dreamed of, or did not even know were in existence. Ah, the sun of prosperity warms into life and engenders a swarm of followers."

"I know that," said Squabshot, reflectively, "I know that, old boy, no one better. Why, I started in life, as the saying is, with a 'silver spoon in my mouth.' It precious soon dropped out of it though, and then when I was pinched by the frost of poverty, my word, but didn't my quandom friends book it. Ah, I've passed through almost every phase in life's drama, and I am going to have a happy denouement, let us hope."

"Let us hope so, indeed. May a bright and glorious future await you," said Colonel Jack, lifting his glass to his lips, and pledging his companion.

"Amen to that," said Ubsdell; "a glorious future."

"You know, colonel," said Squabshot, confidentially, "I have been up to every shift on the board. There was that confounded Emperor of Morocco—"

"Yes, I know, the fighting cock."

"Yes, precisely. Well, if it hadn't have been for him I should not have had to have been whitewashed. But I don't regret it after all, for I've seen life, and what is a man fit for unless he has?"

"Nothing at all," answered our hero, with a slight smile.

"You know I used to have my uncle to fly to," said Squabshot.

"Exactly; after you have visited the 'aunts of dissipation,' you generally have occasion to fly to your uncle's,' as the saying is."

"But they are gone—gone—far away, whither we know not."

Mr. Squabshot was getting sentimental, and sentiment falling from his lips generally elicited laughter from those present. It did so in the present instance.

"Did I ever tell you of my caper to raise the wind once?" said Squabshot, suddenly altering his tone, and brightening up.

"You have had so many," answered our hero.

"Yes, but I mean the dodge I resorted to with my uncle?"

"I don't remember to have heard it. Let's hear it."

"Well, you must know I was hard up, confoundedly hard up. I had backed Luke Larkins, and lost every blessed penny I had in the world, and worse than this, I was over head and ears in debt."

"Well, that's not so unusual a thing," remarked our hero, with a smile.

"No, but I was more than usually so at the time of which I am speaking. I was precious hard up, and that's the truth, but 'necessity is the mother of invention,' is an old adage, and as I had drawn all I could from my uncle's by fair means I thought of a grand expedient. You must know that both my respected relatives had always been harping upon one string, and that was matrimony, so I thought the best thing I could possibly do would be to get married."

"Get married!" exclaimed the colonel, in much surprise.

"Ah, to be sure. When a man is driven to his wit's end, and when he don't know how to support himself, he very often turns to matrimony as a last alternative, and so, you see, I was determined to make mine turn out a profitable investment, as the capitalists say. So I wrote to my uncle Theophilus to say that I had married a Spanish lady by the name of the Donna Juana Baptista. I should have told you that I had been on the continent, and in my letter to my uncle I informed him that I had met with a lady who was a paragon of female perfection—a perfect goddess of beauty and amiability. The old boy was delighted, and I received half of a fifty pound note by the next post and the following half the next morning. He congratulated me upon the step I had taken, wished me happiness, and hoped I should now be steady, as he chose to term it, as if I had ever been anything else. I shed sympathetic tears over his letter, and soon spent the fifty pounds. It didn't last long, no indeed it did not,' said Mr. Squabshot, pathetically. "So as I had found this dodge so successful I thought I would try my other uncle, but as I knew variety was charming, I wrote to him, saying that I had married a young Frenchwoman, by the name of Mademoiselle Victorine Leprais, a distinguished member of the Opera Comique. This letter was addressed to my uncle William; he resided at this time in a farm-house in Gloucestershire."

"What was the result of this application ?" said the colonel, with a smile.

"Oh, another fifty," answered Squabshot, carelessly.

"Which went like the rest, I suppose," said Colonel Jack.

"Yes, just the same way. A few weeks and all was gone, how it would be difficult for me to say just now, but it did go, that is quite certain, and so I was once more on my beam ends, as the saying is. What was to be done now ? I could not marry a second time, that was quite clear, but I was seldom at a loss, either then or at the present time. I hit upon another expedient. What do you think it was ?"

"I haven't the slightest idea."

"The birth of a son and heir."

"Ha, ha, ha," shouted out the colonel and Ubsdell, as they both fell back in their chairs in an immoderate fit of uncontrollable laughter.

"Brilliant idea!" they both exclaimed.

"Nothing could be better," said Squabshot. "I wrote to both my uncles by the same post, and informed them that my good lady had given birth to a fine boy, and there was some doubt as to what name we should choose for him, whether it should be Theophilus or William. The thought had presented itself to my mind that the child might bear both their interesting patronymics. This was rewarded also with a golden shower. My uncle Theophilus came out handsome on the occasion, he sent a cheque for a hundred pounds upon Boody's bank in Cheapside, and my uncle William fifty in bank notes. There was a glorious haul, produced by the fertile imagination of your humble servant. It is not very credible, you will say, but what was to be done, any ruse was pardonable in a starving man. I went on merrily for some time, but, alas, I was again attacked with my old complaint—a shortness of funds —this was bad enough, but what was worse I received a letter from my uncle Theophilus in which he stated that it was his intention

to pay me a visit for the express purpose of seeing my charming wife, and lovely little cherub. Here was a go, what was to be done now ? He was, however, not to start from Wales, where he resided, for a fortnight at the very least. Much might be done before the expiration of that time. In the course of a few days I wrote an agonising letter announcing my wife's death. You see what one lie leads too, we are obliged to tell a hundred others to cover it Never give your mind to lying, Ubsdell," said Squabshot, turning to his companion ; "never do it, my boy, or depend upon it, sooner or later, you will curse the hour you did so. Well, as I was saying, I wrote the letter dispatched it, and received one in reply sympathising with me for my loss, but it contained no money or cheque. In a few weeks after this my other uncle died, leaving all his wealth to his housekeeper. My uncle Theophilus eventually came to London, paid me a visit, and, I regret to say, became aware of the deception practised on him. He was in a monstrous passion, I believe, but he kept it all to himself, and, what was worse, he kept his money to himself. No, not one farthing did I have of it after this, so I paid dear enough in the end for my malpractices, as we all do," said Squabshot, contemplatively ; "as we all do, gentle and simple."

"That was indeed a serious end to the comedy or farce, whichever you please to term it," said Colonel Jack.

"Fact, I assure you, it's every word of it true as I am a sinner."

"I hear that they have been making most anxious inquiries after you," said Colonel Jack, turning towards Ubsdell.

"Indeed !" exclaimed that worthy with a start. "Where did you hear that."

"Oh, it matters little where I heard it, they have advertised you."

"What in ?"

"The 'Hue and Cry' of course. I told you so," said Squabshot, "you had better hook it, my friend, to the continent as soon as possible."

Mr. Ubsdell turned pale with fright.

"Advertised me," he exclaimed. Oh, dear. What shall I do ?'

"Refill your pipe. Mix another stoup of liquor and make your life as happy as you can under existing circumstances," said Colonel Jack.

"What did they advertise in ? ' inquired Ubsdell.

"In the 'Public Ledger.'"

Oh, is that all ?"

After some further discussion, Mr. Ubsdell made up his mind to take his departure from London altogether, and pay a visit to a maiden aunt of his who resided some hundred of miles or so from the metropolis.

Colonel Jack took his departure, promising to call in a day or so, and Mr. Squabshot and his friends were once more left to their own meditations.

"So," exclaimed the former, "that matter is settled."

"What ?'

"The settlement with the colonel."

"It's a goodly sum for the use of a horse and cart," answered Ubsdell.

"Get out with you. You don't mean to grumble, do you ?"

"Ah, no, no."

"We are completely in his power, and of course he has to tip a handsome sum to his companions to ensure their silence."

"Ah, I forgot."

"Yes, you are apt to forget, my friend, like a good many more people, when they have got their own turn served. Nothing is so easy as to forget. Hammer no more upon this head, the matter is settled, and now where do you rest to-night ?"

"Why at my lodgings of course," answered Udsdell.

Since the removal of the box from White-friars, Mr. Ubsdell had rented a couple of rooms within a few doors of his companion Squabshot.

"Ah, I thought you would not like to leave those," said the latter. nodding with his head towards the bags which were lying *perdu* in the press, or cupboard, where Squab-shot had placed them."

"I can take one or two of them with me," said Ubsdell.

"As you please—they are rather heavy," remarked Squabshot, with a laugh. "Better leave them where they are."

His companion hesitated.

"Oh, well," exclaimed Squabshot, "try if you can carry them conveniently."

Ubsdell lifted one up. It was indeed very heavy, but still he managed to carry it with ease.

"Will you have another?" inquired Squab-shot.

"Yes, I can carry them both."

"Put them under your cloak, and then no one will ask any questions."

Luckily Ubsdell had a cloak, and placing the two bags of gold under this, he marched off in triumph, wishing his friend a hasty good night.

Mr. Squabshot carefully locked up his bags of gold, closed the lid of the box, and then ruminated for half an hour or so, laying out his future plans of action, much to his own satisfaction, and reflected upon the future glorious career he was to run, and eventually wound up by retiring to rest, and dreaming of sweet ideal worlds.

———

CHAPTER CVIII.

THE MIDNIGHT SURPRISE.

IF our friend Squabshot had glanced at the small window which was in the door of the bed-room adjoining the parlour which had been the scene of his operations—we say if he had glanced at this said window during that time which saw him occupied in count-ing out the gold belonging to the deceased Gabriel Beechcroft, he would in all proba-bility have been able to distinguish the swarthy features of the servant maid belong-ing to his respectable establishment in Gos-well Street ; but he was too intent upon the glittering pieces which lay before him, to even give a cursory glance to the window in question, against which Matilda, or 'Tilda, as she was more familiarly termed, was flat-tening her nose, as her large goggle eyes were opened to their very utmost degree of tension.

As handful after handful of the precious coins were deposited in the bags, 'Tilda's sur-prise increased. It was with considerable difficulty that she was enabled to put suffi-cient restraint upon herself to forbear from crying out, and it was only by an effort that she remained so passive as she had done during that period which saw her a silent but not unobservant spectatress of the pro-ceedings of the two friends in the front parlour.

'Tilda was certainly not the fairest of Eve's daughters, neither was she the most cleanly of her sex, nevertheless she had a lover or a young man, as she termed it, a follower, in fact, that is, assuming Mrs. Twelvetrees allowed followers, which, un-fortunately for 'Tilda, she did not, for Mrs. Twelvetrees was a hard practical woman, and considered that *gals* had no right to be laying themselves out to attract the male sex.

By a singular coincidence, Tilda had a cousin come up from the country on that very night, and so after work was over she begged of her mistress to spare her for a couple of hours to go to her aunt's, in White Lion Street, Islington.

Mrs. Twelvetrees was impenetrable at first, but after half an hour's coaxing or so, she at length was induced to give a reluctant consent for the maid's absence for the space of two mortal hours, but no longer.

'Tilda was dressed in a few minutes, and was at the end of that time trudging along Goswell Street towards the Angel at Isling-ton. She turned down one of the bye streets on the left side of Goswell Street, which led

in the direction of that spot where Hicks'
Hall stood, and which is now known as the
Clerkenwell Sessions House.

The street was by no means the most respectable one in the metropolis; indeed it
had but an unenviable reputation at the best
of times, which had rather increased than
otherwise at the time of which we write.

However, 'Tilda trotted along gaily enough,
and halted not till she came to a dingy, dilapidated-looking house at the farther end of
it. Here she paused, and knocked at the
door with her knuckles, for there was neither
bell or knocker, such appendages being
considered superfluities.

The inmates of the establishment, if there
were any, did not take any notice of this
summons. 'Tilda knocked again more vociferously, and finding that useless, she rapped

at the dingy window which lent a feeble
light into the kitchen below. In a few minutes after this, an old woman made her
appearance, half opening the door and peering out therefrom. At first she did not
appear to recognise the new comer, but after
a minute or so she exclaimed in a shrill
voice —

"What, 'Tilda, lass!—be it you?"

"Ah, sure," said the girl. "Is Ralph at
home?"

"No, child, he seldom is; home's the last
place you are likely to find him at."

"Ah, I s'pose so," said 'Tilda. "Do you
know when he will return?"

"No; but you'd better walk in."

"Thank you—but my time is short.'

"Well, if you really are anxious to see
Ralph, your best chance to meet with him

will be at the Pickled Egg. You know where that is ? '

" Oh, yes ; in Cow Cross."

" Yes, child."

" Is he there ?"

" He went there an hour or two ago ; but I can't say with any certainty that he's there now."

" Thank you," said 'Tilda, " I'll go there and see. Thank you—good night—thank you."

And off trotted 'Tilda to the public-house in question, which the reader will recollect as the same establishment that our hero resorted to after his escape from Newgate. She had a frightful locality to pass through before she arrived at the house in question. Words and language was uttered by those who happened to be in the street, or at the windows of the houses, which would call up the blush of shame to any female but the most callous and hardened of her sex, and more than one ruffian accosted 'Tilda with coarse epithets ; but she was either used to such scenes, or else did not care about it. At any rate she took her way along with the most perfect self-confidence, and in a short time reached the Pickled Egg.

Going straight up to the bar, she inquired for Ralph Bunkham.

The landlord went into the tap room, and brought out an ill-looking ruffian, who appeared to at once recognise the girl, for his ill-favoured features were lighted up with a grim smile.

" What, 'Tilly, my girl," he exclaimed ; " coom in lass."

" No, Ralph, not now—I have no time."

" What brings you here then ?" inquired Ralph.

" I'll tell you—but not here."

" Oh, that's it, eh ?" said the man. " Well, lass, I'll coom with ye—wait a bit."

And he ducked into the tap-room, said a few words to his companions, and returned to 'Tilda.

The two then left the house, and sauntered together down the dark and miserably-lighted street.

" Ralph," said Tilda, " where have you been ?"

" Where ?" exclaimed the man, stopping short ; " where do you think ?"

" Oh, I don't know, Ralph ; but I have seen very little of you lately."

" Why, Tilly, you ain't jealous, wench ?" said the man. " That is not the business that brought you here ?"

" No," answered 'Tilda, " no, Ralph ; " but hush—somebody may overhear us."

" And what if they do ?"

" Ralph, I have seen such a sight. I have seen hundreds of golden guineas within my very reach."

" Why didn't you bring away a few of them then ?'

" Hush—don't talk so loud. Listen. Our parlour lodger has got in his room heaps of gold—bags full of gold."

" The deuce he has ?"

" Yes ; now don't look so wildly—he has If we could only get a little of it, we might be married, and be happy together for the resf of our lives."

The girl then favoured her lover with the whole of the particulars with which the reader is already acquainted.

The cupidity of Ralph Bunkham was aroused on the instant.

To possess himself of some of these was his first thought. Then came the question of how and when.

It was ultimately agreed by 'Tilda that before she went to bed she would unfasten the door of the house in Goswell Street ; and at the same time that she made this promise, she gave her companion the latch-key of the house.

Ralph Bunkham snatched at it with eagerness, and thrust it hastily in his pocket.

This done, after a little conversation, the lovers, if they could be called so with anything like truth, parted, and 'Tilda returned to the house of Mrs. Twelvetrees.

Upon the girl's return, her first thought was to see that her agreement with Ralph was carried out. It was the custom of Mrs. Twelvetrees to see that her immaculate servant retired to rest before she courted the drowsy god herself, and on the night in question she did not omit so excellent and discreet a practice.

'Tilda was trotted off to bed, but not to sleep.

She half undressed herself, blew out her light, and then waited for half an hour or more after her mistress had retired to rest. When she thought the good lady had fallen off to sleep, she crept softly down stairs, and agreeable to her promise to Ralph Bunkham, she unfastened the bolts of the door one by one, making as little noise as possible, and trembling in every limb as she did so. This done, she crept softly up stairs and tumbled into bed.

It has often been the remark of astute writers and close thinkers, how time lags and halts with some of us, and goes at a railway speed with others.

To the lover waiting for his mistress, every minute seems a day ; to the young girl in a crowded ball room and pleasant parterres, time flies with lightning speed ; and, oh, to the miserable wretch who lies in the condemned cell, waiting the ominous morn to make that fearful leap into that undiscovered and unknown world, how dear time is with him.

It went slowly enough with 'Tilda, as she lay listening for the admit of her lover—it went slowly enough with her, as the beatings of her heart thumped out the hurried seconds. She thought that Ralph never would come. Perhaps he had relented—had been detained by his companions, or persuaded not to make the attempt. What should she do then? Should she wait another hour or so, and then creep down and refasten the door? Her mind wandered off into a rambling and discursive series of reflections, until she became worn out, and was eventually overtaken by sleep.

Her slumber was sound, so sound, indeed, that she did not hear the lock of the outer door gently turned, and then noiselessly opened.

Ralph Bunkham was in the passage of Mrs. Twelvetrees house; he drew his breath thickly—and he was alone.

The hour was nearly two o'clock, and all the inmates of the establishment were fast asleep.

Ralph, when he first set foot in the passage, paused and listened attentively for a minute or so, and then softly closed the door. He was necessitated to do this, as otherwise the watchman in the street would suspect that all was not right. This done, Ralph paused again, after which he crept along the passage towards the door of the parlour. He turned the handle of this, and found it fastened.

Inwardly cursing 'Tilda for misleading him, he tried again.

The girl had told him that the parlour door would be unfastened, and she was justified in saying so, as Mr. Squabshot had never been in the habit of locking it; but on this particular night it appeared that he had done so, much to the chagrin of the burglar.

Ralph Bunkham was now fairly puzzled; but he, although by no means an accomplished housebreaker, was determined not to be baulked at first starting off. In his coat pocket he had several skeleton keys and a jemmy; but before trying the latter, he began to see if any of the keys would answer the purpose. One by one they were tried, and eventually he succeeded in turning the lock; but the door still resisted his efforts. It must be bolted on the inside. He then tried to open it with his jemmy, but could not succeed in doing so.

He remembered that 'Tilda had told him that Mr. Squabshot slept in the back parlour, and consequently he was unwilling to enter there, unless driven to do so by an absolute and imperative necessity.

Again and again he tried, with as little success as before.

He could not imagine what detained 'Tilda, for the girl had promised to come down the moment she heard him enter. He went to the bottom of the stairs and listened; perhaps she knew how the door was fastened; in any case it would be better to see her.

And how was this to be managed? He did not know the exact situation of 'Tilda's bed-room, but supposed it must be either on the second floor or else in one of the garrets above.

He crept softly up stairs. He passed the first floor without deigning to look in either of these rooms, and then made his way up to the second floor.

All this had been done without his disturbing anyone in the house.

When he arrived at the second floor, he was at a loss how to act.

He knew that the girl's room was situated on this storey, but which it was he knew not. He, however, gave a short whistle, and then ventured to call 'Tilda softly two or three times; but the girl took no notice of these demonstrations on the part of her lover.

Ralph Bunkham was puzzled.

There were three doors leading from the passage in which he stood, into three separate apartments.

Through the crevices of one of these, Bunkham perceived a light. This then, was 'Tilda's room. No doubt she had left a light burning with the intention of coming down to his assistance the moment she heard him enter the premises.

Fully impressed with this idea, Ralph entered the bed-room. On a small table therein was a feeble light, which came from one of those known as floating wicks.

The housebreaker took his way up to the bedside, calling upon his 'Tilda.

As he did so, he was suddenly startled by a piercing scream, and before the first surprise had subsided, he found himself grasped by the back of the neck and throat. The figure on the bed rose up and held the housebreaker with a firmness that he could hardly have supposed possible for any woman to have possessed.

He struggled to free himself, and felt in the pocket of his coat.

Then a series of screams were sent forth by the occupant of the bed which awoke the silent echoes of the night, and were appalling in their intensity.

Ralph Bunkham actually trembled with the mighty fear which took sudden possession of him.

What the end of all this would have been it is impossible to tell, that is, had the two been left to themselves; the probability is that Mrs. Twelvetrees, for it was no other than that lady, who held the burglar in his grasp, the probability is that she would have fallen a victim to her temerity, as soon as the man had recovered from his sudden surprise; but while the two were struggling, 'Tilda herself made her way into her mistress's bed-room.

When she caught sight of Ralph and Mrs. Twelvetrees, she sent forth a piercing scream, and run about the room like a mad girl, for she was under the impression that Ralph had been endeavouring to murder her mistress.

Now, although 'Tilda longed to obtain possession of some of the wealth below, she had a religious horror of bloodshed or violence, and she rushed, therefore, upon the impulse of the moment, to her mistresses assistance.

Clutching hold of Ralph Baukham, she dragged him away from Mrs. Twelvetrees' grasp, and besought him in the most moving accents to desist from any further violence.

It was not at all probable that with all this violence and noise that Mr. Squabshot would remain quiet in his own apartment. The noise of the screams found their way into his sleeping room, and he was awakened thereby to the full consciousness that something was going on in the house—some deed of violence which required his immediate attention.

Springing out of his bed, and hastily slipping on his clothes, Mr. Squabshot armed himself with a large horse pistol, and flew up-stairs to the rescue.

The noise soon told him in which apartment the melee was taking place, and without further ceremony the parlour lodger rushed into the bed-room of his landlady.

The moment Mr. Squabshot caught sight of the ill-favoured visage of Ralph Bunkham, he levelled his pistol, and commanded him to yield, upon the pain of instant death. Ralph recoiled from the point of the weapon, and shielded himself behind 'Tilda, who wrung her hands, and appealing to Squabshot, said—

"Oh, don't—pray don't, sir—in mercy's sake, don't fire. He meant no harm. Oh, pray don't."

"Meant no harm! What is the meaning of all this, wench? Speak."

"Oh, if you please, sir, I will speak. It ain't his fault—he came to see me, indeed he did."

"You abandoned hussy!" exclaimed Mrs. Twelvetrees, who, falcon-like, was ready to swoop down upon her maid upon the slightest pretext. "Shameles baggage—to dare to talk thus before a gentleman and a honest woman! Help!—murder!—watch!"

"My dear madam," said Squabshot, in his blandest accents, "I pray of you not to agitate yourself. A shameful breach of the peace has been committed. Who and what is this person—this escaped lunatic—felon, housebreaker, or murderer—who is he?"

"He's my young man," said 'Tilda, with an effrontery and hardihood which perfectly petrified Mrs. Twelvetrees.

"Your young man!" exclaimed the latter, in a paroxysm of ungovernable rage; "your young man, you abominable slut! Oh, is it possible that I have been harbouring a snake—a viper—a scorpion, in my very house. Mr. Squabshot, will you see that both these persons, the girl and her *paramount*, are safely lodged in custody. For my sake, for the sake of society at large, it is not proper that two such atrocious monsters should be allowed to *mislest* honest and innocent persons."

Mr. Ralph Bunkham, during this conversation, had been debating with himself what had best be done in the painful and awkward position in which he was placed. A brilliant idea suddenly occurred to him. The door of the room was partially open and so, on a sudden he made a bolt at this to make his escape.

Mr. Squabshot sprang forward upon the instant, and sought to detain him; but Ralph was strong and active, and more than this, his fears lent him an additional strength. He therefore succeeded in shaking off Squabshot, and proceeded down stairs.

"Don't let him escape!" exclaimed Mrs. Twelvetrees; "pray don't let him escape. Thieves! watch! murder! fire!"

Then turning to 'Tilda, she shook her fist at her, and said—

"Oh, you abominable huzzy—you worthless baggage. Is it for this that I have been as good as a mother to you?"

Mr. Squabshot flew to the head of the stairs.

"Stop!' he exclaimed, as Ralph Bunkham descended; "stop, or I will surely blow your brains out. Do you hear?"

Mr. Bunkham did hear, but he did not heed; he thought that it was a mere empty threat, and so he took his way down the creaking stairs without the least intention of stopping.

A loud report was heard, awaking an old gentleman in the back-room first floor, and alarming more than one neighbour.

Squabshot had fired his horse pistol, but the ball passed within a foot or so of the flying burglar, and then lodged harmlessly in the wall of the staircase.

Bunkham hurried on, and gained the passage, when, upon his making for the door, he found himself in the firm grasp of a powerful man.

The burglar could not see his opponent, for they were both in the dark, with the exception of a dim light which found its way in from the fanlight over the street door.

Ralph struggled desperately; for the moment he believed himself in the grasp of an officer. In a minute or so afterwards. Mr. Squabshot himself came down, wax taper in hand. Judge of his surprise, when he discovered the housebreaker to be in the hands of Colonel Jack.

It was in vain that he endeavoured to make his escape, the highwayman held him too firmly in his grasp.

When Squabshot made his appearance on the scene, our hero dragged Bunkham into the front parlour, into which apartment he was followed by Squabshot.

"This is where you wanted to come to, I suppose," said the colonel to the housebreaker, satirically, "eh ?"

"Let me go—it wasn't my fault," stammered out Bunkham ; "I swear to you it wasn't my fault."

"Oh, of course not," said the colonel ; "but it will be your fault if you come here again. Now look here, Ralph—let us understand each other."

"Very well, colonel."

"This gentleman is a friend of mine, and you must not come upon this lay again. Do you comprehend ?"

"In course I do."

"Then there's nothing more to be said. One word is as good as a hundred. You may go as soon as you please."

"Go !" exclaimed Squabshot.

"Of course ; you don't want him here, do you ?"

"No."

"Then go at once. Keep your word and all will be right," said Colonel Jack.

The man took his departure immediately, and Squabshot turned an inquiring glance at our hero.

"That is the best termination to this night's business," said the colonel. "He will not trouble us again."

"But Mrs. Twelvetrees ?" said Squabshot.

"What of her ?"

"She will want to know what has been done with the culprit."

"Let her imagine that he has escaped. So he would have done had it not have been for me."

"How came you to be here ? Did you know of this ?"

"Yes—private information. I have no time to stay now, but will see you in the morning—or at any rate, some time to-morrow," said Colonel Jack, who then took a hasty departure.

When he had gone, Mr. Squabshot re-assured his landlady that all was right, but to be quite certain, he agreed to sit up for the remainder of the night.

Mrs. Twelvetrees said she could not sleep herself, and moreover declared that she dared not be alone ; consequently she dressed herself, and came down into the front parlour. Mr. Squabshot lighted his pipe, and for the amusement of his landlady, read one of the tales out of the budget left by the deceased Gabriel Beechcroft, which for the reader's behoof, we shall give in three parts.

CHAPTER CIX.

THE VICTIM ; OR, INNOCENCE, VANITY, AND DEATH.

PART I.—INNOCENCE.

ABOUT two miles from that fashionable place, Torquay, on the southern coast of Devonshire, may be seen the village of Babbicomb. It can hardly be distinguished as a village, for the houses it contains are but about seven or eight, which are occupied, with the exception of an inn, by families of gentlemen.

This hamlet of villas, or rather *cottage ornees*, are most romantically situated, being so nestled in a wood, and hidden by the inequalities of the ground, that they are scarcely visable from one another. They are all covered with thatch, and the walls so overgrown with ivy and creeping plants, that only the tops appear even from the heights that shut in this lovely valley.

The spot chosen for these abodes are the most romantic and picturesque it is possible to imagine.

Some stand immediately on the beach, shadowed by thick plantations of forest trees that grow most luxuriously down to the water-edge; others on little platforms that seem designed by nature for their erection. One is cinctured by rocks of the most fantastic forms, that overhang as if about to crush it; whilst, higher up, another home of peace, encircled by a grove of venerable sycamores—the patriarchs of the place—looks down from an extensive paddock over a deep precipice of wood, and commands the whole of the Bay of Babbicomb. Sheltered from all but the easterly winds, the sea is generally calm as a lake; even when they rage with the greatest fury.

In the cottage last mentioned there lived, at the period when this tale begins, Lady Morton, and her daughter. Lady Morton was the sister of an earl, and had been left a widow when Emily was yet a child. Her husband, a younger brother of a noble family, had enjoyed a lucrative sinecure under the government, and, after dissipating her fortune, had left her almost without the means of subsistence. Her connexions on both sides were rich ; but though prodigal, some of their advice, others of their pity, and all of invectives at the imprudence of her husband and her own extravagance, none of them came forward with any substantial assistance.

Her acquaintance—those dear friends who had frequented her routs, and courted her in the pride of her summer days—fell off one by one, and left her in the solitude of a lodging, exchanged for one of the villas looking into the park, to reflect bitterly on the selfishness, the hollowness, the heartlessness, the insincerity, of the world of which she had made a part, and whose example she had all her life, without any compunction, been imitating. It may be supposed, that this her new residence was not the most agreeable to herself, while it was a reproach to her relatives. Their houses, it is true, were open to her ; she was invited by sufferance to their family dinners and splendid balls, and had occasionally the use of their carriages ; but the sense of dependance grew daily more burdensome, from the mode in which these unwilling favours were dispensed ; and when familiarity with her distress had worn away commiseration, she at length found herself gradually sinking into that nondescript and most unfortunate of beings in the scale of society—a humble companion. It was at this time that one of her brothers, a member for a borough, and a staunch supporter of the ministry, bethought him of the Civil List. His application was successful, and Lady Morton obtained the privilege of drawing annually four hundred pounds for herself and Emily. It was part of the family compact that the pensioners should immediately retire (the greater the distance the better) from the metropolis ; and, after many a consultation, Devonshire was chosen for their exile.

It will now be seen by what concurrence of circumstances, it happened that these two principal actors in this drama found themselves at Babbicomb.

Lady Morton, on her arrival at Torquay, had taken an apartment on one of those terraces that present a continual panorama to the eye. But she met at that place none of those families who had been in her visiting list—none of those names familiar to her ear. She discovered, or fancied she should discover, none among its settlers whose society it would not be a lowering of her grade to cultivate. Living at such a distance from the metropolis, they had not, by an occasional attrition with the London world, rubbed off any of the rust of provincialism. Her language and manners would, she thought, be misunderstood and misinterpreted. They would be strangers to all the *demi-mots* that pass current in a *certain* circle—those phrases and allusions which are a mystery to all out of a particular sect or sphere. She, therefore, avoided their intercourse : and, wrapping herself in her *morgue* and *hauteur*, and to avoid the possibility of contagion, settled himself at Babbicomb.

Lady Morton, at an age when most girls are still under the care of a governess, was prematurely formed in the *serrechaude* of fashion ; naturally delicate, had been still more enfeebled by the dissipations of her after-life. Out of London she might, therefore, be considered an exotic ; and did not look as though she had sufficient vigour of constitution to become acclimated under any other sky. She had, indeed, occasionally visited the seats of some of her wealthy relatives ; but they had carried with them the town into the country, and made it only a continuation of the same carnival. She loved flowers, it is true ; but they must be of the rarest and most expensive novelties ; such as the botanical treasures of Chelsea and the Regent's Park supplied. Gardens she loved ; but the parterres must be laid out in the trimmest French order, the beds disposed with the nicest care, and the colours varied so as to make one mosaic. She loved perfumes ; but they must be of the most exquisite and costly kinds. She loved music, and sang and played with great feeling and the nicest ear ; but it must be the music of Rossini. In short, she had acquired a fastidiousness of taste that qualified her for none of the occupations, the amusements, and pleasures, of common life. As to the country—or nature in the abstract, or its details—it had, as may be supposed, no charms for Lady Morton. That she should find the grove, therefore, a desert, is not wonderful ; nor that she continually sighed for those scenes which distance and hopelessness rendered still dearer, and for that circle of which she had once been the admiration and the ornament.

Yet had she one object to relieve her solitude, to employ her thoughts, and almost to make her forget the world from which she had been torn ; it was her daughter.

I shall pass over her years of childhood, when I remember her

"A little elf,
Dancing, singing, to itself,"

and introduce you to Emily as she was at sixteen. We are not going to describe a Venus, as she rose from the salt ooze of the sea. No ; the beauty of Emily was of the soul. It was that which lit her blue eye, with its long silken lashes. It was that which animated her usually pale cheek, rather long than of a perfect oval. That it was which made the smile playing about her mouth almost angelic ; which rendered her every movement and gesture a grace. Emily, if you will have her portrait, was a *blonde*—so blonde, that the fairest beside her seemed almost a brunette ; yet had she none of the *fadeness* so common to such a complexion. It reflected like a mirror her emotions, however profound ; her ideas, however secret.

It was to be feared that at a more advanced age she would inherit from her mother that temperament, that excess of imagination, which had embittered her life—that sensibility which, as it is the greatest of blessings when well regulated, might become the most dangerous of gifts amid the shoals and shallows of the world. But, at the time of which I was speaking, she was the child of nature ; and she adored it almost with the affection of a mother. Babbicomb was, to her the happy valley of Rasselas ; but, unlike him, it comprehended all her hopes and dreams ; she wished for no world beyond its limits. The flowers which she had planted, the birds she had reared—everything about her was associated with some recollection of her childhood. The shrubberies which her mother had formed had grown up with her, and become a part and a portion of herself—the life of her life.

Lady Morton, well remarking how artificial had been her own education, and the unkindness and severity with which the innocent sallies of her young spirits had been repressed, adopted a diametrically opposite system with Emily. It may be said that she had never shed a tear ; she was indeed, the personification of joy, and made all happy that she looked upon. How beautiful was that wild flower ! How lovely that child of sixteen, running wild among the walks and woods of that enchanted land, bounding like a fawn with elastic step, her loose locks playing in the winds !

Gifted with talents that rendered their cultivation a pleasure instead of labour, Emily was thus early mistress of Italian and French, and soon rivalled her mother in her knowledge of music. But she had one advantage which few women possess—to these accomplishments were superadded other and more solid acquirements. For these solid acquirements she was indebted to Herbert Vivyan. Herbert was the only son of a clergyman in the neighbourhood.

He was four years older than Emily, and had distinguished himself at Cambridge by being in the first tripos, and second wrangler of his year. Alas, poor Herbert ! It is a trite quotation—

" The course of true love never did run smooth."

Happy were they in their hours of study. To sit by her, her arm folded round his, in the sweet abandonment of innocent familiarity, her long silken locks brushing his cheek : to see her throw back those ringlets, with a hand whose fingers, to the very ends, were instinct with sensibility, and possessed

that easy and graceful curve we so much admire in the Madonnas of Raphael ! Those shoulders—*toujours a l'air*, winter and summer, covered as with an eternal snow—pressing against his ! And then her eyes, when they met his—when they were sparkling with delight at some trait of heroism or virtue—or flashed with inspiration, caught from some sublime passage of our favourite bards—or filled with tears, as she identified herself with the fictitious sorrows of some pathetic tale. Yet did they never speak of love. Was it not enough that they felt it—the certainty of that mutual love ? To have questioned it would have destroyed the charm—would have been an insult to long years of affection—would have implied a chilling doubt. Was it not enough to listen to her words of endearment ?—any words from her were music.

After these hours of study came, too, other hours. They knew every nook and angle of that romantic land. Sometimes they hunted for madreporas ; at others, explored the mountain-passes, and lost themselves among the tangled thickets that cover their precipitous sides, and overhung their bluff and jagged shores ; or, lower down, between the openings, caught glimpses of the wide extent of the channel ; or followed the curving coast, till the point of Portland melted into the horison. Scenes worthier of inspiring love did never pen nor pencil paint.

Never have there been seen rocks so varied in colour, so admirable in their groups, so fantastic in their forms ; here denuded of vegetation, and there luxuriantly tufted with ivy, or raising from among the brushwood their bare scalps ; whilst the glades and dells were enamelled with flowers and plants, native to that favoured clime, and which are cultivated as exotics in other parts of England. At times he would row her in his little skiff across the bay ; or, suspending his oars, they would float motionless on its marble surface, and watch the sun sink behind the rocky barrier, and the clouds of the western sky reflect themselves in gold on its glassy mirror, till they faded away in the twilight, and the stars warned them unwillingly to return. Sometimes she would take her guitar. He used to mention her singing a song of some old composer, with words not unworthy of Herrick, beginning—

" O sing, sweet bird ! O sing !"

" And," added Herbert, " that single air —her look—the tones of her voice—that sweet, pure simple voice—I seem to hear them still !"

It was during one of their water-excursions they were nearly lost. Babbicomb, and the bays that lie between it and Torquay, are the most treacherous of all that line the coast of Devonshire.

They are environed by cliffs that at once plunge into them precipitously; and the gusts of wind that rush through the gorges of the mountains, as through a tunnel, almost without giving warning, suddenly blacken the surface, and at once spend their fury on those who, incautious and heedless of danger, are, perhaps with all their sails set, scarcely moving through the water.

One day, allured by the lightness of the breeze (for it was midsummer), they had prolonged their voyage further than usual; and, having rounded the Pope's Nose, observed in front two islands which Emily had often desired to visit. They are of small extent. They found one the resort of gulls and other aquatic birds, that make their nest in the inaccessible points of the crags; and as they whirled, their white wings flashing in the sun above the heads of the intruders, made a murmur that, though hoarse and discordant when near, seemed at a distance like that of a musical instrument.

Herbert and Emily did not land here; but having rowed round it, he made for the sister island.

It is of greater extent, and inhabited by two goats, that, with the hardihood of their race, live here winter and summer unsheltered and exposed to the elements. They have for years found a scanty subsistence by browsing on the lichen and marine plants growing luxuriantly among the interstices of the rocks, some of whose fissures retain, as in natural basins, water collected by the rains.

Herbert, as they drew nigh, had been recounting to Emily a circumstance relative to these animals that had much interested her.

The pair had once had young; but, as the place afforded only food for the parents, they, with an instinctive love of self-preservation, which overmasters their other instinct—that affection which has given its name to the stork—had precipitated their offspring into the sea.

It was on this islet on which, with some difficulty, they disembarked. Emily's intention was to carry home to her mother some specimens of the parasite creepers, then in full bloom, many of whose species were unknown to her.

"Look, Herbert," said Emily, "what a beautiful thing."

And she stooped down to pluck up some saxifrage by the root.

But at that moment one of the squalls already mentioned struck the skiff, laid it on its beam ends, and, dashing it violently against the rocks, stove in one of its planks. It filled with water, and in a few moments sunk.

What was now to be done?

On one side stretched the boundless expanse of the Channel, and on the other, the iron-bound and uninhabited coast. All aid seemed hopeless, no fishing-boat was in view, for the mackerel season was over. The idea of passing the night there—perhaps of perishing with hunger—was horrible!

The day was on its decline; they sat with their hands locked in each other's, and gazed wildly on the western sky, whose last orange tint had begun to mingle with the shades of evening.

Emily's thoughts now recurred to home; she thought not of herself, but of her mother —her anxiety at her absence—her despair.

"Emily," at length said Herbert, after a long silence, "have you the courage to trust yourself with me?"

"What do you mean, Herbert?" replied Emily. "Trust myself with you?"

"Do you see," said Herbert, pointing with his hand to a speck among the cliffs, "that little creek? Will you venture thither with me?"

"What fears can I have, Herbert, with you? Should we be drowned, at least we shall perish together," said Emily, with a voice that trembled.

"Yes," said Herbert, with a melancholy smile, "I will not survive you, Emily. But let us entertain better hopes. You will have need of all your presence of mind, dearest friend."

"Do you doubt my courage?" said Emily, upbraidingly. "Do you think me still a child?"

"No, love," whispered Herbert, "you are all gentleness and firmness. But attend to my instructions. You must remain passive —motionless. I must tie your hands."

"Let me," said Emily, affectionately, "throw them round your neck once before I die!"

He clasped her in his arms and pressed her to his heart. Oh, what a moment was that. He bound her hands behind her back.

"And now, Emily," said Herbert, "one thing more."

He loosened her hair, that almost reached her waist, and rolled it into a knot.

This done, they threw themselves on their knees, and prayed fervently to the Almighty for protection. He then plunged her into the deep.

Herbert was a powerful swimmer, and though he could easily have reached the shore alone, as he only had one hand at liberty—the other having to bear the weight of Emily—his strength began by degrees to give way. Still he wrestled with the element and kept her head above the water.

Fortunately the tide was setting in; and, after they had sunk more than once, a wave threw them on the dry land.

He bore her fainting and almost lifeless to her mother's arms.

Nothing is more delightful than to look back on past dangers: and this drew still closer the bonds of their love.

It may be asked whether Lady Morton was blind to this ever increasing attachment. A martyr to a painful complaint, her days were passed on a sofa in her boudoir, where the light was only admitted through a half-closed Venetian.

Long habit had accustomed her to see Herbert Emily's constant companion. She was grateful to him for the progress her daughter made in her education; and, perhaps, might tacitly have whispered to herself the possibility of one day consenting to their union.

Thus had passed years that seemed like

No. 70.

days; and Emily knew not that all this happiness was but for a day—she knew not there must be an end to all these her pure delights, these humble joys—that the world, with all its pomps, and vanities, and danger, must shortly await her. Yet an unforeseen event occurred that at once destroyed all Herbert's hopes, and changed the current of Emily's life.

The family of Lady Morton, though they had not altogether forgotten her. Annual letters communicated the births, deaths, and marriages, of her relations, and contained some trifling souvenirs of their regard. Her sister, Lady Gretnor, was one of the lady patronesses of Almack's and had succeeded, by a manœuvring the envy of the ablest tacticians of them all, in obtaining the most unexceptionable partners for her numerous daughters, whom, with an admirable tact, she had brought out, to use a vulgar phrase, hot and hot, one after the other. Though they were neither remarkably handsome nor particularly talented, she had succeeded in giving them those tinsel accomplishments, and a certain air of fashion, that passed for grace, and classed them successively among the belles of the season.— *C'est le premier pas qui coute.* It is the *debut*, the first spring, that usually decides the prospects, the fate of a girl. Such, at least, was the case with Lady Gretnor's. She was a skilful politician and diplomatist; and knew that dinner-parties, as a sequel to balls, waltzes to the piano, horticultural breakfasts, walks in Kensington Gardens, not to mention boxes at the Opera, tend to bring about that desired event, a declaration. Her daughters had the advantage of being strikingly like each other; and though it was remarked that Ellen was not so pretty as Margaret, nor Anne as Eliza, yet the very resemblance to their wedded sisters ensured them admirers, who were converted into husbands. In short, Lady Gretnor's occupation was gone—she was become a useless wall-flower—had no longer any one to chaperon. The happy selection, the skill, the vigilance required, not only in looking, but gaffing—the conduct of the affair to its *denouement*—had been an excitement; it reminded her of her young days, and she almost lived them over again in her daughters. It was at this time that she remembered she had a niece called Emily Morton. She had never seen her from a child, and, but for some vague and uncircumstantial notice of her in her sister's annuals, would hardly have known whether she were alive or dead. Brought up, as Emily had been, in the wilds of Devonshire, she pictured to herself a *gauche* hoyden, a mere country girl—perhaps a spoiled child. Two things she hoped to find she was not—vulgarly *embonpoint*, or with a fixed colour in her face. The rest of defects, whatever, they might be, she promised herself she could either amend or conceal.

The eyes of Emily were swimming with tears when she first informed Herbert of her being about to leave for London.

"Leave!" he exclaimed, passionately; "you leave—and for—" he would have said "ever," but his emotion stifled the word. Her tears continued to flow on. "You will soon forget me, Emily," said Herbert, bitterly.

"You are cruel to-day. What have I done to deserve this from you, Herbert?" said Emily, still weeping.

"Pardon me, Emily," said Herbert, emphatically; "I cannot command myself—I cannot repress the bitterness of my soul. A thousand thoughts torment me—the thoughts of what I have been—of what I shall be when you are gone—when I no longer see you—hear your step—your voice, that is my music—when, oh, torments! I find that you have forsaken the friend of your youth—that you—"

"Heavens!" said Emily, with one of her smiles, half tears, that no expression can paint, "do you think so ill of me?"

"Poor child!" said Herbert, with a melancholy tone of voice—"not of you—no, but of those with whom you soon will be. I pity you, for you have much to suffer. Oh, if you knew what is passing in my mind—I hardly dare tell you. That world into which you are about to enter, Emily—their women heartless and selfish—their men, those *roues* of fashion, who lie in wait to betray the reputation of the most virtuous —who would not shrink from the idea of ruining even you, innocent as you are—no, not you, for you are of high family, and protected."

"Is it true what you tell me?" she replied, earnestly. "Alas, what am I to do?"

"Nothing," answered Herbert. "You will become like the rest, and forget the obscure being who cannot follow you into this brilliant world that is not made for him."

"Can you believe that I shall be so wicked and ungrateful?" said Emily. "You are *mechant* to-day, Herbert. What would you have me do? Say, and I will do it. I will not go to my aunt—to that odious London. Why are all my cousins married? You promised me, Herbert, we should be friends for ever—and now!"

Emily put her trembling hand into his, that trembled even more. He pressed it against his heart, against his lips.

"You are an angel—forgive me. if you knew!" said Herbert, with fervour. "I have been so long used to see you—to love you—that now!—Ah, Emily, you do not know my day-dreams—my night-dreams! Stay, is there nothing in my silence that your heart has interpreted? Know you not, when alone with you, why I am so absent? Why I am sad when you are sad—joyful when you are joyful? Do you not know the cause of all this?"

"And who has told you that I do not?" replied she, in a whisper, bending her eyes to the ground.

"Is it true, Emily," said Herbert, in rapture, "that you know—you feel?"

"Silence, Herbert," said she, half terrified at the avowal.

Then, in all the abandonment of innocent affection, she leaned her head against his shoulder.

"Emily," said he, pressing her to his heart.

"Herbert!"

At this moment a light step was heard entering the arbour.

She raised her head.

"Ah, are you there, dear child! I thought as much," said Lady Morton. And then with a smile, half amiability, half mockery, she said, "I hope, Mr. Herbert Vivyan, that you will permit a mother also to make her adieus."

Herbert, with his hands folded, followed them with his look till they entered the house, when Emily turned round, and their eyes met—there were tears in both.

Nothing could be more unexpected than Lady Gretnor's propositions. Lady Morton awoke as from a dream. New visions of ambition arose that had long slumbered in her breast—unhoped-for prospects she had never dared to entertain. Emily could not conceal her anguish at the thought of parting with her mother—her despair at being torn from all the scenes of her youth; and in the ingenuousness of her nature, revealed her long attachment for Herbert. She at first put on her *petit air mutin*, and refused to go to London; and it was only when she saw her mother unhappy that she at length consented to depart. It was by kindness that Lady Morton commanded.

Herbert and Emily met no more at Babbicomb.

PART II.—VANITY.

We left Emily Morton on the eve of bidding adieu to her mother and the scenes of her youth. We will pass over the desolation of that parting and take a glance at her when in London.

Lady Gretnor was awaiting with a momentarily increasing impatience the arrival of her niece, when her carriage, well known by its sound, drove up to her door in Grosvenor Square. A wonderful effort for her, she quitted the drawing-room and descended three steps of the staircase to meet Emily. She took her in her arms, kissed her, looked at her again and again and appeared satisfied with the scrutiny.

A family squad was assembled to pass judgment on the new arrival, uncles and aunts and cousins, known only by name and whom she had no desire to know further. What an empty thing is near relationship! Those ready made affections, those ties which the world imposes, but to which the heart responds not. They eyed her as though they expected to find her some curiosity from another planet. One examined her air, another her figure, a third her dress. They lavished on her a profusion of caresses,

kisses and compliments, and called her a flattering likeness of her mother.

But it was only to this circle that Emily was visible. She was to make her *debut* at the approaching ball in Willis's Rooms, and till then, was as carefully guarded as in a convent or Turkish gyneseum from the eyes of the profane.

Lady Gretnor too, had ample employment on her hand, and many a lesson to give to her *protegee*, preparatory to that important event.

But Emily's heart beat with none of the anticipations usual on such an occasion, her thoughts were in Devonshire. The rattle of the carriages, the noise and dust of the streets, the whirl and bustle of that great Babylon served but to recal more forcibly her accustomed occupations the peaceful valley of Babbicomb and its quiet bay; and she sighed for the caresses of her mother, for the daily greeting and affectionate smiles of Herbert. She thought bitterly of their parting interview when their hearts gave utterance to sentiments long felt but never till then expressed. Her memory had carefully stored every word of his, to the inflections of his voice, and expression of his every look—even to the last, when she turned and saw him with his arms folded as though they would never again be unlocked. She looked back on her past life. What a scene of enchantment! And now there was no heart to beat in response with hers!

"Emily," one morning said Lady Gretnor to her, when she found her in tears, "your eyes are red with weeping—you will wear those long silken lashes. Such blue eyes as yours were not made for tears. You don't know what to do with them. I have a mind to scold you, child. You must not keep them fixed on the ground, but give them some expression. You should look timid, my dear, but not abashed. Remember, it is only when you catch the eye of your partner in the dance that you must cast them down; and let him suppose, when you lift them again, that you are thinking of him. It is a very pretty thing to be *naive*; but it should be in some degree studied, or it is apt to be construed into *gaucherie*. You should only blush on occasion, and when it is called for. These shoulders are well turned; but, to display them to advantage, you should show that your scarf will not stay there, and be continually raising it, as though it were falling, with that pretty hand. Nothing is more graceful than such an attitude. Henrietta had a cast of a statue in her room, and profited much from the attitude, but more from her glass. Then that foot, which is like a little bird's—of what use is it to be pretty, if it is not to be shown? There is nothing men admire more. You should contrive to let it appear now and then, and speak. It discourses very elegant music."

"Mamma—" said Emily, somewhat shocked with all this affectation.

"Your mamma," interrupted Lady Gretnor, "has become crystallised, like the mountains about her. You must forget—"

"Forget her!" exclaimed Emily; "no, never!"

"Look on me as your mamma, now," said Lady Gretnor. "But here comes your cousin Arabella. I wish," said Lady Gretnor, addressing her, "that you would give this naughty girl a lesson; she is inclined to be mutinous. My sister writes to me that she has left her heart in Devonshire—indeed, I see it. There—I leave you together." Thus saying, she retired to her boudoir.

"Emily, dear," said Arabella, kissing her cheek—"well, you are the prettiest creature!—you will make such a sensation to-morrow night!"

"But Arabella," replied Emily, "I do not wish to make a sensation. Would I were back a Babbicomb!"

"Why, you sigh, dear, as though you had really—mamma has whispered to me something about one—"

"Whom do you mean, cousin?" interrupted Emily, blushing deeply.

"One Herbert Vivyan," said Arabella, significantly; "perhaps you do not know such a person, eh?"

"Mamma," sighed Emily, "has perhaps written something about him."

"Little hypocrite! What! you never think of him;" said Arabella. "Perhaps you write to him, too."

"No, indeed, Arabella. But if I did think of him," said Emily, innocently, "he was my friend my master."

"And ended by becoming your lover—a natural conclusion," said Arabella archly. "Foolish little thing; he is very handsome, eh?"

"No; but he is so good, so kind, so amiable," said Emily, with earnestness. "I owe him so much. Mamma, too, has often said how grateful she is to him for the pains he took with me."

"One of those Werter-faced youths, I imagine," said Arabella, ironically, "so full of thought, so teaming with sensibility, so melancholy. To listen to him, his heart is a tomb in which are buried all the joys and hopes of life."

"You mock me, cousin," said Emily, seriously. "He is very melancholy. I left him very unhappy."

"On you account, Emily?" said Arabella. "What you would marry him, child?"

"I have no thoughts of marrying; I am too young," replied Emily.

"No thoughts of marrying, coz!" said Arabella—"too young! It is never too soon to make an advantageous match. I was married myself at seventeen; and should have been out earlier, if Jane had—"

"I hope no one will think of me, Arabella," said Emily.

"Why so, my dear?" asked Arabella.

"Why," stammered Emily, playing with the end of her sash, and blushing, "because —I—I—"

"Do you really, seriously dream of such a thing as marrying Mr. Herbert Vivyan?" said Arabella, laughing.

Emily made no reply, but her confusion increased.

Arabella burst into a louder laugh.

"Why do you laugh?" said Emily.

"At the idea of your being a country curate's wife. Think you that my aunt would ever consent to such a union?" replied Arabella.

"Perhaps—she loves me," objected Emily.

"Loves you, dear," said Arabella, throwing her arms round her neck; "and so do I. When I was of your age, I was as silly. It is all very well in the country, those grand passions; it serves to fill up time. *C'est bien gentil.* Adoration and desolation; but as to marriage, that is a serious affair: it is for life."

"Can any one be happy who marries without loving?" said Emily.

"Dear coz, it is very well at first," said Arabella. "But this love, for which everything is to be sacrificed, do you expect it will last? It is a sad truth; but so it is. There was Caroline Aymer, who had been brought up in every luxury, and would have her half pay colonel; and is now living, with six children in a thatched cottage in Hampshire. Jane Grandison, who, against the consent of all her friends, ran away with an ensign in the rifles, who spent her little fortune and left her with scarcely the common necessaries of life. In short, my dear, there is no end to the catalogue. Marriage is, as I said, a serious affair, and does not admit of speculation: there should be no lottery in it. Like all other important matters, we should consider it well—with due judgment, and unblinded with passions. There is nothing so dangerous as to love the man you are to marry. Esteem—respect—are very well; inclination even. Marry first, and love after, my dear, was mamma's maxim with all of us. Marriage is a position in the world, and has nothing to do with sentiment. The advantages that fortune brings, particularly when united with rank, are lasting—substantial."

"And then of love?" sighed Emily.

"They fill up but little of our time," replied Arabella, "or our thoughts. "What are the real occupations of life! Dressing, visiting, walking, driving, the opera, concerts, balls, &c."

"But cousin," said Emily, "supposing all this to be true, when we love, it is not easy to forget."

"Emily," replied Arabella, "that is not so difficult as you imagine. I, for instance—now, I am quite safe with you—I was once in love—the year after my marriage. Oh, if you had seen me. I was in despair! Such sighing and weeping. But it went off I can't tell how; and I have never thought of the man since. I had all sorts of distractions, and could not find time to think of my inamorata. And now I am the happiest of women."

"Heavens, cousin; I don't think I could be ever like you," said Emily.

"Try it, cousin, and you'll see," was the reply.

The conversation was continued in this strain for some time. Arabella joked and quizzed Emily half out of her amour, without wounding her *amour propre*—filled her mind full of doubts and casuistry.

Arabella was a good ally to Lady Gretnor, and left Emily not less disconcerted, but certainly much less disinclined for the ball at Almack's.

"Arabella on quitting Emily went straight to Lady Gretnor.

"Well, mamma," said Arabella, "'tis as you thought; that foolish girl is desperately in love with her tutor."

Lady Gretnor smiled; but with a smile of incredulity—a disbelief in the desperation of Emily's love.

"I tell you, mamma," repeated Arabella, "that she prefers the valley of Babbicomb to all the grandeur of town—a country curate to a coronet."

"You do not know women's hearts so well as I do, dear," said Lady Gretnor, laughingly; "they are like the skins we use in our pocket-books—pass your finger over the writing, and it is soon effaced. Leave her to me. *Laissez-moi faire.*"

"Depend also on me," said Arabella, as they were parting.

"*Nous verrons,*" were the last words of Lady Gretnor.

There was a confidence in their manner of delivery that seemed oracular.

I have no intention of describing a ball at Almack's; so do not be alarmed. Nor do I mean to give a particular account of Emily's dress — whether it was blonde, muslin, or silk, must be left to the imagination; or how she looked; or whether she waltzed at all; or if she made a general sensation or not; sufficient, that Lord Singleton admired her.

And who was Lord Singleton? I will tell you. He was a man who, it may be said, had never been young; for, though scarcely twenty-six, he might have been mistaken for nearly double that age. His tall and emaciated figure corresponded well with his cadaverous and livid face, of an immeasurable length; and both betrayed the effects of early dissipation, or an hereditary taint in his constitution. His father had obtained his title by long services to a party. But his son, who had watched the tide of events, now that the flood was turning, took a diametrically opposite line of politics, and worshipped the rising sun, which, when once well above the horizon, he knew would continue to increase in power.

Principles he had none; but a blind devotion to the cause he had espoused, as is the case with all converts, made him a fit instrument in the hands of a set in whose eyes apostacy was the greatest of merits, as well as a pledge for future honours. Brass glitters more than gold, says the adage. Thus all his talents were rather shining than solid. But his career as a statesman was scarcely at that time begun. He had spoken indeed, occasionally in the Lower House, and with considerable fluency; but his speeches had all the odour of the schoolboy declamations heard in the debating rooms of Oxford or Cambridge, and evidently smelt of the midnight oil consumed in their composition.

His youth had been devoted to two pursuits—or, rather, occupations—horse-racing and acting. But they were the means of giving him *ton* in the circles of fashion. Many of his contemporaries aimed at glassing themselves in his mirror, and becoming his echoes. There was a false smile that continually played about his mouth that was not in harmony with the gravity and seriousness of his other features—a mannerism in his address, an affectation of ease, a theatrical air in his attitudes and gestures, and a lengthened drawl in his pronunciation, that made himself and his imitators almost a caste apart. His language, too, was a jargon unintelligible to the uninhabited,—had an undercurrent, like the writings of the Germans; for his words would always bear a double interpretation, so as completely to mask his real character, if he had any. The sketch is not imaginary nor overdrawn. At the period when Emily made her *debut* he had had a disappointment in love, and vainly sought among the *belles* of the season one who came up to his *beau ideal* of woman—who realised all the perfections with which his imagination had gifted the divinity at whose shrine he had vainly worshipped. Such was the man whom Lady Gretnor, like an able tactician as she was, selected for her future husband.

Nothing is easier, in piscatorial phrase

.han to hook—to catch—your fish; much yet remains to be done, or the trout may slip off the barb, or break away. But Lady Gretnor was an angler whom experience had taught all the resources of the art. She played with the victim, but never slackened her line.

It was now that she never lost sight of Lord Singleton; every day gave birth to some new invention of pleasure, and water parties and picnics followed each other in quick succession. It was so late in the season that general engagements were few; so that he had more time to devote to the family in Grosvenor-square.

The indifference with which Emily received his attentions piqued his vanity; and to be twice refused—for the world began to talk of his admiration—would have been indeed an indignity. Love him, or not love him, at any price she should be his. Such was his rash resolution.

Arabella, meanwhile, was Emily's inseparable companion, and to stifle a predilection hostile to her mother's projects was her unceasing aim. She had found the distractions of society an efficient remedy for her own passion, and into them she plunged deep her cousin. It was not without a secret remorse that Emily confessed to herself the corrupting influence of this new world and its pleasures, and felt herself daily more and more detached from him to whom she had bound herself by the most sacred engagement. But the voice of conscience, like the pressure of the ring of Gyges, grew fainter and more faint. The handsome lifeguardsman whispered in her ear, as they waltzed, that she was beautiful.

She heard, when she sat down, a flattering murmur pursue her; she saw many an eye fixed on her with a look of admiration. In the midst of such seductions to the senses what room was there for melancholy reflection, or sad retrospect? Like an evil genius Arabella was ever by her side, deflowering her soul of its purity—stripping it, leaf by leaf, of its ingenuousness—its candour—its beauty. The hand that laid it bare was adroit and gentle. The voice that whispered in her ear was full of sweet poison. She did not wound her love; with mingled caresses and cajoleries, with pity rather than reproof, she spoke of the happiness of being united with one we love; with a sigh lamented the futility of such Utopian projects—the romance of such ideas—the danger of indulging in such hopes—till Emily herself insensibly believed in the impossibility of happiness.

We soon forget what we can never attain.

What a mystery is the human mind! How waxen to take impressions; how easily warped into wrong. Is it in matter itself that this evil properly resides, or is it but the agent of two rival principles implanted in our nature?

Physicians know our diseases, and can calculate on their effects in others; but are not our vices themselves contagious? Is there not an infection in minds as well as bodies? —or, perhaps, there was in Emily a latent hereditary taint—a lurking ambition—a love of the world, long stifled—dormant, it is true, but whose seeds were ready sown, and waiting to bear their fruit; a bitter one it proved.

The old axiom, that "soft waters wears away the hardest stones," was exemplified in Emily's instance. Her heart was not hard, it was soft, gentle, and, alas, ductile. By degrees she was led to look upon Lord Singleton no longer with eyes of aversion. He was unremitting in his attentions, for he had made up his mind to woo and win Emily—not from any particular love he bore her, for his was a nature utterly incapable of comprehending or sustaining a grand or lofty passion, but as a matter of honour; or more properly speaking, he was bent upon winning Emily—of marrying her.

By determined assiduity on his own part, joined to the persuasive powers of his two female coadjutors, Emily was at length induced to bestow her hand upon Lord Singleton.

Their wedding was what is termed a fashionable one. The *elite* of the aristocratical notabilities honoured the nuptials of the happy pair with their presence; after which the two departed to spend their honeymoon on the continent.

Here Lord Singleton entered into a vortex of dissipation. Night after night did Lady Singleton watch for the return of her absent Lord.

It was generally morning before he made his appearance, and then so disfigured by passion and wine, that she could hardly recognise him as the man in whose care she had given up her happiness to.

On very many of these occasions, Lord Singleton was accompanied by a friend, a Prince Romanckoff.

This gentleman appeared to take a great interest in Lord Singleton. He reasoned with him upon his reckless conduct—told him that he was the dupe of sharpers—and commiserated with Lady Singleton, whom he affected to pity.

By degrees he became a constant attendant, and succeeded in winning the esteem of Lady Singleton—we had almost said her love.

Lord Singleton was utterly neglectful of his young and beautiful wife; in fact, he was tired of her. Prince Romanckoff was, on the contrary, her devoted admirer.

There were not wanting persons who prophesied how all this would end.

Eventually, Lord Singleton upbraided his wife with infidelity—a charge which she indignantly repudiated as false and wicked. But it would be needless to dwell upon all the recriminations of this unhappy pair.

Emily, or more properly speaking, Lady Singleton, was driven to distraction by the brutalities of her husband, who besought her to fly with the prince.

Alas! eventually, in an unhappy hour, goaded almost to madness, she was induced to do so.

Lord Singleton returned to England, and sunk into an early grave.

For some time Lady Singleton lived comparatively happy with Prince Romanckoff. He was kind to her, and she loved him, at any rate much more than she had done her lawful husband. Indeed, in her eyes he was perfection, with one exception, and that was his love of play.

As time advanced, this passion seemed to increase rather than diminish. Nevertheless, she looked with a lenient eye upon what might with justice be termed his leading vice, and one indeed which absorbed much of his time and thoughts.

There is nothing which women hate so much as play, because they know it is a passion stronger than love. Emily often lamented that one so perfect should give way to such a vice.

Among his companions—his inseperable associates—was a baron who had been at Florence the preceding season, and to whom she had from the first a magnetic antipathy. There are certain natures hostile to each other—hatreds innate, as it were—whose manifestations are warnings more sure than reason. Such was the prepossession that Emily felt against this man, and which, in the ingenuousness of her character, she had not concealed from the prince. The baron was quite sensible of her aversion.

One morning, after one of the usual midnight scenes, as Emily was sitting in her boudoir, adjoining the drawing-room, she heard the baron and the prince in loud altercation. Her first impulse was to quit the room; but she must pass through that where they were met. Emily was no spy, no listener; but she could not shut her ears to the conversation that became momentarily more interesting to her.

"Prince," said the baron, "I am come to you for those two hundred sequins that you borrowed of me so long ago at Florence."

"But, my friend—" objected the prince.

"It is now twelve months ago. I was so hard hit last night, that I cannot take any excuse. Had they been lost sùr parole, it would have been another affair; but you know I lent them to my great inconvenience, and now I must have them. Do you hear?" said the baron, with emphasis.

"But, baron," replied Romanckoff, "I have not got them. What can I do?"

"Prince," answered the German, "it is for you to look to the ways and means. At the rate you are going on, you had need have as many serfs as Denudoff; a mine in Siberia would hardly supply this extrvagant mode of living; and we know that you have neither one nor the other. Everything goes on badly with such extravagance. It is your fault that everything goes on badly. Why did you send for me from Milan? At least there were some English to draw upon, and Romanowitz bled freely. The pigeons you thought you had caught here were not worth the plucking. That Steinenburgh, the Hungarian, who is just come of age, is too far north for us."

"I was always doubtful about that mentor of his—a wolf in sheep's clothing—eh?—a—"

"Well, well," said the baron, "that is nothing to the purpose. Money—I must have money, prince."

"A colder air of the Carbonare!" exclaimed the prince, not heeding the appeal made to his purse. "Why, baron, your hand was out last night, your fingers were not so sensitive as usual: you should file them to the quick, that we may never be so again bothered to remove the cursed five."

"I never dealt so vilely," muttered the baron, in an angry tone; "he broke the bank—nay, I owe him some hundred Napoleons, on my word of honour, or 'I owe you,' as the English say. You know as well as I do that he must be paid, or—"

"Call him out, baron, and—"

"Such things have been done," answered the baron, "before now; but the cash must be laid down first, according to the usual rules—afterwards it is not worth while. They tell me he is a good hand at his sword. But I have no mind to try him."

Here the prince laughed gutturally.

"My honour, I say," repeated the baron; "what else have we to depend upon? The Napoleons must be paid in twenty-four hours, or all Vienna will ring with it; besides, I mean to get them back with interest. It will only be a loan. 'Better luck next time,' says an English proverb."

"I repeat," said the prince, stammering, "that I have not fifty Napoleons in the house. The strong coffer I brought with me from Italy is drained nearly dry. It is a bad affair, very bad —"

"You play your cards wretchedly; you let that English heiress at Rome slip out of your hands. She would have been a good partner, although she was a bourgeoise—a cheesemonger's daughter, and helped to make butter ; and instead—"

"I know what you are going to say; cease! no more!" said the prince, with some irritation.

"And my lady, your—"

"Name her not!" interrupted Romanckoff, raising his voice, imperatively.

"What! you love her still," said the baron, sneeringly. "How constant you have grown of late. Ha! ha!"

"I tell you," said the prince, "that I will have no badinage where Emily is concerned. Some writer says, 'The soul is a high celestial light, that comes and goes.'"

"It is a good definition of love, prince; but I have an idea—"

"Your ideas are generally good, baron, on all but love; but there we differ *toto cœlo.*"

"That night you carried her off from the Scal," said the baron, lowering his voice to a whisper, you had been at a fancy dress ball—"

"Well," said the prince, "and what of that?"

"My lady," continued the baron, "wore jewels. Were they diamonds?"

"But—yes," said the prince, after a pause, as though he were reflecting deeply. "But I dare not ; I will not."

"You *will* not?" answered the baron.

"Never!" said the prince.

"Very well," said the baron; "I give till this evening to decide. Think well of it."

"You threaten me, baron!"

"I do not threaten you, but I entreat you, prince, for yourself—for me—to do this deed."

"I will think of it," was the reply.

The baron here abruptly took his leave, but Emily neither heard his retiring step nor the last words of the dialogue. She felt all her strength abandon her, and had fallen senseless on the floor.

When she recovered she found the prince kneeling over her.

He had divined the occasion of her illness.

"You know all—you have heard all," said Romanckoff.

"All," replied Emily; "but you love me, Alexandre!"

"Love you, Emily! et tu me pardounes, ange."

What will a woman not pardon in one she loves? She got up, and in a few minutes returned with the diamonds.

That day, and several successive days, the prince, by a thousand little attentions, endeavoured to efface the recollection of this scene; but it was not to be effaced.

To whom had she linked her destiny? She dared not put the question; her heart answered—to a gambler; but this she knew, and the companion of gamblers. But one thing more she had discovered, to a chevalier d'industre—a felon.

No reproach ever escaped her lips.

The re-unions continued. The bank, strengthened by the sale of Lady Singleton's jewels, attracted a still greater crowd of players. The baron's star had the ascendant; the prince and his croupier put the diamonds to good interest, and ended the season by sharing the profits, which were not inconsiderable.

All the German world were now quitting their capitals. Some went to Baden-Baden, others to Wiss-Baden and the other watering-places, and a few to Spa.

It was the latter place which the lovers chose.

Lost in the crowd of a dissipated city, Lady Singleton had not felt the situation in which she was placed, and had been in some degree insensible to her shame. But at Spa, the resort not only of foreigners, but of her own compatriots—Spa, the watering-place of Brussels and Bruges, where her story was known, without its alleviating circumstances, though the hard, cruel world admits not of such—Spa, where she met some even connected with her family, many acquainted with her numerous and high connections—it required all her fortitude to bear the mortifications that every coming day brought with it. With that extreme sensibility which she inherited from her mother, she interpreted every look and gesture into an insult or a reproach. In the walks and rooms they seemed to shrink from her as though there was leprosy in her touch—contagion in the very atmosphere she breathed. If she went to the public balls, they left the side of the room where she was seated. If she got up to dance, it was difficult to procure a *vis-a-vis.* And even those whom she had known at Vienna seemed to partake of the general influenza, and to receive her coldly, or not at all. In feeling all these "stings and arrows of outrageous fortune" that were darted into her on all sides, her heart failed her, and she bitterly regretted the past.

And Prince Romanckoff, was he, too, marked with the general stigma? No; it is at woman—feeble, helpless, poor, weak woman—that the finger of scorn points; that her own sex take a savage delight in crushing, in trampling on—once overthrown, in levelling with the dust. But man—that lord of the creation, the tempter, the betrayer, the seducer—he, instead of being placed out of the pale of society, walks with head erect, and is more courted, fêted, and admired, than ever.

Reciprocal regard and esteem may enable a woman of great firmness to shelter herself from the neglect or even the scorn of the world in the affection of the object she loves.

But Lady Singleton had neither energy of character nor respect for her paramour. And he, the prince, had originally many good qualities; but they had all fallen down before the shrine of necessity.

He had been warped into wrong by evil associations; and, cast in the mould of that society in which he had lived, he insensibly took the impress of that deformity.

The force of circumstances, and the momentary dominion of the senses, the *eclat* of the intrigue with the most beautiful of the English women on the continent, had, in spite of himself, led him to take a step on the rashness of which he had not calculated; but, having had time to reflect on it with the cold casuistry of prudence, he had serious thoughts, like an able chess-player who had

No. 71.

made a bad move, of regaining the position he had lost.

Satiety had succeeded to passion. Pecuniary embarrassment, from the run of ill-luck into which he had fallen at Spa, where gambling is made a profession, and where, though himself a professor, he met with many an able competitor, tended to strengthen this resolution; and he now only waited for the chances to declare themselves in his favour.

His first object was to corrupt the mind of Lady Singleton; and to that effect he introduced her to a Russian countess, by the name of Pushikoff, whose notorious profligacy made her a fit handle for his purposes. Women are either angels or devils; and not only the heathen mythology has given a female personification to all the evil passions, but the greatest dramatists of all times have, in their profound study of human nature and delineation of character, made them the instruments of crime. If we wish for examples, we have only to take Clytemnestra and Lady Macbeth.

There is a deformity in some minds that make them take a savage delight in vitiating others. It is to them an excitement, like seduction to an impotent *debauchee*. Perhaps jealousy also gave a stimulus to revenge, for she had, a few seasons before, been a favourite of the prince.

The task was, however, a difficult one—more difficult than she had yet encountered. Habits are like ideas—they are never wholly obliterated.

It would be an office from which I should shrink, to trace the system of education practised by this able proficient in the arts of corruption.

But Emily's pupilage was scarcely begun, when Romanckoff was determined on a rupture, on the plea of pressing affairs. He accordingly quitted the Baths for Brussels, leaving Lady Singleton in charge of the Pushikoff.

Before his departure, the following dialogue passed between those ancient confederates—that *par noble fratrum*—Baron Steinenberg and the Prince Romanckoff.

"So, prince, you are going to Brussels?" said the baron, significantly.

"Yes," answered the prince, with a feigned sigh, "my affairs—"

"And Emily?" inquired Steinenberg.

"Well, i'faith, we get tired in time of everything. It is the law of nature—it is not my fault."

"You have profitted at last, as I find, by the quotation of some breviary," remarked the baron, ironically.

"The *liason* was not so dangerous as you predicted, eh, baron?" responded Romanckoff; "but with you for a mentor—"

"You flatter me, prince," said the baron, ironically. "I might take a lesson out of your book myself. We have changed parts, and I am the Telemachus and you the Mentor. May I ask what you propose doing with Lady Singleton?"

"What a question!" replied Romanckoff. "That troubles me. She is beautiful, amiable, and tempting; nevertheless—"

"You are going to leave her. We get tired in time of everything!" said the baron, with an air of mockery.

"Not altogether," said the prince. "But there is at Brussels, as you know, a certain widow, who is enamoured of me—completely in love—"

. "She is rich, is she not?" said the baron, with a sardonic glance.

"Tolerably," said the prince, "a million of francs. You must be aware," added he, "I must be liberal; and I confide to you the office of breaking to Emily our separation—the necessity of our parting. She will be in despair, poor dear! but what can I do?"

"Not so despairing as you imagine," answered Steinenberg. "She will find her consolation—"

"You would console her, baron? Is it not so?" said the prince, doubtingly. "I wish you good luck; but you know she hates you."

"So much the better—extremes meet," observed the baron.

"Yes, you and I," observed Romanckoff, with a half sneer, that implied his now superiority.

"You jest, prince; we shall see. I hope, at least, that in a certain case you will reimburse the value of the diamonds?"

"That is but fair," replied the prince. "I promise it after I have touched the fortune of Madame ——; in the meantime, I have need of money. You will lend me one hundred Napoleons, if I recommend you to the good offices of the countess?"

"Well, I will send you the money," answered the baron.

"You will not fail to send me news?" said the prince. "You have my best wishes for your success."

"It is a bargain," ended the baron.

Two days after this conference, Baron Steinenberg, after a long audience with the Pushikoff, wrote to Lady Singleton a note, requesting an interview with her.

Lady Singleton wondered what the object of this meeting could be; but complied with the request, not without some presentiment of evil.

"I have been desirous, Lady Singleton," said the baron, insinuatingly, "of speaking to you in private; and have a communication to make."

"To me!" said Lady Singleton, somewhat haughtily: "and what can Baron Steinenberg have to say to me?"

"It is of the prince I am come to speak," said the baron, significantly.

"He might have found a more welcome messenger," said Lady Singleton.

"None that takes a livelier interest in you, Lady Singleton," said the baron; "none who more sincerely respects—and—pities you."

"Pities me, baron! To what do you refer?" said Lady Singleton. "Speak—"

"I fear," replied Steinenberg, "that you have always taken a false view of my character—have had a strange predilection against me—an antipathy that nothing could have justified; and I am anxious to set myself right in your opinion. I entreat you to look upon me as your friend, and as such am come to consult with you—to offer you my advice under certain circumstances, as to what may best be done."

"What may all these inuendos mean?" said Lady Singleton, not without alarm. "Explain yourself, sir. To what circumstances do you allude?"

"It is a delicate task I have undertaken," said the baron, "and I could well have been spared a revelation."

"What revelation?" said Lady Singleton, still more alarmed.

"You are aware, Lady Singleton," said the baron, "that Prince Romanckoff is without fortune—that—"

"It was not his fortune, baron, that attached me to him," said Lady Singleton, interrupting him.

"No; you are too noble, too generous," said the baron, with a flattering air. "The sacrifice you made of an enviable position in life is the best proof of your disinterestedness and affection. But Romanckoff is, *entre nous*, an adventurer; and is at this moment utterly without the means of supporting you. In short—"

Lady Singleton wept bitterly. Her waking dream was about to be realised. Desertion, destitution, stared her in the face in all their horrors; and yet she had not expected this. The prince had been cold—neglectful; but that he should abandon her! no; this she never anticipated.

She still had much to learn of mankind. Her emotion was too great for words. She hid her face with her hands, whilst the tears coursed each other down her cheek.

"I sincerely sympathise with you," said the baron, who had succeeded even in forcing out a tear. "But the prince was unworthy of you, Lady Singleton; he is even now—why must I not reveal it?—paying his addresses to another."

"This, then," said Lady Singleton, "was the occasion of his visit to Brussels—of his urgent affairs. Oh, villain—villain!"

"You have applied to him a term that he fully deserves," said the baron, with an air of sincerity. "Nay, if you knew all—"

"What more remains to be known?" she replied. "Have I not heard enough?"

"We have parted, and for ever," said the baron, as if he felt Lady Singleton's wrongs. "I have renounced his friendship. If you had heard my reproach—if you could conceive that I even humiliated myself by entreaties that he should not desert you—and when they failed, by threats; but they were equally unavailing. Oh, Lady Singleton, if you knew the interest I have ever felt for you; if you could be aware of the power you possess over me, of my admiration for your

virtues, of the effect your beauty produced on me from the first moment I saw you. I have gazed on you, unobserved by yourself, till my heart was in my eyes—have watched every turn of your expressive countenance—have suffered all the pangs of jealousy—have dreamed of a life devoted to your happiness —of being your slave, of worshipping you as an idol. Oh, Lady Singleton, have pity on me—have mercy! It shall be my aim and ambition to anticipate your every wish, to purchase you every gratification that the world can bestow. All I ask of you is, that you should, if you cannot love me, look upon me as your friend. Nothing more will I exact of you. I am weary of this life I have so long led—have been driven into it solely from a want of sympathy—from the absence of an object to supply the yearnings of my soul. At this moment," he added, "perhaps it would be indelicate further to urge my suit."

With these words he took her hand, and pressed it respectfully to his lips.

When Baron Steinenberg left her she thought differently of him. She did not love him more, but hated him less.

The baron was right. Extremes meet. Yes, Baron Steinenberg became the prince's successor.

A few days after this conversation, a post chaise was at the door of the prince's house, and the too confiding Lady Singleton was hurried into the same by Steinenberg. The latter was habited in a travelling cloak and cap.

The last rumbling of the carriage wheels were heard by Romanckoff, who had been privy to the whole proceedings, and felicitated himself at having got fairly rid of one who, of late, had been a source of trouble to him.

PART III.—DEATH.

DURING the seven years that had elapsed since the commencement of our tale, Herbert Vivyan had run a glorious career in Parliament, which promised to raise him to one of the first law offices.

During the recess he had, by way of recreation from the labours of the sessions, gone to Paris.

Care, rather than time, had operated a cruel change on his appearance. His face was thin and wan; and the few gray locks that fell on each side of his temples, showed to the full height his ample and wrinkled forehead, in every line of which was deep thought.

He had put up at an hotel in the Rue de la Paix. It was his intention, after seeing the French capital, to take a rapid glance at those of Berlin and Vienna. It was the first time of his setting his foot on the continent.

One day, on entering the porter's lodge, and looking on the table for his letters, he accidentally glanced his eye over the names of the lodgers at the hotel, among which one caught his eye that might well rivet his attention—that name was Lady Singleton.

Her story, which had furnished aliment for the weekly gossip and also scandal of the town, till it gave place to some equally glaring novelty, had of course reached his ears. But her husband—who now filled one of the high offices of the government, from a dread of certain disclosures that might injure him in public opinion, as well as the uncertain success of the process, and the fear of disobliging the family of Lady Singleton, whose powerful interest had assisted effectually his views, as well as the disinclination to another matrimonial connexion—had failed to apply to the tribunals for a divorce. Her ladyship had been long unthought of by the world. Her relatives had forgotten her too; or, if she recurred to their memories, they entertained but one sentiment—that she was dead, or ought to be. But she was not dead in the recollection of Herbert Vivyan: he had staked his happiness on the cast of a die, and lost.

"Emily," he had often said to himself, "with thy love to stimulate my ambition, I should have obtained a name that would have covered thee with its glory. I should have set a glittering star on thy brows—a reflex of my genius. For this I should have become great. I should have made an Eden for thee, and placed myself at the gate of Paradise, like the archangel with his flaming sword, to prevent sorrow from entering. But, instead of that, Emily, thou tookest thy station among the vulgar crowd of the great, and became heartless and abandoned. I now ought to hate thee, Emily, because thou hast destroyed my dream of happiness, blighted my young affections—because thou hast taught me what woman is. Thou didst sell thyself for a vile price—prostitute thyself for a coronet, an empty title. Thou hast thy reward. Rest in thy shame."

Such had often been the bitter reflections that had poisoned his cup of life.

Curiosity, however—perhaps a better feeling—prompted him to question the portress as to her inmate.

"Ah, poor lady!" said the woman, "she has now been some time above. She is very miserable; and what is more, the doctor tells me she has not long to live. She suffers sadly, poor dear creature! and it is now six weeks since she left her room. Her groans are dreadful—so dreadful that we were obliged to carry her to the third story. But,

to tell you the truth," added she, in a whisper, "she is very poor; and it was but yesterday that I took her last bracelet to the Mont de Piété. It is a shame for one so well born to pawn her jewels; for they say she is noble."

"Has she no friend," said Vivyan, anxiously, "no—?"

"Alas! monsieur," replied the woman, "she came here with a foreigner—an Italian, I believe he was. He passed all his nights at the Maison de Jeu, and, when he lost, came home in a bad humour; and sometimes," said she, lowering her voice, "he beat her, because— All they had to live on was, I hear, a little pension—two hundred livres sterling."

"And this Italian?" inquired Vivyan, deeply interested.

"One night he left her. Whether he is at Paris or not, she does not know; but it is three weeks since he left her."

"Did she love him? asked Vivyan.

"Did she love him? Who knows, monsieur. But she cried much: she felt her destitution. Poor creature! she attempted to drown herself."

"Drown herself!" said Vivyan, much shocked.

"Yes monsieur; it is but too true. Two days after his departure—it was a terrible night—the rain fell in torrents—the wind shook her casement—it awoke her from a troubled sleep—the clock struck—she counted the hours as they sounded—it was midnight —she had not left her bed for two days—the fever was strong upon her—when, all at once she rose, wrapped herself up in a shawl, and slipped out without my perceiving her. She knew the way to the Seine—crossed the Place Vendome, and traversed the corner Rue Rivole and the Place Louis Quatorze. It is there where the bridge is—you know the bridge, monsieur? The storm was a terrible one—one of those tempests which we have so often in summer—and the lightning, as it played on the dome of the Hôpital des Invalides, showed her the Seine running darkly through the arch. The parapet of the bridge is high, and, weak as she was, I can't think, monsieur, how she could contrive to get upon it. But she did, monsieur; and was just going to throw herself over, when a gendarme, who happened to be passing at the time, saved her, and brought her back, more dead than alive, to the hotel. Since then she has got worse and worse. Ah, monsieur! it is a terrible thing to be sick and alone, without friends—without—"

"And has she no acquaintance here?—no means?" asked Vivyan, much affected by the simple narrative.

"She has written to her husband, and he sent her some money; but he would not come and see her. They say, monsieur, that she is divorced; and more, that she has not much beauty—even ugly."

"Who is her physician?" asked Vivyan.

"Monsieur Dubois. He is a good doctor, and a good man—and very kind, monsieur; he never takes a fee from her. Yesterday I saw he had been shedding tears when he left her—saw him with my own eyes; and, for myself, I cannot see her without crying; and my niece, who takes care of her, sometimes is obliged to quit her. There are moments when she is delirious, and makes confessions that are really terrible to hear; but—"

"I do not want to hear them," said Vivyan, fearful of her garrulity, and much moved by the relation which, coming from one so hardened as the portress of an hotel, showed the miserable state to which Lady Singleton was reduced.

"Ah, monsieur," continued the woman, "there is not at the hospital a woman more ill than my lady; and when she is dead, monsieur, who will pay the expenses of her interment? That is what my master says. He thinks of sending her to St Jaques; but—"

"My good woman," said Herbert, "I will be responsible for—"

"Oh, you are English," said the portress. "You have a good heart? I told him so."

"I entreat you," said Vivyan, "not to name me."

"Very well," said the woman, as she ran to open the door.

But she did not keep her promise. An hour afterwards she announced Herbert Vivyan.

As he entered the room, Emily made an effort to rise from her bed, but sank back from exhaustion, and covered her eyes with both her hands.

The chamber which Lady Singleton occupied was not the third story, as the portress, for the honour of the hotel, had stated, but the fourth story, and at the back. The only window it possessed opened upon a stable yard, where the neighing and pawing of the horses, and the swearing of the grooms, were audible. That window was in the roof; and the light which it admitted was so feeble that the objects in the room were scarcely distinguishable.

In a sort of alcove was the bed—one of the usual French description; and the once white curtains that hung at both ends from a circular piece of board in the centre, so scanty and tattered that they served neither for ornament nor use. All the furniture that it contained were a table with a marble top, and two or three rush-bottomed chairs. The chimney-piece—a rare thing even in the most miserable apartments in Parisian hotels

—had no clock, but, instead, it was covered with phials of all sizes and shapes, betraying that an ill-attended invalid had long inhabited the room.

It was long before Herbert's eyes became so far accustomed to the obscurity as to distinguish the companion of his youth—the poor, but degraded Emily. Her haggard and yellow face was thin to emaciation; a long string of her hair, which had escaped from her cap, showed that it was thickly interspersed with gray; her eyes, lustreless, and sunken in their sockets; and her lips, thin and livid, were half open, the lower one pinched and contracted, as with some recent convulsion.

Vivyan would not have recognised her—not a trace of her former self remained. She had become old—prematurely old. What has old age to do with years? With some they flow on unperceived, and glide, in an even current, like a stream, with scarcely a ripple on its surface, through a long and continued plain, till lost in the ocean of eternity. Time writes no wrinkle on their brows—lays not a finger on their cheek—his step is inaudible; whilst others—oh, it is misery! it is the mind—it is the mind that preys within, which consumes, and eats, and rusts, and corrodes. This it was that had left its ravages on the once beautiful Lady Singleton.

He approached the alcove, affected almost to tears.

They gazed on each other for some time—neither spoke.

At length, with a broken voice, Herbert said—

"I am come—"

"Oh. it is good, it is kind of you, Mr. Vivyan," said Emily, "to come to me—you, of all persons, who have most cause to hate me. No one comes near me—every one shuns me as they would a pestilence. Oh, Mr. Vivyan, it is strange that I should have been thinking of you; and it is long since you have been the companion of my thoughts. I dared not think of you, Mr. Vivyan; such thoughts, they say, are as warnings before death, like the glare of the lamp about to be extinguished.

Here she wrung her hands; Herbert would have taken them in his.

"No," said she, drawing them away; "their touch would pollute you, Mr. Vivyan. Oh, it was cruel in them to part us; was it not? If you knew all, your hate would turn to pity."

"Think not ill of me. I hate you!—no!" said Vivyan, earnestly.

"But you cannot hate me so much as I hate myself. Oh, I am loathsome! But who made me so? Lady Gretnor. Curses on her!—may—"

"They cannot reach her," said Vivyan, interrupting her; she is—"

"Dead!" exclaimed she, with a hollow, convulsive laugh, which lit up her eye with a momentary lustre—"dead! then my curse was fatal. They tell me curses have the power to drag down to the grave; and mine, even mine have been heard on high. Ha, ha! Have I not cause to curse her? Oh, if you knew the arts by which I was trepanned—was lured into that fatal marriage—the infernal means by which I was beset. My cousin, too, that syren! how she flattered and cajoled me! neither left me night nor day till they had accomplished their hellish purpose—wrung from me my all-unwilling consent. Oh, I loved you, Mr. Vivyan, with all the affection of my young heart! and to be sacrificed to the man I abhorred! Oh, if you knew what it is to be prostituted to the loathsome embraces of one whom we hate—to recoil from his touch as from that of a serpent. All this I have endured. Can hell, in all its ingenuity of torments, have worse in store?"

She shuddered as with some dreadful recollection, and continued, her eyes almost starting from their sockets—

"Think you that the spirits of those who are gone are permitted to revisit this earth—that they continue to feel an interest in those they once loved—those left here in misery? Can they grieve and weep, for the wretchedness they have caused? It seems to me"—and here she looked wildly around her—"that my mother is ever near me, that she haunts my couch—that I hear her voice, sometimes her sobs—never her reproaches. Oh, she was all gentleness; was she not Mr. Vivyan? and now she is in a place where there is no sorrow, and where, alas, I shall never join her."

"Have better hopes," said Vivyan, tenderly; "trust in Heaven and its infinite mercy."

"Hopes! mercy!—oh, what hope," she said bitterly, "is left for me? And yet the Magdalen was pardoned, was she not, Mr. Vivyan? But then she was penitent. Oh, if you could see within. If my sins were graven on my brow, you would shrink from looking at it, as from some infamous picture. Yet are they not written in every feature?—read you not there the traces of guilt?—the lines of sin, debauchery, depravity? Oh, Mr. Vivyan, I wish to live—now that my hour approaches, I wish to live. Shall I tell you a secret?" said she in a low tone. "Twice I have planned my death—my self-destruction—ay, thought of the grave as my best friend; but now—oh, sir, I am unfit to die—to die with all my sins upon my head! Oh, it is a dreadful thing to die, and so young—to hear no more the voice of birds—to see no more the sunshine! Oh, I cannot die—I will not die!"

"Give not way to such thoughts, Lady Singleton. Trust in heaven. Perhaps you may yet—"

"No, no," she replied; "Dubois has said it—Dubois has said it!"

She rolled her head backwards and forwards on the pillow for some time, as a child is rocked in its cradle, as though she could thus still to rest some troublous thought, and repeating—

"Dubois has said it—Dubois has said it!" Vivyan wept.

"Ah, you weep, Mr. Vivyan!—would that I could weep!—but the sources of my tears are dry now. Ah, I have shed tears—floods of tears—have passed a life of tears. It has been a cruel world to me. I have found none good in it—no not one. It is peopled with fiends. They have only the outward form of man, but are like the apples in the Dead Sea—shew beautiful to the sight, but within dust—vile dust and ashes. I sought for happiness in love—I loved, but was cruelly abandoned, betrayed, sold to a villain who made a merchandise of my beauty, and bartered my person for gold. I have herded with gamesters and sharpers, till I ceased to feel shocked at their villany. Nay, myself—it is true; you may well look at me—I have lured others into their nets—assisted in their ruin. Oh, you would loathe me if you knew all. Listen," said she in a whisper, "I will give you the catalogue of my lovers. But no, your ears are too pure—and to you, too—no, no—I could confess, but not to you."

Vivyan shuddered—he had not been prepared for this avowal.

To change the current of his thought, he paced the room backwards and forwards several times. When he again approached her couch, he found that Lady Singleton, exhausted by her exertion, had fallen into a swoon.

He called the nurse; and Dubois at that moment made his appearance.

For many succeeding days Vivyan, by every kind attention, endeavoured to soothe Lady Singleton, and alleviate her sufferings by the tenderest sympathy. But her malady, a rapid pulmonary consumption, hourly gained ground, and baffled the aid of medicine; whilst her mind refused all consolation. As she felt her end draw nigh, she clung with increasing eagerness to life; and Dubois' oracular words were continually on her lips.

Lady Singleton never rallied. She lived for some days after Vivyan's first interview with her. The spirit hovered between two worlds—the flagging pulse—the sunken eye,—and the attenuated frame, told but too surely that she was fading away from the living things of this earth, and Vivyan felt that he would not be permitted to see her for long. He was unremitting in his attentions. He saw that she was provided with every comfort, all that money could purchase. One evening when he called, the woman of the house informed him that the doctor had been there some three or four hours previously, and had declared that it would be impossible for her to last even that night. She was then in a state of syncope, and perfectly unconscious of all that was passing around.

Vivyan expressed a wish to go up to her room, to take a last look at her before her spirit winged its flight.

"It will only pain you, monsieur, and cannot possibly do you any good, for she has not known any one for the last four hours. Indeed, sir," she continued, sinking her voice to a low whisper—"she's gone, poor dear soul, as far as understanding anything, and let us hope that her earthly sufferings are over, and that she will be permitted to pass away in peace."

"I must see her," said Vivyan, firmly.

"Oui, monsieur — as you please. Of course you can go up stairs, but —"

"Ah, never mind whether it pains me or not," answered Vivyan, "I will, with your permission, go up and see her."

"As you please, monsieur," answered the woman," and she led the way up stairs.

When Mr. Vivyan entered the bed room, he found Lady Singleton, as the landlady had stated, calm, rigid, and insensible. As he gazed upon her thin and pale features, they presented the appearance of one who had already passed away, and spoke of recent dissolution.

At first, Vivyan thought that in reality she was dead, but upon a close inspection he discovered that she faintly breathed.

The landlady clasped her hands together, and looked from the face of the dying woman into that of her former lover. She then shook her head.

Vivyan regarded her with a look of inquiry.

"She will never wake from this, monsieur," exclaimed the woman, "never!"

"I will sit down and wait awhile," answered Vivyan.

There was an old woman in the room, who had been hired as a nurse to the invalid. This woman had been engaged at his request, and was paid by him. She came forward and placed a chair for his accommodation, and the landlady softly left the room.

For a long time Vivyan watched the form of the inanimate woman. She appeared to him as though she lay there in her long last sleep—that sleep which knows no waking. It was evident enough that she did not suffer much, for she was perfectly passive, and unconscious to all that was passing around.

Vivyan watched her, and desired the nurse to see if she could not manage to convey a small portion of jelly into her mouth.

The old woman endeavoured to do so, but the effort was not attended with any success. Another half hour or so passed, but the sick woman remained still in a state of unconsciousness.

At the expiration of this time, the doctor who had attended her, made his appearance. He examined the patient carefully, and then slowly shook his head.

"Is there any hope?" Vivyan inquired, eagerly.

"My dear sir," said the surgeon, "I cannot promise you any. I fear that this trance, if I can so term it, is but the precursor of death; nature is fairly exhausted, and the poor dear lady, let us hope, will pass away in peace.

"Do you not think then that she will survive through the night?"

"I think it very improbable that she will," he answered, "but it is barely possible to put the precise limit to the duration of human life, however much the patient may be prostrated. As to her ultimate recovery, that is another impossibility. She is calm and unconscious; let us be thankful for that; it is better than being racked with aching and agonising pains."

The disciple of Esculapius than took his departure.

In about an hour after he had left, a gentle sigh escaped from the sufferer; she slowly and gently opened her eyes, a slight tremor shook her thin lips, and she moved uneasily on one side, and then moaned.

The nurse hastened to her side, and inquired if she wanted anything.

The dying woman shook her head.

"Has Mr. Vivian been here?" she inquired.

"Emily!" said Vivian hastening to her side, and bending over her.

"Ah, Herbert!" she murmured, with something of her old intonation, although so feeble that the words were scarcely audible, ah, Herbert—you here. How kind of you how very kind. Have pity on me—pity!

"My dear, dear Emily," said Vivyan, "would that we had met earlier. To see you thus—"

"Weep not for me," she exclaimed, "I am not fit to live. There is an end to all my happiness in this world. I have sunk too low. An end of all happiness—but the next --, ah, the next!" The miserable woman, closed her eyes, as though with some sudden spasm of pain, and then murmured "the next—the next."

She then looked fixedly on the countenance of Herbert Vivyan, and said, laying her hand upon his—

"Forgive me—I know you will. Say you forgive me, and I die happy."

"Forgive," said her former lover. "Do not talk thus. What have I to forgive?"

"Up—above—Herbert—that name"—exclaimed the dying woman, as she pointed with her thin finger above her head. Her hand fell upon the bed, and without a groan, her spirit had passed away.

Mr. Vivian saw that the last obsequies were attended to. He followed her remains to their last resting-place, and then hastily left for England.

Thus ended the career of one who was a victim to a forced marriage.

CHAPTER CX.

MR. RALPH BUNKHAM.—THE ORDINARY'S NOTES.

MR. RALPH BUNKHAM, when Colonel Jack gave him his release, took his departure, very well satisfied with having escaped so well as he had done. All things considered, he esteemed himself pretty fortunate. He had, however, no reason to felicitate himself upon this for long. Mr. Bunkham, had, as it is termed, many things against him—and, what was worse, he had the eye of Jonathan Wild directed towards him.

Wild had made many inquiries about his whereabouts, and some few evenings after his attempt on the property belonging to the redoubtable Mr. Squabshot, Mr. Wild favoured him with an interview, and what was worse, he did not seem disposed to part with him.

The two—the thief and thieftaker—met in a passage leading to the tap-room of the Pickled Egg.

It is probable that Bunkham might have escaped the renowned thieftaker, for Wild had betaken himself to the parlour, but was attracted to the other public room by the noise and confusion that reigned there, and attracted his notice.

Within the tap-room a number of uproarious men were assembled, who were seated round the table, above which was suspended a tin lamp with two wicks. One of the company, a stout thickset fellow, was squaring his fists, and challenging one of the company to fight. In the right-hand corner of the room crouched a woman, who regarded the proceedings with the utmost complacency—by her side was a child. Another man, on the other side of the table, held in his right hand a bludgeon, while with his left he appealed to heaven.

The noise and confusion was at its height when Wild proceeded to the tap-room ; but before he arrived there he met Bunkham in the passage leading to the room in question.

Wild at once collared him, and effected a capture, and from this place Mr. Bunkham was marched off to Newgate, there to await his trial for forging and passing some Bank of England notes. A true bill was found against him, he was convicted, and sentenced to death.

Previous to his execution, the ordinary brought him to a sense of his position, and he was what might be termed a repentant sinner.

Bunkham expiated his crimes upon the public scaffold.

It would be needless for us to inform our readers what numbers have suffered for the same offence since then ; but as many of them will be interested in two remarkable offenders, we subjoin the following notes by ones of the deputy ordinaries of Newgate, as they can be relied upon as an actual fact.

Although the ordinary of Newgate is the only person engaged and paid by the city authorities, for giving spiritual advice and assistance to prisoners, still there are many gratuitous deputies, and such is the zeal for saving souls in this age, that the authorities at Newgate are daily under the painful necessity of rejecting the pious services of numerous volunteers, who fancy that no crimes are too enormous for their talents in salvation.

We do not intend to tax our good natured readers with a mere abstract of bygone crimes and trials, the interest of which might at the period when the events occured have been sufficiently intense to reach the ears of a school-boy in his first quarter's probation, at an economical establishment of learning in the remotest part of Yorkshire, but which would now be stale and unprofitable reading to all, save some few old ladies whose remaining span of life would be a blank without those condiments of existence—the shocking and the horrible—those who can never find anything in a newspaper to interest and engage their attention, but accidents and offences.

After a certain age, with a certain class of society, when nature begins to flag, and the rigidity or induration of nervous fibre commences, nothing but copious draughts of *aquæ vitæ*, and a Corder's murder can arouse their feelings ; marvellous tales of the shedding of blood, and dram-drinking, are the mustard and cayenne which awaken many into a state of conscious existence ; without the potential or actual cautery, an unintellectual old age is but a foretaste of death, if not death itself.

These papers are known to be genuine,

and penned under circumstances of peculiarity. It appears that the author of the memoranda in question, had a kind of morbid taste throughout his life for visiting prisons and conversing with criminals, more especially when they were ordered for execution, or suddenly snatched from the jaws of a violent death by an unlooked for reprieve; after noting their conduct, it was his practice to sift out the private character and public life of each individual criminal which came under his observation, probably with the laudable view of more accurately accounting for the cause of crime, than has hitherto been done. It is to be regretted, that one who appears to have devoted so great a portion of a life, protracted beyond the usual space of time allowed to man, should not have left us any account of the oject he had

in view, or that he should not in his writings himself have applied them to the solution of the problem he had proposed to himself, or of his own (no doubt) favourite theory. Be it what it may, but which is unknown to us, our posthumous documents are dry matters of fact, which will, however, furnish the curious reader with many amusing anecdotes, and be food for the philosophical man —studies offering him some very knotty questions of inconsistencies in the character of bipeds to reconcile and account for. The effects of punishment in lessening crime, is still a problem, and the individual or generic character of criminals is but very little understood by the legislature. Archbishop Whateley says, that the question is not, what effect punishment has upon the criminals, but what impression it makes upon the unconvicted of any crime; now this sentence is both unphilosophical and unchristianlike. Are we then not to judge of the probable effect punishment, or the dread of it, has upon mankind in general, by the conduct of those who are undergoing it, or of the general impression it makes on society, by the number who are found to disregard it, or who from their course of life seem to do so. Again, does the Christian perform his duty, who makes no effort to reclaim one fallen into crime? Yet, says the archbishop, it is little consequence what they think or say; where did the learned divine obtain his authority for this doctrine—surely not from the scriptures? His charity extends not to those unhappy wretches who in the world and the world's law often find no helper—who are pitied for a moment, and in a moment forgotten: and who perish without leaving any lasting impression of terror from their sufferings, which almost cease to be exemplary, when frequent, excessive, and promiscuous. The archbishop appears to have passed over the fact, that in all countries, the history of criminal man, furnishes as many instances of enormities committed by society, or those who govern it, upon individuals, as individuals have against society, if we omit cases of petty larceny; but if the primary causes of petty theft were known, it is probable that in the majority of cases, the generating causes would be found to be, *poverty*, or the want of proper *instruction* When another question would present itself viz. Whether governments may not be considered *criminis particeps* in many of the delinquencies of the country over which they rule. Legislatures have a trick of covering their want of skill, and more frequently want of honest intentions towards mankind, under the plea of the incorrigibility of man—of his inherent sin, and the inborn wickedness of his heart; they pass over the fact that is this very cause which prevents their making just and equitable laws—no people are happy, because no people have good laws, nor are there any really good men who obtain power to make them; the wickedness of heart they complain of is general. Weakness of judgment, and cruelty of disposition, have in all ages but too frequently been the associates of power; which operating on society, produces a reaction, generating opposition, and leading to the infraction of the laws, proceeding by steps till the greatest enormities are committed, which furnish the rulers of the people with further excuses for committing excesses and violence in legislation, and thus they proceed, accelerating and increasing the mischiefs they affect to counteract.

Man has ever with unrelenting assiduity felt a pleasure in exercising cruelty and torture upon his fellow creatures; sometime crucifying or burning them, at others tearing their limbs asunder, or breaking their bones upon the wheel; now again flaying them, or wrapping criminals in the warm skins of beasts and exposing them to wild dogs to be torn in pieces. The following is extracted from the *Morning chronicle* of September 2d, 1811:—"In May last, some robbers broke open the tomb of the mother of the Sultan Selim, at Constantinople, and robbed it of gold cloths and precious stones to the value of one hundred and fifty thousand piastres. Suspicion alighting on some Sclavonian slaves, they were taken up and put to the torture; two of them refusing to make confession, were impaled in the streets of Constantinople, and remained alive, but in dreadful agony, twenty-two hours."

In our own country, the most barbarous enormities have been perpetrated on man, under the sacred name of religion and justice. Even the pious and wise Sir Thomas More caused the rack to be used in his presence; and judges celebrated in their day for knowledge in all matters of law, and the affairs connected with the existence of man, have not much more than a hundred years since, been allowed to commit with impunity their legal murders. "I know not that Judge Powell was a weak or a hard-hearted man. But I do know that in the Augustan age of English literature and science, when our country was adorned by a Newton, a Halley a Swift, a Clarke, and an Addison, this judge, in 1712, condemned Jane Wenham, at Hertford, who, in consequence, perhaps, of a controversy that arose upon her case, rather than from any interposition of Powell, was not executed; and that four years afterwards, he at Huntingdon condemned for the same crime (witchcraft) Mary Hickes, and her daughter Elizabeth, an infant of eleven years old, who were executed on Saturday the 17th of July, 1716. At the beginning of the same century, of which English philosophers and English scholars talk with triumph, two unhappy wretches were hung at Northampton, the 17th March, 1705; and upon July the 22d, 1712, five other witches suffered the same fate, at the same place."—*Characters of Charles James Fox.*

This subject being introduced for the purpose of showing the prejudices and errors of those who have obtained credit for being wise and great men, I must be allowed to add the following remarkable instance of the influence which the current opinions of the times in which we live will have over the minds of the most enlightened men. I put the reader in mind that Lord Chief Baron Hale was one of the greatest judges of his day, and is quoted as an authority in our courts of law up to the present hour; also that Sir Thomas Brown was an eminent physician, and the author of a work entitled "Vulgar Error."

Amy Duny and Rose Callender were tried and condemned at Bury St. Edmonds, in Suffolk, by the Lord Chief Baron Hale. They were tried upon thirteen several indictments. Amy Duny was charged with bewitching Mr. Pacey's children, and causing them to have fits; and when Sir Thomas Brown, the famous physician of his time, who was in court, was desired by my Lord Chief Baron to give his judgment in the case, he declared 'that he was clearly of opinion that the fits were natural, but heightened by the devil co-operating with the malice of the witches, at whose instance he did the villanies;' and he added, 'that in Denmark there had lately been a great discovery of witches, who used the very same way of afflicting persons, by conveying pins into them.' This it is said, made the great and good judge doubt so much that he would not sum up, but left it to the jury to decide, 'praying that the great God of heaven would direct their hearts in that weighty matter.' The jury, having Sir Thomas Brown's declaration about Denmark for their encouragement, in half an hour brought them in guilty upon all the thirteen indictments. After this my Lord Chief Baron gave the law its course, and they were condemned and died declaring their innocence."

Readers, remember that in those days, as in the present, there were legislators who asserted that the penal laws of England did not admit of any amelioration. It would seem that we are never to approximate any nearer to perfection in the art of legislation, or in teaching the people morality; so long, however, as there are cruel and unjust laws, will the immoral and ignorant plead their severity in justification of revolt against them; just as a rebellious and perverse child reproaches an immoral father with his faults when corrected for those of his own commission. Every statute which enacts cruel and unjust punishment for minor offences, is a heavy crime committed by the legislature against the people; for, independently of the individuals who suffer under its provisions, it never fails of demoralizing the mass of the people. See the effect of the game laws, which were made for the accommodation of a few churlish country gentlemen, who now, when everybody can have game upon their table, disregard it, after having inflicted an irreparable injury upon mankind in general to obtain it.

Any law to be effective must be of that character, that the offender may know when the crime is committed that all his fellow men will exclaim he merits his punishment. On the contrary, it matters not how heavy the punishment may be, it will be disregarded if public commisseration accompanies its infliction.

The man who was boiled in Smithfield for the crime of poisoning, was conscious of having the pity of the public, and therefore braved his fate.

In the reign of Henry the Eighth, when the people were ruled with an iron hand, regardless of the character or feelings of the people, the executions were two thousand a year; but in the reign of Queen Elizabeth, when the Reformation introduced a purer religion and a more humane conduct, they decreased from two thousand to four hundred. All sensible parents are very justly afraid of hardening their children by severity; but government is not afraid of hardening the people by rigorous laws. Yet the maxims of one ought to guide the other; the whole community is but a family.

Burgh, in his "Political Disquisitions," advises us to imitate the conduct of the judicious Quakers, "who do more by their manner of educating their youth, and their treatment of them in consequence of their behaviour, than all the kings of Europe, with their laws and sanctions piled on one another to the height of mountains."

I now turn from these considerations to the subject of criminals as they have been seen and known in more recent days; beginning with those of familiar recollection, cases which afford to those who are curious of information regarding the human heart scope for the deepest contemplation; such as Fauntleroy, the Berner Street Banker, and Captain Montgomery, their cases were somewhat similar, yet were attended with distinct shades of difference.

Fauntleroy suffered for forging the names of the owners of Bank stock, by which he feloniously caused to be transferred into his own hands considerable—nay, enormous sums of money, still however continuing to pay the owners of the stock their half-yearly dividends on the same; it is to be observed, that he forgot no names, or made free with any sums of money belonging to those who were not connected with him in the way of business.

As a banker, he was agent to stock-holders residing in the country, and was authorized by them to receive the bank dividends accruing on their stock. The banking-house in which he was a partner being on one occasion run hard upon and in want of money, Fauntleroy, who was always estimated as a superior financier, undertook to raise the required sum, and this he did the very next morning. What he said to his partners, or how he accounted for his possession of the money, has not yet been known; probably, they were too hurried at the moment, and too glad to have the timely supply to be over-nice in their inquiries.

It is, however, now known that he went to the Bank, and, by means of forgery, transferred the money he obtained from the name of a customer to that of his own, conceiving, that the party would not, probably, so long as he lived, wish to sell out his stock, and therefore would remain unconscious of the use which had been made of it so long as he regularly received his dividends; if, however, it should occur that the stock was required, he calculated, as agent to the party, that he should have time to replace it, even if he should be driven to the necessity of making free with another person's stock in the same way as heretofore. And this he actually subsequently did many times; until he got involved in a labyrinth of transferred stock, and his accounts so built up one on the other, that there was no retreating before the world as an honest man—no path open to him either to stop payment or go on— nothing before him but ultimate ruin, disgrace, and punishment; yet in this state, by plunging desperately, and as it were daring the worst, he maintained the credit of the banking-house for upwards of eight years after the first fraud is supposed to have been committed. All this period, it should be observed, that his partners were totally in the dark as to his proceedings, he being the only real active partner in the firm.

The two men above named, were placed in that class which supposes that their crimes were committed from any other cause than that of poverty; at least that poverty which, in the general acceptation of the term, is considered as the prevailing cause of crime; these offenders therefore suggest the idea whether certain cases of public delinquency, may not, as some say of poetry, be referred to organization; or, as others affirm of the same art, that it may be ascribable to the self-determination of a strong will acting upon the accidents of individual destiny; or, again, may it not be asked, whether it be not a combination of both causes.

It appears that each of these men committed their offences deliberately, were men of education, and, moreover, had the benefit of a strong admonishing internal repugnance to commit crime; that is to say, their consciences were wide awake, and often pulled the check strick, as they themselves have subsequently acknowledged, and that each might, had they timely availed themselves of its warning voice, have been saved, even after the commission of many offences. Each also stated that they had a presentiment of their fate.

It would seem that there could be no traitors in the dominions of the prince of darkness, and that being once naturalised and embodied among his subjects, there is no letting off upon any terms.

Fauntleroy could, every day up to the one of his apprehension, have possessed himself of sufficient money to have carried himself out of danger; and if he could have brought himself to a life of obscurity and seclusion, might have spent the remainder of his days in independence.

This alternative, he said, constantly occurred to him; but although, at last, hourly in anticipation of detection, and notwithstanding the horror which at times came over his mind at his impending fate, he was, as he himself affirmed, spell-bound to the spot, which he never could summon resolution enough to break.

This may in a manner be accounted for by his attachment to more than one female; he was naturally amorous, and ultimately became licentious.

Men with perturbed minds sometimes purchase their *lethe*, or *nepenthe*, from Bacchus; Fauntleroy went to another market for this draught and drug—that of Venus.

A passion of any kind, by excessive indulgence will soon become preternatural, a more striking instance of which never occurred than in this case.

When wearied and oppressed with intensity of reflection, and borne down with the horrors of an ignominious death, and when nothing could rouse him even when in prison, his conduct towards women was remarkable.

Had it been lawful or consistent with the rules of Christian propriety to have made an experiment with him, I am convinced from memoranda in my possession and other facts known to me, that he would, if the opportunity had been allowed him, have gone through all the forms of making love to any female thrown in his way, and have continued so to engage himself up to the last hours perhaps of his existence.

In point of fact, this is not a *postulatum*, it all but did occur, dead as he was to all wordly affairs; while under sentence of death, the sight of a female awakened recollections and associations of the mind producing a manner and conduct on his part which were then incompatible with his then awful situation, and which can only be accounted for upon the principle I have stated; namely, morbid action of the nervous system, occasioned by the associations of the mind touching the chord of former recollections.

But of this presently I shall have something more to say.

During the whole period that he was conscious of being criminal, he never could endure to be left alone to his own thoughts;

when, therefore, disengaged from business, his whole time was spent, if not in visiting and receiving parties, in the company of his kept mistresses.

All persons denounce drunkenness as the most degrading vice—with a propensity for drink it is useless to boast of other virtues—they are but tinkling cymbals; granted, but a sober rogue is a more dangerous character than a drunken honest man.

Had Fauntleroy taken to drinking instead of women to drive away his reflections, his careers would have been short, and the injuries he did very much curtailed.

I do not mean to advocate or patronise drunkenness, but facts are facts, draw what inferences you may from them, and I shall avail myself of this opportunity to state one, without dread of their saintship's ire, namely, that all thorough-paced astute knaves are sober men ; and that they tell everybody of their virtue, wherever they meet them, spending one third of their time in expatiating against drunkenness—one third in sleep—and the other in studying and plotting how they may best cheat their neighbours or fellow men.

Many men have one favourite vice which they are anxious to disguise and cover by the practice of many virtues ; others are proud and ostentatious of a solitary virtue, the possession of which, they have persuaded themselves will carry them through and counterbalance all vices.

Frauds in trade, injustice and oppression of the poor, using divers or false weights and measures, usury, and dealing falsely with your friend, are all nothing, provided the party is a sober man, and has not been yet legally convicted of any offence.

"But God hath chosen the foolish things of the world to confound the wise ; and God hath chosen the weak things of the world to confound the things which are likewise mighty."

Charity, our forefathers thought, covered a multitude of sins.

You have now only to become a member of a temperance society, and you may have a cloak large enough to cover house, garden, orchard and paddock. Drink tea in public, and brandy in private—take especial care not to become inebriated in any place but your own bed-room, or when your wife is in the way to protect you from the public gaze, by answering to all inquiries, that you are not at home ; and, in what it may be asked, is the difference between this and the old mode of taking a bottle? Only, instead of enjoying your glass and the conversation of your friend at one and the same time, he opening his heart, and you your own, as the juice of the Tuscan grape warms its springs —you now, under the new system, have your conversation first at the tea party, and your glass when you return home.

It was a saying of my old grandfather's, (who by the bye knew something of human nature) that he made it a rule never to trust any man until he had, at least once, seen him drunk ; and a celebrated writer says " that the heart of a man is without disguise when in liquor.

Both old and young tradesmen agree in opinion that there is no man now to be known or trusted with safety. If you must give credit to any, it will be better to choose a middle course ; the confirmed drunkard will perhaps spend your money, but the temperance man will most assuredly rob you of it, and laugh at your gullibility afterwards. Avoid the temperance man in commerce as you would a known swindler. Coster was a very temperate man.

There is probably no instance on record, judging from Fauntleroy's education and station in life, of a sensitive mind enduring for so long a period a state of peril and danger, yet keeping up all the external appearance of gaity and self-possession ; though his acquaintance now say that it was evident he laboured to be at ease.

There can be no doubt but that the latter part of his career was spent in making efforts to disengage himself from his own thoughts, the hardest task for man to perform, and it is highly probable, had his detection been protracted much longer, that his mind would have broken down under the energies his unhappy situation called upon him to exert. The force of a fall is always in proportion to the height from which we are hurled ; the truth of this aphorism was illustrated in this case : he had no hope from the moment of his apprehension, his depression was the work of an instant ; the sight of the officer, whom he knew when he came into his presence (Plank, of Marlborough-street Police Office), operated upon him like a *coup soleil*, and he never afterwards rallied ; his heart indeed must always have been like a watch, which knows no repose until it ceases to beat. As regards money, for several years he appears to have been reckless of consequences, his habits were of the most extravagant character ; only a few hours before he was taken into custody, he had given some directions for furniture which was to be sent to Brighton, where he was fitting up a house for the residence of a female in a style unusually superb for any private person. When giving directions for the manufacture of some costly furniture, he said (this was on the very day he was apprehended) " Let every thing be done in a manner to eclipse the king's pavilion ; if my house be not so large as his palace, it may, at least, be as richly decorated "

"What mockery is the tinsel pride of splendour, when the mind is desolate within."

He was a very liberal subscriber to public charities, and often gave a sovereign when asked for alms by casual beggars in the streets; at other times he either was or affected to be very parsimonious; but all inconsistences in a man thus circumstanced may be ascribed to a troubled mind. When first placed before the public as a suspected criminal, at Marlborough-street Police Office, he appeared in a great coat, crouching his head into the collar of it for the purpose of concealing as much as possible his countenance, and with his arms folded. When committed to Newgate, he found favour with some of the City Aldermen, being accommodated contrary to all recent custom with very comfortable apartments in a portion of the prison devoted to the use of one of the turnkeys and his family, in this instance consisting of himself, wife and servant. The turnkey's wife was considered a pretty woman, at least she was a very pleasing and remarkably good natured woman; every thing was done which could, under the circumstances of his distressed situation, to alleviate his sufferings; he underwent none of the privations usually encountered in a prison—all his friends, both male and female, had free ingress and egress to his apartments, which was a favour rarely granted to one charged with so heavy an offence; he ordered his own dinner and drank his wine as usual after it, if he wished it, but nothing could rouse him from dejection, or put enough of the man into him, either to enable him to philosophise upon his situation and the causes which had placed him in it; or on the other hand, to imitate the desperate culprit and brave them. His conduct may be defined to be that of a sulky man, except when spoken to by a female, when, if she were but a servant, he affected politeness and unnecessary attention; perhaps he was not altogether (vain as it was) without a hope that he might make himself interesting enough to induce them to engage in some scheme for his escape; considered in another light, under the circumstances, his conduct was absurd and censurable to the last degree.

His trial is already before the public; it required but the forms of the court to pronounce a verdict of guilty, and for the judge to pass the sentence of the law, viz.—death. After which he gradually wore down by the intensity of internal agony, and the prospect of death before him; towards the last, he declined in flesh so rapidly, losing altogether his animal spirits, that if it had been possible to keep him another day, or even a few hours longer under the same impression of his proximity to the grim monster, it is a question whether pulsation would not have ceased under the mere apprehension of death.

"The weariest and most loathed worldly life,
That age, ache, penury, and imprisonment
Can lay on nature, is a paradise
To what we fear of death."

Even when sentence of death had been passed on him, and after the order for his execution arrived, he was allowed still to remain in the turnkey's apartments, instead of being removed to the cells, as is customary with all prisoners the instant a verdict of guilty for a capital offence is recorded against them.

It may be asked, whether there is either policy or justice in making these distinctions. Fauntleroy, if he could enjoy any bed, had a soft one up to the morning of his execution; besides this he had another indulgence granted him, the companionship of a favourite spaniel dog, upon which he was wont to look when sitting in his chair for hours; this animal he gave to the turnkey's wife, but after he lost his master he pined and wasted rapidly away until he died, when the owner of him (Mrs. H.) caused him to be stuffed, and placed in the turnkey's lodge, which leads to the apartments once occupied by his master in Newgate; and there he was to be seen a short time since, a monument of fidelity to man when deserted by all the rest of the world.

On the evening previous to the execution of Fauntleroy, the turnkey's wife went into his room, after having placed his clean linen, &c., ready for the forthcoming awful event, and asked him if there was anything further she could do for him; upon which he sprang up, and in a most romantic and impassioned manner said, after falling upon his knees before her—

"My dear lady," at the same time taking her hands and kissing them vehemently, "you behold the fallen Fauntleroy before you, I cannot but admire you!—I cannot but adore you!"

The object of this address exclaimed, "for God's sake, Mr. Fauntleroy, don't kneel to me, you, you must have other occasions to kneel."

"But I will," he continued; saying—"what can I do for you? What shall I say to you?" Then turning his pockets inside out, said, "here! this is all" holding out some money, "that is left in the world to Fauntleroy now to bestow on any one, take it for my sake with this purse."

He then handed her his purse, containing three sovereigns, with which, conceiving him to be (as she said) lightheaded, she escaped from the room.

It is very currently reported that his friends, through influence with the city authorities, caused a narcotic draught to be given him the evening before he underwent his sentence. Be this as it may, it is very certain that in the morning he was quite unconscious of what was being done with him.

He was taken from his room at thirty-five minutes after seven, and led between two men to the press-yard, there to be pinioned, and as the clock struck eight the procession which usually accompanies these miserable men to the scaffold, moved through the devious and long winding passages to the fatal drop ; and the way to which he was supported, and also while the finisher of the law performed his duty, being apparently in a perfect stupor during the whole proceedings.

It is very much the practice upon these occasions to say a great deal about penitence and the religious feeling of the culprits, all of which is very much misunderstood, and generally mis-stated.

All malefactors coming under a sentence of death, may be classed under two heads as regards general demeanour.

First—Those who are depressed and rendered so nervous through fear, that at no time can they collect their thoughts, or acquire steadiness of mind enough to calmly contemplate the perilous situation in which they are placed; every time they make an effort to figure death in their minds' eye, in order to reason thereon and prepare for the event, the mental faculties involuntarily refuse to come up to the sticking-place; a violent agitation or vibration of the whole nervous system supervenes, which ends in stupor, during which the patient can only get sleep : every time the effort and relapse takes place, the powers are weakened, the sufferer falling in them into a state of idiotcy, and in that condition is executed.

Fauntleroy was one of these men, in whom fear overpowered reason.

Secondly—Those whose coarser natures or tougher fibre have led them to plunge into crime in defiance of the law; these men, having accustomed themselves to place death in one eye, and licentiousness in the other, have in some measure their nerves ready strung for the issue.

Now the whole business of the ordinary is comprised in preserving public decency. The public must not see men hung up like lambs, or go off from the drop like lions; the feelings engendered in both cases are unfavourable to the end in view.

Example :—

The ordinary's duty, therefore, is simply to break down the spirit of the latter, and cheer up those of the former ; to tell one there is no hope for him of salvation, and the other that there is every hope, and to persuade each to walk quietly to the place of execution, and there submit to their fate.

In 1828, Captain John Montgomery was apprehended and charged with uttering forged notes.

He had been possessed of property, and was of a respectable Irish family ; circumstances connected with extravagant habits, and a fatal attachment to expensive women, reduced a gentleman, once respected as a man of honour, to an utterer of forged notes ; but his case is interesting in other points.

Notwithstanding the certainty of his criminality, (he pleaded guilty,) this man was ill-used.

It must be within the recollection of most readers, that when this crime was more frequently committed, the Governors and Company of the Bank of England were in the habit of consenting to the offenders pleading guilty to the minor offence, which spared their life, and subjected them to transportation only : these terms were conditional—namely, that they made a full disclosure of the means by which they became possessed of the forged notes.

When Montgomery was committed for trial, his attorney waited upon Mr. Freshfield, the attorney of the bank, and offered in case the bank would forego the capital charge, the prisoner should plead guilty to the minor charge of having the forged notes in his possession, and also give the necessary information respecting the manner by which he obtained them.

This proposition was favourably received, which induced him to send in a written confession, and a full statement of all the circumstances connected with his forged bank note transactions.

Notwithstanding this candour, however, a few days before his trial, he received a written notice that the bank intended to proceed against him to the uttermost ; but he had now gone too far to recede, and under the advice of his attorney, he, when brought up for trial, pleaded guilty, in the full hope and belief that the sentence of death would not be carried into effect.

In this hope he was disappointed, the council decided against his claim to mercy, another order came down for his execution.

During his confinement he was allowed to remain in the infirmary until the night preceding the day appointed for his execution, when he was removed to a cell in the press yard; he was locked in one of these dreary abodes by himself; about half-past six the following morning, one of the turnkeys went to warn him of the approaching hour, when he was discovered to be already dead.

On the table were several sealed letters, and a small phial bottle. An inquest was called, when it appeared that he had taken prussic acid, during the night, which was the cause of his death : indeed, his letters explained how he ended his life, with every particular regarding the hour when he took the permanently soporiferous draught, &c.

Men under sentence of death are generally pretty carefully watched during the day time, and at night never permitted to take anything into the cells with which they may commit suicide ; when, however, the order arrives for their execution, they are brought into the keeper's room, belonging to the press or condemned yard, and most rigorously examined—generally, indeed, stripped naked and made to open their mouths to satisfy the searcher that they have nothing about them ; he frequently rips open the collar, &c. of the coat, to further assure himself that his painful duty may be properly performed.

It is no doubt owing to this precaution, that so few suicides in the condemned cells have been committed.

Montgomery, as before noticed, was not placed in the cell until the night before his execution, when he underwent the strictest examination of his person, that he was not examined before and secluded, is accounted for by the very sanguine hope every one had of his being reprieved, in which hope it was well known he himself indulged, and therefore was not likely to destroy himself to defeat, as it is termed the ends of justice ; but in this case *injustice*, because he had although guilty, been deceived and entrapped into a confession under an implied promise sanctioned by previous practice. Now a question has arisen how he could obtain the prussic acid after he was locked up in the condemned cell : and more than one innocent person has been accused of being accessory in conveying it to him ; I can, however, now remove all doubts on the subject.

Long before he was taken into custody he had provided himself with this vehicle to carry himself far out of the reach of the hangman's hands ; and had so concealed it that it was all but impossible, under any search, to discover he had it about his person. Ill usage, family differences, an impatient temper, together with an amorous temperament, irregularly indulged, had plunged him into the commission of crime.

But he had not long been in it before he saw all the horrors of his situation, without, however, having the resolution to remove himself out of it ; affording another instance that unless the battle against the temptation to crime be fought *in limine*, and never allowed to enter the house, victory cannot be obtained.

Montgomery was a remarkable fine, well-built, and handsome man, to which were joined showy talents, agreeable manners, and a good education. He was, moreover, very frank and candid, discussing freely and without disguise his own errors, conversations on which subject with himself these remarks are founded.

He says, that for months before he was apprehended his name was never mentioned that he did not think it was an officer ; he had the sense of wrong-doing, and the consciousness of danger, but in all other respects he describes his mind as being in a mist —in a state of irresolution and confusion— it appeared as if the hand of fate were upon him, and that it was in vain to make an effort to turn his destiny aside ; in this state he thought of the hangman, and resolved to cheat him. His original intention was to have destroyed himself when ever taken into custody, and being aware of the practice of disencumbering all suspected persons of their moveables, he hit upon the scheme which ultimately served his purpose ; having purchased a *l'huile* or scent bottle, about an inch long and one-third of an inch in diameter ; this he caused to be filled with prussic acid, and adroitly managed to keep it about his person, and thus prepared himself for the worst which could happen.

He was a man of undaunted courage, and his letters, which were written only a few minutes before his departure, prove that he shook hands with death as he would with an old acquaintance. The anecdote to which he referred when using the French phrase *une facon de parler*, in his last written letter to a friend, is already before the public, and therefore need not be repeated here.

Montgomery, while in prison, entertained hopes that should his sentence be commuted to transportation, that he should be enabled to escape and reach Persia, where it was his intention to enter the Persian cavalry ; and from the judicious plan he had conceived, and the assistance which was offered him, I have but little doubt he would have succeeded.

A singular occurrence took place whilst he was awaiting his trial.

A lady came in her carriage to the prison —it is said she was possessed of a considerable fortune—and after seeing the governor, was permitted to come and view the person of Montgomery from the roof of the building, as he took exercise in the yard beneath, several days successively.

She was heard to say, that if he escaped, her hand and fortune should be devoted to him, if he would accept them.

She was herself very handsome, and it was understood, had before seen Montgomery ; but he was not aware of the impression he had made, nor was he acquainted before he died of this visit to the prison.

CHAPTER CXI.

COLONEL JACK MEETS WITH A STRANGE ACQUAINTANCE.

SOME few days after the conviction and execution of Mr. Ralph Bunkham, Colonel Jack, who had been out on professional business, with Hackett and Knapp, was returning home in the vening towards London. He had passed over that locality so celebrated for highwaymen and duels, known then, as it is now, by the name of Wormwood Scrubs. He was within an hour's ride of the great metropolis, and was in one of those reflective moods which often came over him when left alone.

After passing the Scrubs, he came in sight

of a closed gate which opened on the highway. As he reached this he walked his horse leisurely towards it ;—as he did so, he descried the figure of a man leaning against its post. He was at once struck with his appearance. His figure was tall, gaunt, and powerful—his face regular in every outline, but singularly repulsive—as to his age, it would have been impossible to have guessed it with any degree of certainty; it might be fifty, or might be five and twenty, its indications were so contrary. His dress was squalid as a mendicant's—his air, when the colonel desired him to open the gate, careless almost to insolence.

He did open it, however, and our hero flung him sixpence in return, which he picked up and pocketted, without any observation.

Colonel Jack passed through the open

gate, and when he had gone a few paces he reflected for a moment upon the strange character of the stranger. There was something curiously attractive about him, and the colonel pulled up and, as a matter of curiosity, addressed him—

"You seem in poverty, my friend,—out of work, I presume?"

"Do I look a man likely to work?"

"Egad, you look like, much like a man who would"—the colonel paused.

"Oh, don't be particular; I'll finish the sentence for you," continued the man—"rather rob, blast it. Eh?"

"You are a strange fellow; you have divined my meaning. Have you no trade?"

"I have fifty," returned the man.

"A soldier in your time, I dare be sworn?"

"You are right."

"And at sea, occasionally, perhaps?"

The man nodded an affirmative.

"Could you name your other callings?"

"Umph, they would be rather tedious to enumerate. I have been a player and a gipsy,—a clown and a quack,—a smuggler and a spy,—a peeler and a pugilist,—touter to an hotel, hound in a hell, a thimble-rigger, swept a crossing, was guard to a coach, mute to an undertaker, and assistant to a pawnbroker."

"And what, then, are you supposed to be doing now?"

"Leaning against this gate, for want of better employment," was the sarcastic reply.

"Have you dined?"

"No, hang me if I have, not for the last fifteen days."

"Have you no home?"

"Yes, the highway."

"The highway!" exclaimed our hero in some surprise.

"Oh, don't be alarmed, your person and money are secure; I am a wanderer, and not a highwayman or footpad."

The colonel smiled, and inquired if he had any relatives.

"I have, no doubt, but I never knew them. For aught I know, I may be the offspring of a pickpocket or a peer."

"You are a strange fellow," said our hero, much struck by the man's answers. "I'll order dinner in the next village, or, rather, the next roadside house we come to, and you shall have a feed at my expense, and a glass of grog afterwards. What say you to that offer?"

"Well, were it but for the novelty of the thing, I will accept of your offer."

The colonel pulled his horse up to a walk, and rode slowly on, the stranger following. On arriving at the nearest house, he gave directions that the man should be accommodated with a substantial repast, and giving his horse to the ostler, the two—our hero

and his companion—took possession of the parlour, in which there were, fortunately enough, no other visitors.

A comfortable dinner seemed to smooth down the ferocity of the stranger's nature, for he actually condescended to thank his patron for the kindness offered him. Not only his features but his feelings had undergone a change, and in the reckless being before him the colonel perceived he could discover relics of manly beauty, which, in wild youth, had been envied by one sex and admired by the other. Our hero offered him brandy—he drank again and again—his rigid features gradually relaxed—the sneer was exchanged for a smile—the harshness of a grating voice softened by degress—and, as he placed the empty glass on the table, he thus addressed the colonel—

"Forgive my rudeness to you when we first met; I was just then smarting under vulgar insolence, and men, who at night have neither breakfasted in the morning, or supped on the previous night, are not apt to be in the best of all possible tempers."

The colonel stared at the outcast. The tone of his voice was gentlemanly and; his language fluent and correct; and yet—there he was, a thing of rags—a walking scarecrow.

"Who and what are you?" exclaimed our hero.

"You ask me more than I find it convenient to answer," was the reply—then after a pause, he said—"Would you like to hear the revelations of an ambitious love?"

"Ambitious love!" exclaimed his companion.

"Ah, no wonder you smile—ambitious love!" More brandy; there's life in that—I feel it course through every vein, and warm this frozen heart. Listen, sir stranger."

The colonel made a signal for him to proceed.

"I never knew my parents," he said with a sigh. "I was left on the steps of Lord——'s mansion, in Grosvenor Square. From the place selected, and the time chosen for my exposure, I am led to the inference that my parentage was genteel."

"I was nursed by the gamekeeper's wife—introduced in due time to the third table of the servants' hall—kicked for a year or two by every menial in the establishment—fancied by the young heir—patronised in consequence by his lady mother—rose rapidly into favouritism — divided the affections of the Marchioness with a French poodle—became playmate of the heir—acquired the education from his tutor which his dull intellects could not receive, and, at eighteen, travelled with him as a companion. After two years we returned — he twenty one, and I a year younger.

"My history, were it detailed at length,

would reach over volumes. For you two or three rough sketches will be sufficient.

"At twenty-one, Lord Adolphus was five feet six, thin, ricketty and consumptive. Like the body, the mind was imbecile. He was cold, proud, and uncompanionable, and from constitutional infirmity unable to enter into the pleasures of the world. No equal sought his friendship—no woman's eye brightened at his approach. Without the tastes and talents which charm a secluded life, Lord Adolphus was, in habit and manner, almost a misanthrope. The father's soul and thoughts were centred in the political movements of the day, and, though the existence of an ancient name and lineage rested on the frail chances of continuance, and hung on the life of a feebly constituted youth, the Marquis of —— strained after wealth and honours with as much avidity as if the foundations of his house had been adamantine.

"To perpetuate the noble name of ——, Lord Adolphus's early marriage had been decided on, and while we were absent on the continent every preliminary had been arranged for an union immediately after his return with the daughter of an earl. That there was the slightest necessity to consult Lord Adolphus on the subject, his noble father never for a moment believed, and the perfect indifference with which the young lord received the intelligence of an early union with a lady he had never seen, justified the Marquis in the opinion he had formed.

"I had, apparently, taken more interest in the projected union of my friend than himself, and had, therefore, made enquiries touching the noble family with whom he was soon to be allied. The world's estimate of the earl was not favourable. In youth a *roue*, in middle age a gambler, he had been driven from society by enormous losses, and obliged to submit to seclusion from the world, which he felt to be intolerable. A tyrant father, he had forced his only son to become an alien—his only crime a refusal to join his infatuated parent in raising sums of money to dissipate in the race-course, or at the hazard table. Darker crimes were imputed to the earl. He had killed unfairly in a duel on the continent a gentleman from whom he had won a heavy sum, and who had openly declared that he had been cheated. And a young lady, his own ward, it was said, had been seduced by her false guardian, and afterwards was missing. With Lord Adolphus's father the political influence, and not the private character of this unworthy nobleman was considered.

"I have described the heir to the title and estates of the ancient house of——, and I may now add a personal sketch of the playmate of his youth and the companion of his manhood, myself. Nay, start not—he was then a model for a statuary—the mould was faultless,—and women said the face had all that wins the favour of the softer sex. He had profitted by early education, and the advantages of early travel had not been lost upon him. To exterior advantages, a daring spirit and latent ambition burning for worldly distinction were united. Such was the companion of Lord Adolphus—such the wreck of manhood—the thing of misery—the ragged outcast on whom you look."

He paused, a burning tear stole down his sun burnt cheek, and every limb and feature quivered as if an ague fit had smitten him. Colonel Jack ordered another glass; he drained a considerable portion of its contents, and in another moment regained his composure and thus continued—

"An early day was named for our departure to the north, when Lord Adolphus was to make acquaintance with the family to whom he was about to be allied, and in due form he was presented to his future bride. Of course I was to accompany him; for, from his nervous temperament every thought and movement was under my direction, and without me Lord Adolphus was as helpless as an infant. His father remarked the infirmity of his son's character and saw in me the stay on which he rested. But it seemed to have escaped the deep penetration of the wily marquis that a more dangerous companion could not have been selected, for mentally and phisically the contrast was glaring the visit to the earl's proved that truth. The indifference which Lord Adolphus had evinced for the hymeneal arrangements concluded by his father gradually gave place to alarm as we drew nearer to the residence of the bride elect; and when we entered the park gates he became painfully excited. To his nervous disposition a new and strange family were always sufficiently formidable, had he been but a common place visitor; but the serious nature of the engagements which we came to ratify to one like Lord Adolphus were absolutely appalling. I used every argument to overcome his timidity; but as to inspiring him with confidence that I found to be an utter impossibility. When we descended to the saloon after making our toilette he actually leaned upon me for support, like some weak trembling girl. To the end we had been already introduced. A footman threw open the drawing-room door, and announced us. With that ceremony all self possession seemed to desert my unfortunate friend, and when we entered the presence of Lady—and her daughter. Lord Adolphus who had fallen back a step or two looked pale and affrighted as though he were about to be led to execution.

"The earl unfortunately was absent and

a painful mistake occured. Our identity was not understood. I was supposed to be the gallant suitor, and Lord Adolphus his humble companion. Under this misconception I was presented to Lady Caroline by the countess ; and to both that introduction occasioned a present embarrassment and a future misery.

" I have seen loveliness of every grade and in every clime and were I to live life over I would declare that she who was there for the first time introduced to me was the most peerless and loveliest of her sex. A detail of beauty from lips like mine would be simply disgusting—a mere outline will suffice for our present purpose. Lady Caroline was nineteen, but you might have imagined her a year or two older. Her charms were perfectly natural and her beauty commanding. To a figure of the finest proportions, a face of singular loveliness was united. Indeed, but she was very beautiful altogether ; and yet if in Lady Caroline there was much to idolise—there was at the same time much to dread. When the first glance of unquallified admiration had ended and the eye was permitted to examine calmly that matchless specimen of Nature's handwork, a heart cold enough to find fault would not be disappointed—the haughty character of the face—a manner which bespoke impatience of contradiction, air, walk, and carriage all demanded admiration. Her beauty's spell was not that steals imperceptibly upon the heart by soft approaches. Homage was required as a right ; but at so proud a shrine, timid love would fear to make his offering. When the countess took my hand and was about to present it to her daughter an approving smile brightened the fair ones eyes and the haughty features of Lady Caroline evinced a secret satisfaction. To me the personal mistake was painfully humiliating, and while vanity was gratified, pride was wounded to the quick.

" ' Pardon me, Lady,' I muttered, ' allow me to introduce my noble friend,' and I turned to Lord Adolphus.

" Never did an unexpected announcement occasion more evident annoyance to all concerned. To me it was an exposure of dependency, and the countess was mortified in having mistaken the shadow for the substance. My nervous companion had marked the flush of approbation with which Lady Caroline had viewed her husband in expectancy ; but all these united fell immeasurably short of the agonised disappointment which the changing features of the bride elect betrayed.

" In a moment the blush of pleasure faded from her cheeks—her rosy lips were bloodless —her brows contracted, and eyes whose language had invited love exchanged it for an expression of scornful indifference. Poor Lord Adolphus timidly advanced—the lady's hand was formally delivered to him by her mother ; he trembled as he took it, and when he strove to speak he muttered unintelligible words. With a contemptuous glance the proud beauty surveyed the person her mother had presented, and then turning her eyes in disgust away as the curling lip told that the impression had been an unfavourable one.

" The evening of that inauspicious day was to all parties anything but agreeable. The earl a proud, scornful, unamiable man, was not a person calculated to remove the constitutional timidity with which his future son-in-law was inflicted. The manners of his lady were cold and unceremonious, and the bride elect seemed to endure but not return the attentions of a suitor whom she evidently despised. Of the party I was the most at ease and when we separated after supper I overheard the earl mention me in flattering terms to Lord Adolphus, while vanity told me that Lady Caroline's ' good night' was strikingly different from the cold formality with which she parted from her lord elect—him whom in a brief month she was to promise, to love, honour, and obey."

" You ought to have gone in and won," said Colonel Jack, with a smile.

" You shall hear how things progressed. If I had won I should not have the honour of sitting opposite a gentleman like yourself," answered the outcast.

" A fortnight passed and I found myself in a position exquisitely painful. At the desire of Lord Adolphus I had wooed a bride by proxy, and the earl perfectly acquainted with the proud and uncompromising nature of his daughter, tacitly intrusted me to the delicate task of removing objections to a union which at times threatened to overturn preliminary arrangements and interpose obstacles fated to the contemplated marriage. A close intimacy between Lady Caroline and myself was the result. When my friend accompanied the earl in his rides I was the escort of the intended bride.

" At first she listened with disgust—again with impatience—and finally she begged of me not to again allude to an union which every day became more and more repulsive and disgusting to her.

" What strange beings men are. From his extreme sensibility, it might be supposed that Lord Adolphus would have recoiled from accepting a hand when the heart which should accompany it was peremptorily engaged ; but by a singular infatuation, an alliance he had contemplated with indifference, became now the engrossing object of his soul. His feelings towards Lady Caroline were inexplicable —he both loved and feared her.

"I had passed an hour in his chamber, and had informed him that the progress of his suit was worse than slow. I left him for the night, and found a *billet* attached to my pillow. I broke the seal—it was brief as 'woman's love,' and ran thus :—

"'At one o'clock meet me in the library.'

"Meet whom? I was puzzled. Who could that peremptory mandate come from? It could only be from one.

"The clock struck twelve when I read this mysterious and singular summons. I sat down, and began to seriously reflect upon my strange position. I, the agent of another, was wooing one whom I loved to desperation —one, so immeasurably removed beyond the possibility of being mine; but that very thought was madness.

"And yet her conduct to me was almost inexplicable. Haughty and impatient, she courted interviews again and again, and after insulting rejections of Lord Adolphus's suit, gave me fresh opportunities of renewing my importunities in his favour.

"I was at no loss to detect the secret motives which influenced the haughty fair one, and though she fancied it was unperceived, I had marked already the struggle between pride and love. The state of her affections was past concealment, and when I had sought Lord Adolphus, I had unconsciously won a heart destined for another.

"'You are true to the appointed time," observed the lady, assuming an indifferent manner, which ill assorted with pale cheeks and heavy eyes. 'My maid succeeded in conveying the billet I entrusted to her care?'

"'She did, my lady,' I answered.

"I would have requested this meeting verbally, but after an interview with my father, I found that you had retired to Lord Adolphus's chamber. I have written to him, and in the morning he will receive my letter.'

"'May I hope that the communication is more favourable than the sentiments you expressed this morning. I do hope and trust, madam, that you will alter your determination with respect to my friend and companion, Lord Adolphus.'

"'He has by this time received my letter,' she answered, with some degree of hauteur, 'or if not now, he will have it the first thing to-morrow morning. In it I have stated my determination, which is merely a repetition of what I told the earl this evening.'

"'And what may that be?' I ventured to inquire, as I awaited her reply with breathless uncertainty for those words to fall from her lips which were to encourage the wildest hopes or doom me to despair.

"For a moment she raised her eyes, and they met mine. Her face became suddenly suffused with a deeper tinge of red—her forehead flushed—and in a voice half smothered with emotion, she exclaimed, passionately—

"'Cold hearted man!—is it for woman to tell the secret of her heart?'

"The spell was broken. The next moment I was kneeling at her feet, while her head drooped upon my shoulder, and a flood of tears followed the avowal of love.

"I can hardly tell you what followed. Hurried on by the sudden declaration of our mutual passion, we became almost delirious. We plighted our troth, and swore that death should alone divide us. Every prudential consideration had vanished—the gulf which rank and fortune had interposed between us, was overlooked. I, a nameless man, a nameless outcast, a dependant, I was to aspire to the hand for which the heir to the haughtiest house in Britain had sued in vain.

"In a dream of felicity that seemed superhuman, an hour passed away. The clock struck two—'twas time to separate—so we both said—but parting's such sweet sorrow, that the chimes had sounded three before I tore myself from my charming companion, and with noiseless steps stole through the corridor and regained my own room.

"As to sleeping, that was out of the question. I lay tossing on my couch, and I asked myself if what had passed was reality or only a dream. The rapture of the moment when we two had exchanged mutual vows of love and constancy had so completely engrossed Lady Caroline and myself that all other matters were disregarded, and all I learned of her interview with the earl was, that the scene had been, on both sides, stormy and disagreeable. We had arranged a meeting for to-morrow, an affair in no way difficult to arrange, from the intimacy which existed. My haughty mistress did not appear at the breakfast table, and I had not much difficulty in guessing the cause of her absence. The gloomy expression of her father's countenance confirmed my suspicions. A letter was placed in Lord Adolphus's hand; as he read it, his agitation was painfully apparent. He rose and left the room; whereupon the earl rose and immediately followed. In an hour I received a summons to the library, and there found my young friend and his father in earnest conversation.

The scene of the preceding night vividly returned as I gazed over the apartment. At the table where the earl and his guest were seated I had knelt at the feet of his proud daughter, and heard her own undying love for one who could not even boast that he possessed a name. Here our vows of eternal attachment were interchanged, her lips were pressed to mine to seal the compact.

"' Sit down, Mr. Fortescue," said the earl, as he pointed to a chair. "We have sent for you as a trusty friend to communicate an unexpected embarrassment which has arisen through the silly caprice of a wayward girl, and beg your assistance and advice in smoothing the difficulty away.'

"I bowed, and Lord Adolphus briefly observed that, from the tone of Lady Caroline's letter he feared that any attempt to remove the ladies objections would be hopeless. I had noticed the stern displeasure of the earl's face at breakfast, for which my recent interview with his daughter had prepared me, but now there was an expression in his features which almost amounted to ferocity, as he bit his pallid lips, and muttered with a deep imprecation that, 'never had the object on which he had fixed his heart been thwarted nor while he had life should it ever be.' I read his character and trembled.

"The earl was a determined and vindictive man, who would throw away every softer feeling to the four winds of heaven, and bend or break the spirit that dared to oppose itself to his.

"A long and unsatisfactory conversation followed—it ended as I had anticipated; the earl would not trust himself a second time with the refractory beauty—Lord Adolphus's pride and timidity forbade him to seek an interview. I was supposed to be the only person who might probably obtain a patient hearing, and so, accreditted by her father and recent suitor, I requested and obtained permission to visit the *boudoir* of the wayward beauty.

"When I entered the apartment her maid retired and we were left tete-a-tete. Victorine undertaking to keep watch, and ward, and secure us from interruption. I will not attempt a description of an interview, where 'madness ruled the hour,' and every prudential consideration was forgotten. Let it suffice to declare that we decided upon an elopement, and had I have had enough common sense to have looked to consequences, the tameless spirit of Lady Caroline would have swept away from before her will every obstacle that would have opposed it. So personal vanity on my part was amply gratified, every better principle should have revolted from the wild prospect that lay before me. To the earl my conduct was at least inhospitable—to Lord Adolphus false and ungrateful—to her the cause of all still more inexcusable. She knew not the circumstances of my disgraceful truth—she never dreamed that the humblest serf that toiled in her father's domains was my superior. I could perceive that to veil her pride and stoop even to be the wife of a private gentleman had caused her a deadly struggle; but were she told that I had been

casually pushed up and was indebted for name to the menial who found me, what would her feelings be at an alliance with a foundling? I was master of a few hundred pounds—whence came they? from the pocket of him whom I was deceiving, and the hand that supported me, and the house which took in the outcast was destined from that base ingrate to receive the deadliest blow which could be inflicted on it."

"How often is such the case throughout life," said Colonel Jack. "How often do we warn into life an adder that turns round and stings us."

"Lady Caroline was in her own right nobly dowered, another year would bring an ample independence, and the liberality of the family I was about to injure supplied the means by which the interval could be passed.

"It was desirable to gain a few days' time, and Lady Caroline yielded to necessity.

"She was but a sorry actress, and her forced endurance of Lord Adolphus's timid assiduities, would have been evident even to a stranger. Upon her father, this compromising conduct was not lost; his suspicions were awakened—he tried Victorine—gold succeeded, and she betrayed us.

"On the succeeding night we were to quit —— Castle for the continent. Every precaution had been made. Victorine, of course, was busy packing her mistress's wardrobe—I had secured post horses, with some difficulty —and, as I fancied, our intended elopement was unsuspected.

"During the morning I had no opportunity of conversing with Lady Caroline; but we met in the drawing-room before dinner, and none but ourselves were present. I fancied that something had flurried the fair fugitive—she was pale—her manner agitated.

"' Be cautious,' she replied, to a hurried inquiry, 'I fear we are betrayed. I saw my father's valet part from Victorine in the shrubbery. To thwart him in a trifling matter would be dangerous; in his present object—one on whose success his heart is fixed—to cross his path were fatal. Observe him—I know his temper well—if he frowns upon me fear nothing, if he smile, then dread the worst. Think not that with woman's timidity, I shrink from the coming trial, and because the sky is clouded, that I would hold back. No! at the appointed hour, come good come ill, I shall be at the park wicket. Until our meeting, be circumspect. The door opens no more. At one we meet for the last time in the library.'

"She ceased. That last concluding sentence was ominous. *For the last time!* Prophetic phrase! It was indeed the last time."

"You had a sort of foreshadowing of what was to follow," said Colonel Jack; "for I take it for granted that you did not succeed in carrying off and espousing the fair young lady."

The narrator continued.

"The dinner passed in dull formality, and never did a less hilarious group assemble round a festive board. Lord Adolphus seemed in wretched spirits, and Lady Caroline's assumed indifference was altogether forced and unnatural. The earl, alone, was perfectly at ease, and did the agreeable to an almost alarming extent.

"Then it was that I thought of his daughter's warning. Danger lurked in every smile, and I felt the wine-pledge, interchanged between the host and me, could wishes have effected it, the liquor would have been deadly poison.

"I never met with a more exquisite dissembler. No word or look betrayed the inward workings of his malignant spirit, and when we deserted the hall for the drawing-room, more than once he addressed his daughter as 'dear Caroline.'

"The evening wore away, chime after chime sounded from the belfry, and at eleven o'clock we parted for the night.

"Lord Adolphus complained of a headache, and retired directly to his chamber; and I, after bidding the ladies a formal 'good night,' sought my own apartment, to wait the trysted hour, and, as I hoped, keep my last secret appointment with my future bride.

"The interval which occurred was a painful one, the gloomiest apprehensions haunted my mind, and at the slightest sound my heart palpitated. A feeling as of some impending calamity oppressed my spirits, and it was in vain that I attempted to rally my courage, and nerve myself for the daring step which was now unavoidable.

"I fancied the stroke from the clock tower, as it beat one, vibrated through the long corridor like a death knell.

"I rose and obeyed the summons, and as I entered the library, Lady Caroline unclosed a private door, and advanced with trembling steps to meet me.

"In a female so young, I had never witnessed a prouder or more daring spirit; but to-night the woman had become paramount, and she was unusually depressed.

"We sat down on an ottoman—I endeavoured to remove her apprehensions, and had partially succeeded. She fancied that Victorine was faithful, and that her interview with the earl's valet, was merely an *affair de cœur*. Still neither of us felt at ease, and the slightest noise created an alarm, which she evinced and I concealed.

"'Caroline,' I whispered, as my arm clasped her waist, and her beautiful head rested on my shoulder, 'one day more, and we shall be beyond the power of those who

sever the union of hearts that love like ours.'

"'Would that we were,' she exclaimed. 'While within my father's reach, the miserable wretch prostrate beneath the lion's paw, is in not more imminent peril. Ah! did you know how at the bare thought of rousing him to vengeance I—and I am no coward—I positively tremble.'

"'Courage!' I exclaimed, 'parental tyranny shall be exchanged for devoted and constant love. This bosom, sweet one, shall be your resting place, and one day more shall make you mine for ever.'

"'Your's! scoundrel—your's! audacious villian!' exclaimed a voice of thunder, as every door of the apartment flew, open, and men with lights and weapons rushed in.

"The earl, with a pistol in each hand, advanced. The ottoman divided us, and although his daughter clung to my arm, he raised and snapped the flint. The pistol did not explode, and, muttering a deep curse he flung it on the carpet, and then changed it for its fellow. I, by a desperate impulse, caught up a book from the table, and as the murderer levelled the second weapon, I flung it at him. At the moment of explosion the book smote him heavily on the arm, the ball diverged—a cry—a fall—too surely told that it had struck his daughter. I know no more—a desperate blow from behind stretched me senseless—and when reason returned— Merciful heavens! I can proceed no further."

The outcast became convulsed, his features writhed, his limbs trembled! He hastily caught up the flask. Poor wretch! the only antidote for misery like his was that balm of consolation for desperate men—brandy.

"Well," said Colonel Jack, kindly. "It's no use dwelling upon the bitter recollection of the past. I have had enough of these myself and have now. Proceed my friend."

After a long pause the wanderer continued his melancholy story.

"When recollection gradually dawned upon me I found myself in a carriage which appeared to travel rapidly; but from the obscurity of the night I could neither ascertain the direction we were driving in, or discover whether I was alone or had companions in the vehicle. I felt my position uneasy—my head was dreadfully painful, and the movement of the carriage increased the agony I suffered when I endeavoured to raise myself in the carriage, I groaned.

"'He is not dead!' remarked a voice beside me, in whose foreign accents I recognised those of the French valet of the earl.

"Then he has a skull not to be broken by a poker, for by Heaven the blow I struck would have felled an ox,' returned a second speaker.

"A confused recollection of the scene in the library recurred. I strove to question my companions, but the words died upon my lips in feeble mutterings—my head swam, and then once more I fainted.

"When consciousness came back and I awoke as if from a fearful dream I found myself stretched ʃupon a matress in a room or rather cell, for the window was grated and the roof arched. A burning thirst tormented me—it was now broard daylight and my dizzy eye fell upon a water pitcher. I strove in vain to reach this vessel, my hand fell powerless by my side after this effort, and like another Tantalus with the means beside me I could slake a thirst which seemed insatiable. As I gazed in agonising despair upon the water, bolts were withdrawn, the door was unclosed and a man of strange and savage appearance entered.

"'Oh, oh!' he exclaimed. 'Umph! calmer, I see. Very well, you choose to live, it seems—"

"'Water!—water! for mercy's sake!' I feebly articulated.

"'Oh, there's no scarcity of that here,' he growled, as he raised the pitcher to my burning lips; and as I drank again and again, the fellow eyed me with a sort of infernal and malignant sneer.

"'Nice, ain't it?' said he.

"'Oh, so refreshing.'

"'Ah, capital beverage, with something else in it just to qualify it,' he answered. 'Lord, Lord, how the world wags—claret yesterday at my lord's table, but to day a humbler beverage serves your turn.'

"'For mercy's sake tell me where I am?' I asked.

"'Bah! ask no impertinent questions. Let's have a look at your head.'

"He turned me roughly, and I expressed the pain I felt by a scream of agony which, at the time, was irresistible.

"'Psha! what ails the man?' said the ruffian, for such he in reality. 'Upon my conscience, the earl has some hard strikers in his establishment, and one of them made an ugly opening in your skull last night. Lie gently'

"With savage indifference, but evidently with some skill, the fellow proceeded to dress and bandage my wounded head; and while the operation proceeded, it seemed to cause him but little anxiety whether he inflicted pain or not, either personal or mental, it was a matter of perfect indifference to him.

"'Umph!' he exclaimed, 'I don't think the skull is fractured after all. And so, nothing but an earl's daughter would content you? Ambitious man Be still, now, the job is nearly completed, and made to look as nice as possible. And so you who were employed to seek my lady for your lord, must needs go and woo her on your own account. Very pretty—very pretty, indeed. There, it is done, and not a surgeon in the whole neighbourhood could patch a damaged skull in shorter time. Pray from whom am I to expect my fee?—you, or your kind host, the earl?'

"'For God's sake give me drink—some more water!'

"'Oh, of that I can give you plenty—drink,' and again he placed the pitcher to my lips.

"'Where am I? Pray tell me! Is this a gaol?'

"'A gaol!' exclaimed the ruffian, with a sneer. 'Would you find the comforts of this chamber in a prison?—and could a gentleman of my polished manners be a gaoler?'

"'Tell me that I am not under restraint,' I returned, passionately. 'I am incarcerated —in a prison—a—'

"He had folded his dressings up, and prepared to quit the cell, but stopped a moment in the doorway.

"'And so you fancy yourself in gaol!' he said.

"'I feel convinced of it.' I replied.

"'Well, how people will deceive themselves; you are only—'

"'Where—where?—quick, do not keep me on the rack.

"'Only in a madhouse,' he answered, and slammed the door—the bolts were turned, and I was left to misery, solitude, and despair.

"Six weeks passed. My recovery was slow, indeed, at one time doubtful; but though the wound was severe, the extensive hæmorrhage prevented fever, and ultimately saved my life. The dietary was also favourable—bread and water, and that in a quantity not over-abundant effected a perfect cure.

"When I remonstrated against the restraint imposed upon me, and demanded to know on what grounds I was placed in my present state of confinement, I received according to my keepers mood, a savage word or else a sneer.

"'Why should I be hear?' I demanded 'I am not mad.'

"'Patience,' replied my comforter. 'One more year and you shall have no cause to make that complaint my friend.'

"In ten days I was able to quit my pallet, and sit beside the grand window. It was but a dreary prospect on which it looked, a dull, desolated garden, with high walls, grass-grown walks, unclipped hedges, and every appearance that indicated former elegance and later neglect.

"Closely imprisoned, a brutal wretch my gaoler, my spirits sunk, my mind became morbid, and no doubt I should have sunk into gloomy madness, had I endured the miserable probation my keeper hinted at.

We are, after all, the mere creatures of circumstances, and accident preserved reason and probably continued life.

"Whatever might have been the general arrangement of the establishment it would seem that the desolate garden my window overlooked, was forbidden ground to the inmates of the prison house. During three long and weary evenings, while I gazed from the grating of my cell, no living thing appeared to disturb my melancholy musings. The singular history of my life was recalled to my memory, its leading incidents passed in shadowy review, the last fatal scene rose to my mind's eye, while wild ambition and wilder love, were sadly contrasted with present sufferings, embitterd by the conviction that death alone would end them. Hours

passed—the last visit of the keeper had been made—and still I gazed in listless misery from the window. I sighed, and was answered. Was it fancy? The night was bright and starry, and I pressed my face against the iron bars, to gain a more extended view up the deserted garden. A minute passed—alas, it was a delusion—and the sigh an echo of my own. No living thing was near. Hush! there is a movement underneath—a foot treads softly on the gravel—a human figure issues into the stream of moonlight which is flung across the parterre below. By heavens, a woman! Ah, shall I ever forget that night, when I first saw thee, poor Mary!

"I attracted her notice, and she informed me that she was in this horrid madhouse a prisoner like myself, but she was permitted to walk in the garden at the rear of the premises. She was pale and wan, but was, even in her misery, very, very beautiful!"

The outcast sighed, and again had recourse to the brandy flask.

"Well, go on," said Colonel Jack.

"You must know that I had by this time but one thought—one absorbing thought; it was, how I could best make my escape from this infernal hole. In the course of a few days after my interview with the unknown, I was permitted to take exercise in one of the lower corridors of the hateful establishment. In this there were two windows which overlooked the deserted garden, from either of these I could converse freely with my new found acquaintance. Our interests were identical. We both wanted to escape, and we discussed the question night after night, and hour after hour, as to how this was to be accomplished.

"As time went on, I appeared to be perfectly resigned to my fate, and bore it patiently, and without a murmur.

"No doubt this deceived my gaoler, for he thought I had sunk into that apathetic, listless state, which was so frequently the case with the miserable inmates of establishments of this description.

"I don't believe that we should either of us ever have succeeded, had it not have been for a circumstance which we could never by any possibility have foreseen; and I do believe, had it not have been for this same circumstance, we should have both been by this time comfortably sent into the other world. And after all," said the outcast, in continuation, "it would have been better, perhaps, if we had. What is life when it is stripped of all that makes it desirable ?'

"Life is sweet, even to the most wretched," answered our hero.

"It may be so, perhaps it is; but mine has been so truly wretched, that I have long since been weary of it."

"What was this circumstance which so strangely favoured your escape ?" inquired Colonel Jack ; "for I take it for granted that you did escape, since you are here to tell me your own story."

"Why, you must know," said the outcast, "that there was—in the establishment in which I was confined—you must know that there was, at the same time, a real live baronet, who had been placed there to be kept out of the way ; and he was no more mad than you and I are at the present moment, although I am sure I have gone through enough to drive twenty people mad."

"A baronet !" exclaimed our hero, starting on his seat. "Why, surely the place you speak of—surely it was not the establishment of a Mr. Hardy ?"

"Indeed but it was !" said the outcast, who in his turn became astonished at the sudden inquiry. "Yes, but it was," he said, in continuation ; "do you know aught about it ?"

"Yes, something—a little," returned our hero. "But go on with your story."

"Well, you must know that this gentleman—the baronet, I mean—"

"Yes, precisely."

"He was planning his escape. But, Lord bless you, it was of no use. He was quite broken down, poor fellow, and hadn't got any life in him. I used to see him at chapel, and anyone could see that he was quite a gone man—clean gone."

"How could he serve your purpose, then?" inquired Colonel Jack, who now became doubly interested as the man began to discourse of an establishment from which, as the reader will no doubt remember, he had managed to make his escape.

"You shall hear," answered the outcast, "you shall hear. It appears that it was the intention of the villain, Hardy, to murder Sir Reginald Fleetwood—that was the name of the baronet of whom I am speaking—yes, murder him, sir, poison him by slow degress, that was his infernal scheme, and not the first time by a good many that he had done so."

"That I am quite aware of," answered the colonel.

"And I believe," continued the outcast, "I believe that the baronet was brought half way on his journey to the other world, when as luck would have it, he met with a friend in Mr. Hardy's establishment. Now, I dare say you have heard of the celebrated Colonel Jack ?" said the narrator, looking hard at our hero; "I'll be bound you have heard of that famous highwayman ?"

As the man said this in a mysterious tone, the colonel found it impossible to repress a smile.

"Oh, yes, I've heard of the rascal," he answered.

"Don't call him a rascal," said the outcast: "he is a thorough first-rate good fellow, and deserves the thanks of more than one person. Had it not have been for him, I should not be here at the present moment to tell you this long and prosy tale. I am not romancing—Colonel Jack was a prisoner at Mr. Hardy's establishment. But, law, I need not tell you that bolts and bars could not confine him ; but to my own share in the business.

"I had promised to make my escape, and at the same time I had assured the young lady, whom I met night after night in the garden, I had promised her to take her with me at the same time. It was to be both or none—I would not go without her.

"I will not weary you with a detail of all the various schemes which we concocted together, and when we had matured our plans, as we thought, there was something or other turned up to knock them on the head. Our last scheme, however was this, and it was the one we had determined upon putting into practice.

"Mary was permitted to have her female friends to see her occasionally; in fact, she was favoured a little more than usually fell to the lot of the inmates of that establishment. Now, I was without weapons of any sort, and it was arranged that one of her female acquaintances should bring in a dagger or short dirk.

"This was done, and at night Mary handed the same to me.

"When I had this deadly weapon in my hand, I felt almost a new man. I concealed it in the interior of my mattress, and a night or two after this, a brace of pistols were handed me by the fair Mary.

Now, the next thing to be done was for me to get into the garden, if possible; and we agreed that if this could be accomplished without any alarm taking place in the establishment, we might, perhaps, succeed in rushing through the gate.

"While the men were at supper, Mary was to watch a fitting opportunity and give me notice, by throwing sand or gravel against the panes of my window. I should have mentioned that I had already succeeded in filing nearly through one of the bars in front of the window, and it only required a sharp blow to remove it from its position, then an opening would be made sufficiently large to admit of the passage of one person."

"And did you receive the desired notice from your female friend?" inquired Colonel Jack.

"No; but a strange and unlooked-for occurrence took place, which rendered this unnecessary. I have already mentioned to you that Colonel Jack, the celebrated highwayman, was a prisoner within the walls of Mr. Hardy's establishment?"

"Yes, I remember; so you said. Well?"

"I waited anxiously enough for Mary to make her appearance in the garden, and for two or three nights after our understanding, I observed her flitting form occasionally, but each time that I saw her, she motioned to me that for the present no opportunity had occurred to put our scheme in practice.

"Well, one night I was suddenly aroused by loud cries, hurried footsteps, the report of two pistols, and looking out of my window, I saw a man run across the grass plat, scale the wall, followed by the celebrated Jonathan Wild.

"You never heard such a noise and clatter. I thought the whole establishment were be-side themselves, and that half of them were about to make their escape, or perhaps had already done so.

"I saw, or rather judged, that no time was to be lost. Hastily snatching up the nearest available weapon, which chanced to be the pistol which Mary had given me, I struck the bar of my window with the same, and after a few blows, had the satisfaction of removing it.

"I was on the grass plat in a few seconds, and then glanced round me.

"From what I had heard, I should have supposed that the garden was in the occupation of numbers of persons; such, however, was not the case.

"I saw two men, followers of Jonathan Wild, making their way through the lobby or gateway in the small habitation where it was customary for the porter to sit. These two individuals were followed by Mr. Hardy and his assistants.

"I had already loaded my pistol, and with this and a long dirk, I felt myself tolerably well armed, and I made up my mind, come what might, that I would sell my life as dearly as possible. It was a question of now or never."

"But were you about to leave without your female companion?" inquired Colonel Jack.

"I looked everywhere for her, and after a pause for a few seconds, had the satisfaction of seeing her emerge from one of the doors which led up to the corridor.

"'Mary,' I said, solemnly, 'have you the courage to make this attempt? Answer me, my dear girl. You must summon up all your courage.'

"'I am but a woman, a weak almost broken-hearted woman,' she answered; 'but I am made strong from desperation. See, my form does not tremble, my cheek does not blanch. Better to meet instant death, than to drag on a miserable existence in these gloomy walls—better to know the worst at once. I am ready; and believe me, my good friend, you will not be compromised by any indiscretion on my part. I will be firm, and am ready to meet my fate, be it for good or for ill.'

"'A trial awaits us. Listen. We must rush into yonder building, and before the first surprise is over, endeavour to make our escape. If there should be any resistance, it is for me to fight till the death.'

"I examined the priming of my pistol as I said this, and then withdrew another from the breast-pocket of my coat, and examined that also.

"I thought I observed the countenance of my female companion undergo a change as I did this, but for the rest, she was wonderfully calm and resolute, considering the weakness of her frame. Taking her by the hand, I led her towards the gateway, and without a moment's hesitation, I flung open the door, and with my companion rushed in. There were two men in the lobby. One was seriously wounded, and the other, one of the keepers of that infernal asylum, turned sharp round upon me, and immediately endeavoured to collar me. I struck him a terrific blow in the face with my clenched fist, but he held on with the utmost tenacity. I then drew one of my pistols, and presenting it to his head, swore that I would blow his brains out there and then if he did not leave go his hold."

" Well, and what said he ?"

" He would not release me from his grasp, and for the moment I can assure you, sir, I had serious thoughts of carrying my threats into execution ; but being unwilling to take the life of a fellow creature, however worthless and despicable a character he might be. I restrained myself as best I could, and endeavoured to shake him off by an almost superhuman effort. I was not successful, for the scoundrel held on like grim death. I felt that not a moment was to be lost. It was a question of life or death, and levelling the pistol I sent the ball through his right shoulder, with a groan of pain and agony he fell to the earth and dragged me with him for he had not even then released his grasp. Exasperated beyond measure, and being fearful that some-one else would make their appearance on the scene. I struck his hands with the butt end of my pistol and eventually he let go his clutch, for I observed as he relaxed his grasp that my assailant had swooned. Bidding Mary follow, we both made towards the outer door. Alas, it was locked ; but upon my looking round I observed a bunch of keys on the table. I lost no time in making myself master of these, and with one of which I succeeded in unlocking the door. We passed through, and I shut it to with a loud slam. When we got on the outside of the building I observed a number of persons in loud and angry altercations. One or two appeared to be badly wounded, and there was a vehicle into which a man was being conveyed ; but I did not wait to see much more, but ran off with Mary in a different direction. I afterwards learnt that Colonel Jack was captured and conveyed to Newgate, being taken prisoner by Jonathan Wild."

" And did you get clear off after this ?" inquired our hero.

" Yes, I managed to make good my retreat, accompanied by my female companion, who, throughout the whole of our adventures, had evinced a firmness and determination which, to say the truth, I should have hardly given her credit for."

" And what became of Colonel Jack ?—did they execute him ?" inquired our hero, with an ill-concealed smile.

" Execute him ! No, I should think not ! The bolts are not forged yet that can confine him. Didn't you know that he made his escape from Newgate ?'

" Well, I ought to know," replied the colonel.

" Of course—so I should have thought. Every gentleman in the land has heard of Colonel Jack's adventures—his education is not complete without it."

" Is he so remarkable a person, then ?"

" One of the most extraordinary men of his time.'

" You have met with him, then ?"

" Never."

" Oh, yes, you have."

" Indeed, sir, I never have. I should have very much liked to have met so celebrated a man."

" What sort of a person do you picture him ?"

The outcast hesitated.

" Oh, he is tall, dark and handsome, and carries in his countenance an open frankness and at the same time a look of determination. Altogether, I feel and know he must be a remarkable personage."

" You are complimentary," said our hero. " You would like to see this Colonel Jack ?"

" Indeed I should.

" You have not far to go, then, behold— him ! Stranger, friend, or chance acquaintance, whichever you please, I am Colonel Jack."

" You !" exclaimed the outcast, as he regarded the speaker with a look of such wonderment, that, for a moment his senses seemed to be taken away. " You, Colonel Jack ! Well I never."

A loud and merry laugh from our highwayman followed this exclamation.

CHAPTER CXII.

THE OUTCAST CONTINUES HIS STORY.

WHEN the first effects of the surprise had somewhat worn off, Colonel Jack begged of his companion to continue his adventures.

" Well, sir, after I left Mr. Hardy's establishment, I managed to procure a horse and cart. The country through which we passed was bleak and desolate, heath and dwarf plantations came in close succession, and for miles we did not meet a farm house. A faster animal I never drove. After two hours' rapid journey, we had reason to believe that pursuit, should any be made, would be unavailing ; and at a little inn, where roads intersected, I pulled the horse, to refresh my wearied companion.

"A half-extinguished lamp glared feebly on the sign-board, for the inmates of this retired hostelry had long since retired to bed. I sounded loudly on the bell—the summons was replied to—the horse was taken from the gig, and introduced to the stable—while a comfortable meal was laid upon the table with reasonable dispatch.

"I cannot describe my feelings, but I can fancy similar ones—those of a reprieved convict or a rescued mariner—some one, in short, with whom hope is over, and to whom, in the last hour assigned for his existence, an unexpected pardon or deliverance had been granted. Such were my feelings when, returning from the stable and I rejoined my fair companion, I laid the earl's cloak on one side, placed the pistols on the table, and referring to the purse I had hidden in my breast, and the weapons at my hand, I felt myself once more a free man."

"What earl's cloak?" inquired Colonel Jack.

"Ah, I forgot to mention that the wounded man I saw in the lobby was none other than the earl himself, and as I made my escape, much to his chagrin, I snatched up his cloak which was lying across a chair.

"This circumstance not a little added to my embarrassment. After the ostler had brought his light, every order I gave was answered by a bow, and on every occasion I was liberally be-lorded. An examination of our vehicle at once explained the causes to which I was indebted for this honourable reception. On the panels of the dog-cart, and the harness of the horse, an earl's coronet was emblazoned.

"However flattering this might be to pride, it was anything but conducive to security, and I determined, on arriving at the next town, to exchange my aristocratic equipage for a humbler carriage.

"When my companion was refreshed, and the horse had rested, we resumed our journey. A couple of hours brought us to the town of ——, a post-chaise was procured, the other trap left in charge of the innkeeper, and with light hearts and fresh horses we took to the road again.

"Having given ample directions to mine host of the Black Swan to assure the safe return of the earl's cart and cloak, we proceeded to the next town, and we determined to obtain some necessary clothing, and consider which course should be adopted for present security and future comfort. It appeared manifest that some singular freak of fortune had linked our destinies together, and that, united by the band of misfortune, the same fate was reserved for both.

"You may think it odd that I have not described the personal appearance of one to whom I had been so strangely introduced, and through whose agency the means of escape from death had perhaps, been afforded. From the first evening I had seen her in the garden, events had followed each other in such rapid succession, which made them seem rather the wild creations of some fearful dream than actual realities, and it was not until safe from pursuit, and we found ourselves seated quietly in a country inn, that I had calmness and opportunity to examine her features, and learn the private history of my fair companion :—

"She was decidedly handsome, but hers was a wreck of beauty. The outline of the face was regular, the eye dark and intelligent, while her raven hair and well arched brows, contrasted with cheeks pale as the marble of a sculptor, the whole expression had a melancholy wildness which might denote unsettled intellect, or have arisen from the painful excitement attendant upon 'hope deferred,' and blighted fortunes. Her figure was particularly graceful, and although attenuated, its proportions were unexceptionable—none could look upon her without mingled feelings, and it was doubtful whether pity or admiration would predominate the most.

"Misfortune, it has often been observed, accustoms men to strange bedfellows, and a community in suffering and danger is still more powerful in uniting persons by the mutual interest which springs from reciprocated sympathy. Such feelings influenced me and the unknown. Our acquaintance, originating in accident, had been hurried into intimacy, and long before we had known each other's history, we had played a desperate game, and tested our mutual fidelity. We felt like isolated beings flung on each other for support—she the protected—I the protector.

"'Mary,' I said, as I took her hand in mine, 'how close the union of our fortunes seem, and yet how little we know of the secret causes which bind our fates together. Would you confide in me, and tell me the story of an early life, in which so much mystery appears to be involved?'

"'Willingly,' she answered. 'The child of misfortune has nothing to blush for, save the villany of others. Mine is a sad tale, but from you concealment would be unnecessary, nay, ungenerous. God knows how heavily I have been wronged—how foully faith plighted to a dying parent has been violated—how villanously was hopeless orphanage abused.'

"She paused for a minute, as if to collect her wandering thoughts, and then commenced her melancholy narrative.

"'I am well descended—my mother wa

heiress to Sir James Stutgard, and my father's family one of the oldest on the borders. In birth my parents were tolerably equal, but fortune was entirely on the lady's side, as Sir James had acquired wealth in the Indies, while my father was left an unportioned orphan. Intended for the church by the bounty of a distant relative, he had passed one of the English universities, and taken the highest honours as a scholar, and as a gentleman, none held a higher reputation; and singular as it may appear, to that proud distinction the misfortunes of his unhappy orphan may be traced.

" 'The Earl of ——, in public estimation, was second to no peer in Great Britain. A favourite with the monarch, he was at the same time an object of general popularity. To great hunting talent, he united the attainments of a scholar; and were one desired to name a noble of the highest cast at that day, the claim of the noble earl to this most honourable pre-eminence would have passed unquestioned. He had an only son, the heir to his ancient title and estates, who had been carefully educated under his parent's eye, and on entering Oxford, the earl made diligent inquiry for one to whom his further literary progress should be entrusted. My father was recommended—the task of completing the young nobleman's education was offered to him—and unfortunately he undertook the task.

" 'The collegiate career of his young pupil was not satisfactory to his tutor. He had talents, but he could not cultivate them, and irregularities in his conduct were often and severely censured. At length Lord ——, graduated,—my father's tutelage ended—and under the charge of a foreigner, of showy accomplishments and fashionable manners, he left his native land to travel.

" 'The new preceptor and pupil were worthy of each other. Without a shade of principle, the Chevalier de Bertram was an infidel and a voluptuary; but the most artful scoundrel in existence, his specious manners and boundless duplicity most effectually masked his real character. No wonder, then, that one, whose disposition was inherently vicious, under such a tutor, became matured in every bad principle. For five years Lord —— continued on the continent, and a shorter probation would have rendered him what he returned, an adept in vice, and familiar with profligacy in all its phases. A more dangerous individual was never loosed upon society. Sensual and cold-blooded, he veiled heartless depravity under an imposing address—bland and open manners lulled the destined victim into a false security—and when about to stab, he concealed his fell purpose with a smile.

" 'During his quondam-pupil's absence on the continent, my father had left the university, obtained a benifice, and married. The income of his living was small, but my mother's fortune was ample; and a year after the union, by the death of Sir James Stutgard, my father succeeded to fifty thousand pounds. Wealth, however, brought no addition to his happiness. His lady's health became seriously impaired—the seeds of consumption manifested themselves—and by medical advice, a warmer clime was resorted to. Change of country failed to arrest the progress of this most insiduous of all diseases, and after lingering a year, my mother left him a widower, and me in infancy an orphan.

" 'The sudden demise of his excellent and deeply lamented parent, called the present earl to England, and when he took possession of the ancient hall, as my father's vicarage was in the immediate vicinity of —— Park, the quandom tutor and his pupil renewed their former intimacy. Never were two beings less adapted for the society of each other. The one confiding, charitable, and unsuspicious—thinking no guile himself, he imputed none to others—and with an open heart and a generous disposition, he looked upon men and women and their actions as they pretended to be, and not as they were. In a word, he was, from his better nature, formed to become the dupe of designing and unprincipled men, and unhappily he fell into the power of one gifted with every evil quality to make him one.

" 'Nothing could surpass the matchless artifice with which the earl led on his victim step by step until he obtained a boundless influence over his acts—nay, over his very thoughts. Years wore on, ' wild youth had passed,' but no change in the character of Lord——In other relations in life he had been tried and found wanting—a cold hearted and grasping landlord his tenantry disliked him—tales of criminality abroad, and profligacy at home were more than whispered. It was reported that he was a confirmed gambler, and anything but a fair one—a cold and brutal husband, and a harsh father.

" 'And yet he maintained over my deluded parent, an ascendency almost magical, and time which might have been expected to dispel the delusion seemed only to strengthen it. Attacked by a chronic disease, tedious but incurable. As my father's health failed and the mind weakened with the body, the earl's power became paramount, and the dying man became a mere puppet in the hands of his betrayer. On his death bed he appointed him my guardian, placed my fortune under his absolute control, committed me silently to his care, and expressed in the full assurance that in his false friend his child had found a second father, and that the look upturned to Heaven with which the earl invoked God to witness how sincerely his duty to the orphan would be performed, indicated the fidelity with which the pledge would be redeemed. Alas, it was but the acting of a finished hypocrite, and his promises to my poor father were false as dicers' oaths!

" ' I was educated at a public school—years passed away. I had never known a parent's care, but falling into kind and able hands, I had become attached to the family, and an order from my noble guardian to remove me occasioned the first severe grief that I can remember. I was now fifteen, full grown, and in appearance almost a woman, in knowledge of what the world was, less than a child.

" ' The house to which I was removed, was situated in a retired neighbourhood and tenanted by a lady by whom as I was informed by my guardian my education was to be completed. My curiosity was much excited by the earl's letter which announced this unexpected intelligence and during my journey to this new abode I amused myself by conjecturing what sort of a person my new protectress would prove. I had secret misgivings that I should not find the motherly kindness, which for eight years I never saw her unruffled temper display, and I had sad cause afterwards to discover that these ominous apprehensions were but too well founded.

" ' When on the second evening of my journey I reached my destination and was introduced to Madame Montelbert, I could not but draw a mental, and I must add, a very unfavourable contrast between my new preceptress, and the gentle and modest personage whose roof I had quitted for ever. In middle age Mrs. Bramby was a favourable specimen of an English wife. Her beauty was matronly, her dress plain, neat, and becoming, the expression of her face mild, and intelligent, and during our intimacy of eight years I never remember temper exhibited. Exemplary as a wife and mother to all in their respective relations. She discharged her duty faithfully, and a happy home and well regulated family attested the value of a pure heart, and a good example. Madame Montelbert was in her thirtieth year. Her beauty was a little *passe*, but still it was more than attractive. Her cast of countenance was decidedly foreign, and her dark hair and lustrous eyes were really magnificent. A figure tall, voluptuous, and commanding, had every advantage which art could bestow upon it, every movement was graceful—every look intended for effect, but nothing had been left to nature—all was studied—all was artificial, and while the eye was fascinated, the heart remained untouched.

" ' When I was introduced to her boudoir, she received me with open arms, kissed me with the warmth of a sister, and lavished praises on my beauty ; but whispered, that the world had trials and temptations for the young, and told me that personal advantage required a closer communion with heaven, to obtain the only true support that would enable me to pass through the ordeal which awaited me.

" ' Mine had been a sound and serious education, and in a few days I discovered the utter incompetency of Madame Montelbert to succeed to the charge my very revered instructress had executed so admirably. Generally uninformed, and almost illiterate, she possessed but two accomplishments—music and dancing ; and she considered that they embraced all that a female should be taught In dress her whole thoughts were concentrated—the business of the toilette was to her the occupation of existence, and ere a fortnight had passed, young as I was, I could not but regard with any feeling but of reverence, a woman whose character was, even in my unexperienced eyes, so thoroughly contemptible.

" ' I had brought with me a small collection of excellent books, mostly prizes and presents given me by Mr. Bramby, and I need scarcely observe that religion and instruction formed their subjects. They were cursorily looked over by madame—some she examined with indifference, while the titles of others excited a sneer. All were thrown aside with the designation ' stupid nonsense,' and a sarcastic observation of what a ridiculous old frump Mrs. Bramby must have been.

" ' She directed, however, my attention to other works—French novels and Italian tales. Never was I so astonished as when I glanced over their contents. All were opposed to morality, and some indelicate, that I felt my cheeks redden as I flung them from me with disgust.

" ' Lonely as the mansion was, still the style of the establishment, though small, was elegant. To the simple comforts I had enjoyed in Mrs. Bramby's parsonage, the luxury of Madame Montelbert's chateau was strongly contrasted. Every meal was attended with display—the few domestics were dressed in the richest liveries—the buffet presented a variety of costly wines—and in her domicile it was evident enough that economy was but little consulted.

" ' With two exceptions the servants were foreigners, and these were the gardener and a very interesting little girl. All besides, the lady of the mansion excepted, spoke

English imperfectly; and in a remote district, whose dialect was remarkable, but for the assistance of these native domestics, the household communications with the peasantry would have been at times with difficulty maintained. Susan, upon my arrival, was named my personal attendant, and only two or three years older than myself, the handsome villager and myself became sincerely attached.

" 'The male attendants on Madame Montalbert were Italians; her maid, in whom unbounded confidence appeared to be reposed, was a Neapolitan; and she exercised a singular and undisputed authority, not only over the mansion, but over the mistress herself.

" 'This favourite domestic was a few years younger than the lady, and with a neat figure and a pretty face, united great shrewdness and decision. She had talents to render her an able ally or a dangerous foe, intuitive insight into character, quick perception, profound cunning, and a determination of purpose rarely found in a woman. In the management of this secluded household, everything was in obedience to her will; and yet, while all were directed like puppets, none could trace the agency by which the movements were effected.

" 'Had I had a knowledge of the world, much of the secret history of the chateau would have been speedily disclosed to me. I had been taught French and Italian—knew both languages literally—but from natural diffidence declined attempting to speak either in the presence of madame. When, in answer to her inquiries, I assured her that I was an indifferent musician, and a most unaccomplished dancer, she lifted her eyes and hands together in perfect astonishment.

" ' 'Do you speak French fluently?'
" ' 'My answer was a decided negative.
" ' 'Nor converse in Italian?'
" ' 'I shook my head.
" ' 'This slight conversation confirmed a previous estimate of my perfect ignorance, and because I did not speak the language, it was never suspected that I understood it; and under this misconception, the lady and her domestics conversed with unreserved freedom in my presence, as they would have done in the case of a young rustic.

" Several months passed. My life was dull and uniform, and excepting at meals, Madame Montelbert and I seldom met. She complained of the climate and the want of covered carriages, and rarely walked farther than the garden. Charlotte, the managing lady of the establishment, was her constant companion both indoors and out of doors; while I, hitherto accustomed to a life of active employment, in which mental and bodily exercise were happily combined, read

and worked if the weather was unpropitious, and if favourable, wandered over the adjacent heaths and sea beach with Susan as my companion.'

" "I must acquaint you," said the outcast, addressing himself to Colonel Jack, "that four-and-twenty years since the coast of —— was the constant scene of wild adventure, and consequently of the crimes to which lawless enterprise will always tend. Smuggling was then at its height—not the sneaking, shuffling system of deception by which it is now carried on, but by a bold brigandage which challenged opposition, and placed the majesty of the law beautifully at defiance. The means taken to prevent it were irregular and imperfect, daring and experience generally evaded detection—cargoes were landed wholesale; while a decoy boat, not worth taking, carried away every official in false chase. The shadow saved the substance."

" "I know something about it," said the colonel, with a smile.

" "I dare say you do, sir," answered the outcast; "I forgot who I was addressing for the moment.

" Well, I will, if you please, follow on with the narrative of Mary.

" 'It was during one of these rambles,' she continued, 'that the first adventure of my life occurred. Susan and myself were returning from an evening stroll by the seaside, and were slowly ascending a pathway that wound from the beach to the moorland, when at a bending of the narrow road, a figure dashed wildly past us. By a sudden impulse he checked his headlong flight, listened for a moment, then in a low but rapid tone of voice, muttered—'Be silent, or my life is sacrificed,' sprang from the pathway, into a fissure in the cliff. All this was the action of half a minute.

" 'I was terror-stricken, and remained rivetted to the spot, with my eyes fixed upon the chasm in the cliff where the stranger had disappeared. Susan, however, was a bolder spirit—she listened.

" ' 'They come,' she said; 'go forward, lady, or the poor fellow will be murdered.'

" 'She caught my arm, hurried me up the pathway, and we had barely cleared the ravine, when half a dozen savage-looking men, armed and well mounted, rushed at a gallop from the beach.

" 'The leader instantly pulled up.

" 'I cowered behind my companion, but Susan's presence of mind did not desert her.

" ' 'So, ho!' he exclaimed, 'you saw a man run past—which way did he bend?'

" ' 'A man run past?' returned my bolder companion, while I nearly sank upon the ground.

" ' 'Ay, a man—not a minute since—speak! What frightens the silly girl?—we will not

harm her. Which way did the fellow take, I say?'

"'No man passed here,' returned the attendant.

"'Hell and furies!' exclaimed a second rider; 'we have completely overrun the chase. I told you he would dodge us at Black Dick's Gap; but you're always so devilish positive.'

"'No,' returned the leader, angrily, 'he passed it—I'll swear he—'

"'Bah!' exclaimed the other; ''tis impossible!—these girls must have seen him.'

"'What in the devil's name is to be done?'

"'Why, we have made a wrong cast, and we must redeem the mistake,' was the reply. 'No chance but one remains. He'll make for Squire Davis's plantations, and skulk there all night. If he gain the wood he's as safe as if on board the lugger. Damnation! had my advice have been followed, we should have shared a hundred pounds. But let us be off, as it is of no use jawing here any longer. If we can cross the heath before him, he can't escape us after all.'

"'As he spoke, the rider turned his horse's head, and spurring over the moorland at full speed, in a few minutes the whole party disappeared.

"'All this passed so rapidly, that I remained in breathless astonishment, and it was only when these wild horsemen vanished in the distance, that I recovered my self-possession. Susan, with fearless determination, watched them out of sight.'"

No. 75.

———

CHAPTER CXIII.

The narrator, after again having recourse to the brandy flask, continued as follows:—

"Thank heaven!" ejaculated Susan, as the hindermost rider disappeared, "he is saved! Come, madam, we must secure him from running again into the danger he has so narrowly avoided."

Turning back, my companion led the way, descended the path, and I followed. Stopping before the chasm where the fugitive had taken shelter, she announced that his pursuers had crossed the heath. Next moment the unknown issued from his concealment, advanced with dignity, took our hands in his, and with the ease and language of a gentleman, thanked us warmly for his deliverance.

"To your fidelity and discretion, I am indebted for my life—and never was a man succoured in his extremity by fairer preservers. Say, lady, he continued, addressing himself to me, "who shall I name as my good angel in my prayer?—and to whom is Will the Ranger bound for ever by a tie of gratitude?"

"Will the Ranger!" exclaimed my companion, as she recoiled.

"Fear nothing, pretty one," said the stranger, with a smile. "What! harm thee! Oh, no; I would shed my heart's blood to prove my gratitude, could it but pay the debt I owe thee."

"And are you the man whom all admire, and all dread?" inquired my attendant, timidly.

"I am indeed him surnamed the Ranger," returned the stranger, with a smile. "Alas! in a lawless life there is little to admire, and were the truth known, perhaps, in me as little to be dreaded. But, say, whom do I address? Where do you reside, and when shall I again have an opportunity to see and thank my fair preservers?"

While this brief conversation passed between Susan and the stranger, I had been eagerly examining a personage who seemed to carry terror with his very name; but in his appearance there was nothing to excite alarm, and whatever dreaded qualities he possessed, were concealed under an exterior calculated to produce very different impressions.

The Ranger was remarkably handsome, his figure tall, active, and commanding, and as he removed his sea cap while addressing us, I could carefully examine his face, and none could be more prepossessing. A laughing eye of brilliant hazel, a high, bold forehead, half hidden by the brown hair which curled profusely around it, nose, mouth, and teeth, all in perfect keeping with each other, united to form a countenance which none could deny to be eminently handsome, but whose expression was even more winning than its regularity.

His dress was the ordinary one worn by seafaring men—probably of superior materials; he was armed, for in a black waistbelt he carried a cutlass and pistols, while the haft of a dagger peeped from a side pocket in his jacket.

At his repeated entreaties, we told him who we were, and pointed out the chateau as the house was termed by its foreign occupants; and when we parted, we gave him an assurance that on the following evening we would revisit the place where this first interview occurred under such singular and alarming circumstances.

As we proceeded home, I need scarcely tell you that the Ranger engrossed our conversation, and that I learned all the particulars of his history and exploits with which Susan was acquainted.

Her information, however, on the subject, was confined to village rumour, and was not very extensive.

He was a smuggler and an outcast, admired vastly by the peasantry, and dreaded by excisemen. For two or three years, during which he infested the coast, his landings had been as successful as his escapes had been miraculous; and until three months before, he managed by ability and fine seamanship to get in safety from the coast; but at last he was chased, overtaken, and would have been captured, had he not have resorted to the desperate alternative of fighting the king's cutter. Here, too, fortune befriended him, for he managed to disable his opponent.

In effecting his escape several of the cutter's crew were wounded, and in consequence the Ranger was declared an outlaw, and a price put upon his head.

On the next evening we were punctual to the promise given, and again met the stranger. These meetings continued daily, and when we separated I shall never forget the impatient feelings with which I looked forward until he came again, and we hastened to the cliff. Unconscious of the truth, I had lost my heart to this wild admirer, and when he announced his immediate departure, and pressed me to meet him and say farewell, a passionate burst of tears was the reply, and told him that I assented.

The evening came, and I set out with Susan to meet the possessor of a heart which had never known a preference, before I had read stories of the master passion—of first love—and, alas, was doomed to feel its intensity. The ranger was waiting for us, and while we sat down together on a bank,

Susan mounted the cliff to guard against surprise.

It would be useless to detail the scene that followed. Kneeling at my feet, my wild admirer avowed his passion, and I artlessly admitted that his love was faithfully reciprocated.

He clasped me to his heart, kissed me again and again, while I reclined sobbing on his breast.

At this moment Susan gave a signal that strangers were approaching.

"One parting kiss, Mary," exclaimed the outlaw, " one parting promise."

As he spoke he drew a ring from his finger and placed it on mine.

"Hear me, Mary," he whispered. "This may be the last time you and I may meet in this world. A trial awaits me. If fortune smiles, the object which brought me to this coast will be accomplished—should I fail I know the penalty, and am prepared to meet it as becomes a man. Within twelve hours I may be cold as stone," and he turned over a pebble with his foot as he made the last observation; "and even in an adventurous career like mine, now while standing probably on the brink of eternity, this is a solemn moment of my life, here, by this emblem, I plight my everlasting love. Wilt thou pledge thine?"

What was my answer? I flung myself into his arms, and in an agony of grief, murmured a promise of eternal constancy and love.

"An amorous young lady," said Colonel Jack, with a smile.

"She was desperately in love," returned the narrator, "or thought she was, which is much about the same thing, I suppose. But I will continue with her narrative. Again Susan gave the signal that we should separate.

"One instant and we part," said my lover. "You will before many hours elapse hear tidings of Will the Ranger; should fortune fail him, his last thoughts and dying prayers will be for you; should he succeed, the wanderer will return ere long, and claim his promised bride."

"Are you mad?" exclaimed a voice, and Susan impatiently waved her arm. "Men have landed from a boat, and come this way," she cried.

"They are no enemies," replied the outlaw, " but the parting moment has come."

Again he pressed me to his heart, and, as if the act required a sudden and determined effort, he placed me gently on the bank, bounded down the cliff, and hurried towards the spot where Susan had observed the men debarking.

"Well," said the attendant, as we slowly crossed the moor. "I half wish that Robert

had been a smuggler. Why, we meet and talk in the garden so quietly, and we reckon how much it will cost to furnish the cottage and buy a cow, and all the time he rests upon his spade and speaks as calmly as we do in the servant's hall, when the work is done. But, lawk! what a different lover the Ranger is. Why, in five minutes you get more kisses than I do in a fortnight. Ah! something has occurred, see a horseman dismounts at the gate. At our dull place we seldom see a visitor. He seems to be a servant. But let us hasten, for madame remarked last night at supper that our walks were longer and more frequent than formally."

Two hours passed, and I was sitting at the fire, listening to Susan's gossip—its theme the exploits of the Ranger—when the door opened, and an unusual visitor came in. It was madame's woman, Carlotta.

"Supper is being served," she said, "and I have news for mademoiselle—the marquis and two visitors come to the chateau to-morrow— But, blessed angels! what a beautiful ring!"

My hand was unconsciously resting on the table, and I had not removed the outlaw's gift.

"A brilliant!" continued the waiting woman, as she raised my hand and examined the ring more closely, " 'tis worth a thousand francs."

Confused and surprised, I made no answer, but Susan's ready wit luckily came to my assistance

"A farewell present from a schoolfellow," she replied. "Is it not sweetly pretty?"

"Ah, paste, of course," returned the attendant to madame; "and yet by candlelight, and in a crowd, it would pass current for a diamond. An excellent imitation, certainly—most excellent."

She quitted the room, and Susan and I, blessing our good genius for thus narrowly evading an awkward discovery. The ring was carefully put aside, and I descended into the parlour.

Madame was unusually thoughtful, and the visit of the marquis seemed to her an important occurrence, for after supper she read the letter the courier had brought thrice over, while at times she was lost in thought, and muttered to herself.

I rose immediately the meal was finished, and as I ascended the stairs, heard the bell rung, and Carlotta summoned to attend her mistress.

The first interview for many years with a guardian whom I but indistinctly recollected, scarcely occasioned a care. One engrossing object occupied my mind—the Ranger was ever present. I thought of him waking—his name was mingled in my prayers—a thousand times his ring was pressed to my lips and my heart—and in my dreams I sat beside him on the cliff, heard him declare his love, and in return plighted mine. No wonder that my slumbers were broken and unfreshing, until nature became exhausted.

I was fast asleep when Susan came to dress me. One glance at the attendant's face told me that something important had happened.

"Oh, Mary," she exclaimed, after bolting the door carefully, "such a scene there was after you left the supper room! There's mischief in this visit of my lord, and you are deeply concerned."

"Then our meetings at the cliff have been discovered, Susan ?"

"No, no, no," was the prompt reply, "not a suspicion of the kind exists. But let me tell you my story my own way."

"Go on," I said ; "you have excited both my fears and my curiosity."

"Well," exclaimed Susan, as she commenced arranging my hair, "as the night was fine, and as Robert and I wished to talk a little to ourselves, I slipped into the garden unperceived, where he was waiting for me. One of the window shutters of the dining-room was half unclosed, and we saw you retire, and presently Carlotta came in. I have often told you, miss, how intimate madame and her maid are, but last night discovered more than I could ever have imagined. When Carlotta entered the room, she pulled a chair to the fire, filled a glass of wine, and seemed to be quite her mistress's equal Robert and myself watched what followed, for, as you know, the windows of the room open on the garden. My lord's letter was read, and rest assured there's mischief in that same. Madame expostulated—Carlotta stormed like a virago—your name was mentioned every minute—matters became worse—and Heaven knows they spoke loud enough, could Robert and I but have understood their gibberish. At last, both started from their seats—Carlotta crossed the table to her mistress—held her clenched hand to madame's face—poured out a volley of abuse—and left the room, darting a look at the lady which made me tremble, and which I shall remember to my dying day."

"What can all this mean, Susan ?" I inquired.

"Heaven alone can tell. But, Miss Mary, there's mischief in the wind, and you are deeply concerned."

"What—what is to be done ? I am at the mercy of strangers—not a friend to pity or assist me."

"That is unkind, Miss Mary," said the attendant, as her eyes filled and her cheeks flushed, "am *I* not to be trusted—*I* who would fly with you to the end of the world ?"

"Forgive me, dear Susan, I spoke without a thought. I know your fidelity, and would trust my life in your hands. Pray forgive me."

"Ay, and you have another friend beside. Robert would follow me through fire and water, through thick and thin. He's but a gardener, it's true ; but there's not a man on the wide border that he would turn his back upon. Come, courage."

I flung my arms round the neck of my pretty and warm-hearted attendant, and presently repaired to the breakfast-room, where I found Madame Montelbert already awaiting me.

If my sleep had been disturbed, I should say her slumbers had been still more unrefreshing. Whether her toilette had been neglected, or that art could not conceal the workings of a mind diseased, certainly Madame Montelbert's features betrayed Time's encroachments, and looked anything but happy.

She had received me with more than ordinary kindness, embraced and kissed me, and complimented me on my looks. Never was a falser compliment paid ; the pier glass reflected cheeks pale as they are now—and the information Susan had given, occasioned an anxious expression, which did not escape the observations of the lady of the mansion.

"How pretty," she said, "and yet how pale. These long walks must be discontinued. Exposure to this horrid clime would rob an angel of her beauty. Would that we were once more in Italy ! This dull and lonely mansion is destructive to one's happiness and looks. Should you not wish to leave it ?"

I started at the question, but in a moment answered that I would.

"And whither, child ?"

"To the guardian of my infancy—to her who proved a second mother to me."

Madame Montelbert started at my reply.

"What, return to school ! Bah ! you jest. No, no, yours will be a happier exchange—a house—a home—a husband !"

"What can you possibly mean !" I inquired in utter astonishment

"Why, that your kind guardian, Lord—— anticipates your wishes," returned the lady, coolly. "and brings a suitor here this evening. All has been already engaged—are you too overjoyed."

"No, madame, I am quite astonished. An union arranged for me, and with a man I am totally unacquainted with. Surely, madame, you are jesting."

"Well, be it so—your guardian will explain matters better than I."

Her woman had answered the bell, and she gave some trifling orders. Susan's disclosures had excited my curiosity, and I observed the bearing of the mistress and her maid. Madame's indifference was affected. Carlotte received her orders with contemptuous silence, while in answer to Madame Montelbert's remark of "I have told Marie that my surveilance will be ended speedily." A look of fearful meaning was directed towards her, and another of deadly hate turned to me. What could all this portend? I consulted Susan but her conjectures were as vain as my own.

While the day passed, an unusual bustle among the domestics, and frequent and angry interviews between madame and her maid, roused Susan's curiosity, like my own, to the highest pitch imaginable. On me more serious thoughts obtruded. Where was my wild lover? and how sped the arduous trial upon which life and death depended?

With the evening visitor's arrival, a carriage rolled across the court yard, and three men closely muffled, alighted from the coach. An hour passed—a message from madame summoned me to the drawing-room, and when I entered it I found the strangers conversing with the ladies of the house.

"Ah, my fair ward," exclaimed the tallest and most *destingue* of the group, as he advanced with an air of authority, and passing his arm round my waist pressed his lips to mine. At this unceremonious liberty my cheek coloured, while from his embrace I recoiled as if by animal instinct. Madame introduced him to me as my guardian the Earl of —— and then in turn presented me to his companions the Chevalier de Belmont, and Count Orliff.

I need not describe the end to you. The chevalier was a man of sixty, of gentlemanly appearance and comely address. The count scarcely half that age with a showy person united to regular and handsome features; but the expression of his face was unfavourable, his manner presumptuous, and from our first introduction I regarded him with feelings of aversion. Unacquainted with society and educated in strict retirement, the manners and social intercourse of the visitors and the lady of the mansion appeared to me at times inharmonious and artificial. There was a softened haughtiness in the earl's bearing to his companions which seemed an effort of condescension, and a placency of address in the chevalier which betrayed dependency. Without the ease of the former, or the tact of the latter, Orliff was unable to keep up a semblance of equality. The earl seemed to tolerate his familiarity with impatience while the chevalier during a trifling argument dissented from a statement of his friend with the indifference of carelessness if not contempt. None seemed at ease, and possibly to judge by circumstances the lady of the mansion was the most comfortable.

The wine circulated freely, and Belmont was the only person who did not indulge freely. The effect of the bottle on the drinkers was remarkable. Madame became free and talkative, the count familiar, as regarded me, in look and manner, almost insolent; on the earl the effect was opposite, and some idle pleasantries of the count and gay sallies of madame were returned with a coldness bordering upon severity.

Coffee was introduced and I was about leaving to retire to my chamber when the door opened and a man entered unannounced. At the same moment by a different door, Carlotta glided in and whispered something to my mistress. Her eyes met Orliff's, and I alone remarked the looks mutually exchanged—one of entreaty and deprecation on his part returned by a threatening glance by the *femme-de-chambre*, in which scorn and hatred intermingled. The high and excited tone with which the earl addressed the stranger at once commanded and obtained attention.

"Well, what news to-night Have you at last succeeded? Fools that you were with the quarry in view to let the game escape ye."

"My lord, I was not to blame. I think the foul fiend saved him; and assuredly nothing but the devil could have stood his friend last night."

"Hell and furies!" cried the earl, "is he not captured?"

The man merely shook his head.

"Go on, fellow! By heaven you madden me! Go on!"

"My lord," said the chevalier, "ladies present—and—"

"Know nothing of what we are talking of at present," was the reply.

The stranger, who was wrapped in a loose riding-coat, with an oil-skin-covered hat, had the appearance of a drover, and at first I did not recognise him; but when he spoke, the remarkable tones of his voice brought him instantly to my recollection, and I recognised him as one of the men who had pursued my lover, and questioned Susan and me upon the cliff, on the evening the Ranger had escaped.

On the stranger's entrance, I was about to retire; but my curiosity was powerfully excited now, and I therefore kept my seat at the table.

"My lord," continued the stranger, "since the evening we lost him on the cliffs, night and day we have continued our search, and every place where he could obtain a shelter has been visited. One trace only could we find; and strange as it may appear, a man who answered the description of the Ranger most accurately, was seen but three evenings since at the very spot where he seemed to vanish when we chased him! He was observed conversing with two women; and so convinced was I that I had recovered the lost scent again, that since daylight I and my companions have been hiding in the rocks. No wonder that we watched in vain, for the Ranger was twenty miles away."

"Ha! and have you found out his retreat?" inquired the earl, passionately.

"Yes, my lord; but too late to profit by the discovery."

The earl growled a curse between his teeth, and the stranger thus continued—

"That my information was correct, circumstances have convinced me. When we lost him at the Dutchman's Cape—as the country people call that opening to the seach beach—I overtook two girls at the very place, and questioned them whether they had seen anything of the Ranger? One appeared frightened and remained silent, but the other denied that anyone had passed. They were both pretty, and when I heard that the Ranger had been seen again, and in company with two females, I at once concluded that love had brought him here. Well—"

The stranger paused.

"Go on!" exclaimed the earl, angrily.

"Never was man more mistaken in his conjectures. Last night, with a dozen desperadoes like himself, he broke into the county prison, overpowered the keepers, liberated and carried off the men whose capture caused us such incessant trouble—and was seen to embark on board a lugger waiting for him, and—"

"Has escaped, and with his companions, too?" exclaimed the earl, in a voice of thunder.

"Too true, my lord. He's once more on the water, and free as any sea bird that breasts the wave."

I had listened with breathless anxiety to every syllable that passed the stranger's lips, and during his short narrative my heart had throbbed to bursting. But when he announced that my lover had escaped—when I was assured that the hazardous trial of which I had been apprised was over—that his adventurous attempt had succeeded, and that the Ranger was at liberty—unable to control the impulse, I uttered an exclamation of delight, fainted, and fell into the arms of Carlotta.

Nothing could surpass, as I was afterwards informed, the confusion my exclamation and fainting fit occasioned.

I was carried from the parlour to my own apartment, and while Susan and madame's confidant used the customary means to recover me, the 'most admired disorder' prevailed among the company assembled in the dining-room. All were astounded, but the earl's rage was not to be described.

"What means all this?" he exclaimed, fiercely, turning a look in which rage and suspicion were united upon the pale countenance of the lady hostess. "Pauline, you have betrayed your trust."

"Not I, by Heaven!" was the reply. "If aught has occurred, it is without my knowledge altogether. I cannot even comprehend it."

"But I can, easily," returned the earl. "She who should have been secluded from the world, as I have been led to believe, was permitted to roam whither she pleased, and to form the acquaintance with the last person living to whom she should have been introduced."

"It is a singular and mysterious occurrence altogether," observed the chevalier. "Was the young lady whom you saw carried from the room just now, one of the females you met upon the cliff when the Ranger made his escape?" he continued, addressing himself to the stranger.

"I cannot pretend to say she was," was the answer.

"Retire my friend," said the earl, "you need refreshment, and we will converse again presently."

The order was obeyed, the door carefully secured, and the secret conclave resumed their deliberations; and, as it turned out, my unguarded exclamation hurried an unfortunate destiny to its crisis.

When the stranger disappeared, the earl addressed himself sharply to the lady of the mansion.

"Pauline," he said, "you have neglected your duty. I might say you have betrayed me, but that I know you *dare not* do. Will you, at least, favour me with the particulars."

Her reply was merely an expression of surprise, and numerous appeals to virgins and saints.

"My lord," said the chevalier, "it is quite evident that the affair is wrapped in mystery. After all, the sudden excitement of the girl may have arisen from other causes. But, looking upon the business in its worst light, the danger may be remedied."

The earl listened attentively.

"Go on, Belmont," he replied, "you have the only cool head in the company. This infernal affair has chafed my temper overmuch. But before we decide on what plans are to be adopted, I should wish to have some private conversation with my friend here. Would you, Monsieur Orliff, attend madame to her boudoir, whither, in a short time, the chevalier and myself will find our way?"

The count led the way from the supperroom with the lady, who seemed by no means flattered with being secluded from the secret conference. Not so Orliff; it offered him an opportunity to converse with madame, and when the door was closed, he threw himself upon the sofa beside the lady of the house, and took her hand in his.

"Pauline," he exclaimed, "how fortunate this *tete-a-tete*. Moments are precious, and while opportunity permits, attend to him who has ever been your friend."

"And why not add lover?"

"Nay, Pauline, this is no time for idle foolery," returned the count.

"Idle, indeed," observed the lady, "if aught involving Orliff's attachments are to be discussed."

"Hear me, Pauline, it is useless to speak of the past, while at the present moment my star is overcharged with all that augurs evil. One thing can avert it, and that is to carry into effect this marriage scheme."

"What, will not one wife suffice for Count Orliff?" replied the lady, with a sneer.

"How now, Pauline. What mean you—what wife?"

"She for whom your mistress was abandoned, Carlotta."

"Then I am betrayed to—"

"One who will take no advantage of the discovery," returned the hostess. "When in her fury last night, as I communicated the earl's intentions respecting his ward and you, she stormed like a fiend, announced herself as your wife, and swore that, even to death, she would maintain her claim; while I despised the weakness which left you at the mercy of such a woman, anger changed to pity, and I forgave you."

"Oh, Pauline, none had ever cause to curse his folly as as I have had. In one brief month I felt the wretched thrall in which I stood, a year, and we were separated, and, as I then hoped and believed, never to meet again. Little did I suppose, when I heard that you and Carlotta were in England, and associated by a singular freak of fortune, that I should be placed dependent on the kindness of one I loved and had neglected, but worse far, thrown upon the way of a fiend whom I had made my wife."

"And which tender relationship, if there be truth in woman, will, on her part, be rigidly maintained? What do you mean to do?"

"See her to-night—reason with her—show her the folly of continuing an union where mutual hatred are the fruits—point out the advantages which wealth will confer on me, and—"

"Through revenge she will tell you that, though the golden apple be within your reach, a touch of hers will wither your arm ere you can pluck it."

"Is she then determined?"

"She is inflexible in that resolve."

"But she cannot effect it, Pauline; the earl is no fool, and he is in my power. How stand you with his lordship? Are those who

were lovers in Palermo but cold friends in England?"

The past might give me reason to distrust you, Orliff, but no partial confidence will answer now. If there be a man on earth I hate, that being is the earl. What did he find me? A woman followed by the crowd, idolised by a husband, high in position, affluent, admired—all these I lost through him, and yet I was scarcely in his power before a dark-browed peasant-girl supplanted me. Far from friends and country no alternative was left but submission. Here for years have I been cooped up, the slave of him who once knelt at my feet—a puppet at his back—a mere agent of his infamy. Will the splendour of her prison reconcile the captive to her thraldom—will the linnet endure the cage because the wires are gilded? No, Orliff, the chains which bind you to Carlotta are not more galling than that which fetters me to a man whom I loathe and despise. Marked you his contemptuous bearing?—the sneer with which his lip curled as he addressed me?"

"Indeed Pauline, I did observe how disrespectful was his manner. But this is mere woman's jealousy. Would you give up the earl's protection?"

"Had I a shelter for my head, however humble it might be, I would fly from a man who has repaid misplaced affections with insult."

"Then assist me through the difficulty which threatens to interrupt my present prospect of obtaining the earl's ward, and share fortune with me in another land."

"Until another and fairer rival wins the volatile heart of Monsieur Orlif, and I become a second time cast upon the world and deserted."

"No, Pauline, never was man's inconstancy followed by more sincere contrition. But did the earl ever discover that you and I were aught to each other than mere acquaintances?"

"Never; himself in England, he believed that the general report spread by my own emissaries was true, and that to evade the arm of justice I had taken shelter in the convent of the Benedictines. And while the Countess Orliff was engaged figuring in the gayest circle of the city where she was residing with her friend and constant lover, the self-created count, he fancied she was mortifying past sins in one of the strictest communities, placed on bread and water regimen, and attired in sackcloth and ashes."

Pauline laughed heartily.

"And now," she continued, "may I inquire for what amiable qualities has the earl selected you to become the husband and obtain the fortune of his ward? Probably he knows not so much of your private history as I do, nor comprehends how Jules Caunat the courier, became Henri Orliff. To confer a wife upon a friend is frequently a great convenience to the donor, a fortune accompanying the present, however, makes it a rather more agreeable gift."

"A hurried disclosure, Pauline, of the relations existing between my lord, will best explain the reason. The lady I shall receive in full, the fortune but in part.

"How so, Jules—nay, I had forgotten—Henri."

"You know the talents I possess, and will not think I make an idle boast when I say, that in every capital in Europe I have played and never been fairly defeated. The earl is, as you know, a daring gambler, and last spring his play transactions were extensive, and, as they afterwards proved, unfortunate. Fortune declared heavily against him, his losses impaired his judgment, and by desperate exertions alone he managed to meet engagements which amounted to a fearful figure. The season was nearly over, when a discovery made at Baden obliged me to quit the continent in haste and seek a temporary residence in London until the affair should blow over. It was my first visit to the British capital, and in the higher circles I was entirely unknown. Belmont and I ran against each other by accident on the second evening of my arrival, and his surprise at meeting me was only equalled by his delight, for I was the very man he wanted—the only person who could retrieve the tottering fortunes of the earl.

"I was immediately taken to Lord ——'s hotel, gave him some specimens of my science, plans were matured, and I was in a day or two introduced to his fortunate associates. None suspected me to be aught but what I had been described. I played among the noblest gamblers, and in two months won back a large portion of the money previously lost, and again set the earl on his legs. Do you wonder now at his being grateful to one who, in the eleventh hour, saved him from ruin all but consummated?"

"Now, indeed," replied madame, "I comprehend the causes which led your noble protector to gift you with a wealthy heiress."

"Probably not all the causes," returned the pseudo count. "The earl generally contrives to keep in the back ground some secret spring which actuates his motives, and believe me that, in the present instance, my dear Pauline, he has not deviated from his usual course."

"Explain yourself, Monsieur Henri."

"Heavy losses were to be met—money was therefore indispensable—and where was it to be obtained? Not a tree was standing which dared be felled, and the earl's son,

with a prudence and determination not to be overcome, refused every entreaty and artifice employed by his affectionate father to induce him to open the estate. Belmont, in the emergency, reminded the hard-pressed noblemen that his ward's property was funded, and by some little ingenuity might be rendered immediately available. It would benefit the orphan, too. The country only paid her three per cent. and the earl would make it four. The plan was carried out, a signature or two was forged, and Miss Meadow's fortune of fifty thousand has crumbled down to exactly a tithe of the original. Now do you comprehend me, Pauline?"

"Why, yes, but still imperfectly. The earl has disposed of the fortune of his ward."

"And has neither the wish, nor the means of replacing it."

"I am all attention. Proceed."

"Well, Belmont has hit on a method of abridging his lordship's guardianship of a pretty girl, and cancelling a large debt at the same time, two very important matters you must allow. I wed the lady with five thousand, and the earl will be relieved of five-and-forty."

"Ah, I understand the business now correctly, and you consent?"

"Why, yes."

"And accept five thousand pounds only?"

"Certainly, Pauline, but it is to make that money a more rapid means of enforcing the other forty-five."

"By heaven, Orliff, I could worship you. Do these island laws afford the means of reaching at a delinquent like my lord?"

"Ay, madame, provided the injured is in a position to set the law machinery into action. My lord's most munificent five thousand will oblige him to disgorge the other five-and-forty. And now that we understand each other will you assist me?"

"Ah, will you a second time deceive?"

"Never, by every hope of happiness—never, by this kiss."

"Ah, steps in the lobby," said Pauline, in a whisper. My Lord Earl, what an absence. Another moment and I should have slept. I cannot compliment the count's amiability to-night. The fogs of England have affected him."

Then turning to Orliff, she drawled out—

"Pray, M. le Comte, what were you last speaking of?"

"Pauline," said the earl, "we have much to speak about to-morrow. Ring for some wine. This room is quiet—? no eavesdroppers?"

The lady bowed an affirmative.

"Ah—all well. And now, madame, we wish you sound repose."

Nothing could have pained a woman once flattered and followed by admirers, more

sensibly than the cold civility with which the earl intimated that her absence was desirable. She rose immediately, bade the earl a good-night, bowed formally to the chevalier, and when she reached the door and caught the eye of Orliff, her look spoke volumes.

What had passed between the earl and his dependent, the chevalier, in the supper-room, I know not; but for the details of the *tete-a-tete* which occurred in madame's boudoir, I was indebted afterwards to the last person upon earth from whom I could have expected either sympathy or information.

"It appears," said the outcast, in continuation, "that since Mary's illness in the parlour, Susan's stay with her was kindly protracted, and she was sitting at the fire, conjecturing a thousand causes for the earl's visit, and wondering whether the Ranger

would redeem his promise and return, when a tap was heard at the bed-room door. Carlotta entered. At that late hour, from her, a visit was most unusual, and the appearance of Madame Montelbert's favourite was absolutely startling. The expression of her face betrayed the stormy workings of her mind too plainly; her cheeks and lips were colourless, her hair partially disordered, and the wildness of her brilliant eyes had all the frenzied excitement of madness in their lightning glances. She seemed at first displeased to find Susan in her chamber.

"What, not in bed yet?" she exclaimed.

"No," returned the young attendant, "so soon after her sudden indisposition, I did not think it proper to leave Miss Meadows by herself."

"You are right, girl," was the reply. "I

come from my most amiable mistress and your accomplished governess, mademoiselle, to make affectionate inquiries after your health. I shall report favourably, and thus relieve the more than maternal anxiety of Madame Montelbert for her pupil's health."

Nothing could surpass the sarcastic tone or the contempt which the curling lip of the lady's *femme-de-chambre* conveyed as she delivered madame's formal message. When retiring, Mary's eyes involuntarily followed her as she was leaving the apartment. Pausing in the doorway, with a meaning look and a slight movement of her finger, she intimated that she would speak to Mary, and she obeyed the summons.

" Do not undress—dismiss your attendant, and expect me in half an hour. Neglect this opportunity, and—*you are ruined !*"

The emphatic whisper in which the last sentence was delivered, had the effect that was intended; and when Mary returned and sat down beside Susan at the fire, her agitation did not escape observation.

Their girlish conversation was brief, and it terminated in Susan's retiring to her own room.

After she had departed, Carlotta entered. Mary handed her a chair. She seated herself, and then asked Mary if she had been the object of the earl's visit.

"He would marry me to a man whose presence here only excites my disgust," was the answer.

Carlotta informed her that such was the case.

" Well, to cut the narrative short, I may as well at once inform you that Carlotta, instead of being Mary's enemy, at once turned and became her friend. She informed her that the count was an imposter, being in fact none other than the notorious Jules Canot. On the following evening a stranger was admitted on the sly into the gardens which surrounded the house. He spoke a few hurried words to Mary, and then it was that she discovered that he was the Ranger. She informed him of her perilous situation. In less than four-and-swenty hours the Ranger made his appearance, with some ten or dozen of his companions, and aided by Carlotta, he succeeded in carrying off Mary. Thus the earl and his two vile companions were outwitted. It was some time after this that I became acquainted with her, but the account of this I will tell you some other time, for to say the truth, I fear I must have exhausted your patience."

"Well," said Colonel Jack, " you are swimming in troubled waters at present— what are you going to do ?"

The outcast gave a shrug, expressive of his utter inability to answer the question put to him.

" Ride on to town with me," said our hero, " and we can talk the matter over."

" I have no horse," answered the man.

" I can manage that; they have one or two spare ones at this house."

The outcast was but too glad to accept of the colonel's offer, and in the course of half an hour they were trotting side by side along the road leading to London.

As they were thus proceeding, they were overtaken by a middle-aged individual, also mounted on horseback, who inquired the way to the great city.

Colonel Jack informed this personage that he was himself journeying thither.

" Might I beg permission to bear you company," said the new comer, who appeared to be particularly loquacious and communicative; " for you must know," he continued, " that I am afraid of meeting with highwaymen or footpads, and for our mutual safety it would be as well for us to travel together."

" I shall be rejoiced to have your company," said the colonel, who could not repress a smile when highwaymen were referred to.

In the course of a few minutes the conversation took a lively turn. The stranger was a man of good education, had seen a good deal of the world, and during their journey to London he related to our hero and his companion the following tale, which we shall reserve for another chapter.

CHAPTER CXIV.

THE GHOST OF THE GALLERY.

" My worthy cousin, Mr. Christopher Oldcourt," said the stranger, " ought certainly to have had the honour of a formal introduction to you. Let me describe him. Cousin Christopher is one of those solitary samples still extant of the beau of the old school. He was the terror of all prudent mothers with grown up daughters—at his approach guardians with rich wards trembled—lovers became jealous—and spinsters of a certain age, the very dragons of virtue, fled in fear.

" Alas ! for Cousin Christopher ! the once gay Lothario—the pride of the assembly, the hero of the hunt, the almost accepted suitor of the divine Lady Margaret (she is now a well-jointured widow, a grandmamma, much afflicted with rheumatism). He is no longer the dangerous young man of fashion, but has dwindled down into a quiet, respectable old gentleman of a country town; patronises long whist, snuff, worsted stockings, lambs' whol socks, capacious shoes, cloth leggings, and after-dinner naps.

" He inhabits a comfortable, unpretending

looking house on the outskirts of L——; it has a garden in front and a garden behind, that boasts of a circular pond, just large enough to hold a couple of sulky swans, that appear always to be in the pouts with each other; a fountain, which, like a great actor, refuses sometimes to play from caprice; a grotto, admirably calculated to catch cold in; a dropsical Bacchus, holding a bunch of bullets, that are intended for grapes; a squabby Cupid, who has outgrown his wings; two fir trees in green tubs; a gigantic-leaved plant, said to be an aloe, and supposed to have blossomed once within the memory of man.

"There is pent up, like Napoleon at St. Helena, that towering spirit, once the delight of the young and fair, and whose time is now employed in directing and finding fault with his man servant Diggory, who is gardener, valet, and butler; and in being himself alternately scolded, snubbed, and coddled by his old housekeeper, Deborah.

"She nurses him during his periodical fits of the gout, superintends the domestic concerns of his establishment, consisting of the said Diggory, a handy servant of all work, and a little fag of a boy, who cleans shoes and knives, runs of errands, does all the mischief generally attributed to that universal scape-goat Mr. Nobody, and is also receiver-general of the various ratings, which are handed down in succession from the higher powers to him.

"Such is now Cousin Christopher, who, except being occasionally prosy, and addicted to stories, is, on the whole, a pleasant old gentleman.

"He is fond of assembling round him the numerous offshoots of the family tree, particularly my mirth-loving cousin Harry, the heir of the manor; my very refined relative Mr. Courtly; besides half a dozen minor torments, male and female, who delight in teasing their uncle Kit, and putting Mrs. Deborah into a passion; and who, on grand occasions, such as a birthday dinner, can only be pacified and prevented from turning the house out of window, by my kind old cousin promising to tell them a story—something horrid and hobgoblinish, that sends them to bed in the shivers, and makes them pop their heads under the clothes if a board creaks.

"Fancy, then, that at some such family réunion the following tale was narrated, which I have taken the liberty of naming— *The Ghost of the Gallery.*"

In the most romantic part of Yorkshire, is situated Merivale Castle, a once immense and magnificent pile, but which is now in many parts crumbling to ruins. The centre, which is still entire, has been transformed from an antique residence into a spacious country dwelling, though an odd mixture of magnificence and inconvenience pervades the whole. Long passages, that would figure in the most incomprehensible romance ever penned; the staircases almost perpendicular; then such roomy apartments, and such apologies for windows; and the little odd holes and corners one was always stumbling on; and the old hall, with its roof of carved oak; and the painted gallery, which still connects the habitable part of the eastern and western turrets; the said turrets, by a contrivance of the builder who superintended the repairs, being unapproachable, save by this long gallery.

The castle was formerly surrounded by majestic woods; it has still in front of it a venerable looking avenue of oak and elm, which was said to have witnessed the nightly rendezvous of every ghost within a walking distance.

Every turret, corridor, or out of the way nook, have its tenants-at-will of the shadowy race, who, from time immemorial, have frightened their descendants, and kept the neighbourhood in awe.

But within the last fifty years, a few of these good people have discontinued their nightly visits. They certainly must have fallen out among each other, for no ghost, of any reasonable expectations, would have taken offence at the treatment they met with. Half of the state apartments, the large white tower, and the fine tapestried chamber, were given up their use. Yet, shortly after the first repairs were commenced, Lady Abigail's ghost took huff, just as the little painted room, bearing her name, was opened, and the large willow tree was cut down that waved its long branches in front of the window; and when the moonlight shone in upon the deserted chamber—which happened to be on the ground floor—dark, undefined shadows appeared, gliding over the walls. These were never seen but on moonlight nights, or when the wind was high; so her ladyship and the old willow walked off together.

The apparition of Sir Reginald Merivale decamped from the damask bed-chamber, because the furniture was removed, the rats dislodged, and the carved pannels refastened, that were dropping from the walls. And his great friend, the fair Elinor, departed in high dudgeon, a short time after, because, forsooth, her haunts underwent a process of white-washing, painting, and glazing, and because her picture was removed from the crazy frame, voted past service, and consigned to the lumber room.

Merivale Castle, in my days, was inhabited by beings of a very different species: a fox-hunting baronet and his fashionable wife presided in its lordly hall, and invariably filled the house with company during the shooting season, keeping up to the very letter the renowned hospitality of old England.

In the autumn of my eighteenth year, I was permitted to accompany a friend, who was going to visit Sir Arthur and Lady Agnes Merivale.

As I was a mere youth, and the castle was crowded with visitors, I was accommodated with an apartment in one of the turrets, in which, by dint of good generalship, I could just turn round without bruising my shins or endangering my limbs.

If my dormitory was not of the most aristocratic dimensions, the castle itself made ample amends.

I can well remember the gothic hall into which the library, dining-room, and magnificent sitting-rooms opened; at that extremity facing the entrance, were the doors of stained glass, leading to the conservatory, through which the guests, who occupied the turret rooms, passed and repassed to their respective chambers.

The conservatory led to the painted gallery, and connected it with the main body of the building, to which the gallery run paralel: at either end of the latter, a low oaken door conducted to a small stone entrance, in which a marvellously inconvenient staircase, led to the apartments above; and a small nail-studded portal, similar to that which gave egress into the gallery, opened on to the old-fashioned plaisance occupying the space once encumbered with ruins.

In my youthful days, when a nobleman or the head of a good family assembled his friends rounds the festive board, or invited them to pass a few weeks within his almost princely mansion, he did not think it sufficient merely to meet them at the dinner table, and leave them to amuse themselves during the day, either by sauntering in the library, and watching the rain drops on the window pane, should it chance to be wet, and riding through dusty roads when the weather permitted.

There was a great demand on the attention of a host in the olden time—such preparations, such studying; where Lady A.. and Mrs. B., should be shown to; and whether Sir C., or plain D., should take the precedence.

When a party of fashionables congregate in these times, they appear to consider the house to which they are bidden in the light of an hotel, where they enjoy as much freedom and double the comfort; they also come and depart without the least apparent ceremony. Captain Suchaone looks irresistible in the drawing-room, and plays the agreeable at the dinner-table: in less than one brief day he is vanishing at the rate of twelve miles an hour, and Cornet Somebody is going through the same part, in the same place.

But when I was young! oh, the ceremony of reception! the presentations, the introduction in all its pristine horrors of propriety; the formal circle, that rose simultaneously at the entrance of a new comer; and the bow! slow, respectful, and geometrical in the superlative degree; with the feet, so exactly placed in the third position, and the queue, tied with a watered ribbon, that rose and sank in the direction of a right angle.

Compared to the modern nod of recognition and salutation, a bow in those days had all the dignity of an eastern salaam.

And then the fair dames, who swam through the rooms and glided in our dreams in hoops of not more than five yards in diameter, with fans a foot and a half in length, and toupees, and sausage-like curls, miscalled ringlets, and looking very captivating in brown powder and black patches.

Then the glories of the ball-room! the graceful minuet—the elegant cotillon—the lively heys, and the country dances, most slanderously called kitchen dances by sundry modern writers.

It was not then considered *bon ton* to saunter through a quadrille; but the perplexity of step; the coupee, the chassee, the rigadoon, were so religiously observed: and the stately, sliding walk, the hand presented so precisely, and the dress hat (never designed to fit human head) secured under the disengaged arm. Those were times to live in!

Here my worthy cousin uttered an indistinct sort of growl, which I dare say he intended for a sigh.

He then continued.

Amongst the guests were two ladies, aunt and neice, distant relations of Sir Arthur. The aunt I can never forget—she always looked so like propriety personified; a Sir Charles Grandison in petticoats walked out of the novel; and morning, noon, and night she was to be seen either netting or knitting, or musing upon satin stitch, or tent stitch, as though every feeling and sentiment were absorbed in silks, worsteds, and chenille. Her manner, too, impressed you with the idea of that negative sort of goodness which is so extremely disagreeable—that hopeless nonentity of mind so often found in the very excellent kind of people, in whose bosoms, if the passions calmer slumber, the soul-stirring and endearing virtues are certainly sound asleep.

They think, they feel, they act mechanically! always wear the same look, and seem so surprised that any one should differ from them in a single iota. Such was Mrs. Margaret Forrester. But her neice Lucy! far better do I remember, though so unequal to the task of describing her.

Lucy was my senior by two years; she was not handsome, though at times she looked almost beautiful; and as she sat in the recess formed by the deep bay window, her guitar at her side, her fair cheek resting on her delicately shaped hand, she might have been a study for Velasquez, that prince of portrait painters. Her hair was of the richest brown, and, in the fashion of those days for young people; it flowed in unrestrained curls over her elegant figure, untouched by powder or pomatum. Her attire, too, though partaking, in a slight degree, of the unbecoming formality of the existing mode, was at once graceful and simple. It appeared, despite of stiff stays, stomachers, and ruffles, to resemble the picturesque costume of Spain and Italy as now portrayed in the paintings of Stephanoff.

Sometimes a sprig of white jesamine, or a cluster of roses, placed amid her luxuriant hair, heightened the likeness. Lucy was an almost portionless orphan; she was also a Catholic, and had been educated in a French convent. The total exclusion in which her early life was passed had given to her pleasing countenance an air of repose, bordering upon melancholy, that was most interesting.

A few days after her arrival at Merivale Castle a new guest made his appearance, who, as I understood, joined the party, as soon as it was notified to him that the Misses Forrester were to be domesticated there for some months. The new comer, Mr. Bradfield, of Bradfield Park, lord of, I forget how many manors, patron of three livings, and who commanded twenty votes for the county, was, without flattery, the most ungainly, and most unpleasing, and the greatest blockhead that ever wrote esquire after his name.

Imagine a tall figure that appeared to be compounded of left limbs, with hair showing through the powder, the doubtful hue between sandy and dirty brown, and which stood up from his head like an ill-fitting wig, you may then picture to yourself Mr. Bradfield, of Bradfield-park, a hunting, shooting, game preserving, cock fighting, horse racing, dog-fancying squire, who could just sign his name to a receipt and a letter when his steward had penned them.

Such was the husband elect of the gentle, the intellectual Lucy Forrester, who, under the rigid surveillance of her aunt Margaret, was brought to Merivale Castle purposely that the match might be concluded.

Novel writers in later years have said much on the subject of match-making mothers, aunts, and chaperones. There were creatures of that stamp in my young days; Mrs. Margaret Forrester was one of them; and her very faculty was on the *qui vive* to forward her niece's marriage with Mr. Bradfield. Lucy Forrester disliked him; nothing

particular in that, for very few people did otherwise; but her aunt would not hear of refusing him. She had no idea how any young lady could possibly reject for a lover or husband a gentleman who kept a train of livery servants, ate off plate, whose carriage was drawn by four long-tailed greys, and who was, moreover, master of Bradfield Park, and possessed a town house of corresponding magnificence.

Then the jewels she would wear, and the envy she would raise, were of themselves sufficient to win the consent of any fair lady. It seemed that Lucy was of quite a different opinion; she thought it very immaterial to her happiness to be drawn in a lumbering chariot by four horses; and whether she dined off delf or dresden, plate or pewter, she was convinced that Mr. Bradfield, of Bradfield Park, would not be a wit less odious.

I often observed the look of abhorence she involuntarily cast on her admirer when he entered the drawing-room in his full dress suit—his head poked forward like an *avant courier*, to announce the approach of the body, and which head might almost have made its way through the very pannels of the folding-doors, without much detriment to its owner.

And poor Lucy had to endure his attentions, and to look resigned; for she had no hope of escape from him, but the cloister, to which alone she looked for refuge. But then aunt Margaret had settled that Lucy was to become Mrs. Bradfield, and, of course, she would always reside with her neice, and it would be so pleasant for her to superintend the servants, and arrange parties, and dress, and visit, and dine out, and be the great lady of the neighbourhood.

I sometimes suspected that Lucy had not always been so averse to her lover; I once surprised her gazing intently on a miniature which she had not time to conceal on my approach; the picture was that of a young and handsome man; a very different sort of a person to Mr. Bradfield. I glanced at it; Lucy, I perceived, had been weeping; she did not remove the miniature, but as if in reply to my inquiring look, she observed, "That is the likeness of a person who was once very dear to me."

"Was?" I exclaimed!

"Yes; he is now dead."

Not another word was said, for the eternal and ever-to-be-met-with aunt Margaret stalked into the parlour, followed by the lover, who forthwith began playing the agreeable; grinning by way of a smile, and disarranging the order of Lucy's work-box, in order to win her admiration.

It was evident to the most unconcerned spectator that Miss Forrester was completely surrounded by kind friends who were determined she should not quit Merivale Castle, but as Mrs. Bradfield, of Bradfield Park.

In this unanimous resolve each had their own selfish feeling.

Sir Arthur looked to the twenty votes; Lady Anne to the delightful parties her friend would give ; aunt Margaret, like many other negotiators, had simply her own interest in view. Lucy, it appears, had previously determined on the line of conduct she would pursue, though she had not, heroine-like, a confidante to whom she could disclose it.

"One evening as it was growing dusk, and the ladies were seated in the damask drawing room, waiting till the gentlemen should join them, Lady Agnes, to amuse her guests, began relating a tradition of two brothers of the Merivale family. I, on account of my youth, was permitted to leave the dining-room, my absence being neither noticed nor cared for. I stationed myself by Lucy, whilst our fair hostess continued her narrative. It was sufficiently interresting to keep up our attention, one part of it apparently recalled to Lucy Forrester some events in her past life; for as my hand rested on her chair, I felt her tears on it. I was about to ask her if she were ill, when begging me, in a whisper, to take no notice of her absence, she rose and left the room, unperceived by the remainder of the party ; and Lady Agnes concluded her story, which had been sufficiently horrifying to gratify all lovers of the marvellous and terrible."

"Yet, really, Lady Agnes," exclaimed one of the young visitors, " it is very disagreeable to listen to such horrid stories, and in the dark, too ; do, pray, let me ring for candles ?"

"Certainly, my dear, and by way of relief to my *triste* narrative, Miss Forrester shall sing us one of her French rondeaus. Lucy, my love, will you not oblige me?" inquired Lady Agnes.

"Miss Forrester has left us," I observed.

"Good heavens !" exclaimed Mrs. Margaret. How extremely rude—how very improper."

"Miss Forrester, I fear, is not well," I replied.

"Dear me," rejoined the aunt, " why not inform me of it : she is in her dressing-room, I suppose ; may I trouble you, Mr. Oldcourt, to ring for my servant ?"

I was rising to obey her orders, when a wild piercing shriek rang through the house ; it was echoed by the ladies, who simultaneously rushed to the door, at which the servants were then entering with lights. Judge of the confusion, the dire confusion that reigned ; of the accidents, of the scuffling, the tearing, the jostling, the pushing, the scrambling that ensued.

The gentlemen had run out from the dining-room, the servants from the hall, the ladies from the drawing-room, one of whom had entangled her sacque in the sword of her admirer ; wigs were flying from heads, heads were huddled against heads, footmen elbowed their masters, and abigails ran foul of their ladies; ladies fainted, and no one pitied them. Mrs. Margaret Forrester exclaimed that the voice was Lucy's, that it seemed to come from the gallery. Sir Arthur instantly rushed down the conservatory; I followed him—so did Mr. Bradfield ; but in his haste he contrived to tumble over an orange-tree that would not get out of his way, and we left him like "love among the roses," on his back, with a stand of flowers overturned on him.

On entering the gallery we beheld poor Lucy, lifeless, as we imagined : she was stretched upon the marble floor—her face was pale as that of a corpse, and the blood welling from her mouth, which in falling, she had struck against the pedestal of a column, at whose base she lay.

We raised her, Lady Agnes and her aunt applied the usual restoratives, and by degrees she recovered ; but she was unable at first to answer our inquiries. Tears at length came to her relief ; she wept so bitterly, that our curiosity might never have been satisfied, had not her gallant lover, Mr. Bradfield, made his appearance in the circle, and, having gathered up his limbs, he advanced with his wonted grace. It seemed that he had suffered by his downfall, (in common with other great men) for his forehead exhibited marks of a severe contusion, insomuch that all the *poudre a la marechale* was literally bumped out of his hair, by the violence with which his head and the stone floor had exchanged salutations; one ruffle of right mechlin, hung in a most maudlin state over his extra sized band, the other was displayed *en etendard* on the hilt of his sword, which one would imagine had been as frightened as its wearer, for, like a cowardly dog, it was seeking shelter between his legs, to the imminent danger of the 'squire's neck.

The moment that Lucy beheld him she drew back in horror, and, in a tone expressive of disgust and hatred, she commanded him not to approach her.

"Very extraordinary upon my word!" muttered the offended lover. " In what can I have offended Miss Forrester ?"

"If you would but remove that man from my sight," continued Lucy, addressing Sir Arthur ; "if I might be permitted to be left with my aunt, with Lady Agnes," she added.

"Certainly, my dear Lucy," replied Sir Arthur, " we will leave you directly ; come, Bradfield, you see they are turning us all out; come, ladies, allow me to escort you to the drawing-room."

"Accordingly, every one but Lady Agnes and Mrs. Margaret returned to the house; I was amongst the last; and as I left the gallery, I heard Lucy exclaim in a low, yet distinct voice, "*I have seen him!*" Seen *him!* "Who, my dear child?" inquired her aunt.

"Who?" cried Lucy in a wild tone. "*He*, who for my sake would have resigned wealth, honours, friends; he whom I loved; he whom *you* said had long since lain in the cold grave, where my hopes and happiness are buried with him. He stood yonder in the pale moonlight; called me by my name; I heard the tone of that voice, which I feared would never have blessed my ear again; I could not answer him, for a chilling horror crept over me; I shrieked and fell."

"Good heavens!" whispered Lady Agnes to the aunt, "she must be either mad or delirious."

"No, I am neither," replied Lucy; "but God forgive you all, I fear you will soon make me so, for my heart is broken; and, oh! aunt, you have only dragged me here to see me die, or, what is worse, to behold me a raving maniac;" and she again burst into tears.

"Sir Arthur must be informed of this," said Lady Agnes rising, and coming into the conservatory, where she espied me as I was quitting it. "Mr. Oldcourt," said her ladyship, "may I trouble you to bring Sir Arthur here; Miss Forrester has been dreadfully alarmed, and I wish her to be persuaded that her fright is needless."

I flew to execute her commission, and returned with Sir Arthur, much against the inclination of the ladies, who had heard that something very terrific had appeared to Lucy; but whether ghost, hobgoblin, or robber, they had not yet determined. Lady Agnes, in a few words, informed Sir Arthur of the cause of Lucy's agitation, which certainly partook in a great measure of the mysterious and the marvellous. He affected to laugh at her terror, and observed, that the ghosts of his ancestors were by far too well bred to frighten a fair lady; he persisted, that probably one of the servants had been loitering in the gallery, and thus innocently caused the terror she felt; without giving her time to reply, he immediately summoned to his presence those servants who were likely to pass through the gallery at that time of the evening. They all denied having been the hero of this adventure, and, in all probability, a very interesting legend, to the full as terrific and appalling as the history of the ghost and Lady Tyconnel, would have been transmitted to posterity, had not

one of the under gardeners begged permission to speak to Sir Arthur. He was admitted, and after many bows and much hesitation, he informed his master that he was commissioned to clear up the mistake which had occasioned so much alarm to the young lady. He then proceeded to tell us, that a poor half-witted man, whom he had, within the last few days, employed in the garden, was the luckless wight who had the misfortune of being mistaken for a ghost, or something worse. He was passing through the gallery into the conservatory, in order to close the sashes, when he beheld Miss Forrester; and at the distance, and in a glimmer of the twilight, he imagined her to be one of the housemaids, named Lucy; he called her, when to his great surprise, the young lady gave a frightful scream; and he, terrified at seeing her fall senseless to the ground, and apprehensive of the anger that he should incur, very naturally thought it would be wiser to make his escape; and accordingly he jumped out of the nearest window. In proof of this statement, the gardener pointed out to us several fragments of glass, and one of the painted casements smashed into atoms—a mischief which no apparition, however formidable, could ever have had the spirit to do.

Sir Arthur desired the culprit might be discharged from his service, but Lucy eagerly pleaded in his behalf, and expressing herself perfectly convinced of her childish folly, she made it her particular request that the whole affair might be forgotten.

Lady Agnes, dismissing the servants, then proposed returning to the company; Miss Forrester, who although she made light of her indisposition, was evidently suffering from the effects of terror, begged of them to excuse her, and, accompanied by her aunt, she retired to her room.

The remainder of the evening was spent in wondering and guessing what could put such silly ideas into Miss Lucy's head; and some of the young ladies protested that not for worlds would they ever venture at nights into that terrible gallery; and, in spite of the explanation we had given them, they were decidedly of opinion that some monstrosity of a raw-head and bloody-bones had shown itself. Although I was very sceptical on the subject of apparitions, I must confess that my belief was somewhat staggered; and I could not imagine that such a trifling occurrence would have alarmed a girl of Lucy's superior character.

That something uncommon was *sur le tapi*, I well know; for during two days she never left her room, and on the third, before she made her appearance, Mrs Margaret was closeted with Sir Arthur and Lady Agnes, and the detestable Mr. Bradfield was of the council ; and, on its breaking up, he was pleased to put on a mighty mysterious look, such as the favourite valet of the favourite minister's favourite mistress may assume, when he wishes to be thought in the secret.

On Lucy's re-appearance, I was surprised to observe that her personal charms seemed rather to have improved during her temporary illness. Certainly, she exhibited no remains of indisposition ; she even received with unusual complaisance the attention of her lover ; and in the course of the day it was conveyed to us by confidential whispers and hints, that Miss Forrester had actually accepted the rich Mr. Bradfield, of Bradfield Park, and in one brief month she had promised to be his bride.

"Oh, woman ! woman !" I mentally ejaculated, when informed of her decision, and comparing it with the confession I had heard from her own lips three evenings since. I could almost have hated her for smiling on the booby, whom in her heart she despised i I was even delighted to find that my stay at the castle was to continue but for a few days, the friend whom I had accompanied having been ordered to join his regiment. We only postponed our departure till after a ball, which Lady Agnes was desirous of giving on Lucy's account, who was then to be introduced in form as a bride elect.

That evening she appeared with all the advantages of the most splendid dress and blazing in diamonds, the gift of her intended —she really looked beautiful ; the animation of her glance, the brilliancy of her expressive eyes, her elegance, charmed and surprised every one. But how far more pleasing to my mind was Lucy in her simple and unadorned attire ; and with those pensive graces, that threw an interest over her ! I have often thought I could discern under that vivacity of manner so foreign to her, a feeling of more than usual melancholy. Like a skilful actress, who assumes some extravagant character, she was evidently playing a part revolting to her feelings ; I observed that amidst the unnatural exuberance of spirits, there was a wild and distressing restlessness of manner that spoke a heart ill at ease ; and it did not escape my penetration, that she was indebted to art for the roses that I will not say *adorned* her countenance.

I was rather anxious to observe her more narrowly, and had the good fortune to obtain her hand for one dance. This priviledged me to give her the support of my arm, as we promenaded the rooms between the dances. After conversing on some uninteresting subject, I ventured to observe, that as I was to leave Merivale Castle on the morrow, I should take the opportunity of paying her my compliments *d'avance* on her approach-

ing marriage, and expressed my best wishes for her happiness in her union with the wealthy 'squire.

"Happiness in my marriage with Mr. Bradfield !" exclaimed Lucy. "Can you think so meanly of me, Mr. Oldcourt ?"

"Yet," I replied, "you appear to-night as his affianced bride, you are spoken of as engaged lovers, and, allow me to add, your behaviour towards the gentleman in question gives me reason to suppose that your sentiments are greatly changed in his favour ?"

"Suspend your judgment for a few hours," said Lucy, "and you will think differently, unless," she added, with a faint smile, "you imagine that my inclinations, my feelings, and my reason can be fettered by these glittering baubles."

Without giving me time to reply, Lucy, under pretence of feeling the heat of the ball-room too oppressive, proposed that we should take a turn in the conservatory, I gave her my arm, and we strolled together down the cool and fragrant apartment. It was brilliantly illuminated, and the groups of gaily dressed dancers dispersed, in different corners, the sweet perfume shed by the flowering exotics, and the soft light of a summer moon, which silvered the gardens and even threw its quivering beams through the lofty sashes upon the marble pavement, mingling its mild lustre with the rich radiance of the many-coloured lamps, gave it the appearance of a fairy scene. We seated ourselves in a recessed window, round which some plants of the fusci t, the red China rose, and the white jessamine, twined and formen a species of bower. We had not remained there many minutes when I heard a slight rustling noise, and I distinctly beheld the tall figure of a man, wrapped in a dark travelling cloak, standing on the step of a glass door near which we were seated. Lucy must have seen him too, for she instantly rose, clung to my arm, and requested I would lead her to the ball-room ; in spite of the rouge she wore, I could perceive her turn of a deadly paleness ; she inquired the hour, and on my telling her it was past midnight, she started, and was for a time seized with such a trembling that I led her to the seat we had quitted.

I unwittingly looked into the garden towards the spot where the stranger had been standing ; he was there still, the moonlight shone full on his countenance, and I beheld the features of the picture which Lucy had mentioned as being the likeness of a deceased friend.

I gazed at her, then again at the figure, but it had disappeared in the gloom of a small plantation of evergreens. I was not a little startled, for I connected all I had

heard on the night of the gallery adventure with what I then saw; I refrained from noticing this to Miss Forrester, who seemed to be aware of my discovery; we returned to the company, and Lucy, who for a few minutes before had almost been fainting, was now leading off the dance with the most graceful animation with her lover, who, be it observed, moved in all the elegance of manner and attitude usually described as pertaining to that fabulous animal, denominated *a hog in armour*. I never saw Lucy Forrester after.

On the next day, which was fixed for our departure, and also for the signing of the

No. 77.

marriage settlement, the party at a later hour than usual, assembled in the breakfast-room. We were discussing the ball of the preceding night, when a servant entered, and whispered Lady Agnes, who rose and left us. There was nothing to wonder at in all this; but shortly after Mrs. Margaret Forrester came in out of breath, and looking as much alarmed as her propriety of feature would allow her, she hastily inquired if we had seen her niece; on being answered in the negative, she at once quitted the apartment.

Sir Arthur next made his appearance, looking particularly puzzled; and the lover, too, walked in with an air of more than common stolidity.

"Very extraordinary !" he said, his usual phrase when his stupidity could not or would not understand what was passing under his eyes. "Miss Lucy has played truant; I propose that we go in search of her immediately—after breakfast," And this devoted adorer sat down to a plentiful repast of cold fowl, ham, eggs, coffee, fruit, and all the et ceteras of a breakfast in those times.

Presently, Lady Agnes, with a look of uneasiness and alarm, accompanied by Mrs. Margaret, who really seemed to be frightened in right earnest, returned and informed us that Lucy Forrester had certainly eloped, for nowhere was she to be found.

"Eloped! eloped!" we all exclaimed.

"Eloped!" repeated Mr. Bradfield, nearly choking with moor fowl and passion. "Eloped! what with my diamonds—the family diamonds. Good heavens! this is dreadful!'

"Oh, horrid! shocking!" vociferated half-a-dozen young ladies, who had a vast penchant for diamonds and for Bradfield Park.

So clamorous was their indignation against Lucy, and their pity for the ill-used swain, that there is no saying what might have happened had not Miss Forrester's maid run in with a parcel, directed in Lucy's writing to Mr. Bradfield, and which *selon les regles* was found upon her dressing-table.

The impatient lover tore it open; it contained the jewels with which he had presented her, but no note—not even a single line which could afford a clue by which her flight might be traced. Mr. B., wonderfully consoled by the unhoped for restoration of his diamonds, was strenuous in his advice to take the matter coolly, and to advertise the runaway in the "County Herald."

Sir Arthur, in consternation, invited the gentlemen to assist him and his servants in the search. We all dispersed through the pleasure grounds and the woods that skirted them, but no vestige could be traced—not the mark of a carriage wheel nor the track of horses could be described. But as my companion and I were passing a rustic bridge which crossed a waterfall in the woods and that rushed down from a considerable height between the ledges of inaccessible rocks, that rose abruptly on either side from the shore of the lake beneath, I saw a white scarf and chip hat, that had caught in the bushwood on the declivity; I recognised them instantly.

We summoned the rest of the party; we pointed them out to Sir Arthur, who, horror-struck at the discovery, exclaimed that she had drowned herself. Yes; poor Lucy, beyond a doubt, perished in the torrent; and the broken heart, fevered by sorrow, disappointed affection, and blighted hopes, was at rest for ever beneath the cold water on which we were gazing.

It was in vain to attempt making any search after the body; the whirlpool into which the waters fell was unfathomable. We returned to the castle with our dreadful tidings, on hearing which our hostess was thrown into convulsions, and the manœuvring aunt, who had sacrificed her niece, was carried off to her apartment in violent hysterics.

Of course this unexpected calamity was the signal for the departure of every guest; we all left the house of mourning. I could not refrain from telling my friend the adventure of the preceding night, and my opinion on the subject; he agreed with me that it certainly was very mysterious.

I have never since met with Sir Arthur nor Lady Agnes, nor in fact with any of the party; my acquaintance with them was entirely through my friend, who went abroad shortly after, and died in battle. Nothing has yet transpired to elucidate this melancholy affair; but I shall ever think that the disappearance of poor Lucy Forrester had some connexion with the *Ghost of the Gallery.*

My cousin concluded his narrative with a deep sigh, that was echoed by the younger part of his audience; but I am grieved to say that Harry Oldcourt and a certain Colonel de Mercourt, a friend of Mr. Courtly (who was passing a week at the Manor House), were very much disposed to laugh at the pathetic conclusion of worthy Christopher's story. Indeed, the latter, though in the main a good-natured old gentleman, was so irritated at their tittering, that he asked them, in no very gentle tone, if they *doubted* his veracity.

Colonel de Mercourt assured him, that, to his knowledge, every fact he had related was perfectly true—except the tragic catastrophe he had so feelingly detailed.

"How, sir!" replied the old beau. "Excuse me, colonel, for reminding you that I was an eye-witness of the fact, and that you, I should imagine, were not in being at the time. As to the fatal end of the heroine of my tale—"

"It is perfectly incorrect," interrupted the colonel, "since the youngest son of that very lady has the honour of assuring you that she is now living at Rome in perfect health, and without the most remote idea of ever having committed, or intending to commit suicide."

"Is it possible !" exclaimed cousin Kit.

"And therefore, my dear sir," resumed Harry, "your flowers of eloquence are quite unnecessary; and the chip hat and scarf, and fevered heart, and cold waters of the lake, and the blighted hopes, and the brushwood, and the inaccessible rocks, and that crowning climax, the *Ghost of the Gallery*, though capital things of their kind, and admirably worked up, must be curtailed the next time you favour your friends with the recital; let me advise you to finish your story with the account of Miss Forrester's flight."

"But, Harry," expostulated the old man, "it will make a very abrupt ending!"

"Oh, Colonel de Mercourt will give you every information in his power."

"With pleasure," replied the colonel.

"Then, in the first place, I am curious to know who it was that Miss Forrester eloped with, and how she planned it, and——in fact, you must tell me everything."

"Then," said the colonel, smiling, "I ought to inform you that my father, the Viscomte de Mercourt, the original of the miniature you mentioned, was really the same person who caused such alarm in the gallery. He had followed Mrs. Margaret and her niece to Merivale Castle, where, in the disguise of a labourer, he obtained admittance to the gardens. He was not aware that a report of his death had been brought to England, and when he accosted Miss Forrester, he was almost as much alarmed as herself at the terror she felt. He escaped, and that prevented his detection; but long ere the next evening, he had found means to convey a letter to her, containing a full explanation, and also detailing the plan he had settled for their escape. Her feigned acceptance of Mr. Bradfield was suggested as a means of blinding the vigilant aunt Margaret; my father, by dint of a liberal bribes to the under gardener, secured his assistance, was admitted into the castle on the night of the ball, and my mother, under pretence of retiring to rest, before the company separated, changed her dress for a plain travelling suit, and having previously made a small parcel of the clothes she would require, she left her apartment unperceived, joined my father in the gardener's cottage, to which she was conducted by the owner, and was privately married by a Catholic priest, to her first love, whilst an old valet of my grandfather's and their host and hostess witnessed the ceremony. Immediately after, their travelling carriage conveyed them to the nearest town, and in a very few days they were quietly established in the Hotel de Mercourt, Rue de *** à Paris."

"Then the hat and scarf?" inquired Mr. Christopher.

"Were thrown there by the confidant, purposely to mislead the baronet."

"And pray what became of aunt Margaret?'

"*She* became Mrs. Bradfield, of Bradfield Park; for as the wedding dresses had been ordered, and Mr. B. had made up his mind to be married, he prevailed on the good lady to change her name, to the great disappointment of a whole regiment of unmarried misses."

"Well, Colonel de Mercourt, though it gives me the greatest pleasure to hear that in one respect my narrative deviates from the truth, you will allow that the denouement of my story is the most romantic."

"Most undeniably so, my dear sir."

The companion a fellow traveller had concluded his story of the "Ghost of the Gallery," which narrative had afforded our hero much amusement. The colonel discovered that the stranger was a man well informed upon most subjects, and one, indeed, who had seen much of the world, and was, moreover, well acquainted with human nature. They chatted as they went along, familiarly enough, until they arrived within three or four miles of the metropolis.

Our travellers were somewhat suddenly alarmed by a loud and piercing shriek, which awoke the silent echoes of the night, putting spurs to their horses they galloped in the direction from whence the sound proceeded, but could not discern aught, that might have occasioned so strange an alarm. They then drew their horses up and paused. Presently another shriek met their ears, and the colonel, whose senses were more acute than those of his companions, concluded that the noise came from a bye lane which led from the road along which they had been travelling. Without waiting for his two companions Colonel Jack clapped spurs to his horse and dashed down the lane in question, he had not proceeded many hundred yards when he discerned an old fashioned lumbering carriage. In this there was a young and beauteous female. And at the door of the vehicle a tall gentleman stood insisting upon the lady's alighting. The moment the latter caught sight of the colonel. She was loud and urgent in her appeals to him for assistance.

The highwayman knew the voice to be that of Miss Langford's, or more properly speaking, Mrs. Osborne. It was impossible for him to get up to the carriage on horseback He therefore dismounted and drawing his sword, hastened to the side of the carriage. The man turned round and disclosed the features of Sir Richard, or rather Mr. Richard Fleetwood. An expression of deep hatred passed over these when he caught sight of Colonel Jack.

"Help—help, mercy!" exclaimed Mrs. Osborne.

"Back, Richard Fleetwood!" exclaimed Colonel Jack. "Back, I say and let the carriage pass."

'Insolent ruffian, whose neck should have

been in the halter long since," answered Mr. Fleetwood. "Perdition! Do I meet you once more. Have at you then. 'Tis the hangsman's duty to rid the world of such a miscreant, but I will anticipate the work," And without further ado he rushed on to the colonel and commenced a vigorous assault,

We have already seen that our hero was one of the most skilful swordsman of his day, and he was more than a match for his adversary. After a sharp encounter he succeeded in breaking Mr. Fleetwood's sword in two. The latter recoiled back a pace or two in evident alarm. Colonel Jack held up the forefinger of his left hand and said—

"Mark me, Richard Fleetwood I will not spare your life for many minutes longer. Go! hence! For by the Lord above, if you do not make the best use of your legs I will stretch you lifeless in the road." Mr. Fleetwood was evidently overawed. Near to where the encounter had taken place there was a small ale-house. Uttering a deep curse, Mr. Fleetwood turned his heel upon our adversary, and hastened towards this.

"Ah, fly—fly! Mr. Halford," exclaimed the lady in the carriage, "fly, Mr. Halford, while there is yet time. This man will give you in custody. There is nothing but what he would do to be revenged."

"Pshaw. I fear him not, my dear madam, I scorn and despise him."

"Ah, but for your own sake, for mine, for Osborne's, do not run any risk.'"

"How is Henry?" enquired the colonel. "I have not seen him since—since his return from the continent."

"He is well. Excellent well in health. Pray come and see us."

"He is happy, I hope," said the colonel with a deep drawn sigh.

"Yes. Ah, dear yes, I hope so."

"Ah, hope!"

"Nay, I am sure of it."

"My dear madam," said our hero, advancing towards the carriage window. "Colonel Jack (he emphasied these words) is no fitting companion for his once kind and valiant friend—"

"Once! and is he not still so?" inquired the fair Honora.

"To the end of my life," exclaimed our hero, suddenly.

He took the lady's hand in his, raised it to his lips, and said—

"I wish you joy, madam. I wish you every happiness it be possible for woman to have. May your life be one of unclouded sunshine—each day fulfilling the promises of yesterday—still promising to-morrow. I know not what the good wishes of Colonel Jack can be to any one, but you have them,

believe me. You have them with all the sincerity of my heart."

"Ah, Mr. Halford!" exclaimed Honora. "You are kind, noble, and generous. Why are you so much a stranger to us? Dost thou not remember that time when, with my poor father, I was in the Oxford coach, and you listened to the pleadings of a poor defenceless woman?"

The colonel held up his hand in a deprecating gesture.

"Let that pass," he exclaimed.

"Nay, but I owe you much—even within this very hour. Where should I have been but for your kind aid and assistance?"

"We will talk about this business hereafter. You had best make good your retreat from this gloomy lane. Permit me to see you into the high road?"

Colonel Jack remounted his horse, and trotted by the side of the carriage until it reached the high road, where he found his two companions awaiting his return, and evincing no small amount of surprise at his prolonged absence. Their surprise was increased when they observed him accompanying a carriage, in which a young and beautiful female was seated. The appearance of the outcast was unprepossessing enough, as we have before stated, his dress consisted of almost rags, and his features were ill-favoured enough. He had, however, been made to look a little better by our hero lending him a horseman's cloak, which in some measure hid his dilapidated garments.

The colonel told him to fall back out of the sight of the lady in the carriage, an order which he promptly obeyed. The colonel then rode by the side of the carriage, so that he might converse with Mrs. Osborn as they proceeded.

"How did this attack from Fleetwood commence?" enquired our hero. "You were journeying alone?"

"Yes, I had been to pay a visit to a friend —an old schoolfellow, who is not expected to live," said Honora. "I was sent for, in fact, and Henry being from home, I had no other alternative but to order the carriage and proceed thither at once. I never dreamt of being molested, and still less did I imagine that it would be Sir Richard Fleetwood who would attack me."

"Mr. Richard Fleetwood!" said her companion.

"Yes, I mean Mr. Fleetwood. And how is it, Mr. Halford, that you have never been to see us—may I enquire once more?"

"I will do so shortly."

"No time like the present. Come, I will not take any refusal. Come this very night; escort me home, for gallantry sake," said Honora, with a smile.

Colonel Jack did not know very well how

to refuse, so when the party arrived in London he made a virtue of necessity, and agreed to accompany Honora home to the house of her husband. Upon arriving in the Oxford-road, he told Honora that he must be excused for a few seconds, as he had to give instructions to a friend. He then fell back, and beckoned the outcast.

"See here," said our hero, when the latter had trotted up to his side. "I must leave you now, having to see this lady home, but I will see you in the morning. Have you any place to sleep at to-night?"

"St. Giles' Workhouse," answered the man.

"I will give you a billet for the night. Do you know Westminster?"

The man replied in the affirmative.

"Good. Do you know the Cow and Cauliflower?"

The man replied in the negative this time.

"Well, no matter; you will have no difficulty in finding it out. It is kept by one whom we call the Badger. Give him this slip of paper, and he will in return give you sleeping accommodation for the night. Now do you understand?"

"Yes."

"Then be off at once, and wait there till I come."

"Good night, sir," said the man, and off he trotted.

The colonel's other companion was not so easily got rid of; he would insist upon giving our hero his address, and inviting him home to his residence. However, the colonel did get rid of him eventually, and accompanied his fair charge on her way without further "let or hindrance," to use a legal phrase.

———

CHAPTER CXV.

STATE OF CRIME IN ENGLAND.—MYSTERIOUS ROBBERY.

WHILE our hero is on his road to the residence of his old friend and schoolfellow, Henry Osborne, we will, for the reader's information, subjoin a few statistical facts on the "progress of crime."

There are people in the present day who are continually exclaiming, that the world is daily becoming worse, and that there is now more crime than there ever was. In answer to this, we give the following brief statement.

We have had occasion, in our narrative of a highwayman's progress, to glance at our criminal laws, and deal with facts as we found them, and have at the same time endeavoured to give as faithful a picture of the times in which Colonel Jack flourished, as it has been possible for us to do, from the facts with which we have been furnished.

Let us now glance at crime in the earlier history of England.

During the time of the Saxons, the predominant crimes of the age were of an atrocious character. Assassinations, the plundering of whole towns and districts, and bare-faced perjuries, were offences of ordinary occurrence by persons of condition. The punishment of delinquents was either shockingly cruel, or strangely inconsistent with modern notions of penal justice. The horrible torture of burning out the eyes was not only inflicted for delinquency, but sometimes merely to incapacitate a rival.

Although theft to the amount of twelvepence was a capital offence, yet the taking away life might be committed for a pecuniary penalty. This varied with the rank of the sufferer. For the murder of a king, the penalty was thirty thousand thrymsas (about eight thousand pounds of our money), for a prince one half, for an alderman, an earl, or a bishop, eight thousand thrymsas, for a thane two thousand, and for a ceoil, or churl, (supposed, by some writers, to have been a slave,) two hundred and sixty.

This account, given by Wade, in his "History of the Middle and Working Classes," may appear somewhat at variance with the generally received opinion of the Saxon character; but the statement is supported by Turner.

Some of the Saxon monarchs maintained better order—Alfred, for instance—but these were exceptions to the general character of the Saxon kings, who were generally too much engaged in war to attend to the domestic management of the country.

After the conquest, this state of things was somewhat improved; but in 1425, an act of parliament was passed, in which it is recited that "Many evils, as murders, robberies, and man-slaughters, have been committed heretofore in the city, by night and by day, and people have been beaten and evil treated, and divers other mischances have befallen, against the king's peace; it is therefore enjoined, that none be so hardy as to be found going or wandering about the streets of the city after curfew tolled at St. Martin's le Grand, with sword or buckler, or other arms, for doing mischief, or whereof evil suspicion might arise; nor any in any other manner, unless he be a great man, or other lawful person of good repute, or their certain messenger, having their warrants to go from one to another, with lanthorn in hand."

How far this statute was effectual, we have no means of determining with certainty; but this and similar provisions could have had but little effect in checking the disorders they were intended to prevent, since we read continually, about this period, of the disturbances that took place in the city, occasioned generally, it appears, by the "apprentices and serving-men."

Sir Walter Scott, in his "Fortunes of Nigel," has given an excellent description of the manner in which a riot frequently commenced; the following account of one of the many that really occurred, and frequently too, is taken from Lambert's "History of London," and will give the reader a good idea of the state of the metropolis at this period :—

A serious commotion broke out in London in the year 1517. The rioters consisted of the apprentices, servants, watermen, and priests, and the foreigners were the objects of their illegal proceeding. The complaints against these men, as set forth in "Hall's Life of Henry the Eighth," were "that there were such numbers of them employed as artificers, that the English could get no work. That the English merchants had little to do, by reason the merchant-strangers bring in all silks, cloths of gold, wine, oil, iron, &c., that no man almost buyeth of an Englishman. They also export so much wool, tin, and lead, that English adventurers can have no living. That foreigners compass the city round about, in Southwark, Westminster, Temple-Bar, Holborn, St. Martin's le Grand. St. John's Street, Aldgate, Tower Hill, and St. Catherine's; and they forestall the market, so that no good thing, for them, cometh to the market, which are the causes that Englishmen want and starve, whilst foreigners live in abundance and pleasure. That the Dutchmen bring over iron, timber, and leather, ready manufactured, and nails, locks, baskets, cupboards, stools, tables, chests, girdles, saddles, and painted cloths."

These accusations throw some light on the commercial condition at this time. Preparatory to this commotion, one John Lincoln, a broker, engaged Dr. Bell who preached the Spital-sermon on Easter Tuesday, to inflame the people by magnifying the grievances under which they laboured. The doctor complied, and took these words for his text : "The heavens to the Lord of heaven ; but the earth is given to the children of men."

From whence the doctor shewed, that as this land was given to Englishmen, and as birds defend their nests, so ought Englishmen to cherish and maintain themselves, and to hunt and drive out aliens, for the good of the commonwealth.

And from another text, "Fight for your country," that by the laws of God they were justified, and therefore it was their duty to clear the city of strangers.

This sermon had such an effect on many weak minds. that they assaulted foreigners as they passed along the streets ; for which offence, on the 28th of April, Stephen Studley, Stephen Betts, and some others, who were principals, were committed by the lord mayor to prison. Soon after which, a report was spread that the citizens intended, on May-day following, to destroy all strangers that should be found in the city or its liberties.

The king's council hearing of this rumour, Cardinal Wolsey sent for the mayor, and advised him to be on his guard, and prevent the like disturbances for the future. To effect which. he summoned the aldermen, about four o'clock in the afternoon preceding May-day, to meet him at Guildhall immediately. The assembly being met, they, with the approbation of the cardinal, came to the following resolution :—

"That every man should be commanded to shut up his doors, and keep his servants within." In consequence of which, an order was made and published, by the aldermen of each respective ward, that no man, after nine o'clock, should stir out of his house, but keep his doors shut and his servants within till nine o'clock in the morning.

Before the order was properly dispersed, it unluckily happened that Sir John Mundy, in his way home, was rudely treated by two young men, playing at bucklers in Cheap, one of whom he ordered to be sent to the Compter. Many 'prentices who were by, rescued the young man from the alderman, crying out—

"'Prentices—'prentices! Clubs—clubs!" on which so great a body assembled with clubs and other weapons. that the alderman was put to flight. These were increased by a number of serving-men, watermen, and others ; and by eleven o'clock at night, there assembled in Cheap about 700, and in St. Paul's Church-yard 300.

They proceeded in a body to the Comptor, which they broke open, and released the rioters, who had been committed there by the mayor for assaulting foreigners ; after which they went to Newgate, and took out Studley and Betts, committed for the like offence. A proclamation was issued by the mayor and sheriffs, in the king's name, but without effect. The mob increasing, they threw sticks and stones at many strangers as they passed, particularly one Nicholas Dennis, a serjeant-at-arms, who, being much wounded, cried out—

"Down with them."

This heightening their resentment, they broke the windows and doors of the houses in St. Martin's le Grand, and plundered the house of one Mewtas, a Frenchman, in Leadenhall Street, whom they intended, had they met with him, to have destroyed. Early in the morning they dispersed, from an apprehension of being overpowered by the forces preparing to march into the city, under the command of the Earls of Shrewsbury and Surrey.

In this time, by the dilligence of the mayor, three hundred of them were taken and committed to the Tower, Newgate, and the Compters; and about five o'clock in the morning the riot subsided.

Among those committed to the Tower was Dr. Bell, for preaching his seditious sermon. A commission of oyer and terminer was immediately made out for the trials of the offenders. On their arraignment, they pleaded not guilty, and their trials were postponed.

The commissioners appointed for this purpose were the lord mayor, the Earl of Surrey, and the Duke of Norfolk, who came into the city escorted by 1300 men; and the prisoners, to the amount of 278, some men, some lads not exceeding fourteen years of age, were brought through the city, tied with ropes. On the first day, John Lincoln and several others were indicted, and found guilty; and the next day thirteen were condemned to be drawn, hanged, and quartered

For this purpose, and to strike a greater terror, ten pair of gallows were set up at the following places:—

Aldgate, Blanchapelton, Grass Street, Leadenhall, opposite each Compter, Newgate, St. Martin's, Aldersgate, and Bishopsgate. They were made to run on wheels, for the better convenience of removing them to such places as might be properly adapted for the execution of so many rioters.

Some little time after sentence was passed, Lincoln, Sherwin, and the two brothers named Betts, were drawn upon hurdles to the standard in Cheapside. The first was executed; but as the others were near being turned off, a reprieve came from the king, to the universal joy of the populace.

The police of the country, says Wade, was also extremely defective, and shows that the community was far from having attained a general state of order and security. This, however, did not result from a lenient infliction of criminal punishment; for never were severe laws issued in greater profusion, nor executed more rigorously, and never did the unrelenting vengeance of justice prove more ineffectual.

Harrison assures us, that Henry VIII. executed his laws with such severity, that 72,000 'great and petty thieves were put to death during his reign." He adds, that even in Elizabeth's reign, 'rogues were trussed up apace;' and that there was not 'one year commonly wherein 300 or 400 of them were not devoured and eaten up by the gallows in one place and another.'

In spite of these sanguinary punishments, the country continued in a dreadful state of disorder. Every part of the kingdom was infested with robbers and idle vagabonds, who, refusing to labour, lived by plundering the peaceable inhabitants; and often strolling about the country in bodies of 300 or 400, they attacked with impunity the sheepfolds and dwellings of the people.

The laws and police were totally inadequate to control these ruthless spirits, who, by rendering both property and persons insecure, checked the rising prosperity of the country. The cause of these outrages may be partly traced to the changes which had just then taken place in society; the abolition of veillenage was undoubtedly both just and beneficial; but the transition of a large body of people, still comparatively barbarous and uninstructed, from bondage to free labour, was naturally attended with transitory outrage and confusion. These statements will enable the reader to make a comparison between the state of crime at former periods and its state at present.

We should be sorry to trespass too much upon the reader's patience by the introduction of what is termed " dry matter," but in glancing at times past by in English history we are, in a measure, almost compelled to diverge from the unbroken thread of our narrative; and as a sequel to the present chapter we give the following extract from a celebrated French work, entitled, " Les Causes Célèbres," or celebrated trials.

Francis Count de Montgomery and M. d'Auglade lived in the same mansion, in the street Royale, in Paris. The house consisted of four floors, the two lowermost of which were occupied by the count, his wife and family, and the two upper by Monsieur and Madame d'Anglade, with their only daughter and servants.

The two families visited each other, and were altogether upon good terms, though there existed no strong or sincere friendship between them. Count de Mongommery was wealthy, and had an establishment corresponding with his rank and means. He even kept a domestic chaplain, or almoner, a person found in houses of the highest distinction. M. d'nAglade, on the other hand, though he made a decent appearance in society, and was received in the best circles, was understood to be rather straightened in circumstances. Such was the condition individually and relatingly of the principal parties in the following unfortunate affair:—

Count de Mongommery and his lady having projected a visit to their country house at Villeboisin, invited Monsieur and Madame d'Anglade to accompany them. The invitation was at first accepted, but afterwards it was declined upon some slight plea.

The count and countess accordingly set out for their estate, attended only by their chaplain, Fancois Eaguard, and other domestics, on Monday, the 22nd of September, 1687, proposing not to return till the evening of the succeeding Thursday. During their absence the town house was left under the charge of a female servant named Formenie, with whom a page and four girls, who worked at embroidery, also remained.

Some trifling presentiment of evil having occurred to Count de Mongommery, who was somewhat superstitious, he returned with his suite to town on Wednesday—a day earlier than he intended. Nothing unusual was observed about the count's aparments at first, excepting that the door of a chamber on the ground floor, in which some of the servants slept, was found to be unlocked, though the chaplain had locked it, and taken the key with him on his departure. Formenie and her companions had never touched the door, and had believed it always to be locked. This circumstance, however, did not excite much notice at the time.

The count and countess took supper after their arrival, and had just finished their repast, when M. d'Anglade entered by the door common to his apartments and those of the count. This was about eleven o'clock. M. d'Anglade had been supping out, and finding the Mongommeries to have returned, he went into the chamber where they were, and chatted with them for a time; after which Madame d'Anglade came down likewise, and joined in the conversation. The domestics of the count afterwards alleged that both the d'Anglades appeared struck with surprise on learning the count's arrival.

On the evening of the following day Count de Mongommery gave information to the authorities that he had been robbed. The lock, he stated, of his strong-box had been forced during his three days' absence, and there had been taken away thirteen bags, containing each 1,000 livres in two-pistole gold pieces, a twisted rouleau of 100 new louis-d'ors, and a pearl necklace, valued at 4,000 livres.

On the announcement of this enormous loss, M. Deffita, one of the heads of the criminal department, and other officials, went to the count's apartments.

The first impression on the mind of every one was, that some person about the house had committed the robbery, and, therefore, a search was resolved upon.

M. d'Anglade and his wife came forward at once, and requested that their chambers might be first examined. This was assented to. The lowermost of the two floors occupied by the D'Anglades was begun with, the master and mistress of the house themselves conducting the officers through all parts of it. Coffers, cabinets, beds, and, in short, everything were turned over and examined, without any vestige being found of what was sought.

After the first floor was ivestigated M. d'Anglade led the way to the upper story, his wife declining to go, on account of an attack of faintness. In the upper flat, on examining an old trunk full of clothes and linens, a twisted rouleau of seventy louis-d'ors was found in it, wrapped up in a paper which contained a printed genealogy. On opening this rouleau to count the money, the hand of M. d'Anglade was seen to tremble, and he himself said, "I tremble."

Count de Mongommery declared the paper containing the genealogy to be his, and said —what he had not said before—that his louis were of the coinage of 1686 and 1687, the same as those found in d'Anglade's rouleau.

Suspicion once thrown, as it now was, upon this unhappy man, other circumstances were not long in occurring to increase it. On descending to the chambers of Count de Mongommery, Madame d'Anglade observed to the judge or officer, M. Deffita, that one room, she had heard, had been found unlocked, and that in it something might perhaps be found; adding, unguardedly, that some of the servants were probably the authors of the act. When, on searching that same room, five of the missing bags of livres were discovered, with a sixth, in which the sum of 1,000 livres was incomplete.

Madame d'Anglade's pointing out the room, and her readiness to accuse others, increased vastly the suspicion against herself and her husband. Moreover, the count declared that he would answer for the honesty of his servants, and seemed firmly persuaded that the d'Anglades were the actors in the robbery. So strong also was the impression against them on the mind of M. Deffita, that he made the remark to M. d'Anglade, shortly after the discovery of the louis-d'ors in the trunk: "Either you or I has committed this robbery." The result of the search was, that at the requisition of the count, with the consent of the public prosecutor, M. and Madame d'Anglade were thrown into prison, confined in separate places, and prevented from seeing anyone. Their effects were all sealed up at the same time.

The following are the chief circumstances, in addition to the discovery of the louis and the genealogical paper, and other grounds of suspicion mentioned, that came out against the prisoners on further inquiry, and led to their condemnation :—

The d'Anglades knew that the count had large sums of money by him; they made a frivolous excuse to break up the engagement to go to the country; on the Tuesday night,

which, in all probability, was the night of the robbery, M. d'Anglade supped in his own house, which was rarely or never the case at other times; he sought and obtained from Count de Mongommery the keys of the street door before the latter's departure, which keys were necessary for the carrying away of the stolen property; and, when interrogated separately about the seventy louis d'ors, the two prisoners contradicted each other—the husband saying that he did not think his wife knew of his having that money, and that he had not touched it for several weeks, while the wife declared that she had several times counted it over along with him, and that the last reckoning of it had taken place three or four days back.

M. d'Anglade's previous character was, besides, inquired into, and report said that

he was a gambler. A robbery was also proved to have taken place in the same house before Count de Mongommery came to it, and while D'Anglade lived in it, the authors of which had never been detected.

All these circumstances, slight as they were singly, were held in the mass to justify the application of the torture to the unfortunate M. d'Anglade, in order to extract from him a confession of that guilt which he persisted in denying. He was a man of a weak frame of body, and of a sensitive spirit.

The torture he bore with extreme firmness, and not a word or sign, in acknowledgment of the charge, could be elicited from him. But this did not, according to the laws of that day, establish his innocence. On the contrary, though never regularly convicted in a court of justice, he and his wife were condemned by an arbitrary decree to all the penalties attending conviction.

On the 16th of February 1688, after undergoing the torture, and lying five months in confinement, M. d'Anglade was sentenced to the galleys for nine years, and his wife to banishment from Paris and its environs for the same period; besides which, all their property was confiscated, in order to make restitution to the Count de Mongommery of the money he had lost. The sums which the D'Anglades were decreed to pay, amounted in all to about 32,000 livres.

M. d Anglade went with a chain of criminals to Marseille, where he died within four months. His health had gradually declined in prison, and the torture gave the crowning blow.

He died, in a resigned and even cheerful frame of mind, with his eyes fixed on another and a better world, praying for forgiveness to all who had injured him. Madame d'Anglade's health also broke up in confinement, and prevented her from being ever removed from Paris, in pursuance of her sentence. But her cares were greatly soothed by the presence of her daughter, a child of five years old, and of a sweet and affectionate disposition.

After the mother recovered in some degree, the child fell ill, chiefly owing to the wretched character of the lodgment to which they were doomed. The mother besought and obtained the favour of being removed to a cell of a somewhat better kind; and here she was occupied in attending upon her child when a great change took place in the condition of this unhappy family.

Within a short period of the decease of M. d'Anglade, certain anonymous letters came into the hands of the criminal authorities, announcing that the writer had retired into a cloister, and that he felt it necessary to unburden his conscience by revealing the true authors of the robbery of Count de Mongommery's property.

These were, the writer said, a man named Vincent Belestre, and the chaplain Gagnard, the latter of whom had been in the count's service at the time, but had since left it. A woman named Comble was also mentioned as one who knew all the particulars. Though the Count de Mongommery's partisans averred these letters to be an invention of Madame d'Anglade, yet inquiries were made into the characters of Belestre and Gagnard, which were found to be of the very worst order. They were discovered also to have exhibited about the time in question a sudden influx of wealth. These circumstances induced a search for them, which was unsuccessful, until, as if providentially, both men came into custody upon other charges. A short time afterwards, the writer of the anonymous letters, who was a needy priest of the name of Fontpeire, and the woman Comble, were brought forward, and a strong body of testimony came out respecting the robbery.

It was brought home beyond all possibility of doubt to Belestre and Gagnard. Gagnard had given his accomplice impressions of all the necessary keys, and Belestre had fabricated false ones, by the aid of which he had committed the robbery. It is unnecessary to enter into all the particulars which came out one by one against the prisoners. Suffice it to say, that in the end Gagnard confessed the whole. He and his associate in guilt paid the penalty of it with their lives. It is remarkable that Gagnard said before his execution, that had he been questioned at the time the house was searched, he was in such a state of agitation as must have made him confess all. A considerable property purchased with the stolen money by Belestre, and the valuable pearl-necklace, were recovered by the Count de Mongommery.

These discoveries could not restore the innocent D'Anglade to life, but his name, at least, might be cleared from reproach. Madame d'Anglade demanded that the justification of her husband's memory and of her own innocence should be pronounced, and also claimed the restitution of their property, as well as damages from the Count de Mongommery for his calumnious accusation. This produced a trial of some importance, as the count justified the proceedings which had taken place, and insisted, among other pleas, that damages might as well be sought from the ministers of the law as from him. The answers made by Madame d'Anglade to his recapitulation of the evidence against her husband and herself, shew clearly that if men could at the time have rid their minds of the unhappy prepossession against the accused, the issue of the case would not have been what it was. Madame d'Anglade shewed, that a slight given by the count's sisters to her husband had caused his refusal to go to the country with the count, and proved from what parties the rouleau of seventy louis had been got by her husband. The printed genealogy, she also proved, had been sold to her by a broker. Many other points were cleared up by her, some of which had been explained at the very first; but the eyes of justice were dimmed by prejudice. Apparently, the court now felt that the Count de Mongommery's rash confidence, in stating that "he would responsible for the honesty of his servants," had prevented the truly guilty parties from being examined and detected. His assertion, also, that the printed genealogy belonged to him, materially influenced the case, and was utterly devoid of foundation. Upon these and other grounds, the court decided that the count should restore all the property of the d'Anglades, and should pay all the expenses, from first to last, which this case had occasioned; which last heavy imposition was regarded by the court as a sufficient assigument of damages against the count.

Thus ended this case, in which an unfortunate man lost his life almost on mere suspicion. We may congratulate ourselves, that such things could not occur in our day, where the accused and accuser have equal facilities. Though the loss of a husband and a father was too severe a one to be ever forgot, Madame d'Anglade and her daughter had the satisfaction, at least, of re-entering society with honour and an unblemished name. The sympathy of the world was so much excited in their fovour, that a portion of livres was collected, and presented to the daughter of the ill-fated d'Anglade. She afterwards married M. des Essarts, counsellor-at-law.

CHAPTER CXVI.

THE COLONEL'S VISIT TO OSBORNE.

AFTER Colonel Jack had parted with his two companions, namely the outcast and the gentleman whom he had met with on the road, he accompanied Honora to her husband's town residence. This proved to be a palatial mansion in Berkeley Square, then one of the most fashionable localities in the metropolis. It has fallen down in repute since the time of which we are writing, although it still retains something of its grandeur and respectability. Honora was in high spirits as she proceeded along towards her home, for she knew that it would not only be an agreeable surprise to Osborne, but a source of infinite delight for him to again behold the friend of his youth. As we progress onwards in what the poet calls "the weary pilgrimage," the faces we have known in our earlier days become doubly dear to us. Henry Osborne's reminiscences were nothing but pleasurable ones with regard to our hero—from his earliest youth he had been accustomed to receive naught but kindness from him, and although he would not, indeed, from motives of delicacy dared not give expression to his deep regret at the colonel's mode of life, he would at the same time willingly have given up half his income to have withdrawn him from the occupation he. was at present following. Shakespeare has observed that "there is a tide in the affairs of men which taken at the

flood leads on to fortune. Omitted, all their lives are spent in shoals and shallows." The tide had passed with Colonel Jack. Early warped to wrong he now found it impossible to be bent back into the straight path. A sadness crept over him as he neared the mansio noccupied by Osborne—a sadness which he found it difficult, nay, almost impossible to cast on one side. Honora's carriage came to a sudden halt and stopped opposite to a house blazing with lights. A loud and prolonged cisserara was given by the footman and in a few seconds the door of the mansion was thrown open disclosing a magnificent hall and vestibule. Colonel Jack dismounted and throwing the reins of his horse to one of the serving men he entered with Honora.

There were several guests in the rooms above, who had dispersed themselves at the various side-tables, and were seated at the same in various groups, some of whom were playing cards, whilst others were discussing the last news and general topics of the day. Henry Osborne himself, was in one of the smaller rooms above. The major-domo of the establishment knocked and then entered, softly announcing the arrival of his mistress and Mr. Halford. Osborne gave a start and caught up a candle-stick bearing a wax candle of colossal dimensions. He walked across the room and with his right hand was about to push open one of the richly panelled folding-doors. The major-domo laid hid hand upon his chest and made a low bows This was such a dignified and profound obeisance that Osborne turned an inquiring glance at his domestic.

"Pardon me, my respected master," said the major-domo. "Pardon me, but—"

Here he placed his hand upon his heart and made another low bow, which was, to say the least of it exquisitely comic.

The man appeared to have all the solemn and grand dignity of the whole establishment upon his shoulders and more than this he seemed well able to bear the weight. He was attired in full court costume—the old fashioned embroidered coat and peruke.

"What is the matter, Biggleswade?" inquired Osborne.

"Pardon me," said the domestic, "but, may it please you, I will bear the luminary."

"Oh, you will carry the candlestick. Well do so, if it please you," said Osborne, handing the same to his servitor, and smiling the while at the latter's punctilios. "Take it, in welcome, I am not at all particular, you know."

"N—o," drawled out Mr. Biggleswade; "but for the honour of the establishment I would rather not see my master wait upon himself or do any menial office."

"Psha! A man is none the worse, Biggleswade—none the worse, believe me, for learning to wait upon himself."

Another low bow was the only reply the domestic vouchsafed to the latter observation, He took the candle from his master, and drawing himself up in an attitude of pomposity, lighted Osborne down the grand staircase.

As the latter descended, he caught sight of his old friend, Halford. He rushed forward and grasped him by the hand, and indulged in a natural but unaristocratic demonstration of friendship.

Mr. Biggleswade shrugged his shoulders in despair. This violent external show of feeling was decidedly objectionable to the major-domo of Osborne's establishment. It was not considered orthodox, or at all the thing, by that worthy, who at all times objected to any undue expression of feeling.

Our hero was conducted by Osborne into an elegant and sumptuously furnished suite of apartments, and introduced by the host to the various guests assembled therein.

Our hero joined one of the parties in a hand at whist; after which, supper was served in an adjoining apartment.

The highwayman felt that he was moving in fashionable society, for most of the guests were persons of distinction. They did not however, mind cheating at cards, so the colonel found out—the old ladies especially. He laughed to himself when he thought of what strange inconsistencies and antagonistic materials the human character is made up.

As the night wore on, one by one the guests began to depart, and eventually Colonel Jack was left alone with Osborne and Honora.

Although the hour was late and the night far advanced, none of the three felt disposed to part company; and as may be readily imagined, the most pleasurable part of the evening was when they sat down to enjoy some social converse.

Colonel Jack's manner was serious, not to say melancholy. Old recollections of his early life came rushing across his brain in rapid succession. Few of us pass through our existence without some painful remembrance in taking a retrospective glance of the road we have travelled. This was more especially so with our hero.

"Frank," said Osborne, slapping his companion on the shoulder, "I need hardly say, my best of friends, that this is the happiest hour I have passed for many and many a day. I have not seen you since my—my marriage."

"You have been on the continent, Harry," answered his visitor.

"Yes, but have returned long since. Did you not know that?"

"I heard that you had returned."

"And yet you have kept yourself so much a stranger?" said Osborne, reproachfully.

"Ah, Harry," said the colonel, thoughtfully, "it is not from any want of friendly feeling, I need hardly assure you of that; but as I told you before, our ways are different, and I should be sorry if the presence of—of Colonel Jack should in any way compromise you. A happy future now lies before you, and no one in the world is more rejoiced at your position than myself; that also I need hardly say."

Then suddenly after a pause, he said—

"You see something of Squabshot, I suppose?"

Honora and Osborne laughed outright at this query.

"Oh, dear yes," exclaimed the latter, "often enough, believe me. Why, do you know, our little friend is madly in love?"

"I shouldn't have supposed it of him," answered the colonel, with an ill-concealed smile.

"It's a fact, then, I assure you."

"And who may the lady be? Do I know her?"

"Perfectly well—Edith Staunton, Honora's old friend and schoolfellow."

"He might do worse than fall in love with Miss Staunton."

"Yes, and it appears Squabshot has got some money somehow or other."

"I shouldn't have supposed that of him either," answered our hero, with another quiet smile; "I might do worse than that."

"And he's not a bad chap," said Osborne.

"Bad!—no; he's a capital fellow. Rather eccentric and crotchetty, but a thorough good fellow in the main. Does the fair lady listen to his suit?"

"Well, she laughed at him in the first instance; but latterly—"

"Well, latterly?"

"Why she don't laugh so much. She finds that he is terribly in earnest."

"It's the first time he ever was."

"No doubt; and so he is, perhaps, making up for lost time. It is really too bad to make game of him, but his agony is so irresistibly comic, although he does not intend it to be so."

"Comedy is Squabshot's forte," said the colonel; "I thought he left money making and love making to others."

"No, he's been trying his hand at both of late," said Osborne, who had not the slightest idea where his friend had obtained the cash he was at present in the enjoyment of.

"Talking of money," continued Osborne, "puts me in mind of something. I dare say you will guess what it is."

The colonel did guess, but did not feel disposed to say so. He therefore made no reply.

"You know Frank, I have now at my

control enough means to satisfy half a dozen men, and, therefore—"

"I know what you would say," answered the colonel. "Rest content upon that subject; I am of the same opinion as when we last conversed about it."

"You might do me the favour of accepting of something. I do not mean to offend you, Frank, I need hardly say that; but I had hoped when you reconsidered the matter, you would have come to a different conclusion."

"I am resolved," answered Colonel Jack, "and do not see anything to cause me to alter my first resolution. Apart from this, did I need worldly wealth, I might without doubt be in possession of the same. You remember that box which I promised to restore to you when myself and companions stopped the Oxford coach?"

This last observation was addressed to Honora.

"Yes, of course," answered Mrs. Osborne, "I remember it well enough; but to say the truth, I had quite forgotten the circumstance till you mentioned it."

"Well, I did not restore it to you, that is quite certain."

"No," said Honora, with a smile.

"And why, think you? Simply because its contents did not concern you; but I am given to understand that they do me."

"Indeed! How so?" inquired Osborne.

"It appears that Lady Reichbeck died immensely rich. She was always reputed to be wealthy, but I believe no one imagined that she was possessed of the vast amount of wealth, from which my lawyer informs me I come into a considerable share of this."

"Then why not prove the will and take possession of your rights?" said Osborne.

"Well, there are many legal impediments at present, and the case is a difficult one to unravel, so Mr. Baintree informs me; all of which requires patience, perseverance, and an outlay of capital, in the shape of legal fees and costs."

"Well you need not stand still for money," said Osborne.

"Oh, no, I do not require any—Mr. Baintree will willingly undertake all that. Besides, even supposing such were not the case, I have ample means at my own disposal."

"And are too proud to be beholden to your friends," answered Osborne, with a smile. "By the way, did you notice that foreign gentleman I introduced you to—the Count de Wilts?"

"What, he with the thick moustache and beard?"

"Yes, the very same."

"I did not take particular notice of him. Why?—does he know me?"

"Not that I am aware of; only a singular circumstances is connected with him. He has but one arm, as no doubt you observed."

"I did not notice it."

"Ah, he's lost an arm," said Honora.

"I made his acquaintance in Paris, and finding him a gentlemanly man—indeed, most particularly so—we became very good friends, and hence his appearance here. But I was going to tell you how he lost his right arm."

"In a duel?"

"No, had it amputated."

"Mortification?"

"No, you would never guess. Listen, and I'll endeavour to give you the history as it was detailed to me. About twenty years ago the house of Monsieur de Luertal was celebrated for the brilliancy of its fêtes and parties. Contrary to the established custom, it was neither in Paris nor in the winter time that these festivities took place. Monsieur de Leurtal possessed a beautiful mansion in the vicinity of Anteuil, and thither were invited the most celebrated people of the day.

"Amongst those who assiduously sought the society of M. de Leurtal at this period was the Count de Wilts, an individual who had attained a considerable degree of military reputation, and who was also well known as a man of intellect and information. Indeed, his fashionable education was superintended and completed by certain ladies, especially those who flourished in the time of the Directory, and who distributed a portion of their own foppery to many an ill-bred clown, and thus the Count de Wilts was considered a polished gentleman."

"And so he appears to be," said Colonel Jack.

"Oh, without a doubt, so he is," answered Osborne. "It is not, however, necessary for me to describe the nature of that passion which he speedily entertained for Madame de Leurtal, nor the particulars of the early stage of their reciprocal affection. Let me hasten to detail to you that event which proved so disastrous to him.- I give it you as it was detailed to me me," said Osborne, and he continued as follows :—

It appears that one morning, it was scarcely two o'clock, and although in the summer season, darkness prevailed around a window was noiselessly opened at one of the angles of M. de Leurtal's mansion, and a man descended from it more noiselessly still.

A female's anxious glances followed him from that casement; and when the object of her solicitude had reached the ground in safety, she made him a sign of tenderness and satisfaction.

Count de Wilts, for it was he, acknowledged the sweet token of adieu, and hastily retreated amongst the labyrinths of shrubs and trees that surround the house.

Amelie—such was the name of Madame de Leurtal—did not leave the window until she had suffered the necessary time to elapse to enable the count to reach the park gate. She then retired; but whether the hinges of the wicket had creaked on their pivots—whether the gate itself had been shut with less care than usual—or whether it was the cry of a human being—Madame de Leurtal knew not; it was, however, certain that an unaccustomed noise fell upon her ears.

She hastily opened her window, and listened once more; but she heard nothing farther to excite her alarms; and the deep silence that ensued entirely calmed her terrors.

The daylight dawned—and at length the breakfast hour arrived. Madame de Leurtal descended to the dining-room to do the honours of the table to her husband and the numerous guests who were staying at the house; and as usual, the conversation was lively and gay; the principal topic of discourse being the ball which was to be given that very evening in honour of Madame de Leurtal's birthday. Every one was prepared to be amiable and agreeable upon so interesting an occasion; when suddenly the gardener, whose name was Antoine, rushed wildly into the apartment, giving vent to the violence of his feelings in loud and hasty exclamations.

"Oh! my God—my God!" cried he; "what have I found? We are all done for now; everything will be laid waste throughout the country! Yes, sir, the robbers have entered the park; but whether they be Jacobins, republicans, or highwaymen, I scarcely know!"

"Who has dared enter my inclosures?" demanded M. de Leurtal, interrupting the ejaculations of Antoine.

"Who has dared to enter your park, sir," repeated Antoine, vehemently; "who has dared? Why, assassins, sir—villains—robbers—with false keys that open the wicket next to the wood."

Amelie felt that her cheeks lost all their colour at this moment. But Antoine cried so lustily that the attention of everyone was directed towards him.

M. de Leurtal again stopped him in the midst of his incongruous lamentations, and demanded what had happened to occasion so extraordinary an ebullition of woe?

"Behold, sir!" cried the unfortunate gardener, now almost angry: "behold what I have discovered!"

And with these words he drew a handkerchief from his pocket, and threw two fingers, horribly smashed and mutilated, upon the table before his master.

Everyone present drew back in unfeigned horror, while Amelie uttered a loud shriek; but in a moment she recollected that her own happiness and that of her lover depended upon her prudence; and she accordingly succeeded in mastering her feelings.

During the silence which succeeded the cry of horror that had escaped the lips of Madame de Leurtal at the sight of the bloody members lying upon the table, the gardener had time to continue his clamorous narrative.

"Yes, sir," said Antoine, in a loud voice —"they were caught in the park gate; and that which proves that the thing was done by robbers, and that the rogues were numerous, is the fact that the wicket had only smashed the fingers, and that they were cut off afterwards with a knife. It is not possible that one man could have courage enough to operate in so terrible a manner upon himself."

M. de Leurtal examined the fingers with gloomy looks and deep attention; and then suddenly glancing hastily round the room, without fixing his eye upon any one in particular, he said with a bitter smile—

"The skin of these mangled fingers is very white, and those nails are kept in too good order to be those of a robber. Is not such your opinion, ladies?"

Every one of these words fell like scorching drops of boiling lead upon the heart of Amelie! Her teeth chattered—she felt that her brain whirled, and that her eyes became dim; but the various opinions which M. de Leurtal's question called forth from the guests present at the breakfast table, created too much confusion to allow her emotions to be perceived. The indignation of her friends concealed the shame of Amelie.

Presently M. de Leurtal, having uttered a sort of half apology to his guests, demanded of Antoine if the traces of blood that was left afforded any particular ground of suspicion?

"Impossible," replied the gardener; "they stop at the foot of the wicket."

"And you have discovered nothing more?" continued M. de Leurtal; "nothing that can put us upon the right scent, as it were —no fragment of a garment, no riding-whip, nor key, or anything, in fine, which the wounded man may have let fall?"

"No, sir, no; I have found nothing," replied the gardener. "But another fact, which proves that the villians were numerous —or rather, that there were more than one —is that the knife, which cut off the fingers, was wiped upon a piece of paper, a thing that no wounded man could think of doing. This is the paper I allude to."

"Give it to me!" cried M. de Leurtal, hastily; and he anxiously seized upon the bloody paper which Antoine handed to him.

He examined it long and attentively; and during his investigation, while every one was silently gazing upon the host, Amelie could hear her heart beating in her breast. Suddenly M. de Leurtal raised his eyes towards her, and said, without exhibiting even the most remote suspicion—

"If you examine this, you will think as I do. Here is the mark where the blade was wiped; and the trace clearly proves that the amputation was performed with a flat poignard, and not with a common knife."

"Exactly what it is!" shouted Antoine. "Those brigands always carry poignards! the villians! the ruffians! the murderers!"

M. de Leurtal ordered his domestic to leave the room, while Amelie took the paper, and mechanically passed it to her right-hand neighbour so soon as she had glanced cursorily over it. This individual scrutinised it with the utmost curiosity, and again awoke the slumbering terrors of the wretched Amelie, by crying—

"Yes; there is something written beneath this blood!"

"Let me see it—let me see it!" exclaimed M. de Leurtal, his eyes flashing fire, and his voice almost choked with emotion.

The paper was passed to him once more, and after a great deal of difficulty, he gradually decyphered these words:—"Monsieur and Madame de Leurtal have the honour to invite—"

He stopped; the paper was torn just *there*. The syllables of this phrase, thus seen through the bloody traces, sounded like the call of Death in the ears Amelie. M. de Leurtal crushed the paper in his hands with terrible violence; and, now for the first time giving vent to the tempest that raged within him, he addressed his wife in a fierce tone, and said—

"'Tis well! This evening we shall see which of our guests will be missing!"

He hastily left the room, followed by his friends, in a state of moody and suspicious silence. Amelie remained alone behind, and for the first time was she now enabled to examine the terrible object of accusrtion. She gazed upon it, and—so well is each beautiful feature of a lover registered in the tablet of his mistress's memory—she speedily recognised those fair fingers, and faultless nails which had also struck her husband. She recognised them—she was alone—and she secured the sad relic!

But, oh, this was not all the devotion of the noble count to the honour of his mistress! To mutilate himself was terrible: but that which he subsequently did, was far more chivalrous still.

It were impossible to depict the misery—the agony—the despair that rent the bosom of Madame de Leurtal throughout that unhappy day! Years—long, long years of woe were outdone by that single day of bitterness—of reckless project—and of unutterable distress! A vain hope—ever attendant upon those cases where the result of misfortune is not yet known—occasionally penetrated to her wounded soul. The sense of her duties, and the necessity of attending to her domestic avocations, also came to her assistance, and she thus partially soothed her agitated mind.

In the evening she appeared in the drawing-room, resplendent and calm! In proportion as the hour of danger advanced, she felt that she gradually became more tranquil. Instead of suffering her misfortune to gain upon her step by step, she calculated its full extent in her imagination; she knew that the lapse of a few minutes would decide her fate—her dishonour, and her death; and she was prepared for so great a catastrophe.

The entertainment commenced, and the guests arrived in crowds. M. de Leurtal, stationed at a little distance from the door, affected to receive them with a degree of politeness which permitted him to count and examine all who passed him.

The hour advanced, and M. de Wilts did not make his appearance; a few other fashionables of the day were also late. Madame de Leurtal was at that period sufficiently beautiful to excite the desires of more than one, and to receive an universal show of homage, so that the suspicions of her husband might, after all, remain undecided and dubious.

The festival continued, and some of the expected guests were still wanting; but they were only ladies or old men—not one on whom suspicion could fall, save M. de Wilts. Amelie was aware of this; and her husband whispered in her ears, as she passed by the place where he was posted—

"The circle of my suspicions gradually becomes smaller; it now includes but three names—and already might I seleet one, and convince myself that Monsieur de—"

At the moment when M. de Leurtal was about to pronounce the fatal name, the drawing-room door was thrown quickly open, and a lacquey announced the Count de Wilts, Monsieur and Madame de Leurtal were each so anxious to devour him with a look, that neither perceived the disorder which was pictured upon the other's countenance. But the appearance of the count excited far different sentiments in the breasts of his entertainers. M. de Wilts came carelessly forward, with his opera-hat under his arm, playing with his shirt-frill with one hand, and dangling his watch-chain with the other—both being covered with milk-white gloves.

"Ah! it is not he, then!" thought Monsieur and Madame de Leurtal, both at the same moment.

"It is not he whom I must suspect," said the husband, feeling himself suddenly embarrassed and ashamed.

"It is not he who was wounded!" said Amelie, within herself.

Oh, from that moment, how everything was changed in her eyes! The magnitude of the danger which menaced her was diminished, her lover was safe, and her agonies of soul were abrogated. These ideas raised her spirits to such a height, that had not M. de Leurtal been occupied in waiting for other guests who did not come, he would have read the truth in the joyous glances of his wife. Several times, when M. de Wilts passed near her, he spoke with that ease and elegance of which he was the model. The ball progressed, and Amelie was relieved of all her fears.

In the course of the evening, according to the custom of the times, the company present proposed to dance a gavot. The most distinguished people in the room were called upon to figure in this dance; so that M. de Wilts soon found himself placed as the *vis-a vis* of Madame de Leurtal. Amelie was in ecstacies at the prospect of being enabled to receive and return the courteous smiles of her lover, and to press the hand so freely tendered in the prescribed mazes of the dance.

Her heart felt lighter than it ever before had seemed ; and even if a remnant of dread had lurked in her mind, it would have fled at the sight of the ease and grace with which M. de Wilts acquitted himself in the gavot, and by which he attracted the attention of all the spectators present. In one of the figures, when the rapidity of the Terpsichorean movements concealed every expression of any passion or particular feeling, Amelie suffered herself to squeeze her lover's hand, as if to felicitate him upon a joy which she supposed he could not comprehend. At that moment a terrible shriek re-echoed around the room.

It did not emanate from M. de Wilts. It escaped from the lips of the unhappy Amelie; for she had felt, as she pressed her lover's hand, the fingers of cotton, so skilfully prepared, yield to her touch, while he was unaware that she had thus intended to convey a token of her esteem.

On the following morning a dreadful fever seized upon Madame de Leurtal ; and every morning did M. de Wilts call to inquire after her health, thus evincing his tenderness to the last. At the expiration of a week, he departed to join the army, carrying his secret with him!

Monsieur and Madame de Leurtal were shortly after informed, that, having been dreadfully wounded in an engagement where he exposed himself with uncalled-for rashness, he was obliged to undergo a shocking operation. On his return, he had lost an arm.

"Heaven!" exclaimed Madame de Leurtal, so soon as she saw him alone, and for the first time—"what have you done?"

"The most prudent thing I could do," was the calm and tranquil reply. "Your honour was in my keeping."

"And to save my reputation you have submitted to this painful operation. What a dreadful sacrifice!" exclaimed Madame de Leurtal. "Kind, generous, noble-hearted creature. How shall I repay you?"

"Madame, I am content," answered the count.

"And is it possible such an amount of chivalry exists in the present day," exclaimed Colonel Jack. "Positively the count deserves a statue erected by a joint subscription from the fair sex."

"Ah, ah ! Honora would subscribe no doubt," said Osborne, laughing. "Would you not, my dear."

"I don't know," answered his wife, with a smile. "I don't know till I am asked."

The night wore on, or more properly speaking, the morning drew on apace and eventually the three friends were compelled to part for a few hours at any rate. Colonel Jack had agreed to take up his quarters at his friend's house for the night, and eventually the three retired to their respective dormitories.

In the morning when Colonel Jack made his appearance at the breakfast-table, he met with a surprise as sudden as it was unexpected. Osborne and Honora were seated in the breakfast-parlour and were rising to greet their guest when our hero's daughter ran up to him with outstretched arms. So completely taken aback was Colonel Jack by this circumstance that he hardly knew how to express himself. He folded the little girl in his arms and embraced her tenderly. Osborne and Honora looked on in silence. Presently the colonel gave a glance of inquiry, at his friends, and Honora was the first to speak.

"I know you will pardon this liberty Mr. Halford," she said in hesitating accents." "For it is a liberty to bring the dear little creature here without your permission, but then the circumstances of the case must be our excuse."

"Madam, Mr. Osborne," stammered out our hero. "I do not deem it a liberty—circumstances of the case?—I do not as yet exactly comprehend your meaning—Rosalie was with her grandmother some hundred or so miles away from London."

"She was, Frank," said Osborne, "but

her grandmother died suddenly some two months ago."

"Dead! Is this possible?" exclaimed our hero.

"It is but too true, and so finding that Rosalie was left alone without any female guardian, I took the liberty, after having consulted with Honora, of taking upon myself the responsibility of bringing her up to London, and, if it please you, we will take charge of her for the future."

"You are very kind," said Colonel Jack, in a hesitating manner. "I am sure, Harry, I am much beholden to you for this unlooked for act of kindness."

"And we are so fond of our dear Rosalie that we never want to part with her," said Honora.

No. 79.

"Yes, Honora has been making up her mind to adopt her," said Osborne.

A heightened colour was observable on Colonel Jack's features at this last observation.

"Adopt my own dear Rosalie," he murmured. "I—that is—Mrs. Osborne would hardly like to take the responsibility upon herself of so onerous a task."

"Aye, but she would; and, indeed it would be the greatest favour you could possibly confer upon her to consent to this arrangement," answered Osborne.

"Oh, as far as I am concerned, I cannot possibly have any objection."

It was eventually agreed that Rosalie should continue under the charge of Honora; and Colonel Jack, in the course of conversation, found that Curson had been brought by Honora to her residence in Berkeley Square, and installed as a domestic in the establishment.

The colonel was much pleased to hear this, as he knew his daughter had become attached to Curson.

Before he left Osborne's residence, he had the latter called up into the parlour, and had a long private and confidential conversation with her, the nature of which it will be hardly necessary to detail, as it merely concerned his own private domestic affairs.

Eventually he took leave of Osborne and Honora, promising at the same time to be more constant in his attendance on them. After which he proceeded to that respectable hostelrie, the Cow and Cauliflower, whither he went to meet the outcast, whom it will be remembered he had billitted upon Mr. Dyson, alias the Badger.

That worthy was in a state of ecstacy at once more beholding Colonel Jack, whom he had not seen for some time past. He ushered him into his own private back parlour, in which was seated a raw-boned athletic-looking man.

"Friend of mine," said Mr. Dyson, in answer to Colonel Jack's look of inquiry; "just come from the north—Mr. MacFergus."

The colonel bowed and sat himself down without further ceremony.

"Well, Bill," he said, "you had some one come from me last night, eh?"

"Yes," answered Mr. Dyson.

"Is he here?"

"He's here, leastways I 'spose so," answered the Badger; "he ain't up yet. He's rather fond of his bed."

"Well, no matter, Dyson—I am in no hurry. Any of my chaps been here?"

"Not for the last day or so. What will you take, colonel?—a drop of brandy?"

"Perhaps the gentleman would like a glass of wine," said MacFergus. "I shall be happy to do a bottle of champagne with him, or any other sort."

"With all my heart," said Colonel Jack, who was at all times pleased with an open frankness of manner in anyone.

Glasses were filled and emptied—they were replenished again with a like result.

"You are from the north, sir, so Dyson informs me. What part, may I inquire?"

"Not far from Inverness," answered the Scotchman.

"Ah, he's been mixed up in a rum sort of case, he has," said Mr. Dyson. "Now we've half an hour to spare, just tell my friend all about it," said the Badger.

Mr. MacFergus cleared his throat, and then gave our hero the following particulars, which we reserve for the next chapter.

CHAPTER CXVII.

MR. MACFERGUS'S ADVENTURE.

"I LIKE to tell a story or narrative in which I have been in some way connected myself," said Mr. MacFergus, "for in that case a man speaks with more freedom and certainty; and with what I am about to relate I was so far connected as to know the two principal characters slightly, and was the first man who brought intelligence of the death of one of them, and raised the hue and cry after his murderers.

It happened, that about the middle of September, 17—, Robert Armstrong, grieve to Mr. Harbottle of Bathwaite, accompanied by four other borderers as common drivers (Robin being what is called topsman on the road), went into the North Highlands to bring a great number of sheep, which had been previously bought by Mr. Harbottle, both for himself and Lord Carlisle.

Robin Armstrong had the sole charge of receiving, paying, and conducting the droves home; so he had a great deal of money to take with him. This he took all in banknotes, for the Highlanders in those days would not look at gold; and even yet they always view it with a jealous eye, and will give a good luck-penny for Scotch banknotes instead.

Robin's way of carrying so much money was rather novel. He put it into his stockings, a stocking in each shoe, tied all in the pack of his plaid, and threw them over his shoulder; and in that way walked barefooted into the middle of the Highlands. In the mean time, he had a book stuffed with waste-paper in his breast-pocket; so that his own associates never knew where his treasure was concealed, but all the while conceived it to be in his breast-pocket. Robin's journey was doomed to be one of adventures, and those not of the most agreeable nature.

He was a man just of ordinary size and strength, but of a hasty temper, and sudden and quick in quarrel. The very first night he was in the Highlands, he and his associates fell in with a band of smugglers, some way about the sources of the Bran, who filled them all drunk. Then Robin began to abuse the men as lawless vagabonds, and threatened not only to thrash them, but to give them up to justice. By this time Robin could with difficulty stand, so the Highlanders gave them a drubbing, and, as a remuneration for the whisky they had drunk, stole Robin's huge pocket-book, which his associates had nick-named Matthew Henry. When he told them the next morning how he had lost it in the fray, their blank looks manifested such vexation and misery that

Armstrong laughed most heartily in his sleeve, as the shoes and stockings were safe, and not one sixpence lost.

They all urged Robin to return, arguing that it was vain to go forward without the money; but he refused to return, saying, they could not go home without the sheep, for that he could draw upon his master, or the Earl of Carlisle, to any amount, at Inverness; or, if that could not be done, they were all five responsible men, and would join in a bond for the price of the sheep. This did not go well down, but, with fallen countenances, they strode on after their commander.

The next night they reached a place called Carnoch, which, though I never saw, must, I think, be about the braes of Tummel It was a small moor-farm, held by one John Menzies, who let it out to droves and boarded the men, selling them plenty of good smuggled whisky at twopence the gill. Our borderers, knowing the habitation and the cheapness of the lodgings well from long experience, made towards it, reached it at a late hour, and found there one Hector Kennedy and three Highlanders with him, who were conducting a great drove of cattle to the south.

This Kennedy, whom I have seen twice or thrice living, and once dead, was a tall, powerful man, rather thin made, but excelling in strength and temerity. He was a perfect ruffian, and was employed as a topsman by the Highland drovers for many years, merely because he was one of those fellows who would not be thwarted in anything.

His will was law, all the way from Cape Wrath to the middle of England. He would turn his cattle off the road to any quiet pasture he choose, nor would he turn them a foot for one until his own time; and when any of the shepherds or farmers were very hard upon him, he thought nothing of knocking them down; indeed, he delighted in it, and thought it fine sport.

He one time came to the south with no fewer than twenty-four men under him, which were a perfect scourge to the country through which they passed.

Menzies' house at Carnoch being small, the Highlanders and borderers came in contact; not a very safe one; little better than a barrel of gunpowder and fire. They supped together sumptuously on venison, bull, trouts, and potatoes, and then fell to drinking Menzies' cheap whisky.

Now I have always noticed, that this Highland whisky has a peculiar facility in stirring up the angry passions.

For several hours the two parties were the best friends in the world, and seemed so happy that they had met; but at length, when they happened to be all speaking at once, a deadly quarrel arose between the two leaders, nobody knew how.

It was indeed said, and sworn to by one man, that Armstrong, being somewhat inebriated, had used very degrading language regarding the Highlanders, as to their ignorance and poverty, and in particular to the debased state of the Kennedy's, whom their chief Glengarry, was obliged to banish from the territory. However, ere ever the rest knew what was going on, Kennedy had knocked Rob Armstrong down, who was lying senseless on the floor.

A furious onset was then made by the Borderers, who cracked the crowns of the Highlanders with their cudgels considerably well. There were now four to four, but Kennedy was a tower of strength, and reckless beyond calculation; so that when they fairly closed, the Borderers were rather overpowered, all save one man, Thomas Little, who had downed his opponent, and was kenelling him with the one hand and choking him with the other. It was at this moment that Menzies came in to see what was the matter, and found Thomas Little stabbed to the heart, and bleeding to death. He never spoke another word! And the *skene-dhu*, or black dirk, was still sticking in his side; while, in the mean time, the tables and lights had all been overturned.

This dreadful catastrophe, of course, put an end to the fray; but Menzies knew not what to do, there being a murdered man lying in his house, and no justice to be had nearer than Perth. He rode first to Mr. Robertson, for a warrant to seize on the aggressors; but that gentleman was not at home. He then sent a man on horseback all the way to Perth, to warn the sheriff, fiscal, and proper officers, to await the drovers at Aberfeldie, as he could not detain the cattle; but he warned neither of the parties of what he had done, but the next morning hurried the Highlanders off his farm, with their cattle.

Armstrong withstood this, and told Kennedy that neither he nor one of his men should leave the spot until they answered to the laws of their country for the murder of his friend. Kennedy began to storm and rage in his usual way, and threatened to stab any man who dared to interrupt his progress without a regular warrant; in the mean time brandishing his dirk.

"You murdering rascal!" said Armstrong, coming close up to him without fear, " touch one of us with that butcher's whittle of yours, if you dare, for your blood! You took me anawares last night, but tit for tat is fair play;" and with his huge cudgel he knocked him down,

Time was it, for Kennedy was just getting

himself to close with him, with his drawn dirk in his hand; but the rest of the Highlanders, whose hearts were chilled by the foul murder of the foregoing night, offered no interference, although the Borderers rather wished and provoked it. They, however, readily assisted their foreman, washing his head with whisky, and binding it up with a napkin; and it was not long till he was able to arise and accompany them though in a very weakly state.

Armstrong still persisted in detaining them by force; but Menzies came and spoke to him, and finding that he could not detain the cattle, he suffered them to proceed; but he and his three followers kept them company, as a guard over the men, that none of them might escape; and yet, strange to tell! for all their vigilance they lost one. The men had let the cattle rest for a while above the old castle of Garth, and when they rose to move forward one of the Highlanders was wanting, and no where to be found; and at Wiems Castle the officers met them, and took them all into custody, with the intention of carrying them to Perth.

But here a new difficulty occurred. What was to become of the cattle? They could not be left on that wild to straggle through the country, and become the prey of all who chose to take possession of them. This was a responsibility the officers durst not take upon themselves; they therefore took them in before Sir Robert Menzies, who called in two other justices of the peace, and examined the prisoners and witnesses. The Highlanders would tell nothing; they would not even tell the name of the man who had so cleverly absconded; nor would they acknowledge to whom the bloody dirk belonged, which Robert Armstrong had brought with him. All the four produced their dirks, fair and clean! and there really was very little variety among them all. In short, there was no proof against any one of them that was at all tangible; and as one man had absconded, it was the opinion of the justices that he was the murderer. They therefore resolved to reprimand the men, and dismiss them to the charge of their valuable drove, and offer a high reward for the man who had made his escape. But just as Sir Robert was addressing Kennedy in a severe reproof for his turbulent and quarrelsome disposition, and for being the beginner of an affray which had cost an innocent stranger his life, behold Mr. Menzies, the landlord at whose house the murdered man lay, arrived to take orders what was to be done. His evidence rather turned the scale, although it was not conclusive. He knew the man who had absconded to be Hector's brother, and generally esteemed as an amiable and mild character. He could not swear that it was

Hector Kennedy who stabbed Thomas Little, but he had strong suspicions of it; for when he entered, the room was dark, save a little light from a wood fire, and he saw Kennedy lying across the breast of one of the Borderers, with his left hand at his throat; and he was much mistaken if he did not see Kennedy withdraw his right hand from the murdered man's breast at that moment. They then examined Kennedy's sleeve, and easily perceived that it had manifestly been sprinkled with blood, although an effort had been made to clean it. The justices and sheriff-substitute for that district then ordered him off to Perth prison directly, to take his trial at the next quarter-sessions.

When he heard what was determined concerning him, he stormed like a lion at bay, and dared the officers and constables to touch him. When they seized him, he laid about him right and left, knocking them down at every blow; and if it had not been for the assistance of the Borderers, he would have overpowered all the four, but they held him down until they handcuffed him. Still he continued to storm and swear most desperately, and when he could no longer get at the officers with his hands, he kicked them and tripped them with his feet, until they were obliged to bind him in a cart. He was about six feet three inches high, rather slenderly formed, but his muscular power was prodigious; and at this time his head being tied round with a red napkin, and his crabbed Highland bonnet above it, he looked much more like a demon than a man, and the justices declared to one another that they deemed him one of the very worst description.

When bound in the cart, he perceived Rob Armstrong's malicious smile; on which he cried, in a voice of fury—

"Base craven of a Sasenach dog! dare you laugh at me? The day may come when we may meet again, and curse me if I don't give you your dichens!"

"Then I assure you we shall see one another again," said Rob; "for I shall come all the way from the border to Perth to see you hanged."

"Me hanged, you Sassenach dog!—me hanged!" exclaimed Kennedy. "There is not a court in Scotland dares condemn me to be hanged! If they dare to hang me, their town will be in ashes before many days are over."

When he was taken into the sheriff-clerk's office, at Perth, to be examined, and have his declaration taken down, he stopped short at the door, and would not move for his two conductors to be placed at the bar.

On being asked by the sheriff what he meant, he said he wanted to know if all were come in who had to come?

The sheriff said all were present that were necessary.

"Then," said he, swearing a great oath, "I promise you that not one of you shall get out again until I am satisfied that I get fair justice."

So saying, he bolted the door, set his back to the bolt, and the prison-officers might as well have tried to remove a rock.

The sheriff and his assistants gazed at one another in silence, astonished at the temerity of the powerful savage; and, as was thought, out of sheer alarm, were very mild in their examination of him.

He would confess nothing, but merely stood and cursed the Sassenachs, and affirmed that they were the beginners of the affray; for that abusing one's kinsmen to his face was much more heinous than giving a broken crown.

There is only one circumstance that I ever heard relating to the final trial of Kennedy, and a very ridiculous story it was; but it is told among the Border Littles, and about Stanegirthside, as a literal fact to this day.

Thomas Little the murdered man's old mother, attended at Perth circuit to hear the trial of Kennedy, and after all the rest were examined, and it was maifest the libel was going to be returned not proven, she came forward and requested to be examined; on which a Mr. Bell, one of the deputy advocates, was requested to examine her in her own broad border dialect, which he did in the following terms. After taking down her name and place of abode, age, &c., he proceeded thus:—

"And now, Bessy Armstrong, what hast thou to tell us anent this same mourder? My name is Mr. Bell, a caontryman o' theyne own, sae joost speak freely to me as to a friend. Where were you on the night the mourder was committed?"

"I was at heame, at mae own fuyer seyde."

"Then what canst thou knaw about the muorder, when thou wert ane hoondred and fourty meyles from the pleace where it happened?"

"I joost kean this mookle about it, Mr. Baill, that I'll take me born and swalem oath—I'll sweer ber all the Holy Treenity, and aw that is sacred on earth or in heaven—I'll sweer with mee hand upon the gospels, that that ruffian, your prisoner, was the mourderer of my swon Tom."

"Whey this is beyound our comprehension, Bessy. The witnesses are all here, and no one of them, though present, can swear to the perpetration of the creyme; and how couldst thou kain? Thou couldst only kain bee the second seyght."

"Ney, but I had ane better witness than any of theyne; I had a witness on whose verity I could trust my leyfe and sowl's salvation. But I maun tell thee a story, Mr. Baill; and if thou dou nae believe me, it will be the worse for thee and thy pragmatical lwords, bwoth in this leyfe and that which is to cwome.

"Weel thou seest, Mr. Baill, as I was sitting at mee own ingle, on the evening of the fourteenth of September last, and croaning to myself the ballant of 'Johnie Armstrang,' the fuyer was burning wi' a clecr lowe, but I had nae light forbye; and when I looks, who should I see but my son Tommy, sitting over against me on the other seyde of the fuyer, hinging his head.

"'Peace be wi' the sowl o' thee, Tammy! What has brought thee heame so soon? I thought thou had engaged wi' Rwobin Airmstrang to gang the feer Heelands, and bring heeame the earl's and Harbottle's droves: what has turned thee again?'

"He still hung down his head, and said neything.

"'Now I'll weager a plack wi' thee, Tommy,' says I, 'that Robin and thou hast had an outeast. Weel do I ken hett-headit thou art baith! And I wish thou maunna hae doone swom deadly ill that thou's sae doore the night.'

"'I returned back to tell thee swome secrets, mwother,' said he, 'lest I should not have unwother chance. Thou kens that I have been an industrious son for thee and I, and I have even made more money than thou kenst or thinkest of; but it is all in good hands, and you will find vouchers for it all in the shottle of my kist, which thou must break open, for I have not the key; and if you do not break it up, and make your claim first, you may lose all. But what I principally wanted to tell thee is, that there is a girl in Burgh, Mrs. Wilson's daughter, of the George and Dragon; she is my wife, and she has a baby. If she apply to you, take her to your home and your bosom, as we were married over the water at Graitney, and naebody kens but oursels twa.'

"'And pray, my dear Tommy,' said I, laughing, 'what is the meaning of all this? Are you going to fly the country, and leave your wife and baby, and take leg-bail for America? Then, Tommy, thou'rt gawn to do a bad thing; and, I fea me, hast done some waur thing already, that thou'rt gawn to leave thy weyfe, and thy baby, and thy ould minny, and aw thy siller. This is no aw for naething, Tommy; so tell me the treuth."

"'Whoy, then, mwother, to tell thee the plain treuth,' said he, 'I was joost now mourdered in the Heelands of Scotland!'

"'Dear Tommy, my man, thou'rt drunk!' said I, laughing until I was like to faw. 'If thou hadst been mourdered, how couldst thou have been here? I confess I never saw thee looking waur aw my leyfe, for there's swomething gash in theyne appearance ; but mourdered thou canst nae be.'

"'I tell thee, mwother, that the beetle has not yet boomed a mile since I was basely stabbed to the heart by a ruffian named Hector Kennedy,' said he. 'Should he be acquitted of my murder, as probably he may, the room being dark and in confusion, go thou and bear this testimony for me, and assure the murderer, that although he may be acquitted by men, he shall not be acquitted of God, for his blood shall be shed for mine. And now remember my charges to you. Farewell.'

"With that my son arose and went out, and I saw the wound in his right side, and the blood streaming from it ; and I fainted, and was not myself again for several days and nights. This is the truth, and if you let the mourderer escape, dear shall be your retribution."

"Indeed, Bessy, yours is a very extraordinary tale," said Mr. Bell ; "and I confess it has deep effect on me, but before a jury I fear it will not avail."

Mr. Bell was right, for the jury returned a verdict of *Not proven*.

I saw Kennedy on the following autumn, conducting once more great droves of cattle to the south, and found him more rude, boisterous, and unreasonable than ever, and swearing in a way that it was dreadful to hear him.

But there is something mysterious in this whole history, for the next summer, or perhaps the next again, I am not sure which, I thought proper to make the tour of the counties of Inverness and Ross on horseback, a mode which, in all my tours, I never tried before or since. I left Inverness on a morning of May, very early, determined to halt at the inn of Abernethy all night, and view the haughs of Cromdale. But the way was longer than I expected, and when I came to the Spey it was long before I could get my horse over ; so that when I reached the inn at Abernethy it was late, and the house was empty ; one family having removed and the other just entering, without meat or drink, corn or hay.

With a sore heart I was obliged to set off, and cross the mountains into Banffshire, to an outlandish place called Tomantoul, which was the nearest stage.

About midnight, after crossing the height, I came into a wood, where there was a complete thicket on each side, so dense that a weasel could scarcely have got through either of them ; and there, all at once, my horse stopped, and refused to proceed a step further. She was a young mare, but I had never seen her start or hesitate before, and was not a little astounded.

I whipped, I spurred, I alighted, and tried to lead and force her on by severe drubbing. It was all in vain : she made ground backward, but none forward.

I was driven desperate, and knew not what to do ; and after calling out several times and receiving no answer, I was obliged to fasten my mare to a bush, and go forward and reconnoitre.

I had not gone far till I perceived a dead man, lying at full length across the road—yes ! a dead man, and a murdered one !

I went up and looked at the body—called, but got no answer—laid my ear to his face, to hear if there was any breathing ; but there was none.

I thought I knew the wan features, but had not the least recollection whose they were.

His hat was lying about three yards behind him ; he had on top-boots and spurs, and his boots were tied above his knees with green tape.

I was in a terrible quandary ; but after I had gone up, my mare, with coaking, condescended to go likewise, but made a spring by the feet of the corpse that had nearly dislocated my arm, and brought me fairly down on the road.

I mounted, galloped to Tomantoul, told the people what I had seen, and proffered to accompany them to the place ; but they refused, and said—"It was as fitter to let sleeping togs lie."

And they informed me further, that there was a gang of gipsies lurking about their woods, who took everything they could get, and they had no doubt that they had murdered the gentleman.

I could sleep none that morning, and mounting at an early hour, I rode straight for the Lowlands; for I had a sort of lurking dread that I might be taken up for the murderer.

It was Kennedy who was killed, and whom I had seen lying dead on the road.

A strict search was set on foot for the murderers, and two of the gipsy gang were taken and tried at Perth.

One of them proved an *alibi*, but the other was condemned and executed, as I saw by the newspapers ; but on what grounds I do not know, as he denied to the last.

For my part I think he was guiltless, for there were upwards of seven hundred pounds found on Kennedy's person, which amounted to more than the price of all the cattle he had sold for his employers in the southern markets.

I think, therefore, that it had been some of the border Armstrongs, or Littles, that slew him ; for, in fact, one-third at least of the culprits of this country are wrongously condemned by ignorant jurymen, influenced by the manifest falsehood of advocates, which now, it seems, is legitimate pleading."

"That is a strange adventure," said Colonel Jack, when his companion had concluded.

"It is a true one," answered Mr. Mac-Fergus, "that I can vouch for, as I was, as I have told you, an actor in it myself."

"Your friend is not stirring yet," said the Badger, in allusion to the outcast, who appeared to enjoy his bed so well that he did not feel disposed to leave it. "Shall I call him?"

"No, let him have his fill of sleep. I suspect, poor chap, that a comfortable bed is a luxury with which he has not been acquainted for a long time past," answered the colonel, with a laugh.

"And we'll e'en take another bottle of the same wine," said Mr. MacFergus. "It's very exhilirating tipple, not so strong and heady as our own Highland whisky, it's true, but nevertheless is better drink for the morning. Your good health, sir. I have not been long in London, and am happy to have been fortunate enough to make your acquaintance. And while we've half an hour or so to spare, I'll tell you another story. I dare say you will think giving way to superstition, but I assure you it's a fact which I am about to relate."

"Oh, as to that," said Colonel Jack, "I am, in truth, not much given to superstitious fears; but nevertheless, go on with your story."

"The people of my country are superstitious," observed Mr. MacFergus, "there can be no doubt of that—more so than the English. I was not connected with any of the parties myself," continued the Scotchman; "it was Mr. David Hunter, only son of the farmer at Clun-keigh, who told me the strange story I am about to relate.

He said that he went to court a very dear and lovely girl, Phemie Hewitt, and spent about three hours with her in the fondest endearment; kissed her, shook hands, and left her about two o'clock on a winter morning. He said he was sometimes whistling a tune to himself—for, like me, he sawed a good deal on the fiddle; but he was all the way thinking and thinking of Phemie, and whether he would take her home to his father's house or get a cottage of his own built on the farm; when, behold! after he was almost close to his father's house, and had walked about three miles and a half, he met with Phemie coming leisurely to meet him, with her gown-skirt drawn over her lovely chestnut locks, as she always had when she went out to the courting.

"Mercy on us, Phemie!" exclaimed he, "but ye surely are keen o' the courting the night, when ye're come a' the gate here for another brash at it."

"I forgot two things," said she; "and as I kenned we were never to meet again, I coudna part wi' you without telling you. In the first place, you are never to gang back to Auchenvew again to the courting; for things are no a' right there."

"What's wrang about Auchenvew, Phemie?"

"O your Margaret's no just as she should be, poor woman—an' I'm very sorry for her; but ye maunna gang back again, else ye're sure to get o'er the fingers' ends."

"Now, Phemie, that's sheer jealousy, for which I am sure you have little reason."

"O, I daresay you gaed for her for an hour or twa's diversion; but you did gang, and mind you're no to do it again."

"Weel, my dear woman, I gie you my word o' honour that I never shall gang back to the courting again. But, Phemie, what was it you said about us never meeting again?"

"O, yes, we'll meet again; but I'll be dead before then! and my principal errand here this morning was to get your blessing; for when you kissed me and parted with me, you did not say 'God bless you, Phemie!' which you never neglected before since ever we met. Now, I could not part with you without your blessing."

"I dinna understand you this morning, Phemie. We are never to meet again—and you are to be dead before we meet again—what is the meaning of all this? Remember you are engaged to meet me on the seventh of next month at the easternmost tree of the Grennam Wood."

"Well, I'll meet you there."

"Well, God bless you, my dear girl; and I'm sure I give that blessing with all my heart and soul."

David stretched out his hand to seize hers, to draw her to him, and kiss her. There was no hand, and no Phemie there! He wheeled round and round, and called her name.

"Phemie!—Phemie Hewit! My dear woman, what's come o' you, or where are ye?"

But he ran with all his speed, and called in vain; there was no Phemie to be seen nor heard.

He stood in breathless astonishment, recommending himself to all the blessed Trinity, and then saying audibly—

"The mercy and grace of Heaven be around me! Is it possible that I have seen my dear Phemie's wraith? No, it is impossible; for it looked and spoke so like her sweet self—it could not be a spirit. But there was something very mysterious about her this morning, in following me so far; nay, in outwalking me, meeting me, and uttering the words she did. But it was herself, there is no doubt of it; and she has given me the slip in a most unaccountable manner."

David went home, and awakened his youngest sister, Mary, who gave him something to drink; but he could not speak an intelligible sentence to her, and she thought he was either drunk or very ill, and sat up with him till day.

He slept none, but sighed, moaned, and turned himself in the bed; and he continued thoughtful and ill for several days; but at length he arose and went about his father's business.

This visionary courting night was on the twenty-eighth of January or February, I have forgot which : and the lovers were engaged to meet on the seventh of next month at their trysting-tree.

Now the families of the two lovers were not on very good terms; they were, I believe, rather averse to one another. They were of different tenets in religion, and never met either at church or in society. But the only son of the one family fell in love with the youngest daughter of the other at a Thornhill fair, trysted her to meet him, courted her, and won her affections, and they engaged themselves to one another.

They were a very amiable pair, and I knew them both very well. David was a handsome, stout fellow, upwards of six feet high, and Phemie a gentle, mild-looking creature, with a face something what one would suppose an angel's to be, but rather pale-looking, and apparently not long for this world. She was, nevertheless, witty, and good-humoured, and had a most affectionate and benevolent heart.

Well, the seventh of the month came, and David attended punctually at the hour. He had not sat a minute and a half until Phemie came, with the skirt of her frock round her head, as usual.

"Come away, Phemie! you are true to your word as ever," said he.

"Yes, you see I have come as I promised; for I would not break my tryste with you; but I have a very short time to stay."

"Well, come and sit under my plaid, for the time that you have to stay, my dear lassie, and let me caress you; for I have had heavy thoughts and sad misgivings about you since I last saw you."

"No, I cannot come under your plaid, nor court to-night, for reasons that you will soon come to know. But I came principally to inform you that you are not to come back to court me till I send you word, or come and tell you myself: yes, I think I'll come and tell you myself, and then you are safe to come."

"You cannot come under my plaid; I must not come to court you again until you come and tell me to do so! Will you really come and tell me that I must come and woo you, Phemie? Phemie, my dear, there is a mystery about you of late which I cannot comprehend."

David was looking down to the ground at this moment, pondering on the words of his beloved; and when he looked up again he saw Phemie gliding away from him. He sprang to his feet and pursued, calling her name in a sort of loud whisper; but she continued to fly on : and, though very near, he could not overtake her till she entered the minister's house by the back gate that led through the kirk-yard.

David's eyes were opened; he saw at once that the elegant and genteel minister had seduced his sweetheart's affections; and he now conceived that he understood all her demeanour, and everything she had said to him.

So he rushed into the kitchen : there were two servant girls in it, and he asked them, with a voice of fury, where Phemie was?

Now, I must tell you, that this parson had got a bad word with some young ladies, both married and unmarried; and though for my part I never believed a word of it, yet the report spread, which weaned the parson's congregation from him, all save a few gentlemen who came to dine at the manse every Sunday.

David was perfectly enraged; for he perceived his road straight before him.

"Where is Phemie?" cried he.

"What Phemie?" said the one girl.

"What Phemie?" said the other.

"Why, Phemie Hewit," cried he, fiercely. "I know how matters are going on, so you need not make any of your confounded pretences of ignorance to me. I followed her in here this minute; so tell me instantly where she is, or bring your master to answer to me."

"Phemie Hewit!" said the one girl.

"Phemie Hewit!" said the other.

And with that one of them, Sarah Robson, ran ben to the minister, and said—

"Gor God's sake, sir, come but an' speak to Mr. David Hunter; he is come in raving mad, and asking for Phemie Hewit, and seems to think that you have her concealed in the house."

Mr. Nevison, with all his usual sauvity of manners, came into the kitchen, asked Mr. Hunter how he was, and how his father and sisters were.

"I'm no that ill, sir; I hae nae grit reason to complain o' ony thing or ony body excepting you. Where is my sweetheart, sir? I followed her in here this minute, and if ye dinna gie her up to me I'll burn the house aboon your head!"

"Your sweetheart, Mr. David?" exclaimed Mr. Nevison. "Whom do you mean, sir? Is it one of my servant girls?—for there is

no other woman in the house, to my knowledge?"

"No, sir, it is Phemie Hewit that I want
—my own Phemie Hewit—my betrothed!
I followed her in here at you back gate this
instant, and I insist on seeing her."

"Phemie Hewit!" exclaimed the two ser-
vant-girls; "Phemie Hewit!" exclaimed
the minister. "My dear sir, you are raving,
and out of your senses; there was but one
Phemie Hewit whom I knew in all this country, the merchant's daughter of Thornhill,
and she is dead, and was buried here, within
six paces of the back of my house, the day
before yesterday."

"Come, now, sir, that is a hoax to get me
off," cried David, in a loud tone, betwixt
laughing and crying. "That winna do;
tell me the truth at aince. That is ower

serious a matter to joke on; therefore, for
the sake of Heaven and this poor heart, tell
me the real truth."

"I tell you the real truth, Mr. Hunter.
I was at her funeral myself, and laid her
left shoulder into the grave, and saw engraved in gold letters on the coffin-lid, 'Eu-
PHEMIA HEWIT, aged 22.'"

David's whole frame grew rigid, his hands
and his eyes turned up convulsively; and
after uttering a few internal groans, or rather
shrieks, he fell backward in a swoon. They
carried him to bed, and he soon came again
to his senses; but the distress of his mind
was deplorable.

He lay at the manse for nearly three weeks,
and though the minister administered every
anodyne to him that he possessed, or could
procure, his patient remained in a very pre-

carious and unsettled state, and continued to exclaim every day—

"O, had I been but warned of it! to have watched by her dying bed, and received her parting blessing, and her parting breath between my lips, and to have laid her head in an unhonoured grave, I would have been satisfied! But to be parted thus! O my Phemie, my Phemie!"

We had some fine curling on the ice after this, therefore I think it must have been about the beginning of February; and we were all astonished to find that our friend David, one of the best and strongest curlers of us all, never appeared on the ice. So one evening I went that way to take my tea with the family, and see what was the matter; for he and I were great cronies, and talked much about religion and the Scriptures, and sometimes about the lasses, but not often. But he had a strong attachment to me, and said one day, before all the club, that there was nothing in the world he would court independence so much for, as to keep me independent.

I found him pale and emaciated, sitting in the kitchen, with his plaid about him. He took no tea; he ate not a bite of bread; he spoke not a word. My blood ran chill to my heart; for he was a good lad, and I loved him. As we were going into the parlour for our tea, his sister Margaret took me aside, and said—

"I am very glad that you have come to-night, for we are perplexed about Davie. Something extraordinary seems to have happened to him; but we know nothing, and he is continually speaking about you. See if you can find out what it is that distresses him."

"He is sadly changed, indeed, for the worse," said I; "and I am very much alarmed about him. He is too retired, and too thoughtful. Could you not persuade Jane Wilson, or Nancy M'Turk, or Jane Armstrong, to come over and stay with you for awhile? I have seen each of these put him into high glee and good humour."

"He would not once look or speak to any of them," said she. "His spirits are broken, and I am afraid he is not long for this world."

"For God's sake, do not say so, Miss Margaret," said I. "But I am sure he will open his mind to me."

He set me on my way as far as the limits of his father's farm that night, and related the above narrative, adding—

"She has, you see, promised to call on me again, and inform me when I am to meet her; and do you not think that when that happens it will be a warning for me to prepare for leaving this world?"

"Yes I do, David," said I. "After what

has already happened, in such a mysterious way, between you and your beloved, I believe that when your Phemie comes and gives you this intimation, even in a dream, it will be a death-warning to you, and that you must prepare to meet her in another and a better world."

"O no, no, not in a dream," said he; "she is with me in every dream, evening, midnight, and morning. I see her, I caress her, kiss her, and bless her, without ever once recollecting that the grave separates us. O no, not in a dream! I shall see her face to face, and speak to her as a man speaketh to his friend; and when that happens, if it should ever happen, I shall send you word."

This was at the laight gate. So we shook hands, and parted; for I durst not let him stand longer in the cold. But he continued to grow worse and worse, until one morning, about the beginning of May, a servant came posting to me on horseback; and requested me to go and see Mr. David Hunter, who was very poorly, and wished particularly to see me. I obeyed the summons with alacrity, and found him in bed, very low indeed. He desired his two sisters to go out, and then, taking my hand, he said—

"Now, my dear.friend, my time is come—the time which I have long desired. I have seen my Phemie again to-day."

"But only in a dream, David, I am sure. Consider yourself; only in a dream."

"No, I was wide awake, and sensible as at this moment while speaking to you. The door was standing open, to give me air. I was all alone, which you know I choose mostly to be, for prayer and meditation, when in glided my Phemie, with the train of her grey frock drawn over her lovely locks. I had no thought, no remembrance that she was dead. It was impossible to think so; for her smile was so sweet, so heavenly, even more beatific than I had ever seen it, and her complexion was that of the pale rose. She threw her locks back from each cheek with her left hand, and said—

"You see I have come to invite you as I promised, David. Are you ready to meet me to-night at our trysting-tree, and at the usual hour."

"I am afraid, my beloved Phemie, that I shall scarcely be able to attend," said I.

"Yes, but you will," said she; "and you must not disappoint me, for I will await your arrival." And with a graceful curtsy and a smile she retired, saying as she left the room—"God be with you till then, David."

This narrative quite confounded me. It was a long time before I could either act or think. At length I sat down on his bedside, and took his hand in mine, it was worn to the hand of a skeleton. I felt his pulse, that strong and manly pulse, had dwindled into a mere stiver. I easily perceived that it was all over with him.

"How do you think my pulse is?" said he.

"The pulse is not amiss," said I; "but you may depend on Phemie's word, for you will meet her to-night at the trysting hour, I have no doubt of it."

"Ah, yes—ah yes! Phemie never told me a lie in her life. Let me have your prayers, my dear friend—let me have your prayers to take with me, and I will trust to my Redeemer for the rest!"

These were the last words he uttered in his life, and he uttered these with a croaking voice perfectly sepulchral. I called in his father and two sisters, and told them that David was dying, and that I wished, by his own desire, to pray with him before parting with him for ever. His sisters were like to burst their hearts with crying, but the old father seemed perfectly resigned. I sang the fifth verse of the thirty-first psalm, I remember it well, and read about half of the fourteenth chapter of the Corinthians. When I had done, he seized my hand feebly, and held it until death loosed his grasp; for the trysting hour was fast approaching, and whether he longed for it, or wished to remain a little longer in this, to him, miserable state of existance I cannot tell, but he turned his eye frequently to the clock, that stood opposite his bed, and exactly at the trysting hour he expired. The two young lovers were virtuous and lovely in their lives, and in their death they were but shortly divided.

As soon as Mr. MacFergus had finished his narrative, the outcast made his appearance in front of Mr. Dyson's bar. Colonel Jack rose, and walked into the public room, followed by his protege.

"Well," said the colonel, "I hope you have slept well, and all the better for a good night's rest."

"Many thanks to you," answered the outcast. "I feel a new man, I have not had such a luxury for many a day, or rather night, for, as I told you when we first met, I have been wandering about without a place to put my head in."

"Well you must have breakfast," answered our hero, rising and ringing the bell.

Dyson's head man made his appearance in answer to the summons, breakfast was ordered and served, much to the satisfaction of the outcast, who made a vigorous assault on the same without further ado, when he had sufficiently satisfied his appetite. Colonel Jack proceeded to interrogate him as to his future prospects. In answer to his queries the outcast said—

It would be ridiculous of me to talk about prospects when I have none. There is no green vista in the distance for me. No shady retreat where I may lay me down and seek rest in so troublesome a world as that we at present inhabit, for it has been, and is, a sad and weary one to me."

"No doubt. Well you know my calling?"

The outcast gave a word of assent to this query.

"It is little that I am able to do for anyone, but if you like to be in my employ, to look after our horses, and do whatever odd jobs may be wanted, well and good, you shall be enrolled as one of our company. We are freebooters, as I have already informed you, at war with the world, which, to say the truth, has used most of us scurvily enough."

"It has me, for one," answered the colonel's companion.

"Then what say you to my proposition?"

"I most cheerfully and gladly accept of it, and shall be but too happy to be enrolled as one of your followers—your faithful followers," added the outcast, with emphasis.

"Good, then now we understand one another. Here is an earnest of my good intentions," said Colonel Jack, in continuation, as he pulled out his purse, and taking several pieces therefrom, handed the same to his companion.

At first the latter did not seem disposed to accept of the money proffered him.

"I have done nothing to deserve this," he answered, hesitatingly.

"Psha! you are wondrous particular for a man in your situation. Take it man; you don't want to starve, I suppose?"

"I have been very near starving of late."

"Get yourself a few things to make a respectable appearance—do you hear?"

"Thank you, sir. I am, in truth, at present a disgrace to any one—not fit to be seen, in fact."

"You are rather in a dilapidated condition, it must be admitted; but that can soon be repaired. Dyson will tell you where you can be rigged out upon the cheapest terms, and some of my companions will be here shortly, when he will introduce you to them. I will leave you a letter to give to Knapp or Hackett, for I am compelled now to take my departure for the present, having some private business to attend to of my own."

Colonel Jack then went to the door of the public room, and glanced at the bar of the Cow and Cauliflower; the Badger was behind this, serving a customer. The colonel betook himself to the bar parlour, where Mr. MacFergus was seated.

The Scotchman expressed his pleasure at our hero's return to the parlour, and seemed disposed to enter upon another story; but Colonel Jack informed him that he had an appointment upon business that morning, and therefore was compelled, however unwillingly, to take his leave for the present.

"But I shall see you again, Mr. Mac-Fergus," said Colonel Jack. "You are staying here, I presume?"

"Oh, yes, my friend—yes; this is my head quarters for the present, and will be for the next week or ten days."

"Good; then I shall have the pleasure of spending an evening or two with you, I dare say."

"With all my heart, sir—I shall be delighted," answered Mr. MacFergus."

"And see here, Dyson," said our hero, addressing the Badger, "when any of my companions come here, I wish you to introduce that worthy in the parlour to their notice. You will give him bed and board for the present."

"All right, colonel, it shall be done," answered Mr. Dyson.

"For the present I am compelled to leave. Good morning, gentlemen."

So saying, the colonel emerged from the very respectable establishment kept by the Badger.

Our hero then wended his way towards the chambers of Mr. Baintree, of whom we have heard so little of late, that we may possibly have forgotten him altogether.

Colonel Jack had placed the papers in his hands which, the reader will no doubt remember, was taken from Miss Langford and her father when the Oxford coach was stopped by our highwaymen. The box containing these papers had been stolen from the residence of the elder Mr. Baintree by the notorious Nobbler; but it will be remembered that it was regained, and had been since then in the safe custody of Colonel Jack's lawyer.

It appeared that Mr. Baintree, junior, had been called to the bar since our hero had paid him a visit, and had maintained a very good position in the profession.

He received our hero most cordially, and apologised for being engaged for the next few hours, as he had to go to the Westminster Court.

"Oh, no matter," said the colonel, "I can call to-morrow, or some more convenient day."

"I shall be at home at four this afternoon. Come round, Halford, and spend the evening with me, and we can talk this matter over at our leisure."

"If it will not be inconvenient, I will do so," answered our hero.

"Not at all so—I particularly wish it," said Mr. Baintree.

"Then I will call after four."

Colonel Jack kept his word, and was with Mr. Baintree, junior, at about six o'clock. The counsellor had dined, and was alone in his private room. He was much pleased to see the colonel, whom he began to think was lost, not having been favoured with a call from him for so long a period.

"Sit down, Halford, my esteemed friend, although of late a stranger," said Mr. Baintree, as he poured out a glass of wine for his visitor.

Our hero thanked him, and at once sat down.

"Well," said Mr. Baintree, "I have gone over the papers left in my charge. They were rather puzzling at first, but I believe I may say that they are now unravelled. It would appear, by the will of the late Lady Reichbeck, that a considerable portion of her wealth, nay, the greatest portion, is left to the present wife of Sir Reginald Fleetwood."

"And her property is immense, I believe?" said Colonel Jack.

"Well, it is something considerable, certainly, but not what is expected. Listen. It appears that she holds, or rather, more properly speaking, did hold, a large amount in trust; and now, to make you more clearly comprehend, I must enter into the particulars of the property, as far as I can understand them. You must know, that very many years ago there resided in Milk Street, Cheapside, an old miser or money scrivener, whose whole thoughts was the amassing of wealth. He scraped, he contrived, he pinched, and denied himself the common necessaries of life, and was thereby enabled to save a considerable sum. Having no family of his own—that is, no direct issue, to use a legal phrase—he conceived a scheme, which, at any rate, has the credit of being an original one. His name was Abel Meech."

"I have heard of the name before," exclaimed our hero.

"Very possible, he was a distant relative of your family. Now mark his singular will. Abel Meech is dead, long, long since; he is passed away from this world, and nothing can touch him further. His will runs thus:—He wills and bequeaths the whole of his property, without reservation, to his next of kin, after two generations have passed away."

"Two generations! I do not understand the meaning of such a bequest," said the colonel.

"No, and entangled as the case is at present, it would be difficult for anyone else to understand it. Indeed, it has been with the greatest difficulty that I have been able to arrive at any conclusion. Let me endeavour, as briefly as may be, to give you the details. Abel Meech leaves a will—his next of kin is not to receive the benefit of his property. His next of kin, as far as I can make out, was your father, who is now dead. He was not to become the recipient of Meech's wealth, neither are you; but your eldest born comes into the whole of this property, that is, supposing I am right in my premises that your father was his nearest relative, which is a fact we have not as yet determined with any degree of certainty, but we will assume, for argument's sake, that such is the case, then by the terms of old Meech, will your eldest child indeed come into the property, upon her coming of age."

" But I have no son," said Colonel Jack.

" No matter; there is no reservation, as far as that is concerned. The will says your eldest born—male issue to take precedure of the female—but in the absence of male issue then it reverts to the females. According to my reading of the case, I am under the full impression that your daughter is the party. There is only one impediment in the way, as far as I can see, and that is to prove the demise of a certain Morgan Halford ; if he be alive, or if he has left any issue, why then, I fear, he or his heirs will come in before your father, yourself, or your daughter."

" Morgan Halford was an uncle of mine," said Colonel Jack.

" Of course ; he was your father's eldest brother."

" Precisely."

" Well, do you know what has become of him ?"

" Dead, years and years ago."

" Has he left any issue ?"

" I should say not ; I never heard of his having any family. Indeed, I don't know that he ever married, but I cannot answer with any certainty as to this, for I don't remember ever having even seen my uncle."

" Well, my good sir, I have traced out the particulars of his history thus far :—he went over to Ireland many years ago, and settled in Leinster."

" I never heard that he did."

" Ah, but I have. Now, it will be absolutely necessary for someone to ferret out his history in Lienster. To obtain proof of his death, and at the same time get whatever attestation may be necessary, of the fact that he died without issue. Now you must under-stand, Mr. Halford," said Mr. Baintree, "that this is a great stake we are playing for ; and as I am about to journey to Ireland on cir-cuit, I propose that you accompany me, and see what can be done in the way of finding out the particulars of the said Morgan, his heirs, or assigns."

Colonel Jack agreed to this proposition, and in a day or two after the foregoing con-versation, he and Mr. Baintree travelled together over to Ireland.

CHAPTER CXVIII.

ADVENTURES IN LEINSTER.

MR. BAINTREE was compelled to attend to one or two cases in which he was retained as counsel, and upon his arriving with our hero in Ireland, he persuaded his companion to accompany him to the law courts, after which they intended to seek out the Colonel's uncle ; or rather, the place where he had resided, for our hero knew that he had long since de-parted from this sublunary sphere.

They who imagine that the experience of a barrister is confined to the dull routine of court practice, or the monotonas details of legal vicissitude, know little either of the realities of the law or the physical conforma-tion of the individuals composing the pro-fession. The worst passions of human nature, and all the follies and vices of mankind, are daily paraded before us ; and dull, indeed, of comprehension must we be, if, from this natural drama, where all the characters are original, and the incidents real, we could not cull something which might be deserving of more than ephemeral notice or casual obser-vation, particularly on circuit, where the sim-ple and unsophisticated bearing of the witness or suitor presents so strong a contrast to the practised complacency or passionless exterior of the individuals frequenting the metropo-litan courts. 'Tis this rapid play of new ideas through the mind, and the ever-varying panorama of scenes and objects, which render " life on circuit" agreeable, though otherwise attended with many inconveniences. Besides that, there are always to be found amongst the members of the bar some who are not averse, by reason of their age or education, to relieve the dry details of litigation by oc-casional deviations "after the picturesque." Hence it happens that to many, if not all, the assizes are a species of legal carnival.

About the middle of the month of July, 17—, the summer assizes for the city and county commenced at Waterford, the Hon. Baron Bluster and Mr. Justice Cramwell being in the commission. Such of the gen-tlemen of " the Leinster" as were not aristo-cratically inclined to travel in chaise and pair, secured to themselves the most ample mode of conveyance which the last assize town afforded. There is no law, rule, or cus-tom on this circuit, as on others, whereby the members are compelled to travel in carriages, for a very sufficient reason—that the supply of four-wheeled vehicles would never equal the demand ; and even though it should, the locomotive power would still be sadly in arrear.

The colonel and Mr. Baintree started for Waterford so as to reach it before breakfast, and experienced no particular accident during the progress of our journey, if we except the usual breakage of traces and mendings thereof, retrograde motions of horses with crablike propensities, and sundry expedients resorted to by jarvey and bystanders to overcome the natural impediments to expeditious travelling—such as setting fire to straw under the abdomens of leaders who seemed tempted rather to develope the theory of the precession of the equinoxes than the laws of rectilinear progression, and various undulations of the Jehu to escape the matutinal salutations of the wheelers, whose legs, from their frequent gyrations, suggested two hypotheses—either they belonged to that class of solids whose external surface is continually flying off in conformity with the eternal laws of transformation, or else there existed some natural chemical affinity between the substance of which the biped's nose and quadruped's hoofs were composed, as they were perpetually in a state of juxtaposition or Mesmeric attraction. Be this as it may, they reached in safety the "*urbs intacta*;" and on inquiring what might be the origin of the worthy citizens adopting this motto, was informed by Mr. Carrotty, a brother Leinster, that it was intended to convey to the mind of the stranger, that the city remained untouched by the hands of a scavenger in all its virgin purity, or, rather impurity, since the day on which Raymond le Gros laid the foundation of his castle on the quays. The appearance of the streets added a great degree of probability to this surmise, reposing, as they did, in a state of primitive Augean tranquillity.

As the vehicle drew up at the hotel, Mr. Baintree had an opportunity of forming an opinion as to what degree of estimation he and his companions were held in as a body by the Munster men, overhearing a conversation between two coach-office loungers.

"I say, Jim," said one to the other, "what are all these gintleman on the car?"

"Counsellors, or torneys," croaked Jim; "the Lord preserve us!"

As if we were impersonations of famine or pestilence.

The notes of "God save the Queen!" emitted by instalments from a battered bugle, inflated twice in the year by a Waterford Boreas, gave us to understand that no time was to be lost in making the necessary changes towards appearing in court, if we wished to hear the judge's charge; though we confess we do not think there ever was much variation or interest in such discourse, from the days of the first justice in eyre, Mr. Judge Samuel, to the period of the present assizes.

The sheriff hands the calender to his lordship, on the bench or in his carriage, which the grand jury have previously perused, as it had been published in a newspaper. His lordship then either condoles or congratulates upon the state of the county; whereupon the grand inquest, as if hitherto they were not exactly certain whether to rejoice or weep, forthwith become distended with county wisdom, and look big, and duck to the judge, and then the judge ducks to them; and every man of them now finds his lordship had expressed in words his own opinion, and so they are all unanimous, though before they had only agreed to differ: the *Blues* swearing the country never was in such a state of insubordination since the days when King Malachi imposed a tax upon noses, though there was then no snuff in them,—most unjustly assessing an aquiline at no higher valuation than a pug, or an elongated skin-flint than a Grecian; and the *Greens* calling Heaven te witness that any man, except a tithe-proctor or a parson, might walk the roads at the *dead* hour of the night.

No case worth recording occurred till that of the Queen *v*, O'Mulligan was called, which appeared to create a sensation. The clerk of the crown read the indictment in a voice so thick and muddy, that one would wager he hadn't tasted anything more substantial than flummery for the last six months.

"You, Thimotheus O'Mulligan, *alias* Tim Mulligan, *alias* Tim with the leg, stand indicted, &c. Are you guilty or not, prisoner?"

To which he replied, to the astonishment of the court—

"Guilty."

The judge then informed him he might withdraw the plea, if he pleased; but the traverser persisted.

"That shure he might as well say he was guilty, kase he had no counsel or torney to defind him, nor no money to get them."

But the last sentence of Mr. O'Mulligan was sadly economical of the truth, as we were given to understand he was horse-doctor, cow-tapster, and man-midwife to half the country; and, though wealthy, resorted to this plea of poverty that he might have counsel assigned to him. Whilst Mr. Baron Bluster was looking over the book of presentments, the following dialogue took place between the accused and one of the gentlemen of the bar, who usually held a fair share of criminal briefs:—

"Mr. Martin Cowslip, acushla, shure your honour won't see a dacent man like me hanged and notomised, and my ould carcase cut up by them blood-thirsty ruffians, the 'sack-'em-ups,' and not say a word for me? Many's the word I gave your honour when you came down to rouse the county, last election, for the Liberator. Your honour's spache from the windy of the hotel *stud* me in a leg, kase

I smashed the ould timber toe on the head of a bloody minded Brunswicker, that wouldn't take off his hat; and if you desart me now, divil a leg at all I'll have to stand on."

Mr. Cowslip, to whom these observations were addressed, was the very *beau ideal* of what a "counsellor" ought to be in the eyes of a Munster man,—about six feet four in height, with a stentorian voice issuing from a mouth whose dimensions brought to one's mind an advertisement of a Dublin joint-stock burial company, by which they startled the entire race of "jackeens" one morning, announcing the awful intelligence, "that their cemetery was open for *general interment*." Above this frightful aperture was a nose, so suddenly and deeply indented near the *terminus*, that the first words of a lease, "this indenture," always occurred to you when you looked at it; as if Nature had ingeniously predestined the wearer of the ornament for a limb of the law, and stamped his profession upon him before he came into the world, to save his parents the anxiety of thinking about what was best to be done with their hopeful boy. However, the counsellor was not to be done by this specious plea, and was determined that the "grave" shouldn't yawn or the nose be indented without the *quiddam honorarium*; and so Mr. Tim was obliged to give directions about having a sufficient sum abstracted from the many folds of a child's caul, wherewith to fee counsel and attorney; and with the more alacrity, as he began to fear his lordship, who had just inquired what was delaying the court, might hang him off hands, or by way of handsel to the sub-sheriff.

The first witness called on the part of the crown to sustain the indictment for manslaughter was as stolid a looking pug as was ever produced in court. Sometimes his head hung down upon his chest, much after the sesquipedalian fashion that black-pudding is exposed for sale; as if Nature had taken a flying shot with a head at a body, and hit it by the merest accident: then the head was raised, and its features were contracted, and a guttural arsenal was opened with such a *chevaux de frise* in front as a shark might envy. The witness gave his name as Patrick Tobacco; but this surname was a *sobriquet* which he had earned by being everlastingly seen with a pipe in his mouth.

Mr. Scutt commenced the direct examination. This gentleman, whenever he intended to be peculiarly emphatic, always pointed with the fore finger of his dexter hand towards the box, as if he were probing the jury to stimulate their attention, just as a bear is poked in a menagerie; or, perhaps, according to Cassiodorus, who calls "pantomimes men whose learned hands had tongues at the end of each finger," he thought he should be more effective by a display of this bilingual eloquence.

But the witness continued obstinately silent, notwithstanding several frightful lounges were made at him with the digital weapon; occasionly exchanging glances with an old grey-headed man who stood below the table.

"Pythagoras redivivus," said a rotund "Leinster" upon a small scale, yclept Roger Hottentot, resembling a note of interrogation turned upside down. He was a most consequential little man; in fact, he strutted about with that degree of self-induced and egotistical pomposity that a person would be disposed to assume who, carrying within his single breast the mighty conviction that he had taken the entire constitution—queen, lords, and commons, under his protection, had thereby discharged the good lieges of the realm from any further anxiety as to its stability and probable duration.

The judge, becoming impatient at this contempt of court, threatened to commit the witness; when, all of a sudden, the animal opened its mouth, and informed his lordship "that he was willing to answer him any question, as he was tould he was a dacent man; but as for thim Dublin jackeens," pointing to the bar, "may be, if I hould any talk with the likes of them, they'll tell me to be—"

With difficulty did we observe the proper degree of court decorum in suppressing our laughter at this most candid acknowledgment of our forensic merits.

The witness, after being assured by Mr. Baron Bluster that no violence should be offered to his exquisitely sensitive feelings, gave his testimony to the following effect, but with sundry digressions which it is not necessary to record.

"Phill Doyle, the disased man, had a pair of legs that were mighty bad with him; and he axes me to what docther I'd recommind him; and I says, 'Phill, darlint, shure you know there's Tim Meull, that flogs the European world for horse-dochoring, accowshering, bone-setting, and bellows-minding. Don't go farther than his door.'"

"Not so fast, my good man," said his lordship; "I can't take down your evidence. Eh, what did you say?—cow-shoeing, bone-setting? That'll do."

"Stay a moment," interposed Mr. Martin Cowslip; "how do you know he united all these branches of trade in his single person?"

"Didn't I see it in print on his boord?" returned he, of Havannah celebrity, darting a look of most ineffable contempt at the counsel.

"'Confirmation strong as page of holy writ,' gentlemen," observed Mr. Cowslip to the jury.

The witness resumed.

"Well, then, he took my advice; and so we sends for the bone-setter there, in the dock, and he comes with his instruments; and with that we tied Phill Doyle on a door, with his face to the wood; and he says to Tim—

"'It's a could mornen, dochter.'

"'And if I said it was,' answered he, ''twouldn't be a lie for me; maybe you'd be after given us a leetle drop of the 'delight,' just to study my hand?'

"'To be shure I will, and plinty of it,' said Phill.

"So he tould me to sarch in an ould churn in the corner of the room, and I'd find some of the raal mountain-dew: and shure enough there it was, smiling like a new pratie. So I hands the piggin full of it to Tim there, and he take a pull at it I thought would reach the bottom, and then he lets me just look into it.'

"I suppose," cried Mr. Cowslip, "the prospect was so charming, you drank it in with the look. "Go on."

"By my sowl, counsellor, I don't think you'd look skew-ways (askew) at it yourself," returned he of pig-tail memory.

"I must protest against this interruption," observed Mr. Scutt; at the same time that he made a fearful pass at the witness with the evil-minded finger.

Mr. Patrick Tobacco, fearing lest the digit might be speedily eclipsed in his body corporate, hastily continued.

"Well, thin, the man with the legs says to Tim—

"'How's your hand, surgeant, after that? Is't study yet?'

"'Not intirely,' says the docthor; 'it thrimbles a little.'

"And with that he takes the piggin from me, and it never left his lips till Moll Thompson's mark was on it.

"'Now,' says he, 'I'd bleed a bull.'

"So he takes a phlames out of his pocket, and gives the leg a little nick, to find out the vein; and whin he had made certain of that, down comes the mallet on the instrument, that I thought the leg was cut off, and out spouts the blood. Sorrow a groan came from the man on the table, only he tould Tim to cut bould, as he gave him great relief afore. So Docthor O'Mulligan says to him—

"'Are you asier now, Mr. Doyle?'

"'Oh, much asier, and a trifle cooler,' says Phill, 'and a little weak; have you ere a drop left?'

"'Not as much as id christen a child,' answered the docthor. 'Paddy there, fornent you, seen the last of it; there warn't much in it.'

"But I'll give my Bible oath, my lord and gentlemen, 'twas himself had the first and last of it; blazes the drop I had but a pint in the middle of it."

Here Mr. Scutt, with a face duly distended to befit the solemnity of this part of the tragedy, asked—

"If any styptics were applied to close the cicatrix?"

The witness, not understanding the question, and thinking it was put to him to make a fool of him, turned to the judge, and complained that it was a burnen shame for an ould counsellor like him, that had been goen the road for forty years, to talk about skip-jacks,' and 'cats'-tricks,' and the sowl leaving a dead man's body."

"I beg, Mr. Scutt," observed Mr. Smartley, as the finger of the former went backward and forward like the piston of a steam engine, moving horizontally, "you'll address the witness in language intelligible to him."

The barrister by whom this last observation was made, from the peculiar adaptability in that region where a man's honour is supposed to reside constantly, suggested the idea what an excellent subject for *royal patronage* he would have been in the days when *flagellations per prox* were more practised than they are now.

"Sir," replied the crown prosecutor, "I shall not simplify the density of my phraseology to suit the obesity of any man's intellect;" and the *dexter digit* seemed to delight itself in numerous gyrations, as if it had made a home thrust.

"Then," rejoined Sir Mungo Malgrowther's double, as he directed his question to the witness, "since the crown oracle is as ambiguous as ever, I shall ask you in plain terms, did you or the prisoner make any effort to stop the blood?"

"To be shure we did," said Mr. Patrick Tobacco, as he took up his tale after this interruption. "Phill Doyle finding himself mighty cool and pleasant, and thinking there was enough of the strame of life outside, axes the docther to stop the bleeding; and with that the docther puts the cobweb of a murthering spider over it, and some die-a-lick-em plaster on that same, and thin binds the whole of it with a bit of an ould felt hat, but it would'nt stay in like a bould gassoon, at all at all. So Phill, and the surgeant, and myself, gets frightened, and we sends for the raal docthur down to the dispensary, but he wasn't to the fore just then; and when he did come, poor Doyle was as dry as a lime-burner's breeches—divil blow the sup that was in him. Mr. O'Mulligan was for houlden a consultation, but the dispensary docther wouldn't have any call to him, but said he murdered the man, and some harm would come to him. With that the prisoner looks as blue as a Brunswicker; and so I said to him, 'I suppose, Tim, you'll send in the same

bill to Phill Doyle's widdy for attindance on her husband, as you sent to the major when you kilt his horse,—eight and three happence for curing his honor's horse till it died!" Off makes the bone-setter as fast as his poplar toe would carry him, afeard of the police."

Thus ended the evidence of the first witness ; the next, which was the dispensary doctor, proved that the popliteal artery had been severed by the energy with which the operator had used the horse-lancet : so Mr. O'Mulligan was found guilty, and sentenced to be incarcerated for twelve months, to deter him for the future from confounding the race of bipeds and quadrupeds in the course of his extensive practice But he didn't continue in prison for a third of the period, as Lord Normanby let him out upon

a representation contained in a memorial to the effect that Tim's wooden leg was becoming emaciated from want of exercise ; besides that, several of the good wives were near their time, and his excellency was too tinderhearted to refuse them the medical gentleman who understood their constitutions.

Mr. Baintree was retained for the next case. He defended a man for keeping an illicit still, and Colonel Jack had the pleasure of listening to an able speech from his friend. He was successful for the man was acquitted. On the next morning they started for Tipperary. They were now approaching the capital of this great country, "four and twenty counsellors all on a car," when they met the representatives of the *posse comitatus* moving in solemn state to meet the judge. They were dressed in long blue coats, one of which would have been amply capacious for any two. This unnecessary profusion of cloth, provided by assessment, could only be accounted for in two ways—either the garments were annually transferable, like the sheriff's wand of office (and, as Nature didn't mould all men in the same shape, it couldn't be expected they would fit an ever-shifting series of *posses*); or, perhaps, the Clonmel snips, like their brethren of Aleppo, measure by azimuth and compass, and so maintain that the body ought to be adapted to the coat, and not the coat to the body. Whatever be the reason of the "space infinite," still there remains the wanton sacrifice of a tailor's favourite vegetable to be accounted for. They were mounted upon animals which cannot fairly be denominated quadruped, seeing that there was only the use of six pair of legs amongst each dozen; and, from the numerous gyrations upon the road, the colonel calculated that eyes were in similar abundance.

The riders kept their seats for a time very well, being of the race of bum-bailiffs, poising in their hands what was intended to represent a halbert of the olden time; but, in reality, was more like the discarded pole of a barber, with a superannuated butcher's knife on the top of it, and the tassel of a bell-pull at the junction of wood and iron. On they marched to guard the majesty of the law, and never had Justice such valiant defenders. The urchins and old women on the roadside quailed to a woman as they passed along; even the very pigs and ducks that, in the "island of saints," seem to have been created for no other earthly purpose than to have their necks broken by public conveyances sneaked into the ditches to escape the terrific presence of these doughty men-at-arms. They soon came up with the carriage in which Mr. Justice Cramwell rode, and superseded the escort which had guarded him from Waterford, duly inflated with an awful sense of the responsibility which now devolved upon them, and determined to shed the last drop of beer in them in defence of her most gracious majesty's representative. His lordship, like the son of Jehoshaphat, delights in quick travelling; in fact, he always proceeds with the rapidity of a man who, fancying he has gotten a new idea under the sun, hastens home to record it, that it may not be lost to the world. The postilions, therefore, urged their horses, who were nothing loath to go, as the corn wasn't far off; the *posse* dug the rowels into the flanks of their gallant steeds, who seemed not to understand this novel application of *acupuncturation* to their rheumatic sides. As the pace increased, the halberts dropped from the perpendicular to the horizontal, and the points of the rear-rank

wandering from their line of direction, stuck into the haunches of the front, and occasionally into the developement of the *posse* himself; and so one *posse* after another was tilted off, tournament-wise, and, biting the dust ingloriously, became a *pulveris posse*, in place of a *comitatus posse*. Last of all, the horses, urged both fore and aft, by heel and halbert, unaccustomed to such warlike treatment, set off a full speed, and then the *stampedo* fairly commenced. Halberts and horsemen flew in all directions; the riders might be seen lying upon the road, the ruling passion strong in death, *moriens dulce reminiscitur Argos*, grasping the official weapons in one hand, and with the other vainly endeavouring to hold on by the dicky of the sheriff's carriage, that they mightn't desert their charge, upon which the eyes of all Ireland were fixed. But no judge could ever speed the queen's writ to equal the rapidity with which such of them as managed to keep their seats were borne over hill and dale, mountain and moor, to Clonmel. And the good citizens, seeing the familiar coats and spears floating through the air, came out to escort Justice, supposing she was to be found amongst the *posse*; and the trumpeters made the welkin ring with the welcoming blast: but great was their amazement to find that not for the first time the sword had outstripped her slow progress.

Rumour mounted her winged steed, and rode furiously through the multitude, giving out as she went along that the maiden with the skewer in one hand and the balance in the other, which they call Justice, had been tossed into a bog-hole, and might be dug out some centuries hence as the fossil remains of an elk or behemoth, or some other unknown animal whose genus the naturalist geologist has not been able to fix. In the midst of all this confusion and dark surmise, in she came, and the astonishment of the lieges was tenfold increased upon discovering that no insult has been offered to her, though she had travelled more than a quarter of a mile unprotected by the *posse*.

"The Leinsters" arrived soon after, but at a snail's gallop compared with the pace at which the flying constables went. The commission opened at four in the afternoon, so Mr. Baintree repaired to the Court-house, which was densely crowded with numerous specimens of the *raal boys*, all attracted by the prospect of *divarsion*, as they call a wedding or an execution. Each man bearing in his own person many badges of distinction, earned in well-contested fields, in which each warrior might say with that old twaddler, Æneas, "*quorum magna pars fui*." One could observe male eyes blacker than the sparkling jets of the Milesian maid; and what brother Jonathan say of a man having so thin a face that there was not space for two individuals to look upon it at the same time, was fully verified here, as the spectator could discover a fragment of a countenance amongst three, and a single feature served for the profile of many.

The colonel turned from the contemplation of human dovetailing in the gallery to listen to the charge of Mr. Justice Cramwell, in which he ignored every thing which Mr. Justice Moore had said of the country-crime statistics six months previously. So true is it that judges' charges consist purely of saying and unsaying, just as the life of man is made up of buttoning and unbuttoning. The only case tried this afternoon was that of the Queen v. O'Shaunessy; or, as the defendant was more familiarly called, *Short-nosey*, though the *sobriquet* was a cruel libel upon the extent of that feature, which was like a hanging terrace to his face. The indictment charged the aforesaid with feloniously robbing a hen-roost, and stealing thereout a cock; and the jury found him guilty, though it was distinctly proved for the defence that the man was hen-pecked; recommending him, however, to mercy—I suppose the mercies of his wife. The court then rose, and we adjourned to mess at the Great Globe. As "the Leinsters" mustered strongly, it required some knowledge of the exact sciences on the part of their host, the *maitre d'hotel*, so to arrange the tables, that the elbows of the individuals dining shouldn't render the intromission of food a work of supererogation by boring holes between their neighbours ribs to let it out again. We would premise that we do not think any assemblaged of men, met together in a given space for the purpose of performing the three great functions of human nature,—demolition, deglutition, and digestion, can compare with a barmess. Talk of your military bivouacs for such an object! Why the very colour of an officer's coat prevents him from enjoying his dinner. An awkward attendant, as he removes a soup-plate, may, by an unlucky trip, put him to the expense of twelve or fourteen guineas by treating the scarlet, to some mock-turtle.

The lieutenant-colonel from the head announces a most important discovery in strategy that there *is* no fifth regiment of light dragoons, and then proceeds to relate to the major on his right some adventure of his which occurred when he was brigadier-general in Ava, which the major can detail much better in the abstract, because the narrator makes sundry additions thereto after each monthly perusal of the *United Service Journal*; and then he cordially wishes the colonel was general of the fifth light-horse, or the noble army of martyrs; and, as he writhes upon his chair from nausea at hearing the "ofttold tale," digs his spurs into the captain; and the captain, wincing from the pain, shoves his epaulet into the lieutenant's mouth, whose face is ever directed towards it; and then the lieutenant, to avenge himself for the insult, snubs the sub, and all the while the discipline of the service must be preserved.

But, at a bar-mess, there is the most perfect equality between the members; or, if there be any distinction of one above the other, 'tis the result of voluntary homage conceded to age, talent, or experience.

The president of this festive republic, and seated at the head, was our worthy father, Mr. Richardson. For many years had his patriarchal reign continued over "the Leinsters," respected and beloved. In his public capacity, not more conspicuous for his erudition as a lawyer, his brilliancy as an orator, and his accomplishments as a scholar, than for his urbanity as a gentleman and total absence of professional jealousy; whilst in private he was not merely in name, but in reality, father to the members of the circuit, abounding with anecdote, and told with such propriety and ease, as left his hearers at a loss whether to admire most the extent and variety of the material, or the elegance of expression by which it was characterised.

Long may he rule over us, and when his time-honoured reign shall have been brought to a period, the highest praise which his successor can hope to attain will be that he resembles Mr. Richardson in the qualities of his head and heart.

At the foot was that most illustrious adjunct to a bar-mess, the junior, Mr. Herbert Monday. The junior, by tenure of his office, is treasurer to the bar, which consists in being the depositary of all the dirty notes upon circuit, to collect which he must display the agility of a lamp lighter, the *reduced dimensions* of a skeleton, so as to occupy as little space as possible in squeezing his way through court, and the *ubiquity* of Sir Boyle Roche's bird.

He is to allow as much wine as the funds in hand will admit of, or more, and charge as little as possible for it; and if ever a doubt should arise in his mind whether he ought to mulct himself or the bar for the matter of a small balance remaining unpaid after the town subscriptions have been exhausted, always to give the latter the benefit of the doubt.

He ought by all means to be born on a Thursday, so as to have each eye turned different ways, and able to see round a corner; that he may note with the precision of a post-office clerk the arrival and departure of mail and stage coaches, and all other machines implying locomotion, having their boxes looking from, and not towards him.

Yea, it would not be amiss after mess to glance into turf-cars, and wheelbarrows, having straw in them, as I recollect to have once seen in one or other of these vehicles a pair of legs which, from their peculiar shape, I suspected to belong to brother Sully, but I didn't satisfy myself of their identity, as I fancied I could distinguish a second pair of more delicate proportions. Not that there ever is a refusal to discharge liabilities on demand, but very few people ever volunteer payment; and, somehow or other, a debt seems not to be incurred until after a formal requisition to meet it.

The junior is also keg-bleeder and cork-drawer to the establishment; and however incompatible those several duties may appear with the dignity of the profession, he has no option of declining them, as their performance is compulsory upon every gentleman admitted of the circuit. Such was the post, the respectable functions whereof Mr. Herbert Monday was doomed to discharge, with infinite dissatisfaction to himself; the amusement of the bar being in inverse ratio with the dislike of the individual to the occupation.

His frame was of such delicate dimensions as to have been evidently designed by nature to be perpetually engaged in that branch of civil engineering which relates to the examination of the intestines of a pump; or certainly, by becoming a temporary inmate, would have exactly suited the purpose of a reverend divine in the city of Cashel, who, having a house to let, posted a placard to that effect upon a *lamp-post*, directing those who were desirous of becoming tenants to nquire *within*.

On the right of the "Father," was Mr. Joshua Hatchment, Q. C., equally remarkable for his loquacity in court and his taciturnity at mess. No doubt concurring with the Bristol alderman, that at dinner the mouth should be opened for no other purpose than to let in food, and that the goddess of gastronomy ought to be worshipped with mute adoration. In court, however, as the crier used to observe. "The strame of wit and humour came as spontaneous from him as smoke from a *dhudecn*."

Not far from him sat Mr. Diogenes Bruin; the play of whose features was so versatile that he never could purchase a *face admission* at a theatre, for it was impossible to recognise him a second time, and that must be a hardy witness who would undertake to identify him.

His practice was not more extensive than his great legal acquirements justified; but, however well read in law, he certainly was not equally familiar with the writings of the prince of dramatic bards, as his memory retained but one line from them, which was

ugged in upon all occasions, like the monopologue of the Epicurean philosopher about "Jupiter in his winged car," whenever a witness who ought to have been produced was held back by the antagonist party. Then did the court re-echo with the words—

"Call the spirits from the vasty deep."

The most recondite application of the favourite line was when a case of pig-stealing was being tried. After due invocation, an addition was made thereto from Virgil, to the surprise of his legal brethren; which was most appropriate, allowing for a slight inaccuracy, occasioned by the exciting nature of the subject—

"Stridunt Aquilone porcelli (procellæ.")

Which was thus interpreted by the junior—

"The pigs they ride on the nor'-west wind,
    As they through the country sweep;
And Bruin, not to be left behind,
    Mounts on ' a spirit from the deep.' "

About the centre of the table had Mr. Smalltalk anchored himself, who was wholesale manufacturer and retail vender of quaint sayings and smart repartees to the fraternity. In the university he was distinguished by an extraordinary classical monomania, which shewed itself in a ceaseless and assiduous anxiety to discover the preterperfect tenses of verbs.

Once had he been known, after a sleepless night of intense verbal agony, to despatch his domestic peripatetic at five o'clock of a bleak winter's morning, with his compliments to Dr. Polyglot (who was more familiarly known by the elegant *sobriquet* of *Ursa Major*), to inquire whether he did not agree in opinion with him that the preterite "insanivi" ought to be deduced from the obsolete verb *insanio*, and not from *furo*. To which the learned professor, indignant at being roused so early, and cordially wishing to the devil all parts of speech, except, perhaps, conjunctions copulative returned for answer— "Semel insanivimous omnes," with the further addition that he believed Mr. Smalltalk's paroxysm was then at its height. This *furor præteritus* changed its venue on his being called to the bar; and the same untiring perseverance which had rescued the occult and lurking perfect from beneath the dust of antiquity was now directed to roam through the chaos of reports, till the lawyer had become quite case-hardened and chagrined.

Every motion in court was made with feverish anxiety for its success; so much so that Mr. Herbert Monday used to affirm, whenever it did please Mr Smalltalk to cut his parchment and die, it would be of a rule *nisi*, and the obituary would contain the melancholy announcement— "Died of a conditional order not made absolute, Jonathan Smalltalk, Esq. barrister."

In close conversation with the friend of the perfects was Mr. Recorder Sky-the Copper, remarkable for one very amiable trait—his hands were never seen outside his pockets, except to close upon a fee.

Colonel Jack and Mr. Baintree sat together at the dinner-table, and the latter pointed out to his companion the notabilities who were then and there present.

"And so, what do you think of Irish life?" inquired the counseller.

"Oh, it's original and amusing, to say the least of it," answered the colonel.

"I have one or two other cases to attend to," said Mr. Baintree, "and then I shall have done, as far as my professional duties are concerned; I shall after then be at your service. I hope I am not making too great a tax upon your patience?"

"Quite the contrary; I am and have been highly entertained," returned our hero, who, in saying this much, only spoke the truth.

"After the trials are over, we will see about the business which more immediately concerns you."

"Thank you, sir," answered Colonel Jack; "I am sure you are very kind."

Space will not admit of our sketching the portraits of "the Leinsters," so we return to the dinner, at which the colonel and Mr. Braintree sat.

The soup and fish had been duly despatched, and they were awaiting in breathless expectation the removes, when distant sounds of altercation reached their ears. Anon they came nearer and nearer; and now the colonel and Mr. Baintree could distinguish the words of the belligerents.

"I say it is for the bar."

To which was fiercely retorted—

"Bad luck to you and the bar together!—I say 'tis not—it's for the grand jury."

First voice again—

"Blazes to your soul if you shall have it."

And then there was a shuffling of feet.

Second voice—

"By the holy farmer! I'll knock the daylights iv you with this rib of beef, if you don't take your dirty claws from it."

And suiting the action to the word, bang went the door, and in came the bar-waiter, toppling down upon a goodly array of soup-plates and fish-sauces, whilst the sirloin of beef, the meritorious cause of action, after grazing his head, was safely deposited in the lap of the junior.

But the junior, becoming enraged at being helped in this wholesale manner, seized in both his hands a tureen of soup, and discharged its contents at the head of the delinquent.

Then was there uproar and confusion.

Some "Leinsters" asking the indignant junior whether he intended to monopolise to himself the entire lap of beef; and others asserting that the offender would be quiet for the rest of the evening, as he had got his "souporific" from Mr. Monday.

In the meantime the prostrate servitor was making several efforts to raise himself, but unsuccessfully, as he went down again, his feet slipping on the greasy floor. At last, planting them against the cornice, he succeeded in getting upon his legs.

Never was seen so ludicrous an appearance as the two recent combatants presented, shaking themselves like dogs out of water.

Our broth of a boy always had a curious sort of amphibious look, like a half-baked crumpet, which was rendered tenfold more ambiguous by the murky streams which flowed from him in every direction.

The other individual was wiping his face with some boiled cabbage-leaves, purloined from a dish in the hall, not daring to enter the room for a napkin, his face being beautifully mosaic, resembling rather the chequered surface of a fruit-pudding or spiced collar, than the countenance of a human being, being studded universally with patches of vegetable and small pieces of calves' head; which latter found themselves upon a kindred substance.

The grand jury messed at the Great Globe much about the same hour as the bar, and were also suffering privations from the war-like attitude which had been assumed by the respective domestics.

Finding that no one appeared to answer the summons of the bell, two of them were despatched to discover a short passage to a dinner; and being attracted by both noise and vapour, they reached the hall just about the time the two sponges were squeezing themselves.

Inquiring into the strange aspect of affairs, they were given to understand, by the being with the tessalated countenance, that the "victuals intended for them had been intercepted by the counsellors, like everything else that was worth taking: and when he riz up for them, he had been sarved with soup till he was as smooth as a soaped pig; but if I was, your sowl to glory, colonel! if I didn't dish one of their saucepans in style!"

The "self and fellows" were not to be satisfied with a mere feast of reason. It was too serious a thing to have nothing more substantial before them, from nine in the morning till seven in the afternoon, than bills of indictment; and then to lose, by forestalling, the best joint which the hotel could afford, or make up their minds to be content with secondhand bones, and something "that was and is not."

So an imparlance was duly prayed of the bar; and the grand inquest, by their deputies, demanded that we should shew cause why a detainer had been laid upon their goods and chattels. Whereupon Messrs Hatchment and Diogenes Bruin were ordered to appear on behalf of the legal community; and, further, to examine witnesses, and ascertain the rights of the litigant parties. The plenipotentiaries on the other side were the Hon. Mr. Blueface and Colonel Purify. Of the latter gentleman rather an amusing anecdote was recorded, which we may as well introduce whilst the evidence is being gone into. It happens at certain seasons of the year in the country of Tipperary, and I suppose in other districts of Ireland likewise, turkey-cocks are in great request; so much so, that it requires the utmost vigilance on the part of the owners to guard them from being abducted by female depredators. Information was given to a Major M'Pherson, commanding a troop of Scots Greys at Caher, that a trespass *vi et armis*, of a most aggravated nature, had been committed upon the premises of a farmer, and property to a large amount feloniously carried off by the White-boys. The military were ordered to assist the police, as the country was not very tranquil; and the major headed tne troop in person. It was alleged that the depredators had been seen to take the road to Bansha; and that one of them could be easily identified by the party who had been robbed. After a hot pursuit of some hours, they came up with a person on the road, whose dress answered the description previously given of one of the plunderers; and having taken the "epicene" into custody, and examined it, it proved to be of the same sex as mother Eve, carrying in a basket a fine specimen of a turkey, not of the feminine gender, which the farmer, who acted as guide, swore to belong to him. The culprit was immediately dragged before a magistrate, Colonel Purify, and information whereon to ground a committal tendered; but he refused to take them, knowing that it was never intended to steal the property, but that it would be honestly returned after a forced loan thereof. However, seeing that the major had acted with praiseworthy promptitude, he thought it right to compliment him for it; and assured him "that he might always reckon upon his countenance and protection."

The dinner being over, and after most if not all present, had succeeded in satisfying their carnal appetites, Mr. Baintree and our hero rose therefrom, and took a stroll through the town of Tipperary. We have already given the reader a slight sketch of Irish life, and will therefore spare him any further details of the most distinctive features of this uncertain, strange, but warm-hearted race.

CHAPTER CXIX.

THE SEARCH FOR MORGAN HALFORD.

"Now," said Mr. Baintree to Colonel Jack, after he had finished his professional business. "Now comes a question as to how it is possible to find out the settlement of this Morgan Halford. I have been informed that he settled in some village a few miles from Tipperary, but whether such was the case I am unable to say with any degree of certainty. However, there is a crier in the town, as also a postman. Possibly one of these worthys will be able to afford us some information upon the subject. At any rate, there is no harm in trying. We have had a good dinner —thanks to our host, and our own industry in collaring hold of whatever came in our way."

"Ah, ah!" laughed Colonel Jack. "It was a scrambling repast, to say the least of it."

"Well, we will see if we can find out the crier."

And so saying, Mr. Baintree went to the Court-house, where the Petty Sessions was held. The counsellor entered the entrance-hall of this building, and saw a lazy porter in the vestibule.

"Where abouts shall I find the crier of the town?" said Mr. Baintree.

"Och, sure now, and is it the crier you'd be after seeing," inquired the man, scratching his head.

"Yes."

"Oh, and may be ye've lost something?" said the man, not giving an answer to the question, but as is usual with his countrymen, asking another instead.

"Yes, I have lost a man, or rather, I want to find one," said Mr. Baintree, with a smile.

"Ah, indeed! It's a man you've lost, eh?" said the porter, opening his eyes in astonishment.

"Ah, sure; is there anything astonishing in that?"

"May be he belongs to the light infantry?"

"No, no—he's no deserter."

"Och, murder! but I don't mean a soger," said the Irishman. "It isn't that same at all, at all; but he's just had on a clean pair of heels of his own, and may be he's given ye the slip."

"Well, he's slipped off into the other world, my friend," said Mr. Baintree, with a smile.

"Oh, bad luck to me then, it's no crier

that'll qring him back agin then. Ye'd better go to a priest."

Mr. Baintree was getting tired of the man's circumlocution, and then said, somewhat sharply.

"Come, my good fellow, never mind what I want him for. Tell me where it is likely I shall find the crier."

"He was here not an hour ago," answered the man, "but I think you'll find him at the House of Detention, for you see he's just gone there to indemnify a prisoner."

"Identify you mean, I suppose. Well, that's near enough for our purpose. Come, Halford, we'll go there at once. It's not a quarter of a mile from here," said Mr. Baintree, turning towards Colonel Jack.

The two then took their way to the building in question. Upon arriving there they saw the head turnkey, who introduced them to a ward where the crier was. The unfortunate crier was in a terrible position. He was on the stone pavement of a large square yard, the walls of which were surmounted with a *chevaux de frise,* and one of the prisoners, a strong dark looking man was striking at him with his fists in a most unmerciful manner. Several other prisoners were in the yard, and cheered on their comrade as he continued to assault the crier in a most unmerciful manner.

"Hilloa! What's all this about? I'll give you a taste of the cat-o'-nine-tails," exclaimed the turnkey in a voice of thunder, which it was necessary to assume to be heard above the din and uproar. The prisoner desisted from his attack, and turned towards the turnkey, breathless and half abashed.

"The lying spalpeen; what right has he to come here and indemnify me as a rick-burner?" exlaimed the man, savagely.

The crier picked himself up, and came by the side of the turnkey for protection. He then entered into a long account of the injuries he had received, and wound up by saying—

"Och and sure now, the only thing that supports a man in all this is to know that he is serving his Majesty the king."

"Of course," said the turnkey, who then went out of the yard, followed by the crier, who it appeared was not much hurt after all, and as these scenes were of daily, nay, almost hourly occurrence, very little more notice was taken of the transaction.

The four—the turnkey, the crier, our hero, and Mr. Baintree then adjourned to the lobby of the former.

"These gentlemen wish to speak to you," said the turnkey.

"Yes, my man," said Mr. Baintree. "I am anxious to know where the late Mr. Morgan Halford resided?"

"Morgan Halford," said the crier. "And sure I don't know the name at all, at all. Was it in the town he resided? Did he kape a shop, or was he a rale gentleman?"

"That is more than I can tell you, but he's dead now. All we want to know is where he resided when alive."

"And is it his ghost ye'd be afther taking?" inquired the man, in some surprise.

"No, all we want is to ascertain if he left any issue."

"Any what?"

"Son or daughter."

"Ah!" exclaimed the crier, as a light appeared to suddenly break in upon him, "I see!"

"Well, do you happen to know anything of the party?" inquired Mr. Baintree, once more.

"There has been a chap by the name of Halford used to come into the town," said the man, reflectively, and scratching his head, "and I do believe that he must be the same of whom you are in search. Let me see, how can we find out? I never did know his address—but, bedad! I tell yer what yer can do—and sure, man, it's the best thing for yer to be afther."

"And what may that be, my man?"

"Why, jest this. Ye must mind that it's market-day, is this same."

"Yes."

"And being market-day, of course every one all round the country will be—why, jest lonely, in a manner of speaking."

"What, the people from the surrounding districts."

"To be sure; ivery man to his business," said the crier, in continuation, "and sure un' it's mine I am afther thinking of, and please ye, gentlemen."

"Well, go on," exclaimed Mr. Baintree.

"And what say ye to my journey into the market, and offering a handsome reward to anyone who may give information of this—what's his nane?"

"Morgan Halford."

"Ah! that's it, Morgan Halford."

"I think your suggestion an excellent one," answered Mr. Baintree; "about it at once; the market is pretty full, just now."

"Oh, quite full, yer honour; and, indeed, ye may say that, too, without a telling of any lie."

Agreeable to the means suggested, the three left the house of detention, and proceeded at once to the market, which they found quite full of an heterogenous throng of persons. Mr. Baintree gave directions to the crier to offer a reward of two guineas to whomsoever would give information respecting one Major Halford.

In a short time, the tintilabury clatter of the crier's bell called the attention of those assembled in the market-place. Then followed the "Oh yes! oh yes! this is to give notice to all persons in or near Limerick, that the sum of two guineas will be given to any person who will give information of the late Mr. Morgan Halford, who was supposed to reside—"&c. &c.

This was repeated at various points of the market-place, without any other effect than attracting the attention of a gaping lot of idlers. At length, however, when the parties were about to give the matter up in dispair, when as the crier was repeating the words he had been instructed to bawl out for the last time, a man who had hitherto remained concealed in the bustle of the market, stepped forward and listened attentively to what the crier was saying; he suddenly cried out in a stentorian voice—

"Bad luck to ye, yer noisy spalpeen! and hould yer row for a few seconds! and do yer want to be after splitting people's ears?"

"Now then!" said the crier," and who may you bay, that ye stop people in their business?'

"Who is it ye are wanting?"

"Mr. Morgan Halford."

"Thin ye can't have him;—he's gone to 'the place.'"

"Did you know him, my friend?" inquired Mr. Baintree, who had been following the crier during the whole of his proceedings, and watching the issue of the same.

"And sure I did, yer honour, as well as I know'd my own son, Pat. Why, he lived close by me."

"You are the very man we want, then;" said Mr. Baintree. "How far do you reside from here, my friend?"

"Oh, it will be about twelve miles."

Colonel Jack and the lawyer consulted together, and came to the conclusion that it would be better for them to go to the village where the farmer (for such he turned out to be) resided.

Mr Baintree asked him how long it would be before he started home, and was informed by that individual that it would be in about two hours. He offered at the same time to drive the counseller and his companion to the village in question; and things being arranged satisfactorily thus far, Colonel Jack gave the crier a guinea for his trouble, and with many thanks he took his departure.

"Now, how are we to eke out the time till our friend is ready, that is the next question," said Mr. Baintree.

"You had better go to the "Black Boy," where my horse is put up," said the farmer; "and if you'll wait there awhile I will join you, and then we can drive over together; and sure now, they've excellent whiskey at the "Black Boy," or indeed it is not myself that would put up at that same house."

"We will go there, my friend," said Mr.

Baintree. "Our time's our own, but I hope you will keep your appointment, for I don't want to lose sight of a man who promises to be of such essential service to us. I have not inquired your name as yet."

"And sure now, it's my name you are wanting?" said the man with an inquiring look; and ye don't think now that I am likely to be ashamed o' the name I bear?"

"Oh, I am sure you are not," said Mr. Baintree. "You'll excuse my asking. I meant no offence, only in the event of your not coming or being detained you know—"

"Not coming! and do ye think that O'Callagan's iver made a promise that they didn't perform," exclaimed the man, indignantly. "Ye want to find out something about Morgan Halford, what's gone to 'tother world, don't ye?"

"Yes."

"Well, then, look here now. It's myself that'll show you the home he lived in, and may be, for the matter of that, the praste who knows better than any mother's son of us where he's gone to."

"You are the man for my money, Mr. O'Callagan," said Mr. Baintree. "We will not take you from your business, but will wait for you at the Black Boy."

"Very well, and good luck to ye till I see ye again," said Mr. O'Callagan who disappeared into the thick of the market.

Mr. Baintree and Colonel Jack took their way to the "Black Boy," which they found in one of the principal streets of the town. They went into the chief room of this respectable hostelry, and ordered some whiskey punch. When this was brought in, and a portion of it swallowed, the two friends felt a little more at their ease. What with the crowded court-house, and following the crier about the town, they felt positively jaded, or what we should term in the present day, "seedy," a term then unknown in the vernacula.

"Our friend will keep his word, I do not doubt," said Mr. Baintree, "and we may esteem ourselves particularly fortunate that we have progressed thus far. Now comes the question, whether this said Morgan Halford thought proper to get married and leave issue."

"Let us hope not," returned our hero.

"Did I ever tell you the adventure I had abroad? You know I have been to most parts of the continent since I saw you, I suppose?" said Mr. Baintree.

"No, I did not know it."

"Oh, yes; I left my father and the clerks to look after our professional business, while I went for a vacation ramble, as we term it. It seems that some men are fated to meet with adventures—the burglary at Dulwich, for instance."

"Ah, that was an unmatched piece of heroism," said the colonel. "But what was this one to which you allude?"

"You shall hear," said Mr. Baintree. "We have some difficulty in filling up the time till our friend Mr. O'Callagan's return, and I will give you an account of the adventure."

"With all my heart," said the colonel.

———

CHAPTER CXX.

MR. BAINTREE'S ADVENTURE.

"You must know," said the lawyer, "that after a day's ramble among the winding passes of the Pyrennees, I came towards

No. 82.

evening to a lonely *auberge* situated in the line of one of the rough and broken roads which connect the French and Spanish frontiers. I can tell you I was vastly pleased when I caught sight of this habitation, for I was jaded, and had been seeking for a place of shelter for some time.

"Well, on reaching the inn in question, I found it to be small, but to bear an air of comfort and neatness which gave promise of comfortable accommodation, a good repast, and a pleasant night's rest.

"The worn out traveller can sleep upon a hard bed if needs be.

When I arrived at the house in question, the appearance of the persons inside its walls were at variance with the promising external appearance. I was received and kindly welcomed by a young woman, who was extremely good looking, and had a pretty child of about a year old in her arm. She was habited in the costume usually worn in those regions, which is a perpetual combination of bright colours: a red handkerchief was bound round her head, and her vest, petticoat, and stockings were all stuffs striped and tinted with various dyes.

When I mentioned to her my wants, she called a young girl from another apartment, and giving her the child, began herself actively to prepare refreshments for me.

The respectable animal called the goat was of great service on this occasion, for in a short time after I sat down to flesh, milk, and cheese, all provided by that rock-loving and four-footed hardy mountaineer.

As the main apartment, namely, the kitchen, is the only place where travellers abide under such circumstances—for you must know, the house did not boast of a room like the "Black Boy"—so, situated as I was, I had opportunities of conversing with my hostess during the preparation of the meal.

She seemed to be cheerful, though not too gay. Her husband, she told me, was out on the hills, along with a lad who assisted him in the management of the little spot of ground attached to their residence.

By the time that I sat down to my repast, the shades of evening had begun to fall in, and while I ate—as I did most voraciously—I observed my hostess beginning to shew signs of impatience. Ever and anon she went to the door and looked abroad, returning each time with visible anxiety on her countenance.

I was tempted at length to ask—

"If a storm was at hand, or if she feared any impending evil?"

"Ah, sir," said she, "I am only a little distressed that Miguel, my husband, should be out so long. It will soon be dark."

"Is there any danger?" I asked; "has the neighbourhood a bad name?"

"Oh, no, sir," replied she; "the country is now thought to be quite safe, and I am perhaps foolish to be uneasy; but it was once very unsafe, and we suffered so much from it in consequence, that I cannot rid myself of fear at times."

She bent down her head as she spoke, and appeared to lose for a moment the sense of present uneasiness in the revived recollection of the past.

At this instant the door opened, and a tall, strapping, sun-burnt fellow entered, whom I immediately conjectured to be the husband, from his being followed by a young peasant. My hostess had sprung to her feet, and I thought it augured well for her husband's marital tenderness, that he at once noticed

her to have been discomposed, and exclaimed—

"What, Inez, at thy old terrors!"

Then, noticing me for the first time in the growing dusk, he continued—

"And strangers with thee, too!"

He then saluted me civilly, and we were soon engaged in conversation.

I stayed two days with Miguel and his wife, and became excellent friends with them. I found an opportunity to gratify my curiosity, by inquiring into the misfortunes which my hostess had alluded to as having arisen from the former insecurity of the country, and I heard the whole story from her. I will tell it you.

"But a few years ago," said Inez, which was my hostess's name, "my father was the tenant of this house, where we now live. Here I was born, and here had the misfortune to lose my mother in my youth; in short, all my days have been spent here. When I was about eighteen, I became first acquainted with Miguel, who had hired himself as conductor of wagon that passed regularly by this road from one side of the mountains to another. The wagon always stopped a night here as it passed, and Miguel and I began to love each other. Nor was it long ere we were both aware that this was the case. My father saw the state of our affections as well as we did, and he was not averse to our union, for he was growing old, and, even at the best, he always required a lad to assist him with the little farm, upon which our support depended much more than on the visits of travellers to the house. It was at length settled, that Miguel and I should be married as soon as he had completed his term in his present occupations.

"When this arrangement was made, Miguel had but three journeys backwards and forwards to perform. These were long journeys to be sure, and, what was worse, there were reports of recent robberies at no great distance, which made travelling dangerous. The first journey, however, was performed in safety. When Miguel came to us on his way over the mountains a second time, some circumstances took place which after events caused us to remember. A traveller had come to our house that day, before Miguel reached us with his wagon. That traveller was a dark, active-looking man, dressed in the ordinary Spanish fashion, and seemingly in the prime of life. Before Miguel arrived, this visitor addressed himself to me in such a manner as was very disagreeable. I at first indeed paid little attention to his words, for my thoughts that day were occupied with another subject. When, at length, encouraged it may be by my silence, he would have carried his freedoms further. I regarded him civilly, but firmly, and told him plainly that my affections and hand were engaged to another. The dark malignant smile which passed over his countenance when I said this, gave me new and unpleasing ideas of our guest, whom I had hitherto regarded as only a man of a light and sportive temperament. He did not alter his conduct, nor, even when Miguel came, did he desist from annoying me. This gave me much alarm, for I perceived Miguel's brow to darken on observing his behaviour. Nor was my alarm groundless, for, on the traveller's seizing and holding me by the arm as I accidentally passed him, Miguel sprang up, and threw him violently to the further end of the room, where he fell heavily on the floor. In an instant the man was on his feet, had his long knife drawn from his belt, and seemed about to spring upon Miguel. But my father chanced to enter at that moment, and the traveller, uttering a violent threat, hastily left the house. Though he had spoken of resting all night, he did not return.

"On being informed of what had passed, my father, who had been in a weak state of health for some time, said to Miguel · "I grow weaker and weaker every day, my dear son. It is time that you were here to protect Inez—and myself also, Heaven help me! Had you not been here accidentally just now, we might have been exposed to any insult from such a rude visitor as this." Miguel was so much struck by the truth of the remark: "You are right; I ought to be here to guard over those whose lives are so dear to me; and I will be here without delay, if I can get a trust-worthy substitute to perform the rest of this journey for me when I reach the town of Ai.' We talked long on these subjects before going to rest. Little rest indeed fell to my lot that night, for the dark looks and dagger of the man whom Miguel had made his enemy for my sake, came over between me and slumber.

"In the morning, Miguel departed with his wagon, under the promise to return soon, if it was in his power. I had never before felt so much anxiety at his departure, though, when I told him so, he smiled at my fears on his account, and showed me his double-barrelled gun, calling it his sure protector. Nothing occured for two days afterwards, though, during that interval, many fears came over me relative to the possible return of the traveller, the man who had so hurriedly disappeared. Our household at this time, it is to be understood, consisted of my father, a lad who assisted him out of doors, and myself. This lad went always first to rest, my father next, and I last. After they had both retired, on the second night from Miguel's departure, I closed the door, and

went into my own little room to seek repose. But I had not yet undressed myself, when I heard a noise, seemingly outside of the house. I listened and heard it repeated, nearer at hand as it appeared to me. Though much disturbed, I resolved to satisfy myself that there was a true cause for alarm before I called my father. With this view, I took up my light, and went into the kitchen, when I saw a sight that rooted me for an instant to the spot. The under part of the window had been raised, and a man, having got in with his feet foremost, was in the act of extricating his head and shoulders from the window. I, unguardedly, screamed, and fled in the direction of my father's sleeping-place; but before I had gone a few steps, I found myself in the grasp of the man who had entered, and who dragged me back into the kitchen. A faintness came over me, when, by means of the light which I had dropped on receiving the first alarm, I discovered that my captor was the traveller of the former day. He gave me a look of such triumphant malice, mingled with more hateful feelings, as made me shudder. Meanwhile, one man after another entered rapidly by the window, to the number of six, as it seemed to my confused senses. "Oh! my poor father! what is to be our fate?" was my first thought on seeing this; and so oppressive was the prospect to my spirit, that I received a temporary relief from all care by sinking into insensibility.

"How long I lay in this condition, I cannot tell. It must, however, have been a considerable time, for, on recovering my consciousness, I found my father hanging over me, in the state in which he had been dragged by the ruffians from his bed. The poor youth who lived with us was there in the same condition. Besides, the wretches had had time to discover and seize the little money and valuables which had been gathered by my father, the fruits of his long toils. Matters were in this state when my father raised me. I clung to his breast almost unconsciously, to preserve myself from the grasp of another who stood by me—the traveller—or rather the chief of the robbers, for such he seemed to be. "Divide, divide, men!" said he; "for me, I will take nothing; this is my prize!" laying his hand at the same time upon my shoulder. "O! Miguel, Miguel!" was the thought that passed through my shrinking soul at that instant, "little knowest thou what Inez in now suffering!"

"Look at that open space, sir," said my hostess at this part of her story, pointing at the same time to the end wall of the kitchen where we were sitting. A portion of the space above the level of the side walls was open, being evidently an entrance into a hayloft that lay over the stable of the *auberge*, and which stable was continuous with the dwelling, the whole being of one story. "As I thought upon Miguel at that awful moment," continued Inez, "my eyes—as my head lay upon my father's shoulder—were raised to that space, and there I beheld the head of Miguel! It struck me at first that my excited fancy had conjured up an illusion, and I closed my eyes for a moment. It was well that I did so, for the thought that the image was a deception, gave me time also to consider that a word or a scream would betray him, if what I saw was real. All this passed in an instant. Again I opened my eyes, and I saw not only that Miguel was really there, but that he was about to attempt something for our delivery, for his gun was stretched out before him. He motioned to me with his hand, and I understood his motion and his purpose—his terrible yet necessary purpose!—I bowed my head low, and, in another second of time, a sound as of thunder filled the apartment, followed by groans and curses. Another reverberation almost instantly followed, and amid the smoke which filled the room, I saw nothing, though I heard my brave Miguel leap down into the chamber, shouting (to deceive the robbers, doubtless, respecting the number of their assailants), "Here! this way, my friends! Down with the plunderers!" I beheld some of the latter escaping from the room by the way they had entered, and all was erelong quiet!

"What a scene, however," continued my hostess, whose emotion was greatly exicted by what she described; "what a scene, sir, this place where we now sit presented after that awful struggle! Two men, killed by one ball, lay prostrate on the floor, and another beside them mortally wounded, so well had the weapon been aimed. Miguel's first thought, after pursuing for a short way the men who had fled in fear and confusion, was to close the house more carefully for the night, the remainder of which we spent in thanking Heaven for our deliverance. Miguel informed us that, having procured a faithful substitute at the town of Ai, he had rapidly retraced his steps on foot, being oppressed with fears for us, arising out of the late adventure with the traveller. When he reached our house, he had discovered the state of things through the window, which had been but partially closed by the robbers after their entrance. He then went to the stable, burst open the door, and was in time to save us, as has been been described.

"In the morning, the lad was sent to Ai, to bring the officers of justice. When they came, the poor wounded wretch (to whom we paid every attention) was still living to disclose the fact hat the six men, of whom he had been one, composed the band who had for a time annoyed and plundered the country, and that the *traveller*, one of those who had fallen by Miguel's rifle, had been their captain. When I stooped my head, the bullet had passed over me to his heart! The bodies were removed from our house, and an anxious search made in the neighbourhood for the other three. They were all ultimately taken, and punished.

"The fastening of the window," continued the hostess, "by which the robbers had entered, must have been secretly loosened by their captain on the day when he was our guest, with a view to future plunder. For his courageous conduct in destroying this band, Miguel received the thanks of the whole country. But, alas! sir, my poor father never recovered from the shock which he got on this occasion. He lived, however, to see Miguel and myself united, and then he died happy. Although none of the band concerned in that attack are any longer to be feared, yet can you wonder, sir, after this relation, that I should sometimes tremble when the recollection of these things comes across me, and when Miguel is abroad at night on these lonely hills?"

I paid the comely Inez many compliments on the bravery of her husband, which the affectionate wife blushed with pleasure to hear. Such was the story, which I heard in my wanderings among the lofty Pyrenees.

CHAPTER CXXI.

THE SEARCH FOR TRACES OF MORGAN HALFORD, AND THE RESULT.

MR. O'CALLAGAN's two hours proved to be long ones—"They had been beaten out," so he averred. An Irishman is seldom at a loss for an excuse. Some of the Irish miles are long and narrow ones, and it would appear that some of their hours were much the same—at least, so Mr. Baintree and Colonel Jack thought.

However, in the due course of time, Mr. O'Callagan did eventually make his appearance. He was very much out of breath, and in a great state of flustration, when he presented himself to Mr. Baintree in the parlour of the Black Boy.

"Bad luck to me, but I've been a long time," said Mr. O'Callagan, addressing himself to our hero and Mr. Baintree.

"It's no fault of yours I dare say," answered the latter. "Besides, my friend, it is our duty to wait for you. Come, what will you take?"

"Anything yer honour is drinking."

"Whiskey toddy is the order of the day,"

answered Mr. Baintree. " We have chosen this according to your advice."

Mr. O'Callagan sat himself down, and having disposed of a tolerable amount of whiskey, he rose, and desired the ostler to put to his horse; and in the course of half an hour or so he was driving Mr. Baintree and the colonel along the road which he averred led to the village near to which he resided.

The roads were in anything but a good condition—the vehicle itself was without springs—and as to the horse, he had a pace and movement peculiarly his own; it might be termed eccentric, so that Mr. O'Callagan's two companions found it anything but easy travelling. However, they were well content to arrive at their destination by almost any means.

Steam was not invented at the time of which we write, neither were cabs then in existence.

When they had got a little way on their journey, and Mr. O'Callagan had exhausted himself in expatiating upon the beauty of his horse, Mr. Baintree began to broach the subject which was to him and his companion of much more importance.

"So you knew Mr. Morgan Halford, eh?" said the lawyer. "And pray can you inform me if he had any family?"

"Not that I ever heard of," answered O'Callagan.

"Was he married?"

"Oh, dear yes; his wife's alive now—at least, his widder, more properly speaking. No, but it's wrong that I am there, for she can't be widder, seeing that she married again."

"Then where does she reside now?" was Mr. Braintree's next inquiry.

"Close to where her first husband lived, although not in the same house."

"It's fortunate we met with you," exclaimed Mr. Baintree.

"An' sure now, all the information I can give you you are welcome to," answered the good-natured Irishman.

And after chatting along the road, they arrived in the due course of time at the residence of Mr. O'Callagan. It was situated some quarter of a mile from a very primitive village. It would hardly be dignified by that appellation in England, for it consisted only of some dozen or two straggling houses.

Mr. O'Callagan pointed out to his two companions the house occupied by the late Morgan Halford. It was a small, low habitation, and seemed to be more like one that would be suited for the residence of an English labouring man.

Colonel Jack expressed a wish to alight when the vehicle arrived opposite the house in question, but as it was getting late, Mr. Baintree deemed it advisable to put up somewhere for the night, and pursue their inquiries on the following day.

Mr. O'Callagan upon hearing this, insisted upon their partaking of his hospitality; and after several refusals, the two friends were at length persuaded to accept of his offer.

They found themselves in tolerably comfortable quarters, and after the day's fatigue, slept the sleep of the just.

In the morning they sat down to an excellent breakfast, for their host had given orders to his better half to place before his guests the best the house afforded.

After the meal was over, Mr. O'Callagan inquired how they intended to proceed?

"I mane, gentlemen, with regard to your inquiries," said Mr. O'Callagan.

"First and foremost, I must tell you what we are in need of," said Mr. Baintree. "We want proofs of the death of Morgan Halford."

"An sure it's the praste as can give you that same," answered O'Callagan."

"Do you know him?"

"Sure I do, as weil as I know my ownself and a deal better for the matter of that. It was Father Ryan as took charge of poor Morgan's soul, the saints protect him."

"Does he live far hence?" inquired the counsellor.

"Devil a bit, an' it'll be afther seeing his house ye'd be, if ye'll jist look out of the side window."

"Very well, Mr. O'Callagan," "we'll, just step over and see Mr. Ryan."

"An' it'll be myself as will show you his house," said the farmer, as he prepared to accompany his two guests.

They arrived at Mr. Ryan's residence, the owner of which was a little man, with thin livid features.

Upon their explaining the nature of their visit, he at once entered into the particulars of the death of Morgan Halford. He was with him during his last hours, and he knew where he was buried of course, the parish register would prove his burial.

Upon this Colonel Jack and Mr. Baintree paid a visit, in company with the priest, to the churchyard, which served as the last resting-place for the former's uncle. Mr. Ryan pointed out a tombstone on which the name of Morgan Halford was chiselled, together with his age and the date of his death. While they were contemplating this memorial of him who had passed away from all earthly suffering, the parish clerk made his appearance on the scene. The church itself was very ancient, one of those primitive edifices which had stood the test of corroding and all-destroying time. Without doubt it was some hundreds of years old.

Mr. Baintree, who was something of an

antiquarian knew enough to be assured of this fact.

"Whose grave may you be looking for, gentlemen?" said the parish clerk, as he came up to the side of the two strangers.

"Colonel Jack pointed to the tombstone in front of where he and his companion was standing."

"Oh, that same is where Mr. Morgan Halford was buried. Did you know him?"

"Yes; we want an extract from your books, as an attestation of his death," said Mr. Baintree.

"That you shall have, sir," answered the clerk.

"This is a very old church I should say," remarked the lawyer.

"Yes, some hundreds of years old. Indeed I believe no one really knows how far it dates back, but we have monuments of persons who have died and were buried here before the reign of Richard the First of England. Now yonder," continued the speaker, pointing to a spot about twenty paces from the church porch. "Yonder is an old monument which has attracted the notice of numbers of visitors, antiquarians who take a delight in inspecting monumental brasses. Its records may at any time be deciphered, but the most favourable time for the purpose (supposing you are an enthusiastic student of romance) is at night when the full autumn moon from an altitude of ninety degrees pours in its slanting rays at the eastern window. Then the scenery and circumstances of the locality so contrive it that a flood of light falls upon the pavement stone in question, while around you all is buried in comparative darkness."

"Oh, then the tomb you are speaking of is inside the church," said Mr. Baintree, who was led to suppose from the clerk's manner that it was in the churchyard.

"Oh, yes, inside. You want the register of Morgan Halford's death and burial. If you will follow me, I will copy it out, and at the same time you will be able to inspect the monumental brass of which I have already spoken."

Mr. Baintree, Colonel Jack, and Father Ryan made their way into the old village church. The clerk first proceeded to turn over the leaves of the parish book, and in the course of a few minutes he had the satisfaction of finding the name in question. He then showed the book for satisfaction sake to Colonel Jack and Mr. Baintree, and made a copy of the entry.

After this he took them to the tomb he had named. It consisted of two figures reposing in a devoted attitude, so characteristic of the old faith and sentiments of our sires. —one was a stalwart knight, and the other his peerless wife. An inscription surrounding the whole, records a dark and bloody legend, and ends with an humble supplication that the reader may pray for the souls of Sir Rufus de Gildenhame, and Alice his lady. Mr. Baintree was curious to know the history of these people and the clerk at his request repeated the following legend—

CHAPTER CXXI.

THE CLERK'S STORY—THE UNNATURAL COMBAT.

"No braver knight," said the clerk, "ever donned spur and buckler or lent lustre to the bright names of the Anglo-Norman chivalry, than Sir Rufus de Gildenhame. When in the year of our redemption one thousand one hundred and ninety—the negotiations then pending that ended in freeing the Lion-hearted King from his loathsome and galling captivity, and restoring him to his beloved subjects—an honourable and worthy escort for so brave a monarch was needed to reconduct him to his home. Ardent, impetuous, generous to a fault, Sir Rupert was the first to fly to horse. Heading the glittering train of knights, he bade a tender, but hasty, adieu to his newly-wedded lady, and, confiding her to the keeping of his half brother, Hugh, together with his castles and demesnes, he sought the inhospitable shores of the Teuton a week later he hailed the hated towers of Tycrnsteign.

It is matter of history how the perfidious tyrant Leopold, bound by no oath, however sacred, violated again and again his solemn engagements—how the Lion-heart was bent, crushed, by the unparalleled venality of his gaolers—how, sold and resold, the king held even the very hope of liberty as a chimera—and how, at length, freedom came a thousand-fold sweeter from its deprivation. It is pending these negotiations that the events occurred which we are about to relate. Let us return home to England.

Hugh de Gildenhame was, as we have said, Sir Rufus's half-brother. In him were united the worst ingredients of a semi-savage nature, with a few of those brighter parts that adorn our kind. Thus he was brave and bold as the Nubian lion; but cruelty and a boundless rapacity rendered him a terror to all such as, possessing the advantages of nature or fortune, lacked the power to retain them against aggression. Wild, wayward, and untutored—for he had scorned as a boy the gentle whisperings of instruction; as a man he despised the subtleties of *meum* and *tuum* —his will in his own sphere was law, and his appetite his rule of conduct. Sir Rufus was the only being he feared; he had served with him and under his eye, had learned to acknowledge the superior force of intellect combined with virtue and moderation. It remained to be seen what course he would follow now that the talisman of his brother's presence was withdrawn.

The Lady Alice, apart from the grief that a bereaved bride must need nourish in her bosom at the absence of its liege lord, had to encounter all the deep distrust of her heart for the conduct of her allotted keeper. She had seen more than once the utter abandonment of shame, or a sense of justice where in the case of those less powerful than himself, his brutal will had been attempted to be resisted. She had witnessed with what unblushing effrontery the poor man's lamb had been slain and eaten; the sanctuary of his hearth invaded; and even the ecclesiastical censure scorned. The worst apprehension filled her mind, the more as weeks rolled over without tidings of Sir Rufus, and the insolence of Hugh grew more and more unbearable.

The continued absence of his brother first sowed in the Castellan's mind the seeds of ambition; the appetite for unlimited power, of which he had now enjoyed a kind of foretaste, took possession of his mind. He yearned for possession, and his own mind speculated on the chances of its acquisition.

But this was not all. He had cast his unholy eyes upon the fair person of its pure-hearted mistress. Her charms for the nonce presented to the brute mind of her jailer an even still more tempting object, and, unschooled as yet in repulse, he made his first vile advances. Deep was the scorn, and bitter the reproaches, the beauteous Lady Alice showered upon her persecutor. In vain, day after day brought their repetition. Vainly she sought the protection of her reverend confessor. The sanctity of the castle chapel afforded no protection, and its holy walls re-echoed with the ruffian's threats. Upon one occasion the aged priest ventured to remonstrate, and received a stunning blow which deprived him of sensation. Awestruck, she fled from the desecrated spot, and sought the privacy of her turret, where, throwing herself at the foot of the little crucifix, which adorned her oratory, she besought the assistance of heaven.

Having recovered from the shock her feelings had sustained, the Lady Alice bethought herself that possibly artifice would yet avail to ward off the hated advances of her treacherous keeper, till such time as her beloved lord should return and with this intention, summoning her page, she despatched him to Hugh, with a message to the effect that the Lady Alice marvelled greatly at the somewhat rude wooing of Hugh de Gildenhame, whose virtue were, sooth to say, obscured by the over roughness of his spirit. She did not deny that his bold bearing and knightly prowess were greatly to be loved; but she begged that he would not urge his suit until his image had grown more pleasing to her fancy, which, she doubted not, it would soon do. Above all she desired to be left in quiet for a brief term.

The wily Hugh smiled grimly at the message, but was not entirely unmoved at it. The prize was worth the pursuit; and as he knew no artifice could elude his vigilance, the brief deprivation of his wishes only heightened their anticipated triumph. He bade her by the page prepare to receive him at the end of two days. Meantime, the agonised gaze of the distressed lady was bent towards those points of the horizon whence Sir Rufus, or a messenger from him, might be expected to appear.

Not with more pain or dread flows the lifeblood from the gored and dying hunter, far removed from leech or friends, than flew the hours by the affrighted watcher. Still, no signs of help came. A day hath passed; the second dawns—it passes; 'tis evening—night; still, no hope!

Hugh de Gildenhame had well prepared himself for any event that might fall out. The castle was rendered proof against surprise; and having dismissed, or got rid of in other ways, all such of the retainers of Sir Rufus as he could not trust, he "laughed a siege to scorn." The aged priest had indeed sought and obtained permission to retire to a hermitage at some distance from the castle, but with that exception none had been permitted either to enter or to quit the fortress.

And now the rude, savage heart of Hugh exulted in its pride as the third day from that of the interview with Lady Alice in the chapel dawned. His passions, from suffering a repulse, however slight, had, like the stream, which, obstructed by a huge rock, becomes a torrent, only acquired an additional impetus; and, as he paced his gloomy hall alone, his brow flushed, his teeth ground together, his hair bristled, and his hands clenched—he looked the very incarnation of pride, rapine, and every malevolent passion. Occasionally he would pause at the hall-door, and listen with an air of attention, as though expecting a message or summons. Then, turning again, he would resume his walk.

The figure of Hugh de Gildenhame presented, on the occasion in question, no unimposing appearance. Although, in the legitimate order of rank he had but attained to that of squire, or armourer, in his vanity he had donned the habiliments of a knight. What cared he whether or not a royal hand had bestowed the title. He was a knight in his own right, and in contempt of kings. He braced on his brawny thighs the glittering sword. A visor and helmet encased the head, and there he stood to maintain his knighthood.

A page entered—

"How now, knave?" exclaimed the Castellan, in accents of rage and impatience.

"May it please you," answered the youth, kneeling, in terror, at his feet, "my lady craves a boon!"

"A boon! speak quickly, what would she?"

"My lady craves, for her health's sake, yet two more days repose."

"Repose! beshrew my soul, hath she run too lustily at the quintain? or hath the morris-tripping tired her?—repose!"

"My lady is sick!" added the trembling page.

"I will go and visit!" answered the furious Hugh—and, bidding the page lead the way, he strode in the direction of the turret.

On the way a retainer met him with the intelligence that Father Anselm had craved admission.

"'Tis well!" he replied, "admit him; and bid him await my orders in the chapel."

The retainer disappeared, and Hugh de Gildenhame proceeded to the turret.

Lady Alice met him at its threshold, grief, horror, and despair had tortured her fair features, and the lapse of two days had worked the common effects of many years. She stood for a moment a statue of sorrow, then falling at his feet, she besought him to cease so unhallowed a pursuit. But the distraction of her manner only aroused in the bosom of the Castellan the worst emotions. He had never beheld anything so lovely. Her golden hair released from its bands fell in lengthened tresses over her snowy bosom, which heaved and throbbed with violent emotions, and half disclosed its delicate beauties to his gloating eyes.

Heedless of her words, he endeavoured to raise her from the ground, but she shrank from his touch as from the taint of a leper, and sprang through the open door of the apartment in the turret.

She was quickly followed by Hugh, who, at one stride reached an opposite door in the tapestry at the moment when Lady Alice was in the act of darting through it. With a scream of terror and adjuring the name of God, she sank, in a swoon, to the earth. The treacherous Hugh now saw himself possessed of all he desired. Helpless at his feet lay the victim of his treachery, and with a fiendish laugh of exultation, he contemplated the beauteous ruin. At that moment a noise, as if an attack upon the castle, met his ears, and, he fled to place himself at the head of his retainers.

It was Sir Rufus, who had been apprised of the perfidy of his half-brother; and had returned with a powerful body of knights to the rescue of the place.

The capture was soon accomplished. A secret entrance into the castle was opened by Father Anslem; the opposition of its defenders melted away at the presence of its legitimate lord; and but a short time had elapsed when the brothers found themselves face to face in deadly conflict.

By superior skill and prudence in the use of the sword Sir Rufus succeeded in disarming his antagonist, and, delivering him to the custody of his brother-knights, to be confined in the dungeon of the keep, he sought the bower of his beloved Alice.

"Alice! dear Alice!" cried Sir Rufus, as he threaded the intricacies of the castle. But although with each step he redoubled his cries, no answer met his ears. He reached the gallery leading to the turret—all was still. At length he gained the apartment of the Lady Alice—but it was unoccupied. Alarmed—nigh distracted—he flew through each chamber usually occupied by her; but he had regained the bower without finding any traces of his beloved. A window in the bower opened upon the western part of the moat. He sprang upon its sill, and the sight that met his gaze nearly turned him to stone. Beneath, at the distance of a hundred feet, lay the mangled corpse of Lady Alice. The truth flashed upon him. Recovering from her swoon, she heard the martial sound without the castle; and, seeking to descry her liege lord, she had climbed to, and fallen from, the window, into the moat, and died.

*   *   *   *   *

It is night; the castle is still; the solitary figure of a knight is seen to descend the staircases leading to the lower dungeons of the keep; he reaches the door of one—applies a ponderous key to the lock, and enters.

There are now two figures in the dungeon. The first named has locked the door, and throwing away the key, approaches the other figure, raises his steel-gloved hand, and smites him in the face, who starts up, receives a sword from the other, and they place themselves in the attitudes of combat. They fight—fiercely—desperately; there is no sign of pity or remorse in either. They have drawn the sword, and thrown away the scabbard. Ten minutes have elapsed, and the deadly fight is continued—ten minutes more, and they have not ceased—in another ten minutes, the corses of the two brothers filled that cell! The race of De Gildenhame became extinct by the issue of the unnatural combat.

"Such is the legend, gentlemen," said the clerk, "which has been handed down from generation to generation, and has awakened

the curious inquirer to listen to this chronicle of a past age."

"And one deserving of remembrance," said Father Ryan, in a prophetic tone of voice, at the same time crossing himself.

"Well, I believe we have all we require for the present," said Mr. Baintree, pulling out his purse, and giving the clerk a handsome gratuity therefrom.

After lingering some little time longer, and noticing several other features of the ancient ecclesiastical edifice, Colonel Jack, the priest, and lawyer took their departure.

"The widow of Morgan Halford lives hard by,' said Mr. Baintree to the priest.

"She does, sir. Not a quarter of a mile from this spot."

"Ah, so Mr. O'Callagan informed me. It would be as well for us to see her."

No. 83.

"She is no longer a widow," answered Ryan. "She has taken to herself another husband."

"No matter, she may afford us some information."

"Might I make so bould as to inquire the object of this visit," asked Ryan. "Morgan Halford has gone to his account, he died a repentant sinner."

"Did he leave any children ?"

"Not that I iver heard of, sir. No, not that I iver heard of, but that's neither here nor there, he might have done—"

"But none that you knew anything of."

"Certainly not. Shall I take you to her house?'

"If you please. I shall be obliged by your doing so."

"Her present husband isn't to say a particularly obliging man, that is, he's short and testy."

" Oh, that matters not."

" He's rather unperlite," continued the priest in a low tone of voice, and glancing round in all quarters to see that there were no listeners. "And more than that he's rather fond of—"

" Of what ?"

" His drafths."

" Oh, that's rather a common feeling with his countrymen."

" Ye may say that, sir. It is—by the powers but it is, and bad luck to me, all that I can do won't stop them at that same sort of business ; but O'Flake is a very head-strong man—oh very."

" Who is O'Flake ?"

" Och murder, now didn't I tell ye that he was the husband of Mrs. O'Flake," said the priest indignantly.

" Indeed, but you did not, my friend," retorted Mr. Baintree, " and even assuring that you had, I should have been as wise as ever, seeing that I don't know who Mrs. O'Flake is."

" Oh, but you bother me entirely," said Ryan, " and isn't this Mrs. O'Flake ye would be afther saying ?"

" Not that I know of. It's the wife of the late Morgan Halford that I am inquiring for."

" To be sure it is."

" Well then."

" Well then, and isn't she now Mrs. O'Flake ?"

" Oh, I understand," said Mr. Baintree, looking at Colonel Jack, and indulging in a quiet smile at the priest's expense.

In a short time they came in sight of a sort of Irish cabin which Mr. Ryan declared to be the present residence of Mr. and Mrs. O'Flake, whereupon the three hastened towards it.

CHAPTER CXXIII.

THE INTERVIEW WITH THE O'FLAKE'S

WHEN the priest had come within a res-pectable distance of the O'Flake mansion, he came to a rather sudden, and, to Colonel Jack, an unexpected halt.

" It's afther leaving that I'd be now," said Ryan.

" Leaving my friend, and wherefore ?" inquired the colonel.

" Oh, but O'Flake ain't a man I be afther saying at all, at all."

" Oh, I understand, you are not friends."

" We are all friends and brothers," said Ryan, laying his hand upon his breast, " friends and brothers."

" Possibly so ; but why your objection then, to go with us ?"

" And sure, now ain't I here ?" said the priest.

" Yes, but I mean inside his habitation."

" Oh, I understand. Well, now as I was afther saying, this O'Flake ain't a man who is likely to resave me well. Indeed, but he's an ungodly man and that's the truth of it."

" Ah, and don't like gentlemen of your cloth. Is that it ?" inquired Mr. Baintree.

" Well, it's something afther that same fashion."

" Oh, then in that case we will not trouble you. After our interview we will do our-selves the pleasure of calling again at your residence to let you know how we have suc-ceeded."

" It's obliged to you I am for that same promise," said Mr. Ryan, as he took an abrupt departure.

" By my faith," said Mr. Baintree, with a smile, " this O'Flake seems to have im-pressed our friend with a strange and un-accountable fear. At any rate we do not share the same feeling, I suppose."

" Indeed, I should think not," answered Colonel Jack.

The two friends presently came in front of Mr. O'Flake's respectable habitation. It was evidently dirty enough, and untidy on the outside, and they found it still more so upon entering the inside thereof. The door was open so there was not much trouble in obtaining admission. The counsellor knocked at the door with his stick, and a shrill voice called out—

" An' sure can't ye find yer way in, who-ever ye are ?"

Without further ceremony, the two friends entered.

When they did so, they observed a raw-boned, large-framed woman with a low beet-ling brow, engaged in some domestic occupa-tion. She stared with surprise as she ob-served two strangers.

" Have I the pleasure of addressing Mrs. O'Flake ?" inquired the lawyer.

" An' sure enough my name's O'Flake," retorted the woman.

" You will excuse the liberty we have taken as strangers," said the attorney. " But you see, madam, I believe I am justified in as-serting that my friend is a relative of yours, that is, if we have been rightly informed."

" Of what ?" inquired the woman.

" A relative by marriage." answered Mr. Baintree.

" I do not know this gentleman," she re-plied, staring at our hero.

" You were the wife of Mr. Morgan Hal-ford, I believe,"

" An' sure I was that same."

" Ah, then we are not mistaken. This

gentleman's name is. Halford also, and he was a nephew of Mr. Morgan Halford."

" ' Och, by the powers and was he though ? ' exclaimed Mrs. O'Flake, who appeared to be so surprised at this unexpected announcement that she did not know very well how to comfort herself. "And it 'ell be sitting down, gentlemen," said Mrs. O'Flake. "Dear me, and only look at that now, the nephew of my first husband, what's dead and gone, and the likes of who I shan't and can't say again. Well, then you are right welcome, and good luck to ye, and may the blessed Virgin kape watch ov'r ye here and hereafter."

She crossed herself reverently as she gave utterance to this last observation. "An' it's glad I am to say ye anyhow. An' sure now it's the nephew of Morgan Halford that ye are."

"It is that same without a shadow of doubt," answered Colonel Jack.

"An' sure now you've not been long in Ireland," said Mrs. O'Flake.

"No, not long."

"An' what might have brought you over, then."

"My friend came on professional business, and I accompanied him," answered Colonel Jack.

"Oh, I see now."

"Mr. Morgan Halford has passed away," said Mr. Baintree, "and you are now Mrs. O'Flake."

"An' sure I am," answered the woman. "And it's sad an' sorry I am that I lost as good a husband as iver sinful woman had, an' I may say that sure enough."

"I think I heard you had no family, no children," said the lawyer, carelessly."

"Yes, we had one son."

"Oh, indeed. And is he alive, pray ?"

"Alas, sir, he fell into misfortune—very misfortunate he was."

"How so?"

"Well, you must know that, foolish young man, he was misled, and—oh, but it's a long story, and I would wish to forget that same, for it does my heart no good to remember it. He was misled, he joined the rebels, was taken, tried and condemned to death," said Mrs. O'Flake, in a low tone of voice.

"And did he suffer?" inquired Colonel Jack.

"The Lord be praised ! no. He managed to make his escape from the sojers who kept guard over him, and shipped himself in a vessel, and went abroad."

"And what became of him after this?" inquired the colonel.

"Oh, sure now, afther that he died of a faver."

"What evidence have you of this?"

"Och, and by the powers haven't I the very best of ividence? Didn't two of his fellow prisoners who escaped along with him come back and tell me how poor Dennis died on board ship, and how they tied the poor lad up in a cloth and cast him into the say? And that's evidence enough; and it's sick and sorry I am when I think of that same ividence, and bad luck to the government, which drove my poor boy from his native home, and whom I may niver say more."

And the disconsolate mother began to shed tears when she came to this part of her description.

Mr. Baintree turned to Colonel Jack, and regarded him for a moment with a look of inquiry.

"What was the name of the vessel in which your son died?" inquired the lawyer.

"Oh, I'm bothered if I can ever remember it's name," said the woman; "it's such a hard one to pronounce."

"Can't you give me any idea ?"

"I'faith, no. It was a Syrus—nighus, or some such a name as that same now. I'm bothered intirely when I try to think of it. But what matters? Dennis is gone, poor fellow ! Why do you ask?—sure ye didn't know Dennis, did ye ?"

"Oh, dear, no," said the colonel; we did not even know that such a person was ever in existence till we heard it from you."

"An' sure now, you same to be very particular in your inquiries afther him, I'm thinking," said the woman, who, however, was suddenly cut short in her observations by the apdearance of a stalwart man of no very prepossessing appearance.

He glanced at Mrs. O'Flake's two visitors, with no very pleasant looks, and then fixed his glance on his wife.

"It's a nephew of mine, this same gentleman," said the woman by way of explanation, and at the same time glancing at our hero.

"Och, by the powers, ye're good at an excuse, that ye are, ye double-dealing hussy. It's lies ye are afther telling me, and ye know it. Nephew, indade ! It's a fine nephew ye've brought home. And ye're a fine gentleman to come to a man's house when he is away, to say his wife."

"Come, my friend," said Mr. Baintree, "there is no occasion for you to put yourself out of the way. This gentleman is really and truly the nephew of the late Mr. Morgan Halford."

"Psha!" exclaimed Mr. O'Flake, giving his shoulder a graceful twirl. "I'm sick of the very name of that same Halford: bad luck to the man who mentions it in my pre- and so you may take your change out of that both of ye. An' look here now," he continued, still more violently, and walking up to Colonel Jack; "look here now, if you are the nephew of that spalpeen, you are not welcome here at all, at all, and don't you darken my doors again."

"You are a very unpolite man, Mr. O'Flake, that is all I have to say," said our hero, without moving a muscle of his countenance.

"Och, murder! would ye insult a man in his own house," said Mr. O'Flake, putting himself in a warlike attitude. "It'll be a broken head that ye'll be afther getting, if ye don't show a clean pair of heals."

"For shame of you, Mr. O'Flake," said Mr. Baintree, "you ought to know better than to conduct yourself in this way. I thought your countrymen were remarkable for hospitality."

"It's hospitality ye're talking about, is it?" exclaimed O'Flake, "and do you think now that we are going to show hospitality to two snakes like you."

"Come, come," said Colonel Jack. "If you begin to be insolent we will find a way to stop your tongue. If you don't know how to conduct yourself it is time you were taught"

"Oh, mercy on me it's jealous he is," exclaimed Mrs. O'Flake, tossing up her hands. "Don't take any notice of him, gentleman—for my sake don't take notice of him."

"Hold yer tongue ye lying hypocritical canting hussy," said Mr. O'Flake, turning like a savage upon his wife. "Gentlemen, indade; as much gentlemen as my fat sow. Not so much. Be off wid ye at once, do ye hear."

"Oh. it's a drafth of drink he has in him," said the woman.

"Yer lie," said her husband, then turning to Colonel Jack he again said in a still louder voice—

"Be off wid ye at once. Do ye hear?"

"You are a very ill-conducted fellow," said our hero, not moving an inch.

"I'm better than the likes of ye, with all ye're fine clothes. Mine are come by honestly which is more than you can say."

"Now look here, my friend," said Colonel Jack with aggravating coolness. "Just you look here, if you give me any of your insolence, I'll make an example of you on the spot."

"Hush, hush," exclaimed Mr. Baintree, "let him alone."

"A pair of cowardly snaking rascals," said O'Flake, flourishing his shilalegh. "It 'ell be myself that will give ye a good sound thrashing," and without further ado he aimed a blow at Colonel Jack, which luckily caught him on the shoulder, instead of the head, as was intended by the ill-mannered O'Flake.

Colonel Jack laid hold of the weapon with his left hand, while with his right he knocked his assailant down. Mr. O'Flake got up and flew at the colonel in a furious state; but the latter closed with him and after a short struggle, our hero threw Mr. O'Flake very ignominiously to the farther end of his room.

"Och murder, but I'll be aven wid ye!" exclaimed Mr. O'Flake, once more coming to the attack this time without his shilalegh, for Colonel Jack had succeeded in wresting it from him, and had flung it outside the cabin. When Mr. O'Flake came again, Colonel Jack collered him and held him firmly in his clutches.

"This time Mr. O'Flake," said the colonel, "you do not go, for you are my prisoner."

"Presinir!" exclaimed the irritated Irishman, "presinir! och murther, but we'll soon say that. And it's prisinir that ye'd be afther talking about, and bad luck to me," and he made desperate efforts to disengage himself from his adversary's grasp; these were however in vain, Colonel Jack held him with the firmness of a vice.

"You had better fetch a constable," he said, to Mr. Baintree. "This man has committed an unwarrantable assault upon me in the first place, and he is evidently disposed to continue on with his uncalled for and infamous conduct."

At this Mr. O'Flake became somewhat more subdued in his manner and bearing. His better half begged of the colonel not to give her husband in charge, alleging at the same time that he was under the influence of drink, and more than this, his temper was such, that he forgot all discretion or rules of guidance for his good behaviour.

"He has committed a most unwarrantable assault upon my friend," said Mr. Baintree. "But I think I may take upon myself to say that no further notice will be taken of his conduct if he promises to be peaceable."

The woman besought her husband to promise to conduct himself better, and as he found himself firmly clasped in Colonel Jack's iron grip, he was fain to make a virtue of necessity, and apologised for his misconduct in his own rough uncouth way.

The colonel then released him, and he and Mr. Baintree took a hasty departure from the inhospitable roof of Mr. O'Flake. As they did so, Mrs. O'Flake followed them to the door, and extracted a promise from our hero that he would pay her another visit before he returned to England.

"By my faith," said Mr. Baintree, when they had got some little distance from the house where the affray had taken place, "but I am not surprised at Father Ryan having so great an objection to go to our friend's domicile. What is to be done now?"

"About what?" inquired our hero.

"Respecting this young man—their son."

"Ah, he is dead, it seems."

"We must have proof of that."

"How is it to be obtained?"

"I was going to ask her when we were so suddenly interrupted. I was going to inquire if the fellow-culprits who went out with him were in the neighbourhood."

"Perhaps Mr. Ryan will be able to tell us that," suggested Colonel Jack.

With this the two took their way to the priest's house, and then and there made him acquainted with what had taken place in Mr. O'Flake's residence.

The priest informed them that in all probability they would meet with one of these said parties at a small roadside public-house, some mile or so down the road, but it would be evening before they were likely to be there.

Under these circumstances, Colonel Jack and the lawyer filled up their time as they best could, and towards evening went in company with Mr. Ryan to the house in question.

It was a small, old-fashioned, low public-house, and when the three individuals entered the parlour, there was in it but one occupant, an old man of some three-score years or so.

The new comers sat themselves down, ordered some whisky toddy, and prepared to wait the coming of the party whom they wished to see.

Father Ryan inquired of the landlord if it was likely that young Jebb would be there? The landlord replied in the affirmative, and Mr. Ryan returned to the room and informed his companions of the landlord's statement.

"Then we will wait," remarked Mr. Baintree.

As it was a fine evening, the three drew their chairs up to the bay window in the room, and amused themselves by gazing out therefrom, at the few stray passengers which ever and anon took their way along the road, making at the same time comments on each, as is the custom, I am afraid, with most of us.

In the course of half an hour or so, a very pretty young Irish girl took her way along the road on the opposite side.

"See," said Colonel Jack to Mr. Baintree, "the Irish women are sometimes very beautiful."

And he pointed out to his friend the one in question.

"Ah," exclaimed Father Ryan, "she is very pretty; not unlike a girl I knew. She was known by the name of the Lady of Ligswell."

"Ah," exclaimed the colonel, "some fair damsel, I suppose, who inspired you with a tender passion in your earlier days, eh?"

"No," answered the priest. "If you wish to hear her history, I can tell it you."

"We have not much better to do till this Jebb comes," answered Mr. Baintree, "and so let us hear her history, if it be not too sad."

The three then sat themselves down, and Father Ryan began his narrative which we reserve for another chapter.

CHAPTER CXXIV.

THE IRISH PRIEST'S STORY

It is still common in many villages," said Father Ryan, "to give the prettiest girl the complementary name of some flower; if fair she is called the lily, if florid the rose, and "fair as the lily-flower," is a comparison found in many writings showing that these simple similes, which everybody understands, outlive in popularity the loftier images of poetry. The "Lily of Ligswell," as she was called, was christened plain Edith at the time-worn font of the ancient village church, the grey walls of which had many a Sabbath echoed back her silver voice—the sweetest voice in the rural choir. It was a pretty picture to see her sitting in the rustic cottage porch, embowered with green and fragrant climbing plants, in that morning-dawn of maidenhood when the girl was budding into the youthful woman, as Spring, unseen, merges into Summer. Prettier still was it, as the sound of the church-bells came and went over the hills and down the dales, to see her in her cheap, clean, white dress and pink sash, with hymn and prayer-book in her hand, on her way to church, as she curtsied to the kind greeetings of her village neighbours—old men and women, who, when their winter-aches and pains left them, sunned themselves, as they leant against the moos-covered garden-palings, and talked about those they had known, long since dead and gone, and who were once as fair as the Lily of Ligswell. "Ah! do you 'mind' her grandmother?" one would say, when that old inhabitant, a churchyard cough, which had possession of him years back, allowed him permission to speak; "they call her the Lily in her young days, but that was long ago, long ago! She died when plums came in, fifteen summers back. I mind it well: for Squire Langley, that was so good to the poor, deceased the same year: he was buried about peascod—rest his soul!'

Both Edith's father and mother did much towards spoiling her, for they were ever praising her beauty before here face and behind her back; and on a Sunday the fond mother would stand and watch her at the garden-gate on her way to church, to which her parents seldom went; and if any neighbours chanced to pass, the vain mother was sure to inquire "what they thought of her Lily?" Instead of "enjoying himself," as he called it, at home, her father was too fond of taking his pipe and pint at the "Barley-mow"—a well-to-do road side village inn, which brewed the best ale in Brampstone, and furnished "good entertainment for men and horses," as the sign announced which spanned above the entrance of the inn-yard. The Lilly had frequently succeeded in getting her tipsy father to leave the "Barley-mow" when her mother's mission had failed, for she had only to send a meassage saying that "she was waiting for him outside," when, no matter who were his pot-companions, he would lay down his pipe, empty his pint at a draught, and, though not with the steadiest steps, at once accompany her home. One night, however, a sudden shower of rain came heavily down while she waited, and as the landlady was standing at the door, she invited Edith into the bar-parlour, which was only occupied by her own daughter, there to wait until it ceased raining. From what apparent trifles —though they are not so—do the greatest evils springs! After this, Edith constantly went into the private bar, and seemed in no greater hurry to leave her female companions than her father did his smoke-a-pipe acquaintance. Nor did he obey her summons as he had done beforetime, but seemed to feel a pride in telling all who came in that "his Lily was waiting for him in the bar, and was quite 'thick' with the landlady." From the bar to the drinking-room was but another downward step, and although at first it was only taken with the intention of hastening the departure of her father, yet it ended by her sitting down beside him, though "only for a mintue" at the commencement; but those short intervals were too soon prolonged.

There was a small market-town some five miles beyond Ligswell, and many of those who came from the country places that lie behind the village halted to rest and refresh themselves at the "Barley-mow," as they returned from market. Thus, a large company often met in the spacious kitchen or tap-room—for the clean parlour, with its sanded floor, was only thrown open at the village-feast, statutes (when servants come to be hired), or on some rare occasion. Butchers, millers, drovers, farmers, labourers. hawkers, tinkers, beggars, gipsies, and travellers of every descriptions, besides the worst of characters, assembled on this neutral ground, where one man's shilling was considered just as good as another's, and all were, if they chose to enter into the "well-

met fellowship," during their stay, equal. With many of these Edith's father drank and shook hands, and some of the young fellows who had seen the Lily, jocularly proposed to become his son-in-law; to which, when in his cups, he always consented. Many thought that the young blacksmith, who had succeeded to his father's old-established business, stood highest in the Lily's favour; but his widowed mother, a firm, God-fearing woman, had called down the anger of Margaret's mother through commenting upon the impropriety of her daughter sitting down in a common public-house.

"Two blacks don't make a white," said the blacksmith's stern widow, turning her back and walking away, as the other began to enumerate the many farmers' wives and daughters who occasionally halted at the "Barley-mow." She told her son that, unless the Lily changed, she would soon be unworthy of her fair name; whereat he hammered harder at his iron, and sighed like his furnace,—for he knew that the sweet voice which he had so often accompanied in the villiage choir on the holy Sabbath, had at her father's request, backed by the solicitation of his boon companions, been tempted to sing amid the beer and smoke of the "Barley-mow." It was soon noticed by the neighbours, that instead of hurrying off at a moment's notice without her bonnet, and her long silken ringlets blowing loose in the wind, but she now took great pains in arranging her dress, more like one going out on a visit, than as before, on a disagreeable errand. Though she never drank with anyone, many concluded that the company she found there was quite as agreeable to her taste as it was to that of her father. Her singing often caused her to receive invitations to the sheep-shearing feasts and Harvest-homes of the neighbouring farmers, and at last drew down a reprimand from the village pastor, as well as myself," said Mr. Ryan. "Would that she had listened to my advice! Many, who in their hearts had blessed that sweet, fair face, as it looked out like a burst of sudden sunshine from under the warm pink lining of her pretty rustic bonnet, now passed by with averted head. Yet, with her parent's approval of what she did—with hints from others, that it was only envy of her fine voice that called down those cold looks,— added to her own natural vanity, which had never been curbed, but on the contrary, encouraged,—it was not to be wondered at that such youthful errors sat lightly on her inexperienced mind·

"Gipsy Jem," as he was always called, was a regular visitor at these rural merrymakings, and a great favourite among the customers of the "Barley-mow," especially with Edith's father. He was a wild-looking, handsome fellow, with olive complexion, and black hair that curled into scores of bright ringlets—the longest of which hung about his face like those of a woman ; he also wore round silver ear-rings, could sing a good song, dance, fiddle, fight, run, wrestle : he looked like a picturesque Italian bandit. He was never without money, which he carried in a purse made out of the skin of a mouldi-warp—one the largest moles ever caught, as he boasted." He was clever at curing and breaking-in young dogs, was a good judge of horses, and no doubt picked up a little money at times among the sporting farmers. Sometimes he would encamp with his tribe ; then remain away from them for weeks together ; though it was noticed by close observers, that during his stay at Ligswell, there was generally a gipsy or two prowling about the neighbourhood, with whom he was in communication. There was something about this man that struck the beholder at once, and you thought at first that it was the strange costume which attracted attention, but when the eye had wandered from the gaudy-coloured neckerchief which was tied loosely around the well-formed throat, to the flowered waistcoat and leather small-clothes, that fitted him as if they were glued on,—it became again fixed on those dark restless eyes, which turned aside the instant you looked at them, and before your glance was half-averted, were again full upon you. You felt that you could no more trust him than you could have done a beautiful tiger that had escaped from its den, sheathed its claws, and instead of tearing and rending, as you expected, began playing with you. It was strange to watch those fierce eyes soften down, and to see the natural sneer fade from his face whenever he looked at the Lily ; while she coloured at first, and with downward gaze, beat the floor unconsciously with her restless foot, looked at him again from under her long eye-lashes without raising her head, then turned away her bewildered glance, like a dove fascinated by a hawk that draws nearer and nearer, and has not the power to fly away. He spoke but little to her at first, but like the fabled basilisk, seemed to smite her by his gaze.

After a time, he would take a part with her while singing, or become her partner in a dance on the village green, while her foolish father would join in the applause they received, vow that they were the handsomest couple on that side the country, and looked as if they were made for one another ; It was noticed at such times that the young Blacksmith would turn away with a sigh, or take a part in the dance, though solicited by the greatest beauties when the Lily was expected.

Before long it was whispered through the village that Gipsy Jem and the Lily had been seen together in the solitudes of the forest, that the gamekeeper had come upon them unaware seated together in the deepest and darkest recess of the forest ;

The old woodman had seen them in untrodden places, such as only himself and the earth-stopper visited ; and when these tidings reached her father's ears, he only said 'He wished there were no worse fellows in the world than Gipsy Jem, and that as she made her bed, so she must lie.'

"When remonstrated with by her mother, she blushed, sighed, hung down her head, and said " it was her fate."

"What reeked she of the future ? For there is a future in store for all of us, my friends," said Mr. Ryan, putting down his pipe for a moment. "How many a young swain has sworn eternal constancy to the too credulous and listening maiden. She might have been the wife of the honest young blacksmith, who said, as his voice trembled with emotion, ' that he loved the ground she walked upon,' while this gipsy was, by nature not adapted for her. Psha ! What is the use of reasoning in such a case ?"

She had always been, when a girl, a lover of nature, fond of hearing the birds sing, of watching the bees and butterflies, and I often thought, in after-days, that in their wanderings together, he pictured their gipsy-tent as standing in some of the sweet solitudes which they visited, catching the summer sunshine, filled with the aroma of the forest, or blown upon by the gentle winds. I knew that she was uneducated—a creature of impulse—a simple child of nature, easy of belief—a fanciful, foolish, trustful thing, wishing she were a bird, a bee, or a flower, and often in her reckless, innocent, and thoughtless buoyancy, condemning what she called " a homely, in-door, humdrum life ;" and I believe that he, in his cunning watchfulness, seized upon her in one of these weak-minded moods, and bore her away in heartless triumph.

There was something ominous in the wedding, though a lovelier morning never broke through the golden bars of the gates of heaven, than that which dawned upon her bridal-day ; but while the sad-hearted clergyman was reading the marriage ceremony—sad-hearted on her account—a sudden storm burst out, and the lightning struck and shattered the church-spire. The villagers said it was because the gipsy was a heathen, and had polluted God's altar by his presence ; for that old satanic sneer was on his lip all the time the ceremony was performed. She walked back to the " Barley-mow," where the wedding was kept, in her white dress, through the pouring rain. A lily beaten and broken down to the grand by the rain, could not have been more soiled than she was as she returned from church.

Although several gipsies were hanging about the village during the three days that he kept up the wedding-feast, it was remarked that none of them drank with him, neither would they partake of his food. They came and went, exchanged a few words with him in private, but nothing more. After these interviews, he was always excited and angry, and drank large portions of raw brandy, as if to drown his thoughts, before he could again make himself agreeable to his guests. On the fourth day, he had high words with two men of his tribe, in the field that fronted the "Barley-mow," and he would have fought had not his wife rushed across the road. They parted from him scowling and uttering threats. In the evening, an old gipsy-woman came; she but beckoned to him with her hand, and he obeyed. Their interview was short, and when he returned, he was silent for the rest of the night. Some said that the old dark woman was his mother, others that she was the Queen of the Gipsies. He told his young wife that she must get ready to go away with him that night; when she asked "where to ?" he said "she will see soon enough." He packed all her clothes up in a large bundle, and staggering, through the quantity of spirits he had drunk, walked out with them strapped across his back, a little before midnight, followed by Edith to go she knew not whither.

"What a silly girl," said Mr. Baintree, "to wed a wandering scamp like that!"

"Silly, sir!" exclaimed Father Ryan, "I really hadn't patience with her, for she was indeed very beautiful—far a-head in that respect of the one who passed this window a few minutes ago. Well, to continue, it appears that after a long hour's walk, Edith found great difficulty in keeping pace with her husband, they came to where a fire was burning, and which was kept alight by two bare-footed gipsy children; this was at the corner or skirts of a wood. He spoke to the children in a language which Edith did not comprehend. The boy answered him, and pointed across a dark common. In reply to another question, the girl put her hand into the bosom of her ragged frock, took out a pair of antique ear-rings, and gave them to him. He told the children to return into the tent. As they stood making faces at Edith through the opening of the tent, she saw that their coarse hair was matted together like a colt's mane that had been left to run all its life on a wild, hedgeless, and furze-covered moor; she heard them say "that pale face shan't be our mother; we will run away to Barbara:" and a strange sickening of the heart came over her. As for her gipsy

husband, he sat with a large brandy flask in his hand, drinking, and looking into the fire, until at last, overpowered, he fell back, and there lay until the sun was high above the wild and houseless common.

"On the following morning, he left her with the children, and came not back until the evening of the fourth day.

"He might as well have left her a couple of wild cats of the wood to tame, as to keep guard over those two children: the only peace she had was whilst they went away to steal whatever they could lay hands on; they uttered such language as made her shudder. She had had no occasion to ask them about their mother, for when not abusing and making faces at her, they were talking of Barbara 'who some day would come back, and tear her pale face to pieces!'

"Days passed away, and he came and went without telling her whither he was going, or when he should return; she lay all alone in her cold tent, listening to the roaring of the trees, and the barking of the foxes from the wood.

"When he came back, he swore at the children if they brought no plunder to the camp, partook of the eggs, fowls, and fruit they had stolen, and if Edith remonstrated, told her she was a fool, and unfit for a gipsy's wife.

"Still there were, for the first few days, moments when he seemed kind to her; he placed the gold rings in her ears, and in her presence threatened to kill the children if ever they named Barbara again.

"Well, poor girl, she did pay a dear penalty for her indiscretion," said Mr. Baintree. "The fellow was already married, then ?"

"Oh, he was a wild, reckless, good-for-nothing scoundrel," answered Father Ryan. "And how often do we see such as him creep round the heart of a girl sooner than a straightforward, upright man."

"Too often indeed," exclaimed the old gentleman, who had been in the room when our hero, Mr. Baintree, and Father Ryan entered.

"Well," said the latter, in continuation, "weeks passed away. When he came one night drunk, and broke up the encampment, he swore such horrible oaths as made his wife tremble; said that his money was all gone, and his tribe had deserted him, and cursed her as the cause of it all. He told her that she must steal, tell fortunes, and become in every way a gipsy, or she would not do for him.

"But she would neither drink nor steal, though she went with him from village to village, carried his tinker's wallet, knocked at the cottage and farm-house doors to see if they had any pots or pans to mend."

"What a life to lead!"

"Ah, you may well say that; but she behaved well through it though. In spite of his threats and abuse, she behaved as though he were the most affectionate of husbands; and many who admired her sweet careworn face, gave her work out of charity; but her husband did it so badly, that she was sometimes ashamed to take it back.

"He became idle, stern, silent, and, when in drink, brutal. He left her for days in the hut, to get work as she could. He had long threatened to bring back another who would do his bidding in all things, and at last he fulfilled his threat."

"He never had the effrontery to do that, surely?" exclaimed Mr. Baintree.

"Oh, but he did though. He had the very effrontery of—saving your presence—the very devil.

No. 84.

"It was one morning, after the brute had struck her—though she was then heavy with the innocent burthen that she bore—that he returned, and overthrowing the tent, at the entrance of which she sat weeping and watching the fire, he with an oath and a blow bade her arise and begone. He had a bold, brazen, black-eyed woman with him, whose hair was dark as the longest night, and who wore a string of large glass-beads around her neck, and who, while cursing, in her deep, disgusting voice, tore the gold rings from Edith's ears. It was Barbara, the children's mother,—the villanous gipsy's wife, according to the heathen forms which were considered binding by their tribe.

It was on a late, cold autumn morning, while the frost already hung white on the few bean "stouks" that stood blackening in the silent fields, when, heavy with child, heart-broken, faint, hungry and foot-sore, the once-fair Lily of Ligswell sat with her face buried in her hands, in the grey dawning, on the churchyard-steps of her native village. The young blacksmith, always early at work, was the first to approach her. She tried to rise when he spoke to her, but was unable,—so staggered and fell. With eyes so blinded by tears that he could scarcely see his way, he raised her in his brawny arms—for she was senseless—and carried her to his own home, and consigned her to the care of his mother. When he had placed her upon his mother's bed, he fell on the floor as if shot suddenly through the heart, moaning unconsciously. It was pitiable to see that strong man in his great mental agony, for his pity and sorrow then seemed stronger than his love. She lingered on through a few painful weeks, but never expressed a wish to visit her own home again. The blacksmith's widow was kinder to her than her own mother had ever been, for she led her to seek comfort at the foot of that Holy Cross where the sincerely penitent never plead in vain. The presence of her ever-drunken and maudlin father seemed to give her pain. All pitied her, and I never missed a day, gentlemen, without kneeling in prayer by her bed side. Indeed, it is some comfort to me when I reflect upon her truly contrite heart. I believe she had as good a heart as ever beat in a woman's breast; but a weak heart, a too trusting nature, a delicate frame and a susceptible organisation. She was to be pitied, if ever woman was, and had she listened earlier to good advice she would not have been cut down in the spring time and flower of her youth ; but I must do justice to my countrymen, they have many faults, but they are warm-hearted, and when sorrow and trouble presses heavily upon anyone they respect the same. Everyone did so in the case of poor Edith. The rude hawker would cease to whistle as he passed the chamber where she lay, and the drunken reveller would stop suddenly in the midst of his deafening song, as he saw the light streaming across the road which flashed from her curtained casement.

"At last, the window was darkened, mother and child were launched like a ship into that unknown sea where many a human barque has voyaged, under His guidance who can alone moor them in the undisturbed tranquillity of eternity, where the waves of trouble cease to roll, and the sighs of sorrow are heard no more.

"The white day-lilies which the true-hearted blacksmith had planted around her grave were shedding their flowers, when Gipsy Jem accompanied the shameless Barbara to the village feast which took place about that time. The blacksmith was present. He and the gipsy fought a fierce and deadly battle. After that day the gipsy never held up his head again. It was said by the villagers that the burning words uttered by the blacksmith had more to do in killing Gipsy Jem, than the blows he had received, though the latter could be heard by those who were standing in the churchyard. A few weeks after the feast he was found dead in the wood beside the nest of the large black ant, and those who found him said that but for his clothes they should never have known that it was Gipsy Jem, so altered was he who had married and by wickedness murdered the Lily of Ligswell.

"And what became of the blacksmith?" inquired Mr. Baintree.

"He stayed for some months after this in the village, but his manner was reserved, and it was easy to be seen that the canker-worm was at his heart; but, however, he endeavoured to bear up against the great trial which he had been subjected to. Somehow or other, there was always something turning up to remind him of the lost and ill-fated Edith, and eventually he embraced an opportunity afforded him and emigrated to America. What became of him after this, I never heard. He had lost his mother before he left England, or else he would never have thought of emigrating. However, he settled there, so I was informed, and may be alive now, for aught I know," said Mr. Ryan. "Be this as it may, there has been a blight in his existence."

"How often do we find this to be the case," said Mr. Baintree ; "too often, indeed, that a young girl chooses the very man of all others that she ought not to do, when an honourable suitor might make her happy for life."

The room door was now opened, and an uncouth-looking man presented himself.

He exchanged a familiar nod of recognition with Father Ryan, who rose from his seat, and shook hands with the new comer.

"Be seated, Mr. Jebb—pray be seated," said Father Ryan. "These gentleman and myself are desirous of questioning you upon one or two matters which deeply concern them."

Mr. Jebb looked rather suspiciously at Colonel Jack and Mr. Baintree, and did not at first seem disposed to fraternise with them as readily as might have been supposed.

The fact was, that the Irishman began to have some very serious and grave doubts as to his own safety. He had transgressed the laws on more than one occasion, and was half afraid that Mr. Baintree and Colonel Jack were officers.

Some such idea crossed the mind of Father

Ryan, for he said, in a half whisper to the new comer—

"English gentlemen, Mike. You have no occasion to be afraid. They are friends—good men and true. They are here to see if you can afford them any information of the departed."

"Of the departed?" said Mike Jebb, with a half sneer. "An' sure now, and isn't it the praste as can tell them of that same, for bad luck to me, but it's a poor hand that I shall make of it."

"Sit down, my boy, and take a drop of the crathur," said Father Ryan, soothingly.

The man did as he was desired, and drained off a respectable quantity of the whisky toddy, drinking the health of the two strangers at the same time.

"Mike, my lad," said Father Ryan, gaily, "ye know that I wouldn't ask you to do aught that might in any way compromise you; but at the same time I know also that it's a good heart that you've got, Mike, although you've been a bit of a scapegrace."

"Oh, don't," exclaimed Mr. Jebb, "pray don't."

"Well, then, I won't touch upon that subject, my man—bygones are bygones; only ye'll just say that these same gentlemen—rale, downright gentlemen, Mike—want to know something about Dennis Halford, he that went on board ship along with you, Mike."

"Ah," said Mike, crossing himself; "and it's gone that Dennis is, heaven rest his sowl."

"He died on board ship his mother told me," said Colonel Jack.

"Oh, it's his mother that you've been seeing, is it?"

"Yes, my friend, we saw her this very day."

"Maybe ye know her, then?"

"Well, we know her now, of course; but this is our first introduction to her. The fact is," said the colonel, in continuation, "the fact is, that I am a relative of hers—her nephew, in fact."

At this declaration, the Irishman's eyes became dilated to nearly double their size.

"Och, murder, but ye don't mane that?" he exclaimed.

"Aye, but I do mean it, Mr. Jebb. My name is Halford, and Morgan Halford was my own father's brother; consequently you see that Mrs. Halford that was, and Mrs. O'Flake that is, must of necessity be my aunt by marriage—don't you see that?"

"Oh, sure now, I say that plane enough now. Oh, that's thrue enough, that same. Her nephew! Well now, I'm just bothered entirely."

"You didn't think that I was so respect-ably connected, perhaps," said our hero, with a smile.

"Oh, bedad, but it isn't altogether that," said Mr. Jebb, scratching his head in a puzzled manner. "Och, no, it isn't altogether that, but ye'll say I didn't altogether expect this."

"Neither did you expect us, I suppose?"

"Well, now, and sure that's true enough," answered Mike Jebb.

"Now," said Mr. Baintree, "you say you were on board of the vessel in which Dennis Halford died."

"An' sure I was," answered the Irishman.

"You saw him pass away perhaps?"

"What?"

"You were with him at the time of his death?"

"Sure, not exactly that."

"At his funeral?"

"Yes, I saw poor Dennis sewn up in a hammock, and thrown into the say. Bad luck to them as did that same."

"What was the name of the vessel?"

"The Semeramis," answered Mr. Jebb.

Mr. Baintree turned to Colonel Jack and gave a nod of satisfaction.

"That is enough for our purpose."

"It is evidence, I suppose?" said our hero.

"Quite sufficient, backed with the other collateral testimony we can obtain," answered the lawyer.

He then turned to Mike Jebb, and said—

"You will have no objection to make this statement in writing?"

Mr. Jebb had again recourse to his invariable practice, when puzzled, that of scratching his head.

"I am not much of a fist at writing," he observed, in a subdued tone of voice.

"No, possibly not, but I will write what it is necessary for you to state, and you can sign it."

The man glanced at Father Ryan.

"You can sign your own name, I suppose, Mike. You can do that I know," said Father Ryan. "Or, at any rate, you used to be able to do so."

"Oh yes, I can do that same, if I ought."

"Of course you ought. All these gentlemen want is an attestation of the death of Dennis Halford. There can be no certificate of his burial, seeing that he died on the high seas."

Mr. Baintree took a sheet of paper from his pocket-book, laid the same on the table, and then proceeded to write.

"What is your proper appellation, my friend?" inquired the lawyer.

"My what?" said the party so addressed.

"Your right name," chimed in Mr. Ryan.

"Oh, an' it's my name ye want?'

"To be sure."

"Mike Jebb," answered the man.

"Michael Jebb, I suppose ?" enquired the lawyer.

"Ah, and sure that's it."

Mr. Baintree wrote. In a few minutes he read this over out loud—

"I, Michael Jebb, do hereby certify that I sailed from Dublin in the Semiramis, a merchant vessel of 1,000 tons burthen, and that on board this same ship there was one passenger by the name of Dennis Halford, who died on board some three weeks after we had been out at sea; the said Dennis Halford died of a fever he caught on board; and I further certify, that I saw him several times during the progress of his malady, and that I also was present at his burial, he having been sewn up in a sack, was cast into the sea, the ship-chaplain reading the service of the dead previous to the body being cast into the deep; and hereby further declare that the said Dennis Halford was the only son of Morgan and Mary Halford, of St. Asaph, a small village, a few miles from Limeric."

"Signed—Michael Jebb."

The lawyer paused, and looked at Mr. Jebb, and then at Father Ryan.

"Nothing can be clearer than that," exclaimed the latter. "You understand the meaning of what this gentleman has been reading?" said the priest, in continuation, turning to Mike Jebb.

"Och, and sure it's aisy enough to understand that same, an' it would be strange indeed if a man with a head on his shoulders could not understand that."

"Well, then, all you have to do is to sign it, my friend," said Father Ryan.

Mr. Jebb hesitated for a moment. He glanced at the pen and ink, and then at the colonel and Mr. Baintree.

"Och and sure, it's no harm that I'll be doing by signing that same ?"

"Of course not. I will answer for that," said the priest.

Upon this Mr. Michael Jebb took up the pen, looked at the nib of it, and then ran his eye down the quill—much the same as a carpenter might do with a plane or saw. After he had done this he began trying the pen upon the newspaper which happened to be in the room, and the "weapon," as he termed it, appearing satisfactory, he, with many strange, uncouth flourishes, did eventually sign his name to the document which the counsellor had written.

"So far all is satisfactory," said Mr. Baintree, folding up the paper, and putting it into his pocket.

"Mr. Jebb, I am much obliged to you, but as I don't like to work myself without being paid for the same, you must permit me

to offer you some slight recompense for the trouble we have put you to."

"Och, murder! but ye don't think I expect to be paid at all at all," said Mr. Jebb, indignantly. "Bad luck to me, but I don't want a scurrick from ye."

"There now, don't be a foolish man," cried Mr. Baintree. "Never refuse a good thing," and at the same time handing the Irishman a couple of guineas, by way of recompense. The latter was loth to accept of the same, but upon Mr. Baintree informing him that he might want his services again at some future period, he at length was prevailed upon to pocket them. In the course of half an hour or so Colonel Jack, Mr. Baintree, and Father Ryan left the house and proceeded to the hospitable dwelling of Mr. O'Callagan.

The colonel and his two companions walked gaily along the dark road which they had to go to reach Mr. O'Callagan's residence. They had not proceeded for more than half a mile when their ears were saluted with a confused murmur of sounds. A man's voice was heard speaking with great volubility, and then the plaintive tones of a woman, who appeared to be making some sort of appeal to the latter

"What is the matter?" said the colonel.

"Ah, that's hard to say," answered Mr. Ryan.

The three hastened on towards the disturbance, if it could be so called.

When they had arrived at the spot, and Colonel Jack had ignited the small lantern he generally carried with him, they soon saw the cause of the disturbance. An Irish jaunting car lay in the road upset, one of the wheels having come off. An old lady had evidently been thrown into a ditch, for her clothes were covered with mud, and she was in a terrible flight, indeed it might be said, "more frightened than hurt."

"Oh, dear, kind gentlemen," exclaimed the old lady, who was evidently an Englishwoman, and one of superior breeding. "Oh, dear, kind gentlemen, have pity on a distracted and unfortunate female, who has been half killed by this careless man."

"What, O'Ruke, is it you?" said Father Ryan. "Why, what has been the matter?"

"Are sure now, an' saving your riverence's presence, the baste, you say, is knowing what a rare laddy he had behind him, would be afther showing what mettle he's made of, and consequently yer riverence the whale came off."

"Yes, I see, and pitched the lady out."

The man gave a nod of assent to this, and Colonel Jack had by this time been assisting and consoling the female as best he could. It was eventually agreed that our hero should take the lady in question to the house of Mr.

O'Callagan, and inquire of that worthy if he could accommodate her with a lodging for the night, for the colonel learnt that she was an English maiden lady who had been on a visit to a relative who had settled in Ireland, and she was making the best of her way back when the accident already described occurred.

The colonel was ever mindful of the softer sex, even if they were as old as Methuselah, consequently he and Mr. Baintree accompanied the old maid, for such she proved to be, to the house of O'Callagan. That gentleman at once declared that it would afford him infinite delight to have the English lady as his guest, and in the morning one of his men would drive her to the place she wished to go. So all was arranged satisfactorily enough, and Miss Cary, that was the lady's name, proved to be a very sociable old soul and a charming companion.

Warmed by some whiskey-toddy, Miss Cary entered into the full particulars of her life, and as they are possessed of considerable interest, we shall reserve them for a separate chapter.

CHAPTER CXXV.

PAST AND PRESENT.—THE OLD MAID'S TALE.

"I have already told you that I am an old maid," said Miss Cary.

"Yes, indeed," said O'Callagan. "I hope it ain't your fault."

"You shall hear. When at home, I lived in an old-fashioned country town. I am old, as you see, so old indeed, that when the census papers came round a few years since, I found that I had forgotten to register the flight of time. As a good and loyal subject, I did not consider myself justified in evading (as many younger folks did) the polite request of the enumerator, but diligently searched the Family Bible, in which the domestic archives of the Brumbridges are enrolled for many past generations. I must confess that the result of my research rather startled me; nor do I think I should have said anything about my age here, but that from what I am about to tell you, the veriest tyro at arithmetic could easily calculate it.

"Market Mowbray is the name of the quiet town in which I live. I call it a town, because, as its name testifies, it once was so; but long ago it subsided into that last stage of town, as of other, life—"mere oblivion." It consists of one long, straight, and broad street, half a-mile in length perhaps, with labourers' cottages, tradesmens' shops, and gentlefolks' residences, jumbled together in great confusion; and an old grey church rising in the midst, and casting its cool shadow across the quiet sunny street. Some of these houses are very large; and, with their aid, the town still holds out a proud bearing to the world at large, and stands resolutely on the memory of its former dignity. Indeed, it strongly reminds strangers (so I have been told) of the "lean pantaloon's youthful hose, a world too wide for his shrunk shank;" for many of these houses are rented at sums which would be moderate for cottages elsewhere. I have whole Bluebeard suites of rooms unfurnished and unused; while our church is large enough to give a separate pew to every member of its congregation for life, and provide him with a dry, roomy vault, all to himself, when dead.

"In explanation of this decay, the Market Mowbray people will tell you, with just pride, that before the time of the Great Plague, their town was a thriving, populous place, which for its sins God thought fit to visit with just though heavy affliction, so that it became the plague-spot of the surrounding country: and if you are antiquarian enough to visit us for that purpose, I will point out the bridges at either end of the town, across which chains were slung, and upon which great fires were kept blazing, that the dreaded infection should not spread. During which terrible season the market was held in an adjoining place, then a mere village; but which, having naturally forgotten to return its temporary privileges, has since grown into a large and populous town, still showing traces of its low birth; for its square and chief streets are shrunken and paltry, while it has large misshapen limbs in the form of suburbs.

"Therefore, Market Mowbray never recovered from the shock which deprived it of its population and its privileges; and its upstart neighbour soon carried away all our trade and business, leaving us what we are as well pleased with—respectability, and the memory of former dignity. You may be inclined to smile at the feud of two hundred years ago smouldering now, but I assure you we are still very jealous of the Stownham people, and seldom receive them; the less, perhaps, that they are mostly connected with trade, while we justly pride ourselves on being of good families.

"I live in a very small house, in which everything, from my little maid to my minute garden, is in minature. The doorways are so low, that I am in unspeakable dread when an ordinarily tall gentleman calls to see me, ever since our new curate, who is high-church, and has the 'grand monarque' manner, stooped to bow his parting salute on the threshold, and so injured his head from contact with the jambs, that he was compelled to walk home, hat in hand.

"For all its want of size and grandeur, great carriages and good people—I mean well-connected people—stop before that little door—for is not its mistress a Brumbridge? and are not their chronicles to be read in every County History that has ever been written? Therefore, I am by no means a dull or lonely old maid, although I have undergone trials and suffered afflictions. Indeed, I lead on the whole what sometimes appears to me a rather dissipated life, and indulge in more rubbers of whist and quadrilles than I shall be able satisfactorily to account for, I am afraid. But I give my winnings to the poor-box and shall continue to hope for the best.

"Moreover, did I not bear a county name, I should never be long lonely, for I have a large and cheerful family circle, by whom—as by less partial connoisseurs—my Christmas bowl of punch is pronounced a miracle of art. I think I should like to tell you a few particulars about my family—the Brumbridges of Burton Manor. My father lived, and died, as many a Brumbridge had before him—in the pleasant old manor house, about a mile from Market Mowbray.

"If I had time to introduce you to the family portraits in the old hall, I should point out two or three of my father's predecessors who made more free with the manor property than a due regard for their successors' interests would justify; and so it happened that my father had to farm the estate for his family's support instead of his own amusement, after the good old Brumbridge fashion. And, to add to his life's embarrassments, he had a son, a sad wild scapegrace—never so wicked, however, as thoughtless—whose good qualities might be said to have run to waste so that from flowers they had grown into weeds, and who gave us much trouble that (much as through all evil report we still loved him) his departure for foreign parts was a great relief. Something sobered him in Heaven's own good time (perhaps a melancholy episode of his romantic life, which I have no time to narrate now), and, like some other scapegraces, he turned his former dear-bought experience of the world to good account, and prospered and grew rich; and came home, the rich prodigal, some time before his father's death, no longer young, and with a large family; to whom, when the family vault opened its portals to receive another tenant, I resigned my mistress-ship of the manor, and retired to my own little home.

"Who dares to libel life by calling old age selfish, and denying to it the warmth and nobility of youth? Is youth never selfish? or beauty never wayward and fickle? I know that we grey-haired folks (of course, my dears, I should be grey if I did not wear a wig) love each other as warmly and honestly as when I was a young lass, and he wild

Harry Brumbridge, and our lives went a-maying in the spring-tide of youth. And by this time his sons and daughters have become men and women—fathers and mothers, and a new generation is springing up at our feet; to every one of whom I am "Aunt Cary—dear old Aunt Cary," in turn their playmate, confidante, and first friend in need.

"I happen to be an old maid who dearly loves children. I am confident that most of my unjustly maligned class do, and that I am no exception to the general rule. I consider Harry Brumbridge, my brother, as great a child (if this be not an anomaly) as his smallest grandson, for all his grey head and sun-tanned face; and on those happy nights when my little house is handed over to the youngsters, he is sure to be amongst the merriest and noisiest. On such nights, I give juvenile parties—that is, parties to which the adults consent to be invited, and, when there, ruled by the juveniles. My work had been harder than usual this past year, for we had been pleasantly toiling in our little town in the manufacture of woollen comforters for the brave fellows who were keeping their Christmas so gloriously three thousand miles from home. Ah, how gloriously! My old heart throbs as we speak of it, with something of that wild youthful ardour with which it beat when the fathers of these brave hearts were working out God's will in another land, and against another foe, so many, many years ago! Ah, did you grant me patience, what a strange homily I would weave for your young folks—spun from the experiences of a single life of three-score years and—There, I very nearly let my age slip out then.

"So, from this and some other minor reasons, my Christmas party was postponed to a later period of the season; much to their pleasure, I hope—otherwise I should never have told my little story of what we did and said on the night of the last of January in the present year.

"Of course, we formed a merry party on that evening. I may as well state that fact at once, positively, to avoid repetition. We laughed enough to sweeten the cups of our lives for another year, at least; and were altogether as merry, reckless, idle, good-for-nothing a party of young and old folks as you would be likely to meet with even in the great world beyond Market Mowbray.

"I happen to know a few rigidly Pharisaical people, who would shake their wise heads at our good-for-nothing gaiety, and tell us we had better have been singing penitential psalms and imbibing the bitter (though wholsesome) Waters of Marah, than carolling worldly ditties and drinking my famous brew of punch—but I care little what these think or say.

"Old as I am, standing on the threshold of a new existence, I can better bear to look back upon the gay and healthful moments of my life, than upon the serious and bilious ones. And between relatives and friends, joy and merriment together shared, forge the links which mutual grief and sorrow, sooner or later, will firmly weld into a chain. There! will you excuse an old maid's moralising? I promise to be better in future, if you will.

"I intend giving you a Sun-picture (if I may call it so) of my guests young and old, taken by the glowing light of the bright wood fire—as it cracked and sparled, in its honest glee sending up whole legions of messenger sparks to the dark night without, where large flakes of snow were falling thick, veiling the stars from sight—as it sometimes sent a bouncing spark among the merry youngsters on the hearth, from which they scattered and fled to return with glowing cheeks and timid yet trustful eyes, to bask in the good friend giant's warmth again.

"Facing me sat my tropical-sun-tanned brother. From his long residence abroad, he has a foreign look: he wears a well-trimmed beard and long grizzly grey moustachios, every hair of which was glistening in the blaze of the cheering fire. Beside him sat his youngest daughter, who is the *unfortunate* of the family—in all large families there is always such an one—who has lived a long life in a few short years, and sunk into welcome repose and retirement long before the rich bloom has faded from her cheeks, or the dark hair become more than streaked with silver. She is the mistress of the old manor now—my brother's housekeeper, and an universal favourite.

About the room were seated two or three dark whiskered men, who called me "Aunt," and from their memories of auld lang syne, roused up recollections of similar evenings, when they filled the places of that deluge of merry-faced, bright-eyed children, who were romping in detachments, being fondled on knees, or secluded in quiet corners, after their several inclinations. These are my grand nephews and neices—Heaven bless their rosy cheeks and bright eyes! Amongst them is a yellow-haired, blue-eyed young fellow, who, although he has passed the stage of childhood, and is passing the rubicon of boy-manhood, delights to forego his dignity and head the youngster's riot. He is a lad of spirit, is this Eric Brumbridge, and worthy of the good Saxon name he bears. He waits the passing of a few more months ere he dons the queen's uniform, and carries the name wherever bold hearts assemble for brave purposes.

They wanted to make a lawyer of this handsome madcap, but he resolutely clung to the prospect of a sailor's life, and will tread the plank like a true son of "Old Ocean's Island child." When I die, my little carefully-husbanded patrimony will belong to this light-hearted youngster; for, is he not an orphan—poor, and—my love? If for no other reason, I confess I should like to enjoy it myself for a few years longer, until Time, among her other lessons, shall have taught this bright trifler the value of money.

Were he placed in possession of my small fortune now, I am not at all sure that he would not sink it in collars, through which phase of social life he is at present wearing, or invest it in toffy for all the juveniles in Market Mowbray. When he sails on his first voyage, and I lose his bright face and merry smile, I almost fear my old heart may break, for all that it is pretty tough by this time, and has stood a great deal of wear and tear.

I do not think, that for the purposes of this short tale, I need particularize any more of my visitors.

We generally put the young people down to a round game, for the purpose of steadying them, for digestive and other reasons, before supper. I am bound to confess that our plan frequently fails; but this night it succeeded tolerably well. Once only the universal harmony was disturbed. Almost immediately after the matrimony pool had been emptied by an eager young gambler, the poor privilege fell to my lot. Eric tried to still the uproar of laughter which followed the exposure of my good fortune, and failing, took up weapons in my behalf.

"Never mind, Aunt Cary—deal round again, young Crœsus. I shall find wedding cards for Eric Brumbridge, Esq., H.M.S., Firebrand, some day yet."

"You silly fellow," I answered, "you should rather be looking for my death in the papers."

At which unfortunate speech, a nephew, an articled clerk in a London attorney's office, gave a loud, prolonged guffaw.

I am not so fond of this nephew as I should be; and as he is in noways disinclined to give himself airs, I am afraid anything but a proper cousinly regard exists between him and Eric.

Indeed, I was very much alarmed by Eric's flushed face and angry eyes, and a hasty threat, having reference to the punching of heads, which was neither gentlemanly nor quite appropriate.

But my brother, Harry Brumbridge, averted the threatened storm.

"You may laugh, young fellows," he said; "but Aunt Cary might have drawn many a prize in the lottery of marriage, had she listed."

"Hush, brother, hush!" I quickly said—for although green grass grows above graves, we care not to tread upon them; and it is the same with buried hopes. Eric stole to my side in the momentary silence which ensued. The angry flush was gone; he sent it back, as he tossed the long yellow curls from his fair forehead, and clothed his face with sunny smiles instead.

"Dear Aunt Cary!" he whispered, "after supper, we always guess riddles and act proverbs. Let us tell tales to-night, and do you begin." I knew well what the dear fellow meant; for had I not, like a garrulous old woman, told him more of my youth than any of the others; and full, still, of the morning's thoughts, I nodded Yes. But my heart misgave me the moment after I had given this promise, and I grew very serious and quiet during supper-time, which happily interfered in no degree with the young folks' appetites. And, supper over, we grew very merry when we clustered around the wood fire, and the punch circulated, and songs were sung, and toasts proposed and duly honoured. The young lawyer, who had sung a humourous but, I am afraid, not very select, chant, was beginning to give a long speech, when my impetuous and impatient heir broke in—

"Oh, confound the spouting, Tom! Here is good luck to the brave fellows, and God bless 'em! Hurrah!"

And my little room rang with his boyish voice, and the children's shrill accompaniment.

"Hurrah! again and again! That's better than all the long winded jaw of Westminster Hall put together."

The clouds of another storm were gathering fast, when I mustered up courage to say, "I am going to tell you a tale of war, my dears, when these noisy boys will be a little quieter."

"Slip your cable and clap on all sail then, Aunt Cary. Pipe all hands on deck. Now then, youngsters, silence—Aunt Cary *loquitur*."

"I am going back, you good-for-nothing fellow, to a time when I as little dreamed of being old Aunt Cary as you think of gout or indigestion—to a time when your grandfather was what you are now, as young, good-for-nothing, and as troublesome. Do you remember, brother?"

"And you were a gay little flirt, Cary, and broke the hearts of half the country-side. Am I likely to forget it?"

"Harry Brumbridge! Harry Brumbridge! will you never be more sober? I am asking you to remember when war was as familiar to us as it is to these youngsters now; only its battle-fields were nearer home, and none could tell how soon their household gods might be shattered on their own hearths. Well, my dears, I was a young girl then, and

I dare say giddy; but I warn none of you to follow my example, for the punishment equalled the offence. And I dare say I did flirt—a little—and tried to break a heart or so, perhaps; in which, of course, I failed, giving only pain instead.

"At this time the country swarmed with soldiers, and in our little town were billeted some companies of a cavalry regiment. You may be sure the officers were made welcome everywhere; and nowhere more so than at the Manor. Of these, there were two who from acquaintance soon became familiar friends. They were cousins, and fondly attached to one another; for all that, they differed as much in disposition as in personal appearance. The elder was a tall, staid, soldierly man, with a grave face, seamed and scarred from exposure to worse foes than 'winter and rough weather:' but which, when lit up by a smile, that was the expression of no single feature, but shone from every one, was what even a young girl would call handsome. The younger was gay and thoughtless, with an ever-sunny smile and a light heart, that bore down thought or care without an effort. To be in his presence, was to bask in continual sunshine: and so his senior officer felt, for he loved his gay young cousin with a noble, manly earnestness, 'passing the love of woman.' It was strange to be in the society of these two, so dissimilar and yet so disseparable—to hear the grave words of advice which fell from the lips of the one, telling of duty, and honour, and self-respect no less to oneself than to the world at large, met with the sparkling jest and merry repartee that forced from the moralist a smile.

"But I think the feeling which the younger cousin returned for this care and forethought was tinged with a little reverential awe of virtues he might never share, and mental qualities he could hope to reach. I may be wrong, but I think respect for acknowledged superiority, and real love, can seldom exist together. Anyhow, however wrong, I thought so then; and, much as I loved to linger by Lionel Balmer's side, and listen to tales of foreign lands and dangers undergone and bold deeds done—recited with a modesty that set them off as simple settings do rich jewels—I trembled when my heart whispered one question, and the time came when an answer must be given. For this noble-hearted soldier stooped to win the young girl's heart; and those whose duty it was to counsel me, said—how truly!—what a proud and happy girl I ought to be; and how rich I should feel in the possession of such a heart! And while I was with him, and the smile was on his face, I felt that this was true: but when sometimes the grave brow spoke gentle reproof of some childish folly or trivial absurdity, I trembled again at the prospect of a prison with even the best of husbands for a gaoler.

"I think he saw this the first of anyone, but forebore to speak. I am sure, now, that he saw how freely I revelled in the careless gaiety of his young companion; and how naturally our hearts, in their mutual youth and folly, flowed into one stream of thought and action.

"But he bore all patiently, and never relaxed in his tender thought for either of us, but seemed to watch over and guard us with the care and patience of a fond father.

"At length he spoke. I am not likely to forget the day. It was a bright summer morn, and I was watching the sunlight chasing the cloud-shadows over the fields of yellow grain, when I saw the two cousins walk up the avenue; and while Lionel Balmer crossed the porch alone, his friend paced backwards and forwards along the terrace walk.

"I need not tell you what he said, or how I answered him. Every word he spoke on that well remembered morning was true to his gentle nature. I know I wept as he probed my heart; but through my tears I could see Harold Linton pacing too and fro in measured strides. The terrace was dotted with rose bushes, and as he passed them I could see him clutch at the buds, and scatter the petals about his path.

"Lionel Balmer was watching my glance, and I saw him smile sadly, almost compassionately.

"Then my evil spirit rose, and, forgetting what I owed him, I spoke like a silly wayward fool, and sobbed my anger out. He answered me sorrowfully and with deep compassion, and soothed me as one would a spoiled and petted child, and left me to rejoin his cousin on the terrace walk, with whom he spoke long and earnestly, pacing too and fro the while.

"All this I saw through my tears, which flowed freely. I had banished him, with his strong mind and noble heart; and already misgivings arose. Could I not have learned to love him—did I not love him already? Could I bear to think that he had left me in sorrowful anger, never to return? Was I prepared for this?

"They were on the terrace still, but Harold had dropped the rosebuds, and was talking with eager vehemence. I saw them part friendly, but with haste. I saw Lionel look back, as his figure faded into the distance, and wave his hand; while Harold, with his eyes shaded, gazed long and earnestly down the path he had taken. He passed down the long avenue, with the streaks of sunlight through the trees dancing on his receding form, into the bright light beyond,

No. 85.

and was gone. In another moment, Harold Linton was by my side, and—I was a happy woman.

"We were both so young that my father would not give his consent to our marriage then, and as Harold's company was still stationed here, the summer months flew pleasantly by. Although this is a love-story, I am not going to send you gentlemen to bed to dream of romance and sentiment and nonsense of that sort; so I shall merely say that we lapsed into the humdrum life of recognised *fiancés*, and were very happy in our own selfish way. Lionel, we found, had obtained leave of absence, and, without often saying so, we missed him very much; and grieved terribly when we found he had exchanged into a regiment proceeding abroad on active service. I think I shed many tears, at the thought that I had been the means of sending him into the midst of that strife he had wished to forego for ever; and used to feel very wretched, until Harold charmed my sorrow away. But, although this soothing did very well for a time, I found my remorse had deeper root; and then a terrible struggle ensued.

"I am too much ashamed of this period of my life, to dwell upon its memories unnecessarily long. It is sufficient to say that, wayward as ever, my thoughts followed more and more that grave gentleman who was fighting his country's battles on a foreign soil, carrying from his home his vexed heart, wounded by my hand. Harold was ever good and kind,—but so he was to every one. Nothing could ruffle his easy good-temper; but that is virtue sometimes nigh akin to a fault. He wanted energy and spirit. While every heart was throbbing to share in the glory which was laurelling so many brows, he seemed content to bask in the sunshine of inglorious ease. And yet you will see that this graceful idler, when his time came, fought and bled with the bravest of them.

"Well, the more clearly I perceived the life-long error I had committed, the more I strove to love him whom I had blindly endowed with so many virtues. And in some degree (for there was much to love and admire in Harold Linton) I succeeded. But, I acknowledged, that while with him, I might be a happy woman—with Lionel Balmer, I should have been a good wife.

"We heard of Lionel only through the public prints. We read there how he was distinguishing himself, and how rapidly he was rising in public esteem. We saw his name returned as 'wounded,' and then I hoped he would have written, but he never did; and when Harold was at length ordered abroad, my last request was that he should seek his cousin, and offer him the friendship he had cast away,

"Months passed away. I heard frequently from Harold; and, at last, his latent spirit seemed fairly aroused, and the nobility of his nature showed itself. At the point of his sword, he bore off honour and reward; and many a night, sitting in the Old Manor Hall by the winter's fire, have we read and re-read his letters, brother, until we could fancy ourselves bivouacking amidst the mountains of Spain, and hear the shout of victory, as the chivalry of England hurled themselves upon the legions of France.

"To make a short tale still shorter, I will pass over all our sorrow and anxiety, when, step by step, every one dearly purchased by the enemy, an English army stepped backward (I will not say retreated), with their face to the foe. We suffered as others did who had dear ones in that army. In a return of casualties, I read the name of Harold Linton, known to be severely wounded and supposed to have fallen a prisoner into the hands of the French. On that dreary day of mourning, all my love for him returned with tenfold force. And when I read in the next *Gazette* the name of Lionel Balmer, returned as 'dangerously wounded,' I was nearly wild with grief. So long as Lionel was alive, and near him, I felt hope; but now the dark waters closed above my head. So the dreary days passed by and became weeks, and the weeks grew into long months, and still we heard nothing more. We made many inquiries, and sought for information eagerly; but the authorities returned the same answer that they 'had reason to believe Harold was a prisoner, and that Lionel was struggling with death.'

"Spring came. I had given up all hope now. I had been very ill, and Heaven had kindly ordained that my senses should be deadened by the shock I had sustained; so that I passively breathed the pure spring breezes, and they and the bright early summer suns had a cheering effect upon my enfeebled frame. One day, when I was sitting screened within a window of the old room, gazing down the avenue, across which the shadows were glaring as when Lionel Balmer passed from their sunny network into the light beyond, I saw a carriage wind up the path and stop before the porch. I could not move nor speak, as I saw the steps lowered, and a tall figure—upright, for all that he was pale and thin, and wore his right arm in a sling —stepped out into the sunlight, and, dismissing the carriage, entered the house. He must have seen me at the window, for he crossed the hall familiarly as of old, and laid his hand upon the handle of the door; but ere he entered, I had mustered strength to rise. I think he was as much struck with my pallid face, as I was grieved at his altered frame; for his lips trembled with the words

they could not pronounce, and I saw his eyes fill will with a rush of tears. I was the first to speak.

"'You need not tell me, Major Balmer; I—I have long known that he was dead.'

"'Need I say,' he answered—and I cannot express to you the depth of feeling evinced in his tone and manner—'need I say how well pleased I am that the cruel blow has not to be inflicted by my hand. Yes, he died a soldier's death. I am glad that my sad tidings have been forestalled, and yet almost sorry—'

"I would not undeceive him, but bent my head in answer.

"'For I need not say how terrible I felt this task would be, both for you and for me; and that nothing but a sense of duty, and a promise given, would have induced me to shock you with my presence at this time.'

"Still I could find no words to answer him.

"'To bring to your mind folly bitterly repented of by me, and wild dreams madly indulged in at so terrible a cost, would be far from my wish; but indeed I undertook this mission at a time when the promise I gave was the only compensation God allowed me to make for much wrong done, and unjust anger borne.'

"I struggled to ask him what he meant, in vain.

"'And, in fulfilment of this sacred charge, I have much to say to you. Will you allow me to see you again, when you are better— stronger?'

"He was going, when he turned back and came to where I stood, and said, for I had not yet spoken—

"'Do you forgive me? When his young life was ebbing fast away—he did; and— and promised that you should, too.'

"'What!' I gasped out, 'you were with him when he died?—you were reconciled? you parted in your old love? I—I never knew the manner of his death. Oh, thank God—thank God for this!'

"'I reeled, and should have fallen, but that he caught me with his one strong arm and laid me in my chair. On that day I could hear no more, nor on many future days; but, when I grew better, Lionel Balmer, in several interviews, told me all. And thus—

"'When I heard that he had fallen, I hastened to the rear.' We were hard pressed then, and many of our wounded fell into the hands of the enemy. I had to ride no great distance, before I came to an old ruined convent, of which our men had made a temporary hospital, and where they had been compelled to leave the dying and the dead. I had small hope of seeing him alive; but, after some search, I found him in a sheltered nook of the old ruins, wrapped up in his cloak, and sinking fast. With the aid of my brandy-flask, I restored him to consciousness, and then gently raising him, I carried him into the fresh night air. There was a little fountain, all chipped and moss covered; and it was strange, amid the horrors and desolation of the scene, to hear the soft plash of its waters, and see them glimmer in the moon's rays. Beside this I laid him, and putting back the clotted locks from his young brow, allowed the cool spray to dash upon his face. After a time, he revived still more, and knew me, although his mind wandered back to a time when—when we were all happy together. From that he spoke of you, and of his love, never stronger than in that last agony—strong enough to make him repent the glorious death he was dying. And, as his mind cleared, we talked long and earnestly of you, and of the sorrow you would feel; and then I promised to bear you his latest words, and assure you that these, and his last thoughts, were of you alone. And then he pardoned the part I had played in my old keen sorrow; and—by this time, the night was far advanced—he repeated the simple prayers of his childhood; so do extremes meet; and, with my hand fast clasped in his, and your name upon his lips, his noble spirit passed away. I could not give him even a soldier's burial. By this time, I could hear and see the French videttes in the little village below me; and I had too many duties to perform, to sacrifice life or liberty needlessly. But I escaped from this peril to fall into a greater. Before I could write to you—before I could make any return of Harold's fate, I was stricken down, and lay for many a day unconscious, trembling between life and death. When I recovered, I returned home and fulfilled my mission.'

"And not a word in this sad tale of the dangers he had undergone and the honour he had won. Those, with that modesty which ever accompanies true bravery, he only recognised as the simple consequences of that path of duty he ever trod. I have said, he gave me these particulars in many interviews. He conversed with me with the ease and freedom of an old friend; and indeed, as he truly said, he had buried the old hopes and follies long ago; while I, without forfeiting any of my loyalty to the memory of my young hero, felt my heart drawn closer every day to the dear friend who had closed his eyes and received his latest breath. But Lionel Balmer never again spoke words of love. And, sitting by the same old window, I watched him once more pass through the slanting shadows on the grassy avenue path, and stop on the border of the sunny light beyond, to wave his last adieu. And so I became an old maid, and old 'Aunt Cary.'"

"And what became of brave Lionel Balmer?" inquired Colonel Jack.

"I have taken the liberty of giving fictitious names to the heroes of my true story," answered Miss Cary, or "Aunt Cary," as she was more familiarly termed. "He bore a more common place and less novel-like name than Lionel Balmer. Did I tell you his right name, you would find it mentioned often in the chronicles of his country's glory. He lived for many years after this, and died not long ago, of gout in the stomach, leaving a large family. This is the end of my romance, gentlemen."

"Wife, stir the fire, and fill up the glasses," said Mr. O'Callagan.

"And if you will credit the experience of a long life," said Miss Cary, "believe me that war like other misfortunes, sows the seeds of manifold blessing's. Beside the nettle ever blooms the cure, and it's the same with human nature. I told the youngsters this on the night of my party, and I gave the toast "of our brave army." And while the youngsters waved the banners, and shouted till the walls trembled, we drank the toast with enthusiasm that greater folks might rival, but could not excel."

My little party was over. The merry voices were hushed in slumber, and the bright faces were smiling in childhood's pleasant dreams, and once more I was left to the solitude of my own quiet home. As I pulled aside the blind, and gazed down the broad street of Market Mowbray, the moon's rays shone upon a calm and peaceful scene. From a few windows long streaks of light gleamed on the white snow, and I knew that within those rooms sat watchers beside the sick and weary. Swiftly the thick flakes fell, and covered the far off hills as with a pall—I saw and thought all this while my mind was far away.

"Then as I drew the curtains around my couch, I said to myself—

"'When I was a girl, I used to pray for God's vengeance on those who had slain my love; and now, in my old age I bless them. Well, His will be done.'

"Amen!" said Father Ryan, who had entered the hospitable parlour of Mr. O'Callagan. "His will be done," repeated the priest, with a devotional reverence. "Madam, your story does honour to your head and heart. 'Whom the Lord loveth he chasteneth. Blest be the name of the Lord.'"

"And so, here I am, in the company of several gentlemen, to whose gallantry, I owe so much—my present safety, and perhaps my life—here I am, a confirmed old maid," said Miss Cary, with a smile.

"Well, ma'am, and wasn't it myself that said it couldn't be your own fault, and sure enough it ain't."

"Let bygones be bygones, Mr. O'Callagan," said the priest. "Let the past be passed away; the most fortunate of us have some painful recollections in taking a retrospective glance at our past lives. Madam, I have the pleasure of drinking your very good health, and long life and happiness to you."

This last observation was addressed to Aunt Cary, who pledged the priest in return, and said she had not passed a more pleasant evening for many a day.

"An' sure now," said Mr. O'Callagan, "it won't be for long that ye'll be staying in old Ireland ?"

"No; I came here only on a short visit," said Miss Cary, "and was taking my way back, when I met with that accident, which, to say the truth, I do not regret, seeing that it has been the means of introducing me to such very excellent company."

"Bravo !" shouted out several voices.

"By the powers, but ye've kissed the blarney stone," exclaimed O'Callagan, "an' good luck to ye for that spache."

"You saw that man, the old gentleman, who was in the parlour when we first went in ?" said Father Ryan, addressing himself to Colonel Jack and Mr. Baintree.

"Most certainly we did," they both answered.

"That is Mr. Timothy Dabblebrush, the celebrated artist," said the priest.

"I never heard of him," answered the colonel. "But that is not to be wondered at, seeing that I know very little about art or its professors. Is he one of Ireland's famous artists, then ?"

"He is an Englishman, only settled here, but he was born in England."

"Well, if you've got anything to tell us about him, out with it," said Mr. Baintree. "We are tiled in here for the night, and have nothing to do but to amuse ourselves as best we can."

Thus encouraged, Mr. Ryan gave his companions the following sketch of the gentleman in question.

CHAPTER CXXV.

MR. RYAN'S NARRATIVE.

"Now, I must observe on the outset of my narrative," said the Irish priest, "that it is not an Irish story I am about to tell you; the honest artist whom we have seen some hour or so ago is a man of great talent and renown in his profession, of which he was always proud to acknowledge he was a member. He had laboured and studied much, and though not born of one of the most opulent families, still, through considerable exertion and perseverance, he had, by the time he was sixty, amassed a sufficient sum, as he would philosophically remark, to support a wife; for be it known that Mr. Timothy Dabblebrush was a right down bachelor up to that period. He then led to the altar a 'young and blooming bride.'

"Mr. Timothy had always been a man of prudence (at least so he wished to be considered), and did not admire the principle of coupling off too early; but though a sound philosopher on that point, still he forgot that "young wives, like changing winds, their power display, by shifting points, and varying day by day." Not that I mean to impeach, in the slightest degree, the fidelity of Mrs. Timothy, or to hint even, that Mr. Timothy himself was wrong, because Mr. Timothy had lived a life of strict chastity, and single blessedness, up to the period of his matrimonial alliance. Mr. Timothy was a man of good conduct and integrity, and above all, a man of affluence, and therefore, as Mrs. Timothy saw all those sterling qualities, and had repeatedly vowed that he was the only man on whom she had deigned to bestow an approving glance, it was not likely that Mr. Timothy had united himself to one, for whom (in after years) he might have reason to sigh.

Having proceeded so far, it will be seen that Mr. Timothy Dabblebrush was a married man, and proud, too, he was of the appellation, as it was not unusual for him (when sauntering from his bed-chamber of a morning) to exclaim, that he really thought he was the happiest man in existence—not forgetting, at the same time, to observe, in an under key, that, although so happy, yet he was morally inclined to think he should be happier still, if the scene of his bliss were graced by the smiles of a little son and heir; but these ideas would soon be over-ruled by his questioning the probability of such a thing ever being the case, as they had already been married for two years.

Mr. Timothy, as I have before remarked, was a man of honest principles, and morals indisputable; and he was a man altogether of the most unsophisticated habits, and still pursued his daily toils with equally as much energy and perseverance as he had done even before his happy marriage.

Mrs. Timothy was the *mignonne* of both her mamma and papa (who, it must be understood, were retailers in tripe), in consequence of which it did not fail to disturb their peace of mind for some weeks, nay months, after she had been made the happy Mrs Timothy Dabblebrush—not because they thought that her happiness was at stake, but solely on account of the sacrifice they presumed she had made, by tying herself to one whose years were so considerably in advance of her own. His circumstances were never for a moment questioned, his affluence being so well known, which in some degree compensated for the very spiteful inroad the old gentleman had made in their domicile. Concluding, therefore, that Mrs. Timothy was perfectly pleased with her bargain, it is nothing but natural for one to suppose that her youthful husband, and her parents in law, were happy also.

In order, however, to avoid being too prolix in the description of Mr. and Mrs. Timothy Dabblebrush, we shall but slightly turn again to the subject of my hero, just hinting, as I proceed, that Mr. Timothy (as I previously remarked) was a man of reputation, and a man also of great respectability; at least, so I should judge, from the fact of his renting a large establishment, where I cannot exactly call to mind; but certain it is, that it was a house, and containing, perhaps, ten or twelve rooms, three or four of which he contrived to let out to single juvenile lodgers.

There was a room, too, by itself, which overtopped all the others; and this garret, for such it was, being somewhat large and lofty, appeared to be the favourite place of Mr. Timothy Dabblebrush to carry on his daily avocations.

Mr. Timothy, too, was an artist exceedingly partial to sketching scenes of rusticity, and, consequently, it was not unusual for him, during the summer season, to take a solitary tour, for months together, round the suburban parts of our metropolis, in order that he might carry out his ideas to their greatest and fullest extent; and it was during one of these trips that Mr. Timothy Dabblebrush was seen bringing his little bark towards the margin of the lake, being, as we for a moment or two imagine, somewhat fatigued with his day's work.

It might have been another reason or purpose that induced Mr. Timothy to take this precipitate step; and it might have been, at the same time, on account of the gloomy appearance of the sky, and not impossibility of there being a smart shower of rain, which, to say the least, if at this very critical period such a disaster did occur, it would not only considerably disturb his well-regulated peace of mind, but, possibly, somewhat destroy the produce of his day's labour, for it was intended for an immense painting, and quite unlikely that such a thing could be put into his coat pocket.

Bearing, therefore, all such possibilities in mind, Mr. Timothy first looked here, and then there—then above, and then below—till at length he began to doubt whether or not it would rain, and then afterwards openly confessed to himself that he really thought it would: so that, in order to come to a full determination on the point, he fixed his oars at the stem and stern of his boat, and then very composedly brought himself to a perpendicular position. His spectacles (which were a pair of large green ones) were now taken off and wiped; being, as quickly replaced upon his nose; then, like Phaeton, when startled by the approaching thunderbolt from Jupiter, for setting the heavens on fire, he stretched forth his gaze towards the dusky sky. Here a few moments elapsed, when there came such a flash of forked lightning, that, without any notice, cruelly prostrated the lean and lanky form of poor Mr. Timothy on the bottom of his little boat.

Being nearly killed by this sudden commotion in the heavens, he had only sufficient time to raise himself to witness a similar flash, but followed by a heavy and deafening peal of thunder.

"Hollo! help there!" cried out the timerous Mr. Timothy, as he beheld a man in the distance; "help me"—beckoning at the same time for the man to approach—but here the rain came down in such torrents, that he foolishly thought the best thing he could do was to take care of his painting, and not caring exactly what he did, instantly pulled off his coat (the only one he had on), and carefully wrapping it up—applying himself the next moment to the unfastening of the boat—but the water, like poor Mr. Timothy's mind, being somewhat disturbed, kept incessantly splashing him in the face (much to his annoyance and vexation), and after considerable labour in his endeavour to disentangle the sculls, which he had forced in the mud to secure the boat, he at length made one desperate tug, and up it came; but so sudden was the shock that off flew his hat and spectacles, which were carried away by the wind for many yards, and in another moment he was capsized into the "boiling waters of the lake."

"Me—Me—, Mrs. Timothy," spluttered out the drowning artist— "Mrs. Timothy, Mrs. Timothy, I—I am"—and down he went, his mouth being at the same moment completely filled with mud and water. "Whe—, whe—, where's my painting," he bawled as he again came to the surface of the water. "Me—Me—Mrs.—," and down he popped his head again, entirely overpowered. Just, however, at this time the man whom he had hailed in the distance, arrived: and not being far from the water's edge, he soon extricated the unfortunate old gentleman from his perilous situation, when, after collecting his things together, hastened him to the nearest inn to be taken care of.

Leaving the host and his mistress to attend to the wants of the luckless Mr. Timothy, Dabblebrush, I shall now revert to the position in which Mrs. Timothy had been left, and the manner also in which she conducted herself and her establishment during the absence of her poor but faithful partner.

Now, some ladies have a great *penchant* for company, and particularly in the absence of their lords. Some ladies, too, have a most uncommon taste for the exhibition of their lungs when at all put out of temper; and some ladies also (in spite of all remonstrance) will not only do what they like, but by little manœuvring induce their husbands to do what they like also.

Mrs. Timothy now was not exactly a character of this description, but still there was a something in her conduct at times which certainly made it appear analogous, inasmuch, as she really was to a little extent wayward in her ideas, chiding, and withal, particularly partial to company; and I have authority for stating these peculiarities of Mrs. Timothy, partly from the fact of her having accepted of an invitation to a ball, once or twice in the absence of her Timothy, and also once or twice being seen to accept the arm of a young gentleman who had kindly offered (upon her quitting the ball-room) to see her home.

This, however, was a circumstance quite excusable and to be accounted for, inasmuch, as the young gentleman in question turned out, upon inquiry, to be her only and affectionate cousin.

Taking this, therefore, for granted, there could be no great objection or impropriety on the part of Mrs. Timothy, for acquiescing in this, particularly under existing circumstances—I mean, as Mr. Timothy was not there, to fill that office—and Mrs. Timothy seeing this, and feeling, too, that her cousin was somewhat an agreeable companion, was not by any means offended to hear that he had called now and then to inquire after the exact state of her health.

Considering, then, that Mrs. Timothy and her cousin became in time upon the most intimate terms of friendship, it was not at all out of the way to find him now and then mingling with a party of her young friends.

On one of those occasions, when every one was elated to the highest pitch of merriment, Mr. Walker, the penny postman, arrived, and, with the greatest *nonchalence* and *devil-mecarishness*, audacity knocked with such violence at the door, that he nearly frightened poor Mrs. Timothy and her party into fits; and then thrusting the letter under the bottom of the door, quite as quickly darted off. The servant, however, was soon on the spot, and spying the letter, instantly picked it up, and conveyed it forthwith to her mistress.

Mrs. Timothy, finding the letter sealed with a most laughable patch of black wax, and the edges being enveloped in mourning line, hastily withdrew, and breathlessly tearing it open, read as follows:—

"My dear Sophia,—Prepare my flannel drawers and nightcap with all possible dispatch, and from the time you receive this, keep the warming-pan constantly hot in my bed, for the day after to-morrow I shall be home for certain.

"Have a good fire in readiness, for the water—oh! the dreadful calamity!—has chilled, and nearly killed me.

"Until then, with every affection and esteem, I remain your fond and doting husband,—TIMOTHY."

Now, whether Mrs. Timothy imagined that his brain was at all defective when she had perused this strange, wild, and unsatisfactory effusion (stating neither where he was, where he had been, or what he had done), we are not prepared to state; suffice it, however, to observe, that no sooner had she conned its contents, than she calmly folded it together, and put it into the fire, remarking, as she again mournfully entered the apartment, "that her poor Timothy had been taken suddenly ill, and so serious was the attack, that it behoved her to leave town, and join him, if possible, early on the morrow."

The evening having passed away, though rather more indifferently than was anticipated, the company separated.

Next morning there was a most unusual scene in the street wherein resided Mr. and Mrs. Timothy, for, just as the church clock was chiming the three-quarter past seven, in rolled a very suspicious-looking vehicle, drawn by four horses, with out-riders to boot; ere they had proceeded far the chaise halted, and after a little inquiry, it made a dead stop at the house of Mr. Timothy Dabblebrush.

Now, as far as regards the mystery as to who this chaise was for, that was soon cleared up by the fact of the artist's wife being seen to rush from her domicile, full-dressed and blooming, followed close to her heels by her young cousin, who, after giving their instructions to the postillions, instantly sprang into the chaise, and were soon wheeled away and lost in the distance.

Such an occurrence as this was naturally quite sufficient to rouse any well thinking person to inquire who they were—what names, and above all, the nature of such proceeding. All these inquiries, as a matter of course, were nothing but natural. Now, as to who they were, and what were their names, that was soon answered; but as to what their object was, that was a problem not easily solved, thus, leaving them to ponder, question, doubt, and determine. We find Mrs. Timothy and her companion in a very short time dashing along one of the quiet little country villages, bordering on the south-side of a certain coast, and it being considered necessary by this time to have a change of horses and a little refreshment, it was determined at once to rein in their steeds, and drive gently up to the first inn on the roadside—proceeding somewhere about half-a-mile further, a snug little place presented itself to their view, and it was here that master, mistress, horses, and men soon found themselves partaking of some of the best things the place could afford.

Having refreshed themselves, Mrs. Timothy and her cousin now suggested the propriety of again proceeding on their journey ; but a sudden thought striking them, they forthwith called for pens, paper, and ink, and Mrs. Timothy, by her cousin's dictation, began to write to her husband in the following very peculiar and interesting strain :—

"My dear and ever affectionate Timothy,—I—" but here they were somewhat interrupted by a pair of green spectacles falling rather heavily from off the nose of an old gentleman upon the table, at which he had for some time been very quietly and unobservedly seated, conning an old newspaper, but Mrs. Timothy and her cousin, not taking the trouble to look round, again commenced their epistle :—

"My dear and ever affectionate Timothy—I trust sincerely you will pardon me for taking the present step."

"No, no!' laughingly, exclaimed her cousin, "that won't do, let us proceed again ; say it in an off-hand way, that you have taken nothing but your white satin dress for the occasion, and a few other articles of the same description, together with a few trinkets and bank notes, which, being entirely your own, you hope he will not —"

"D—n it, what do you mean?" vociferated an elderly gentleman, springing from his seat, in a paroxysm of passion, on hearing what had passed. "I—I—I'll be—here, landlord! waiter! constables!" And having brought himself by this time near to where they were seated, with one leap he totteringly threw himself completely on the back of his apparent rival.

The suddenness of the transaction altogether so flabbergasted the cousin of Mrs. Timothy, that it quite disabled him to demand even an explanation of his assailant; so that, first twisting this way, and then that, he at last lost all equilibrium, and they both tumbled into the middle of the room together, with a tremendous crash.

"Murder!" screamed Mrs. Timothy, "murder!"

"Zounds!" cried the landlord, as he hurriedly approached the scene of confusion. "Zounds, men, what are you doing there together ; get up, get up."

But the old gentleman was hugging his victim so unmercifully, that the only answer or satisfaction obtained, was loud cries of "Let me go," intermingled with pitiable snorting and puffing from the old gentleman : independent, however, of which a most awful demoniacal grin was playing upon his sallow and withered countenance. At length a desperate struggle ensued, and, after many laughable rolls, staggers, and flounderings, the old gentleman was quietly deposited under a table, being minus his hat, his wig, and spectacles.

The affair having thus terminated in favour of the younger party, he instantly joined his fair companion, Mrs. Timothy, who had but just recovered from a slight faint, and being determined upon having an explanation for this rude behaviour, significantly approached the old gentleman for that purpose ; but ere they had made one right down good look at him, to their horror and vexation, they discovered that the fallen hero was no less a personage than the poor chapfallen artist, Mr. Timothy Dabblebrush. For a moment or two each party stood perfectly aghast ; and poor Mrs. Timothy, knowing her *innocence* so well, and the *good intent* she had for going to the place, immediately on discovering the fact, darted to her husband, and implanting *an affectionate kiss* upon his quivering lips, threw out her arms, and violently exclaimed :

"Is it you, Timothy ? Oh, heavens ! then have I found you at last !"

Behold now, then, this poor old man, with glassy eyes and trembling limbs, raised to his feet by the hands of his immaculate and wrongly-suspected sposa.

Behold him, as the wreck of misfortune, fated, for a time, to undergo at an age of sixty-five, all the pangs of jealousy (for such it was), and ill-requited love.

How hard, indeed, has been his fate ! He had suspected his wife (that doating, fond wife) of inconstancy—of her eloping in his absence—vile, perfidious suspicion that it was. But let me not dilate any further on this painful affair, for I am sure you cannot for a moment suppose that amiable, that kind, that affectionate soul, Mrs. Timothy (after the description of her estimable qualities), guilty of the slightest impropriety, under any circumstances ; and now, like a faithful historian, I shall conclude my little narrative by remarking that, however ill-used, as the old gentleman thought he had been, with all the patience of Father Job did he attend to the explanation of both parties ; and quite as patiently, too, did they listen to his, and, everything proving satisfactory, with the greatest of cordiality and kindness shook hands, forgave and forgot.

"And no wonder," said Father Ryan, "you will see from this little episode that matrimonial life is not all honey."

"Was that the same party we saw in the

parlour of the house where we met our friend, Michael Jebb?" enquired Colonel Jack.

"The very same," answered the priest.

"He seemed pleased enough, then," said our hero; "does he live with the immaculate Mrs. Timothy, now?"

"Oh, dear yes, and they are supposed to be the happiest couple for miles round."

"More happy than our friends, Mr. and Mrs. O'Flake?"

"Hist!" said the priest. "It's there that you beat me. Oh, but O'Flake is a terrible fellow—a most terrible fellow. How did you get on with him? But I'll not ask."

"We got into a row, that's all," answered Colonel Jack.

"Oh, I am not surprised at that; it's no more than I expected. He is a rough customer."

"Your countryman may be rough at times," said Miss Cary. "No matter for that, they have warm hearts, and are very hospitable and kind to strangers—at least I have every reason to say so. This is the first time I have ever been in Ireland, and I assure you I am much pleased with my reception."

Most of the gentleman bound in acknowledge of this, and Mr. Baintree said—"that he was happy to have met with a lady of so much intelligence and affability." At the same time adding that two persons had favoured the company with a story—the one a very graphic sketch of an episode in her own life, and the other, Father Ryan, with a somewhat comic version of the woes of an ill-used artist—he supposed he must add his quota to the evening's entertainment; "but," said Mr. Baintree, "you must know that I am a lawyer, and there is very little romance about gentlemen of my cloth; however, I will just detail to you what actually occurred to me some few years ago."

"By all means, hear! hear!" exclaimed those present. "Proceed."

Mr. Baintree then gave to his friends the following sketch—

CHAPTER CXXVI.

THE VAMPIRE—A FRAGMENT.

"In the year 17—" said Mr. Baintree, "having for some time determined on a journey through countries not hitherto much frequented by travellers, I set out, accompanied by a friend, whom I shall designate by the name of Augustus Darvell. He was a few years my elder, and a man of considerable fortune and ancient family—advantages which an extensive capacity prevented him alike from undervaluing or overrating.

Some peculiar circumstances in his private history had rendered him to me an object of attention, of interest, and even of regard, which neither the reserve of his manners, nor occasional indications of an inquietude at times nearly approaching to alienation of mind, could extinguish.

I was yet young in life, which I had begun early; but my intimacy with him was of a recent date; we had been educated at the same schools and university; but his progress through these had preceded mine, and he had been deeply initiated into what is called the world, while I was yet in my noviciate. While thus engaged, I had heard much both of his past and present life; and although in these accounts there were many and irreconcileable contradictions, I could still gather from the whole that he was a being of no common order, and one who, whatever pains he might take to avoid remark, would still be remarkable. I had cultivated his acquaintance subsequently, and endeavoured to obtain his friendship, but this last appeared to be unattainable; whatever affections he might have possessed seemed now, some to have been extinguished, and others to be concentred; that his feelings were acute, I had sufficient opportunities of observing; for, although he could control, he could not altogether disguise them; still he had a power of giving to one passion the appearance of another in such a manner that it was difficult to define the nature of what was working within him; and the expressions of his features would vary so rapidly, though slightly, that it was useless to trace them to their sources. It was evident that he was a prey to some cureless disquiet; but whether it arose from ambition, love, remorse, grief, from one or all of these, or merely from a morbid temperament akin to disease, I could not discover; there were circumstances alleged, which might have justified the application to each of these causes; but as I have before said, these were so contradictory and contradicted, that none could be fixed upon with accuracy. Where there is mistery, it is generally supposed that there must also be evil. I know not how this may be, but in him there certainly was the one, though I could not ascertain the extent of the other—and felt loth, as far as regarded himself, to believe in its existence. My advances were received with sufficient coldness; but I was young, and not easily discouraged, and at length succeeded in obtaining, to a certain degree, that commonplace intercourse and moderate confidence of common and every-day concerns, created and cemented by similarity of pursuit and frequency of meeting, which is called intimacy, or friendship, according to the ideas of him who uses those words to express them.

Darvell had already travelled extensively; and to him I applied for information with regard to the conduct of my intended journey. It was my secret wish that he might be prevailed on to accompany me; it was also a probable hope, founded upon the shadowy restlessness which I observed in him, and to which the animation which he appeared to feel on such subjects, and his apparent indifference to all by which he was more immediately surrounded, gave fresh strength. This wish I first hinted, and then expressed; his answer, though I had partly expected it, gave me all the pleasure of surprise—he consented; and, after the requisite arrangements, we commenced our voyage. After journeying through the various countries of Europe, our attention was turned towards the East, according to our original destination;

No. 86.

and it was in my progress through those regions that the incident occurred upon which will turn what I may have to relate.

The constitution of Darvell, which must, from his appearance, have been in early life more than usually robust, had been for some time gradually giving way, without the intervention of any apparent disease; he had neither cough nor hectic, yet he became daily more enfeebled; his habits were temperate, and he neither declined nor complained of fatigue, yet he was evidently wasting away. He became more and more silent and sleepless, and at length so seriously altered, that my alarm grew proportionate to what I conceived to be his danger.

We had determined, on our arrival at Smyrna, on an excursion to the ruins of Ephesus and Sardis, from which I endeavoured to dissuade him in his present state of indisposition—but in vain. There appeared to be an oppression on his mind, and a solemnity in his manner, which ill corresponded with this eagerness to proceed on what I regarded as a mere party of pleasure, little suited to a valetudinarian; but I opposed him no longer—and in a few days we set off together, accompanied only by a serrugee and a single janizary.

We had passed halfway towards the remains of Ephesus, leaving behind us the more fertile environs of Smyrna, and were entering upon that wild and tenantless track through the marshes and defiles which lead to the few huts yet lingering over the broken columns of Diana—the roofless walls of expelled Christianity, and the still more recent but complete desolation of the abandoned mosques—when the sudden and rapid illness of my companion obliged us to halt at a Turkish cemetery, the turbaned tombstones of which were the sole indication that human life had ever been a sojourner in this wilderness. The only caravansera we had seen was left some hours behind us, not a vestige of a town or even cottage was within sight or hope, and this "city of the dead" appeared to be the sole refuge for my unfortunate friend, who seemed on the verge of becoming the last of its inhabitants.

In this situation, I looked round for a place where he might most conveniently repose;—contrary to the usual aspect of Mahometan burial-grounds, the cypresses were in this few in number, and these thinly scattered over its extent; the tombstones were mostly fallen, and worn with age. Upon one of the most considerable of these, and beneath one of the most spreading trees, Darvell supported himself, in a half-reclining posture, with great difficulty. He asked for water. I had some doubts of our being able to find any, and prepared to go in search of it with hesitating despondency—but he desired me to remain; and turning to Suleiman, our janizary, who stood by us, smoking with great tranquillity, he said—

"Suleiman, verbana su," (i. e. bring some water,) and went on describing the spot where it was to be found with great minuteness, at a small well for camels, a few hundred yards to the right. The janizary obeyed.

I said to Darvell, "How did you know this?"

He replied, "From our situation; you must perceive that this place was once inhabited, and could not have been so without springs. I have also been here before."

"You have been here before!—How came you never to mention this to me? and what could you be doing in a place where no one would remain a moment longer than they could help it?"

To this question I received no answer. In the meantime Suleiman returned with the water, leaving the serrugee and the horses at the fountain. The quenching of his thirst had the appearance of reviving him for a moment; and I conceived hopes of his being able to proceed, or at least to return, and I urged the attempt. He was silent, and appeared to be collecting his spirits for an effort to speak. He began—

"This is the end of my journey, and of my life—I came here to die; but I have a request to make, a command—for such my last words must be. You will observe it?"

"Most certainly; but have better hopes."

"I have no hopes, nor wishes, but this—conceal my death from every human being.'

"I hope there will be no occasion; that you will recover, and—"

"Peace!—it must be so; promise this."

"I do."

"Swear it by all that—"

He here dictated an oath of great solemnity.

"There is no occasion for this. I will observe your request; and to doubt me is—"

"It cannot be helped; you must swear."

I took the oath; it appeared to relieve him. He removed a seal ring from his finger, on which were some Arabic characters, and presented it to me. He proceeded—

"On the ninth day of the month, at noon precisely (what month you please, but this must be the day), you must fling this ring into the salt springs which run into the Bay of Eleusis; the day after, at the same hour, you must repair to the ruins of the Temple of Ceres, and wait one hour."

"Why?"

"You will see."

"The ninth day of the month, you say?"

"The ninth."

As I observed that the present was the ninth day of the month, his countenance changed, and he paused. As he sate, evidently becoming more feeble, a stork, with a snake in her beak, perched upon a tombstone near us; and without devouring her prey, appeared to be steadfastly regarding us. I know not what impelled me to drive it away, but the attempt was useless; she made a few circles in the air, and returned exactly to the same spot. Darvell pointed to it, and smiled; he spoke—I know not whether to himself or to me—but the words were only—

"'Tis well!"

"What is well? what do you mean?"

"No matter; you must bury me here this evening, and exactly where that bird is now perched. You know the rest of my injunctions."

He then proceeded to give me several directions as to the manner in which his death might be best concealed. After these were finished, he exclaimed—

" You perceive that bird ?"

" Certainly."

" And the serpent writhing in her beak ?"

" Doubtless ; there is nothing uncommon in it ; it is her natural prey. But it is odd that she does not devour it."

" He smiled in a ghastly manner, and said, faintly—

" It is not yet time !"

As he spoke, the stork flew away. My eyes followed it for a moment, it could hardly be longer than ten might be counted. I felt Darvell's weight, as it were, increase upon my shoulder, and, turning to look upon his face, perceived that he was dead !

I was shocked with the sudden certainty which could not be mistaken. His countenance in a few minutes became nearly black. I should have attributed so rapid a change to poison, had I not been aware that he had no opportunity of receiving it unperceived. The day was declining, the body was rapidly altering, and nothing remained but to fulfil his request. With the aid of Suleiman's ataghan and my own sabre, we scooped a shallow grave upon the spot which Darvell had indicated ; the earth easily gave way having already received some Mahometan tenant. We dug as deeply as the time permitted us, and, throwing the dry earth upon all that remained of the singular being so lately departed, we cut a few ends of greener turf from the less withered soil around us, and laid them upon his sepulchre.

Between astonishment and grief I was tearless.

" And did you keep your promise ?" inquired Colonel Jack.

" Yes, I cast the ring in the salt springs as he desired, and after this I waited in the ruins of the Temple of Ceres.

" With what result ?"

" A man came ; a stranger to me. He thanked me on behalf of Darvell, and said that all was well.

" And what followed ?"

" I went away, having performed my mission ; and as I did so, strange thoughts rushed through my brain. I was told afterwards that my friend and companion was a Vampire."

" Good heavens ! do such beings exist ?" exclaimed the priest, crossing himself.

" We have most of us heard of such things," said Colonel Jack ; " for my own part, I never believed in the existence of such fabulous beings. One's mind revolts at such monsters, and we are apt to comfort ourselves with the assurance that such things are in reality fabulous."

" What I have related actually occurred, that I can vouch for," said Mr. Baintree.

" And did you never see or hear anything of him afterwards ?" inquired Father Ryan.

" Never from that day to the present moment," replied Mr. Baintree.

" A friend of mine, a Mr. Osborne, was mentioning to me a somewhat similar circumstance," said Miss Cary.

" Mr. Osborne ?" exclaimed Colonel Jack ; " not Mr. Henry Osborne ?"

" Yes," said Miss Cary.

" Do you know him then ?"

" Yes, perfectly well, and his amiable wife and their adopted daughter."

" You astonish me !" exclaimed our hero. " Why Henry Osborne is an old and valued friend of mine. I have known him since his boyhood."

Miss Cary was in her turn astonished, and she stared at Colonel Jack with so great an expression of surprise, that the latter could not refrain from bursting out in a loud laugh.

" Well this is singular !" he exclaimed. " Why we are old friends, or rather you are a friend's friend, which is much the same thing, madam ; it gives me infinite pleasure to have become acquainted with you."

" The feeling is reciprocal," answered the lady, with a smile.

" And how long have you known my friend Osborne ?"

" Oh, for some years ; I knew him when at Oxford, when he was a despairing suitor for the hand of the fair Honora Langford. The Langfords I had known some time before that. I became acquainted with Mr. Langford through the family of the Briggs'. Did you ever hear Miss Langford mention the name of the latter ?"

" No, never."

" They used to be very intimate at one time, but afterwards there was a coldness between them."

" The Briggs family. I never heard of them."

" Well, for your entertainment I will give you a sketch of them—that is, if you do not think me a foolish, gossiping old woman," said Miss Cary, with a comical expression of countenance.

" Very far from it, my dear madam ; I see in you a lady of acute perceptions, and more than that, you are endowed with a graphic power of description."

The lady made a sort of mock reverence as the colonel passed this compliment on her, she then commenced her narrative of the Briggs family, which we shall reserve for another chapter.

———

CHAPTER CXXVII.

THE BRIGGS FAMILY. AS SKETCHED BY "AUNT CARY."

"THE people I am going to tell you about are the types of a very large section of the community," said Miss Cary ; "society, as you most of you know, is divided into classes, each of a distinctive character, and differing in very many degrees from one another.

"Now, I must tell you that in 1740, the accession of the Honourable Theophilus Briggs to the property of a maternal uncle, in a central English country, caused a prodigious excitement at the time.

"Mr. Briggs was the younger brother of an Irish peer, and having been previously limited to a very small income for the support of a large family, he had repaired to the continent in order to educate his daughters with less expense than would have been incurred at home.

This circumstance, however, did not transpire, and he entered upon his estate with all the *eclat* of his connection with an old baronial family, unalloyed by the stigma of previous poverty.

"The eldest of Mr. Briggs' growing-up daughters had reached her twenty-second year ; the youngest was about fifteen ; there was a baby besides, and three or four sons. All the girls were remarkably handsome ; their beauty was of that striking and attractive kind which is recognized at once, and cannot be disputed. The three elder girls were out, the fourth coming out, and the two others ready to come out whenever a marriage in the family should afford a vacant seat in Mrs. Briggs' carriage.

"Thirty-two years ago, the quiet society of the English counties was comparatively little acquainted with foreign manners. The admiration, therefore, excited by the Misses Briggs, was not unmingled with surprise. Their natural vivacity, aided by a French education, rendered them very different from the pattern young ladies of their circle.

"Fortunately, they were very good-tempered and obliging ; and though they waltzed to excess, and wore shorter petticoats than ever had been seen before, it was only the very rigid and censorious who ventured any disparaging remark. Mr. Briggs commenced his career in England by keeping open house. He made no invidious distinctions respecting his visitors, receiving all comers with a hearty hospitality worthy of old times.

"The family took possession of the estate in the month of August, and immediately a scene of festivity commenced, which lasted without intermission until the return of the season called them to London.

"Such riding, and driving, and picnicing to every place in the neighbourhood where there was anything to be seen ! It was thought nothing to go fifteen or twenty miles to a ball ; and the intention of the Briggs's to be present was sure to congregate all the beauty, fashion, and bachelorhood of the vicinity.

"The place in which public assemblies were held at Singleton, at the period of which I am speaking, was a building erected over the market, and rather oddly constructed—no unusual circumstance in a country town. It had at first been approached by an outside-stair ; but this being found very inconvenient, another entrance had been opened under cover, and the company now walked through the butcher's shambles into a small dark vestibule, which led, in the first instance, to a large kitchen, in which, on market-days, the farmers usually dined from the smoking joints roasted at immense fireplaces at either end. On ball-nights, this apartment was dedicated to the tea-kettles which supplied boiling water for that beverage which cheers but not inebriates, together with negus and lemonade, forming the liquid refreshments provided on such occasions.

"A gloomy, ill-lighted staircase led to a suite of four apartments, one being a small ante-chamber, in which stood the persons who received the tickets of the subscribers ; the largest of the remaining three formed the ball-room, the two others being dedicated to tea and cards.

"All were dismal enough, being panelled with dark wood, or hung with dingy paper, and badly illuminated by a few very old-fashioned chandeliers, and girandoles, made of an uncouth mixture of glass and brass, and calculated to hold a very small number of candles.

"In 1740, the balls at Singleton had fallen off considerably.

"They had been for the most part limited to the genteeler sort among the townspeople who were eligible to be subscribers ; and in consequence of the lame manner in which quadrilles were executed, contra-dances had maintained their ascendancy upon the floors long after they had been exploded from every other town.

"Six or eight lugubrious-looking couples would take their places in the centre of the dismal ball-room, and go through the evolutions in that spiritless manner, which a paucity of numbers upon any occasion of hilarity generally produces.

"The arrival of the Briggs family in the county changed the aspect of affairs.

"Mr. Briggs, senior, to oblige his daughters, consented to take the office of steward upon himself ; and in consequence, a vast concourse of people were collected together—crowds which brought to mind the good old times in the remembrance of the oldest inhabitants of the place.

"Previously to this era, the Misses Tollemache had led the fashion in the neighbourhood of Singleton.

"They were very fine girls; very correct in their deportment, and had the character of being proud and difficult

"Hitherto an attendance at the balls at Singleton had been considered too great a condescension by these young ladies; and their absence kept many others away, few liking to go to a place which the Tollemaches despised.

"A spirit of rivalry now operated as a stimulant, and determined them to take the field against the Briggs's.

"The latter family were at first wholly unconscious of the jealous feelings which they excited; they entered the ball-room solely in pursuit of pleasure, and gave themselves up to the unrestrained indulgence of the gaiety of their hearts.

"They were constantly surrounded by all the beaux, while the Tollemaches were comparatively neglected, being only asked to dance by those who had failed in securing a hand of the Misses Briggs.

"Three of the four sisters—for the one who was coming out in London had come out in the country—were nearly equally the objects of admiration; but Miss Briggs, the eldest, was universally pronounced to bear away the palm, and to her standard the *elite* of the male portion of the assembly flocked.

"Amongst many others, she attracted the great man of the neighbourhood, Sir Charles Dorrington, a young baronet of large fortune, who was supposed to be looking out for a wife. This gentleman had paid some attention to the elder Miss Tollemache, and had been universally set down as her admirer; but before matters had gone too far, the appearance of Miss Briggs changed the spirit of his dream, and he now exhibited himself as the devoted slave of the new beauty.

"The card-players of the balls at Singleton had been, time out of mind, subjected to two distinct species of annoyance—the one being the smoke, which, when the wind set in a particular direction, poured down the chimney, whether there was any fire in the apartment or not; the other, the irruptions of young ladies with their partners, who would sit down and talk, sometimes in a loud key, about nonsense, which distracted the attention of all the whist-players, and sometimes in a low tone, which would occasion some very inquisitive old lady or gentleman, anxious to catch the purport of the conversation, to revoke.

"Upon the present evening, Miss Briggs and Sir Charles Dorrington proved the greatest delinquents. After almost every dance, they bolted in, seated themselves behind the door, and talked incessantly.

"Some people averred that an offer was certainly made and accepted; but as the parties had never met before, this seemed premature.

"Miss Tollemache looked on with suppressed rage. The tide of popularity ran so strongly in favour of the Briggs's, that prudence dictated a pacific appearance, since any show of hostility would have been attributed to jealousy; and, therefore, the Misses Tollemache admitted at once, that the Briggs were very fine girls, with exceedingly enviable spirits.

"'It was certainly merely a matter of taste,' they continued, 'but, for their part, they liked less display; these foreign manners did not quite suit them.'

"The Misses Tollemache had a brother, with whom they waltzed in turn; thus showing off their figures without incurring the odium which attached itself to those who were less scrupulous in the choice of a partner.

"Young Tollemache, who would rather have danced with one of the Briggs, thought the duty a bore, and wished that his mother would take the girls to France, to get rid of their starch; but Lady Jane Tollemache loudly expressed her determination that her daughters should never make such an exhibition of themselves.

"She drew a small circle around her, who fully concurred in her views of propriety, and who felt assured, that the example of a few persons like herself would check the progress of that general licence which threatened to change the face of society.

"The balls at Singleton were generally over by two o'clock, in the morning; it seemed quite impossible to sustain life till a later hour upon tea, bread and butter, and weak negus. At an early hour in the evening, Sir Charles Dorrington had suggested the scheme of a supper at a neighbouring inn. The Briggs's eagerly acceded to the plan, and a few choice spirits were collected for the purpose. The Tollemache family were invited as a matter of form; but Lady Jane gave a dignified refusal, and looked daggers at her son, who, having packed up his sisters in the family-coach, ran to offer his arm to Emily Briggs's, who skipped across the street and over the gutters in her white satin shoes, with some flimsy thing of a shawl over her head. It was reported next day that the Misses Briggs's sang after supper, which, though allowable in the mansion of a friend, was deemed highly improper at a public inn. The party, however, was a very joyous one, and it led to the proposal of a ball to be given by the bachelors at the same place.

So brilliant an affair had never been heard of at Singleton before. The Briggs's were the queens of the evening, while the eldest daughter might be called the empress; their dresses had come direct from Paris, and were unlike anything that had been seen in England before, while it was remarked that the eternal white satin of the Tollemaches had a very heavy appearance. If any doubt could have remained upon the minds of the spectators respecting the intention of Sir Charles, they were now dissipated. It was very certain that he desired nothing so much as to become the husband of the beautiful girl, whom, against all the rules of etiquette, he led to the supper-room, and seated at his right hand at the top of the table, above all the matrons and dowagers of the party. Henrietta Tollemache almost made up her mind to the loss of the young baronet, and by everybody the marriage of the happy pair was looked upon as a settled thing.

No such marriage, however, took place. Miss Briggs's, having the vision of a ducal baronet flitting before her eyes, refused the baronet. Sir Charles, though at first disposed to give way to despair, consoled himself with the idea, that time and assiduity would work a change in his favour. He was not aware of the ambition which lurked in the bosom of the lady of his affections, while she, satisfied with having assured him of her determination, considered herself at liberty to receive attentions paid under, what she chose to consider, a full knowledge of the state of the case. Mrs Briggs's, who was of an indolent disposition, and had no voice in the family, regretted this rejection. With so many daughters, she thought it a good thing to get one off her hands, and was of opinion that Geraldine's marriage with Sir Charles would save a great deal of trouble. Other offers were made, and refused; and some of the cavaliers, either more or less sensitive than the baronet, withdrew upon the failure of their hopes; the remainder, assured of the consequences of hazarding a proposal, contented themselves with laughing, and talking, and flirting, and in this manner time sped upon its lightest pinions. The shooting-season brought quantities of young men to Mr Briggs's manors, to the great detriment of the game, and the no small diminution of the contents of the cellar. Everybody went out in the morning, either to knock down the hares and the partridges, or to lunch with the sportsmen in some approved spot. Riding and driving occupied the remainder of the day until dinner, and in the evening there was music and dancing. With the addition of the female visitors, the Briggs's could always get up a ball without extraneous aid: and the arrival of Christmas brought with it fresh sets of company, and

fresh methods of beguiling time. Meanwhile, Mr Briggs's grown-up sons thought themselves entitled to live in the style becoming their expectations. One, who was with his regiment, kept up a very gay establishment; and the eldest being the heir, divided his time between Melton Mowbray and home, with occasional visits to distant parts of the country, in which good hunting was to be had.

"At length Easter arrived, and the Briggs's took their departure for London, leaving the county in a state of quietude which it had not enjoyed for many a long day. Intelligence of the festivities in which the family had been engaged in the great metropolis, was duly forwarded to Singleton through the medium of the fashionable papers.

"The coteries of the town learned that four of the Misses Briggs had been presented at court; and though rather puzzled by the mystical language in which the account of their dresses was conveyed, understood that they made a very brilliant appearance. Frequent mention was subsequently made of the beautiful sisters; and in the course of a few weeks, the following announcement showed that the expectations entertained by the family of an alliance with the peerage were not without foundation:— 'Married at St George's Church, Hanover Square, by the Hon. and Rev. the Dean, &c., Lord Viscount Rossallan, &c., to Letitia Eugenia, third daughter of the Honourable Augustus Theophilus Braggs, of —— Hall, in ——shire.'

"This was rather a surprise to the good folks of the country, since, according to their unsophisticated notions, Letitia Briggs seemed to be the least amiable of the family. There was an expression in her countenance which might be taken for a sneer; she had not the vivacity which characterised her sisters, and there were some persons who went so far as to say, that they thought her a little stupid, and rather ill-tempered. How it so happened that the qualities of her mind which were thus stigmatised in the country; procured her more favour in London than was accorded to the other Misses Briggs's, they could not make out.

"In the simplicity of their hearts, the Singletonians felt quite assured that, as the third daughter had become a viscountess, the eldest would be a marchioness at least, and might look up to a ducal coronet. Geraldine, unfortunately, thought the same, and the illusion was fostered by the attentions of a young duke, which, however, never came to anything; and at the end of the London season, Mr. Briggs returned into the country, with all his family about him, Lady Rossallan alone excepted.

"Soon after their arrival, Lady Jane Tollemache discovered, greatly to her vexation, that her only son George, who was just of age, had engaged himself to Emily Briggs. She had perceived a good deal of dancing and flirting going on between the parties during the spring; but as she had given her opinion pretty strongly regarding the young lady, she concluded that an only son, so well brought up, and so fully warned respecting the consequences of such an alliance, would never think of doing so mad a thing.

"She was mistaken; and George proclaimed that he had arrived at the age of indiscretion, by leading Emily to the altar, which proved a severe blow to Lady Jane and her daughters.

"Sir Charles Dorrington was observed to be as attentive as ever to Miss Briggs; but with the success of Lady Rossallan before her eyes, and a young duke in her head, she could not be prevailed upon to listen to him.

"The recess passed away nearly in the same manner that the preceding one had done; the two younger girls came out, so that there were still four Misses Briggs to be seen at the balls and races; Geraldine, however, continuing to be considered the flower of the family.

"The next London season produced nothing, at least nothing of consequence; the young duke who had been so attentive, married somebody else, but his place was supplied by an earl, who, it was thought, would certainly propose.

"This nobleman had promised to spend a part of the shooting season at Brigg Hall; consequently, there could be no hope for Sir Charles Dorrington; and, either tired of his pursuit, or convinced of the utter heartlessness of its object, he withdrew his pretensions. In a mood of mind to be grateful for the flattering conviction that he had been long favourably regarded by another, he fell in with Henrietta Tollemache, who very adroitly drew him into matrimony.

"The earl did not fulfil his engagement, and Miss Briggs, for the first time in her life, found herself without any professed dangler.

"She determined to make good use of the following season; but it brought out some formidable competitors. Lady Rossallan was on the continent, and the circle which George Tollemache drew around him, did not offer anything of sufficient consequence to induce her to relinquish the chances of another season.

"People now began to reckon the number of years during which Miss Briggs had been out.

"Her sister Stella had deemed it full time to marry, and, failing to procure a suitable establishment, accepted the hand of an officer who held a high command in a South American service, and who, having been well introduced, and covered with orders, had passed himself off as a very great personage at Nataxcampaia, or some such place.

"Mr. Briggs's estate was now discovered to be not quite equal to the demands made upon it. The family, therefore, not finding it convenient to return to the country, went to rusticate at Boulogne.

"A winter in Paris was subsequently tried, and some very ruinous expenditure incurred, and, after various chances and changes, the family settled at Cheltenham.

"It happened, shortly afterwards, that Miss Briggss, in paying a visit to her sister, Mrs. Tollemache, came to Singleton by the stage coach, and, while waiting for the carriage, which her brother-in-law had promised to send for her, gazed upon the site of the theatre of her former glories.

"The site only remained, for, in the progress of improvement, the market-place and the clumsy building above it had disappeared, the former being removed to another part of the town.

"Some bitter feelings passed across her mind, and, turning from the window, her eyes encountered a looking-glass. The form reflected there was certainly very different from that which, years before, had been displayed upon its surface. All its youth and freshness were gone—the face was haggard and careworn—the figure had lost it roundness—and she sighed as she reflected upon the waste of years, and the foolish ambition which had led her to despise the blessings within her reach.

"Her mortifications did not end here, for she was obliged to meet Sir Charles and Lady Dorrington very frequently, and many a bitter tear did she shed in secret over the wreck of all her hopes.

"On her return to Cheltenham, she found it impossible to settle down. The appearance of the house, its mean decayed furniture, bearing marks of the destructive propensities of many a former tenant, the apology for a man-servant, the ill-served dinner, and the difficulty of procuring fitting apparel for the parties, which still formed the sole amusement of her life, impressed her with the necessity of striking some bold stroke.

"There were still two sisters besides herself unmarried—one was a confirmed invalid, and upon whose account they were obliged to continue at Cheltenham; and another, the baby mentioned in a preceding paragraph, who had grown up into rather a fine girl, but very inferior in personal attractions to her elder sisters.

"This young person, who had never known the splendour formerly enjoyed by the family, was quite as eager after amusement as her sisters had been, and carried on the same sort of pursuits, though in a very limited sphere.

"During a visit to Lady Rossallan, Geraldine had succeeded in captivating a man of large property, and hopes which had long lain dormant, now revived. She was, unfortunately, obliged to return home before the affair could be settled, but was speedily followed by her admirer.

"He had been charmed by the spirit, elegance, and intelligence of Miss Briggs; but the sight of her youngest sister, who, though immeasurably inferior to what she had been, had now, with some resemblance, the advantages of youth and natural brilliancy, changed the object of his pursuit, and he made an offer to Elizabeth.

"Mr. Briggs, too happy to marry a daughter so well, gave his consent. The young lady had been brought up in a school in which self-interest was more considered than any finer sentiment; she, therefore, made no objection, and Geraldine was obliged to conceal her feelings of mortification as best she might.

"I cannot conclude the history of this Briggs family without expressing my deep regret, that in the superior spheres of English society the love of splendour and distinction should be so absorbing a passion. With all the advantages of the present state of society, it is to be feared that the more generous and unselfish feelings have yet but little play amongst us, for the very arts which seem most to raise and embellish life, introduce in their train habits of effeminacy and self-indulgence. They create new wants, which become in turn from servants masters. They concentrate the entire being—with self-sacrifice, an absurdity—duty, a difficulty—they add to riches a fictitious value, measured by the lowest passions of our nature. These are sad truths, nor do we see in existing institutions the means of giving a different current of mind in the superior circles of society."

"Yours is a very graphic sketch of a large class of individuals," said Colonel Jack, "and you deserve the thanks of the whole company."

Miss Cary gave a nod of approval, as our hero passed this compliment upon her descriptive powers.

After some further conversation, Mr. Baintree entered into the particulars of a murder done in Scotland, which had come to his knowledge during his professional career.

CHAPTER CXXVIII.

MR. BAINTREE'S NARRATIVE OF WILLIAM BEGBIE.

"In the year 17—," said Mr. Baintree, "when what is now considered the inferior parts of the town, still retained many respectable tenants; the banking affairs of the British Linen Company were conducted in a large house which had formerly belonged to the Marquis of Tweeddale, within a court connected with the street called the Netherbow. A narrow covered close or alley (called, from its original possessors, Tweeddale's Close), of about fifteen yards in length, and usually somewhat dark, leads from the street into the spacious court where this building is situated.

"About five o'clock of the evening, on the 13th of November, when the short midwinter day had just closed, a child who lived in a house accessible from the close, was sent by her mother, with a little kettle, to obtain a supply of water for tea from the neighbouring well.

The little girl, stepping with her kettle in her hand out of the public stair into the close, stumbled in the dark over something which lay there, and which proved to be the body of a man just expiring.

On an alarm being given, it was discovered that this was William Begbie, a porter connected with the bank, in whose heart a knife was stuck up the haft, so that he bled to death before uttering a word which might tend to explain the dismal transaction. He was, at the same time, found to have been robbed of a package of notes to the value of above four thousand pounds, which he had been intrusted with, in the course of his ordinary duty, to carry from the branch of the bank at Leith to the head quarters. The blow had been given with an accuracy, and a calculation of consequences, shewing the most appalling deliberation of the assassin; for not only was the knife directed straight into the most vital part, but its handle had been muffled in a bunch of soft paper, so as to prevent, as was thought, any sprinkling of blood from reaching the person of the murderer, by which he might have been, by some chance, detected.

The knife was one of those with broad thin blades and wooden handles which are used for cutting bread, and its rounded front had been ground to a point, apparently for the execution of this horrible deed. The unfortunate man left a wife and four children to bewail his loss.

The singular nature and circumstances of Begbie's murder occasioned much excitement in the public mind, and every effort was of

course made to discover the guilty party. No house of a suspicious character in the city was left unsearched, and parties were despatched to watch and patrol all the various roads leading out into the country. The bank offered a reward of 500*l* for such information as might lead to the conviction of the offender or offenders; and the government further promised the king's pardon to any except the actual murderer, who, having been concerned in the deed, might discover their accomplices. The sheriff of Edinburgh, Mr. Clerk Rattray, displayed the greatest zeal in his endeavours to ascertain the circumstances of the murder, and to detect and seize the murderer, but with surprisingly little success.

All that could be ascertained was, that Begbie, in proceeding up Leith Walk on his

fatal mission, had been accompanied by 'a man ;' and that, about the supposed time of the murder, 'a man' had been seen by some children to run out of the close into the street, and down Leith Wynd, which is a lane leading off from the Netherbow, at a point nearly opposite from the close. There was also reason to believe that the knife had been bought in a shop about two o'clock on the day of the murder, and that it had been afterwards ground upon a grinding-stone, and smoothed on a hone.

A number of suspicious characters were apprehended and examined ; but all, with one exception, produced satisfactory proofs of their innocence. The exception was a carrier between Perth and Edinburgh, a man of dissolute and irregular habits, of great bodily strength, and known to be a dangerous and desperate character. He was kept in custody for a considerable time, on suspicion, having been seen in the Canongate, near the scene of the murder, a very short time after it was committed. It has since been ascertained, that he was then going about a different business, the disclosure of which would have subjected him to a capital punishment.

It was in consequence of the mystery he felt himself impelled to preserve on this subject that he was kept so long in custody; but at length facts and circumstances came out to warrant his discharge, and he was discharged accordingly.

Months rolled on without eliciting any evidence respecting the murder, and, like other wonders, it had ceased in a great measure to engage public attention, when, on the 10th of August, a journeyman mason, in company with two other men, passing through the Bellevue grounds, in the neighbourhood of the city, found, in a hole in a stone enclosure, by the side of a hedge, a parcel containing a large quantity of banknotes, bearing the appearance of having been a good while exposed to the weather. After consulting a moment, the men carried the package to the sheriff's office, where it was found to contain about 3,000*l* in large notes, being those which had been taken from Begbie. The British Linen Company rewarded the men with 200*l* for their honesty, but the circumstance passed without throwing any light on the murder itself.

Up to the present day, the murder of Begbie has not been discovered; nor is it probable, after the space of time which has elapsed (forty-seven years), that it ever will be so. It is most likely that the grave has long closed upon him. The only person on whom public suspicion alighted with any force, during the sixteen years ensuing upon the transaction, was a medical practitioner in Leith, a dissolute man and a gambler, who put an end to his own existence not long after the murder. But I am not acquainted with any particular circumstance on which this suspicion was grounded, beyond the suicide, which might spring from other causes. Some further light was thrown on this mysterious case. On a work published under the title of *The Life and Trial of James Mackoull*; there was included a paper by Mr. D—, the Bow Street officer, the object of which was to prove that Mackoull was the murderer, and which contained at least one very curious statement.

Mr. D— had discovered in Leith a man, then acting as a teacher, but who, in 17—, was a sailor boy, and who had witnessed some circumstances immediately connected with the murder. The man's statement was as follows:—‘ I was at that time (November,

17—) a boy of fourteen years of age. The vessel to which I belonged had made a voyage to Lisbon, and was then lying in Leith Harbour. I had brought a small present from Portugal for my mother and sister, who resided in the Netherbow, Edinburgh, immediately opposite to Tweeddale's Close, leading to the British Linen Company's Bank. I left the vessel late in the afternoon, and as the articles I had brought were contraband, I put them under my jacket, and was proceeding up Leith Walk, when I perceived a tall man carrying a yellow-coloured parcel under his arm, and a genteel man, dressed in a black coat, dogging him. I was a little afraid: I conceived the man who carried the parcel to be a smuggler, and the gentleman who followed him to be a custom-house or excise officer. In dogging the man, the supposed officer went from one side of the Walk to the other (the Walk is a broad street), as if afraid of being noticed, but still kept about the same distance behind him. I was afraid of losing what I carried and shortened sail a little, keeping my eyes fixed on the person I supposed to be an officer, until I came to the head of Leith Street, when I saw the smuggler take the North Bridge, and the custom-house officer go in front of the Register Office; here he looked round him, and imagining he was looking for me, I hove to, and watched him. He then looked up the North Bridge, and, as I conceive, followed the smuggler, for he went the same way. I stood a minute or two where I was, and then went forward, walking slowly up the North Bridge. I did not, however, see either of the men before me; and when I came to the south end or head of the bridge, supposing that they might have gone up the High Street, or along the South Bridge, I turned to the left, and reached the Netherbow, without again seeing either the smuggler or the officer. Just, however, as I came opposite to Tweeddale's Close, I saw the custom-house officer come running out of it, with something under his coat; I think he ran down the street. Being much alarmed, and supposing that the officer had also seen me, and knew what I carried, I deposited my little present in my mother's with all possible speed, and made the best of my way to Leith, without hearing anything of the murder of Begbie until next day. On coming on board the vessel, I told the mate what a narrow escape I conceived I had made; he seemed somewhat alarmed, having probably, like myself, smuggled some trifling article from Portugal, and told me, in a peremptory tone, that I should not go ashore again without first acquainting him. I certainly heard of the murder before I left Leith, and concluded that the man I saw was the murderer; but the idea of waiting on a magistrate, and communicating what I had seen, never struck me. We sailed in a few days thereafter from Leith, and the vessel to which I belonged having been captured by a privateer, I was carried to a French prison, and only regained my liberty at the last peace. I can now recollect distinctly the figure of the man I saw; he was well dressed, had a genteel appearance, and wore a black coat. I never saw his face properly, for he was before me the whole way up the Walk; I think, however, he was a stont, big man, but not so tall as the man I then conceived to be a smuggler.'

This description of the supposed customhouse officer coincides exactly with that of the appearance of Mackoull; and other circumstances are given, which almost make it certain that he was the murderer.

This Mackoull was a London rogue of unparalleled effrontery and dexterity, who for years haunted Scotland, and effected some daring robberies. He resided in Edinburgh at this period, and during that time frequented a coffee-room in the Ship Tavern at Leith. He professed to be a merchant, expelled by the threats of the French from Hamburgh, and to live by a new mode of dyeing skins, but in reality practised the arts of gambler and a pickpocket. He had a mean lodging at the bottom of New Street, in the Canongate, near the scene of the murder of Begbie, and to which, it is remarkable, that Leith Wynd was the readiest, as well as most private access from that spot.

No suspicion, however, fell upon Mackoull at this period, and he left the country for a number of years, at the end of which time he visited Glasgow; and there effected a robbery of one of the banks. For this crime he did not escape the law. He was brought to trial at Edinburgh, was condemned to be executed, but died in jail while under reprieve from his sentence.

The most striking part of the evidence which Mr. D— adduced against Mackoull, is the report of a conversation which he had with that person in the condemned cell of the Edinburgh jail, when Mackoull was very doubtful of being reprieved. To pursue his own narrative, which is in the third person— ' He told Captain Sibbald (the superior of the prison) that he intended to ask Mackoull a single question relative to the murder of Begbie, but would first humour him by a few jokes, so as to throw him off his guard, and prevent him from thinking he had called for any particular purpose (it is to be observed, that Mr. D— had a professional acquaintance with the condemned man); but desired Captain Sibbald to watch the features of the prisoner, when he (D—) put his hand to his chin, for he would then put the question he

meant. After talking some time on different topics, Mr. D— put this very simple question to the prisoner—" By the way, Mackoull, if I am correct, you resided at the foot of New Street, Canongate, in November, did you not?"

' He stared—he rolled his eyes; and as if falling into a convulsion, threw himself back upon his bed. In this condition he continued for a few moments, when, as if recollecting himself, he started up, exclaiming wildly— "No—! I was then in the East Indies—in the West Indies. What do you mean?"

" I mean no harm, Mackoull," he replied; " I merely asked for my own curiosity; for I think when you left these lodgings, you went to Dublin—is it not so?"

" Yes, yes, I went to Dublin," he replied; and I wish I had remained there still—I won ten thousand pounds there at the tables, and never knew what it was to want cash, although you wished the folks here to believe that they locked me up in Old Start (Newgate), and brought down your friend Adkins to swear he saw me there—this was more than your duty."

' He now seemed to rave, and lose all temper, and his visitor bade him good-night, and left him.'

It appears extremely probable, from the strong circumstantial evidence which has been offered by Mr. D— that Mackoull was the murderer of Begbie.

" I should suppose that there could be but little doubt of that," said Colonel Jack.

After some further conversation the whole party retired to rest in the hospitable house of Mr. O'Callagan.

CHAPTER CXXIX.

THE RETURN TO LONDON.

MR. BAINTREE and our hero had fulfilled the mission which had brought them to Ireland. They were now possessed of sufficient evidence to prove, beyond dispute, the death of Morgan Halford and his only son. The lawyer told his client that there was now a certainty of his daughter inheriting the property left by the miser—or money scrivener —Abel Meech by name, the nature of whose will the reader is already acquainted with. Mr. Baintree was now anxious to return to London, and intimated his wish to Colonel Jack, who, to say the truth, was nothing loth to return to his old companions.

On the following morning, therefore, after the incidents of the last chapter, Colonel Jack informed his friend, Mr. O'Callagan, that he and his companion were necessitated to start for their own home.

"An' sure now," said the warm-hearted Irishman. "It's sorry I am to part wid ye, gentlemen, seeing as how I was in good hopes that ye were going to do me the honour of staying wid me for a few days longer."

"My good friend," said Mr. Baintree, "business calls us back ; and, indeed, to say the truth, I have already protracted my stay longer than I had intended, and business calls are imperative. I must of necessity return. I do not doubt but you will say that now we have our turn served, that we care little for the rest, and are anxious to get back ; but, at the same time, Mr. O'Callagan, you must permit me, on behalf of both myself and my friend Halford, to offer you some slight remuneration for the services you have so promptly rendered us in the furtherance of our object."

Mr. O'Callagan gave such a dramatic start as the lawyer came to this part of his speech that the latter paused suddenly.

The Irishman assumed an air of wonderful dignity.

"And it's afther payment that ye'd be talking about?" said Mr. O'Callagan, deprecatingly. "An' sure it's not myself that would accept of a single skirrick—not, not if I was without a meal's victuals."

"My good friend," continued the lawyer, "you really must—nay, you ought not to be offended with my suggestion. Take a business view of the transaction. I confess, I am apt to do so in most transactions of my life. We were perfect strangers to you when we first met in the market-place. What claim have we upon you?"

"Who said ye had any claim?" returned the Irishman, sharply.

"Nobody has said so, neither have we," answered Mr. Baintree, " and such being the case, you really must accept of some recompense for the trouble we have put you to."

Mr. O'Callagan again declared his determination of not accepting one farthing, and finding him inexorable, the lawyer and Colonel Jack did not press the matter further.

Before leaving Ireland our hero paid another visit to his aunt, and he was received by her husband, who happened to be at home at the time, with much more civility than he had chosen to display on the occasion of his first visit.

The interview over, the Colonel and the lawyer returned to the house of Mr. O'Callagan. Miss Cary, or " old aunt Cary," as she was called, was also bent upon returning to her own quiet home, and as Mr. Baintree and the Colonel were taking an immediate departure, they offered to escort her back to London, which offer she was but too glad to accept.

Matters being thus arranged, the three prepared to take their departure. Father Ryan expressed his willingness to ferret out any further evidence respecting the death of Major Halford's son, if such were needed, but Mr. Baintree assured the priest that there was already sufficient for his purpose. Still, at the same time, he told the priest that, should there by any chance more be required, he would avail himself of his services, and so, thanking him for his kind offer, the lawyer presented Mr. Ryan with several pieces of gold, which, after a little hesitation, the priest accepted. The saver of souls was less scrupulous than the honest farmer.

Mr. Baintree, our hero, and Miss Cary, soon found themselves again in England. The latter before she went to her country seat called upon Mr. and Mrs. Osborne, who prevailed upon her to stay for a few days at their town residence.

Colonel Jack rejoined his friends Knapp and Hackett, who had met with considerable success on " the road," since his absence. After this Colonel Jack called at the chambers of Mr. Baintree to learn some further particulars of the inheritance under the will of the late Abel Meech.

The lawyer had been busy enough since his return, but luckily he was disengaged when our hero waited upon him.

"I am glad you have called, Halford, very glad," said Mr. Baintree. "Be seated."

Colonel Jack drew a chair up to the fireplace, and seated himself thereon."

"Well," he said, "what's the news now. Do you think that there is any chance for Rosalie ?"

"For whom ?" inquired the lawyer.

"For my daughter, Rosalie," returned Colonel Jack.

"Oh, pardon me, I forgot her name at the moment," answered Mr. Baintree. "True, I have no doubt now of your daughter's being the real heir of the deceased man, Abel Meech. There will, of course be many legal forms to be gone through. The certificate of your own baptism, as also of—I beg pardon, what did you say is your daughter's christian name ?"

"Rosalie—Rosalie Halford is her name?"

The lawyer opened a book, and made an entry of the same thereon.

"You must understand," he said, reflecting, "that this property was held in trust by the late Lady Reichbeck. Naturally enough it seemed to swell the amount of her possessions to an enormous extent, and her ladyship was reputed to be immensely wealthy, much more so than she was in reality was, for I believe Sir Richard Fleetwood, had he succeeded in keeping his brother out of the way, and thereby have been enabled to produce a certificate of his death, he, Sir Richard, would have administered to the will of the late Lady Richbeck, and the probability is that, unscrupulous man as he is, the probability is, my dear sir, that he would, in conjunction with his friend, Sharpthorne, have laid his hands upon the amount of money left by Abel Meech ; had this been the case, we should have had some difficulty in wresting it from him."

"But we have no cause to fear that now," returned Colonel Jack. "Sir Richard, or rather, Mr. Richard Fleetwood, has been baffled in his designs, and is, comparatively, harmless."

"Have you seen or heard of him lately ?" inquired Mr. Baintree.

"No, strange to say, he has kept himself quiet," returned our hero, "and more than that, he has chosen to preserve a strict incognito. Indeed, to speak the truth, I am surprised at the close secresy which Mr. Richard Halford has chosen to assume. I cannot learn from any one where he is located, and what are, or have been, his movements."

"He's a bold bad man," said Mr. Baintree, and depend upon it, that although he may be baffled at present, he will not rest without endeavouring to put some new scheme in practice for his own aggrandizement."

"But I hope it's out of his power to interfere with the inheritance which is to come to my daughter, for I need hardly tell you, after what has occurred," said the Colonel, sinking his voice to a much more subdued tone, "that for myself 1 care but little—my dear Rosalie inherits all the graces and sweet disposition of her mother." He sighed deeply, and paused for a moment, as he gave expression to this sentiment. "Yes, all those natural graces that distinguished her mother," he said, dwelling upon his words as though he loved to record the virtues of her who, in the life, had been to him all that faithful woman could be to a loving, but at the same time, an erring husband.

Mr. Baintree saw that his visitor was visibly affected.

"She does not know ought of her father's position in life, Mr. Baintree," said our hero, in continuation, "and I would wish that she never should know. My friend, Harry Osborne has taken charge of her, and under the guidance of his amiable wife, Rosalie will be brought up with the strictest moral principles, and her intellect will be cultivated under efficient teachers. What more can be desired? Perhaps she may become estranged from her father. Well, it's a natural sequence, perhaps. In any case, it would not be possible for me to take charge of her, situated as I am—no, it is better as it is."

"She will inherit a large fortune," said Mr. Baintree, "and a sunny future lies before her."

"Yes,—perhaps," sighed the colonel.

"Well, there is every reason to believe so," answered the lawyer.

"Unless—"

"Unless what ?" inquired Mr. Baintree. "Let us not anticipate troubles."

"Unless her pure ears should be assailed by her father's sullied reputation," returned Colonel Jack, and wishing the lawyer a hasty good morning, he abruptly left the office.

Pulling his hat over his brows, the colonel threaded his way through the dingiest and most obscure thoroughfares he could pick out towards the residence of his friend, Henry Osborne. A sort of heavy weight seemed to oppress him and weigh down his spirits. He felt ill at ease with himself and the whole world. Strange that the fact of his daughter's prosperity should awake such feelings, but so it was. None of us can probe the depth of the human heart. None of us can account for the strange contracts which diversify the character of man. Colonel Jack's thoughts wandered off upon a variety of subjects, as he took his way to his friend Henry Osborne's. The centre, if it could be so termed, of these thoughts, was his daughter, whom he began already to view as a being removed from himself—a sort of separate being, living in a different atmosphere—in almost a different world.

As time went on, so the colonel thought she would become more estranged from him. It was a natural consequence that such should be the case—he could not see her after, and if he did, as she grew up to womanhood she would perhaps not desire to be much with him, for, affectionate as she was, the colonel felt, and indeed knew, that her taste would become refined, and possibly she might,—and this thought was agonising to him. Perhaps she might become ashamed of her parent. Such things had taken place, and why not so with him ? No matter, he thought. She will be happy, and what more do I desire ? As for myself, why let me rough it on the road of life as has been my wont.

He turned into a neighbouring house, and drank off a bumper of brandy to keep up his spirits, for he felt that they were below water-mark at that moment.

Then once more he proceeded on towards Osborne's. Upon his arrival he found that his friend and Honora were out, but the servant informed him that his master and mistress would be both back in the course of an hour or so, and he was shown up into the first floor front room.

CHAPTER CXXX.

THE COLONEL'S INTERVIEW WITH OSBORNE.

WHEN our hero found himself in the room into which he had been conducted by Osborne's obsequious servant, the first person that met his eyes was Aunt Cary, and the next was his own daughter. Miss Cary was giving the latter so... instruction in water-colour painting. She rose up upon the colonel's entrance, and advanced towards him.

"My dear Mr. Halford," said the good-natured old maid. "Indeed, but this is a pleasure. We have been wondering what had become of you, and I was only saying to my friend, Mrs. Osborne, that you had treated both her and myself in a very cavalier sort of way. Ah! but I was," continued Miss Cary, shaking her fan menacingly at the new comer, who could not refrain from indulging in a smile at the naive manner of the lady.

"You must pardon me, my dear madam, pressing business must be my excuse."

"Oh, if that be the case, I am answered," said Miss Cary, handing the visitor a seat, which, however, he was not permitted to take, for his daughter Rosalie ran up to him, and clasped her little arms round him. The colonel was surprised to observe how she had grown, and what a visible alteration there was in her appearance, an alteration for the better, so he thought, for she looked more happy. Her face no longer wore that anxious expression which the colonel had oftentimes observed on it immediately preceding and after his wife's death. There was now a contented, happy expression on it.

"Ah," thought the colonel, "troubles sit lightly upon the young."

He took his daughter in his arms, and embraced her fondly. He felt happy as she wound her soft and placid arms round his neck, and laid her cheek against his. Yes, he felt happy, although some fearful thoughts flitted ever an anon through his brain. Placing her by his side, he sat down.

"You are happy, my dear child?" he inquired, hardly knowing why he should put such a question to her.

"Oh, yes, father. How can I be otherwise. Mr. and Mrs. Osborne are so kind to me—so very kind, no one can be kinder—"

She paused.

"Except—"

"Except my mother," she said, sadly.

As she gave expression to this, she observed a change come over her father's features. She ran to the table, and brought him a water-colour sketch she had been making.

"See," she said, assuming a cheerfulness which perhaps she did not feel at the time.

"See what I have been [doing—dear good Miss Cary has been teaching me."

"It is very kind of her, and you ought to be grateful, Rosalie," said Colonel Jack, taking the painting from his daughter, and inspecting it with the eyes of a connoiseur. He then entered into a rigid criticism of it—much to the astonishment of his daughter, who did not know that he was so well versed in the fine arts. She, however, listened complacently enough, and shook her curls, and hung down her head, when he found fault with certain parts.

"And what a time you have been away," said Rosalie, reproachfully. "I thought you had forgotten me altogether."

"No, no, my love. You should not imagine that," said Miss Cary. "It's wrong to say so. I am quite sure your father is too proud of his little treasure to forget."

"Oh, yes, of course, I know that," answered Rosalie, half ashamed of what she had been saying.

"Rosalie, my dear, your father has had business to attend to—important business."

Rosalie made no other reply than again embracing her parent, after which she ran on in her own childish way, giving her own account of many, and indeed most of her proceedings since his absence.

Miss Cary took an opportunity at this time of leaving the room, so that Colonel Jack might be left to converse with his daughter alone.

Rosalie again expressed herself deeply attached to her kind protectors, Mr. and Mrs. Osborne. She gave her father a detailed account of their various acts of kindness towards herself.

Some half hour elapsed when the colonel's interview with his daughter was brought to an end by the sudden appearance of Osborne himself.

"Frank!" exclaimed the latter, hastening up to Colonel Jack, and shaking him warmly by the hand; this is indeed an honour."

"What?"

"Your visit here."

"Pshaw! you are jesting."

"No, indeed ; but at the same time I am bound to observe that it is an honour I have seldom conferred on me, and all the more prized, perhaps, on account of its rarity."

"You are satirical, Harry," said our hero.

"And you have been too much of a stranger," was the reply.

"Well, how do you think Rosalie looks."

"Oh, charming, I find her wonderfully improved, in health and spirits."

"I hope she is happy."

"I am sure she is, Harry. I cannot sufficiently express my gratitude for all your kindness towards her."

"Pshaw! you are talking like a very silly

man. What gratitude do you owe me? None at all. There, a truce to this. To tell the truth, Honora is so fond of her little Rosalie, that I do believe it would break her heart to part with her."

"There is no reason for her to be alarmed. Rosalie will stay as long as you choose to keep her, until you are tired of her."

"That will never be; will it my child," said Osborne.

This last inquiry was addressed to Rosalie herself.

"I don't know," she replied coquettishly.

Osborne led Colonel Jack into his library, where they could be to themselves. Placing him in one arm-chair, he seated himself in the opposite one.

"Harry," said our hero, "I have been wishing to see you, for you must know, my dear fellow, that Rosalie's future prospects are likely to be fair ones, much more fair than I had anticipated. You remember that I mentioned to you that there was a considerable amount of property left under a will, which I believed would, or rather ought to come to me?"

"Yes, I remember you were talking about the same when I last saw you. Have you done any more in the matter? Miss Cary mentioned to Honora that you had been over to Ireland upon a matter of business."

"That is true enough," said the colonel. "Listen, it appears that Rosalie is the heir to property left by an old miser by the name of Abel Meech. This property was to be left to his nearest of kin, three generations removed."

"I do not understand you," said Osborne.

"Why, his will runs thus: the whole of his property falls to his nearest relative's son's son. Now, supposing my father was alive, he would be his nearest relative, but such not being the case, I should be."

"Well, then, the property comes to you, I suppose."

"No; neither would it have come to my father, even if he was alive at the present time. By the will of Abel Meech the money he bequeathed is not for his nearest relative's use, nor for his children's, but for his children's children, three generations removed. Now do you understand?"

"What a singular will," said Osborne. "What could be the man's object in making so strange a bequest?"

"Vanity, I suppose."

"How so?"

"I cannot say, but Mr. Baintree seems to think that he made this will under the idea that the property would accumulate to an enormous sum in the course of time, and it was a sort of vanity, if I may so term it, which made him put off the inheritance for three generations."

"And is Rosalie the third remove?"

"Yes. My father had an elder brother who settled in Ireland; had he been living, or had he left any issue, male or female, then no member of my family would come in for the property left by the late Abel Meech, but Morgan Halford is dead, his only son is dead, consequently my daughter—my own dear Rosalie, is heir-at-law."

"My good friend, I am delighted at this," said Osborne. "Rosalie will be a rich heiress."

"Unquestionably," reiterated the Colonel, "and now, Harry, I would have her kept in entire ignorance of her father's antecedents —a time may come," said the colonel, sadly —"a time may come when perchance she may have cause to blush for her father. Pray heaven that this may be deferred as long as possible. She will be brought up under the guidance of yourself and Mrs. Osborne. In the atmosphere with which she is at present surrounded, there is nothing that can pollute the most chaste of her sex. I would have her remain thus pure and undefiled. For myself, I shall visit her as often as may be, but for the rest she will be well cared for. Of course, I put no restrictions as to any expense for her education. Let it be as liberal as possible, such an one as will make her the most accomplished of her sex, so that when she moves in those select circles which her position and education will command, no one will suspect Rosalie Halford to be the highwayman's daughter."

Colonel Jack paused, he pressed his hand uneasily across his brow, and leaning forward was for some time lost in reflection.

Osborne did not disturb him, but rose from his seat, and placed decanters and wine-glasses on the table. This movement recalled our hero once more to himself.

"You are happy, Henry, and have a glorious future before you," he said, somewhat suddenly.

"I have no reason to complain of Dame Fortune," answered Osborne, "nor of my marriage," he continued after a pause.

"I did not allude to that," answered the colonel, sadly. "You are blessed in the choice you have made, of that I am well assured."

"And then, Honora is so devotedly attached to Rosalie," said Osborne, "she takes such an interest in her education. You'll see what an accomplished young lady we shall make. Wait a bit, you'll see by-and-bye."

"Ah, by-and-bye, that is easily said," returned the colonel. "No doubt we shall see."

He leant his forehead on his hand, and was again lost in reflection.

By-and-bye. There is music enough in these words for the burden of a song. There is a hope wrapped up in them, and an articulate beat of a human heart.

"By-and-bye." We heard it as long ago as we can remember, when we made brief but perilous journeys from chair to table and from table to chair again. We heard it the other day, when two parted that had been "loving in their lives,"—one to California, the other to her lonely home.

Everybody says it—some time or other, The boy whispers it to himself, when he dreams of exchanging the stubbed little shoes for boots like a man's. The man murmurs it —when in life's middle watch he sees his plans half finished, and his hopes yet in the bud waving in a cold late spring. The old man says it, when he thinks of putting off the mortal for the immortal—to-day for to-morrow. The weary watcher for the morning whiles away the dark hours with "by-and-bye —by—and-bye."

Sometimes it sounds like a song; sometimes there is a sigh or a sob in it. What would not the world give to find it in the almanacs set down somewhere, no matter if in the dead of December—to know it would surely come. But fairy-like as it is, flitting like a star-beam over the dewy shadows of the years, nobody can snare it; and when we look back upon the many times those words have beguiled us, the memory of that silver "by-and-bye" is like the sunrise of Ossian—"pleasant, but mournful to the soul."

It was mournful enough to Colonel Jack, for it called up to his mind what his own position might be with regard to his daughter in years to come; and this thought seemed to strike him with a sudden and unaccountable sadness.

Strange mutations are caused by Time! and then its flight—how different is it with us, at various periods of our existence!

How beautifully the widening and brightening days of the year would look if we could only lay them down in mosaic along the halls of time—gold and silver, and shadow.

Time is a strange thing to be sure! A week ago we witnessed the blossoming of the century plant. It was nothing but the opening of a flower, but it was, nevertheless, a thought-provoking scene. There it was, one of Flora's own chronometers, marking no such paltry fractions as your life or ours, but silently marking the flight of centuries. Near it, nestled in the moss asleep, was the flower that lives and dies a dozen times a day, while within our own bosom was the heart that beat out the moments like kernels beneath the falling flails.

Everybody is warring against Time; every lengthened lever—every new combination of which is a weapon against Time—prolonging, abridging, quickening or retarding it. The Press is the mightiest engine yet brought to bear against it. It is the "Polyglott of Human thought." It enables us to repeat a million times what otherwise we could only say but once. It unseals the lips of the dead, and keeps them speaking ages, audibly and eloquently, through the dumb and long-gone years.

"You seem melancholy, Frank," said Osborne, after a pause.

"No—no," answered the colonel, suddenly called to himself. "Indeed, I know not why I should be so, seeing that this accession of fortune will be the means of placing Rosalie in a proud position hereafter. Harry, you must pardon me; but I do grow melancholy, and that's the truth—I mean at times. When I reflect upon her who was so gentle and faithful to me, my spirits become depressed in spite of myself. Psha! there's an end of such dismal thoughts!"

So saying, Colonel Jack poured himself out a bumper of wine, and drained it off, pledging his companion therein.

"By the way," said Colonel Jack, "I have not inquired after our friend Squabshot. How is he? Have you seen anything of him?"

"Oh, yes, he has been here constantly to see Miss Staunton, but as she is now away, our worthy little friend has not deemed it worth while to give us a call lately."

"Away!" said the colonel, in some surprise. "Has Miss Staunton left then?"

"No, only she has been rusticating at our country house at Twickenham."

"And is she there now?"

"Yes. She has been located there for the last five weeks."

"And Squabshot?"

"He is continually going down there, so I hear."

"Is the fellow as madly in love as ever?"

"Yes, over head and ears. He's well nigh distracted, for he imagines he has a rival."

"Ah! And is there any truth in such a supposition?"

"I can hardly tell you. There is a party —a clergyman, in fact—who has been dangling after Edith, but what his intentions are it is impossible for me to say."

"Poor Squabshot!" said the colonel, with a laugh. "I should like to see the little fellow, for he is not a bad sort."

"On the contrary. He is a very excellent sort," said Osborne. "I have every reason to speak well of him."

While this conversation was taking place, a servant entered the room, and announced to Osborne that his mistress had returned, and when convenient, she would be glad to see

the gentlemen. Osborne looked at Colonel Jack, who at once rose from his seat and prepared to accompany his host. The two then took their way into the drawing-room, where they found two or three other visitors assembled, besides Miss Cary and Honora, who expressed her delight in no measured terms at seeing our hero. The lady introduced her visitors one after the other to Mr. Halford (Colonel Jack) in due form. One of them was a Mr. Rioden from the county Cork.

He was very much of a gentleman and Irish by birth. He was seated on a couch between two young ladies, with whom he was engaged in an animated conversation. It was arranged that all present should stay to dinner, and the colonel himself acceded to this request.

Now we most of us know that the hour before dinner is generally an awkward one. People meet, and they don't know what to talk about. There is a chilliness, until the midday meal has been partaken of. However, Aunt Cary. and Mr. O'Rioden managed to keep the company pretty well entertained by their sketches of Ireland and its inhabitants. The company was not a little amused at the colonel's account of the hall of justice, and the cases he heard there.

"Oh, my countrymen have strange ways and manners with them," remarked Mr. O'Rioden. "What a piece of work is man! a riddle—a mystery; inexplicable even to himself; his firmest convictions perpetually contradicted by his actions; half of his little hour fretted away in repenting, and the other half in sinning ; and then he goes, in my country, to the priest, who gives him absolution for that same."

"Perhaps in no action of man's wayward career on this sorry planet does this melancholy and humiliating truth appear so strongly as in the circumstance of his not rising early in the morning. No one can be more persuaded than he is of all the advantages that attend the practice : the lovely morning, the abundance of time afforded, the healthful walk, the cheerful spirits, the fine appetite, the cleanliness, the freshness, the consciousness of doing right, the comfort in every respect, are all fully before his mind, yet is the present enjoyment of a pair of miserable sheets and blankets, the wretched animal gratification of comparative insensibility, enough to make this "noblest work of God" sink all those rational considerations, "weigh his eyelids down, and steep his senses into forgetfulness !

"Now for my own part," said Mr. O'Rioden, "I candidly confess that I cannot rise early. No, I positively cannot."

"Nor I," said another of the party present.

"Nor I," repeated Aunt Cary.

"Well now, I'll just tell you how a friend of mine cured himself of that same bad habit," said Mr. O'Rioden. "He was an Irishman, like myself, but for the life of him could not contrive to get up at even decent time. He hit upon an expedient. Shall I give you the history of this same ?"

"By all means," said Colonel Jack.

"Well then, the Honourable Effingham Snoreaway—the surname is fictitious, for I don't want to expose my friend."

"No, that is near enough."

The Honourable Effingham Snoreaway was a man who, though fully impressed with a sense of all the pleasures and advantages of early rising, could never bring himself to get up. When he did rise at ten or eleven, or it might be twelve, o'clock in the morning, nothing could exceed his contrition ; he looked back on the lovely morning that had rolled five or six delightful, sunny hours over him, while he was buried in a shameful stupor ; he thought of all the fine things which he might have been (as they say in Ireland) after doing during that "sweet hour of prime ;" but as all was now unavailing with respect to the past, the only thing left for him, by way of silencing the reproaches of his better judgement, was a firm resolution to "bounce" the next morning—which firm resolution, need it be said ? melted away when the morning came before the heating influence of a few stone of feathers ! Over and over, did the Honourable Mr. Effingham Snoreaway resolve and resolve, yet still stay in bed ; over and over did he fret and blush and reproach himself, yet still slept away ; over and over, did he promise and vow and swear that he

would never be found in bed late any more, yet when morning came, there he was.

Alas, human nature ! still, still, was poor Mr. Snoreaway held from executing all these fine resolves by the slender walls of mere furniture calico !

Notwithstanding all his resolutions, all his frettings, all his remorses, all his self-reproach and sense of shame, all his promises ; notwithstanding all his sincere and earnest desires and wishes, backed by bringing before his mind, as he was going to bed at night, all the most powerful arguments that he could suggest (enough to make him stay up all night in order to be up early in the morning) —alas, notwithstanding all, there he was the next morning, long after the matin hour, "as fast as a rock !"

What was to be done ? Several expedients were resorted to, but they were all, at the very moment of their effectual operation, stopped by his own hands.

A machine which raised up the bed at an appointed hour (he set it to five), so as to gently throw the sleeper out on his feet—a thing like the spout of a gardener's watering pot, which was kept to drop cold water on his face, at a given hour, in like manner—an alarm clock—a bell, just over his head—all, as I have said before, although all his own delicate designs, were prevented from discharging their respective and sanatory functions by his own suicidal hands ; one quick jump out of bed, between asleep and awake, the instant that any one of them gave the smallest awakening note of preparation, and a still quicker snap at the moving principle either of the machine, the spout of the gardener's watering pot, the alarm clock, or the bell, whichever he happened the night before to have set upon duty, soon taught the busy and impertinent little intruder manners, at that hour of the morning, and in half the twinkling of an eye was poor and ever-to-be-pitied Mr. Snoreaway more closely, if possible, than before, gathered up in his bed-clothes to repay himself, as it were, by augmented enjoyment for the momentary sensation of pain he had suffered in the little transit which has been just alluded to.

At length, all ordinary and indeed extraordinary expedients having been unsuccessfully appealed to, one desperate resolution was taken to triumph over his hitherto unconquerable propensity. He hired an Irish servant, named Terry Oulahan, to whom was committed the important task, and that only, of awakening him at half-past five o'clock every morning.

"Now," said he, to Terry, "remember I hire you for one single purpose, and for nothing else whatever, namely, to call me up every morning at half-past five o'clock, and to be sure that I get up. This is all you will have to do, and for this I will pay you £20 a year.

Terry promptly closed with an engagement which appeard to him a perfect sinecure, little conjecturing what was to await him, even on his very first or second essay ; and making every protestation of attention and regularity, he looked impatiently for the hour which was, in the course, as he thought, of a few minutes, to see him through his day's work.

At half past five to the moment, Terry was at his master's bed-room door. He gave a gentle tap—no answer ; two or more —a little louder—not a word. Terry peeped in through the key-hole, gave another tap, and then put his ear to the same, and hearing no reply, exclaimed, "Murther! murther! but I believe he's one of the seven sleepers." He stopped awhile, but before he could give another knock, he was started off his legs by a tremendous noise which came from the bed-room ; it was the grand winding up, or finale of a most discordant snore—"Oh, blessed and holy Saint Monica," cried out Terry, " the Lord between us and harm, but the divil the like of such a snore as that did I ever hear afore. No matther at any rate, I must thry and get him up."

The fear of being unsuccessful in his first morning's work, and that without any fault of his, emboldened poor Terry to throw a little more force in his knocks. At length he succeeded ; a response was given to his appeal. Terry followed up his advantage quickly, and gave a couple of brisk raps more, louder and louder ; another response from within ; but no articulate or satisfactory indication to Terry that his man was fairly on his legs.

" Humh."

" It's me, sir ; its Terry that cum to call you sir."

" Humph, Humph."

" I'm here sense half afther five, sir."

" Humph.!"

" And its now just six—it's six o'clock, sir ; it's a fine morning sir."

" Humph—humph—hah."

" With expressions such as these, intermingled with a knock and a listen, was poor Terry engaged, turning his right side one time to the door, and then his left, and receiving only that sleepy response through the nasal organ, which those are familiar with that have to deal with heavy sleepers, when to his expressible mortification, even that sound which had evidently been an acknowledgement of his call, died altogether away, and was succeeded by one which left no doubt at all on his mind, that his drowsy master had relapsed into a dead slumber.

Terry now gave a tremendous knock ; if any one has ever heard the sudden stopping of a Scotch bagpipes, or a good grunt from a pig, or a violent sneeze at an unsuspected moment, he may be able in a small way, to form some idea of the noise produced by the sudden interruption which Terry's loud knock had given to the running tones of the Honourable Effingham Snorcaway's snoring. Terry would not be taken in again, but rattled like a man, until to his great joy, about a quarter after six o'clock, he heard a "Who's there?"

" By the powers o' Moll Kelly," said Terry to himself, smiling with joy, at the idea of succeeding so far, " but it's well you wakened.

" It's me, sir; it's Terry. I'm calling you these two hours" (and, although he was not yet an hour at his day's work, it was little wonder he should think it two). " It's me, sir," again repeated Terry louder," and it's half past six now instead of five sir."

" Bad luck to you," was the silent reply ; how infernally punctual the rascal is !"

Terry heard something ; he listened ; some sleepy voice from within articulated—

" That will do, Terry ; you're an excellent servant. You may go away this morning. Go down now, You're a very regular man. Now that's what I like."

What could the poor man do under these circumstances but go away, a little reluctantly, certainly, as he did, consoling himself at the same time, with the fact of not only having punctually discharged his duty, but much more, with the ready testimony which his master had borne to it. All went on for the present as before, with Mr. Snoreaway. He was left to the undisturbed enjoyment of his bed, until a quarter after twelve o'clock, at noon, when upon looking at his watch, and faintly recollecting the early occurrences of the morning, a series of feelings ran across his mind, of such a nature as by no means to be envied.

The first thing that he did, when he came down stairs, was to call for Terry, Terry appeared immediately.

" Well, Terry," said he, " what did I hire you for ?"

" Sure I called you, sir," replied Terry.

" Yes," answered Mr. Snoreaway, " you called me, but that is not enough ; it was not merely to call me that I hired you, it was to call me until you found me out of bed— until you found me completely up."

" I was ever so long rappin' at the door, sir, afore I could get you to spake," added Terry.

" Well, let it pass for the present, but don't let it happen again," said Mr. Snoreaway ; " if I don't answer when you rap, open the door and come in, and come over to me and rouse me, and shake me, no matter what I say to you. If I threaten you—no matter what excuses I make, don't mind me ; don't attempt, for your life, to go away, or leave me, until you have me out on my legs. If I find to-morrow morning, that you go away without having me up at five o'clock, I'll have no further business for you. I will instantly discharge you."

Terry heard this with very curious feelings, and replied—

"Oh, very well, sir; it's myself that sees now what your honour wants: I'll be bail, if I've life in my body, it's to-morrow morning your honour's up wid the cock."

So saying, and receiving another and a still stronger caution from Mr. Snoreaway, under all circumstances and at all hazards not to fail next morning, Terry slowly turned about, and closed the door after him.

The next morning found him again at his post. It was worse than the morning before; so, as he had not only been authorised, but commanded, he boldly opened the door and went in—

"It's me, sir," said Terry (again a Humh). "Lord deliver my sowl, what a sleeper; he bangs Banagher! Up he gets, anyhow, wid all his snoring; I'm his boy," saying which, he went to the bed and at first gave him two or three gentle stirs

"Humh, humh," was the only fruit of these; and upon two or three stirs more, backed by—

"Get up, sir; get up, sir."

Terry began to shake him in sound earnest, and continued so until he had him clean awake.

"Oh," said Mr, Snoreaway, after rubbing his eyes and recognising Terry. "That's very right now; you have done all that I wished; that will do, Terry; you may go down now, I'm fully awake, and I consider myself the same as up."

"Oh, sir," answered Terry, "you know you bid me not leave you, no matter what you'd say, until I saw you completely up, and if I go away now, and you fall off again, you'll be blaming me, sir, for not doing as you bid me."

"You're very right, Terry," replied Mr. Snoreaway; "I know I bid you not go away until you had me up, but I'm now the same as up; at all events I won't blame you, so you may go down—there now—go, Terry, go;" and saying this he turned round on his right side.

"Faith, sir, axing your pardon, there's no use in you turning that way," said Terry; "I'll not go a foot till you're out o' bed; see there now, sir, you're dropping off again (oh, murther, what'll I do!). Sir, sir!" exclaimed Terry, giving him again several shakes. "Arrah, tunder and ages, sir, there you're beginning to snore again, and you'll be as bad as yesterday if you don't get up now at once."

The snoring continued and increased. Terry was now beginning to lose all patience, and his tone of voice was getting angry and reproving. He again shook his master, without any regard to etiquette, until he had him well awake, when he wheeled round, and, addressing Terry in a manner that startled him a good deal, as quickly as he could utter it.

"Didn't I tell you to go away, sir? didn't I tell you there would be no blame to you? I've no fault to find with you;" and getting a little gentle, " you have done all that has pleased me. Go down now, I'm broad awake, and I'll get up and dress myself the moment you shut the door after you ;"

"Sure I know, sir," added Terry, "that it will be just the same way with you as yesterday, if I go without seeing you out of bed; so I may as well tell you I'll not leave the room till you get out of bed."

"Oh, my heavens!" exclaimed Mr. Snoreaway to himself; "well, I believe this rascal will have me out: what, you rascal," said he, "do you dare to refuse to do what I desire you? Go out of the room immediately."

Terry was firm, and exclaimed—

"The devil a foot he'd go, till he had him out," and accordingly he began to pull the clothes off him, and gave him a thrust here and there to keep him awake—but all in vain.

"Do you mean, you audacious vagabond, to give me the lie; don't I tell you I'm up," exclaimed Mr. Snoreaway, most furiously; "I tell you I'm up; I don't wish to gratify you, by getting up before you, when I tell you you've nothing to do but go away and let me dress myself ; or I'll tell you what it is, for I see now you are an impudent fellow —as soon as I go down stairs, if you do not go away in one instant, I'll immediately discharge you."

The latter observations wrought powerfully on Terry. Every thing wore the air of such deliberate earnestness on the part of Snoreaway; his positive promises that he would not blame Terry ; Terry's conviction that he made him sensible; his partial belief that he, by being then awake, " was all as one as up," as he said himself, and that he could not, after all he said, have the conscience to go to sleep again, added to his positive command to leave him ; all prevailed upon poor Terry to go away, which he did very slowly, and very heavy-hearted, and with too melancholy a consciousness that his occupation was not of that easy or pleasant character which in the first instance he had imagined.

Of course, as soon as he had gone, Snoreaway fell off immediately into a sounder sleep than ever; and, as usual, or rather worse than usual, did not get up until twenty minutes past one that day. He was ready to tear himself. He could hardly bring himself to look at his face in the glass—eight dead hours lost—precious hours. He blamed Terry—he excused him. He certainly must have terrified the poor man—but why had not the villain the perseverance—and the indifference to any thing he might say, as he had warned him. Once more he would give a stronger caution and try him again ; and if this failed, he would abandon himself to despair.

"Terry, the master wants you !" announced one of the servants to him.

"Me !" said Terry.

"Yes," answered the servant : " he's just now after coming down from his bed-room."

"And what o'clock is it now ?" said Terry.

"Why, it's going to three," answered the servant.

Terry put the sign of the cross on his forehead—had a melancholy foreboding of what he was summoned for, and, with fear and trembling, went as he was ordered.

"Well, Terry, this is the second morning, and you have not done what I agreed with you for."

"Oh, sir," said Terry, I declare to God, it 'ant my fault."

"But, I tell you," said Mr. Snoreaway, "it is your fault."

"As I hope to be saved, your honour, but I worked as hard at you as if the good people had you in a trance, and you frightened the life out o' me, and damned and sunk me, and said that you'd discharge me, and that I was an impudent rascal, and was giving your honour the lie, and towld me you were as good as up, and to be off with myself—I wondher what was I to do."

"Well, now, I'll look over this, too. I'll give you one trial more ; and now mark me, and mark me again—whatever I say to you or do, it is not I that say it, or do it ; do not believe me to be fully awake, though I tell you that I am, and you may think so. If I damn you, or curse you, I do not mean it, so don't mind me—do anything and everything until you have me up. If you find all won't do, pull the clothes off me, and throw cold water on me ; and now mind, Terry, besides your wages, I'll give you a guinea, if you do as I tell you, to-morrow morning."

"Say no more, sir," said Terry, "that'll do ;" and away he went, determined to have Snoreaway up the next morning, if he was to lose his life.

The third and last morning came.

The scenes of the two preceding mornings were fully gone through—the snorings, the sighings, the shakings, the get up, sirs, gentle and angry replies, threats, promises of pardon, &c. ; but Terry was not to be trifled with "this going off."

Away went the quilt.

"Oh, you infernal rascal—you scoundrel, are you going to rob and murder me ; I'll call the police, and have you sent this instant to gaol."

Here Snoreaway gave a sudden pull to the bell handle ; but, as the servants knew what was going on, not one of them came up.

He was now in a truly deplorable way.

Terry made a grasp at the blankets ; but Snoreaway had them—fearing an assault on this part of the citadel, after the quilt had been captured—so tucked under him and round him, that it was impossible to pull the blankets off without dragging him out along with them. Terry pulled hard—Newgate was threatened ; there were two loaded pistols in the room, and if he dared to persist in assaulting him in this way, he would blow his brains out before he left the room. It would not do ; all manner of abusive names, curses, oaths, discharges, Newgate. transportation, kickings, and shooting—all fell harmless against the decided determination of Terry to succeed or fall in the action.

Terry was a man of powerful strength—seizing a deadly grasp of the blankets, sheets and all, in his athletic hands, he dislodged his man, who, to save himself from the utter evacuation of his drowsy territory, put out one of his hands and caught the bed-post. Terry still held on, amid a tempest of curses, shrieking, and roaring now loud cries of "Murder, murder," until at length, overpowered by superior strength, the victim of a constitutional, but not a willing, laziness gave up the ghost, and found himself, in an instant, sprawling about the floor. Reviving and self-applauding reason was now beginning, with the glorious sun, to shine bright upon the mind of Snoreaway, and to assert her prerogative.

He now began to lend his own free co-operation to this great work, brought at last to so successful an issue, and, pitching the fragments of the sheet which he had kept lazily adhering to him, from about him, jumped up, and. giving a most hearty laugh, took Terry by the two hands, and shook them, saying—

"Now, Terry, you're my own man—you have now done as I wished, and you see now that I am up and awake—so far from being angry, I applaud you."

He had not proceeded further in dressing himself than having put on his trousers, when he took out his purse, and honourably kept his word with Terry by handing him a guinea in gold. The double joy of poor Terry, upon going down stairs, may be more easily imagined than described

You will be glad to learn that his well-paid pertinacity was of essential benefit to his master, and the day of this glorious victory an epoch in both ther lives.

"Well, I frankly confess," remarked Osborne, "that I never was an early riser, and I don't think it likely I ever shall be."

"You should have recourse to the same means as Mr. Snoreaway," suggested Miss Cary. "It seems to have been very efficient in his case."

At this period of the conversation, dinner was announced, and the whole party wheeled off to partake of the mid-day meal, which, however, in this case, as in many others in fashionable life, was a misnomer, for it was certainly nearer night than mid-day when Osborne's guests were ushered into the dining room to partake of his hospitality.

CHAPTER CXXXI.

SQUABSHOT AND HIS RIVAL.

IT will be necessary for us to leave the palatial mansion of Henry Osborne, for the purpose of taking a glance at the proceedings of our friend Squabshot, whom, it will be remembered, had been supposed to be still rusticating at Osborne's country seat, near Twickenham.

This was delightfully situated close to the banks of the Thames, which was, at the time of which we are writing, veritably a pure and limpid stream. Indeed it was, at Twickenham, as pure as crystal.

Miss Staunton had been located at this delightful retreat for many weeks. Although she possessed an income of her own amply sufficient to maintain herself in the highest degree of respectability, she nevertheless seemed to be almost like one of the family in Osborne's establishment. She had been from girlhood the constant companion of Honora Langford, and when the latter married, she could not bear to part with her old schoolfellow and playmate.

Edith Staunton had neither father or mother living at the time we first made her acquaintance, and although she had a number of relations residing in the West of England, she preferred being with her friend, Mrs. Osborne, than taking up her abode amongst them.

She loved the country and nature's haunts, and the house at Twickenham was in accordance to her tastes.

Squabshot had hovered about her like a shadow. He had taken her out on boating excursions—for Osborne owned a trim built yacht, which Squabshot managed to perfection.

There were, of course, numbers of droppers in at Mr. Osborne's country seat, and Miss Staunton was high priestess of this establishment. Among the most constant of these

visitors was a dissenting minister, the Rev. Ozius Meek by name.

This gentleman had been a bitter thorn in the side of Squabshot; in fact he was an endless source of annoyance to him.

Hour after hour would Meek sit nursing one of his knees, as his eyes followed the movements of the graceful Edith Staunton, as she flitted about the room. Then his voice was so soft and mellifluous—his periods so well rounded. It was not what he said, but the manner of saying it.

His manner was so soft, so insinuating, that Squabshot trembled lest he should be worsted in the conflict by a superior opponent. He hated the Reverend Ozius Meek—most cordially hated him; in truth, hate is too mild a term to express his feelings towards his clerical rival—for rival he felt certain he was.

Let us take a glance at the house where Miss Staunton was located.

The time is in the after part of a summer's day—the long, slant shadows of the tall trees upon the velvetty lawn, gave indications that the sun had lost its meridian power. Miss Staunton is walking on the smooth grass plat at the rear of the house. This plat runs down to the water side.

The gardens which surround Osborne's country seat are beautiful to the last degree —the well-kept lawn, the neatly cut hedges, and pretty parterres, are all that the most fastidious could desire.

By her side may be seen a sleek-looking gentleman dressed in black. This is the Reverend Ozius Meek.

It would appear, from the lady's manner, that she was not aware of the presence of her visitor, for upon her first entering the grounds she started when her eyes lighted upon the well-known features of the clergyman. She drew back for a moment, and then said—

"Oh, pardon me, Mr. Meek, I did not know you were here."

"I was but taking the liberty of enjoying a walk in your grounds," said Mr. Meek, in his most mellifluous tones; "admiring the beauties of nature, which attune the mind to holy thoughts, far removed from this sublunary sphere. The face of nature harmonizes the soul. Miss Staunton, I was awhile lost in reflection."

"I am sorry I have broken in upon your meditations," answered Miss Staunton, who seemed inclined to return.

"Nay, pardon me, madam," said the clergyman, "every place is enhanced in its beauty by the presence of one of Eve's fairest daughters."

"Mr. Meek," said the lady, "you flatter, sir."

"It is not my wont to do so, believe me.

Woman's presence lends a charm to the most arid and desolate scene."

"You are eloquent, sir."

"Nay, I am but just. I should be unworthy the name of man did I not acknowledge this great truth, that your sex are sent to bless and comfort the stern nature of man. Nothing so strongly indicates the possession of a little mind in man, as an appearance of contempt for the intellectual qualifications of the opposite sex; for how absurd it is to observe some coxcomb, vain of the little modicum of knowledge he possesses, or some antiquated pedant, proud of the learned lumber he has obtained, endeavouring to impress upon their auditors the utter hopelessness, uselessness, and ignorance of the fairest portion of the creation! And how repugnant to our feelings it is to hear the libertine repeating the hacknied instances of the evils women have brought upon the earth from the creation of the world to the period of his own useless existence; and I fear me much that there are many such—alas, very many," said Mr. Meek, in a deprecatory tone of voice, as he crossed his hands behind him, and proceeded to walk by the side of his fair companion.

"By such people," said the parson, in continuation, for Miss Staunton had not chosen to make any reply to his homily; "by such people the mother of mankind is abused for having devoted all her posterity to sin and misery, by setting the first example of wickedness and disobedience to the divine commandment. They impute to Helen the shedding of the noblest blood of Greece and Ilium—they denounce Semerimus and Catherine of Russia as demons, whose cruelties caused some of the most fertile portions of the globe to be rendered a solitude and a desert. The murder of John the Baptist, and the revolting cruelty of Amestris, are brought forward as the actions of beings who delighted in blood; while Catherine of Russia and Elizabeth of England, are spoken of as tyrants whose beauty and ambition were the cause of death and disgrace to some of the most excellent and most innocent of their fellow creatures. But are the whole sex to be condemned for the crimes of a few?—and is man to be considered an innocent and perfect being? Justice, Miss Staunton, compels me to say no! If Eve was the first to commit sin, Cain was the first to perpetrate murder."

The Reverend Ozius Meek paused. He looked up into the face of her who he had been addressing, as though he were anxious to obtain an expression of approval. He was, however, doomed to disappointment, for Miss Staunton had thought but little of his high flown defence and eulogism of women.

"Besides, what man could believe aught but high honour and purity could dwell in one of Nature's fairest forms," he added with a sigh.

"There are good and bad of both men and women, Mr. Meek," said Edith Staunton, sententiously.

"Without a doubt, my dear madam, without a doubt," added the clergymen. "Examples of female cruelty are, thank Heaven, but of rare occurrence; but the attrocities committed by mankind have been too numerous to find chroniclers.

To the latter we are indebted for the invention of torture to extract confession—for all punishments which power has created and innocence suffered; and man it was who first practised murder for the sake of the dead body.

History records no instances of cruelty in a woman so revolting as that of Nero, Caligula, and the rest of the Roman tyrants; of Robespierre, Danton, and the other despots of the French revolution; or of the innumerable wretches who in all ages have disgraced the shape of man, and delighted in the destruction of their species.

The scholar who is determined to seek in classical literature for evidence to back his arguments against the excellence of the female character, will possibly find what he may consider sufficient authority for his opinions by a careful examination of some of the Greek and Latin authors; but we object to their evidence, for two reasons—first, because they did not understand sufficient of the subject to judge correctly; and, secondly, causes have influenced their opinion, and rendered their judgment partial.

Euripides acknowledged his dislike of the sex, but he is supposed to have had some reasonable ground in his objections; for he married twice, and his wives turned out abominable shrews.

Socrates possessed but an unfavourable sample of womankind in the vociferous Xanthippe—he may, therefore, be supposed to have had a similar reason for complaining.

Susarion gives some shrewd advice to his countrymen on the absolute necessity of female society; for, although he declares that women are a torment, he acknowledges that it would be as great a torment to be obliged to live without their assistance.

In works of both historians and poets we meet with some severe reflections on the character of the Roman ladies. Tacitus gives us vivid and revolting descriptions of feminine depravity; in Livy we find similar scenes; and Sallust forcibly delineates the criminal licentiousness which then disgraced female society.

From such writers as Ovid and Catullus we cannot expect to gain any favourable information on the subject; and the minor poets, whose works are of a similar nature, follow the examples of their greater contemporaries, and speak of woman but as an instrument of pleasure. But when the Roman's lost the primitive simplicity of manners which adorned their early history, it could not be expected otherwise than that their women should partake of their degeneracy; and the profligacy of the males is always a sufficient excuse for the licentiousness of the females.

In approaching nearer to our own times, we find that the early dramatists were fond of having an occasional fling at the failings of the softer sex.

Heywood, who was jester to Henry VIII., and is supposed to be the first person who introduced the legitimate drama into England, in an interlude written by him, called "The Four P's," which is a humourous dialogue in verse, between a palmer, a pardoner, a pothecary, and a pedlar, makes these worthies come to a determination of having their individual claims to pre-eminence settled by a trial of their qualifications as relaters of the marvellous and improbable; and, in the very spirit of Munchausen, they state the most incredible fictions that were ever invented; but at last this happy talent (of which many of our modern travellers are no contemptible professors) is universally allowed to belong to the palmer.

"Why even our great poet, Milton," said Mr. Meek, in continuation, "has written one of the severest satires against women."

"Milton!" exclaimed Miss Staunton, in some surprise. "One of our greatest poets."

"Yes, Miss Staunton, Milton. You must bear in mind that few men experienced so many vexations in domestic life. From brooding over his own unhappiness, and from the continued state of moral torture in which his highly sensitive feelings were kept by the sight of his desolate hearth and comfortless house, while his disappointment preyed upon his spirits till their action produced a morbid sensibility on his mind. He began to imagine that a woman's heart was the source of malice, hypocrisy, and wickedness, instead of being a fountain of living waters, possessed of all the sweet humanities of life; and the troubled bard, sinking under his domestic afflictions, seems to have called into question the wisdom of the Deity for forming a creature so fair to view, and so false to know, as woman, when he exclaims—

"Oh! why did God,
Creator wise, that peopled highest heaven
With spirits masculine, create at last
This novelty on earth, this fair defect
Of nature, and not fill the world at once
With men, as angels, without feminine,
Or find some other way to generate
Mankind? This mischief had not then befallen,

And more that shall befall, innumerable
Disturbances on earth through female snares."

"When we remember the misery of the husband, Miss Staunton," said the parson, "we must pardon the injustice of the poet. Milton found his felicity shipwrecked and fancied that the happiness of mankind must founder on the same shores. Could he for a moment have known the brilliance of the different phases of the female character, woman's tender solicitude as a mother, wonderful affection as a daughter. Her gentle kindness as a sister. Her sincere disinterestedness as a friend, and the earnestness of her devotion to the object of her idolatry—as a being capable of conferring happiness upon another—he would have been more anxious to prove that she was created to be honoured and respected, to be careful and loved. Yes, loved, my dear young lady!"

The lady made no reply, whereupon the gentleman handed her to a rustic seat, which was placed under an umbrageous tree. Miss Staunton seated herself, the gentleman also; after a few minutes the latter sighed.

"You are an eloquent defender of the female portion of the community," said Edith Staunton, not knowing what to say, for to speak the truth, she felt uncomfortable when left alone with the immaculate and sanctified Ozius Meek.

He was so very good—or professed to be; he entered into such learned disquisitions; he picked his words, and occasionally let fall such high-sounding phrases—that Edith felt herself under a certain restraint in his presence.

More than this, with woman's keen perception, she had divined that the marvel of perfection, Meek, had some lurking, a sneaking fondness for her—the latter term will be the best one, perhaps, to convey to the reader's mind the peculiar manner of Ozius. For a moment he made no reply to Honora's last observation. His mind seemed pre-occupied, as he gazed out abstractedly upon the silver Thames, which flowed and ebbed within a few yards from where he and his companion were seated.

"I beg your pardon, Miss Stanton, "he exclaimed, somewhat suddenly. "What were you observing. You must really pardon my inattention, but the fact is I was thinking of —shall I confess it—of you."

"Of me?" exclaimed Honora in some surprise.

"Yes my dear lady of you. I dont think I have told you that I have an offer to go abroad. When I say an offer I am perhaps not speaking correctly. I should with greater truth say a command!"

"Indeed! from whom?"

"From that inward monitor which tells me that it is my bounden duty to fulfil that

mission for which I am sent on the earth. That mission which has been entrusted to me by him who sees and knows all hearts. Permit me to briefly explain. You must know, Miss Staunton, that there are a certain number of our clergymen whose duty it is to go abroad to savage regions and there to publish the gospel and words of eternal truth."

"Yes, I have heard of that before," answered Edith.

"Well, my dear young lady, these men, are devoted warriors on the Lord's side. They are our conscript, a chosen few, who are to wrestle with bigotry, ignorance, and paganism. Theirs is a glorious mission—most glorious!" exclaimed the eloquent Meek, casting his eyes up to the blue vault above. The sun came into his eyes, so he was fain to lower his enraptured gaze.

No. 89.

"Some of them get killed sometimes, do they not, Mr. Meek."

"Alas, yes. I regret to say that our missionaries have been peculiarly unfortunate, but it does not deter us. It does not deter others from following in their wake. Well, I was observing but just now that I was thinking about you. That was strange you thought. Shall I confess it. I was also thinking about myself"

"Oh, indeed. Well, there is no harm in that."

"But I much fear me there is harm in it," said the soft-spoken and oily tongued Meek. "Listen. It has almost become an imperative necessity for me to leave the country."

"My dear Mr. Meek, I am sorry to hear you say so," said Edith, in her own natural and ingenious manner. " Very sorry to lose you."

"Oh, what entrancing music it is to hear you say those words," said the clergyman, with rapture. "It's sweeter than the noise of gushing waters to the parched traveller in a sandy desert! Sweet and delicious."

"As I was observing," said the wily priest in continuation; "as I was observing, my dear young lady, my duty prompts me to journey far away from a place which is endeared to me by a thousand recollections, but none will remain so permanent and so dear to my recollections as the memory of yourself. Miss Staunton, it has been reserved for you to awake in my heart the deep and enduring passion of love."

"Of love!" exclaimed Edith, in unfeigned surprise, as she drew back some short distance from the side of her admirer.

If the Reverend Ozius Meek had turned his head towards a clump of Portugal laurels, which were situated some dozen or fifteen yards from where he and Edith were seated. —if the reverend lover had cast his eyes in that direction—he would have observed an apparition which might have somewhat discomposed him. It was none other than our old friend Squabshot, who had sought Miss Staunton in the garden, and had just come up in time to hear the latter part of Mr. Meek's discourse. Our little friend was awestruck. He stood transfixed with horror—dark and desperate thoughts rushed through his brain. Should he immolate the sanctimonious Meek then and there upon the spot? He stood irresolute, not daring to trust himself to break in upon the scene. From the position he occupied he could only see the backs of the two persons seated on the garden chair; but he knew well enough who they both were. The well-known tones of the parson's voice would have at once declared his identity. Squabshot's eyes were rivetted on these two individuals. Presently, to his horror, he observed the parson kneel down upon one knee, take Miss Staunton's hand in his, and pour forth a passionate declaration of love.

Squabshot's knees knocked together, he felt a sort of choking sensation in his throat. At first he thought of suddenly quitting the spot, but he found that retreat was impossible; there was a degree of fascination which rivetted him to the spot. He must stay and hear the end of this, to him, agonising interview. He gathered some small crumbs of comfort from the fact, that Edith Staunton was evidently an unwilling actor in the scene. She endeavoured to disengage her hand from the grasp of her clerical admirer, who persisted in retaining it, pressing the same to his lips with the fervour of a passionate admirer. Squabshot felt like a man

suddenly struck by lightning—a violent paroxysm shook his frame. He could contain himself no longer, but suddenly emerging from the clump of evergreens, he walked up in front of the two individuals. Miss Staunton uttered a slight scream, and struggled in vain to release herself from the grasp of her admirer.

Squabshot uttered a groan of anger as he presented himself. Mr. Meek looked up to where he stood, and it is probable that he was—we were going to say, overwhelmed with shame, but, perhaps this would be too strong an expression. He was certainly humiliated to a certain extent.

"Ah, ah!—our esteemed friend, Mr. Squabshot," said the Reverend Ozius Meek, rising from his kneeling posture, and endeavouring to look as little discomposed as possible, "our friend, Mr. Squabshot," he iterated, in his most bland accents.

"Don't friend me, sir," cried Squabshot, drawing himself up to his full height, which, to say the truth, was never very great, "don't friend me, sir—I am no friend to hypocrites and impostors."

"Hypocrites and impostors!" exclaimed the priest, "Mr. Squabshot, I pity you."

"Pity me! D—n your pity!" yelled out Squabshot, who was boiling over with ill-concealed rage; who wants your pity? the pity of a sneak and a—ah—an impostor!"

"Young man," said the Reverend Ozius Meek, who endeavoured to assume an air of injured innocence, although he was, in reality, boiling over with ill-suppresed rage, "Young man, I cannot feel at my heart to be angry with you, no, indeed I cannot, although you have given utterance to unseemly expressions, which, I know, your calmer judgment will teach you to repudiate and regret; I know this, and therefore I am not angry—no, indeed I am not."

This was uttered with such a meek manner, and such a bland, rolling, sonorous voice, that, as he proceeded he seemed to become more satisfied and naturally contented, as though pleased to hear the music of his own voice.

"Yes, I am sure Mr. Squabshot," he said, in continuation, "I am quite sure that you will have reason to regret having given utterance to those expressions which have inadvertently fallen from your lips. I know that you will castigate yourself for having poured forth your vials of wrath upon the Lord's annointed. I am not angry with you, but I am rather moved to pity. Repent, young man, ere it be too late—repent and turn from your wickedness."

"Insolent impostor!" said Squabshot. "Don't seek to come any of your hypocritial whinings over me. I despise and contemn you. And mark ye sir, it will not be long before I unmask you. It will not be long before I expose the wolf in sheep's clothing. Do you hear that, sir," said Squabshot, stamping on the ground in a violent rage.

Mr. Ozius Meek was astonished; so much so, that he actually turned white, almost as white as his spotless cravat; his coutenance underwent such a sudden change, and he looked so threateningly at his rival, that Miss Staunton rose from the seat she had been occupying and interposed between them.

"Gentlemen, for my sake, pray do not lose your tempers. Mr. Squabshot, I am surprised at you!"

Poor Squabshot, when he heard this fall from the lips of her whom he loved to distraction, did not know how to bear up against the accumulated mass of misfortunes which seemed to come, all at once, upon him. He reeled back, and, after a pause of a few seconds duration, exclaimed "Surprised at *me*, Miss Staunton,—Edith! I—that is—I am perfectly petrified myself. Can it be possible?—is it possible?"

"What?" inquired Edith.

Mr. Squabshot could not find it in his heart to reply to this query, he only looked at his rival, and then turned away in disgust, and, indeed, to say the truth, his looks were, perhaps, much more eloquent than words.

"You must pardon me, my dear Miss Staunton," said the very Reverend Ozius, "you must pardon me for being the unwwitting cause of some annoyance to yourself. I deeply regret this, I was not aware at the time, I was giving utterance to words which came from my heart, that there was any eves-dropper near." Will you permit me to have the pleasure of conducting you to the house."

"No, sir," cried Squabshot, "she will not permit you, at least, I won't hang your impudence, so you think to carry it off with a high head, do you? If any one is to conduct Miss Staunton into her own house it shall be myself, who is an older, and, I should hope, a more trusty friend than you."

"If you are a gentleman," answered the clergyman, "you will not interfere in this matter"

"And if you are a gentleman, which I much doubt," said Squabshot; "you will leave these grounds at once. You are an intruder here. I had an appointment with Miss Staunton to take her on the water; and when she wants to go into her own residence, I can escort her without your assistance or interference."

"It is for the lady to decide," said Mr. Meek, as he turned his glance upon Edith.

"I certainly had an appointment with Mr. Squabshot," said Edith Staunton.

"Ah, indeed!" exclaimed the parson, somewhat staggered. Then raising his head respectfully, he said "I should be sorry to interfere with any appointment Miss

Staunton had made, and therefore, although I have been the subject of personal remarks—and, I may add, of personal abuse—although such has been the case, I will, my dear young lady, take my departure, if such is your wish; for I need not say that your wish is to me law, as unalterable as those of the Medes and Persians. But before I leave, I hope I may crave a few minutes' conversation with you in private."

Edith Staunton hesitated.

Mr. Squabshot was the first make a reply to this request of his clerical adversary. It will be seen plainly enough that Squabshot was quite out of order in all he had been doing and saying, but he was out of temper as well as out of order, and hardly knew how to be disagreeable enough with the amatory parson.

"You have had quite enough conversation with Miss Staunton, sir. She has heard quite enough of your smooth-tongued hypocrisy."

"You are an insolent fellow," said the parson, in quite a different tone of voice to the one he usually assumed, "and deserve chastisement on the spot for the insults you have chosen to heap upon me in the presence of a lady; and were it not for my respect for Miss Staunton, I would not be here to listen to your insulting vituperations. But I pity your ignorance, although, at the same time, I am free to confess that I contemn and despise the man who can so far forget himself as to be utterly regardless of the conduct which is due to the character of a gentleman."

"I am not a hypocrite," said Squabshot.

"You are an ungodly man and a sinner," answered the parson.

"I don't take money from people, to give away in charity, and put it in my own pocket," said Squabshot.

"Mr. Squabshot, really this is too bad!" exclaimed Edith Staunton. "You are positively insulting. If you cannot conduct yourself better, pray leave us."

"Leave you with him?," said Squabshot. "Oh, Miss Staunton, you know nothing about this man's doings. You believe in his smooth-tongued discourse. A time will come when you will have cause to regret your credulity."

"Hush! Silence! I conjure you to say no more," said Edith.

"I am silent," answered Squabshot, folding his arms, casting a withering look at the priest, and walking to the farther end of the grounds.

Mr. Meek then advanced to the side of Miss Staunton.

"My dear and esteemed young lady," he said, in his blandest accents. "If I have evinced any temper, I am sure your own generous nature will pardon and forgive me. I little deemed that so abrupt, so unpleasant a termination would have been put to our converse. I love you—I have already told you this much. May I hope. Do not doom me to despair. For you I would forego my sacred mission. It is selfish, you will say, for me to do so; perhaps it is, but oh! Miss Staunton—Miss Edith, if you will permit me to call you so, we are none, not even the best of us, masters of ourselves. It is reserved for you to either make or mar my happiness for life. I do not ask you to return me an answer now, all I would beg of you is this, to consider what I have said, which, believe me, has been spoken in all the sincerity of my heart. All I would ask is this. I dare not hope—I cannot hope that so poor and plain a man as myself should have won the love of one of the fairest and gentlest of her sex—I cannot hope that; but when you learn more of me, when you are fully acquainted with that deep and devoted feeling of sincere attachment which I feel towards you, and will only cease with my life, I think then—that is, assuming your heart is not already engaged— I do think that you may possibly be brought to look more favourably on me than you do at present."

"You have surprised me, Mr. Meek. I must confess, that this morning you have very much surprised me." answered Edith Staunton. "I have always looked upon you as a gentleman who has commanded my respect, and, I may add, my esteem; but within the last hour you have assumed quite a new character—and, indeed, to say the truth, Mr. Meek, you have been somewhat sudden in your declaration."

"And is that all Miss Staunton has to say upon the subject?" inquired the Reverend Ozius Meek.

"Well, for the present, I do not know what more I have, or, indeed, need be said," answered Edith.

"Do you bid me hope?"

"Well, Mr. Meek, I must deal frankly with you; I am not a romantic girl—never was."

"All the better—I like you the more on that very account."

"And being a practical girl, or woman— for, to say the truth, although not married, I am no longer a girl, but rather more like a staid woman—"

"Precisely," said the reverend gentleman, with a smile, "a woman, if it please you better."

"Well, then, I must frankly confess that I do not feel myself justified in accepting of your offer; that is, I do not consider that I ought to receive you as a suitor."

"Ought not! Pardon me, my dear young lady, but I suppose the truth is—that—I mean, I am to imagine that you are already engaged."

"I do not say that," answered Edith Staunton.

"Ah!" exclaimed the reverend gentleman, with a deep-drawn sigh of relief; "then what is to be the interpretation to your words?"

"Our tastes are dissimilar, in the first place."

"My dear Miss Staunton, I should hope not. Wherefore, pray?"

"Oh, it's impossible for us to discuss this question now—some other time," said Edith Staunton, wishing, evidently enough, to bring their interview to a close as soon as possible.

"Well, some other time—so be it," said the clergyman. "I would not be importunate—I would not trespass upon your forbearance—only I am somewhat hurt at the last expression which has fallen from your lips."

"Which one do you mean?" inquired Edith, with surprise.

"That one in which you declare our tastes are dissimilar."

"I fear they are."

"What should make you imagine that? It would and, indeed, should be, my most constant care to consult your wishes and taste in everything—in every action of my life."

"Well," said Edith, "such has been and is my impression."

"You do not like my calling, perhaps?" said Mr. Meek.

"Nay, I should be wrong to object to so sacred an one—but—"

"But what?"

"Why, I am not sufficiently good, or sanctified—there, it will out—to become the wife of a clergyman," said Edith, with a slight smile upon her beauteous countenance.

"You are an ornament, and add a grace to any household," said Mr. Meek.

"Ah, you flatter, Sir Priest," answered his companion. "But we have all our fancies, and my sex are, in truth, the most capricious of the two."

"Our fancies!—of course we have," answered her companion, not a little discomposed at the declaration, for it would appear that he was not her fancy—at least, that was the inference he deduced from her observation. "Yes, we have certainly our fancies, Miss Staunton. We have more than that— at least, I have—a deep, devoted, and—I fear, hopeless love!" he added, sadly, as his voice became suddenly broken. "Yes, I fear a love which is hopeless—utterly hopeless. What say you, Miss Staunton? Yours is a gentle nature, and you might have pity on me."

"We cannot talk further on this subject at present," answered Edith. "You know,

Mr. Meek, we are but recent acquaintances, and I have, that is, I have known but little of you further than your occasional visits to the house of my friend, Mr. Osborne."

"I am aware of that. I do not wish you to do anything precipitate—anything that your calmer reason would have cause to regret. No, I would not wish that. Let us become better acquainted, and in time, perhaps, you may relent."

"I know not what I have to relent," answered Edith.

"You may learn to view me with more favourable eyes, that is my meaning."

"Oh, I understand," said Edith Staunton, with a slight laugh. "Well, for the present, Mr. Meek, I will bid you farewell."

She extended her hand as she said this. The parson raised it to his lips, and took his departure.

Edith Staunton was delighted to see him emerge through the green-gate which led into the garden at the rear of Osborne's house.

All this while, our friend Squabshot had been at the extreme end of the said garden. He made hideous faces at the priest as he took his departure. After which he strolled to where Miss Staunton was standing.

"Well, sir," said that lady, as he approached, "are you not ashamed of your rude conduct? What have you to say for yourself?"

Squabshot hung down his head. We have seen during our acquaintance with him that he was not, or rather, used not to be a particularly bashful man. Neither was he so now, save when in the presence of Edith Staunton.

"Can you not answer, sir?" said his companion.

"Miss Staunton—my dear Miss Staunton, I was mad. I did not know what I was saying. Ah, if you could only imagine the agony I have endured, you would not only forgive, but pity me."

"The Reverend Ozias Meek pitied you; what more do you desire?"

"Hang his pity!" exclaimed Squabshot. "Oh, I beg your pardon," he added, in continuation, as he observed a transient expression of displeasure cross the face of Edith. "I beg you ten thousand pardons. The fact is, ahem! I don't think I know very clearly what I am about, and that's the truth."

"Well, I don't think you do, Mr. Squabshot, or you would never have forgotten yourself so, and used such insulting expressions to the very Reverend Ozius Meek," answered Edith Staunton.

"I hate and despise him," exclaimed Squabshot; "yes, hate and despise him. Oh, Miss Edith, judge of my horror, my agonised state of mind, when I beheld that fellow on his knees before you. It's enough to drive anyone mad."

"And wherefore, sir, I pray?" inquired Miss Staunton.

"Can you ask?" said Squabshot.

"Yes, I do ask, of course. Haven't you heard me?"

"Oh, Edith, I have never spoken before—"

"Never spoken!" exclaimed the lady, in surprise. "My dear Mr. Squabshot, you are certainly mad."

"I don't mean that—"

"No, I should think not. What do you mean then?"

"I say I have not spoken of the volcano that lies smothered in this breast."

"Dear me, that is sad. A volcano?"

"Yes, my heart is in flames. Morning, noon, and night I have but one thought, it is the deep and unalterable attachment I bear towards yourself. I could have immolated that smock-faced deceiver upon the spot. By heavens! I know not what restrained me—unless it was your presence," he added, a little more calmly.

"I am glad I was here, then."

"Miss Edith, I am not an eloquent man. I hardly know how to give expression to my feelings, but tell me—oh, in mercy tell me, have you listened to the suit of that reptile?"

"Reptile!"

"Yes, madam, reptile. I can call him nothing else. If you knew one half of his duplicity you would stand appalled. He is a reptile of the very worst character, for he comes under the garb of sanctity."

"Mr. Squabshot, I shall not stay to listen to these slanders. You ought to know yourself better—you ought to have greater respect for his calling. There, I am not angry with you, only drop these personalities."

"You defend him!" exclaimed Squabshot, retreating back some paces—"you defend him!"

"No, I do not, but I like not to forget the rights of hospitality."

"Miss Staunton, the fellow is a robber. I'll prove it. He is treasurer of a fund and has cheated numbers of persons out of their little all."

"Nonsense, man, you are dreaming."

"Ah, you defend him."

"No, I do not."

"Pardon me, I thought you did."

"He bears an excellent character from all who know him. You must be altogether mistaken in your surmise."

"He may bear a character good enough, for the matter of that, by those who do not know him, but I happen to have it from the very best authority that he was about to fly from his native town in consequence of having cheated and robbed everybody. There, what do yov say to that? The very best authority—indisputable authority."

"And pray who may that be ? Some person who is, like yourself, jealous of him, perhaps."

"Miss Staunton, I am not jesting now—I am serious in what I am saying. The fellow is a hypocrite, a cheat, and a scoundrel."

"Bah ! Your passion gets the better of your discretion. We must not—ought not —to believe what people say in their detraction of others."

"I believe my informant," answered the other.

"Who is he, or she, perhaps."

Jonathan Wild, the most celebrated thieftaker of the day," said Squabshot, putting himself in a tragic attitude.

"Jonathan Wild," iterated Miss Staunton, for the very mention of the thieftaker's name caused an alarm to the fair Edith. "Do you know Jonathan Wild, then ?"

"Yes, perfectly well," answered her companion.

Miss Staunton drew back a pace or two, and regarded the speaker with a look of amazement.

"Perfectly well," said Squabshot, in continuation, "and more than this, I hear from him that the very Reverend Ozius Meek was very nearly being taken in custody by the thieftaker. It was only because he had managed matters so artfully as to avoid the charge of embezzlement, by making himself a partner, that he escaped being punished for his crime."

"Surely, my friend, you must be mistaken —misinformed," said Edith.

"But I tell you I am not. I'll swear it— swear to the truth of what I have given utterance to."

"How long have you known this ?"

"Oh, a long time."

"Why did you not mention it before ?" said Edith.

"Because I am not fond of picking holes in other persons' coats, particularly when it is a parson who wears the coat. Don't you see that ? And I should not have done so now, only I heard that you might be taken in by the rascal, and that with his bland manner he might win your affection."

"Oh, that's it, eh ?" said Edith, as she burst out in a loud and long continued laugh. "I am sure I ought to be much obliged to you."

"And when you know, or if you don't know you ought, that's all I have to say, that I doat on the very ground you walk upon— that you are to me the very sun of my existence—the air I breathe—the food I live on— my life—my soul—my world," exclaimed Squabshot, with a vehement burst of passion and tenderness that surprised Miss Staunton,

and which, to say the truth, did even more than that, it surprised himself.

"There, that will do," said Edith. "Come, your arm, I would go into the house. We will, if you please, drop the curtain upon this scene, and at the same time endeavour to forget it."

Squabshot offered his arm to the lady, and escorted her into the house.

———

CHAPTER CXXXII.

SHOWS HOW THE RIVAL SUITORS WERE TREATED.

SOME two or three days after the incidents we have already described had occurred, the Reverend Ozius Meek once more presented himself at the residence of Henry Osborne.

It was evening when he came, and as it happened, there were several persons assembled in the drawing room. Mr. Meek was invited up stairs, *sans ceremony.*

Squabshot, at the time of his entrance, was seated at the piano, singing a comic song.

The entrance of Mr. Meek, so completely discomposed Squabshot, that he had some difficuilty in getting through his song at all. However he did manage to finish it, and rose from the music stool on which he had been seated.

Edith Staunton, cast upon him a look, indicating that she expected him to comport himself with something like courtesy.

The Reverend Ozius Meek bowed stifly to Squabshot, who did just condescend to return his salutation, that was all. Most of the other guests were known to the clergyman ; and he therefore shook hands with one after the other in due form.

There was a sort of depression, after the entrance of Mr. Meek, which Edith Staunton in vain endeavoured to dispel.

Squabshot was, of course, not at his ease, neither did the conversation flow with that degree of merriment, as it had done before the parson's entrance. Perhaps he saw this, for he took an opportunity, after about half-an-hour had elapsed, to speak privately to Miss Staunton.

"I fear me much, I am intruding here," said Meek.

"Oh, dear no, not at all. What should make you imagine that ?" inquired his fair hostess.

"Well, I know not, it was but a suggestion. Your friend, Mr. Squabshot."

"Oh, he regrets having made use of the expressions he did—I assure you he does. Let me hasten to apologise for him."

"You are good and kind," answered the

clergyman. "May I beg a few minutes' conversation with you ?'

Edith Staunton hesitated, but as she thought Meek seemed pained at her want of promptitude in answering his query, she at once granted his request, and led him into an ante-room, contiguous however to the one they were then occupying.

"Now sir," said Miss Staunton, when she had arrived at the ante-room, and handed her companion a seat.

"Now, Mr. Meek, I am at your service."

This was said as though she wished him to be as breif as possible.

A shade of displeasure pased over the features of the reverend gentleman.

"Miss Staunton, I had hoped to have found you disengaged and alone; in this however I am disappointed," said Meek. "I need hardly say, why I desire an interview with you ; I have, as you have nodoubt divined, not deemed it expedient to intrude myself upon your notice, since that unpleasant interuption we had in the garden. May I inquire if you have thought of what I have said, of those words which fell from my lips, of the deep—"

"Yes I know," said Miss Staunton, suddenly interrupting him, which was certainly not over polite. "I know. Have I thought anything of the declaration you were pleased to make, and of the great honour you have done me."

"Nay, the honour it would be to me if—"

"Yes, I understand, I feel greatly flattered. Of course no woman could do otherwise under such circumstances."

"I do not say that."

"But I do. Well, no woman could do otherwise. Permit me to proceed, if you please."

The clergyman bowed submission to this mandate.

"I have considered," said Miss Staunton.

"Oh, you have, well that is a relief. A relief to think that you even condescended to bear in your mind so unworthy an object as myself. And what have you determined. Am I to hope ? Will you consent to know more of me?"

"I shall of course be always glad to receive you as a friend," answered Edith Staunton, emphasising the last word in a marked manner, which was painful to the Reverend Ozius Meek.

"A friend !" he exclaimed. "And in time ?"

"Well, in time. What else."

"I hope to visit you in a more distinct character—as a lover, in fact."

The lady gently shook her head.

"I fear not, Mr. Meek. You must not take it unkindly, but in fact I like frankness—"

"So do I, madam," answered her companion,

so sharply, and in such a different tone of voice to the one he had hitherto assumed, that Miss Staunton was quite surprised thereat.

"Well, then," said Edith, in continuation, "I must at once declare that, although I am greatly flattered by your offer, I am at the same time bound in honour to refuse it."

"Bound in honour I did not understand that you were engaged to anyone," said the clergyman, in surprise, as there was an expression of deep meaning in his eye—a meaning which declared that there was certain smouldering passions beneath the outer encrustations of his calm exterior.

"I cannot say that I am," said Miss Staunton.

"Well, then, am I to understand that I am repulsive to you?" exclaimed the clergyman.

"Nay, do not imagine that for a moment," answered Edith, in a kinder and more gentle tone of voice.

"What am I to divine, then? Simply this, that there has been some malicious, scandalising knave who has come betwixt yourself and me. I can guess the cause of this strange alteration in your tone and manner. In justice to myself, I must ask of you as you possess so much candour, if such be not the case."

"Your assumption must be evidently incorreet to yourself. Is not my bearing and manner precisely the same as it was when you first broached this subject in the garden ? Assuredly you cannot find anything inconsistent in my conduct. I told you then, Mr. Meek, that I did not, nay, could not look upon you in any other light than as a friend."

"Nay, I think not—you did not say that much. Come now, deal candidly with me. There has been some traducer in this business, and I will tell you who the individual is—Mr. Squabshot !" exclaimed Meek, with anything but a meek manner. "Mr. Squabshot, madam, and none other !" iterated the now much-moved clergyman, "and he shall answer for it—I will make him answer for it—I will indict him for scandal—for wicked and despicable scandal !"

So loud did Mr. Meek utter these words, that they reached the ears of Squabshot himself.

Edith Staunton endeavoured to pacify the irritated saint as well as she could, but he seemed to have lost himself as much as his rival had two or three days previous.

Squabshot could remain passive no longer. He emerged from the front room on to the landing which led to the staircase, and as he made his appearance there, Mr. Meek called out, in a loud voice—

"Stand forth, thou vile traducer ! Thou despicable slanderer !"

This time our friend Squabshot assumed his own natural bantering tone, which, in truth, was at all times the more natural to him.

Does any gentleman call me?" inquired Squabshot, now assuming an oleagenous tone of voice, not unlike that in which his rival indulged when in his more placid moods.

"Ah, don't, pray don't!" said Edith Staunton; "gentlemen! for my sake—do not pursue the subject further!"

"But it must be pursued further," said Meek. "One of the elect has been scandalised—and there stands the brazen-fronted individual—an ungodly man—a wordly man, without, ah, without the fear of the Lord before his eyes. Answer me, thou sinful man, answer me!"

"What do you want?" said Squabshot, not in the least discomposed. "Do you wish me to answer for you?"

"You have already heaped insult upon me in the presence of this lady, sir," said the irritated Meek.

"I am aware of it," answered Squabshot, "and permit me, Mr. Meek, to offer you every apology for having let fall expressions which in my calmer moments I see good reason to sincerely regret."

"But you have done worse than this, sir," said Meek, rising and advancing threateningly towards his rival; "you have done worse than this—you have poured poison in the ear of one who is much dearer to me than my own life."

"Beg pardon, but I think you are mistaken," answered Squabshot, who was, however, under the impression that Miss Edith Staunton had repeated all he had said to her.

"No, sir, I am not mistaken, and you cannot—you dare not—look me in the face and deny the allegation!"

Mr. Squabshot did look his companion in the face, and very hard too.

They stood scowling at one another for a few moments, when Squabshot said, with the utmost coolness—

"Mr. Ozius Meek, do not lose your temper, I pray—it is unseemly for a gentleman of your persuasion, of your holy calling. Whatever I have said of you or anybody else, is the truth. • I know you are an expounder of the truth, and you cannot complain of so humble an individual as myself endeavouring to follow so worthy an example."

The Reverend Ozius Meek was pale with rage.

"You shall answer for this, you insolent scoundrel," he exclaimed; "you shall answer for this."

"Shall I?"

"Yes, sir, you shall answer for this."

"For what?" inquired Squabshot.

"For the malicious lies you have given utterance to."

"Lies?"

"Yes, sir."

"What do you mean?"

"What I have said," replied Mr. Ozius Meek.

"Now, look here," said Squabshot, "I do not want to expose you before any one, but if you don't be a little more civil, I certainly will."

"Expose me?"

"Yes."

"Expose me, thou miserable and wretched imposter! What do you mean?"

"Simply this, that those who live in glass houses themselves should not throw stones at their neighbours—that is what I mean."

"Oh, gentlemen, gentlemen, let this discussion drop," exclaimed Edith Staunton. "We are breaking in upon the amusements of the evening, and—"

"I am sorry that this should be so, madam," said Meek, "but you must pardon me when I say *my* character is of far greater importance to me than any amusement, and much as I regret being the cause of any inconvenience either to yourself or your guests, I am bound, as a man of honour, were it before fifty persons, to shame the traducer."

Squabshot gave vent to a loud laugh as the reverend gentleman finished this little speech, and pointed towards our little friend.

"Oh, you'll take a long time to shame me," said Squabshot.

"I fear so," answered his rival. "But I can expose you, I can hold you up to the execration of all good persons," said Meek.

"Ask him if he knows Mary Curtis," said a voice from the door of the front drawing-room.

It would be impossible for us to depict or even give a faint idea of the varied expressions on the countenances of those present as the words dropped from a stranger or comparative stranger to those in the back room. Mr. Meek actually reeled back at the mention of the name of Mary Curtis.

Edith Staunton stared from one to the other in mute surprise, and Squabshot gazed in the direction from whence the voice proceeded.

"Beg your pardon," exclaimed the latter, after a pause, "but I think some gentleman spoke."

"Ask the Reverend Ozius Meek if he knows the name of Mary Curtis," said the same voice.

"You hear, sir," exclaimed Squabshot, looking at the clergyman.

"I do hear," replied that individual, who by this time had somewhat recovered him-

self. "Yes, sir, I do hear. And what of that?"

"Know Mary Curtis!" inquired Squabshot·

"I did such an individual once."

"Ah, I thought so," said the person who had asked the question, "and she has good cause to know you."

"I do not understand the meaning of these interrogations," exclaimed the Reverend Ozius Meek.

The young man who had been so inquisitive now emerged from the doorway of the front drawing-room. The Reverend Ozius Meek regarded him with an inquiring, and at the same time a defiant look. The parson did not seem to recognise the new comer.

"Come," said the latter, "we have met before, and I do not seek to expose you."

No. 90.

And as he said this he looked hard at the sanctified Meek, as much as to say, it would be better to take himself off without bringing on what is termed "a scene."

Mr. Meek returned his look, and, from the expression of his countenance, it might be divined that he was inclined to enact the part of a bully.

"Your interruption is an impertinent one, to say the least of it, sir!" exclaimed Mr. Meek. And hark ye, sir! the impertinent questions you have thought proper to put to me before this lady, would admit of an unfavourable construction. The implication would be that there was some disreputable conduct on the part of myself. I am well aware that you have done this only for the purpose of annoying me, and in the hope of humbling me in the eyes of my fair hostess. But my mission in this world is an errand of peace, and I hope and trust that I shall not be tempted to forget my sacred calling. You take advantage of this, otherwise, from anyone else the probability is that you would have met with personal chastisement on the spot, which your conduct so well merits. However, I pity and forgive you—and now you will, perhaps, oblige me by leaving the room."

"Ah, ah!" laughed Squabshot and his friend, for the young man in question was a particular young friend of his. "Really this is a good joke. You are pleased to be facetious, Mr. Meek."

"You are pleased to be insulting, sir," answered the clergyman. "How dare you conduct yourself thus in the presence of a lady!' Then turning to Edith he said, "My dear Miss Staunton, I must pray of you to pardon this unpleasant scene, I deeply regret that my presence here should have been the cause of any annoyance to yourself; but at the same time permit me to hope and trust that no observation of these persons will weigh with you for a moment, as I am sure neither of them are worthy of credit."

"You had better ask Mr. Jonathan Wild for your own character," said Squabshot's friend.

"Mr. Wild! I do not even know such a person," answered Meek, at the same time, however, turning unnaturally pale.

"There, that will do," said the same speaker. "Mr. Meek you had better go. It is in my power to unmask you."

"Insolent fellow! What do you mean?'

"Simply that you are an impostor, and, under the cloak of religion, are enabled to do that which would subject me or my friend to punishment at the hands of the law. There, you know my meaning. Let there be an end to this, or it will be the worse for you."

"I will remain here no longer, to be insulted!" exclaimed Meek, as he at once left the room, wished Miss Staunton a hurried good night, descended the stairs, and disappeared.

CHAPTER CXXXIII.

THE PARTY AT OSBORNE'S.—MR. O'RIODEN'S TALE.

WE left the guests at Henry Osborne's seated at dinner. A sumptuous repast furnished by the liberal and hospitable host, and after the party had pledged each other in sundry glasses of wine, the conversation flowed in a lively stream.

Mr O'Rioden discoursed with Aunt Cary and Colonel Jack upon the peculiar charac-

teristics of his own countrymen, and he was a fund of information and entertainment for the whole company.

After the dessert the ladies retired, with the exception of Miss Cary, whom the warm-hearted Irishman had insisted upon retaining. He had promised a story of Irish life, and Miss Cary was anxious to hear the narrative. Mr. O'Rioden was about to make a commencement, when Osborne said—

"Now, I tell you what it is, O'Rioden. You see, I think, as well as my friend Halford, that it is hardly fair to exclude our other female friends from listening to your tale, and therefore I submit to you whether it would not be as well for us to adjourn up stairs, for I should presume that there is nothing in your story but what ladies may listen to."

"Oh, dear no," answered O'Rioden. "I'm always too glad to have the bright eyes shining upon me like a light from heaven."

Upon this the gentleman and Miss Cary rejoined the ladies, and Mr. O'Rioden commenced the story of Irish life, which he gave in his own words.

"I am going to tell you," said Mr. O'Rioden, "about a queer chap called Sam. Well, you must know that this youth had a thirst for knowledge. In some senses, this one Sam was a remarkable individual. Strictly speaking, he was anonymous, and passed through life as a myth. All that could be known of his origin may be comprised in a few words. His uncle, or at least the man who passed as such, was a stranger in the parish of Ballymacfun, in which he had settled, bringing Sam along with him on his first appearance there, the aforesaid Sam being then a monkey of about twelve years of age. Old Sam, who was a kind of jack-of-all-trades in his way, was as great a myth as his nephew, with the single exception, of his having been known to admit the fact, that he had had a father and mother; an advantage for which his nephew always envied him, as he staunchly affirmed that he himself had never either the one nor the other. The uncle, who was a frolicsome and amusing man, was nevertheless a most mysterious one. Nobody was ever yet able to ascertain his name, the only length to which he was known to go on the subject being, that his Christian name was Sam; but as to his surname, he disclaimed all knowledge of it himself—quoting the old proverb, so complimentary to the ladies, 'that it is a wise child who knows his own father.'

Soon after his settlement in Ballymacfun, however, the neighbours, in consequence of his lively and humourous character, bestowed on him the name of "Company," in consequence of the extraordinary powers which he exhibited in their entertainment. It must be known to you all that it is usual to say of a lively and facetious man, "he is excellent company."

"That is a common expression in English," said Colonel Jack.

"Is it? Well, of the uncle Sam's origin and pedigree this was all that could ever be known; but of young Melchizedic and his strange fate I intend giving you a brief account—

Young Sam felt a singular ambition for becoming a schoolmaster—an ambition, however, that had much to contend with, a peculiar fate, with which you will become acquainted, having stood fearfully in the way of his success. At fourteen years of age he was sent to school, but in consequence of an impression which had gone abroad respecting him, and the peculiar structure of his frame, he found himself the subject of much mystery and dread to both master and scholars. His face was small and withered—his eyes deeply in his head, and his head so deeply sunk between his shoulders, that the hump upon his back was nearly on a level with it. Complexion he had none, unless you can call the colour of a drumhead a complexion; his stature, even for one of his years, was much below the usual size, but although graced with a large hump behind, as I have said, yet this was matched by a protuberance of abdomen, which betokened a vast capacity for food. The back part of his head, especially the *cerebellum*, was inordinately large, whilst the front was rather under the average of the intellectual developments. His mouth, in proportion to the rest of his face, was large, and in conjunction with a full and firm set of grinders, betokened a ready but destructive *penchant* for whatever description of unlucky nutriment might enter that fearful aperture. Such was Sam the second; when about the age of fourteen he was sent to Pat Frayne's hedge school to be "indoctrinated," as Pat himself would say on the subject.

Sam's first appearance at school was hailed, both by master and scholars, as something scarcely within the category of ordinary humanity—a general opinion having gone abroad, that "he wasn't right;" and, indeed, what else could be inferred from his unnatural appearance, and the undoubted fact, that he never had father or mother. This his uncle—if he was his uncle—stoutly affirmed, and when questioned as to what he could be, or how he was generated, requested his neighbours not to press him on that fearful subject, assuring them that it might be as much as his life was worth to make any further disclosures with regard to him.

Under these circumstances an alarming notion began to creep about, that he must necessarily belong to the "good people,"—an impression which kept both young and old

from obtruding their companionship upon him.

Although formed as I have said, he possessed the strength of youngsters twice his age, and as for his activity, it was not only astonishing, but almost beyond the powers of nature. No monkey could climb a tree with half his agility, and it was solemnly asserted, as a well-known fact, that if he were locked and double-bolted in the strongest house in the parish, give him but five minutes, and he might be seen dancing a hornpipe before the door! Another circumstance that wrapped both himself and his reputed uncle in mystery, was the pertinacity with which they avoided any place of worship. Instead of frequenting church, chapel, or meeting-house, they used to spend their Sundays in some Fairy Rath in the neighbourhood—but how engaged, or what communion they may have held whilst there, nobody could tell—for nobody had courage to ascertain.

In truth, the points which constituted their character, and marked their habits, were at once both strange and numerous. When a storm, for instance, occurred—especially of wind, young Sam was seen running about shrieking with delight, clapping his hands and dancing with all the wild ecstasy of an elf.

There was one night in the year, however, on which neither Sam nor his uncle were ever visible. This was Hallow-eve, the very night which leaves ghosts, and fairies, and all supernatural spirits at liberty to appear and hold communion with mankind. But although our hero and his uncle became invisible on that night, it was uniformly observed that they appeared fatigued and jaded to death the next morning.

What this meant could be very easily unriddled, without the aid of a conjuror. Nothing could be more evident than the fact, that on that *eirie* night, as the Scotch say, they took part in the *saturnalia* held by the fairies in the celebration of their great anniversary.

Be this as it may, old Sam took the *weird* youth by the hand, and on a Monday morning brought him along to Pat Frayne's celebrated establishment.

The uncle and young Sam had no sooner entered, than the loud buzz of the school was immediately hushed into silence, like the works of a noisy piece of machinery suddenly brought to a stand-still; the youngsters gazed on Sam, as upon some supernatural mystery that filled them with awe. All the bye-play and bye-battles—all the secret punchings in the ribs—all the thrustings of pins into each other's flesh—all the fightings of ink-bottles—together with a long catalogue of hedge-school freaks, were instantly suspended, and every eye was turned with a kind of uneasy curiosity upon the wild-looking and misshapen object before them. The master himself, indeed, was not at all free from an apprehension of the risk which might attend the education of the young myth.

He stared at the uncle and him for a considerable time without speaking, and you need not feel surprised that he did so, inasmuch as he had shortly before that precise period become impressed with a sincere belief in the malevolent power and existence of the *fairies;* the cause of his impression being as follows :

It was only during the preceding winter that he had, with a good deal of rodomontade and swagger, dared to cut down a fairy whitethorn on Kilrudden rock, during an extraordinary scarcity of fuel. This tree he splintered into faggots and carried home on his own back, scorning the influence and defying the vengeance of the *Dinnashee* with derision and contempt. The neighbours, of course, were shocked at this daring and impious outrage upon the " good people," and failed not to throw out many prophetic hints as to the disastrous consequences which must necessarily fall upon either him or his. These he laughed to scorn, assuring his friends that he defied them, and threatening that if any injury resulted to himself, his family, or his property, he would get a hatchet and cut down every whitethorn on the rock. This magnanimous threat, however, was very far from his heart. What, in the meantime, was the upshot ? In six months afterwards his youngest child was carried off by the meazles, and within the course of a year his only cow died of the fairy malady ; for the neighbours in general stoutly asserted that she had been *elf-shot.* Mary McQuade, the *Pisthrouge* woman, was brought to examine her, and she solemnly assured them that the unfortunate animal had been struck in the flank by an *elf-stone*—that she could feel the hole made by it under the skin ; for an elf-stone never cuts the skin ; and that, of course, it was the fairies that did the deed. This made the weight of testimony too strong against Pat ; his courage was completely borne down ; but he was not insensible to conviction, and was consequently forced to admit his profanity, and cry *peccavi.* In this state was Pat when young Sam and his uncle entered the school.

I have already described the sensations which their appearance created in both master and scholars ; but as every man claiming the character of a genuine Philomath is bound to exhibit a lofty indifference to both danger and fear, he felt himself called upon to give those who looked up to him for protection an unquestionable proof of his courage, resulting, as they believed it did, from his wonderful knowledge of every subject on the face of the earth.

" Good morrow, masther," said Sam senior, taking off his hat ; " by dad, sir, you have a lot o' the youngsters here, sure enough."

" Good morrow, Misther Company, and good luck," replied Pat ; " why yes, I have as many as ould Plato himself could manage, if he sat upon my tripod, and perhaps a score or two more if it went to that. Indeed, Mr. Company, I think it will become compulsory on me to make a number of them scarce of the establishment. If I had as many eyes as Argus, and as many hands as Briareus, I could not manage the Lilliputian crew that I have to dale with."

" And I'm bringing you another, sir, to increase your trouble."

" Troth, Mr. Company, it would delight me to indoctrinate the same youth in the elements of sound larning ; but, as I said, you see I've got more than I can manage. In the course of this winter, at least a score of them must travel. But this is the curse of celebrity. If I was a blockhead or an *ignoramus*, I dare say my seminary would be as thin as wather-gruel ; but once a larned man gets a reputation for high scholastic ability, he's nothing else than a victim to the extraordinary thirst of knowledge which his presence occasions for miles around him."

" Well, but you'll take this lad in ? You won't refuse him, Mr. Frayne ?"

" If it could be done, Mr. Company ; but you see it can't. With the greatest pleasure I would take him in ; but the thing's impossible."

" And now, what's your objection, may I ask ? You got three new scholars to-day, and you sent none o' them back. Come, you won't be worse with him—give the *shingawn* a thrial. If you do, I tell you luck will flow on you, and if you don't—but no matther—we must only lave it to yourself—hem !"

This implied threat was rather a puzzle to Pat ; but still he resisted, though with anything but firmness, at heart, if the truth was known.

" Well, Mr. Company," said he, proposing a kind of compromise, " suppose you wait till I get my seminary cleared of all the dunces and vagabones ; I may have it in my power to do what you wish ; at present, the thing isn't within the bounds of my ability."

" Oh, very well," replied the other, " if you're made up against it, there's no harm done—yet. Sam," said he, addressing the little fellow, " ask Mr. Frayne, will we have a hard winther, and if there will be much occasion for firing."

" Mr. Frayne," said Sam, " will we have a hard winther, and will there be much occasion for firin', sir ?" and as he put the question, he gave a significant grin, that startled the whole school.

It is impossible to describe that grin nor the

fearful chuckle, half malignant and half derisive, with which it was accompanied.

Poor Pat felt his hair stir under his hat, and courage ooze out of his heart, at the urchin's words and manner, for his conscience told him that the two interrogatories had reference to the vengeance which the fairies had taken upon him by the death of his child and cow.

The interrogatories were to him significant enough, but the grin and chuckle with which they were uttered, made him feel at once that he was in anything but safe hands. He now fell back upon concession, or rather he felt himself forced into it by what he had heard and seen.

"Well, Mr. Company," said he, with a nervous quaver in his voice. "I would feel sorry, after all, to turn the—hem—hem—the—the—fine little fellow out—is he fond of larning? for there's a great dale in that."

"Sam," said his uncle, "are you fond of larning?"

"Ay, am I," replied Sam, "and I must have it—now!"

"Well, then," proceeded Pat, "I will take down his name—I will put him on the list. What's his name, Mr. Company?"

"Hem!—I'd rather you wouldn't ask me, masther—just write down 'Sam,' and that will do."

"Very good; but I have another question to ask him. 'Come here my fine lad, were you ever christened?'"

To this, Sam replied with an eldritch scream of laughter, so loud, contemptuous and piercing, that a gloomy sense of fear settled upon the whole school as before, and the master's very hands trembled at the godless and unnatural sounds.

"Me christened—ha, ha, ha! No, nor never will. Christen me!—ha, ha, ha!"

"Suppose you were to come with him next week," said Frayne, once more attempting to get out of the difficulty.

"Masther," said his uncle, "you're humbuggin' him and me. I see it—me you may humbug, but don't try it on him, if you're wise. He wants to be a school-masther, and to teach his own people something when he goes home to them; and above all things, he has a rason for wishing to manage the multiplication table. Masther a word with you outside. Now," he added, when they had gone out, "be advised by me and tache this creature, if you can; you don't know how he may stand your friend with them that don't like a bone in your skin, for good rasons. I know a sartin quarther, and so does he; betther than I do, where there's a rod in pickle for you; but if you're kind to him you may escape it. I'll say no more, but lave the whole matther to yourself. Your doom's in it, Mr. Frayne."

"Well, Mr. Company," replied Pat, "if that be the case, let the lad tackle to his business; and if it be in the power of man to inoculate him with the genuine principles of profound larning, I will do it."

Now I must tell you that Pat Frayne was a young man at this time, not long married. Like most hedge-schoolmasters of this day, he was fond of the mountain dew, and indulged in it whenever and wherever it came in his way. He was also a man who, notwithstanding the hazardous feat of cutting down the fairy thorn, was almost proverbially afraid of ghosts, spirits, black dogs, and white women; in short, of the supernatural world and all its inhabitants. He possessed an active and exaggerating imagination in those matters that was as extraordinary as it was ludicrous, and we need scarcely say that among the wags of the neighbourhood, he was looked upon as an excellent subject for the several pranks they played on him. As for his cutting down the "thorn," this piece of heroism was accomplished when he was fuddled, as was the case in the conditional threat he uttered, when he assured his neighbours that he would cut down every thorn on the Rath, which consisted of a large mass of rock known far and near in the country as "Kilrudden Rock."

This rock was in a very lonely situation, and crested the edge of a deep and solitary glen, in the centre of which, and at the root of a large thorn, was a deep and beautiful well, known as the "Fairies' Well."

Now it is a peculiar but well-known fact, in connection with wells in general, that whenever the adjoining village becomes depopulated and dessert, that is to say, when water is no longer drawn from them, they dry up and die away. This is indisputably true, with some rare exceptions.

The well in question, however, was always in a clear and crystal state, so much so, that of a bright summer day a person might stand over it, and on looking down, find that the water was invisible, in consequence of its transparency; he could see nothing but the bottom from a little aperature in which it kept perpetually bubbling up a bright chain of limpid water like molten silver. All these circumstances put together, convinced the people of the neighbourhood that it belonged exclusively to the Dinashee or "Good people;" and the consequence was, that not a soul for miles around would have drawn or tasted a drop of water from it, no more than if it had been so much aquafortis. Such, then, was Pat Frayne, and such was a portion of the scenery contiguous to his residence.

Pat, on that day, felt uneasy, anxious. A singular struggle between two terrors was going on within him, to wit, a natural apprehension against having anything whatsoever to do or say with the unaccountable being before him, and a fear of exciting his enmity should he neglect him. In order, however, to relieve himself from this anomalous state of feeling, he resolved to hand him over for instructions to the hardiest and most intrepid boy in the school. This cowardly manœuvre, however, proved a dead failure; neither that nor any other boy in the school would consent to come in contact with the *shingawn*, which signifies a diminutive person, who is supposed to look *like* a fairy, or to be connected *with* them. Pat was consequently obliged to hear him his first lessons himself; but, as he did so, he experienced a singular and strange feeling, for which he could not account. On examining Sam's face when close to him, he thought he could plainly see that in it which was unquestionably not human ; and what confirmed him in this was, that whenever he ventured, no matter how furtively, to scrutinise his features, the piercing and sinister eye of the other instantly detected him with such a quick and forbidding glance, that he actually knew not whether he sat or stood, and almost began to think that the whole thing was an unpleasant dream or nightmare under which he laboured.

In the course of the day, notwithstanding all this, he seemed to feel as if fascinated by the being before him ; he could scarcely take his eyes off his person, and what made matters worse, he sometimes imagined, after a long look at him, that the little *shingawn* was enveloped in a thin cloud or haze from which he peered out at him with a mocking expression that was without parallel in merely human faces. On one occasion, when he was in the act of pointing out the disagreeable peculiarity of his figure to one of the larger boys whom he spoke to in a low whisper, the other shouted out, although his back was towards him.

"Quit pointin' me out, you had betther ; and don't make game of me, or it'll be the worst for you. Dan Devlin won't be the betther for it, anyhow."

Dan flew like an arrow to his seat, and the master called up another class in order to escape his observation, and, if possible to avoid its malignity. What, however, were his sensations when Dan's two brothers came to school the next day as usual, but unaccompanied by Dan.

"Where is your brother, Mick ?"

"Is it Dan, sir ?"

"Yes, Dan—why didn't he come to school wid you?"

"Bedad, he couldn't sir ; he strained his foot yestherday on his way home from school, an' my mother's rubbing it with a 'coction of dwarf eldher."

The master involuntarily turned his eyes upon the *shingawn*, and witnessed a malignant and triumphant chuckle, which at once satisfied him as to the origin of the accident if accident it could be called.

Sam went on in his efforts to acquire knowledge, but they were exceedingly slow. The master, however, attributed his stupidity to what he considered to be the right cause. He could not, for instance, suppose that a lad so knowing, quick, and unusually precocious in everything else, should be so unpenetrably dull at his learning, if his original capacity had been bestowed on him from a human source. He consequently inferred that he had the obstacles arising from his own mysterious nature to contend with ; and on this principle, and with this impression, he continued to instruct him as well as he could.

Everything about Sam was mysterious. On his way to school, and home again, he never was accompanied by any of his schoolfellows, and when some of the boldest of them wanted to offer him companionship, he refused it with threats and indignation. He passed his school hours, therefore, among them, but with the evident conviction of one who felt that he was not of them, and could not mingle with them as one of themselves.

In the meantime, he became a great and absorbing idea in the alarmed mind of the schoolmaster—a prominent but painful fact in his already heated imagination. Like some hypochondriacal and disagreeable impression, he appeared to have established a permanent existence in his being, and, what seemed still worse, he was every day and every night gaining an expanding and predominant influence over all his faculties. In fact, he began to feel, with something like horror, that their fates were fast approaching to a state of coalition, and that there was an identity of destiny between them that was threatening to become unavoidable. He spoke of Sam, he dreamt of Sam, and when drunk he sang of Sam, or made strange and wild orations upon him and his inconceivable attributes. Nay, such an empire had Sam got over him, that he felt an hallucination—something between horror and delight—that led him sometimes to fear and sometimes to wish that he should get fond of Sam. In this state of mind he consulted several fairymen and fairywomen upon the peculiarity of his condition, but the moment Sam's name was mentioned they declared off—nothing could induce them to take any steps that might offend or contravert either him or his friends.

By the period when Pat had arrived at this state of mind, Sam had been with him about five years, but during all that time he had never got further than he had the first. During the last four he had attended him only during the winter ; but what was equally extraordinary and unaccountable, it was found that whatever he had learned during any one winter, he forgot during the ensuing summer. This stood alone as a fact in the mind of man, as well as in its education. Like Penelope's web, the whole fabric of knowledge which had been woven into his memory during the winter, had been unravelled during his absence from school, to which he only returned to go over the same process with the same result.

At this time a circumstance occurred at the close of winter, when Sam had made a more successful progress than usual. He had his slate and "Gough" under his arm, for he was now commencing figures, and, turning to the master, as he was about to leave school until the next season, he said—

"Well, masther, I have done well this winther at all events, and only for something that you don't know, but that you will know, I could get on just as well as another, and wouldn't forget in summer what I larn in winther, but above all things the multiplication table. But as regards yourself, mind my words—there will come a heavy complaint upon all kinds of cattle about next June, and several of the neighbours will lose a good many; your cow in the meanwhile will escape, that I tell you."

He then danced out of the school, and left the master to ponder over what he had said and predicted. In the meantime, let us follow up the prophecy. Summer came as usual; it was dry and burning; the wells, small rivers, and brooks were nearly, if not altogether dried up, and an usual mortality set in amongst the cattle. Fortunate Pat saw them die on each side of him, and listened to the lamentations of his neighbours with an easy heart, because he knew that he, or at least his cow, was exempted from the prevailing calamity. And such was the fact; during the whole summer his cow had never enjoyed better health, nor given so much milk and butter.

Now this, though in a temporal point of view, was certainly a consolation, still, when taken in connection with Pat's singular state of mind regarding Sam, we must admit that the comfort he derived from it was more than counterbalanced by his knowledge of the questionable, if not unlawful means by which it had been brought about.

Pat was now seldom sober, and I need scarcely say that, with respect to him, the circumstances I have just related were not calculated to diminish the influence of that extraordinary being over him. The fact is, he felt that a secret knowledge of the forbidden and the supernatural was forced upon him through Sam's agency; and that he was very likely, if matters went on as they did, to be withdrawn from humanity, and transferred to a new but inexplicable state of existence.

Circumstances soon occurred to confirm this formidable apprehension, and we shall relate them.

Sam, it seems, ever since he had entered into figures, felt such extreme pride in the progress he had made, that he seldom went anywhere without carrying his "Gough" and slate under his arm, observing to his neighbours, that no man except Pat Frayne could ever have taught him so successfully.

"And for that," said he, "I will make a new man of Pat."

These words he repeated so frequently, that they became the burthen of every conversation he entered into.

He did not, however, stop here, but sang them to a wild and startling tune, unlike anything of the kind ever heard before.

"And I say that for that—for that—
I'll make a new man of Pat,"

became so well known in the neighbourhood, that they were taken up by the people at large, who frequently amused themselves by singing them even in Pat's presence, and afterwards in congratulating him upon the happy prospects which Sam had predicted for him.

Sam had now been ten years with him, but found himself, so far as his education went, exactly in the same state in which he left school at the close of his second winter; and what puzzled Pat beyond all his powers of investigation into this unexampled privation of memory was the extraordinary fact itself which stood naked before him, although the causes of it were involved in the most inexplicable mystery.

This mystery, however, was soon to be solved—very little, it is true, to his own satisfaction, but much to his dismay.

One night he disappeared from his wife and family, who waited for him with considerable anxiety until the hours of three or four o'clock, when, despairing of him until morning, they at length retired to their beds. They knew, however, that he had been in the habit of visiting several of the private stills which were at work in various parts of the neighbouring moors and glens; and he took it for granted that he had remained there during the night, as had been occasionally the case before.

This consequently relieved them a good deal, and after their long watch for him, they were soon asleep.

In this supposition, however, they were only partially correct, but they soon had an opportunity of becoming thoroughly acquainted with the true cause of his protracted absence.

The next morning, about daybreak, he

knocked at the door, and when it was opened, presented to them, in his own person, as wet, shivering, and woe-begone a spectacle as human eye could witness.

His wife and children, startled into alarm, asked what was the matter, and what had reduced him to such an extraordinary condition?

All, however, was in vain. Under these circumstances, they very properly concluded that the best thing to be done was immediately to put him into his warm bed, and leave him to get a good sound sleep.

It was past dark when Pat awoke, and called for a drink of whiskey-and-water. With this he was immediately supplied, and after having swallowed a large draught, he smacked his lips, now no longer parched; and observing several of his neighbours, who had called to make friendly inquiries, sitting about the fire, he commenced his narrative:—

"Nancy," said he, "shut the door. I'm willing to narrate what I have to say to you and our friends here, but not to a certain class of our neighbours that shall be nameless. This day's Sunday, may the Lord stand between us and harm!"

These last words he used as the popular exorcism against fairy influence.

"You see, neighbours," he proceeded, "on last evening, which being that of Saturday, it occurred to me that I would spend an hour or two up in Claghliem, wid Hugh Roe M'Cahy, under the hospitable roof of his own still-house.

"I felt a good deal fatigued after the larned labours of the week, and I said to myself, 'Pat, you are both a social and convivial spirit, and a compotation rather than a mere solitary potator—the last being a character that you do not relish unless you fail in procuring the society of a genial companion.

Then what would you say to the proposal of spending a couple of hours with your friend Hugh Roe, around whose still-house hearth there will be assembled a goodly number of the neighbours, to indulge in the relation of many a pleasant anecdote—story and legend, not pretermitting a copious libaiion of the mountain dew.' 'I close with the proposal, Pat,' said I, 'inasmuch as it is both agreeable and pleasant, and affords a delightful opportunity of filling up a space.' I accordingly proceeded to the 'Valley of the Mountain Water,' where the still-house stands, and there, just as I had expected, were seated on stones and sacks of malt about the hearth, half-a-dozen friends and acquaintances, all engaged in pleasing conversation, and the enjoyment of the native.

"Many a pleasant story was told, and many a bumper went round, and among other narratives was one related by old Harry Connolly, the fairyman, concerning a castle of grandeur, that is said to be within Kilrudden Rock, and that it was well known by the world at large, that young Sam was often seen both going into it and coming out of it. Well, I simulated infidelity on that subject, although I felt the very veracity of it in my heart. At all events the conversation went on, enlivened and stimulated by the liquor.

"In the course of our compotations I felt my courage revive, and I began (God pardon me) to swagger upon the subject, and to show them that no man of profound larning, as I was, could, with a good grace, allow himself to become a believer in such legendary hobgoblinism.

"They shook their heads, however, and said —'I might yet live to be convinced to my cost.' By degrees, as the time grew late, they bade me good-night one by one, until there was nobody left behind but Hugh Rowe, two of his assistants, and myself. After their departure there is *lapsus memoriæ*, which I cannot fill up ; but be that as it may, I must have proceeded homewards, and you all know that Kilrudden Rock stands in a right line between this and the still-house. Now I knew this myself well enough, but I had no notion of taking that right line, but to come home by Ballylastra, as I went. At all events, the first thing I remember, was to find myself at the rock ; and sure enough I would have given a king's ransom to be ten miles from its vicinity. I stood, and at once felt my hat rising on my head, and by that I knew that they were near me. 'I have nothing for it now,' said I, 'but to travel as fast as possible,' which I was about to do, when I heard a well-known voice whisper to me—

"'It is too late, Pat, you must enter the rock, and see the Castle of Grandeur—if you don't, you're lost ; be advised by a friend.'

"'Ah! Sam, darling,' says I, 'be a friend to me ; you know the pains I've taken for the last ten years in accomplishing your education.'

"'I do,' he replied, 'and the fine progress I made under you—ten years now, and I'm not aiquil to the multiplication table yet! Isn't that creditable to you, Pat?'

"'But you know, Sam, darling,' said I, 'there is no working impossibilities—no making a silk purse out of a—'

"I couldnt' finish the words, but I felt myself drawn forward by some secret power that I hadn't strength to resist, and, what was odd, all this time I couldn't see Sam, for indeed the night was as dark as pitch. At length I found myself standing against a part of the rock that was like the side wall of a house, and Sam again said—

"'Come, Pat, have courage ; it is do or

die with you —if you don't enter, you are a lost man, and neither Nancy nor your childre will ever see you more, but if you have a stout heart you will get out of it."

"'Ay, Sam, but how am I to get into it?'

"'By the words that I will tell you,' said Sam; 'strike the rock three times with your knuckles, and say, kid eat ivy, mare eat hay; then the rock will open, and you'll see the Castle of Grandeur. If you don't do this, you will be transmogrified where you stand, and neither friend nor enemy will ever see you more in this world. Come have courage, and I'll stand your friend.'

" Well, I found that I had nothing else for it; so, after making him repate the words over again, I struck the rock three times

with my knuckles, when a voice said to me out of it, 'who wants to come into the Castle of Grandeur?' 'I do,' said I—'one Pat Frayne, a famous Philomath, and instructor of the rising generation.'

"'Ay! but can you give the word, Pat?' he asked.

"'Kid eat ivy, mare eat hay,' I replied. The words were no sooner out of my mouth than the rock flew open like a pair of folding-doors, and I saw before me far inside the wonderful and magnificent Castle of Grandeur. 'Walk in, Pat, said the person, 'and you're welcome amongst us! But now listen: I am your friend, and Sam's your enemy; be guided by me, and do no single thing that he desires you. Neither eat nor drink here, or if you do, you will never get out of this. The king's daughter's in love with Sam, and has promised to marry him as soon as he's master of the multiplication table, but her father's against the match and would rather give her to me a thousand times. I'm one Dan Corrigan, that was stolen from my mother when I was a child, and I have lived here ever since.'

" 'Blood and compunction!' said I, 'the king's daughter fall in love with Sam ! What a beautiful specimen of taste !'

" ' Ay,' replied Dan Corrigan, 'such is the melancholy fact, Pat ; but you must know that Sam's the white-headed boy among the girls here, and when the king's daughter saw that they were tearing one another's caps about him, begad, she took into her head to fall in love with him too, and he's now known to be her favourite. The truth is, Pat, he danced her out of her senses; for you must know that he dances "Liggerhumcush" and " Kiss my Lady" better than e'er a fairy in his majesty's dominions. And now, Pat, listen hether again : her father knows that she has a *grah* for him, and the law of the land here is, that any male person who can master the multiplication table may claim the king's daughter for his wife. Sam, under your learned instructions, would have done that long ago; but his majesty gives him a gaulioque of fairy wine that makes him forget during the summer whatever he has larned in the winter from you ; and Sam's object now is, to get you kept here to teach him—and for this reason, that anything in the shape of drink his majesty may give him has no effect until he goes out into the world—so there, now, is a hint for you, and look to it ; but, come, I must introduce you to his majesty.'

" ' But has his majesty no queen at all ?' I asked.

" 'Oh, yes,' said he, ' Biddy Bradley is his queen for the last fourteen years, and has borne him a fine family. Poor Lanty, her husband, thinks her dead ; she departed, poor woman, they thought, in a fit (of drink,) and if Lanty was to search her grave, he wouldn't find her body there at any rate. In the meantime I have told you enough—so now step out and have the honour of being introduced to the king.'

" Well, if any tongue could describe the grandeur of that place, I think that of Pat Frayne could ; that's all I say. Such gardens and meadows, and orchards, eye never saw ; and as for the palace itself, there was a window in it for every day in the year. The king was sitting on his throne, when Dan Corrigan introduced me.

" ' Plase your majesty,' said Dan, ' this is Pat Frayne, the great Philomath that all the world wonders at for his larning ; but above all parts of knowledge, he shines at the multiplication table and poteen.'

" 'I could forgive him the poteen,' said the king, ' but do you tell me, Dan, that this is the vagabone who is doing his best to tache " Sam" the multiplication table ! By the bells of Shandon, Dan, I 'll make an example of him.' His majesty was smoking a dudeen and helping himself to a glass of poteen as he spoke, and to say the truth I felt myself anything but comfortable.

" ' Please your majesty,' said I, 'you do me injustice ; it never was either my wish or inclination to tache Sam anything—and it 's not my wish that ever he should show his comely face in my seminary again, and I hope your majesty will rid my hands of him altogether.'

" ' That's not in my power, Pat,' replied the king, ' but you must know he's a great thorn in my side. He's what they call a radical, and wishes to introduce reform and education in order to corrupt my subjects; and he's such a devil of a fellow among the ladies, that my daughter, Nora, has fallen in love with him, and expects in spite of me, to have him for her husband, and to send Dan Corrigan, my favourite and prime minister, to the right about. Now, if you make me a solemn promise, and swear by the rock of Kilrudden, that you will give him no more instruction, and above all branches in that confounded multiplication table, I will allow you, after you see the grandeur of my palace, to go home safe in spite of Sam.'

" I readily made the promise, and glad I was to make it ; and when I did so, I heard a confounded chuckle behind me, that I knew, proceeded from Sam.

" ' Pat,' says his majesty, " we give a grand ball and supper to-night, and we expect to have the honour of your company. In the meantime, Dan Corrigan will show you everything worth seeing, and do you the honours of the palace. I'm going myself to join the lords of the court for an hour or two at a game of spoil-five and a jug of scaltheen.'

" Dan then took me with him, through all parts of the palace ; but such wonders I never dreamt of. Everything was gold and silver, jewels and precious stones—up stairs and down stairs—curtains, carpets, silks, velvets, and satins. In the kitchen, all the vessels were of gold and silver ; and the number of cooks, and the fizzing and frying, the roasting and boiling, the skimming and basting, the running here and the running there, the squalling and the brawling, could never enter the mind of man, unless he saw it as I did. Dan then brought me out into the grounds, and there I saw the good people dancing and amusing themselves in a thousand ways. They were the prettiest little creatures In the world and were all elegantly dressed in green. Pipes and fiddles and all kinds of music were going on, and such happiness, if one could believe their eyes, could scarcely be found in paradise itself. These were the real fairies, and Dan whispered to me that they had once been angels in heaven, and said, that when Lucifer fought against God, all those spirits that took his part were sent with him into hell; and all those that fought for God were promoted to greater happiness in heaven. 'The third class,' said he, (I mean the fairies) 'that were too cowardly to fight on either side were cast out of heaven, and it will not be known until the day of judgment whether they are to be saved or not. They have great power, and only for the fear of not being saved, it is thought, they would destroy the world.'

"But, besides the real fairies, there were a great many persons who had been stolen when young, and who were the same size as men and women with us, and a great many too were there whom their friends considered dead; but although they seemed to die, it was the fairies that took them; and if their coffins were opened, a log of bog oak would be found in each. I saw a great number of our old neighbours there, and spoke to some of them. It is true, I could give you their names, and would, but that I don't wish to make their friends uneasy by hearing of their imprisonment. These persons didn't seem quite at their ease, and one of them said to me, when I was admiring all the grandeur and gold that I saw about me.

"'Ah, Pat, avourneen; all isn' gold that glitters.'

"But above all things, what do you think I saw with my own eyes? Oh, you'd never guess—why, devil a thing but our own cow Drimmindhoo; for that's the way with them, they steal everything they can lay their hands on. I went over to the poor beast, and she licked me with kindness, and as far as I could judge from her appearance, she was both glad and sorry to see me.

"Well, after looking at all these things, we were sent for to the ball. The king and queen opened it, with Jig Polthogue, and well they did it—for I couldn't think the ould couple had such mettle in them. Next came Sam and the princess to the tune of 'Morgan Rattler;' but although I thought the shingawn couldn't be outdone, he wasn't a flaybite to the princess. If she jumped an inch off the floor she jumped a yard, and with one hand on her side, she cracked her fingers with the other, and did the trepling steps, that it would do your heart good to see her. A fine pair of legs she had, and, begad, she wasn't a bit backward in showing them. At this rate they were going on—not an idle pair of feet among them—all at it—helter-skelter—up and down—criss and cross, backwards and forwards to that degree, that you would think they were all mad. In this way I say, they diverted themselves for a couple of hours, when at last a servant in frieze livery came to say that supper was on the table. I thought I had seen enough of grandeur before, but when I entered the supper-room, I thought the very eyes were dazzled out of my head with the light, and the brilliancy of everything about me. I thought I'd get blind, and began to think I must be in a dream; but just at this moment when I was desired by the king to set on his left hand and partake of supper, Dan Corrigan whispered to me once more—

"'Pat, taste nothing here, or you're lost.'—

"'Come, Pat,' said the king, 'sit beside myself, and take a bit o' supper. Her Majesty, Bid, and I, am going to dig our way into a dish o' calcannon, and you will have the honour of joining us. Sit down, my hearty—and after that we'll drink scaltheen till we're black in the face.'

"'Plase your Majesty,' said I, 'the honour is great that you offer me—but unfortunately I can neither eat nor drink in regard that this is a fast day with me.'

"'But, Pat, my worthy,' he replied, 'we have a rule here, that no man can leave our palace without both eating and drinking, and although, Patrick, we have all heard of fast days, for indeed you have too many of them out in your Irish world—still I ask you, who ever heard of fast nights? Come, come, no nonsense, you must eat and drink with us—or if not, worse will happen you; here's a good horn spoon for you—or you may take your choice between gould and silver if you like—come, sirra, sit down and help yourself.'

"The old sinner began to look crusty, but knowing as I did, that if I neither ate nor drank they had no power over me, I said, just as stiff as he seemed stout—

"'Devil resave the bit or sup I'll taste with you or yours to-night.'

"'Hello!' he shouted; 'call in the blackguards and off wid him to the Dark Dungeon.'

"The words were scarcely out of his lips, when I was carried heels foremost to the prison he mentioned, where I was locked up within bolts and bars that would keep in a giant. 'Militia, murther!' thought I, 'what's to become o' me now?'

"'Ah! you may well ask, you villain,' said the cursed voice of Sam through the bars; 'but be it known to you, Pat, that until you make me master of the multiplication table, and so gain me the princess for my wife, I'll haunt you wherever you go, and as long as life's in your miserable carcase, and when we're both dead—for I must die as well as you—I'll hunt you with my slate and Gough undher my arm till the day of judgment.'

"How long I remained in that prison I can't say, for I must have gone asleep to keep myself comfortable. All I know is, that I felt very cold, and awoke shivering. And now, where do you think I found myself, why, lying on the wet ground outside the rock, drenched to the skin—stiff almost as a corpse—and hardly able to rise. Indeed it was as much as I could do to stagger home ; but home I got—and here I am—and now let me hint to you, is it to be wondered at, after what I saw and heard last night, that I should ask for a drink of whiskey-and-water ?"

This was procured for him, and as he was about to put it to his lips, "Here," said he ".is disappointment and confusion to Sam !" At this moment the wild and well-known chuckle, something between a scream and a laugh, was heard outside the door, which was knocked at three times, and it was felt by all present that the knocks had a hollow and supernatural sound. Two or three of the neighbours, however, had courage to open the door, but on examining the premises around the house closely and thoroughly, no sign or trace of Sam could be found; not the slightest appearance of a human being was visible. Poor Pat's face could not become much paler than it was—but, at all events, he felt it necessary to recruit his failing courage, by an additional stimulus of whiskey-and-water, after which his neighbours wished him good night, and he went to bed.

The next morning he got up, and breakfasted in silence. His family observed that he was anxious and gloomy. The whole neighbourhood had by this time been made acquainted with the scenes he had witnessed in Kilrudden Rock—and the whole neighbourhood believed them. Be this as it may, Pat addressed his wife as follows :—

"Nancy," said he, "this vicinity is not for me ; I must get away as well as I can from the designs of the *shingawn*. I heard him calling me this morning, while you were all asleep—to get up and prepare to go to school —that he wanted to buckle once more to the multiplication table. There is nothing for it now, but to leave the country as quietly as possible, so as that he may have no trace of me. I will sell my house, furniture, and bit of land, and go up to the county of Sligo, where I have a brother in good circumstances and there I will open a new school, where that devil Sam won't annoy me. I will now go to the school-house, and give them a fortnight's holidays, and in the meantime we'll start for the county Sligo. Here I will not stay, because, if I do, I'm sure to be transmogrified, which means being metamorphosed into a fairy."

Pat's plan succeeded very well. He lost no time in disposing of his property, and within the allotted period he found himself and his family residing in a comfortable cottage on his brother's property. In a short time he procured a school-house, and soon had the satisfaction to see it well filled with a young crew of jabbering Sligonians. His mind had now become more sedate and composed, everything was proceeding favourable —his school was crowded, and from the mixture of guttural Irish and broken English, one might well imagine that Pat gave instruction somewhere in the vicinity of the Tower of Bable, after the confusion of tongues had taken place. This, however, was no way disagreeable to Pat, who spoke Irish and English equally well, and was beginning to feel himself extremely comfortable in his new locality.

In this agreeable state of mind, he was sitting one morning quite at his ease, and a a good deal inflated with a consciousness of his authority, when who should walk in with his Gough and slate under his arm, but his old friend "Sam." "Alas, poor Yorick !" said Sterne—no, but, alas, poor Pat ! say we.

To describe his consternation and dismay is quite beyond any powers of description we possess.

His eyelids expanded, his eyes projected, his hands became tremulous, his sympathetic hat once more rose upon his head, and his hair, in raising it, seemed to display that courage which Pat had not. He would have spoken, but his voice treacherously abandoned him, and his cowardly tongue took refuge in the roof of his mouth.

His eyes, however, were riveted upon Sam with an expression of terror that astonished and alarmed the whole school. The youngsters, on looking at the master, and then at Sam, whose unnatural figure and aspect justified Pat's terror, began by degrees to settle down from their noise ; an awe, a kind of chill, an undefinable fear fell upon them, which gained ground until the whole obstreperous gabble of the school was hushed into a solemn and wondering silence. Pat, however, felt the necessity of speaking ; the manner of the strange being before him rendered it imperative on him to do so. He saw at once the impression which Sam's presence and appearance had made upon his scholars.

From both, it was evident that they were old acquaintances, that there was besides some mystery between them, that the master was afraid of him, and that he appeared to be able to "cow" the master—a feeling which stripped them of all confidence in Pat's learning, honesty, or courage, as the case might be.

They saw at once, that Pat's eye quailed under that of the *shingawn* ; and although they themselves felt a sense of dread, yet that was no reason why a learned man who knew so much as Pat did, should make such a pitiful appearance in the case.

Pat, however, at length somewhat recovered himself, and was able to ask—

"Sam, what brought you here?"

"The *Multiplication table*," replied Sam, with a sardonic grin.

"But, my good fellow, can you get no one else to teach you the Multiplication table?"

"No," replied Sam, "you are doomed to it, and you know it."

"Try writing love-letters," said Pat, "you'll find it pleasanter, Sam; the truth is, you haven't brains for the Multiplication table. How is Miss Nora, the princess?"

"She's not far from where you sit," replied Sam; "but if you take my advice, you'll make no particular inquiries about her."

"Well, may I not ask how is his majesty the King, her father?"

"He and Biddy the Queen are helping themselves to a good dish of calcanon in the Rath above there—keep yourself quiet then, and show me where I'll take my seat."

"Sam," said Pat, making a desperate effort, "I have borne with you long enough, but I'm determined to bear with you no longer. Go about your business—devil a lessin either in multiplication or anything else ever you'll get from me! Make the best of that you can!"

"Oh, very well," replied Sam, looking up significantly at the slight roof of the house, "there is a smart breeze out, Pat, and I'm of opinion we'll have a gale that will try the roof of your school-house at any rate. In the meantime, I'll step up to the Rath and chat to Miss Biddy, the Princess."

He accordingly disappeared, and unfortunate Pat felt glad of his disappearance, and was beginning to congratulate himself on having got rid of him so easily when, by-and-bye, the wind began to blow rather briskly; in a quarter of an hour afterwards, it increased considerably, rising and powerful gales swept over the house, and the slight ribs and rafters began to shake and quiver. So did Pat, and so did the whole school literally, both mental and material; but Pat, from a different principle. At length a portion of the thatch was blown off, and after whirling about in the wind, was diven into the door.

"I can't bear this," thought Pat, "it's too bad to have the school blown about our ears; I'll try if I can see him and bring him back; I must only bear with him for a time, but, at all events, I will soon slip my cable from this neighbourhood. Nancy and the children have a free house and a bit o' land from my brother; that, thank God, gives me a loose leg, and accordingly I'll soon start for some *terra incognita* that he won't find out—I'll

travel disguised, and by coach, so that the devil's in it if he can trace me; I'll change my name, too, as I go along, and then let him hunt my trail if he can."

Now it so happened that there was a Rath about a hundred and fifty yards above the school-house, and as Sam had alluded to it, he turned his eyes on going out in that direction. Judge of his astonishment when he saw Sam dancing in the storm for the bare life and uttering screams of wild and frantic delight. He immediately beckoned to him, with an inviting motion of the right arm, and in a couple of minutes Sam was beside him.

"You know what I mean, Sam," said he; "be a good boy, and come in to your business."

Sam nodded, and had not been five minutes under the roof when the tempest lulled, and then fell away by degrees, until it was succeeded by a perfect calm.

At present we have nothing further to say of Pat than, that on the day but one afterwards he had disappeared from the neighbourhood, and no human being could tell what had become of him. In the course of some months, however, after his mysterious absence, a little man of dark complexion and careworn features, was seated upon his scholastic throne in a school situated in the county of Kerry, renowned for classics and science.

We have said that his face was care-worn, but, nevertheless, a keen observer could mark a faint gleam of satisfaction, or it may be of hope that struggled with the solemnity of his visage, reminding one of those sickly glimpses of sunshine which came out faintly from the lowering clouds of an April sky.

The unhappy individual in question was Pat, who had once more a flourishing seminary, the vernacular language of which was in general Latin. There he sat, meditating upon the adventures of his past life, and making strong calculations upon the probability of his escape from the misshapen Frankenstein, who had tormented him so long, when, about the hour of twelve o'clock, in walks Sam with Gough and slate as usual under his arm. To detail what occurred upon this occasion would be only a repetition of what we have observed before. We shall not, therefore, attempt it, but only inform our readers that, in the course of a day or two, Pat had once more disappeared from Kerry.

It is useless to go over the same ground, and only sufficient to say that Pat migrated from one county to another, pursued by Sam, still bearing the identical Gough and slate under his arm, until the latter had coursed him through the thirty-two counties that constitute the length and breadth of the kingdom.

This, to be sure, was a chase of years. Pa^t was now an aged man ; but what constituted the most extraordinary feature in the life of Sam, was the fact that, in proportion as he grew old, he appeared to reverse the effect of time and to grow backwards; by which we mean that every year added to the appearance of his youth, or as it is commonly expressed, he seemed to get younger and younger every day.

This juvenility, however, was all in vain—their distiny was one and the same ; Sam's mortal existence was bound up with and contained in Pat.

The latter, now sensible that no change of locality, no disguise, no change of name, could protect him from recognition by his pupil, at length reached Kilrudden once more, just as the hare, when pursued, takes her flight through every variety of the neighbourhood, but is sure to double back to her own, in which she prepares to meet her fate. So it was with Pat : he reached Kilrudden in a state of health completely broken down and ruined by Sam.

"I hope," said he, " I will be free from him now ; he can have no longer any object in pursuing me, unless he intends to die along with me,"

He was now confined to his bed, and at the end of a week was at the last gasp, when who walks into him, but Sam.

"Ah, Sam," said Pat, "why will you persecute me in this way? Don't you see I'm dying ?"

"So am I," replied Sam, "for I intend to die with you. But whisper, Pat—I'm scarcely able to speak—but whisper; we'll meet again, and I'll have the *multiplication table* out of you yet."

Poor Pat turned on his right side and breathed his last, and when his family came to see how he was, they found Sam and him both dead.

Now one might very naturally conclude that death should close this extraordinary catastrophe ; but this, as it happened, was not to be. They were buried in different churchyards, where it would seem they lay quietly enough for some weeks, as if to take rest after the busy chase and anxious flight of the last twenty years. After the expiration of a couple of months, however, they were once more seen always near the hour or midnight—Pat running at the top of his speed, and Sam eagerly pursuing him, with his Gough and slate as usual under his arm. And thus they are to be seen up to the present time—the one in flight and the other giving strong chase ; and it is the opinion of everyone who sees them, that this strange pursuit is to continue till the Day of Judgment, or at least until the fairies are banished out of the kingdom.

"We have most of us heard of innumerable instances of the pursuit of knowledge under difficulties, but I am opinion," said Mr. O'Rioden, "that there is no case on record equal to that which I have related of Sam and Pat Frayne."

"Ah, ah ! a very excellent story, Mr. O'Rioden," exclaimed Miss Cary. "You are really quite a chronicler of your countrymen's peculiarities."

"Madam," exclaimed O'Rioden, "if my narrative has afforded you any pleasure, I am amply repaid."

All the company present declared that they had been highly entertained with O'Rioden's history of Sam and Pat Frayne.

"A comic enough incident occurred to a friend of mine," said Mr. O'Rioden. "When I say a friend, I should, with greater truth, say an acquaintance. I dare say you have most of you heard of the celebrated highwayman, Colonel Jack ?"

As these words fell from the lips of the Irishman, a sudden spasm seemed to pass through Osborne. He did not know well how to reply.

Our hero was nearly losing his self-possession. He rose from his seat, and strolled towards the window. Osborne followed him. None of the company, however, seemed to notice the movements of the two.

"Does he know me, think you?" inquired Colonel Jack.

"Oh, dear no. Be under no fear. I feel convinced that he knows nothing about you. He's one of the best fellows I know ; and of course, it is not at all likely that he would think of mentioning your name, if he had the slightest idea of your identity."

This somewhat reassured our hero, who was, however, much vexed at the turn the conversation had taken. Nevertheless, he made a virtue of necessity, and sat down once more, and listened to Mr. O'Rioden's account of his own doings with Mr. Sheriff Underwood—consisting of his own imprisonment in the cage at Barnet, and how he had escaped therefrom—likewise the account of his visit to the sheriff in the dead of the night, when our hero drew his pistol and presented it to the head of the astonished and terrified sheriff.

All this, and much more, Mr. O'Rioden recounted with great gusto, and Colonel Jack laughed most heartily as the narrator proceeded, seeming to enjoy the description with infinite relish.

"Ah, a rare fellow—a rare fellow, is this Colonel Jack," said Mr. O'Rioden, when he had finished his tale; "I wish I could become acquainted with him. We ought not to say so in genteel socity, but, to tell you the truth, I have rather an admiration for these knights of the road, especially one so celebrated and chivalrous as the one in question."

"And so have I," said Osborne.

"Oh, but it must be very dreadful to be stopped by a highwayman," exclaimed Miss Cary, with a shudder. "And yet, I think, after all, that I should just like to meet with one—of course, a gentlemanly highwayman."

"Oh, yes," answered Mr. O'Rioden, "a gentlemanly one, of course. But to say the truth, they are most of them courteous enough to the ladies."

After this, much to our hero's satisfaction, the conversation dropped, and took a different turn; for Osborne, who began to see that it was neither a pleasant or a palatable one to our hero, had the good judgment to propose a song from his wife, who immediately set down to the piano and complied with his request. After this, there was no recurrence to the unpleasant subject.

That night Osborne gave a large party, and his brilliantly lighted saloons were filled with a galaxy of beauty and fashion.

CHAPTER CXXXIV.

MR. RICHARD FLEETWOOD AND HIS DISTINGUISHED COMPANION.

WE have taken but little notice for some time past, of the Fleetwood family.

Mr. Richard Fleetwood was, as we have already seen, a disappointed man. Foiled in his attempt to cheat his brother out of the title and property, he had contented himself with driving him to almost a state of absolute despair by abstracting his child. In vain Sir Reginald Fleetwood sought out the hiding-place of his little girl—in vain had he besought Mr. Sharpthorne to use his utmost endeavours to learn some traces of the missing fugitive.

Sharpthorne tried his utmost, but all to no purpose, and Sir Reginald and his sweet wife mourned hopelessly the loss of their only child.

They had wealth, and all that it could purchase, nevertheless there was an air of gloom and settled melancholy in their house at Acton, which they in vain endeavoured to dispel.

As to Mr. Richard Fleetwood, he was a disappointed man, he was more than this, he was a reckless, nay, a lost man. He lived only for revenge. He had, in truth, loved Honora Langford, and the loss of her was perhaps more supremely bitter than being foiled in the possession of his estates—or rather his brother's.

As is often the case, Mr. Fleetwood, always rather a dissipated man, now became more so.

He took to drinking, gambling, and wasted his money—for he had some in his own right independent of his brother—and became one of the most notorious roués, or men about town.

Still, with all, he kept his brother's child snug and quiet, far removed from its parents.

We must now call the reader's attention to a small, low public-house, in St. Giles's-in-the-Fields. In the parlour of this establishment sat two personages, both of whom we have seen before.

The first of these was the once lofty and aristocratic baronet, Sir Richard Fleetwood; but oh, how changed from what he was when first we made his acquaintance. His hair is prematurely grey, his eyes are sunken, and have that restless, unsettled look, which declares at once that their owner is ill at ease with himself and all the world. From a strong, robust man, too, he would appear to have shrunk to a mere shadow of his former self. His attire had become neglected, and he looked, indeed, the very personification of a man regardless of himself and the world's opinions. Such was in reality the case.

As to his companion, it is scarcely possible to imagine a more unprepossessing ruffian. The reader may imagine this when we say it was the Nobbler who was indulging in a *tete-a-tete* with the quondam baronet.

"It's all werry well, your talking," said the Nobbler, "but I thinks as how I've suffered enough on your account. Vot's gone of all my pals, I should like to know?—vere are they? Scragged! and all about that 'ere business at Dulwich. Who was the cause of that?"

"Not me," said Mr. Fleetwood.

"Not you? Oh, thank ye. I begs pardon, Muster Fleetwood, but I takes it that it was you; leastways, that's my view of the matter, and a werry correct view it is, to my thinking. Why, when we were all together, we were as purty a lot o' magsmen as ever cracked a crib, we were. And now, what has become of all my chaps? Gone, and I've been playing the game of hide and seek ever since. I ain't half, not a quarter the man I was. Why, I used to be looked up to—now I'm looked upon with contempt. It's hard to see a man, who was the first in his perfession, quite knocked off his stump—dooced hard."

The Nobbler after this declaration, dipped his nose in a tankard of ale, and drained off a large draught of its contents.

"It is no fault of mine, I tell you," repeated Mr. Fleetwood. "You undertook the task for a consideration, and if it turned out an unfortunate affair, I am not to blame."

"Ugh! I wish I had never seen that parchment-faced lawyer, that's all I have to say in the matter," retorted the Nobbler. "Howsomever, it ain't of no use hollaring now; but they were a purty lot o' chaps, and that's the truth—a werry purty lot o' chaps."

"Well, I have got no good by the affair. The papers and the will are out of my reach, and it seems that my enemies are to triumph as they have done before. Have you seen the child ?"

"Yes, saw her last week."

"She's well, I suppose ?"

"Purty middling."

"And well taken care of ?"

"Oh, dear yes—they treat her like one of their own."

"That is well. I have to give you some cash for her board and lodging. Now mind, if by chance any one should come to inquire after her—"

"Darks the word," said the Nobbler, significantly.

"Precisely. Do not let any one see her. I don't suppose any body will take the trouble to inquire about her, but I am only giving you a caution."

"All right," ejaculated the Nobbler; "you may rely on my—or, at least, their—being fly to your moves. It ain't very likely, though, that any one will care to take much notice of an outcast, a cross child," said the Nobbler, looking hard at Mr. Fleetwood, who, however, did not seem disposed to take much notice of the observation. Both parties puffed away at their pipes—for Mr. Fleetwood seemed to have lost all pride, and had commenced smoking pipes instead of cigars, as was his wont. The Nobbler regarded his companion from beneath his shaggy eyebrows for some time. There was no light in the room, save that which came from the fitful and uncertain gleam of the fire.

"It's a rum world," said the Nobbler, after a silence for some time, "a precious rum world. Leastways I have found it so, and so, I suppose, have you."

Mr. Fleetwood looked up. We say up, for his eyes had been cast down in deep reverie.

"Well, what if I have ?" he said, sharply, and with something of his old manner.

"No offence, guv'nor; no offence, I hope. What I meant was just this 'ere. You've been, like myself, knocked out of time. That's just it. It ain't always the best man as wins."

Mr. Fleetwood did not like the simile, but he did not say anything. He contented himself with looking somewhat angrily at the speaker, and then relapsed into silence.

"He doesn't appear to come, this man," said Mr. Fleetwood, after another pause.

"Oh, he'll be here without a doubt," said the Nobbler. "Give him time; he'll be here, I'll answer for that."

"Humph, so much the better," answered the ci devant baronet, in a sharp tone. "But

I have not given you the money for the girl's board."

Whereupon he drew from his pocket a purse—and told out upon the table several pieces of money. The Nobbler pocketed these in silence. After another pause, he said slowly—

"I must ask you for something myself."

Mr. Fleetwood looked hard at the speaker.

"What do you mean ?"

"I'm cursedly short of the ready !"

"Well, what of that ?"

"Why, a good deal of it. You and your sapient lawyer cove have knocked up my profession, and I tell you I'm short, and so that's all about it !"

"Well, what of that ? I'm sorry for it. That's all I can say."

"Ah ! it ain't what you say, it's what you do."

"I really don't understand you, my friend," said Richard Fleetwood, drawing his chair a few inches from his companion.

"Well, I'm sorry I don't speak plain enought. The fact is, I want money, and what is more, I must have it."

"Must !"

"Aye. That was my word. So, you see, the quickest way to settle the matter, will be for you to dub up !"

"If you expect any more money from me, I must tell you frankly, it is not in my power to oblige you. I am already deeply involved, and to much crippled to let you or anyone else have a shilling—so now you have your answer."

"Won't do," said the Nobbler, sententiously.

"What do you mean by talking in that way, fellow. Take your answer, and have done with it."

"Now you look here. We had better not quarrel; at least, it would be better for you not to put me out."

"S'death, do you presume to threaten me," exclaimed Richard Fleetwood, rising from his chair, and growing somewhat alarmed, for he had a certain indescribable dread of the Nobbler.

"Oh, there's no call to move. You've always found me act fair and square, and I ain't a going to alter now. So sit down, Master Fleetwood. I say it won't do for either on us to quarrel, so you clearly understand that,"

"Zounds, man ! who is talking of a quarrel but yourself."

"True; so I begs pardon. Come, sit down. You must let me have a fifty, so that's all about it."

"I don't understand your dictatorial tone, and once for all must inform you that it is utterly out of my power to oblige you."

"You know that may be all werry well,"

retorted his companion; "but we've been a rowing together, and you see I'm fly to your moves; and I think you will oblige me."

Richard Fleetwood turned suddenly pale at this last observation.

"Fly to my moves!" he exclaimed, somewhat suddenly. "You are impertinent enough, to say the least of it."

"Well, you know there's this 'ere girl. In course she's expensive," said the housebreaker, in a voice half oleaginous and half husky.

"And to a gentleman so short of the ready as yourself; why in course she would be better out of the world than in it. So that's about the price of that 'ere as far as it goes. Then, you see, the child seems as though she would not die. Children of that sort never will. It's wery hard, but, you see they

won't sometimes. Well, then, there's this 'ere chap, him as is a coming here. He is up to his work usually, and, no doubt, will be in this instance."

"How much money do you want?" exclaimed Mr. Fleetwood, suddenly.

"You can blue a fifty, I dare say," said the Nobbler, looking at the fire, and speaking quite in a contemplative manner.

Mr. Richard Fleetwood said no more. He drew a fifty-pound note from his pocket-book, and placed it, without a word, in the hands of his companion, who, without a single observation, transferred the same to his own pocket.

"Ah, I always had a respect for you," said the housebreaker, still looking at the fire, and making his observation in quite a contemplative and desultory manner. "Because

No. 92.

why, you can take a hint and understand business, and that's all about it. I have not been very fortunate as yet in having anything to do with you, but, I dare say, the time will come when I shall be; and so Mr. Fleetwood, here's your health; and better luck to both of us. I'm sure it's needed. At least, I know it is with me; I can answer for that."

So saying the housebreaker tossed off a portion of the contents of the tankard, and then handed the same to his companion.

It has been well said that there is a freemasonry in crime, for in the present case it caused a gentleman and an unquestionable ruffian to be on the most familiar terms of companionship. In a few minutes after the two had been so familiar and friendly as to drink each other's health out of the same tankard, the door of the dingy room in which they sat was cautiously opened, and the face of a man peered in. It was a thin face—a worn, cadaverous face—a face upon which sat a multitude of strange expressions to the curious observer. The face belonged to an old man without a doubt, for it was rugose—the eyes were sunken, although they did not appear to have lost anything of their pristine lustre, for these expressions were positively hawk-like, if such a term could with propriety be used in describing the human countenance. Mr. Fleetwood turned his eyes in the direction of the parlour-door, and recognised the individual who was taking a survey of the room and its two occupants.

"Ah, it's you, Mr. Newt," said Fleetwood. "You are somewhat behind your time, are you not?"

"Pardon me, Mr. Fleetwood," said the party so addressed, "but other business, which to say the truth I had not at all expected, has detained me longer than I had anticipated."

"Punctuality is the soul of business," remarked the Nobbler.

"Oh, how do you do this evening," said Mr. Newt, courteously enough to the housebreaker.

"Purty well for an ill-used man," remarked the ruffian, with something of an injured tone in his voice and manner.

"Umph! ill-used!" exclaimed Mr. Newt. "We are all badly treated in this world!"

"You two gentleman have business matters to discuss. So I'll not intrude," said the Nobbler, rising from his seat.

"No, don't go," answered Mr. Newt. Mr. Fleetwood and myself are off, so pray don't disturb yourself."

"Oh, that's it, is it," growled the housebreaker, once more resting himself in his chair, and refilling his pipe.

"When you are ready, Mr. Fleetwood, I am at your service," said Newt, who had not set down.

"I 'spose you are in hurry?" remarked the Nobbler.

"Well, my time is pretty well occupied as you know," answered Newt, and in the course of two or three more minutes, he and Fleetwood left the public-house together. Not, however, before the latter had requested the housebreaker to call upon him on the morrow.

CHAPTER CXXXV.

THE HOUSEBREAKER'S HANDY MAN.

THE cracksman, burglar, housebreaker, Nobbler, or general ruffian was left alone in the dingy room of that dingy, and unprepossessing house. He was a little better satisfied since he had made—for that is the proper term—since he had made Mr. Richard Fleetwood "blue" a fifty flimsy. The first thing the ruffian did, after Fleetwood's departure, was to ring the bell, and upon the waiter making his appearance, he ordered a stiff glass of brandy-and-water, hot, strong, and sweet. The Nobbler puffed away at his pipe, and very soon despatched the brandy-and-water, which had been brought by a patriarchal looking waiter. Another was ordered, and then a visitor came into the room. He caught sight of the Nobbler's back as the latter was seated before the fire, and this appeared to give him the greatest satisfaction, for a smile actually passed over his features, which, to say the truth, upon the first glance, would have led a superficial observer.

"Oh, it's you, Ned; sit down," said the housebreaker, in a satisfactory tone of voice.

The man so addressed was tall and thin, being, in fact, more than six feet in height. He was the same individual whom the reader may possibly remember we had occasion to take a cursory glance of in the earlier portion of this work.

"Sit down," again repeated the housebreaker, in a patronising tone, "and take a sip of that."

Whereupon he handed to the new comer the steaming glass of brandy-and-water. The man took it and conveyed the same to his lips in a sort of humble and subservient manner. He had always looked upon the Nobbler as a superior being, and consequently stood in considerable awe of him.

"Thank you; much obliged, I'm sure," said Long Ned, for that was his cognomen. "Here's jolly good health, gov'ner, and jolly good luck to both on us, and I'm sure that's needed."

" "You're right, Ned. Amen to that, say I."

"Mister Fleetwood ain't here, then," said Long Ned, inquiringly.

"No: gone about—about half an hour ago."

"Ah, glad on it."

"Why?"

"Don't like him. He's so cursedly proud."

"Oh, he ain't a bit proud now; that's all knocked out of him," remarked the house-breaker.

"Ah, gone with the title, 'spose," returned his companion.

"Yes, with the title and a lot of other things as well. Oh, he's a rum 'un—a queer fish."

"Well, but I say," remarked Long Ned, in a sort of hoarse whisper, "do you know who this child belongs to?"

"Yes, in course," said the housebreaker, sharply, taking the pipe out of his mouth; "in course I do—it's Muster Richard Fleetwood's."

"Is it?"

"Most certainly."

"You are out this time, master," said Long Ned, with a look of deep mystery.

"Hang me if I understand you," exclaimed the housebreaker, "and that's all about it. She ain't yours, I 'spose?"

"No, I'll answer for that; leastways, not as I knows on," he added, correctively.

"Ah, that's all right."

"Well, then, I say as how you are not," repeated Ned. "I've learnt some very important imformation—quite promiscuously, like."

"Oh, have you; so much the better."

"Well it appears that this 'ere little girl is the only child of Sir Reginald and Lady Fleetwood—brother and sister-in-law to Mr. Richard."

"You don't mean that?" exclaimed the burglar, starting back, and looking hard at his companion.

"I just do though. Mr. Richard Fleetwood has been up to a lot of tricks; and one on 'em was to imprison his brother, and keep him locked up in a madhouse for two or three years; his next little game was to march off this child. Arter that, his brother, Sir Reginald managed to get out of this 'ere madhouse, not, however, before Mr. Richard had well-nigh poisoned him."

"Ye don't mean that, Ned?" exclaimed the burglar.

"Aye, it's true enough," returned his companion.

"Vell I never!"

"And he was well nigh doing it—there's no mistake about that 'ere; and what's more, he would have done so, had it not have been for Colonel Jack."

"What had the colonel to do in the mat-ter, then? Did he know Sir Reginald?"

"Lor' bless ye, he knows the whole lot on 'em. Vy, he's a relative, the colonel is."

"Gammon and all!" exclaimed the house-breaker.

"No gammon in the matter," answered his companion. "I tell ye it's all true what I'm saying, every bit on it."

"Vell, go on, Ned; let's have the whole true and pertikler account of the matter."

"Ye see," said Long Ned, in continuation, Mr. Richard Fleetwood was Sir Richard, at this time. His brother was supposed to be dead. He was well nigh so, but no matter for that—he's alive, and all right enough now. Vell, as I vos a saying, he was supposed to be dead. What does his wife do, but give birth to this 'ere little girl. What does Sir Richard do—he was Sir Richard then—what does he do, but he walks the babby off, in quick sticks. He's stuck to her ever since."

"What, with the wife's consent?"

"Oh, he humbugged her somehow or other. She's a poor soft thing, so I've been told."

"Well, you get before me," said the bur-glar; "you've got right before me, Ned, and that's the truth."

"This girl is the child of the present Sir Reginald Fleetwood. There's not the slightest mistake about that 'ere," said Long Ned. And now you know the upshot of the whole matter."

"Well, I'm blest! This is glorious news, and no flys," remarked the housebreaker.

"And you'll make something of it?"

"I should hope so. Oh, that's why he wants the child put out of the way."

"Does he want her put out of the way?"

"In course he does. I knows that—but thinks I, she is too profitable a spec'lation to lose all in a hurry—so I sees that her cordial ain't administered to her, that's about the price of it. It's dooced lucky I have acted as I have. Oh, she must be looked arter—there, waiter! two more glasses of brandy-and-water!"

The last observation, or order, was given to the patriarchal servitor of the establish-ment.

The liquor was brought, for the Nobbler was in high spirits at the information his confidential man had given him, and he was determined to enjoy himself at the prospect which the new and unexpected information had opened to him.

"Now, I tell you what it is," remarked Ned. "I don't presume to know better than you do; but it's my humble opinion that the best game would be to take the kid away. Ye know, Sir Reginald Fleetwood would come down handsome—ah, jolly handsome he woud, only just to catch a sight of her sweet face, for she has a sweet face of her own."

The Nobbler gave an approving nod.

"And then you know as to Mr. Richard Fleetwood. I, for my own part, wouldn't care a straw about him, eh ?"

"Oh, you are a bit too fast," said the Nobbler, reflectively.

"Vy ?"

"Pshaw ! vy, indeed ! Mr. Fleetwood ain't a man to be trifled with. In course, he could hang both on us."

"Oh !" exclaimed Long Ned, suddenly altering his tone. "I never thought of that !"

"It's rather an important thing to think of, nevertheless," returned his superior.

"It is so."

"And you see, Ned, I have had several transactions with Mr. Richard. I've made him blue a fifty not two hours ago."

"Oh, a fifty, eh !"

"Yes, a fifty flimsy—but that's neither here or there. There ain't any call to stick to him any longer than it answers our purpose."

"In course not."

"Only I must put the stopper on, as I have done, agin his doing anything upon the cross, that's all. We'll wait a bit, and then see what can be made of this. The cards seem to be turning up trumps, and we must mind how we play them. You are quite certain that you are correct in your information ?"

"I'll stake my life on it."

"Do they know anything about it ?"

"Not a word—not a syllable. They believe her to be really the child of Mr. Richard Fleetwood."

"That is well. Do not mention a word of what you have heard to them—keep dark!"

"Trust me for that, master," answered Long Ned. "I'm as close as an oyster upon that head."

The Nobbler gave a satisfactory nod of assent to this declaration of his companion, and re-filled his pipe, and had the glasses replenished : and so we must leave him to follow the footsteps of Mr. Richard Fleetwood and the worn and cadaverous individual who accompanied him.

—

CHAPTER CXXXVI.

THE CHEMIST'S LABORATORY.

THROUGH dingy streets, through narrow courts, where the sun of Heaven seldom found an entrance, through winding and numerous alleys, reeking with unwholesome and pestilential odour, did Mr. Richard Fleetwood and his strange companion take their way. They had not, during their progress, exchanged half-a-dozen words or so, and they

still continued on their course in comparative silence, for Mr. Fleetwood himself did not appear to be on a very familiar footing with the person who strode by his side. Occasionally, and as the footway narrowed here and there, he fell back, and walked behind There was an air of mystery about the passage of these two men, which reminded you of a couple of conspirators, who avoided the most frequented thoroughfares, and shrunk from "the gaudy, garish eye of day." Presently Mr. Fleetwood said, inquiringly—

"Is it far now ?"

His companion looked at him for a moment, and said—

"No, not far. Have patience, and we shall be there in a few minutes," and so saying, the speaker strode on at a somewhat accelerated pace.

In a short time the two individuals found themselves before a large old-fashioned house, whose overhanging front, deep bayed windows, high pitched roof, and quaint architecture, at once declared it to have been built a century or so before, at the very least. Fleetwood's companion paused at the doorway of this residence ; and pulling from his doublet a large curiously formed key, he inserted it into the lock, and opened the door. A strange mephitic odour found its way to the nostrils of Mr. Richard Fleetwood—an odour made up of a combination of smells, none of which was agreeable—an odour as of the charnel house and grave. Mr. Fleetwood shuddered as the door of the house was thrown back by his companion. A large dingy hall was visible, and beyond this a wide staircase dimly perceptible in the gloom.

"Enter," said Fleetwood's companion. "Enter, my friend !"

For a moment the ci devant baronet hesitated He was not naturally a timid man, as we have had proofs of on more than one occasion. Nevertheless, there seemed to come over him some strange and undefined sensation of fear.

His companion regarded him with a curious inquiring sort of glance, upon which, Mr. Fleetwood hesitated no longer, but entered without further hesitation. The chemist, or leech, for such he in reality was, closed the door after him, when the two were in the passage in all but total darkness, for there was no other hall-lamp or luminary of any sort to dissipate the gloom, which, to say the truth, became painful to Fleetwood.

The chemist walked towards a bracket fixed in the side of the wall, from this he took a small taper, which he ignited by inserting a match into some chemical compound, for lucifers were unknown in those days. This done he led the way to a room in the rear of the premises, bidding his companion follow.

Mr. Fleetwood then found himself in a room, which appeared to be more like a cell or vault of some necromancer of the middle ages. In it were numerous philosophical instruments, skeletons of animals, stuffed birds, human skeletons, heaps of bones, cabalistic-looking books—ponderous volumes in black letter and the dead languages, phials and bottles of various shapes and sizes, chemical retorts, various specimens of *lusus naturæ* preserved in spirits in well-corked and hermetrically sealed bottles, and a variety of other objects, the nature of which it was impossible for Mr. Fleetwood to guess with any degree of certainty, as to their use and object.

The chemist ignited a large sized lamp, which was placed on his table, and then desired his companion to be seated, at the same time he threw himself into a large easy chair, which was placed in front of his table. Mr. Fleetwood did as he was desired, after which there was a pause of a few moments duration.

"Now, sir, I am entirely and completely at your service," said the chemist. "We are on hallowed ground, sir. On this spot where we are now seated once dwelt one of the most celebrated masters of his craft. Yes, the most celebrated. In this, or rather the spot upon which this house is built, was once the cave of the celebrated Merlin."

The reader, or, rather, the more learned in the antiquities of London, need not be apprised that Mr. Fleetwood and his companion were not far from where Northampton Square, Pentenville, now stands.

Mr. Fleetwood started, and fidgetted somewhat uneasily in his chair. There was an air of mystery about the individual who sat opposite to him, that was such as to occasion him considerable misgivings. What these were, in what direction they pointed, he was at a loss to determine.

"You need my services," said the chemist. "Already have you been a purchaser of a potent compound—what would you more? Does the elixir fail to do its work? My friend, I hold here, in this room, numbers of keys which open the door to that dark and mysterious future—that undiscovered country. I hold the keys which open the portals of death. By subtle essence—by all but impalpable powder—the spirit is made to wing its flight to realms of peace and happiness, and removed far from this world of sin and trouble. Such is the work of science—of that mighty science which is enabled to sap the very life springs, noiselessly, with certainty, and which defies detection. But I think it was not human life you were desirous of taking," said the chemist to his companion, at the same time fastening on him a look at once inquiring and incredulous.

"Ahem! no," exclaimed Fleetwood, "oh, dear no. It was for the destruction of horses that I first consulted you."

"Precisely. And did you succeed?"

"I regret to say that I did not."

"That is strange. Did you administer the potion I gave you?"

"Yes."

"And what was the effect?"

"Two were made ill, but they did not die. I suspect that the groom who had charge of them did not act fairly."

"Act fairly!" exclaimed the old man. "What do you mean? He did not put the draught I gave you in the water?"

"I saw that done myself, and what is more, saw it administered."

"How then? The draught was potent enough."

"Some antidote—"

"You want one?"

"No; but I suspect that the groom gave some antidote to the animals after I had taken my departure."

"Pshaw!" exclaimed the leech, indignantly; "you are dreaming, friend. Dost thou think that I am so errant a bungler in my profession as to be outwitted by a mere groom? There is not a man in this city who would be able to furnish an antidote to the poison I furnished you with. By-the-way, you have not tried its efficacy upon any human subject, I suppose?" inquired the leech, with apparent carelessness.

Fleetwood gave a sudden, although, truth to say, not an unexpected start at this interrogatory.

"Dear me, no!" he exclaimed. "What could make you imagine such a thing?"

The leech smiled.

"Ah, my friend," he said, slowly, and with painful distinctness; "ah, it is not a very extraordinary supposition, to say the least of it. More than this, with all due defference to your veracity, I am led to the very natural conclusion that it is human life you are desirous of taking."

Mr. Richard Fleetwood rose from his seat, a shade of indignation passed over his features, and he appeared as though he was about to take an abrupt departure from his companion's house.

The latter quietly awaited the issue. Leaning his chin upon one of his hands, he calmly contemplated the embarrassment of his visitor. He seemed rather to enjoy it than otherwise—to take a savage delight, in fact, in Fleetwood's acting, for it was nothing else, after all.

"Pray be seated, Mr.—Mr. Bryant," said the leech, without moving a muscle of his cadaverous countenance. "Let us be friends —let us understand one another. What do you desire now? We are alone, but I know not how long we may be so; for, to say the truth, I have so many call upon me, that I cannot be certain of my time."

Mr. Richard Fleetwood once more seated himself in the chair opposite to his companion.

"So, that is well!" exclaimed the latter. "These affairs are better transacted with a cool head, and at the same time without any disguise from the party who consults the man of science. One person is doomed—I take that for granted."

"What do you mean ?—one person!"

"Yes ; one person is to be sent to another sphere than the one we at present inhabit. It may be more than one. I do not inquire if it be child or adult—male or female. It suffices for me that you need my services for a special purpose—I know, or at least I can guess, what that is. You say it is to poison horses—I accept the statement as truth. I am not bound to inquire further, and I must, or ought to apologise for having indulged in the observations which have already fallen from me. So be it—you would poson one or more of the lower animals. Now," and here the speaker opened a small drawer of the table by which he was seated, and took therefrom a phial. "Now, here I hold in my hand a liquid so potent, that a drop, the merest infinitesimal scruple, will in the space of a few, a 'very few seconds, will destroy life in the largest and strongest animal in the creation. This poison is a legacy bequeathed to me by a celebrated Italian chemist. Poor man, he perished on the scaffold."

Mr. Fleetwood gave another start.

"Perished on the scaffold !" he exclaimed, turning suddenly very pale, and trembling slightly.

"Yes, is there anything so astonishing in that ?" inquired his companion.

"No, perhaps not, but—"

"But what ?"

"It's not much of a recommendation—not a pleasant reminiscence."

"You only want to poison horses," said the leech, with an icy manner.

"Ah, no—certainly."

"Besides, this said Italian was a bungler ; not in his art or profession, but in the practice of it. He confided in a woman, and was betrayed."

"He was to be pitied."

"Without a doubt. But you are not here to listen to his history, and so to business. I will now prove to you the efficacy of this drug."

The speaker rose from his seat, went to the door of his apartment, and called out the name of " Adrian."

A voice was heard from below answering the call, and in another minute a youth of apparently about seventeen or eighteen years of age made his appearance. He was very handsome, and seemed to be dressed in foreign costume, Italian, so Mr. Fleetwood thought. His long hair hung over his polished brow in thick ringlets, and his features were of that peculiar mould so often depicted by Italian and Roman sculptors.

He stood on the threshold of the door awaiting his master's orders.

"Adrian," said the latter, "bring me Nero."

The boy took his departure, and in a few minutes returned with a moderately-sized dog.

At a motion from his master, he again disappeared, closing the door after him as he left.

Mr. Ephriam Tospeck, that was the chemist's name, called the dog to his side. In another minute the faithful quadruped was on his knee. With one hand he opened the mouth of the animal, and inserting the feather of a quill in the phial, he drew the same once or twice across the tongue of the dog, and then placed him on the floor.

Mr. Richard Fleetwood was watching these proceedings with a considerable amount of interest.

For a few seconds the dog trotted about the apartment as though nothing had happened. It might be from about twenty to thirty seconds that he did this—hardly so much as that, so Fleetwood thought—when all of a sudden a tremor shook his frame— he staggered—then once more endeavoured to regain his equilibrium—then staggered again and finally turned on his side—a slight spasm passed through his frame once more, and then all was still—the dog was dead !

Mr. Tospeck looked hard at his visitor.

"Now, my friend, you do not doubt the efficacy of this, I suppose ?" he said, pointing to the small phial he still held in his hand.

"I should be an idiot to do so," was the prompt reply.

"Good ; and what is more, this *defies detection.* Make what post-mortem examination you like, there will be no traces of poison found in the stomach, blood or the tissues. It tells no tales, keeps your own secret, and dies with you."

There was an eager, hungry, horrible look upon the countenance of Richard Fleetword as these words fell from the lips of Ephraim Tospeck.

"This is not the same drug you furnished me with when I saw you before ?" he inquired hastily.

A smile passed over the countenance of the chemist.

"No," he answered.

There was then a pause.

"But you would let me have it now, or at least a portion of it, I suppose ?"

"It's very expensive," answered Tospeck.

"No matter for that. Have your own terms."

"And what is more I do not entrust it to everyone."

"No; I should suppose not."

"I must know the name and quality of the purchaser."

"Undoubtedly—that is but fair—you know my name."

The leech smiled.

"His real name," he said, slowly, and in that peculiar dry manner which discomposed Fleetwood, who fidgetted in his chair, but made no immediate reply. "Yes, his real name. But I need hardly inquire in the pre- present instance. Mr. Richard Fleetwood."

The party so addressed looked at the speaker in perfect amazement.

"You know my name, then," he said.

The leech nodded an assent to this query.

"And now your purpose?"

"What do you mean?"

"Your purpose. For whom and for what do you require this potent poison?"

"I have already told you."

"Is it the child, or is it your brother?"

Mr. Fleetwood was so perfectly astonished at this inquiry, so unlooked for and so unex- pected, that his strong frame shook as though he were struck by a palsy.

"I—my—good God! What is the meaning of this?" he gasped forth, as though he were choking.

"Mr. Richard you are known to me," said Tospeck, turning round, and proceeding to arrange divers and sundry bottles containing medicaments of various sorts, more it must be confessed for the destruction rather than the preservation of human life."

"Known to you?" stammered forth Fleet- wood.

"Ay, surely—not personally, it is true, but by name—by repute."

"I was not aware of this."

"Possibly not, but you remember Mr. Hardy's establishment, I suppose?"

"Certainly," answered Fleetwood, in perfect astonishment. "Mr. Hardy, at Wandsworth."

"The very same."

"Yes, I know the place well enough. What of that? Numbers of others know it besides myself."

"No doubt. Myself for one. Ah, we went to work too slowly there," exclaimed Tospeck, in a hissing, horrid whisper.

"Too slowly?"

"Yes; that was the mistake; Colonel Jack outwitted the lot of us."

"I do not understand you."

"I am plain enough."

"Not to my comprehension."

"Indeed. You are dull, my friend. Colonel Jack outwitted us. Am I not right? You nearly lost your life. You did what to you was almost worse, perhaps, you lost position, title, wealth, and all that could make life de- sirable. Had a stronger mixture have been given to Sir Reginald Fleetwood you would have not been here to-day."

If Mr. Richard Fleetwood had been pos- sessed of the power of resolution at this par- ticular time, the probability is that he would have risen from the chair upon which he was seated, rushed through the door of the doctor's laboratory, and from thence into the street, and never again set foot in his house; but unfortunately he was not possessed of the capability of moving. He was so completely thunderstruck at the revelations which had been made to him one after the other, and all in such a cool and non-emotional manner by the terrible dealer in drugs, whose assist- ance he had blindly sought, that he was completely frustrated, and felt himself over- matched by the superior intelligence of his companion.

"No," repeated the leech. "You would not have done me the honour of paying me the present visit. You would have been still Sir Richard Fleetwood, the lofty baronet, surrounded with all those appliances which wealth can purchase and position command. Well, we can't all succeed in the world. We can't all reach the topmost round of the ladder. You are a baffled and disappointed man. No wonder you should be disappointed —you laid your schemes well—and to say the truth, up to a certain point you carried them out well—but where's the end? Here you are seeking my advice. Shall I give it you?"

"I am here for the purpose of consulting you," remarked the astonished Fleetwood, for he knew and felt that the strange, mysterious being opposite to him was reading his very thoughts, plumbing his very soul, seeing into his actions as plainly as though he were a book.

"You are here, if I take it rightly, to pur- chase a certain drug of me. Is it not so?"

"Most certainly."

"Well, my answer to you is simply this. You have failed hitherto. You are ambi- tious. You would be restored to your rights, I was going to say, but you would be placed in the same position you were before, Sir Reginald Fleetwood had escaped from Mr. Hardy's establishment? Is this not so?"

"Well, what if it is?"

"Simply this. You must act in concert with me—if you feel so disposed—for I must tell you frankly, that unless I am made fully acquainted with your proceedings, I shall decline serving you in any way."

"Humph!" ejaculated Fleetwood. "You are candid—nay, dictatoral."

"My friend, you are playing for a great stake; and mark me, you will not be able to win the prize by yourself. Rest assured of that; without we act in concert, you may as well bid farewell to your dream of ambition."

Mr. Richard Fleetwood looked at the speaker in utter amazement. He made no reply, but regarded the cruel features of the leech with something like horror. Unprincipled as he was himself, he did not dream of such gigantic villany as that which was but too plainly made manifest by the words which had fallen from the lips of his companion.

"You see I speak plain enough," exclaimed the latter, still in the same cold sepulchral voice which he had assumed during the whole of the interview, and which, to say the truth, was habitual to him.

"You do, indeed!" said Fleetwood. "But I am still at a loss to conjecture your precise meaning."

"Let me explain more fully. Your brother is in the way. We must all die some time or other, and it is only a question of time as to when and how. Let your brother be cut off, and then—but you know the rest."

Fleetwood turned so fearfully pale at this suggestion, that even the leech became alarmed.

"There, there," he exclaimed; "I meant not to pain you. Forgive me. We men of science are materialists, and are, I frankly confess, but too apt to reason coldly. Come, sit down and we may come to a better understanding."

Mr. Fleetwood reseated himself on the chair he had previously occupied upon his first entrance.

"What will you give me if I join issue with you?" inquired Tospeck.

"Name your terms."

"An annuity. A good round sum annually, so long as you are in full and undisturbed possession of the property of your ancestors"

"An annuity!"

"Certainly the labourer is worthy of his hire. I will make a bargain with you. Leave me to work out the business. Leave me to remove all impediments, and stumbling blocks in your way, and then when you are reinstated into your own good position. I shall call upon you for my share. What can be fairer than this? No cure no pay!"

"You are very kind, I'm sure," remarked Fleetwood, half satirically.

The man of drugs smiled.

"Well, you consider over my proposition and see me again. To-morrow, if convenient—say about the same time as we met this evening."

"I will do so," answered Fleetwood, rising again from the seat which he had not, since his first entrance, been able to sit upon with anything like comfort to himself.

"Yes, consider the matter over, and by the time you come again I will reduce to paper my terms. You can then please yourself, either refuse or accept the same; and at the same time I pledge my word that this conversation between ourselves is strictly confidential. No other ear will it fall upon but our own."

"Accept my thanks for this pledge, as also for the interest you take in my affairs," said Fleetwood, as he sallied towards the door of the doctor's museum or laboratory. Mr. Tospeck saw him to the outer door, closed it after him, and then returned to his back room. As he did so, he indulged in a quiet chuckle; and rubbing his hands together in evident satisfaction, he seated himself in what he chose to term his consulting chair.

"Ah—ah! Mr. Richard Fleetwood. I have you on the hip. The fox is snared. You'll be back here to-morrow, without a doubt. Oh, yes—back here ready to sign the pretty little document. I will take care to have it prepared. Hark! what was that?"

The leech turned suddenly towards a glass door, which led out to a smaller apartment than the one he then occupied. He thought he had heard some sound proceed from this. Hastily rising from his seat, he cautiously and quietly opened the door, and made a careful inspection of the farther apartment. No one was visible, and Mr. Tospeck returned to his laboratory much better satisfied. He, however, still had misgivings, for he exclaimed, hastily—

"I could have sworn I heard some sound, as of a person in yonder room; but no, it must be fancy—mere fancy after all. How conscience makes us cowards. Surely it could not have been Adrian—oh, no, I should think not."

He went to the other door of his room, the one which led into the passage, and shouted out the youth's name.

As before, the summons was answered immediately, and Adrain made his appearance.

"Did you call?" he said.

"Ah—yes—I—that is— Did you not hear a noise?"

"No," answered the youth.

"Has any one come in?"

"No, master. The gentleman has been gone out a few minutes."

"Pshaw! dost thou think I did not know that? There, take away this carrion," and, as he said this, he pointed to the dead dog which lay upon the hearth rug.

The youth stooped down, and took the remains of the poor animal in his arms, and conveyed it down stairs.

"And, harkye!" exclaimed Tospeck, as he heard the lad descending the stairs, "I would speak to thee."

In a few more minutes the lad returned, and stood before his master, with that peculiar look of passive submission upon his features which by long habit he had acquired.

"You have have been listening—have been playing the eves-dropper."

The lad gave an indignant look, but did not reply.

"Do you hear me, Adrian?"

"Yes, I hear you," he answered.

"And what answer have you to make? None, it appears——you confess?"

"I have not been listening. I was down stairs until you called me. Ask Isabella."

"Bah! she's about as much to be relied on as yourself. Now, mark me, I will have no spies in my establishment. I have told you this over and over again—in fact, I know not how often."

No. 93.

"Very often, I know that," said the youth, sadly.

"Well, then, you know my orders. Dare to infringe them, and it will be worse for you, mind that."

"I not seek to pry into your secrets," answered the youth. "I already know enough —too much for my own happiness."

"Silence!—would you dare!" exclaimed the doctor, in a violent and sudden rage.

Then, after a pause, he said, more calmly—

"Have I not saved you from destruction? —brought you up, lodged, fed, and clothed you?"

"I do not deny it," answered Adrian. "I ought to be grateful, and I hope I strive to be so."

"See that I have not warmed into life an adder—nurtured a scorpion to sting me."

" I am no adder," said the lad, indignantly. " I do your bidding, and say nothing. In return for what you give me, I keep your secrets."

" We have both our secrets, mind you that, Adrian. Have I not taught you mysteries which your young mind never dreamt of till I opened to you the springs of knowledge ?"

" You gave me a taste for knowledge, I own," answered Adrian, sadly ; " and in the knowledge you have communicated, I have felt a charm that at times seemed almost fatal. You have confounded in my mind evil and good, or rather you have left both evil and good, as dead ashes, as the dust and cinder in your own crucible. You have made intellect the only conscience. Of late, I wish my tutor had been my own village priest."

" You murmur. What were you when we were first acquainted ?—an innocent girl, I suppose ?"

" I was early warped to wrong, by one who is gone to answer for his crimes."

" Psha ! while yet a child you were made the instrument to bring death to the innocent."

" I do not deny it. I knew no better—I was but a mere puppet in the hands of others."

" You would be no longer a puppet—you would act for yourself ?"

" I have not said so. I am content as I am."

" Adrian," exclaimed the leech, " there is treason in the camp. Do not think that I am blind to your aspirations. You would throw off the shackles which bind you. I read it in your eye—in your very looks. Seek not to deceive me. Bah ! it is hopeless for you to endeavour to do so. Hear me !" and as the man of drugs uttered these words, he regarded his beauteous companion with an eye of flame. " Hear me—I love you !"

His companion started back with a sudden movement.

" Yes," he continued, " you have youth, and, ah, a more than ordinary beauty—I, the old, withered, and worn man of science—I love you !"

" Oh, say not so ! say not so ! this is worse than all !" exclaimed his companion, in a plaintive and troubled voice. " You cannot mean it—surely you do not !"

" But I do," exclaimed the doctor, in a hissing tone, " I do ! It sounds unmusical to your ears. Listen, Adrian—nay, turn not from me—it is in your power to command me, to make me your devoted slave. The time has come when we must both throw off the mask. In me, behold an ardent and passionate lover. From almost childhood you have been under my charge. I have saved your life—I would open to you a happy and glorious future. I am rich, and shall shortly have a considerable accession of wealth ; but what is all this without a companion to share it ? Nothing, positively nothing. For you I have toiled. I shall shortly retire from my profession ; we will then go abroad to your own country ; you will throw aside your present garb, and stand revealed as your own sex."

The girl shuddered—for the supposed boy, Adrian, was in reality a young Italian girl of nineteen summers. She shuddered, and placed her hands before her eyes, as though she would shut out the hideous reality. She stood for a minute thus, and then burst out into a passionate flood of tears.

" You weep, child," said Tospeck, approaching her, and laying his hand kindly upon her shoulder. " Poor girl ! Perhaps if some handsome gallant had said as much as myself you would have smiled, eh ? Is it not so ?"

" Alas ! alas ! I have been too much the child of sorrow to listen to the honied words which fall from the lips of men when addressing the opposite sex. No, my heart is a tomb, in which lies buried the hopes of youth."

" I love you !" iterated the doctor with passionate earnestness.

He bent over as he said this and kissed her cheek, she shrunk from his touch. He observed this and suddenly thrust her from him.

" Go !" he exclaimed " I see my touch is pollution. Go ! ungrateful girl, wayward, capricious, and uncertain like your sex. Go now ! think of what I have said. It rests with yourself either to make me your most devoted and attached of husbands, or your bitterest enemy, make your own election. You know me. Go ! I would be alone."

Adrian quickly left the room and the chemist threw himself in his chair—flung himself forward on the table and buried his face in his hands. He remained thus for sometime.

" Foiled ! foiled !" he presently exclaimed, in wild and passionate accents. " Oh fool ! fool ! with all thy science, with all thy skill, thou knowest not any drug, or medicament to warp or bend the mind of wayward and wilful woman !"

———

CHAPTER CXXXVI.

ISABELLA AND ADRIAN.

EPHRAIMK TOSPEC was right in his surmises as to the existence of treachery in his camp. After Adrian as she was called, left the doctors museum or studio, she went down stairs to the housekeepers room ; and Mistress Isabella, when she observed the features of her young charge, was able to make a pretty shrewd guess as to the nature of her interview with her master. With a woman's tact Isabella had observed enough within the last few months to understand how matters were likely to turn out.

It was a strange establishment that of the chemist, singular in many respects. The house itself was of large dimensions, much larger than could possibly be required for its present occupants for Mr. Tospeck was without wife or child.

Now it generally happens however bad a man may be, whatever strange dealings he may have, he generally succeeds in having a few faithful followers. The woman Isabella was one, in the case of Topspeck she had been in his service for years. It would be absurd to suppose that she was in entire and complete ignorance of her masters backslidings. No matter, he was good to her, treated her with considerable kindness. It is true his ways were strange, his manner was frigid, nay oftentimes severe, but in the main he was not an unkind master.

Adrian set herself down in the housekeeper's room, and looked the very personification of utter wretchedness and despair. She had not remained long thus, when she heard Tospeck make his exit through the front door of his house.

"Master's gone out!" exclaimed Mistress Isabella. "Did he say he was about to leave?"

"No" answered Adrian.

"You seem sad, child. Has the master been angry with you?"

"No" again answered the young Italian girl.

"Why what ails you?" said Isabella, looking at her young companion inquiringly over her spectacles.

"He has been too kind" ejaculated Adrian, for we must still call her so "much too kind."

"People are not generally displeased at too much kindness," answered the old dame.

"Oh Mistress Isabella" said the young girl in chocking accents " you know what a fond slave I have been here, ever since I was a child, scarcely having a will of my own."

"I know that, child, well enough. My master's will is all-in-all here."

"Indeed it is, or he would wish it to be. Isabella, you have been my only friend since I left my own country; and, my dear lady, I know you will not desert the poor lonely orphan now."

"Hoity, toity! No. What does the girl mean?"

"Mr. Tospeck has declared that he is in love with me."

"Well, there's nothing extraordinary in that; for to say the truth, my child, you are in sooth, a comely looking lass."

"Would that I were as hideous as sin"

"Hush, hush, dear. Don't make use of such dreadful expressions. It's sinful."

"Oh, I am the most wretched being in the world," exclaimed the young Italian. "I want to leave this house. Nay, I will leave it, Isabella; for if I remain in it, I shall die!"

"Die! And wherefore?"

Adrian explained the nature of her interview with Mr. Tospeck, and pointed out to her companion that in the event of her refusing to become the mistress or wife of Tospeck, he would in all probability take a signal revenge, the nature of which Mistress Isabella was at no loss to surmise, although she pretended ignorance to her young companion.

"Nay, never fear, my dear, he will never harm you, believe me," exclaimed Mistress Isabella, "never, believe me, I will answer for that. He loves you too well."

"You do not know him," answered the young Italian.

"I ought to do so by this time," said Isabella, bridling up.

"Oh, you know not half—not one twentieth part of his dark secrets. I tell you, Isabella, that if I thwart him, I shall share the same fate as this poor brute."

She pointed as she said this, to the dog which lay almost at her feet.

"You know more about the master than I do," said Isabella, with a shrug, "but I suppose you owe him a debt of gratitude. You were an orphan and proscribed in your own country, and he kindly brought you over disguised as a lad, which attire you have continued to wear ever since. Is that not true?"

"It is," exclaimed Adrian, bursting into tears. "Would that I had suffered the worst to have befallen me before I had sought these shores."

"Why? You have been treated kindly enough, I hope."

"By you I have."

"And by Mr. Tospeck. Yours has been a strange connection with him. How did you become acquainted with him in the first instance?"

"Hush!" exclaimed Adrian; "promise me that you will never breathe a syllable to human ear of what I am about to divulge."

Mistress Isabella looked alarmed, but she gave the required promise.

"I was as I am still, an orphan," she continued.

"Were you so at the time of your first acquaintance with Mr. Tospeck?" said Mistress Isabella.

"Yes, from my earliest childhood. It is true I have a dim recollection of a kind and gentle face bending over me in my earliest dreams of infancy. A face the features of which I even now distinctly remember."

"You did not know her for long, I suppose."

"No."

"And your father ?"

"Died soon after my poor mother, and how I but too shrewdly guess. They fell victims to a monster in the shape of a man. A wretch wearing the garb of humanity. Oh, Mistress Isabella, you know not half; the miseries which cruel fate, sad destiny has made me subject to. Listen, I was, after the death of my parents, under the charge of their murderer—yes, their murderer!"

"Good Heavens! can this be possible ?"

"This man taught me his wicked acts; or rather made me instrumental in carrying them out. It was from my hand that the poison which sapped the springs of life was taken."

"From your hand! Poison!" exclaimed Isabella. "Impossible."

"Yes; not one, not two, not a dozen victims only fell before this man and his agents. I learnt afterwards that my own parents received their death at his hands; and at least, one hundred and seventy other persons."

"Great heavens, and he had charge of you ?"

"Yes. But oh, it's a long, long, dreary and sad story the history of my early life. I do not know if I was not in reality the daughter of my protector, or guardian, if such can be termed of a man who teaches the young mind nought but ill. He was the most celebrated Italian poisoner of his day. My mother was a very beautiful woman. Perhaps one of the most beautiful women of the time. At least, so I have been told, and judging from the portrait I have seen of her, I should judge such to be the case. Well, you must know that Signor Alberti—that was the wretche's name—conceived a violent passion for my mother. He had an amour with her. Eventually my father grew jealous; he was easily disposed of; the signor gave him one night, a sleeping potion. He then carried on his intrigue with my mother without fear of an enraged husband's interference. He taught her his terrible secret. I cannot enter into the particulars or the catalogue of their crimes. It is enough to know that week after week, month after month, strange sudden, and mysterious deaths followed one after the other until it was the signor's turn to become jealous."

"Ah, and serve him right, too," resumed Isabella.

"It happened," said her companion, in continuation—"it happened at that time that a young and handsome Englishman came over to Italy. He became acquainted with my mother, paid her considerable attention at the several parties where he was in the habit of meeting her, for I should observe that my mother and the Signor Alberti moved in the very highest circles of Italian fashionable life. Well, the young Englishman was persistent in his attentions to my mother, eventually he declared his love, she listened to him, and, in fact, so I have been told, was in reality smitten with him. The probability is that she was wearied and sick of the Signor Alberti. The latter it seems had observed the marked attentions of Sir Richard Fleetwood."

"Sir Richard Fleetwood," exclaimed Isabella. "Why, my dear, you do not mean to say that the young Englishman of whom you have been speaking was Sir Richard Fleetwood ?"

"Yes, certainly. What makes you so astonished ?"

"Astonished! Well I may be. Why, do you know that the very person of whom you were speaking was here this very evening. In fact that is the gentleman who came in with master."

"Impossible!" exclaimed Adrian.

"It is true, my dear. But go on with your story."

"Where was I—let me see? Oh, I was saying that the Signor Alberti had watched the proceedings of Sir Richard Fleetwood and my mother. It appears that they had agreed to fly together to England, for I suppose my mother knew well enough that her life would not be worth a day's purchase if the signor suspected her. So they flew together to Paris; there they lived for some months. One night Sir Richard Fleetwood returned home to the house in which he resided when in Paris; he inquired of the maid if her mistress had gone to bed, and upon the latter answering in the negative, he proceeded up stairs into their sitting-room. My mother had not gone to bed. She was seated by the fire in her arm-chair as though she were waiting for the return of Sir Richard, who, of course, then passed as her husband. The English baronet observed the figure of my mother seated in her usual seat; she had apparently fallen off to sleep, for her head and body were bent forward. Sir Richard Fleetwood approached her, he called her by name; there was no reply—no movement on the part of the sleeper. An opened letter lay upon the table. Sir Richard glanced at this and shook the sleeper. There was a rigidity and a coldness which struck him. He peered curiously into her face. There was no mistake then—it was the long, long, long sleep of death which the woman of sin had dropped off into. Sir Richard caught hold of the letter, which she had evidently been reading, for one of her icy hands were still on it. As the baronet endeavoured to trace the characters in this epistle, a faintness came over him, and eventually he swooned, falling upon the floor in a senseless state. How long he remained in that position he was unable to tell, but upon regaining his consciousness, he found himself stretched upon his bed, and upon inquiring for his lady he was informed by the doctor in attendance that she was buried, and, added that person—

"'You may esteem yourself very lucky in escaping as you have. This will be a lesson to you, my friend, I hope.'

"'What do you mean?' inquired Sir Richard.

"'Why, just this, that you chose to make off with the mistress of one of the most subtle and celebrated poisoners of his day.'

"Poisoners!" exclaimed Sir Richard.

"'Just so; and I again say you have had a lucky escape. Had you inhaled the smallest portion more of the subtle essence in which that letter had been steeped you would have been no longer of the living things of this world.'

"'The letter! ah! I remember feeling sick and ill the moment I took it into my hand,' returned the baronet.

"'No wonder, since it contained a potent and deadly poison, the fumes of which had killed your mistress. Have a care my friend, how you make the acquaintance of a skilled and unscrupulous Italian poisoner. Again I say you have had a lucky escape.

"Sir Richard Fleetwood as soon as he had sufficiently recovered had the prudence to leave Paris for England.

"I must tell you" said the young Italian girl in continuation "I must tell you that all this while I was under the charge of Signori Albert he had taught me to administer the fatal draught to the unconscious victims on very many occasions, but sooner or later crimes such as his must naturally lead to condign punishment. He was arrested tried and condemned."

"I should in all probability have shared the same fate, had it not been for the intervention of you and my master. It appears, that he had, while in Italy, made the acquaintance of the Signor. They were very intimate and when the officers of justice made their appearance at the house of my protector the Signor who had recognised them as they approached the door of his domicile had more pity on me or my probable fate. Mr. Tospeck was in the front room at the time, the Signor begged and implored of him to take charge of me, to carry me away to England, anywhere rather than submit me to the tender mercies of an Italian Court perhaps he was afraid that I, child as was, might be induced to give evidence damnatory to himself. Be

that as it may, I was placed under the care of Mr. Tospeck, and luckily he succeeded in reaching England. I passed off as his daughter during our journey, and the probability is that I should never have been able to have been got clear off unless that had been the case."

"But how did you and my master manage to escape from the signor's house?" inquired Adrians companion.

"The signor desired his servants not to answer the summons of the officers; they knocked in vain to obtain admittance. The door of the house was not opened, and after exhausting their patience in repeated knocks, they eventually, so we afterwards learned, broke it open, ascended the stairs, and captured the signor."

"And you, and master?"

"We had already made our escape at the rear of the premises."

"Alas!" exclaimed the young Italian girl, with a shudder, "he died a dreadful death; but, perhaps, after all, it was no more than his crimes had deserved."

"Yours is a fearful tale," exclaimed her companion.

"Ah, you do not know half, one quarter of the history of my early life. I shudder when I contemplate it. And now, now another murder is about to be perpetrated! Would that I could warn the unfortunate victim, or victims—for there is more than one—would that I could warn them in time."

As the young girl said this, she suddenly burst into tears.

Isabella did all she could to sooth her, and promised, at the same time, to aid her in her humane task, if it were possible. And so that night passed over, both the old and young woman being too much excited to obtain the rest of the weary and the just.

CHAPTER CXXXVIII.

AT RICHMOND.—MR. SQUABSHOT'S TALE.

WE left our friend Squabshot with his friend, and Miss Staunton, in the back-room of the latter lady's, or, rather, Henry Osborne's house. When the very Reverend Ozius Meek had taken his departure, Mr. Squabshot's spirits rose to an alarming pitch. He could not be happy, nay, not even comfortable, while the curer of souls was "darkening the doors," as he expressed it, of his adored Edith Staunton.

When the clergyman was fairly out of the house, Squadshot burst out into a fit of laughter, in which he was joined by his friend, who had played so conspicuous a part in the interview.

"For shame, gentlemen," exclaimed Miss Staunton, "for shame. Pray do not laugh at the clergy."

"Clergy, indeed," said Squabshot's friend. "He is a black sheep in the fold, a disgrace to his calling, a hypocrite, an imposter!"

"Well, we will not indulge in vituperations," said Miss Staunton. "Let us return to our guests, who, to say the truth, must by this time be somewhat astonished at our protracted absence."

The two gentlemen and Edith Staunton took their way into the front room, and to stop any inquiries respecting their absence, Squabshot rattled on from one subject to another in rapid succession.

After hovering over one topic of conversation and another, he eventually launched forth and told the company the following comic story which we give to the reader.

"The story I am about to narrate," said Squabshot, "is, in reality, no story at all, for it is a fact, 'pon honour it is—yes, a positive fact. The gentleman who was the hero of the adventure was a Mr. Addlepate, a naturalist. He was pursuing his discoveries in Africa, when he was overcome by the intense heat, and having lost his companions, he thought, before he sought for them, that he would have a bathe. A tempting river was at hand—he stripped, and jumped in."

"Oh, dear!" exclaimed several of the ladies.

"Yes, he jumped in. All at once he was pursued by a crocodile. What does Addlepate do, but he runs up on to the bank of the river, and succeeded in climbing an adjacent palm tree. For hours he was perched up there, while the rapacious crocodile kept watch below."

"Ah," remarked one of the guests, "that puts me in mind of when I was in India. Two of our officers went out on a hunting excursion, but lost each other during the day. Towards evening one of them found himself in close proximity to a large crocodile, and had to take refuge in a tall palm tree. Just as he was ascending the trunk of the tree, the monster made a snap at his legs, but fortunately for him, his brother officer came up at the time, and discharging his rifle, succeeded in saving his friend's life."

"Well," resumed Squabshot, looking rather indignant at the interruption, "all day Mr. Addlepate remained thus a prisoner in a state of nudity. Night came on, but he dared not descend. Luckily he hit upon an expedient to quench his thirst, which had become intolerable. He curled up several of the palm-tree leaves, and caught the dew in them; these he licked.

"Having satisfied one great want of life, Addlepate began to grow luxurious. He recollected the trifling circumstance of his having ascended the tree in bathing costume, and bethought himself of the expediency of guarding against the chills of another tropical night, by providing some sort of covering for his naked person. Another consideration, too, was favourable to this intention. Decency appeared to demand some attention; and though the professor could not clothe himself, like Robinson, with a goat-skin dress, yet there were materials at hand which might serve the same purpose.

"'A pretty figure I should cut,' thought Addlepate, 'if any lucky chance were to send a passing boat to rescue me. The natives would stare at the last importation of civilised life, and chronicle the circumstance that an English traveller was found on the banks of the Nile with less clothes on his back than even african fashion renders indispensable.'

"No sooner did the idea occur to him, than he carried it into execution. In his airy dressing-room, the Professor gathered a sufficient quantity of palm leaves and with a skill worthy of an accomplisped tailor, soon finished a vegetable paletôt, which, without any pretensions to elegance, had a very primitive cut about it, and was decidedly picteresque. With two more leaves he made a capital nightcap, which might even lay claim to some elegance of shape, and was at all events far more comfortable than the black hat which he had been condemned to wear in the haunts of civilised society.

"After these ingenious operations, Addlepate folded his arms with the air of a man who is pleased with himself. Indeed, he deserved all the happiness that a man can feel who has made the best of his position in life. He had provided himself with food, lodging, and clothing, under circumstances in which a desponding spirit might well have abandoned himself to exaustion and misery. All happiness is comparative. Addlepate now compared his situation with that of Robinson Crusoe, very much to the disadvantage of the latter. He would not have exchanged his palm-tree for the island Crusoe has rendered famous, even with the Man Friday and all other advantages to boot.

"But his reflections were interrupted by a movement on the part of the enemy. There was some mischief brewing at the foot of the tree.—No doubt of it.—The crocodile looked extremely vicious, and seemed to be contemplating an assault. Poor animal! he was growing tired of the blockade.

"The result of the crocodile's deliberations soon became apparent. Not being able to climb the tree, or to drive the traveller from his stronghold by assault or even blockade, he had recourse to the expedient of snapping and mining, after the usual plan of seige operations. The enormous teeth of the monster were vigorously applied to the tree, which shook with the violent efforts he made to overturn it. There was a determined air about his proceedings that seemed to say, "It is high time to bring matters to a close." And Addlepate heard with terror the grinding of those powerful jaws against the hard fibres of the palm. Being a good Catholic, the Professor was struck with the happy idea of offering up his vows to St. Simeon Stylites, the anchorite of the pedestal, which he did with the utmost fervour.

The construction of a crocodile's mouth is very unfavourable to the operation attempted by the specimen whose history is connected with that of the Drivelmore Professor. The molar and incisory teeth are so arranged, that to gnaw at the base of a tree is nearly impossible; the teeth can only make an impression on each side. They may graze the surface of the object attacked, but cannot bite a hole in it. Nature has thus wisely provided a refuge for unhappy travellers in the impregnable stronghold of a palm-tree! But Addlepate with all his scientific knowledge, was ignorant of this natural weakness in the forces of the enemy. Pliny, and other writers, have alluded to the fact; but the Professor could not turn to their writings, and read over the chapter, "Crocodile." Had this been possible, he would not have had quite such a miserable time of it as he spent while the snapping and mining was going on. His hair stood on end within the leafy head-dress, at the thought that he might yet be destined to reward the laborious crocodile with the materials of a good supper. Unwept and unburied, without an epitaph to mark his grave or a paragraph in the "Drivelmore Gazette" to chronicle his loss—to descend peacemeal into the interior of the horrible scaly quadruped, on which his eyes were fixed as if by fascination—was indeed a sad prospect.

A further respite was, however, granted. After some hours' exertion, the crocodile abandoned the snapping and mining process, and adopted a new mode of attack. He began to batter the tree with his powerful tail. The tree stood the shocks bravely, but the professor was almost frightened out of his senses. The ground shook with the violent blows administered by the scaly appendage of the infuriated animal, and Addlepate's dressing-room quivered from top to bottom in a way that threatened seriously to disarrange his toilet. Every now and then, a shower of dates from some of the branches fell upon the head of the crocodile and increased his rage, like darts from a citadel on the bodies of the beseigers. This struck a new terror into Addlepate. If the battery

continued to play much longer, all the dates on the tree might be shaken off, and what could he then find to eat? Horrible surmise! It nearly drove him distracted. Several times he endeavoured to persuade himself that death was preferable to the tortures of suspense, and life not worth preserving amidst such continued terrors. At last, in the height of his despair, he descended from his perch in the top of the tree to the lowest bough, put one foot out in order to spring to the ground, where certain death awaited him, and then—drew it back again very hastily. A sudden and salutary reflection prevented him from anticipating his fate.

The professor had no relations, no wife, children, brothers or sisters, to lament his loss. It was his duty, therefore, to preserve the last hope of his family—the sole representative of the House of Addlepate. How ingenious was this logic, which arrived at a very satisfactory conclusion from premises that might have been open to dispute. Had our hero been a husband or a father, he would have lived for the sake of his family. As a bachelor, the value of half-a-dozen lives was concentrated in his solitary person.

He clambered back to his former position, determined to await the event of the siege like a philosopher and a Briton.

His feelings now underwent a great change, He had passed the crisis of despair, and became composed, not to say light-hearted. He thought himself an idiot for having given way to despondency; and sitting comfortably in his leafy recess, took the most careful precautions to secure himself against the possibility of a fall.

As the crocodile still continued to work his caudal battery against the tree, without producing much effect upon it, Addlepate began to derive amusement from the swinging exercise which it afforded to himself. At each concussion, he gave a cheer, which awakened the echoes from the rocks on the opposite side of the river, and astonished the enemy considerably. Finding the sound of his own voice very agreeable, he next delivered himself of an address to his antagonist, which, though extremely vituperatory and personal, might be considered, under the circumstances, quite pardonable.

Whether the crocodile understood the English language, clothed in a slight Hibernian brogue, may appear doubtful. At all events, he did not seem satisfied with the progress of the siege, and rattled his tail about in a bounceable manner that was scarcely justified by any advantage he had hitherto gained.

The palm-tree was decidedly impregnable The professor was triumphant. He recalled to his memory the chapter of Seneca in which that learned philosopher exhorts his readers to find materials for happiness in every situation of life. Addlepate resolved to carry out his precept. He looked forward to a long residence in the tree, and felt quite reconciled to the prospect. What better abode could he desire? Here he had discovered a fine climate, frugal but healthy diet, charming solitude; and ample supplies of water. There was even a chance some day or other of catching wood-pigeons on their flight, and roasting them in the sun. So much for necessaries. On the score of luxuries, he had also reason to be satisfied. At his feet lay a noble river, flanked by some splendid ruins, guarded by a lively crocodile —a combination of objects. animate and inanimate, that could not fail to prove interesting to him. Moreover, he had now ample leisure for preparing an important treatise on the antiquities of the country that lay around him, extending to the far-famed Emerald mountains and the mountains of Ajas—those immense deserts in which travellers have found the ruined temples of Jupiter and Apollo, between Berenice and Nechesia.

Supported by these reflections, the professor saw the necessity of making his residence more comfortable. He divided it accordingly into three separate rooms, separated by screens of leaves. He next clambered about from one room to another, both in order to give exercise to his limbs and also to indulge in the pleasant feeling of proprietorship. His library contained a vast number of leaves on various branches of knowledge, which he hoped soon to cover with writing by the aid of a pointed stick. His dining-room was full of dates, both green and dry, ready to drop into his mouth. One corner of this apartment was occupied by the hydraulic machine, which had now been brought to perfection. There was only one luxury which Addlepate sighed for—a pair of gloves. Perfect happiness is seldom met with.

A musical entertainment was provided for him every morning. when he awoke at sunrise, by the harmonious sounds issuing from the Colossus of Memnon. His next occupation was to " chaff" the crocodile, and pelt him with dates, which the monster swallowed eagerly, as he would have done Addlepate himself, had an opportunity presented itself. After these recreations, the time for study arrived.

The professor then engaged in the most profound meditations. He opened the volume of his memory, and, reading Herodotus, he visited with that historian the Labyrinth, or the shores of the lake Mœris, or Arsinöe, the Province of Roses. At another time he followed the progress of the Emperor Adrian along the course of the Nile, to his town of Antinöus.

When any brilliant thought crossed his mind, he scratched it down on a palm-leaf; and the frequent perusal of these fragments afforded him the greatest pleasure.

While taking his short walks on an extended branch of the tree, he strained his eyes to look for the distant valley of Cambyses, and shed a tear to the memory of those learned and unhappy Egyptians, so barbarously treated by the ignorant and cruel Persians.

Before retiring to rest, he went through a course of astronomical observations, beneath those splendid constellations which had been the delight of the Chaldean astrologers.

No jealous neighbours could watch the actions or defame the character of our hero ; no newspaper was likely to libel him ; no policeman, tax-gatherer, or collector of water-rates, could intrude upon him.

He was as free as the air in which his abode was placed ; and he bestowed a smile of pity on the sarcasms which the author of Hudibras has levelled at human pursuits.

" Why didn't he go and live on a pedestal, or up in a palm-tree, like Simeon Stylites or myself ?" said Addlepate. " His contemplations would have been more serene, and his mind more vigorous."

Leaving the contented professor in his tree for a moment, let us pass down the left bank of the Nile, where we may observe a party of three persons, whose arrival at the scene of action will probably prove disastrous to the crocodile, and at all events raise the siege.

Mr. Daffodil, a learned English botanist, was engaged in looking for a yellow species of the lotus plant, which he believed to exist on the deserted shores of the Nile.

Herodotus saw yellow lotuses, it is true ; but then Herotodus had the privilege of seeing many things that never existed ; for instance, the two pyramids, six hundred feet high, in the middle of Lake Mœris, Therefore we may venture to doubt the existence of the yellow lotus, though, of course, we cannot disbelieve Herodotus. Perhaps the species has become extinct since his time.

This conjecture, unfortunately, may incline many people to waste their time in searching for it, as Mr. Daffodil did.

He was now wandering across the neighbouring chain of mountains, peeping into every crevice of rock or verdant spot where his treasure might lie hid. Two Arabs, armed with long muskets, accompanied Mr. Daffodil.

There are some objects which strike us with astonishment when we meet them in the desert, though at home they are familiar enough. That distinguished traveller Paul Bouncer, F.R.S., describes his sensations as quite overpowering, when he discovered forty pyramids situated on the peninsula of

Meroe (which probably disappeared after his visit, as nobody has ever seen them since.) Bouncer was quite wrong in being overpowered on the occasion. He was looking for pyramids, and he found them, (or says he did). Had he discovered in the middle of the desert of Sahara a pastry-cook's shop all alone in its glory, or an electric clock, or even a pump of European construction, he might have had some excuse for being astonished. Now, Daffodil had much more reason for uttering the exclamation which he did when he saw something on the bank of the Nile before him.

It was a pair of Wellington boots that arrested his horror-struck gaze. One standing upright, the other leaning a little on one side, as if resting itself.

There is nothing remarkable about a pair of boots in civilised society! but the feelings which their unexpected presence on the banks of the Nile would inspire are inexpressible. How did they get there? Where were the legs belonging to them, and the body which might also be reasonably argued to have existed with those legs? the reflection was one full of horror!

I may remark that Addlepate's clothes, which had been placed on the bank of the river when he stripped for bathing, had disappeared! whether washed away by the stream, or devoured by an omnivorous crocodile, we cannot say. The boots alone remained having been placed by themselves, on a large stone. These were the objects which met Daffodil's eye. He thought them at first to be a part of the rock, fantastically shaped; but, as he drew nearer, he saw that they were made of leather; and this made him shrink back with alarm, as is there were a spectre before him, whose boots alone were visible.

The two faithful Arabs, natives of Ombos, had never seen a pair of boots in their life. They shared the alarm of the botanist, and levelled their muskets at the dangerous objects, which fell pierced by two bullets. Daffodil did not quite see the use of this proceeding; however, he thanked the Arabs for their devotion to him, and walking up to the boots, examined them carefully. Beyond the discovery, that they were rather trodden down at the heels and sadly in need of blacking, Daffodil was more puzzled than ever.

From the top of his palm tree, Addlepate heard the discharge of fire-arms, and started up. He left his bed-room and entered the sitting-rooom, which had an east.ern aspect Looking out between the leaves, the professor saw three men standing on the bank of the Nile. His first impulse was one of discontent at this invaion of his meditative solitude; but human weakness proved too strong for him, an he determined to hold

No. 94.

out signals of distress to the travellers. For this purpose, he tore off a long branch and waved it below the tree; while with the other hand, he threw bunches of dates into the the water, being the only misiles which he had at hand.

Daffodil was still more surprised than he had been by the sight of the boots. He saw before him a palm-tree, from which waved an enormous branch, and that, too, when there was not a breath of air stirring. Here was a discovery in the vegetable world! Joy succeeded surprise; and the botanist felt that the wonderful palm-tree quite made up for the absence of the yellow lotus.

Opening his note-book, Daffodil proceeded to chronicle his discovery in the following words:—"There is found in Upper Egypt, a species of palm which resembles the aloe in its form; with this difference, however, that the stem of the aloe, after growing to the height of twenty feet or so from the grouud, remains fixed in an upright position, whilst the palm of Upper Egypt moves the top of its stem about in a vertical direction with a wonderful regularity of motion, like the pendulum of a clock. We have given to this tree the name of the Palma Daffodilis.

After committing these observations to paper, the botanist made a sketch of the palm-tree, and showed it to the Arabs, having no other person to consult. Their sharper eyes, however, had just discovered a human form in the thick foliage of the tree, and they made signs to this effect to Daffodil, who was absorbed in the pleasure of his discovery, and only thinking of the sensation which would be created in the scientific world by the *Palma Daffodilis*. However, the Arabs persisted in assuring him, as clearly as gestures could do, that on the little island before them, there was a human creature, crouched in the top of the tree, probably in some danger, and desiring succour.

Daffodil put up his eye-glass, and shrugged his shoulders with the air of a man who does not liked to be bored. On looking at the tree, however, his two former surprises had been nothing to what he now felt. He saw distinctly a face, and that an unmistakeably English one, encased in leaves. A hand, too, which seemed to belong to the face, was holding a branch with a bunch of leaves at the top of it, and shaking it about vigorously.

The botanist put down his glass with a sigh of regret—read his notes over again—looked at his sketch—and after having reflected, like Brutus, on the dreadful choice between inclination and duty, the one urging him to leave the palm-tree undisturbed, the other pleading for an effort to save the traveller's life, he determined on the more humane course.

"However," he said, "though my discovery may have been premature, it is not improbable. So, as I have written it in my note-book, I shall stick to it. As there is no doubt about the existence of the aloe-tree, I don't see why the *Palma Daffodilis* should not also exist, if Nature finds it a useful species. I think it extremely useful, and shall maintain its existence accordingly."

After this resolution had been formed, the party took counsel together. They wanted a boat in order to cross over to the island, but on the advice of one of the Arabs, they walked to Assouan, a few miles distant across the desert, and after a broiling journey of two hours they reached this village, which was a town in the time of Herodotus. Mr. Daffodil held up a piece of gold to the first fisherman he met, pointing to a boat at the same time—a pantomimic action easy to comprehend. The boat was started down the river, and the botanist, pointing in the direction, said with an air of pride, as if the boatman could understand him—

"Land me at the island where the *Palma Daffodilis* grows."

His finger indicated the route more clearly than his speech.

They soon approached the island, and the Arabs began to show signs of impatience and surprise, as if there was something to be seen which they had not expected.

As they drew nearer, there was no doubt about it. An enormous crocodile was prowling round the tree. This was the fourth surprise of the day, and Daffodil thought it the most disagreeable one of all. A chill of horror came over him, though he took care not to compromise the dignity of a British subject by showing any signs of it to the Arabs. The latter, however, were not alarmed themselves, and therefore did not trouble themselves about their companion. They primed their muskets, took a careful aim, and fired at the same moment.

The unfortunate crocodile had come to meet the intruders, and the balls entered his mouth, almost the only vulnerable part of his body and—came out at his tail. So Addlepate says; who was anxiously watching events, as may be imagined; but of the latter circumstance there appears some doubt. However, the effect of the bullets was striking, whatever their course may have been. The monster went through a series of convulsions, which amused the professor extremely, and caused sounds of laughter to proceed from his perch at the top of the tree.

Vomiting blood in large quantities from his mouth, the crocodile ended the siege and his existence at the same moment.

Addlepate adjusted his leafy paletot, looked about for his gloves, but found that he had none, and then descended the tree with great

care, lest his fellow-countryman's delicacy should be shocked by any exposure arising from the nature of his dress.

The Arabs are remarkable for their gravity, but the sight of the object before them was too ridiculous.

They roared with laughter, and said funny things to each other in unintelligible gibberish. Even Daffodil was obliged to bite his lips in order to welcome the English traveller, without appearing to poke fun at him in any way that might not have been appreciated.

The botanist and the professor embraced each other most cordially, and told their several adventures. Addlepate begged Daffodil to stop the cachinnations of the Arabs, which was not done without some difficulty; and perhaps their complete restoration to tranquillity was owing to the charitable conduct of Daffodil in enveloping Addlepate in his own grey over-coat, which amply covered his entire person. He also took care to recover his boots, which wore a sadly scorched, blackingless appearance, but were nevertheless in good working condition.

The crocodile was placed in the boat as a testimony to their adventures; and the travellers took a solemn leave of the locality, after the examples of Byron and other sentimental poets, who have taught us to leave places with regret which we hope never to see again. Addlepate, in particular, showed considerable emotion on leaving his Palm-tree—the place where he spent (as he now says) so many happy hours—and shed some tears on its scorched stem. He also carried away with him all the leaves which had formed his furniture and library. These precious relics were destined to ornament the Egyptian Gallery, in London, where Addlepate, for several years afterwards, held an exhibition, entitled, "The Ascent of the Nile." But we are anticipating.

On returning to the village of Assouan, a journey which the travellers accomplish by land, Addlepate donned an entire native costume, which he purchased for a trifling consideration from the patriarch under whose roof they found food and entertainment. Had the professor entered any town in Europe in the light dress he had constructed in his palm-tree, he would doubtless have been taken up as an indecent rogue and vagabond. But the African natives were not so particular.

From this time the botanist and the professor were united in bonds of the closest friendship. Each gave up his hobby—the one his Peninsula of Meroe, and the other his yellow lotuses; and this mutual sacrifice made both appear more rational beings. On their way back to Cairo, Addlepate remembered the vows he had made while in danger

—an uncommon effort of human memory. To make up for past inattention, he kissed the sacred feet of the Colossus of Osimandias, and ween he saw the Pyramids, made them a most gracious bow.

At Alexandria the two friends found a steamer for Malta, and soon reached that delightful island, where they rested for a short time after their fatigues and dangers. They were not inattentive to the cause of science, however, in the meantime. By a happy division of labour, Addlepate wrote, in the " Malta Times," an admirable account of the *Palma Daffodilis* by the intrepid botanist whose name it bore, accompanied by a sketch of the tree as it existed in the imagination of Daffodil, with its leafy plume frisking in the air. On the other hand, Daffodil furnished the public with particulars of the perilous adventures of Professor Addlepate, who had ventured up the Nile as far as the third cataract, had made several valuable additions to Bruce's map, and killed two crocodiles by means of a galvanic battery.

These two accounts reached London before the travellers had set foot in England. Consequently when they did arrive in the metropolis, they became lions of the first magnitude.

The Horticultural Society of London applied to Daffodil for specimens of his newly-discovered palm; and even offered to pay the expenses of his making a journey back to Africa for the purpose of procuring them; but he wisely declined to accede to this appeal. There is a vacant space yet kept in one of the conservatories at Kew Gardens for the palm in question; and the managers still entertain hopes of procuring it.

Addlepate had his crocodile stuffed, so as rather to exaggerate, if anything, its original dimensions, which were none of the smallest. The authorities of the British Museum, with their usual sagacity, offered him a handsome price for it, which he accepted; though we grieve to inform our readers, in confidence, that the crocodile which they received from him was not the hero of the siege, but one which the professor bought through a friend at Alexandria. The veritable animal was for several years exhibited at the Egyptian Hall, in the professor's popular entertainment, " The Ascent of the Nile." This, as thousands of our readers may recollect, was the favourite exhibition of the day, some time since. The stage was decorated with a fine show of palm-trees, waving on an imaginary island, in the midst of an artificial Nile.

It would be superfluous for us to allude to the various attractive features of that entertainment—the professor's able imitations of the rattling of the crocodile's tale, and the music that proceeded from the statue of Memnon in the desert—the crocodile polka played by his band, or that irresistibly comic song, " My airy home amid the leaves," which always sent the visitors away laughing. Above all, a pair of boots, with two little holes in them, stated to be the identical Wellingtons which the native guides made a target of, used to excite the interest of the public, and add confirmation to Addlepate's story.

The public got tired of " The Ascent of the Nile " at last, but not before Addlepate had realised by it a considerable addition to his previous wealth. His objections to matrimony disappeared soon after his return to England; indeed, we are inclined to believe that he repented of celibacy from the time that he was so nearly making a false step from the palm-tree into the jaws of the crocodile. He has several children, but the eldest boy need only be noticed, as bearing the name of Daffodil.

Occasionally when his better-half is in her less amiable moods, or any domestic trouble disturbs his equanimity, Addlepate speaks regretfully of his quiet habitation in the palm-tree, and wishes himself back there again.

Such is the perverseness of man! Now that the danger is over; he will persuade himself that he enjoyed his hunger, thirst, nakedness, and the terrors of a devouring crocodile, better than the luxuries of a house in London, and a country seat near Drivelmore—to the scientific institutions of which place, it may be stated to his honour, the professor still affords his countenance.

However, notwithstanding this delusion which occasionally possesses him, Addlepate is a very worthy member of society; and there are many less agreeable ways of spending an evening than meeting him and Daffodil at dinner, and hearing these two travellers, under the influence of port wine, killing their crocodile over again, and comparing their reminiscences of the whole adventure from beginning to end.

The company had interrupted Squabshot in his narrative with repeated bursts of laughter; and when he brought it to a conclusion, they felt themselves licensed to indulge in a still more vociferous and noisy demonstration of mirth.

" You may smile, ladies," said Squadshot; " but what I have been relating is strictly true, upon my word it is."

" No one doubts it," exclaimed half-a-dozen pretty damsels; " no one for a moment doubts it, Mr. Squabshot. We only wish you had some more such tales to tell us."

" I dare say I shall think of something more, if our friend here will amuse the company for a few minutes," said Squabshot.

This latter observation was addressed to the gentleman who had interrogated the Reverend Ozius Meek. Thus challenged, he was not the man to refuse.

"Well, ladies, I will just give you a sketch of my courting days."

"Oh, how nice!" they exclaimed. "But we did not know you were a married man."

"You hoped not," said Squabshot.

"Oh, for shame, Mr. Squabshot."

"Well, ladies," commenced the young man, "those were delicious days when I used to go a courting Emily, indeed they were. Yes, go a courting. It is an old-fashioned phrase; but it explains, what I am sorry to see is growing to be an old fashioned idea. Now-a days, a young gentleman pays his addresses—a poor, spiritless term, borrowed from a people who do not know what love is, and which we in vain strive to attach to an honest, warm-hearted, English sentiment. Paying your addresses, is an affair of politeness—unacceptable timidity, and cold ceremonial—not at all what the dear creatures (who do not even hint at their little wishes) approve of. But going a courting, as our fathers used to go a courting, was a much more pleasat proceeding. Let me see. It is— No; my heart beats, and my tongue falters so at the bare thought, that I dare not pronounce the words. Your sentimentalists will lament over this spring-time of passion. I should be sorry to endure such an ecstacy, were it prolonged beyond the period usually affixed, with equal good sense and humanity, by the objects of adoration. What more unfortunate being, than a man who is engaged, but to whom his embodied fate postpones the fulfilment of his engagement beyond that very proper period—ranging from one to three months?

I once knew a hapless one, who was thus held suspended between heaven and earth during nine years. Poor fellow! He seemed, to my imagination, to personify the two most awful ideas of suffering ever conceived by the human soul. He was at once Tantalus, and the Wandering Jew. The unhappy wretch was cut off from the rest of his kind. He was neither bachelor nor married man; he had the wishes of the one, with the ties of the other, and the pleasures of neither. And when at last the period of his torture expired, he had become a melancholy wreck of a lover—an attenuated victim of misplaced romanticism—a living warning to imprudent young ladies.

It is my fixed opinion, derived from experience, that the period of courtship cannot be too short. I have good reason to say, when you have hooked your fish, the sooner you use your landing net the better. And remember, what you lose in one way, you gain in the other. Is retrospect nothing? If you put an end to Hope, you secure Memory. Think of the pleasures of recollection; from the warm and passionate or honeymoon-ish stage, up to the calm delight of the John Anderson-my-Jo-ish.

I courted Emily in the old-fashioned way. She liked it the best.

"The course of true love never did run smooth." As for mine, it was a succession of eddies, rapids, torrents, and cataracts; nay, for a time, it lost itself in a cavernous gloom of worse than jealousy. I will not say whether at last it found a placid, unruffled rest.

Emily was a decided beauty, of the dark-haired, bewitching order, with flashing eyes, a transparent skin, and a form it was intoxication to look at: but I must confess it, she had what is called "a spirit." I would not say that she ever lost her temper, for I would not vulgarise those sudden tempests of passion which rendered her ten times more beautiful, and somewhat difficult to manage.

She had a noble heart, and her very faults were magnanimous.

Among them were a pride of sex, an almost morbid sensitiveness as to the delicacy which she conceived to be the soul of love, and a tenacity of all those marks of deference, even of adoration, which the chivalresque code exacted from a lover towards his mistress. Out of these sprung all the troubles of my courting days, which well nigh had a tragical end.

I had my faults, too. I was so full of love that it over-brimmed in little amatory follies. For these her heart forgave me, thought her taste reproved. Her high-wrough delicacy shrunk from this involuntary proclamation of our love.

She would have been a thousand times more tender when we were alone, had I been more able to control myself in public.

From my unconquerable habit of giving eloquent expression to my passion, she almost suspected that I confided to some friend the artless confessions of her soul. In this she did me injustice; for, though I had a friend, to whom I told most things, everything relating to her was sacred. Still, there lurked the thought; and, if once confirmed, such was her exaltation on those points, my case was from that hour hopeless. She might still love me, but marry me—never!

Nor was this all. Women must be wooed more or less through the imagination. With the true ones, love is worship.

Now, I had a kind of reputation; was looked up to by her circle as somebody: so she was thus far proud of her lover. But I rested too much on the intensity and sincerity of my love, and I too much neglected the romantic part of my duties, and I was thoughtless in the trifles which insensibly form the atmosphere of life; and out of these things it came to pass that there was ever a struggle between these high-wrought sentiments of my charming mistress, and her innate sense of the value of my manly, straightforward, absorbing passion.

Among my bad habits was one which much irritated her. Like many men of impetuous nature, I was a careless, slovenly writer. My love-letters were a disgrace to me, and a torture to her. I will do the dear girl the justice to say, that this was chiefly because she could not read them, and so was deprived of the pleasure of contemplating an ardour of passion which personally she affected to repress.

But also her pride was wounded. What! would he not even take the trouble to write like a gentleman? Was it respectful to send a lady a scrap of paper, covered with hopeless hieroglyphics, as if a spider had crawled over it out of an ink-bottle, and defiled it with blot upon blot? She was right, and I knew it; but still I sinned.

At length one day she brought me to my senses. I had sent her one of these palpitating enigmas, incomprehensible enough to have puzzled a Delphic priest. Emily must have looked fearfully lovely that morning; indeed, I heard of her pretty fury. But she rose with the occasion. There was nothing little in the soul of that graceful stormflower. She left her breakfast untasted—she went out. She returned in about half-an-hour with a small packet; and, in five minutes after, her faithful maid was on her way to my house. As for myself, I almost kissed the girl, I was so delighted at this quick answer to my impassioned note, which—I may as well confess—was an audacious request that Emily would "name the day."

To my dismay, I received back my own scrawl, and an elegant little writing-case filled with blotting-paper. There was an additional hint in the shape of a sheet of delicate cream-laid, and a lover-like envelope.

The mute poetry of this reproof went straight to my heart. And, it was Emily's first present! I dare not think what follies I committed over it. I can only guess them from the grinning gusto of the servant girl. From that hour I reformed. The blotting-case was always on my table, and I never put pen to paper, without it being carefully inserted between two leaves of the blotting paper, and gently pressed, so as to absorb the ink. Perhaps it had been better for us both if I had gone on sinning; or if my reformation had extended to all the little weaknesses which irritated Emily, and perpetually disfigured her ideal. In all the other things which offended her pride and her delicacy, I was, I regret to say, as bad as

ever, so much so, that she almost grew cold, when I talked about "the day." On the other hand, her sister, her brother, her mother (dear old soul), were always encouraging me, so that I went on floundering and blundering in an agitated sea of bliss.

I have said that I had a friend, or supposed I had, which in this world is too often the same thing. He had much influence over my mind, being a man of superior powers, who flattered my vanity, by looking up to me. To him I confided most of my affairs; and of course he knew that I was engaged to Emily; but, on my honour, no more. He had not even seen her. I had no reason for not introducing him, save, perhaps, an unconscious selfishness, or a desire to hide my treasure from one who looked at women with the eye of an artist, but coveted them for their beauty, not for the love which sanctifies.

"You are mightily afraid to let your little dark beauty be seen," he said to me one day. "One would almost think you were jealous."

"Not of you at all events, my dear fellow," said I.

"Then why don't you make an excuse to take me there some day? Recollect, if I don't get into her good graces before marriage, I shall be put on the list of bachelor friends, and be proscribed afterwards."

There was some sense in this. Indeed, I had divined that Emily would give me some trouble on that head. It was not the petty tyranny of an English wife that she contemplated; but her dominating delicacy shrunk from the thought of knowing those who had been my companions in unsanctified days. My friend, too, seemed somewhat piqued at my closeness in all that related to Emily—I, who was so frank and confiding on all other matters.

"I would give something to read your love-letters, old fellow," said he to me one day. "They must be rare things for a lady's eye."

I shook my head.

"It would be more than my chance with the little dark beauty, as you call her, is worth, if I did! I verily believe she would tear my eyes out, if she thought I even went so far as to talk of her."

"Indeed! Then what would she say if she knew you had let another man see one of her own love-letters?"

And this was said with a most peculiar smile of triumph, which flashed across my memory long, long afterwards.

"Good heaven! what do you mean?" I cried, really alarmed, for I had some time before missed one of the rare but cherished epistles of my mistress, and had been nervous ever since.

"I mean," said he, "that it provokes one

to death to see you smacking your lips as you do after coming from this beauty of whom you are so jealous. I am determined to see your honey-pot, you bear; and the day when you introduce me to her, you shall have back the dear girl's letter, which you dropped in one of your careless fits one day. Egad! if that girl has a shadow of the passion in her eyes that she puts into her love-letters, she ought to be worth fighting for. It's short, to be sure, but it's sweet! I know it by heart. I can repeat every word of it. It is perfect—a love-blossom, a sonnet, a—"

And so he went on, heaping coals of fire on my head. I capitulated. I introduced him to Emily, and he gave me up her letter. But every now and then, when he was spitefully disposed, which was always when I was " close " (as he termed it) on the subject of Emily, he would annoy and alarm me by repeating it aloud—literally word for word.

Now this friend of mine—I do not name him, because he came like a shadow over my life and happiness, and like a shadow let him pass away—was certainly my superior in many things. I have described my faults, and their effect upon Emily; he was accomplished in everything wherein I was deficient —I think I may add, that he was deficient in all the qualities which women prefer when they give themselves time to reflect.

How can we blame them if they are sometimes deceived by externals, and superficial claims on their admiration ? We over-stimulate their imagination, and under-cultivate their sense.

And even would we do otherwise, how ? Knowledge of mankind and wisdom, come but from experience; and the utmost we could do would be to plant suspicion in their minds—thank Heaven, an uncongenial soil !

This friend of mine, then, had many striking qualities, calculated to fascinate the imagination of women; and it was not to me surprising, therefore, that he should soon have become a favourite with the family of Emily.

He came almost as often to see them, as I did to see her. I felt flattered by his undisguised admiration of her beauty.

Meanwhile, all went auspiciously enough for me. My speedy marriage with Emily seemed to be a settled thing; and the more certain seemed my happiness, the more intoxicated I became with joy.

My future mother and sister-in-law laughed at my amorous follies; but Emily, the more I doated, the more she grew dignified. Possibly the presence of a third person, and that person a keen observer, with an undertone of the satirical in his gestures, sometimes in his words, made her more sensitive to my weaknesses.

My head and heart were both too full to allow either observation or reflection. I saw Emily through my passion, not as she was. This friend of mine was necessarily often a witness of these clumsy transports.

" Miss Emily ought to be proud of so much love, old boy," he said to me, one day. " I never saw a fellow so devoted. I wish I could work myself up to the concert pitch. Really, I think I shall begin with the little sister."

" So much the better, my dear friend ; I should like to have you for a brother-in-law."

And I felt fraternal already.

I was full of these sentiments when I paid my next visit to Emily. I met her sister on the stairs. She smiled, with a meaning.

" What is it ?"

" Oh, you will know soon enough. Your passion-flower, as you call her, is in full bloom this morning !"

And she tripped away laughing.

I found Emily in the drawing-room. I ran to embrace her. She drew back. I saw at a glance there was something wrong. She was in one of her tropical moods, and there was danger under all that ravishing beauty.

" There, sir—stay, if you please. We can talk as well at a distance."

I advanced.

" Stay, sir ; I command you !" And she stamped her little foot with such graceful rage that I wanted to kiss it all over. " You make yourself ridiculous, sir !"

I gazed at her—not all in astonishment. The truth is, that when she had one of these rare storm-fits, there was such a strange beauty in her, that I drew an exquisite pleasure even from my suffering.

" Yes, sir ; you make yourself ridiculous— and you make me ridiculous, too !" The rich mantling blood rushed to her temples as she trembled under the stress of her passion. " Do you know what your friend said yesterday to Clara ?"

I still gazed. I was not thinking of my friend, or of Clara, but of the divine type before my eyes.

" He said, that you love me like a lap-dog! —yes, like a lap dog !" And the blood rushed back again, till she was as pale and as beautiful as night.

" That, then, was what the little wicked witch was smirking at on the stairs ?"

" Yes; and that's not all !" Here the blood came back again, but not in such force. The storm was about to burst in rain. " He said it was quite refreshing to see a fellow so over head and ears, and hat, too—yes, and hat, too—in love ! He said you were like a bo—bo—boy in a treacle-barrel."

And down came the shower. I thought to profit by the sobs to put my arm where it had grown to have a sort of natural right to be.

But I was repulsed, and told never to come near her any more. As I knew she hated to be seen with red eyes, I left. On the stairs I met the provoking little Clara again. She laughed outright, enjoying the fun. Alas! she did not know that she was playing with edged tools.

When I returned home, I found the friend there. As I entered he was carelessly turning over the leaves of a blotting-book which lay on the table. I remonstrated with him on what he had had said to Clara, but he only laughed. It was only afterwards that I remembered that laugh. He promised, however, to be more careful in future.

As for Emily, Clara made my peace with her. Still, there was a something, an indefinable something, between us. The poison of ridicule had worked.. Her pride, her delicacy, her taste, had all been wounded. Between her and my honourable devotion was the image—now of a lap-dog, now of a boy in a treacle barrel.

"The sooner you put an end to all this folly, by getting her to name the day the better," said Clara to me, after this last incident. And my mother-in-law elect smiled approval..

After the narrator had finished his story, or rather, more properly speaking, his brief sketch, Mr. Squabshot cleared his throat, by tossing off one or two glasses of wine, and commenced his narrative of what he termed a "Smart chase." This we reserve for another chapter.

——

CHAPTER CXXXIX.

THE RUINED MERCHANT.

"WELL, you must know," said Squabshot, "that my friend, Singleton Bowles, had got himself into a terrible mess. It is hardly worth while entering into all the particulars; it is enough to know that they were of so overwhelming a nature, that he had not the courage to look matters in the face, and he—in fact, he bolted, to use a vulgar phrase. He had gone on one of the Thames hatch boats, and was going down to Gravesend, and after then, the Lord knows where. I was coming from the city, having hired a hackney coach; just as I was getting into this, I was accosted by a naval-looking man whom I knew.

"How lucky!" he exclaimed; "you are the very identical man I want to see."

"My dear fellow," said I, "I am on business, next door to life and death. You must really defer—"

"Defer!" he exclaimed. "You're a wise man, and crafty. Why, my ship's gone down to Gravesend, this morning, and I sail to-morrow, or next day, at the latest. Defer, quotha! Why, I must join this evening, and in eight-and-forty hours may be in blue water."

Well, I told him to jump into the hackney coach. He did so, and off we drove. A stoppage occurred on our road; we came to a dead lock in one of the streets. While this was going on, my attention was attracted to a man who emerged from the side-door of a public-house close to us. He was rather remarkably dressed, in a foreign fashion; high-crowned, broad-brimmed hat, a profusion of red hair and beard, and baggy trousers gathered tight at the waist.

"I say, do you know that fellow?—he stared hard at us," said I, to my companion.

"What, the man with the felt hat and red beard?"

"Yes."

"I should rather think I do. He's a queer fish, a foreigner, but speaks good English. He asked me if I would call for him at Plymouth—no; then would I pick him up in the channel—"

At this I felt almost sick, for I must tell you, ladies and gentlemen, I had good reason to be so; but of this hereafter.

My nautical friend, who was with me in the hackney coach, was captain of a fine emigrant ship, bound to the shores of the New World.

I was about to call upon Singleton's wife, previous to my going in search of her husband. In a short time the hackney coach drew up to the door of the house in which she resided.

It was early in the morning, much earlier than it was usual for me to favour either her or her husband with a call, and she looked startled and anxious when she caught sight of me, and scarcely allowed the ordinary salutations to conclude, before she eagerly inquired to what she was indebted for so early a call?—was there not something wrong in the city? She had been fearing so for some time. Would I tell her all about it at once?

I had resolved how to frame my announcement, and begging her not to worry herself, explained simply thus much—that her husband had left town without providing for some bills coming due during his absence—which I had no doubt he had forgotten—(Heaven forgive me for that lie!)—and it was of the greatest importance that Singleton should return immediately, and be in the city on the following day.

"Oh! then," remarked Marian, much relieved, "it is not one of those horrible speculations of poor Singleton's—those dreadful mining shares and patent concerns, about which he always in such a fever. I declare, my life has been miserable for the last three months—but what to do now?"—and she mused, with her eyes fixed on the carpet and the point of a pretty kid slipper playing with the tassel of a footstool. "You want to see him and see him about this sad *contre-temps*—how could he be so careless?—and make him come back at once."

"And I want you to tell me how I can find him out quickest," I broke in.

"That is the most difficult part of the matter. To be frank with you—when Singleton started, he made me promise (he does so hate to be pestered with letters forwarded on any business when he is out on an excursion) that I would not give anybody a clue to his whereabouts."

"But he never could have anticipated, when he made you give him that promise, what has actually come to pass."

"No! But the worst of it is, if I gave you the clue, you would find yourself almost as far off your point as you are now."

"Marian, every moment's delay is fraught with peril. I do assure you, solemnly, that I consider the crisis so momentous, that I must, at any risk and expense, set myself on Singleton's track without a moment's delay."

"Then the matter is more serious than you would have had me believe at first; and those dreadful speculations——"

"I believe in my heart, and that from actual inquiry—to tell you the truth at once—they are utterly valueless, if not worse. Remember, I may be wrong here, and things might take a favourable turn; but I should be unkind not to say I think the whole set of the chances is the other way.

"Poor, poor dear Singleton!" she murmured, deeply moved; for her first thoughts were still for him, not for herself, and for a moment she gave way, as woman must do, to her feelings; then, starting up—"Of course, now I see—you must seek him out without loss of another moment; I am sorry I have kept you here so long as it is, but you should have told me more at first. Now, the worst of it is, the only clue I can give you is this—Singleton is gone on a cruise down the river somewhere; he said he should hire one of those—what do you call them—the boats he is so fond of sailing in down to Whitstable and Margate?"

"Hatch-boats?"

"That is the name!"

"One more question—do you know the name of the boat he has hired?"

"Something—*Swallow*."

"Good-bye, Marian! and if mortal energy can do it, I'll have him in London to-morrow."

I was through the door, when I heard her light step behind me. She laid her hand on my arm. I turned to meet a gaze more anxious, more piteous, more haggard than ever I had seen before.

"Tell me the whole truth," she said, in a voice scarcely audible from suffocation—"Is Singleton—is—he—*ruined?*"

"My dear girl," I cried, "God bless your loving heart, and sustain you in all trials. The exact extent of the disaster I cannot yet tell—no one can; but I am sure things are very, very bad. Keep quiet; don't worry yourself, it can do no good; and you shall soon hear more."

"Oh! tell Singleton," she exclaimed, joyously, as a smile flitted over her wan face like a gleam of sunshine over an April cloud, "tell him, if he loves me, to come back at once; have done with all these dreadful speculations; sell the house and furniture—everything—and we can go down into some quiet country place and live so happily and contentedly on my own income. Why, in the country it would be quite a little fortune."

I could stand no more, and muttering I know not what, broke away.

By a series of manœuvres familiar to my legal friends—but which I mean to keep, as I hope they will ever continue to be, a sealed mystery from the present company—by the superhuman exertions of certain unfortunate clerks and law stationers—and by the energetic assiduity of a learned counsel—by the kind attention of a good-natured Vice-Chancellor—and by some little contempt in the ordinary trick-track—I became possessed, in the course of the afternoon, of certain documents of extraordinary and mystic power, having various minutory, compulsory, and restraining aspects on the direction of Mr. Singleton Bowles, and the trustees of a settlement—a small corps of soldiers of the law, who were to mind that one Singleton Bowles left not the kingdom until he answered certain charges of a grave character. To these mute but powerful myrmidons of the law I attach a living creature, likewise an emanation from the same source—a gentleman who, though, if you asked him his profession, he would tell you he was an "offisher," was, in fact, neither in the army or navy. But I must endeavour to describe to you this Judas Creepely.

"Why, you were going to arrest your own friend then?" exclaimed one of Squabshot's audience.

"Certainly—a friendly arrest, of course."

Singleton was about to leave the country. Had he done so, he would never, in all probability, have held up his head afterwards. He had been the victim of designing men. It is not worth while to enter into all his business transactions. Let it suffice, that it was to his own interest for him to be detained. I knew that he would be able to surmount the difficulties; in fact, I held in my possession certain documents which materially

altered the face of affairs; but let me proceed. Where was I? Ah! Mr. Judas Creepely.

He was a wonderful man in his line—small, and remarkable in person, pale and unhealthy in aspect, his small eyes rendered still smaller by a habit of keeping them ever half-shut—his immovable mouth, and hanging under-jaw, and his incorrigible stoop, gave Judas the appearance of a dull, timid man. On this deceptive appearance, he traded largely and successfully. No haughty debtor or absconding bankrupt, hiding in parlours of obscure and dingy public-houses in back streets and holes, a thousand miles from everywhere, ever suspected until he had become familiar with Judas' person, that the quiet, stupid, looking man was reckoning up every one upon whom he cast his eye. Mr. Judas Creepely, and I found ourselves stepping on board a Gravesend boat at four o'clock in the afternoon; I had been too

excited and eager to think about eating and drinking, and should have shod all the blandishments of the most civil and persuasive steward that ever lived, had it not have been for a quiet hint conveyed to my ear in an undertone by Judas. This was to the effect that the best way to get through work well and prosperously, was to "take your meals regular," and that irregularity in that particular had a tendency to impair the energies, &c. This one word for his neighbour and two for himself, delivered in a phraseology of his own, was the prelude to our descending into the cabin.

Here, on a long table composed of a series of small ones placed side by side, and running down one-half of the cabin was laid out a banquet of no mean order. The guests consisted of a group of "regulars," who, herded together at one end of the table, confined their conversation to their own circle, and called the steward and his assistants by their

Christian names—a group of pilots, returning from taking ships up to the docks, who evidently looked on dinner in something the same light as Rene d'Anjou did, and would by no means hazard the accurate performance of the solemnity by any undue levity or unnecessary conversation, and a sprinkling of cockneys bent on an excursion in search of a little fresh air and diversion—both which objects are, according to the creed of Cheapside, attainable, it would seem, chiefly by an inordinate share of a sumptuous entertainment in a close cabin, and next by an equally liberal course of questionable cigars and bottled porter after.

We had ploughed our way steadily through half our task, when one of the pilot guests, who had interrupted himself occasionally in his serious avocation to half rise from his seat and glance through the ports to see what was going on on the river, exclaimed—

"What's Tom Marks about this afternoon, I wonder ?"

"*Saucy Swallow* goin' down ?" inquired another.

"Yes, there she goes, with Tom at the helm, Excursion, I expect. Leastways, there's a queer-looking swell with a beard on board; one of the cockney-yachtman tribe, I guess."

I started to my feet with a plunge which sent my stool spinning between the legs of one of the waiters, and, peering through one of the ports, caught sight of an object which made my heart bounce up into my throat.

Close to us—so close that I could have tossed a biscuit on board of her—one of the larger sized Thames hatch-boats was sailing along, with all sail set to a briskish N.W. breeze, steering the same course with ourselves ; and though ours was reckoned a fast vessel, even on that play-ground of fast boats, the Thames, holding her own well with us, which, by the way, from her position she was sure to do for awhile, on principles familiar to frequenters of the river, but which I never heard satisfactorily explained by philosophers. Besides her master and usual complement of hands, she carried—as the reader as already guessed—the identical fellow whom I had met in the morning, attired at all points as then, save only that he had exchanged his felt broad brim for a glazed rowing-hat.

"Judas," I eagerly whispered, "the strange-looking passenger on board that vessel, now smoking a cigar, is our man—take notice of him."

Judas's mode of receiving the intelligence was remarkable.

"Never could see no fun in it, sir," he said aloud, as though replying to my observation. "Please to pass me the salt. Here, steward, don't take my plate away. I'm

only going up-stairs for a moment ;" and he lounged carelessly out of the cabin.

"Up-stairs," remarked the pilot who had first spoken, with unspeakable contempt ; "it is plain that young man of yours ain't been much at sea, sir."

"Why not ?" I inquired.

"Most people calls it goin' on deck, not up stairs—up-stairs, indeed !"

The rest of the pilots grinned as Judas returned, and, reseating himself, merely observed to me, in an under-tone—

"Beard and mustarshers is a get-up from Nathan's, I take it ;" and resumed his dinner with the utmost tranquillity.

After we had concluded and paid, I went on deck, and sought to propitiate my friend the pilot, by the sacrifice of an unexceptionable Havannah.

After the few stereotyped sentences of dialogue appropriate to the transaction, I ventured to remark—

"Remarkably fast some of those hatchboats are."

"I believe you, sir. Look at that vessel we passed in Galleons. Why, I'd back her for a long run in any weather; and a long run, such as I call a real long 'un, is—say from London Bridge to Eddystone Light and back; for that I'd back the "Swallow" and Tom Marks against most any craft that leaves the Thames—yacht-clubs not excluded."

"The "Saucy Swallow" is reckoned fast, then ?"

"A 1, and no mistake. And I guess Tom Marks don't make a bad thing out of her neither. Why, Tom gets all sorts of out-of-the-way jobs all along, of her character, and nothing else. 'Twasn't two months ago come next spring, that he begged a twenty pun' note for landing a run-away couple on the coast of France, spite of a steam-tug the pursuers had chartered, but which Tom—the wind being a-beam and the sea high, you see—dropped many a mile a-starn."

"Of course, so fast a vessel as ours will easily beat him ?"

"Well, I hardly know. Let's see—whereabouts is she now ? Oh! there she is, just roundin' into the Rands, and we're not half way down Long Reach yet. She won't be ten minutes a-starn of us at Gravesend now."

All too short for the project I had been forming ever since I had caught sight of Singleton in the hatch-boat—namely, to obtain some further assistance at Gravesend—for I suspected he might make a fight of it, and board him as he passed. I therefore started a fresh idea.

"Surely there must be something else on the river as fast as the Swallow."

"Well, we reckon Charley Wolf's Swift about a match even for the Swallow—now, a run between them two over the course I've mentioned already—good tobacco this of yours, sir—a run over that course, I say, would be a sight better worth seein' than all this year's yacht-club matches put together."

" Where is the Swift—do you know ?"

" I saw her lying off the Town Pier, as I went up ; but why do you want to know ?"

" I had some thoughts of taking a run out to sea for a day or two," I returned, carelessly.

" Well, you couldn't have a better vessel under you than the Swift ; nevertheless," he added, taking a glance at the sky, " I doubt you'll have but a greasy sort of a night of it, if you put to sea this evening ; it looks queer all round—and, if you'd take my advice, you'd sleep ashore to-night, and see how matters look in the morning."

" I don't mind a bit of sea," said I, valiantly.

" It's not a bit of sea, but a great deal of sea, I'm thinking you'll have—but if you are bent on it, ask the cap'en to hail Charley Wolf as he passes."

I did so, and the result was, that within two minutes of our getting alongside the long black barges moored against the columns of the Terrace Pier, I was in conversation with Mr. Charles Wolf, a fine, bluff, red-faced John Bull-looking fellow, who wore a claret-coloured coat, with an alarming wide collar, and an accurately brushed hat of wonderful nap, and could not keep his hands out of his trousers' pockets.

Now, the Annersley was lying in the stream, and I knew full well that I had only to step on board her, and accompany her down channel, to secure my prize ; but during my run down the river, several considerations had occurred to me, which made me anxious, if possible, to attain my object in some other way—the principal one, of course, was the publicity—the unavoidable publicity—which must attach to the arrest of a man on the deck of an emigrant ship, in the presence of some scores, if not hundreds, of people ; and as by way of *dernier ressort*, I could always do as Singleton proposed to do, board the Annersley in the channel, if the Swallow should prove too fast : and as (to confess the truth) I began to wax chivalrous and romantic over the scheme of pursuing the run-away in his own way, and beating him with his own weapons, I had resolved to try the scheme of a chase, with a view of bringing the enemy to a parley where none but the few " hands " who managed the hatch-boats, and any stray fishes near the surface, were likely to be cognisant of our meeting.

" Mr. Wolf," said I, " time is precious ; you see that hatch-boat coming round the point out of Northfleet Hope ?"

" *Saucy Swallow*, sir."

" I know. She's going down Channel. Can you catch her ? Mind, we may have to chase her to Land's End, and further. And what shall I have to pay you ?"

" Can we ? Nothin' I should like better than to try ; but we must get summut on board first, and look sharp, too. Will ten guineas hurt you, sir ?"

" Twenty—"

" Here, Villiam, you run up to—"—but no matter for the orders given—suffice it to say, that ere the Swallow had reached Coal-house Point, which marks the beginning of the next bend of the river below Gravesend, the gallant little Swift was, by a miraculous effort of energy on the part of her master and crew, manned and victualled for a week's cruise at least ; and as ready and eager to bound on her course as a greyhound in a leash when puss is sighted.

There was something behind, however. Wolf's broad, honest countenance had more than once been turned with a doubtful expression on the unmistakeably Israelitish features of my companion. Just as all was ready, Wolf took me aside with a mysterious air—

" Excuse me, sir, nothing in the Bum Bailey line this 'here, I hope ; your young man's—excuse me again—a queerish-looking sort of a chap."

" Look you, Mr. Wolf, if a young lady, say a daughter of your own, had married a cunning rascal—had trusted every sixpence she had in the world to him, in faith that he would do what was right and manly by her —and if you knew he was bolting to Australia with that sacred deposit, and had hired the Swallow to put him on board-ship in the Channel, and so evade pursuit, what would you—"

" Set your fores'l, Villiam ! Now, young man, look alive ;" and we jumped into the cockle-shell of a punt, and in another minute were on board.

It was striking seven by the Gravesend clocks when we hauled the Swift clear of the surrounding craft, eased her well out in the stream, got sail on her, and laid our course as nigh as we could fetch for Coalhouse Point. Saucy Swallow we could easily see working through the Lower Hope, but standing so carelessly and so heedlessly over to the Kentish shore that Wolf began seriously to doubt whether she would weather the Blighe Flats without making a board—a proceeding which (for the benefit of you who are, I suppose, not nautical) I explain. It resembles the doubling of a hare, and in the present case, would have the effect of most materially shortening the distance between us. Suddenly I observed the Swallow luff close up to the wind, steer a steadier course, and as was evident from the increased tension of her sails, take an extra pull on her sheets, which, being interpreted, is—so arrange her sails as to keep much closer to the wind than before.

"What's the meaning of that?" I inquired of Wolf. "Do you think he begins to smell a rat at that distance?"

"Don't you go to be angry, sir," replied Charley, very deliberately. "Ve has our customs on this 'ere river, and ve respects 'em, under any circumstances; ve've undertook to do the best for you as lays in our power, and ve'll do it, never fear; nevertheless, customs is customs, and as such must be respected."

"Now, what in the name of wonder, does all this mean?" I inquired.

Trust thee sir. You've engaged us for to ketch the Saucy Swallow. Good! ve'll do it if mortal man can; and I think ve can; but all that 'ere don't pervent the usual customs of the river, which is fair warning, which I've just give Tom the signal, 'I'm arter you,' that's all."

"Oh, I see! Then, Mr. Thomas Marks may be considered at this moment as perfectly wide awake?"

"Werry.'

From this moment the chase assumed an interest, which to a mere landsman, was almost intelligible. Here were the two craft (of their kind) on the river, under the guidance of two of the ablest and most experienced captains—each master of his business—engaged in a trial of speed and skill than which no regatta ever furnished one more exciting.

I had not observed the signal in question, and to this day have not a notion how it was made; but that Tom Marks had seen and thoroughly understood it, was pretty clear. The Saucy Swallow, with her sails as flat as boards, hugging the wind as close as she possibly could, was doing her utmost to weather the extreme corner of the flats I have mentioned and which were now nearly dry, the tide being at low ebb. This point turned, a glance at the map will show the reader that the Swallow had a straight run before her, down Sea Reach, past the Nore, and (if she pleased) straight away to the coast of Holland, or anywhere else almost. This, with a good two miles start, which it would give her over us, would render our chances of catching her but small.

Meanwhile the prognostications of my friend, the river pilot, were being rapidly verified. The sun was fast going down through a lurid, wild-looking mass, composed of equal parts of cloud and London smoke and smother; a dirty, ragged drift was whirling through the air high overhead; and ever and anon an eddy of wind driving downwards out of the rack above, would catch our

sails would lay us over for a few seconds with ominously resistless force All the notice however, which Charley Wolf took of these or any other symptoms of the impending bad weather was an occasional rapid glance upwards and to windward, accompanied, when the gust caught us, by a slight alteration of the helm, just enough to bring the vessel close to the wind, and so moderate its effects on the sails without deadening her way for her yard, With these exceptions his attention, as well as that of the rest of us, was rivetted on the Swallow which was now close on to the point, her mode of turning which was to "Make or mar her quite."

Suddenly she heeled over till the end of gaff seemed almost to dip in the water, at the same time turning half round—broaching to, as it is called.

"He's touching the pint," ejaculated Charley, chuckling immensely; "he's touched the pint—I thought you was a runnin' of it a little too fine, Master Tommy. Now scrape her across if you can," he added, as we could could spy the hands setting to work with the great oars, as well as poling and pushing with everything and anything that came handy.

"But the is running down still," I suggested. "He'll not get off till it turns."

"It's running down still, sir—but it won't fall no lower. This 'ere's all clear country water a comin' down now. Tom'll scrape over, never fear; he ain't one to run a risk of that kind; he knows what he's after, does Tom; but whilst he's poling we're sailing, that's all."

And sure enough, after a few vigorous tugs at the oars, and some see-sawing and working of the poles, and, above all, after a heavier gust than had hitherto struck us, the Swallow slid over the tongue of the bank, and was in deep water again. The delay, however, had enabled us to gain a good half-mile on her, and so we entered Sea Reach.

"And now we're in for a starn chase, which every fool knows is a long chase," said Mr. Wolf. "So, open one of them 'ere bottles of porter, and look out for squalls, Master Villiam."

As we scampered down the Reach, the scene a-head was a study for a painter. A background of dark lead-coloured clouds piling and clambering and hurtling along, one over another, in the wildest confusion, over the dark, roughening line of the seaward horizon, now becoming rapidly indistinct in the deepening darkness; against this gloomy background the sails of the Saucy Swallow, catching what light the vanishing sun still sent over our heads from the west, looked like a rose pinned on a black curtain; whilst in the foreground the water was seething and hissing in a fussy fidgetty way, as though working itself up for the bustle that was coming.

"Mr. Wolf," said I, after a more than ordinarily careful survey of the heavens, "will you be so good as to detach your lips from that mug of porter just long enough to give me your candid opinion on one point. What sort of a night are we going to have?"

"In my humble opinion, sir, which I may say it's a certainty, as nigh as anything can be in this 'ere world, it'll be blowing a gale o' wind afore three o'clock to-morrow morning, from nor'-west or thereabouts."

"And do you consider the Swift is able to hold her own through a north-wester round the Foreland?" I inquired.

"Is the Swift able to—here, Villiam! come aft and tell the gentleman our adventure. He'd beat a parson at jawin, sir, would Villiam. Our adwenture the time the gale took us up on the north coast o' Scotland; he'll tell you wot the Swift can do. Tell the gentleman the adwenture."

"Villiam, though I cannot compliment him on his powers of relation quite so highly as Wolf did, certainly managed in the course of a curiously interwoven story, which lasted to Southend, to impress me with a very exalted opinion of the duck-like qualities of the Swift; and my confidence in that vessel's powers, and in the safety of our position generally, was finally established by Wolf's corollary to Villiam's proposition.

"And after all, sir, mind this 'ere first; we've got the Sallow afore us—where she goes we can follow, I think. Next, if it should come on us too cruel at last, why we've got Margate this side, and Broadstairs and Ramsgate t'other side the Foreland to run for, when the worst comes to the worst; but let's see the Swallow run first. While she lives we can live—when she runs we'll run, and for the same port. Tom Marks, as I have told you afore, sir, knows what he's about, does Tom Mark; and wot's more, he's a family man, and I know he ain't insured his life."

All this time Judas remained a perfectly passive spectator and auditor. What we were about was now no business of his, his time was to come, and like a wise and thoughtful man he was husbanding his energies for the occasion. My speculations on the weather, and Villiam's tale of thrilling interest, alike fell unheeded on his ear. It is true he now and then cast a keen glance in the direction of the Swallow, as if to assure himself that his scene of action was still in sight; but with this exception he was a mere inactive, unimpressible log, reclining on one of the rough benches which ran along the sort of well-hole in which we sat. Our cutwater—stupid piece of dead wood though it

was—as it hissed and swirled and bustled through the water, was a lively animal compared with Judas. Wolf had eyed him once or twice in the same half-puzzled, half contemptuous way in which one may picture a mastiff sniffing at a rattlesnake.

At length Judas seemed roused to thought and action. After a consultation with a turnip-sized and shaped machine doing duty for a watch, he remarked to me in his usual confidential whisper—

"How about tea?"

This was absolutely the first word he had spoken since we left Gravesend.

"Wot's wrong with the young man?" inquired the watchful Wolf.

"He wants his tea," I explained.

"His tea!" repeated Charley, with unutterable contempt. "Do you know what a—but o' course he don't, how should he? Here, Villiam, bile some water and make the young man a sup o' cocoa—it's the nighest thing we got."

Villaim dived, and in an incredible short space of time produced a steaming biggin of cocoa, with which and some biscuit Mr. Creepeley seemed well satisfied.

So we jogged on. At length, after a somewhat longer look to windward than I had yet seen him give, Mr. Wolf summoned the anecdotical "Villaim" to take his place at the helm, and diving into the low cabin, emerged in about a couple of minutes metamorphosed in a marvellous manner. The well-brushed, long-napped hat had given way to a sou'-wester, with a fan spreading extensively over his broad shoulders; a large garment, like a black bed-gown, made of canvas, and "dressed" by a water-proofing colouring and varnishing process, peculiar to pilots and others, and the valuable recipe for which I possess, supplied the place of the smart mulberry coat; whilst a pair of fisherman's boots, drawn over gigantic grey stocking, encased his lower man.

Casting his eye over my own garment, as he rejoined us, he made some inquiry about my means of resisting rough weather, and finding me totally unprovided—for the excitement of the morning had driven every idea but the leading one out of my head, he offered me sundry "baps" (as the Scotch call them)—spare ones of his own—equipped with which I bade defiance at once to the elements and to any attempt at recognition on the part of my most intimate friend.

Mr. Creepeley was given his choice; to roll himself up in a sail or ensconce himself in one of the queer little shelves five feet six by two feet nothing, on which Messrs. Wolf and Co. were supposed to woo sleep in the cabin, "dirty weather comin' on," as he was informed. He chose the latter alternative, after a parting glance at the Swallow, and a confidential one at myself, and I may here add, was seen no more that night, though occasionally heard in paroxysms of woe, which would almost have led one to believe that the spirit of Judas was taking a reluctant leave of its earthly tenement; or, as Wolf maliciously expressed it, "as though he know'd wot was afore him, and was dyin' proportionate hard."

"It's coming now, sir, and no mistake," suddenly exclaimed Wolf, in a much sharper and louder key than he had hitherto used, "ve'll have the mains'l down, Villaim; jump about now and be sharp, Sam, you young scamp!" (this to a hobbadehoy of whose presence I had a general impression, but who never seemed to be anywhere in particular), "stand by, to help him get it in, and be smart, d'ye hear!"

Our principal sail was speedily hauled down and secured; and all eyes now turned to windward, where, in front of, and relieved in an almost distorted manner by the dark, slate-coloured background of cloud, a long wide mass of greyish white vapour, in shape not unlike an enormous bolster, (I can compare it to nothing more opposite), appeared sensibly climbing the north-western sky, and that at a sweeping pace. I looked around to see whence the unnatural light came which made it so brilliant, for the sun had quite gone down now, and the heavens were black with clouds. Far away down on the eastern horizon the broad disc of the moon was ploughing its way up amid the most extraordinary jumble of whirling clouds I ever beheld, spreading a pale hazy light through the whole atmosphere in general; but, as it peeped between the scraps of dirty scud, illuminating the long mass of vapour I had been watching with an almost unnatural brilliancy.

There was a lull, too, in the gusty wind; and long before the storm caught us, we could hear far up in Essex the trees literally screaming as they bent to the blast.

At last we got it. "Come down like the side of a house, didn't it, sir?" was Mr. Wolf's poetical description of it afterwards. For myself, I must confess that, although I had resolved to note with great accuracy all the phenomena of the gale, and though I was far from unused to rough weather, yet, after holding on for a minute or so to the weather gunwale, which seemed suddenly elevated almost perpendicularly over the the other, and being sensible of nothing but a hurricane of sharp, driving, misty spray, which stopped my breath and blinded my eyes, I fairly dived under the lee of the gunwale aforesaid, and there cowered till the first rough blast was over.

I am not going to bore any of you here with a "log" of that most exciting night's

cruise. Suffice it to say the first onrush of the gale was repeated with a terrible sameness all through the night; blinded squalls of wind (rain there was none; the drenching showers which flew over us being but the driving spray), succeeded by comparative lulls, made up the whole account of the night's weather; and Wolf explained to me that in all probability the gale "wouldn't settle to his work regular" until this gusty business had continued for some hours longer. So we whirled along, past many a heavy ship, riding bravely with a couple of anchors down, and none can tell how many fathoms of chain out, and glancing past us like a phantom mammoth in the half light; past many a tight fishing-smack, snugly lying-to, and caring as little for a gale of wind as a barrel of herrings; past—most wonderful to me of all—many a lumbering coasting-lighter, sturdily breasting the rising sea and throwing it off in clouds of spray from its broad flat bow, and now and then hailing in tones utterly incomprehensible to me, some sister craft, caught like ourselves in the hurly-burly.

Wolf contrived to run his vessel in under a bank, and there let go his anchor till the fury of the squall had passed over.

During this manœuvre he had been straining his eyes through the darkness in search of the chase; and as soon as a partial clearing-off admitted a stray moonbeam through the scud, he turned to me with his usual self-satisfied chuckle—

"There she is, sir—there she is. I thought he'd do it, too. Now, it's a curious thing the way these two wessels has been managed since we came out. I has my ideas about steering a wessel, you see, and Tom Marks has his n; sometimes we has our differences —what wonder? But, notwithstan'in, here's him and me been out so far in a matter of some seven or eight hours of the most tryingest weather I recklect, and so far ve've been managin' these 'ere two craft as tho' they was wun—wen I run he runs—wen I luff he luffs—wen I lays-to he does the same; and now when I let's my anchor go there he is a ridin' too—it is wonderful—arn't it? and to a man who has that respec' towards Tom Marks as I entertains, gratifyin', I should say. Here, Villaim, open a bottle o' stout, I'm dry."

Morning—such a morning! broke as we rounded the North Foreland. The Swallow still held her own, or if anything, perhaps we had slightly gained on her; but the sea was getting up fearfully; we could see the waves plashing up the chalk cliffs on shore, as though they would climb into the corn-fields, and one or two "dosers," as Mr. Wolf called them, and which to me bore a strong resemblance to being suddenly and forcibly dragged through a cold bath, began to carry conviction to the sturdy mind of even Mr. Wolf.

"I'll tell you wot, sir," he said, suddenly, at last, "Tom must run—that's my opinion; run for Broadstairs, I think—Ramsgate, at any rate—it's getting too hot this 'ere; and Tom's a born lunatic if he perseweres—which he won't, I'm thinking."

"And if he carries on?" I inquired.

The honest fellow seemed to be making vast efforts to swallow a bullet, and at length with a most woful countenance managed to growl out only these words—"Won't do."

We were nearly abreast of Broadstairs, when a squall came down on us more fierce and crashing than any we had yet met with; for some minutes even the rag of sail we carried seemed likely either to bear us down into the bowels of the waves, or carry us off bodily, parachute fashion, into the interior.

However, by dint of superhuman exertions and most dexterous management on the part of Wolf, Villiam and the hobbadehoy, we soon began to right; but had searcely done so ere a shout from Wolf started us.

"By——! Tom's got into grief at last. It's all up with the Swallow, or I'm a nigger. Poor Tom!"

We looked in the direction in which he pointed. The last squall had carried away the Swallow's mast about eight feet above the deck; the broken half of the mast, with the rigging and half the mainsail, were hanging over the side in the water, and banging and bumping against the vessel at every heave of the waves, threatening to knock no end of holes in her side. Mr. Marks had let go his anchor (his only chance), and, we were near enough to see, was himself actively engaged, axe in hand, in cutting away all that remained of mast and rigging. But he was alarmingly near the back of the pier, towards which he had drifted in the squall, and on which a surf was breaking, which we could hear above all the din of the gale, and which we could plainly see sending showers of spray right up the face of the cliff and into the garden and windows of the coast-guard station above.

All this we had a speedy opportunity of observing more closely, for Wolf's determination had been taken the moment he espied the catastrophe; and the Swift was now dashing straight for the harbour's mouth. A few terrific heaves on the cliff-like waves near the shore—sundry hoarse directions from excited figures on the pier, which seemed quite comprehensible to Wolf, but sounded to me like nothing but "Bow wow, wobble bobble, bauw wauw," or something of the sort; some hurling of ropes and scrambling; and we were safely riding in about three bucketsfull of water (the tide was low) inside the harbour.

This was not a moment, however, for us or the Broadstairs boatmen to think of anything about ourselves or the Swift. We scrambled on the pier without a moment's delay (Judas emerging from his lair for the first time, limp and woe-begone, but otherwise very little altered), and ran down to the nook at the back, where it was now too evident the poor Swallow must soon lay on her bones.

For though it would have been a positive insult to Mr. Marks, and gross injustice besides, to suppose that the Saucy Swallow was not "found in" the best of everything, and so that, inter alia, the cable at which she was now tugging with all her might and main was not sufficient to hold her, yet it must be remembered not only that this was a gale which for force and fury had not had an equal in the memory of that respected mythical person, the "oldest inhabitant" of Broadstairs, but that (and this was the worst of it) the doomed little barkie had let go of her anchor at so short a distance from the shore, there was no room, or hardly any, to veer out any more cable, and she was all too short as it was.

The only question, therefore, was how long it would be ere the inevitable catastrophe should take place, the Saucy Swallow be ground into firewood against the chalk rocks and the groins, and Mr. Thomas Marks, his crew and passenger, roughly hauled into the arms of the forty or fifty stout fellows, and conjectures were even beginning to be hazarded about her riding out the tide.

Meanwhile I had leisure to look after my companions. Wolf, his sturdy, bluff features, lit up with unnatural excitement, was moving rapidly about among the boatmen, suggesting this, pointing that, and in a fever lest any precaution should be omitted which might by any remotest chance to secure the safety of the hatch-boat's crew when she came ashore; and though the local boatmen knew berter than he did what to do, and he was as well aware of it as they were, yet on the one hand he could not help fidgetting about and telling them twenty times over what they knew right well long before, nor could they on the other hand refrain from giving a sort of half-contemptuous, half good-humoured assent to his suggestions, fully sympathising in the fellow-feeling which made him so anxious about his neighbour and rival.

Mr. Creepeley had taken up a position at once sheltered and commanding, under the lee of a building devoted to the storings of masts, cordage, &c., &c., so placed as to give a clear view of the only path from the beach to the back of the pier. Here this judicious functionary had gravely seated himself, and was discussing with much nonchalance a meal of roll and butter, coffee and bloater, brought for his especial behoof from the neighbouring inn.

The crash came at last rather unexpectedly. As the Swallow was lifted for the hundredth time her cable suddenly parted, so sharply that the broken end—it having gone but some ten or twelve feet from the bow—flew up into the air, and fell back in-board, narrowly missing Mr. Marks head, who, however, deftly dodging it, began kicking off his big boots and divesting himself of all superfluous clothing—a proceeding in which he was as very quickly followed by the rest of the crew, Singleton alone, whom I had watched all the morning with intense interest, sitting still in exactly the same position I had first spied him in, apparently lost in stupor. We could see Marks shaking his shoulder, bawling to him, and pointing to the shore, but he did not appear to heed it, and the moment had now arrived when the word must be " every man for himself."

How the Swallow melted away from our vision, I am quite unable to say. All I know is, that at this moment I saw a trim neat vessel all complete save a stump of a mainmast, riding buoyantly on the crest of an enormous wave, and that the very next moment there was swept up to my feet, as that wave thundered down on the beach, a confused jumble of seething foam, bits of broken wood, and struggling men. Of the poor Swallow this was the last that was ever seen.

We were all ready ashore—half-a-dozen strong ropes had been made fast to good holdings, and as many strong men held on to each ready to dash into the surf on the slightest provocation; and so, as the gigantic wave swept back, it left the whole crew of the Swallow safely lodged in the not over delicate gripe of four or five pairs of hands each.

Marks won his way above the reach of the waves with very little assistance, but Singleton hung like a log on the hands of the men who had seized him, and who had to carry him along altogether; they bore him so up the short path to the back of the pier, and oddly enough, laid him down at the feet of Mr. Creepeley, who hung fondly over him, muttering something which sounded very much like, "I arresht you,"—but perhaps I was mistaken, for the wind was noisy.

I had Singleton carried to the inn, undressed, and put into a hot bed as speedily as might be; but finding the stupor not yield to the remedies I applied, I sent for medical assistance.

Meanwhile, my faithful myrmidon was near falling a victim to popular fury. It seems that Wolf, who had, it will be remembered, expressed some repugnance at the outset to Mr. Creepeley's calling, and to whom I had been obliged to explain some part of the story, had kept a sharp eye and ear for the Israelite's movements all through, and had overheard the same expression which I had.

This information, hastily communicated to the congregated boatmen, had roused a smouldering fire, which, on the chambermaid's casually mentioning that Judas had been searching the gentleman's pockets (which was perfectly true) whilst I was putting him to bed, burst out into an open flame. So just as Judas had seated himself snugly at the bed's-head, grasping with a complacent air a pocket-book, the door of the room swung roughly open, and I, jumping up to meet the doctor, ran into Wolf's arms, who, with an inflamed countenance, and backed by a whole lobby-full of infuriated boatmen, fiercely demanded that the Jew should be then and there handed over to the summary justice of himself and friends. I did not at all like the looks of these rough administrators of fair-play; but Judas didn't seem to think much of it.

"Itsh the vay they allus treatsh us offishers," he muttered; and then sidling up to me, strove to slip the pocket-book into my hand, whispering—"Take holt o' dish 'ere, mind."

"None o' that now," roared the excited Wolf; "no pickin' o' dead men's pockets—you wrecker."

And he made a rush at Judas, who dodged him round the small table; a hoarse growl from the mob below, expressive of a desire to witness the terrific descent of the Jew from the window, seemed to goad Wolf to fresh exertions; and in spite of my entreaties to regard the sufferer, affairs were fast coming to a crisis; when fortunately the parish clergyman—who was also a justice of the peace—made his appearance; and with his assistance, articles were soon drawn up, and an armistice agreed on. Creepeley was to remain in the room with his prisoner, but was to refrain from approaching or molesting his person, and the pocket-book was handed to the parson, and sealed up by him to abide further proceedings.

Weeks, however, elapsed ere these further proceedings could be put in train. The violent excitement had brought on the culprit a stern brain fever, which brought him to the brink of the grave, but from which he arose at last a sadder, a wiser, and a better man.

Who nursed him through it all? Who but the ever-patient, the ever-affectionate Marian? I had her down at once, and contrived—the parson kindly conniving—to keep the real state of the case from her altogether; and though some things her husband let drop during his wanderings puzzled her not a little, she never guessed the truth.

Meanwhile, the trustees were changed, and the money was re-invested. Bowles's violent illness, old Ledgerall and I traded on so successfully in the city, that we actually got matters straight for him; and though he lost cruelly by his speculations, yet we pulled something out of the fire for him, and so managed, that on his return to the city, he found his legitimate business—to which he has steadily stuck ever since—but very little injured.

"Six months after the adventure I have described," said Squabshot, "we went in great state down the river to assist at the launch of Mr. Thomas Marks' new hatch-boat, built at the sole expense of Singleton Bowles Esq., and which, though we all suggested should, in name, as well as everything else, be a legitimate successor of the Saucy

No. 96.

Swallow. Mr. Marks, with pertinacious gallantry, insisted on calling her the "Marian," and so Marian named her, with the assistance of a bottle of port."

"And your friend had good reason to thank you for the part you had played," said Edith Staunton

"I hope so," answered Mr. Squabshot, with an expression of satisfaction on his countenance.

"Who is this painting by?" inquired a lady of the party, addressing herself to her fair hostess.

"Ah, that's by Vandyck," answered Miss Staunton, "and it is considered a very good specimen."

"It's very beautiful!" exclaimed another of the company, and immediately there was a rush of persons round the picture in question.

"Ah! talking of Vandyck," said Squab-shot's friend. "I will just tell you a story, or rather a slight sketch, which was given to me by an artist a few years ago."

The whole of the company seated themselves once more, when the voluntary tale teller narrated the following, which we reserve for another chapter.

CHAPTER CXL.

RUBENS AND VANDYCK.—A SCENE IN AN ATELIER IN ANTWERP, 1616.

"A PARTY of young men," said the narrator, "were on one fine June afternoon in one of the stateliest mansions in the city of Antwerp. It is many years ago now since the scene I am about to describe took place, as it occurred in the year of Our Lord 1616.

"Do pray open the master's *atelier*, M. Ruys, and let us go into it," said several of students, for such they in reality were.

The old man they were addressing was a servitor of the celebrated painter's tutor, whose work we have all been just admiring. He was busily engaged in mixing colours. He shook his head, and replied—

"Oh, no; I have promised that I would do no such thing; and when I have made a promise, I always keep it."

"Ah, ah," laughed the students; "you are jesting, Monsieur Ruys."

"I am serious. I say, when I give a promise I always keep it, or at least, endeavour to do so."

"Ah, that's better," exclaimed one of the party; "you endeavour, but don't always succeed. Well, no matter, the attempt is creditable."

"Bravo Frantz!" exclaimed the companions of the last speaker.

"I generally do succeed in keeping my word," answered the old man, somewhat testily.

"Then you keep the promises you make to yourself better than those you make to other people," replied one of the young men, in a jesting tone; "at least, I have heard it affirmed that you make a vow every day to your wife that you will drink no more beer, and yet indulge before night in such copious libations that both head and legs refuse to perform their accustomed office."

"Nonsense, Master Diepenbeke; you must not believe all you hear; and even supposing it to be true, that has nothing to say to my opening my master's *atelier*."

"Come, come, Master Ruys, you must open the door for us," cried another of the young students; "what are you afraid of?"

"Afraid of, Master Van Dyck—I afraid!"

replied the old man, drawing himself up. "I have served at sea in my youth, gentlemen; and a man who has served at sea is not generally a coward, I would beg you to understand; he sees death face to face every day of his life—he becomes acquainted with death."

"Well, we don't envy you that acquaintance," rejoined Van Dyck; "but we do want to make acquaintance with the style of Master Rubens, and for this purpose it is a matter of actual necessity that you should admit us into his *atelier*, in order that we may examine his works in their different stages of progress—we really cannot get on without doing so."

"Certainly, Master Van Dyck," replied the old man, tranquilly proceeding with his occupation; "if you only wished to visit the *atelier* from such praiseworthy motives as these, I should not like to refuse you; but you see, when you all get in, you begin to play instead of studying, and then something gets broken. It was only yesterday that little statuette of Diana was knocked down; and when Master Rubens came in I was obliged to say it was the wind had done it. 'What! the wind!' he exclaimed, 'there was not air enough to-day to stir a leaf.' So he gave me the credit of breaking his statue. No, no, gentlemen, I cannot stand that; you abuse my kindness."

The students were not, however, so easily to be diverted from their purpose. They gathered round the old man, and assailed him with cries of "My dear Ruys!—my good Ruys!—do give us the key—you shall have a packet of tobacco for the key—you shall have my beautiful amber pipe, if you will only give us the key!"

At last the old man, utterly bewildered, clapped his hands to his ears. The young men took advantage of the favourable opportunity thus afforded them, and, seeing the key peep forth from his pocket, they seized upon it, and were in the *atelier* before he knew what he was about. "My dear young gentleman," exclaimed the faithful servitor, who saw that all further attempt at resistance would now be fruitless, "my dear young gentlemen—do, out of pity for me, take care not to do mischief—look at everything you like, but do not touch them. Promise me that you will not touch them."

But all were too busy either to reply to the old man, or to give much heed to his words. Some were looking at a mere sketch; others at a finished painting; whilst the largest group were gathered around an easel, on the outstretched canvas of which the painter had commenced his now celebrated picture, "The Descent from the Cross," which forms an object of attraction in the Cathedral Church of Notre Dame at Antwerp.

All, however, appeared to be in a silent and contemplative mood; and Ruys was about to leave them to themselves, when a sudden thought seemed to occur to the old man's mind, and returning on his steps, he encountered a very young man, of dark complexion, whose countenance breathed at once the fire of genius and of youth, and addressing him in a whisper, said:

"Master Van Dyck, I trust to you; you are the steadiest and most studious young man in the school. Will you keep an eye upon those young madcaps?"

Van Dyck smiled and nodded assent, whilst the old man slowly retired.

Rubens' *atelier* opened upon one of the handsomest streets in Antwerp; and the young students loved to frequent its forbidden precincts as much for the purpose of gazing upon the *beau monde* who thronged the busy thoroughfare, as for that of studying the secrets of the great master's art.

For some time after the aged servitor had taken his departure, their conduct, it must be allowed, was most exemplary. They discussed the tone of the colouring, the effect of such and such draperies, &c., with the gravity of older heads.

"What a great master Rubens is!" exclaimed one,

"And such a brilliant career!" added another.

"Yes," rejoined Van Dyck; "my father was telling me, the other day, that when Rubens was Ambassador at Vienna, a nobleman, on hearing his paintings highly praised at the table of Prince Kaunitz, the Austrian Minister, inquired from one of the guests whether Rubens was not an Ambassador who amused himself by painting?" Casanova replied with a smile: "Your Excellence is mistaken. Rubens is a painter who amuses himself by acting as Ambassador."

During this conversation one of the young students, wearied with his morning's work, retired from the group, and began to throw into the air an elastic ball which he had discovered in a corner of the room. Once, it escaped his grasp, and rolled to the feet of his companions, who immediately caught it up and laughingly threw it at its owner's head. Immediately, all joined in the game, and, totally forgetting where they were, they rushed hither and thither, heedless of the treasures of art by which they were surrounded, until, at length,—none could tell how the catastrophe occurred, but so it was—Diepenbeke stumbled against the master's easel; it fell to the ground, and Diepenbeke falling with it, lay extended at full length upon the canvass. He sprang to his feet without a single moment's delay; but a cry of consternation burst

from every lip; the arm of the beautiful Magdalen is effaced, and the Virgin's chin is entirely obliterated.

A dead silence ensued, until, at length, looking at each other in dismay, they exclaimed, "Oh, what *have* we done!"

"We are lost," cried another. "We shall certainly be dismissed from the school to-morrow."

"I shall not wait to be dismissed," said a third; "I shall leave at once."

"And so will I," added a fourth.

"And where, in that case, should we go, gentlemen?" interposed Van Dyck. "Where should we find a second master like Rubens? No; we must make up our minds to bear his anger, and remain."

"His very look frightens me," said Diepenbeke.

"Yes," resumed Van Dyck, in a mournful tone; "I feel my heart die within me when he even raises his voice a little higher than usual."

"I think we had better restore everything to its place, and slip away without saying anything," suggested Richard, who had been the originator of all the mischief by first throwing the unlucky ball.

"For shame!" exclaimed Van Dyck. "This poor Ruys would then have all the credit of the mischief we have done; and we should have to reproach ourselves with having caused the old man's ruin."

"But what, then, is to be done?" asked Diepenbeke, in a tone of dismay.

"Gentlemen, an idea has just occurred to me" exclaimed the youngest of the group. "We have done the mischief, and we must repair it. Let us set to work, and do the best we can."

"Cohen's advice is not bad," replied Diepenbeke, "The cleverest fellow amongst us had better seat himself at the easel, and repair the mischief as quickly as he can."

"And which is the cleverest?" inquired one of the young artists.

"Van Dyck!" exclaimed his comrades, as with one voice.

"I!" rejoined Van Dyck, terrified at the task they were seeking to impose upon him.

"Yes; *you?*" replied his fellow-students; "you alone can do it; you have three hours before you. Put a good heart to the work, and save us."

With a trembling hand, Van Dyck seized the palette, and seated himself at the easel; but, as he was about to touch the masterpiece which lay before him, his heart failed him; he laid down the brush, and exclaimed—

"It is too great a piece of audacity for me to attempt to put a finger to it."

"Come, come, Van Dyck, you must not

forsake us, indeed you must not," cried his friends in an imploring tone; and at length, yielding to their entreaties, he reseated himself before the painting.

The more he feared the displeasure of his master, the greater were his efforts to equal him, if possible.

"Only three hours of daylight left!" he exclaimed, "and I must seek to reproduce this fresh colouring, these unequalled tints of Rubens—may God help me, or I am a lost man!"

The arm of the Magdalen grows rapidly beneath the young artist's touch—the cheek of the Virgin is next retouched—his friends press round him with admiring congratulations, and just as the shades of evening close around, his task is accomplished; and Van Dyck, his brow streaming with perspiration, and his face flushed with anxiety, rises from his seat.

One of the greatest difficulties was thus happily vanquished: but to-morrow, when Rubens sees his painting and discovers that an unknown hand has touched it, what will he say? Not one of his pupils we may be well assured, closed an eye that night.

"Well, I am satisfied with your conduct this evening, young gentlemen," said Ruys, when the elder pupil returned him the key he had entrusted to them—"you have been as quiet as so many mice. I should not have guessed you were in the *atelier*, if I had not known it.

Not a smile lighted up the countenance of any one of the youthful group at this *naive* expression of praise on the part of the old servant; and the succeeding morning, when they repaired to the school, anxiety was depicted on every face.

At length, Reubens entered the room, and many a fearful and inquiring glance was directed towards the master's countenance. He wore an unusually smiling aspect,—it was evident that he, as yet, knew nothing of what had occurred, He went from easel to easel, addressed a word of encouragement to one, of reproof to another, of instruction to each.

Suddenly, however, he paused, and addressing himself to the whole body of students, he said,—

"Gentlemen, I wish to show you my picture; a Church picture, which I am now painting—follow me,"

At these words, a shudder passed through the veins of the conscience-stricken pupils —they rose, and followed the master in silence. On entering the studio, Rubens walked straight towards his now celebrated painting of the "Descent from the Cross," and pointing towards that portion of his great work which he imagined he had completed on the preceding day, he observed:

"That is not the worst part of my work —look at it."

But suddenly interrupting himself, he stepped hastily towards the picture—gazed at it intently, and passed his hand across his eyes as though he could scarcely believe he saw aright.

This was a terrible moment. Van Dyck's heart might almost have been heard to beat.

"It is strange," said Rubens, at last "it is passing strange.

This work is mine, and it is not mine. It is admirably painted—that I must allow; but a strange hand has been at work on my painting."

And turning towards his pupils, the consternation visible in every countenance betrayed to him, in part, at least, the true state of the case.

"You must have made your way into my *atelier* yesterday!" exclaimed the Master, in a impetuous tone. "You meddled with everything, like a set of young madcaps as you are, and you met with a misfortune—is not that the truth? Speak out—tell me what happened? This part of the painting was effaced," he continued, pointing to the arm of the Magdalen; "and one of you young gentlemen took upon himself to repair the damage? Will you have the goodness to answer me?—you set me mad with your silence. Which of you painted this? Tell me directly." Then looking round upon the astounded circle, he exclaimed, "Are you afraid of telling me? Do you think I am going to scold the man who painted that arm? No: I would rather clasp him to my heart, and proclaim him my successor. Yes; he who has painted this, will one day excel us all. Tell me, then, what is his name?"

"Van Dyck!" exclaimed the pupils with one accord as they made way for the young artist, who retreated into the back-ground overwhelmed with confusion.

"Van Dyck!" repeated Rubens, at the same time holding out his hand to his youthful pupil, "I might have guessed as much. You may now bid farewell to my *atelier*. I can teach you nothing more—absolutely nothing. You must now go to Italy, my lad, and study the great masters there. Only one word of advice would I give you: devote yourself to portrait painting—that will be your forte. Gentlemen," added Rubens, "I forgive you your folly in consideration of the manner in which its effects have been repaired."

When the aged Ruys saw the whole band of young men coming out of the studio with smiling faces, and the Mater himself leaning in a familiar manner on the shoulder of Van Dyck, he said to himself—

"Well at all events, my remonstrances yesterday proved of some use. Master Rubens is pleased with them to day, good youths! I will not refuse them the key another time—no, that I will not."

Van Dyck, born at Antwerp in 1599, was at this time seventeen years of age. In compliance with the wishes of his master, he shortly afterwards quitted Rubens, and repaired to Italy. Previous to his departure, he painted three historical pieces, which he presented to Rubens in token of his gratitude, and this great Master of the art esteemed them so highly that he was wont to point them out as the gems of his collection.

The after career of the young artist is well known. On his return from Italy, he remained for a short time in his native land; but, in a moment of disappointment, he repaired to the Hague, whither strangers used to flock in order to have their portraits executed by his hand. The same success attended him in England, where he came on the invitation of Charles I., whose love of art is well known. Van Dyck's portraits were in such demand at the Court of that Prince, that he might have demanded almost any sum he pleased for them; but still his wealth did not accumulate. He kept open house, had a numerous establishment of servants, and was ever ready to open his purse to friends, whether real or pretended. In addition to this, he was much given to the study of alchemy, and no inconsiderable portion of the sums which he earned by the pencil, did he afterwards melt away in the crucible.

Van Dyck married the daughter of Lord Ruthven, the head of an ancient and illustrious Scottish family; but his wife brought him no other dower save her noble birth and exceeding beauty. He died of consumption, at the early age of forty-two.

"They were both wonderfully clever men," said a gentleman of the party, whose observations upon works of art had at once proved him to be a connoiseur."

"Van Dyck is supposed to be one of the best portrait painters of either his own or any other country, was he not?" inquired Edith Staunton.

"Unquestionably, he stands in the foremost rank."

"Before Rubens!"

"No, not as an allegorical painter, or indeed as a painter of Scripture subjects, Van Dyck was essentially a portrait painter and nothing more. All these men have their own particular walk, or rather branch of the arts; and, as our friend here has given us a very graphic account of these two great painters, I will go back to a still earlier date, nearly two hundred years before the existence of either of the other two celebrities. I dare say some of you have heard of the celebrated Albert Durer, who was, in the early history of art, so remarkable for his designs for books, and still more so for his engravings of the same. Listen, therefore, to my sketch of this celebrated man.

"On a beautiful day in October, 1498," said the narrator, "a large number of persons, under the influence of idleness, curiosity, or some better motive, had assembled opposite the Hotel de Ville of Nuremberg, attracted apparently by a placard affixed to one of its pillars, which bore the following announcement:—

"'Joseph Durer, Goldsmith of this city, acquaints his fellow citizens that he will this afternoon at his shop on the Place de l'Horloge, sell by auction all the works of art in gold and silver that he possesses, and which are too numerous to be detailed —the sale will commence at four o'clock precisely.'"

"What!" exclaimed one of the bystanders, who had just arrived, and who, from the style and magnitude of his attire, was apparently a person of some distinction; "what! the rich goldsmith Durer selling off all his celebrated works of art! what can have reduced him to such an extremity?"

"You are evidently a stranger, sir," replied a citizen to whom the question had been addressed, "or you would have known that Joseph Durer has made the greatest sacrifices to sustain his son-in-law, who was a short time since considered one of the principal merchants of Lubeck, but who has lately fled, leaving behind him debts to a considerable amount. It is to meet this disaster to save the honour of his grandchildren, and to preserve their names pure and unblemished, that the worthy man is now about to part with those beautiful works that were the pride and delight of his old age, of those masterpieces the possession of which has, so to say, identified itself with his very existence—such noble and disinterested conduct has called forth a general sympathy from his fellow citizens, and has done much to remove a prejudice which existed against him, in consequence of an event which occurred some years since.

"May I, without being deemed indiscreet, ask to what you allude?" said the stranger.

"You must know, seigneur, that Joseph Durer had three sons and a daughter; the daughter he gave in marriage, with a large fortune, to the Lubeck merchant of whom I just spoke; his two elder sons, he, by the sacrifice of enormous sums of money, succeeded in procuring appointments for, at the Courts of Bavaria and Weimar, where their progress was so rapid that they soon learnt to despise their plebeian father, and contrived to exchange his humble name for titles of nobility."

"And the youngest son—what became of him?"

"Albert, poor fellow!" replied the citizen; "Albert wished to become a painter, his father, however, refused to gratify this desire, wishing that the lad should follow his own calling of Goldsmith, and threatened that if he did not he should be turned into the streets—in fact, behaved so unkindly to the poor boy, that one day he fled from home and has never again been heard of—many years have since passed, but so general a favourite was poor Albert, that even now his loss is remembered, and reproaches are still uttered against his father for the ill-treatment that caused the departure and perhaps the death of his youngest boy. Poor Albert!"

At this moment the clock struck four, the Goldsmith's ware rooms were thrown open, and the crowd rushed in to examine and to admire the costly articles that were submitted to their curious inspection.

The sale began—massive dishes, ewers, and flagons of silver and gold were first offered—then came the more precious wares, the master-pieces of the craft—chalices exquisitely carved, Gothic temples enriched with tracery of marvellous delicacy and fineness, jewelled shrines with scriptual subjects in relievo of wondrous beauty, figures from the antique of admirable perfection.

So long as the more common-place though costly things only were offered for sale, the Goldsmith sat quietly and calmly at the back of his shop, but when he heard the master-pieces of his skill named, and their worth and excellence extolled in the hackneyed terms of praise usual on such occasions, he could no longer maintain his attitude of resignation, but hastily rising, as if under the influence of some invisible power, he hovered round the various articles that were offered, with all the anxiety of a parent round the cradle of her offspring.

The crier now announced for sale six statuettes in gold and silver from the antique.

"A thousand ducats," said a voice.

"A thousand and fifty," said another.

"Eleven hundred," exclaimed the first, there was no higher bidding and the statuettes were sold.

The old Goldsmith breathed heavily, his features were white as his venerable locks, and a convulsive movement agitated every limb. He nevertheless persisted in remaining near the official whose duties it was to register the purchases made. When all was sold the poor old man looked around him with a feeling of terror—the fatal moment approached when the purchases were to bear away all those rich productions of his art which had so long surrounded him, those household gods which were to him part and parcel of his own life.

"Let the purchasers of the last twenty-three lots come forward," called out the official register.

"They were all bought by one person," exclaimed a voice in reply.

"Let him come forward then and state his name."

At these words a young cavilier of some six or seven and twenty years of age, and whose handsome features bore the stamp of intellectuality and mildness, stepped forward. He was richly dressed, and beneath an embroidered mantle, which was artistically and gracefully thrown over him, might be seen a massive chain of gold, that hung round his neck, and from which was suspended a miniature portrait, set in diamonds, of the Emperor Maximilian. His hat was looped up in front, and his flowing curls redolent of perfume, fell upon a collar of rich lace.

"Here is the amount of my purchases," said, in a tremulous voice, the young stranger, "be pleased to verify its correctness."

The sum was found exact, and the officer then requested the name of the buyer in order that it might be inscribed in the register.

Meanwhile the old Goldsmith, mute and downcast, awaited with the anxiety of despair the removal of the treasures no longer his.

"Write," said the young stranger in faltering accents, "write Albert Durer."

At this name the old man sprang up with all the energy of boyhood, and in an instant was locked in the embrace of his son.

"Albert!" he exclaimed, "my poor Albert! is it indeed you that I see—you that I hold to my heart! My poor boy, and you have not then forgotten your old father—and you have forgiven him?"

"Forgiven you, my dear father," replied the youth kneeling, "it is I who have to solicit forgiveness for my disobedience to your wishes and commands."

"All is forgotten, all is pardoned, my dear Albert—at such a moment can I think of aught else than your return, and of the happiness restored to me?"

"And that happiniss will be increased, sir," said a stranger, who now approached, and whose dress bespoke him to be a man of high rank, "when you learn that your son and my dear friend Albert is now one of the most renowned artists of Germany —that he is not only a painter of the highest order, but one of the most skilful engravers, an architect and engineer of the greatest eminence—that he is at this moment chief painter to the Emperor Maximilian—that the Republic of Venice is anxious to engage his services, and that the King of France, Louis the 12th, has entreated him to proceed to Paris, to undertake the embellishment of that capital—what say you to this, worthy sir?"

"Say," exclaimed the old Goldsmith, again embracing his son, "say! that great talents are rarely unaccompanied by a noble heart, and that my Albert is a proof that the man of genius and the man of worth may, and ever should be, one and the same."

Having concluded this slight sketch of an incident in the lives of the two great painters, Miss Stauton favoured the company with the following short story of the early days of Henri Quatre, the celebrated French King whose history is generally known in our country.

CHAPTER CXLI.

THE FIRST LOVE OF HENRI QUATRE.

"All the world has heard of the fair Gabrielle," said Edith Staunton, but it is not of her I am about to speak, she was exactly fitted for what she was, *a maitresse en titre,* and by no means fitted for the heroine of a tale of true and devoted love, such as mine is going to be. My story is one of those whose name has never been recorded in history, but I had it from a French lady upon whom I can rely. My heroine, if she can be so called, was little known and less remembered, sweet and lovely as a violet, she resembled it also, being hidden from the light of day.

When Henri Quatre was about fifteen, Charles the Ninth came to pay a visit to the court of Navarre. He was then Prince of Béarn, and was already distinguished for brilliancy and enterprise, and graceful courage. During the stay of the French King, there were all kinds of games and fêtes, to celebrate his visit to Nérac. In all these Henri shone.

One day there was a match of archery. Charles IX. was fond of this exercise—perhaps to keep himself in practice to shoot his subjects out of window. When kings play at bowls they give the lie to the proverb, and seldom meet with rubbers. When Louis XIV. danced in the ballets at Versailles, no dancer could cut so high by several inches. In like manner, when his ancester drew his bow at Nérac, no arrow went half so near the mark as his. But Henri was sadly deficient in knowledge of the *bienséances* due to royal competitors, and made no scruple of outshooting the king. An orange was the mark, and the young prince's arrow pierced it through and through.

The next day the game was to be renewed; and all the inhabitants of the country around flocked to see the sport. But great was the disappointment when it was announced that the king did not intend to shoot, or even to honour the assembly with his presence. The arrow of the young prince which carried away the orange, had carried away the king's temper also; he remained within. But the Duc de Guise stepped forth as his representative. He had no idea that provincial clods, and Huguenots into the bargain, should bear away the prize from Parsians and true Catholics,—so he draws his arrow to the head, and away flies the orange into two pieces.

It was now Henri's turn—he looks round for another mark to be erected, but there is no second orange to be found. What is to be done? The spirit of fifteen prompts him with an expedient.

In the inner circle of spectators stood a young girl of perhaps fourteen years. Her hair and brows were dark like those of her country, but she had the blue eye of the north. The face and arms were embrowned with a hue of healthful labour, but the kerchief gave a glimpse of a downy whiteness of skin, which showed how delicate nature had meant that this creature should be. The limbs, it is true, wanted their full roundness, but there was certain indication that they would not want it long; and the kerchief, which I have mentioned, was swelled gently forth (like a sail softly breathed into by the wind) in a way which gave token of the commencement of maidenly beauty. Where this was crossed upon the bosom, rested a rose, shedding a reflected tint upon the white breast, like the hues of sunset upon the snow of the Alps. I don't know how it is that young eyes catch such objects readily, but it is certain that, as Henri looked around for something to replace the orange, he glanced upon this rose; in an instant, he sprang to the young girl, took it from her bosom without saying a word, and placed it upon the target. The Duc de Guise shoots first —the arrow passes the flower, only shaking its leaves by the disturbance of the surrounding air. Henri now shoots himself—

his shaft now pierces the stalk—he takes it with the rose sticking to its point, and presents it to the blushing and delighted owner.

There are few sensations more delicious than those two young people experienced, when they looked *into* each other's eyes; and though Henri and the young peasant did not know this, they felt it as their eyes flashed with consciousness upon each other,

The first love-beat
Of the youthful heart

was at that moment experienced by both of them. Love verified the proverb concerning him, expressed so often in the alliterative antithesis, "he made equal the prince and the peasant."

Henry lost no time in learning who it was whose rose had become the rose of love. It appeared that she was the daughter of the gardener of the castle, and was most appropriately named Fleurette. She lived in a cottage at the end of the garden, which cottage still exists at Nèrac, The next day, the prince suddenly discovered that gardening was the most delightful of all studies and occupations, and that he had for it a peculiar taste. A portion of ground was marked out as his own, close to the fountain in the centre of the garden. He chose this spot, perhaps, on account of the ease it afforded him to fetch water for his plants, for it was hither that the attendants employed in the garden came for water—Fleurette among the rest.

About a month after this time the setting sun one evening cast upon the suaface of the fountain the shadow of two figures, seated upon its bank. They were slender and youthful, but as the reflection appeared in the water, it was not very easy to distinguish the respective outlines of each. These were Henri and Fleurette; his arm supporting her form, his shoulder was the cushion to her cheek. It might be the reflection of the sunset, but the cheek appeared more flushed than usual, and her eyes swam in a glistening moisture, which was unknown to it at the archery contest. One would think that two young persons thus placed would love to gaze upon each other, especially if it be so delightful as I have before mentioned. His eye is bright with love and joy, but not with fervour; with happiness, but not with hope. His tone seems now to be that of soothing and entreaty. He kisses the tears from her cheek, and they flow the faster for the very kisses.

How different were the feelings of the two when they parted that night! He bounded along at a pace between running and leaping, *walking* was too quiet and

vapid for him *now*. His heart expanded and danced within his breast, with all the bright and exquisite joy of certainty and *irrevocableness*. He was raised in his own eyes—he almost pittied all others. He could remain in no place, he could continue in no occupation. He could not sleep from excitement and joy. When she parted from him, she walked to her humble home with a trailing and melancholy step, and paused before she crossed its threshold. When she entered she slunk from her father's notice, and seated herself in a dark part of the room. Her tears again began to overflow her eyes, and trickle down her hot cheeks, if not with bitterness, at least with deep mournfulness. She was sunken in her own esteem, and feared the loss of the esteem of all the world. She even envied a deformed and half-diot girl, who came into the cottage to beg a little milk. She, also, could not sleep; but, oh, how different was her sleeplessness from his?

For above two months, every evening, or nearly so, beheld the young prince and the young peasant together at the fountain. Fleurette's father had never been in the habit of watching the motions of his daughter, and if she now stayed rather later in the garden than usual, it attracted no notice, or at least no suspicion. Not so the prince's tutor. Old La Gaucherie was well versed in human nature; and the sudden and violent addiction of his pupil to gardening led him to suspect that there was in the case some other goddess besides Pomona. Accordingly, one day, he made the garden the scene of his evening walk, and the appearance of the mortal Pomona was quite sufficient to enable him to make up his opinion on the subject. I have said that La Gaucherie had considerable knowledge of human nature; he, therefore, was fully aware that any remonstrances that he could make to his pupil would have about the same effect "as if he were very heartily and earnestly to entreat a moth not to fly into a candle." The next day he accordingly told the prince, that, on the following morning, they were to set out for Pau, and then to proceed to Bayonne, where the French court at that time was.

To say that Henri was pleased with this would be doing him injustice—to say he was sorry would be more than the truth. His were mixed feelings, in a case where there always ought to be, but never was nor will be, unmingled regret. To a young mind, burning with enterprise and ambition, and not averse from pleasure, the announcement that he was at once to go forth into the world, and that world a court, and that court the most brilliant and

powerful of the time, conveyed a feeling of hope and gladness, which, I am afraid, was far from being counterbalanced by the regret he really did experience in parting from Fleurette. Still it would be less than justice if I did not say that that regret was a considerable alloy to the golden expectations of the future hero of Ivry. And at the moment when he was to take leave of her, I question whether, just at that instant, he would not have given up all to remain.

"You leave me," she said, "you leave me and then you are lost to me for ever! It is vain to expect, that in the midst of the court, you should continue to love me, a poor lonely creature, who is far away. It is vain to expect it, and I do not expect it, and yet it will wring my heart to think that you do not love me. Your love is all

I have in the world: if I lose it I lose everything;" and she wept bitterly as she hung upon his neck.

These things are, I believe, always said in substance, whatever may be the words, by woman at the moment of separation. But trite as they may on that account be considered, they are to me inexpressibly touching nevertheless. It is the truth of these fears which makes them affecting. Degrading and painful as it may be to confess it, out of a hundred cases there are not two in which the prophecy is not accomplished. I am far from saying that all parting is necessarily followed by inconstancy; but a parting like this, when the lover is very young, and has been a favoured one—when he is to go into the world for the first time, and his qualities alike, and his defects, fit him to shine in that world and to love it; when she who is left has yielded up the best and strongest hold of her lover's heart—the power of inspiring hope; when she has nothing to give as reward, and nothing to withhold as punishment, above all, when the parting is for a long and indefinite period, then, alas, and alas for her heart and hope and happiness! she has no chance indeed!

Henri said what are equally the universal parting words of men; but which are not in the least touching, because they are not true. He tried to persuade her that her fears were vain—he promised, he swore eternal love. She neither swore nor promised; but she kept the promise and the oath which he broke. He was to leave the castle early in the morning, but earlier still they were together at the fountain. It was now the rising sun which shone upon it, but its beams of increasing brightness were to them far more saddening than its waning light had been of old.

"You are going, Henri," she said; "you will have novelty and motion and change to cheer your spirits and dissipate your sorrow. But I shall remain; I shall every day see again and again the places which you have made so dear to me, by being in them with me—I shall have everything to remind me of past happiness and present pain. Dear, dear Henri, do not forget me—if you do," and she lowered her voice as she spoke, "if you do, I shall die."

At that moment his vow of increasing affection was a true one, for it was made in the spirit of truth; at that moment the tears which he shed were as heart-gushing as her own.

"And this fountain," she added, looking upon its loved waters, "this fountain—I shall always be there; when you are away, or when you are near me, it will be still the same—you will always find me there."

These were the last words, and he remembered the expression afterwards.

At length, about fifteen months after his departure from Nèrac, Henri returned thither. He accompanied the queen-mother's court. His walks in the garden were renewed, but his companion was not the same; and to the shame of his heart be it spoken, he never saw or asked for her who had been so formerly. As he paced the walks by the side of Mademoiselle d'Ayelle, one of the maids of honour of Catherine de Medicis, enthralled by her beauty, and fascinated by her wit, he never cast a thought on the simple maiden who had given him all the affection of an unpractised heart, and loved him with a strong, unmingled passion, which this courtly creature could never feel. As he passed the fountain, I cannot believe that the image of Fleurette did not rise before his mind; but, if it did, it was merely for him to chase it from his thought, as the sultan in the eastern story flung from him the talismanic ring, which reminded him that he was doing wrong.

And where was Fleurette herself? Her heart had swelled and bounded with joy when she heard of Henri's return; but the news which she heard almost as soon (for scandal has a winged tongue), cast at once the icy chill of death upon her heart. Her long, long hope had been for his return, and now that he was returned—oh, heaven! how that hope was crushed and blasted!—she did not seek Henri, she conveyed to him no reproach—she suffered, suffered on.

Gracious heaven! did men but know the pangs which even the lightest of their conduct occasions, unless they were very fiends, they could not continue to act thus! But they never *can* know what a woman feels on desertion or even slight, It is not in our nature to feel such things in the same manner as they do; the early doubt—the gradual decline of hope—and at last the sick despair of certainty—are their hearts human, that they can inflict these things on the beings who love them to very madness, and, as it were, a punishment for that love itself?

Fleurette had once or twice seen the prince and Mademoiselle d'Ayelle walking together in the garden; but she always shrank from their way and hid herself among the trees. Her heart rose in her throat, and she felt almost as if it would choke her as she looked upon her former lover. The time which he had been away had wrought great improvement upon his person; he was more formed, his statue more increased, his figure had become more manly, and his eye and brow more determined. Still his smile (who can forget the smile of one they have loved?) was the same; and poor Fleurette felt sick at heart as she saw it given to another. She watched them—their manner, their looks. "She does not love him as I did; no one can ever do that," the poor girl said to herself! "and he does not look on her face as he did on mine; he does not love her as he did me; but he does love her, and he loves me no longer, and that is enough."

But one day, Fleurette found herself close to them on a sudden, and she felt an irresistible temptation not to avoid them this time. They met; and as they passed, she looked up (it was indeed an effort) into Henri's face. His eyes met hers, and the blood sprang in volumes to his cheeks. He passed on without speaking; but that day he came to the door of her cottage, as she was sitting at her wheel (but not spinning), and in a hurried and embarrassed tone begged her to be at the fountain the next night. Without raising her eyes from her work she answered. "At eight o'clock, *I will be there.*"

It was now the autumn of the year, and the evening was chill and gloomy. As Henri walked through the garden, his spirits felt the effect of the season—his conduct rose upon his heart, and smote him. The wind sighed and swept the fallen leaves in eddies; and the trees, which had yet a few discoloured leaves upon them, looked, perhaps, still more melancholy and uncheering than if they had been wholly bare. He saw the fountain at a distance, and perceived that she was not yet come. His feelings were not exactly such as to lead him to prefer that spot to wait—it accused him too strongly.—He walked once more round the garden. The night now began to close in; and the wind, as it struck chill upon him, seemed to shoot its coolness into his heart also. He again came in sight of the fountain, and still no one was there. Was this like Fleurette? He went towards it slowly, expecting every moment to see her approach through the gloom. But he got close to the brink, and still she did not appear. As he reached it, however, he saw, on the spot where they had always been accustomed to sit, a short wand stuck into the earth. He approached it— he recognised it well! It was the arrow with the rose, long since withered, still adhering to its barb! He took it up with a deep sigh, when suddenly he found a paper fastened to the feather. He tore it open, but it had become too dark for him to distinguish a line. He flew to the castle; the note contained these words :—

"You have ceased to love me; but I do not reproach you! May God Almighty bless you and make you happy!—May He, and His great goodness, forgive me!—I promised to meet you this night at the fountain; I have kept my trust—If you seek, *you will find me there!*"

The truth flashed across him in a moment —he rushed back to the fountain: the unfortunate *was indeed there!*

"Ah, the narrative you have just been relating, bears upon it the impress of truth, Miss Staunton," said the gentleman who had related the anecdote of Rubens and Van Dyck; "and just to restore the equillibrium of us all, after so touching a story, I will narrate to you Palazzi's last adventure."

All declared their willingness to hear it, and the middle-aged gentleman, for he was no longer a youth, related the following :—

CHAPTER CXLII.

AN EXIT THROUGH THE WINDOW.

IN an ancient castle, and in a front room of this said castle, the Count di Palazzi, a handsome young Neapolitan nobleman, sat at breakfast.

The view from the window of the apartment was superb, but as for the apartment itself, though there were some fine fragments of statues in the niches, and though it was hung with tapestry, still we can't help thinking that a furnishing upholsterer might have employed himself in it for a day or two, much to the improvement of its general appearance and comfort.

The count poured himself out another cup of coffee: no vile decoction of roasted horse beans, but deduced from the genuine berry of Mocha, in all the aroma of its oriental fragrance.

Palazzi, who had within the last few months led to the altar a young and blooming bride, resided at Naples, and was now on a visit to an estate he possessed about sixty miles distant. His ancestral castle was in a very dilapidated state on which account his wife's accompanying him thither was quite out of the question; still, as his steward did not collect, or, at any rate, never remitted the rents, go he must, and go he consequently did, having made up his mind to cashier the unjust steward, and then hasten back to the arms of his beloved Maria with all possible expedition.

Various circumstances, however, contributed to detain him longer than he at first intended; and it was already the fourth morning of his stay that he was seated at breakfast in the manner described.

Suddenly a loud rat-tat-tat disturbed the Neapolitan in the enjoyment of his coffee, and a man, covered with dust and perspiration, entered the room.

"Ha, Matteo! what brings you hither?" exclaimed the count, in an anxious tone of voice.

"Your brother, most noble count, sent me with this letter," gasped Matteo; and the man sank exhausted on a chair, fatigue overcoming the respect with which the other's rank inspired him.

Palazzi ran his eye over the words of the letter, and his cheeks grew paler than the paper they were written on. Without any other symptoms of agitation he perused it several times, and thrusting it into his bosom, rose, without a word, and left the room.

Matteo seated himself at the deserted breakfast-table as soon as the sound of horses' hoofs assured him of his master's departure, and, it is to be hoped, found the coffee to his liking.

The rain poured down in torrents: the lightning flashed with unusual brightness; and the thunder rolled in fearful harmony—still Palazzi spurred on his jaded steed. In the rain that drenched him he felt but the foretaste of tears of agony, henceforward to be shed: in the lurid lightning was reflected the fire that consumed his own tortured soul; and the roar of the thunder sounded like the laugh of demons, triumphing in his ineffable misery.

He was now within a mile of his home, when his horse, totally incapable of proceeding a step further, sank beneath him. Thrice had the noble animal saved its master's life in battle, never had it betrayed one vicious trick; but now he forsook its body, heedless whether it lived or died; though but the day before he would probably have given a fourth part of his possessions to have preserved its life.

In two minutes—such is the superhuman vigour passion excited imparts to the mortal frame—he stood at the private door of his palace, which he immediately opened; and, without letting any one know of his arrival, ascended the stairs leading to his dressing-room. Thence, taking care to make no noise, he proceeded through several other rooms, until he reached a spacious saloon, on one side of which were three windows opening to a balcony, the rail-work of which had been recently removed in order to undergo repairs, and had not yet been put up again.

Palazzi threw the centre window open to admit the cool evening breeze. Was it the moonlight or the fatigue he had undergone that gave the Neapolitan's features so unearthly a hue? We shall see.

Footsteps approached; hastily the count concealed himself behind the curtains of one of the other windows. His right hand was thrust into his bosom—it grasped the hilt of a dagger.

"Dear Francisco," said a tall and exquisitely beautiful woman, who now entered the saloon, leaning on the arm of a dark, thick-set man, of about six-and-thirty. "Dear Francisco, let me entreat you to cease your visits, to relieve me of the terrible apprehensions I constantly labour under. Let the past be forgotten!—think but of the fearful vengeance of Palazzi!"

"His vengeance!" replied her companion, scornfully. "I know well his uncle is a cardinal, and he himself the best swordsman in Naples—what of that? A purse of gold can guide the bravo's dagger to his proud heart. Oh, Maria! why, why did you allow yourself to be persuaded into marrying this accursed Palazzi! when, had you waited but

one short month, my hand and newly-inherited riches might have been yours?"

"Alas, Francisco! could I have foreseen?"

"True! dearest, true! pardon my peevishness," interrupted the lover; but why not quit these scenes of misery, and fly with me to regions where there are no Palazzi's to disturb us!"

And Francisco encircled her waist with his arm, and pressed his lips to hers. At this moment Maria gave a loud shriek, and fell, half senseless, on the ground.

"Good even!" said a voice, soft and musical, but vindictively ironical.

A tall, dark figure stood in the centre of the room; it advanced, and Francisco recognised the injured Palazzi.

Francisco was a man of great courage; but, nevertheless, he felt his flesh creep and his blood run cold, as Palazzi repeated his greeting, in a voice still more musical, and gently laid his hand on his shoulder. There was a calmness unnaturally horrible about the demeanour of the latter, which checked the words of defiance Francisco would gladly have given utterance to.

"No bravo's dagger can reach my heart," said Palazzi, in the same fearful tone. "Ha, ha, ha!—laugh Francisco! it is for the last time!"

And grasping him firmly, he dragged him towards the open window.

Francisco was a powerful man—he writhed and struggled to escape; but the proud smile of conscious superiority on Palazzi's countenance banished all doubt as to his fate.

"At least," muttered Francisco, "we will perish together!"

And, ceasing to struggle, he in his turn, grappled with his relentless adversary.

"The noble Palazzi dies not with the dog Francisco," said the former, and with a tremendous effort hurled his victim through the open window.

The wretched man tottered for an instant on the edge of the balcony, and, with a piercing cry, fell at least twenty feet into the street below.

"You have murdered my lover!" cried the phrenzied Maria; "prepare for your fate!"

And she aimed a stiletto at his heart; but Palazzi arrested her arm before the blow could descend; and, calmly throwing her from him, left the apartment in silence. What words can express the thoughts that filled the soul of that man?

"The Countess di Palazzi entered a nunnery, of course?" asked one of the guests, as the narrator paused.

"No, not exactly. She eloped with the eldest son of an Irish lord, making the grand tour, three weeks after the occurrence I have narrated."

"Dear me! you don't say so?" exclaimed Miss Staunton.

"Fact."

"And what became of Francisco?"

"Oh, he survived his exit through the window, and used to limp about Naples on two wooden legs, or cork, I really forget which—a living example to succeeding generations not to make love to other people's wives when the husbands were out of town."

"And Palazzi?"

"Poor fellow! broken-hearted at his beloved Maria's faithlessness, he travelled to the far east, and made friends with Bedouin Arabs and hyenas. The last news I heard of him was that he had taken lodgings in the town of Petra, and strayed through its deserted streets, cutting the letter M, with his pocket-knife, on all the houses. Much pleasure may the occupation afford him, say I."

"How can you jest on such serious subjects."

"Better to laugh than to weep. Life's a jest."

"And is this life?"

"Upon my honour, I can't say; but I fancy so."

"As we have had stories of all sorts tonight," said a smooth faced gentleman, as soon as the exit through the window had been concluded. "As we have had a variety of entertainments, I will, 'an it please you, repeat to you what I remember of an imaginary German legend; but, mind, I do not vouch for the truth of it."

All present declared their willinness to listen to the narrative, and thus encouraged, the smooth faced gentleman related the following.

CHAPTER CXLIII.

THE FORGET-ME-NOT.

Two tiny elves sat by the moss-bedecked borders of a sparkling rivulet, watching the wavelets bubbling and plashing at their feet. One was a little, broad-shouldered, short-necked, withered, hump-backed old man, and his thin legs, which he carefully drew up under him out of reach of the waters, added to the oddity of his appearance. His dress was brown, rather prim, and his head was covered with a hat or cap of brown leather, which cast a shadow over his plain, pale, but still good-natured and pleasant face. His companion was an elegant, delicate fairy; her yellow hair fell in ringlets over her shoulders and arms—her lovely but roguish face was mirrored in the waters where her naked feet were playing, and she

was amusing herself, as often as she could find the opportunity, by flirting the drops in her neighbour's face. She wore an auricula for head-gear, and carried a wand made from the stalk of a flower.

"Ah! Heinzelman," cried the pretty creature, "are you still afraid of the water?"

"I have got my best shoes on," answered the other, drawing still farther from the stream; "but," he continued, in hopes of turning the conversation, "don't call me Heinzelman, my family name sounds strangely in my ears; call me Littlecap, as mankind do when they want to coax me."

"Very good," replied the fay; "and you are always to call me Lilli, as we are old friends."

And they really were so, in the regular course of events. First they made acquaintance during the bathing season; from that sprung up a season's intimacy, and from this, a friendship which outlasted the time in which alone they met. They had no means of keeping up a correspondence, but perhaps they thought the oftener of each other on that account. They had this evening come to the stream, which had been their meeting-place for some years, and Littlecap was bent on going regularly through a course of bathing, in order to clear himself of the dust and dirt in which his life was passed. Lilli was come for amusement, on account of the society one meets in those places, and also to revisit the flowers she found at the spring, and cherished so dearly, although Littlecap often assured her that the same species and genera were to be found in a thousand similar places.

Littlecap had painfully toiled thither on foot, but Lilli had spread out her butterfly, dragonfly, or firefly wings (I am not quite sure which sort were most in vogue that season), and had pleasantly flown through the soft air, arriving at the selfsame time with her companion.

Littlecap at once began to bathe, and to drink his morning draught of dew from the most wholesome or medicinal flowers; while Lilli paid her visits, gossiped, fluttered about, and inquired if any other fairy had made any fresh discoveries in the important art of turning flower-stalks into fairy wands. But of evenings the friends invariably met, and recounted to each other the day's adventures, or their opinions of time present, past, and future. We will listen to them—

"You are looking pale, Littlecap," said the fairy, and her merry face was clouded for a moment. "You have been working too hard in your dusty, close room."

"I have really much to do. There is a great deal stirring just now amongst books and printing. We are overwhelmed with those abominable political pamphlets. Now and then we come upon a fresh poetical story, or a stately, large, and learned folio. I am but a printer's Brownie, and so I have plenty of work this year. Many letters and printer's signs have been brought to light which had long lain useless in their cases; they were covered with dust, which gets down one's throat and injures the lungs; so the bathing season was most essential for me this year."

Lilli burst out laughing.

"I don't pity you a bit," she cried. "What are all those books, letters, and pamphlets to you, or to mankind even?"

"You know nothing about it, my pretty friend. Every one must work in the place appointed to him by fate; the bee must build it's cell, and the ant it's hill, and if you destroy their works, they immediately set about replacing them. I must work as they do—it is so ordained. Do you do nothing?"

"I? no; I dance in the moonbeams, I prattle with the flowers, I listen to the glow-worms, I live, I enjoy—"

"You are like a butterfly, it is your nature; and yet this enjoyment is your labour. You see, there are also many differences among men with whom I am so constantly in contact; some are industrious, like me, and work themselves to death; others enjoy themselves as you do—they live in nature, they listen to and learn from her; these are the poets; their work is to amuse; their fellow-men call them dreamers, and laugh at them, because they live in a world of their own creation, and which none others know. If they succeed, however, by means of words, sounds, or colours, in giving mankind a glimpse of their world, they are called poets, or artists, and are extolled, although their state is not one jot changed. Your lot is to live in the poetry of nature; to imprint the Creator in your heart through His works; be thankful for it, but do not jeer at mine."

Did the fairy understand him? Perfectly, and she was flattered by his words.

"It may be so," she said; "I must believe that it is your place to work; but, my poor fellow, it must be very hard, very tiresome!"

"Not in the least," replied Littlecap, drawing himself up; "you would hardly fancy how pleasant it is. There lie the black letters each in order in its own little compartment; it is my business to watch that they do not get mixed up together; and at night, as I sit on the case, I sometimes hear a doleful sigh—that is, when something is out of order, and a poor letter is complaining that he has got into strange company; some poor little *a* is being teased and laughed at by the great *A's*, or a vowel is plagued by the stiff consonants, for every one lives apart, or with his own set—then I come to their help and put them all in order, and when the compositor comes in the morning he little thinks what care I have taken all night; he picks them up from their cases and sets them together; and as the looker-on may see, they fall into terrible confusion; but he does it all according as men have written it for him; and when the letters are printed on paper, they speak such beautiful and clever things, that everyone takes pleasure in them. I read all the proofs; that is my recreation."

"A fine recreation," said Lilly, contemptuously.

Heinzelman grew more earnest, coughed as if he had taken some resolution, and said—

"We are friends, Lilli, and that gives me a right to speak freely to you; you are clever. you have mother wit."

"I should think so!"

"Do not interrupt me—but you want cultivation, and you despise science, and literature, because you know nothing about them —that is not right."

"Heinzelman," cried Lilli, turning away pouting, "you are ungallant."

"Let that be," said the elf, cosily rubbing his hands; "you know it is not ill-meant— you are so intellectual—what would you not do if you could but read, and you have so much leisure for it in winter."

"In winter?" said the fairy, still rather sulky; "it is just in winter that I have least time; then it is that I visit my dear flowers in the earth's bosom, as they sleep in their brown, hard, little seedling shells. I sit by them and talk to them about the sweet spring and sunny summer, when they will joyfully rouse themselves, and spring out in new life of fragrance, and bright tints; then I peep into the souls of the growing buds, and set them thinking, and they learn how they too must blossom, and blow, and adorn the world."

"The souls of the flowers?" asked Littlecap, in a tone of unbelief.

"Do you know nothing of them? Away then with your book-learning," cried Lilli; "if the flowers had no souls, how could they know what to do when they first appear above the sod?"

"You must tell me more about this," said Littlecap, with increasing faith. "In earlier times they used to write in books about the souls of the dead, but lately we have not heard much about them—go on."

"When the flowers wither," Lilli began, "the soul is in the fragrance (for the perfume is the flower's soul, as thought is man's), which still lies hidden in the dried up calyx It long hovers round the dead flower, and then spreads in the air. If man took more notice of these things, he might perceive how often a sweet fragrance steals through the air when the blossoms are opening, though he cannot trace its source. The dead flowers perish, the buds grow till they almost mingle with the earth in their turn ; but their souls reappear, and watch like faithful guardians over their new-born sisters, to whom they tell all they have seen in the course of their lives, all they have learnt of the wondrous ways of nature or of man ; they sing this softly to their charge, and it steals into the heart of the yet unformed flower. Thus, in the bosom of the silent earth, life and intelligence are constantly growing and renewing, but man cares not a doit for anything beyond the blossoms' colour, and make, yet they open to love and to serve him."

" You are poetical, Lilli," remarked Littlecap.

" Will you have a proof?" asked Lilli ; and leaning back, she broke a forget-me-not from the flowers that shaded her seat " Look at this flower—you know the meaning that man attaches to it, it is a Forget-me-not."

" *Myosotis pratensis*, or mouse-ear," said Littlecap, correcting her

" What do I care for your learned names ?" continued Lilli ; " we and man's feelings have called it Forget-me-not. It is a flower sacred to friendship and fidelity ; she knows that much now, while she is growing on her little green stalk ; but she is still untaught, and wants feeling ; on opening, she will be of a red colour, love's own tint ; this is her first dress, but in good time her soul teaches her better, and she paints herself of a deep blue, and her petals rise up from her deep yellow cup, like a prayer to the true hearted, as a solace in the hour of separation. Why should she do this if she did not know her name and its meaning ?"

Littlecap, who had studdied all the botanical literature in the world, could not, with all his science answer that question.

" And yet you look down upon me because I cannot read," continued Lilli ; " you think perhaps that there are no other books than those made out of your ugly black letters. Poor Littlecap, you know more of your stupid printer's room than of all the rest of the world. The Creator has a thousand other ways of writing, but you cannot read them. I understand many of them : see this Forget-me-not leaf ; look at this soft blue velvet ; and see, when I hold it against the sun, the tiny veins—how they cross each other—so complicated, and yet so regular—do you think they have no sense or plan when the flower springs open so full of meaning ? Do you think that Nature's handwriting is less legible than your compositor's, when he picks up his letters from

the cases which you keep tidy for him ? Every stroke has a sense, each fibre a plan, each breath a thought ; something is legibly printed on each petal. I can read it, and so could you, if you were a poet instead of a printer."

Heinzelman pondered between curiosity and unbelief over the fairy's words. He would not ask her to read to him, lest she should think he believed her ; and yet he would have liked much to know what was written on the leaves. He expected it would be a scientific classification of the species, a catalogue that each had in their possession He winked his eyes as if he knew all about it, and let drop a half-question—" But all these flowers say exactly the same things ?"

" Not at all," answered Lilli ; " the Creator's rich invention never repeats itself. Since you are so clever and highly-educated," she continued, with some irony, " I will tell you more about it. You know how the souls of flowers watch over the germinating root ; when the flower itself appears, a story is written on each leaf, so that for those who have learned to read it, it is a book with many pages. I read these in my leasure hours, and yet you mock at me because I do not cultivate literature. What should I know about mankind, with whom I never associate, if the flowers did not teach me ?"

" Well, then, tell me what is written on this Forget-me-not," cried Littlecap.

" Very simple things. What adventures can happen to a poor Forget-me-not ?"

" Only just what is on the five leaves of the one you are now holding—do, do, my clever, pretty little friend."

Lilli silently studied the leaf for so long a time, that Littlecap expected that she would not be able to decipher anything.

" This is not like one of your books, where one begins at the first opening," she remarked. " We must first find the clue ; the rest quickly follows."

" Like soothsayers, who predict the future from the lines in a man's hand," Littlecap observed.

" Pretty nearly," she replied ; " but my art is more certain. Listen : on this leaf is the story of a Forget-me-not's soul. She says—

" On the meadow where I blossomed, two dear children were running and playing about ; a girl, with light waving curls, a brown-haired boy, some years older ; they were hunting butterflies—at least the girl was ; but the boy thought more of her than of his sports. They were born in the same village.

" Oh, dear," cried the girl, " it is muddy here in this deep ditch, and there is such a beautiful butterfly, a peacock's eye, flown across it, and I cannot get over."

She stood mournfully at the edge of the ditch, as if a large fortune had vanished from her before she had had time to enjoy it. Who knows if her grief and loss were not quite as great?"

"Don't try it," said the boy, "I will carry you across."

"No, no, you will let me fall," she answered.

But the peacock's eye was still fluttering on the other side; she could nearly reach him with her net. The boy wanted to lead her away; but the fair child, still intent on her butterfly, waved him back.

"Quick, quick!" she cried, "there he is again."

At this, the boy took her in his arms, and leaped into the ditch, where he stood with his dear little burden.

"What will you give me for my help," he asked.

"Nothing; but do make haste, I am too heavy for you."

"Nothing! Then, I will stop here."

"Stupid fellow! you will stick fast. What do you want?"

"A kiss!"

"Oh! silly," and she suddenly turned her head.

"Ah, what beautiful flowers!" and, forgetting her chase and her attendant's request—"you must pick them for me."

And she lightly sprung from his arms, and stood on the other side; the boy still remained in the water.

"Do you want the Forget-me-nots?" he asked.

"Yes, yes!"

So he began to pick them while she joyfully clapped her hands.

"What are you going to do with those flowers?"

"I will set them in a vase full of water, with a stone at the bottom, there their stems will take root; and I will keep them in my mother's room, where they will grow and open."

Soon after, they were seated side by side on the bank.

The girl was arranging a nosegay from the flowers he had gathered for her, her apron was full of them; the boy was thoroughly happy, and had forgotten that she had cheated him of his kiss.

"Give me a flower to keep for your sake," he petitioned.

"No! why did you want to steal a kiss from me just now?" and catching up the corners of her apron, she raced off towards her home.

The boy frowned, doubled up his fist, and shook it at her; the next moment he walked off on his way as if nothing had crossed him. We Forget-me-nots were treated as they had settled; we grew up, opened our budding flowrets, and began to prattle to each other, and to wonder what had become of the boy whom we had never again seen: but our thoughtless little owner had quite forgotten us, the butterfly, and the coveted kiss.

At last the boy came on a message from his mother, and as he was waiting for an answer, his eye fell on us, his cheek flushed, and when her mother's back was turned, he stepped over to us, and, plucking me from the vase, hid me in his breast.

"What are you doing?" asked the lady.

"Nothing!" he answered; but he grew still redder, and drew his coat over me.

As soon as possible, I was placed between the leaves of his Latin grammar, and there remained till winter. When the snow was deep on the ground, the school-boys began snowballing each other one day, and the books were laid on a stack of wood, when I, slipping out, was carried in with the logs, and was burnt in the school-room stove, as the boy was reprimanded for continually turning over the pages of his book in lesson time, and would not say what he was looking for. I never could discover, however, why he blushed when he stole me from the vase."

"That is the story of the first leaf," said Lilli, pulling it off, and letting it fall into the stream; "it is finished. There are four more on the cup."

Littlecap was not quite certain what he ought to say about the story, and had sat the whole time in painful impatience; he was half waiting for the point, half inclined to give a criticism which might gently guide his friend to it.

"Very good, very pretty indeed," he remarked; "but you must just once read my books. There is so much more in them, and there would have been written a heap of wonderful circumstances which occurred between the children before they became a pair; I have been expecting something of the sort all along."

"I know no more about that than my Forget-me-not does," replied Lilli; "it is no book, it is but a leaf, and my poor flower's soul has told no more than the adventures she herself experienced: shall I go on?"

"It will be all the same to the end," replied Littlecap, "just what happens to Forget-me-nots, and a few other flowers."

"Let us see."

She held the second leaf against the sun, studied it a few moments, and then began fluently to translate what the other soul related.

"I was born on the banks of a sparkling river, though I could not see its waters, for a small meadow, damp with the water drops which the rolling waves scattered over it, and with the tiny streams which glided along it through sand and pebbles, was the place where I, with many sisters, first sprung from the earth.

I used to hear a rushing, rumbling noise, but I never saw anything, perhaps because I was scarcely full blown, and it was but a day since my leaves had unfolded themselves; but on the other side I saw the high cliffs, to which three ruined castles still clung, rising from the valley, and the only sunset I witnessed cast a ruddy glow over them. He soon sunk, and I was yet watching the still beauty of the evening, when I heard a confused sound of men's voices, the tramping of horses, and the measured plash of oar's in the water; I turned with all my might from the old towers, towards which my flowery eyes had been directed, in the hope of seeing more.

I felt my curiosity increasing, and pushed my head between my sisters, till I had space to see all that was going on in the road behind me.

A long procession of young men arrived on horses and in carriages. First came three horsemen in boots high above the knees and fitting close to them, and swords by their sides, their scarfs fluttered across their breasts, their heads hardly covered by the little gold embroidered cap. Then came a carriage drawn by six horses, and more riders with swords; these were followed by some carriages-and four, and then came many two-horse concerns.

A loud halt! was sounded: the young men, all with the tiny student's cap on their flowing locks, descended, while the carriages and horses were left in utter disorder to get home as they could.

A boat, with streamers of the same colour as the scarfs and caps, and further decked with garlands of flowers and branches of oak, was waiting for them at the river's edge, while its band welcomed their arrival with its strains.

Most of them embarked immediately, but some wandered with gleesome steps along the bank; the ferry-boat started, the music struck up a student's song, and the young voices mingled with it, and echoed through the air; the oars moved in time to the melody; and I again wistfully turned my looks towards the old castle, which, in the sun's rays, and in the glory that the song threw over them, braved the festive groups. I was suddenly withdrawn from my profound meditations. The students who had remained behind had each gathered some flowers or sprays, and wound them round their caps. One cap alone wanted this ornament; its owner remembered it just as he came opposite to us; he stooped, and with one grasp I and many others were plucked; a large gar-

land of forget-me-nots was fastened on his cap, and I rejoiced at it, as now I should join in the feast, and help to grace an assembly of students.

They soon all left the boat, and roamed over mountain or dale, as chance or pleasure directed.

I bent over my wearer's brow from the castle which I had watched so curiously from afar; he bore me through ivy and brambles to the highest point of the old tottering walls. I saw the wide, wide world before me, and looked—to my shame be it spoken—with aversion, on the lowly spot where I was born.

The students who had followed us went further. My friend clambered all over the loose masonry; my head turned and swam. A yellow wall flower, whom I had offended in climbing up, mocked at me.

"What are you doing here, you flower of the dale?"

I looked at her with a proud smile, but was far above her; and before I could answer, my friend sat himself astride the wall, threw his arm round an old tree, whose roots had crept down deep in the damp stones, and gazed as I did on the wide earth outspread beneath us.

He had heated himself in climbing, so he took off his cap, on which I still waved, and laid it on a large stone by his side; the first surprise was over, and I rocked myself into such an uncommonly-melancholy train of thought, and was in such a lyrical mood, that I was inclined to compose a poem, which should reflect back the deep tone engendered by the ruins in my neighbourhood. The same idea must have struck my student, for he took out his pocket-book, laid himself on the stone beside his cap, and began to write with his pencil.

I was most anxious to look over him, for I felt sure that he had taken my poem from me before I had even begun it, and of which I felt not a little proud; but the cap, and I with it, were too far away; the sun fell straight on the paper; the student thought a moment, and then placed his cap so that its flower shaded his writing, and I was thus enabled to read. I was full of joy and admiration—not a bit like my song—no tears for the past, no expectations for the future—nothing but admiration for the rich scenery! Undoubtedly its writer was a student—a student! that is a reason for every eccentricity.

"What are you doing up there?" cried a voice from below.

"Nothing," answered my student, who, looking very red, clasped his pocket-book, threw his cap on his head, and swung himself quickly from the tower, whilst many loose stones rolled after him. Then he went with hasty steps down the mountain to the inn by the water side, where the whole company had joyfully aassembled in one room.

A long table was laid out with many bottles on it, and at each end two naked swords formed a cross; the musicians were in the orchestra, and opposite to them was a gay transparency, on which the students' arms were painted. Flowers were spread over the tables and hung from the walls; their coats were thrown aside; but each wore the three coloured ribbon across his breast; a sign was given with the swords, everyone took his place, and the repast began.

All was felicity, brimming over with joy, youthful energy, youthful pleasure, youthful riches! their glasses were quickly emptied and re-filled; they were pledging each other on all sides.

The music now struck up one of their songs; the swords again clashed against the table.

"Silentium!" shouted their president.

Their talking ceased, and their voices joined in the inspiring burden of their song. The first was sacred to friendship; and I, the flower of friendship, waved to the melody as they sung; and I glanced proudly on the other flowers that garnished the caps, tables, and walls, as if I myself were the hero of the song; and when, at the last verse, they all stood up and their glasses clinked against each other, while each hand was firmly grasped by some cordial friend, and each sought the other's eye.

I felt as happy as if every drop of melancholy had been pressed from my cup; I was no longer a sentimental floweret. Thus they went on deep into the night, ever growing louder and more jocund, and many a true outpouring was then whispered to a friendly ear.

My student passed his arm round a friend's neck, and they went out together on the balcony. Above us were the starry heaven's beneath, the flowing Neckar; behind us, the old castles were dimly shadowed forth in the decreasing light; near us the jingling glasses, the song of many voices. My student pressed his friend's hand; I knew he was full of happiness, for I had read his lay.

Once more the swords clashed, and "Silentium," resounded through the room; all were silent, and resuming their coats, returned to their places. After the storm of merriment came a dead calm.

"Our fatherland!" cried the president, and then that glorious air began.

The first verse was sung just as the preceding songs had been; at the second, the two students, who presided at each end of the table, rose and brandished their swords in time to the music.

As each took his oath, he leaned his hands on the crossed swords with which his cap had been run through.

Then they passed the swords to their next neighbours; and as the song proceeded, the caps were pierced in time to the music, until the four swords met in the middle of the table. It fared ill for us poor flowers, and I fell off, severed by the steel; but I pushed my head up among the caps, and thus saw how the swords travelled round the table. The song was over, and now the President began another.

Each student caught up his own cap, and placed it on his head; and as soon as all were covered, the president put on his own, and waving his sword, exclaimed, '*Ex est commercium, initium fidelitatis!*" A hurrah, which they seemed to have with some difficulty repressed during the previuos ceremony now burst forth; the walls shook, the glasses jingled. We had been first shaken off or cut from the caps, and now we were strewn about the floor and tables. Even the Forget-me-nots were forgotten; and he who had plucked me and sworn eternal friendship by our name, cared not, knew not of our fate. My neighbour fell on the stem of his glass, and hung there, and when he drank his last pledge, she gave him a farewell kiss and dropped exhausted at his feet. I envied her. But yet, torn and mangled as we were, we were not quite unobserved. His friend saw me; a sudden memory struck him; he picked me up. "A Forget-me-not!" he murmured; it is just such another as the one she refused me long ago, and she is grown up and is very lovely. Would she refuse it to me now? As if she would give it to me now? He sighed, and laid me between the leaves of his song book.

There I breathed my last. If the youth opened his book again that year, of what did the poor shrivelled Forget-me-not remind him? Of the maiden at home, or of the student's revel at Necker Steinach?"

Littlecap had listened attentively to the end, whether from interest, gallantry, or resignation, we cannot say. "Yes, men have wonderful Tom-fooleries," he remarked; "especially when they happened to be students."

"Our Forget-me-not appears to be quite full of it," said Lilli; "it almost drew tears from her."

"A Forget-me-not cannot want subjects to cry over" Littlecap resumed.

"And what dreadful things happened to it!" interrupted Lilli.

"Ah, poor Forget-me-not—and such nonsense too? the train of carriages, the drinking, and then spoiling their caps, making holes in them!"

"May be so" Lilli replied; "I am not going to defend my tale;" and she let the second leaf fall into the rivulet.

Perhaps Littlecap meant to improve its contents, for he stooped forward to prevent her, but the stream carried the leaf far from his reach.

"That's a pity," he said, "I should like to have written out the description of the student's party."

"What's the use ?" asked the fairy; "there are a thousand prettier stories than this written on the leaves."

"I might have made use of it, perhaps, when I had managed to find time to write it off on the blank side of a proof sheet. It is good enough for that, though it is not worth much. We have this sort of stories handsomely printed, and bound up with gold edges and fine vignettes. These books stand upon tables now, instead of the other baubles mankind used to be so fond of setting out for show. They like their outsides, and sometimes turn over the pages, but I do not think they care much for their contents."

"A queer race, they are," laughed Lilli; "and so you call that having a taste for literature ?"

The sun had now sunk, the twilight spread over all, and the evening mist rose from the damp ground, and hung over the place where the pair sat, like a broad moist veil stretching out in the night air. Littlecap pulled his hat over his ears, and buttoned up his coat, while Lilli, making herself a seat of the floating thistle-down, prepared to read the third page.

"You will spoil your eyes," said her friend, endeavouring to take the flowers from her.

She laughed, and, half rising from her seat, called out in a clear, silvery voice—

"Now glow-worms, wake up, trim your lamps, and light me !"

Immediately the sparkles began to twinkle through the grass till the meadow grew lighter and lighter; the little torches moved through the mist, first slowly, then more quickly, till they glittered and shone all around.

"Come here to me," the fairy again cried, "and those who stand quite still, and light me nicely, shall hear my story."

Then the rays shone about them, some from their mossy seat, others from the flowers which overhung it, till the friends were in a flood of light.

* * * * *

I was not born in the free air of nature. A lofty and spacious room, with glazed walls and roof, saw me burst forth into existence. It was very pretty there; but we sadly missed the pure free air.

We were a large party of flowers, collected from all parts of the world. The stately palm waved its branches there; the wonderful butterfly-orchis of the Orcades hung from the roof, and threw its tendrils and perfume around; the coquettish camellia contrasted her rich waxen flowers with her shining leaves; the pomegranate displayed her vivid fiery tints.

How they all were called, and if they ever conversed with each other on the home-sickness plants and flowers can feel, I really cannot tell you. I will own that I had no regrets for my own home; but I heard that I had left it many years since; that I had been taken from it in my earliest youth. The sunbeams told me this. They used to visit us when the matting was taken off our windows, and we could look out on a world covered with ice and flaky snow.

"But why should they set us ?" I used often to ask of a clump of violets who stood near me; "why should they place us, of whom they generally think so little, in the company of so many choice, highborn, foreign plants ?"

We had not much time to ponder over the question, for the gardener, our guardian and nurse, came one day and cut flowers and branches away, and carried us all off. Tender hands bound us together in small posies, laid us in a crystal vase, covering us up well against the winter, and carried us away all at once.

I was half-frozen by the blast which pierced through our protecting cloth, and yet half-rejoiced in the free pure air; and occupying myself with myself, I at last attained the same resignation with which a dark camellia braved the wintry breezes. I also heard the soft moans of an orange blossom, who was tightly bound up and lay helpless under the leaves, while a hardy erica endeavoured to console her.

But suddenly a warm and perfumed air stole upon us—a dazzling light burst through our prison—its cover was removed—the wonders of a ball-room were revealed to my astonished gaze—light streamed from the dazzling chandelier which hung from the roof—radiance glittered along the walls—a crowd of elegantly-dressed and beautiful young people were collected together—the melodious tones of the orchestra resounded through the room, and the couples moved in unison to its electric measure.

We must have been brought in as the revelry was drawing to an end; a myrtle spray which had escaped from a lady's bouquet, and, being carelessly tossed into the vase, had fallen near me, explained all the mysteries which had so suddenly burst upon and bewildered me.

We flowers were set down in a corner, and no one seemed to pay any attention to us; we stood in a window-niche on a jardinière, so that I could see everything.

At first, I was entirely occupied with the blaze of light which, with the softest tones of the music, pervaded equally every corner of the room, with the brilliant dresses, and the lovely faces.

At last I became sufficiently composed to look into particulars, and my friendly myrtle was ready to answer my minutest questions. How wonderfully they moved about! How softly the young men stepped up to the ladies—how lowly they bowed before them—how reverently they received the yielded hand!

In a second more, the same couple were rushing past us, their eyes laughing, their bosoms heaving. and the fragile form of the lady trembling on the arm that was clasped round her. But when they returned to their place, there was the same low bow, the same stately cerimonial. It was a sudden blazing up—as suddenly extinguished. And now a longer pause ensued. At last, the instruments began a few sounds; people hurried up and down; the chairs were all pushed up together; the ladies were conducted to their places; those who did not dance seated themselves. The first couple opened the dance—the lady was the queen of the night; she was a beautiful girl, tall, and slightly made; her fair hair hung down in ringlets; her almost regal brow was crowned with the fuchsia's delicate bells; her eyes sparkled through the room brighter than the diamonds which shone on her bosom. and her lovely arm, with its heavy-jewelled bracelet, lay lightly on her partner's. The myrtle twig soon remarked my curiosity:

" She is the daughter of the house, and they were celebrating her betrothal," he said: " her partner is her betrothed. I know it because I belonged to her bouquet; and that, and her whole dress, were presents, from him." " How happy she must be!" I sighed. Near the recess sat an old lady and her daughter, who, most probably had found no partner; they were talking to a gentleman standing by them. " Her mother caught him immediately; the task was easy enough; he is not over bright;" " We were most intimate friends at school," said the daughter. " It is scarcely a week since she told me how excessively tiresome she found him; but she is such a flirt and—" " It is a capital match for her," said the gentleman. Two young officers came near us in the dance.

" She is lovely!" said one " But utterly heartless," replied the other. A young man, dressed in black, stood opposite me, leaning against a door-post; he did not dance, and spoke but little; but his dark eye constantly followed the bewitching creature, who was the theme of conversation—the observed of observers. I pitied him, though I knew not what for. I had thought we flowers were

entirely forgotten; but they placed the vase in which we lay so quietly, on a little table in the middle of the room. A gentleman stepped up to it, took out a nosegay, and presented it to a lady; a look, a dance, were the return for his gift. The vase was soon empty; the last dancer had made his choice; and the nosegay in which I was, lay neglected at the bottom.

The young man who had so watched the affianced beauty now left his place for the first time. He hurried up to the vase.

"A Forget-me-not!" he cried : and hastily seizing us, carried us to the daughter of the house.

As he bowed before her, his dark eye cast a penetrating glance at her. She could not bear his look; hers bent beneath his; she took the flowers; and, as if to evade observation, said,—

"A Forget-me-not! Do you remember the time when we were children, and used to gather them in the fields ?"

"And later still," he answered; "but we have no need of memories to-night."

He took her hand, and they danced round the room. I looked for him a few minutes after, but his place was empty—he had vanished. The dance came to an end, the company disappeared, the room was empty. The beautiful girl tossed away her many nosegays, trophies of the admiration she had elicited; but she still held mine fast in her hand. She left the room, looking indifferently on the dazzling lights and the flowers that strewed the floor. Her step was firm, her eye clear, her head as proudly raised as ever. She went to her room, where her maid was waiting for her; the garland was quickly removed from her hair, the diamonds unfastened, the costly bracelets unclasped, she threw them on the table without a second look.

She hurriedly dismissed her maid, who left her standing in the middle of the room: but she did not turn to her couch She again drew near to the table where all her ornaments lay. Was it to take another joyful look at the elegance and value of the jewels in which she had shone ?

She snatched up the poor nosegay; her fingers trembled as they sought among the leaves and flowers. I felt for her; I knew she was looking for me. She thrust everything on her dressing-table on one side; a costly brooch rolled on the ground; she never heeded it, but caught up her scissors, severed the string which bound us together, pushed the other flowers away, and seized on me. She bowed her head over me.

My heart too sunk withered, for a hot drop fell in my cup, and as I looked up once more, how I wondered that they should have called her cold and haughty! Her head was bent, tears rolled from her beautiful eyes over her pale cheeks ; her whole countenance was changed. Was she not happy, then ? Had she a heart ?

She sank in her chair, and laid her head on her hand. How long she laid there I know not. The taper was burnt out, day was peeping in through the shutters. I fancied I saw a dark shadow pass before the window. She started up, took an unpretending little locket from her dressing-table, and unclasped it. A lock of hair fell from it. She laid me, who, till then, she had held in her hand, in the case. I felt it; but first she pressed me to her lips—and I died in that kiss.

Lilli was silent.

" Is it over ? " asked Littlecap ; " your stories always finish just as one thinks they are beginning."

The fairy made no answer, but let the third leaf fall into the water. Fortunately, the stars were coming out, or she would not have been able to read, for the glowworms had fallen asleep.

" They are a lazy set," said Lilli, and she stirred up the grass until the worms were frightened, and their lamps began to sparkle on all sides as they swarmed about.

" I pay you for your trouble," she continued. " I am reading a story to you ; mind, you help me through it."

After all, what interest could the poor little glowworms, born in a meadow, take in the pleasures of a ball-room ? Littlecap himself could not see what they had to do with it.

" Do you know," he asked, " why the glow-worms have lights ?"

" That we fairies may see on nights when the moon does not shine, and when the stars are hidden behind the clouds," was the answer.

Littlecap laughed in his sleeve. He had a touch on the tip of his tongue at the elfin egotism which only saw a provision for its own especial comforts in the Creator's handiwork ; but he kept back these remarks, and prepared to give a scientific explanation of this fact in natural history.

" I do not ask for the reason," he said, " but for the producing causes."

" I know them," Lilli replied.

Littlecap was astonished and rather disappointed to find that he could not bring out his vast stock of knowledge respecting electricity and phosphorescent emanations ; but Lilli chattered away without attending to him.

" The caterpillars had a wedding, and all the moths, beetle, and chafer tribe were invited to it. Many had a long journey to make, and grew tired on the road. It was night, for the moths travel best at that time,

just as the butterflies prefer to go out in the sunshine. The travellers were near the place which they had settled to reach, before the first rays of morning ; but between them and it lay a bog, on which the wildfire was merrily dancing. The party stopped short, and began to consult as to what must be done.

" We cannot cross over," said a prudent cockchafer, " this wandering flame will burn our wings."

" Then let us fly round the marsh," said a moth ; but the smaller travellers would not agree to that ; they were tired, and did not like to go out of their way.

" Let us take a dragon-fly for guide ; they are all well acquainted with this bog," advised a ladybird.

But the little ones would hear of no roundabout paths. After some more debating, the larger beetles endeavoured to fly over the marsh, and the little ones remained melancholy behind, fearing to lose the wedding-feast. Time passed on; a will-o'-the-wisp came nearer to them ; the poor things stood undecided; at last the glowworms, who were then nothing but common grey beetles, spoke up—

" We have courage ; we will go on, and see if the flames will injure us ; stay on the edge of the bog, and watch the issue of our adventure."

And thus it happened. The grey beetles cautiously and softly crawled on to the shining fiery sprite. At first, when he danced up to them, they were frightened, and turned back to the spectators, who were already triumphing over their defeat. But this spurred them up to new attempts. They soon surrounded the jack o'-lantern, and rejoiced to find that there was nothing to fear from the flames which had so alarmed them; for they had expected to be blinded by the rays which he sent right against them, and yet not one of them was in the least injured. Again they fearlessly attacked the enemy, who was soon so environed, cut at, and bound, that he was obliged to yield himself prisoner, and was dragged in triumph to the firm ground. The other insects would now have taken part in the war, and shared the poor prisoner as common booty; but the little beetles claimed their entire right to him, as they alone had attacked him.

He was laid upon an old trunk of a tree, and hewn in pieces with a long blade of grass, whose sharp edge served them as a saw, so that each could have a little bit of his clear ray, which they securely fastened to their tails.

The travellers now proceeded securely over the bog, uninjured by the wild-fires, who, frightened at their brother's fate, left the place free for them. And what rejoicings there were, as the little insects came up to the bride, and paid her their compliments long before the big ones arrived, tired and worn out with their long flight, for the dragon-fly had carelessly led them astray, and mischievously left them to find their way as they best could. When the others asked them how they had managed to cross the burning marsh, they bent their feelers, and mumbled out a few unintelligible words, the glowworms having begged them not to say a word about their prowess, for they love quiet better than anything; so they wished to be silent about the resolution they had displayed.

They day passed on, and the high feasting of the nuptial evening began; the big moths and chafers had been resting, and rose quite recovered; everyone was making their toilet; the glowworms alone looked shabby in their plain grey coats, and were scarcely distinguishable in the grass. A golden beetle, who had taken some time to dress himself, looked down contemptuously on them, in his green and gold clothes, and said—

"Poor fellows, you really cannot set off those dusty cloaks of yours, or else I would offer you some gold filings which I cannot use, and which you will find on a grassy knoll beside a dewdrop, which serves me for a looking-glass."

"We are much obliged to you," answered a glowworm, offended by his airs of patronage; "but though we have no gold embroidery to boast of as you have, we have a still more brilliant ornament, which you are in want of."

With these words they all lifted their wings up, the bright rays shone out, and there was no end to the wonder and admiration they excited when they whizzed into the marriage party. They were the heroes of the company; and the caterpillar, the blushing bride, was lighted to her home by them. That is a long while ago, but the glowworms have kept their sparkling rays ever since; and if by chance they are extinguished, they go and find a jack-o'-lantern, and share him between them."

"Stuff!" shouted Heinzelman, losing patience, at last; "it is sheer nonsense."

"No, indeed," the fairy earnestly replied, "it is quite true; I have heard it from creditable authority, just as I give it to you; and if you should happen to go through the wood at night, you may judge for yourself. There stands many an old trunk of a tree in the damp grass, shining and glittering through the darkness—some think that a treasure lies buried there; but they must dive deep who come to take it up. The glowworms bind the will-o'-the-wisp on these stumps, and then they shine for a long, long time, for neither rain nor dew can ex-

tinguish them, since they spring from boggy places, and water does not injure them. There lies a splinter of this sort of wood; I will take it at once and fasten it by our seat, so that it may light us while I read you what the fourth petal says. The stars also are coming to help me; so I think I shall manage it."

Before Littlecap could make the least opposition, Lilli was in full career, and thus she deciphered the fourth story.

"I am the latest born, the last bud of a large family. Many of my sisters, who had blown in the same year with me, had reached their appointed time; many had lost their last leaves; and the bare green stem, bereft of its blue crown, stood up ungracefully on the plain. They were born in the bright days of spring and summer; I came forth on a cold, foggy, autumnal day; so veiled, I scarcely saw the few rays the sun sent through the alders and willows which grew about the barren land where my lot was cast. As far as I could see, there was nothing but damp, marshy ground, and a few full-blown flowers, whose leaves were brushed off by the cold breezes. The colours and perfume accorded to my predecessors, the children of a happier time, were faint and dead with us. My eyes shed tears as I first opened them, for I felt my loneliness, though I could scarcely understand it. The sun sunk—its blood-red and shapeless ball hid itself behind the fog, which hung, heavy and moist, from the trees, who shook their branches angrily, as if they would chase it away.

I was expecting a dreary, solitary night; when I suddenly heard the regular tread of many steps in the distance, and the booming roll of metal, interrupted by words of command. It came nearer and nearer, falling more muffled on the mossy ground, and I soon saw the glitter of weapons glistening through the twilight. A division of soldiers came up in compact, close array, just like a strong wall, and quite near to the place where I was growing; and I shrunk behind a large stone, so as not to be crushed under foot.

"Halt!" cried their captain; and they stood as if rooted to the ground. A few more words were spoken, but the wind bore them from me.

A small division were sent off, who began to scour the ground, and were soon lost to my gaze, nor could my ear long follow the sound of their steps, but the ranks of those who remained were soon dispersed; a part went so far away, that I could scarcely discern their figures in the grey background, and those who remained began to disencumber themselves of their weapons and knapsacks. The dead silence, which had only been broken by the word of command, was followed by an unrestrained merry hum of voices, all busy and free. As in my neighbourhood alone the ground was level, and thickly strewn with large stones. some seated themselves there; others wandered into the elder thicket, and many rolled themselves up in their cloaks, and rummaged in their knapsacks. The officers formed themselves into a circle; but I could not discover whether they were still under command, or whether entire liberty of speech prevailed amongst them.

"At a little distance, I remarked the serjeants, who were noting down the adjutant's whispered directions. Again all was quiet, but not for long. We heard the sound of horses' hoofs in the distance, and of clattering swords, and a squadron of Hussars galloped up. They halted and dismounted; stakes were run into the ground, that they might make their horses fast; man and beast were busy. I could not notice everything for it grew darker and darker, and my attention soon became absorbed in what took place in my immediate neighbourhood. The soldiers, who had been wandering through the wood, now came in with large faggots, and laid them on the ground which the others had cleared from the stones. From all sides of the heath fires were beginning to burn up. At first, the smoke from the green fuel whirled thickly round; then the flames burst out, and the light sparks shot up high in the black night. It was a wet, cold evening; rain-drops fell on us, and the wind blew roughly and dispersed the smoke of the bivouac fires on all sides. Every one was now at rest; a cheerful chat began among all the parties; the smart jest was interchanged and applauded by a laughing chorus; the soldier's flask was handed round, and here and there a soldier's song rose over the moor, and won a new outbreak of praise; the trumpeter tuned some merry lay; the officers joked with each other by their fire, or, seated on the drums, formed a still smaller circle. It was a many-coloured, moving picture; the groups of men lying about now seen clearly by the fire-light, now half hidden in the smoke and night; the numerous uniforms mixed up, but contrasting with each other, and for a background the glistening weapons standing in clusters, and the horses, who, with their backs to the fire, were busily emptying their nosebags.

Gradually the place became quieter; one after another they coiled themselves up more tightly in their cloaks, and, stretched at full length, or leaning their backs against the trees, fell soundly asleep.

The rain ceased; we could hear the sentries' footsteps, and distinguish the patrols' cries. The fire had burned down; only two remained by it, and they were quite close to me; a lieutenant of infantry, and a doctor in an Hussar regiment, who sat in confidential talk.

They were old friends, and had met at that fire after a long separation. I had noticed them from a distance, and was glad when they came so near to me. The lieutenant seated himself on the very stone which sheltered me; the surgeon, wrapped in a woollen mantle, lay at his feet. I could hear them so nicely.

The surgeon looked well, and well pleased with the world; the officer's face and voice, even in the pleasure of seeing an old friend, and talking of old times, bore the tokens of deep sorrow.

Among other memories, they recalled the years when they had studied together in Heidelberg. Happy hours were brought to mind; the rollicking drinking-parties which they had celebrated; and many a name was mentioned whose owner had formed part of their jovial crew, before fate dispersed them all; and then they wondered at being brought together, most likely but for a few hours, in a situation of which they had once little thought.

The earnest soldier service, and the swords at their sides, reminded them of their playing at soldiers in their college days, and they smiled over those bygone moments.

The surgeon asked the lieutenant what had induced him to enter the service. This question cast a deep shade over his face, he made no answer. and both sank into silence. A noise, a loud call roused them from this pause. Some weapons had fallen down a little way off. The noise and the sudden glare of the fire had startled one of the horses; it had broken loose and severely injured the soldier who was grooming it, and the surgeon was called from his friend's side. The other remained alone, looking silently and wistfully into the dreary night. I felt that I understood what was passing within him. The happy remembrance of earlier years, when he was full of hope and exultation, were constrating themselves with those of later days, over which he was still grieving. At last he woke up from his reverie; he shook his dark locks from his brow, as if he could shake his cares off also, and opening his coat, pulled out his watch. Something shining clinked against the stone on which he sat, and fell amongst the grass —his watch chain had broken. He bent down and holding his glimmering cigar as a light, felt about for it. One of its rings had entangled itself so completely in my leaves, that he picked us up together. "A Forget-me-not?" he said, "whch chance thus places in my hand. It is strange—again this little flower; I will accept it, as an omen of the approaching battle.

He placed me in his waistcoat pocket, and drawing his cloak more tightly around him, laid himself down to sleep by the expiring embers. There I lay on a man's beating heart; how it stirred and heaved with secrets close locked within it! I listened at the silent chamber, and followed each pulsation, as they beat higher or more gently, according to the sleeper's dream. Morning broke, the fog rolled sullenly away, dispersed by a sharp wind. The sun rose—rose to open a day full of fatal destines. The beat of the drum roused the sleepers; the trumpets summoned men and horses. They were all quickly armed and ready, in the same perfect order I had admired on the preceding evening.

"March !" cried the commanders, and the foot-soldiers stepped with measured tread over the heath, and I with them, still resting on my bearer's heart. We soon reached a high-road, and then we went on, with a quick but cautious step, till we gained a rising ground, where we were once more bid to halt. I could peep over a wide expanse of plain; a bushy ground lay before us; behind that a high wall protecting a village, from whence rose a hill thickly covered with trees. The walls and village were in the enemy's hands in the foreground. The line of battle was marked out. The troops whom I accompanied formed the right wing.

"Third rank forwards !" was the word of command. The riflemen withdrew within the lines, and the officer who had taken charge of me offered to lead them on again.

We stood some time in silent expectation. The fight had already begun on the left wing; the enemy's artillery thundered from the heights, and our men were twice repulsed in an attack on them. The signal was given for us; the light infantry moved on, and I at the head of them, on their leader's breast. The ground was nearly gone over; the enemy should not drive them back. Firmly, manfully, my officer showed his spirit; his orders were given clearly, his eye was bright, his step steady; nothing betrayed his inward emotion. I only knew it, I only felt what was passing in that throbbing heart. Was it the excitement of the battle-field, the foreboding of death, the parting from life, which thus moved him? I know not. We had hardly crossed the ground, when a terrible fire was opened on us. Here and there one of our ranks fell, but "On, on !" was our leader's cry—forwards, was his example. The sharpest conflict was immediately under the walls; we mounted them, but our ranks were now much thinner.

The officer bid them fall in, and again the assault began. Then I could plainly hear his heart beating. Did he fear death, or was he seeking for it? The attack was repulsed this time, and again renewed. Death gaped at us from innumerable iron throats; I trembled for myself and my friend. A bayonet-thrust sank deep in his heart, and carried me far into the wound. He fell; the torn heart gave one last throb, one sigh escaped the bleeding chest, and all was still; he cared no more for earthly joys or sorrows. I died in his life-blood.

The fourth petal followed its predecessors; it clung for a moment to a stone on which it had fallen, but a dew-drop rolled from the moss, and washed it into the stream.

Lilli had something obscuring her eyes, and was obliged to rub them; but when Littlecap good-naturedly asked what was the matter with her, she began to scold at the stars for shining so dimly, and to complain of the difficulty of reading by their light. This was what he had already told her; but just as he was reminding her of it, and congratulating himself on his prudent forethought, she turned round, praised the stars, and assuring him that theirs was the very light for study, prepared herself to reveal the story of the fifth leaf.

Littlecap saw that all his reasoning would be thrown away, and therefore resigned himself once more to his friend's caprices, and to her course of reading.

But Lilli really seemed puzzled this time, as she bent over the leaf; and a look of mischievous joy, which was seldom seen in him, stole over Littlecap's features, as she owned that he was in the right, by saying——

"There really must have been something the matter with my eyes, for I have torn the golden cup, and part of the fifth leaf, in pulling away the fourth. Half the story is gone."

"Then, do not let us go on," said Littlecap, rising from his seat.

"Nonsense !" cried Lilli, detaining him. "I mean to read my story to an end; and you, who are so clever, and have studied so many books, and know all about mankind, and their concerns—you can clear up what is obscure. We shall soon have finished; there is nothing wanting after here. Now, listen:

The maiden stood at the window, and held me tightly. She passed her hand across her brow and eyes, and looked out into the distance. I followed her glance: a rider was galloping along the dale; it was he who—

"How are we to understand this, Lilli ?" Littlecap impatiently asked. "Who is the maiden ? How came the forget-me-not in her hand ? Who is he ? We don't know anything of all this."

Lilli had taken it into her head that she would decipher her flower from beginning to end.

"Don't interrupt me, dear friend," she said, "it is quite clear. It is a young maiden to whom a young man has, I should say, given a Forget-me-not. He is riding off, and she is looking after him. What else would you want? Now, let us go on; and the end will show if I am not right.

When he had vanished in the distance, she withdrew from her lattice; you might have thought that she had repressed her tears as long as he was in sight, lest they should obscure her gaze, for now, as she stood in her room, they fell in a stream over her cheeks. Then she smiled, even as she wept, and pressing me, whom she still held in her hands, to her lips, she murmured—

"Is it possible—is it really, really true—he loves me?"

She stepped across the room, her foot fell lightly, she was full of inexpressible delight. She stood before her mirror; she saw her features so full of soul, and they seemed dearer to her since he loved them. She was surprised to see traces of her tears.

"I weep," she cried, "now that I am happier than I ever was in my whole life."

She smiled and dried her eyes, but they still overflowed; and between crying and laughing, the tears stood like diamonds on her cheeks. She paced the room to and fro; then she became more composed, and her thoughts, that had only been occupied with one object, appeared at length to take a farther range. She suddenly stood quite still.

"And grandmamma!" she cried, "my grandmother will never allow it; I can never tell her of it!" Her blood seemed to turn cold; she stood there, so deadly pale, her tears frozen up, her eyes staring wildly, her lip quivering, her heart wildly beating. She listened, she heard steps slowly approaching, she shrunk together, flew to the work table, caught the first work that came to hand, and seated herself. I had fallen from her hand, and lay on the table before her. The door opened, and a venerable matron entered. Her unbroken figure, piercing eyes—shaded by her grey hair, and firmly-compressed lips, betokened pride and resolution. Her face was a book, on which Life had traced many pages. I saw this at the first glance, as she silently kissed her grandchild, who softly sunk her head before her. Her eyes had long forgotten how to weep. She looked anxiously at the girl, who felt her gaze, and bowed her head still lower. The matron's features never changed, but her searching glance read the lovely girl's countenance like an open book.

"You have been weeping," she said; "he is gone—you love him."

The poor child had never thought of revealing her sweet secret, but how could she deny him; he, the first, the sacred master

of her heart! She was silent; fresh tears answered for her. The grandmother, after a short pause, continued in a milder tone—"This is, most likely, the first battle of your life; but all who live must learn to fight with the world—and with their own hearts. You must forget him!"

The maiden's heart beat wildly.

"Forget!" she cried; "forget! No, never, never!"

"Child!" said the grandmother, "what must we not overcome in this life—what must we not forget?"

The grandchild softly shook her head. The feeling that had so newly sprung up in her young heart defied the sorrowful experience of old age.

"Has he spoken of anything to you? What did he say when he took his leave?" the old woman asked.

"Nothing," her grandchild answered. "But I feel sure of him—from his looks, from his touch, from his trembling hand, as he gave me these flowers for a farewell present."

She had let her work fall, and took me from the table. She held me out so proudly, so carefully to her; I embodied her lover's confession.

"A Forget-me-not!" said the matron; "a Forget-me-not!"

She sank back in her easy chair, and looked long and silently at me; her features worked, her heart began to heave, her thoughts were conjuring up, in the vacant space before her, things that were long, very long gone by. Her grandchild still stood by her side and watched her—half hoping, half fearing. She had never seen her thus, and she waited her decision.

"Go to my bureau," said the old woman; and the trembling girl heard her in silence: "open the little drawer—not that one; there, to the left. Move the letters! Do you see a little gold locket? That is it. Bring it to me, my child!"

The girl obeyed her. The grandmother took the locket in her thin, white hands; she pressed it—it opened; and a withered, yellow Forget-me-not lay within it.

"You love," she said. "Oh, you are happy!"

And her tears fell over the poor flower in her hands. The grandchild had never before seen her grandmother weep; the party-wall between them was destroyed; the crust melted off the old and frozen heart; she knelt at her feet, and, astonished at the unexpected secret revealed to her, exclaimed—

"You, too, have loved, grandmamma—you have loved!"

The grandmother drew her nearer to her, and kissing her forehead, whispered—

"You shall be his; you shall be happy!"

The maiden twined her arms tighter and tighter round the matron's neck, and in their embrace, I fell from her hands. They sat in silence for a long time. At length the grandmother rose, and closing the locket, which had never left her hands, carefully replaced it, with the withered Forget-me-not, in the drawer, where the girl had found it. I was forgotten, and perished on the floor. Love, in its happiness, wants no memorial!

The last leaf sunk into the rivulet, and Lilli rose from her seat. The dawning day was blushing over the horizon; the long grasses and flowers were raising their heads; the dew was sparkling cheerily.

"You must drink your waters,' said the fairy; "and I, who have been gossiping here with you the whole night, must see what the other elves are about. Let us go."

Littlecap also rose, and offered his arm to his friend to help her from her stone and over the meadows.

"Take care how you tread," he said, and don't hurt the Forget-me-nots at your feet."

Lilli laughed, and went off without further adieu. She stepped carefully and slowly along, winding in and out among the blue flowers, so as not to injure one of them.

CHAPTER CXLV.

MR. SQUABSHOT IS DEMONSTRATIVE.

THE guests who had formed the party at Mr. Osborne's country seat, had, after their several narratives, one by one, taken their departure. Our friend Squabshot, however, lingered on that spot, where to use his own phraseology, sat "the altar of his affections." He was loth to leave—so loth, indeed, that after several broad hints had been dropped by Miss Stanton, he still pertinaciously and obstinately persisted in remaining, looking the very picture of woe and despair—lovers generally do—according to the approved custom in poem, romance, and, indeed, in real life. The hour was growing late; nay, it had already done so—nevertheless Mr. Squabshot remained immovable, a very monument of woe.

"Mr. Squabshot," said Edith Staunton, after a pause. "You—that is—do you know the time?"

"The time," exclaimed the gentleman. "What care I for time. Time was made for slaves."

"Yes, but—"

"But what? You want to get rid of me. Is that your meaning, Miss Stanton?"

"Oh, dear no; I am pleased to be in your society; but you have to get home and—"

"Home!" exclaimed Squabshot. "I have no home, I am a waif and stray upon the ocean of life—a remnant—a salvage. What to me is the air I breathe—the sun, the moon, and stars? Nothing! positively and absolutely nothing! Worse than nothing."

"Law, Mr. Squabshot. Don't talk in that manner," exclaimed Miss Staunton.

"But I must talk in that way—I will!" said Squabshot, with sudden energy, which surprised his fair companion. "Look at me!"

Miss Staunton did look at him, and was compelled to bite her lips in the vain attempt to repress a smile.

"Am I not a wretched object?"

"I don't know—I should hope not," answered the lady.

"But I am, madam—I am most deplorably wretched."

"I am sorry to hear you say so. What can there possibly be to make you so wretched? You have youth, hope, and expectations. As yet you have but tasted half the sweets of life."

"Ah!" exclaimed Squabshot, with a prolonged emphasis, and then with a deep drawn sigh he said in hollow tones, "That is true enough—but too true!"

"Well, then, why grieve, Mr. Squabshot?"

"Why, madam? why? Great Heaven! can you ask such a question?"

"Yes, you see I do ask the question."

"Hang it," answered Squabshot, "I am choking, choking. Yes, madam, I cannot breathe."

He rose from his seat and paced the room twice or thrice with hurried footsteps. He paused suddenly, and confronted Miss Staunton.

"You love this man?" he exclaimed.

"Love who?"

"This reptile—this viper—this smooth-tongued, perfidious, double-dealing, hypocritical Meek."

"Hush! do not speak so loud—you are very rude, I must say so—you are very rude, and have been so on several occasions when you have met the Reverend Ozius Meek. He has not done anything to offend you that I am aware of." She could not help smiling when she made this last observation. Squabshot cast upon her a look of withering scorn.

"You defend him," he said suddenly." Oh, yes, of course you defend him!"

"And why not, if I think he is in the right," said Miss Staunton.

"In the right!" said her companion, as he recoiled back several paces and threw himself into the arm chair in which he had been previously seated. He muttered to himself several unintelligible sentences for some time, and then relapsed into silence. Miss Staunton saw plainly enough that her companion was in what might be termed a troublesome state, and she began to wish that he had taken it into his head to have taken his departure with the other guests, some hour or so earlier.

"It is somewhat late to enter into a discussion, which, to say the truth, at any time, and all times seems to vex and irritate you," she said gently.

"And enough to irritate me," answered her companion. "To see a fellow like that—ah—trying to—to—warp your affections, to gain the love of one who is to me my light and life."

"Mr. Squabshot!" ejaculated Miss Staunton; "Mr. Squabshot, what do you—what can you mean?"

"Oh, Edith!" replied Squabshot, as he now rose from the chair on which he was seated and threw himself at the feet of his enchanttress. "Oh, Edith Staunton, is it nothing to have watched you for weeks, for months, to have passed sleepless nights and wretched days for your sake—is it nothing to have found awakened within my heart a love deep-burning and passionate—a love which must and will last to the latest hour of my existence. Is it nothing to live on the smile of one who holds me in the most perfect thraldom that ever mortal man was subject to—is this nothing, think you? Have some small share of pity for me. If I can never own your love, I know that I am not deserving of so high an honour, I know that I am entirely and completely unworthy of you. I know that—no one knows it better—I am, as I always was, a plain man ; I have not the gift of speech, the smooth and persuasive tongue of him who, I know, has supplanted me in your affections, I know that daily and hourly I have this truth more vividly impressed upon me. Well, what then ? What remains ? I must suffer in silence. I must learn to endure my real fate as I best may, but oh, Edith, my dearest, my most adored Edith, I love you as no man ever loved woman before. Have pity on me, have mercy, I know not what I say, but I love you!"

He clasped her hand as he gave utterance to this passionate speech, and raised it respectfully to his lips. In spite of all his sincerity, which was self-evident enough to the fair being by his side, there was at the same time an irresistable comicality about his appearance and manner which would naturally have excited the risibility of most females ; but Miss Staunton, although she was in some measure struck with humour at the scene, was, nevertheless, too good-natured and too kind-hearted to make a jest of what was evidently a serious affair with her admirer. She gently released her hand from his grasp and looked kindly down upon his upturned face, which wore so agonised an expression that she could not find it in her heart but to

do aught else than pity him—"Pity," says the poet, "is akin to love."

"My very excellent and esteemed friend," said Miss Staunton, as she retired back a few paces. "I fear me much that your ardour is getting the better of your judgment ; you are saying a little more than perhaps your more sober reason would dictate. Rest content now. It is, as I have before observed, now very late. In the morning—to-morrow, or some more convenient day—we will discuss this matter at our leisure: for the present let it drop. We have had a long evening, and, I hope, a pleasant one ; and, to say the truth, I little dreamed that the *finale* would be of so serious a character as this. There, believe me, Mr. Squabshot, I have a great esteem for you—a very great esteem, and I look upon you as one of my most particular friends. More than that I cannot say."

To have seen the expression of Mr. Squabshot's countenance, when these words fell from his enslaver, would have done your heart good—to have seen the alternations in that index of thought and mind, would have been worth a journey of miles and miles. When Miss Staunton had come to a conclusion, he stood like one on the very brink of despair—he did not move from the position he had chosen to assume, but remained still upon his knees.

"I will never rise until I have the answer, which is to either bid me hope, or doom me to utter despair."

"Now pray don't!" exclaimed the lady. "Pray be a little reasonable. At some other time we will discourse more fully upon this subject, but, for the present, pray let it drop. What would you have me say ?"

"What? Bid me hope," answered her companion. "I know I am a rough, and, it may be, an uncouth fellow. I am little schooled in those arts which win the love of a young and beautiful female, and, oh, so beautiful that to merely gaze on her is happiness, so supreme that I can hardly deem that I am deserving of such. I know that I do not either in face, form, or speech possess anything that would recommend me to your notice. All I have is a sincere heart, a simple, honest disposition—such an one as would scorn to pain or injure any of your sex, either by word or deed. This is not much you will say—neither is it. To some one less radiant and accomplished than yourself it might be something, but to you who are so fair that—"

"There, that will do, Mr. Squabshot," exclaimed Edith Staunton, hastily. "I pray you not to indulge in those compliments. I am as Nature made me, possessed of none of those attributes which your too-faced imagination is disposed to assign to me—I pray you cease. Rise, and—"

"Never !" exclaimed Squabshot. "I will never rise until the fiat has gone forth which is to make or mar me."

"Oh, dear me! what shall I do with this man ?" exclaimed Miss Staunton, who now began to perceive that she had a gentleman to deal with who certainly was not of a very pliant disposition upon this one question at any rate. "Do rise, Mr. Squabshot !" she ejaculated now more vehemently.

"Never !" answered her obstinate lover; "I already anticipate your answer. Keep me no longer in torturing and agonising suspense. Say at once that you cast me off, and I shall know the worst better that, than this dreadful incertitude. You care nought about me. You throw back my love with scorn, even to my very face. You refuse to listen to my suit, for your heart is already engaged to him—to that man—I know it, I see it all. Why hesitate ? why refrain from inflicting the last blow which is to sever me from you and hope for ever ?"

"What do you mean?" exclaimed Edith Staunton. "Of a surety you are the most unreasonable man that was ever born. I again beseech you to rise. Surely if you love me, as you profess—love me so much that there cannot be found a parallel for the same among the whole human race—surely, you cannot consistently refuse me this small request. Rise!"

Mr. Squabshot mechanically rose to his feet. At a motion from Edith Staunton, he seated himself in a chair close to the one she herself occupied.

"I obey you," said Squabshot; "and now—what now, Edith."

He endeavoured to lay hold of her hand again, as he said this, but she withdrew it from his hold. At this he again put on a look of blank despair. He then sighed, and looked inquiringly into her face, For a minute or so neither spoke There was an awkward pause. Presently Miss Staunton broke the silence, which was becoming painful—

"Mr. Squabshot," said the lady, "I was not aware that I had awakened so deep a passion in your breast which it has pleased you to declare, a few minutes ago. To deal frankly with you, I am free to confess that I am flattered by your declaration, but, at the same time, I am much surprised."

"Mercy on me! and wherefore ?" he ejaculated.

"Well, I am, and that's the truth."

"Can you have misunderstood my attentions? Is it possible that you have not devised the state of my feelings towards you ? It is true that I have never spoken out before, but then women—and especially one of your superior perceptions and discernment—could never have been blind to that which, although the tongue refused to declare the looks and manner but too plainly indicated. Ah, no! Edith, I never will—I never can believe that you were dead to a sense of that deep attachment which has taken strong root in my breast."

"You forget, my friend, that men are but too apt to fancy themselves in love with females whom chance or circumstances may place in their way Woman never loves but once ; but man—ah, he roves from flower to flower."

"Not me—I swear it !"

"Yes ; you men are always ready to swear upon this subject."

"Do you doubt my sincerity ?"

"No."

"I thank you for that acknowledgment, at all events."

"No, I do not doubt your sincerity ; on the contrary, I am free to confess that I look upon you as a free, open-hearted gentleman ; a little too prone, perhaps, to indulge in hyperbole, but nevertheless, in the main, of a truthful and a gentle nature. I esteem you, Mr. Squabshot."

"But you can never love me? Is that what you mean ?" he inquired, hastily.

She made no reply.

"You have promised to become the bride of the Reverend Ozius Meek ?—is it not so ?"

"You are too hasty. We will discuss the question some other time. For the present you must really leave me. What will the servants say, at our conference, at this unseasonable hour. Why, it is nearly two o'clock."

"There is no rest for me to-night, or rather morning," exclaimed Squabshot. "I care not for the time."

"Possibly not; but I do. You would not wish to compromise me, I should hope ?"

"No, certainly not," answered her companion. "But it will not take you long to put me out of my misery. All I want is an answer; an answer, Edith, which is perhaps to doom me to despair."

"By my faith, you seem most anxious to be doomed to utter despair, as you term it," answered Miss Staunton, with a scarcely perceptible smile.

"Answer me one question—are you engaged to the Reverend Ozius Meek ?"

"To a plain question I give a plain answer—no ! So let that suffice for this night. And now, pray leave me."

Mr. Squabshot indulged in another deep-drawn sigh, which seemed to rend his very heart.

"I thank you for that !" he exclaimed, suddenly. "At any rate there is some small scrap of comfort in that. I would rather see you—see you—"

He paused suddenly.

"Well, sir?" she said, inquiringly.

"I would rather see you wedded to the meanest in the land, than be sacrificed in marrying one who is so utterly unworthy of you."

"I know not why it is that you should please to abuse this unfortunate clergyman."

"Unfortunate!" he ejaculated. "It is they who are connected with him that are unfortunate."

"Let there be an end to this discussion. You have been, in my opinion, exceedingly rude to Mr. Meek. This, I think, you must admit. I do not know anything about the accusation which your friend has chosen to make against him. It may be true, or false."

"It is true!" exclaimed Squabshot. "I swear to you, Miss Staunton, that every word of it is true. If you wish it—if you disbelieve me or my friend—I can, nay, I will, bring you a witness who will at once convince you that every word is true."

"It is hardly worth while our discussing that question now. He has not, at any rate, injured either you or myself; and he has, since my acquaintance with him, always conducted himself as a gentleman, which is more than he will say, perhaps, of either yourself or your friend."

"A gentleman, forsooth!" Squabshot exclaimed; "a ruffian, when it suits him, and a hypocrite. But I have done—I see I pain you. Good Heavens, what is there in this man that he should find so much sympathy, and so able and determined a defender? But I am done."

"I am glad to hear it."

"Ah, Miss Edith, am I to hope? Say one kind word to me."

"I hope I have said many kind words to you," she answered; "and more than this, I am still disposed to say kind words to you. There, now, what more would you ask? Now leave me—I charge you to leave me."

"Ah," exclaimed Squabshot, "if you knew the pleasure I feel at the present moment—if you knew the pleasure it gives me to be thus—to be by the side of her who holds me so enchained, that I feel the most desponding wretch in the world when out of your presence—"

"I should hope, Mr. Squabshot," answered the lady, "that you had no occasion to become a despairing wretch, as you term it. But, to say the truth, I believe that we shall each of us present but a miserable appearance to-morrow if we protract this conversation any longer. Once more let me beg of you to take your departure. You force me to use no ceremony, and to speak my mind thus freely. 'Stand not upon the order of going, but go at once.'"

"Your commands shall, nay, must be obeyed," answered her companion. "I will at once take my departure. But, oh, Edith, before I do so, say, am I to hope?"

"Of course, we all hope; it is the only solace sometimes left to the afflicted," she said, with a smile.

Mr. Squabshot brightened up, and kneeling at her feet, took her hand in his, and covered it with burning and passionate kisses.

"There, that will do," exclaimed Miss Staunton. "Really, there never was such a man, I do believe."

"Never one who loved so sincerely," answered Squabshot, who was now half delirious with joy.

After some further protestations, he at length took his departure, much to the satisfaction of his fair companion.

CHAPTER CXLVI.

Mr. Squabshot returned home to the house in which he had taken lodgings since Miss Staunton had become an occupant of Henry Osborne's mansion at Richmond. He was, as we have observed, in much better spirits, for the result of the interview with his enslaver augured a better prospect for the success of his suit; consequently, Mr. Squabshot was too much excited to think of laying himself quietly down and doing what any other reasonable man might be supposed to do, namely, to seek repose.

But lovers never were, and we suppose never will be, reasonable, and so the tortured lover sat himself down in his bed-room, lit his pipe, and began that airy, dreamy process of building castles in the air—a process pleasant enough, it is presumed, but certainly not conducive to health at past three o'clock in the morning. Nevertheless, Mr. Squabshot chose to do so.

After several vigorous puffs at his pipe, a smile of satisfaction passed over his features.

"So," he exclaimed to himself, "she does not, then, after all, love this reverend gentleman. I think that is quite certain, and yet she has listened to his soft whisperings, and, at times, seems to defend him. We were rude though—I suppose we were. Oh, yes, certainly. There can be no doubt of that—we were most unquestionably rude. But, then the fellow is—bah!—a viper! a scorpion! a sycophant! a demon in human form! Oh!' and here the speaker ground his teeth and made up a face expressive of scorn and defiance. "She's certainly a charming creature—an angel! there can be no doubt of that either. One of the fairest of God's creation—the most amiable of her sex. Well, what then? She drives me mad, and that's the truth. Psha! What fools men are; here am I, who made up my mind to forswear the sex, over head and ears in love—madly, distractedly, hopelessly in love? Who would have believed that this would ever have come to pass? Can't believe it myself hardly—were it not for—for —for that—for my sufferings. What good does it do a man to be so eggregrious a fool? that's what I want to know. What use is there in his sighing and groaning, of his hanging upon the words, and watching the looks of another being? None—positively none. And yet there's no help for it, I suppose—not in my case, that is quite certain. I am in love, I'm quite sure of it. I have thought myself so once or twice, fully believed myself to be so at the time, but law that was nothing like this passion, which devours, consumes me. Oh, nothing in comparison—oh, no, I am in love, I am quite sure of it. I have argued, I have reasoned with myself, I have used philosophy, and I have enough of that, quite enough to bring to bear upon the subject, but it has all been of no avail—all knocked over by a woman —all scattered to the four winds of heaven. All gone!—philosophy, discretion, good sense, inflexible determinations, or what should be inflexible—but, alas! it's as insubstantial as stairs of sand or ropes of water!"

Again Mr. Squabshot had recourse to several vigourous puffs at his pipe. For a long time he sat watching the dying embers of the fire which his landlady had caused to be lighted in his bedroom, and after being lost in reflection for some time, he, as morning began to dawn, retired to rest.

When Mr. Squabshot did stretch himself upon his downy couch his sleep was sound as that of a chamois hunter, but the sun was high in the heavens before he arose, and then his head ached a trifle and his hand was rather shaky, and so, feeling himself rather *blase*, or seedy, he thought he would endeavour to refreshen himself up a little before presenting himself before the fair Edith.

It is one thing to say refreshen yourself up, and another thing to do it. How was it to be set about? The first thing Mr. Squabshot did was to treat his aching limbs with a bath. The next thing he did was to call upon a friend of his who had been at Miss Staunton's party, on the night previous. This gentleman's name was Boxall—Phil Boxall, as he was more familiarly termed by his intimate companions—and so, after his bath, Mr. Squabshot called at his friend's lodgings. The landlady's daughter opened the door and informed Squabshot that his friend was as yet not up. Mr. Squabshot, however, being naturally an unceremonious gentleman, at once proceeded up stairs to his friend's bed-room, and knocked at the door thereof, whenupon his receiving no answer to the summons, he unceremoniously entered the room.

"Hilloa!" exclaimed Squabshot. "It's the early bird that gathers the worm, my friend."

Mr. Boxall started up in his bed at the sound of a man's voice in his room, and for a moment or so stood in some surprise.

"Well, how goes it?" inquired Mr. Squabshot.

"Ah, it's you, Squabby," exclaimed Mr. Boxall "How are you, old boy?"

"Oh, amongst the middlings. And you?"

"Got a confounded headache. My head has been spinning round for these last four hours."

"I am not in first rate trim myself," answered Squabshot, "and so thought I would come round to you, and have a turn on the water together."

"With all my heart," said Mr. Boxall, jumping out of bed and proceeding to dress himself with an alacrity which would have suggested to the mind of a superficial observer that Mr. Boxall was called out upon "urgent business."

In less than half an hour he had dressed, and had swallowed a hasty breakfast, and in a quarter of an hour after that, he and Mr. Squabshot were sailing in a yacht on the bosom of "old Father Thames." Their brave built skiff cleared the waters, and glided rapidly over the silver stream. The two occupants of the barque reclined at their ease, and lighting their pipes, prepared to enjoy themselves.

"Do you know, Squabby, my boy," said Mr. Boxall, "that I have been tossing about the best part of the night, and have not been able to rest."

"What's that been about?" inquired his companion. "You are not in love, I hope?"

"Psha! I should hope not. But the fact is, I have had the incidents of a work I have been reading running in my head all the night through."

"What was it about then?"

"Oh, all about fairies."

"Fairies?"

"Yes, fairies. Shall I enter into an explanation of this mystical volume?"

"Yes, do; it will amuse me. Proceed. Drive on, Phil."

"Well, you must know," said Mr. Boxall, "that the work I have been speaking of treats of the gambols of Puck. He chooses for the groundwork of his tale the quarrel between Oberon and Titania, about the changling boy, which Shakespeare has rendered familiar to us."

"Oh, that's been his game, has it?" said Squabshot.

"Yes; the author represents the fairy court to be the scene of domestic strife on this subject, this state of things being chiefly owing to the love of mischief of Master Puck; but he at last outwits himself, by carrying his mischievous pranks at Queen Titania's expense, too far. He is banished from Fairy Land, and Titania vows he shall never return until he has solved the enigma of 'What is it that most pleases a woman?'"

"Ah," exclaimed Squabshot, "he had a difficult task assigned to him."

"Well, Puck proceeds with a heavy heart to the realms of earth to undergo his punishment, intending to make the best use of his time to discover the riddle. The successive frolics he is engaged in are undertaken for this purpose. By way of giving you idea, I shall give you an outline of frolic the first."

"All right. I am all attention, Phil," answered Squabshot.

"Puck, when he reaches the earth, takes upon himself the appearance of a gipsy boy. After some adventures he gets into the service of an old veteran, who has a beautiful daughter, called Jessie, who has a spirited young sailor for a lover, whose name is Frank Monkton. This son of Neptune stands higher in Jessie's good graces than he does with her father. Puck's singular conduct, and deliberate mischief speedily makes his quarters too hot to hold him, but he does not leave the family before he has become deeply interested in the success of Frank's suit for the hand of Jessie. Frank, at this time, formally makes proposals to the old soldier for his daughter's hand. He is rejected on the score of poverty, but the old man promises to give his consent whenever Frank can satisfy him that he is possessed of five hundred pounds. He considers this as tantamount to a complete rejection of his suit. Puck flies to his assistance in this dilemma, and informs him that he has been at Calshot Castle, and that Lord Cloud has arrived, and taken up his residence there, and that he had seen his lordship, told his tale to him, and that his lordship had promised to furnish him with the sum required to satisfy the old soldier's scruples."

"Very kind of him, I'm sure," exclaimed Squabshot. "And did he do so? or was it only a promise?"

"You shall hear the result," answered his companion. "Puck and the lover proceeded to the castle together—Puck at the castle-gate, disengages himself from Frank, and Puck himself, seeing Lord Clovel, prepares himself for receiving the sailor. He is ushered into his lordship's presence, when the following scene ensues:—

His lordship was sitting by himself at a table placed in the deep embrasure of one of the windows, from which he could, when he thought proper, by drawing back the curtain, look out on the water, that was tossing and sparkling in the brilliant moonlight. He was a little, rotund gentleman extremely well, and even delicately, proportioned, notwithstanding the roundness of a certain part of his figure, which it is not necessary to particularise. Nor was this defect, or rather this augmentation, of the natural man, by any means so excessive as to give the idea of bloatedness, or to be at all unpleasant to the eye. It rather added to the humourous expression of his handsome face, which with its hooked nose, and eagle eyes, bore so strong a resemblance to Howleglass, as at once, in Frank's mind, to solve the mystery of their connection. The only material difference between them was that which a few years would naturally make, or which arose from the darker complexion of the gipsy, who, exposed as he must have been by his way of life to all weathers, could not be supposed to have the fair tints of one bred up in the shade of luxury. It was evident, Frank thought, that the lad was a wild slip of his lordship's grafting, and, if so, it was easy to see why they should be on a familiar footing, a riddle which it had sorely puzzled him to untie till that moment. The young lord, it was true, could not be more than thirty, while the son, thus liberally bestowed upon him, wore the appearance of fifteen at least; but then the former had all the appearance of a wild companion, who would not lose any time in enjoying life, and so by a very little stretch of fancy the thing might be. If not probable, it was at least possible.

The dress of this merry, rosy-cheeked lordling, with some trifling exceptions borrowed from his own whimsical fancy, was the costume of his age, being the time of Charles the First. His coat was a frock of crimson velvet, with gold buttons and rolled collar, the shoulders full and curiously slashed; his waistcoat and nether habit were of the same material, but white, and his loose boots, or rather buskins of Spanish leather, reached nearly to the knee. Down his right cheek hung the love-lock, that indispensable characteristic of a gay cavalier, and the object of unceasing scorn and hatred to the puritans, who, amongst other equally sage doctrines, held religion and long hair to be inconsistent, and as little like to meet as Whitsuntide and Christmas.

The appearance of Frank did not for some moments withdraw his attention from the more serious business of the table. He continued drinking his wine and munching his fruits from the various dishes before him, without apparently being conscious that any addition had been made to his company, and when after a time he did notice him, it was only by a nod, and a significant pointing of the hand to a chair, which gesture Frank interpreted into a desire that he should be seated. The bottle was then pushed towards him with the same silence, and, though somewhat surprised at this dumb scene, he did not the more hesitate to avail himself of the offer, but, conforming himself to his lordship's humour, he filled a glass without ceremony, and returned the decanter as silently as it had been sent to him. A second gesture invited him to take an orange from the plate near him. Frank shook his head by way of declining the offer, and, having cast his eyes curiously over the table, found no dish so much to his fancy as a noble pineapple, which his lordship seemed incilned to reserve to himself exclusively.

But the guest had no notion of any such distinctions. Since he had been received on a footing of good-fellowship, he was determinep not to lose any of its privileges from a silly bashfulness; besides, he wished to let his host see that the son of Lieutenant Monkton held himself equal to any lord in Christendom, though not quite so rich—rather an ill-judged display, considering the nature of his embassy to Calshot Castle, but pride will play reason strange tricks at times.

Accordingly he was drawing the desired fruit over to his own side, when a sudden embargo was laid upon it by his eccentric host, who, without saying a word, thrust his fork into the pine-apple, and having conveyed it to his own plate, pushed the empty dish towards the visitor.

This action Frank thought proper to interpret in a way most agreeable to his own interests. He got up, coolly rang the bell, and, on the appearance of the butler, gave him the empty plate, with a sign that it should be replenished.

The servant looked at his master, and having received a signal, the import of which Frank could not understand, though he fancied it boded mischief, immediately made his exit.

In a few minutes the man returned with a dish of withered crab-apples, that he set before the guest with infinite ceremony, and while the latter eyed it in some doubt whether to fling it at the bearer's head or not, the little lord was leering at him with a most provoking expression of intelligence.

"Is it so?" said Frank, to himself; "I'll be even with you, however. I think, friend,"—this was addressed to the butler—"I think, friend, you might have the grace to offer the dish to your master first."

At this grave rebuke of his servant's want of manners, the eccentric host seemed to be mightily tickled. He burst into a hearty laugh, and, for the first time, broke his silence to order his butler to fetch the best

pine-apple in the store-room. Then, turning to Frank, whose humour seemed to jump so admirably with his own, he exclaimed—

"By my faith, rogue Howleglass told me no lie, when he said you were a free, careless fellow, who recked neither for king nor kaiser. You make yourself as much at home in a nobleman's drawing-room, as if you stood on the deck of your own ship But I like you all the better, if it were only for the variety of the thing, for the most of my visitors have so much respect for me, that they have none left for themselves, and are so prodigiously civil, that I am forced to turn them over to Harry Huntsman; push about the bottle though, with a little more spirit, for I have two rules,—two standing rules of my house wherever I may be, and which I hold in no less respect than a Turk holds his koran: The first is always to go to bed at midnight, for I love good hours; and the next is never to go to bed sober. Now, by that clock over the door, it is hard upon eleven, and, as you see I am only just beginning to be merry, so we have no time to lose."

"Your lordship is getting on pretty well though," said Frank, who himself began to feel the effects of the choice Burgundy and the sparkling Champagne.

"Well?" repeated the little lord in disdain, "how is it well? There are six stages, according to my calculation, between the first bottle, and that comfortable state when a man is fit for bed, and I have only gone through two of them as yet. You found me on the second, dumb as a dog that won't bark and can't talk; but thank heaven, that part of the road is over, for it is the dullest in the whole journey. In another bottle or so,—I wish though you would keep the bottle so long on your side of the table."

"Is she aground with me?" said Frank; "I was not aware of it. But we'll soon shove her off again."

"Yes, but fill, first. Fill man, a bumper, that's right. And, if we only keep on briskly in another bottle or so, I shall be at the half way house."

"I'm afraid, then," said Frank, "you'll leave me behind on the way, though I'll do my best to keep up with you. But your lordship was speaking just now of Howleglass. He was the pilot on the cruize hither to your castle, and I should be sorry if he came to any harm, not that I mean to say a word against his getting a round dozen from your huntsman, which I have no doubt will be better than silver to him, for he is a sad rascal, that's the truth of it. A tight flogging, if it goes no farther, will, maybe, teach him to keep his hands in his own pocket for the future, and save his neck a stretching."

"Have you no fear for him," replied his

lordship; "he is as well off with me as with his best friends. Marry! I should be sorry as any one that he got into more trouble than his wit could get him out of again."

"Why, I think you owe him a good turn," said Frank, "if it were only for the likeness between you. He might call himself your son, and no one, who had seen you both, would cast the proverb in his teeth, as if he did not know his father."

The little lord laughed, and nodded his head significantly, as much as to say, "folks would not be far out in their guesses."

From this time the bottle circulated with a rapidity truly alarming to an inexperienced toper; and very soon both guest and host might be said, in his lordship's phrase, to have reached the half-way house, or, in other words, to be at least half-drunk. They talked

loud, and swore louder, interspersing their dialogue, like a modern opera, with songs more distinguished for rhyme than reason, or rather with snatches of songs, for neither of them could get beyond a few bars before he was interrupted by the other. Then, as their spirits waxed higher, and their judgment proportionately decreased, they began to play off sundry practical jokes, neither very wise nor very witty, and would no doubt have shocked those, had any such been present, who have learnt the art of carrying their liquor with discretion. Amongst other mad freaks, for example, his lordship condescendingly flung a bumper of old hock into Frank's face, and Frank showed his sense of the favour by hurling half-a-dozen of the glasses nearest to him out of the window.

"Bravo, Mr. Frank!" cried his lordship

"I could not have done better myself ; but, by all the gods and goddesses in the heathen pantheon. you pay for that smash, either with a song, or with broken bones. So choose."

"I'll have no broken bones—I am going to get married," said Frank, with drunken gravity—" and your lordship is to pay the parson."

"Sing, then ; sing," exclaimed his lordship; "and I'll bear a part : and so shall John Chinaman—won't you, old boy?"

This interrogatory was addressed to a little porcelain figure, that stood, or rather sate cross-legged, on the mantel-piece, with the sly simper on its face usual to such images, and which makes them appear as if they were cheating an European in a bargain of tea. But the figure thus invoked had a quality not quite so common to his porcelain brethren —he actually seemed to hear and understand the question put to him, opened his mouth, rolled his eyes, and bowed his head in acquiescence.

"Aha!" shouted the little nobleman, in infinite glee. "I was sure he could not say no. John Chinaman is an excellent hand at a glee or catch, though I would not vouch much for him in a bravura, or in any of your Italian quavers and demiquavers, he's half an Englishman for that."

Frank stared, as well he might, in no slight astonishment. He looked, and looked, but could make nothing of it, while his lordship sipped his wine as if it had all been a matter of course. Suddenly a bright idea struck him that he might possibly be drunk, and have fancied it all. To be certain of the fact, he applied to his host.

"Will your lordship oblige me by just answering a single question ?"

"Any question you like, Mr. Frank, for, if I can't tell the truth of it, I can at all events tell a lie."

"Much obliged to your lordship," replied Frank ; "the one will do just as well as the other. And now. pray tell me, am I not very tolerably drunk?"

"Not a jot of it—as sober as myself."

"Yes, but are you quite sure myself—by which I mean your lordship—is not half seas over ? you seem to have a queer roll with your eyes, and don't sit too steady."

"No such thing. I am never in decent trim 'till the fifth bottle, and I have had but four to my share yet."

"Humph !" said Frank ; "that being the case, I must have a better acquaintance with the little fellow on the mantle-piece."

"What the deuce are you about now?" cried his lordship.

"Going to do as the proverb tells us we should—hold a candle to the devil ;—for that gentleman must be the devil, or a limb of him, and so I have a mind to throw a light upon his face."

He rose accordingly, and made a sort of zig-zag approach to the fire-place, when, taking the mandarin in his hand, he turned him right and left, held the candle before him and behind him, and examined him from head to foot, but it did not appear that he learnt much from the investigation. Replacing the figure on the mantel-piece with as much care as a nurse would set down a pet child, he exclaimed in a tone of high admiration—

"Gosh ! you are the drollest fellow I ever met with. This is the first time I ever heard of a Chinaman singing—that is, a Chinaman, like yourself of clay. Dost know the catch of, *I love old October's liquor !*"

"I'll be sworn for him he does," replied his lordship—" so to it, my lads, like French falconers. You may take the first part, for neither he nor I will have anything to do with your malt potations, and they are the burthen of it, he shall undertake for the second ; and I'll lift up my voice for brandy. Now, boys ! now !"

At this challenge, the mandarin started off at once into the proposed catch, without giving himself any of the airs of a fine singer, and requiring to be pressed. Though his voice was somewhat thin, and not very melodious, he acquitted himself with infinite spirit, while the host and his guest bore their parts in it with no less taste and energy. It is only a pity that the picture of the three cannot be as easily and faithfully transferred to paper as the words of the catch, for the latter loses half its merit when taken out of its connection with the singer, songs being as little meant for the eye as the music of them, and for the most part not conveying much more intelligence. Such as it was, however, it is here transcribed, and the reader will do well to fill up the necessary accompaniment from his own imagination. Let him fancy the little figure chirping away as if he had drunk his three bottles instead of having played the part of a looker-on only, yet all the time perfectly motionless, except with his lips and eyes, while his Lordship roared like a bacchanal under the inspiration of his deity, and Frank, assuming all the gravity of an amateur, beats time as he sings, with hand and foot, and occasionally casts an angry glance at the Chinaman, when, according to his idea of the matter, the little fellow is not rapid enough with his quavers.

THE CHINAMAN'S CATCH.

1st Voice. I love old October's liquor.
2nd Voice. Wine for me, sirs, with the vicar,
It will stir the blood much quicker

3rd Voice. Fill me brandy, there and then,
        That's your only drink for men.

1st }
2nd } Voices. No, no, no.

3rd Voice. I swear 'tis so.

1st Voice. 'Tis ale!

2nd Voice.   'Tis wine!

3rd Voice.   'Tis brandy!

All.   No! no! no!

        But ne'er mind what drink it be,
        So the cup brims merrily.
        Ale, wine, brandy—'tis all one,
        We'll be jovial ere night's done,
        Hal, and Dick, and every one.

            Swill! swill! swill!
        Be the liquor what it will—
            Swill! swill! swill!

"John Chinaman for ever!" shouted Frank, tossing off a bumper as the catch ended. "I should like him better though if he were to spare us some of those outlandish flourishes. It's like a bad cook overdoing a dish with cayenne pepper. The one takes away the taste of the meat, and the other destroys the air of the song. What think you, my lord?"

"Think," exclaimed his lordship—"how dare you talk of thinking to a man who has nearly emptied his fourth bottle? A bumper of salt water for the word by all the laws of honest potation. I will not spare you a drop of it."

"I'll take two brimmers of Burgundy instead," cried Frank: "won't that do as well?"

"It shall suffice," replied his lordship; "for this once I am content to be merciful. Fill—opseys!"

Both host and guest were now in that blissful state, in which the future is nothing and the present moment everything, and it was saying not a little for the excellence of the wine, as well as the strength of their own constitutions, that they were able to keep their places at the table. As to the object of Frank's visit, that seemed to have glided altogether from their memories. Even the pine-apple had been brought in and laid before them without either taking any notice of it. Yet at times a glimmering of the truth would steal across the sailor's brain, like a ray of light peeping through a crevice into a closely shut-up chamber, but it served to no useful purpose. It only showed, without dispelling, the inward darkness.

So rapid and so frequent had been their applications to the bottle, that the store of wine provided for their debauch and it was no niggard supply, was exhausted, while yet it wanted a quarter to twelve, before which hour, as the host had already informed his guest, he never thought of going, or, to speak it more correctly, of being carried to bed.

The key of the cellar hung on a brass hook to the right of him, for he was one of those exemplary managers, who are much too jealous to allow a butler to intrude into the sacred recesses of the wine vault, the penetralia, as it were, of the temple, in which their deity resides. But on the present occasion, though he made many efforts to rise, and take the key, for the purpose of visiting the cellar in person, and drawing thence a fresh supply of potables, he found himself unable to quit his seat; a weight of lead seemed to pull him back again whenever, with much effort and many groans, he had contrived to lift himself up a few inches, by the support of his hands upon the elbows of the chair. Frank, who saw his patron's condition, though he could not see his own, and had at the same time a very high notion of his superior sobriety, volunteered his services to fetch up the wine, an offer which was graciously accepted by the little lord.

"Go," he said; "go, son Frank, and prosper; for you are my son—are you not? I'll swear you are my son—the heir of all your father's virtues: and your mother was —let me see—your mother was the queen of the gipsies. I met her once in the forest, picking blackberries, and thereby hangs a tale."

"Yes, I remember you were married in St. Mary's church, and I was born six weeks afterwards," replied Frank.

"So we were, boy," exclaimed his host, "so we were; and you shall inherit my wine, and my castle, and my lands, and I'll make haste and die like a loving father, that you may step into my shoes the sooner. As to rogue Howleglass, he is a drunkard—a wine-bibber and a brandy-bibber; I wash my hands of him, I disown him, I abandon him. He may hang, drown, or starve, as best pleases himself. But fetch the wine, lad, and make haste about it, for the clock's going at a devil of a rate—tick! tick! tick! Fie on it—he's drunk—he can't stand still a moment."

"Horribly drunk," said Frank; the hour hand is running a race with the minute hand. Bravo, little one! never mind his long shanks, you'll beat him yet."

"But the wine, son Frank, the wine!"

"Aye, aye," replied the son of wonderful memory; "I am ready to start: only give me the bearings of the cellar, and I'll steer right for it, though the tide's running against one at the rate of six knots an hour. Gosh! I never knew it set so strong before."

"The way to the cellar?" said his lordship, in profound meditation; "I should know something of the geography of those parts; but I have a bad head, a very bad head; let me see—oh, I have it. First you go straight forward, as straight as you can go; then you turn to the right or left—I'm not sure which, but it's one or the other; then down stairs, then right or left again, and the cellar is before you."

"That will do very well," replied Frank, making for the side of the room, opposite to that in which the door was.

"Yes, but you'll not get out of the room the way you are going, unless you mean to knock down the wall first."

"You are a fool, father mine—father mine you are a fool. Can't you see the wind's right against me? and how then do you think I shall ever make cellar point, if I don't tack, and keep her well away. Gosh! I should like to know where you got your schooling; they were not conjurors who taught you."

His lordship stared at this rebuke of his ignorance, without seeming much to comprehend its meaning, and, shaking his head very wisely, like one who agrees with some sage maxim, he returned to his Burgandy. In the meantime his dutiful son, candle in hand, pursued his course as well as he could to the wine-cellar.

Frank meets with sundry extraordinary sights in the cellar, he is not successful, however, in his search for more wine. And, by some means or other, which is unaccounted for, he finds himself at daybreak lying in the castle moat.

How had he got there? for, supposing all the rest to have been no more than a drunken dream, he felt assured that he had partaken of his lordship's hospitality, and remembered perfectly well having been commissioned by him to fetch more wine from the cellar. The recollection of this was much too vivid to be mistaken, for the effect either of sleep or intoxication, though he could not help attributing the whole scene of the goblins with their elfish freaks to one or the other of these causes. Or perhaps he still slept? No!—he saw and felt everything too plainly: there was the skiff rocking at anchor before the eastern stairs; there was the island lying before him with its white cliffs and thick woods; there was the castle as distant as ever castle could be; and, to make all yet more certain, there too was his lordship, sested at an open window, in his flowered dressing-gown, inhaling the freshness of the day as he sipped his chocolate.

"Soh!" exclaimed the little nobleman, when he saw that Frank moved, and began to look about him—"Soh, you are awake at last, are you? And pray what do you think of yourself and of your pranks last night? You come to a nobleman's castle to borrow his money, or rather to beg it; for, unless guineas were to be caught like mackerel, I see little chance of your ever repaying five

hundred pounds; and, by way of recommending yourself to his good graces, you get intolerably drunk, break a little porcelain mandarin, a particular rarity, because the image won't sing when you wisely call upon it to join you in a catch; and, to conclude the evening as you began it, insist upon visiting his cellar, where you upset half-a-dozen wine-buts, and would not have left a whole cask amongst them had not the butler, with the help of his fellows, seized you by the neck, and turned you head over heels out of the castle."

At this complication of charges, so much at variance with his own recollection of the night's adventures, Frank was utterly astounded. That he had been intoxicated, like enough; but as to the breaking of the little mandarin, or the overthrowing of the wine casks! Heavens and earth! if it were not a dream, as he had been willing to imagine, yet what was he to think of such a version of the story? His lordship seemed to be mightily amused at his bewildered looks, and the visible efforts he made to recall and reconcile what he thought had happened with this statement, and called out to him again, though in a more good-humoured tone than at first—

"I suppose you imagined because I indulged somewhat freely, you might do the same; but I would have you to observe there are two good reasons why that which is well enough in me, may be very bad when you come to practise it. In the first place, you are no more than a plebian, a mere salt-water Jack, while I am a nobleman. In the next, your brain, not being used to the acquaintance of claret, champagne, and burgundy, is liable to be confounded by a few bumpers, while I, from better practice in such mysteries, have learnt to carry my wine with discretion."

Now this, like the other assertions, flatly contradicted all that the sailor could remember of the late transactions. His lordship, as well as he could recollect, was incomparably the more drunk of the two, and by the same token was utterly unable to rise and go himself to the wine-cellar. He ventured to remind his host of this part of the story; but the observation was received just as might have been expected, that is, with an exceedingly ill-grace, few people liking to be rebuked by those who come to solicit their favour.

"Why, how now, you deboshed fish!" exclaimed the little nobleman; "do you pretend to bandy words with such as I? Suppose I did somewhat exceed in my libations, is it for you, in your blue jacket, to remark upon it? Go to, sirrah! Let me tell you, you must change your notes, or you are not like to stumble on a patron in a hurry. It may require a hard blow to draw sparks from a flint. but it is the soft word and the supple neck that must extract gold from a rich man's pocket."

The blood of Frank fired at this insult. He sent his quondam entertainer to the devil in no very measured terms, declaring that he cared neither for his rank nor his money, and only regretted his ever having come on so beggarly an errand. "But," he added, in a low tone, not intended for his lordship's ear, though it did happen to reach it, "but, when once a man has got a girl in his head, he generally contrives to play some foolish prank or another."

"Very sagely remarked," said the nobleman, who seemed to be more amused than irritated by his violence; "very sagely remarked indeed! This girl in your head shall be a sufficient excuse for the follies of last night, as I dare say she has been, and will be, for many others. You shall have the money, you drunken dog; but I will not trust it into your hands, lest it should slip between the fingers, as my poor mandarin did. Send up your Jessie—I think you called her Jessie—to the castle this evening, or sooner if you like it better, and she shall have the gold."

"No, truly," said Frank, "she comes not here with my good will."

"She's no true woman, then, if she does not come without it," replied his lordship. "But be it as you can settle it between you."

Without vouchsafing any reply to this observation, the sailor flung himself into his skiff, with a firm resolution that Jessie should learn no more of the transaction than that he had failed in his endeavours to procure the money.

Puck takes good care that this resolution shall be foiled, and he accordingly informs Jessie that her presence is required at Calshot Castle. Mr. Frank, much against his inclination, is commissioned to convey Jessie and her father to the castle; they are well received at the castle gates by the domestics, but Frank is refused admittance; they proceed, leaving him behind.

The room into which they were shown was the same that had witnessed the orgies of the preceding night, but in the person of the nobleman they found one they had least expected to see under such circumstances. Instead of the round. lusty figure, described by Frank, it was Howleglass (Puck) himself who stood before them—not with the light, fantastic carriage he had been wont to put on when playing the part of a gipsy, but with the air and bearing of one who is fully sensible of his elevation above the generality of mankind. He seemed, too, to have grown five years older since they had last seen him, but this might in some measure be accounted for by the difference of dress and manners between his past and his present state; the one being as much calculated to take from the appearance of years, as the other to add to it. He was now splendidly habited in white satin slashed with crimson, with silk stocking rolled above the knee, and large roses in the shoe composed of precious stones of inestimable price. The clasp too of his sword belt, as well as the belt itself, was studded with diamonds, and the large jewels that fastened the feathers in his hat were scarcely of less value. From his neck, suspended by a golden chain, and on his breast he wore the various orders peculiar to different countries, so that his fame was evidently not limited to one land. With these appliances, he, who before had only seemed handsome, was now a perfect model of manly beauty, so much had dress and the assumption of a higher character added to the natural graces of his person.

At this unexpected sight, Jessie blushed and smiled, while a thousand vague fancies chased each other across her little brain, like the shadows of spring-clouds scudding across the fields; and some of them of a nature which, if Frank could have been aware of them, would by no means have tended to allay the fever of his jealousy.

As to the sergeant, he commenced sundry exclamations without having the power to finish them, looking from the ceiling to his daughter, and from his daughter back again to the ceiling. If, however, he hoped to gain anything in the way of elucidation from either, he was sorely disappointed, and even the large fly, that buzzed upon the latter, seemed to be mocking his embarrassment.

After having enjoyed their confusion for some time, his lorpship at last condescended to be his own interpreter.

"You seem surprised, old man, at my transformation, and truly it is something, from a vagrant to a lord; but yet I should imagine that you, who are so experienced a gardener, and so fond of tulips, must ere this have seen a grub unfold himself into a butterfly? And you, Jessie—women are generally more keen-sighted than men in these matters—can you not guess what it is that has made a nobleman descend from his state, and take upon him the beggarly character of a gipsy for so many weeks?—must I say in so many words, that I love you, and am ready to share with you my name and fortune? Nay, answer me not till you have heard all that I can offer."

"Good, my lord," exclaimed the impatient veteran, who was wrapt into the seventh heaven at this confirmation of his best hopes; "good, my lord; what should she wish to hear more than she has heard?—or what other answer should she make than by going on her knees and taking the hand you are pleased to hold out to her? Swoons! if she had not been beside herself with joy, she had done so much already. But you must forgive her, my lord; you must forgive her. She is young and foolish, faults that she will mend of in time."

"You are too hasty," replied the nobleman, smiling at his eagerness to catch a coronet for his daughter. "Leave me to argue this point with our Jessie, and I trust things will fall out to both our wishes. Look here, maiden; look at these treasures—enough to buy a county, though that county were your own Hampshire Only say you are mine, and all this is yours, to lend or to give, to use or to waste, at your own good pleasure, without rendering a reason for it to anyone."

As he said this, he opened drawer after drawer of a large ebony case, each of which was filled with gold coins, that lay loosely in it as a thing of no account.

The eye of the sergeant glowed like a living ember as he gazed on all this wealth, and his transports were still greater when their noble host turned to a second case, of less dimensions, in which diamonds, emeralds, rubies, and every sort of precious stones, were displayed on black velvet, in the various shapes of rings, clasps, bracelets, necklaces, and the other forms best suited to show off their rare brilliance.

"These, too, are yours when you are mine," said the tempter.

Jessie sighed, but it is hard to say whether that sigh proceeded from a wish to possess what she had seen, or from a consciousness that her truth to Frank was not quite so fixed as her feelings told her it ought to be.

"These, too, are yours, when you are mine," repeated the tempter. "But answer me not yet. You have not seen all. Here is the picture of my estate in the west—one out of many—and from it you may judge what life she may hope to lead who calls herself my bride."

He led her up to a large mirror, and passed his handkerchief over the glass as if clearing away the dust from it, when there immediately appeared a magnificent villa, or rather a palace, in the midst of a noble park and grounds, that extended on all sides as far as the eye could reach. Nothing in nature could be more beautiful. This immense space was a continued succession of wood and water, hill and dale, those parts which were not covered with trees, being a mixture of fields highly cultivated and of the richest downs, where herds of cattle were grazing whose sleek sides bore witness to the fatness of the pasture. To complete the scene, a splendid equipage was visible rolling up the avenue between the oaks to the mansion.

"Now hear me, Jessie," said the owner of all this magnificence, who had attentively watched the effect produced by the picture of it on the simple fancy of the maiden. "What you have seen does but coldly express the half of what awaits you in being mine. Let me try to eke out the picture by words. As many days as there are in the year, so many shall be your dresses, and each more magnificent than the other. As many weeks as there are in the year, so many shall be your servants. As many months as there are in the year, so many shall be your horses. No queen when she rises shall rise to such a banquet; nor, when she lies down to sleep, shall her day have been of so much pleasure. And tell me, Jessie, is there anything in myself to make such an offer less worthy than it would be from another? Am I deformed, that a maiden should slight my love?"—He drew up his finely-proportioned figure to its full height, and flung out his hand as if challenging her eye to find a defect—"Or is there any blemish in these features, that I need be ashamed to show them?"

"No, by G—d!" exclaimed the serjeant, forgetting the person he spoke to in the warmth of his conviction; "I never saw a more proper man in all my born days, and I think an old soldier ought to know something of such matters."

Even Jessie could not help stealing a glance at the challenger, and her eyes, though she spoke not, plainly enough confessed that he was well worthy of a maiden's dearest affection. This did not escape the lover. He saw he was on the eve of triumphing, and pressed the final question—

"Will you be mine, Jessie?"

"To be sure she will," cried the sergeant, whose own heart was more than sufficiently captivated by the gold and jewels; "to be sure she will, or she must have taken leave of her senses."

Poor Jessie! Again she sighed more deeply than before—she herself could not tell why. Her head seemed to swim. She looked up a second time from the jewels and the picture to cast a timid glance on her wooer, whose appearance, if anything could have excused a woman's fickleness, must have pleaded her pardon for that moment of frailty; for, truth to say, though it may injure the poor maiden with the lovers of idle fiction, she was more than half won.

"Will you be mine, Jessy?" he repeated, taking her hand, and speaking in those soft, persuasive tones, which sound so sweetly to the ear of woman.

Jessie blushed, drooped her head, and fairly wept; but her fingers returned the pressure of his hand, though so faintly as not to have been sensible to anything less apprehensive than the quick touch of a lover.

Emboldened by this token that his suit was fast prospering, he put one arm round her waist, and drawing her more closely to him, again said—

"Will you not be mine, Jessie?"

The little maiden held both hands to her eyes, and sobbed aloud, exclaiming, as if in sorrow at her own weakness—

"Oh, Frank, Frank!"

It would seem that her voice was a spell to conjure up the absent, for no sooner had the words escaped her lips, than a voice close behind her answered, "I am here, Jessie—mine own true Jessie."

Jessie, whose back was to the window, hastily turned round at this exclamation, and there, sure enough, was Mr. Frank, who on his passion having cooled, which it did not fail to do when the gates were closed behind him, became anxious to know what was going on with his mistress.

As the doors were absolutely closed against his return by the barbarity of the chief huntsman, who had no idea, he said, of a fellow like him coming in and out of his lordship's castle as if it were a tap-room, he could think of no better means to gratify his curiosity than by clambering up to the window. This to a sailor was a task of little difficulty, time having destroyed in many places the even surface of the soft stone, and left sundry cavities and rough points, which afforded, if not a safe, at least a sufficient footing for one of his habits. In this way he heard, to his great joy, the last appeal of his mistress, though had he reached the window a minute sooner than he did, it is possible his admiration of her constancy might have been much more temperate. But in love, as in war, it is the right timing of matters that brings fame or shame, victory or defeat.

The sergeant, of course, viewed this interruption of his quondam friend with no very favourable eyes. In his heart he wished him at Jericho, and, as he was seldom restrained by any considerations from giving words to his thoughts, he exclaimed, in great ire—

"I wonder—that, is, I should wonder, if I had not known your impudence of old—what brings you here, stealing in like a thief at the window. Away with your dog's face the same way you came, and as much faster as may be. If his lordship were of my way of thinking, he would have you ducked in the castle moat, and then hung up on the flagstaff to dry again."

"It might be no easy matter for half a score of popinjays to do as much, even though he had an old fool to help him, with a heart as tough as his own wooden leg," replied Frank, who was in no mood to pick his phrases. "But, Jessie, do you," the words

seemed to choke him, "do you sing to the same tune? If so, say but the word, and I am gone, not to trouble you again in a hurry."

"No, no!" cried Jessie, eagerly; "save me, Frank, save me from myself. And may heaven forgive you, my lord, for tempting a poor girl so cruelly. Say not a word to me me, father. If I was weak enough to to be dazzled for a moment, it was only for a moment; I am come to my better senses again, and know the wrong I did to myself and to the truest heart that ever owned love for a maiden. Point not to the gold, my lord, or the picture of your large estates; I can now look on both as a woman should do whose faith is given to another."

"Her faith, perhaps, but not her love," replied the young nobleman, sarcastically.

"Yes, my lord, her love, too," replied Jessie, her feelings too deeply agitated for her to stand on the wonted reserve of female bashfulness; "her love, too, or she never had plighted her faith."

Till this moment, Frank had hesitated to enter the room, though he had forced open the window; but no sooner did he hear this plain avowal of love from the lips of his mistress, than he sprang from the sill into the chamber, and grasping her firmly round the waist with one hand, with the other he brandished his trusty cudgel in defiance.

"After that word let me see who will take her from me," he said, looking to his rival as to the quarter whence he expected an answer to his challenge.

"Not I, by the rood!" replied his lordship, laughing. "Yours she is, and yours she shall be, if my best wishes can make her so."

"What!" cried the sergeant, disappointed at the baffling of his own hopes, and no less shocked at the pusillanimity indicated, as he thought, in this ready surrender; "will your lordship suffer yourself to be bearded after this fashion by a fellow who can't bring his wife even a snail's portion, for the poor snail has a house to his back, if he can boast of nothing else. Come hither, Jessie—come hither from his side this instant."

"Not so, father," replied Jessie, firmly, but modestly. "A little while since and I was at your disposal, but when you gave my hand to Francis you lost the right to command and I the power to obey you."

"Why how now, jade!" exclaimed the indignant veteran; do you mutiny? do you fight against orders? fire and fury—"

"Leave the fire to the furies, and the furies to the fire," said the gypsy-lord; "they are well matched. And let us see if we cannot contrive another match equally fitting, and not so ominous. Come, come, old soldier; you must relent, and the rather as you have been mistaken all along in this matter. What I have said to our little Jessie in the way of love, was but to try how woman's word and woman's faith would hold together, and glad am I to find they twist into a line that will bear some straining before it breaks. The trial I grant was a sore one, but the reward shall be proportioned. Give me your hand, fair and faithful, for you deserve that title ; and do you, my worthy rival, smooth, if you can, those jealous wrinkles, which will else make an old man of you before your time. If I ask a maiden's hand, it is to return it to you, not richer indeed, for wealth gilds not beauty, but with the only addition that was wanting to ensure your happiness."

He gave Jessy a key, and pointing to a little iron chest, desired Frank to take it up.

" It is yours," he continued, " and contains the sum you asked for twice told. Bear witness, old man, that I give it freely, both interest and principal."

The serjeant was too deeply absorbed in certain calculations of his own to attend to this appeal, and it was clear they must have been of a very profound nature, for they had ploughed half a-dozen additional wrinkles in his forehead, each an inch deep, besides drawing down his brows like an extinguisher over his solitary optic. Frank, too, hesitated, in doubt, whether to avail himself of his patron's generosity, but a single glance from, and into, the bright blue eyes of Jessy decided him.

" I will not refuse your lordship's bounty," he said, in his usual brief, manly manner ; " but it's on the condition that, if it should chance to prosper in my hands, I may consider it as a loan to be without offence returned. Should it fail, no unlikely matter where the hazard is so great, I can only say, I thank your lordship for your kindness, and am sorry I cannot return it better."

" Sorrow not about it, honest Frank, as far as the loss may concern me only. I would rather give the gold than lend it, and, if the terms are changed, it will be because you choose to have it so."

" Twice five hundred make a thousand," suddenly exclaimed the sergeant, having duly come to this undeniable conclusion, after a long and laborious consultation with his fingers—" children, you have my blessing ; my lord, I thank you heartily ; and the marriage takes place to-morrow."

" Such is the history of Mr. Puck's doings," said Phill Boxall ; " and the affair has been so running in my head, that to say the truth, as I have before said, my nights' rest has been disturbed thereby."

" Ah, that's a sad job, Phill—very sad," said Mr. Squabshot, " because you see you are so very delicate !"

Mr. Phill Boxall was the very personification of robust health, and he laughed long and loud at the observation of his friend.

" Ah !" sighed Mr. Squabshot, after a pause. " *You* are to be envied."

" Me !" exclaimed Mr. Boxall, with a start ; " me—and why pray ?"

" You are not in love !"

" Oh, thank you for that information."

" Ah ! you are in love, then."

" I have not said so. Don't measure other peoples corn by your own bushel, Squabby."

" Ah !" again sighed Mr. Squabshot.

" There, don't look so melancholy, old chap," said Mr. Boxall. " Look yonder ! we are observed."

" Where ? What do you mean ?" inquired Squabshot.

" We are observed," answered his companion, and before Squabshot had time to make any further inquiry, his ears were saluted with a stentorian voice calling out " Phill, Phill, confound you, old fellow—put her head in shore !"

Mr. Boxall, who happened to be at the helm, did put the head of the little skiff towards where the party who had called out so vociferously was, at that particular time, standing.

" It's Jem Turvey," said Mr. Boxall, explanatively to his friend Squabshot.

" Who is he ?" inquired the latter.

" Oh, an old pal of mine. I promised to go down with him to the fens."

" To the fens ?"

" Yes."

" What for ? Does he live there ?"

" No. He's a great sportsman, and I was to form one of a party to go fishing in the fens. Turvey has only just got back I expect, and with your permission we will land and hear how he got on."

By this time the yacht had gained the bank of the river. Its two occupants moored it off the shore and landed. The gentleman who had called out so vociferously laid down his fishing-rod, and grasped the proffered hand of Mr. Phill Boxall who returned his grasp and evinced considerable pleasure at meeting with his quandom companion. In the space of a few more minutes the three gentlemen repaired to a neighbouring hoslery to partake of a hearty lunch, with divers and sundry bottles of ale.

" You never came according to your promise," said Mr. Turvey to Boxall.

" My dear boy," returned the latter " I could not, upon my word I could not, the loss was mine. How did you get on ?"

" Oh, gloriously."

" Well, we've half-an-hour to spare—tell us all about it. Did the Reverend Charles go with you ?" inquired Boxall.

" Oh, yes : he was true to his word. Well,

after a long journey, we entered the first level of the fens, and, as night had come on, we entered a comfortable room, and were welcomed by a kindly-faced, bright-eyed landlady. We take formal possession of our quarters, and set down to a substantial dinner, tea and supper all in one, with the fabled appetite of hunters. That dispatched, and digestion consummated with the aid of a whiff of tobacco, we are a-bed betimes.

Awakened by the first sunbeams on the morrow, seven o'clock finds us clothed and shod ; and while breakfast is preparing, we take a survey of the localities.

B—— Creek is the confluence of two fen rivers, between which, on the point at the angle of their junction, is built our hostelrie. I find that, in the event of desperate weather, I could angle from the parlour window with my twenty-four-foot bamboo. Out-houses, stables, a walled garden, and a smithy, occupy a fair area.

A strong white bridge crosses one of the rivers, carrying over it the continuation of the road by which we came last night. The ground about the house is bare of trees and covered with a short turf, which a one-eyed horse, some relation to the rusty little pony, is cropping diligently.

B—— Creek is a considerable barge station ; and, from the number of those black lumbering craft moored about the point, whose burly navigators are just cooking their breakfasts, and coming ashore for their morning beer, we augur favourably of the convivial capabilities of the "Ship."

The water seems in pretty good order, though somewhat clear : and having gazed into its depths at the gambolling fry, and contributed our expectorated mites to its tranquil current from the rail of the bridge, we return to breakfast.

We find that noblest meal prepared on a prodigious scale; and engage upon it with commensurate zeal.

At its close, the landlord is summoned for consultation.

He enters—big, phlegmatic, shrewd, and civil, half Hollander in face and build. By his advice we shall take the lesser river for the worm to-day, and he will get us leave for some preserved jack-fishing on the main one, being the Ouse, about a mile below the house.

While I pack up the materials for an *alfresco* lunch—with great store of beer, first approved jointly by the imbibition of a pint sample, taken medicinally, to counteract the nervous effects of the théine and caféine—the Reverend Charles orders in the baits, which were sent over night to the cool shades of the cellar.

The great camlet bag is opened, and displays about half-a-bushel of moist, green

No 101.

moss ; at the bottom whereof—the same being lifted up—lie, in some loose, light mould, a mass of huge, obscene lob-worms, that would weigh many pounds, and fill a half-gallon measure.

About a third of the quantity, with plenty of moss, but without mould, is placed in a flannel bag of more convenient size, for the day's supply, and two handfuls are separately deposited in two lesser flannel bags, to be carried in the hand for current use.

These preparations completed, and my town supply of smaller annelideans and gentles rejected, as unfit for fen fishing, we start on the day's campaign.

As we ascend the stream of B——, which gives its name to the creek, I have a good opportunity of noting the peculiar features of this country of the Fens.

High embankments guide and restrain the once vagabond waters of its rivers ; their turf sides sloping on one side to the level of the country, on the other to the marge of the stream, which is fringed with flags and sedge.

Along the ridge of one bank runs the towing-way, along the other we are steadily trudging on a path of loose dusty silt. Planted at intervals of about a hundred yards in the banks, along the edge of the water, are great bare posts, mostly the dead butts of old pollard willows, as moorings for belated craft.

The stream is clear, pretty deep, and flows with a steady current ; and so, in the picture of one you may see all fen-rivers ; treeless, monotonous, and artificial-looking, they differ only in width or flow ; or, in the directness or sinuosity of their course, according as art has been satisfied to assist nature, or has struck out a better course for itself.

On this eight or twelve-foot bank we out-top the whole landscape around, save the distant high lands of Ely, and the undulating mounds crowned by a village on our left.

But I am wandering from my subject ; and the Reverend Charles, who dwells on the skirt of the Fen himself, and has seen it all before, is anxious to get to work.

We descend the inner slope of the bank, and my admiration is soon concentrated on the very finny-looking water, that laves the line of sedges at its base.

Rods are soon fitted, and tackle fastened ; a stout float that shall breast the water gallantly under ballast of shot and freight of heavy lob, a fair large hook, and, borne thereon, seven struggling inches of worm.

An underhand swing of the long rod, and my companion's bait has plumped into the middle of the stream, between two ambuscades of weed.

Ere the float has well righted, a telegraphic dip beneath the surface gives intelligence from the depths below. Again it signals—this time by total disappearance ; and, more eagerness than discretion—for once—impelling the Reverend Charles's arm, is recalled by a hearty jerk, which brings the line up with a clip and a jar—electric in its significance—followed by instant relaxation ; and the bait swings up uninjured.

"Ass that I am," quoth the Reverend Charles. "Why was I born to miss ?"

"Ah, if a man should never miss his aim, how invincible he would be," I moralise.

"How little he would care about fishing," responds my companion ; and my own bait being also in the water, a heavy bite thereat terminates the dialogue, even were I disposed to dispute the position involved in the Rev. Charles's rejoinder, viz., that one-half at least of the sweet charms of angling arise out of its small disappointments. The first blood is drawn, as usual, by my companion ; a royal three-quarter pound perch, after much fight, being compelled to yield to his inexorable fate. For a time the Rev. Charles seems to have fixed his day's average by the first specimen, while I am doomed to keep testifying to the truth of the landlord's dictum, "that the smallest perch in the river will take the biggest worm." But fortune is at length propitious ; and after a brief but severe struggle, I landed a two pounder—the finest fish before lunch.

By this time we have walked and fished a good three miles, nor is a brief rest ungrateful. Reclining at the prandial hour, the rods are carefully laid over the rushes to fish for themselves, and the big perch and B—— river are toasted in Berserk draughts of brown ale. By an invariable coincidence, fish leave off feeding when the angler feeds (or *vice versa*) ; so that we eat our morsel in peace, and it is not until we are half through a very indolent postprandial cigar, that a succession of importunate bites, disturbing our placid smoke-wreaths, recalls us to the business of the day. *Quid plura ?* As the morning, so the afternoon. We love variety ; and there are few of the cyprinidæ that B—— does not yield us from his crystal depths, now ruffled by the strong south wind. By the close of the day we have well worked four miles of his tortuous waters, and set our faces homeward with full baskets and whetted appetites. The creels are emptied on a charger in the parlour of our hostel ; and the glad and tired anglers count with contending eyes a glittering heap of orange-finned bright roach, burnished kingly rudd, perch striped and spined like chiefs of the Ojibbeways, tawny, flat-sided bream, and long, lubberly chub—nine dozen and one in all ; weight, fifty-three pounds. A dish of perch for to-morrow's breakfast is picked out, and the rest are committed to the kindly

landlady for distribution among the poor, the sick, and the needy of our little neighbourhood.

So passed the first day of fen-fishing ; but the second was not like unto it, as I shall show you in a brief conclusion.

Morning breaks with a keen wind and a clear sky. In defiance of his own prognostications, the Rev. Charles sallies forth before breakfast, firing shots from Dr. Watts at sluggards in general, and assailing me with opprobrious language, for acting on his prophecies of failure by refusing to incur the shame. Descending an hour-and-a-half later, I meet him just returning, with a solitary, lantern-jawed chub, dangling from his dexter hand. Breakfast over, I move for a trial of the pike-fishing on the great river below. The Rev. Charles, however, regarding all trolling and angling for pike as a kind of hard labour, and "work fitted only for desperate convicts," doth, in spite of the inauspicious meteorological aspects towards the same determine to adhere to worm-fishing.

So it is agreed that I shall go downwards and try the jack preservss, while he will re-tread our steps of yesterday up the banks of B——, and that I shall return and join him at the hour of lunch, calling at the inn for the commissariat stores on my way. Efforts are made for an hour to catch me some small fish for bait ; but the water is clear and the sky bright, and, at the first shadow of the cast-net, they flee to shelter. I am obliged to depart on my experimental trip with five baits only in the can—three gudgeon and two little roach. However, I have no expectation of catching anything, and saunter, well-satisfied and lazily, in the hot sunshine, along the top of the embankment. The big river is like unto the little river, save that the channel is as wide again, the water deeper, and the turf ramparts on either side larger in proportion. About a mile and three quarters below, I find the spot to which I have been directed—a great sullen bay of the river, indented by small promontories of turf ; its water of black depth, outside a ledge of weeds, which skirts along the shore. A more perfect lair for fierce, pirate pikes, those Dyaks of fresh water, could not be. I recline indolently on the sunny inner slope of the embankment as I prepare my tackle—a stiff rod, long and strong line, a float as big as a ripstone pippin, much gimp and swivels below, ballasted with a small bullet, and terminating in a single large hook. The latter is passed through both fleshless cartilaginous lips of a gudgeon—(I declare on the faith of my studies in comparative anatomy, it hurts him not)—and the vivacious little prisoner is hurled, at the end of forty feet of line, afar into the river, where he swims about at mid-water, buoyed up by the great float, and vainly endeavouring to drag it below the surface. I lay the rod down and my body likewise, and begin meditatively to inhale the fumes of the Indian weed.

The sun is hot and high, and the glassy water is ruffled only at rare intervals by little flaws and puffs of the cold East, hostile to anglers. As they come, the tall sedges and broad-bladed flags bow their green heads, and whisper and talk so pleasingly, that I strive to comprehend their speech, and more than once seem to catch familiar words. The swallows are circling wide and dizzily overhead, and occasionally a fen-kite flaps slowly across the sky. A kingfisher turns the bend of the river, and passes me, swift and silent, like a ball of blue electric light. Small river-birds are hopping with chirps and whistlings all around. Insects of curious form and colour are parading and hovering about the hedges; and beautiful minute beetles glint back the sunbeams from their burnished armour in the grass. I notice many species peculiar to the Fens, especially some prodigious fellows of the aquatic kind among the weed-stems in the shallows. (One of the hugest of the latter I capture for a microscopical friend of the Reverend Charles, who has offered half-a-crown for one two inches long, that he may have the pleasure of inspecting his digestive apparatus under a two-million magnifier.) My view is limited in front to the green slope of the opposite bank, and the tops of some scrubby pollards peering above it. A road runs along its base on the other side (as usual in the fen-country), and I can just see the hat of any vehicular or equestrian traveller glide along behind the ridge. A couple of barges came down the stream, from B—— Creek; the horse dragging them, from the tow-path on the top of the bank, by a rope fastened to a high mast in the foremast; while the driver encourages him with a musical cry peculiar to the fen-bargees, ending in a long shake—yo, ho-o-o-o·q-o-o yodling, which breaks the sunny silence exquisitely. Horse and man stand in fine clear relief against the azure sky. The barges sweep gurgling by; and, as the eddies subside. I glance towards my long-neglected float, and finding it to have utterly disappeared, I give a minute or two, raise my rod cautiously, and strike. A heavy, sluggish motion, like that of a live post at the end of my line, tells me that, in Waltonian parlance, I have got him. I wind in the slack, and essay to lift my unseen captive. Shade of Walton! what a fish is here! I feel one jarring wag of his huge, lithe body, and up flies the resilient line, as my bent rod suddenly straightens, broken at the arming of the strong gimp, luckily below the float,

Old Father Ouse only knows against what leviathan of his oozy flood I had been trying the strength of tackle, that would have tethered a donkey; my own convictions on the subject I shall decline to state.

It is possible that the catastrophe was mercifully arranged; for who can say what might not have been the tragical issue of a prolonged contest—the water so deep, so tenanted, and no help at hand.

However, I light the cigar of resignation and lie down to refit. A second hapless bait is attached to the securely-knotted line and heaved half across the river like his predecessor. Soon the tossing voyage of my copulent indicator is arrested; swift and straight it descends to the depths below. In two minutes I am engaged in lively fight with a six-pounder. As I draw him towards the bank, scared probably by the apparition of my wide-awake hat, he makes a convulsive plunge; and the bait, released from his Acherontian jaws, returns terribly mangled to me twice-disappointed. Still I smoke the tobacco of placidity. A third time my line is cast upon the waters, and a third time they close over the cork pippin. Patience, and caution! I strike deliberately. Eh! What! Can it be him again? Yes. Stay! No. I can lift this, whatever it is that answers pull with pull, and from the profound depths of Ouse bends my strong rod like a willow switch. Now a rush, and the obedient line spins wildly from my reel; and now I wind it in again, as the strain relaxes. Every minute gives me fresh confidence. Still the struggle is long. It is twelve minutes ere I catch a glimpse of my dear cork pippin; and fourteen ere I behold for the first time the dimensions of my foe. Drawn at last to the surface, I see a bulk like that of old Pontoppidan's sea-snake, which, with a sweep of its huge tail, disappears below the flood again, in a maelstrom of its own creation. I will have him, I feel that he is mine.

But now the real horror of my situation strikes me. How on earth am I to land him? No landing net, no gaff-hook, and nobody to help me. To drag him to the side among the weeds—from which I have been sedulously restraining him were fatal folly. Accoutred as I am, to plunge in after him would argue an enthusiasm which I fail to effect, even fanatic angler as I am. Must I wait unknown hours till the monster, effectually choked with his own element, may safely be towed to land. Strange anomaly a drowned fish! Can I much longer resist the horrible fascination of those hideous jaws, which are fast luring me to resign a finger or two to their mild nemesis, in a desperate attempt to catch the levithan single-handed? I will lift up my voice and shout; peradventure assistance may be nigh though I know it not.

A moment. The sound of wheels on the road behind the opposite bank. I see a black hat gliding along beyond the ridge—It must be a gentleman, then—perhaps a parson ; everybody else wears wide-awakes here—and being a gentleman, he will help me. No ; is is a shabby hat, a shocking bad hat, in fact; and as he isn't a gentleman. therefore, he shall help me. I utter loud cries in the vocative. The wheels stop and I lose the hat for a minute or two. Presently it re-appears ; then a face, a blue garberdine. and two fustian legs become, seriatim, visible below it. A butcher's man, on his way, doubtless, with mutton chops for the luncheon of some pampered farmer's wife—that class dine at fashionable hours hereabouts, I assure you. Well ; lunch at Dogdike Farm must wait a bit.

The butcher is an understanding man, and sees my meaning—in spite of my explanation probably, which is very blatant and intermittent, owing to renewed struggles on the pike's part, demanding my full attention. There is a little punt lying in a creek on the other side, which I have noticed before, but have taken to be a wreck. It seems, however, to be one of those selfish ferries occasional on these rivers. In these the boat is free, and the person crossing poles or paddles himself across, and fastens his craft to the bank he has reached, leaving the next comer on the same route to wait for his return, or the advent of a passenger from the other side.

There is one advantage attending this arrangement, which is, that a man coming to the ferry, and seeing the boat on the opposite shore, knows his fate at once, and need never scream himself hoarse to an adder-deaf Charon. On one side or the other, however, there is commonly a cottage or two, whose inmates have established the punt to shorten the route to market.

Into this same punt then does my butcher cautiously descend, and paddles over to my assistance.

New terrors animate the pike, who seems to have had a reserve fund of energy for the last emergency.

My butcher, grinning with delight and astonishment, makes several grabs at him, striking the strained line every time, while I gnash my teeth and dance with anxiety at his awkwardness. At last he kneels down in the boat, and plunging both arms into the water, fairly hugs the slipery monster to his breast, lifts him out, and heaves him far up the bank.

Three blows on his broad, ugly head, administered with grim satisfaction, and he lies the corpse of a fish, which in aspect and dimensions seems rather the denizen of some vast stygian lake than of a narrow river of East Anglia. The butcher says he weighs "two stone ;" and holding him up by the gills, I find that he is a foot at least more than half my length ; and I am of sesquipedalian stature.

After being duly admired and reviled, the butcher at last re-enters his frail pinnace ! while I, athirst for more blood, cast another bait to mid chanel as before.

A five-pounder is soon vanquished and lifted out—this time scientifically, by the eyes—and laid on the sunny grass beside his fellow. My fifth and last bait is sent after the rest, and my butcher, filled with staring wonder at my success, lingers yet awhile for another summons.

However, it comes not ; and with many a look behind, he docks the punt, clambers over the bank, and disappears.

Scarce has the rattle of his wheels died upon my ear, when I have established a link of union between piscator and pike for the fifth time. My perplexity is as great as before. I shout aloud, for the chance of a rustic audience within hail. Five minutes pass. My cries become frantic. Presently a distant yell in reply ; and two bacon-eating tillers of the soil come tumbling out or breath, over the embankment behind me.

The pike is not landed until one of them casts off his brogues and gaiters, and wading through the weeds clutches him fairly by the gills.

I reluctantly close my morning's work, having expended all my baits, and stringing my prizes on an old handkerchief, prepare to carry them to our hostelrie.

A curious spectacle I presented to fen-men and bargees as I plodded along the silty path of the embankment, bearing the captives of my rod on my back under a broiling sun ; the tail of the biggest flapping below the skirt of my fishing coat, while his head rose over my shoulder.

"As for my pike, his length being marked on the floor of the room, his weight noted over twenty pounds, he was that very night packed in a deal coffin, and sent up to town by the coach to be stuffed, and now leers at me with half-open jaws, from a covert of stained paper sedges and cocoa-nut fibre weed in a glass case over my mantel-piece.

The sporting gentleman having concluded, Mr. Squabshot and Mr. Boxall made a motion to retire from the comfortable parlour in which they had spent a social hour or two. In the course of a few more minutes, the three individuals rose and, after settling the reckoning, sallied forth, and in a short time the two friends parted with their sporting companion after having promised to join him in an excursion on some future occasion.

"Well," exclaimed Mr. Boxall, "thus far have we marched into the day. Bless me, I had no idea it was so late."

"Pleasant company adds speed to the flight of time," said Squabshot.

"Thank you," retorted his companion.

"Oh, you take the compliment to yourself, eh?"

"Ahem! I suppose it was intended for this perverse and wayward individual?"

"If the cap fits wear it."

"Good. You can quote Shakespeare—not a very apt quotation, but no matter for that. It was well intended, no doubt."

"And, no doubt, is also well appreciated. A knavish speech sleeps in a foolish ear."

"Shakespeare again, I do declare. Why, Squabby, old boy, you are getting classical."

"It's more than I ever aspired to, and it's too late to begin, I'm thinking. But a truce to this badinage. Whither are you now bound for?"

"Home," said Mr. Boxall. "And you?"

"Well, there you puzzle me. I am undecided."

"Miss Staunton, I suppose?"

"Miss Staunton!" exclaimed Squabshot, with a sigh. "My own Edith."

"Whew!" exclaimed his companion. "Has it come to that. My own Edith. You are a lucky fellow—a very lucky fellow. My own Edith. That's the way you talk. Oh, 'tis love that makes the world go round."

"It makes my head spin round," answered Squabshot, mournfully.

"Come, muster up courage, man, and pop the question at once. Faint heart never won fair lady."

"I have popped the question."

"Well, and with what result?"

"She bids me hope."

"Oh, that is all. How about Meek?"

"Hang him!" exclaimed Squabshot.

"Oh, he will be hung one fine day or other; you may take your oath of that."

"So much the better."

"Miss Staunton is not sweet upon the fellow?" inquired Boxall.

"Oh, dear no."

"You are sure of that?"

"Quite certain."

"Ah, I fancy we settled his business the other night."

"Don't know; but should suppose so."

"Gracious goodness," suddenly ejaculated Mr. Boxall, "as I live, if there is not Jonathan Wild."

"Where?" inquired Squabshot.

"Why, yonder; and he's making this way. Ah, he catches sight of us—see!"

Mr. Squabshot turned his glance in the direction pointed out by his friend, and beheld Jonathan Wild taking his way down the leading street in Richmond. He telegraphed to Squabshot and his companion, and hastened towards them.

In the space of a few minutes, Mr. Wild was by the side of the two friends. He shook Squabshot cordially by the hand, hailing him as a comrade.

"Well, I declare," exclaimed the thief-taker, "and who would have dreamt of seeing you? Rusticating for the benefit of your health, I suppose?"

"Ahem! yes; and you?"

"Business — professional business," answered Mr. Wild, with a low chuckle.

"Anything up in this neighbourhood, then?" inquired Squabshot. "I hope you have not come for either of us?"

Wild laughed.

"No, you are not worth my notice; you are all the petty larceny way."

"Thank you."

"And you know I sweep at greater game."

"Precisely. And who may the gentleman be? But it's a secret, I suppose?"

"No. I have come down here to look after a fellow—a scamp, a blackguard, a wholesale robber—a clergyman, in fact."

"A clergyman—and in this neighbourhood. Why, surely it is not our friend?" said Mr. Boxall, turning towards Squabshot.

"And who may your friend be?" inquired Wild.

"The very Reverend Ozius Meek," said Squabshot.

"The very identical man, and none other," answered Wild. "And so you know him, then?"

"I should think we do," said Boxall. "We have good reason to know him."

"Capital. Then I at once enlist your services in the cause," returned Wild, addressing himself to Squabshot. "We have already had dealings together, and I always said you would make a smart officer. Lend us a hand in this business, and it shall be made worth your while."

"I know the liberality of my friend, Mr. Wild," said Squabshot, "I know that from my own personal experience; but in this matter I must keep dark."

"Indeed! And wherefore?"

"For very special reasons."

"Oh, he is a friend of yours, perhaps."

"On the contrary, he is one of my most bitter enemies."

"Whence this unwillingness, then."

"He is a sort of rival."

"A rival! What! you have not been on the same tack?"

"You are speaking in enigmas! What tack do you mean?"

"Swindling," returned Wild, sententiously.

"I should hope not," said Squabshot, drawing himself up to his full height, and giving the thief-taker an indignant look, which, to say the least, was half comic and half serious.

"Oh, I beg pardon," answered Wild, with a smile. "You know I am only joking."

"Oh, I know that—there's not the least doubt of it. Only you should be more guarded in your observations—you really should, Wild. It's of no consequence in the company we are at present; but it might have been, my friend—you see that. So, for the future, pray be more guarded."

"I stand corrected," answered the thief-taker. "I am sure you will believe me when I say there was no offence meant, and so now to business."

"Well, drive on. What is this fellow charged with?"

"Forgery!" answered Wild, "forgery of the worst description. He has swindled, robbed, and cheated hundreds of poor persons out of their all—ruined them and brought them to wretchedness and beggary in their old age."

"That is bad enough."

"Bad, sir! Highway robbery, housebreaking, or shop-lifting is a respectable calling to what this sanctified blackguard has been guilty of."

"And so you want him."

"I do; and what is more, I intend to have him."

"Good; I hope you will succeed."

"But you must know," said the thieftaker, "that the rascal knows me, and is as cunning as the very old one himself. I have been already to his house, but have not succeeded in seeing him, although I am quite certain he was at home."

"Well, you can force an entrance, I suppose."

"That won't do at present, no. Now suppose you were to call—you know him, you say."

Mr. Squabshot shook his head.

"Can't be done at the price, Wild," he answered; "can't be done at any price at all."

"The devil it can't. You are getting scrupulous."

"I must have no hand in this business," said Squabshot.

"Why not?"

"It would not be generous."

"Generous be hanged?" exclaimed the theiftaker.

"Well, I tell you it can't be done, by no manner of means, as we say in the classics. I must be plain with you."

"Well, that's what I like."

"Yes, I know; and so, my friend, you must know, in the first place, that this fellow has had the audacity to try and supplant me in the affections of one who—whose love I hold dearer than anything else in the world."

"Ah, that's the way the feline quadruped jumps, is it?"

"That's the way. And as a man of refinement and delicate appreciation of honour —as a man gifted—"

"Oh, I say, draw it mild," said the thieftaker.

"Well, as a man of the world, then, you will see the impossibility, the utter impossibility of my having any hand in this business. It would not look generous, you know."

"And pray do you want to look generous?" inquired Wild. "Be just before you are generous, is an old adage."

"You must fight your own way in this business," answered Squabshot.

"Very well; if it must be so, it must, I suppose. But here's your friend, he is not bound to remain passive, if you are, I suppose?"

"I would rather he would not interfere in the matter. He knows all parties, like myself; and it would be sure to be said that I had urged him on to the business, if he were to lend himself to effect a capture of the Reverend Ozius Meek. However, do not let me influence you, Boxall. Do as you please."

"Oh, as for the matter of that, I so utterly despise and contemn the fellow, that I care not what may be done to bring him to the bar of justice. He has robbed a relative of mine to a considerable extent, and I am ready and willing to lend a helping hand to Mr. Wild, or anyone else, who may be commissioned to take him into custody."

"Spoken like a man!" exclaimed Wild. "You and I will understand each other in less than a quarter of an hour, I'll be bound. Come, let us go and have a glass of wine together."

And the thieftaker made a movement in the direction of a large hotel which stood some hundred yards or so from the spot where the three were conversing. Mr. Squabshot did not respond to the movement of his companions, at which Wild looked somewhat surprised.

"What!" he exclaimed, "are you not game for a glass of wine?"

"I have already had some, and, to say the truth, I feel my head none of the strongest to-day, and therefore, with your permission, I will decline for the present; but do you go and discuss the business on hand with my friend Boxall, and may you succeed in the undertaking in hand is my most cordial wish. You will not be leaving the town for the present, I suppose, and so I will, with your permission, see you in the evening, and we will do a social glass together then. By that time you will be able to tell me the result of your labours."

"Very good; so be it," answered Wild.

"I will give you a look round in the course of the evening," said Phil Boxall, "and let you know how we have sped. And also where we are to be found. Where shall I find you?"

"At Miss Staunton's; if not there, I will leave word with the servant where I am to be found."

"Good; so be it; and for the present farewell."

"Adieu! Remember me," said Squabshot, with a theatrical air. "You are in good company, Phil."

"No better in England," answered Wild, and so the three separated.

Mr. Squabshot, when he saw his friends enter the hotel, remained for a minute or so irresolute. He looked to the right, then to the left, then up and down the chief street of Richmond in a dubious and uncertain sort of way. To say the truth, he would much rather not have had this little affair come off, as he termed it, at this particular juncture of affairs. It must militate against him with his beloved Edith Staunton, the goddess of his idolatry. Indeed, Mr. Squabshot was not anxious that Mr. Meek should be handed over to the officers of justice, not that he bore the man in question any good will, on the contrary: nevertheless, it might look suspicious. Miss Staunton would perhaps imagine it was a planned thing of his, Squabshot's.

"Confound the fellow," exclaimed the latter. "I wish, after all, he may show them a clear pair of heels. He's a miscreant, a ruffian, an unhung thief, nevertheless, I do not seek his life. His game is up as far as Edith is concerned, and I do not want any dark cloud hanging over the bright sunshine I am in hopes of basking in. Well, he must take his chance like the rest of us, I suppose. A poor one, I'm thinking with such a chap as Wild at his heels; however, here goes to break the news to Edith."

And so, pulling up his shirt collar, arranging his locks, and attending generally to his toilette, Mr. Squabshot sallied forth in the direction of that domicile which contained all that he held dear on this earth. Such was his figurative language of expressing himself when speaking of one who held his happiness in her keeping.

CHAPTER CXLVII.

SQUABSHOT CALLS UPON MISS STAUNTON.—UNEXPECTED APPEARANCE OF HENRY OSBORNE.

"Miss Staunton is at home," was the reply he received, when he inquired of the footman, who opened the door of Mr. Osborne's country mansion. Squabshot, *sans ceremonie*, took his way up into the first floor, where he had parted from his lady love on the previous night, or rather morning. He gave a gentle rap at the door, and a gentle answer was returned thereto, in the dulcet and well-known tone of Miss Staunton herself. In another second or so, Squabshot was by her side. Edith Staunton was busily engaged at her embroidery frame. She looked up when her lover presented himself, and a slight smile curled about the corners of her mouth, as she inquired half sportingly and half satirically, "If he was better?"

"Better," said Squabshot. "My dear Edith, I am not, nor have I been unwell."

"Oh, I thought you talked of dying, or something of the sort, when I last had the pleasure of seeing you," returned the lady.

"Oh, Edith, do not trifle with me," exclaimed the sighing lover. "In good sooth were I to think that you—ah, that you did not view me with eyes of favour. I verily believe I shall die—in reality."

"Oh, don't do that, sir, I pray. I wish you to live."

"Then live I will," exclaimed Mr. Squabshot, with sudden and surprising energy. "Yes, Miss Staunton—live for you alone."

"As long as you can, I suppose.'"

"Yes, as long as I can."

"Ah, there's a good man. How very accommodating; but you really are not looking too well, I must confess. Doubtless it is late hours which takes the rose from your cheek."

Mr. Squabshot drew back. He glanced in the large mirror, which hung over the mantelpiece, and saw but too plainly that his face and features wore an anxious and jaded look. He tried to call up a smile and put on an appearance of ease and satisfaction he was far from feeling.

"Pray be seated," said Miss Staunton. "You look tired, and I presume you are not about to depart immediately."

Mr. Squabshot drew a chair by the side of the one on which Edith Staunton was seated, and sat by her side without another word. After this there was a pause for a minute or so—Squabshot was the first to break the silence.

"Have you considered of—I mean about—that is, upon the matter we were conversing last evening."

"Oh, dear, yes. It took you so long a time to express yourself, that it is not at all likely I should forget it," answered the lady, in a tone somewhat mocking. "Do you know, Mr. Squabshot, that I positively think you don't know your own mind."

"I shall go out of my mind if you talk thus," answered her admirer. "I know that without you life would be robbed of half its charms. In fact, there would be nothing in the world worth living for."

"Tush, man, there are plenty of things worth living for; there's ambition, the thirst for reputation. We all live, or most of us live for a purpose, or should do so."

"I live but for you," answered Squabshot.

"Well, then, shall I tell you a plain piece of honest truth?—I am not worth living for."

"My dear Edith, you do yourself an injustice. Besides, I am the best judge of that."

"Of what?"

"Whether you are worth living for."

"Are you?"

"Yes, I should suppose so."

"So Mr. Meek says."

Squabshot started.

"Meek!" he exclaimed, indignantly. "But law, I don't know why I should bear him any animosity—I pity him!"

"Pity him! By my faith, you have very much altered your tone, then, since last night," said Miss Staunton.

"He deserves our pity," said Squabshot, solemnly.

"Ah, and wherefore, pray?"

"He is likely to be in great trouble."

"How so?"

"He is chaged with a heavy crime," said Squabshot.

"How do you know this?"

"As I and my friend Boxall were strolling through the high-street this morning, we met by mere chance, the celebrated Jonathan Wild."

"I have heard of him. What then?" inquired Edith.

"He informed us that he was in search of the Reverend Ozius Meek, who was charged with the capital charge of forgery."

Miss Staunton changed colour as these observations fell from the lips of her companion, who could not fail to observe that she was visibly affected.

"I am sorry for this," she said, in a low voice.

"And so am I," chimed Squabshot.

"You?"

"Yes; I bear him no ill will, or, at least, none that would cause me to wish him to be in so sad a position as he is likely to find himself."

Edith Staunton then looked hard at Squabshot. She hesitated, then, after a pause, she said, somewhat suddenly—

"You have had no hand in bringing this about?"

"Me!" exclaimed Squabshot. "My dear Miss Staunton, I hope you have a better opinion of me."

"Answer my question."

"No, a thousand times no!" returned Squabshot. "I should scorn such an action. I should hate myself if I could be guilty of such baseness. Me any hand in bringing it about? I swear to you, most solemnly, that

I had not the most remote notion that Mr. Meek was in such a predicament until we met Wild this morning in the High Street."

"I am satisfied," said Miss Staunton. "I should be sorry indeed if you had any hand in bringing this unfortunate man into difficulties."

"I hope you will do me the justice to believe what I have asserted. I have had nothing to do with the serious charge which hangs over the Reverend Mr. Meek."

"I believe you are the last in the world to do so," said Miss Staunton, extending her hand, which Mr. Squabshot lost no time in tenderly embracing.

While thus pleasantly engaged a servant suddenly put a stop to the proceedings by announcing Mr. Henry Osborne. The lovers started, Miss Staunton rose, and Mr. Osborne himself entered the room in which they were seated, a pleasant smile lighted up his handsome and good natured features as he advanced to where Miss Staunton stood; he kissed her and handed her to the chair from which she had so suddenly risen, then turning to Squabshot he said—

"Well how speeds your wooing?"

Squabshot looked sleepish, whereupon Mr. Osborne slapped him on the shoulder and said—

"There that will do—I am answered, you have arranged matters by this time I should hope."

"Mr. Osborne!" exclaimed Edith Staunton deprecatingly.

"Well, what?"

"How can you talk so?"

"Well I am going to have the pleasure of giving you away."

"Ah, I shall never be married, if that's what you mean," replied Edith, with that peculiar perverseness which is so characteristic of her sex.

"Never be married! Pshaw! I know better than that—we both know better than that, Eh Squabshot?"

"I should hope Miss Staunton is only speaking in jest, which, to say the truth, would be a cruel one if it were true—or intended to be so.

"Edith," said Henry Osborne, "take a fool's advice—I dare say I know you as well as most persons.—If you do not actually despise and detest this man, put him out of his misery at the earliest opportunity."

"Put him out of his misery?"

"He is not a bad chap and dotes upon you. Honora and myself know this perhaps better than you do, for it very often happens that those most deeply concerned in matters of this sort are the least informed upon the case. I tell you that he loves you."

"Oh sir, he has told me that I know not how many times."

"Until you are wearied of hearing it, I suppose, eh?" said Osborne.

She made no reply to this, whereupon Osborne laughed.

"There, I see how the case stands," he exclaimed.

Then walking up to Edith Staunton, he took her by the hand, and drew her towards Squabshot, whose hand he then took, and placed it in that of Edith's.

"There," said Osborne, "take her, Squab-shot—she's yours. Bless thee, my children."

And then, with a mock theatrical gesture,

No. 102.

he placed his hands upon the heads of the two lovers.

Squabshot knelt down with mock gravity, to receive the blessing of Mr. Osborne, who was for the nonce, playing the part of a theatrical parent.

"And now, my children, sit down like a good boy and girl, and we will converse of your future prospects. In the first place. When is the happy day to come off?"

"Law, Mr. Osborne," exclaimed Edith Staunton. "You are positively carrying the joke too far."

"There's no joke about the matter," replied Osborne. "On the contrary, you are now betrothed; nay, more than this, you must perforce be married as soon as possible."

"Mr. Osborne," said Edith, laughing. "No one has asked me whether it be agreeable to me or not."

"We'll chance that."

"Yes, but consider my future happiness."

"All that has been considered over and over again. Honora and myself have continually talked the matter over, and we have settled it. There, now, it is of no use your making any wry faces. So swallow the pill with the best grace you may—if pill it can be termed."

"Matrimony is a very bitter pill; at least, so it proves but too often," answered Edith.

While she was yet speaking, she gave a loud scream, and turned suddenly pale. She seemed as though about to fall, but Squabshot caught her round the waist, and supported her drooping form. He then glanced through the window of the apartment to which her eyes were directed. Mr. Squabshot then became aware of the cause of her sudden excitement. A hackney coach was passing on the outside of which was seated Mr. Phill Boxall, and inside the vehicle Squabshot could distinguish the well-known features of Jonathan Wild. By the side of him there was seated the Reverend Ozius Meek—the very picture of woe, despair and humiliation. As he caught sight of those persons, who were gazing at him from the two French windows of Osborne's house, he drew back for very shame. Mr. Boxall caught sight of Squabshot, and waving his hand several times to attract the attention of his friend. He then pointed significantly towards the interior of the vehicle until it was lost to sight.

"What is the meaning of all this?" inquired Mr. Osborne. "It is not a wedding party, I should suppose,"

"No, more like a funeral cortege," answered Squabshot. "The person in the coach whom you may have observed drawing himself back when he caught sight of us was no other than the very Reverend Ozius Meek, a clergyman of this town. He is being conveyed to Newgate on the charge of forgery, and the party by his side was no other than the celebrated Jonathan Wild."

"Ah! I know that gentleman," said Osborne. "I have good reason to remember him."

"Ah, yes of course, I forgot." said Squabshot, suddenly.

"Pray heaven he may be able to prove his innocence."

"That I fear he will not be able to do."

"Is he guilty then?"

"I have every reason to believe so."

"Poor fellow!"

Edith Staunton hurried away and retired to the interior of the room. She sat down in one of the easy chairs and for a few moments wept.

Henry Osborne himself looked melancholy enough, the circumstances served to call to his recollection the time when he himself was in Newgate upon the grave and terrible charge of murder.

There was a pause of some minutes duration, during which period Sqabshot endeavoured to sooth the ruffled feelings of his lady love. In the course of another quarter of an hour or so all parties had managed to shake off the gloom which this incident had occasioned, and in the course of the day our friend Squabshot had the satisfaction to hear from the lips of Edith Staunton herself that an early day should be appointed for their wedding. And perhaps no man in the three kingdoms was ever in such a state of delight as was Squabshot himself when he heard this pleasing intelligence, and it was a happy evening that Edith, Osborne, and Squabshot passed on that occasion,

---

CHAPTER CXLVIII.

IN WHICH A STEP IS TAKEN TOWARDS CONCLUSION.

"Time runs on," is an old adage, and in good truth we most of us find out the truth of this trite saying, in our passage through life.

Live as long as we may the first twenty years of our existence will always appear the longest ones. As we advance in life, time seems to run on with the greatest rapidity as though the old adage be as anxious to hasten us to our end.

How beautifully has the poet expressed himself in the following lines—

Time rolls his ceaseless course. The race of yore,
  Who danced our infancy upon their knee,
And told our marvelling boyhood legends store,
  Of their strange 'ventures happ'd by land or sea
How are they blotted from the things that be!
  How few all weak and withered of their force,
Wait on the verge of dark eternity,
  Like stranded wrecks, the tide returning hoarse
To sweep them from our sight! Time rolls his ceasless course.

And now the ever flowing and restless ocean of time brings us to another place in our highwayman's history.

We will pass over a few years.

Let us see what time has done. Squabshot, as the reader may very shrewdly guess, has married Edith Staunton. He has cut the greater, or rather the worser, portion of his town acquaintance, and indeed, to say the truth, these were the greater portion.

Well, after his marriage Squabshot cut them. He turned his attention to agricultural pursuits, settled in the country and became a pattern for husbands.

We have said time runs on: it did run on with the characters in our tale. Rosalie Halford, as we have already seen, was under the tender and assiduous care of Mrs. Osborne, already she had began to bloom into lovely womanhood.

As she was known to be a rich heiress—for the money left by the old miser of Milk Street was by this time all her own; that is, it was placed in trust till she became of age—and being possessed of a rare and exquisite beauty, of an amiable and gentle disposition, and having moreover a princely fortune in perspective, it is not to be wondered at that she should have numerous ardent admirers, who fluttered about as moths round the candle's flame, and who sighed and sued, and sighed in vain.

Amongst these, however, there was one, the most modest and undemonstrative of the throng, who was regarded by the fair Rosalie with eyes of greater favour. This gentleman was the son of a nobleman, the Honourable Augustus Fairfax, by name. He was highly accomplished, having received a liberal education, and was possessed of a more than ordinary share of intellect than usually falls to the share of scions of the aristocracy.

Rosalie Halford was by this time verging upon eighteen, and it has been truly said that if a girl or woman is not beautiful at that period of her existence, she never will be.

Augustus Fairfax loved Rosalie Halford—loved her with all the warmth of man's first pure and unsullied attachment.

As months passed on, Mr. and Mrs. Osborne became aware of the state of Mr. Fairfax's feelings towards their adopted daughter. In fact, the Honourable Augustus Fairfax had himself fully declared the passionate love he bore towards Rosalie, to Mrs. Osborne herself.

The latter made Rosalie aware of this fact, and soon after this the young aristocrat became an accepted suitor of the highwayman's daughter.

Little did he deem, at the time, that he was wooing the only child of one of the most celebrated highwaymen of his day.

Rosalie herself might have had her own suspicions as to her birth and parentage, but she was entirely ignorant of the fact, or the identity of Mr. Halford and Colonel Jack being one and the same person. Had she

have known this fact, the probability, nay, the certainty is, that she would not have accepted the Honourable Augustus Fairfax as a suitor for her hand.

CHAPTER CXLXII.

THE LAST HEIR OF FLEETWOOD.

WE think that the readers of this somewhat discoursive history must have lost sight of many of the characters who have played either more or less conspicuous parts in our tale.

It will doubtless be remembered that the last time we took a glance at the Nobbler, he was discussing with his companion, Long Ned, a lucrative speculation respecting the child of Sir Reginald and Lady Fleetwood.

The speculation did turn out a lucrative one to the now unemployed housebreaker, for since the affair at Dulwich, the Nobbler had been compelled, unwillingly enough, from continuing the leading star or luminary in his own particular circle.

Mindful as he was of the fate of his less fortunate companions in front of Newgate, and having a most particular dread of Mr. Wild, the Nobbler had deemed it expedient to withdraw from the conspicuous position he had been accustomed to occupy, and had therefore only been able to undertake a "few quiet jobs," as he termed them.

The Nobbler, like many better men, had lost his position in the world. He knew this, and felt it acutely, and like a hungry, disappointed wolf, growled his menaces and discontent from an obscure corner. He was no longer the leading cracksman of his day; no longer able to figure in burglaries which startled and astonished the inhabitants of the great world of London by the adroitness with which they had been managed, and the amount of courage and resolute determination by which they had been carried out; and the Nobbler was a disappointed man.

He laid most of his troubles to Sir Richard Fleetwood, whom he hated and despised, nevertheless he condescended to take his money; nay, more than this, he condescended to threaten the baronet, as he termed him, for the Nobbler liked to indulge in the pleasing fiction that he was associated with the aristocracy, if it were only for the pleasure of robbing them.

He had caused the child of Sir Reginald to be removed from the persons who had charge of it, and he did not deem it expedient to let Mr. Richard Fleetwood know whither it was conveyed. He, however, drew a pretty considerable sum every month from the latter for the maintenance of the little girl, and at the same time for his own support ; for the Nobbler was a man of rather extravagant habits, and his income was by no means commensurate with his wants.

In vain had Sir Reginald and Lady Fleetwood sought and caused to be sought every means to discover the missing fugitive ; they could discover no traces of her. Mr. Sharpthorne had been consulted on very many occasions—advertisements had been inserted in the papers—all to no effect.

Jonathan Wild had been consulted, and even this astute officer was at fault ; he could learn little or no intelligence.

Now and then, from time to time, he fancied he had hit upon some clue : but each one turned out a myth, and so poor Sir Reginald and his gentle, simple-minded wife, mourned the loss of their only child, even as fathers and mothers are wont to mourn the loss of a dear beloved one.

One evening Sir Reginald and his lady were seated in their own apartment, in that now gloomy mansion at Acton. They had been conversing upon that subject which was continually uppermost in their thoughts, and there was an expression of sadness on the countenance of both husband and wife—a certain air of dejection which long and continued sorrow is wont to produce.

A grey twilight found its way into the room in which they were seated, a gloomy twilight, just enough to half-enshroud the room in partial darkness, and deepen the shadows on the faces of its occupants. The nodding trees in the garden at the rear of the house cast their shadows fantastically on the wainscotted walls—night was coming on apace.

The two occupants of that gloomy chamber remained seated in comparative silence. They had been conversing, however, but at the time we take a glance at them, they were each occupied with their own thoughts ; what these were, the reader may guess, for the last words which had passed between them was relative to their lost child.

Lady Fleetwood was the first to break the silence, which had at length become almost painful.

"Strange!" exclaimed her ladyship, "very strange that we never hear anything of your brother."

The baronet sighed.

"Ah!" he exclaimed, sadly enough, "my brother! A strange brother, forsooth!"

"Will he never come here again, think you?"

Sir Richard shrugged his shoulders doubtfully.

"You parted with him on good terms. He surely does not bear so deep an animosity as to be estranged from his relations for the remainder of his life?"

"When a man has done another so much injury as Richard has me, it seldom happens that he likes to look the man he has so injured in the face."

"But that is all over now, Reginald," answered her ladyship. "Let the past be buried in oblivion. You are restored to your rights, you are happy, and—"

She paused suddenly, for she became aware that she was treading upon dangerous ground, and that she was, moreover, stating that which was not the case, for it struck her suddenly that her liege lord looked the very picture of unhappiness.

"My brother Richard has injured both of us too deeply ever to become a happy and contented inmate of our house," said the baronet, solemnly. "I would that the past could be forgotten, but I fear me much that it is not possible to bury the remembrance of it in oblivion. Ah, no! I fear worse than this, my own dear wife—I fear much worse than this."

"What!" exclaimed Lady Fleetwood, with sudden energy.

"I can hardly tell you what I fear," her companion replied, "for all is vague—all is doubt. I sometimes think that it would be well for all of us if memory's pictures were not so vivid."

"What do you mean, Reginald?"

"Our dear child," said the baronet, sadly. "If she be in existence, which, to say the truth, I much doubt—"

"Doubt! Have you any reason to imagine that she is dead, that she—"

The speaker paused suddenly.

"Alas, I fear so! All inquiries seem to have been useless, and I fear—I fear the worst."

Lady Fleetwood made no reply, but her eyes silently filled with tears.

"My brother," said her husband, in continuation, "my brother is as unscrupulous as—"

Here he paused suddenly.

"Unscrupulous?" echoed his wife.

"Of a surety, yes," he answered.

"What of that, he never, surely—"

"Well, dearest?"

"He never would be monster enough to harm the dear innocent?"

Sir Reginald made no other reply than a deep drawn sigh.

"Ah, no," said his wife, in continuation : "I never will believe that he could be inhuman enough to swoop at such heartless villainy as that."

"Pray Heaven that your opinion may be a true one," answered Sir Reginald.

A footman entered the room with noiseless

and stealthy steps,—he came near to where his master was seated, looked dubiously at him for a moment, but said nothing.

"Well, Stephen?" said the baronet.

"I beg pardon, Sir Reginald, but are you disengaged?"

"Yes, certainly. What is it?"

"A party wishes to see you."

"Who? Any one you know? Lady or gentleman?"

"It's a party, if you please, sir. Not a lady."

"Oh, show him into the library."

"Yes, sir," answered the domestic, whereupon he disappeared from the room in which husband and wife had been so long conversing. In a few minutes he reappeared, and said the party awaited the appearance of Sir Reginald, in his library. The baronet rose and took his way to the room in question. Upon his arrival there, he found an odd-looking individual, with small grey eyes, a piercing nose, and pinched features. There was a restless expression about the eyes themselves, which were what might be called painful. They wandered about the room, as though in search of some missing object, and then wandered over the face and form of the baronet himself."

"Pray be seated, sir," said the latter, handing his visitor a chair. "What might be your business?"

"Well, you see, Sir Reginald," said the individual, after he had seated himself on the extreme edge of the library chair. "You see, Sir Reginald—"

Sir Reginald did not see anything but a plain, ordinary, not to say repulsive looking man, before him, but he did not interrupt him.

"You see that I am in the employ of Mr. Wild."

"Oh!" exclaimed the baronet, significantly.

"Yes, sir, Mr. Jonathan Wild."

"I know."

"And consequently you'll excuse my making so bold."

"Go on, my man," said the baronet, impatiently this time, for he saw that the gentleman before him seemed inclined to indulge in unnecessary preliminaries.

"Mr. Wild," said the man in continuation, "thought as how it would be better to come to you at once—"

Here he paused.

"I am much obliged," said the baronet.

"And so see," continued the man, "we may be mistaken, but the governor thinks he has a clue—he's on the scent."

"I pray of you to be more explicit. What is your meaning?"

"The child," said the man.

At this, the baronet, in spite of himself, turned suddenly pale.

"Oh," he exclaimed, and then staggered back a pace or two, and dropped into a chair.

"Shall I go on?" said Wild's man.

"By all means. You are keeping me in suspense unnecessarily, so it appears to me."

Upon this the man poked his head on one side, and proceeded to lay his case before the baronet.

"I dare say you have heard of a chap as we call the Nobbler."

Sir Reginald nodded his assent.

"Well, he's—leastways, that is the Nobbler, has been up a tree for a long time past. Not a trace could be found of him, or he would have been sent to his account long ago. The fellow has kept as close as an oyster in his shell. We ain't even been able to ascertain what he has been about, when luck would have it, that we have heard a little about him within these last few days."

"Oh, you have?"

"Yes, we have, Sir Reginald; a chap as does the light-fingered business now lies in Newgate, and he says to Mr. Wild, says he, 'Don't you want to know something about a child belonging to Sir Reginald Fleetwood?' Well, in course the governor says 'I just do, and no mistake.' 'Well,' says he, 'I'm your man for that job.' 'Are you?' says Wild? 'Yes,' says he. 'Well, then, out with all you know at once,' says the governor. 'What for?' says he. 'If you can put me in the way of finding out this ere child,' says the governor, 'I'll put you in the way of getting outside these walls.' 'That's a bargain,' says the cut-purse. 'It is,' says the governor. Well, then, to cut the story short, Sir Reginald, he ups and tells Mister Wild how he knowed the child—your child you must understand."

"Yes, yes," answered the baronet, impatiently.

"He ups and tells all he knowed about her."

"And what was that?"

"Well, it appears, Sir Reginald, that this ere man lived in a house, where a lot of other chaps like himself lived, and in the place there was a family—an Irish family—so he says, who had charge of a little girl, who was yourn. He knowed this, 'cause Mr. Richard Fleetwood used to come sometimes with the Nobbler and see her."

A groan escaped from the baronet at this part of the story.

"I believe the Nobbler paid for her board, so the man says; and he says as how Mr. Richard and the Nobbler were not always first cousins in the matter. Well, somehow or other, it so turned out—mind I don't say it's true, sir, but this is what has been stated, it so turned out that there was an intention on the part of Mr. Fleetwood to put the child away for good and for all."

"What do you mean ?" inquired the baronet.

"Get rid of it."

"Where ?"

"Poison it !"

"Good God ! Can this be possible ?"

"So the fellow in Newgate says," answered the man. "So he says. In course, it is impossible for us to say if he speaks the truth or not, but there is every reason for us to think so."

"Tell me, does the child live ?" exclaimed the unhappy father.

"Yes, I should say so."

"Where is it then ?"

The man shook his head.

"You had better hear me to the end," he answered.

"Yes, go on."

"Well, then, whether it was to prevent Mr. Fleetwood from carrying out his wicked designs, or whether it was done for any other purpose I am unable to say, but this thing is quite certain, the little girl was suddenly taken away from the drunken Irish family with whom she had been living, and taken to some friend or acquaintance of the Nobbler."

"And my brother Mr. Richard ?"

"Has not the slightest notion of what has become of her," answered the man.

"You are sure of that ?"

"Quite certain."

"Where is she now ?"

"Ah ! there we are at fault Sir Reginald. One fact is quite certain, she is placed somewhere by the Nobbler. The Nobbler has her under his especial care, once get hold of him and we are all right for the rest."

"And do you know where he is likely to be found ?"

"Ah, that would puzzle a wiser head than mine to tell,,' answered the man.

"Then we are as far off as ever," returned the servant.

"No, no, certainly not, far from that, Mr. Wild told me to come down and see you. He said as how it would be better for me to explain all to you, and most likely you would be able to tell him where to find your brother."

"Indeed I am unable to do that," answered Sir Reginald.

"Ah, you are."

"Quite unable, I have no more notion than you have yourself."

"He never comes here."

"Never."

"Strange. Don't you know where he resides ?"

"Ah, that's unfortunate, most unfortunate, he's a slippery customer too. Do you know Colonel Jack ?"

"Yes, why do you ask ?" said the baronet, in some surprise.

"Why because he and Sir, leastways, Mr. Richard used to be intimate "

"They are sworn enemies now. At least they were some short time since."

"Well we must work it our own way then," returned the man. "I dare say we shall be able to find out where the Nobbler is to be pitched upon—sooner or later."

"Look here my man," said Sir Reginald. "I will give you or anyone else anything you may demand, in reason of course, if you can find out my child and restore her to me. Tell Wild from me—tell him that five-hundred—a thousand pounds shall be given to him if he can succeed in this the dearest object of my life. More than this, I will besides reward you handsomely for the same. Now remember this."

"I will not forget it," answered the officer.

He had been a thief, but he was an officer now.

There is an old saying of "set a thief to catch a thief," and Wild had, on more than one occasion, acted in accordance with this wise and discreet doctrine.

After some fruther conversation the man with the restless eyes took his departure from the country seat of the Fleetwoods.

Before reporting progress to his master, Wild, he went to all the parties he knew to try and find out the Nobbler. He even visited the man in Newgate, who had given the information respecting the child, but he could extract nothing further from him but what was known already. As he said Wild had "pumped him dry." After he had satisfied himself that there was little or nothing more that he could gather which might lead him to the Nobbler's whereabouts, the quondam thief and present officer betook himself to his master's quarters in Cold Arbour Lane. He then and there informed Wild of the result of his visit to Acton.

The celebrated theiftaker listened to all his man had to say, and then bid him use every endeavour to find out the notorious housebreaker who had for so long a time eluded his search.

Two days after this Mr. Jonathan Wild took his way to a small tavern in Islington which, at the time of which we write, was in reality the country. Wild seemed to be on excellent terms with the landlord, for he was greeted by that worthy as an old friend, and at once betook himself to the bar-parlour. When quietly ensconced there, he turned to the landlord and said—

"Well?"

Now, there's not much to be gathered from the simple expression " Well," but there was a great deal of significance in it under existing circumstances.

The landlord said—

" Has not been here."

" Likely?" said Wild.

" Can't tell," was the rejoinder.

" I'll wait," answered the thieftaker; and he sat himself down in a dark corner of the bar-parlour.

And so he did wait. An hour passed away, then another, and another. Still the thieftaker kept his station, watching the bar customers, not a few of whom he recognised, but he took no notice. The landlord took no notice, and, like a cat waiting for a mouse, Jonathan Wild sat with exemplary patience all that evening for no purpose.

When it had passed, and the clock of old Islington church had chimed out a quarter to one, Wild took his departure.

The next night saw him at the same spot quietly ensconced in the bar-parlour. Hour after hour passed, but there he sat like a harpy waiting for his prey.

" I am afraid," said the landlord, quietly.

" Of what?" inquired Wild.

" Oh, not of you," returned boniface.

" I should hope not, Barker," returned Wild.

" Oh, no, not of you."

" What then?"

" That you'll have all your trouble for nothing."

" That's my business."

" Unquestionably. But he don't come here often."

" S'pose not. He's too wide awake for that."

" More than that, he may never come here again."

" That's true. But then he may, you see."

" Oh, most certainly."

" Why, you are not going to show the white feather, Barker."

" I should hope not!" exclaimed the landlord, indignantly.

" That's all right."

" Only, you see, it's such a chance."

" What is?"

" About his coming here at all."

" And I don't intend to throw a chance away. Do you happen to see that, my friend?"

" Just like you," returned the landlord, with a laugh, which however was hollow like many of his own butts, for, to say the truth, Mr. Barker did not like the business on hand although he dare not hint at such a thing to Wild. " Ah, just like you, there never was such a man."

" Gammon !" said Wild.

The landlord looked puzzled.

" I shall wait," continued the thieftaker, " to-night, next night, the night after that, and so on—"

" Until—"

" Until I find him."

" Oh!" exclaimed Mr. Barker.

" But you've kept it quiet, I suppose?" said Wild, fastening a look upon the landlord which pierced him through.

" Quiet! I should think so."

" I should hope so."

" I am sure so."

" So much the better. That will do," and Wild nodded his head to the landlord to proceed about his business.

The latter left the bar-parlour, and began serving his customers. As he passed to and fro, Wild watched him carefully.

" Come here," he said, after about another half-hour had passed. The landlord entered.

" He will be here, unless he has been put on his guard," said Wild, significantly.

" You think so?" returned Barker.

" I don't think, I am sure."

" Oh."

" Unless he has been prevented. Do you understand?"

" Well—yes—that is—not exactly."

" Let me explain. You know, Barker, there is a little affair—"

" Oh, don't mention it."

" Oh, but I must. I say there is a little affair."

" Yes, yes, I know to what you are alluding."

" I'm glad you do, because it is not necessary for me to remind you, or go over the ground again."

" Not the least occasion I assure you."

" Very well. Now you know what I was just saying. He will be here, unless he has been prevented."

" I should hope he has not—that's all I have to say."

" Now look here, Barker," said Wild. " You'd better be upright and straightforward with me, mind you that. Have you been acting as you ought to do?"

" Goodness me, yes! Why you don't— you don't, surely, suspect—"

" I suspect everyone !"

" What me?"

" Hark ! what was that?" said the thieftaker, in a hoarse whisper.

" His voice, I do believe," exclaimed the landlord, turning suddenly pale, for he was an arrant coward. " His voice, as I am a living man !"

Wild looked through a chink in the room in which he was seated, and a look of demoniacal satisfaction passed across his ill-favoured features. He clapped one of his horny hands on his knee.

"It is him," said Mr. Barker, who felt as though his own knees were about to give way beneath him.

"Aye, him sure enough. Stay where you are."

"Why."

"You look frightened, that's all," returned Wild, and you might frighten some one else. Do you see that, my friend."

"Do I look frightened?"

"Of course you do."

The Nobbler, for it was he, took his way into a small room in the rear of the premises. It was not altogether the public room generally used by the frequenters of the establishment, but was a sort of side room where persons occasionally went into to be quiet and have a cold collation, served in the midday, or a cup of chocolate in the afternoon.

"Now, Mr. Barker, you'll sit down there, if you please," said Wild, rising from the arm-chair on which he had been seated, and placing the landlord in the same."

"Oh," said the latter.

He was pale as a parsnip with fright, being, as we have before observed, a notorious coward, and the idea of an affray with one of the most desperate burglars and the most celebrated thieftakers of the time taking place in his own house actually made him tremble like an aspen bough agitated by the wind.

"You will keep quiet till I come back," said Wild, authoritatively. "Do you mark that?"

"I am your servant," said Mr. Barker.

"Then mind what I say."

And the thieftaker left the bar parlour, went to the side of the bar itself, and then gave utterance to a note which was between a whistle and a whisper. He did this near to a window which was in the passage, which ran from the side of the bar itself to the kitchen and staircase, which led to the bedrooms above. Upon this two heads made their appearance at the window in question. Some telegraphic signs passed between Wild and the owners of those two heads, and then the thieftaker walked quietly in front of the bar. There were several persons there, some of whom knew him well enough, but they said nothing, only regarded him with a look of surprise and fear. Walking quietly round the bar, Wild bent his steps towards the room into which the Nobbler had gone but a few minutes before. The thieftaker opened the door of this room so quietly that the probability is that he would not have disturbed anyone had it not have been for one circumstance. It was this. The Nobbler was seated in front of the fire with his back towards the door of the room.

He would not have observed the thieftaker in the position he then occupied, had it not have been for the circumstance to which we have alluded—it was this: there was a looking-glass, a dingy one enough, over the mantel-piece—in this the well-known features of Wild became reflected.

The Nobbler glanced up at them, and to have seen the expression of his countenance then, would have been worth journeying many miles for.

Turning sharp round, and flinging his chair from him, he confronted his enemy—that enemy who had been so often at his heels—with a look of deep hate and fearful ferocity.

A half-growl, more like a wild beast than anything else, escaped from his throat, and came through his clenched teeth. With one wild spring he made towards the door, before which Wild stood with indomitable resolution. In another moment he had the thieftaker by the throat, and endeavoured to fling him on one side.

"You'd better take it quietly," said the latter, laying hold of the Nobbler's throat in return.

"D——n!" exclaimed the housebreaker.

"I tell you that it will be better for you to take it quietly," repeated Wild, almost breathless with the struggle which was going on. "Listen—you shall have a pardon upon one condition!"

At these words the grasp of the ruffian relaxed.

"Pardon?" he exclaimed.

"Of course," answered Wild. "I'm your best friend, after all."

The Nobbler recoiled a few paces and gazed at the speaker with surprise, and well he might.

"Now, sit down," said Wild. You are caught, and if you had ten times the strength and twenty times the daring, you couldn't give me the slip."

As he said this he removed his back a trifle from the door to admit into the room two of his followers.

"Clap on the darbies," said Wild, to the new comers.

"Not if I know it," said the Nobbler, assuming an attitude of defence.

"Now look here, what's the use of your coming any of your capers," said Wild. "We ain't at Bill Dyson's."

"Ugh! ain't we—what if we ain't," returned the housebreaker.

"And you know," continued Wild, "we must all on us come to the full length of our tether some time or other, and you have come to yours, and a pretty long one you've had my friend, that's what I have to say upon that head."

The Nobbler gave a sort of howl of defiance. He stood glaring at his enemies with his drawn knife in his hand.

"And so that being the case," said Wild

in continuation, "I don't see that you've much to complain of, especially as we don't want to have you scragged. No, we really don't."

"Get out—what do you want?" inquired the Nobbler.

"Well, in the first place you are our prisoner," answered Wild. "And now, sit down and listen to me. I will offer you terms such as you will not refuse."

The Nobbler sat sulkily down upon one of the chairs in the room.

"Now, look here, my hearty," said Wild; "I need not tell you that if there ever was a chap who deserved a hempen noose, you are the man, and no mistake."

"Oh, stow that," exclaimed the housebreaker, 'cause I can't stand it."

"Very well, I won't hurt your feelings, only, you see, we all of us have something or other to bring us to our end. However, that's neither here nor there. I ain't a going to harrow up your feelings, that is, supposing you have any; and so, let us to business. You want your life, I suppose?"

The Nobbler gave a nod of assent.

"Good; and I want a certain child, about whom you are the right party to inquire of, I should suppose."

The housebreaker gave another nod of acquiescence.

"Well, then, the case stands thus:—it's as simple as—as prigging. You give up the child, and I promise you that you shall go your ways as soon as you please."

"I ain't got the child," returned the Nobbler.

"No, my friend, but you know where she is. Do you see that?"

"I hear you say so. What of that? But s'posing it to be true?"

"Which it is."

"I say s'posing it to be true," returned the Nobbler, "I ain't a going to give up the kid without being tipped something. I can't live upon the air, can I? and I am knocked out of time in my professional capacity. Well, what's the consequence?—why, just this, I must starve. Better to be scragged at once than starve."

"Oh, you won't starve, I dare say," retorted Wild. "A man of your ready wit is not likely to starve in a land of plenty."

"That may be all very well, but I tell you I ain't a going to give up the kid without you blue something."

Jonathan Wild considered for some few minutes.

"Well," he said, after a little reflection, "I am not a hard dealer. Come, I will deal liberally with you. You shall have a handsome sum down upon the nail upon the production of the child."

"Done! then I am your man. Give me

No 103.

my liberty, and make any appointment you like, and I will keep it and bring the child with me."

"Give you your liberty!" exclaimed the thieftaker; "give you your liberty! Gammon and all. You shall have your liberty only when you produce the child; and more than this I cannot promise. You are my prisoner, and must remain so until you do as I desire."

The Nobbler gave a sulky, discontented look at his captor, but made no reply.

Jonathan Wild, without another word, drew a pair of handcuffs from his pocket, and slipped them on the wrists of the burglar, who submitted to the operation with a calmness which perfectly astonished the occupants of the room.

"One, two, and all told," said Wild, with the utmost *sang froid.* "Now we understand one another. I shan't take you to Newgate, nor to the Compter; only to my own house."

"Thank you," said the Nobbler.

"And," said Wild, in continuation, "you will there remain till such time as you produce the kid."

"And what do you stand for her?" asked the burglar.

"Oh, something handsome—a couple of hundred. Suppose we say a couple of hundred."

"Oh, is that all?" said the Nobbler, discontentedly.

"And quite enough too, considering you have your liberty, which is worth to you many thousands."

"A couple of hundred?" said the burglar, once more.

"Well, we won't quarrel upon that score. Suppose we say three, or even four hundred? I dare say the parties belonging to the child won't be too particular."

"As they happen to be very rich," suggested the Nobbler.

"Well, they are not particularly rich, but they are not poor—certainly not poor."

"I should think not," said the Nobbler; "anything but that."

"You know them, then?"

"I should just think I did."

In the course of a few minutes the Nobbler was taken in a hackney coach to the house of the celebrated thieftaker in Cold Arbour Lane, and in a few days after this, he emerged from that respectable establishment, with five hundred golden guineas in his pocket, and beat a hasty retreat through the narrow courts and alleys which abounded in that objectionable locality.

The child had been brought to Wild's house by Long Ned, at the Nobbler's request. The poor little thing was so miserably clad, and altogether she presented such a woeful appearance, that it would be impossible for anyone to have supposed for one moment that she was the daughter of a baronet.

Wild did not think it expedient to take her to Acton in her miserable plight, and consequently he had her cleansed and fitted out with some fresh things, and when this had been done, he took her to her desponding parents.

It would be difficult for us to give anything like an adequate description of the scene which took place upon the re-union of parents and child. Even the callous Jonathan Wild was moved at its contemplation.

CHAPTER CL.

A CRUSHING BLOW TO THE LOVER'S HOPES. DEATH OF COLONEL JACK AND RICHARD FLEETWOOD.

OUR tale is drawing to a conclusion. But a few last scenes yet remain to be discovered. As time went on the attentions of the noble Augustus Fairfax became more and more protestant. He pressed both Rosalie and Mr. and Mrs. Osborne to name an early day for his marriage with the former. This was put off from time to time until at last the ardour of the young aristocrat would admit of no denial and reluctantly enough, Mr. Osborne and our hero after having consulted together, consented to the day being named for the nuptials.

After this, as our readers may imagine, the minds of all were fully occupied in preparations for the coming ceremony, for the wedding was to be on a grand scale of magnificence. Several of the proudest of England's proud nobles were to be present. The earl himself was to support his son, and Mr. Osborne was to give the bride away.

It was a few days before the ceremony was appointed to take place that a scene occurred which dashed the hopes of the lovers to the ground, and well nigh drove them to despair.

The scene we are about to relate took place at Richmond. The Honourable Augustus Fairfax and Rosalie Halford were returning home along a road which ran through a small wood which led to Richmond, when they were suddenly confronted by a tall dark individual who stood before them and glanced at both of them in a most malignant manner. Rosalie became alarmed, for the shades of evening were beginning to descend, and the first thought, naturally enough, suggested the possibility of the mysterious stranger being in reality a robber, she uttered a slight scream and clung to the arm of her companion who looked at the intruder with some surprise.

"Oh!" exclaimed the latter between his clenched teeth, "a pretty couple forsooth!"

"Insolence!" ejaculated the young nobleman, "stand back sir,"

"Lovers!" returned the man with an agravating sneer in his tone and manner, which was galling to the last degree. Lovers, ah, ah! lovers! a pretty pair forsooth. The young scion of the Fairfax family is about to wed the daughter of a highwayman a precious choice truly. Really—Ah, ah! The daughter of a highwayman excellent jest!"

As these words fell from the lips of the stranger in bold and bitter satire, the colour came and went in quick and transient succession. Augustus Fairfax felt the weight on his arm become heavier every minute and the form of poor Rosalie shook as with a sudden palsy.

"Who and what are you?" exlclaimed Fairfax. "If you have any spark of gentlemanly or manly feeling, you will leave this spot, and not seek to insult those who have never harmed you. Go, at once, and we will forgive the libels you have uttered."

"You are jesting, my friend," returned the stranger, in slow accents, so that every word might fall upon the ears of his listeners with painful distinctness. "Do you know, Augustus Fairfax, that the woman or girl you have on your arm is none other than the daughter of the celebrated highwayman Colonel Jack."

"Insolent liar!" exclaimed Fairfax. "Were it not for the presence of this lady, I would chastise you on the spot."

"Young man," said the stranger, solemnly, "I have spoken the truth. You are about to marry the daughter of the celebrated Colonel Jack. I have said it—and I swear it—as I hope for mercy hereafter. So mind you look to it."

Augustus Fairfax looked at the speaker in a perfect state of stupefaction. At first he had doubted the truth of which the latter had uttered; but by degrees, when he heard the same statement repeated—by degrees he began to waver in his first impression and opinion.

"You doubt what I have given utterance to, sir," said the stranger. "Listen to me for a moment. If you do not believe me, put the question to your friend Henry Osborne, who is to give the fair bride away—the same Henry Osborne who was in Newgate some years ago upon the charge of murder."

"Murder! In Newgate!" exclaimed Augustus Fairfax. "Am I dreaming? Am I awake?"

"It is time you awoke to a sense of your situation," answered the stranger. "Awake before it is too late."

"Mr. Osborne is a gentleman, and my most particular friend."

"Then I have no reason to congratulate you upon your choice of acquaintance," returned the stranger. "You are about to wed the daughter of a notorious highwayman, and you rank among your acquaintances the sycophant and hypocrite Henry Osborne."

"Unsay those words, or by Heaven I will chastise you in spite of this lady's presence!" exclaimed Fairfax.

"Oh, mercy! Let us go. Take no heed of him, Augustus!" exclaimed Rosalie Halford. "Take no heed of him, dearest."

Her voice was so week that it surprised her lover, as he felt assured that she was about to faint. The stranger still kept regarding the two lovers with a look of half satisfaction and half malignantly.

"You will do well, young man, to remember my words. Is it fitting? Is it proper for one in your exalted position in life, to wed the daughter of a highwayman? Answer that?"

"The daughter of a highwayman! Begone! Liar and slanderer! Begone, and remove your hated presence from our sight. "This young lady is the purest and gentlest of her sex. What matters it to me whose daughter she is? Do you think I would consent to listen to your vile aspersions?"

"Ask Henry Osborne whose daughter she is?" returned the stranger.

"Who and what are you?" exclaimed Fairfax.

"My name is Fleetwood," answered the stranger.

"Sir Reginald Fleetwood?"

"No, Richard Fleetwood—plain Richard Fleetwood."

"I have heard of the name; I know your brother, sir."

"And I know the earl, your father," answered Mr. Richard Fleetwood. "Mark what I have said. Do not marry that girl. You will repent it for the remainder of your life, if you are imprudent enough to do so. Mark you that. If you have one spark of consideration for your family name, avoid this disgrace—a disgrace which you will never be able to retrace. Her name is Rosalie Halford—daughter of Frank Halford, more commonly known as the celebrated Colonel Jack. My cheek blushes when I acknowledge that this hardened ruffian is related to myself—a worthless scion of an honourable house. It is humiliating to be forced to confess this much—it is painful to the last degree; but in doing so, I am only doing an act of justice to a young man who is ignorant of the knowledge of these glaring and painful facts, it is a pity he should be so longer. Young man, be not deceived, the woman you are about to wed is the daughter of a villain, a ruffian, a wholesale plunderer and robber, whose name is a bye-word in the three kingdoms. Remember that! Take heed of it, ere it be too late. It would look pretty to have quartered on the Fairfax arms a couple of pistols, a mask, and a well-filled purse; it would look marvellously pretty. The proud earl, your father, would be pleased to learn this fact. The probability is that it would bring his grey head with sorrow to the grave—stoop it with shame—bring desolation and ruin on his house. If not for yourself, you might have consideration for him whose proud nature could ill brook so deep a blow to his family pride."

Young Fairfax was deadly pale. He looked at Mr. Richard Fleetwood in perfect astonishment. His lip trembled as he became aware that the beauteous Rosalie had swooned. He caught her in his arms, to prevent her from falling to the ground, and gave a beseeching look towards Fleetwood.

"As a gentleman," exclaimed Fairfax, "I charge you to leave us. This poor girl has swooned at the dreadful recital you have chosen to indulge in—swooned, sir. Good Heavens! she scarcely breathes. Rosalie, dear—dear Rosalie, speak!"

But Rosalie made no reply, she had fairly swooned.

Her lover was well-nigh distracted. He again besought Mr. Richard Fleetwood to leave the spot, and proceeded with Rosalie in his arms to the nearest seat.

"If you doubt my word, Mr. Fairfax, I shall be happy to meet you at any time to prove the allegations I have made. I am to be heard of at the Old Hummums, Covent Garden."

"I will write to you, sir," said Mr. Fairfax, whose chief anxiety was to get rid of his persecutor.

Mr. Fleetwood turned upon his heel, and proceeded in an opposite direction to the one taken by Fairfax. He had not advanced more than a hundred and fifty yards or so, when he felt a hand laid roughly on his shoulder. He turned suddenly round, and to his surprise and alarm he beheld the tall figure of Colonel Jack, who had emerged from the dense part of the forest.

"Scoundrel! wretch! inhuman monster?" exclaimed Colonel Jack, in a paroxism of rage. "Is it thus that you malign and injure one who never did you any harm? Is it thus that you seek to destroy the prospects of my only child—and for what?—from a pure spirit of fiendish delight. Dastard and reptile as thou art!"

As the speaker gave utterance to these words he struck Fleetwood so severe a blow that he staggered some paces.

"Draw sir—draw and defend your worthless life, for one of us two must fall!" exclaimed Colonel Jack, who had been a silent listener to the latter part of the conversation between Mr. Fairfax and Fleetwood. His blood boiled, and his brain reeled as he listened to the words which fell from Fleetwood, who did as our hero requested, and, drawing his sword, he stood upon the defensive.

"Follow me," said the colonel, "and we can try this matter hilt to hilt! This time one us leaves not this place alive."

Fleetwood followed in silence to a glade in the forest, where there was an open part covered with green sward.

The moon which had now risen lighted this partially up, save here and there, where the slanting shadow of the trees crossed and re-crossed the otherwise bright spot. It was a spot, however, which was destined to be the scene of a deadly conflict.

The swords of the combatants were crossed in silence, for neither of them spoke after the ground had been chosen tacitly, as though by mutual consent, for them both to settle the quarrel of a life. They both fought well —cautiously enough at first, although Colonel Jack was by far the most impetuous of the two, and made several terrific lunges, which were, however, skilfully parried by Fleetwood, who then, in his turn, assumed the offensive. As he rushed upon his assailant, his foot struck against the root of a tree, and he fell forward. Colonel Jack might then have satiated his vengeance, and killed him on the spot, but with a generosity even to so great an enemy as the one before him—a generosity which was one of the leading characteristics of his nature; he scorned to take any undue advantage of a prostrate foe. He, therefore, quietly waited till Fleetwood regained his footing ; this done, the two combatants were once more engaged in deadly and desperate strife.

Again the swords flashed, tipped by the silver rays of the moon. Again, eye to eye, and point to point, were they opposed. Another quarter of an hour passed over, during which time Fleetwood had received two slight wounds, one in his sword arm, a few inches above the wrist, and the other in his left shoulder. The colonel also was wounded slightly in the chest—the point of Fleetwood's weapon having struck against the breast-bone glanced off, leaving a long narrow gash. Fleetwood made a sudden and more desperate assault upon his adversary, the fierce nature of which somewhat surprised our hero. Fleetwood was under the impression that the colonel was weak and faint from loss of blood, for he thought that the latter had received a much more serious wound than he had in reality, who parried his well-directed thrusts with a skill and address which proved him to be what in reality he was, an accomplished swordsman and a dangerous adversary.

In one of these lunges the colonel succeeded in striking his adversary's sword from his hand, and flinging it some dozen yards or so behind him. Fleetwood prepared himself for the worst, fully expecting to meet his death on the instant, but Colonel Jack stood with his arms crossed, and said—

"Go! pick up your weapon. I strike not an unarmed man!"

Fleetwood rushed past his adversary, and sought for his lost weapon, which had become embedded in some tangled underwood. Colonel Jack quietly awaited his return, not even deigning to turn his head to watch the *ci devant* baronet's movements.

It would have been well for our hero if he had done so, for it would in all probability have saved him his life. Fleetwood crept into the underwood in search of his weapon. As he did so his form was lost to view by the deep shadows of the trees, which kept the place he occupied in all but total darkness. The colonel, however, stood in the bright moonlight—that moon whose rays lighted up his handsome but care-worn features for the last time on this earth.

Presently the barrel of a pistol is seen from the underwood, then a flash, a sharp and ringing report, and Colonel Jack lay upon the green sward without life or motion. Richard Fleetwood had drawn a pistol from his breast coat-pocket, levelled it at our hero, and the shot found its way to his heart with deadly and unerring certainty.

Thus perished Colonel Jack—thus perished the highwayman of the last century. He fell, after all, by treachery—his life, like every other man's, is not without its moral teachings. He was, without doubt, an erring man, but with generous promptings, however, and immeasurably superior in character to his dastardly adversary, whose life he had spared on more than one occasion.

A terrible and awful grin of satisfaction sat upon the features of Richard Fleetwood. His greatest enemy lay dead a few paces from where he then stood—he who had been the main cause of thrusting him from the position he held in life—he who had exposed and humbled him.

A demoniacal smile of delight was visible on Fleetwood's countenance, who emerged from the underwood, and silently and cautiously took his way to the spot where Colonel Jack lay on his face. When he arrived there he turned the body over. The features were set and fixed as by the hand of death.

There was no mistake about it—the spirit of the highwayman had passed away, and there was a calm placidity about the countenance of the murdered man which surprised Fleetwood himself.

As he stood contemplating the prostrate body at his feet, who had worked so much for good and for ill in this world, as he stood contemplating his relative and his victim, a sudden alarm occurred to the guilty man which froze his blood and shook his limbs. He heard the rustling of the leaves, not agitated by the wind, his ears were sufficiently accustomed to that sound, no, this time it was though as if they were agitated by some person creeping through them. The murderer shuddered; his first thought was of flight, but, guilty wretch as he was, he had not the courage to move. He was not, however, kept long in suspense; in the space of a few seconds more a loud growl was heard, and the dog Slott had sprung up and fastened his fangs in Fleetwood's throat.

"Heaven have mercy on me!" exclaimed the now truly miserable man, who dreaded, perhaps, this enemy more than all others in the world.

"Help me Heaven, I shall die!" exclaimed Richard Fleetwood, now in a perfect agony of despair. "Ah, mercy—the hound—oh, this brute!"

He felt the blood trickling down his neck—he struck Slott with all the force he was master of, but to say the truth that was not much, for he was weak from loss of blood, and the great excitement he had been under, which had now passed away, had left him trembling and weak as a girl. He, however, fought with his canine assailant, struck him again and again, and ultimately fell with him on the ground. He rolled over, in the hope of being able to crush him, but all to no purpose, Slott clung the more tenaciously to him. Cold drops of perspiration stood upon the clammy forehead of the miserable man.

His very flesh crept. To die thus torn to pieces by a hound. Ah, how he longed to be possessed of a weapon wherewith to destroy the dog. But this thought was a vain and foolish one, he had naught about him, for the sword for which he had been in search, he had dropped when Slott first sprang upon him.

Suddenly, to his infinite surprise he heard the voice of men calling the hound by name. Slott perched up his short ears and listened, and at the same time slightly relaxed his grasp for which the baronet was thankful. Again the name of Slott was pronounced by two voices, and the animal then relaxed his hold.

Fleetwood streaming with his blood rose to his feet and beheld Knapp and Hackett who were not unknown to him, as the reader may guess. One glance sufficiently explained to these two how the case stood. They beheld the lifeless body of their captain stretched upon the green sward they knew Richard Fleetwood was his bitter enemy.

As the latter rose upon the impulse of the moment, the swords of both the highwaymen were passed through his body. He uttered a piercing shriek, and stood for a moment balancing himself on his legs as he best could, and then fell forward. His features became horribly convulsed, and he clawed at the dank grass as though he were suffering acute agony which without doubt he was. He turned up his eyes towards the two highwaymen.

"This your work, Richard Fleetwood?" said Hackett. "Your work? He was your kinsman. You it was who ruined his prospects in early life—drove him to be what he was, and now, as a finish to all the injuries you have heaped upon him, you take his life. A curse light on your head for that!" exclaimed Hackett, suddenly evincing a deep feeling which almost stopped his utterance.

"Oh, mercy! some water!" exclaimed Fleetwood. "He sought my life. Indeed he did, or this would not have occurred."

"You never slew him in fair combat. I'll answer for that," said Knapp, contemptuously.

"We fought for a full half-an-hour with swords," exclaimed Fleetwood. "If he could speak he would tell you so. Oh—water!"

"How is it then that he met his death by a pistol shot, then?" said Knapp, who had knelt down by the side of the colonel and examined him carefully.

"Ah, I don't know. Water gentlemen," exclaimed Richard Fleetwood, writhing in agony, as the green sward became dyed with his blood.

"Wretch," exclaimed Hackett. "Your hour has arrived. Repent of the accumulated mass of wrongs you have done to this noble-hearted fellow, who was your superior in eery way."

"Ah, mercy—pity!" exclaimed the dying man.

"I have no pity for such as you," answered Hackett. "The sooner all such are out of the world the better."

"Oh, you have murdered me!" ejaculated Fleetwood, "What harm did I ever do you—I am a murdered man."

A low plaintive whine was now set forth by the dog Slott, it was prolonged and continuous, it appeared to worry and vex the dying man more than anything else, for as he heard the dog he groaned in anguish.

"Ah the brute," he exclaimed.

"He's more humanity in his disposition than you ever had," said Knapp, who had been engaged with his companion in constructing a litter on which they were about to place the body of the murdered highwayman. As they placed the dead body of their comrade on this Richard Fleetwood, who had not lost all consciousness, which was a matter of surprise considering the amount of blood he had lost, turned to the two living highwaymen a beseeching look, and begged of them, in the most abject terms, not to leave him, but to procure the services of some leeh to attend to his wounds.

"Psha!" exclaimed Knapp, "there is not half an hour's life in you—maybe not a quarter of an hour's. Tell your sins and repent."

Richard Fleetwood presented a most ghastly and sickening sight to look upon. His countenance was livid, and fast changing to the hue of death. It was smeared and bedabbled with blood.

He called so piteously for water, that Hackett, from feelings of common humanity, went to his side, and placing the mouth of his brandy-flask to his lips, bid him drink. The dying man took a deep draught, which somewhat revived him.

He opened his eyes, which were gathering with the thick films of death, and smiled a certain amount of satisfaction upon the good Samaritan who had thus ministered to him in his extreme hour of suffering.

In a few more minutes the guilty Richard Fleetwood had ceased to live.

"There is an end of as great a scoundrel as the world ever saw," said Knapp, to his companion.

"I suppose then it was he who slew the colonel?" retorted the latter.

"Yes, and in cold blood, I'll be bound," said Knapp. "What are we to do with the body, Ned? It will never do to leave it here."

"No, no," returned Hackett, sadly. "Ah, me, I never thought that I should live to see this day. I believed that he would have outlived us two. No, I never thought to see so sad a sight as this. How calm he looks, poor fellow. Confound the dog!" exclaimed the speaker, as Slott set up another of his long, low, melancholy howls. "Silence sir! lay down Slott!"

The dog looked up into the eyes of the speaker, as though he would inquire the cause of the sad catastrophe which had taken place, and uttered a lower and more suppressed howl or whine.

The two highwaymen exchanged glances with one another. Their countenances were indicative of the deepest woe, and neither cared to speak harshly to Slott, who kept by the side of his master even in death.

Well, a great deal has been said about the faithfulness of dogs Panegyrics have been written by numbers of writers, but not half has been said yet.

Reader, when you are deserted by old friends—when you find out the hollow heartlessness of the world—when you become the sport and toy of fate—look into the wistful eyes of a faithful hound, and you will find no treachery there.

"His daughter is somewhere in the neighbourhood, is she not?" said Hackett

"Don't know whether she is here or at the town house of the Osbornes," answered Knapp. "She was to have been married in a week or so."

"Was she, though?"

"Yes."

"Well, she won't be married now for some time, I should imagine."

"I should suppose not, for she was very fond of her father, poor soul."

"Why poor, she is very rich, I understand —a great heiress."

"Ah, that's all true enough, but when I say poor girl it is in allusion to this," and here the speaker pointed to the dead body of Colonel Jack.

"How shall we convey the body? and, indeed, where shall we take it to?"

"Ah, that is a question which I have some difficulty to answer at present," said Hackett. "Crawley will be down here with the cart early to-morrow morning. If he were here now there would be no difficulty in the matter. Then, again, it's a puzzle to say if it be advisable to see and find out the daughter and Mr. Osborne. He told me when we parted that he was going to Osborne, and, if I mistake not, it was to meet his daughter—at any rate, I know he was going there."

"Then I tell you what we had better do."

"What?"

"Why, stay in Richmond to-night."

"That, of course, I have already arranged that."

"Well, then, don't you think it would be better to stow the body somewhere for the present, and then I or you, which you like, will go round to Mr. Osborne's house and acquaint either him or Miss Halford, if she is there—and if not her, why Miss Staunton will do as well—of the sad event which has taken place."

"I would not be too fast in breaking the news to Miss Halford," said Hackett.

"No, we will see how that may be. Possibly she is not there."

"Well, you can go if you like," said Hackett.

"Oh, no, you," returned the other.

"You have been the most used to genteel society my boy," returned Hackett; "and more than that, your appearance is decidedly best adapted for the purpose."

"Then there's the body," said the other highwayman. "What is to be done with the body?"

"We will endeavour to conceal it in some obscure part of the forest, and return when we have made the necessary arrangements, and remove it at our leisure."

Upon this the two highwaymen carried the body of Colonel Jack some distance in the forest. Placing it in a copse, they covered it over as best they could, and after marking the spot by notching the trunk of the nearest tree, they left the spot sadly enough. Betaking themselves to a small roadside public-house, they sat down in the parlour previous to their indulging in any further actions. They were both melancholy to the last degree. The loss of the leader who by his presence had always animated them, and inspired them with confidence—the loss of that leader now dashed their spirits and weighed them down with a melancholy it was impossible for them to shake off. They sat silently down and mechanically lighted their pipes more from old habit than from any enjoyment they found therefrom. They both puffed away for some time and remained seated in silence.

"When do you think of going up yonder?" inquired Hackett, nodding at the same time in the direction of the hill.

"What, to Osborne?"

"Yes."

"Oh, presently; but to tell you the truth Ned, I don't half like the job. My nerves are unstrung, and somehow or other I don't feel the right sort of thing to go and see that pretty-faced lass. Not in my present state at all events."

"Have a stoup of brandy—that will put you in better spirits, old boy."

"Fictitious courage produced by artificial means! Oh, no," exclaimed Knapp. "It won't set me right, Ned—only for an hour or so perhaps."

"Well, that is all you want to go up yonder. You will be back in less than an hour, I'll be sworn."

"Possibly so."

"Well, then?"

"You think I had better be off—is that what you mean?"

"Oh, please yourself. The sooner a bitter pill is swallowed the better, to my thinking; but if you don't feel up to the mark just now, why wait awhile, there's no particular hurry. He will wait quietly enough for us now, poor chap."

"Ah, he'll wait sure enough," said Ned. "It seems impossible that such a restless spirit as the colonel's should lay so still and quiet."

"It does. I wonder if that scoundrel murdered him, after all," said Hackett.

"Impossible to say, with anything like certainty; but we did well to send him to his account, if it was only to pay off old scores. He was a bitter enemy to the colonel, surely."

"He was so—he was all that."

Knapp rose to his feet, looked out through the window, and then turned to his companion.

"Well," said the latter, "what do you make of it?"

"Of what?"

"How do you feel?"

"Well, I have made up my mind to be off at once."

"Well done resolution."

"I am a trifle better now, and if I wait any longer, perhaps my courage may ooze out. So, I'll be off at once."

And so saying, Knapp pulled up the collar of his coat, and without more ado walked out of the room. He put his head in for a moment, however, to say to his companion—

"You'll wait here till I return!"

"Oh, of course," exclaimed the latter. "Certainly, you will find me here."

Knapp then departed. He took his way up the hill, in the direction of Henry Osborne's house, and in the space of about twenty minutes he was at the front entrance thereof.

CHAPTER CLI.

THE TERRIBLE ANNOUNCEMENT—GENEROSITY OF FAIRFAX.

It was with a beating heart that Knapp found courage enough to knock at the door of Henry Osborn's mansion. He hardly knew how to break the intelligence, besides which he was quite at a loss to know who he should see. Possibly neither Osborne nor Miss Halford were there. In that case, he would ask for Miss Staunton—he knew her, and consequently, there would be no difficulty in that matter. He knew Mr. Osborne, too, well enough, and so he hoped and prayed that either one or the other of them might be at home.

A footman answered the door to his summons.

"Mr. Osborne at home?" inquired Knapp.

"Yes, sir. What name?" returned the servant.

"Captain Knapp," said the highwayman—for such he had always called himself, when waiting upon great folks.

"Ah," returned the servant. "Please to walk in."

Knapp did as he was requested, and was shown into a room on the basement of the house. The footman took his way up stairs, and returning, informed the highwayman that his master awaited his presence up stairs. Knapp followed the servant, and was shown into a small back room where he found two individuals with very long faces. One of these was Mr. Osborne himself, and the other was a stranger to the highwayman. He is no stranger to the reader however, for the last named individual was the Honourable Augustus Fairfax.

"Oh," exclaimed Osborne, advancing towards the highwayman. "Captain Knapp How are you, Knapp?"

"But middling, Mr. Osborne—only middling."

"Umph! We are all much the same it would seem. You have business with me, perhaps. Any letter from—from Halford?"

At this inquiry Knapp changed colour. He was so visibly effected that it could not escape the notice of both the gentleman present.

"I do wish to speak to you, sir," said Knapp; "but perhaps you are engaged?"

"No, not at all; say on. Is it relating to the colonel?"

At this question, Knapp regarded the speaker with a look of perfect surprise and wonderment.

"Oh, you need not be afraid of speaking before this gentleman," said Osborne. "This is the Honourable Augustus Fairfax, and he now knows all. It is well that he does, for it has removed a great weight off my mind, which, to say the truth, hung like an incubus over me. How about the colonel?"

"Mr. Osborne," said Knapp, sadly, "I know you were always very kind to him—I know well enough that he esteemed and loved you beyond any other man in the world—I feel assured of that, and my tongue falters to tell you the sad, sad news respecting our esteemed and valued friend."

"Gracious heavens Knapp, what is the matter? Speak out man, keep me no longer this agonizing suspense."

"Mr Osborne, the career of Colonel Jack is closed, the volume of his life is closed and sealed with the signet of death!"

Henry Osborne made no reply, he staggered to a chair, fell into it, fell forward with his face on the table and cried like a child.

Fairfax looked at his friend, and gently laying his hand upon Osborne's shoulder he said, in gentle accents—

"Nay—nay, Osborne, my very good friend, be not thus moved. It might have been worse, much worse. It might have been—"

He paused suddenly.

"True," exclaimed Osborne, "you are right, Fairfax. It might indeed have been much worse. You must pardon me this emotion, but it has come so sudden on me, this news, and immediately on the heels of the other, that I am quite unnerved. How did the colonel meet his death?" inquired Osborne of the highwayman.

"We have every reason to believe by foul means," said Knapp.

"How so, my friend?"

"We found Colonel Jack stretched lifeless on the green sward in an open part of the wood, on t'other side of the town. He was lying on his face, quite dead."

"Gracious Heavens! Any wounds?"

"Yes one bullet wound and two slight wounds as though inflicted by the point of a sword. The bullet wound had evidently been given from behind, for it had gone through the left shoulder blade and entered the cavity of the chest. I should suppose that death must have been instantaneous for the face wore a placid expression, and I should suppose that the pistol bullet entered his heart."

"Who do you suppose has done this deed?" inquired Osborne.

"We found near to where the colonel lay Mr. Richard Fleetwood, also badly wounded with the colonel's dog Slott holding him down by the throat. Indeed it was the dog which at first drew our attention to the spot."

"Richard Fleetwood!" exclaimed Fairfax. "What time was this, sir?"

"It must have been about a quarter after nine when we first made the discovery of the dead body of the colonel."

"Not much more than half an hour after I had parted with him," exclaimed Fairfax. "Yes, nearly three quarters of an hour it must have been."

"And where is Mr. Fleetwood now, then?" inquired Osborne.

"He is dead!" answered the highwayman.

"Richard Fleetwood dead?"

"Yes, sir; he was wounded when we came upon the scene; and Slott, the colonel's dog, having inflicted several severe bites on his throat, Mr. Fleetwood died some quarter of an hour after our arrival. He informed us that there had been a duel between himself and the colonel, and I should imagine that the latter was like to become victor, when, as I suspect, the cowardly Fleetwood took some advantage of him, and fired his pistol from behind."

"Did he admit this?"

"Who sir?"

"Mr. Richard Fleetwood."

"No, he is not—or rather was not—a man likely to do that; but I think myself there can be no doubt as to how all this occurred. I can see it as plainly as though I had been there."

"This is, indeed, sad intelligence," exclaimed Mr. Osborne.

"Poor dear Rosalie!" ejaculated Fairfax.

"We must keep this intelligence from her for the present," said Henry Osborne. "It would be madness to inform her of her father's death in her present state."

"Worse than madness—it would be positive cruelty."

"What shall we do with the body?" inquired Knapp. "The last remains of Colonel Jack."

"Where is the body now?"

"We left it concealed in a copse near to where he fell."

"Better give notice to the authorities," suggested Fairfax.

Knapp shook his head.

"We thought of removing him to town," he said, slowly.

"I will go with you, my friend, and see to that," answered Henry Osborne. "It will be a painful ordeal for me to undergo, a very painful one, to see the companion of my boyhood and the friend of my youth and early manhood stretched lifeless by the hand of death, but I must nerve myself to the task. Mr. Fairfax, you will pardon me, I am sure, one horrible revelation comes so soon on the heels of another, that I hardly know what I am about. I pray you pardon me."

"Listen," said Fairfax. "Avoid exposure. Not for my sake, for I am ready to dare all for her whom I love—more than this, or anything else that may occur; but avoid exposure, for the sake of my family."

He spoke these last words in a half-whisper to his companion, and Knapp, who imagined that perhaps the two friends had something to say without a third party's presence, deemed it prudent to retire. He told Mr. Osborne that he would await his orders in the room below—the one he had at first been shown into.

"Thank you, Knapp—thank you. I will attend you presently."

Knapp left the apartment immediately.

"Now, Fairfax," said Osborne, "you know all. As a friend, I should advise you to reconsider the matter. This will be for us to discuss hereafter; but I, for one, would not press this suit upon you. The marriage has been appointed to take place, it is true; but what of that? Hundreds of other marriages have been broken off, even at the eleventh hour, for some trifling cause or other, consequently, no reasonable person could possibly complain of your doing so in the present instance, when there is so great and deep a cause for your doing so. How is it possible that a scion of a noble house could ever expect happiness in espousing the daughter of a highwayman. The world would say it was an impossibility.

"My friend, what the world says is a matter of little moment. I have lived long enough to know that; the world, we generally wrong in these conclusions.

"At any rate, I should presume that every man is, or ought to be, a judge of his own happiness better than the world. I love Rosalie Halford, be she whom she may, I see in her virtues and qualities, which I search in vain for among those of my own class. I do not tell you that I wish everyone to know who she is, or rather who her father was. No one will know, I should presume. It is not likely if all is managed with discretion. You had better not be seen

in the matter. There will be an inquest, of course. Well, what then? both parties were slain. There were no seconds. It is presumed that the quarrel broke out suddenly, from some cause or other, which cannot be ascertained. Swords were drawn. Wounds were received. Colonel Jack fell, not without honour, seriously wounding his adversary. What then? A dog—the colonel's dog, comes up, and tears the neck and throat of the wounded Richard Fleetwood, in such a manner that he too, yields up his life. The case is as simple as possible. Let that man—What's his name?"

"Who?"

"The one who has just gone down stairs."

"Captain Knapp."

"Well let him give evidence, let him state as to how he found the combatants, the one dead and the other wounded; and all will be well. The jury will return a verdict of 'justifiable homicide,' or some such verdict and there will be an end of the matter The body will be given up to their relations, who will of course claim them, and then this tragedy will end—for it is a tragedy, and a deep one to!" exclaimed Fairfax, sadly.

"It is, indeed."

"But again I must impress upon you, Osborne, not to be too forward in the matter. Tell this man—can he be relied on."

"Who, Knapp?"

"Yes."

"Ah, dear yes, relied on for anything."

"Very good, tell him not to bring your name—mine, or our sweet Rosalie forward in any way. Of course it will be useless to endeavour to conceal the fact that one of the dead bodies is that of Colonel Jack."

"He is too well known for us to endeavour to do that."

"So I should presume. Very well, acknowledge it at once. The jury may come to what conclusion they please. They cannot bring either of these to life again. No one can know them in this world, so let them bring in their verdict. Let this Knapp or someone else, claim the body of Colonel Jack, and you and I need not be seen in the business. Indeed, my dear Osborne, if you would take my advice, I should say you had better not go to the corpse at all, leave it to Knapp—let him remove the body or else give notice to the authorties."

CHAPTR CLII.
THE INQUEST ON COLONEL JACK AND RICHARD FLEETWOOD.

AGREEABLE to the instructions of the Hon. Augustus Fairfax, Henry Osborne instructed Hackett and Knapp to communicate with the High Sheriff of the County and inform him of the two dead bodies which were lying dead in the copse at Richmond.

The last remains of Colonel Jack and Mr. Richard Fleetwood were taken to the nearest public house or hotel, as it was called by courtesy. The establishment rejoiced in the sign of the "Potter's Wheel," and here it was that the two dead bodies were conveyed, there to await the coroner's inquest. The neighbourhood of Richmond, as may be supposed, was in a state of considerable excitement, for it soon became bruited about that a gentleman of high birth had met his death at the hands of one of the most celebrated highwaymen of his day, and numerous reports were current at the time, few, if any, of them being near the truth.

There is an old saying "that report is a great liar," and it would appear that such was the case in the present instance. Curiosity is one of the most marked characteristics of the human race, and the inhabitants of the surburban district of Richmond were in a state of feverish anxiety until the day of the inquest.

When the day arrived for the coroner and jury to " sit upon the bodies," as it is termed, the Potter's Wheel was crowded to excess. Mr. Osborne had not yet made his appearance, but Knapp and Hackett were the chief witnesses.

It was the first time that either of these two persons were in a court of justice or inquiry room, properly speaking, in the present instance, and both Knapp and Hackett felt that they had an onerous, not to say a painful, part to play in the drama which was about to be enacted. Most of the human family have these feelings. Let man be ever so callous, let him be sunk into the lowest abyss of crime, he, nevertheless, has some tender chords in his heart, he has some touch of pity for a companion and compatriot.

Such was the case with both the living highwaymen. They loved their distinguished commander—he whose daring spirit had led them into dangers the most imminent, and in so very many instances had brought them out scathless.

They revered his memory. It may appear strange to many of our readers to say thus much, but nevertheless such was the case. Colonel Jack, with all his faults, and they were many, possessed a nobleness of character and a generosity in his disposition, which could hardly fail to command those under him, and enlist their sympathies in his behalf.

As an instance of this, we have only to mention one of his followers, Crawley, who almost worshipped him. It is true that the latter was an unsophisticated man, gifted with but small powers of ratiocination, and was, in fact, a child of nature, and a rough

child too ; but he was tender hearted, strong in his attachments, weak and almost as susceptible as a child. When he was taken by Knapp and Hackett to the side of his revered commander, he wept like an infant. Indeed, he was so completely overcome, that his brother highwaymen were perfectly astonished at the effect that the sight of the dead body of our hero had on him.

Despite all their efforts, he would not be pacified. He knelt closer over the dead body of the colonel and blubbered like some great girl.

Yes, this rough man—a modern Hercules in physical strength—was quite broken down, and played the woman for the nonce.

Knapp and Hackett led him from the spot, and only regretted their own imprudence in bringing him there at all.

During the time which elapsed between the first taking the two bodies to the Potters' Wheel, up to that period when the jury sat upon them, the landlord of that respectable and tolerably well frequented hostelry, drove a thriving and lucrative trade.

In his heart, he wished that a highwayman and a gentleman might fight a duel every month, at the very least, that is, with this proviso—that the authorities would choose his house in which to hold their inquests. But, alas, for landlords, and mankind in general, the longest week will have an end, and so, in the course of less than that time, some fourteen gentlemen—tradesmen in the neighbourhood—were assembled in the first floor room of the Potters' Wheel, there and then awaiting, with exemplary patience, the appearance of Mr. Lynxy, the coroner, who in the due course of time made his appearance. He was a gentleman of considerable weight, both as regards his own corporeal proportions, and his social position. He rejoiced in an amplitude of abdomen, a double chin, and eyes which suggested to the glance of a superficial observer that they might by chance drop out of their sockets, and roll over the large white waistcoat which their owner usually wore. In fact, they were eyes which seemed to have a difficulty to be managed, for they appeared as though starting out of their sockets.

Mr. Lynxy was in a great bustle—he was always in a great bustle—it was habitual to him ; the wonder is that he kept himself in such good condition, considering the immense amount of physical and mental labour he had diurnally to perform.

He was attended by a little man in a rusty suit of black, the very opposite to himself in every respect. This gentleman was his clerk. He had held this respectable situation for years, until he had grown old in the service. His features were very much pinched and lineal, his body was also very much pinched and attenuated, and it must be confessed that his means were also very much pinched.

His name was Baffles—he had a small salary and a large family—nine at the very least, so that the life of Baffles was not that of a bed of roses. The world had used him somewhat badly, and he had endeavoured to return the compliment. Upon Mr. Lynxy making his appearance in the first floor room of the Potters' Wheel, Mr. Baffles, after a preliminary cough, proceeded to read over the names of the jury—fourteen gentlemen answered to their respective names, as they were called over, in the mild tones of the coroner's clerk, for Mr. Baffles assumed a mild tone of voice in all his professional duties. The jury then went to view the bodies. The countenance of Colonel Jack wore a placid expression, while that of his late enemy and persecutor gave evidences of that last struggle which told of some acute agony. It was remarkable the contrast between the two, so the jury thought. After they had made an examination of the two bodies, they once more returned to the chief room of the Potters' Wheel, then and there to hear what evidence was to be offered to account in any way for the death of the two unfortunate gentlemen.

The first person examined was Mr. Drastic, the village surgeon, who had made a *post mortem* examination of the two bodies. This gentleman indulged in a series of technicalities, which were, of course, not understood by any of the jurymen present. He gave it as his opinion that the death of our hero was caused by the entrance of a foreign body into the chest of Colonel Jack—this foreign body had entered the left scapula, passed through the right ventricle of the heart, and then lodged between the third and fourth ribs. Death must have been instantaneous. The cavity of the chest was filled with blood, little of which had found its way out. Mr. Drastic gave it his opinion that the wound must have been caused by some person firing from behind the deceased man. The wound so received was the immediate cause of death. There could be no question of this.

Respecting the body of Mr. Richard Fleetwood, the learned doctor informed the intelligent jury that he had discovered his wounds—one on the right side, and the other on the left, made by a weapon which had evidently passed through the body, for the orifice could be traced in one of them to the opposite side, but neither of these wounds were of a nature to cause immediate death. It was quite certain that anyone receiving such, could not ever recover therefrom; but as no vital part, neither heart, lungs, or liver were injured, the probability is, that the un-

fortunate gentleman might live for some short period, say half an hour after he had been so wounded, that is, assuming that these were the only wounds on the body, which, however, was not the case in the present instance, for the throat of the unfortunate sufferer had eventually been lacerated to a fearful extent, as though he had been bitten by some animal. No doubt he eventually died from excessive hæmorrhage, consequent upon the severe nature of his wounds. Edward Hackett was then called. Both he and Knapp had at the suggestion of the Honourable Augustus Fairfax, deemed it advisable to have the assistance of a legal gentleman in their case.

Mr. Lynxy cleared his throat so that he might roll out his words with a majesty befitting the occasion.

"Your name is Edward Hackett, I believe?' said the coroner.

"Yes sir."

"Repeat it, what is your name?

"Edward Hackett."

Ah, now sir, will you tell us how you first discovered the bodies of these two gentlemen?'

Hackett then proceeded to inform Mr. Lynxy that he and his friend Knapp were by chance making their way along that part of the forest near to where the bodies were found they were somewhat surprised to hear the smothered cries of a man as though he were endeavouring to call out for help, but from some cause or other were prevented from from doing so. They hastened to the spot and there found the prostrate form of what afterwards turned out to be Mr. Richard Fleetwood and at the same time beheld the dog Slott, who was known to them, at the throat of the then dying man. They lost no time in calling the animal off.

"Was Mr. Fleetwood dead at the time?" inquired Mr. Lynxy.

"No sir."

"Did he speak?"

"Yes sir, we asked him the cause of his situation, and he informed us that he had had a quarrel with Mr. Halford about some family matters, as we understood, in consequence of this they had drawn swords and fought for nearly an hour and that Mr. Halford wounded him so severely that he knew he should never recover.

"Did he say how Halford had come by his death?" inquired the coroner.

"We accused him of having murdered Mr. Halford, sir."

"And what said he?"

"He denied it at first."

"At first? Did he afterwards admit it, then?"

"He did not positively admit it, but upon

our repeating the question, and accusing him more determinedly, he ceased to deny it, but would not reply."

"Did he say how he received the two wounds himself?"

"In combat, so we understood."

"It seems to have been a strange sort of a duel," remarked the foreman of the jury. "One of the combattants receives a wound which evidently must have been given from behind, and the other has two wounds which it is hardly possible for his opponent to have inflicted."

"You are quite sure, Mr. Hackett," said the coroner, "that there was no other person on or near the spot where this fatal encounter took place?"

"I am quite certain upon that point," answered Hackett.

"No seconds?"

"No, sir."

The coroner looked hard at the speaker.

"I suppose you need not be told, gentlemen," he remarked, turning towards the jury, "that this Mr Halford is none other than the celebrated Colonel Jack."

Of course, every one in the room knew that as well as Mr. Lynxy did himself. The foreman at once acknowledged this fact.

Knapp was then examined. His evidence was, of course, much the same in substance as that of his companion's. He corroborated Hackett's testimony in every particular.

The probability is that both the highwaymen would have been roughly handled by the coroner had it not been for one fact, which was simply this, the name and position of Mr. Osborne and the Honourable Augustus Fairfax had their influence upon the immaculate and self-sacrificing Mr. Lynxy. This gentleman like many of his predecessors, and it must be successors, was open, we won't say to bribery, for that is a harsh term, but he was extremely open to influence. He had received a hint to pass lightly over the history and antecedents of both the two chief witnesses his duty it was to examine. The affair was to be hushed up as well as it could. The Honourable Augustus Fairfax wished it hushed up, Sir Reginald Fleetwood wished it hushed up, in fact everybody. wished it hushed up. What could be plainer? Two gentlemen had had a duel—they had fought for an hour at the very least—both were slain—what could be done? It was impossible to ask either of these who was to blame, that is, it was impossible to do so with any chance of getting an answer, for as the old saying is "dead men tell no tales," what was—what could be the natural inference? Why the two gentlemen had slain one another, or at any rate the colonel had half killed his antagonist, and his faithful hound had completed the business. Should they examine

Slott? This was a question which occurred at once to the intelligent and enlightened jury who had been empanelled to sit upon the body. They must examine the dog!—oh, yes; the foreman of the jury—the jury themselves—the coroner—all of them came to the conclusion that there was a necessity, a vital necessity, to examine the dog, Slott.

"Whose dog was he?" inquired Lynxy.

"Mr. Halford's," said Hackett.

"How came he to spring upon Mr. Fleetwood?"

"For very special reasons: the dog assumed that Mr. Fleetwood had murdered his master."

There was a shuffling of feet in the room, a confused murmur of voices. A space was cleared In the crowd, and then one or two individuals informed the coroner that a dog had been dodging about for some time past, ever since the coroner's jury had began to sit.

Some one, at the request of the coroner, endeavoured to collar the animal, and bring him forward. To this Slott decidedly objected. He growled and showed his teeth, and gave demonstrations that this was a source of proceeding to which he had a most decided objection. Upon this the coroner requested Hackett to see if he could lay hold of the dog. The highwayman called Slott, and in a second or two the animal was by his side. Hackett then laid hold of his collar, and drew him in front of the table at which the coroner and the jury were seated. To have painted Slott then would have immortalised an animal painter. The expression which sat upon his features could hardly be translated. It was a mixed expression—he regarded the jurymen from the corner of his eye with a half-defiant, half-frightened, and, at the same time, half-contemptuous look...

"Oh, this is the dog, is it?"

"Yes, sir."

"Ah, a terrible-looking brute, it must be confessed," remarked one of the jurymen; "a terrible-looking brute, without doubt."

"Ah, this is the animal," said the foreman.

They most of them leant forward and, from a feeling of curiosity, looked hard at Slott, who returned their stare, but did not at all appear to like the close inspection to which he was being subjected.

What could they do? It would be impossible to ask the animal his motives for having been so bloodthirsty as to spring at the wounded man's throat, although they could be shrewdly guessed at by the least intelligent of the body of gentlemen.

There was a sad expression on Slott's countenance which spoke of long vigils, sleepless nights, and a miserable mind. There was a haggard and an anxious look about the quadruped that, even ugly as he was, enlisted the sympathy of those who sat on the body of his master in his behalf.

"He liked his master, I suppose?" asked the foreman of the jury.

"He was devoted to him, sir," answered Hackett.

"It would be as well to have the dog shot," remarked one of the jurymen who did not like the appearance of Slott.

At this, Hackett and Knapp started back, and there was a sort of smothered groan from the assembled crowd who had been spectators of the scene.

"Shot!" exclaimed the counsel employed to see to the interests of Knapp and Hackett. "Shot! and what for, may I ask?"

"Oh, I don't know. He might be dangerous."

Another sort of murmur of discontent ran through the crowd.

"I do not at all agree with you," remarked the coroner, who saw plain enough which was the popular side of the question. "The dog has only been guilty of what, after all must be considered, a very natural act. It was his business to protect his master, and I only wish that everyone of us gentlemen, may always have so faithful a follower as this rough looking brute appears to have been."

"He is a rough looking brute," remarked the same person, who had proposed shooting Slott. "He is certainly a very—I may say, ugly animal."

The coroner did not seem to think, it worth, while prolonging the discussion. He ran over the leading facts, touching the deaths of the two unfortunate men—the intelligent jury brought in a verdict of "Justifiable homicide," with a deodand of ten pounds upon the dog at the suggestion of the juror, whom it would appear had taken a most decided prejudice against the highwayman's dog.

"A deodand of ten pounds upon the dog?" said Serjeant Fiat, the gentleman engaged to defend Knapp and Hackett.

"A deodand! and for what?"

"That is their business," remarked the coroner.

"But really, Mr. Lynxy, I must object to this. Who is to pay the deodand?"

"That is the dog's business, or rather the owner of the quadruped," remarked the coroner, with a smile.

"Why, nobody will deem the animal worth ten pounds," said Fiat.

"Yes, I do," said Hackett. "Oh, don't trouble yourselves, gentlemen, the money will be paid."

And the money was paid. The Honourable Augustus Fairfax expressed a wish to Hackett that the dog should become his pro-

perty, so he paid the deodand, and Slott was transferred to the custody of Mr. Fairfax's groom, who tied him up the stable. But the animal managed to break loose, and after going to all the colonel's old haunt's, Hackett and Knapp were surprised to find him at our old friend the Badger's. Of course they took him back to the residence of the Honourable Augustus Fairfax, who caused him to be more carefully watched; and so he was chained up and locked in the harness room.

While here, he remained as sulky as possible, never condescending to look with favour on the groom, but took the food brought him sulkily enough.

One day the Honourable Augustus Fairfax took the animal, led by a chain, to the residence of Mr. Osborne. This was done at the request of Rosalie Halford, Colonel Jack's only surviving daughter.

When Slott caught sight of Rosalie, he evinced violent and unmistakeable evidences of joy and satisfaction. In fact, he became quite a different quadruped—pricked up his ears—disported himself about—and was altogether more lively and affectionate in his manner.

Rosalie begged permission of her lover to take charge of him, which request, we need hardly say, was cheerfully and promptly granted.

Days, weeks, and months passed on, and still the Honourable Augustus Fairfax was a persevering suitor for the hand of the beauteous and amiable Rosalie. Despite the death of her father, and the fearful discovery consequent thereon, Mr. Fairfax did not waver from his first intentions. He would marry Rosalie, or in the event of her persistence in refusing him, he would never marry anyone else. But Rosalie herself was obstinate; she felt that she was asking the young man to make too great a sacrifice in espousing her.

Mr. and Mrs. Osborne interposed, they besought her to consent to an union, and as time went on, her objections gradually faded away, and about a year and three months after the death of our hero, she was led a young and blushing bride to the altar by one of the most amiable and self-sacrificing of England's proud aristocracy. They were married, and then went for some time on the continent, and were esteemed the happiest pair in the three kingdoms.

"What remains to be told? Our hero was buried with all due honours in the same grave as her who had been to him a devoted and gentle partner. Dyson, the "Badger," retired from business, after having amassed a tolerable fortune. He took to farming in his old age, and became a noted character in the neighbourhood he had chosen to settle in for the remainder of his days. He did not quite drop the sporting business, for after he had been established for a year or so, he found farming rather slow, as he termed it, and in consequence he was induced to buy a roadside public-house, and here numbers of the "fancy" would resort; foot races, pigeon shooting, and cock-fighting were frequently occurring at the house of Mr. Dyson, and his old friend Squabshot would occasionally pay him a visit.

The Nobbler met his death from the hands of a ruffianly companion. They had some dispute about the swag, and in crossing a field early one morning after a job, the Nobbler received two severe stabs from a clasp knife carried by his companion. No one was ever able to make out the precise nature of the affray.

All that was known about the affair may be told in a few words. The Nobbler and his ruffianly companion were taking their way across the fields, after having "cracked a crib," they were heard by a drover in angry altercations, and in the morning a cow-boy discovered the prostrate form of the once formidable housebreaker, lying on his side bathed in his own blood. He was not quite dead then, and upon the cow-boy giving the alarm the nearest sergeant came to the spot.

The almost lifeless body of the Nobbler was conveyed to the nearest public house, where he expired in about two hours afterwards. He never spoke, but groaned once or twice, and then lay insensible for some time and eventually expired.

The body of Mr. Richard Fleetwood found a last resting-place in the family vault of his ancestors, and bad man as he had been, his brother, Sir Reginald mourned his loss and felt his loss for a considerable period.

Mr. Sharpthorne was eventually struck off the rolls, and became in his old age a miserably poor man, proving that the old adage, "honesty is the best policy," is a true one.

Mr. Baintree, jun., became a distinguished ornament to his profession, and was looked up to as a great legal authority. In the course of years he was created a judge.

Crawley became a waiter at Mr. Dyson's establishment.

Hackett and Knapp retired from the road after the death of their leader, and, through the instrumentality of Osborne and the Honourable Mr. Fairfax, they were placed in a position in life to secure them a comfortable competency.

And now nothing remains to be told.

THE END.